T0348913

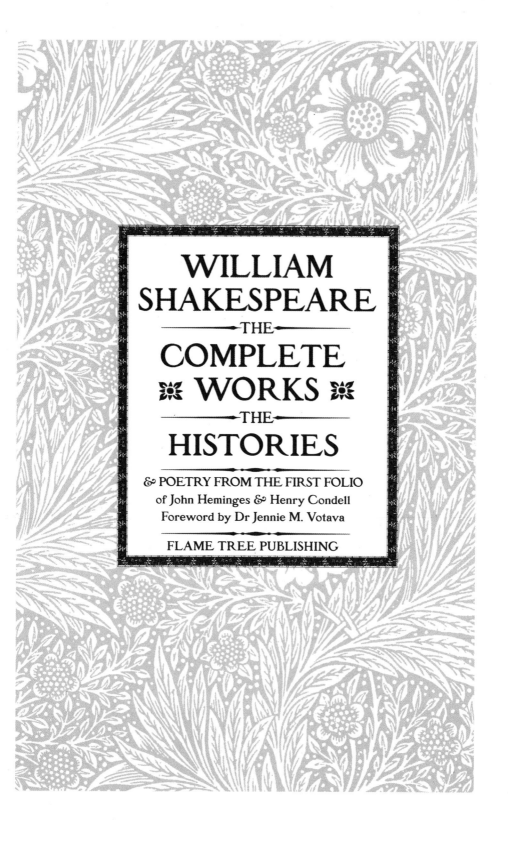

WILLIAM SHAKESPEARE

THE

COMPLETE

❀ WORKS ❀

THE

HISTORIES

& POETRY FROM THE FIRST FOLIO
of John Heminges & Henry Condell
Foreword by Dr Jennie M. Votava

FLAME TREE PUBLISHING

This is a FLAME TREE Book

Publisher & Creative Director: Nick Wells
Editorial Director: Catherine Taylor
Project Editor: Jemma North

Publisher's Note: Due to the historical nature of the classic text, we're aware that there may be some language used which has the potential to cause offence to the modern reader. However, wishing overall to preserve the integrity of the text, rather than imposing contemporary sensibilities, we have left it unaltered.

FLAME TREE PUBLISHING
6 Melbray Mews, Fulham, London SW6 3NS, United Kingdom
www.flametreepublishing.com

First published 2025

Copyright © 2025 Flame Tree Publishing Ltd

25 27 29 28 26
1 3 5 7 9 10 8 6 4 2

ISBN: 978-1-83562-251-3
Special ISBN: 978-1-83562-506-4

All rights reserved. No part of this publication may be reproduced, stored in a retrieval system, or transmitted in any form or by any means, electronic, mechanical, photocopying, recording or otherwise, without the prior written permission of the publisher.

The cover image is created by Flame Tree Studio based on the *Marigold* design by William Morris, 1875. The images on: pages 79, 429, 432, 474 are by Florence Harrison (1877–1955) from *Early Poems of William Morris*, Dodge Pub. Co., 1914; pages 8, 116 is from *The dramatic works of William Shakespeare: accurately printed from the text of the corrected copy left by the late George Steevens, Esq.*, 1830; page 272 is a 19th-century engraving of King Henry V of England at the Battle of Agincourt; page 314 is Thomas W. Keene as Richard III, from *The Haymarket Theatre Souvenir*, Chicago, 1887; pages 405–425 are by George Wharton Edwards, from *A Book of Old English Love Songs*, 1897; page 427 is from *Shakespeare's Sonnets*, ed. William Role, 1883.
Other smaller incidental images are courtyesy of Shutterstock.com and the following: Hein Nouwens, Vector_Line, Barashkova Natalia, Artskrin, Morphart Creation, Arthur Balitskii, PackagingMonster, Marta Leo.
Other decorations created by Flame Tree Studio.

A copy of the CIP data for this book is available from the British Library.

Printed and bound in China

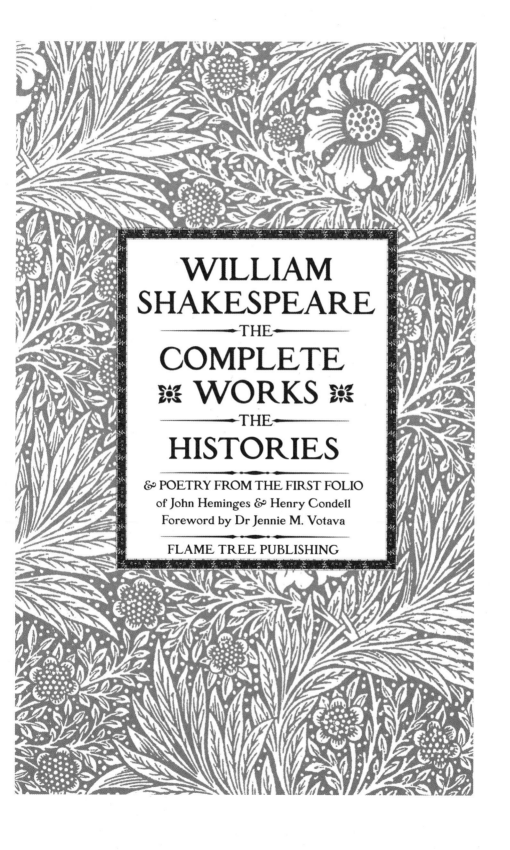

WILLIAM SHAKESPEARE

— THE —

COMPLETE
❁ WORKS ❁

— THE —

HISTORIES

& POETRY FROM THE FIRST FOLIO
of John Heminges & Henry Condell
Foreword by Dr Jennie M. Votava

FLAME TREE PUBLISHING

Contents

Foreword

AT THIS PIVOTAL twenty-first-century moment, reading Shakespeare's plays and poems is more important than ever, both for the many pleasures they provide and as a means of understanding their enduring role in our contemporary world. This is especially the case with Shakespeare's histories. Since their composition in (primarily) the 1590s, these dramatizations of key episodes in England's mediaeval past have repeatedly surged in popularity during crises in British national consciousness, signalling not only the aesthetic and historical value of these texts but also their significance in urgent conversations about power, the nature of history and the formation of national identity. More recently, screen adaptations of the histories – such as the BBC and NBC Universal's miniseries *The Hollow Crown* (2012-16) and the all-Black American adaptation *H4* (2012) – have become broadly accessible through streaming platforms. Through such performances, the histories have become a global means of grappling with these vital issues and their intersections with race, class, sexuality, disability and gender.

In a foreword to a volume that combines Shakespeare's histories with his sonnets and other poems, it is worth noting that *Henry V*, one of Shakespeare's most frequently performed history plays, concludes with an epilogue in the form of a Shakespearean sonnet. On one hand, these two genres represent polar opposites within the considerable range of the author's craft – the histories' concern with public, political questions spanning multiple centuries, versus the sonnets' focus on personal, private reflections within a single speaker's mind. On the other hand, these two seemingly disparate forms embody forces that over the past four hundred years have helped shape categories of identity that are at once both public and deeply personal.

Inventing a Genre, Imagining a Nation

While Renaissance comedy and tragedy were modelled on ancient Greek and Roman drama, the history play emerged as a novel genre in Shakespeare's era. The main source for these plays was a new form of history writing: long prose accounts such as Raphael Holinshed's *Chronicles of England, Scotland, and Ireland*, the second edition of which appeared in 1587.

In the process of helping create a new genre, Shakespeare contributed to a new understanding of both history and England itself. Written in the bloody aftermath of the Protestant Reformation, these ten plays are less about accurately recreating past events than managing a tumultuous present – enabling England to imagine itself not as a kingdom or realm but as a new kind of collective known as a nation. By the 1590s that nation, which eventually became Britain and later the British Empire, had already incorporated non-English Celtic peoples under its rule, including the Welsh, the Scots, and, of course, the Irish. In *Henry V*, the Irishman Captain Macmorris, fighting for the English on French territory, pointedly asks, 'What ish my nation?' His query reveals how the notion of a uniform national identity was questioned from its very inception.

Another innovative aspect of Shakespeare's histories is their connection to one another. While *King John* and *Henry VIII* are standalone dramas, the remaining eight history plays are typically grouped into two tetralogies. The first tetralogy consists of the three parts of *Henry VI* and *Richard III*. These plays describe the disastrous civil wars – usually called the Wars of the Roses – that befell England after the death of Henry V, when his nine-month-old son became King Henry VI. The tetralogy ends with the defeat of the hunchbacked tyrant, Richard III, by Elizabeth I's grandfather Henry VII, the first Tudor king.

Experimental in both form and content, the three *Henry VI* plays are not often performed outside the United Kingdom. They include, however, some of Shakespeare's most memorable unconventional women – such as Joan of Arc and Queen Margaret, who respectively lead their countries' armies – as well as his most quotable line about the legal profession from an insurgent butcher named Dick: 'The first thing we do, let's kill all the lawyers'. *Richard III*, on the other hand, with its disabled, ostracized, yet seductive protagonist, has long been one of Shakespeare's most popular plays. This was especially true in early America, where in 1821 it was the first Shakespeare play performed – to great protest by white Americans – by the all-Black African Grove Theatre company. *Richard III* likely appealed to early white Americans because of their sympathies with a story about overthrowing a tyrant, and to early Black Americans because of their identification with a main character marginalized due to his bodily appearance.

In Britain the first tetralogy is generally associated, at least in its early performances, with the more conservative politics of what E.M.W. Tillyard famously called the 'Tudor myth' – endorsing the defeat of Richard III at Bosworth Field and the subsequent reign of Tudor kings and queens as the manifestation of divine providence. The second tetralogy, however, openly questions the very idea of monarchy. These four plays, written in the second half of the 1590s – *Richard II, Henry IV, Parts 1* and *2*, and *Henry V* – recount the earlier events leading up to the Wars of the Roses, beginning with the deposition of the hereditary monarch, Richard II, by his cousin, the eventual Henry IV. Structured, like a tragedy, around its title character's fall, *Richard II* also raises the critical question, as Russ McDonald and Lena Cowen Orlin point out in *The Bedford Shakespeare*, of what to do when the rightful king is unfit to rule. The play clearly struck a chord with Elizabeth I, who is said to have remarked, in the wake of an unsuccessful rebellion against her own reign, 'I am Richard II, know ye not that?'

In contrast, the two *Henry IV* plays are more concerned with Prince Hal, who later becomes Henry V, than with Henry IV himself. As much coming-of-age story as history, these plays depict the prince stuck between two very different father figures: his actual father the king, and the famous, fallen, fat knight Falstaff. Falstaff's wry and often hilarious commentary on a political world in which he exists on the margins initially aligns the *Henry IV* plays with the genre of comedy. However, Falstaff's role takes a tragic turn at the end of *Henry IV, Part 2*, when Hal, now king, fulfils his promise from the prior play to banish his plump friend. This treatment of Falstaff forecasts what has often been seen as the young king's troubling duality in the seemingly celebratory, nationalistic *Henry V*, in which he wages war on France and delivers, in the process, some of the most stirringly pro-English speeches in Shakespeare. Yet the play can also be convincingly interpreted as an anti-war play that questions the actions and rhetoric used in the service of nationalism.

Although each tetralogy's four plays potentially follow a sequential plot, Graham Holderness notes (in *Shakespeare: The Histories*) that they were likely performed individually in Shakespeare's time. In contrast, mid-twentieth-century practices introduced the performance of all four plays in a tetralogy – or all eight plays in both tetralogies – as a single cycle, transforming these originally distinct yet interconnected works into a continuous 'national epic'. This change demonstrates the fluidity of Shakespeare's plays in performance and how their meanings change through time.

More recently, a crucial aspect of such shifts in meaning has been the performance of Shakespeare's histories with nontraditional casts. While, as above, Black actors performed in *Richard III* in the 1800s, only since the 1990s in the United States and the 2000s in the United Kingdom have actors of colour routinely taken on the other histories' lead monarchical roles. Performances from the non-English-speaking world such as the Brazilian *Henry IV* film adaptation *Faustão* (1971), which features a Black Falstaff, similarly testify to the histories' cultural versatility. Since these plays were designed not to depict the past accurately but to link the present with the past and envision a collective national future, Shakespeare scholars increasingly emphasize the importance of representing all races, ethnicities, creeds and genders in that national story, regardless of the nation.

Refining a Form, Reframing the Future

Unlike the histories, Shakespeare's 154 sonnets were not intended for public performance and focus on more personal themes. However, they too play an ongoing role in shaping both personal and political identity. First published together in 1609, these poems flout the established Renaissance sonnet convention of a male speaker pining for the love of an unavailable woman. That Shakespeare's first 126 sonnets are, instead, love poems addressed by a male speaker to an unidentified young man, sometimes called the 'Fair Youth', always surprises my students, who are fascinated by the fluidity of gender and desire in an era they initially assume was more rigid than our own. Similarly, students are surprised by the sauciness of the subsequent poems to the so-called 'Dark Lady', who is anything but unavailable.

It is also essential to point out, however, the problematic racial language embedded in the sonnets, which consistently associate whiteness with purity and blackness with corruption. This is especially clear in Sonnet 144, which begins, 'Two loves I have of comfort and despair, / Which like two spirits do suggest me still, / The better angel is a man right fair: / The worser spirit a woman coloured ill'. The racial implications of such language – especially the ubiquitous word 'fair' and its combined meanings of beautiful, white and noble – went largely unmarked by critics until Kim F. Hall's 1995 intervention in her book, *Things of Darkness*. Because of its combined pervasiveness and invisibility, this aspect of the sonnets undoubtedly has helped shape how speakers of English see black and white.

Indeed, for good and for ill, Shakespeare's works continue to be a testimony to the enduring power of language. This is certainly true of the still-popular Shakespearean sonnet form, three quatrains followed by a rhyming couplet. This form provides a potent structure for working through a complex idea or emotion, and then, in the couplet, simultaneously offering closure and subverting expectations.

As an extreme example, the sonnet that ends *Henry V* serves as a conclusion to both tetralogies, as its final six lines look both forward and backward toward the violent future depicted in the earlier plays:

> *Henry the Sixth, in infant bands crown'd King*
> *Of France and England, did this King succeed;*
> *Whose state so many had the managing*
> *That they lost France and made his England bleed;*
> *Which oft our stage hath shown; and, for their sake,*
> *In your fair minds let this acceptance take.*

The key word 'fair' in the phrase 'fair minds' carries multiple important connotations, including those of justice, beauty, and whiteness. While the epilogue implores its viewers, like so many reluctant beloveds, to 'accept' an inadequate performance, it also invites them to embrace a complex, shared theatrical and national history.

As you read the plays and poems that follow, I hope that part of your enjoyment of some of Shakespeare's most compelling creations will involve considering their role in shaping that ever-evolving tapestry of personal and political stories. Rather than simply 'accepting' these texts as unassailable monuments, I encourage you to approach them critically, questioning the injustices they perpetuate as well as recognizing those they challenge. In this way, reading Shakespeare can contribute not only to a deeper understanding of the past but to positive change in our present world.

Dr Jennie M. Votava, Allegheny College

Further Reading

Hall, Kim. F., *Things of Darkness: Economies of Race and Gender in Early Modern England* (Cornell University Press, 1995)

Holderness, Graham, *Shakespeare: The Histories* (Palgrave Macmillan, 2000)

Howard, Jean E. and Phyllis Rackin, *Engendering a Nation: A Feminist Account of Shakespeare's English Histories* (Routledge, 1997)

McDonald, Russ and Lena Cowen Orlin (eds)., *The Bedford Shakespeare: Based on the New Cambridge Edition* (Bedford/St. Martin's, 2015)

Pittman, L. Monique, *Shakespeare's Contested Nations: Race, Gender, and Multicultural Britain in Performances of the History Plays* (Routledge, 2022)

Thompson, Ayanna (ed.), *The Cambridge Companion to Shakespeare and Race* (Cambridge University Press, 2021)

Tillyard, E.M.W., *Shakespeare's History Plays* (Penguin Books, 1944)

Vendler, Helen, *The Art of Shakespeare's Sonnets* (Harvard University Press, 1999)

Votava, Jennie M., *Shakespeare's Histories on Screen: Adaptation, Race and Intersectionality* (Bloomsbury, 2023)

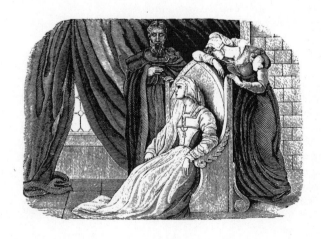

Publisher's Note
on the Three-Edition Set

OUR AIM has been to create beautiful gift editions of the complete works of Shakespeare that look good and read well. This involved hundreds of hours of editing, proofing and picture researching before achieving the first illustrated edition, and then these luxury text-only editions. It is important to highlight that the books are intended for the general reader and expressly not for scholarly use: our desire to keep the books within a set number of pages, while retaining readability, has driven a number of editorial decisions, but generally we have strived for accessibility. Our primary source for decision-making has been the work of two of William Shakespeare's friends and fellow actors in the acting troupe to which he dedicated the majority of his productive life as a dramatist, The King's Men. John Heminges' and Henry Condell's First Folio, published in 1623, was the first authoritative publication of Shakespeare's plays; to that we've added *Pericles, Prince of Tyre* (included in the Third Folio of 1663), *The Two Noble Kinsmen* (now acknowledged as a collaboration between Shakespeare and John Fletcher), the sonnets and the main poetic works, much of which were published under Shakespeare's own auspices. Notwithstanding the various authorship, textual and dating controversies of the last five hundred years, these editions represent our balanced judgment of the language, use of stage directions and specific content for a complete works for the modern reader. In the course of the exciting and demanding project we mediated between several great historical texts, including the 1951 Alexander Shakespeare text, the original Oxford University Press (OUP) single-volume text edited by W.J. Craig (1905) and the subsequent Stanley Wells and Gary Taylor OUP text of 1988. The Penguin Shakespeare and Arden Shakespeare multi-volume libraries have also been invaluable in resolving issues of clarity.

Line decorations from the seventeenth, eighteenth and nineteenth centuries, with typography designed by William Morris in the early 1890s add interest to the text to offer the reader a pleasing experience.

Finally, it is worth saying that we sincerely hope that *The Comedies*, *The Tragedies* and *The Histories* in this edition of *William Shakespeare: The Complete Works* will inspire you to see the work of its author as it was originally intended: in the theatre, where the intoxication of language, music and physical movement blend together to create fantastic worlds, reveal ultimate truths and, above all, offer sublime entertainment.

A Note on Dates

Broadly, we have presented the plays in the order of the First Folio, with the dates (years) above the titles. In academic circles it is not wholly respectable to allocate a specific date to each of these works, as there are disputes about the performance versus license and publication dates. The plays and their reviews, as well as references in other plays and contemporary publications, occasionally provide contradictory evidence for dating. The dates are therefore provided as a rough guide only.

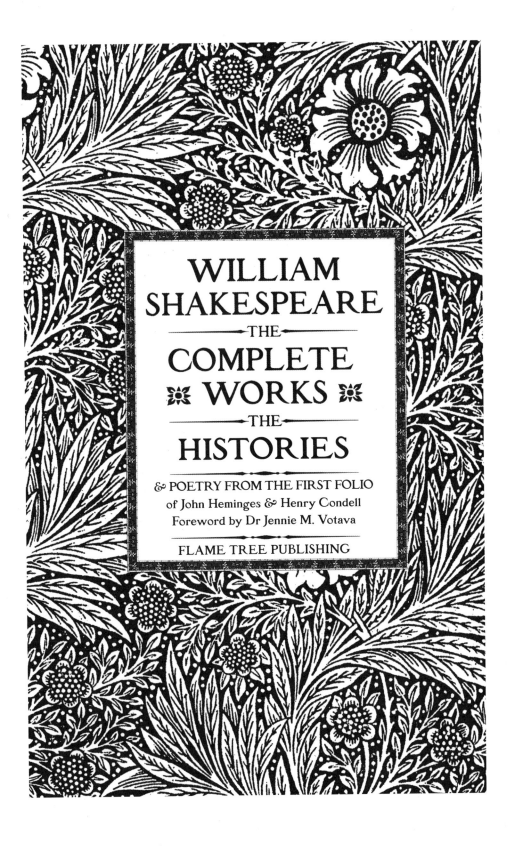

WILLIAM SHAKESPEARE

·THE·

COMPLETE

❈ WORKS ❈

·THE·

HISTORIES

& POETRY FROM THE FIRST FOLIO
of John Heminges & Henry Condell
Foreword by Dr Jennie M. Votava

FLAME TREE PUBLISHING

1594

King John

Dramatis Personae

KING JOHN
PRINCE HENRY, his son
ARTHUR, DUKE OF BRITAINE, son of Geffrey, late
Duke of Britaine, the elder
brother of King John
EARL OF PEMBROKE
EARL OF ESSEX
EARL OF SALISBURY
LORD BIGOT
HUBERT DE BURGH
ROBERT FAULCONBRIDGE, son to
Sir Robert Faulconbridge
PHILIP THE BASTARD, his half-brother
JAMES GURNEY, servant to Lady Faulconbridge
PETER OF POMFRET, a prophet

KING PHILIP OF FRANCE
LEWIS, the Dauphin
DUKE OF AUSTRIA (Lymoges)
CARDINAL PANDULPH, the Pope's legate
MELUN, a French lord
CHATILLON, ambassador from France
to King John

QUEEN ELINOR, widow of King Henry II and
mother to King John
CONSTANCE, Mother to Arthur
BLANCH OF SPAIN, daughter to the King
of Castile and niece to King John
LADY FAULCONBRIDGE, widow of
Sir Robert Faulconbridge

Other Lords, Citizens of Angiers,
Sheriff, Heralds, Officers,
Soldiers, Executioners,
Messengers, Attendants

SCENE
England and France

ACT I

SCENE I
KING JOHN'S palace

Enter KING JOHN, QUEEN ELINOR, PEMBROKE,
ESSEX, SALISBURY, and others, with CHATILLON

KING JOHN. Now, say, Chatillon, what would
France with us?
CHATILLON. Thus, after greeting, speaks the
King of France
In my behaviour to the majesty,
The borrowed majesty, of England here.
ELINOR. A strange beginning-'borrowed majesty'!
KING JOHN. Silence, good mother; hear
the embassy.
CHATILLON. Philip of France, in right and
true behalf
Of thy deceased brother Geffrey's son,
Arthur Plantagenet, lays most lawful claim
To this fair island and the territories,
To Ireland, Poictiers, Anjou, Touraine, Maine,
Desiring thee to lay aside the sword
Which sways usurpingly these several titles,
And put the same into young Arthur's hand,
Thy nephew and right royal sovereign.
KING JOHN. What follows if we disallow of this?
CHATILLON. The proud control of fierce and
bloody war,
To enforce these rights so forcibly withheld.
KING JOHN. Here have we war for war, and blood
for blood,
Controlment for controlment-so answer France.
CHATILLON. Then take my king's defiance from
my mouth-
The farthest limit of my embassy.
KING JOHN. Bear mine to him, and so depart
in peace;
Be thou as lightning in the eyes of France;
For ere thou canst report I will be there,
The thunder of my cannon shall be heard.
So hence! Be thou the trumpet of our wrath
And sullen presage of your own decay.
An honourable conduct let him have-
Pembroke, look to 't. Farewell, Chatillon.
Exeunt CHATILLON and PEMBROKE
ELINOR. What now, my son! Have I not ever said
How that ambitious Constance would not cease
Till she had kindled France and all the world

Upon the right and party of her son?
This might have been prevented and
made whole
With very easy arguments of love,
Which now the manage of two kingdoms must
With fearful bloody issue arbitrate.

KING JOHN. Our strong possession and our right
for us!

ELINOR. Your strong possession much more than
your right,
Or else it must go wrong with you and me;
So much my conscience whispers in your ear,
Which none but heaven and you and I shall hear.

Enter a SHERIFF

ESSEX. My liege, here is the strangest controversy
Come from the country to be judg'd by you
That e'er I heard. Shall I produce the men?

KING JOHN. Let them approach. *Exit SHERIFF.*
Our abbeys and our priories shall pay
This expedition's charge.

*Enter ROBERT FAULCONBRIDGE and PHILIP, his
bastard brother*

What men are you?

BASTARD. Your faithful subject I, a gentleman
Born in Northamptonshire, and eldest son,
As I suppose, to Robert Faulconbridge-
A soldier by the honour-giving hand
Of Coeur-de-lion knighted in the field.

KING JOHN. What art thou?

ROBERT. The son and heir to that
same Faulconbridge.

KING JOHN. Is that the elder, and art thou
the heir?
You came not of one mother then, it seems.

BASTARD. Most certain of one mother,
mighty king-
That is well known-and, as I think, one father;
But for the certain knowledge of that truth
I put you o'er to heaven and to my mother.
Of that I doubt, as all men's children may.

ELINOR. Out on thee, rude man! Thou dost
shame thy mother,
And wound her honour with this diffidence.

BASTARD. I, madam? No, I have no reason for it-
That is my brother's plea, and none of mine;
The which if he can prove, 'a pops me out
At least from fair five hundred pound a year.
Heaven guard my mother's honour and my land!

KING JOHN. A good blunt fellow. Why, being
younger born,
Doth he lay claim to thine inheritance?

BASTARD. I know not why, except to get the land.
But once he slander'd me with bastardy;
But whe'er I be as true begot or no,

That still I lay upon my mother's head;
But that I am as well begot, my liege-
Fair fall the bones that took the pains for me!-
Compare our faces and be judge yourself.
If old Sir Robert did beget us both
And were our father, and this son like him-
O old Sir Robert, father, on my knee
I give heaven thanks I was not like to thee!

KING JOHN. Why, what a madcap hath heaven
lent us here!

ELINOR. He hath a trick of Coeur-de-lion's face;
The accent of his tongue affecteth him.
Do you not read some tokens of my son
In the large composition of this man?

KING JOHN. Mine eye hath well examined
his parts
And finds them perfect Richard. Sirrah, speak,
What doth move you to claim your
brother's land?

BASTARD. Because he hath a half-face, like
my father.
With half that face would he have all my land:
A half-fac'd groat five hundred pound a year!

ROBERT. My gracious liege, when that my
father liv'd,
Your brother did employ my father much-

BASTARD. Well, sir, by this you cannot get
my land:
Your tale must be how he employ'd my mother.

ROBERT. And once dispatch'd him in an embassy
To Germany, there with the Emperor
To treat of high affairs touching that time.
Th' advantage of his absence took the King,
And in the meantime sojourn'd at my father's;
Where how he did prevail I shame to speak-
But truth is truth: large lengths of seas
and shores
Between my father and my mother lay,
As I have heard my father speak himself,
When this same lusty gentleman was got.
Upon his death-bed he by will bequeath'd
His lands to me, and took it on his death
That this my mother's son was none of his;
And if he were, he came into the world
Full fourteen weeks before the course of time.
Then, good my liege, let me have what is mine,
My father's land, as was my father's will.

KING JOHN. Sirrah, your brother is legitimate:
Your father's wife did after wedlock bear him,
And if she did play false, the fault was hers;
Which fault lies on the hazards of all husbands
That marry wives. Tell me, how if my brother,
Who, as you say, took pains to get this son,
Had of your father claim'd this son for his?

In sooth, good friend, your father might
have kept
This calf, bred from his cow, from all the world;
In sooth, he might; then, if he were
my brother's,
My brother might not claim him; nor
your father,
Being none of his, refuse him. This concludes:
My mother's son did get your father's heir;
Your father's heir must have your father's land.

ROBERT. Shall then my father's will be of no force
To dispossess that child which is not his?

BASTARD. Of no more force to dispossess me, sir,
Than was his will to get me, as I think.

ELINOR. Whether hadst thou rather be
a Faulconbridge,
And like thy brother, to enjoy thy land,
Or the reputed son of Coeur-de-lion,
Lord of thy presence and no land beside?

BASTARD. Madam, an if my brother had my shape
And I had his, Sir Robert's his, like him;
And if my legs were two such riding-rods,
My arms such eel-skins stuff'd, my face so thin
That in mine ear I durst not stick a rose
Lest men should say 'Look where three-
farthings goes!'
And, to his shape, were heir to all this land-
Would I might never stir from off this place,
I would give it every foot to have this face!
I would not be Sir Nob in any case.

ELINOR. I like thee well. Wilt thou forsake
thy fortune,
Bequeath thy land to him and follow me?
I am a soldier and now bound to France.

BASTARD. Brother, take you my land, I'll take
my chance.
Your face hath got five hundred pound a year,
Yet sell your face for fivepence and 'tis dear.
Madam, I'll follow you unto the death.

ELINOR. Nay, I would have you go before
me thither.

BASTARD. Our country manners give our
betters way.

KING JOHN. What is thy name?

BASTARD. Philip, my liege, so is my name begun:
Philip, good old Sir Robert's wife's eldest son.

KING JOHN. From henceforth bear his name
whose form thou bearest:
Kneel thou down Philip, but rise more great-
Arise Sir Richard and Plantagenet.

BASTARD. Brother by th' mother's side, give me
your hand;
My father gave me honour, yours gave land.
Now blessed be the hour, by night or day,

When I was got, Sir Robert was away!

ELINOR. The very spirit of Plantagenet!
I am thy grandam, Richard: call me so.

BASTARD. Madam, by chance, but not by truth;
what though?
Something about, a little from the right,
In at the window, or else o'er the hatch;
Who dares not stir by day must walk by night;
And have is have, however men do catch.
Near or far off, well won is still well shot;
And I am I, howe'er I was begot.

KING JOHN. Go, Faulconbridge; now hast thou
thy desire:
A landless knight makes thee a landed squire.
Come, madam, and come, Richard, we
must speed
For France, for France, for it is more than need.

BASTARD. Brother, adieu. Good fortune come
to thee!
For thou wast got i' th' way of honesty.

Exeunt all but the BASTARD.

A foot of honour better than I was;
But many a many foot of land the worse.
Well, now can I make any Joan a lady.
'Good den, Sir Richard!'-'God-a-mercy, fellow!'
And if his name be George, I'll call him Peter;
For new-made honour doth forget men's names:
'Tis too respective and too sociable
For your conversion. Now your traveller,
He and his toothpick at my worship's mess-
And when my knightly stomach is suffic'd,
Why then I suck my teeth and catechise
My picked man of countries: 'My dear sir,'
Thus leaning on mine elbow I begin,
'I shall beseech you'-That is question now;
And then comes answer like an Absey book:
'O sir,' says answer, 'at your best command,
At your employment, at your service, sir!'
'No, sir,' says question, 'I, sweet sir, at yours.'
And so, ere answer knows what question would,
Saving in dialogue of compliment,
And talking of the Alps and Apennines,
The Pyrenean and the river Po-
It draws toward supper in conclusion so.
But this is worshipful society,
And fits the mounting spirit like myself;
For he is but a bastard to the time
That doth not smack of observation-
And so am I, whether I smack or no;
And not alone in habit and device,
Exterior form, outward accoutrement,
But from the inward motion to deliver
Sweet, sweet, sweet poison for the age's tooth;
Which, though I will not practise to deceive,

Yet, to avoid deceit, I mean to learn;
For it shall strew the footsteps of my rising.
But who comes in such haste in riding-robes?
What woman-post is this? Hath she no husband
That will take pains to blow a horn before her?

Enter LADY FAULCONBRIDGE, and
JAMES GURNEY

O me, 'tis my mother! How now, good lady!
What brings you here to court so hastily?
LADY FAULCONBRIDGE. Where is that slave, thy
  brother? Where is he
That holds in chase mine honour up and down?
BASTARD. My brother Robert, old Sir
  Robert's son?
Colbrand the giant, that same mighty man?
Is it Sir Robert's son that you seek so?
LADY FAULCONBRIDGE. Sir Robert's son! Ay,
  thou unreverend boy,
Sir Robert's son! Why scorn'st thou at Sir Robert?
He is Sir Robert's son, and so art thou.
BASTARD. James Gurney, wilt thou give us
  leave awhile?
GURNEY. Good leave, good Philip.
BASTARD. Philip-Sparrow! James,
There's toys abroad-anon I'll tell thee more.

Exit GURNEY.

Madam, I was not old Sir Robert's son;
Sir Robert might have eat his part in me
Upon Good Friday, and ne'er broke his fast.
Sir Robert could do: well-marry, to confess-
Could he get me? Sir Robert could not do it:
We know his handiwork. Therefore,
  good mother,
To whom am I beholding for these limbs?
Sir Robert never holp to make this leg.
LADY FAULCONBRIDGE. Hast thou conspired
  with thy brother too,
That for thine own gain shouldst defend
  mine honour?
What means this scorn, thou most
  untoward knave?
BASTARD. Knight, knight, good mother, Basilisco-
  like.
What! I am dubb'd; I have it on my shoulder.
But, mother, I am not Sir Robert's son:
I have disclaim'd Sir Robert and my land;
Legitimation, name, and all is gone.
Then, good my mother, let me know my father-
Some proper man, I hope. Who was it, mother?
LADY FAULCONBRIDGE. Hast thou denied thyself
  a Faulconbridge?
BASTARD. As faithfully as I deny the devil.
LADY FAULCONBRIDGE. King Richard Coeur-de-
  lion was thy father.

By long and vehement suit I was seduc'd
To make room for him in my husband's bed.
Heaven lay not my transgression to my charge!
Thou art the issue of my dear offence,
Which was so strongly urg'd past my defence.
BASTARD. Now, by this light, were I to get again,
Madam, I would not wish a better father.
Some sins do bear their privilege on earth,
And so doth yours: your fault was not your folly;
Needs must you lay your heart at his dispose,
Subjected tribute to commanding love,
Against whose fury and unmatched force
The aweless lion could not wage the fight
Nor keep his princely heart from Richard's hand.
He that perforce robs lions of their hearts
May easily win a woman's. Ay, my mother,
With all my heart I thank thee for my father!
Who lives and dares but say thou didst not well
When I was got, I'll send his soul to hell.
Come, lady, I will show thee to my kin;
And they shall say when Richard me begot,
If thou hadst said him nay, it had been sin.
Who says it was, he lies; I say 'twas not. *Exeunt.*

ACT II

SCENE I
France. Before Angiers

Enter, on one side, the Duke of AUSTRIA and Forces; on the
other, KING PHILIP OF FRANCE, LEWIS the Dauphin,
CONSTANCE, ARTHUR,
and Forces

KING PHILIP. Before Angiers well met,
  brave Austria.
Arthur, that great forerunner of thy blood,
Richard, that robb'd the lion of his heart
And fought the holy wars in Palestine,
By this brave duke came early to his grave;
And for amends to his posterity,
At our importance hither is he come
To spread his colours, boy, in thy behalf;
And to rebuke the usurpation
Of thy unnatural uncle, English John.
Embrace him, love him, give him
  welcome hither.
ARTHUR. God shall forgive you Coeur-de-
  lion's death
The rather that you give his offspring life,
Shadowing their right under your wings of war.
I give you welcome with a powerless hand,

But with a heart full of unstained love;
Welcome before the gates of Angiers, Duke.
KING PHILIP. A noble boy! Who would not do
  thee right?
AUSTRIA. Upon thy cheek lay I this zealous kiss
  As seal to this indenture of my love:
  That to my home I will no more return
  Till Angiers and the right thou hast in France,
  Together with that pale, that white-fac'd shore,
  Whose foot spurns back the ocean's
    roaring tides
  And coops from other lands her islanders-
  Even till that England, hedg'd in with the main,
  That water-walled bulwark, still secure
  And confident from foreign purposes-
  Even till that utmost corner of the west
  Salute thee for her king. Till then, fair boy,
  Will I not think of home, but follow arms.
CONSTANCE. O, take his mother's thanks, a
  widow's thanks,
  Till your strong hand shall help to give
    him strength
  To make a more requital to your love!
AUSTRIA. The peace of heaven is theirs that lift
  their swords
  In such a just and charitable war.
KING PHILIP. Well then, to work! Our cannon
  shall be bent
  Against the brows of this resisting town;
  Call for our chiefest men of discipline,
  To cull the plots of best advantages.
  We'll lay before this town our royal bones,
  Wade to the market-place in Frenchmen's blood,
  But we will make it subject to this boy.
CONSTANCE. Stay for an answer to your embassy,
  Lest unadvis'd you stain your swords with blood;
  My Lord Chatillon may from England bring
  That right in peace which here we urge in war,
  And then we shall repent each drop of blood
  That hot rash haste so indirectly shed.

Enter CHATILLON

KING PHILIP. A wonder, lady! Lo, upon thy wish,
  Our messenger Chatillon is arriv'd.
  What England says, say briefly, gentle lord;
  We coldly pause for thee. Chatillon, speak.
CHATILLON. Then turn your forces from this
  paltry siege
  And stir them up against a mightier task.
  England, impatient of your just demands,
  Hath put himself in arms. The adverse winds,
  Whose leisure I have stay'd, have given him time
  To land his legions all as soon as I;
  His marches are expedient to this town,
  His forces strong, his soldiers confident.

With him along is come the mother-queen,
An Ate, stirring him to blood and strife;
With her the Lady Blanch of Spain;
With them a bastard of the king's deceas'd;
And all th' unsettled humours of the land-
Rash, inconsiderate, fiery voluntaries,
With ladies' faces and fierce dragons' spleens-
Have sold their fortunes at their native homes,
Bearing their birthrights proudly on their backs,
To make a hazard of new fortunes here.
In brief, a braver choice of dauntless spirits
Than now the English bottoms have waft o'er
Did never float upon the swelling tide
To do offence and scathe in Christendom.
  [Drum beats]
The interruption of their churlish drums
Cuts off more circumstance: they are at hand;
To parley or to fight, therefore prepare.
KING PHILIP. How much unlook'd for is
  this expedition!
AUSTRIA. By how much unexpected, by so much
  We must awake endeavour for defence,
  For courage mounteth with occasion.
  Let them be welcome then; we are prepar'd.
  Enter KING JOHN, ELINOR, BLANCH, the BASTARD,
    PEMBROKE, and others
KING JOHN. Peace be to France, if France in
  peace permit
  Our just and lineal entrance to our own!
  If not, bleed France, and peace ascend
    to heaven,
  Whiles we, God's wrathful agent, do correct
  Their proud contempt that beats His peace
    to heaven!
KING PHILIP. Peace be to England, if that
  war return
  From France to England, there to live in peace!
  England we love, and for that England's sake
  With burden of our armour here we sweat.
  This toil of ours should be a work of thine;
  But thou from loving England art so far
  That thou hast under-wrought his lawful king,
  Cut off the sequence of posterity,
  Outfaced infant state, and done a rape
  Upon the maiden virtue of the crown.
  Look here upon thy brother Geffrey's face:
  These eyes, these brows, were moulded out
    of his;
  This little abstract doth contain that large
  Which died in Geffrey, and the hand of time
  Shall draw this brief into as huge a volume.
  That Geffrey was thy elder brother born,
  And this his son; England was Geffrey's right,
  And this is Geffrey's. In the name of God,

How comes it then that thou art call'd a king,
When living blood doth in these temples beat
Which owe the crown that thou o'er-masterest?
KING JOHN. From whom hast thou this great
    commission, France,
To draw my answer from thy articles?
KING PHILIP. From that supernal judge that stirs
    good thoughts
In any breast of strong authority
To look into the blots and stains of right.
That judge hath made me guardian to this boy,
Under whose warrant I impeach thy wrong,
And by whose help I mean to chastise it.
KING JOHN. Alack, thou dost usurp authority.
KING PHILIP. Excuse it is to beat usurping down.
ELINOR. Who is it thou dost call usurper, France?
CONSTANCE. Let me make answer: thy
    usurping son.
ELINOR. Out, insolent! Thy bastard shall be king,
That thou mayst be a queen and check
    the world!
CONSTANCE. My bed was ever to thy son as true
As thine was to thy husband; and this boy
Liker in feature to his father Geffrey
Than thou and John in manners-being as like
As rain to water, or devil to his dam.
My boy a bastard! By my soul, I think
His father never was so true begot;
It cannot be, an if thou wert his mother.
ELINOR. There's a good mother, boy, that blots
    thy father.
CONSTANCE. There's a good grandam, boy,
    that would blot thee.
AUSTRIA. Peace!
BASTARD. Hear the crier.
AUSTRIA. What the devil art thou?
BASTARD. One that will play the devil, sir,
    with you,
An 'a may catch your hide and you alone.
You are the hare of whom the proverb goes,
Whose valour plucks dead lions by the beard;
I'll smoke your skin-coat an I catch you right;
Sirrah, look to 't; i' faith I will, i' faith.
BLANCH. O, well did he become that lion's robe
That did disrobe the lion of that robe!
BASTARD. It lies as sightly on the back of him
As great Alcides' shows upon an ass;
But, ass, I'll take that burden from your back,
Or lay on that shall make your shoulders crack.
AUSTRIA. What cracker is this same that deafs
    our ears
With this abundance of superfluous breath?
King Philip, determine what we shall
    do straight.

KING PHILIP. Women and fools, break off
    your conference.
King John, this is the very sum of all:
England and Ireland, Anjou, Touraine, Maine,
In right of Arthur, do I claim of thee;
Wilt thou resign them and lay down thy arms?
KING JOHN. My life as soon. I do defy
    thee, France.
Arthur of Britaine, yield thee to my hand,
And out of my dear love I'll give thee more
Than e'er the coward hand of France can win.
Submit thee, boy.
ELINOR. Come to thy grandam, child.
CONSTANCE. Do, child, go to it grandam, child;
Give grandam kingdom, and it grandam will
Give it a plum, a cherry, and a fig.
There's a good grandam!
ARTHUR. Good my mother, peace!
I would that I were low laid in my grave:
I am not worth this coil that's made for me.
ELINOR. His mother shames him so, poor boy,
    he weeps.
CONSTANCE. Now shame upon you, whe'er she
    does or no!
His grandam's wrongs, and not his
    mother's shames,
Draws those heaven-moving pearls from his
    poor eyes,
Which heaven shall take in nature of a fee;
Ay, with these crystal beads heaven shall
    be brib'd
To do him justice and revenge on you.
ELINOR. Thou monstrous slanderer of heaven
    and earth!
CONSTANCE. Thou monstrous injurer of heaven
    and earth,
Call not me slanderer! Thou and thine usurp
The dominations, royalties, and rights,
Of this oppressed boy; this is thy eldest
    son's son,
Infortunate in nothing but in thee.
Thy sins are visited in this poor child;
The canon of the law is laid on him,
Being but the second generation
Removed from thy sin-conceiving womb.
KING JOHN. Bedlam, have done.
CONSTANCE. I have but this to say-
That he is not only plagued for her sin,
But God hath made her sin and her the plague
On this removed issue, plagued for her
And with her plague; her sin his injury,
Her injury the beadle to her sin;
All punish'd in the person of this child,
And all for her-a plague upon her!

ELINOR. Thou unadvised scold, I can produce
  A will that bars the title of thy son.
CONSTANCE. Ay, who doubts that? A will, a
  wicked will;
  A woman's will; a cank'red grandam's will!
KING PHILIP. Peace, lady! pause, or be
  more temperate.
  It ill beseems this presence to cry aim
  To these ill-tuned repetitions.
  Some trumpet summon hither to the walls
  These men of Angiers; let us hear them speak
  Whose title they admit, Arthur's or John's.
     Trumpet sounds. Enter citizens upon the walls
CITIZEN. Who is it that hath warn'd us to
  the walls?
KING PHILIP. 'Tis France, for England.
KING JOHN. England for itself.
  You men of Angiers, and my loving subjects-
KING PHILIP. You loving men of Angiers,
  Arthur's subjects,
  Our trumpet call'd you to this gentle parle-
KING JOHN. For our advantage; therefore hear
  us first.
  These flags of France, that are advanced here
  Before the eye and prospect of your town,
  Have hither march'd to your endamagement;
  The cannons have their bowels full of wrath,
  And ready mounted are they to spit forth
  Their iron indignation 'gainst your walls;
  All preparation for a bloody siege
  And merciless proceeding by these French
  Confront your city's eyes, your winking gates;
  And but for our approach those sleeping stones
  That as a waist doth girdle you about
  By the compulsion of their ordinance
  By this time from their fixed beds of lime
  Had been dishabited, and wide havoc made
  For bloody power to rush upon your peace.
  But on the sight of us your lawful King,
  Who painfully with much expedient march
  Have brought a countercheck before your gates,
  To save unscratch'd your city's
    threat'ned cheeks-
  Behold, the French amaz'd vouchsafe a parle;
  And now, instead of bullets wrapp'd in fire,
  To make a shaking fever in your walls,
  They shoot but calm words folded up in smoke,
  To make a faithless error in your ears;
  Which trust accordingly, kind citizens,
  And let us in-your King, whose labour'd spirits,
  Forwearied in this action of swift speed,
  Craves harbourage within your city walls.
KING PHILIP. When I have said, make answer to
  us both.

  Lo, in this right hand, whose protection
  Is most divinely vow'd upon the right
  Of him it holds, stands young Plantagenet,
  Son to the elder brother of this man,
  And king o'er him and all that he enjoys;
  For this down-trodden equity we tread
  In warlike march these greens before
    your town,
  Being no further enemy to you
  Than the constraint of hospitable zeal
  In the relief of this oppressed child
  Religiously provokes. Be pleased then
  To pay that duty which you truly owe
  To him that owes it, namely, this young prince;
  And then our arms, like to a muzzled bear,
  Save in aspect, hath all offence seal'd up;
  Our cannons' malice vainly shall be spent
  Against th' invulnerable clouds of heaven;
  And with a blessed and unvex'd retire,
  With unhack'd swords and helmets
    all unbruis'd,
  We will bear home that lusty blood again
  Which here we came to spout against
    your town,
  And leave your children, wives, and you,
    in peace.
  But if you fondly pass our proffer'd offer,
  'Tis not the roundure of your old-fac'd walls
  Can hide you from our messengers of war,
  Though all these English and their discipline
  Were harbour'd in their rude circumference.
  Then tell us, shall your city call us lord
  In that behalf which we have challeng'd it;
  Or shall we give the signal to our rage,
  And stalk in blood to our possession?
CITIZEN. In brief: we are the King of
  England's subjects;
  For him, and in his right, we hold this town.
KING JOHN. Acknowledge then the King, and
  let me in.
CITIZEN. That can we not; but he that proves
  the King,
  To him will we prove loyal. Till that time
  Have we ramm'd up our gates against
    the world.
KING JOHN. Doth not the crown of England
  prove the King?
  And if not that, I bring you witnesses:
  Twice fifteen thousand hearts of
    England's breed-
BASTARD. Bastards and else.
KING JOHN. To verify our title with their lives.
KING PHILIP. As many and as well-born bloods
  as those-

BASTARD. Some bastards too.

KING PHILIP. Stand in his face to contradict
his claim.

CITIZEN. Till you compound whose right
is worthiest,
We for the worthiest hold the right from both.

KING JOHN. Then God forgive the sin of all
those souls
That to their everlasting residence,
Before the dew of evening fall shall fleet
In dreadful trial of our kingdom's king!

KING PHILIP. Amen, Amen! Mount, chevaliers;
to arms!

BASTARD. Saint George, that swing'd the dragon,
and e'er since
Sits on's horse back at mine hostess' door,
Teach us some fence! [To AUSTRIA] Sirrah, were
I at home,
At your den, sirrah, with your lioness,
I would set an ox-head to your lion's hide,
And make a monster of you.

AUSTRIA. Peace! no more.

BASTARD. O, tremble, for you hear the lion roar!

KING JOHN. Up higher to the plain, where we'll
set forth
In best appointment all our regiments.

BASTARD. Speed then to take advantage of
the field.

KING PHILIP. It shall be so; and at the other hill
Command the rest to stand. God and our right!

Exeunt.

Here, after excursions, enter the HERALD OF FRANCE, with
trumpets, to the gates

FRENCH HERALD. You men of Angiers, open
wide your gates
And let young Arthur, Duke of Britaine, in,
Who by the hand of France this day hath made
Much work for tears in many an
English mother,
Whose sons lie scattered on the
bleeding ground;
Many a widow's husband grovelling lies,
Coldly embracing the discoloured earth;
And victory with little loss doth play
Upon the dancing banners of the French,
Who are at hand, triumphantly displayed,
To enter conquerors, and to proclaim
Arthur of Britaine England's King and yours.

Enter ENGLISH HERALD, with trumpet

ENGLISH HERALD. Rejoice, you men of Angiers,
ring your bells:
King John, your king and England's,
doth approach,
Commander of this hot malicious day.

Their armours that march'd hence so silver-bright
Hither return all gilt with Frenchmen's blood.
There stuck no plume in any English crest
That is removed by a staff of France;
Our colours do return in those same hands
That did display them when we first
march'd forth;
And like a jolly troop of huntsmen come
Our lusty English, all with purpled hands,
Dy'd in the dying slaughter of their foes.
Open your gates and give the victors way.

CITIZEN. Heralds, from off our tow'rs we
might behold
From first to last the onset and retire
Of both your armies, whose equality
By our best eyes cannot be censured.
Blood hath bought blood, and blows have
answer'd blows;
Strength match'd with strength, and power
confronted power;
Both are alike, and both alike we like.
One must prove greatest. While they weigh
so even,
We hold our town for neither, yet for both.

Enter the two KINGS, with their powers, at
several doors

KING JOHN. France, hast thou yet more blood
to cast away?
Say, shall the current of our right run on?
Whose passage, vex'd with thy impediment,
Shall leave his native channel and o'erswell
With course disturb'd even thy confining shores,
Unless thou let his silver water keep
A peaceful progress to the ocean.

KING PHILIP. England, thou hast not sav'd one
drop of blood
In this hot trial more than we of France;
Rather, lost more. And by this hand I swear,
That sways the earth this climate overlooks,
Before we will lay down our just-borne arms,
We'll put thee down, 'gainst whom these arms
we bear,
Or add a royal number to the dead,
Gracing the scroll that tells of this war's loss
With slaughter coupled to the name of kings.

BASTARD. Ha, majesty! how high thy glory tow'rs
When the rich blood of kings is set on fire!
O, now doth Death line his dead chaps
with steel;
The swords of soldiers are his teeth, his fangs;
And now he feasts, mousing the flesh of men,
In undetermin'd differences of kings.
Why stand these royal fronts amazed thus?
Cry 'havoc!' Kings; back to the stained field,

You equal potents, fiery kindled spirits!
Then let confusion of one part confirm
The other's peace. Till then, blows, blood,
  and death!
KING JOHN. Whose party do the townsmen
  yet admit?
KING PHILIP. Speak, citizens, for England; who's
  your king?
CITIZEN. The King of England, when we know
  the King.
KING PHILIP. Know him in us that here hold up
  his right.
KING JOHN. In us that are our own great deputy
And bear possession of our person here,
Lord of our presence, Angiers, and of you.
CITIZEN. A greater pow'r than we denies all this;
And till it be undoubted, we do lock
Our former scruple in our strong-barr'd gates;
King'd of our fears, until our fears, resolv'd,
Be by some certain king purg'd and depos'd.
BASTARD. By heaven, these scroyles of Angiers
  flout you, Kings,
And stand securely on their battlements
As in a theatre, whence they gape and point
At your industrious scenes and acts of death
Your royal presences be rul'd by me:
Do like the mutines of Jerusalem,
Be friends awhile, and both conjointly bend
Your sharpest deeds of malice on this town.
By east and west let France and England mount
Their battering cannon, charged to the mouths,
Till their soul-fearing clamours have
  brawl'd down
The flinty ribs of this contemptuous city.
I'd play incessantly upon these jades,
Even till unfenced desolation
Leave them as naked as the vulgar air.
That done, dissever your united strengths
And part your mingled colours once again,
Turn face to face and bloody point to point;
Then in a moment Fortune shall cull forth
Out of one side her happy minion,
To whom in favour she shall give the day,
And kiss him with a glorious victory.
How like you this wild counsel, mighty states?
Smacks it not something of the policy?
KING JOHN. Now, by the sky that hangs above
  our heads,
I like it well. France, shall we knit our pow'rs
And lay this Angiers even with the ground;
Then after fight who shall be king of it?
BASTARD. An if thou hast the mettle of a king,
Being wrong'd as we are by this peevish town,
Turn thou the mouth of thy artillery,

As we will ours, against these saucy walls;
And when that we have dash'd them to
  the ground,
Why then defy each other, and pell-mell
Make work upon ourselves, for heaven or hell.
KING PHILIP. Let it be so. Say, where will
  you assault?
KING JOHN. We from the west will
  send destruction
Into this city's bosom.
AUSTRIA. I from the north.
KING PHILIP. Our thunder from the south
Shall rain their drift of bullets on this town.
BASTARD. [Aside] O prudent discipline! From
  north to south,
Austria and France shoot in each other's mouth.
I'll stir them to it.-Come, away, away!
CITIZEN. Hear us, great Kings: vouchsafe awhile
  to stay,
And I shall show you peace and fair-fac'd league;
Win you this city without stroke or wound;
Rescue those breathing lives to die in beds
That here come sacrifices for the field.
Persever not, but hear me, mighty Kings.
KING JOHN. Speak on with favour; we are
  bent to hear.
CITIZEN. That daughter there of Spain, the
  Lady Blanch,
Is niece to England; look upon the years
Of Lewis the Dauphin and that lovely maid.
If lusty love should go in quest of beauty,
Where should he find it fairer than in Blanch?
If zealous love should go in search of virtue,
Where should he find it purer than in Blanch?
If love ambitious sought a match of birth,
Whose veins bound richer blood than
  Lady Blanch?
Such as she is, in beauty, virtue, birth,
Is the young Dauphin every way complete-
If not complete of, say he is not she;
And she again wants nothing, to name want,
If want it be not that she is not he.
He is the half part of a blessed man,
Left to be finished by such as she;
And she a fair divided excellence,
Whose fulness of perfection lies in him.
O, two such silver currents, when they join,
Do glorify the banks that bound them in;
And two such shores to two such streams
  made one,
Two such controlling bounds, shall you
  be, Kings,
To these two princes, if you marry them.
This union shall do more than battery can

To our fast-closed gates; for at this match
With swifter spleen than powder can enforce,
The mouth of passage shall we fling wide ope
And give you entrance; but without this match,
The sea enraged is not half so deaf,
Lions more confident, mountains and rocks
More free from motion-no, not Death himself
In mortal fury half so peremptory
As we to keep this city.

BASTARD. Here's a stay
That shakes the rotten carcass of old Death
Out of his rags! Here's a large mouth, indeed,
That spits forth death and mountains, rocks
and seas;
Talks as familiarly of roaring lions
As maids of thirteen do of puppy-dogs!
What cannoneer begot this lusty blood?
He speaks plain cannon-fire, and smoke
and bounce;
He gives the bastinado with his tongue;
Our ears are cudgell'd; not a word of his
But buffets better than a fist of France.
Zounds! I was never so bethump'd with words
Since I first call'd my brother's father dad.

ELINOR. Son, list to this conjunction, make
this match;
Give with our niece a dowry large enough;
For by this knot thou shalt so surely tie
Thy now unsur'd assurance to the crown
That yon green boy shall have no sun to ripe
The bloom that promiseth a mighty fruit.
I see a yielding in the looks of France;
Mark how they whisper. Urge them while
their souls
Are capable of this ambition,
Lest zeal, now melted by the windy breath
Of soft petitions, pity, and remorse,
Cool and congeal again to what it was.

CITIZEN. Why answer not the double majesties
This friendly treaty of our threat'ned town?

KING PHILIP. Speak England first, that hath been
forward first
To speak unto this city: what say you?

KING JOHN. If that the Dauphin there, thy
princely son,
Can in this book of beauty read 'I love',
Her dowry shall weigh equal with a queen;
For Anjou, and fair Touraine, Maine, Poictiers,
And all that we upon this side the sea-
Except this city now by us besieg'd-
Find liable to our crown and dignity,
Shall gild her bridal bed, and make her rich
In titles, honours, and promotions,
As she in beauty, education, blood,

Holds hand with any princess of the world.

KING PHILIP. What say'st thou, boy? Look in the
lady's face.

LEWIS. I do, my lord, and in her eye I find
A wonder, or a wondrous miracle,
The shadow of myself form'd in her eye;
Which, being but the shadow of your son,
Becomes a sun, and makes your son a shadow.
I do protest I never lov'd myself
Till now infixed I beheld myself
Drawn in the flattering table of her eye.

Whispers with BLANCH

BASTARD. *[Aside]* Drawn in the flattering table
of her eye,
Hang'd in the frowning wrinkle of her brow,
And quarter'd in her heart-he doth espy
Himself love's traitor. This is pity now,
That hang'd and drawn and quarter'd there
should be
In such a love so vile a lout as he.

BLANCH. My uncle's will in this respect is mine.
If he see aught in you that makes him like,
That anything he sees which moves his liking
I can with ease translate it to my will;
Or if you will, to speak more properly,
I will enforce it eas'ly to my love.
Further I will not flatter you, my lord,
That all I see in you is worthy love,
Than this: that nothing do I see in you-
Though churlish thoughts themselves should be
your judge-
That I can find should merit any hate.

KING JOHN. What say these young ones? What say
you, my niece?

BLANCH. That she is bound in honour still to do
What you in wisdom still vouchsafe to say.

KING JOHN. Speak then, Prince Dauphin; can you
love this lady?

LEWIS. Nay, ask me if I can refrain from love;
For I do love her most unfeignedly.

KING JOHN. Then do I give Volquessen,
Touraine, Maine,
Poictiers, and Anjou, these five provinces,
With her to thee; and this addition more,
Full thirty thousand marks of English coin.
Philip of France, if thou be pleas'd withal,
Command thy son and daughter to join hands.

KING PHILIP. It likes us well; young princes, close
your hands.

AUSTRIA. And your lips too; for I am well assur'd
That I did so when I was first assur'd.

KING PHILIP. Now, citizens of Angiers, ope
your gates,
Let in that amity which you have made;

For at Saint Mary's chapel presently
The rites of marriage shall be solemnis'd.
Is not the Lady Constance in this troop?
I know she is not; for this match made up
Her presence would have interrupted much.
Where is she and her son? Tell me, who knows.

LEWIS. She is sad and passionate at your
  Highness' tent.

KING PHILIP. And, by my faith, this league that we
  have made
Will give her sadness very little cure.
Brother of England, how may we content
This widow lady? In her right we came;
Which we, God knows, have turn'd another way,
To our own vantage.

KING JOHN. We will heal up all,
  For we'll create young Arthur Duke of Britaine,
And Earl of Richmond; and this rich fair town
We make him lord of. Call the Lady Constance;
Some speedy messenger bid her repair
To our solemnity. I trust we shall,
If not fill up the measure of her will,
Yet in some measure satisfy her so
That we shall stop her exclamation.
Go we as well as haste will suffer us
To this unlook'd-for, unprepared pomp.

          Exeunt all but the BASTARD.

BASTARD. Mad world! mad kings!
  mad composition!
John, to stop Arthur's tide in the whole,
Hath willingly departed with a part;
And France, whose armour conscience
  buckled on,
Whom zeal and charity brought to the field
As God's own soldier, rounded in the ear
With that same purpose-changer, that sly devil,
That broker that still breaks the pate of faith,
That daily break-vow, he that wins of all,
Of kings, of beggars, old men, young
  men, maids,
Who having no external thing to lose
But the word 'maid', cheats the poor maid
  of that;
That smooth-fac'd gentleman,
  tickling commodity,
Commodity, the bias of the world-
The world, who of itself is peised well,
Made to run even upon even ground,
Till this advantage, this vile-drawing bias,
This sway of motion, this commodity,
Makes it take head from all indifferency,
From all direction, purpose, course, intent-
And this same bias, this commodity,
This bawd, this broker, this all-changing word,

Clapp'd on the outward eye of fickle France,
Hath drawn him from his own determin'd aid,
From a resolv'd and honourable war,
To a most base and vile-concluded peace.
And why rail I on this commodity?
But for because he hath not woo'd me yet;
Not that I have the power to clutch my hand
When his fair angels would salute my palm,
But for my hand, as unattempted yet,
Like a poor beggar raileth on the rich.
Well, whiles I am a beggar, I will rail
And say there is no sin but to be rich;
And being rich, my virtue then shall be
To say there is no vice but beggary.
Since kings break faith upon commodity,
Gain, be my lord, for I will worship thee.

                      Exit.

ACT III

✿ SCENE I ✿
France. The FRENCH KING'S camp

Enter CONSTANCE, ARTHUR,
and SALISBURY

CONSTANCE. Gone to be married! Gone to swear
  a peace!
False blood to false blood join'd! Gone to
  be friends!
Shall Lewis have Blanch, and Blanch
  those provinces?
It is not so; thou hast misspoke, misheard;
Be well advis'd, tell o'er thy tale again.
It cannot be; thou dost but say 'tis so;
I trust I may not trust thee, for thy word
Is but the vain breath of a common man:
Believe me I do not believe thee, man;
I have a king's oath to the contrary.
Thou shalt be punish'd for thus frighting me,
For I am sick and capable of fears,
Oppress'd with wrongs, and therefore full
  of fears;
A widow, husbandless, subject to fears;
A woman, naturally born to fears;
And though thou now confess thou didst
  but jest,
With my vex'd spirits I cannot take a truce,
But they will quake and tremble all this day.
What dost thou mean by shaking of thy head?
Why dost thou look so sadly on my son?
What means that hand upon that breast of thine?

Why holds thine eye that lamentable rheum,
Like a proud river peering o'er his bounds?
Be these sad signs confirmers of thy words?
Then speak again-not all thy former tale,
But this one word, whether thy tale be true.
SALISBURY. As true as I believe you think
    them false
That give you cause to prove my saying true.
CONSTANCE. O, if thou teach me to believe
    this sorrow,
Teach thou this sorrow how to make me die;
And let belief and life encounter so
As doth the fury of two desperate men
Which in the very meeting fall and die!
Lewis marry Blanch! O boy, then where art thou?
France friend with England; what becomes
    of me?
Fellow, be gone: I cannot brook thy sight;
This news hath made thee a most ugly man.
SALISBURY. What other harm have I, good
    lady, done
But spoke the harm that is by others done?
CONSTANCE. Which harm within itself so
    heinous is
As it makes harmful all that speak of it.
ARTHUR. I do beseech you, madam, be content.
CONSTANCE. If thou that bid'st me be content
    wert grim,
Ugly, and sland'rous to thy mother's womb,
Full of unpleasing blots and sightless stains,
Lame, foolish, crooked, swart, prodigious,
Patch'd with foul moles and eye-
    offending marks,
I would not care, I then would be content;
For then I should not love thee; no, nor thou
Become thy great birth, nor deserve a crown.
But thou art fair, and at thy birth, dear boy,
Nature and Fortune join'd to make thee great:
Of Nature's gifts thou mayst with lilies boast,
And with the half-blown rose; but Fortune, O!
She is corrupted, chang'd, and won from thee;
Sh' adulterates hourly with thine uncle John,
And with her golden hand hath pluck'd
    on France
To tread down fair respect of sovereignty,
And made his majesty the bawd to theirs.
France is a bawd to Fortune and King John-
That strumpet Fortune, that usurping John!
Tell me, thou fellow, is not France forsworn?
Envenom him with words, or get thee gone
And leave those woes alone which I alone
Am bound to under-bear.
SALISBURY. Pardon me, madam,
I may not go without you to the kings.

CONSTANCE. Thou mayst, thou shalt; I will not go
    with thee;
I will instruct my sorrows to be proud,
For grief is proud, and makes his owner stoop.
To me, and to the state of my great grief,
Let kings assemble; for my grief's so great
That no supporter but the huge firm earth
Can hold it up. *[Seats herself on the ground]* Here I and
    sorrows sit;
Here is my throne, bid kings come bow to it.
    Enter KING JOHN, KING PHILIP, LEWIS, BLANCH,
        ELINOR, the BASTARD, AUSTRIA,
            and Attendants
KING PHILIP. 'Tis true, fair daughter, and this
    blessed day
Ever in France shall be kept festival.
To solemnise this day the glorious sun
Stays in his course and plays the alchemist,
Turning with splendour of his precious eye
The meagre cloddy earth to glittering gold.
The yearly course that brings this day about
Shall never see it but a holiday.
CONSTANCE. *[Rising]* A wicked day, and not a
    holy day!
What hath this day deserv'd? what hath it done
That it in golden letters should be set
Among the high tides in the calendar?
Nay, rather turn this day out of the week,
This day of shame, oppression, perjury;
Or, if it must stand still, let wives with child
Pray that their burdens may not fall this day,
Lest that their hopes prodigiously be cross'd;
But on this day let seamen fear no wreck;
No bargains break that are not this day made;
This day, all things begun come to ill end,
Yea, faith itself to hollow falsehood change!
KING PHILIP. By heaven, lady, you shall have
    no cause
To curse the fair proceedings of this day.
Have I not pawn'd to you my majesty?
CONSTANCE. You have beguil'd me with
    a counterfeit
Resembling majesty, which, being touch'd
    and tried,
Proves valueless; you are forsworn, forsworn;
You came in arms to spill mine enemies' blood,
But now in arms you strengthen it with yours.
The grappling vigour and rough frown of war
Is cold in amity and painted peace,
And our oppression hath made up this league.
Arm, arm, you heavens, against these
    perjur'd kings!
A widow cries: Be husband to me, heavens!
Let not the hours of this ungodly day

Wear out the day in peace; but, ere sunset,
Set armed discord 'twixt these perjur'd kings!
Hear me, O, hear me!

AUSTRIA. Lady Constance, peace!

CONSTANCE. War! war! no peace! Peace is to me
a war.
O Lymoges! O Austria! thou dost shame
That bloody spoil. Thou slave, thou wretch,
thou coward!
Thou little valiant, great in villainy!
Thou ever strong upon the stronger side!
Thou Fortune's champion that dost never fight
But when her humorous ladyship is by
To teach thee safety! Thou art perjur'd too,
And sooth'st up greatness. What a fool art thou,
A ramping fool, to brag and stamp and swear
Upon my party! Thou cold-blooded slave,
Hast thou not spoke like thunder on my side,
Been sworn my soldier, bidding me depend
Upon thy stars, thy fortune, and thy strength,
And dost thou now fall over to my foes?
Thou wear a lion's hide! Doff it for shame,
And hang a calf's-skin on those recreant limbs.

AUSTRIA. O that a man should speak
those words
to me!

BASTARD. And hang a calf's-skin on those
recreant limbs.

AUSTRIA. Thou dar'st not say so, villain, for
thy life.

BASTARD. And hang a calf's-skin on those
recreant limbs.

KING JOHN. We like not this: thou dost
forget thyself.

Enter PANDULPH

KING PHILIP. Here comes the holy legate of
the Pope.

PANDULPH. Hail, you anointed deputies
of heaven!
To thee, King John, my holy errand is.
I Pandulph, of fair Milan cardinal,
And from Pope Innocent the legate here,
Do in his name religiously demand
Why thou against the Church, our holy mother,
So wilfully dost spurn; and force perforce
Keep Stephen Langton, chosen Archbishop
Of Canterbury, from that holy see?
This, in our foresaid holy father's name,
Pope Innocent, I do demand of thee.

KING JOHN. What earthly name
to interrogatories
Can task the free breath of a sacred king?
Thou canst not, Cardinal, devise a name
So slight, unworthy, and ridiculous,
To charge me to an answer, as the Pope.
Tell him this tale, and from the mouth
of England
Add thus much more, that no Italian priest
Shall tithe or toll in our dominions;
But as we under heaven are supreme head,
So, under Him that great supremacy,
Where we do reign we will alone uphold,
Without th' assistance of a mortal hand.
So tell the Pope, all reverence set apart
To him and his usurp'd authority.

KING PHILIP. Brother of England, you blaspheme
in this.

KING JOHN. Though you and all the kings
of Christendom
Are led so grossly by this meddling priest,
Dreading the curse that money may buy out,
And by the merit of vile gold, dross, dust,
Purchase corrupted pardon of a man,
Who in that sale sells pardon from himself-
Though you and all the rest, so grossly led,
This juggling witchcraft with revenue cherish;
Yet I alone, alone do me oppose
Against the Pope, and count his friends
my foes.

PANDULPH. Then by the lawful power that I have
Thou shalt stand curs'd and excommunicate;
And blessed shall he be that doth revolt
From his allegiance to an heretic;
And meritorious shall that hand be call'd,
Canonised, and worshipp'd as a saint,
That takes away by any secret course
Thy hateful life.

CONSTANCE. O, lawful let it be
That I have room with Rome to curse awhile!
Good father Cardinal, cry thou 'amen'
To my keen curses; for without my wrong
There is no tongue hath power to curse
him right.

PANDULPH. There's law and warrant, lady, for
my curse.

CONSTANCE. And for mine too; when law can do
no right,
Let it be lawful that law bar no wrong;
Law cannot give my child his kingdom here,
For he that holds his kingdom holds the law;
Therefore, since law itself is perfect wrong,
How can the law forbid my tongue to curse?

PANDULPH. Philip of France, on peril of a curse,
Let go the hand of that arch-heretic,
And raise the power of France upon his head,
Unless he do submit himself to Rome.

ELINOR. Look'st thou pale, France? Do not let go
thy hand.

CONSTANCE. Look to that, devil, lest that
    France repent
    And by disjoining hands hell lose a soul.
AUSTRIA. King Philip, listen to the Cardinal.
BASTARD. And hang a calf's-skin on his
    recreant limbs.
AUSTRIA. Well, ruffian, I must pocket up
    these wrongs,
    Because-
BASTARD. Your breeches best may carry them.
KING JOHN. Philip, what say'st thou to
    the Cardinal?
CONSTANCE. What should he say, but as
    the Cardinal?
LEWIS. Bethink you, father; for the difference
    Is purchase of a heavy curse from Rome
    Or the light loss of England for a friend.
    Forgo the easier.
BLANCH. That's the curse of Rome.
CONSTANCE. O Lewis, stand fast! The devil
    tempts thee here
    In likeness of a new untrimmed bride.
BLANCH. The Lady Constance speaks not from
    her faith,
    But from her need.
CONSTANCE. O, if thou grant my need,
    Which only lives but by the death of faith,
    That need must needs infer this principle-
    That faith would live again by death of need.
    O then, tread down my need, and faith
    mounts up:
    Keep my need up, and faith is trodden down!
KING JOHN. The King is mov'd, and answers not
    to this.
CONSTANCE. O be remov'd from him, and
    answer well!
AUSTRIA. Do so, King Philip; hang no more
    in doubt.
BASTARD. Hang nothing but a calf's-skin, most
    sweet lout.
KING PHILIP. I am perplex'd and know not what
    to say.
PANDULPH. What canst thou say but will perplex
    thee more,
    If thou stand excommunicate and curs'd?
KING PHILIP. Good reverend father, make my
    person yours,
    And tell me how you would bestow yourself.
    This royal hand and mine are newly knit,
    And the conjunction of our inward souls
    Married in league, coupled and link'd together
    With all religious strength of sacred vows;
    The latest breath that gave the sound of words
    Was deep-sworn faith, peace, amity, true love,
Between our kingdoms and our royal selves;
    And even before this truce, but new before,
    No longer than we well could wash our hands,
    To clap this royal bargain up of peace,
    Heaven knows, they were besmear'd
    and overstain'd
    With slaughter's pencil, where revenge did paint
    The fearful difference of incensed kings.
    And shall these hands, so lately purg'd of blood,
    So newly join'd in love, so strong in both,
    Unyoke this seizure and this kind regreet?
    Play fast and loose with faith? so jest
    with heaven,
    Make such unconstant children of ourselves,
    As now again to snatch our palm from palm,
    Unswear faith sworn, and on the marriage-bed
    Of smiling peace to march a bloody host,
    And make a riot on the gentle brow
    Of true sincerity? O, holy sir,
    My reverend father, let it not be so!
    Out of your grace, devise, ordain, impose,
    Some gentle order; and then we shall be blest
    To do your pleasure, and continue friends.
PANDULPH. All form is formless, order orderless,
    Save what is opposite to England's love.
    Therefore, to arms! be champion of our church,
    Or let the church, our mother, breathe
    her curse-
    A mother's curse-on her revolting son.
    France, thou mayst hold a serpent by
    the tongue,
    A chafed lion by the mortal paw,
    A fasting tiger safer by the tooth,
    Than keep in peace that hand which thou
    dost hold.
KING PHILIP. I may disjoin my hand, but not my
    faith.
PANDULPH. So mak'st thou faith an enemy
    to faith;
    And like. a civil war set'st oath to oath.
    Thy tongue against thy tongue. O, let thy vow
    First made to heaven, first be to
    heaven perform'd,
    That is, to be the champion of our Church.
    What since thou swor'st is sworn against thyself
    And may not be performed by thyself,
    For that which thou hast sworn to do amiss
    Is not amiss when it is truly done;
    And being not done, where doing tends to ill,
    The truth is then most done not doing it;
    The better act of purposes mistook
    Is to mistake again; though indirect,
    Yet indirection thereby grows direct,
    And falsehood cures, as fire cools fire

Within the scorched veins of one new-burn'd.
It is religion that doth make vows kept;
But thou hast sworn against religion
By what thou swear'st against the thing
  thou swear'st,
And mak'st an oath the surety for thy truth
Against an oath; the truth thou art unsure
To swear swears only not to be forsworn;
Else what a mockery should it be to swear!
But thou dost swear only to be forsworn;
And most forsworn to keep what thou
  dost swear.
Therefore thy later vows against thy first
Is in thyself rebellion to thyself;
And better conquest never canst thou make
Than arm thy constant and thy nobler parts
Against these giddy loose suggestions;
Upon which better part our pray'rs come in,
If thou vouchsafe them. But if not, then know
The peril of our curses fight on thee
So heavy as thou shalt not shake them off,
But in despair die under the black weight.
AUSTRIA. Rebellion, flat rebellion!
BASTARD. Will't not be?
Will not a calf's-skin stop that mouth of thine?
LEWIS. Father, to arms!
BLANCH. Upon thy wedding-day?
  Against the blood that thou hast married?
  What, shall our feast be kept with
    slaughtered men?
  Shall braying trumpets and loud
    churlish drums,
  Clamours of hell, be measures to our pomp?
  O husband, hear me! ay, alack, how new
  Is 'husband' in my mouth! even for that name,
  Which till this time my tongue did
    ne'er pronounce,
  Upon my knee I beg, go not to arms
  Against mine uncle.
CONSTANCE. O, upon my knee,
  Made hard with kneeling, I do pray to thee,
  Thou virtuous Dauphin, alter not the doom
  Forethought by heaven!
BLANCH. Now shall I see thy love. What
  motive may
  Be stronger with thee than the name of wife?
CONSTANCE. That which upholdeth him that
  thee upholds,
  His honour. O, thine honour, Lewis,
  thine honour!
LEWIS. I muse your Majesty doth seem so cold,
  When such profound respects do pull you on.
PANDULPH. I will denounce a curse upon
  his head.

KING PHILIP. Thou shalt not need. England, I
  will fall from thee.
CONSTANCE. O fair return of banish'd majesty!
ELINOR. O foul revolt of French inconstancy!
KING JOHN. France, thou shalt rue this hour
  within this hour.
BASTARD. Old Time the clock-setter, that bald
  sexton Time,
  Is it as he will? Well then, France shall rue.
BLANCH. The sun's o'ercast with blood. Fair
  day, adieu!
  Which is the side that I must go withal?
  I am with both: each army hath a hand;
  And in their rage, I having hold of both,
  They whirl asunder and dismember me.
  Husband, I cannot pray that thou mayst win;
  Uncle, I needs must pray that thou mayst lose;
  Father, I may not wish the fortune thine;
  Grandam, I will not wish thy wishes thrive.
  Whoever wins, on that side shall I lose:
  Assured loss before the match be play'd.
LEWIS. Lady, with me, with me thy fortune lies.
BLANCH. There where my fortune lives, there
  my life dies.
KING JOHN. Cousin, go draw our
  puissance together.

                  Exit BASTARD.
  France, I am burn'd up with inflaming wrath,
  A rage whose heat hath this condition
  That nothing can allay, nothing but blood,
  The blood, and dearest-valu'd blood, of France.
KING PHILIP. Thy rage shall burn thee up, and
  thou shalt turn
  To ashes, ere our blood shall quench that fire.
  Look to thyself, thou art in jeopardy.
KING JOHN. No more than he that threats. To
  arms let's hie!   *Exeunt severally.*

✲ SCENE II ✲

France. Plains near Angiers

Alarums, excursions. Enter the BASTARD with
AUSTRIA'S head

BASTARD. Now, by my life, this day grows
  wondrous hot;
  Some airy devil hovers in the sky
  And pours down mischief. Austria's head
  lie there,
  While Philip breathes.
    Enter KING JOHN, ARTHUR, and HUBERT
KING JOHN. Hubert, keep this boy. Philip,
  make up:

My mother is assailed in our tent,
And ta'en, I fear.
BASTARD. My lord, I rescued her;
Her Highness is in safety, fear you not;
But on, my liege, for very little pains
Will bring this labour to an happy end. *Exeunt.*

✿ SCENE III ✿

France. Plains near Angiers

*Alarums, excursions, retreat. Enter KING JOHN, ELINOR,
ARTHUR, the BASTARD, HUBERT,
and Lords*

KING JOHN. *[To ELINOR]* So shall it be; your
Grace shall stay behind,
So strongly guarded. *[To ARTHUR]* Cousin, look
not sad;
Thy grandam loves thee, and thy uncle will
As dear be to thee as thy father was.
ARTHUR. O, this will make my mother die
with grief!
KING JOHN. *[To the BASTARD]* Cousin, away for
England! haste before,
And, ere our coming, see thou shake the bags
Of hoarding abbots; imprisoned angels
Set at liberty; the fat ribs of peace
Must by the hungry now be fed upon.
Use our commission in his utmost force.
BASTARD. Bell, book, and candle, shall not drive
me back,
When gold and silver becks me to come on.
I leave your Highness. Grandam, I will pray,
If ever I remember to be holy,
For your fair safety. So, I kiss your hand.
ELINOR. Farewell, gentle cousin.
KING JOHN. Coz, farewell. *Exit BASTARD.*
ELINOR. Come hither, little kinsman; hark,
a word.
KING JOHN. Come hither, Hubert. O my
gentle Hubert,
We owe thee much! Within this wall of flesh
There is a soul counts thee her creditor,
And with advantage means to pay thy love;
And, my good friend, thy voluntary oath
Lives in this bosom, dearly cherished.
Give me thy hand. I had a thing to say-
But I will fit it with some better time.
By heaven, Hubert, I am almost asham'd
To say what good respect I have of thee.
HUBERT. I am much bounden to your Majesty.
KING JOHN. Good friend, thou hast no cause to
say so yet,

But thou shalt have; and creep time ne'er
so slow,
Yet it shall come for me to do thee good.
I had a thing to say-but let it go:
The sun is in the heaven, and the proud day,
Attended with the pleasures of the world,
Is all too wanton and too full of gawds
To give me audience. If the midnight bell
Did with his iron tongue and brazen mouth
Sound on into the drowsy race of night;
If this same were a churchyard where we stand,
And thou possessed with a thousand wrongs;
Or if that surly spirit, melancholy,
Had bak'd thy blood and made it heavy-thick,
Which else runs tickling up and down the veins,
Making that idiot, laughter, keep men's eyes
And strain their cheeks to idle merriment,
A passion hateful to my purposes;
Or if that thou couldst see me without eyes,
Hear me without thine ears, and make reply
Without a tongue, using conceit alone,
Without eyes, ears, and harmful sound of
words-
Then, in despite of brooded watchful day,
I would into thy bosom pour my thoughts.
But, ah, I will not! Yet I love thee well;
And, by my troth, I think thou lov'st me well.
HUBERT. So well that what you bid
me undertake,
Though that my death were adjunct to my act,
By heaven, I would do it.
KING JOHN. Do not I know thou wouldst?
Good Hubert, Hubert, Hubert, throw thine eye
On yon young boy. I'll tell thee what, my friend,
He is a very serpent in my way;
And wheresoe'er this foot of mine doth tread,
He lies before me. Dost thou understand me?
Thou art his keeper.
HUBERT. And I'll keep him so
That he shall not offend your Majesty.
KING JOHN. Death.
HUBERT. My lord?
KING JOHN. A grave.
HUBERT. He shall not live.
KING JOHN. Enough!
I could be merry now. Hubert, I love thee.
Well, I'll not say what I intend for thee.
Remember. Madam, fare you well;
I'll send those powers o'er to your Majesty.
ELINOR. My blessing go with thee!
KING JOHN. *[To ARTHUR]* For England,
cousin, go;
Hubert shall be your man, attend on you
With all true duty. On toward Calais, ho! *Exeunt.*

✿ SCENE IV ✿
France. The FRENCH KING'S camp

Enter KING PHILIP, LEWIS, PANDULPH,
and Attendants

KING PHILIP. So by a roaring tempest on
   the flood
   A whole armado of convicted sail
   Is scattered and disjoin'd from fellowship.
PANDULPH. Courage and comfort! All shall yet
   go well.
KING PHILIP. What can go well, when we have
   run so ill.
   Are we not beaten? Is not Angiers lost?
   Arthur ta'en prisoner? Divers dear friends slain?
   And bloody England into England gone,
   O'erbearing interruption, spite of France?
LEWIS. What he hath won, that hath he fortified;
   So hot a speed with such advice dispos'd,
   Such temperate order in so fierce a cause,
   Doth want example; who hath read or heard
   Of any kindred action like to this?
KING PHILIP. Well could I bear that England had
   this praise,
   So we could find some pattern of our shame.
      Enter CONSTANCE
   Look who comes here! a grave unto a soul;
   Holding th' eternal spirit, against her will,
   In the vile prison of afflicted breath.
   I prithee, lady, go away with me.
CONSTANCE. Lo now! now see the issue of
   your peace!
KING PHILIP. Patience, good lady! Comfort,
   gentle Constance!
CONSTANCE. No, I defy all counsel, all redress,
   But that which ends all counsel, true redress-
   Death, death; O amiable lovely death!
   Thou odoriferous stench! sound rottenness!
   Arise forth from the couch of lasting night,
   Thou hate and terror to prosperity,
   And I will kiss thy detestable bones,
   And put my eyeballs in thy vaulty brows,
   And ring these fingers with thy
   household worms,
   And stop this gap of breath with fulsome dust,
   And be a carrion monster like thyself.
   Come, grin on me, and I will think thou smil'st,
   And buss thee as thy wife. Misery's love,
   O, come to me!
KING PHILIP. O fair affliction, peace!
CONSTANCE. No, no, I will not, having breath to cry.

O that my tongue were in the thunder's mouth!
Then with a passion would I shake the world,
And rouse from sleep that fell anatomy
Which cannot hear a lady's feeble voice,
Which scorns a modern invocation.
PANDULPH. Lady, you utter madness and
   not sorrow.
CONSTANCE. Thou art not holy to belie me so.
   I am not mad: this hair I tear is mine;
   My name is Constance; I was Geffrey's wife;
   Young Arthur is my son, and he is lost.
   I am not mad-I would to heaven I were!
   For then 'tis like I should forget myself.
   O, if I could, what grief should I forget!
   Preach some philosophy to make me mad,
   And thou shalt be canonis'd, Cardinal;
   For, being not mad, but sensible of grief,
   My reasonable part produces reason
   How I may be deliver'd of these woes,
   And teaches me to kill or hang myself.
   If I were mad I should forget my son,
   Or madly think a babe of clouts were he.
   I am not mad; too well, too well I feel
   The different plague of each calamity.
KING PHILIP. Bind up those tresses. O, what love
   I note
   In the fair multitude of those her hairs!
   Where but by a chance a silver drop hath fall'n,
   Even to that drop ten thousand wiry friends
   Do glue themselves in sociable grief,
   Like true, inseparable, faithful loves,
   Sticking together in calamity.
CONSTANCE. To England, if you will.
KING PHILIP. Bind up your hairs.
CONSTANCE. Yes, that I will; and wherefore will
   I do it?
   I tore them from their bonds, and cried aloud
   'O that these hands could so redeem my son,
   As they have given these hairs their liberty!'
   But now I envy at their liberty,
   And will again commit them to their bonds,
   Because my poor child is a prisoner.
   And, father Cardinal, I have heard you say
   That we shall see and know our friends
   in heaven;
   If that be true, I shall see my boy again;
   For since the birth of Cain, the first male child,
   To him that did but yesterday suspire,
   There was not such a gracious creature born.
   But now will canker sorrow eat my bud
   And chase the native beauty from his cheek,
   And he will look as hollow as a ghost,
   As dim and meagre as an ague's fit;
   And so he'll die; and, rising so again,

When I shall meet him in the court of heaven
I shall not know him. Therefore never, never
Must I behold my pretty Arthur more.
PANDULPH. You hold too heinous a respect
  of grief.
CONSTANCE. He talks to me that never had
  a son.
KING PHILIP. You are as fond of grief as of
  your child.
CONSTANCE. Grief fills the room up of my
  absent child,
Lies in his bed, walks up and down with me,
Puts on his pretty looks, repeats his words,
Remembers me of all his gracious parts,
Stuffs out his vacant garments with his form;
Then have I reason to be fond of grief.
Fare you well; had you such a loss as I,
I could give better comfort than you do.
I will not keep this form upon my head, [Tearing
  her hair]
When there is such disorder in my wit.
O Lord! my boy, my Arthur, my fair son!
My life, my joy, my food, my all the world!
My widow-comfort, and my sorrows' cure! Exit.
KING PHILIP. I fear some outrage, and I'll
  follow her.
                                        Exit.
LEWIS. There's nothing in this world can make
  me joy.
Life is as tedious as a twice-told tale
Vexing the dull ear of a drowsy man;
And bitter shame hath spoil'd the sweet
  world's taste,
That it yields nought but shame and bitterness.
PANDULPH. Before the curing of a strong disease,
Even in the instant of repair and health,
The fit is strongest; evils that take leave
On their departure most of all show evil;
What have you lost by losing of this day?
LEWIS. All days of glory, joy, and happiness.
PANDULPH. If you had won it, certainly you had.
No, no; when Fortune means to men most good,
She looks upon them with a threat'ning eye.
'Tis strange to think how much King John
  hath lost
In this which he accounts so clearly won.
Are not you griev'd that Arthur is his prisoner?
LEWIS. As heartily as he is glad he hath him.
PANDULPH. Your mind is all as youthful as
  your blood.
Now hear me speak with a prophetic spirit;
For even the breath of what I mean to speak
Shall blow each dust, each straw, each little rub,
Out of the path which shall directly lead

Thy foot to England's throne. And
  therefore mark:
John hath seiz'd Arthur; and it cannot be
That, whiles warm life plays in that infant's veins,
The misplac'd John should entertain an hour,
One minute, nay, one quiet breath of rest.
A sceptre snatch'd with an unruly hand
Must be boisterously maintain'd as gain'd,
And he that stands upon a slipp'ry place
Makes nice of no vile hold to stay him up;
That John may stand then, Arthur needs
  must fall;
So be it, for it cannot be but so.
LEWIS. But what shall I gain by young Arthur's fall?
PANDULPH. You, in the right of Lady Blanch
  your wife,
May then make all the claim that Arthur did.
LEWIS. And lose it, life and all, as Arthur did.
PANDULPH. How green you are and fresh in this
  old world!
John lays you plots; the times conspire with you;
For he that steeps his safety in true blood
Shall find but bloody safety and untrue.
This act, so evilly borne, shall cool the hearts
Of all his people and freeze up their zeal,
That none so small advantage shall step forth
To check his reign but they will cherish it;
No natural exhalation in the sky,
No scope of nature, no distemper'd day,
No common wind, no customed event,
But they will pluck away his natural cause
And call them meteors, prodigies, and signs,
Abortives, presages, and tongues of heaven,
Plainly denouncing vengeance upon John.
LEWIS. May be he will not touch young
  Arthur's life,
But hold himself safe in his prisonment.
PANDULPH. O, sir, when he shall hear of
  your approach,
If that young Arthur be not gone already,
Even at that news he dies; and then the hearts
Of all his people shall revolt from him,
And kiss the lips of unacquainted change,
And pick strong matter of revolt and wrath
Out of the bloody fingers' ends of John.
Methinks I see this hurly all on foot;
And, O, what better matter breeds for you
Than I have nam'd! The bastard Faulconbridge
Is now in England ransacking the Church,
Offending charity; if but a dozen French
Were there in arms, they would be as a can
To train ten thousand English to their side;
Or as a little snow, tumbled about,
Anon becomes a mountain. O noble Dauphin,

Go with me to the King. 'Tis wonderful
What may be wrought out of their discontent,
Now that their souls are topful of offence.
For England go; I will whet on the King.
LEWIS. Strong reasons makes strong actions. Let
us go;
If you say ay, the King will not say no.*Exeunt.*

ACT IV

SCENE I
England. A castle

Enter HUBERT and EXECUTIONERS

HUBERT. Heat me these irons hot; and look
thou stand
Within the arras. When I strike my foot
Upon the bosom of the ground, rush forth
And bind the boy which you shall find with me
Fast to the chair. Be heedful; hence, and watch.
EXECUTIONER. I hope your warrant will bear out
the deed.
HUBERT. Uncleanly scruples! Fear not you.
Look to't.

Exeunt EXECUTIONERS.

Young lad, come forth; I have to say with you.

Enter ARTHUR

ARTHUR. Good morrow, Hubert.
HUBERT. Good morrow, little Prince.
ARTHUR. As little prince, having so great a tide
To be more prince, as may be. You are sad.
HUBERT. Indeed I have been merrier.
ARTHUR. Mercy on me!
Methinks no body should be sad but I;
Yet, I remember, when I was in France,
Young gentlemen would be as sad as night,
Only for wantonness. By my christendom,
So I were out of prison and kept sheep,
I should be as merry as the day is long;
And so I would be here but that I doubt
My uncle practises more harm to me;
He is afraid of me, and I of him.
Is it my fault that I was Geffrey's son?
No, indeed, ist not; and I would to heaven
I were your son, so you would love me, Hubert.
HUBERT. *[Aside]* If I talk to him, with his
innocent prate
He will awake my mercy, which lies dead;
Therefore I will be sudden and dispatch.
ARTHUR. Are you sick, Hubert? You look pale
to-day;

In sooth, I would you were a little sick,
That I might sit all night and watch with you.
I warrant I love you more than you do me.
HUBERT. *[Aside]* His words do take possession of
my bosom.-
Read here, young Arthur. *[Showing a paper]*
[Aside] How now, foolish rheum!
Turning dispiteous torture out of door!
I must be brief, lest resolution drop
Out at mine eyes in tender womanish tears.-
Can you not read it? Is it not fair writ?
ARTHUR. Too fairly, Hubert, for so foul effect.
Must you with hot irons burn out both
mine eyes?
HUBERT. Young boy, I must.
ARTHUR. And will you?
HUBERT. And I will.
ARTHUR. Have you the heart? When your head
did but ache,
I knit my handkerchief about your brows-
The best I had, a princess wrought it me-
And I did never ask it you again;
And with my hand at midnight held your head;
And, like the watchful minutes to the hour,
Still and anon cheer'd up the heavy time,
Saying 'What lack you?' and 'Where lies
your grief?'
Or 'What good love may I perform for you?'
Many a poor man's son would have lyen still,
And ne'er have spoke a loving word to you;
But you at your sick service had a prince.
Nay, you may think my love was crafty love,
And call it cunning. Do, an if you will.
If heaven be pleas'd that you must use me ill,
Why, then you must. Will you put out mine eyes,
These eyes that never did nor never shall
So much as frown on you?
HUBERT. I have sworn to do it;
And with hot irons must I burn them out.
ARTHUR. Ah, none but in this iron age would
do it!
The iron of itself, though heat red-hot,
Approaching near these eyes would drink
my tears,
And quench his fiery indignation
Even in the matter of mine innocence;
Nay, after that, consume away in rust
But for containing fire to harm mine eye.
Are you more stubborn-hard than
hammer'd iron?
An if an angel should have come to me
And told me Hubert should put out mine eyes,
I would not have believ'd him-no tongue
but Hubert's.

HUBERT. *[Stamps]* Come forth.
   Re-enter EXECUTIONERS, with cord, irons, etc.
Do as I bid you do.
ARTHUR. O, save me, Hubert, save me! My eyes
  are out
Even with the fierce looks of these bloody men.
HUBERT. Give me the iron, I say, and bind
  him here.
ARTHUR. Alas, what need you be so
  boist'rous rough?
I will not struggle, I will stand stone-still.
For heaven sake, Hubert, let me not be bound!
Nay, hear me, Hubert! Drive these men away,
And I will sit as quiet as a lamb;
I will not stir, nor wince, nor speak a word,
Nor look upon the iron angrily;
Thrust but these men away, and I'll
  forgive you,
Whatever torment you do put me to.
HUBERT. Go, stand within; let me alone
  with him.
EXECUTIONER. I am best pleas'd to be from
  such a deed. *Exeunt EXECUTIONERS.*
ARTHUR. Alas, I then have chid away my friend!
He hath a stern look but a gentle heart.
Let him come back, that his compassion may
Give life to yours.
HUBERT. Come, boy, prepare yourself.
ARTHUR. Is there no remedy?
HUBERT. None, but to lose your eyes.
ARTHUR. O heaven, that there were but a mote
  in yours,
A grain, a dust, a gnat, a wandering hair,
Any annoyance in that precious sense!
Then, feeling what small things are
  boisterous there,
Your vile intent must needs seem horrible.
HUBERT. Is this your promise? Go to, hold
  your tongue.
ARTHUR. Hubert, the utterance of a brace
  of tongues
Must needs want pleading for a pair of eyes.
Let me not hold my tongue, let me not, Hubert;
Or, Hubert, if you will, cut out my tongue,
So I may keep mine eyes. O, spare mine eyes,
Though to no use but still to look on you!
Lo, by my troth, the instrument is cold
And would not harm me.
HUBERT. I can heat it, boy.
ARTHUR. No, in good sooth; the fire is dead
  with grief,
Being create for comfort, to be us'd
In undeserved extremes. See else yourself:
There is no malice in this burning coal;

The breath of heaven hath blown his spirit out,
And strew'd repentant ashes on his head.
HUBERT. But with my breath I can revive it, boy.
ARTHUR. An if you do, you will but make it blush
And glow with shame of your
  proceedings, Hubert.
Nay, it perchance will sparkle in your eyes,
And, like a dog that is compell'd to fight,
Snatch at his master that doth tarre him on.
All things that you should use to do me wrong
Deny their office; only you do lack
That mercy which fierce fire and iron extends,
Creatures of note for mercy-lacking uses.
HUBERT. Well, see to live; I will not touch
  thine eye
For all the treasure that thine uncle owes.
Yet I am sworn, and I did purpose, boy,
With this same very iron to burn them out.
ARTHUR. O, now you look like Hubert! All
  this while
You were disguis'd.
HUBERT. Peace; no more. Adieu.
Your uncle must not know but you are dead:
I'll fill these dogged spies with false reports;
And, pretty child, sleep doubtless and secure
That Hubert, for the wealth of all the world,
Will not offend thee.
ARTHUR. O heaven! I thank you, Hubert.
HUBERT. Silence; no more. Go closely in
  with me.
Much danger do I undergo for thee. *Exeunt.*

✣ SCENE II ✣
England. KING JOHN'S palace

Enter KING JOHN, PEMBROKE, SALISBURY, and other
LORDS

KING JOHN. Here once again we sit, once
  again crown'd,
And look'd upon, I hope, with cheerful eyes.
PEMBROKE. This once again, but that your
  Highness pleas'd,
Was once superfluous: you were crown'd before,
And that high royalty was ne'er pluck'd off,
The faiths of men ne'er stained with revolt;
Fresh expectation troubled not the land
With any long'd-for change or better state.
SALISBURY. Therefore, to be possess'd with
  double pomp,
To guard a title that was rich before,
To gild refined gold, to paint the lily,
To throw a perfume on the violet,

To smooth the ice, or add another hue
Unto the rainbow, or with taper-light
To seek the beauteous eye of heaven
  to garnish,
Is wasteful and ridiculous excess.
PEMBROKE. But that your royal pleasure must
  be done,
This act is as an ancient tale new told
And, in the last repeating, troublesome,
Being urged at a time unseasonable.
SALISBURY. In this the antique and well-
  noted face
Of plain old form is much disfigured;
And like a shifted wind unto a sail
It makes the course of thoughts to fetch about,
Startles and frights consideration,
Makes sound opinion sick, and truth suspected,
For putting on so new a fashion'd robe.
PEMBROKE. When workmen strive to do better
  than well,
They do confound their skill in covetousness;
And oftentimes excusing of a fault
Doth make the fault the worse by th' excuse,
As patches set upon a little breach
Discredit more in hiding of the fault
Than did the fault before it was so patch'd.
SALISBURY. To this effect, before you were
  new-crown'd,
We breath'd our counsel; but it pleas'd
  your Highness
To overbear it; and we are all well pleas'd,
Since all and every part of what we would
Doth make a stand at what your Highness will.
KING JOHN. Some reasons of this
  double coronation
I have possess'd you with, and think them strong;
And more, more strong, when lesser is my fear,
I shall indue you with. Meantime but ask
What you would have reform'd that is not well,
And well shall you perceive how willingly
I will both hear and grant you your requests.
PEMBROKE. Then I, as one that am the tongue
  of these,
To sound the purposes of all their hearts,
Both for myself and them-but, chief of all,
Your safety, for the which myself and them
Bend their best studies, heartily request
Th' enfranchisement of Arthur, whose restraint
Doth move the murmuring lips of discontent
To break into this dangerous argument:
If what in rest you have in right you hold,
Why then your fears-which, as they say, attend
The steps of wrong-should move you to
  mew up

Your tender kinsman, and to choke his days
With barbarous ignorance, and deny his youth
The rich advantage of good exercise?
That the time's enemies may not have this
To grace occasions, let it be our suit
That you have bid us ask his liberty;
Which for our goods we do no further ask
Than whereupon our weal, on you depending,
Counts it your weal he have his liberty.
KING JOHN. Let it be so. I do commit his youth
To your direction.

Enter HUBERT

[*Aside*] Hubert, what news with you?
PEMBROKE. This is the man should do the
  bloody deed:
He show'd his warrant to a friend of mine;
The image of a wicked heinous fault
Lives in his eye; that close aspect of his
Doth show the mood of a much
  troubled breast,
And I do fearfully believe 'tis done
What we so fear'd he had a charge to do.
SALISBURY. The colour of the King doth come
  and go
Between his purpose and his conscience,
Like heralds 'twixt two dreadful battles set.
His passion is so ripe it needs must break.
PEMBROKE. And when it breaks, I fear will
  issue thence
The foul corruption of a sweet child's death.
KING JOHN. We cannot hold mortality's
  strong hand.
Good lords, although my will to give is living,
The suit which you demand is gone
  and dead:
He tells us Arthur is deceas'd to-night.
SALISBURY. Indeed, we fear'd his sickness was
  past cure.
PEMBROKE. Indeed, we heard how near his
  death he was,
Before the child himself felt he was sick.
This must be answer'd either here or hence.
KING JOHN. Why do you bend such solemn
  brows on me?
Think you I bear the shears of destiny?
Have I commandment on the pulse of life?
SALISBURY. It is apparent foul-play; and
  'tis shame
That greatness should so grossly offer it.
So thrive it in your game! and so, farewell.
PEMBROKE. Stay yet, Lord Salisbury, I'll go
  with thee
And find th' inheritance of this poor child,
His little kingdom of a forced grave.

That blood which ow'd the breadth of all
  this isle
Three foot of it doth hold-bad world the while!
This must not be thus borne: this will break out
To all our sorrows, and ere long I doubt.

Exeunt LORDS.

KING JOHN. They burn in indignation. I repent.
There is no sure foundation set on blood,
No certain life achiev'd by others' death.

Enter a MESSENGER

A fearful eye thou hast; where is that blood
That I have seen inhabit in those cheeks?
So foul a sky clears not without a storm.
Pour down thy weather-how goes all in France?
MESSENGER. From France to England. Never
  such a pow'r
For any foreign preparation
Was levied in the body of a land.
The copy of your speed is learn'd by them,
For when you should be told they do prepare,
The tidings comes that they are all arriv'd.
KING JOHN. O, where hath our intelligence
  been drunk?
Where hath it slept? Where is my
  mother's care,
That such an army could be drawn in France,
And she not hear of it?
MESSENGER. My liege, her ear
Is stopp'd with dust: the first of April died
Your noble mother; and as I hear, my lord,
The Lady Constance in a frenzy died
Three days before; but this from
  rumour's tongue
I idly heard-if true or false I know not.
KING JOHN. Withhold thy speed,
  dreadful occasion!
O, make a league with me, till I have pleas'd
My discontented peers! What! mother dead!
How wildly then walks my estate in France!
Under whose conduct came those pow'rs
  of France
That thou for truth giv'st out are landed here?
MESSENGER. Under the Dauphin.
KING JOHN. Thou hast made me giddy
With these ill tidings.

Enter the BASTARD and PETER OF POMFRET

Now! What says the world
To your proceedings? Do not seek to stuff
My head with more ill news, for it is full.
BASTARD. But if you be afear'd to hear the worst,
Then let the worst, unheard, fall on your head.
KING JOHN. Bear with me, cousin, for I
  was amaz'd
Under the tide; but now I breathe again

Aloft the flood, and can give audience
To any tongue, speak it of what it will.
BASTARD. How I have sped among
  the clergymen
The sums I have collected shall express.
But as I travell'd hither through the land,
I find the people strangely fantasied;
Possess'd with rumours, full of idle dreams.
Not knowing what they fear, but full of fear;
And here's a prophet that I brought with me
From forth the streets of Pomfret, whom
  I found
With many hundreds treading on his heels;
To whom he sung, in rude harsh-
  sounding rhymes,
That, ere the next Ascension-day at noon,
Your Highness should deliver up your crown.
KING JOHN. Thou idle dreamer, wherefore didst
  thou so?
PETER. Foreknowing that the truth will fall
  out so.
KING JOHN. Hubert, away with him;
  imprison him;
And on that day at noon whereon he says
I shall yield up my crown let him be hang'd.
Deliver him to safety; and return,
For I must use thee.

Exit HUBERT with PETER.

O my gentle cousin,
Hear'st thou the news abroad, who are arriv'd?
BASTARD. The French, my lord; men's mouths
  are full of it;
Besides, I met Lord Bigot and Lord Salisbury,
With eyes as red as new-enkindled fire,
And others more, going to seek the grave
Of Arthur, whom they say is kill'd to-night
On your suggestion.
KING JOHN. Gentle kinsman, go
And thrust thyself into their companies.
I have a way to will their loves again;
Bring them before me.
BASTARD. I will seek them out.
KING JOHN. Nay, but make haste; the better
  foot before.
O, let me have no subject enemies
When adverse foreigners affright my towns
With dreadful pomp of stout invasion!
Be Mercury, set feathers to thy heels,
And fly like thought from them to me again.
BASTARD. The spirit of the time shall teach
  me speed.
KING JOHN. Spoke like a sprightful
  noble gentleman. *Exit BASTARD.*
Go after him; for he perhaps shall need

Some messenger betwixt me and the peers;
And be thou he.

MESSENGER. With all my heart, my liege. *Exit.*

KING JOHN. My mother dead!

Re-enter HUBERT

HUBERT. My lord, they say five moons were seen
  to-night;
  Four fixed, and the fifth did whirl about
  The other four in wondrous motion.

KING JOHN. Five moons!

HUBERT. Old men and beldams in the streets
  Do prophesy upon it dangerously;
  Young Arthur's death is common in
    their mouths;
  And when they talk of him, they shake
    their heads,
  And whisper one another in the ear;
  And he that speaks doth gripe the
    hearer's wrist,
  Whilst he that hears makes fearful action
  With wrinkled brows, with nods, with
    rolling eyes.
  I saw a smith stand with his hammer, thus,
  The whilst his iron did on the anvil cool,
  With open mouth swallowing a tailor's news;
  Who, with his shears and measure in his hand,
  Standing on slippers, which his nimble haste
  Had falsely thrust upon contrary feet,
  Told of a many thousand warlike French
  That were embattailed and rank'd in Kent.
  Another lean unwash'd artificer
  Cuts off his tale, and talks of Arthur's death.

KING JOHN. Why seek'st thou to possess me
  with these fears?
  Why urgest thou so oft young Arthur's death?
  Thy hand hath murd'red him. I had a
    mighty cause
  To wish him dead, but thou hadst none to
    kill him.

HUBERT. No had, my lord! Why, did you not
  provoke me?

KING JOHN. It is the curse of kings to
  be attended
  By slaves that take their humours for a warrant
  To break within the bloody house of life,
  And on the winking of authority
  To understand a law; to know the meaning
  Of dangerous majesty, when perchance
    it frowns
  More upon humour than advis'd respect.

HUBERT. Here is your hand and seal for what I
  did.

KING JOHN. O, when the last account 'twixt
  heaven and earth

Is to be made, then shall this hand and seal
Witness against us to damnation!
How oft the sight of means to do ill deeds
Make deeds ill done! Hadst not thou been by,
A fellow by the hand of nature mark'd,
Quoted and sign'd to do a deed of shame,
This murder had not come into my mind;
But, taking note of thy abhorr'd aspect,
Finding thee fit for bloody villainy,
Apt, liable to be employ'd in danger,
I faintly broke with thee of Arthur's death;
And thou, to be endeared to a king,
Made it no conscience to destroy a prince.

HUBERT. My lord-

KING JOHN. Hadst thou but shook thy head or
  made pause,
  When I spake darkly what I purposed,
  Or turn'd an eye of doubt upon my face,
  As bid me tell my tale in express words,
  Deep shame had struck me dumb, made me
    break off,
  And those thy fears might have wrought fears
    in me.
  But thou didst understand me by my signs,
  And didst in signs again parley with sin;
  Yea, without stop, didst let thy heart consent,
  And consequently thy rude hand to act
  The deed which both our tongues held vile
    to name.
  Out of my sight, and never see me more!
  My nobles leave me; and my state is braved,
  Even at my gates, with ranks of foreign pow'rs;
  Nay, in the body of the fleshly land,
  This kingdom, this confine of blood and breath,
  Hostility and civil tumult reigns
  Between my conscience and my cousin's death.

HUBERT. Arm you against your other enemies,
  I'll make a peace between your soul and you.
  Young Arthur is alive. This hand of mine
  Is yet a maiden and an innocent hand,
  Not painted with the crimson spots of blood.
  Within this bosom never ent'red yet
  The dreadful motion of a murderous thought
  And you have slander'd nature in my form,
  Which, howsoever rude exteriorly,
  Is yet the cover of a fairer mind
  Than to be butcher of an innocent child.

KING JOHN. Doth Arthur live? O, haste thee
  to the peers,
  Throw this report on their incensed rage
  And make them tame to their obedience!
  Forgive the comment that my passion made
  Upon thy feature; for my rage was blind,
  And foul imaginary eyes of blood

Presented thee more hideous than thou art.
O, answer not; but to my closet bring
The angry lords with all expedient haste.
I conjure thee but slowly; run more fast. *Exeunt.*

⚜ SCENE III ⚜

England. Before the castle

Enter ARTHUR, on the walls

ARTHUR. The wall is high, and yet will I
  leap down.
  Good ground, be pitiful and hurt me not!
  There's few or none do know me; if they did,
  This ship-boy's semblance hath disguis'd
  me quite.
  I am afraid; and yet I'll venture it.
  If I get down and do not break my limbs,
  I'll find a thousand shifts to get away.
  As good to die and go, as die and stay.
  [Leaps down]
  O me! my uncle's spirit is in these stones.
  Heaven take my soul, and England keep
  my bones!
                                    Dies.

Enter PEMBROKE, SALISBURY, and BIGOT

SALISBURY. Lords, I will meet him at
  Saint Edmundsbury;
  It is our safety, and we must embrace
  This gentle offer of the perilous time.
PEMBROKE. Who brought that letter from
  the Cardinal?
SALISBURY. The Count Melun, a noble lord
  of France,
  Whose private with me of the Dauphin's love
  Is much more general than these lines import.
BIGOT. To-morrow morning let us meet
  him then.
SALISBURY. Or rather then set forward; for
  'twill be
  Two long days' journey, lords, or ere we meet.

Enter the BASTARD

BASTARD. Once more to-day well met,
  distemper'd lords!
  The King by me requests your
  presence straight.
SALISBURY. The King hath dispossess'd himself
  of us.
  We will not line his thin bestained cloak
  With our pure honours, nor attend the foot
  That leaves the print of blood where'er
  it walks.
  Return and tell him so. We know the worst.

BASTARD. Whate'er you think, good words, I
  think, were best.
SALISBURY. Our griefs, and not our manners,
  reason now.
BASTARD. But there is little reason in your grief;
  Therefore 'twere reason you had
  manners now.
PEMBROKE. Sir, sir, impatience hath
  his privilege.
BASTARD. 'Tis true-to hurt his master, no
  man else.
SALISBURY. This is the prison. What is he
  lies here?
PEMBROKE. O death, made proud with pure
  and princely beauty!
  The earth had not a hole to hide this deed.
SALISBURY. Murder, as hating what himself
  hath done,
  Doth lay it open to urge on revenge.
BIGOT. Or, when he doom'd this beauty to
  a grave,
  Found it too precious-princely for a grave.
SALISBURY. Sir Richard, what think you? Have
  you beheld,
  Or have you read or heard, or could
  you think?
  Or do you almost think, although you see,
  That you do see? Could thought, without
  this object,
  Form such another? This is the very top,
  The height, the crest, or crest unto the crest,
  Of murder's arms; this is the bloodiest shame,
  The wildest savagery, the vilest stroke,
  That ever wall-ey'd wrath or staring rage
  Presented to the tears of soft remorse.
PEMBROKE. All murders past do stand excus'd
  in this;
  And this, so sole and so unmatchable,
  Shall give a holiness, a purity,
  To the yet unbegotten sin of times,
  And prove a deadly bloodshed but a jest,
  Exampled by this heinous spectacle.
BASTARD. It is a damned and a bloody work;
  The graceless action of a heavy hand,
  If that it be the work of any hand.
SALISBURY. If that it be the work of any hand!
  We had a kind of light what would ensue.
  It is the shameful work of Hubert's hand;
  The practice and the purpose of the King;
  From whose obedience I forbid my soul
  Kneeling before this ruin of sweet life,
  And breathing to his breathless excellence
  The incense of a vow, a holy vow,
  Never to taste the pleasures of the world,

Never to be infected with delight,
Nor conversant with ease and idleness,
Till I have set a glory to this hand
By giving it the worship of revenge.

PEMBROKE and BIGOT. Our souls religiously
confirm thy words.

Enter HUBERT

HUBERT. Lords, I am hot with haste in
seeking you.
Arthur doth live; the King hath sent for you.

SALISBURY. O, he is bold, and blushes not
at death!
Avaunt, thou hateful villain, get thee gone!

HUBERT. I am no villain.

SALISBURY. Must I rob the law?*Drawing his sword*

BASTARD. Your sword is bright, sir; put it
up again.

SALISBURY. Not till I sheathe it in a
murderer's skin.

HUBERT. Stand back, Lord Salisbury, stand back,
I say;
By heaven, I think my sword's as sharp
as yours.
I would not have you, lord, forget yourself,
Nor tempt the danger of my true defence;
Lest I, by marking of your rage, forget
Your worth, your greatness and nobility.

BIGOT. Out, dunghill! Dar'st thou brave
a nobleman?

HUBERT. Not for my life; but yet I dare defend
My innocent life against an emperor.

SALISBURY. Thou art a murderer.

HUBERT. Do not prove me so.
Yet I am none. Whose tongue soe'er
speaks false,
Not truly speaks; who speaks not truly, lies.

PEMBROKE. Cut him to pieces.

BASTARD. Keep the peace, I say.

SALISBURY. Stand by, or I shall gall
you, Faulconbridge.

BASTARD. Thou wert better gall the
devil, Salisbury.
If thou but frown on me, or stir thy foot,
Or teach thy hasty spleen to do me shame,
I'll strike thee dead. Put up thy sword betime;
Or I'll so maul you and your toasting-iron
That you shall think the devil is come
from hell.

BIGOT. What wilt thou do,
renowned Faulconbridge?
Second a villain and a murderer?

HUBERT. Lord Bigot, I am none.

BIGOT. Who kill'd this prince?

HUBERT. 'Tis not an hour since I left him well.
I honour'd him, I lov'd him, and will weep
My date of life out for his sweet life's loss.

SALISBURY. Trust not those cunning waters of
his eyes,
For villainy is not without such rheum;
And he, long traded in it, makes it seem
Like rivers of remorse and innocency.
Away with me, all you whose souls abhor
Th' uncleanly savours of a slaughter-house;
For I am stifled with this smell of sin.

BIGOT. Away toward Bury, to the
Dauphin there!

PEMBROKE. There tell the King he may inquire
us out.   *Exeunt LORDS*

BASTARD. Here's a good world! Knew you of
this fair work?
Beyond the infinite and boundless reach
Of mercy, if thou didst this deed of death,
Art thou damn'd, Hubert.

HUBERT. Do but hear me, sir.

BASTARD. Ha! I'll tell thee what:
Thou'rt damn'd as black-nay, nothing is
so black-
Thou art more deep damn'd than
Prince Lucifer;
There is not yet so ugly a fiend of hell
As thou shalt be, if thou didst kill this child.

HUBERT. Upon my soul-

BASTARD. If thou didst but consent
To this most cruel act, do but despair;
And if thou want'st a cord, the smallest thread
That ever spider twisted from her womb
Will serve to strangle thee; a rush will be
a beam
To hang thee on; or wouldst thou
drown thyself,
Put but a little water in a spoon
And it shall be as all the ocean,
Enough to stifle such a villain up
I do suspect thee very grievously.

HUBERT. If I in act, consent, or sin of thought,
Be guilty of the stealing that sweet breath
Which was embounded in this beauteous clay,
Let hell want pains enough to torture me!
I left him well.

BASTARD. Go, bear him in thine arms.
I am amaz'd, methinks, and lose my way
Among the thorns and dangers of this world.
How easy dost thou take all England up!
From forth this morsel of dead royalty
The life, the right, and truth of all this realm
Is fled to heaven; and England now is left

To tug and scamble, and to part by th' teeth
The unowed interest of proud-swelling state.
Now for the bare-pick'd bone of majesty
Doth dogged war bristle his angry crest
And snarleth in the gentle eyes of peace;
Now powers from home and discontents
  at home
Meet in one line; and vast confusion waits,
As doth a raven on a sick-fall'n beast,
The imminent decay of wrested pomp.
Now happy he whose cloak and cincture can
Hold out this tempest. Bear away that child,
And follow me with speed. I'll to the King;
A thousand businesses are brief in hand,
And heaven itself doth frown upon the land.

Exeunt.

✑ ACT V ✑

✿ SCENE I ✿
England. KING JOHN'S palace

Enter KING JOHN, PANDULPH,
and Attendants

KING JOHN. Thus have I yielded up into
  your hand
  The circle of my glory.
PANDULPH. *[Gives back the crown]* Take again
  From this my hand, as holding of the Pope,
  Your sovereign greatness and authority.
KING JOHN. Now keep your holy word; go meet
  the French;
  And from his Holiness use all your power
  To stop their marches fore we are inflam'd.
  Our discontented counties do revolt;
  Our people quarrel with obedience,
  Swearing allegiance and the love of soul
  To stranger blood, to foreign royalty.
  This inundation of mistemp'red humour
  Rests by you only to be qualified.
  Then pause not; for the present time's so sick
  That present med'cine must be minist'red
  Or overthrow incurable ensues.
PANDULPH. It was my breath that blew this
  tempest up,
  Upon your stubborn usage of the Pope;
  But since you are a gentle convertite,
  My tongue shall hush again this storm of war
  And make fair weather in your blust'ring land.
  On this Ascension-day, remember well,

Upon your oath of service to the Pope,
Go I to make the French lay down their arms.
  Exit.
KING JOHN. Is this Ascension-day? Did not
  the prophet
  Say that before Ascension-day at noon
  My crown I should give off? Even so I have.
  I did suppose it should be on constraint;
  But, heaven be thank'd, it is but voluntary.

Enter the BASTARD

BASTARD. All Kent hath yielded; nothing there
  holds out
  But Dover Castle. London hath receiv'd,
  Like a kind host, the Dauphin and his powers.
  Your nobles will not hear you, but are gone
  To offer service to your enemy;
  And wild amazement hurries up and down
  The little number of your doubtful friends.
KING JOHN. Would not my lords return to
  me again
  After they heard young Arthur was alive?
BASTARD. They found him dead, and cast into
  the streets,
  An empty casket, where the jewel of life
  By some damn'd hand was robbed and
  ta'en away.
KING JOHN. That villain Hubert told me he
  did live.
BASTARD. So, on my soul, he did, for aught
  he knew.
  But wherefore do you droop? Why look you sad?
  Be great in act, as you have been in thought;
  Let not the world see fear and sad distrust
  Govern the motion of a kingly eye.
  Be stirring as the time; be fire with fire;
  Threaten the threat'ner, and outface the brow
  Of bragging horror; so shall inferior eyes,
  That borrow their behaviours from the great,
  Grow great by your example and put on
  The dauntless spirit of resolution.
  Away, and glister like the god of war
  When he intendeth to become the field;
  Show boldness and aspiring confidence.
  What, shall they seek the lion in his den,
  And fright him there, and make him
  tremble there?
  O, let it not be said! Forage, and run
  To meet displeasure farther from the doors
  And grapple with him ere he come so nigh.
KING JOHN. The legate of the Pope hath been
  with me,
  And I have made a happy peace with him;
  And he hath promis'd to dismiss the powers

Led by the Dauphin.
BASTARD. O inglorious league!
Shall we, upon the footing of our land,
Send fair-play orders, and make compromise,
Insinuation, parley, and base truce,
To arms invasive? Shall a beardless boy,
A cock'red silken wanton, brave our fields
And flesh his spirit in a warlike soil,
Mocking the air with colours idly spread,
And find no check? Let us, my liege, to arms.
Perchance the Cardinal cannot make your peace;
Or, if he do, let it at least be said
They saw we had a purpose of defence.
KING JOHN. Have thou the ordering of this
present time.
BASTARD. Away, then, with good courage!
Yet, I know
Our party may well meet a prouder foe. *Exeunt.*

⚜ SCENE II ⚜
England. The DAUPHIN'S camp at Saint
Edmundsbury

Enter, in arms, LEWIS, SALISBURY, MELUN,
PEMBROKE, BIGOT, and Soldiers

LEWIS. My Lord Melun, let this be copied out
And keep it safe for our remembrance;
Return the precedent to these lords again,
That, having our fair order written down,
Both they and we, perusing o'er these notes,
May know wherefore we took the sacrament,
And keep our faiths firm and inviolable.
SALISBURY. Upon our sides it never shall be broken.
And, noble Dauphin, albeit we swear
A voluntary zeal and an unurg'd faith
To your proceedings; yet, believe me, Prince,
I am not glad that such a sore of time
Should seek a plaster by contemn'd revolt,
And heal the inveterate canker of one wound
By making many. O, it grieves my soul
That I must draw this metal from my side
To be a widow-maker! O, and there
Where honourable rescue and defence
Cries out upon the name of Salisbury!
But such is the infection of the time
That, for the health and physic of our right,
We cannot deal but with the very hand
Of stern injustice and confused wrong.
And is't not pity, O my grieved friends!
That we, the sons and children of this isle,
Were born to see so sad an hour as this;
Wherein we step after a stranger-march

Upon her gentle bosom, and fill up
Her enemies' ranks-I must withdraw and weep
Upon the spot of this enforced cause-
To grace the gentry of a land remote
And follow unacquainted colours here?
What, here? O nation, that thou couldst remove!
That Neptune's arms, who clippeth thee about,
Would bear thee from the knowledge of thyself
And grapple thee unto a pagan shore,
Where these two Christian armies
might combine
The blood of malice in a vein of league,
And not to spend it so unneighbourly!
LEWIS. A noble temper dost thou show in this;
And great affections wrestling in thy bosom
Doth make an earthquake of nobility.
O, what a noble combat hast thou fought
Between compulsion and a brave respect!
Let me wipe off this honourable dew
That silverly doth progress on thy cheeks.
My heart hath melted at a lady's tears,
Being an ordinary inundation;
But this effusion of such manly drops,
This show'r, blown up by tempest of the soul,
Startles mine eyes and makes me more amaz'd
Than had I seen the vaulty top of heaven
Figur'd quite o'er with burning meteors.
Lift up thy brow, renowned Salisbury,
And with a great heart heave away this storm;
Commend these waters to those baby eyes
That never saw the giant world enrag'd,
Nor met with fortune other than at feasts,
Full of warm blood, of mirth, of gossiping.
Come, come; for thou shalt thrust thy hand
as deep
Into the purse of rich prosperity
As Lewis himself. So, nobles, shall you all,
That knit your sinews to the strength of mine.
Enter PANDULPH
And even there, methinks, an angel spake:
Look where the holy legate comes apace,
To give us warrant from the hand of heaven
And on our actions set the name of right
With holy breath.
PANDULPH. Hail, noble prince of France!
The next is this: King John hath reconcil'd
Himself to Rome; his spirit is come in,
That so stood out against the holy Church,
The great metropolis and see of Rome.
Therefore thy threat'ning colours now wind up
And tame the savage spirit of wild war,
That, like a lion fostered up at hand,
It may lie gently at the foot of peace
And be no further harmful than in show.

LEWIS. Your Grace shall pardon me, I will
  not back:
  I am too high-born to be propertied,
  To be a secondary at control,
  Or useful serving-man and instrument
  To any sovereign state throughout the world.
  Your breath first kindled the dead coal of wars
  Between this chastis'd kingdom and myself
  And brought in matter that should feed this fire;
  And now 'tis far too huge to be blown out
  With that same weak wind which enkindled it.
  You taught me how to know the face of right,
  Acquainted me with interest to this land,
  Yea, thrust this enterprise into my heart;
  And come ye now to tell me John hath made
  His peace with Rome? What is that peace to me?
  I, by the honour of my marriage-bed,
  After young Arthur, claim this land for mine;
  And, now it is half-conquer'd, must I back
  Because that John hath made his peace
  with Rome?
  Am I Rome's slave? What penny hath
  Rome borne,
  What men provided, what munition sent,
  To underprop this action? Is 't not I
  That undergo this charge? Who else but I,
  And such as to my claim are liable,
  Sweat in this business and maintain this war?
  Have I not heard these islanders shout out
  'Vive le roi!' as I have bank'd their towns?
  Have I not here the best cards for the game
  To will this easy match, play'd for a crown?
  And shall I now give o'er the yielded set?
  No, no, on my soul, it never shall be said.
PANDULPH. You look but on the outside of
  this work.
LEWIS. Outside or inside, I will not return
  Till my attempt so much be glorified
  As to my ample hope was promised
  Before I drew this gallant head of war,
  And cull'd these fiery spirits from the world
  To outlook conquest, and to will renown
  Even in the jaws of danger and of death.
      [Trumpet sounds]
  What lusty trumpet thus doth summon us?
      Enter the BASTARD, attended
BASTARD. According to the fair play of the world,
  Let me have audience: I am sent to speak.
  My holy lord of Milan, from the King
  I come, to learn how you have dealt for him;
  And, as you answer, I do know the scope
  And warrant limited unto my tongue.
PANDULPH. The Dauphin is too wilful-opposite,
  And will not temporise with my entreaties;

He flatly says he'll not lay down his arms.
BASTARD. By all the blood that ever fury breath'd,
  The youth says well. Now hear our English King;
  For thus his royalty doth speak in me.
  He is prepar'd, and reason too he should.
  This apish and unmannerly approach,
  This harness'd masque and unadvised revel
  This unhair'd sauciness and boyish troops,
  The King doth smile at; and is well prepar'd
  To whip this dwarfish war, these pigmy arms,
  From out the circle of his territories.
  That hand which had the strength, even at
  your door.
  To cudgel you and make you take the hatch,
  To dive like buckets in concealed wells,
  To crouch in litter of your stable planks,
  To lie like pawns lock'd up in chests and trunks,
  To hug with swine, to seek sweet safety out
  In vaults and prisons, and to thrill and shake
  Even at the crying of your nation's crow,
  Thinking this voice an armed Englishman-
  Shall that victorious hand be feebled here
  That in your chambers gave you chastisement?
  No. Know the gallant monarch is in arms
  And like an eagle o'er his aery tow'rs
  To souse annoyance that comes near his nest.
  And you degenerate, you ingrate revolts,
  You bloody Neroes, ripping up the womb
  Of your dear mother England, blush for shame;
  For your own ladies and pale-visag'd maids,
  Like Amazons, come tripping after drums,
  Their thimbles into armed gauntlets change,
  Their needles to lances, and their gentle hearts
  To fierce and bloody inclination.
LEWIS. There end thy brave, and turn thy face
  in peace;
  We grant thou canst outscold us. Fare thee well;
  We hold our time too precious to be spent
  With such a brabbler.
PANDULPH. Give me leave to speak.
BASTARD. No, I will speak.
LEWIS. We will attend to neither.
  Strike up the drums; and let the tongue of war,
  Plead for our interest and our being here.
BASTARD. Indeed, your drums, being beaten, will
  cry out;
  And so shall you, being beaten. Do but start
  And echo with the clamour of thy drum,
  And even at hand a drum is ready brac'd
  That shall reverberate all as loud as thine:
  Sound but another, and another shall,
  As loud as thine, rattle the welkin's ear
  And mock the deep-mouth'd thunder; for
  at hand-

Not trusting to this halting legate here,
Whom he hath us'd rather for sport than need-
Is warlike John; and in his forehead sits
A bare-ribb'd death, whose office is this day
To feast upon whole thousands of the French.
LEWIS. Strike up our drums to find this
danger out.
BASTARD. And thou shalt find it, Dauphin, do
not doubt.   *Exeunt.*

✤ SCENE III ✤
England. The field of battle

Alarums. Enter KING JOHN and HUBERT

KING JOHN. How goes the day with us? O, tell
me, Hubert.
HUBERT. Badly, I fear. How fares your Majesty?
KING JOHN. This fever that hath troubled me
so long
Lies heavy on me. O, my heart is sick!
Enter a MESSENGER
MESSENGER. My lord, your valiant
kinsman, Faulconbridge,
Desires your Majesty to leave the field
And send him word by me which way you go.
KING JOHN. Tell him, toward Swinstead, to the
abbey there.
MESSENGER. Be of good comfort; for the
great supply
That was expected by the Dauphin here
Are wreck'd three nights ago on Goodwin Sands;
This news was brought to Richard but even now.
The French fight coldly, and retire themselves.
KING JOHN. Ay me, this tyrant fever burns me up
And will not let me welcome this good news.
Set on toward Swinstead; to my litter straight;
Weakness possesseth me, and I am faint.*Exeunt.*

✤ SCENE IV ✤
England. Another part of the battlefield

Enter SALISBURY, PEMBROKE, and BIGOT

SALISBURY. I did not think the King so stor'd
with friends.
PEMBROKE. Up once again; put spirit in
the French;
If they miscarry, we miscarry too.
SALISBURY. That misbegotten
devil, Faulconbridge,

In spite of spite, alone upholds the day.
PEMBROKE. They say King John, sore sick, hath
left the field.
Enter MELUN, wounded
MELUN. Lead me to the revolts of England here.
SALISBURY. When we were happy we had
other names.
PEMBROKE. It is the Count Melun.
SALISBURY. Wounded to death.
MELUN. Fly, noble English, you are bought
and sold;
Unthread the rude eye of rebellion,
And welcome home again discarded faith.
Seek out King John, and fall before his feet;
For if the French be lords of this loud day,
He means to recompense the pains you take
By cutting off your heads. Thus hath he sworn,
And I with him, and many moe with me,
Upon the altar at Saint Edmundsbury;
Even on that altar where we swore to you
Dear amity and everlasting love.
SALISBURY. May this be possible? May this
be true?
MELUN. Have I not hideous death within
my view,
Retaining but a quantity of life,
Which bleeds away even as a form of wax
Resolveth from his figure 'gainst the fire?
What in the world should make me
now deceive,
Since I must lose the use of all deceit?
Why should I then be false, since it is true
That I must die here, and live hence by truth?
I say again, if Lewis do will the day,
He is forsworn if e'er those eyes of yours
Behold another day break in the east;
But even this night, whose black
contagious breath
Already smokes about the burning crest
Of the old, feeble, and day-wearied sun,
Even this ill night, your breathing shall expire,
Paying the fine of rated treachery
Even with a treacherous fine of all your lives.
If Lewis by your assistance win the day.
Commend me to one Hubert, with your King;
The love of him-and this respect besides-
For that my grandsire was an Englishman-
Awakes my conscience to confess all this.
In lieu whereof, I pray you, bear me hence
From forth the noise and rumour of the field,
Where I may think the remnant of my thoughts
In peace, and part this body and my soul
With contemplation and devout desires.

SALISBURY. We do believe thee; and beshrew
  my soul
But I do love the favour and the form
Of this most fair occasion, by the which
We will untread the steps of damned flight,
And like a bated and retired flood,
Leaving our rankness and irregular course,
Stoop low within those bounds we
  have o'erlook'd,
And calmly run on in obedience
Even to our ocean, to great King John.
My arm shall give thee help to bear thee hence;
For I do see the cruel pangs of death
Right in thine eye. Away, my friends! New flight,
And happy newness, that intends old right.
            Exeunt, leading off MELUN.

⚜ SCENE V ⚜
England. The French camp

Enter LEWIS and his train

LEWIS. The sun of heaven, methought, was loath
  to set,
But stay'd and made the western welkin blush,
When English measure backward their
  own ground
In faint retire. O, bravely came we off,
When with a volley of our needless shot,
After such bloody toil, we bid good night;
And wound our tott'ring colours clearly up,
Last in the field and almost lords of it!
          Enter a MESSENGER
MESSENGER. Where is my prince, the Dauphin?
LEWIS. Here; what news?
MESSENGER. The Count Melun is slain; the
  English lords
By his persuasion are again fall'n off,
And your supply, which you have wish'd so long,
Are cast away and sunk on Goodwin Sands.
LEWIS. Ah, foul shrewd news! Beshrew thy
  very heart!
I did not think to be so sad to-night
As this hath made me. Who was he that said
King John did fly an hour or two before
The stumbling night did part our weary pow'rs?
MESSENGER. Whoever spoke it, it is true, my lord.
LEWIS. Well, keep good quarter and good care
  to-night;
The day shall not be up so soon as I
To try the fair adventure of to-morrow.
                   Exeunt.

⚜ SCENE VI ⚜
An open place wear Swinstead Abbey

Enter the BASTARD and HUBERT, severally

HUBERT. Who's there? Speak, ho! speak quickly,
  or I shoot.
BASTARD. A friend. What art thou?
HUBERT. Of the part of England.
BASTARD. Whither dost thou go?
HUBERT. What's that to thee? Why may I
  not demand
Of thine affairs as well as thou of mine?
BASTARD. Hubert, I think.
HUBERT. Thou hast a perfect thought.
I will upon all hazards well believe
Thou art my friend that know'st my tongue
  so well.
Who art thou?
BASTARD. Who thou wilt. And if thou please,
Thou mayst befriend me so much as to think
I come one way of the Plantagenets.
HUBERT. Unkind remembrance! thou and
  eyeless night
Have done me shame. Brave soldier, pardon me
That any accent breaking from thy tongue
Should scape the true acquaintance of mine ear.
BASTARD. Come, come; sans compliment, what
  news abroad?
HUBERT. Why, here walk I in the black brow
  of night
To find you out.
BASTARD. Brief, then; and what's the news?
HUBERT. O, my sweet sir, news fitting to
  the night,
Black, fearful, comfortless, and horrible.
BASTARD. Show me the very wound of this
  ill news;
I am no woman, I'll not swoon at it.
HUBERT. The King, I fear, is poison'd by a monk;
I left him almost speechless and broke out
To acquaint you with this evil, that you might
The better arm you to the sudden time
Than if you had at leisure known of this.
BASTARD. How did he take it; who did taste
  to him?
HUBERT. A monk, I tell you; a resolved villain,
Whose bowels suddenly burst out. The King
Yet speaks, and peradventure may recover.
BASTARD. Who didst thou leave to tend his
  Majesty?

HUBERT. Why, know you not? The lords are all
  come back,
And brought Prince Henry in their company;
At whose request the King hath pardon'd them,
And they are all about his Majesty.
BASTARD. Withhold thine indignation,
  mighty heaven,
And tempt us not to bear above our power!
I'll tell thee, Hubert, half my power this night,
Passing these flats, are taken by the tide-
These Lincoln Washes have devoured them;
Myself, well-mounted, hardly have escap'd.
Away, before! conduct me to the King;
I doubt he will be dead or ere I come. *Exeunt.*

⚜ SCENE VII ⚜

The orchard at Swinstead Abbey

Enter PRINCE HENRY, SALISBURY, and BIGOT

PRINCE HENRY. It is too late; the life of all
  his blood
Is touch'd corruptibly, and his pure brain.
Which some suppose the soul's frail dwelling-
  house,
Doth by the idle comments that it makes
Foretell the ending of mortality.
          Enter PEMBROKE
PEMBROKE. His Highness yet doth speak, and
  holds belief
That, being brought into the open air,
It would allay the burning quality
Of that fell poison which assaileth him.
PRINCE HENRY. Let him be brought into the
  orchard here.
Doth he still rage?   *Exit BIGOT*
PEMBROKE. He is more patient
Than when you left him; even now he sung.
PRINCE HENRY. O vanity of sickness!
  Fierce extremes
In their continuance will not feel themselves.
Death, having prey'd upon the outward parts,
Leaves them invisible, and his siege is now
Against the mind, the which he pricks
  and wounds
With many legions of strange fantasies,
Which, in their throng and press to that
  last hold,
Confound themselves. 'Tis strange that death
  should sing.
I am the cygnet to this pale faint swan
Who chants a doleful hymn to his own death,

And from the organ-pipe of frailty sings
His soul and body to their lasting rest.
SALISBURY. Be of good comfort, Prince; for you
  are born
To set a form upon that indigest
Which he hath left so shapeless and so rude.
    Re-enter BIGOT and Attendants, who bring in
         KING JOHN in a chair
KING JOHN. Ay, marry, now my soul hath elbow-
  room;
It would not out at windows nor at doors.
There is so hot a summer in my bosom
That all my bowels crumble up to dust.
I am a scribbled form drawn with a pen
Upon a parchment, and against this fire
Do I shrink up.
PRINCE HENRY. How fares your Majesty?
KING JOHN. Poison'd-ill-fare! Dead, forsook,
  cast off;
And none of you will bid the winter come
To thrust his icy fingers in my maw,
Nor let my kingdom's rivers take their course
Through my burn'd bosom, nor entreat
  the north
To make his bleak winds kiss my parched lips
And comfort me with cold. I do not ask
  you much;
I beg cold comfort; and you are so strait
And so ingrateful you deny me that.
PRINCE HENRY. O that there were some virtue in
  my tears,
That might relieve you!
KING JOHN. The salt in them is hot.
Within me is a hell; and there the poison
Is as a fiend confin'd to tyrannise
On unreprievable condemned blood.
         Enter the BASTARD
BASTARD. O, I am scalded with my violent motion
And spleen of speed to see your Majesty!
KING JOHN. O cousin, thou art come to set
  mine eye!
The tackle of my heart is crack'd and burnt,
And all the shrouds wherewith my life
  should sail
Are turned to one thread, one little hair;
My heart hath one poor string to stay it by,
Which holds but till thy news be uttered;
And then all this thou seest is but a clod
And module of confounded royalty.
BASTARD. The Dauphin is preparing hitherward,
Where God He knows how we shall answer him;
For in a night the best part of my pow'r,
As I upon advantage did remove,

Were in the Washes all unwarily
Devoured by the unexpected flood.

The KING dies.

SALISBURY. You breathe these dead news in as
dead an ear.
My liege! my lord! But now a king—now thus.
PRINCE HENRY. Even so must I run on, and even
so stop.
What surety of the world, what hope, what stay,
When this was now a king, and now is clay?
BASTARD. Art thou gone so? I do but stay behind
To do the office for thee of revenge,
And then my soul shall wait on thee to heaven,
As it on earth hath been thy servant still.
Now, now, you stars that move in your
right spheres,
Where be your pow'rs? Show now your
mended faiths,
And instantly return with me again
To push destruction and perpetual shame
Out of the weak door of our fainting land.
Straight let us seek, or straight we shall
be sought;
The Dauphin rages at our very heels.
SALISBURY. It seems you know not, then, so
much as we:
The Cardinal Pandulph is within at rest,
Who half an hour since came from
the Dauphin,
And brings from him such offers of our peace
As we with honour and respect may take,
With purpose presently to leave this war.
BASTARD. He will the rather do it when he sees
Ourselves well sinewed to our defence.
SALISBURY. Nay, 'tis in a manner done already;
For many carriages he hath dispatch'd
To the sea-side, and put his cause and quarrel
To the disposing of the Cardinal;
With whom yourself, myself, and other lords,
If you think meet, this afternoon will post
To consummate this business happily.
BASTARD. Let it be so. And you, my noble Prince,
With other princes that may best be spar'd,
Shall wait upon your father's funeral.
PRINCE HENRY. At Worcester must his body
be interr'd;
For so he will'd it.
BASTARD. Thither shall it, then;
And happily may your sweet self put on
The lineal state and glory of the land!
To whom, with all submission, on my knee
I do bequeath my faithful services
And true subjection everlastingly.

SALISBURY. And the like tender of our love
we make,
To rest without a spot for evermore.
PRINCE HENRY. I have a kind soul that would give
you thanks,
And knows not how to do it but with tears.
BASTARD. O, let us pay the time but needful woe,
Since it hath been beforehand with our griefs.
This England never did, nor never shall,
Lie at the proud foot of a conqueror,
But when it first did help to wound itself.
Now these her princes are come home again,
Come the three corners of the world in arms,
And we shall shock them. Nought shall make
us rue,
If England to itself do rest but true.

Exeunt.

The End

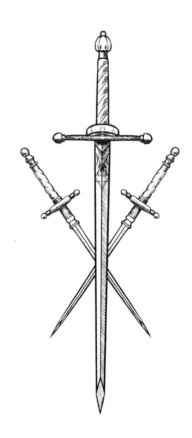

1594

King Richard II

Dramatis Personae

KING RICHARD THE SECOND
JOHN OF GAUNT, Duke of Lancaster-
uncle to the King
DUKE OF YORK (Edmund Langley)-
uncle to the King
HENRY, surnamed BOLINGBROKE, Duke
of Hereford, son of John of Gaunt, afterwards
King Henry IV
DUKE OF AUMERLE, son of the Duke of York
THOMAS MOWBRAY, Duke of Norfolk
DUKE OF SURREY
EARL OF SALISBURY
EARL BERKELEY

Favourites of King Richard:
BUSHY, BAGO, GREEN

EARL OF NORTHUMBERLAND
HENRY PERCY, surnamed HOTSPUR, his son
LORD ROSS
LORD WILLOUGHBY
LORD FITZWATER BISHOP OF CARLISLE
ABBOT OF WESTMINSTER
LORD MARSHAL
SIR STEPHEN SCROOP
SIR PIERCE OF EXTON
CAPTAIN of a band of Welshmen
TWO GARDENERS

QUEEN to King Richard
DUCHESS OF YORK
DUCHESS OF GLOUCESTER, widow
of Thomas of Woodstock, Duke
of Gloucester
LADY attending on the Queen

Lords, Heralds, Officers, Soldiers, Keeper,
Messenger, Groom, and other Attendants

SCENE
England and Wales

ACT I

SCENE I
London. The palace

*Enter RICHARD, JOHN OF GAUNT, with other NOBLES
and Attendants*

KING RICHARD. Old John of Gaunt, time-
honoured Lancaster,
Hast thou, according to thy oath and band,
Brought hither Henry Hereford, thy bold son,
Here to make good the boist'rous late appeal,
Which then our leisure would not let us hear,
Against the Duke of Norfolk, Thomas Mowbray?
GAUNT. I have, my liege.
KING RICHARD. Tell me, moreover, hast thou
sounded him
If he appeal the Duke on ancient malice,
Or worthily, as a good subject should,
On some known ground of treachery in him?
GAUNT. As near as I could sift him on
that argument,
On some apparent danger seen in him
Aim'd at your Highness-no inveterate malice.
KING RICHARD. Then call them to our presence:
face to face
And frowning brow to brow, ourselves will hear
The accuser and the accused freely speak.
High-stomach'd are they both and full of ire,
In rage, deaf as the sea, hasty as fire.
Enter BOLINGBROKE and MOWBRAY
BOLINGBROKE. Many years of happy days befall
My gracious sovereign, my most loving liege!
MOWBRAY. Each day still better
other's happiness
Until the heavens, envying earth's good hap,
Add an immortal title to your crown!
KING RICHARD. We thank you both; yet one but
flatters us,
As well appeareth by the cause you come;
Namely, to appeal each other of high treason.
Cousin of Hereford, what dost thou object
Against the Duke of Norfolk, Thomas Mowbray?

BOLINGBROKE. First-heaven be the record to
 my speech!
In the devotion of a subject's love,
Tend'ring the precious safety of my prince,
And free from other misbegotten hate,
Come I appellant to this princely presence.
Now, Thomas Mowbray, do I turn to thee,
And mark my greeting well; for what I speak
My body shall make good upon this earth,
Or my divine soul answer it in heaven-
Thou art a traitor and a miscreant,
Too good to be so, and too bad to live,
Since the more fair and crystal is the sky,
The uglier seem the clouds that in it fly.
Once more, the more to aggravate the note,
With a foul traitor's name stuff I thy throat;
And wish-so please my sovereign-ere I move,
What my tongue speaks, my right drawn sword
 may prove.
MOWBRAY. Let not my cold words here accuse
 my zeal.
'Tis not the trial of a woman's war,
The bitter clamour of two eager tongues,
Can arbitrate this cause betwixt us twain;
The blood is hot that must be cool'd for this.
Yet can I not of such tame patience boast
As to be hush'd and nought at all to say.
First, the fair reverence of your Highness
 curbs me
From giving reins and spurs to my free speech;
Which else would post until it had return'd
These terms of treason doubled down
 his throat.
Setting aside his high blood's royalty,
And let him be no kinsman to my liege,
I do defy him, and I spit at him,
Call him a slanderous coward and a villain;
Which to maintain, I would allow him odds
And meet him, were I tied to run afoot
Even to the frozen ridges of the Alps,
Or any other ground inhabitable
Where ever Englishman durst set his foot.
Meantime let this defend my loyalty-
By all my hopes, most falsely doth he lie
BOLINGBROKE. Pale trembling coward, there I
 throw my gage,
Disclaiming here the kindred of the King;
And lay aside my high blood's royalty,
Which fear, not reverence, makes thee
 to except.
If guilty dread have left thee so much strength
As to take up mine honour's pawn, then stoop.
By that and all the rites of knighthood else

Will I make good against thee, arm to arm,
What I have spoke or thou canst worst devise.
MOWBRAY. I take it up; and by that sword
 I swear
Which gently laid my knighthood on
 my shoulder
I'll answer thee in any fair degree
Or chivalrous design of knightly trial;
And when I mount, alive may I not light
If I be traitor or unjustly fight!
KING RICHARD. What doth our cousin lay to
 Mowbray's charge?
It must be great that can inherit us
So much as of a thought of ill in him.
BOLINGBROKE. Look what I speak, my life shall
 prove it true-
That Mowbray hath receiv'd eight
 thousand nobles
In name of lendings for your Highness' soldiers,
The which he hath detain'd for
 lewd employments
Like a false traitor and injurious villain.
Besides, I say and will in battle prove-
Or here, or elsewhere to the furthest verge
That ever was survey'd by English eye-
That all the treasons for these eighteen years
Complotted and contrived in this land
Fetch from false Mowbray their first head
 and spring.
Further I say, and further will maintain
Upon his bad life to make all this good,
That he did plot the Duke of
 Gloucester's death,
Suggest his soon-believing adversaries,
And consequently, like a traitor coward,
Sluic'd out his innocent soul through streams
 of blood;
Which blood, like sacrificing Abel's, cries,
Even from the tongueless caverns of the earth,
To me for justice and rough chastisement;
And, by the glorious worth of my descent,
This arm shall do it, or this life be spent.
KING RICHARD. How high a pitch his
 resolution soars!
Thomas of Norfolk, what say'st thou to this?
MOWBRAY. O, let my sovereign turn away
 his face
And bid his ears a little while be deaf,
Till I have told this slander of his blood
How God and good men hate so foul a liar.
KING RICHARD. Mowbray, impartial are our eyes
 and cars.
Were he my brother, nay, my kingdom's heir,

As he is but my father's brother's son,
Now by my sceptre's awe I make a vow,
Such neighbour nearness to our sacred blood
Should nothing privilege him nor partialise
The unstooping firmness of my upright soul.
He is our subject, Mowbray; so art thou:
Free speech and fearless I to thee allow.
MOWBRAY. Then, Bolingbroke, as low as to
    thy heart,
Through the false passage of thy throat,
    thou liest.
Three parts of that receipt I had for Calais
Disburs'd I duly to his Highness' soldiers;
The other part reserv'd I by consent,
For that my sovereign liege was in my debt
Upon remainder of a dear account
Since last I went to France to fetch his queen:
Now swallow down that lie. For
    Gloucester's death-
I slew him not, but to my own disgrace
Neglected my sworn duty in that case.
For you, my noble Lord of Lancaster,
The honourable father to my foe,
Once did I lay an ambush for your life,
A trespass that doth vex my grieved soul;
But ere I last receiv'd the sacrament
I did confess it, and exactly begg'd
Your Grace's pardon; and I hope I had it.
This is my fault. As for the rest appeal'd,
It issues from the rancour of a villain,
A recreant and most degenerate traitor;
Which in myself I boldly will defend,
And interchangeably hurl down my gage
Upon this overweening traitor's foot
To prove myself a loyal gentleman
Even in the best blood chamber'd in his bosom.
In haste whereof, most heartily I pray
Your Highness to assign our trial day.
KING RICHARD. Wrath-kindled gentlemen, be
    rul'd by me;
Let's purge this choler without letting blood-
This we prescribe, though no physician;
Deep malice makes too deep incision.
Forget, forgive; conclude and be agreed:
Our doctors say this is no month to bleed.
Good uncle, let this end where it begun;
We'll calm the Duke of Norfolk, you your son.
GAUNT. To be a make-peace shall become
    my age.
Throw down, my son, the Duke of
    Norfolk's gage.
KING RICHARD. And, Norfolk, throw down his.
GAUNT. When, Harry, when?

Obedience bids I should not bid again.
KING RICHARD. Norfolk, throw down; we bid.
    There is no boot.
MOWBRAY. Myself I throw, dread sovereign, at
    thy foot;
My life thou shalt command, but not my shame:
The one my duty owes; but my fair name,
Despite of death, that lives upon my grave
To dark dishonour's use thou shalt not have.
I am disgrac'd, impeach'd, and baffl'd here;
Pierc'd to the soul with slander's
    venom'd spear,
The which no balm can cure but his heart-blood
Which breath'd this poison.
KING RICHARD. Rage must be withstood:
Give me his gage-lions make leopards tame.
MOWBRAY. Yea, but not change his spots. Take
    but my shame,
And I resign my gage. My dear dear lord,
The purest treasure mortal times afford
Is spotless reputation; that away,
Men are but gilded loam or painted clay.
A jewel in a ten-times barr'd-up chest
Is a bold spirit in a loyal breast.
Mine honour is my life; both grow in one;
Take honour from me, and my life is done:
Then, dear my liege, mine honour let me try;
In that I live, and for that will I die.
KING RICHARD. Cousin, throw up your gage; do
    you begin.
BOLINGBROKE. O, God defend my soul from
    such deep sin!
Shall I seem crest-fallen in my father's sight?
Or with pale beggar-fear impeach my height
Before this outdar'd dastard? Ere my tongue
Shall wound my honour with such feeble wrong
Or sound so base a parle, my teeth shall tear
The slavish motive of recanting fear,
And spit it bleeding in his high disgrace,
Where shame doth harbour, even in
    Mowbray's face.

                                    Exit GAUNT.

KING RICHARD. We were not born to sue, but
    to command;
Which since we cannot do to make you friends,
Be ready, as your lives shall answer it,
At Coventry, upon Saint Lambert's day.
There shall your swords and lances arbitrate
The swelling difference of your settled hate;
Since we can not atone you, we shall see
Justice design the victor's chivalry.
Lord Marshal, command our officers-at-arms
Be ready to direct these home alarms. *Exeunt.*

✤ SCENE II ✤

London. The DUKE OF LANCASTER'S palace

Enter JOHN OF GAUNT with the DUCHESS OF GLOUCESTER

GAUNT. Alas, the part I had in Woodstock's blood
  Doth more solicit me than your exclaims
  To stir against the butchers of his life!
  But since correction lieth in those hands
  Which made the fault that we cannot correct,
  Put we our quarrel to the will of heaven;
  Who, when they see the hours ripe on earth,
  Will rain hot vengeance on offenders' heads.
DUCHESS. Finds brotherhood in thee no
  sharper spur?
  Hath love in thy old blood no living fire?
  Edward's seven sons, whereof thyself art one,
  Were as seven vials of his sacred blood,
  Or seven fair branches springing from one root.
  Some of those seven are dried by
  nature's course,
  Some of those branches by the Destinies cut;
  But Thomas, my dear lord, my life,
  my Gloucester,
  One vial full of Edward's sacred blood,
  One flourishing branch of his most royal root,
  Is crack'd, and all the precious liquor spilt;
  Is hack'd down, and his summer leaves all faded,
  By envy's hand and murder's bloody axe.
  Ah, Gaunt, his blood was thine! That bed,
  that womb,
  That mettle, that self mould, that fashion'd thee,
  Made him a man; and though thou livest
  and breathest,
  Yet art thou slain in him. Thou dost consent
  In some large measure to thy father's death
  In that thou seest thy wretched brother die,
  Who was the model of thy father's life.
  Call it not patience, Gaunt-it is despair;
  In suff'ring thus thy brother to be slaught'red,
  Thou showest the naked pathway to thy life,
  Teaching stern murder how to butcher thee.
  That which in mean men we entitle patience
  Is pale cold cowardice in noble breasts.
  What shall I say? To safeguard thine own life
  The best way is to venge my Gloucester's death.
GAUNT. God's is the quarrel; for God's substitute,
  His deputy anointed in His sight,
  Hath caus'd his death; the which if wrongfully,
  Let heaven revenge; for I may never lift
  An angry arm against His minister.

DUCHESS. Where then, alas, may I
  complain myself?
GAUNT. To God, the widow's champion
  and defence.
DUCHESS. Why then, I will. Farewell, old Gaunt.
  Thou goest to Coventry, there to behold
  Our cousin Hereford and fell Mowbray fight.
  O, sit my husband's wrongs on Hereford's spear,
  That it may enter butcher Mowbray's breast!
  Or, if misfortune miss the first career,
  Be Mowbray's sins so heavy in his bosom
  That they may break his foaming courser's back
  And throw the rider headlong in the lists,
  A caitiff recreant to my cousin Hereford!
  Farewell, old Gaunt; thy sometimes
  brother's wife,
  With her companion, Grief, must end her life.
GAUNT. Sister, farewell; I must to Coventry.
  As much good stay with thee as go with me!
DUCHESS. Yet one word more-grief boundeth
  where it falls,
  Not with the empty hollowness, but weight.
  I take my leave before I have begun,
  For sorrow ends not when it seemeth done.
  Commend me to thy brother, Edmund York.
  Lo, this is all-nay, yet depart not so;
  Though this be all, do not so quickly go;
  I shall remember more. Bid him-ah, what?-
  With all good speed at Plashy visit me.
  Alack, and what shall good old York there see
  But empty lodgings and unfurnish'd walls,
  Unpeopled offices, untrodden stones?
  And what hear there for welcome but my groans?
  Therefore commend me; let him not come there
  To seek out sorrow that dwells every where.
  Desolate, desolate, will I hence and die;
  The last leave of thee takes my weeping eye.

Exeunt.

✤ SCENE III ✤

The lists at Coventry

*Enter the LORD MARSHAL and the
DUKE OF AUMERLE*

MARSHAL. My Lord Aumerle, is Harry
  Hereford arm'd?
AUMERLE. Yea, at all points; and longs to enter in.
MARSHAL. The Duke of Norfolk, spightfully
  and bold,
  Stays but the summons of the
  appelant's trumpet.

AUMERLE. Why then, the champions are prepar'd, and stay

For nothing but his Majesty's approach.

The trumpets sound, and the KING enters with his nobles, GAUNT, BUSHY, BAGOT, GREEN, and Others. When they are set, enter MOWBRAY, Duke of Norfolk, in arms, defendant, and a HERALD

KING RICHARD. Marshal, demand of yonder champion

The cause of his arrival here in arms;

Ask him his name; and orderly proceed

To swear him in the justice of his cause.

MARSHAL. In God's name and the King's, say who thou art,

And why thou comest thus knightly clad in arms;

Against what man thou com'st, and what thy quarrel.

Speak truly on thy knighthood and thy oath;

As so defend thee heaven and thy valour!

MOWBRAY. My name is Thomas Mowbray, Duke of Norfolk;

Who hither come engaged by my oath-

Which God defend a knight should violate!-

Both to defend my loyalty and truth

To God, my King, and my succeeding issue,

Against the Duke of Hereford that appeals me;

And, by the grace of God and this mine arm,

To prove him, in defending of myself,

A traitor to my God, my King, and me.

And as I truly fight, defend me heaven!

The trumpets sound. Enter BOLINGBROKE, Duke of Hereford, appellant, in armour, and a HERALD

KING RICHARD. Marshal, ask yonder knight in arms,

Both who he is and why he cometh hither

Thus plated in habiliments of war;

And formally, according to our law,

Depose him in the justice of his cause.

MARSHAL. What is thy name? and wherefore com'st thou hither

Before King Richard in his royal lists?

Against whom comest thou? and what's thy quarrel?

Speak like a true knight, so defend thee heaven!

BOLINGBROKE. Harry of Hereford, Lancaster, and Derby,

Am I; who ready here do stand in arms

To prove, by God's grace and my body's valour,

In lists on Thomas Mowbray, Duke of Norfolk,

That he is a traitor, foul and dangerous,

To God of heaven, King Richard, and to me.

And as I truly fight, defend me heaven!

MARSHAL. On pain of death, no person be so bold

Or daring-hardy as to touch the lists,

Except the Marshal and such officers

Appointed to direct these fair designs.

BOLINGBROKE. Lord Marshal, let me kiss my sovereign's hand,

And bow my knee before his Majesty;

For Mowbray and myself are like two men

That vow a long and weary pilgrimage.

Then let us take a ceremonious leave

And loving farewell of our several friends.

MARSHAL. The appellant in all duty greets your Highness,

And craves to kiss your hand and take his leave.

KING RICHARD. We will descend and fold him in our arms.

Cousin of Hereford, as thy cause is right,

So be thy fortune in this royal fight!

Farewell, my blood; which if to-day thou shed,

Lament we may, but not revenge thee dead.

BOLINGBROKE. O, let no noble eye profane a tear

For me, if I be gor'd with Mowbray's spear.

As confident as is the falcon's flight

Against a bird, do I with Mowbray fight.

My loving lord, I take my leave of you;

Of you, my noble cousin, Lord Aumerle;

Not sick, although I have to do with death,

But lusty, young, and cheerly drawing breath.

Lo, as at English feasts, so I regreet

The daintiest last, to make the end most sweet.

O thou, the earthly author of my blood,

Whose youthful spirit, in me regenerate,

Doth with a twofold vigour lift me up

To reach at victory above my head,

Add proof unto mine armour with thy prayers,

And with thy blessings steel my lance's point,

That it may enter Mowbray's waxen coat

And furbish new the name of John o' Gaunt,

Even in the lusty haviour of his son.

GAUNT. God in thy good cause make thee prosperous!

Be swift like lightning in the execution,

And let thy blows, doubly redoubled,

Fall like amazing thunder on the casque

Of thy adverse pernicious enemy.

Rouse up thy youthful blood, be valiant, and live.

BOLINGBROKE. Mine innocence and Saint George to thrive!

MOWBRAY. However God or fortune cast my lot,

There lives or dies, true to King Richard's throne,

A loyal, just, and upright gentleman.

Never did captive with a freer heart

Cast off his chains of bondage, and embrace
His golden uncontroll'd enfranchisement,
More than my dancing soul doth celebrate
This feast of battle with mine adversary.
Most mighty liege, and my companion peers,
Take from my mouth the wish of happy years.
As gentle and as jocund as to jest
Go I to fight: truth hath a quiet breast.
KING RICHARD. Farewell, my lord, securely I espy
Virtue with valour couched in thine eye.
Order the trial, Marshal, and begin.
MARSHAL. Harry of Hereford, Lancaster,
   and Derby,
Receive thy lance; and God defend the right!
BOLINGBROKE. Strong as a tower in hope, I
   cry amen.
MARSHAL. [To an Officer] Go bear this lance to
   Thomas, Duke of Norfolk.
FIRST HERALD. Harry of Hereford, Lancaster,
   and Derby,
Stands here for God, his sovereign, and himself,
On pain to be found false and recreant,
To prove the Duke of Norfolk,
   Thomas Mowbray,
A traitor to his God, his King, and him;
And dares him to set forward to the fight.
SECOND HERALD. Here standeth Thomas
   Mowbray, Duke of Norfolk,
On pain to be found false and recreant,
Both to defend himself, and to approve
Henry of Hereford, Lancaster, and Derby,
To God, his sovereign, and to him disloyal,
Courageously and with a free desire
Attending but the signal to begin.
MARSHAL. Sound trumpets; and set forward,
   combatants. [A charge sounded]
Stay, the King hath thrown his warder down.
KING RICHARD. Let them lay by their helmets and
   their spears,
And both return back to their chairs again.
Withdraw with us; and let the trumpets sound
While we return these dukes what we decree. [A
   long flourish, while the KING consults his Council]
Draw near,
And list what with our council we have done.
For that our kingdom's earth should not
   be soil'd
With that dear blood which it hath fostered;
And for our eyes do hate the dire aspect
Of civil wounds plough'd up with
   neighbours' sword;
And for we think the eagle-winged pride
Of sky-aspiring and ambitious thoughts,

With rival-hating envy, set on you
To wake our peace, which in our
   country's cradle
Draws the sweet infant breath of gentle sleep;
Which so rous'd up with boist'rous
   untun'd drums,
With harsh-resounding trumpets' dreadful bray,
And grating shock of wrathful iron arms,
Might from our quiet confines fright fair peace
And make us wade even in our kindred's blood-
Therefore we banish you our territories.
You, cousin Hereford, upon pain of life,
Till twice five summers have enrich'd our fields
Shall not regreet our fair dominions,
But tread the stranger paths of banishment.
BOLINGBROKE. Your will be done. This must my
   comfort be-
That sun that warms you here shall shine on me,
And those his golden beams to you here lent
Shall point on me and gild my banishment.
KING RICHARD. Norfolk, for thee remains a
   heavier doom,
Which I with some unwillingness pronounce:
The sly slow hours shall not determinate
The dateless limit of thy dear exile;
The hopeless word of 'never to return'
Breathe I against thee, upon pain of life.
MOWBRAY. A heavy sentence, my most
   sovereign liege,
And all unlook'd for from your Highness' mouth.
A dearer merit, not so deep a maim
As to be cast forth in the common air,
Have I deserved at your Highness' hands.
The language I have learnt these forty years,
My native English, now I must forgo;
And now my tongue's use is to me no more
Than an unstringed viol or a harp;
Or like a cunning instrument cas'd up
Or, being open, put into his hands
That knows no touch to tune the harmony.
Within my mouth you have engaol'd my tongue,
Doubly portcullis'd with my teeth and lips;
And dull, unfeeling, barren ignorance
Is made my gaoler to attend on me.
I am too old to fawn upon a nurse,
Too far in years to be a pupil now.
What is thy sentence, then, but
   speechless death,
Which robs my tongue from breathing
   native breath?
KING RICHARD. It boots thee not to
   be compassionate;
After our sentence plaining comes too late.

MOWBRAY. Then thus I turn me from my
  country's light,
To dwell in solemn shades of endless night.
KING RICHARD. Return again, and take an oath
  with thee.
  Lay on our royal sword your banish'd hands;
  Swear by the duty that you owe to God,
  Our part therein we banish with yourselves,
  To keep the oath that we administer:
  You never shall, so help you truth and God,
  Embrace each other's love in banishment;
  Nor never look upon each other's face;
  Nor never write, regreet, nor reconcile
  This louring tempest of your home-bred hate;
  Nor never by advised purpose meet
  To plot, contrive, or complot any ill,
  'Gainst us, our state, our subjects, or our land.
BOLINGBROKE. I swear.
MOWBRAY. And I, to keep all this.
BOLINGBROKE. Norfolk, so far as to
  mine enemy.
  By this time, had the King permitted us,
  One of our souls had wand'red in the air,
  Banish'd this frail sepulchre of our flesh,
  As now our flesh is banish'd from this land-
  Confess thy treasons ere thou fly the realm;
  Since thou hast far to go, bear not along
  The clogging burden of a guilty soul.
MOWBRAY. No, Bolingbroke; if ever I were traitor,
  My name be blotted from the book of life,
  And I from heaven banish'd as from hence!
  But what thou art, God, thou, and I, do know;
  And all too soon, I fear, the King shall rue.
  Farewell, my liege. Now no way can I stray:
  Save back to England, all the world's my way.

Exit.

KING RICHARD. Uncle, even in the glasses of
  thine eyes
  I see thy grieved heart. Thy sad aspect
  Hath from the number of his banish'd years
  Pluck'd four away. [To BOLINGBROKE] Six frozen
  winters spent,
  Return with welcome home from banishment.
BOLINGBROKE. How long a time lies in one
  little word!
  Four lagging winters and four wanton springs
  End in a word: such is the breath of kings.
GAUNT. I thank my liege that in regard of me
  He shortens four years of my son's exile;
  But little vantage shall I reap thereby,
  For ere the six years that he hath to spend
  Can change their moons and bring their
  times about,

My oil-dried lamp and time-bewasted light
Shall be extinct with age and endless night;
My inch of taper will be burnt and done,
And blindfold death not let me see my son.
KING RICHARD. Why, uncle, thou hast many
  years to live.
GAUNT. But not a minute, King, that thou
  canst give:
  Shorten my days thou canst with sullen sorrow
  And pluck nights from me, but not lend
  a morrow;
  Thou canst help time to furrow me with age,
  But stop no wrinkle in his pilgrimage;
  Thy word is current with him for my death,
  But dead, thy kingdom cannot buy my breath.
KING RICHARD. Thy son is banish'd upon
  good advice,
  Whereto thy tongue a party-verdict gave.
  Why at our justice seem'st thou then to lour?
GAUNT. Things sweet to taste prove in
  digestion sour.
  You urg'd me as a judge; but I had rather
  You would have bid me argue like a father.
  O, had it been a stranger, not my child,
  To smooth his fault I should have been
  more mild.
  A partial slander sought I to avoid,
  And in the sentence my own life destroy'd.
  Alas, I look'd when some of you should say
  I was too strict to make mine own away;
  But you gave leave to my unwilling tongue
  Against my will to do myself this wrong.
KING RICHARD. Cousin, farewell; and, uncle,
  bid him so.
  Six years we banish him, and he shall go.

Flourish. Exit KING with train.

AUMERLE. Cousin, farewell; what presence
  must
  not know,
  From where you do remain let paper show.
MARSHAL. My lord, no leave take I, for I
  will ride
  As far as land will let me by your side.
GAUNT. O, to what purpose dost thou hoard
  thy words,
  That thou returnest no greeting to thy friends?
BOLINGBROKE. I have too few to take my leave
  of you,
  When the tongue's office should be prodigal
  To breathe the abundant dolour of the heart.
GAUNT. Thy grief is but thy absence for a time.
BOLINGBROKE. Joy absent, grief is present for
  that time.

GAUNT. What is six winters? They are
quickly gone.
BOLINGBROKE. To men in joy; but grief makes
one hour ten.
GAUNT. Call it a travel that thou tak'st
for pleasure.
BOLINGBROKE. My heart will sigh when I
miscall it so,
Which finds it an enforced pilgrimage.
GAUNT. The sullen passage of thy weary steps
Esteem as foil wherein thou art to set
The precious jewel of thy home return.
BOLINGBROKE. Nay, rather, every tedious
stride
I make
Will but remember me what a deal of world
I wander from the jewels that I love.
Must I not serve a long apprenticehood
To foreign passages; and in the end,
Having my freedom, boast of nothing else
But that I was a journeyman to grief?
GAUNT. All places that the eye of heaven visits
Are to a wise man ports and happy havens.
Teach thy necessity to reason thus:
There is no virtue like necessity.
Think not the King did banish thee,
But thou the King. Woe doth the heavier sit
Where it perceives it is but faintly home.
Go, say I sent thee forth to purchase honour,
And not the King exil'd thee; or suppose
Devouring pestilence hangs in our air
And thou art flying to a fresher clime.
Look what thy soul holds dear, imagine it
To lie that way thou goest, not whence
thou com'st.
Suppose the singing birds musicians,
The grass whereon thou tread'st the
presence strew'd,
The flowers fair ladies, and thy steps no more
Than a delightful measure or a dance;
For gnarling sorrow hath less power to bite
The man that mocks at it and sets it light.
BOLINGBROKE. O, who can hold a fire in
his hand
By thinking on the frosty Caucasus?
Or cloy the hungry edge of appetite
By bare imagination of a feast?
Or wallow naked in December snow
By thinking on fantastic summer's heat?
O, no! the apprehension of the good
Gives but the greater feeling to the worse.
Fell sorrow's tooth doth never rankle more
Than when he bites, but lanceth not the sore.

GAUNT. Come, come, my son, I'll bring thee on
thy way.
Had I thy youth and cause, I would not stay.
BOLINGBROKE. Then, England's ground,
farewell; sweet soil, adieu;
My mother, and my nurse, that bears me yet!
Where'er I wander, boast of this I can:
Though banish'd, yet a trueborn English man.

Exeunt.

SCENE IV

London. The court

*Enter the KING, with BAGOT and GREEN, at one door; and
the DUKE OF AUMERLE at another*

KING RICHARD. We did observe.
Cousin Aumerle,
How far brought you high Hereford on his way?
AUMERLE. I brought high Hereford, if you call
him so,
But to the next high way, and there I left him.
KING RICHARD. And say, what store of parting
tears were shed?
AUMERLE. Faith, none for me; except the
north-east wind,
Which then blew bitterly against our faces,
Awak'd the sleeping rheum, and so by chance
Did grace our hollow parting with a tear.
KING RICHARD. What said our cousin when you
parted with him?
AUMERLE. 'Farewell.'
And, for my heart disdained that my tongue
Should so profane the word, that taught
me craft
To counterfeit oppression of such grief
That words seem'd buried in my
sorrow's grave.
Marry, would the word 'farewell' have
length'ned hours
And added years to his short banishment,
He should have had a volume of farewells;
But since it would not, he had none of me.
KING RICHARD. He is our cousin, cousin; but
'tis doubt,
When time shall call him home
from banishment,
Whether our kinsman come to see his friends.
Ourself, and Bushy, Bagot here, and Green,
Observ'd his courtship to the common people;
How he did seem to dive into their hearts
With humble and familiar courtesy;

What reverence he did throw away on slaves,
Wooing poor craftsmen with the craft of smiles
And patient underbearing of his fortune,
As 'twere to banish their affects with him.
Off goes his bonnet to an oyster-wench;
A brace of draymen bid God speed him well
And had the tribute of his supple knee,
With 'Thanks, my countrymen, my
  loving friends';
As were our England in reversion his,
And he our subjects' next degree in hope.
GREEN. Well, he is gone; and with him go
  these thoughts!
  Now for the rebels which stand out in Ireland,
  Expedient manage must be made, my liege,
  Ere further leisure yield them further means
  For their advantage and your Highness' loss.
KING RICHARD. We will ourself in person to
  this war;
  And, for our coffers, with too great a court
  And liberal largess, are grown somewhat light,
  We are enforc'd to farm our royal realm;
  The revenue whereof shall furnish us
  For our affairs in hand. If that come short,
  Our substitutes at home shall have
  blank charters;
  Whereto, when they shall know what men
  are rich,
  They shall subscribe them for large sums
  of gold,
  And send them after to supply our wants;
  For we will make for Ireland presently.
Enter BUSHY
  Bushy, what news?
BUSHY. Old John of Gaunt is grievous sick,
  my lord,
  Suddenly taken; and hath sent poste-haste
  To entreat your Majesty to visit him.
KING RICHARD. Where lies he?
BUSHY. At Ely House.
KING RICHARD. Now put it, God, in the
  physician's mind
  To help him to his grave immediately!
  The lining of his coffers shall make coats
  To deck our soldiers for these Irish wars.
  Come, gentlemen, let's all go visit him.
  Pray God we may make haste, and come
  too late!
ALL. Amen.   *Exeunt.*

ACT II

☙ SCENE I ☙
London. Ely House

*Enter JOHN OF GAUNT, sick, with the DUKE OF YORK,
etc.*

GAUNT. Will the King come, that I may breathe
  my last
  In wholesome counsel to his unstaid youth?
YORK. Vex not yourself, nor strive not with
  your breath;
  For all in vain comes counsel to his ear.
GAUNT. O, but they say the tongues of dying men
  Enforce attention like deep harmony.
  Where words are scarce, they are seldom spent
  in vain;
  For they breathe truth that breathe their words
  in pain.
  He that no more must say is listen'd more
  Than they whom youth and ease have taught
  to glose;
  More are men's ends mark'd than their
  lives before.
  The setting sun, and music at the close,
  As the last taste of sweets, is sweetest last,
  Writ in remembrance more than things
  long past.
  Though Richard my life's counsel would
  not hear,
  My death's sad tale may yet undeaf his ear.
YORK. No; it is stopp'd with other flattering
  sounds,
  As praises, of whose taste the wise are fond,
  Lascivious metres, to whose venom sound
  The open ear of youth doth always listen;
  Report of fashions in proud Italy,
  Whose manners still our tardy apish nation
  Limps after in base imitation.
  Where doth the world thrust forth a vanity-
  So it be new, there's no respect how vile-
  That is not quickly buzz'd into his ears?
  Then all too late comes counsel to be heard
  Where will doth mutiny with wit's regard.
  Direct not him whose way himself will choose.
  'Tis breath thou lack'st, and that breath wilt
  thou lose.
GAUNT. Methinks I am a prophet new inspir'd,
  And thus expiring do foretell of him:

His rash fierce blaze of riot cannot last,
For violent fires soon burn out themselves;
Small showers last long, but sudden storms
 are short;
He tires betimes that spurs too fast betimes;
With eager feeding food doth choke the feeder;
Light vanity, insatiate cormorant,
Consuming means, soon preys upon itself.
This royal throne of kings, this scept'red isle,
This earth of majesty, this seat of Mars,
This other Eden, demi-paradise,
This fortress built by Nature for herself
Against infection and the hand of war,
This happy breed of men, this little world,
This precious stone set in the silver sea,
Which serves it in the office of a wall,
Or as a moat defensive to a house,
Against the envy of less happier lands;
This blessed plot, this earth, this realm,
 this England,
This nurse, this teeming womb of royal kings,
Fear'd by their breed, and famous by their birth,
Renowned for their deeds as far from home,
For Christian service and true chivalry,
As is the sepulchre in stubborn Jewry
Of the world's ransom, blessed Mary's Son;
This land of such dear souls, this dear dear land,
Dear for her reputation through the world,
Is now leas'd out-I die pronouncing it-
Like to a tenement or pelting farm.
England, bound in with the triumphant sea,
Whose rocky shore beats back the envious siege
Of wat'ry Neptune, is now bound in with shame,
With inky blots and rotten parchment bonds;
That England, that was wont to conquer others,
Hath made a shameful conquest of itself.
Ah, would the scandal vanish with my life,
How happy then were my ensuing death!
 Enter KING and QUEEN, AUMERLE, BUSHY, GREEN,
  BAGOT, Ross, and WILLOUGHBY
YORK. The King is come; deal mildly with
 his youth,
 For young hot colts being rag'd do rage
  the more.
QUEEN. How fares our noble uncle Lancaster?
KING RICHARD. What comfort, man? How is't
 with aged Gaunt?
GAUNT. O, how that name befits my composition!
 Old Gaunt, indeed; and gaunt in being old.
 Within me grief hath kept a tedious fast;
 And who abstains from meat that is not gaunt?
 For sleeping England long time have I watch'd;
 Watching breeds leanness, leanness is all gaunt.

The pleasure that some fathers feed upon
 Is my strict fast-I mean my children's looks;
 And therein fasting, hast thou made me gaunt.
 Gaunt am I for the grave, gaunt as a grave,
 Whose hollow womb inherits nought but bones.
KING RICHARD. Can sick men play so nicely
 with their names?
GAUNT. No, misery makes sport to mock itself:
 Since thou dost seek to kill my name in me,
 I mock my name, great King, to flatter thee.
KING RICHARD. Should dying men flatter with
 those that live?
GAUNT. No, no; men living flatter those that die.
KING RICHARD. Thou, now a-dying, sayest thou
 flatterest me.
GAUNT. O, no! thou diest, though I the sicker be.
KING RICHARD. I am in health, I breathe, and see
 thee ill.
GAUNT. Now He that made me knows I see
 thee ill;
 Ill in myself to see, and in thee seeing ill.
 Thy death-bed is no lesser than thy land
 Wherein thou liest in reputation sick;
 And thou, too careless patient as thou art,
 Commit'st thy anointed body to the cure
 Of those physicians that first wounded thee:
 A thousand flatterers sit within thy crown,
 Whose compass is no bigger than thy head;
 And yet, incaged in so small a verge,
 The waste is no whit lesser than thy land.
 O, had thy grandsire with a prophet's eye
 Seen how his son's son should destroy his sons,
 From forth thy reach he would have laid
  thy shame,
 Deposing thee before thou wert possess'd,
 Which art possess'd now to depose thyself.
 Why, cousin, wert thou regent of the world,
 It were a shame to let this land by lease;
 But for thy world enjoying but this land,
 Is it not more than shame to shame it so?
 Landlord of England art thou now, not King.
 Thy state of law is bondslave to the law;
 And thou-
KING RICHARD. A lunatic lean-witted fool,
 Presuming on an ague's privilege,
 Darest with thy frozen admonition
 Make pale our cheek, chasing the royal blood
 With fury from his native residence.
 Now by my seat's right royal majesty,
 Wert thou not brother to great Edward's son,
 This tongue that runs so roundly in thy head
 Should run thy head from thy
  unreverent shoulders.

GAUNT. O, spare me not, my brother
  Edward's son,
  For that I was his father Edward's son;
  That blood already, like the pelican,
  Hast thou tapp'd out, and drunkenly carous'd.
  My brother Gloucester, plain well-meaning soul-
  Whom fair befall in heaven 'mongst
  happy souls!-
  May be a precedent and witness good
  That thou respect'st not spilling Edward's blood.
  Join with the present sickness that I have;
  And thy unkindness be like crooked age,
  To crop at once a too long withered flower.
  Live in thy shame, but die not shame with thee!
  These words hereafter thy tormentors be!
  Convey me to my bed, then to my grave.
  Love they to live that love and honour have.

Exit, borne out by his Attendants

KING RICHARD. And let them die that age and
  sullens have;
  For both hast thou, and both become the grave.
YORK. I do beseech your Majesty impute his words
  To wayward sickliness and age in him.
  He loves you, on my life, and holds you dear
  As Harry Duke of Hereford, were he here.
KING RICHARD. Right, you say true: as Hereford's
  love, so his;
  As theirs, so mine; and all be as it is.

Enter NORTHUMBERLAND

NORTHUMBERLAND. My liege, old Gaunt
  commends him to your Majesty.
KING RICHARD. What says he?
NORTHUMBERLAND. Nay, nothing; all is said.
  His tongue is now a stringless instrument;
  Words, life, and all, old Lancaster hath spent.
YORK. Be York the next that must be bankrupt so!
  Though death be poor, it ends a mortal woe.
KING RICHARD. The ripest fruit first falls, and
  so doth he;
  His time is spent, our pilgrimage must be.
  So much for that. Now for our Irish wars.
  We must supplant those rough rug-
  headed kerns,
  Which live like venom where no venom else
  But only they have privilege to live.
  And for these great affairs do ask some charge,
  Towards our assistance we do seize to us
  The plate, coin, revenues, and moveables,
  Whereof our uncle Gaunt did stand possess'd.
YORK. How long shall I be patient? Ah, how long
  Shall tender duty make me suffer wrong?
  Not Gloucester's death, nor
  Hereford's banishment,

Nor Gaunt's rebukes, nor England's
  private wrongs,
Nor the prevention of poor Bolingbroke
About his marriage, nor my own disgrace,
Have ever made me sour my patient cheek
Or bend one wrinkle on my sovereign's face.
I am the last of noble Edward's sons,
Of whom thy father, Prince of Wales, was first.
In war was never lion rag'd more fierce,
In peace was never gentle lamb more mild,
Than was that young and princely gentleman.
His face thou hast, for even so look'd he,
Accomplish'd with the number of thy hours;
But when he frown'd, it was against the French
And not against his friends. His noble hand
Did win what he did spend, and spent not that
Which his triumphant father's hand had won.
His hands were guilty of no kindred blood,
But bloody with the enemies of his kin.
O Richard! York is too far gone with grief,
Or else he never would compare between-
KING RICHARD. Why, uncle, what's the matter?
YORK. O my liege,
Pardon me, if you please; if not, I, pleas'd
Not to be pardoned, am content withal.
Seek you to seize and gripe into your hands
The royalties and rights of banish'd Hereford?
Is not Gaunt dead? and doth not Hereford live?
Was not Gaunt just? and is not Harry true?
Did not the one deserve to have an heir?
Is not his heir a well-deserving son?
Take Hereford's rights away, and take from Time
His charters and his customary rights;
Let not to-morrow then ensue to-day;
Be not thyself-for how art thou a king
But by fair sequence and succession?
Now, afore God-God forbid I say true!-
If you do wrongfully seize Hereford's rights,
Call in the letters patents that he hath
By his attorneys-general to sue
His livery, and deny his off'red homage,
You pluck a thousand dangers on your head,
You lose a thousand well-disposed hearts,
And prick my tender patience to those thoughts
Which honour and allegiance cannot think.
KING RICHARD. Think what you will, we seize
  into our hands
His plate, his goods, his money, and his lands.
YORK. I'll not be by the while. My liege, farewell.
What will ensue hereof there's none can tell;
But by bad courses may be understood
That their events can never fall out good. *Exit*
KING RICHARD. Go, Bushy, to the Earl of

Wiltshire straight;
Bid him repair to us to Ely House
To see this business. To-morrow next
We will for Ireland; and 'tis time, I trow.
And we create, in absence of ourself,
Our Uncle York Lord Governor of England;
For he is just, and always lov'd us well.
Come on, our queen; to-morrow must we part;
Be merry, for our time of stay is short.

Flourish. Exeunt KING, QUEEN, BUSHY, AUMERLE,
GREEN, and BAGOT.

NORTHUMBERLAND. Well, lords, the Duke of
Lancaster is dead.
ROSS. And living too; for now his son is Duke.
WILLOUGHBY. Barely in title, not in revenues.
NORTHUMBERLAND. Richly in both, if justice had
her right.
ROSS. My heart is great; but it must break
with silence,
Ere't be disburdened with a liberal tongue.
NORTHUMBERLAND. Nay, speak thy mind; and
let him ne'er speak more
That speaks thy words again to do thee harm!
WILLOUGHBY. Tends that thou wouldst speak to
the Duke of Hereford?
If it be so, out with it boldly, man;
Quick is mine ear to hear of good towards him.
ROSS. No good at all that I can do for him;
Unless you call it good to pity him,
Bereft and gelded of his patrimony.
NORTHUMBERLAND. Now, afore God, 'tis shame
such wrongs are borne
In him, a royal prince, and many moe
Of noble blood in this declining land.
The King is not himself, but basely led
By flatterers; and what they will inform,
Merely in hate, 'gainst any of us all,
That will the King severely prosecute
'Gainst us, our lives, our children, and our heirs.
ROSS. The commons hath he pill'd with
grievous taxes;
And quite lost their hearts; the nobles hath
he find
For ancient quarrels and quite lost their hearts.
WILLOUGHBY. And daily new exactions
are devis'd,
As blanks, benevolences, and I wot not what;
But what, a God's name, doth become of this?
NORTHUMBERLAND. Wars hath not wasted it, for
warr'd he hath not,
But basely yielded upon compromise
That which his noble ancestors achiev'd
with blows.

More hath he spent in peace than they in wars.
ROSS. The Earl of Wiltshire hath the realm in farm.
WILLOUGHBY. The King's grown bankrupt like a
broken man.
NORTHUMBERLAND. Reproach and dissolution
hangeth over him.
ROSS. He hath not money for these Irish wars,
His burdenous taxations notwithstanding,
But by the robbing of the banish'd Duke.
NORTHUMBERLAND. His noble kinsman-most
degenerate King!
But, lords, we hear this fearful tempest sing,
Yet seek no shelter to avoid the storm;
We see the wind sit sore upon our sails,
And yet we strike not, but securely perish.
ROSS. We see the very wreck that we must suffer;
And unavoided is the danger now
For suffering so the causes of our wreck.
NORTHUMBERLAND. Not so; even through the
hollow eyes of death
I spy life peering; but I dare not say
How near the tidings of our comfort is.
WILLOUGHBY. Nay, let us share thy thoughts as
thou dost ours.
ROSS. Be confident to speak, Northumberland.
We three are but thyself, and, speaking so,
Thy words are but as thoughts; therefore
be bold.
NORTHUMBERLAND. Then thus: I have from Le
Port Blanc, a bay
In Brittany, receiv'd intelligence
That Harry Duke of Hereford, Rainold
Lord Cobham,
That late broke from the Duke of Exeter,
His brother, Archbishop late of Canterbury,
Sir Thomas Erpingham, Sir John Ramston,
Sir John Norbery, Sir Robert Waterton, and
Francis Quoint-
All these, well furnish'd by the Duke of Britaine,
With eight tall ships, three thousand men of war,
Are making hither with all due expedience,
And shortly mean to touch our northern shore.
Perhaps they had ere this, but that they stay
The first departing of the King for Ireland.
If then we shall shake off our slavish yoke,
Imp out our drooping country's broken wing,
Redeem from broking pawn the
blemish'd crown,
Wipe off the dust that hides our sceptre's gilt,
And make high majesty look like itself,
Away with me in post to Ravenspurgh;
But if you faint, as fearing to do so,
Stay and be secret, and myself will go.

ROSS. To horse, to horse! Urge doubts to them
   that fear.
WILLOUGHBY. Hold out my horse, and I will first
   be there. *Exeunt.*

✣ SCENE II ✣
Windsor Castle

Enter QUEEN, BUSHY, and BAGOT

BUSHY. Madam, your Majesty is too much sad.
   You promis'd, when you parted with the King,
   To lay aside life-harming heaviness
   And entertain a cheerful disposition.
QUEEN. To please the King, I did; to please myself
   I cannot do it; yet I know no cause
   Why I should welcome such a guest as grief,
   Save bidding farewell to so sweet a guest
   As my sweet Richard. Yet again methinks
   Some unborn sorrow, ripe in fortune's womb,
   Is coming towards me, and my inward soul
   With nothing trembles. At some thing it grieves
   More than with parting from my lord the King.
BUSHY. Each substance of a grief hath
   twenty shadows,
   Which shows like grief itself, but is not so;
   For sorrow's eye, glazed with blinding tears,
   Divides one thing entire to many objects,
   Like perspectives which, rightly gaz'd upon,
   Show nothing but confusion-ey'd awry,
   Distinguish form. So your sweet Majesty,
   Looking awry upon your lord's departure,
   Find shapes of grief more than himself to wail;
   Which, look'd on as it is, is nought but shadows
   Of what it is not. Then, thrice-gracious Queen,
   More than your lord's departure weep not-more
   is not seen;
   Or if it be, 'tis with false sorrow's eye,
   Which for things true weeps things imaginary.
QUEEN. It may be so; but yet my inward soul
   Persuades me it is otherwise. Howe'er it be,
   I cannot but be sad; so heavy sad
   As-though, on thinking, on no thought I think-
   Makes me with heavy nothing faint and shrink.
BUSHY. 'Tis nothing but conceit, my
   gracious lady.
QUEEN. 'Tis nothing less: conceit is still deriv'd
   From some forefather grief; mine is not so,
   For nothing hath begot my something grief,
   Or something hath the nothing that I grieve;
   'Tis in reversion that I do possess-
   But what it is that is not yet known what,

I cannot name; 'tis nameless woe, I wot.
Enter GREEN
GREEN. God save your Majesty! and well
   met, gentlemen.
   I hope the King is not yet shipp'd for Ireland.
QUEEN. Why hopest thou so? 'Tis better hope
   he is;
   For his designs crave haste, his haste
   good hope.
   Then wherefore dost thou hope he is
   not shipp'd?
GREEN. That he, our hope, might have retir'd
   his power
   And driven into despair an enemy's hope
   Who strongly hath set footing in this land.
   The banish'd Bolingbroke repeals himself,
   And with uplifted arms is safe arriv'd
   At Ravenspurgh.
QUEEN. Now God in heaven forbid!
GREEN. Ah, madam, 'tis too true; and that is worse,
   The Lord Northumberland, his son young
   Henry Percy,
   The Lords of Ross, Beaumond, and Willoughby,
   With all their powerful friends, are fled to him.
BUSHY. Why have you not
   proclaim'd Northumberland
   And all the rest revolted faction traitors?
GREEN. We have; whereupon the Earl
   of Worcester
   Hath broken his staff, resign'd his stewardship,
   And all the household servants fled with him
   To Bolingbroke.
QUEEN. So, Green, thou art the midwife to
   my woe,
   And Bolingbroke my sorrow's dismal heir.
   Now hath my soul brought forth her prodigy;
   And I, a gasping new-deliver'd mother,
   Have woe to woe, sorrow to sorrow join'd.
BUSHY. Despair not, madam.
QUEEN. Who shall hinder me?
   I will despair, and be at enmity
   With cozening hope-he is a flatterer,
   A parasite, a keeper-back of death,
   Who gently would dissolve the bands of life,
   Which false hope lingers in extremity.
Enter YORK
GREEN. Here comes the Duke of York.
QUEEN. With signs of war about his aged neck.
   O, full of careful business are his looks!
   Uncle, for God's sake, speak
   comfortable words.
YORK. Should I do so, I should belie
   my thoughts.

Comfort's in heaven; and we are on the earth,
Where nothing lives but crosses, cares,
 and grief.
Your husband, he is gone to save far off,
Whilst others come to make him lose at home.
Here am I left to underprop his land,
Who, weak with age, cannot support myself.
Now comes the sick hour that his surfeit made;
Now shall he try his friends that flatter'd him.

Enter a SERVINGMAN

SERVINGMAN. My lord, your son was gone before
 I came.
YORK. He was-why so go all which way it will!
 The nobles they are fled, the commons they
 are cold
 And will, I fear, revolt on Hereford's side.
 Sirrah, get thee to Plashy, to my
 sister Gloucester;
 Bid her send me presently a thousand pound.
 Hold, take my ring.
SERVINGMAN. My lord, I had forgot to tell
 your lordship,
 To-day, as I came by, I called there-
 But I shall grieve you to report the rest.
YORK. What is't, knave?
SERVINGMAN. An hour before I came, the
 Duchess died.
YORK. God for his mercy! what a tide of woes
 Comes rushing on this woeful land at once!
 I know not what to do. I would to God,
 So my untruth had not provok'd him to it,
 The King had cut off my head with my brother's.
 What, are there no posts dispatch'd for Ireland?
 How shall we do for money for these wars?
 Come, sister-cousin, I would say-pray, pardon me.
 Go, fellow, get thee home, provide some carts,
 And bring away the armour that is there.

Exit SERVINGMAN

Gentlemen, will you go muster men?
If I know how or which way to order these affairs
Thus disorderly thrust into my hands,
Never believe me. Both are my kinsmen.
T'one is my sovereign, whom both my oath
And duty bids defend; t'other again
Is my kinsman, whom the King hath wrong'd,
Whom conscience and my kindred bids to right.
Well, somewhat we must do.-Come, cousin,
I'll dispose of you. Gentlemen, go muster up
 your men
And meet me presently at Berkeley.
I should to Plashy too,
But time will not permit. All is uneven,
And everything is left at six and seven.

Exeunt YORK and QUEEN

BUSHY. The wind sits fair for news to go
 to Ireland.
 But none returns. For us to levy power
 Proportionable to the enemy
 Is all unpossible.
GREEN. Besides, our nearness to the King in love
 Is near the hate of those love not the King.
BAGOT. And that is the wavering commons; for
 their love
 Lies in their purses; and whoso empties them,
 By so much fills their hearts with deadly hate.
BUSHY. Wherein the King stands
 generally condemn'd.
BAGOT. If judgment lie in them, then so do we,
 Because we ever have been near the King.
GREEN. Well, I will for refuge straight to
 Bristow Castle.
 The Earl of Wiltshire is already there.
BUSHY. Thither will I with you; for little office
 Will the hateful commons perform for us,
 Except like curs to tear us all to pieces.
 Will you go along with us?
BAGOT. No; I will to Ireland to his Majesty.
 Farewell. If heart's presages be not vain,
 We three here part that ne'er shall meet again.
BUSHY. That's as York thrives to beat
 back Bolingbroke.
GREEN. Alas, poor Duke! the task he undertakes
 Is numb'ring sands and drinking oceans dry.
 Where one on his side fights, thousands will fly.
 Farewell at once-for once, for all, and ever.
BUSHY. Well, we may meet again.
BAGOT. I fear me, never.   *Exeunt*

✦ SCENE III ✦
Gloucestershire

Enter BOLINGBROKE and NORTHUMBERLAND, Forces

BOLINGBROKE. How far is it, my lord, to
 Berkeley now?
NORTHUMBERLAND. Believe me, noble lord,
 I am a stranger here in Gloucestershire.
 These high wild hills and rough uneven ways
 Draws out our miles, and makes
 them wearisome;
 And yet your fair discourse hath been as sugar,
 Making the hard way sweet and delectable.
 But I bethink me what a weary way
 From Ravenspurgh to Cotswold will be found
 In Ross and Willoughby, wanting your company,

Which, I protest, hath very much beguil'd
The tediousness and process of my travel.
But theirs is sweet'ned with the hope to have
The present benefit which I possess;
And hope to joy is little less in joy
Than hope enjoy'd. By this the weary lords
Shall make their way seem short, as mine
  hath done
By sight of what I have, your noble company.
BOLINGBROKE. Of much less value is
  my company
Than your good words. But who comes here?

Enter HARRY PERCY

NORTHUMBERLAND. It is my son, young
  Harry Percy,
Sent from my brother
  Worcester, whencesoever.
Harry, how fares your uncle?
PERCY. I had thought, my lord, to have learn'd
  his health of you.
NORTHUMBERLAND. Why, is he not with
  the Queen?
PERCY. No, my good lord; he hath forsook
  the court,
Broken his staff of office, and dispers'd
The household of the King.
NORTHUMBERLAND. What was his reason?
He was not so resolv'd when last we
  spake together.
PERCY. Because your lordship was
  proclaimed traitor.
But he, my lord, is gone to Ravenspurgh,
To offer service to the Duke of Hereford;
And sent me over by Berkeley, to discover
What power the Duke of York had levied there;
Then with directions to repair to Ravenspurgh.
NORTHUMBERLAND. Have you forgot the Duke
  of Hereford, boy?
PERCY. No, my good lord; for that is not forgot
Which ne'er I did remember; to my knowledge,
I never in my life did look on him.
NORTHUMBERLAND. Then learn to know him
  now; this is the Duke.
PERCY. My gracious lord, I tender you
  my service,
Such as it is, being tender, raw, and young;
Which elder days shall ripen, and confirm
To more approved service and desert.
BOLINGBROKE. I thank thee, gentle Percy; and
  be sure
I count myself in nothing else so happy
As in a soul rememb'ring my good friends;
And as my fortune ripens with thy love,

It shall be still thy true love's recompense.
My heart this covenant makes, my hand thus
  seals it.
NORTHUMBERLAND. How far is it to Berkeley?
  And what stir
Keeps good old York there with his men
  of war?
PERCY. There stands the castle, by yon tuft
  of trees,
Mann'd with three hundred men, as I
  have heard;
And in it are the Lords of York, Berkeley,
  and Seymour-
None else of name and noble estimate.

Enter Ross and WILLOUGHBY

NORTHUMBERLAND. Here come the Lords of
  Ross and Willoughby,
Bloody with spurring, fiery-red with haste.
BOLINGBROKE. Welcome, my lords. I wot your
  love pursues
A banish'd traitor. All my treasury
Is yet but unfelt thanks, which, more enrich'd,
Shall be your love and labour's recompense.
ROSS. Your presence makes us rich, most
  noble lord.
WILLOUGHBY. And far surmounts our labour to
  attain it.
BOLINGBROKE. Evermore thanks, the exchequer
  of the poor;
Which, till my infant fortune comes to years,
Stands for my bounty. But who comes here?

Enter BERKELEY

NORTHUMBERLAND. It is my Lord of Berkeley,
  as I guess.
BERKELEY. My Lord of Hereford, my message is
  to you.
BOLINGBROKE. My lord, my answer is-
  'to Lancaster';
And I am come to seek that name in England;
And I must find that title in your tongue
Before I make reply to aught you say.
BERKELEY. Mistake me not, my lord; 'tis not
  my meaning
To raze one title of your honour out.
To you, my lord, I come-what lord you will-
From the most gracious regent of this land,
The Duke of York, to know what pricks you on
To take advantage of the absent time,
And fright our native peace with self-
  borne arms.

Enter YORK, attended

BOLINGBROKE. I shall not need transport my
  words by you;

Here comes his Grace in person. My
noble uncle!

Kneels

YORK. Show me thy humble heart, and not
thy knee,
Whose duty is deceivable and false.
BOLINGBROKE. My gracious uncle!-
YORK. Tut, tut!
Grace me no grace, nor uncle me no uncle.
I am no traitor's uncle; and that word 'grace'
In an ungracious mouth is but profane.
Why have those banish'd and forbidden legs
Dar'd once to touch a dust of
England's ground?
But then more 'why?'-why have they dar'd
to march
So many miles upon her peaceful bosom,
Frighting her pale-fac'd villages with war
And ostentation of despised arms?
Com'st thou because the anointed King
is hence?
Why, foolish boy, the King is left behind,
And in my loyal bosom lies his power.
Were I but now lord of such hot youth
As when brave Gaunt, thy father, and myself
Rescued the Black Prince, that young Mars
of men,
From forth the ranks of many thousand French,
O, then how quickly should this arm of mine,
Now prisoner to the palsy, chastise thee
And minister correction to thy fault!
BOLINGBROKE My gracious uncle, let me know
my fault;
On what condition stands it and wherein?
YORK. Even in condition of the worst degree-
In gross rebellion and detested treason.
Thou art a banish'd man, and here art come
Before the expiration of thy time,
In braving arms against thy sovereign.
BOLINGBROKE. As I was banish'd, I was
banish'd Hereford;
But as I come, I come for Lancaster.
And, noble uncle, I beseech your Grace
Look on my wrongs with an indifferent eye.
You are my father, for methinks in you
I see old Gaunt alive. O, then, my father,
Will you permit that I shall stand condemn'd
A wandering vagabond; my rights and royalties
Pluck'd from my arms perforce, and given away
To upstart unthrifts? Wherefore was I born?
If that my cousin king be King in England,
It must be granted I am Duke of Lancaster.
You have a son, Aumerle, my noble cousin;

Had you first died, and he been thus
trod down,
He should have found his uncle Gaunt a father
To rouse his wrongs and chase them to the bay.
I am denied to sue my livery here,
And yet my letters patents give me leave.
My father's goods are all distrain'd and sold;
And these and all are all amiss employ'd.
What would you have me do? I am a subject,
And I challenge law-attorneys are denied me;
And therefore personally I lay my claim
To my inheritance of free descent.
NORTHUMBERLAND. The noble Duke hath been
too much abused.
ROSS. It stands your Grace upon to do him right.
WILLOUGHBY. Base men by his endowments are
made great.
YORK. My lords of England, let me tell you this:
I have had feeling of my cousin's wrongs,
And labour'd all I could to do him right;
But in this kind to come, in braving arms,
Be his own carver and cut out his way,
To find out right with wrong-it may not be;
And you that do abet him in this kind
Cherish rebellion, and are rebels all.
NORTHUMBERLAND. The noble Duke hath
sworn his coming is
But for his own; and for the right of that
We all have strongly sworn to give him aid;
And let him never see joy that breaks that oath!
YORK. Well, well, I see the issue of these arms.
I cannot mend it, I must needs confess,
Because my power is weak and all ill left;
But if I could, by Him that gave me life,
I would attach you all and make you stoop
Unto the sovereign mercy of the King;
But since I cannot, be it known unto you
I do remain as neuter. So, fare you well;
Unless you please to enter in the castle,
And there repose you for this night.
BOLINGBROKE. An offer, uncle, that we
will accept.
But we must win your Grace to go with us
To Bristow Castle, which they say is held
By Bushy, Bagot, and their complices,
The caterpillars of the commonwealth,
Which I have sworn to weed and pluck away.
YORK. It may be I will go with you; but yet
I'll pause,
For I am loath to break our country's laws.
Nor friends nor foes, to me welcome you are.
Things past redress are now with me past care.

Exeunt.

✿ SCENE IV ✿
A camp in Wales

Enter EARL OF SALISBURY and a
WELSH CAPTAIN

CAPTAIN. My Lord of Salisbury, we have stay'd
  ten days
  And hardly kept our countrymen together,
  And yet we hear no tidings from the King;
  Therefore we will disperse ourselves. Farewell.
SALISBURY. Stay yet another day, thou
  trusty Welshman;
  The King reposeth all his confidence in thee.
CAPTAIN. 'Tis thought the King is dead; we will
  not stay.
  The bay trees in our country are all wither'd,
  And meteors fright the fixed stars of heaven;
  The pale-fac'd moon looks bloody on the earth,
  And lean-look'd prophets whisper
  fearful change;
  Rich men look sad, and ruffians dance and leap-
  The one in fear to lose what they enjoy,
  The other to enjoy by rage and war.
  These signs forerun the death or fall of kings.
  Farewell. Our countrymen are gone and fled,
  As well assur'd Richard their King is dead.*Exit.✿*
SALISBURY. Ah, Richard, with the eyes of
  heavy mind,
  I see thy glory like a shooting star
  Fall to the base earth from the firmament!
  The sun sets weeping in the lowly west,
  Witnessing storms to come, woe, and unrest;
  Thy friends are fled, to wait upon thy foes;
  And crossly to thy good all fortune goes.*Exit.✿*

❧ ACT III ❧

✿ SCENE I ✿
BOLINGBROKE'S camp at Bristol

Enter BOLINGBROKE, YORK, NORTHUMBERLAND,
PERCY, ROSS, WILLOUGHBY, with BUSHY and
GREEN, prisoners

BOLINGBROKE. Bring forth these men.
  Bushy and Green, I will not vex your souls-
  Since presently your souls must part your bodies-
  With too much urging your pernicious lives,

For 'twere no charity; yet, to wash your blood
From off my hands, here in the view of men
I will unfold some causes of your deaths:
You have misled a prince, a royal king,
A happy gentleman in blood and lineaments,
By you unhappied and disfigured clean;
You have in manner with your sinful hours
Made a divorce betwixt his queen and him;
Broke the possession of a royal bed,
And stain'd the beauty of a fair queen's cheeks
With tears drawn from her eyes by your
  foul wrongs;
Myself-a prince by fortune of my birth,
Near to the King in blood, and near in love
Till you did make him misinterpret me-
Have stoop'd my neck under your injuries
And sigh'd my English breath in
  foreign clouds,
Eating the bitter bread of banishment,
Whilst you have fed upon my signories,
Dispark'd my parks and fell'd my
  forest woods,
From my own windows torn my
  household coat,
Raz'd out my imprese, leaving me no sign
Save men's opinions and my living blood
To show the world I am a gentleman.
This and much more, much more than twice
  all this,
Condemns you to the death. See them
  delivered over
To execution and the hand of death.
BUSHY. More welcome is the stroke of death
  to me
  Than Bolingbroke to England. Lords, farewell.
GREEN. My comfort is that heaven will take
  our souls,
  And plague injustice with the pains of hell.
BOLINGBROKE. My Lord Northumberland, see
  them dispatch'd.
  Exeunt NORTHUMBERLAND, and Others, with BUSHY
  and GREEN.✿
  Uncle, you say the Queen is at your house;
  For God's sake, fairly let her be entreated.
  Tell her I send to her my kind commends;
  Take special care my greetings be delivered.
YORK. A gentleman of mine I have dispatch'd
  With letters of your love to her at large.
BOLINGBROKE. Thanks, gentle uncle. Come,
  lords, away,
  To fight with Glendower and his complices.
  Awhile to work, and after holiday.
  Exeunt.✿

✍ SCENE II ✍

The coast of Wales. A castle in view

Drums. Flourish and colours. Enter the KING, the BISHOP OF CARLISLE, AUMERLE, and Soldiers

KING RICHARD. Barkloughly Castle call they this
at hand?
AUMERLE. Yea, my lord. How brooks your Grace
the air
After your late tossing on the breaking seas?
KING RICHARD. Needs must I like it well. I weep
for joy
To stand upon my kingdom once again.
Dear earth, I do salute thee with my hand,
Though rebels wound thee with their
horses' hoofs.
As a long-parted mother with her child
Plays fondly with her tears and smiles
in meeting,
So weeping-smiling greet I thee, my earth,
And do thee favours with my royal hands.
Feed not thy sovereign's foe, my gentle earth,
Nor with thy sweets comfort his ravenous sense;
But let thy spiders, that suck up thy venom,
And heavy-gaited toads, lie in their way,
Doing annoyance to the treacherous feet
Which with usurping steps do trample thee;
Yield stinging nettles to mine enemies;
And when they from thy bosom pluck a flower,
Guard it, I pray thee, with a lurking adder,
Whose double tongue may with a mortal touch
Throw death upon thy sovereign's enemies.
Mock not my senseless conjuration, lords.
This earth shall have a feeling, and these stones
Prove armed soldiers, ere her native King
Shall falter under foul rebellion's arms.
CARLISLE. Fear not, my lord; that Power that
made you King
Hath power to keep you King in spite of all.
The means that heaven yields must be embrac'd
And not neglected; else, if heaven would,
And we will not, heaven's offer we refuse,
The proffered means of succour and redress.
AUMERLE. He means, my lord, that we are
too remiss;
Whilst Bolingbroke, through our security,
Grows strong and great in substance and
in power.
KING RICHARD. Discomfortable cousin! know'st
thou not
That when the searching eye of heaven is hid,

Behind the globe, that lights the lower world,
Then thieves and robbers range abroad unseen
In murders and in outrage boldly here;
But when from under this terrestrial ball
He fires the proud tops of the eastern pines
And darts his light through every guilty hole,
Then murders, treasons, and detested sins,
The cloak of night being pluck'd from off
their backs,
Stand bare and naked, trembling at themselves?
So when this thief, this traitor, Bolingbroke,
Who all this while hath revell'd in the night,
Whilst we were wand'ring with the Antipodes,
Shall see us rising in our throne, the east,
His treasons will sit blushing in his face,
Not able to endure the sight of day,
But self-affrighted tremble at his sin.
Not all the water in the rough rude sea
Can wash the balm off from an anointed king;
The breath of worldly men cannot depose
The deputy elected by the Lord.
For every man that Bolingbroke hath press'd
To lift shrewd steel against our golden crown,
God for his Richard hath in heavenly pay
A glorious angel. Then, if angels fight,
Weak men must fall; for heaven still guards
the right.

Enter SALISBURY

Welcome, my lord. How far off lies your power?
SALISBURY. Nor near nor farther off, my
gracious lord,
Than this weak arm. Discomfort guides
my tongue,
And bids me speak of nothing but despair.
One day too late, I fear me, noble lord,
Hath clouded all thy happy days on earth.
O, call back yesterday, bid time return,
And thou shalt have twelve thousand
fighting men!
To-day, to-day, unhappy day, too late,
O'erthrows thy joys, friends, fortune, and
thy state;
For all the Welshmen, hearing thou wert dead,
Are gone to Bolingbroke, dispers'd, and fled.
AUMERLE. Comfort, my liege, why looks your
Grace so pale?
KING RICHARD. But now the blood of twenty
thousand men
Did triumph in my face, and they are fled;
And, till so much blood thither come again,
Have I not reason to look pale and dead?
All souls that will be safe, fly from my side;
For time hath set a blot upon my pride.

AUMERLE. Comfort, my liege; remember who
    you are.
KING RICHARD. I had forgot myself; am I
    not King?
Awake, thou coward majesty! thou sleepest.
Is not the King's name twenty thousand names?
Arm, arm, my name! a puny subject strikes
At thy great glory. Look not to the ground,
Ye favourites of a king; are we not high?
High be our thoughts. I know my uncle York
Hath power enough to serve our turn. But who
    comes here?

                Enter SCROOP
SCROOP. More health and happiness betide
    my liege
Than can my care-tun'd tongue deliver him.
KING RICHARD. Mine ear is open and my
    heart prepar'd.
The worst is worldly loss thou canst unfold.
Say, is my kingdom lost? Why, 'twas my care,
And what loss is it to be rid of care?
Strives Bolingbroke to be as great as we?
Greater he shall not be; if he serve God,
We'll serve him too, and be his fellow so.
Revolt our subjects? That we cannot mend;
They break their faith to God as well as us.
Cry woe, destruction, ruin, and decay-
The worst is death, and death will have his day.
SCROOP. Glad am I that your Highness is
    so arm'd
To bear the tidings of calamity.
Like an unseasonable stormy day
Which makes the silver rivers drown
    their shores,
As if the world were all dissolv'd to tears,
So high above his limits swells the rage
Of Bolingbroke, covering your fearful land
With hard bright steel and hearts harder
    than steel.
White-beards have arm'd their thin and
    hairless scalps
Against thy majesty; boys, with women's voices,
Strive to speak big, and clap their female joints
In stiff unwieldy arms against thy crown;
Thy very beadsmen learn to bend their bows
Of double-fatal yew against thy state;
Yea, distaff-women manage rusty bills
Against thy seat: both young and old rebel,
And all goes worse than I have power to tell.
KING RICHARD. Too well, too well thou tell'st
    a tale so in.
Where is the Earl of Wiltshire? Where is Bagot?
What is become of Bushy? Where is Green?

That they have let the dangerous enemy
Measure our confines with such peaceful steps?
If we prevail, their heads shall pay for it.
I warrant they have made peace
    with Bolingbroke.
SCROOP. Peace have they made with him indeed,
    my lord.
KING RICHARD. O villains, vipers, damn'd
    without redemption!
Dogs, easily won to fawn on any man!
Snakes, in my heart-blood warm'd, that sting
    my heart!
Three Judases, each one thrice worse
    than Judas!
Would they make peace? Terrible hell make war
Upon their spotted souls for this offence!
SCROOP. Sweet love, I see, changing his property,
Turns to the sourest and most deadly hate.
Again uncurse their souls; their peace is made
With heads, and not with hands; those whom
    you curse
Have felt the worst of death's destroying wound
And lie full low, grav'd in the hollow ground.
AUMERLE. Is Bushy, Green, and the Earl of
    Wiltshire dead?
SCROOP. Ay, all of them at Bristow lost
    their heads.
AUMERLE. Where is the Duke my father with
    his power?
KING RICHARD. No matter where-of comfort no
    man speak.
Let's talk of graves, of worms, and epitaphs;
Make dust our paper, and with rainy eyes
Write sorrow on the bosom of the earth.
Let's choose executors and talk of wills;
And yet not so-for what can we bequeath
Save our deposed bodies to the ground?
Our lands, our lives, and all, are Bolingbroke's.
And nothing can we call our own but death
And that small model of the barren earth
Which serves as paste and cover to our bones.
For God's sake let us sit upon the ground
And tell sad stories of the death of kings:
How some have been depos'd, some slain
    in war,
Some haunted by the ghosts they have depos'd,
Some poison'd by their wives, some
    sleeping kill'd,
All murder'd-for within the hollow crown
That rounds the mortal temples of a king
Keeps Death his court; and there the antic sits,
Scoffing his state and grinning at his pomp;
Allowing him a breath, a little scene,

To monarchise, be fear'd, and kill with looks;
Infusing him with self and vain conceit,
As if this flesh which walls about our life
Were brass impregnable; and, humour'd thus,
Comes at the last, and with a little pin
Bores through his castle wall, and farewell, king!
Cover your heads, and mock not flesh and blood
With solemn reverence; throw away respect,
Tradition, form, and ceremonious duty;
For you have but mistook me all this while.
I live with bread like you, feel want,
Taste grief, need friends: subjected thus,
How can you say to me I am a king?
CARLISLE. My lord, wise men ne'er sit and wail
  their woes,
But presently prevent the ways to wail.
To fear the foe, since fear oppresseth strength,
Gives, in your weakness, strength unto your foe,
And so your follies fight against yourself.
Fear and be slain-no worse can come to fight;
And fight and die is death destroying death,
Where fearing dying pays death servile breath.
AUMERLE. My father hath a power; inquire of him,
And learn to make a body of a limb.
KING RICHARD. Thou chid'st me well. Proud
  Bolingbroke, I come
To change blows with thee for our day of doom.
This ague fit of fear is over-blown;
An easy task it is to win our own.
Say, Scroop, where lies our uncle with
  his power?
Speak sweetly, man, although thy looks be sour.
SCROOP. Men judge by the complexion of the sky
The state in inclination of the day;
So may you by my dull and heavy eye,
My tongue hath but a heavier tale to say.
I play the torturer, by small and small
To lengthen out the worst that must be spoken:
Your uncle York is join'd with Bolingbroke;
And all your northern castles yielded up,
And all your southern gentlemen in arms
Upon his party.
KING RICHARD. Thou hast said enough.
  [To AUMERLE] Beshrew thee, cousin, which didst
  lead me forth
Of that sweet way I was in to despair!
What say you now? What comfort have we now?
By heaven, I'll hate him everlastingly
That bids me be of comfort any more.
Go to Flint Castle; there I'll pine away;
A king, woe's slave, shall kingly woe obey.
That power I have, discharge; and let them go
To ear the land that hath some hope to grow,

For I have none. Let no man speak again
To alter this, for counsel is but vain.
AUMERLE. My liege, one word.
KING RICHARD. He does me double wrong
That wounds me with the flatteries of
  his tongue.
Discharge my followers; let them hence away,
From Richard's night to Bolingbroke's fair day.
                                    Exeunt.

✿ SCENE III ✿
Wales. Before Flint Castle

Enter, with drum and colours, BOLINGBROKE, YORK,
NORTHUMBERLAND, and Forces

BOLINGBROKE. So that by this intelligence
  we learn
The Welshmen are dispers'd; and Salisbury
Is gone to meet the King, who lately landed
With some few private friends upon this coast.
NORTHUMBERLAND. The news is very fair and
  good, my lord.
Richard not far from hence hath hid his head.
YORK. It would beseem the Lord Northumberland
To say 'King Richard'. Alack the heavy day
When such a sacred king should hide his head!
NORTHUMBERLAND. Your Grace mistakes; only
  to be brief,
Left I his title out.
YORK. The time hath been,
  Would you have been so brief with him,
  he would
Have been so brief with you to shorten you,
For taking so the head, your whole
  head's length.
BOLINGBROKE. Mistake not, uncle, further than
  you should.
YORK. Take not, good cousin, further than
  you should,
Lest you mistake. The heavens are over
  our heads.
BOLINGBROKE. I know it, uncle; and oppose
  not myself
Against their will. But who comes here?
                          Enter PERCY
Welcome, Harry. What, will not this castle yield?
PIERCY. The castle royally is mann'd, my lord,
Against thy entrance.
BOLINGBROKE. Royally!
  Why, it contains no king?
PERCY. Yes, my good lord,

It doth contain a king; King Richard lies
Within the limits of yon lime and stone;
And with him are the Lord Aumerle,
  Lord Salisbury,
Sir Stephen Scroop, besides a clergyman
Of holy reverence; who, I cannot learn.
NORTHUMBERLAND. O, belike it is the Bishop
  of Carlisle.
BOLINGBROKE. [To NORTHUMBERLAND]
  Noble lord,
Go to the rude ribs of that ancient castle;
Through brazen trumpet send the breath
  of parley
Into his ruin'd ears, and thus deliver:
Henry Bolingbroke
On both his knees doth kiss King
  Richard's hand,
And sends allegiance and true faith of heart
To his most royal person; hither come
Even at his feet to lay my arms and power,
Provided that my banishment repeal'd
And lands restor'd again be freely granted;
If not, I'll use the advantage of my power
And lay the summer's dust with showers
  of blood
Rain'd from the wounds of
  slaughtered Englishmen;
The which how far off from the mind
  of Bolingbroke
It is such crimson tempest should bedrench
The fresh green lap of fair King Richard's land,
My stooping duty tenderly shall show.
Go, signify as much, while here we march
Upon the grassy carpet of this plain.
  [NORTHUMBERLAND advances to the Castle, with
  a trumpet]
Let's march without the noise of
  threat'ning drum,
That from this castle's tottered battlements
Our fair appointments may be well perus'd.
Methinks King Richard and myself should meet
With no less terror than the elements
Of fire and water, when their thund'ring shock
At meeting tears the cloudy cheeks of heaven.
Be he the fire, I'll be the yielding water;
The rage be his, whilst on the earth I rain
My waters-on the earth, and not on him.
March on, and mark King Richard how he looks.
  [Parle without, and answer within; then a flourish.]
    Enter on the walls, the KING, the BISHOP
      OF CARLISLE, AUMERLE, SCROOP,
        and SALISBURY
See, see, King Richard doth himself appear,

As doth the blushing discontented sun
From out the fiery portal of the east,
When he perceives the envious clouds are bent
To dim his glory and to stain the track
Of his bright passage to the occident.
YORK. Yet he looks like a king. Behold, his eye,
As bright as is the eagle's, lightens forth
Controlling majesty. Alack, alack, for woe,
That any harm should stain so fair a show!
KING RICHARD. [To NORTHUMBERLAND]
  We are amaz'd; and thus long have we stood
To watch the fearful bending of thy knee,
Because we thought ourself thy lawful King;
And if we be, how dare thy joints forget
To pay their awful duty to our presence?
If we be not, show us the hand of God
That hath dismiss'd us from our stewardship;
For well we know no hand of blood and bone
Can gripe the sacred handle of our sceptre,
Unless he do profane, steal, or usurp.
And though you think that all, as you have done,
Have torn their souls by turning them from us,
And we are barren and bereft of friends,
Yet know-my master, God omnipotent,
Is mustering in his clouds on our behalf
Armies of pestilence; and they shall strike
Your children yet unborn and unbegot,
That lift your vassal hands against my head
And threat the glory of my precious crown.
Tell Bolingbroke, for yon methinks he stands,
That every stride he makes upon my land
Is dangerous treason; he is come to open
The purple testament of bleeding war;
But ere the crown he looks for live in peace,
Ten thousand bloody crowns of mothers' sons
Shall ill become the flower of England's face,
Change the complexion of her maid-pale peace
To scarlet indignation, and bedew
Her pastures' grass with faithful English blood.
NORTHUMBERLAND. The King of Heaven forbid
  our lord the King
Should so with civil and uncivil arms
Be rush'd upon! Thy thrice noble cousin,
Harry Bolingbroke, doth humbly kiss thy hand;
And by the honourable tomb he swears
That stands upon your royal grandsire's bones,
And by the royalties of both your bloods,
Currents that spring from one most
  gracious head,
And by the buried hand of warlike Gaunt,
And by the worth and honour of himself,
Comprising all that may be sworn or said,
His coming hither hath no further scope

Than for his lineal royalties, and to beg
Enfranchisement immediate on his knees;
Which on thy royal party granted once,
His glittering arms he will commend to rust,
His barbed steeds to stables, and his heart
To faithful service of your Majesty.
This swears he, as he is a prince, is just;
And as I am a gentleman I credit him.
KING RICHARD. Northumberland, say thus the
  King returns:
His noble cousin is right welcome hither;
And all the number of his fair demands
Shall be accomplish'd without contradiction.
With all the gracious utterance thou hast
Speak to his gentle hearing kind commends.
[To AUMERLE] We do debase ourselves, cousin,
  do we not,
To look so poorly and to speak so fair?
Shall we call back Northumberland, and send
Defiance to the traitor, and so die?
AUMERLE. No, good my lord; let's fight with
  gentle words
Till time lend friends, and friends their
  helpful swords.
KING RICHARD. O God, O God! that e'er this
  tongue of mine
That laid the sentence of dread banishment
On yon proud man should take it off again
With words of sooth! O that I were as great
As is my grief, or lesser than my name!
Or that I could forget what I have been!
Or not remember what I must be now!
Swell'st thou, proud heart? I'll give thee scope
  to beat,
Since foes have scope to beat both thee and me.
AUMERLE. Northumberland comes back
  from Bolingbroke.
KING RICHARD. What must the King do now?
  Must he submit?
The King shall do it. Must he be depos'd?
The King shall be contented. Must he lose
The name of king? A God's name, let it go.
I'll give my jewels for a set of beads,
My gorgeous palace for a hermitage,
My gay apparel for an almsman's gown,
My figur'd goblets for a dish of wood,
My sceptre for a palmer's walking staff,
My subjects for a pair of carved saints,
And my large kingdom for a little grave,
A little little grave, an obscure grave-
Or I'll be buried in the King's high way,
Some way of common trade, where
  subjects' feet

May hourly trample on their sovereign's head;
For on my heart they tread now whilst I live,
And buried once, why not upon my head?
Aumerle, thou weep'st, my tender-
  hearted cousin!
We'll make foul weather with despised tears;
Our sighs and they shall lodge the summer corn
And make a dearth in this revolting land.
Or shall we play the wantons with our woes
And make some pretty match with
  shedding tears?
As thus: to drop them still upon one place
Till they have fretted us a pair of graves
Within the earth; and, therein laid-there lies
Two kinsmen digg'd their graves with
  weeping eyes.
Would not this ill do well? Well, well, I see
I talk but idly, and you laugh at me.
Most mighty prince, my Lord Northumberland,
What says King Bolingbroke? Will his Majesty
Give Richard leave to live till Richard die?
You make a leg, and Bolingbroke says ay.
NORTHUMBERLAND. My lord, in the base court
  he doth attend
To speak with you; may it please you to
  come down?
KING RICHARD. Down, down I come, like
  glist'ring Phaethon,
Wanting the manage of unruly jades.
In the base court? Base court, where kings
  grow base,
To come at traitors' calls, and do them grace.
In the base court? Come down? Down, court!
  down, king!
For night-owls shriek where mounting larks
  should sing.
                              Exeunt from above.
BOLINGBROKE. What says his Majesty?
NORTHUMBERLAND. Sorrow and grief of heart
Makes him speak fondly, like a frantic man;
Yet he is come.
          Enter the KING, and his Attendants, below
BOLINGBROKE. Stand all apart,
And show fair duty to his Majesty. [He kneels down]
My gracious lord-
KING RICHARD. Fair cousin, you debase your
  princely knee
To make the base earth proud with kissing it.
Me rather had my heart might feel your love
Than my unpleas'd eye see your courtesy.
Up, cousin, up; your heart is up, I know,
[Touching his own head] Thus high at least, although
  your knee be low.

BOLINGBROKE. My gracious lord, I come but for
mine own.
KING RICHARD. Your own is yours, and I am
yours, and all.
BOLINGBROKE. So far be mine, my most
redoubted lord,
As my true service shall deserve your love.
KING RICHARD. Well you deserve. They well
deserve to have
That know the strong'st and surest way to get.
Uncle, give me your hands; nay, dry your eyes:
Tears show their love, but want their remedies.
Cousin, I am too young to be your father,
Though you are old enough to be my heir.
What you will have, I'll give, and willing too;
For do we must what force will have us do.
Set on towards London. Cousin, is it so?
BOLINGBROKE. Yea, my good lord.
KING RICHARD. Then I must not say no.

Flourish. Exeunt.

❧ SCENE IV ❧
The DUKE OF YORK'S garden

Enter the QUEEN and two LADIES

QUEEN. What sport shall we devise here in
this garden
To drive away the heavy thought of care?
LADY. Madam, we'll play at bowls.
QUEEN. 'Twill make me think the world is full
of rubs
And that my fortune runs against the bias.
LADY. Madam, we'll dance.
QUEEN. My legs can keep no measure in delight,
When my poor heart no measure keeps in grief;
Therefore no dancing, girl; some other sport.
LADY. Madam, we'll tell tales.
QUEEN. Of sorrow or of joy?
LADY. Of either, madam.
QUEEN. Of neither, girl;
For if of joy, being altogether wanting,
It doth remember me the more of sorrow;
Or if of grief, being altogether had,
It adds more sorrow to my want of joy;
For what I have I need not to repeat,
And what I want it boots not to complain.
LADY. Madam, I'll sing.
QUEEN. 'Tis well that thou hast cause;
But thou shouldst please me better wouldst
thou weep.
LADY. I could weep, madam, would it do you good.

QUEEN. And I could sing, would weeping do
me good,
And never borrow any tear of thee.

Enter a GARDENER and two SERVANTS

But stay, here come the gardeners.
Let's step into the shadow of these trees.
My wretchedness unto a row of pins,
They will talk of state, for every one doth so
Against a change: woe is forerun with woe.

QUEEN and LADIES retire.

GARDENER. Go, bind thou up yon
dangling apricocks,
Which, like unruly children, make their sire
Stoop with oppression of their prodigal weight;
Give some supportance to the bending twigs.
Go thou, and like an executioner
Cut off the heads of too fast growing sprays
That look too lofty in our commonwealth:
All must be even in our government.
You thus employ'd, I will go root away
The noisome weeds which without profit suck
The soil's fertility from wholesome flowers.
SERVANT. Why should we, in the compass of
a pale,
Keep law and form and due proportion,
Showing, as in a model, our firm estate,
When our sea-walled garden, the whole land,
Is full of weeds; her fairest flowers chok'd up,
Her fruit trees all unprun'd, her hedges ruin'd,
Her knots disordered, and her
wholesome herbs
Swarming with caterpillars?
GARDENER. Hold thy peace.
He that hath suffer'd this disorder'd spring
Hath now himself met with the fall of leaf;
The weeds which his broad-spreading leaves
did shelter,
That seem'd in eating him to hold him up,
Are pluck'd up root and all by Bolingbroke-
I mean the Earl of Wiltshire, Bushy, Green.
SERVANT. What, are they dead?
GARDENER. They are; and Bolingbroke
Hath seiz'd the wasteful King. O, what pity is it
That he had not so trimm'd and dress'd
his land
As we this garden! We at time of year
Do wound the bark, the skin of our fruit trees,
Lest, being over-proud in sap and blood,
With too much riches it confound itself;
Had he done so to great and growing men,
They might have liv'd to bear, and he to taste
Their fruits of duty. Superfluous branches
We lop away, that bearing boughs may live;

Had he done so, himself had home the crown,
Which waste of idle hours hath quite
thrown down.
SERVANT. What, think you the King shall
be deposed?
GARDENER. Depress'd he is already,
and depos'd
'Tis doubt he will be. Letters came last night
To a dear friend of the good Duke of York's
That tell black tidings.
QUEEN. O, I am press'd to death through want
of speaking! [Coming forward]
Thou, old Adam's likeness, set to dress
this garden,
How dares thy harsh rude tongue sound this
unpleasing news?
What Eve, what serpent, hath suggested thee
To make a second fall of cursed man?
Why dost thou say King Richard is depos'd?
Dar'st thou, thou little better thing than earth,
Divine his downfall? Say, where, when,
and how,
Cam'st thou by this ill tidings? Speak,
thou wretch.
GARDENER. Pardon me, madam; little joy have
To breathe this news; yet what I say is true.
King Richard, he is in the mighty hold
Of Bolingbroke. Their fortunes both
are weigh'd.
In your lord's scale is nothing but himself,
And some few vanities that make him light;
But in the balance of great Bolingbroke,
Besides himself, are all the English peers,
And with that odds he weighs King
Richard down.
Post you to London, and you will find it so;
I speak no more than every one doth know.
QUEEN. Nimble mischance, that art so light
of foot,
Doth not thy embassage belong to me,
And am I last that knows it? O, thou thinkest
To serve me last, that I may longest keep
Thy sorrow in my breast. Come, ladies, go
To meet at London London's King in woe.
What, was I born to this, that my sad look
Should grace the triumph of great Bolingbroke?
Gard'ner, for telling me these news of woe,
Pray God the plants thou graft'st may
never grow!
Exeunt QUEEN and LADIES.
GARDENER. Poor Queen, so that thy state might
be no worse,
I would my skill were subject to thy curse.

Here did she fall a tear; here in this place
I'll set a bank of rue, sour herb of grace.
Rue, even for ruth, here shortly shall be seen,
In the remembrance of a weeping queen.
Exeunt.

ACT IV

SCENE I
Westminster Hall

*Enter, as to the Parliament, BOLINGBROKE, AUMERLE,
NORTHUMBERLAND, PERCY, FITZWATER,
SURREY, the BISHOP OF CARLISLE, the ABBOT OF
WESTMINSTER, and others; HERALD, Officers, and BAGOT*

BOLINGBROKE. Call forth Bagot.
Now, Bagot, freely speak thy mind-
What thou dost know of noble
Gloucester's death;
Who wrought it with the King, and
who perform'd
The bloody office of his timeless end.
BAGOT. Then set before my face the
Lord Aumerle.
BOLINGBROKE. Cousin, stand forth, and look
upon that man.
BAGOT. My Lord Aumerle, I know your
daring tongue
Scorns to unsay what once it hath deliver'd.
In that dead time when Gloucester's death
was plotted
I heard you say 'Is not my arm of length,
That reacheth from the restful English Court
As far as Calais, to mine uncle's head?'
Amongst much other talk that very time
I heard you say that you had rather refuse
The offer of an hundred thousand crowns
Than Bolingbroke's return to England;
Adding withal, how blest this land would be
In this your cousin's death.
AUMERLE. Princes, and noble lords,
What answer shall I make to this base man?
Shall I so much dishonour my fair stars
On equal terms to give him chastisement?
Either I must, or have mine honour soil'd
With the attainder of his slanderous lips.
There is my gage, the manual seal of death
That marks thee out for hell. I say thou liest,
And will maintain what thou hast said is false
In thy heart-blood, through being all too base

To stain the temper of my knightly sword.

BOLINGBROKE. Bagot, forbear; thou shalt not
  take it up.

AUMERLE. Excepting one, I would he were
  the best
In all this presence that hath mov'd me so.

FITZWATER. If that thy valour stand on sympathy,
There is my gage, Aumerle, in gage to thine.
By that fair sun which shows me where
  thou stand'st,
I heard thee say, and vauntingly thou spak'st it,
That thou wert cause of noble
  Gloucester's death.
If thou deniest it twenty times, thou liest;
And I will turn thy falsehood to thy heart,
Where it was forged, with my rapier's point.

AUMERLE. Thou dar'st not, coward, live to see
  that day.

FITZWATER. Now, by my soul, I would it were
  this hour.

AUMERLE. Fitzwater, thou art damn'd to hell
  for this.

PERCY. Aumerle, thou liest; his honour is as true
In this appeal as thou art an unjust;
And that thou art so, there I throw my gage,
To prove it on thee to the extremest point
Of mortal breathing. Seize it, if thou dar'st.

AUMERLE. An if I do not, may my hands rot off
And never brandish more revengeful steel
Over the glittering helmet of my foe!

ANOTHER LORD. I task the earth to the like,
  forsworn Aumerle;
And spur thee on with full as many lies
As may be halloa'd in thy treacherous ear
From sun to sun. There is my honour's pawn;
Engage it to the trial, if thou darest.

AUMERLE. Who sets me else? By heaven, I'll throw
  at all!
I have a thousand spirits in one breast
To answer twenty thousand such as you.

SURREY. My Lord Fitzwater, I do remember well
The very time Aumerle and you did talk.

FITZWATER. 'Tis very true; you were in
  presence then,
And you can witness with me this is true.

SURREY. As false, by heaven, as heaven itself
  is true.

FITZWATER. Surrey, thou liest.

SURREY. Dishonourable boy!
That lie shall lie so heavy on my sword
That it shall render vengeance and revenge
Till thou the lie-giver and that lie do lie
In earth as quiet as thy father's skull.

In proof whereof, there is my honour's pawn;
Engage it to the trial, if thou dar'st.

FITZWATER. How fondly dost thou spur a
  forward horse!
If I dare eat, or drink, or breathe, or live,
I dare meet Surrey in a wilderness,
And spit upon him whilst I say he lies,
And lies, and lies. There is my bond of faith,
To tie thee to my strong correction.
As I intend to thrive in this new world,
Aumerle is guilty of my true appeal.
Besides, I heard the banish'd Norfolk say
That thou, Aumerle, didst send two of thy men
To execute the noble Duke at Calais.

AUMERLE. Some honest Christian trust me with
  a gage
That Norfolk lies. Here do I throw down this,
If he may be repeal'd to try his honour.

BOLINGBROKE. These differences shall all rest
  under gage
Till Norfolk be repeal'd-repeal'd he shall be
And, though mine enemy, restor'd again
To all his lands and signories. When he
  is return'd,
Against Aumerle we will enforce his trial.

CARLISLE. That honourable day shall never
  be seen.
Many a time hath banish'd Norfolk fought
For Jesu Christ in glorious Christian field,
Streaming the ensign of the Christian cross
Against black pagans, Turks, and Saracens;
And, toil'd with works of war, retir'd himself
To Italy; and there, at Venice, gave
His body to that pleasant country's earth,
And his pure soul unto his captain, Christ,
Under whose colours he had fought so long.

BOLINGBROKE. Why, Bishop, is Norfolk dead?

CARLISLE. As surely as I live, my lord.

BOLINGBROKE. Sweet peace conduct his sweet
  soul to the bosom
Of good old Abraham! Lords appellants,
Your differences shall all rest under gage
Till we assign you to your days of trial

Enter YORK, attended

YORK. Great Duke of Lancaster, I come to thee
From plume-pluck'd Richard, who with
  willing soul
Adopts thee heir, and his high sceptre yields
To the possession of thy royal hand.
Ascend his throne, descending now from him-
And long live Henry, fourth of that name!

BOLINGBROKE. In God's name, I'll ascend the
  regal throne.

CARLISLE. Marry, God forbid!
  Worst in this royal presence may I speak,
  Yet best beseeming me to speak the truth.
  Would God that any in this noble presence
  Were enough noble to be upright judge
  Of noble Richard! Then true noblesse would
  Learn him forbearance from so foul a wrong.
  What subject can give sentence on his king?
  And who sits here that is not Richard's subject?
  Thieves are not judg'd but they are by to hear,
  Although apparent guilt be seen in them;
  And shall the figure of God's majesty,
  His captain, steward, deputy elect,
  Anointed, crowned, planted many years,
  Be judg'd by subject and inferior breath,
  And he himself not present? O, forfend it, God,
  That in a Christian climate souls refin'd
  Should show so heinous, black, obscene a deed!
  I speak to subjects, and a subject speaks,
  Stirr'd up by God, thus boldly for his king.
  My Lord of Hereford here, whom you call king,
  Is a foul traitor to proud Hereford's king;
  And if you crown him, let me prophesy-
  The blood of English shall manure the ground,
  And future ages groan for this foul act;
  Peace shall go sleep with Turks and infidels,
  And in this seat of peace tumultuous wars
  Shall kin with kin and kind with kind confound;
  Disorder, horror, fear, and mutiny,
  Shall here inhabit, and this land be call'd
  The field of Golgotha and dead men's skulls.
  O, if you raise this house against this house,
  It will the woefullest division prove
  That ever fell upon this cursed earth.
  Prevent it, resist it, let it not be so,
  Lest child, child's children, cry against you woe.
NORTHUMBERLAND. Well have you argued, sir;
  and, for your pains,
  Of capital treason we arrest you here.
  My Lord of Westminster, be it your charge
  To keep him safely till his day of trial.
  May it please you, lords, to grant the
  commons' suit?
BOLINGBROKE. Fetch hither Richard, that in
  common view
  He may surrender; so we shall proceed
  Without suspicion.
YORK. I will be his conduct.   *Exit.*
BOLINGBROKE. Lords, you that here are under
  our arrest,
  Procure your sureties for your days of answer.
  Little are we beholding to your love,
  And little look'd for at your helping hands.

Re-enter YORK, with KING RICHARD, and Offciers
bearing the regalia

KING RICHARD. Alack, why am I sent for to
  a king,
  Before I have shook off the regal thoughts
  Wherewith I reign'd? I hardly yet have learn'd
  To insinuate, flatter, bow, and bend my knee.
  Give sorrow leave awhile to tutor me
  To this submission. Yet I well remember
  The favours of these men. Were they not mine?
  Did they not sometime cry 'All hail!' to me?
  So Judas did to Christ; but he, in twelve,
  Found truth in all but one; I, in twelve
  thousand, none.
  God save the King! Will no man say amen?
  Am I both priest and clerk? Well then, amen.
  God save the King! although I be not he;
  And yet, amen, if heaven do think him me.
  To do what service am I sent for hither?
YORK. To do that office of thine own good will
  Which tired majesty did make thee offer-
  The resignation of thy state and crown
  To Henry Bolingbroke.
KING RICHARD. Give me the crown. Here,
  cousin, seize the crown.
  Here, cousin,
  On this side my hand, and on that side thine.
  Now is this golden crown like a deep well
  That owes two buckets, filling one another;
  The emptier ever dancing in the air,
  The other down, unseen, and full of water.
  That bucket down and full of tears am I,
  Drinking my griefs, whilst you mount up
  on high.
BOLINGBROKE. I thought you had been willing
  to resign.
KING RICHARD. My crown I am; but still my griefs
  are mine.
  You may my glories and my state depose,
  But not my griefs; still am I king of those.
BOLINGBROKE. Part of your cares you give me
  with your crown.
KING RICHARD. Your cares set up do not pluck
  my cares down.
  My care is loss of care, by old care done;
  Your care is gain of care, by new care won.
  The cares I give I have, though given away;
  They tend the crown, yet still with me they stay.
BOLINGBROKE. Are you contented to resign
  the crown?
KING RICHARD. Ay, no; no, ay; for I must
  nothing be;
  Therefore no no, for I resign to thee.

Now mark me how I will undo myself:
I give this heavy weight from off my head,
And this unwieldy sceptre from my hand,
The pride of kingly sway from out my heart;
With mine own tears I wash away my balm,
With mine own hands I give away my crown,
With mine own tongue deny my sacred state,
With mine own breath release all
 duteous oaths;
All pomp and majesty I do forswear;
My manors, rents, revenues, I forgo;
My acts, decrees, and statutes, I deny.
God pardon all oaths that are broke to me!
God keep all vows unbroke are made to thee!
Make me, that nothing have, with
 nothing griev'd,
And thou with all pleas'd, that hast all achiev'd.
Long mayst thou live in Richard's seat to sit,
And soon lie Richard in an earthly pit.
God save King Henry, unking'd Richard says,
And send him many years of sunshine days!
What more remains?
NORTHUMBERLAND. No more; but that
 you read
These accusations, and these grievous crimes
Committed by your person and your followers
Against the state and profit of this land;
That, by confessing them, the souls of men
May deem that you are worthily depos'd.
KING RICHARD. Must I do so? And must I
 ravel out
My weav'd up follies? Gentle Northumberland,
If thy offences were upon record,
Would it not shame thee in so fair a troop
To read a lecture of them? If thou wouldst,
There shouldst thou find one heinous article,
Containing the deposing of a king
And cracking the strong warrant of an oath,
Mark'd with a blot, damn'd in the book
 of heaven.
Nay, all of you that stand and look upon me
Whilst that my wretchedness doth bait myself,
Though some of you, with Pilate, wash
 your hands,
Showing an outward pity-yet you Pilates
Have here deliver'd me to my sour cross,
And water cannot wash away your sin.
NORTHUMBERLAND. My lord, dispatch; read
 o'er these articles.
KING RICHARD. Mine eyes are full of tears; I
 cannot see.
And yet salt water blinds them not so much
But they can see a sort of traitors here.

Nay, if I turn mine eyes upon myself,
I find myself a traitor with the rest;
For I have given here my soul's consent
T'undeck the pompous body of a king;
Made glory base, and sovereignty a slave,
Proud majesty a subject, state a peasant.
NORTHUMBERLAND. My lord-
KING RICHARD. No lord of thine, thou haught
 insulting man,
Nor no man's lord; I have no name, no tide-
No, not that name was given me at the font-
But 'tis usurp'd. Alack the heavy day,
That I have worn so many winters out,
And know not now what name to call myself!
O that I were a mockery king of snow,
Standing before the sun of Bolingbroke
To melt myself away in water drops!
Good king, great king, and yet not
 greatly good,
An if my word be sterling yet in England,
Let it command a mirror hither straight,
That it may show me what a face I have
Since it is bankrupt of his majesty.
BOLINGBROKE. Go some of you and fetch a
 looking-glass.   *Exit an Attendant.*
NORTHUMBERLAND. Read o'er this paper while
 the glass doth come.
KING RICHARD. Fiend, thou torments me ere I
 come to hell.
BOLINGBROKE. Urge it no more, my
 Lord Northumberland.
NORTHUMBERLAND. The Commons will not,
 then, be satisfied.
KING RICHARD. They shall be satisfied. I'll
 read enough,
When I do see the very book indeed
Where all my sins are writ, and that's myself.
          Re-enter Attendant with glass
Give me that glass, and therein will I read.
No deeper wrinkles yet? Hath sorrow struck
So many blows upon this face of mine
And made no deeper wounds? O flatt'ring glass,
Like to my followers in prosperity,
Thou dost beguile me! Was this face the face
That every day under his household roof
Did keep ten thousand men? Was this the face
That like the sun did make beholders wink?
Is this the face which fac'd so many follies
That was at last out-fac'd by Bolingbroke?
A brittle glory shineth in this face;
As brittle as the glory is the face; [*Dashes the glass
against the ground*]
For there it is, crack'd in a hundred shivers.

Mark, silent King, the moral of this sport-
How soon my sorrow hath destroy'd my face.
BOLINGBROKE. The shadow of your sorrow
hath destroy'd
The shadow of your face.
KING RICHARD. Say that again.
The shadow of my sorrow? Ha! let's see.
'Tis very true: my grief lies all within;
And these external manner of laments
Are merely shadows to the unseen grief
That swells with silence in the tortur'd soul.
There lies the substance; and I thank thee, King,
For thy great bounty, that not only giv'st
Me cause to wail, but teachest me the way
How to lament the cause. I'll beg one boon,
And then be gone and trouble you no more.
Shall I obtain it?
BOLINGBROKE. Name it, fair cousin.
KING RICHARD. Fair cousin! I am greater than
a king;
For when I was a king, my flatterers
Were then but subjects; being now a subject,
I have a king here to my flatterer.
Being so great, I have no need to beg.
BOLINGBROKE. Yet ask.
KING RICHARD. And shall I have?
BOLINGBROKE. You shall.
KING RICHARD. Then give me leave to go.
BOLINGBROKE. Whither?
KING RICHARD. Whither you will, so I were from
your sights.
BOLINGBROKE. Go, some of you convey him to
the Tower.
KING RICHARD. O, good! Convey! Conveyers are
you all,
That rise thus nimbly by a true king's fall.
Exeunt KING RICHARD, some LORDS and a Guard.
BOLINGBROKE. On Wednesday next we solemnly
set down
Our coronation. Lords, prepare yourselves.
Exeunt all but the ABBOT OF WESTMINSTER, the
BISHOP OF CARLISLE, and AUMERLE.
ABBOT. A woeful pageant have we here beheld.
CARLISLE. The woe's to come; the children
yet unborn
Shall feel this day as sharp to them as thorn.
AUMERLE. You holy clergymen, is there no plot
To rid the realm of this pernicious blot?
ABBOT. My lord,
Before I freely speak my mind herein,
You shall not only take the sacrament
To bury mine intents, but also to effect
Whatever I shall happen to devise.

I see your brows are full of discontent,
Your hearts of sorrow, and your eyes of tears.
Come home with me to supper; I will lay
A plot shall show us all a merry day *Exeunt.*

ACT V

SCENE I

London. A street leading to the Tower

Enter the QUEEN, with her Attendants

QUEEN. This way the King will come; this is
the way
To Julius Caesar's ill-erected tower,
To whose flint bosom my condemned lord
Is doom'd a prisoner by proud Bolingbroke.
Here let us rest, if this rebellious earth
Have any resting for her true King's queen.
Enter KING RICHARD and Guard
But soft, but see, or rather do not see,
My fair rose wither. Yet look up, behold,
That you in pity may dissolve to dew,
And wash him fresh again with true-love tears.
Ah, thou, the model where old Troy did stand;
Thou map of honour, thou King Richard's tomb,
And not King Richard; thou most beauteous inn,
Why should hard-favour'd grief be lodg'd
in thee,
When triumph is become an alehouse guest?
KING RICHARD. Join not with grief, fair woman,
do not so,
To make my end too sudden. Learn, good soul,
To think our former state a happy dream;
From which awak'd, the truth of what we are
Shows us but this: I am sworn brother, sweet,
To grim Necessity; and he and I
Will keep a league till death. Hie thee to France,
And cloister thee in some religious house.
Our holy lives must win a new world's crown,
Which our profane hours here have
thrown down.
QUEEN. What, is my Richard both in shape
and mind
Transform'd and weak'ned? Hath
Bolingbroke depos'd
Thine intellect? Hath he been in thy heart?
The lion dying thrusteth forth his paw
And wounds the earth, if nothing else, with rage
To be o'erpow'r'd; and wilt thou, pupil-like,
Take the correction mildly, kiss the rod,

And fawn on rage with base humility,
Which art a lion and the king of beasts?
KING RICHARD. A king of beasts, indeed! If aught
  but beasts,
I had been still a happy king of men.
Good sometimes queen, prepare thee hence
  for France.
Think I am dead, and that even here thou takest,
As from my death-bed, thy last living leave.
In winter's tedious nights sit by the fire
With good old folks, and let them tell thee tales
Of woeful ages long ago betid;
And ere thou bid good night, to quit their griefs
Tell thou the lamentable tale of me,
And send the hearers weeping to their beds;
For why, the senseless brands will sympathise
The heavy accent of thy moving tongue,
And in compassion weep the fire out;
And some will mourn in ashes, some coal-black,
For the deposing of a rightful king.

Enter NORTHUMBERLAND attended

NORTHUMBERLAND. My lord, the mind of
  Bolingbroke is chang'd;
You must to Pomfret, not unto the Tower.
And, madam, there is order ta'en for you:
With all swift speed you must away to France.
KING RICHARD. Northumberland, thou
  ladder wherewithal
The mounting Bolingbroke ascends my throne,
The time shall not be many hours of age
More than it is, ere foul sin gathering head
Shall break into corruption. Thou shalt think
Though he divide the realm and give thee half
It is too little, helping him to all;
And he shall think that thou, which knowest
  the way
To plant unrightful kings, wilt know again,
Being ne'er so little urg'd, another way
To pluck him headlong from the
  usurped throne.
The love of wicked men converts to fear;
That fear to hate; and hate turns one or both
To worthy danger and deserved death.
NORTHUMBERLAND. My guilt be on my head,
  and there an end.
Take leave, and part; for you must
  part forthwith.
KING RICHARD. Doubly divorc'd! Bad men,
  you violate
A twofold marriage-'twixt my crown and me,
And then betwixt me and my married wife.
Let me unkiss the oath 'twixt thee and me;
And yet not so, for with a kiss 'twas made.

Part us, Northumberland; I towards the north,
Where shivering cold and sickness pines
  the clime;
My wife to France, from whence set forth
  in pomp,
She came adorned hither like sweet May,
Sent back like Hallowmas or short'st of day.
QUEEN. And must we be divided? Must we part?
KING RICHARD. Ay, hand from hand, my love,
  and heart from heart.
QUEEN. Banish us both, and send the King
  with me.
NORTHUMBERLAND. That were some love, but
  little policy.
QUEEN. Then whither he goes thither let me go.
KING RICHARD. So two, together weeping, make
  one woe.
Weep thou for me in France, I for thee here;
Better far off than near, be ne'er the near.
Go, count thy way with sighs; I mine
  with groans.
QUEEN. So longest way shall have the
  longest moans.
KING RICHARD. Twice for one step I'll groan, the
  way being short,
And piece the way out with a heavy heart.
Come, come, in wooing sorrow let's be brief,
Since, wedding it, there is such length in grief.
One kiss shall stop our mouths, and
  dumbly part;
Thus give I mine, and thus take I thy heart.
QUEEN. Give me mine own again; 'twere no
  good part
To take on me to keep and kill thy heart.
So, now I have mine own again, be gone.
That I may strive to kill it with a groan.
KING RICHARD. We make woe wanton with this
  fond delay.
Once more, adieu; the rest let sorrow say.

Exeunt.

✤ SCENE II ✤
The DUKE OF YORK'S palace

Enter the DUKE OF YORK and the DUCHESS

DUCHESS. My lord, you told me you would tell
  the rest,
When weeping made you break the story off,
Of our two cousins' coming into London.
YORK. Where did I leave?
DUCHESS. At that sad stop, my lord,

Where rude misgoverned hands from
  windows' tops
Threw dust and rubbish on King Richard's head.
YORK. Then, as I said, the Duke, great Bolingbroke,
  Mounted upon a hot and fiery steed
  Which his aspiring rider seem'd to know,
  With slow but stately pace kept on his course,
  Whilst all tongues cried 'God save
    thee, Bolingbroke!'
  You would have thought the very windows spake,
  So many greedy looks of young and old
  Through casements darted their desiring eyes
  Upon his visage; and that all the walls
  With painted imagery had said at once
  'Jesu preserve thee! Welcome, Bolingbroke!'
  Whilst he, from the one side to the other turning,
  Bareheaded, lower than his proud steed's neck,
  Bespake them thus, 'I thank you, countrymen.'
  And thus still doing, thus he pass'd along.
DUCHESS. Alack, poor Richard! where rode he
  the whilst?
YORK. As in a theatre the eyes of men
  After a well-grac'd actor leaves the stage
  Are idly bent on him that enters next,
  Thinking his prattle to be tedious;
  Even so, or with much more contempt,
    men's eyes
  Did scowl on gentle Richard; no man cried 'God
    save him!'
  No joyful tongue gave him his welcome home;
  But dust was thrown upon his sacred head;
  Which with such gentle sorrow he shook off,
  His face still combating with tears and smiles,
  The badges of his grief and patience,
  That had not God, for some strong
    purpose, steel'd
  The hearts of men, they must perforce
    have melted,
  And barbarism itself have pitied him.
  But heaven hath a hand in these events,
  To whose high will we bound our calm contents.
  To Bolingbroke are we sworn subjects now,
  Whose state and honour I for aye allow.
DUCHESS. Here comes my son Aumerle.
YORK. Aumerle that was
  But that is lost for being Richard's friend,
  And madam, you must call him Rutland now.
  I am in Parliament pledge for his truth
  And lasting fealty to the new-made King.

            Enter AUMERLE

DUCHESS. Welcome, my son. Who are the
  violets now
That strew the green lap of the new-come spring?

AUMERLE. Madam, I know not, nor I greatly
  care not.
  God knows I had as lief be none as one.
YORK. Well, bear you well in this new spring
  of time,
  Lest you be cropp'd before you come to prime.
  What news from Oxford? Do these justs and
    triumphs hold?
AUMERLE. For aught I know, my lord, they do.
YORK. You will be there, I know.
AUMERLE. If God prevent not, I purpose so.
YORK. What seal is that hangs without thy bosom?
  Yea, look'st thou pale? Let me see the writing.
AUMERLE. My lord, 'tis nothing.
YORK. No matter, then, who see it.
  I will be satisfied; let me see the writing.
AUMERLE. I do beseech your Grace to pardon me;
  It is a matter of small consequence
  Which for some reasons I would not have seen.
YORK. Which for some reasons, sir, I mean to see.
  I fear, I fear-
DUCHESS. What should you fear?
  'Tis nothing but some bond that he is ent'red into
  For gay apparel 'gainst the triumph-day.
YORK. Bound to himself! What doth he with
  a bond
  That he is bound to? Wife, thou art a fool.
  Boy, let me see the writing.
AUMERLE. I do beseech you, pardon me; I may not
  show it.
YORK. I will be satisfied; let me see it, I say. *[He plucks*
  it out of his bosom, and reads it]
  Treason, foul treason! Villain! traitor! slave!
DUCHESS. What is the matter, my lord?
YORK. Ho! who is within there?

            Enter a Servant

  Saddle my horse.
  God for his mercy, what treachery is here!
DUCHESS. Why, York, what is it, my lord?
YORK. Give me my boots, I say; saddle my horse.

            Exit Servant.

  Now, by mine honour, by my life, my troth,
  I will appeach the villain.
DUCHESS. What is the matter?
YORK. Peace, foolish woman.
DUCHESS. I will not peace. What is the
  matter, Aumerle?
AUMERLE. Good mother, be content; it is
  no more
  Than my poor life must answer.
DUCHESS. Thy life answer!
YORK. Bring me my boots. I will unto the King.

      His Man enters with his boots

DUCHESS. Strike him, Aumerle. Poor boy, thou
art amaz'd.

Hence, villain! never more come in my sight.

YORK. Give me my boots, I say.

DUCHESS. Why, York, what wilt thou do?

Wilt thou not hide the trespass of thine own?

Have we more sons? or are we like to have?

Is not my teeming date drunk up with time?

And wilt thou pluck my fair son from mine age

And rob me of a happy mother's name?

Is he not like thee? Is he not thine own?

YORK. Thou fond mad woman,

Wilt thou conceal this dark conspiracy?

A dozen of them here have ta'en the sacrament,

And interchangeably set down their hands

To kill the King at Oxford.

DUCHESS. He shall be none;

We'll keep him here. Then what is that to him?

YORK. Away, fond woman! were he twenty times
my son

I would appeach him.

DUCHESS. Hadst thou groan'd for him

As I have done, thou wouldst be more pitiful.

But now I know thy mind: thou dost suspect

That I have been disloyal to thy bed

And that he is a bastard, not thy son.

Sweet York, sweet husband, be not of that mind.

He is as like thee as a man may be

Not like to me, or any of my kin,

And yet I love him.

YORK. Make way, unruly woman! *Exit.*

DUCHESS. After, Aumerle! Mount thee upon
his horse;

Spur post, and get before him to the King,

And beg thy pardon ere he do accuse thee.

I'll not be long behind; though I be old,

I doubt not but to ride as fast as York;

And never will I rise up from the ground

Till Bolingbroke have pardon'd thee. Away,
be gone.

Exeunt.

✿ SCENE III ✿
Windsor Castle

Enter BOLINGBROKE as King, PERCY, and other LORDS

BOLINGBROKE. Can no man tell me of my
unthrifty son?

'Tis full three months since I did see him last.

If any plague hang over us, 'tis he.

I would to God, my lords, he might be found.

Inquire at London, 'mongst the taverns there,

For there, they say, he daily doth frequent

With unrestrained loose companions,

Even such, they say, as stand in narrow lanes

And beat our watch and rob our passengers,

Which he, young wanton and effeminate boy,

Takes on the point of honour to support

So dissolute a crew.

PERCY. My lord, some two days since I saw
the Prince,

And told him of those triumphs held at Oxford.

BOLINGBROKE. And what said the gallant?

PERCY. His answer was, he would unto the stews,

And from the common'st creature pluck a glove

And wear it as a favour; and with that

He would unhorse the lustiest challenger.

BOLINGBROKE. As dissolute as desperate; yet
through both

I see some sparks of better hope, which elder years

May happily bring forth. But who comes here?

Enter AUMERLE amazed

AUMERLE. Where is the King?

BOLINGBROKE. What means our cousin that he
stares and looks
So wildly?

AUMERLE. God save your Grace! I do beseech
your Majesty,

To have some conference with your
Grace alone.

BOLINGBROKE. Withdraw yourselves, and leave
us here alone. *Exeunt PERCY and LORDS.*

What is the matter with our cousin now?

AUMERLE. For ever may my knees grow to the
earth, *[Kneels]*

My tongue cleave to my roof within my mouth,

Unless a pardon ere I rise or speak.

BOLINGBROKE. Intended or committed was
this fault?

If on the first, how heinous e'er it be,

To win thy after-love I pardon thee.

AUMERLE. Then give me leave that I may turn
the key,

That no man enter till my tale be done.

BOLINGBROKE. Have thy desire.

The DUKE OF YORK knocks at the door and crieth

YORK. *[Within]* My liege, beware; look to thyself;

Thou hast a traitor in thy presence there.

BOLINGBROKE. *[Drawing]* Villain, I'll make
thee safe.

AUMERLE. Stay thy revengeful hand; thou hast no
cause to fear.

YORK. *[Within]* Open the door, secure,
foolhardy King.

Shall I, for love, speak treason to thy face?
Open the door, or I will break it open.

Enter YORK

BOLINGBROKE. What is the matter, uncle? Speak;
Recover breath; tell us how near is danger,
That we may arm us to encounter it.

YORK. Peruse this writing here, and thou
shalt know
The treason that my haste forbids me show.

AUMERLE. Remember, as thou read'st, thy
promise pass'd.
I do repent me; read not my name there;
My heart is not confederate with my hand.

YORK. It was, villain, ere thy hand did set it down.
I tore it from the traitor's bosom, King;
Fear, and not love, begets his penitence.
Forget to pity him, lest thy pity prove
A serpent that will sting thee to the heart.

BOLINGBROKE. O heinous, strong, and
bold conspiracy!
O loyal father of a treacherous son!
Thou sheer, immaculate, and silver fountain,
From whence this stream through
muddy passages
Hath held his current and defil'd himself!
Thy overflow of good converts to bad;
And thy abundant goodness shall excuse
This deadly blot in thy digressing son.

YORK. So shall my virtue be his vice's bawd;
And he shall spend mine honour with his shame,
As thriftless sons their scraping fathers' gold.
Mine honour lives when his dishonour dies,
Or my sham'd life in his dishonour lies.
Thou kill'st me in his life; giving him breath,
The traitor lives, the true man's put to death.

DUCHESS. [*Within*] What ho, my liege, for God's
sake, let me in.

BOLINGBROKE. What shrill-voic'd suppliant
makes this eager cry?

DUCHESS. [*Within*] A woman, and thine aunt, great
King; 'tis I.
Speak with me, pity me, open the door.
A beggar begs that never begg'd before.

BOLINGBROKE. Our scene is alt'red from a
serious thing,
And now chang'd to 'The Beggar and the King'.
My dangerous cousin, let your mother in.
I know she is come to pray for your foul sin.

YORK. If thou do pardon whosoever pray,
More sins for this forgiveness prosper may.
This fest'red joint cut off, the rest rest sound;
This let alone will all the rest confound.

Enter DUCHESS

DUCHESS. O King, believe not this hard-
hearted man!
Love loving not itself, none other can.

YORK. Thou frantic woman, what dost thou
make here?
Shall thy old dugs once more a traitor rear?

DUCHESS. Sweet York, be patient. Hear me,
gentle liege.

Kneels

BOLINGBROKE. Rise up, good aunt.

DUCHESS. Not yet, I thee beseech.
For ever will I walk upon my knees,
And never see day that the happy sees
Till thou give joy; until thou bid me joy
By pardoning Rutland, my transgressing boy.

AUMERLE. Unto my mother's prayers I bend
my knee.

Kneels

YORK. Against them both, my true joints bended
be. [*Kneels*]
Ill mayst thou thrive, if thou grant any grace!

DUCHESS. Pleads he in earnest? Look upon
his face;
His eyes do drop no tears, his prayers are in jest;
His words come from his mouth, ours from
our breast.
He prays but faintly and would be denied;
We pray with heart and soul, and all beside.
His weary joints would gladly rise, I know;
Our knees still kneel till to the ground
they grow.
His prayers are full of false hypocrisy;
Ours of true zeal and deep integrity.
Our prayers do out-pray his; then let them have
That mercy which true prayer ought to have.

BOLINGBROKE. Good aunt, stand up.

DUCHESS. Nay, do not say 'stand up';
Say 'pardon' first, and afterwards 'stand up'.
An if I were thy nurse, thy tongue to teach,
'Pardon' should be the first word of thy speech.
I never long'd to hear a word till now;
Say 'pardon,' King; let pity teach thee how.
The word is short, but not so short as sweet;
No word like 'pardon' for kings' mouths
so meet.

YORK. Speak it in French, King, say
'pardonne moy.'

DUCHESS. Dost thou teach pardon pardon
to destroy?
Ah, my sour husband, my hard-hearted lord,
That sets the word itself against the word!
Speak 'pardon' as 'tis current in our land;
The chopping French we do not understand.

Thine eye begins to speak, set thy
tongue there;
Or in thy piteous heart plant thou thine ear,
That hearing how our plaints and prayers
do pierce,
Pity may move thee 'pardon' to rehearse.
BOLINGBROKE. Good aunt, stand up.
DUCHESS. I do not sue to stand;
Pardon is all the suit I have in hand.
BOLINGBROKE. I pardon him, as God shall
pardon me.
DUCHESS. O happy vantage of a kneeling knee!
Yet am I sick for fear. Speak it again.
Twice saying 'pardon' doth not pardon twain,
But makes one pardon strong.
BOLINGBROKE. With all my heart
I pardon him.
DUCHESS. A god on earth thou art.
BOLINGBROKE. But for our trusty brother-in-law
and the Abbot,
With all the rest of that consorted crew,
Destruction straight shall dog them at
the heels.
Good uncle, help to order several powers
To Oxford, or where'er these traitors are.
They shall not live within this world, I swear,
But I will have them, if I once know where.
Uncle, farewell; and, cousin, adieu;
Your mother well hath pray'd, and prove
you true.
DUCHESS. Come, my old son; I pray God make
thee new.   *Exeunt.*

✣ SCENE IV ✣
Windsor Castle

Enter SIR PIERCE OF EXTON and a Servant

EXTON. Didst thou not mark the King, what
words he spake?
'Have I no friend will rid me of this living fear?'
Was it not so?
SERVANT. These were his very words.
EXTON. 'Have I no friend?' quoth he. He spake
it twice
And urg'd it twice together, did he not?
SERVANT. He did.
EXTON. And, speaking it, he wishtly look'd on me,
As who should say 'I would thou wert the man
That would divorce this terror from my heart';
Meaning the King at Pomfret. Come, let's go.
I am the King's friend, and will rid his foe *Exeunt.*

✣ SCENE V ✣
Pomfret Castle. The dungeon of the Castle

Enter KING RICHARD

KING RICHARD. I have been studying how I
may compare
This prison where I live unto the world
And, for because the world is populous
And here is not a creature but myself,
I cannot do it. Yet I'll hammer it out.
My brain I'll prove the female to my soul,
My soul the father; and these two beget
A generation of still-breeding thoughts,
And these same thoughts people this
little world,
In humours like the people of this world,
For no thought is contented. The better sort,
As thoughts of things divine, are intermix'd
With scruples, and do set the word itself
Against the word,
As thus: 'Come, little ones'; and then again,
'It is as hard to come as for a camel
To thread the postern of a small needle's eye.'
Thoughts tending to ambition, they do plot
Unlikely wonders: how these vain weak nails
May tear a passage through the flinty ribs
Of this hard world, my ragged prison walls;
And, for they cannot, die in their own pride.
Thoughts tending to content flatter themselves
That they are not the first of fortune's slaves,
Nor shall not be the last; like silly beggars
Who, sitting in the stocks, refuge their shame,
That many have and others must sit there;
And in this thought they find a kind of ease,
Bearing their own misfortunes on the back
Of such as have before endur'd the like.
Thus play I in one person many people,
And none contented. Sometimes am I king;
Then treasons make me wish myself a beggar,
And so I am. Then crushing penury
Persuades me I was better when a king;
Then am I king'd again; and by and by
Think that I am unking'd by Bolingbroke,
And straight am nothing. But whate'er I be,
Nor I, nor any man that but man is,
With nothing shall be pleas'd till he be eas'd
With being nothing. *[The music plays]* Music do
I hear?
Ha, ha! keep time. How sour sweet music is
When time is broke and no proportion kept!

So is it in the music of men's lives.
And here have I the daintiness of ear
To check time broke in a disorder'd string;
But, for the concord of my state and time,
Had not an ear to hear my true time broke.
I wasted time, and now doth time waste me;
For now hath time made me his
  numb'ring clock:
My thoughts are minutes; and with sighs
  they jar
Their watches on unto mine eyes, the
  outward watch,
Whereto my finger, like a dial's point,
Is pointing still, in cleansing them from tears.
Now sir, the sound that tells what hour it is
Are clamorous groans which strike upon
  my heart,
Which is the bell. So sighs, and tears,
  and groans,
Show minutes, times, and hours; but my time
Runs posting on in Bolingbroke's proud joy,
While I stand fooling here, his Jack of the clock.
This music mads me. Let it sound no more;
For though it have holp madmen to their wits,
In me it seems it will make wise men mad.
Yet blessing on his heart that gives it me!
For 'tis a sign of love; and love to Richard
Is a strange brooch in this all-hating world.

Enter a GROOM of the stable

GROOM. Hail, royal Prince!
KING RICHARD. Thanks, noble peer!
  The cheapest of us is ten groats too dear.
  What art thou? and how comest thou hither,
  Where no man never comes but that sad dog
  That brings me food to make misfortune live?
GROOM. I was a poor groom of thy stable, King,
  When thou wert king; who, travelling
  towards York,
  With much ado at length have gotten leave
  To look upon my sometimes royal
  master's face.
  O, how it ern'd my heart, when I beheld,
  In London streets, that coronation-day,
  When Bolingbroke rode on roan Barbary-
  That horse that thou so often hast bestrid,
  That horse that I so carefully have dress'd!
KING RICHARD. Rode he on Barbary? Tell me,
  gentle friend,
  How went he under him?
GROOM. So proudly as if he disdain'd
  the ground.
KING RICHARD. So proud that Bolingbroke was
  on his back!

That jade hath eat bread from my royal hand;
This hand hath made him proud with
  clapping him.
Would he not stumble? would he not fall down,
Since pride must have a fall, and break the neck
Of that proud man that did usurp his back?
Forgiveness, horse! Why do I rail on thee,
Since thou, created to be aw'd by man,
Wast born to bear? I was not made a horse;
And yet I bear a burden like an ass,
Spurr'd, gall'd, and tir'd, by
  jaunching Bolingbroke.

Enter KEEPER with meat

KEEPER. Fellow, give place; here is no
  longer stay.
KING RICHARD. If thou love me, 'tis time thou
  wert away.
GROOM. What my tongue dares not, that my
  heart shall say.

Exit.

KEEPER. My lord, will't please you to fall to?
KING RICHARD. Taste of it first as thou art wont
  to do.
KEEPER. My lord, I dare not. Sir Pierce of Exton,
  Who lately came from the King, commands
  the contrary.
KING RICHARD. The devil take Henry of
  Lancaster and thee!
  Patience is stale, and I am weary of it.

Beats the KEEPER

KEEPER. Help, help, help!

*The murderers, EXTON and servants, rush
  in, armed*

KING RICHARD. How now! What means death in
  this rude assault?
Villain, thy own hand yields thy death's
  instrument. *[Snatching a weapon and killing one]*
Go thou and fill another room in hell. *[He kills
  another, then EXTON strikes him down]*
That hand shall burn in never-quenching fire
That staggers thus my person. Exton, thy
  fierce hand
Hath with the King's blood stain'd the King's
  own land.
Mount, mount, my soul! thy seat is up on high;
Whilst my gross flesh sinks downward, here
  to die.

Dies.

EXTON. As full of valour as of royal blood.
  Both have I spill'd. O, would the deed
  were good!
  For now the devil, that told me I did well,
  Says that this deed is chronicled in hell.

This dead King to the living King I'll bear.
Take hence the rest, and give them burial here.

Exeunt.

✦ SCENE VI ✦
Windsor Castle

Flourish. Enter BOLINGBROKE, the DUKE OF YORK,
with other LORDS and Attendants

BOLINGBROKE. Kind uncle York, the latest news
we hear
Is that the rebels have consum'd with fire
Our town of Ciceter in Gloucestershire;
But whether they be ta'en or slain we hear not.

Enter NORTHUMBERLAND

Welcome, my lord. What is the news?
NORTHUMBERLAND. First, to thy sacred state
wish I all happiness.
The next news is, I have to London sent
The heads of Salisbury, Spencer, Blunt,
and Kent.
The manner of their taking may appear
At large discoursed in this paper here.
BOLINGBROKE. We thank thee, gentle Percy, for
thy pains;
And to thy worth will add right worthy gains.

Enter FITZWATER

FITZWATER. My lord, I have from Oxford sent
to London
The heads of Brocas and Sir Bennet Seely;
Two of the dangerous consorted traitors
That sought at Oxford thy dire overthrow.
BOLINGBROKE. Thy pains, Fitzwater, shall not
be forgot;
Right noble is thy merit, well I wot.

Enter PERCY, with the BISHOP OF CARLISLE

PERCY. The grand conspirator, Abbot
of Westminster,
With clog of conscience and sour melancholy,
Hath yielded up his body to the grave;
But here is Carlisle living, to abide
Thy kingly doom, and sentence of his pride.
BOLINGBROKE. Carlisle, this is your doom:
Choose out some secret place, some
reverend room,
More than thou hast, and with it joy thy life;
So as thou liv'st in peace, die free from strife;
For though mine enemy thou hast ever been,
High sparks of honour in thee have I seen.

Enter EXTON, with Attendants, bearing a coffin

EXTON. Great King, within this coffin I present

Thy buried fear. Herein all breathless lies
The mightiest of thy greatest enemies,
Richard of Bordeaux, by me hither brought.
BOLINGBROKE. Exton, I thank thee not; for thou
hast wrought
A deed of slander with thy fatal hand
Upon my head and all this famous land.
EXTON. From your own mouth, my lord, did I
this deed.
BOLINGBROKE. They love not poison that do
poison need,
Nor do I thee. Though I did wish him dead,
I hate the murderer, love him murdered.
The guilt of conscience take thou for thy labour,
But neither my good word nor princely favour;
With Cain go wander thorough shades of night,
And never show thy head by day nor light.
Lords, I protest my soul is full of woe
That blood should sprinkle me to make
me grow.
Come, mourn with me for what I do lament,
And put on sullen black incontinent.
I'll make a voyage to the Holy Land,
To wash this blood off from my guilty hand.
March sadly after; grace my mournings here
In weeping after this untimely bier.

Exeunt.

The End

1597

King Henry IV, Part I

Dramatis Personae

KING HENRY THE FOURTH

Sons to the King:
HENRY, PRINCE OF WALES
PRINCE JOHN OF LANCASTER

EARL OF WESTMORELAND
SIR WALTER BLUNT
THOMAS PERCY, EARL OF WORCESTER
HENRY PERCY, EARL OF NORTHUMBERLAND
HENRY PERCY, surnamed HOTSPUR, his son
EDMUND MORTIMER, Earl of March
RICHARD SCROOP, Archbishop of York
ARCHIBALD, Earl of Douglas
OWEN GLENDOWER
SIR RICHARD VERNON
SIR JOHN FALSTAFF
SIR MICHAEL, a friend to the Archbishop of York
POINS, GADSHILL, PETO, BARDOLPH

LADY PERCY, wife to Hotspur, and sister
to Mortimer; LADY MORTIMER, daughter to
Glendower, and wife to Mortimer; MISTRESS
QUICKLY, hostess of the Boar's Head in Eastcheap

Lords, Officers, Sheriff, Vintner, Chamberlain,
Francis (a Drawer), two Carriers, Travellers,
Thieves, Messengers and Attendants

SCENE
England and Wales

ACT I

⚜ SCENE I ⚜
London. The palace

*Enter the KING, LORD JOHN OF LANCASTER, EARL
OF WESTMORELAND, with Others.*

KING. So shaken as we are, so wan with care,
Find we a time for frighted peace to pant
And breathe short-winded accents of new broils
To be commenc'd in stronds afar remote.
No more the thirsty entrance of this soil
Shall daub her lips with her own
  children's blood.
No more shall trenching war channel her fields,
Nor bruise her flow'rets with the armed hoofs
Of hostile paces. Those opposed eyes
Which, like the meteors of a troubled heaven,
All of one nature, of one substance bred,
Did lately meet in the intestine shock
And furious close of civil butchery,
Shall now in mutual well-beseeming ranks
March all one way and be no more oppos'd
Against acquaintance, kindred, and allies.
The edge of war, like an ill-sheathed knife,
No more shall cut his master. Therefore, friends,
As far as to the sepulchre of Christ-
Whose soldier now, under whose blessed cross
We are impressed and engag'd to fight-
Forthwith a power of English shall we levy,
Whose arms were moulded in their
  mother's womb
To chase these pagans in those holy fields
Over whose acres walk'd those blessed feet
Which fourteen hundred years ago were nail'd
For our advantage on the bitter cross.
But this our purpose now is twelvemonth old,
And bootless 'tis to tell you we will go.
Therefore we meet not now. Then let me hear
Of you, my gentle cousin Westmoreland,
What yesternight our Council did decree
In forwarding this dear expedience.
WESTMORELAND. My liege, this haste was hot
  in question
And many limits of the charge set down
But yesternight; when all athwart there came
A post from Wales, loaden with heavy news;
Whose worst was that the noble Mortimer,
Leading the men of Herefordshire to fight

Against the irregular and wild Glendower,
Was by the rude hands of that Welshman taken,
A thousand of his people butchered;
Upon whose dead corpse there was
  such misuse,
Such beastly shameless transformation,
By those Welshwomen done as may not be
Without much shame retold or spoken of.
KING. It seems then that the tidings of this broil
  Brake off our business for the Holy Land.
WESTMORELAND. This, match'd with other, did,
  my gracious lord;
For more uneven and unwelcome news
Came from the North, and thus it did import:
On Holy-rood Day the gallant Hotspur there,
Young Harry Percy, and brave Archibald,
That ever-valiant and approved Scot,
At Holmedon met,
Where they did spend a sad and bloody hour;
As by discharge of their artillery
And shape of likelihood the news was told;
For he that brought them, in the very heat
And pride of their contention did take horse,
Uncertain of the issue any way.
KING. Here is a dear, a true-industrious friend,
Sir Walter Blunt, new lighted from his horse,
Stain'd with the variation of each soil
Betwixt that Holmedon and this seat of ours,
And he hath brought us smooth and
  welcome news.
The Earl of Douglas is discomfited;
Ten thousand bold Scots, two-and-
  twenty knights,
Balk'd in their own blood did Sir Walter see
On Holmedon's plains. Of prisoners,
  Hotspur took
Mordake Earl of Fife and eldest son
To beaten Douglas, and the Earl of Athol,
Of Murray, Angus, and Menteith.
And is not this an honourable spoil?
A gallant prize? Ha, cousin, is it not?
WESTMORELAND. In faith,
  It is a conquest for a prince to boast of.
KING. Yea, there thou mak'st me sad, and mak'st
  me sin
In envy that my Lord Northumberland
Should be the father to so blest a son-
A son who is the theme of honour's tongue,
Amongst a grove the very straightest plant;
Who is sweet Fortune's minion and her pride;
Whilst I, by looking on the praise of him,
See riot and dishonour stain the brow
Of my young Harry. O that it could be prov'd

That some night-tripping fairy had exchang'd
In cradle clothes our children where they lay,
And call'd mine Percy, his Plantagenet!
Then would I have his Harry, and he mine.
But let him from my thoughts. What think
  you, coz,
Of this young Percy's pride? The prisoners
Which he in this adventure hath surpris'd
To his own use he keeps, and sends me word
I shall have none but Mordake Earl of Fife.
WESTMORELAND. This is his uncle's teaching,
  this Worcester,
Malevolent to you in all aspects,
Which makes him prune himself and bristle up
The crest of youth against your dignity.
KING. But I have sent for him to answer this;
And for this cause awhile we must neglect
Our holy purpose to Jerusalem.
Cousin, on Wednesday next our council we
Will hold at Windsor. So inform the lords;
But come yourself with speed to us again;
For more is to be said and to be done
Than out of anger can be uttered.
WESTMORELAND. I will my liege. *Exeunt.*

SCENE II

London. An apartment of the Prince's

Enter PRINCE OF WALES and SIR JOHN FALSTAFF

FALSTAFF. Now, Hal, what time of day is it, lad?
PRINCE. Thou art so fat-witted with drinking of
  old sack, and unbuttoning thee after supper,
  and sleeping upon benches after noon, that
  thou hast forgotten to demand that truly
  which thou wouldest truly know. What a devil
  hast thou to do with the time of the day,
  unless hours were cups of sack, and minutes
  capons, and clocks the tongues of bawds,
  and dials the signs of leaping houses, and the
  blessed sun himself a fair hot wench in flame-
  coloured taffeta, I see no reason why thou
  shouldst be so superfluous to demand the
  time of the day.
FALSTAFF. Indeed you come near me now, Hal;
  for we that take purses go by the moon And
  the seven stars, and not by Phoebus, he, that
  wand'ring knight so fair. And I prithee, sweet
  wag, when thou art king, as, God save thy
  Grace-Majesty I should say, for grace thou wilt
  have none-
PRINCE. What, none?

FALSTAFF. No, by my troth; not so much as will serve to be prologue to an egg and butter.

PRINCE. Well, how then? Come, roundly, roundly.

FALSTAFF. Marry, then, sweet wag, when thou art king, let not us that are squires of the night's body be called thieves of the day's beauty. Let us be Diana's Foresters, Gentlemen of the Shade, Minions of the Moon; and let men say we be men of good government, being governed as the sea is, by our noble and chaste mistress the moon, under whose countenance we steal.

PRINCE. Thou sayest well, and it holds well too; for the fortune of us that are the moon's men doth ebb and flow like the sea, being governed, as the sea is, by the moon. As, for proof now: a purse of gold most resolutely snatch'd on Monday night and most dissolutely spent on Tuesday morning; got with swearing 'Lay by', and spent with crying 'Bring in'; now ill as low an ebb as the foot of the ladder, and by-and-by in as high a flow as the ridge of the gallows.

FALSTAFF. By the Lord, thou say'st true, lad-and is not my hostess of the tavern a most sweet wench?

PRINCE. As the honey of Hybla, my old lad of the castle-and is not a buff jerkin a most sweet robe of durance?

FALSTAFF. How now, how now, mad wag? What, in thy quips and thy quiddities? What a plague have I to do with a buff jerkin?

PRINCE. Why, what a pox have I to do with my hostess of the tavern?

FALSTAFF. Well, thou hast call'd her to a reckoning many a time and oft.

PRINCE. Did I ever call for thee to pay thy part?

FALSTAFF. No; I'll give thee thy due, thou hast paid all there.

PRINCE. Yea, and elsewhere, so far as my coin would stretch; and where it would not, I have used my credit.

FALSTAFF. Yea, and so us'd it that, were it not here apparent that thou art heir apparent-But I prithee, sweet wag, shall there be gallows standing in England when thou art king? and resolution thus fubb'd as it is with the rusty curb of old father antic the law? Do not thou, when thou art king, hang a thief.

PRINCE. No; thou shalt.

FALSTAFF. Shall I? O rare! By the Lord, I'll be a brave judge.

PRINCE. Thou judgest false already. I mean, thou shalt have the hanging of the thieves and so become a rare hangman.

FALSTAFF. Well, Hal, well; and in some sort it jumps with my humour as well as waiting in the court, I can tell you.

PRINCE. For obtaining of suits?

FALSTAFF. Yea, for obtaining of suits, whereof the hangman hath no lean wardrobe. 'Sblood, I am as melancholy as a gib-cat or a lugg'd bear.

PRINCE. Or an old lion, or a lover's lute.

FALSTAFF. Yea, or the drone of a Lincolnshire bagpipe.

PRINCE. What sayest thou to a hare, or the melancholy of Moor Ditch?

FALSTAFF. Thou hast the most unsavoury similes, and art indeed the most comparative, rascalliest, sweet young prince. But, Hal, I prithee trouble me no more with vanity. I would to God thou and I knew where a commodity of good names were to be bought. An old lord of the Council rated me the other day in the street about you, sir, but I mark'd him not; and yet he talked very wisely, but I regarded him not; and yet he talk'd wisely, and in the street too.

PRINCE. Thou didst well; for wisdom cries out in the streets, and no man regards it.

FALSTAFF. O, thou hast damnable iteration, and art indeed able to corrupt a saint. Thou hast done much harm upon me, Hal-God forgive thee for it! Before I knew thee, Hal, I knew nothing; and now am I, if a man should speak truly, little better than one of the wicked. I must give over this life, and I will give it over! By the Lord, an I do not, I am a villain! I'll be damn'd for never a king's son in Christendom.

PRINCE. Where shall we take a purse tomorrow, Jack?

FALSTAFF. Zounds, where thou wilt, lad! I'll make one. An I do not, call me villain and baffle me.

PRINCE. I see a good amendment of life in thee-from praying to purse-taking.

FALSTAFF. Why, Hal, 'tis my vocation, Hal. 'Tis no sin for a man to labour in his vocation.

Enter POINS

Poins! Now shall we know if Gadshill have set a match. O, if men were to be saved by merit, what hole in hell were hot enough for him? This is the most omnipotent villain that ever cried 'Stand!' to a true man.

PRINCE. Good morrow, Ned.

POINS. Good morrow, sweet Hal. What says Monsieur Remorse? What says Sir John Sack and Sugar? Jack, how agrees the devil and thee about thy soul, that thou soldest him on Good Friday last for a cup of Madeira and a cold capon's leg?

PRINCE. Sir John stands to his word, the devil shall have his bargain; for he was never yet a breaker of proverbs. He will give the devil his due.

POINS. Then art thou damn'd for keeping thy word with the devil.

PRINCE. Else he had been damn'd for cozening the devil.

POINS. But, my lads, my lads, to-morrow morning, by four o'clock early, at Gadshill! There are pilgrims going to Canterbury with rich offerings, and traders riding to London with fat purses. I have vizards for you all; you have horses for yourselves. Gadshill lies to-night in Rochester. I have bespoke supper to-morrow night in Eastcheap. We may do it as secure as sleep. If you will go, I will stuff your purses full of crowns; if you will not, tarry at home and be hang'd!

FALSTAFF. Hear ye, Yedward: if I tarry at home and go not, I'll hang you for going.

POINS. You will, chops?

FALSTAFF. Hal, wilt thou make one?

PRINCE. Who, I rob? I a thief? Not I, by my faith.

FALSTAFF. There's neither honesty, manhood, nor good fellowship in thee, nor thou cam'st not of the blood royal if thou darest not stand for ten shillings.

PRINCE. Well then, once in my days I'll be a madcap.

FALSTAFF. Why, that's well said.

PRINCE. Well, come what will, I'll tarry at home.

FALSTAFF. By the Lord, I'll be a traitor then, when thou art king.

PRINCE. I care not.

POINS. Sir John, I prithee, leave the Prince and me alone. I will lay him down such reasons for this adventure that he shall go.

FALSTAFF. Well, God give thee the spirit of persuasion and him the ears of profiting, that what thou speakest may move and what he hears may be believed, that the true prince may (for recreation sake) prove a false thief; for the poor abuses of the time want countenance. Farewell; you shall find me in Eastcheap.

PRINCE. Farewell, thou latter spring! farewell, All-hallown summer!   *Exit Falstaff.*

POINS. Now, my good sweet honey lord, ride with us to-morrow. I have a jest to execute that I cannot manage alone. Falstaff, Bardolph, Peto, and Gadshill shall rob those men that we have already waylaid; yourself and I will not be there; and when they have the booty, if you and I do not rob them, cut this head off from my shoulders.

PRINCE. How shall we part with them in setting forth?

POINS. Why, we will set forth before or after them and appoint them a place of meeting, wherein it is at our pleasure to fail; and then will they adventure upon the exploit themselves; which they shall have no sooner achieved, but we'll set upon them.

PRINCE. Yea, but 'tis like that they will know us by our horses, by our habits, and by every other appointment, to be ourselves.

POINS. Tut! our horses they shall not see-I'll tie them in the wood; our vizards we will change after we leave them; and, sirrah, I have cases of buckram for the nonce, to immask our noted outward garments.

PRINCE. Yea, but I doubt they will be too hard for us.

POINS. Well, for two of them, I know them to be as true-bred cowards as ever turn'd back; and for the third, if he fight longer than he sees reason, I'll forswear arms. The virtue of this jest will be the incomprehensible lies that this same fat rogue will tell us when we meet at supper: how thirty, at least, he fought with; what wards, what blows, what extremities he endured; and in the reproof of this lies the jest.

PRINCE. Well, I'll go with thee. Provide us all things necessary and meet me to-night in Eastcheap. There I'll sup. Farewell.

POINS. Farewell, my lord.   *Exit.*

PRINCE. I know you all, and will awhile uphold
The unyok'd humour of your idleness.
Yet herein will I imitate the sun,
Who doth permit the base contagious clouds
To smother up his beauty from the world,
That, when he please again to lie himself,
Being wanted, he may be more wond'red at
By breaking through the foul and ugly mists
Of vapours that did seem to strangle him.
If all the year were playing holidays,
To sport would be as tedious as to work;
But when they seldom come, they wish'd-
for come,
And nothing pleaseth but rare accidents.
So, when this loose behaviour I throw off

And pay the debt I never promised,
By how much better than my word I am,
By so much shall I falsify men's hopes;
And, like bright metal on a sullen ground,
My reformation, glitt'ring o'er my fault,
Shall show more goodly and attract more eyes
Than that which hath no foil to set it off.
I'll so offend to make offence a skill,
Redeeming time when men think least I will.

Exit.

⚘ SCENE III ⚘

London. The palace

*Enter the KING, NORTHUMBERLAND, WORCESTER,
HOTSPUR, SIR WALTER BLUNT, with Others*

KING. My blood hath been too cold
  and temperate,
  Unapt to stir at these indignities,
  And you have found me, for accordingly
  You tread upon my patience; but be sure
  I will from henceforth rather be myself,
  Mighty and to be fear'd, than my condition,
  Which hath been smooth as oil, soft as
  young down,
  And therefore lost that title of respect
  Which the proud soul ne'er pays but to
  the proud.
WORCESTER. Our house, my sovereign liege,
  little deserves
  The scourge of greatness to be us'd on it-
  And that same greatness too which our
  own hands
  Have holp to make so portly.
NORTHUMBERLAND. My lord-
KING. Worcester, get thee gone; for I do see
  Danger and disobedience in thine eye.
  O, sir, your presence is too bold
  and peremptory,
  And majesty might never yet endure
  The moody frontier of a servant brow.
  You have good leave to leave us. When we need
  'Your use and counsel, we shall send for you.

Exit Worcester.

You were about to speak.
NORTHUMBERLAND. Yea, my good lord.
  Those prisoners in your Highness'
  name demanded
  Which Harry Percy here at Holmedon took,
  Were, as he says, not with such strength denied
  As is delivered to your Majesty.

Either envy, therefore, or misprision
Is guilty of this fault, and not my son.
HOTSPUR. My liege, I did deny no prisoners.
  But I remember, when the fight was done,
  When I was dry with rage and extreme toll,
  Breathless and faint, leaning upon my sword,
  Came there a certain lord, neat and
  trimly dress'd,
  Fresh as a bridegroom; and his chin new reap'd
  Show'd like a stubble land at harvest home.
  He was perfumed like a milliner,
  And 'twixt his finger and his thumb he held
  A pouncet box, which ever and anon
  He gave his nose, and took't away again;
  Who therewith angry, when it next came there,
  Took it in snuff; and still he smil'd and talk'd;
  And as the soldiers bore dead bodies by,
  He call'd them untaught knaves, unmannerly,
  To bring a slovenly unhandsome corse
  Betwixt the wind and his nobility.
  With many holiday and lady terms
  He questioned me, amongst the rest demanded
  My prisoners in your Majesty's behalf.
  I then, all smarting with my wounds being cold,
  To be so pest'red with a popingay,
  Out of my grief and my impatience
  Answer'd neglectingly, I know not what-
  He should, or he should not; for he made
  me mad
  To see him shine so brisk, and smell so sweet,
  And talk so like a waiting gentlewoman
  Of guns and drums and wounds-God save
  the mark!-
  And telling me the sovereignest thing on earth
  Was parmacity for an inward bruise;
  And that it was great pity, so it was,
  This villanous saltpetre should be digg'd
  Out of the bowels of the harmless earth,
  Which many a good tall fellow had destroy'd
  So cowardly; and but for these vile 'guns,
  He would himself have been a soldier.
  This bald unjointed chat of his, my lord,
  I answered indirectly, as I said,
  And I beseech you, let not his report
  Come current for an accusation
  Betwixt my love and your high majesty.
BLUNT. The circumstance considered, good
  my lord,
  Whate'er Lord Harry Percy then had said
  To such a person, and in such a place,
  At such a time, with all the rest retold,
  May reasonably die, and never rise
  To do him wrong, or any way impeach

What then he said, so he unsay it now.

KING. Why, yet he doth deny his prisoners,
  But with proviso and exception,
  That we at our own charge shall ransom straight
  His brother-in-law, the foolish Mortimer;
  Who, on my soul, hath wilfully betray'd
  The lives of those that he did lead to fight
  Against that great magician, damn'd Glendower,
  Whose daughter, as we hear, the Earl of March
  Hath lately married. Shall our coffers, then,
  Be emptied to redeem a traitor home?
  Shall we buy treason? and indent with fears
  When they have lost and forfeited themselves?
  No, on the barren mountains let him starve!
  For I shall never hold that man my friend
  Whose tongue shall ask me for one penny cost
  To ransom home revolted Mortimer.

HOTSPUR. Revolted Mortimer?
  He never did fall off, my sovereign liege,
  But by the chance of war. To prove that true
  Needs no more but one tongue for all
    those wounds,
  Those mouthed wounds, which valiantly he took
  When on the gentle Severn's sedgy bank,
  In single opposition hand to hand,
  He did confound the best part of an hour
  In changing hardiment with great Glendower.
  Three times they breath'd, and three times did
    they drink,
  Upon agreement, of swift Severn's flood;
  Who then, affrighted with their bloody looks,
  Ran fearfully among the trembling reeds
  And hid his crisp head in the hollow bank,
  Bloodstained with these valiant cohabitants.
  Never did base and rotten policy
  Colour her working with such deadly wounds;
  Nor never could the noble Mortimer
  Receive so many, and all willingly.
  Then let not him be slandered with revolt.

KING. Thou dost belie him, Percy, thou dost
    belie him!
  He never did encounter with Glendower.
  I tell thee
  He durst as well have met the devil alone
  As Owen Glendower for an enemy.
  Art thou not asham'd? But, sirrah, henceforth
  Let me not hear you speak of Mortimer.
  Send me your prisoners with the
    speediest means,
  Or you shall hear in such a kind from me
  As will displease you. My Lord Northumberland,
  We license your departure with your son.-
  Send us your prisoners, or you will hear of it.

Exeunt KING, BLUNT, and Train.

HOTSPUR. An if the devil come and roar for them,
  I will not send them. I will after straight
  And tell him so; for I will else my heart,
  Albeit I make a hazard of my head.

NORTHUMBERLAND. What, drunk with choler?
  Stay, and pause awhile.
  Here comes your uncle.

Enter WORCESTER

HOTSPUR. Speak of Mortimer?
  Zounds, I will speak of him, and let my soul
  Want mercy if I do not join with him!
  Yea, on his part I'll empty all these veins,
  And shed my dear blood drop by drop in
    the dust,
  But I will lift the downtrod Mortimer
  As high in the air as this unthankful King,
  As this ingrate and cank'red Bolingbroke.

NORTHUMBERLAND. Brother, the King hath
    made your nephew mad.

WORCESTER. Who struck this heat up after I
    was gone?

HOTSPUR. He will, forsooth, have all
    my prisoners;
  And when I urg'd the ransom once again
  Of my wife's brother, then his cheek look'd pale,
  And on my face he turn'd an eye of death,
  Trembling even at the name of Mortimer.

WORCESTER. I cannot blame him. Was not
    he proclaim'd
  By Richard that dead is, the next of blood?

NORTHUMBERLAND. He was; I heard
    the proclamation.
  And then it was when the unhappy King
  (Whose wrongs in us God pardon!) did set forth
  Upon his Irish expedition;
  From whence he intercepted did return
  To be depos'd, and shortly murdered.

WORCESTER. And for whose death we in the
    world's wide mouth
  Live scandalis'd and foully spoken of.

HOTSPUR. But soft, I pray you. Did King
    Richard then
  Proclaim my brother Edmund Mortimer
  Heir to the crown?

NORTHUMBERLAND. He did; myself did hear it.

HOTSPUR. Nay, then I cannot blame his
    cousin king,
  That wish'd him on the barren mountains starve.
  But shall it be that you, that set the crown
  Upon the head of this forgetful man,
  And for his sake wear the detested blot
  Of murtherous subornation-shall it be

That you a world of curses undergo,
Being the agents or base second means,
The cords, the ladder, or the hangman rather?
O, pardon me that I descend so low
To show the line and the predicament
Wherein you range under this subtile King!
Shall it for shame be spoken in these days,
Or fill up chronicles in time to come,
That men of your nobility and power
Did gage them both in an unjust behalf
(As both of you, God pardon it! have done)
To put down Richard, that sweet lovely rose,
And plant this thorn, this canker, Bolingbroke?
And shall it in more shame be further spoken
That you are fool'd, discarded, and shook off
By him for whom these shames ye underwent?
No! yet time serves wherein you may redeem
Your banish'd honours and restore yourselves
Into the good thoughts of the world again;
Revenge the jeering and disdain'd contempt
Of this proud King, who studies day and night
To answer all the debt he owes to you
Even with the bloody payment of your deaths.
Therefore I say-
WORCESTER. Peace, cousin, say no more;
And now, I will unclasp a secret book,
And to your quick-conceiving discontents
I'll read you matter deep and dangerous,
As full of peril and adventurous spirit
As to o'erwalk a current roaring loud
On the unsteadfast footing of a spear.
HOTSPUR. If he fall in, good night, or sink
  or swim!
Send danger from the east unto the west,
So honour cross it from the north to south,
And let them grapple. O, the blood more stirs
To rouse a lion than to start a hare!
NORTHUMBERLAND. Imagination of some
  great exploit
Drives him beyond the bounds of patience.
HOTSPUR. By heaven, methinks it were an
  easy leap
To pluck bright honour from the pale-
  fac'd moon,
Or dive into the bottom of the deep,
Where fadom line could never touch
  the ground,
And pluck up drowned honour by the locks,
So he that doth redeem her thence might wear
Without corrival all her dignities;
But out upon this half-fac'd fellowship!
WORCESTER. He apprehends a world of
  figures here,

But not the form of what he should attend.
Good cousin, give me audience for a while.
HOTSPUR. I cry you mercy.
WORCESTER. Those same noble Scots
  That are your prisoners-
HOTSPUR. I'll keep them all.
  By God, he shall not have a Scot of them!
  No, if a Scot would save his soul, he shall not.
  I'll keep them, by this hand!
WORCESTER. You start away.
  And lend no ear unto my purposes.
  Those prisoners you shall keep.
HOTSPUR. Nay, I will! That is flat!
  He said he would not ransom Mortimer,
  Forbade my tongue to speak of Mortimer,
  But I will find him when he lies asleep,
  And in his ear I'll holloa 'Mortimer'.
  Nay;
  I'll have a starling shall be taught to speak
  Nothing but 'Mortimer', and give it him
  To keep his anger still in motion.
WORCESTER. Hear you, cousin, a word.
HOTSPUR. All studies here I solemnly defy
  Save how to gall and pinch this Bolingbroke;
  And that same sword-and-buckler Prince
    of Wales-
  But that I think his father loves him not
  And would be glad he met with
    some mischance,
  I would have him poisoned with a pot of ale.
WORCESTER. Farewell, kinsman. I will talk to you
  When you are better temper'd to attend.
NORTHUMBERLAND. Why, what a wasp-stung
  and impatient fool
  Art thou to break into this woman's mood,
  Tying thine ear to no tongue but thine own!
HOTSPUR. Why, look you, I am whipp'd and
  scourg'd with rods,
  Nettled, and stung with pismires when I hear
  Of this vile politician, Bolingbroke.
  In Richard's time-what do you call the place-
  A plague upon it! it is in Gloucestershire-
  'Twas where the madcap Duke his uncle kept-
  His uncle York-where I first bow'd my knee
  Unto this king of smiles, this Bolingbroke-
  'Sblood!
  When you and he came back from Ravenspurgh-
NORTHUMBERLAND. At Berkeley Castle.
HOTSPUR. You say true.
  Why, what a candy deal of courtesy
  This fawning greyhound then did proffer me!
  Look, 'when his infant fortune came to age',
  And 'gentle Harry Percy', and 'kind cousin'-

O, the devil take such cozeners!-God forgive me!
Good uncle, tell your tale, for I have done.
WORCESTER. Nay, if you have not, to it again.
We will stay your leisure.
HOTSPUR. I have done, i' faith.
WORCESTER. Then once more to your
Scottish prisoners.
Deliver them up without their ransom straight,
And make the Douglas' son your only mean
For powers in Scotland; which, for divers
reasons
Which I shall send you written, be assur'd
Will easily be granted. [To Northumberland] You,
my lord,
Your son in Scotland being thus employ'd,
Shall secretly into the bosom creep
Of that same noble prelate well-belov'd,
The Archbishop.
HOTSPUR. Of York, is it not?
WORCESTER. True; who bears hard
His brother's death at Bristow, the Lord Scroop.
I speak not this in estimation,
As what I think might be, but what I know
Is ruminated, plotted, and set down,
And only stays but to behold the face
Of that occasion that shall bring it on.
HOTSPUR. I smell it. Upon my life, it will do well.
NORTHUMBERLAND. Before the game is afoot
thou still let'st slip.
HOTSPUR. Why, it cannot choose but be a
noble plot.
And then the power of Scotland and of York
To join with Mortimer, ha?
WORCESTER. And so they shall.
HOTSPUR. In faith, it is exceedingly well aim'd.
WORCESTER. And 'tis no little reason bids
us speed,
To save our heads by raising of a head;
For, bear ourselves as even as we can,
The King will always think him in our debt,
And think we think ourselves unsatisfied,
Till he hath found a time to pay us home.
And see already how he doth begin
To make us strangers to his looks of love.
HOTSPUR. He does, he does! We'll be reveng'd
on him.
WORCESTER. Cousin, farewell. No further go
in this
Than I by letters shall direct your course.
When time is ripe, which will be suddenly,
I'll steal to Glendower and Lord Mortimer,
Where you and Douglas, and our pow'rs at once,
As I will fashion it, shall happily meet,

To bear our fortunes in our own strong arms,
Which now we hold at much uncertainty.
NORTHUMBERLAND. Farewell, good brother. We
shall thrive, I trust.
HOTSPUR. Uncle, adieu. O, let the hours be short
Till fields and blows and groans applaud our sport!

Exeunt.

ACT II

SCENE I

Rochester. An inn yard

Enter a CARRIER with a lantern in his hand

FIRST CARRIER. Heigh-ho! an it be not four by
the day, I'll be hang'd. Charles' wain is over the
new chimney, and yet our horse not pack'd.-
What, ostler!
OSTLER. [Within] Anon, anon.
FIRST CARRIER. I prithee, Tom, beat Cut's saddle,
put a few flocks in the point. Poor jade is wrung
in the withers out of all cess.

Enter another CARRIER

SECOND CARRIER. Peas and beans are as dank
here as a dog, and that is the next way to give
poor jades the bots. This house is turned
upside down since Robin Ostler died.
FIRST CARRIER. Poor fellow never joyed since the
price of oats rose. It was the death of him.
SECOND CARRIER. I think this be the most
villanous house in all London road for fleas. I
am stung like a tench.
FIRST CARRIER. Like a tench I By the mass, there
is ne'er a king christen could be better bit than
I have been since the first cock.
SECOND CARRIER. Why, they will allow us ne'er a
jordan, and then we leak in your chimney, and
your chamber-lye breeds fleas like a loach.
FIRST CARRIER. What, ostler! come away and be
hang'd! come away!
SECOND CARRIER. I have a gammon of bacon
and two razes of ginger, to be delivered as far as
Charing Cross.
FIRST CARRIER. God's body! the turkeys in my
pannier are quite starved. What, ostler! A plague
on thee! hast thou never an eye in thy head?
Canst not hear? An 'twere not as good deed
as drink to break the pate on thee, I am a very
villain. Come, and be hang'd! Hast no faith
in thee?

Enter GADSHILL

GADSHILL. Good morrow, carriers.
What's o'clock?

FIRST CARRIER. I think it be two o'clock.

GADSHILL. I prithee lend me this lantern to see
my gelding in the stable.

FIRST CARRIER. Nay, by God, soft! I know a trick
worth two of that, i' faith.

GADSHILL. I pray thee lend me thine.

SECOND CARRIER. Ay, when? canst tell? Lend
me thy lantern, quoth he? Marry, I'll see thee
hang'd first!

GADSHILL. Sirrah carrier, what time do you mean
to come to London?

SECOND CARRIER. Time enough to go to bed
with a candle, I warrant thee. Come, neighbour
Mugs, we'll call up the gentlemen. They will
along with company, for they have great charge.

Exeunt CARRIERS

GADSHILL. What, ho! chamberlain!

Enter CHAMBERLAIN

CHAMBERLAIN. At hand, quoth pickpurse.

GADSHILL. That's even as fair as-'at hand, quoth
the chamberlain'; for thou variest no more from
picking of purses than giving direction doth
from labouring: thou layest the plot how.

CHAMBERLAIN. Good morrow, Master Gadshill.
It holds current that I told you yesternight.
There's a franklin in the Wild of Kent hath
brought three hundred marks with him in
gold. I heard him tell it to one of his company
last night at supper-a kind of auditor; one that
hath abundance of charge too, God knows
what. They are up already and call for eggs and
butter. They will away presently.

GADSHILL. Sirrah, if they meet not with Saint
Nicholas' clerks, I'll give thee this neck.

CHAMBERLAIN. No, I'll none of it. I pray thee
keep that for the hangman; for I know thou
worshippest Saint Nicholas as truly as a man of
falsehood may.

GADSHILL. What talkest thou to me of the
hangman? If I hang, I'll make a fat pair of
gallows; for if I hang, old Sir John hangs with
me, and thou knowest he is no starveling. Tut!
there are other Troyans that thou dream'st
not of, the which for sport sake are content to
do the profession some grace; that would (if
matters should be look'd into) for their own
credit sake make all whole. I am joined with no
foot land-rakers, no long-staff sixpenny strikers,
none of these mad mustachio purple-hued
maltworms; but with nobility, and tranquillity,
burgomasters and great oneyers, such as can
hold in, such as will strike sooner than speak,
and speak sooner than drink, and drink sooner
than pray; and yet, zounds, I lie; for they pray
continually to their saint, the commonwealth,
or rather, not pray to her, but prey on her, for
they ride up and down on her and make her
their boots.

CHAMBERLAIN. What, the commonwealth their
boots? Will she hold out water in foul way?

GADSHILL. She will, she will! Justice hath liquor'd
her. We steal as in a castle, cocksure. We have
the receipt of fernseed, we walk invisible.

CHAMBERLAIN. Nay, by my faith, I think you are
more beholding to the night than to fernseed
for your walking invisible.

GADSHILL. Give me thy hand. Thou shalt have a
share in our purchase, as I am a true man.

CHAMBERLAIN. Nay, rather let me have it, as you
are a false thief.

GADSHILL. Go to; 'homo' is a common name to
all men. Bid the ostler bring my gelding out of
the stable. Farewell, you muddy knave. *Exeunt*

✦ SCENE II ✦
The highway near Gadshill

Enter PRINCE and POINS

POINS. Come, shelter, shelter! I have
remov'd Falstaff's horse, and he frets like a
gumm'd velvet.

PRINCE. Stand close.   *They step aside*

Enter FALSTAFF

FALSTAFF. Poins! Poins, and be hang'd! Poins!

PRINCE. *[Comes forward]* Peace, ye fat-kidney'd rascal!
What a brawling dost thou keep!

FALSTAFF. Where's Poins, Hal?

PRINCE. He is walk'd up to the top of the hill. I'll
go seek him.   *Steps aside*

FALSTAFF. I am accurs'd to rob in that thief's
company. The rascal hath removed my horse
and tied him I know not where. If I travel but
four foot by the squire further afoot, I shall
break my wind. Well, I doubt not but to die
a fair death for all this, if I scape hanging for
killing that rogue. I have forsworn his company
hourly any time this two-and-twenty years, and
yet I am bewitch'd with the rogue's company. If
the rascal have not given me medicines to make
me love him, I'll be hang'd. It could not be else.
I have drunk medicines. Poins! Hal! A plague

upon you both! Bardolph! Peto! I'll starve ere I'll rob a foot further. An 'twere not as good a deed as drink to turn true man and to leave these rogues, I am the veriest varlet that ever chewed with a tooth. Eight yards of uneven ground is threescore and ten miles afoot with me, and the stony-hearted villains know it well enough. A plague upon it when thieves cannot be true one to another! *[They whistle]* Whew! A plague upon you all! Give me my horse, you rogues! give me my horse and be hang'd!

PRINCE. *[Comes forward]* Peace, ye fat-guts! Lie down, lay thine ear close to the ground, and list if thou canst hear the tread of travellers.

FALSTAFF. Have you any levers to lift me up again, being down? 'Sblood, I'll not bear mine own flesh so far afoot again for all the coin in thy father's exchequer. What a plague mean ye to colt me thus?

PRINCE. Thou liest; thou art not colted, thou art uncolted.

FALSTAFF. I prithee, good Prince Hal, help me to my horse, good king's son.

PRINCE. Out, ye rogue! Shall I be your ostler?

FALSTAFF. Go hang thyself in thine own heir-apparent garters! If I be ta'en, I'll peach for this. An I have not ballads made on you all, and sung to filthy tunes, let a cup of sack be my poison. When a jest is so forward-and afoot too-I hate it.

Enter GADSHILL, BARDOLPH and PETO with him

GADSHILL. Stand!

FALSTAFF. So I do, against my will.

POINS. *[Comes forward]* O, 'tis our setter. I know his voice. Bardolph, what news?

BARDOLPH. Case ye, case ye! On with your vizards! There's money of the King's coming down the hill; 'tis going to the King's exchequer.

FALSTAFF. You lie, ye rogue! 'Tis going to the King's tavern.

GADSHILL. There's enough to make us all.

FALSTAFF. To be hang'd.

PRINCE. Sirs, you four shall front them in the narrow lane; Ned Poins and I will walk lower. If they scape from your encounter, then they light on us.

PETO. How many be there of them?

GADSHILL. Some eight or ten.

FALSTAFF. Zounds, will they not rob us?

PRINCE. What, a coward, Sir John Paunch?

FALSTAFF. Indeed, I am not John of Gaunt, your grandfather; but yet no coward, Hal.

PRINCE. Well, we leave that to the proof.

POINS. Sirrah Jack, thy horse stands behind the hedge. When thou need'st him, there thou shalt find him. Farewell and stand fast.

FALSTAFF. Now cannot I strike him, if I should be hang'd.

PRINCE. *[Aside to Poins]* Ned, where are our disguises?

POINS. *[Aside to Prince]* Here, hard by. Stand close.

Exeunt PRINCE and POINS.

FALSTAFF. Now, my masters, happy man be his dole, say I. Every man to his business.

Enter the TRAVELLERS

TRAVELLER. Come, neighbour.
The boy shall lead our horses down the hill;
We'll walk afoot awhile and ease our legs.

THIEVES. Stand!

TRAVELLER. Jesus bless us!

FALSTAFF. Strike! down with them! cut the villains' throats! Ah, whoreson caterpillars! bacon-fed knaves! they hate us youth. Down with them! fleece them!

TRAVELLER. O, we are undone, both we and ours for ever!

FALSTAFF. Hang ye, gorbellied knaves, are ye undone? No, ye fat chuffs; I would your store were here! On, bacons, on! What, ye knaves! young men must live. You are grandjurors, are ye? We'll jure ye, faith!

Here they rob and bind them. Exeunt.

Enter the PRINCE and POINS, in buckram suits.

PRINCE. The thieves have bound the true men. Now could thou and I rob the thieves and go merrily to London, it would be argument for a week, laughter for a month, and a good jest for ever.

POINS. Stand close! I hear them coming.

They stand aside

Enter the THIEVES again

FALSTAFF. Come, my masters, let us share, and then to horse before day. An the Prince and Poins be not two arrant cowards, there's no equity stirring. There's no more valour in that Poins than in a wild duck.

As they are sharing, the PRINCE and POINS set upon them. They all run away, and Falstaff, after a blow or two, runs away too, leaving the booty behind them.

PRINCE. Your money!

POINS. Villains!

PRINCE. Got with much ease. Now merrily to horse.
The thieves are scattered, and possess'd with fear

So strongly that they dare not meet each other.
Each takes his fellow for an officer.
Away, good Ned. Falstaff sweats to death
And lards the lean earth as he walks along.
Were't not for laughing, I should pity him.
POINS. How the rogue roar'd!   *Exeunt.*

⚜ SCENE III ⚜
Warkworth Castle

Enter HOTSPUR solus, reading a letter

HOTSPUR. 'But, for mine own part, my lord, I
could be well contented to be there, in respect
of the love I bear your house.' He could be
contented-why is he not then? In respect of
the love he bears our house! He shows in this
he loves his own barn better than he loves our
house. Let me see some more. 'The purpose
you undertake is dangerous'-Why, that's
certain! 'Tis dangerous to take a cold, to sleep,
to drink; but I tell you, my lord fool, out of this
nettle, danger, we pluck this flower, safety.
'The purpose you undertake is dangerous, the
friends you have named uncertain, the time
itself unsorted, and your whole plot too light
for the counterpoise of so great an opposition.'
Say you so, say you so? I say unto you again,
you are a shallow, cowardly hind, and you lie.
What a lack-brain is this! By the Lord, our plot
is a good plot as ever was laid; our friends
true and constant: a good plot, good friends,
and full of expectation; an excellent plot, very
good friends. What a frosty-spirited rogue is
this! Why, my Lord of York commends the plot
and the general course of the action. Zounds,
an I were now by this rascal, I could brain him
with his lady's fan. Is there not my father, my
uncle, and myself; Lord Edmund Mortimer, my
Lord of York, and Owen Glendower? Is there
not, besides, the Douglas? Have I not all their
letters to meet me in arms by the ninth of the
next month, and are they not some of them set
forward already? What a pagan rascal is this! an
infidel! Ha! you shall see now, in very sincerity
of fear and cold heart will he to the King and
lay open all our proceedings. O, I could divide
myself and go to buffets for moving such
a dish of skim milk with so honourable an
action! Hang him, let him tell the King! we are
prepared. I will set forward to-night.

Enter his LADY

How now, Kate? I must leave you within these
two hours.
LADY PERCY. O my good lord, why are you
thus alone?
For what offence have I this fortnight been
A banish'd woman from my Harry's bed,
Tell me, sweet lord, what is't that takes
from thee
Thy stomach, pleasure, and thy golden sleep?
Why dost thou bend thine eyes upon the earth,
And start so often when thou sit'st alone?
Why hast thou lost the fresh blood in thy cheeks
And given my treasures and my rights of thee
To thick-ey'd musing and curs'd melancholy?
In thy faint slumbers I by thee have watch'd,
And heard thee murmur tales of iron wars,
Speak terms of manage to thy bounding steed,
Cry 'Courage! to the field!' And thou hast talk'd
Of sallies and retires, of trenches, tent,
Of palisadoes, frontiers, parapets,
Of basilisks, of cannon, culverin,
Of prisoners' ransom, and of soldiers slain,
And all the currents of a heady fight.
Thy spirit within thee hath been so at war,
And thus hath so bestirr'd thee in thy sleep,
That beads of sweat have stood upon thy brow
Like bubbles in a late-disturbed stream,
And in thy face strange motions have appear'd,
Such as we see when men restrain their breath
On some great sudden hest. O, what portents
are these?
Some heavy business hath my lord in hand,
And I must know it, else he loves me not.
HOTSPUR. What, ho!

Enter a SERVANT

Is Gilliams with the packet gone?
SERVANT . He is, my lord, an hour ago.
HOTSPUR. Hath Butler brought those horses
from the sheriff?
SERVANT . One horse, my lord, he brought
even now.
HOTSPUR. What horse? A roan, a crop-ear, is
it not?
SERVANT. It is, my lord.
HOTSPUR. That roan shall be my throne.
Well, I will back him straight. O esperance!
Bid Butler lead him forth into the park.

Exit SERVANT.

LADY PERCY. But hear you, my lord.
HOTSPUR. What say'st thou, my lady?
LADY PERCY. What is it carries you away?
HOTSPUR. Why, my horse, my love-my horse!
LADY PERCY. Out, you mad-headed ape!

A weasel hath not such a deal of spleen
As you are toss'd with. In faith,
I'll know your business, Harry; that I will!
I fear my brother Mortimer doth stir
About his title and hath sent for you
To line his enterprise; but if you go-
HOTSPUR. So far afoot, I shall be weary, love.
LADY PERCY. Come, come, you paraquito,
answer me
Directly unto this question that I ask.
I'll break thy little finger, Harry,
An if thou wilt not tell me all things true.
HOTSPUR. Away.
Away, you trifler! Love? I love thee not;
I care not for thee, Kate. This is no world
To play with mammets and to tilt with lips.
We must have bloody noses and crack'd crowns,
And pass them current too. Gods me, my horse!
What say'st thou, Kate? What wouldst thou have
with me?
LADY PERCY. Do you not love me? do you
not indeed?
Well, do not then; for since you love me not,
I will not love myself. Do you not love me?
Nay, tell me if you speak in jest or no.
HOTSPUR. Come, wilt thou see me ride?
And when I am a-horseback, I will swear
I love thee infinitely. But hark you. Kate:
I must not have you henceforth question me
Whither I go, nor reason whereabout.
Whither I must, I must; and to conclude,
This evening must I leave you, gentle Kate.
I know you wise; but yet no farther wise
Than Harry Percy's wife; constant you are,
But yet a woman; and for secrecy,
No lady closer, for I well believe
Thou wilt not utter what thou dost not know,
And so far will I trust thee, gentle Kate.
LADY PERCY. How? so far?
HOTSPUR. Not an inch further. But hark you, Kate:
Whither I go, thither shall you go too;
To-day will I set forth, to-morrow you.
Will this content you, Kate,?
LADY PERCY. It must of force.   *Exeunt.*

✣ SCENE IV ✣
Eastcheap. The Boar's Head Tavern

Enter PRINCE and POINS

PRINCE. Ned, prithee come out of that fat-room
and lend me thy hand to laugh a little.

POINS. Where hast been, Hal?
PRINCE. With three or four loggerheads amongst
three or fourscore hogsheads. I have sounded
the very bass-string of humility. Sirrah, I am
sworn brother to a leash of drawers and can call
them all by their christen names, as Tom, Dick,
and Francis. They take it already upon their
salvation that, though I be but Prince of Wales,
yet I am the king of courtesy; and tell me flatly I
am no proud Jack like Falstaff, but a Corinthian,
a lad of mettle, a good boy (by the Lord, so they
call me!), and when I am King of England I shall
command all the good lads Eastcheap. They
call drinking deep, dying scarlet; and when you
breathe in your watering, they cry 'hem!' and
bid you play it off. To conclude, I am so good a
proficient in one quarter of an hour that I can
drink with any tinker in his own language during
my life. I tell thee, Ned, thou hast lost much
honour that thou wert not with me in this action.
But, sweet Ned-to sweeten which name of Ned, I
give thee this pennyworth of sugar, clapp'd even
now into my hand by an under-skinker, one that
never spake other English in his life than 'Eight
shillings and sixpence', and 'You are welcome',
with this shrill addition, 'Anon, anon, sir! Score a
pint of bastard in the Half-moon', or so-but, Ned,
to drive away the time till Falstaff come, I prithee
do thou stand in some by-room while I question
my puny drawer to what end be gave me the
sugar; and do thou never leave calling 'Francis!'
that his tale to me may be nothing but 'Anon!'
Step aside, and I'll show thee a precedent.
POINS. Francis!
PRINCE. Thou art perfect.
POINS. Francis!   *Exit POINS.*
Enter FRANCIS, a Drawer
FRANCIS. Anon, anon, sir.-Look down into the
Pomgarnet, Ralph.
PRINCE. Come hither, Francis.
FRANCIS. My lord?
PRINCE. How long hast thou to serve, Francis?
FRANCIS. Forsooth, five years, and as much as to-
POINS. *[Within]* Francis!
FRANCIS. Anon, anon, sir.
PRINCE. Five year! by'r Lady, a long lease for the
clinking of pewter. But, Francis, darest thou
be so valiant as to play the coward with thy
indenture and show it a fair pair of heels and
run from it?
FRANCIS. O Lord, sir, I'll be sworn upon all the
books in England I could find in my heart-
POINS. *[Within]* Francis!

FRANCIS. Anon, sir.

PRINCE. How old art thou, Francis?

FRANCIS. Let me see. About Michaelmas next I shall be-

POINS. *[Within]* Francis!

FRANCIS. Anon, sir. Pray stay a little, my lord.

PRINCE. Nay, but hark you, Francis. For the sugar thou gavest me-'twas a pennyworth, wast not?

FRANCIS. O Lord! I would it had been two!

PRINCE. I will give thee for it a thousand pound. Ask me when thou wilt, and, thou shalt have it.

POINS. *[Within]* Francis!

FRANCIS. Anon, anon.

PRINCE. Anon, Francis? No, Francis; but to-morrow, Francis; or, Francis, a Thursday; or indeed, Francis, when thou wilt. But Francis-

FRANCIS. My lord?

PRINCE. Wilt thou rob this leathern-jerkin, crystal-button, not-pated, agate-ring, puke-stocking, caddis-garter, smooth-tongue, Spanish-pouch-

FRANCIS. O Lord, sir, who do you mean?

PRINCE. Why then, your brown bastard is your only drink; for look you, Francis, your white canvas doublet will sully. In Barbary, sir, it cannot come to so much.

FRANCIS. What, sir?

POINS. *[Within]* Francis!

PRINCE. Away, you rogue! Dost thou not hear them call?

Here they both call him. FRANCIS stands amazed, not knowing which way to go.

Enter VINTNER

VINTNER. What, stand'st thou still, and hear'st such a calling? Look to the guests within. *[Exit FRANCIS]* My lord, old Sir John, with half-a-dozen more, are at the door. Shall I let them in?

PRINCE. Let them alone awhile, and then open the door.

Exit VINTNER

Poins!

POINS. *[Within]* Anon, anon, sir.

Enter POINS

PRINCE. Sirrah, Falstaff and the rest of the thieves are at the door. Shall we be merry?

POINS. As merry as crickets, my lad. But hark ye; what cunning match have you made with this jest of the drawer? Come, what's the issue?

PRINCE. I am now of all humours that have showed themselves humours since the old days of goodman Adam to the pupil age of this present twelve o'clock at midnight.

Enter FRANCIS

What's o'clock, Francis?

FRANCIS. Anon, anon, sir. *Exit*

PRINCE. That ever this fellow should have fewer words than a parrot, and yet the son of a woman! His industry is upstairs and downstairs, his eloquence the parcel of a reckoning. I am not yet of Percy's mind, the Hotspur of the North; he that kills me some six or seven dozen of Scots at a breakfast, washes his hands, and says to his wife, 'Fie upon this quiet life! I want work.' 'O my sweet Harry,' says she, 'how many hast thou kill'd to-day?' 'Give my roan horse a drench,' says he, and answers 'Some fourteen,' an hour after, 'a trifle, a trifle'. I prithee call in Falstaff; I'll play Percy, and that damn'd brawn shall play Dame Mortimer his wife. 'Rivo!' says the drunkard. Call in ribs, call in tallow.

Enter FALSTAFF, GADSHILL, BARDOLPH, and PETO; FRANCIS follows with wine

POINS. Welcome, Jack. Where hast thou been?

FALSTAFF. A plague of all cowards, I say, and a vengeance too! Marry and amen! Give me a cup of sack, boy. Ere I lead this life long, I'll sew nether-stocks, and mend them and foot them too. A plague of all cowards! Give me a cup of sack, rogue. Is there no virtue extant?

He drinks.

PRINCE. Didst thou never see Titan kiss a dish of butter? Pitiful-hearted butter, that melted at the sweet tale of the sun! If thou didst, then behold that compound.

FALSTAFF. You rogue, here's lime in this sack too! There is nothing but roguery to be found in villanous man. Yet a coward is worse than a cup of sack with lime in it-a villanous coward! Go thy ways, old Jack, die when thou wilt; if manhood, good manhood, be not forgot upon the face of the earth, then am I a shotten herring. There lives not three good men unhang'd in England; and one of them is fat, and grows old. God help the while! A bad world, I say. I would I were a weaver; I could sing psalms or anything. A plague of all cowards I say still!

PRINCE. How now, woolsack? What mutter you?

FALSTAFF. A king's son! If I do not beat thee out of thy kingdom with a dagger of lath and drive all thy subjects afore thee like a flock of wild geese, I'll never wear hair on my face more. You Prince of Wales?

PRINCE. Why, you whoreson round man, what's the matter?

FALSTAFF. Are not you a coward? Answer me to that-and Poins there?

POINS. Zounds, ye fat paunch, an ye call me coward, by the Lord, I'll stab thee.

FALSTAFF. I call thee coward? I'll see thee damn'd ere I call thee coward, but I would give a thousand pound I could run as fast as thou canst. You are straight enough in the shoulders; you care not who sees your back. Call you that backing of your friends? A plague upon such backing! Give me them that will face me. Give me a cup of sack. I am a rogue if I drunk to-day.

PRINCE. O villain! thy lips are scarce wip'd since thou drunk'st last.

FALSTAFF. All is one for that. *[He drinks]* A plague of all cowards still say I.

PRINCE. What's the matter?

FALSTAFF. What's the matter? There be four of us here have ta'en a thousand pound this day morning.

PRINCE. Where is it, Jack? Where is it?

FALSTAFF. Where is it? Taken from us it is. A hundred upon poor four of us!

PRINCE. What, a hundred, man?

FALSTAFF. I am a rogue if I were not at half-sword with a dozen of them two hours together. I have scap'd by miracle. I am eight times thrust through the doublet, four through the hose; my buckler cut through and through; my sword hack'd like a handsaw-ecce signum! I never dealt better since I was a man. All would not do. A plague of all cowards! Let them speak, If they speak more or less than truth, they are villains and the sons of darkness.

PRINCE. Speak, sirs. How was it?

GADSHILL. We four set upon some dozen-

FALSTAFF. Sixteen at least, my lord.

GADSHILL. And bound them.

Peto. No, no, they were not bound.

FALSTAFF. You rogue, they were bound, every man of them, or I am a Jew else-an Ebrew Jew.

GADSHILL. As we were sharing, some six or seven fresh men set upon us-

FALSTAFF. And unbound the rest, and then come in the other.

PRINCE. What, fought you with them all?

FALSTAFF. All? I know not what you call all, but if I fought not with fifty of them, I am a bunch of radish! If there were not two or three and fifty upon poor old Jack, then am I no two-legg'd creature.

PRINCE. Pray God you have not murd'red some of them.

FALSTAFF. Nay, that's past praying for. I have pepper'd two of them. Two I am sure I have paid, two rogues in buckram suits. I tell thee what, Hal-if I tell thee a lie, spit in my face, call me horse. Thou knowest my old ward. Here I lay, and thus I bore my point. Four rogues in buckram let drive at me.

PRINCE. What, four? Thou saidst but two even now.

FALSTAFF. Four, Hal. I told thee four.

POINS. Ay, ay, he said four.

FALSTAFF. These four came all afront and mainly thrust at me. I made me no more ado but took all their seven points in my target, thus.

PRINCE. Seven? Why, there were but four even now.

FALSTAFF. In buckram?

POINS. Ay, four, in buckram suits.

FALSTAFF. Seven, by these hilts, or I am a villain else.

PRINCE. *[Aside to Poins]* Prithee let him alone. We shall have more anon.

FALSTAFF. Dost thou hear me, Hal?

PRINCE. Ay, and mark thee too, Jack.

FALSTAFF. Do so, for it is worth the list'ning to. These nine in buckram that I told thee of-

PRINCE. So, two more already.

FALSTAFF. Their points being broken-

POINS. Down fell their hose.

FALSTAFF. Began to give me ground; but I followed me close, came in, foot and hand, and with a thought seven of the eleven I paid.

PRINCE. O monstrous! Eleven buckram men grown out of two!

FALSTAFF. But, as the devil would have it, three misbegotten knaves in Kendal green came at my back and let drive at me; for it was so dark, Hal, that thou couldst not see thy hand.

PRINCE. These lies are like their father that begets them-gross as a mountain, open, palpable. Why, thou clay-brain'd guts, thou knotty-pated fool, thou whoreson obscene greasy tallow-catch-

FALSTAFF. What, art thou mad? art thou mad? Is not the truth the truth?

PRINCE. Why, how couldst thou know these men in Kendal green when it was so dark thou couldst not see thy hand? Come, tell us your reason. What sayest thou to this?

POINS. Come, your reason, Jack, your reason.

FALSTAFF. What, upon compulsion? Zounds, an I were at the strappado or all the racks in the world, I would not tell you on compulsion. Give you a reason on compulsion? If reasons were as plentiful as blackberries, I would give no man a reason upon compulsion, I.

PRINCE. I'll be no longer guilty, of this sin; this sanguine coward, this bed-presser, this horseback-breaker, this huge hill of flesh-

FALSTAFF. 'Sblood, you starveling, you elf-skin, you dried neat's-tongue, you bull's sizzle, you stockfish-O for breath to utter what is like thee!- you tailor's yard, you sheath, you bowcase, you vile standing tuck!

PRINCE. Well, breathe awhile, and then to it again; and when thou hast tired thyself in base comparisons, hear me speak but this.

POINS. Mark, Jack.

PRINCE. We two saw you four set on four, and bound them and were masters of their wealth. Mark now how a plain tale shall put you down. Then did we two set on you four and, with a word, outfac'd you from your prize, and have it; yea, and can show it you here in the house. And, Falstaff, you carried your guts away as nimbly, with as quick dexterity, and roar'd for mercy, and still run and roar'd, as ever I heard bullcalf. What a slave art thou to hack thy sword as thou hast done, and then say it was in fight! What trick, what device, what starting hole canst thou now find out to hide thee from this open and apparent shame?

POINS. Come, let's hear, Jack. What trick hast thou now?

FALSTAFF. By the Lord, I knew ye as well as he that made ye. Why, hear you, my masters. Was it for me to kill the heir apparent? Should I turn upon the true prince? Why, thou knowest I am as valiant as Hercules; but beware instinct. The lion will not touch the true prince. Instinct is a great matter. I was now a coward on instinct. I shall think the better of myself, and thee, during my life-I for a valiant lion, and thou for a true prince. But, by the Lord, lads, I am glad you have the money. Hostess, clap to the doors. Watch to-night, pray to-morrow. Gallants, lads, boys, hearts of gold, all the titles of good fellowship come to you! What, shall we be merry? Shall we have a play extempore?

PRINCE. Content-and the argument shall be thy running away.

FALSTAFF. Ah, no more of that, Hal, an thou lovest me!

Enter HOSTESS

HOSTESS. O Jesu, my lord the Prince!

PRINCE. How now, my lady the hostess? What say'st thou to me?

HOSTESS. Marry, my lord, there is a nobleman of the court at door would speak with you. He says he comes from your father.

PRINCE. Give him as much as will make him a royal man, and send him back again to my mother.

FALSTAFF. What manner of man is he?

HOSTESS. An old man.

FALSTAFF. What doth gravity out of his bed at midnight? Shall I give him his answer?

PRINCE. Prithee do, Jack.

FALSTAFF. Faith, and I'll send him packing. *Exit*

PRINCE. Now, sirs. By'r Lady, you fought fair; so did you, Peto; so did you, Bardolph. You are lions too, you ran away upon instinct, you will not touch the true prince; no-fie!

BARDOLPH. Faith, I ran when I saw others run.

PRINCE. Tell me now in earnest, how came Falstaff's sword so hack'd?

PETO. Why, he hack'd it with his dagger, and said he would swear truth out of England but he would make you believe it was done in fight, and persuaded us to do the like.

BARDOLPH. Yea, and to tickle our noses with speargrass to make them bleed, and then to beslubber our garments with it and swear it was the blood of true men. I did that I did not this seven year before-I blush'd to hear his monstrous devices.

PRINCE. O villain! thou stolest a cup of sack eighteen years ago and wert taken with the manner, and ever since thou hast blush'd extempore. Thou hadst fire and sword on thy side, and yet thou ran'st away. What instinct hadst thou for it?

BARDOLPH. My lord, do you see these meteors? Do you behold these exhalations?

PRINCE. I do.

BARDOLPH. What think you they portend?

PRINCE. Hot livers and cold purses.

BARDOLPH. Choler, my lord, if rightly taken.

PRINCE. No, if rightly taken, halter.

Enter FALSTAFF

Here comes lean Jack; here comes bare-bone. How now, my sweet creature of bombast? How long is't ago, Jack, since thou sawest thine own knee?

FALSTAFF. My own knee? When I was about thy years, Hal, I was not an eagle's talent in the waist; I could have crept into any alderman's thumb-ring. A plague of sighing and grief! It blows a man up like a bladder. There's villanous news abroad. Here was Sir John Bracy from

your father. You must to the court in the
morning. That same mad fellow of the North,
Percy, and he of Wales that gave Amamon
the bastinado, and made Lucifer cuckold,
and swore the devil his true liegeman upon
the cross of a Welsh hook-what a plague call
you him?

POINS. O, Glendower.

FALSTAFF. Owen, Owen-the same; and his son-
in-law Mortimer, and old Northumberland, and
that sprightly Scot of Scots, Douglas, that runs
a-horseback up a hill perpendicular-

PRINCE. He that rides at high speed and with his
pistol kills a sparrow flying.

FALSTAFF. You have hit it.

PRINCE. So did he never the sparrow.

FALSTAFF. Well, that rascal hath good metal in
him; he will not run.

PRINCE. Why, what a rascal art thou then, to
praise him so for running!

FALSTAFF. A-horseback, ye cuckoo! but afoot he
will not budge a foot.

PRINCE. Yes, Jack, upon instinct.

FALSTAFF. I grant ye, upon instinct. Well, he is
there too, and one Mordake, and a thousand
bluecaps more. Worcester is stol'n away to-
night; thy father's beard is turn'd white with
the news; you may buy land now as cheap as
stinking mack'rel.

PRINCE. Why then, it is like, if there come a hot
June, and this civil buffeting hold, we shall
buy maidenheads as they buy hobnails, by
the hundreds.

FALSTAFF. By the mass, lad, thou sayest true;
it is like we shall have good trading that way.
But tell me, Hal, art not thou horrible afeard?
Thou being heir apparent, could the world
pick thee out three such enemies again as that
fiend Douglas, that spirit Percy, and that devil
Glendower? Art thou not horribly afraid? Doth
not thy blood thrill at it?

PRINCE. Not a whit, i' faith. I lack some of
thy instinct.

FALSTAFF. Well, thou wilt be horribly chid to-
morrow when thou comest to thy father. If
thou love me, practise an answer.

PRINCE. Do thou stand for my father and examine
me upon the particulars of my life.

FALSTAFF. Shall I? Content. This chair shall be my
state, this dagger my sceptre, and this cushion
my crown.

PRINCE. Thy state is taken for a join'd-stool, thy
golden sceptre for a leaden dagger, and thy

precious rich crown for a pitiful bald crown.

FALSTAFF. Well, an the fire of grace be not quite
out of thee, now shalt thou be moved. Give me
a cup of sack to make my eyes look red, that it
may be thought I have wept; for I must speak in
passion, and I will do it in King Cambyses' vein.

PRINCE. Well, here is my leg.

FALSTAFF. And here is my speech. Stand
aside, nobility.

HOSTESS. O Jesu, this is excellent sport, i' faith!

FALSTAFF. Weep not, sweet queen, for trickling
tears are vain.

HOSTESS. O, the Father, how he holds
his countenance!

FALSTAFF. For God's sake, lords, convey my
tristful queen!
For tears do stop the floodgates of her eyes.

HOSTESS. O Jesu, he doth it as like one of these
harlotry players as ever I see!

FALSTAFF. Peace, good pintpot. Peace, good
tickle-brain.-Harry, I do not only marvel where
thou spendest thy time, but also how thou
art accompanied. For though the camomile,
the more it is trodden on, the faster it grows,
yet youth, the more it is wasted, the sooner
it wears. That thou art my son I have partly
thy mother's word, partly my own opinion,
but chiefly a villanous trick of thine eye and
a foolish hanging of thy nether lip that doth
warrant me. If then thou be son to me, here
lies the point: why, being son to me, art thou
so pointed at? Shall the blessed sun of heaven
prove a micher and eat blackberries? A question
not to be ask'd. Shall the son of England prove
a thief and take purses? A question to be ask'd.
There is a thing, Harry, which thou hast often
heard of, and it is known to many in our land by
the name of pitch. This pitch, as ancient writers
do report, doth defile; so doth the company
thou keepest. For, Harry, now I do not speak to
thee in drink, but in tears; not in pleasure, but
in passion; not in words only, but in woes also:
and yet there is a virtuous man whom I have
often noted in thy company, but I know not
his name.

PRINCE. What manner of man, an it like
your Majesty?

FALSTAFF. A goodly portly man, i' faith, and a
corpulent; of a cheerful look, a pleasing eye,
and a most noble carriage; and, as I think,
his age some fifty, or, by'r Lady, inclining to
threescore; and now I remember me, his name
is Falstaff. If that man should be lewdly, given,

he deceiveth me; for, Harry, I see virtue in his looks. If then the tree may be known by the fruit, as the fruit by the tree, then, peremptorily I speak it, there is virtue in that Falstaff. Him keep with, the rest banish. And tell me now, thou naughty varlet, tell me where hast thou been this month?

PRINCE. Dost thou speak like a king? Do thou stand for me, and I'll play my father.

FALSTAFF. Depose me? If thou dost it half so gravely, so majestically, both in word and matter, hang me up by the heels for a rabbit-sucker or a poulter's hare.

PRINCE. Well, here I am set.

FALSTAFF. And here I stand. Judge, my masters.

PRINCE. Now, Harry, whence come you?

FALSTAFF. My noble lord, from Eastcheap.

PRINCE. The complaints I hear of thee are grievous.

FALSTAFF. 'Sblood, my lord, they are false! Nay, I'll tickle ye for a young prince, i' faith.

PRINCE. Swearest thou, ungracious boy? Henceforth ne'er look on me. Thou art violently carried away from grace. There is a devil haunts thee in the likeness of an old fat man; a tun of man is thy companion. Why dost thou converse with that trunk of humours, that bolting hutch of beastliness, that swoll'n parcel of dropsies, that huge bombard of sack, that stuff'd cloakbag of guts, that roasted Manningtree ox with the pudding in his belly, that reverend vice, that grey iniquity, that father ruffian, that vanity in years? Wherein is he good, but to taste sack and drink it? wherein neat and cleanly, but to carve a capon and eat it? wherein cunning, but in craft? wherein crafty, but in villany? wherein villanous, but in all things? wherein worthy, but in nothing?

FALSTAFF. I would your Grace would take me with you. Whom means your Grace?

PRINCE. That villanous abominable misleader of youth, Falstaff, that old white-bearded Satan.

FALSTAFF. My lord, the man I know.

PRINCE. I know thou dost.

FALSTAFF. But to say I know more harm in him than in myself were to say more than I know. That he is old (the more the pity) his white hairs do witness it; but that he is (saving your reverence) a whoremaster, that I utterly deny. If sack and sugar be a fault, God help the wicked! If to be old and merry be a sin, then many an old host that I know is damn'd. If to be fat be to be hated, then Pharaoh's lean kine are to be loved. No, my good lord. Banish Peto, banish Bardolph, banish Poins; but for sweet Jack Falstaff, kind Jack Falstaff, true Jack Falstaff, valiant Jack Falstaff, and therefore more valiant being, as he is, old Jack Falstaff, banish not him thy Harry's company, banish not him thy Harry's company. Banish plump Jack, and banish all the world!

PRINCE. I do, I will.

A knocking heard. Exeunt HOSTESS, FRANCIS, and BARDOLPH

Enter BARDOLPH, running

BARDOLPH. O, my lord, my lord! the sheriff with a most monstrous watch is at the door.

FALSTAFF. Out, ye rogue! Play out the play. I have much to say in the behalf of that Falstaff.

Enter the HOSTESS

HOSTESS. O Jesu, my lord, my lord!

PRINCE. Heigh, heigh, the devil rides upon a fiddlestick! What's the matter?

HOSTESS. The sheriff and all the watch are at the door. They are come to search the house. Shall I let them in?

FALSTAFF. Dost thou hear, Hal? Never call a true piece of gold a counterfeit. Thou art essentially mad without seeming so.

PRINCE. And thou a natural coward without instinct.

FALSTAFF. I deny your major. If you will deny the sheriff, so; if not, let him enter. If I become not a cart as well as another man, a plague on my bringing up! I hope I shall as soon be strangled with a halter as another.

PRINCE. Go hide thee behind the arras. The rest walk, up above. Now, my masters, for a true face and good conscience.

FALSTAFF. Both which I have had; but their date is out, and therefore I'll hide me. *Exit*

PRINCE. Call in the sheriff.

Exeunt all but the PRINCE and PETO

Enter SHERIFF and the CARRIER

Now, Master Sheriff, what is your will with me?

SHERIFF. First, pardon me, my lord. A hue and cry Hath followed certain men unto this house.

PRINCE. What men?

SHERIFF. One of them is well known, my gracious lord-
A gross fat man.

CARRIER. As fat as butter.

PRINCE. The man, I do assure you, is not here, For I myself at this time have employ'd him. And, sheriff, I will engage my word to thee

That I will by to-morrow dinner time
Send him to answer thee, or any man,
For anything he shall be charg'd withal;
And so let me entreat you leave the house.

SHERIFF. I will, my lord. There are two gentlemen
Have in this robbery lost three hundred marks.

PRINCE. It may be so. If he have robb'd these men,
He shall be answerable; and so farewell.

SHERIFF. Good night, my noble lord.

PRINCE. I think it is good morrow, is it not?

SHERIFF. Indeed, my lord, I think it be two o'clock.

Exit, with CARRIER.

PRINCE. This oily rascal is known as well as Paul's.
Go call him forth.

PETO. Falstaff! Fast asleep behind the arras, and
snorting like a horse.

PRINCE. Hark how hard he fetches breath. Search
his pockets. [PETO *searcheth his pockets and findeth certain
papers*] What hast thou found?

PETO. Nothing but papers, my lord.

PRINCE. Let's see what they be. Read them.

PETO. [*Reads*]

Item, A capon	2s. 2d.
Item, Sauce	4d.
Item, Sack two gallons	5s. 8d.
Item, Anchovies and sack after supper	2s. 6d.
Item, Bread	0b.

PRINCE. O monstrous! but one halfpennyworth
of bread to this intolerable deal of sack! What
there is else, keep close; we'll read it at more
advantage. There let him sleep till day. I'll to the
court in the morning . We must all to the wars,
and thy place shall be honourable. I'll procure
this fat rogue a charge of foot; and I know,
his death will be a march of twelve score. The
money shall be paid back again with advantage.
Be with me betimes in the morning, and so
good morrow, Peto.

PETO. Good morrow, good my lord.

Exeunt.

ACT III

SCENE I

Bangor. The Archdeacon's house

*Enter HOTSPUR, WORCESTER, LORD MORTIMER,
OWEN GLENDOWER*

MORTIMER. These promises are fair, the
parties sure,

And our induction full of prosperous hope.

HOTSPUR. Lord Mortimer, and cousin Glendower,
Will you sit down?
And uncle Worcester. A plague upon it!
I have forgot the map.

GLENDOWER. No, here it is.
Sit, cousin Percy; sit, good cousin Hotspur,
For by that name as oft as Lancaster
Doth speak of you, his cheek looks pale,
and with
A rising sigh he wisheth you in heaven.

HOTSPUR. And you in hell, as oft as he hears
Owen Glendower spoke of.

GLENDOWER. I cannot blame him. At my nativity
The front of heaven was full of fiery shapes
Of burning cressets, and at my birth
The frame and huge foundation of the earth
Shak'd like a coward.

HOTSPUR. Why, so it would have done at the
same season, if your mother's cat had but
kitten'd, though yourself had never been born.

GLENDOWER. I say the earth did shake when I
was born.

HOTSPUR. And I say the earth was not of
my mind,
If you suppose as fearing you it shook.

GLENDOWER. The heavens were all on fire, the
earth did tremble.

HOTSPUR. O, then the earth shook to see the
heavens on fire,
And not in fear of your nativity.
Diseased nature oftentimes breaks forth
In strange eruptions; oft the teeming earth
Is with a kind of colic pinch'd and vex'd
By the imprisoning of unruly wind
Within her womb, which, for
enlargement striving,
Shakes the old beldame earth and topples down
Steeples and mossgrown towers. At your birth
Our grandam earth, having this distemp'rature,
In passion shook.

GLENDOWER. Cousin, of many men
I do not bear these crossings. Give me leave
To tell you once again that at my birth
The front of heaven was full of fiery shapes,
The goats ran from the mountains, and the herds
Were strangely clamorous to the frighted fields.
These signs have mark'd me extraordinary,
And all the courses of my life do show
I am not in the roll of common men.
Where is he living, clipp'd in with the sea
That chides the banks of England,
Scotland, Wales,

Which calls me pupil or hath read to me?
And bring him out that is but woman's son
Can trace me in the tedious ways of art
And hold me pace in deep experiments.
HOTSPUR. I think there's no man speaks better
  Welsh. I'll to dinner.
MORTIMER. Peace, cousin Percy; you will make
  him mad.
GLENDOWER. I can call spirits from the
  vasty deep.
HOTSPUR. Why, so can I, or so can any man;
  But will they come when you do call for them?
GLENDOWER. Why, I can teach you, cousin, to
  command the devil.
HOTSPUR. And I can teach thee, coz, to shame
  the devil-
By telling truth. Tell truth and shame the devil.
If thou have power to raise him, bring
  him hither,
And I'll be sworn I have power to shame
  him hence.
O, while you live, tell truth and shame
  the devil!
MORTIMER. Come, come, no more of this
  unprofitable chat.
GLENDOWER. Three times hath Henry
  Bolingbroke made head
Against my power; thrice from the banks of Wye
And sandy-bottom'd Severn have I sent him
Bootless home and weather-beaten back.
HOTSPUR. Home without boots, and in foul
  weather too?
How scapes he agues, in the devil's name
GLENDOWER. Come, here's the map. Shall we
  divide our right
According to our threefold order ta'en?
MORTIMER. The Archdeacon hath divided it
Into three limits very equally.
England, from Trent and Severn hitherto,
By south and east is to my part assign'd;
All westward, Wales beyond the Severn shore,
And all the fertile land within that bound,
To Owen Glendower; and, dear coz, to you
The remnant northward lying off from Trent.
And our indentures tripartite are drawn;
Which being sealed interchangeably
(A business that this night may execute),
To-morrow, cousin Percy, you and I
And my good Lord of Worcester will set forth
To meet your father and the Scottish bower,
As is appointed us, at Shrewsbury.
My father Glendower is not ready yet,
Nor shall we need his help these fourteen days.

[*To* GLENDOWER] Within that space you may
  have drawn together
Your tenants, friends, and
  neighbouring gentlemen.
GLENDOWER. A shorter time shall send me to
  you, lords;
And in my conduct shall your ladies come,
From whom you now must steal and take
  no leave,
For there will be a world of water shed
Upon the parting of your wives and you.
HOTSPUR. Methinks my moiety, north from
  Burton here,
In quantity equals not one of yours.
See how this river comes me cranking in
And cuts me from the best of all my land
A huge half-moon, a monstrous cantle out.
I'll have the current in this place damm'd up,
And here the smug and sliver Trent shall run
In a new channel fair and evenly.
It shall not wind with such a deep indent
To rob me of so rich a bottom here.
GLENDOWER. Not wind? It shall, it must! You see
  it doth.
MORTIMER. Yea, but
Mark how he bears his course, and runs me up
With like advantage on the other side,
Gelding the opposed continent as much
As on the other side it takes from you.
WORCESTER. Yea, but a little charge will trench
  him here
And on this north side win this cape of land;
And then he runs straight and even.
HOTSPUR. I'll have it so. A little charge will do it.
GLENDOWER. I will not have it alt'red.
HOTSPUR. Will not you?
GLENDOWER. No, nor you shall not.
HOTSPUR. Who shall say me nay?
GLENDOWER. No, that will I.
HOTSPUR. Let me not understand you then;
  speak it in Welsh.
GLENDOWER. I can speak English, lord, as well
  as you;
For I was train'd up in the English court,
Where, being but young, I framed to the harp
Many an English ditty lovely well,
And gave the tongue a helpful ornament-
A virtue that was never seen in you.
HOTSPUR. Marry,
And I am glad of it with all my heart!
I had rather be a kitten and cry mew
Than one of these same metre ballet-mongers.
I had rather hear a brazen canstick turn'd

Or a dry wheel grate on the axletree,
And that would set my teeth nothing on edge,
Nothing so much as mincing poetry.
'Tis like the forc'd gait of a shuffling nag,
GLENDOWER. Come, you shall have Trent turn'd.
HOTSPUR. I do not care. I'll give thrice so
  much land
To any well-deserving friend;
But in the way of bargain, mark ye me,
I'll cavil on the ninth part of a hair
Are the indentures drawn? Shall we be gone?
GLENDOWER. The moon shines fair; you may
  away by night.
I'll haste the writer, and withal
Break with your wives of your departure hence.
I am afraid my daughter will run mad,
So much she doteth on her Mortimer. *Exit.*
MORTIMER. Fie, cousin Percy! how you cross
  my father!
HOTSPUR. I cannot choose. Sometimes he
  angers me
With telling me of the moldwarp and the ant,
Of the dreamer Merlin and his prophecies,
And of a dragon and a finless fish,
A clip-wing'd griffin and a moulten raven,
A couching lion and a ramping cat,
And such a deal of skimble-skamble stuff
As puts me from my faith. I tell you what-
He held me last night at least nine hours
In reckoning up the several devils' names
That were his lackeys. I cried 'hum', and 'Well,
  go to!'
But mark'd him not a word. O, he is as tedious
As a tired horse, a railing wife;
Worse than a smoky house. I had rather live
With cheese and garlic in a windmill far
Than feed on cates and have him talk to me
In any summer house in Christendom.
MORTIMER. In faith, he is a worthy gentleman,
Exceedingly well read, and profited
In strange concealments, valiant as a lion,
And wondrous affable, and as bountiful
As mines of India. Shall I tell you, cousin?
He holds your temper in a high respect
And curbs himself even of his natural scope
When you come 'cross his humour. Faith,
  he does.
I warrant you that man is not alive
Might so have tempted him as you have done
Without the taste of danger and reproof.
But do not use it oft, let me entreat you.
WORCESTER. In faith, my lord, you are too
  wilful-blame,

And since your coming hither have done enough
To put him quite besides his patience.
You must needs learn, lord, to amend this fault.
Though sometimes it show greatness,
  courage, blood-
And that's the dearest grace it renders you-
Yet oftentimes it doth present harsh rage,
Defect of manners, want of government,
Pride, haughtiness, opinion, and disdain;
The least of which haunting a nobleman
Loseth men's hearts, and leaves behind a stain
Upon the beauty of all parts besides,
Beguiling them of commendation.
HOTSPUR. Well, I am school'd. Good manners be
  your speed!
Here come our wives, and let us take our leave.
  Enter GLENDOWER with the LADIES
MORTIMER. This is the deadly spite that
  angers me-
My wife can speak no English, I no Welsh.
GLENDOWER. My daughter weeps; she will not
  part with you;
She'll be a soldier too, she'll to the wars.
MORTIMER. Good father, tell her that she and my
  aunt Percy
Shall follow in your conduct speedily.
  *GLENDOWER speaks to her in Welsh, and she answers him
    in the same*
GLENDOWER. She is desperate here. A peevish
  self-will'd harlotry,
One that no persuasion can do good upon.
  The LADY speaks in Welsh
MORTIMER. I understand thy looks. That
  pretty Welsh
Which thou pourest down from these
  swelling heavens
I am too perfect in; and, but for shame,
In such a Barley should I answer thee. *[The LADY
  again in Welsh]*
I understand thy kisses, and thou mine,
And that's a feeling disputation.
But I will never be a truant, love,
Till I have learnt thy language: for thy tongue
Makes Welsh as sweet as ditties highly penn'd,
Sung by a fair queen in a summer's bow'r,
With ravishing division, to her lute.
GLENDOWER. Nay, if you melt, then will she
  run mad.
  The LADY speaks again in Welsh.
MORTIMER. O, I am ignorance itself in this!
GLENDOWER. She bids you on the wanton rushes
  lay you down
And rest your gentle head upon her lap,

And she will sing the song that pleaseth you
And on your eyelids crown the god of sleep,
Charming your blood with pleasing heaviness,
Making such difference 'twixt wake and sleep
As is the difference betwixt day and night
The hour before the heavenly-harness'd team
Begins his golden progress in the East.
MORTIMER. With all my heart I'll sit and hear
her sing.
By that time will our book, I think, be drawn.
GLENDOWER. Do so,
And those musicians that shall play to you
Hang in the air a thousand leagues from hence,
And straight they shall be here. Sit, and attend.
HOTSPUR. Come, Kate, thou art perfect in lying
down. Come, quick, quick, that I may lay my
head in thy lap.
LADY PERCY. Go, ye giddy goose.

The music plays

HOTSPUR. Now I perceive the devil
understands Welsh;
And 'tis no marvel, be is so humorous.
By'r Lady, he is a good musician.
LADY PERCY. Then should you be nothing but
musical; for you are altogether govern'd by
humours. Lie still, ye thief, and hear the lady
sing in Welsh.
HOTSPUR. I had rather hear Lady, my brach, howl
in Irish.
LADY PERCY. Wouldst thou have thy
head broken?
HOTSPUR. No.
LADY PERCY. Then be still.
HOTSPUR. Neither! 'Tis a woman's fault.
LADY PERCY. Now God help thee!
HOTSPUR. To the Welsh lady's bed.
LADY PERCY. What's that?
HOTSPUR. Peace! she sings. [*Here the LADY sings a
Welsh song*]
Come, Kate, I'll have your song too.
LADY PERCY. Not mine, in good sooth.
HOTSPUR. Not yours, in good sooth? Heart! you
swear like a comfit-maker's wife. 'Not you, in
good sooth!' and 'as true as I live!' and 'as God
shall mend me!' and 'as sure as day!'
And givest such sarcenet surety for thy oaths
As if thou ne'er walk'st further than Finsbury.
Swear me, Kate, like a lady as thou art,
A good mouth-filling oath; and leave 'in sooth'
And such protest of pepper gingerbread
To velvet guards and Sunday citizens.
Come, sing.
LADY PERCY. I will not sing.

HOTSPUR. 'Tis the next way to turn tailor or be
redbreast-teacher. An the indentures be drawn,
I'll away within these two hours; and so come
in when ye will.   *Exit.*
GLENDOWER. Come, come, Lord Mortimer. You
are as slow
As hot Lord Percy is on fire to go.
By this our book is drawn; we'll but seal,
And then to horse immediately.
MORTIMER. With all my heart.

Exeunt.

⚘ SCENE II ⚘
London. The palace

Enter the KING, PRINCE OF WALES, and Others

KING. Lords, give us leave. The Prince of Wales
and I
Must have some private conference; but be near
at hand,
For we shall presently have need of you.

Exeunt Lords.

I know not whether God will have it so,
For some displeasing service I have done,
That, in his secret doom, out of my blood
He'll breed revengement and a scourge for me;
But thou dost in thy passages of life
Make me believe that thou art only mark'd
For the hot vengeance and the rod of heaven
To punish my mistreadings. Tell me else,
Could such inordinate and low desires,
Such poor, such bare, such lewd, such
mean attempts,
Such barren pleasures, rude society,
As thou art match'd withal and grafted to,
Accompany the greatness of thy blood
And hold their level with thy princely heart?
PRINCE. So please your Majesty, I would I could
Quit all offences with as clear excuse
As well as I am doubtless I can purge
Myself of many I am charged withal.
Yet such extenuation let me beg
As, in reproof of many tales devis'd,
Which oft the ear of greatness needs must hear
By smiling pickthanks and base newsmongers,
I may, for some things true wherein my youth
Hath faulty wand'red and irregular,
And pardon on lily true submission.
KING. God pardon thee! Yet let me
wonder, Harry,
At thy affections, which do hold a wing,

Quite from the flight of all thy ancestors.
Thy place in Council thou hast rudely lost,
Which by thy younger brother is supplied,
And art almost an alien to the hearts
Of all the court and princes of my blood.
The hope and expectation of thy time
Is ruin'd, and the soul of every man
Prophetically do forethink thy fall.
Had I so lavish of my presence been,
So common-hackney'd in the eyes of men,
So stale and cheap to vulgar company,
Opinion, that did help me to the crown,
Had still kept loyal to possession
And left me in reputeless banishment,
A fellow of no mark nor likelihood.
By being seldom seen, I could not stir
But, like a comet, I was wond'red at;
That men would tell their children, 'This is he!'
Others would say, 'Where? Which
 is Bolingbroke?'
And then I stole all courtesy from heaven,
And dress'd myself in such humility
That I did pluck allegiance from men's hearts,
Loud shouts and salutations from their mouths
Even in the presence of the crowned King.
Thus did I keep my person fresh and new,
My presence, like a robe pontifical,
Ne'er seen but wond'red at; and so my state,
Seldom but sumptuous, show'd like a feast
And won by rareness such solemnity.
The skipping King, he ambled up and down
With shallow jesters and rash bavin wits,
Soon kindled and soon burnt; carded his state;
Mingled his royalty with cap'ring fools;
Had his great name profaned with their scorns
And gave his countenance, against his name,
To laugh at gibing boys and stand the push
Of every beardless vain comparative;
Grew a companion to the common streets,
Enfeoff'd himself to popularity;
That, being daily swallowed by men's eyes,
They surfeited with honey and began
To loathe the taste of sweetness, whereof a little
More than a little is by much too much.
So, when he had occasion to be seen,
He was but as the cuckoo is in June,
Heard, not regarded-seen, but with such eyes
As, sick and blunted with community,
Afford no extraordinary gaze,
Such as is bent on unlike majesty
When it shines seldom in admiring eyes;
But rather drows'd and hung their eyelids down,
Slept in his face, and rend'red such aspect

As cloudy men use to their adversaries,
Being with his presence glutted, gorg'd, and full.
And in that very line, Harry, standest thou;
For thou hast lost thy princely privilege
With vile participation. Not an eye
But is aweary of thy common sight,
Save mine, which hath desir'd to see thee more;
Which now doth that I would not have it do-
Make blind itself with foolish tenderness.
PRINCE. I shall hereafter, my thrice-gracious lord,
  Be more myself.
KING. For all the world,
  As thou art to this hour, was Richard then
  When I from France set foot at Ravenspurgh;
  And even as I was then is Percy now.
  Now, by my sceptre, and my soul to boot,
  He hath more worthy interest to the state
  Than thou, the shadow of succession;
  For of no right, nor colour like to right,
  He doth fill fields with harness in the realm,
  Turns head against the lion's armed jaws,
  And, being no more in debt to years than thou,
  Leads ancient lords and reverend Bishops on
  To bloody battles and to bruising arms.
  What never-dying honour hath he got
  Against renowmed Douglas! whose high deeds,
  Whose hot incursions and great name in arms
  Holds from all soldiers chief majority
  And military title capital
  Through all the kingdoms that
   acknowledge Christ.
  Thrice hath this Hotspur, Mars in
   swathling clothes,
  This infant warrior, in his enterprises
  Discomfited great Douglas; ta'en him once,
  Enlarged him, and made a friend of him,
  To fill the mouth of deep defiance up
  And shake the peace and safety of our throne.
  And what say you to this?
   Percy, Northumberland,
  The Archbishop's Grace of York,
   Douglas, Mortimer
  Capitulate against us and are up.
  But wherefore do I tell these news to thee
  Why, Harry, do I tell thee of my foes,
  Which art my nearest and dearest enemy?
  Thou that art like enough, through vassal fear,
  Base inclination, and the start of spleen,
  To fight against me under Percy's pay,
  To dog his heels and curtsy at his frowns,
  To show how much thou art degenerate.
PRINCE. Do not think so. You shall not find it so.
  And God forgive them that so much have sway'd

Your Majesty's good thoughts away from me!
I will redeem all this on Percy's head
And, in the closing of some glorious day,
Be bold to tell you that I am your son,
When I will wear a garment all of blood,
And stain my favours in a bloody mask,
Which, wash'd away, shall scour my shame
 with it.
And that shall be the day, whene'er it lights,
That this same child of honour and renown,
This gallant Hotspur, this all-praised knight,
And your unthought of Harry chance to meet.
For every honour sitting on his helm,
Would they were multitudes, and on my head
My shames redoubled! For the time will come
That I shall make this Northern youth exchange
His glorious deeds for my indignities.
Percy is but my factor, good my lord,
To engross up glorious deeds on my behalf;
And I will call him to so strict account
That he shall render every glory up,
Yea, even the slightest worship of his time,
Or I will tear the reckoning from his heart.
This in the name of God I promise here;
The which if he be pleas'd I shall perform,
I do beseech your Majesty may salve
The long-grown wounds of my intemperance.
If not, the end of life cancels all bands,
And I will die a hundred thousand deaths
Ere break the smallest parcel of this vow.
KING. A hundred thousand rebels die in this!
Thou shalt have charge and sovereign
 trust herein.

Enter BLUNT

How now, good Blunt? Thy looks are full
 of speed.
BLUNT. So hath the business that I come to
 speak of.
Lord Mortimer of Scotland hath sent word
That Douglas and the English rebels met
The eleventh of this month at Shrewsbury.
A mighty and a fearful head they are,
If promises be kept onil every hand,
As ever off'red foul play in a state.
KING. The Earl of Westmoreland set forth to-day;
With him my son, Lord John of Lancaster;
For this advertisement is five days old.
On Wednesday next, Harry, you shall
 set forward;
On Thursday we ourselves will march.
 Our meeting
Is Bridgenorth; and, Harry, you shall march
Through Gloucestershire; by which account,

Our business valued, some twelve days hence
Our general forces at Bridgenorth shall meet.
Our hands are full of business. Let's away.
Advantage feeds him fat while men delay.

Exeunt

⚜ SCENE III ⚜
Eastcheap. The Boar's Head Tavern

Enter FALSTAFF and BARDOLPH

FALSTAFF. Bardolph, am I not fall'n away vilely
 since this last action? Do I not bate? Do I not
 dwindle? Why, my skin hangs about me like an
 old lady's loose gown! I am withered like an old
 apple John. Well, I'll repent, and that suddenly,
 while I am in some liking. I shall be out of heart
 shortly, and then I shall have no strength to
 repent. An I have not forgotten what the inside
 of a church is made of, I am a peppercorn,
 a brewer's horse. The inside of a church!
 Company, villanous company, hath been the
 spoil of me.
BARDOLPH. Sir John, you are so fretful you
 cannot live long.
FALSTAFF. Why, there is it! Come, sing me a
 bawdy song; make me merry. I was as virtuously
 given as a gentleman need to be, virtuous
 enough: swore little, dic'd not above seven
 times a week, went to a bawdy house not above
 once in a quarter-of an hour, paid money that I
 borrowed-three or four times, lived well, and in
 good compass; and now I live out of all order,
 out of all compass.
BARDOLPH. Why, you are so fat, Sir John, that
 you must needs be out of all compass-out of all
 reasonable compass, Sir John.
FALSTAFF. Do thou amend thy face, and I'll
 amend my life. Thou art our admiral, thou
 bearest the lantern in the poop-but 'tis in
 the nose of thee. Thou art the Knight of the
 Burning Lamp.
BARDOLPH. Why, Sir John, my face does you
 no harm.
FALSTAFF. No, I'll be sworn. I make as good use
 of it as many a man doth of a death's-head or a
 memento mori. I never see thy face but I think
 upon hellfire and Dives that lived in purple;
 for there he is in his robes, burning, burning.
 if thou wert any way given to virtue, I would
 swear by thy face; my oath should be 'By this
 fire, that's God's angel.' But thou art altogether

given over, and wert indeed, but for the light
in thy face, the son of utter darkness. When
thou ran'st up Gadshill in the night to catch
my horse, if I did not think thou hadst been
an ignis fatuus or a ball of wildfire, there's no
purchase in money. O, thou art a perpetual
triumph, an everlasting bonfire-light! Thou
hast saved me a thousand marks in links and
torches, walking with thee in the night betwixt
tavern and tavern; but the sack that thou hast
drunk me would have bought me lights as good
cheap at the dearest chandler's in Europe. I
have maintained that salamander of yours with
fire any time this two-and-thirty years. God
reward me for it!

BARDOLPH. 'Sblood, I would my face were in
your belly!

FALSTAFF. God-a-mercy! so should I be sure to
be heart-burn'd.

Enter HOSTESS

How now, Dame Partlet the hen? Have you
enquir'd yet who pick'd my pocket?

HOSTESS. Why, Sir John, what do you think, Sir
John? Do you think I keep thieves in my house?
I have search'd, I have enquired, so has my
husband, man by man, boy by boy, servant by
servant. The tithe of a hair was never lost in my
house before.

FALSTAFF. Ye lie, hostess. Bardolph was shav'd
and lost many a hair, and I'll be sworn my
pocket was pick'd. Go to, you are a woman, go!

HOSTESS. Who, I? No; I defy thee! God's light, I
was never call'd so in mine own house before!

FALSTAFF. Go to, I know you well enough.

HOSTESS. No, Sir John; you do not know me,
Sir John. I know you, Sir John. You owe me
money, Sir John, and now you pick a quarrel to
beguile me of it. I bought you a dozen of shirts
to your back.

FALSTAFF. Dowlas, filthy dowlas! I have given
them away to bakers' wives; they have made
bolters of them.

HOSTESS. Now, as I am a true woman, holland
of eight shillings an ell. You owe money
here besides, Sir John, for your diet and
by-drinkings, and money lent you, four-and-
twenty pound.

FALSTAFF. He had his part of it; let him pay.

HOSTESS. He? Alas, he is poor; he hath nothing.

FALSTAFF. How? Poor? Look upon his face. What
call you rich? Let them coin his nose, let them
coin his cheeks. I'll not pay a denier. What,
will you make a younker of me? Shall I not

take mine ease in mine inn but I shall have
my pocket pick'd? I have lost a seal-ring of my
grandfather's worth forty mark.

HOSTESS. O Jesu, I have heard the Prince
tell him, I know not how oft, that that ring
was copper!

FALSTAFF. How? the Prince is a Jack, a sneak-cup.
'Sblood, an he were here, I would cudgel him
like a dog if he would say so.

Enter the PRINCE and POINS, marching; and FALSTAFF
meets them, playing upon his truncheon like a fife

How now, lad? Is the wind in that door, i' faith?
Must we all march?

BARDOLPH. Yea, two and two, Newgate fashion.

HOSTESS. My lord, I pray you hear me.

PRINCE. What say'st thou, Mistress Quickly? How
doth thy husband? I love him well; he is an
honest man.

HOSTESS. Good my lord, hear me.

FALSTAFF. Prithee let her alone and list to me.

PRINCE. What say'st thou, Jack?

FALSTAFF. The other night I fell asleep here
behind the arras and had my pocket pick'd.
This house is turn'd bawdy house; they
pick pockets.

PRINCE. What didst thou lose, Jack?

FALSTAFF. Wilt thou believe me, Hal? Three or
four bonds of forty pound apiece and a seal-ring
of my grandfather's.

PRINCE. A trifle, some eightpenny matter.

HOSTESS. So I told him, my lord, and I said I
heard your Grace say so; and, my lord, he
speaks most vilely of you, like a foul-mouth'd
man as he is, and said he would cudgel you.

PRINCE. What! he did not?

HOSTESS. There's neither faith, truth, nor
womanhood in me else.

FALSTAFF. There's no more faith in thee than
in a stewed prune, nor no more truth in thee
than in a drawn fox; and for womanhood, Maid
Marian may be the deputy's wife of the ward to
thee. Go, you thing, go!

HOSTESS. Say, what thing? what thing?

FALSTAFF. What thing? Why, a thing to thank
God on.

HOSTESS. I am no thing to thank God on, I would
thou shouldst know it! I am an honest man's
wife, and, setting thy knighthood aside, thou art
a knave to call me so.

FALSTAFF. Setting thy womanhood aside, thou art
a beast to say otherwise.

HOSTESS. Say, what beast, thou knave, thou?

FALSTAFF. What beast? Why, an otter.

PRINCE. An otter, Sir John? Why an otter?

FALSTAFF. Why, she's neither fish nor flesh; a man knows not where to have her.

HOSTESS. Thou art an unjust man in saying so. Thou or any man knows where to have me, thou knave, thou!

PRINCE. Thou say'st true, hostess, and he slanders thee most grossly.

HOSTESS. So he doth you, my lord, and said this other day you ought him a thousand pound.

PRINCE. Sirrah, do I owe you a thousand pound?

FALSTAFF. A thousand pound, Hal? A million! Thy love is worth a million; thou owest me thy love.

HOSTESS. Nay, my lord, he call'd you Jack and said he would cudgel you.

FALSTAFF. Did I, Bardolph?

BARDOLPH. Indeed, Sir John, you said so.

FALSTAFF. Yea. if he said my ring was copper.

PRINCE. I say, 'tis copper. Darest thou be as good as thy word now?

FALSTAFF. Why, Hal, thou knowest, as thou art but man, I dare; but as thou art Prince, I fear thee as I fear the roaring of the lion's whelp.

PRINCE. And why not as the lion?

FALSTAFF. The King himself is to be feared as the lion. Dost thou think I'll fear thee as I fear thy father? Nay, an I do, I pray God my girdle break.

PRINCE. O, if it should, how would thy guts fall about thy knees! But, sirrah, there's no room for faith, truth, nor honesty in this bosom of thine. It is all fill'd up with guts and midriff. Charge an honest woman with picking thy pocket? Why, thou whoreson, impudent, emboss'd rascal, if there were anything in thy pocket but tavern reckonings, memorandums of bawdy houses, and one poor pennyworth of sugar candy to make thee long-winded-if thy pocket were enrich'd with any other injuries but these, I am a villain. And yet you will stand to it; you will not pocket up wrong. Art thou not ashamed?

FALSTAFF. Dost thou hear, Hal? Thou knowest in the state of innocency Adam fell; and what should poor Jack Falstaff do in the days of villany? Thou seest I have more flesh than another man, and therefore more frailty. You confess then, you pick'd my pocket?

PRINCE. It appears so by the story.

FALSTAFF. Hostess, I forgive thee. Go make ready breakfast. Love thy husband, look to thy servants, cherish thy guests. Thou shalt find me tractable to any honest reason. Thou seest I am pacified.-Still?-Nay, prithee be gone. *[Exit*

HOSTESS] Now, Hal, to the news at court. For the robbery, lad-how is that answered?

PRINCE. O my sweet beef, I must still be good angel to thee. The money is paid back again.

FALSTAFF. O, I do not like that paying back! 'Tis a double labour.

PRINCE. I am good friends with my father, and may do anything.

FALSTAFF. Rob me the exchequer the first thing thou doest, and do it with unwash'd hands too.

BARDOLPH. Do, my lord.

PRINCE. I have procured thee, Jack, a charge of foot.

FALSTAFF. I would it had been of horse. Where shall I find one that can steal well? O for a fine thief of the age of two-and-twenty or thereabouts! I am heinously unprovided. Well, God be thanked for these rebels. They offend none but the virtuous. I laud them, I praise them.

PRINCE. Bardolph!

BARDOLPH. My lord?

PRINCE. Go bear this letter to Lord John of Lancaster,
To my brother John; this to my Lord of Westmoreland. *[Exit BARDOLPH]*
Go, Poins, to horse, to horse; for thou and I
Have thirty miles to ride yet ere dinner time.
[Exit POINS]
Jack, meet me to-morrow in the Temple Hall
At two o'clock in the afternoon.
There shalt thou know thy charge. and
there receive
Money and order for their furniture.
The land is burning; Percy stands on high;
And either they or we must lower lie.*Exit.*

FALSTAFF. Rare words! brave world! Hostess, my breakfast, come.
O, I could wish this tavern were my drum!

Exit.

◈ ACT IV ◈

✽ SCENE I ✽
The rebel camp near Shrewsbury

Enter HOTSPUR, WORCESTER, and DOUGLAS

HOTSPUR. Well said, my noble Scot. If speaking truth
In this fine age were not thought flattery,
Such attribution should the Douglas have

As not a soldier of this season's stamp
Should go so general current through the world.
By God, I cannot flatter, I defy
The tongues of soothers! but a braver place
In my heart's love hath no man than yourself.
Nay, task me to my word; approve me, lord.
DOUGLAS. Thou art the king of honour.
No man so potent breathes upon the ground
But I will beard him.

Enter MESSENGER with letters

HOTSPUR. Do so, and 'tis well.-
What letters hast thou there?-I can but
thank you.
MESSENGER. These letters come from
your father.
HOTSPUR. Letters from him? Why comes he
not himself?
MESSENGER. He cannot come, my lord; he is
grievous sick.
HOTSPUR. Zounds! how has he the leisure to
be sick
In such a justling time? Who leads his power?
Under whose government come they along?
MESSENGER. His letters bears his mind, not I,
my lord.
WORCESTER. I prithee tell me, doth he keep
his bed?
MESSENGER. He did, my lord, four days ere I
set forth,
And at the time of my departure thence
He was much fear'd by his physicians.
WORCESTER. I would the state of time had first
been whole
Ere he by sickness had been visited.
His health was never better worth than now.
HOTSPUR. Sick now? droop now? This sickness
doth infect
The very lifeblood of our enterprise.
'Tis catching hither, even to our camp.
He writes me here that inward sickness-
And that his friends by deputation could not
So soon be drawn; nor did he think it meet
To lay so dangerous and dear a trust
On any soul remov'd but on his own.
Yet doth he give us bold advertisement,
That with our small conjunction we should on,
To see how fortune is dispos'd to us;
For, as he writes, there is no quailing now,
Because the King is certainly possess'd
Of all our purposes. What say you to it?
WORCESTER. Your father's sickness is a maim
to us.
HOTSPUR. A perilous gash, a very limb lopp'd off.

And yet, in faith, it is not! His present want
Seems more than we shall find it. Were it good
To set the exact wealth of all our states
All at one cast? to set so rich a man
On the nice hazard of one doubtful hour?
It were not good; for therein should we read
The very bottom and the soul of hope,
The very list, the very utmost bound
Of all our fortunes.
DOUGLAS. Faith, and so we should;
Where now remains a sweet reversion.
We may boldly spend upon the hope of what
Is to come in.
A comfort of retirement lives in this.
HOTSPUR. A rendezvous, a home to fly unto,
If that the devil and mischance look big
Upon the maidenhead of our affairs.
WORCESTER. But yet I would your father had
been here.
The quality and hair of our attempt
Brooks no division. It will be thought
By some that know not why he is away,
That wisdom, loyalty, and mere dislike
Of our proceedings kept the Earl from hence.
And think how such an apprehension
May turn the tide of fearful faction
And breed a kind of question in our cause.
For well you know we of the off'ring side
Must keep aloof from strict arbitrement,
And stop all sight-holes, every loop from whence
The eye of reason may pry in upon us.
This absence of your father's draws a curtain
That shows the ignorant a kind of fear
Before not dreamt of.
HOTSPUR. You strain too far.
I rather of his absence make this use:
It lends a lustre and more great opinion,
A larger dare to our great enterprise,
Than if the Earl were here; for men must think,
If we, without his help, can make a head
To push against a kingdom, with his help
We shall o'erturn it topsy-turvy down.
Yet all goes well; yet all our joints are whole.
DOUGLAS. As heart can think. There is not such
a word
Spoke of in Scotland as this term of fear.

Enter SIR RICHARD VERNON

HOTSPUR. My cousin Vernon! welcome, by
my soul.
VERNON. Pray God my news be worth a
welcome, lord.
The Earl of Westmoreland, seven
thousand strong,

Is marching hitherwards; with him Prince John.

HOTSPUR. No harm. What more?

VERNON . And further, I have learn'd
The King himself in person is set forth,
Or hitherwards intended speedily,
With strong and mighty preparation.

HOTSPUR. He shall be welcome too. Where is
his son,
The nimble-footed madcap Prince of Wales,
And his comrades, that daff'd the world aside
And bid it pass?

VERNON . All furnish'd, all in arms;
All plum'd like estridges that with the wind
Bated like eagles having lately bath'd;
Glittering in golden coats like images;
As full of spirit as the month of May
And gorgeous as the sun at midsummer;
Wanton as youthful goats, wild as young bulls.
I saw young Harry with his beaver on
His cushes on his thighs, gallantly arm'd,
Rise from the ground like feathered Mercury,
And vaulted with such ease into his seat
As if an angel dropp'd down from the clouds
To turn and wind a fiery Pegasus
And witch the world with noble horsemanship.

HOTSPUR. No more, no more! Worse than the
sun in March,
This praise doth nourish agues. Let them come.
They come like sacrifices in their trim,
And to the fire-ey'd maid of smoky war
All hot and bleeding will we offer them.
The mailed Mars shall on his altar sit
Up to the ears in blood. I am on fire
To hear this rich reprisal is so nigh,
And yet not ours. Come, let me taste my horse,
Who is to bear me like a thunderbolt
Against the bosom of the Prince of Wales.
Harry to Harry shall, hot horse to horse,
Meet, and ne'er part till one drop down a corse.
O that Glendower were come!

VERNON . There is more news.
I learn'd in Worcester, as I rode along,
He cannot draw his power this fourteen days.

DOUGLAS. That's the worst tidings that I hear
of yet.

WORCESTER. Ay, by my faith, that bears a
frosty sound.

HOTSPUR. What may the King's whole battle
reach unto?

VERNON. To thirty thousand.

HOTSPUR. Forty let it be.
My father and Glendower being both away,
The powers of us may serve so great a day.

Come, let us take a muster speedily.
Doomsday is near. Die all, die merrily.

DOUGLAS. Talk not of dying. I am out of fear
Of death or death's hand for this one half-year.

Exeunt.

✦ SCENE II ✦
A public road near Coventry

Enter FALSTAFF and BARDOLPH

FALSTAFF. Bardolph, get thee before to Coventry;
fill me a bottle of sack. Our soldiers shall march
through. We'll to Sutton Co'fil' to-night.

BARDOLPH. Will you give me money, Captain?

FALSTAFF. Lay out, lay out.

Bald. This bottle makes an angel.

FALSTAFF. An if it do, take it for thy labour; an if
it make twenty, take them all; I'll answer the
coinage. Bid my lieutenant Peto meet me at
town's end.

BARDOLPH. I will, Captain. Farewell. *Exit.*

FALSTAFF. If I be not ashamed of my soldiers, I
am a sous'd gurnet. I have misused the King's
press damnably. I have got in exchange of
a hundred and fifty soldiers, three hundred
and odd pounds. I press me none but good
householders, yeomen's sons; inquire me
out contracted bachelors, such as had been
ask'd twice on the banes-such a commodity
of warm slaves as had as lieve hear the devil
as a drum; such as fear the report of a caliver
worse than a struck fowl or a hurt wild duck.
I press'd me none but such toasts-and-butter,
with hearts in their bellies no bigger than
pins' heads, and they have bought out their
services; and now my whole charge consists
of ancients, corporals, lieutenants, gentlemen
of companies-slaves as ragged as Lazarus in
the painted cloth, where the glutton's dogs
licked his sores; and such as indeed were
never soldiers, but discarded unjust serving-
men, younger sons to younger brothers,
revolted tapsters, and ostlers trade-fall'n; the
cankers of a calm world and a long peace;
ten times more dishonourable ragged than
an old fac'd ancient; and such have I to fill
up the rooms of them that have bought out
their services that you would think that I had
a hundred and fifty tattered Prodigals lately
come from swine-keeping, from eating draff
and husks. A mad fellow met me on the way,

and told me I had unloaded all the gibbets and press'd the dead bodies. No eye hath seen such scarecrows. I'll not march through Coventry with them, that's flat. Nay, and the villains march wide betwixt the legs, as if they had gyves on; for indeed I had the most of them out of prison. There's but a shirt and a half in all my company; and the half-shirt is two napkins tack'd together and thrown over the shoulders like a herald's coat without sleeves; and the shirt, to say the truth, stol'n from my host at Saint Alban's, or the red-nose innkeeper of Daventry. But that's all one; they'll find linen enough on every hedge.

Enter the PRINCE and the LORD OF WESTMORELAND

PRINCE. How now, blown Jack? How now, quilt?

FALSTAFF. What, Hal? How now, mad wag? What a devil dost thou in Warwickshire? My good Lord of Westmoreland, I cry you mercy. I thought your honour had already been at Shrewsbury.

WESTMORELAND. Faith, Sir John, 'tis more than time that I were there, and you too; but my powers are there already. The King, I can tell you, looks for us all. We must away all, to-night.

FALSTAFF. Tut, never fear me. I am as vigilant as a cat to steal cream.

PRINCE. I think, to steal cream indeed, for thy theft hath already made thee butter. But tell me, Jack, whose fellows are these that come after?

FALSTAFF. Mine, Hal, mine.

PRINCE. I did never see such pitiful rascals.

FALSTAFF. Tut, tut! good enough to toss; food for powder, food for powder. They'll fill a pit as well as better. Tush, man, mortal men, mortal men.

WESTMORELAND. Ay, but, Sir John, methinks they are exceeding poor and bare- too beggarly.

FALSTAFF. Faith, for their poverty, I know not where they had that; and for their bareness, I am sure they never learn'd that of me.

PRINCE. No, I'll be sworn, unless you call three fingers on the ribs bare. But, sirrah, make haste. Percy 's already in the field. *Exit.*

FALSTAFF. What, is the King encamp'd?

WESTMORELAND. He is, Sir John. I fear we shall stay too long. *Exit.*

FALSTAFF. Well,
To the latter end of a fray and the beginning of a feast
Fits a dull fighter and a keen guest. *Exit.*

✤ SCENE III ✤

The rebel camp near Shrewsbury

Enter HOTSPUR, WORCESTER, DOUGLAS, VERNON

HOTSPUR. We'll fight with him to-night.

WORCESTER. It may not be.

DOUGLAS. You give him then advantage.

VERNON. Not a whit.

HOTSPUR. Why say you so? Looks he not for supply?

VERNON. So do we.

HOTSPUR. His is certain, ours's doubtful.

WORCESTER. Good cousin, be advis'd; stir not to-night.

VERNON. Do not, my lord.

DOUGLAS. You do not counsel well. You speak it out of fear and cold heart.

VERNON. Do me no slander, Douglas. By my life-
And I dare well maintain it with my life-
If well-respected honour bid me on
I hold as little counsel with weak fear
As you, my lord, or any Scot that this day lives.
Let it be seen to-morrow in the battle
Which of us fears.

DOUGLAS. Yea, or to-night.

VERNON. Content.

HOTSPUR. To-night, say I.
Come, come, it may not be. I wonder much,
Being men of such great leading as you are,
That you foresee not what impediments
Drag back our expedition. Certain horse
Of my cousin Vernon's are not yet come up.
Your uncle Worcester's horse came but to-day;
And now their pride and mettle is asleep,
Their courage with hard labour tame and dull,
That not a horse is half the half of himself.

HOTSPUR. So are the horses of the enemy,
In general journey-bated and brought low.
The better part of ours are full of rest.

WORCESTER. The number of the King
exceedeth ours.
For God's sake, cousin, stay till all come in.

The trumpet sounds a parley. Enter SIR WALTER BLUNT

BLUNT. I come with gracious offers from the King,
· If you vouchsafe me hearing and respect.

HOTSPUR. Welcome, Sir Walter Blunt, and would to God
You were of our determination!
Some of us love you well; and even those some
Envy your great deservings and good name,

Because you are not of our quality,
But stand against us like an enemy.
Blunt. And God defend but still I should stand so,
So long as out of limit and true rule
You stand against anointed majesty!
But to my charge. The King hath sent to know
The nature of your griefs; and whereupon
You conjure from the breast of civil peace
Such bold hostility, teaching his duteous land
Audacious cruelty. If that the King
Have any way your good deserts forgot,
Which he confesseth to be manifold,
He bids you name your griefs, and with all speed
You shall have your desires with interest,
And pardon absolute for yourself and these
Herein misled by your suggestion.
HOTSPUR. The King is kind; and well we know
   the King
Knows at what time to promise, when to pay.
My father and my uncle and myself
Did give him that same royalty he wears;
And when he was not six-and-twenty strong,
Sick in the world's regard, wretched and low,
A poor unminded outlaw sneaking home,
My father gave him welcome to the shore;
And when he heard him swear and vow to God
He came but to be Duke of Lancaster,
To sue his livery and beg his peace,
With tears of innocency and terms of zeal,
My father, in kind heart and pity mov'd,
Swore him assistance, and performed it too.
Now, when the lords and barons of the realm
Perceiv'd Northumberland did lean to him,
The more and less came in with cap and knee;
Met him in boroughs, cities, villages,
Attended him on bridges, stood in lanes,
Laid gifts before him, proffer'd him their oaths,
Gave him their heirs as pages, followed him
Even at the heels in golden multitudes.
He presently, as greatness knows itself,
Steps me a little higher than his vow
Made to my father, while his blood was poor,
Upon the naked shore at Ravenspurgh;
And now, forsooth, takes on him to reform
Some certain edicts and some strait decrees
That lie too heavy on the commonwealth;
Cries out upon abuses, seems to weep
Over his country's wrongs; and by this face,
This seeming brow of justice, did he win
The hearts of all that he did angle for;
Proceeded further-cut me off the heads
Of all the favourites that the absent King
In deputation left behind him here

When he was personal in the Irish war.
BLUNT. Tut! I came not to hear this.
HOTSPUR. Then to the point.
In short time after lie depos'd the King;
Soon after that depriv'd him of his life;
And in the neck of that task'd the whole state;
To make that worse, suff'red his kinsman March
(Who is, if every owner were well plac'd,
Indeed his king) to be engag'd in Wales,
There without ransom to lie forfeited;
Disgrac'd me in my happy victories,
Sought to entrap me by intelligence;
Rated mine uncle from the Council board;
In rage dismiss'd my father from the court;
Broke an oath on oath, committed wrong
   on wrong;
And in conclusion drove us to seek out
This head of safety, and withal to pry
Into his title, the which we find
Too indirect for long continuance.
BLUNT. Shall I return this answer to the King?
HOTSPUR. Not so, Sir Walter. We'll
   withdraw awhile.
Go to the King; and let there be impawn'd
Some surety for a safe return again,
And in the morning early shall mine uncle
Bring him our purposes; and so farewell.
BLUNT. I would you would accept of grace
   and love.
HOTSPUR. And may be so we shall.
BLUNT. Pray God you do.   *Exeunt.*

❧ SCENE IV ❧
York. The ARCHBISHOP'S palace

Enter the ARCHBISHOP OF YORK and SIR MICHAEL

ARCHBISHOP. Hie, good Sir Michael; bear this
   sealed brief
With winged haste to the Lord Marshal;
This to my cousin Scroop; and all the rest
To whom they are directed. If you knew
How much they do import, you would
   make haste.
SIR MICHAEL. My good lord,
I guess their tenour.
ARCHBISHOP. Like enough you do.
To-morrow, good Sir Michael, is a day
Wherein the fortune of ten thousand men
Must bide the touch; for, sir, at Shrewsbury,
As I am truly given to understand,
The King with mighty and quick-raised power

Meets with Lord Harry; and I fear, Sir Michael,
What with the sickness of Northumberland,
Whose power was in the first proportion,
And what with Owen Glendower's absence thence,
Who with them was a rated sinew too
And comes not in, overrul'd by prophecies-
I fear the power of Percy is too weak
To wage an instant trial with the King.
SIR MICHAEL. Why, my good lord, you need
  not fear;
There is Douglas and Lord Mortimer.
ARCHBISHOP. No, Mortimer is not there.
SIR MICHAEL. But there is Mordake, Vernon, Lord
  Harry Percy,
And there is my Lord of Worcester, and a head
Of gallant warriors, noble gentlemen.
ARCHBISHOP. And so there is; but yet the King
  hath drawn
The special head of all the land together-
The Prince of Wales, Lord John of Lancaster,
The noble Westmoreland and warlike Blunt,
And many moe corrivals and dear men
Of estimation and command in arms.
SIR MICHAEL. Doubt not, my lord, they shall be
  well oppos'd.
ARCHBISHOP. I hope no less, yet needful 'tis
  to fear;
And, to prevent the worst, Sir Michael, speed.
For if Lord Percy thrive not, ere the King
Dismiss his power, he means to visit us,
For he hath heard of our confederacy,
And 'tis but wisdom to make strong against him.
Therefore make haste. I must go write again
To other friends; and so farewell, Sir Michael.
                                    Exeunt.

ACT V

SCENE I
The King's camp near Shrewsbury

*Enter the King, Prince of Wales, Lord John of Lancaster, Sir
Walter Blunt, Falstaff*

KING. How bloodily the sun begins to peer
Above yon busky hill! The day looks pale
At his distemp'rature.
PRINCE.   The southern wind
Doth play the trumpet to his purposes
And by his hollow whistling in the leaves
Foretells a tempest and a blust'ring day.

KING. Then with the losers let it sympathise,
For nothing can seem foul to those that win.
  The trumpet sounds. Enter WORCESTER and VERNON
How, now, my Lord of Worcester? 'Tis not well
That you and I should meet upon such terms
As now we meet. You have deceiv'd our trust
And made us doff our easy robes of peace
To crush our old limbs in ungentle steel.
This is not well, my lord; this is not well.
What say you to it? Will you again unknit
This churlish knot of all-abhorred war,
And move in that obedient orb again
Where you did give a fair and natural light,
And be no more an exhal'd meteor,
A prodigy of fear, and a portent
Of broached mischief to the unborn times?
WORCESTER. Hear me, my liege.
For mine own part, I could be well content
To entertain the lag-end of my life
With quiet hours; for I do protest
I have not sought the day of this dislike.
KING. You have not sought it! How comes
  it then,
FALSTAFF. Rebellion lay in his way, and he
  found it.
PRINCE. Peace, chewet, peace!
WORCESTER. It pleas'd your Majesty to turn
  your looks
Of favour from myself and all our house;
And yet I must remember you, my lord,
We were the first and dearest of your friends.
For you my staff of office did I break
In Richard's time, and posted day and night
To meet you on the way and kiss your hand
When yet you were in place and in account
Nothing so strong and fortunate as I.
It was myself, my brother, and his son
That brought you home and boldly did outdare
The dangers of the time. You swore to us,
And you did swear that oath at Doncaster,
That you did nothing purpose 'gainst the state,
Nor claim no further than your new-fall'n right,
The seat of Gaunt, dukedom of Lancaster.
To this we swore our aid. But in short space
It rain'd down fortune show'ring on your head,
And such a flood of greatness fell on you-
What with our help, what with the absent King,
What with the injuries of a wanton time,
The seeming sufferances that you had borne,
And the contrarious winds that held the King
So long in his unlucky Irish wars
That all in England did repute him dead-
And from this swarm of fair advantages

You took occasion to be quickly woo'd
To gripe the general sway into your hand;
Forgot your oath to us at Doncaster;
And, being fed by us, you us'd us so
As that ungentle gull, the cuckoo's bird,
Useth the sparrow-did oppress our nest;
Grew, by our feeding to so great a bulk
That even our love durst not come near
  your sight
For fear of swallowing; but with nimble wing
We were enforc'd for safety sake to fly
Out of your sight and raise this present head;
Whereby we stand opposed by such means
As you yourself have forg'd against yourself
By unkind usage, dangerous countenance,
And violation of all faith and troth
Sworn to us in your younger enterprise.
KING. These things, indeed, you have articulate,
  Proclaim'd at market crosses, read in churches,
  To face the garment of rebellion
  With some fine colour that may please the eye
  Of fickle changelings and poor discontents,
  Which gape and rub the elbow at the news
  Of hurlyburly innovation.
  And never yet did insurrection want
  Such water colours to impaint his cause,
  Nor moody beggars, starving for a time
  Of pell-mell havoc and confusion.
PRINCE. In both our armies there is many a soul
  Shall pay full dearly for this encounter,
  If once they join in trial. Tell your nephew
  The Prince of Wales doth join with all the world
  In praise of Henry Percy. By my hopes,
  This present enterprise set off his head,
  I do not think a braver gentleman,
  More active-valiant or more valiant-young,
  More daring or more bold, is now alive
  To grace this latter age with noble deeds.
  For my part, I may speak it to my shame,
  I have a truant been to chivalry;
  And so I hear he doth account me too.
  Yet this before my father's Majesty-
  I am content that he shall take the odds
  Of his great name and estimation,
  And will to save the blood on either side,
  Try fortune with him in a single fight.
KING. And, Prince of Wales, so dare we
  venture thee,
  Albeit considerations infinite
  Do make against it. No, good Worcester, no!
  We love our people well; even those we love
  That are misled upon your cousin's part;
  And, will they take the offer of our grace,

Both he, and they, and you, yea, every man
Shall be my friend again, and I'll be his.
So tell your cousin, and bring me word
What he will do. But if he will not yield,
Rebuke and dread correction wait on us,
And they shall do their office. So be gone.
We will not now be troubled with reply.
We offer fair; take it advisedly.
                    Exit WORCESTER with VERNON.
PRINCE. It will not be accepted, on my life.
  The Douglas and the Hotspur both together
  Are confident against the world in arms.
KING. Hence, therefore, every leader to
  his charge;
  For, on their answer, will we set on them,
  And God befriend us as our cause is just!
                Exeunt all but PRINCE and FALSTAFF.
FALSTAFF. Hal, if thou see me down in the battle
  and bestride me, so! 'Tis a point of friendship.
PRINCE. Nothing but a Colossus can do thee that
  friendship. Say thy prayers, and farewell.
FALSTAFF. I would 'twere bedtime, Hal, and
  all well.
PRINCE. Why, thou owest God a death. *Exit.*
FALSTAFF. 'Tis not due yet. I would be loath
  to pay him before his day. What need I be so
  forward with him that calls not on me? Well,
  'tis no matter; honour pricks me on. Yea, but
  how if honour prick me off when I come on?
  How then? Can honour set to a leg? No. Or an
  arm? No. Or take away the grief of a wound?
  No. Honour hath no skill in surgery then? No.
  What is honour? A word. What is that word
  honour? Air. A trim reckoning! Who hath it?
  He that died a Wednesday. Doth he feel it?
  No. Doth he bear it? No. 'Tis insensible then?
  Yea, to the dead. But will it not live with the
  living? No. Why? Detraction will not suffer it.
  Therefore I'll none of it. Honour is a mere
  scutcheon-and so ends my catechism. *Exit.*

SCENE II

The rebel camp

Enter WORCESTER and SIR RICHARD VERNON

WORCESTER. O no, my nephew must not know,
  Sir Richard,
  The liberal and kind offer of the King.
VERNON. 'Twere best he did.
WORCESTER. Then are we all undone.
  It is not possible, it cannot be

The King should keep his word in loving us.
He will suspect us still and find a time
To punish this offence in other faults.
Suspicion all our lives shall be stuck full
   of eyes;
For treason is but trusted like the fox
Who, ne'er so tame, so cherish'd and
   lock'd up,
Will have a wild trick of his ancestors.
Look how we can, or sad or merrily,
Interpretation will misquote our looks,
And we shall feed like oxen at a stall,
The better cherish'd, still the nearer death.
My nephew's trespass may be well forgot;
It hath the excuse of youth and heat of blood,
And an adopted name of privilege-
A hare-brained Hotspur govern'd by a spleen.
All his offences live upon my head
And on his father's. We did train him on;
And, his corruption being taken from us,
We, as the spring of all, shall pay for all.
Therefore, good cousin, let not Harry know,
In any case, the offer of the King.

Enter HOTSPUR and DOUGLAS

VERNON. Deliver what you will, I'll say 'tis so.
   Here comes your cousin.
HOTSPUR. My uncle is return'd.
   Deliver up my Lord of Westmoreland.
   Uncle, what news?
WORCESTER. The King will bid you
   battle presently.
DOUGLAS. Defy him by the Lord of Westmoreland.
HOTSPUR. Lord Douglas, go you and tell him so.
DOUGLAS. Marry, and shall, and very willingly.

Exit

WORCESTER. There is no seeming mercy in
   the King.
HOTSPUR. Did you beg any, God forbid!
WORCESTER. I told him gently of our grievances,
   Of his oath-breaking; which he mended thus,
   By now forswearing that he is forsworn.
   He calls us rebels, traitors, and will scourge
   With haughty arms this hateful name in us.

Enter DOUGLAS

DOUGLAS. Arm, gentlemen! to arms! for I
   have thrown
   A brave defiance in King Henry's teeth,
   And Westmoreland, that was engag'd, did
   bear it;
   Which cannot choose but bring him
   quickly on.
WORCESTER. The Prince of Wales stepp'd forth
   before the King

And, nephew, challeng'd you to single fight.
HOTSPUR. O, would the quarrel lay upon
   our heads,
   And that no man might draw short breath to-day
   But I and Harry Monmouth! Tell me, tell me,
   How show'd his tasking? Seem'd it
   in contempt?
   No, by my soul. I never in my life
   Did hear a challenge urg'd more modestly,
   Unless a brother should a brother dare
   To gentle exercise and proof of arms.
   He gave you all the duties of a man;
   Trimm'd up your praises with a
   princely tongue;
   Spoke your deservings like a chronicle;
   Making you ever better than his praise
   By still dispraising praise valued with you;
   And, which became him like a prince indeed,
   He made a blushing cital of himself,
   And chid his truant youth with such a grace
   As if lie mast'red there a double spirit
   Of teaching and of learning instantly.
   There did he pause; but let me tell the world,
   If he outlive the envy of this day,
   England did never owe so sweet a hope,
   So much misconstrued in his wantonness.
HOTSPUR. Cousin, I think thou art enamoured
   Upon his follies. Never did I hear
   Of any prince so wild a libertine.
   But be he as he will, yet once ere night
   I will embrace him with a soldier's arm,
   That he shall shrink under my courtesy.
   Arm, arm with speed! and, fellows,
   soldiers, friends,
   Better consider what you have to do
   Than I, that have not well the gift of tongue,
   Can lift your blood up with persuasion.

Enter a MESSENGER

MESSENGER. My lord, here are letters for you.
HOTSPUR. I cannot read them now.-
   O gentlemen, the time of life is short!
   To spend that shortness basely were too long
   If life did ride upon a dial's point,
   Still ending at the arrival of an hour.
   An if we live, we live to tread on kings;
   If die, brave death, when princes die with us!
   Now for our consciences, the arms are fair,
   When the intent of bearing them is just.

Enter another MESSENGER

MESSENGER. My lord, prepare. The King comes
   on apace.
HOTSPUR. I thank him that he cuts me from
   my tale,

For I profess not talking. Only this-
Let each man do his best; and here draw I
A sword whose temper I intend to stain
With the best blood that I can meet withal
In the adventure of this perilous day.
Now, Esperance! Percy! and set on.
Sound all the lofty instruments of war,
And by that music let us all embrace;
For, heaven to earth, some of us never shall
A second time do such a courtesy.

Here they embrace. The trumpets sound.

Exeunt.

✣ SCENE III ✣
Plain between the camps

The KING enters with his power. Alarum to the battle.
Then enter DOUGLAS and SIR WALTER BLUNT

BLUNT. What is thy name, that in the battle thus
Thou crossest me? What honour dost thou seek
Upon my head?
DOUGLAS. Know then my name is Douglas,
And I do haunt thee in the battle thus
Because some tell me that thou art a king.
BLUNT. They tell thee true.
DOUGLAS. The Lord of Stafford dear to-day
hath bought
Thy likeness; for instead of thee, King Harry,
This sword hath ended him. So shall it thee,
Unless thou yield thee as my prisoner.
BLUNT. I was not born a yielder, thou
proud Scot;
And thou shalt find a king that will revenge
Lord Stafford's death.

They fight. DOUGLAS kills BLUNT.

Then enter HOTSPUR

HOTSPUR. O Douglas, hadst thou fought at
Holmedon thus,
I never had triumph'd upon a Scot.
DOUGLAS. All's done, all's won. Here breathless
lies the King.
HOTSPUR. Where?
DOUGLAS. Here.
HOTSPUR. This, Douglas? No. I know this face
full well.
A gallant knight he was, his name was Blunt;
Semblably furnish'd like the King himself.
DOUGLAS. A fool go with thy soul, whither
it goes!
A borrowed title hast thou bought too dear:
Why didst thou tell me that thou wert a king?

HOTSPUR. The King hath many marching in
his coats.
DOUGLAS. Now, by my sword, I will kill all
his coats;
I'll murder all his wardrobe, piece by piece,
Until I meet the King.
HOTSPUR. Up and away!
Our soldiers stand full fairly for the day.

Exeunt.

Alarum. Enter FALSTAFF solus

FALSTAFF. Though I could scape shot-free
at London, I fear the shot here. Here's no
scoring but upon the pate. Soft! who are
you? Sir Walter Blunt. There's honour for
you! Here's no vanity! I am as hot as molten
lead, and as heavy too. God keep lead out of
me! I need no more weight than mine own
bowels. I have led my rag-of-muffins where
they are pepper'd. There's not three of my
hundred and fifty left alive; and they are for
the town's end, to beg during life. But who
comes here?

Enter the PRINCE

PRINCE. What, stand'st thou idle here? Lend me
thy sword.
Many a nobleman lies stark and stiff
Under the hoofs of vaunting enemies,
Whose deaths are yet unreveng'd. I prithee
Lend me thy sword.
FALSTAFF. O Hal, I prithee give me leave to
breathe awhile. Turk Gregory never did such
deeds in arms as I have done this day. I have
paid Percy; I have made him sure.
PRINCE. He is indeed, and living to kill thee.
I prithee lend me thy sword.
FALSTAFF. Nay, before God, Hal, if Percy be
alive, thou get'st not my sword; but take my
pistol, if thou wilt.
PRINCE. Give it me. What, is it in the case?
FALSTAFF. Ay, Hal. 'Tis hot, 'tis hot. There's
that will sack a city. *[The PRINCE draws it out and
finds it to be a bottle of sack.]*
What, is it a time to jest and dally now?

He throws the bottle at him. Exit.

FALSTAFF. Well, if Percy be alive, I'll pierce
him. If he do come in my way, so; if he do
not, if I come in his willingly, let him make
a carbonado of me. I like not such grinning
honour as Sir Walter hath. Give me life;
which if I can save, so; if not, honour comes
unlook'd for, and there's an end.

Exit.

✣ SCENE IV ✣

Another part of the field

Alarum. Excursions. Enter the KING, the PRINCE, JOHN
OF LANCASTER, EARL OF WESTMORELAND

KING. I prithee,
  Harry, withdraw thyself; thou bleedest
  too much.
  Lord John of Lancaster, go you unto him.
JOHN. Not I, my lord, unless I did bleed too.
PRINCE. I do beseech your Majesty make up,
  Lest your retirement do amaze your friends.
KING. I will do so.
  My Lord of Westmoreland, lead him to his tent.
WESTMORELAND. Come, my lord, I'll lead you to
  your tent.
PRINCE. Lead me, my lord, I do not need
  your help;
  And God forbid a shallow scratch should drive
  The Prince of Wales from such a field as this,
  Where stain'd nobility lies trodden on,
  And rebels' arms triumph in massacres!
JOHN. We breathe too long. Come,
  cousin Westmoreland,
  Our duty this way lies. For God's sake, come.
                    Exeunt JOHN OF LANCASTER and
                         WESTMORELAND.✣
PRINCE. By God, thou hast deceiv'd
  me, Lancaster!
  I did not think thee lord of such a spirit.
  Before, I lov'd thee as a brother, John;
  But now, I do respect thee as my soul.
KING. I saw him hold Lord Percy at the point
  With lustier maintenance than I did look for
  Of such an ungrown warrior.
PRINCE. O, this boy
  Lends mettle to us all!   *Exit.✣*
           Enter DOUGLAS
DOUGLAS. Another king? They grow like
  Hydra's heads.
  I am the Douglas, fatal to all those
  That wear those colours on them. What art thou
  That counterfeit'st the person of a king?
KING. The King himself, who, Douglas, grieves
  at heart
  So many of his shadows thou hast met,
  And not the very King. I have two boys
  Seek Percy and thyself about the field;
  But, seeing thou fall'st on me so luckily,
  I will assay thee. So defend thyself.
DOUGLAS. I fear thou art another counterfeit;

And yet, in faith, thou bearest thee like a king.
But mine I am sure thou art, whoe'er thou be,
And thus I win thee.
          They fight. The KING being in danger, enter
                    PRINCE OF WALES
PRINCE. Hold up thy head, vile Scot, or thou
  art like
  Never to hold it up again! The spirits
  Of valiant Shirley, Stafford, Blunt are in
  my arms.
  It is the Prince of Wales that threatens thee,
  Who never promiseth but he means to pay.
          [They fight. DOUGLAS flieth]
  Cheerly, my lord. How fares your Grace?
  Sir Nicholas Gawsey hath for succour sent,
  And so hath Clifton. I'll to Clifton straight.
KING. Stay and breathe awhile.
  Thou hast redeem'd thy lost opinion,
  And show'd thou mak'st some tender of
  my life,
  In this fair rescue thou hast brought to me.
PRINCE. O God! they did me too much injury
  That ever said I heark'ned for your death.
  If it were so, I might have let alone
  The insulting hand of Douglas over you,
  Which would have been as speedy in your end
  As all the poisonous potions in the world,
  And sav'd the treacherous labour of your son.
KING. Make up to Clifton; I'll to Sir
  Nicholas Gawsey.
                              Exit.✣
           Enter HOTSPUR
HOTSPUR. If I mistake not, thou art
  Harry Monmouth.
PRINCE. Thou speak'st as if I would deny
  my name.
HOTSPUR. My name is Harry Percy.
PRINCE. Why, then I see
  A very valiant rebel of the name.
  I am the Prince of Wales; and think not, Percy,
  To share with me in glory any more.
  Two stars keep not their motion in one sphere,
  Nor can one England brook a double reign
  Of Harry Percy and the Prince of Wales.
HOTSPUR. Nor shall it, Harry; for the hour
  is come
  To end the one of us and would to God
  Thy name in arms were now as great as mine!
PRINCE. I'll make it greater ere I part from thee,
  And all the budding honours on thy crest
  I'll crop to make a garland for my head.
HOTSPUR. I can no longer brook thy vanities.
                    They fight

Enter FALSTAFF

FALSTAFF. Well said, Hal! to it, Hal! Nay, you shall
find no boy's play here, I can tell you.

*Enter DOUGLAS. He fights with FALSTAFF, who falls down
as if he were dead*

Exit DOUGLAS. The PRINCE kills PERCY.

HOTSPUR. O Harry, thou hast robb'd me of
my youth!
I better brook the loss of brittle life
Than those proud titles thou hast won of me.
They wound my thoughts worse than thy sword
my flesh.
But thought' the slave of life, and life time's fool,
And time, that takes survey of all the world,
Must have a stop. O, I could prophesy,
But that the earthy and cold hand of death
Lies on my tongue. No, Percy, thou art dust,
And food for-   *Dies.*

PRINCE. For worms, brave Percy. Fare thee well,
great heart!
Ill-weav'd ambition, how much art thou shrunk!
When that this body did contain a spirit,
A kingdom for it was too small a bound;
But now two paces of the vilest earth
Is room enough. This earth that bears thee dead
Bears not alive so stout a gentleman.
If thou wert sensible of courtesy,
I should not make so dear a show of zeal.
But let my favours hide thy mangled face;
And, even in thy behalf, I'll thank myself
For doing these fair rites of tenderness.
Adieu, and take thy praise with thee to heaven!
Thy ignominy sleep with thee in the grave,
But not remem'red in thy epitaph! *[He spieth
FALSTAFF on the ground]*
What, old acquaintance? Could not all this flesh
Keep in a little life? Poor Jack, farewell!
I could have better spar'd a better man.
O, I should have a heavy miss of thee
If I were much in love with vanity!
Death hath not struck so fat a deer to-day,
Though many dearer, in this bloody fray.
Embowell'd will I see thee by-and-by;
Till then in blood by noble Percy lie.*Exit.*

FALSTAFF rises up

FALSTAFF. Embowell'd? If thou embowel me
to-day, I'll give you leave to powder me and
eat me too to-morrow. 'Sblood, 'twas time to
counterfeit, or that hot termagant Scot had paid
me scot and lot too. Counterfeit? I lie; I am no
counterfeit. To die is to be a counterfeit; for he
is but the counterfeit of a man who hath not
the life of a man; but to counterfeit dying when
a man thereby liveth, is to be no counterfeit,
but the true and perfect image of life indeed.
The better part of valour is discretion; in the
which better part I have saved my life. Zounds,
I am afraid of this gunpowder Percy, though he
be dead. How if he should counterfeit too, and
rise? By my faith, I am afraid he would prove the
better counterfeit. Therefore I'll make him sure;
yea, and I'll swear I kill'd him. Why may not he
rise as well as I? Nothing confutes me but eyes,
and nobody sees me. Therefore, sirrah *[Stabs
him]*, with a new wound in your thigh, come you
along with me.

He takes up HOTSPUR on his back

Enter PRINCE, and JOHN OF LANCASTER

PRINCE. Come, brother John; full bravely hast
thou flesh'd
Thy maiden sword.

JOHN. But, soft! whom have we here?
Did you not tell me this fat man was dead?

PRINCE. I did; I saw him dead,
Breathless and bleeding on the ground. Art
thou alive,
Or is it fantasy that plays upon our eyesight?
I prithee speak. We will not trust our eyes
Without our ears. Thou art not what
thou seem'st.

FALSTAFF. No, that's certain! I am not a double
man; but if I be not Jack Falstaff, then am I a
Jack. There 's Percy. If your father will do me
any honour, so; if not, let him kill the next
Percy himself. I look to be either earl or duke, I
can assure you.

PRINCE. Why, Percy I kill'd myself, and saw
thee dead!

FALSTAFF. Didst thou? Lord, Lord, how this
world is given to lying! I grant you I was down,
and out of breath, and so was he; but we rose
both at an instant and fought a long hour by
Shrewsbury clock. If I may be believ'd, so; if
not, let them that should reward valour bear
the sin upon their own heads. I'll take it upon
my death, I gave him this wound in the thigh. If
the man were alive and would deny it, zounds! I
would make him eat a piece of my sword.

JOHN. This is the strangest tale that ever I heard.

PRINCE. This is the strangest fellow, brother John.
Come, bring your luggage nobly on your back.
For my part, if a lie may do thee grace,
I'll gild it with the happiest terms I have. *[A retreat
is sounded]*
The trumpet sounds retreat; the day is ours.
Come, brother, let's to the highest of the field,

To see what friends are living, who are dead.

Exeunt PRINCE HENRY and PRINCE JOHN.

FALSTAFF. I'll follow, as they say, for reward. He
that rewards me, God reward him! If I do grow
great, I'll grow less; for I'll purge, and leave
sack, and live cleanly, as a nobleman should do.

Exit, bearing off the body.

⚜ SCENE V ⚜
Another part of the field

*The trumpets sound. Enter the KING, PRINCE OF WALES,
JOHN OF LANCASTER, and WESTMORELAND, with
WORCESTER and VERNON prisoners.*

KING. Thus ever did rebellion find rebuke.
Ill-spirited Worcester! did not we send grace,
Pardon, and terms of love to all of you?
And wouldst thou turn our offers contrary?
Misuse the tenour of thy kinsman's trust?
Three knights upon our party slain to-day,
A noble earl, and many a creature else
Had been alive this hour,
If like a Christian thou hadst truly borne
Betwixt our armies true intelligence.
WORCESTER. What I have done my safety urg'd
me to;
And I embrace this fortune patiently,
Since not to be avoided it fails on me.
KING. Bear Worcester to the death, and
Vernon too;
Other offenders we will pause upon.

Exeunt WORCESTER and VERNON, guarded.

How goes the field?
PRINCE. The noble Scot, Lord Douglas, when
he saw
The fortune of the day quite turn'd from him,
The Noble Percy slain and all his men
Upon the foot of fear, fled with the rest;
And falling from a hill, he was so bruis'd
That the pursuers took him. At my tent
The Douglas is, and I beseech your Grace
I may dispose of him.
KING. With all my heart.
PRINCE. Then brother John of Lancaster, to you
This honourable bounty shall belong.
Go to the Douglas and deliver him
Up to his pleasure, ransomless and free.
His valour shown upon our crests today
Hath taught us how to cherish such high deeds,
Even in the bosom of our adversaries.
JOHN. I thank your Grace for this high courtesy,

Which I shall give away immediately.
KING. Then this remains, that we divide
our power.
You, son John, and my cousin Westmoreland,
Towards York shall bend you with your
dearest speed
To meet Northumberland and the
prelate Scroop,
Who, as we hear, are busily in arms.
Myself and you, son Harry, will towards Wales
To fight with Glendower and the Earl of March.
Rebellion in this land shall lose his sway,
Meeting the check of such another day;
And since this business so fair is done,
Let us not leave till all our own be won.

Exeunt.

The End

King Henry IV, Part II

Dramatis Personae

RUMOUR, the Presenter
KING HENRY THE FOURTH

Sons to the King:
HENRY, PRINCE OF WALES, afterwards KING
HENRY THE FIFTH
PRINCE JOHN OF LANCASTER
PRINCE HUMPHREY OF GLOUCESTER
THOMAS, DUKE OF CLARENCE,

Of the King's party:
EARL OF WARWICK
EARL OF WESTMORELAND
EARL OF SURREY
GOWER
HARCOURT
BLUNT

Opposites against King Henry IV:
EARL OF NORTHUMBERLAND
SCROOP, ARCHBISHOP OF YORK
LORD MOWBRAY
LORD HASTINGS
LORD BARDOLPH
SIR JOHN COLVILLE
TRAVERS and MORTON, retainers
of Northumberland

LORD CHIEF JUSTICE
SERVANT, to Lord Chief Justice

Irregular humourists:
SIR JOHN FALSTAFF
PAGE, to Falstaff
EDWARD POINS
BARDOLPH
PISTOL, PETO

ROBERT SHALLOW and SILENCE,
country Justices
DAVY, servant to Shallow
FANG and SNARE, Sheriff's officers

Country soldiers:
RALPH MOULDY
SIMON SHADOW
THOMAS WART
FRANCIS FEEBLE
PETER BULLCALF

FRANCIS, a drawer

LADY NORTHUMBERLAND
LADY PERCY, Percy's widow
HOSTESS QUICKLY, of the Boar's
Head, Eastcheap
DOLL TEARSHEET

Lords, Attendants, Porter, Drawers, Beadles,
Grooms, Servants, Speaker of the Epilogue

SCENE
England

INDUCTION

Warkworth. Before NORTHUMBERLAND'S Castle

Enter RUMOUR, painted full of tongues

RUMOUR. Open your ears; for which of you
will stop
The vent of hearing when loud
Rumour speaks?
I, from the orient to the drooping west,
Making the wind my post-horse, still unfold
The acts commenced on this ball of earth.
Upon my tongues continual slanders ride,
The which in every language I pronounce,
Stuffing the ears of men with false reports.
I speak of peace while covert emnity,
Under the smile of safety, wounds the world;
And who but Rumour, who but only I,
Make fearful musters and prepar'd defence,
Whiles the big year, swoln with some
other grief,

Is thought with child by the stern tyrant war,
And no such matter? Rumour is a pipe
Blown by surmises, jealousies, conjectures,
And of so easy and so plain a stop
That the blunt monster with uncounted heads,
The still-discordant wav'ring multitude,
Can play upon it. But what need I thus
My well-known body to anatomise
Among my household? Why is Rumour here?
I run before King Harry's victory,
Who, in a bloody field by Shrewsbury,
Hath beaten down young Hotspur and
 his troops,
Quenching the flame of bold rebellion
Even with the rebels' blood. But what mean I
To speak so true at first? My office is
To noise abroad that Harry Monmouth fell
Under the wrath of noble Hotspur's sword,
And that the King before the Douglas' rage
Stoop'd his anointed head as low as death.
This have I rumour'd through the
 peasant towns
Between that royal field of Shrewsbury
And this worm-eaten hold of ragged stone,
Where Hotspur's father, old Northumberland,
Lies crafty-sick. The posts come tiring on,
And not a man of them brings other news
Than they have learnt of me. From
 Rumour's tongues
They bring smooth comforts false, worse than
 true wrongs.

Exit.

ACT I

SCENE I

**Warkworth. Before NORTHUMBERLAND'S
Castle**

Enter LORD BARDOLPH

LORD BARDOLPH. Who keeps the gate here, ho?
 [The PORTER opens the gate]
 Where is the Earl?
PORTER. What shall I say you are?
LORD BARDOLPH. Tell thou the Earl
 That the Lord Bardolph doth attend him here.
PORTER. His lordship is walk'd forth into
 the orchard.
 Please it your honour knock but at the gate,
 And he himself will answer.

Enter NORTHUMBERLAND
LORD BARDOLPH. Here comes the Earl.
 Exit PORTER.
NORTHUMBERLAND. What news, Lord Bardolph?
 Every minute now
 Should be the father of some stratagem.
 The times are wild; contention, like a horse
 Full of high feeding, madly hath broke loose
 And bears down all before him.
LORD BARDOLPH. Noble Earl,
 I bring you certain news from Shrewsbury.
NORTHUMBERLAND. Good, an God will!
LORD BARDOLPH. As good as heart can wish.
 The King is almost wounded to the death;
 And, in the fortune of my lord your son,
 Prince Harry slain outright; and both the Blunts
 Kill'd by the hand of Douglas; young
 Prince John,
 And Westmoreland, and Stafford, fled the field;
 And Harry Monmouth's brawn, the hulk
 Sir John,
 Is prisoner to your son. O, such a day,
 So fought, so followed, and so fairly won,
 Came not till now to dignify the times,
 Since Caesar's fortunes!
NORTHUMBERLAND. How is this deriv'd?
 Saw you the field? Came you from Shrewsbury?
LORD BARDOLPH. I spake with one, my lord, that
 came from thence;
 A gentleman well bred and of good name,
 That freely rend'red me these news for true.

Enter TRAVERS
NORTHUMBERLAND. Here comes my servant
 Travers, whom I sent
 On Tuesday last to listen after news.
LORD BARDOLPH. My lord, I over-rode him on
 the way;
 And he is furnish'd with no certainties
 More than he haply may retail from me.
NORTHUMBERLAND. Now, Travers, what good
 tidings comes with you?
TRAVERS. My lord, Sir John Umfrevile turn'd
 me back
 With joyful tidings; and, being better hors'd,
 Out-rode me. After him came spurring hard
 A gentleman, almost forspent with speed,
 That stopp'd by me to breathe his
 bloodied horse.
 He ask'd the way to Chester; and of him
 I did demand what news from Shrewsbury.
 He told me that rebellion had bad luck,
 And that young Harry Percy's spur was cold.
 With that he gave his able horse the head

And, bending forward, struck his armed heels
Against the panting sides of his poor jade
Up to the rowel-head; and starting so,
He seem'd in running to devour the way,
Staying no longer question.
NORTHUMBERLAND. Ha! Again:
Said he young Harry Percy's spur was cold?
Of Hotspur, Coldspur? that rebellion
Had met ill luck?
LORD BARDOLPH. My lord, I'll tell you what:
If my young lord your son have not the day,
Upon mine honour, for a silken point
I'll give my barony. Never talk of it.
NORTHUMBERLAND. Why should that gentleman
that rode by Travers
Give then such instances of loss?
LORD BARDOLPH. Who-he?
He was some hilding fellow that had stol'n
The horse he rode on and, upon my life,
Spoke at a venture. Look, here comes
more news.

Enter MORTON

NORTHUMBERLAND. Yea, this man's brow, like
to a title-leaf,
Foretells the nature of a tragic volume.
So looks the strand whereon the
imperious flood
Hath left a witness'd usurpation.
Say, Morton, didst thou come from Shrewsbury?
MORTON. I ran from Shrewsbury, my noble lord;
Where hateful death put on his ugliest mask
To fright our party.
NORTHUMBERLAND. How doth my son
and brother?
Thou tremblest; and the whiteness in thy cheek
Is apter than thy tongue to tell thy errand.
Even such a man, so faint, so spiritless,
So dull, so dread in look, so woe-begone,
Drew Priam's curtain in the dead of night
And would have told him half his Troy
was burnt;
But Priam found the fire ere he his tongue,
And I my Percy's death ere thou report'st it.
This thou wouldst say: 'Your son did thus
and thus;
Your brother thus; so fought the noble Douglas'-
Stopping my greedy ear with their bold deeds;
But in the end, to stop my ear indeed,
Thou hast a sigh to blow away this praise,
Ending with 'Brother, son, and all, are dead.'
MORTON. Douglas is living, and your brother, yet;
But for my lord your son-
NORTHUMBERLAND. Why, he is dead.

See what a ready tongue suspicion hath!
He that but fears the thing he would not know
Hath by instinct knowledge from others' eyes
That what he fear'd is chanced. Yet
speak, Morton;
Tell thou an earl his divination lies,
And I will take it as a sweet disgrace
And make thee rich for doing me such wrong.
MORTON. You are too great to be by me gainsaid;
Your spirit is too true, your fears too certain.
NORTHUMBERLAND. Yet, for all this, say not that
Percy's dead.
I see a strange confession in thine eye;
Thou shak'st thy head, and hold'st it fear or sin
To speak a truth. If he be slain, say so:
The tongue offends not that reports his death;
And he doth sin that doth belie the dead,
Not he which says the dead is not alive.
Yet the first bringer of unwelcome news
Hath but a losing office, and his tongue
Sounds ever after as a sullen bell,
Rememb'red tolling a departing friend.
LORD BARDOLPH. I cannot think, my lord, your
son is dead.
MORTON. I am sorry I should force you to believe
That which I would to God I had not seen;
But these mine eyes saw him in bloody state,
Rend'ring faint quittance, wearied and out-
breath'd,
To Harry Monmouth, whose swift wrath
beat down
The never-daunted Percy to the earth,
From whence with life he never more
sprung up.
In few, his death-whose spirit lent a fire
Even to the dullest peasant in his camp-
Being bruited once, took fire and heat away
From the best-temper'd courage in his troops;
For from his metal was his party steeled;
Which once in him abated, an the rest
Turn'd on themselves, like dull and heavy lead.
And as the thing that's heavy in itself
Upon enforcement flies with greatest speed,
So did our men, heavy in Hotspur's loss,
Lend to this weight such lightness with their fear
That arrows fled not swifter toward their aim
Than did our soldiers, aiming at their safety,
Fly from the field. Then was that noble Worcester
Too soon ta'en prisoner; and that furious Scot,
The bloody Douglas, whose well-labouring sword
Had three times slain th' appearance of the King,
Gan vail his stomach and did grace the shame
Of those that turn'd their backs, and in his flight,

Stumbling in fear, was took. The sum of all
Is that the King hath won, and hath sent out
A speedy power to encounter you, my lord,
Under the conduct of young Lancaster
And Westmoreland. This is the news at full.
NORTHUMBERLAND. For this I shall have time
  enough to mourn.
In poison there is physic; and these news,
Having been well, that would have made
  me sick,
Being sick, have in some measure made
  me well;
And as the wretch whose fever-weak'ned joints,
Like strengthless hinges, buckle under life,
Impatient of his fit, breaks like a fire
Out of his keeper's arms, even so my limbs,
Weak'ned with grief, being now enrag'd
  with grief,
Are thrice themselves. Hence, therefore, thou
  nice crutch!
A scaly gauntlet now with joints of steel
Must glove this hand; and hence, thou
  sickly coif!
Thou art a guard too wanton for the head
Which princes, flesh'd with conquest, aim
  to hit.
Now bind my brows with iron; and approach
The ragged'st hour that time and spite
  dare bring
To frown upon th' enrag'd Northumberland!
Let heaven kiss earth! Now let not
  Nature's hand
Keep the wild flood confin'd! Let order die!
And let this world no longer be a stage
To feed contention in a ling'ring act;
But let one spirit of the first-born Cain
Reign in all bosoms, that, each heart being set
On bloody courses, the rude scene may end
And darkness be the burier of the dead!
LORD BARDOLPH. This strained passion doth
  you wrong, my lord.
MORTON. Sweet Earl, divorce not wisdom from
  your honour.
The lives of all your loving complices
Lean on your health; the which, if you give o'er
To stormy passion, must perforce decay.
You cast th' event of war, my noble lord,
And summ'd the account of chance before
  you said
'Let us make head.' It was your pre-surmise
That in the dole of blows your son might drop.
You knew he walk'd o'er perils on an edge,
More likely to fall in than to get o'er;

You were advis'd his flesh was capable
Of wounds and scars, and that his forward spirit
Would lift him where most trade of
  danger rang'd;
Yet did you say 'Go forth'; and none of this,
Though strongly apprehended, could restrain
The stiff-borne action. What hath then befall'n,
Or what hath this bold enterprise brought forth
More than that being which was like to be?
LORD BARDOLPH. We all that are engaged to
  this loss
Knew that we ventured on such dangerous seas
That if we wrought out life 'twas ten to one;
And yet we ventur'd, for the gain propos'd
Chok'd the respect of likely peril fear'd;
And since we are o'erset, venture again.
Come, we will put forth, body and goods.
MORTON. 'Tis more than time. And, my most
  noble lord,
I hear for certain, and dare speak the truth:
The gentle Archbishop of York is up
With well-appointed pow'rs. He is a man
Who with a double surety binds his followers.
My lord your son had only but the corpse,
But shadows and the shows of men, to fight;
For that same word 'rebellion' did divide
The action of their bodies from their souls;
And they did fight with queasiness, constrain'd,
As men drink potions; that their weapons only
Seem'd on our side, but for their spirits
  and souls
This word 'rebellion'-it had froze them up,
As fish are in a pond. But now the Bishop
Turns insurrection to religion.
Suppos'd sincere and holy in his thoughts,
He's follow'd both with body and with mind;
And doth enlarge his rising with the blood
Of fair King Richard, scrap'd from
  Pomfret stones;
Derives from heaven his quarrel and his cause;
Tells them he doth bestride a bleeding land,
Gasping for life under great Bolingbroke;
And more and less do flock to follow him.
NORTHUMBERLAND. I knew of this before; but,
  to speak truth,
This present grief had wip'd it from my mind.
Go in with me; and counsel every man
The aptest way for safety and revenge.
Get posts and letters, and make friends
  with speed-
Never so few, and never yet more need.

Exeunt.

✿ SCENE II ✿

London. A street

Enter SIR JOHN FALSTAFF, with his PAGE bearing his sword and buckler

FALSTAFF. Sirrah, you giant, what says the doctor to my water?

PAGE. He said, sir, the water itself was a good healthy water; but for the party that owed it, he might have moe diseases than he knew for.

FALSTAFF. Men of all sorts take a pride to gird at me. The brain of this foolish-compounded clay, man, is not able to invent anything that intends to laughter, more than I invent or is invented on me. I am not only witty in myself, but the cause that wit is in other men. I do here walk before thee like a sow that hath overwhelm'd all her litter but one. If the Prince put thee into my service for any other reason than to set me off, why then I have no judgment. Thou whoreson mandrake, thou art fitter to be worn in my cap than to wait at my heels. I was never mann'd with an agate till now; but I will inset you neither in gold nor silver, but in vile apparel, and send you back again to your master, for a jewel-the juvenal, the Prince your master, whose chin is not yet fledge. I will sooner have a beard grow in the palm of my hand than he shall get one off his cheek; and yet he will not stick to say his face is a face-royal. God may finish it when he will, 'tis not a hair amiss yet. He may keep it still at a face-royal, for a barber shall never earn sixpence out of it; and yet he'll be crowing as if he had writ man ever since his father was a bachelor. He may keep his own grace, but he's almost out of mine, I can assure him. What said Master Dommelton about the satin for my short cloak and my slops?

PAGE. He said, sir, you should procure him better assurance than Bardolph. He would not take his band and yours; he liked not the security.

FALSTAFF. Let him be damn'd, like the Glutton; pray God his tongue be hotter! A whoreson Achitophel! A rascally yea-forsooth knave, to bear a gentleman in hand, and then stand upon security! The whoreson smooth-pates do now wear nothing but high shoes, and bunches of keys at their girdles; and if a man is through with them in honest taking-up, then they must stand upon security. I had as lief they would put ratsbane in my mouth as offer to stop it with security. I look'd 'a should have sent me two and twenty yards of satin, as I am a true knight, and he sends me security. Well, he may sleep in security; for he hath the horn of abundance, and the lightness of his wife shines through it; and yet cannot he see, though he have his own lanthorn to light him. Where's Bardolph?

PAGE. He's gone into Smithfield to buy your worship horse.

FALSTAFF. I bought him in Paul's, and he'll buy me a horse in Smithfield. An I could get me but a wife in the stews, I were mann'd, hors'd, and wiv'd.

Enter the LORD CHIEF JUSTICE and SERVANT

PAGE. Sir, here comes the nobleman that committed the Prince for striking him about Bardolph.

FALSTAFF. Wait close; I will not see him.

CHIEF JUSTICE. What's he that goes there?

SERVANT. Falstaff, an't please your lordship.

CHIEF JUSTICE. He that was in question for the robb'ry?

SERVANT. He, my lord; but he hath since done good service at Shrewsbury, and, as I hear, is now going with some charge to the Lord John of Lancaster.

CHIEF JUSTICE. What, to York? Call him back again.

SERVANT. Sir John Falstaff!

FALSTAFF. Boy, tell him I am deaf.

PAGE. You must speak louder; my master is deaf.

CHIEF JUSTICE. I am sure he is, to the hearing of anything good. Go, pluck him by the elbow; I must speak with him.

SERVANT. Sir John!

FALSTAFF. What! a young knave, and begging! Is there not wars? Is there not employment? Doth not the King lack subjects? Do not the rebels need soldiers? Though it be a shame to be on any side but one, it is worse shame to beg than to be on the worst side, were it worse than the name of rebellion can tell how to make it.

SERVANT. You mistake me, sir.

FALSTAFF. Why, sir, did I say you were an honest man? Setting my knighthood and my soldiership aside, I had lied in my throat if I had said so.

SERVANT. I pray you, sir, then set your

knighthood and your soldiership aside; and give me leave to tell you you lie in your throat, if you say I am any other than an honest man.

FALSTAFF. I give thee leave to tell me so! I lay aside that which grows to me! If thou get'st any leave of me, hang me; if thou tak'st leave, thou wert better be hang'd. You hunt counter. Hence! Avaunt!

SERVANT. Sir, my lord would speak with you.

CHIEF JUSTICE. Sir John Falstaff, a word with you.

FALSTAFF. My good lord! God give your lordship good time of day. I am glad to see your lordship abroad. I heard say your lordship was sick; I hope your lordship goes abroad by advice. Your lordship, though not clean past your youth, hath yet some smack of age in you, some relish of the saltness of time; and I most humbly beseech your lordship to have a reverend care of your health.

CHIEF JUSTICE. Sir John, I sent for you before your expedition to Shrewsbury.

FALSTAFF. An't please your lordship, I hear his Majesty is return'd with some discomfort from Wales.

CHIEF JUSTICE. I talk not of his Majesty. You would not come when I sent for you.

FALSTAFF. And I hear, moreover, his Highness is fall'n into this same whoreson apoplexy.

CHIEF JUSTICE. Well, God mend him! I pray you let me speak with you.

FALSTAFF. This apoplexy, as I take it, is a kind of lethargy, an't please your lordship, a kind of sleeping in the blood, a whoreson tingling.

CHIEF JUSTICE. What tell you me of it? Be it as it is.

FALSTAFF. It hath it original from much grief, from study, and perturbation of the brain. I have read the cause of his effects in Galen; it is a kind of deafness.

CHIEF JUSTICE. I think you are fall'n into the disease, for you hear not what I say to you.

FALSTAFF. Very well, my lord, very well. Rather an't please you, it is the disease of not listening, the malady of not marking, that I am troubled withal.

CHIEF JUSTICE. To punish you by the heels would amend the attention of your ears; and I care not if I do become your physician.

FALSTAFF. I am as poor as Job, my lord, but not so patient. Your lordship may minister the potion of imprisonment to me in respect of poverty; but how I should be your patient to follow your prescriptions, the wise may make some dram of a scruple, or indeed a scruple itself.

CHIEF JUSTICE. I sent for you, when there were matters against you for your life, to come speak with me.

FALSTAFF. As I was then advis'd by my learned counsel in the laws of this land-service, I did not come.

CHIEF JUSTICE. Well, the truth is, Sir John, you live in great infamy.

FALSTAFF. He that buckles himself in my belt cannot live in less.

CHIEF JUSTICE. Your means are very slender, and your waste is great.

FALSTAFF. I would it were otherwise; I would my means were greater and my waist slenderer.

CHIEF JUSTICE. You have misled the youthful Prince.

FALSTAFF. The young Prince hath misled me. I am the fellow with the great belly, and he my dog.

CHIEF JUSTICE. Well, I am loath to gall a new-heal'd wound. Your day's service at Shrewsbury hath a little gilded over your night's exploit on Gadshill. You may thank th' unquiet time for your quiet o'erposting that action.

FALSTAFF. My lord-

CHIEF JUSTICE. But since all is well, keep it so: wake not a sleeping wolf.

FALSTAFF. To wake a wolf is as bad as smell a fox.

CHIEF JUSTICE. What! you are as a candle, the better part burnt out.

FALSTAFF. A wassail candle, my lord-all tallow; if I did say of wax, my growth would approve the truth.

CHIEF JUSTICE. There is not a white hair in your face but should have his effect of gravity.

FALSTAFF. His effect of gravy, gravy,

CHIEF JUSTICE. You follow the young Prince up and down, like his ill angel.

FALSTAFF. Not so, my lord. Your ill angel is light; but I hope he that looks upon me will take me without weighing. And yet in some respects, I grant, I cannot go-I cannot tell. Virtue is of so little regard in these costermongers' times that true valour is turn'd berod; pregnancy is made a tapster, and his quick wit wasted in giving reckonings; all the other gifts appertinent to man, as the malice of this age shapes them, are not worth a gooseberry. You that are old consider not the capacities of us that are young; you do measure the heat of our livers with the bitterness of your galls; and we that are in

the vaward of our youth, must confess, are
wags too.

CHIEF JUSTICE. Do you set down your name in
the scroll of youth, that are written down old
with all the characters of age? Have you not a
moist eye, a dry hand, a yellow cheek, a white
beard, a decreasing leg, an increasing belly? Is
not your voice broken, your wind short, your
chin double, your wit single, and every part
about you blasted with antiquity? And will you
yet call yourself young? Fie, fie, fie, Sir John!

FALSTAFF. My lord, I was born about three of
the clock in the afternoon, with a white head
and something a round belly. For my voice-I
have lost it with hallooing and singing of
anthems. To approve my youth further, I will
not. The truth is, I am only old in judgment
and understanding; and he that will caper with
me for a thousand marks, let him lend me the
money, and have at him. For the box of the ear
that the Prince gave you-he gave it like a rude
prince, and you took it like a sensible lord. I
have check'd him for it; and the young lion
repents-marry, not in ashes and sackcloth, but
in new silk and old sack.

CHIEF JUSTICE. Well, God send the Prince a
better companion!

FALSTAFF. God send the companion a better
prince! I cannot rid my hands of him.

CHIEF JUSTICE. Well, the King hath sever'd
you. I hear you are going with Lord John of
Lancaster against the Archbishop and the Earl
of Northumberland.

FALSTAFF. Yea; I thank your pretty sweet wit
for it. But look you pray, all you that kiss my
Lady Peace at home, that our armies join
not in a hot day; for, by the Lord, I take but
two shirts out with me, and I mean not to
sweat extraordinarily. If it be a hot day, and
I brandish anything but a bottle, I would I
might never spit white again. There is not a
dangerous action can peep out his head but
I am thrust upon it. Well, I cannot last ever;
but it was alway yet the trick of our English
nation, if they have a good thing, to make it
too common. If ye will needs say I am an old
man, you should give me rest. I would to God
my name were not so terrible to the enemy as
it is. I were better to be eaten to death with
a rust than to be scoured to nothing with
perpetual motion.

CHIEF JUSTICE. Well, be honest, be honest; and
God bless your expedition!

FALSTAFF. Will your lordship lend me a thousand
pound to furnish me forth?

CHIEF JUSTICE. Not a penny, not a penny; you
are too impatient to bear crosses. Fare you well.
Commend me to my cousin Westmoreland.

Exeunt CHIEF JUSTICE and SERVANT.

FALSTAFF. If I do, fillip me with a three-man
beetle. A man can no more separate age and
covetousness than 'a can part young limbs and
lechery; but the gout galls the one, and the pox
pinches the other; and so both the degrees
prevent my curses. Boy!

PAGE. Sir?

FALSTAFF. What money is in my purse?

PAGE. Seven groats and two pence.

FALSTAFF. I can get no remedy against this
consumption of the purse; borrowing only
lingers and lingers it out, but the disease is
incurable. Go bear this letter to my Lord of
Lancaster; this to the Prince; this to the Earl of
Westmoreland; and this to old Mistress Ursula,
whom I have weekly sworn to marry since I
perceiv'd the first white hair of my chin. About
it; you know where to find me. *[Exit PAGE]* A
pox of this gout! or, a gout of this pox! for the
one or the other plays the rogue with my great
toe. 'Tis no matter if I do halt; I have the wars
for my colour, and my pension shall seem the
more reasonable. A good wit will make use of
anything. I will turn diseases to commodity.

Exit.

❧ SCENE III ❧
York. The ARCHBISHOP'S palace

Enter the ARCHBISHOP, THOMAS MOWBRAY
the EARL MARSHAL, LORD HASTINGS, and
LORD BARDOLPH

ARCHBISHOP. Thus have you heard our cause
and known our means;
And, my most noble friends, I pray you all
Speak plainly your opinions of our hopes-
And first, Lord Marshal, what say you to it?

MOWBRAY. I well allow the occasion of our amis;
But gladly would be better satisfied
How, in our means, we should
advance ourselves
To look with forehead bold and big enough
Upon the power and puissance of the King.

HASTINGS. Our present musters grow upon
the file

To five and twenty thousand men of choice;
And our supplies live largely in the hope
Of great Northumberland, whose bosom burns
With an incensed fire of injuries.

LORD BARDOLPH. The question then, Lord
  Hastings, standeth thus:
Whether our present five and twenty thousand
May hold up head without Northumberland?

HASTINGS. With him, we may.

LORD BARDOLPH. Yea, marry, there's the point;
  But if without him we be thought too feeble,
  My judgment is we should not step too far
  Till we had his assistance by the hand;
  For, in a theme so bloody-fac'd as this,
  Conjecture, expectation, and surmise
  Of aids incertain, should not be admitted.

ARCHBISHOP. 'Tis very true, Lord Bardolph;
  for indeed
It was young Hotspur's case at Shrewsbury.

LORD BARDOLPH. It was, my lord; who lin'd
  himself with hope,
  Eating the air and promise of supply,
  Flatt'ring himself in project of a power
  Much smaller than the smallest of his thoughts;
  And so, with great imagination
  Proper to madmen, led his powers to death,
  And, winking, leapt into destruction.

HASTINGS. But, by your leave, it never yet
  did hurt
To lay down likelihoods and forms of hope.

LORD BARDOLPH. Yes, if this present quality
  of war-
  Indeed the instant action, a cause on foot-
  Lives so in hope, as in an early spring
  We see th' appearing buds; which to prove fruit
  Hope gives not so much warrant, as despair
  That frosts will bite them. When we mean
  to build,
  We first survey the plot, then draw the model;
  And when we see the figure of the house,
  Then we must rate the cost of the erection;
  Which if we find outweighs ability,
  What do we then but draw anew the model
  In fewer offices, or at least desist
  To build at all? Much more, in this great work-
  Which is almost to pluck a kingdom down
  And set another up-should we survey
  The plot of situation and the model,
  Consent upon a sure foundation,
  Question surveyors, know our own estate
  How able such a work to undergo-
  To weigh against his opposite; or else
  We fortify in paper and in figures,

Using the names of men instead of men;
Like one that draws the model of a house
Beyond his power to build it; who, half through,
Gives o'er and leaves his part-created cost
A naked subject to the weeping clouds
And waste for churlish winter's tyranny.

HASTINGS. Grant that our hopes-yet likely of
  fair birth-
  Should be still-born, and that we now possess'd
  The utmost man of expectation,
  I think we are a body strong enough,
  Even as we are, to equal with the King.

LORD BARDOLPH. What, is the King but five and
  twenty thousand?

HASTINGS. To us no more; nay, not so much,
  Lord Bardolph;
  For his divisions, as the times do brawl,
  Are in three heads: one power against
  the French,
  And one against Glendower; perforce a third
  Must take up us. So is the unfirm King
  In three divided; and his coffers sound
  With hollow poverty and emptiness.

ARCHBISHOP. That he should draw his several
  strengths together
  And come against us in full puissance
  Need not be dreaded.

HASTINGS. If he should do so,
  He leaves his back unarm'd, the French
  and Welsh
  Baying at his heels. Never fear that.

LORD BARDOLPH. Who is it like should lead his
  forces hither?

HASTINGS. The Duke of Lancaster
  and Westmoreland;
  Against the Welsh, himself and
  Harry Monmouth;
  But who is substituted against the French
  I have no certain notice.

ARCHBISHOP. Let us on,
  And publish the occasion of our arms.
  The commonwealth is sick of their own choice;
  Their over-greedy love hath surfeited.
  An habitation giddy and unsure
  Hath he that buildeth on the vulgar heart.
  O thou fond many, with what loud applause
  Didst thou beat heaven with
  blessing Bolingbroke
  Before he was what thou wouldst have him be!
  And being now trimm'd in thine own desires,
  Thou, beastly feeder, art so full of him
  That thou provok'st thyself to cast him up.
  So, so, thou common dog, didst thou disgorge

Thy glutton bosom of the royal Richard;
And now thou wouldst eat thy dead vomit up,
And howl'st to find it. What trust is in
these times?
They that, when Richard liv'd, would have
him die
Are now become enamour'd on his grave.
Thou that threw'st dust upon his goodly head,
When through proud London he came
sighing on
After th' admired heels of Bolingbroke,
Criest now 'O earth, yield us that king again,
And take thou this!' O thoughts of men accurs'd!
Past and to come seems best; things
present, worst.

MOWBRAY. Shall we go draw our numbers, and
set on?

HASTINGS. We are time's subjects, and time bids
be gone. *Exeunt.*

ACT II

SCENE I

London. A street

Enter HOSTESS with two officers, FANG and SNARE

HOSTESS. Master Fang, have you ent'red
the action?

FANG. It is ent'red.

HOSTESS. Where's your yeoman? Is't a lusty
yeoman? Will 'a stand to't?

FANG. Sirrah, where's Snare?

HOSTESS. O Lord, ay! good Master Snare.

SNARE. Here, here.

FANG. Snare, we must arrest Sir John Falstaff.

HOSTESS. Yea, good Master Snare; I have ent'red
him and all.

SNARE. It may chance cost some of our lives, for
he will stab.

HOSTESS. Alas the day! take heed of him; he
stabb'd me in mine own house, and that most
beastly. In good faith, 'a cares not what mischief
he does, if his weapon be out; he will foin like
any devil; he will spare neither man, woman,
nor child.

FANG. If I can close with him, I care not for
his thrust.

HOSTESS. No, nor I neither; I'll be at your elbow.

FANG. An I but fist him once; an 'a come but
within my vice!

HOSTESS. I am undone by his going; I warrant
you, he's an infinitive thing upon my score.
Good Master Fang, hold him sure. Good Master
Snare, let him not scape. 'A comes continuantly
to Pie-corner-saving your manhoods-to buy
a saddle; and he is indited to dinner to the
Lubber's Head in Lumbert Street, to Master
Smooth's the silkman. I pray you, since my
exion is ent'red, and my case so openly known
to the world, let him be brought in to his
answer. A hundred mark is a long one for a
poor lone woman to bear; and I have borne,
and borne, and borne; and have been fubb'd
off, and fubb'd off, and fubb'd off, from this day
to that day, that it is a shame to be thought on.
There is no honesty in such dealing; unless a
woman should be made an ass and a beast, to
bear every knave's wrong.

Enter SIR JOHN FALSTAFF, PAGE, and BARDOLPH

Yonder he comes; and that arrant malmsey-nose
knave, Bardolph, with him. Do your offices, do
your offices, Master Fang and Master Snare; do
me, do me, do me your offices.

FALSTAFF. How now! whose mare's dead? What's
the matter?

FANG. Sir John, I arrest you at the suit of
Mistress Quickly.

FALSTAFF. Away, varlets! Draw, Bardolph. Cut
me off the villian's head. Throw the quean in
the channel.

HOSTESS. Throw me in the channel! I'll throw
thee in the channel. Wilt thou? wilt thou? thou
bastardly rogue! Murder, murder! Ah, thou
honeysuckle villain! wilt thou kill God's officers
and the King's? Ah, thou honey-seed rogue!
thou art a honey-seed; a man-queller and
a woman-queller.

FALSTAFF. Keep them off, Bardolph.

FANG. A rescue! a rescue!

HOSTESS. Good people, bring a rescue or two.
Thou wot, wot thou! thou wot, wot ta? Do, do,
thou rogue! do, thou hemp-seed!

PAGE. Away, you scullion! you rampallian! you
fustilarian! I'll tickle your catastrophe.

Enter the LORD CHIEF JUSTICE and his Men

CHIEF JUSTICE. What is the matter? Keep the
peace here, ho!

HOSTESS. Good my lord, be good to me. I
beseech you, stand to me.

CHIEF JUSTICE. How now, Sir John! what, are you
brawling here?
Doth this become your place, your time,
and business?

You should have been well on your way to York.
Stand from him, fellow; wherefore hang'st thou
upon him?

HOSTESS. O my most worshipful lord, an't please
your Grace, I am a poor widow of Eastcheap,
and he is arrested at my suit.

CHIEF JUSTICE. For what sum?

HOSTESS. It is more than for some, my lord; it
is for all-all I have. He hath eaten me out of
house and home; he hath put all my substance
into that fat belly of his. But I will have some
of it out again, or I will ride thee a nights like
a mare.

FALSTAFF. I think I am as like to ride the mare, if I
have any vantage of ground to get up.

CHIEF JUSTICE. How comes this, Sir John? Fie!
What man of good temper would endure this
tempest of exclamation? Are you not ashamed
to enforce a poor widow to so rough a course
to come by her own?

FALSTAFF. What is the gross sum that I owe thee?

HOSTESS. Marry, if thou wert an honest man,
thyself and the money too. Thou didst swear
to me upon a parcel-gilt goblet, sitting in my
Dolphin chamber, at the round table, by a sea-
coal fire, upon Wednesday in Wheeson week,
when the Prince broke thy head for liking his
father to a singing-man of Windsor-thou didst
swear to me then, as I was washing thy wound,
to marry me and make me my lady thy wife.
Canst thou deny it? Did not goodwife Keech,
the butcher's wife, come in then and call me
gossip Quickly? Coming in to borrow a mess
of vinegar, telling us she had a good dish of
prawns, whereby thou didst desire to eat some,
whereby I told thee they were ill for green
wound? And didst thou not, when she was
gone down stairs, desire me to be no more so
familiarity with such poor people, saying that
ere long they should call me madam? And didst
thou not kiss me, and bid me fetch the thirty
shillings? I put thee now to thy book-oath. Deny
it, if thou canst.

FALSTAFF. My lord, this is a poor mad soul, and
she says up and down the town that her eldest
son is like you. She hath been in good case,
and, the truth is, poverty hath distracted her.
But for these foolish officers, I beseech you I
may have redress against them.

CHIEF JUSTICE. Sir John, Sir John, I am well
acquainted with your manner of wrenching the
true cause the false way. It is not a confident
brow, nor the throng of words that come with

such more than impudent sauciness from
you, can thrust me from a level consideration.
You have, as it appears to me, practis'd upon
the easy yielding spirit of this woman, and
made her serve your uses both in purse and
in person.

HOSTESS. Yea, in truth, my lord.

CHIEF JUSTICE. Pray thee, peace. Pay her the
debt you owe her, and unpay the villainy
you have done with her; the one you may
do with sterling money, and the other with
current repentance.

FALSTAFF. My lord, I will not undergo this sneap
without reply. You call honourable boldness
impudent sauciness; if a man will make curtsy
and say nothing, he is virtuous. No, my lord,
my humble duty rememb'red, I will not be your
suitor. I say to you I do desire deliverance from
these officers, being upon hasty employment in
the King's affairs.

CHIEF JUSTICE. You speak as having power to
do wrong; but answer in th' effect of your
reputation, and satisfy the poor woman.

FALSTAFF. Come hither, hostess.

Enter GOWER

CHIEF JUSTICE. Now, Master Gower, what news?

GOWER. The King, my lord, and Harry Prince
of Wales
Are near at hand. The rest the paper tells.

Gives a letter

FALSTAFF. As I am a gentleman!

HOSTESS. Faith, you said so before.

FALSTAFF. As I am a gentleman! Come, no more
words of it.

HOSTESS. By this heavenly ground I tread on, I
must be fain to pawn both my plate and the
tapestry of my dining-chambers.

FALSTAFF. Glasses, glasses, is the only drinking;
and for thy walls, a pretty slight drollery, or the
story of the Prodigal, or the German hunting,
in water-work, is worth a thousand of these
bed-hangers and these fly-bitten tapestries. Let
it be ten pound, if thou canst. Come, and 'twere
not for thy humours, there's not a better wench
in England. Go, wash thy face, and draw the
action. Come, thou must not be in this humour
with me; dost not know me? Come, come, I
know thou wast set on to this.

HOSTESS. Pray thee, Sir John, let it be but twenty
nobles; i' faith, I am loath to pawn my plate, so
God save me, la!

FALSTAFF. Let it alone; I'll make other shift. You'll
be a fool still.

HOSTESS. Well, you shall have it, though I pawn my gown. I hope you'll come to supper. you'll pay me all together?

FALSTAFF. Will I live? *[To BARDOLPH]* Go, with her, with her; hook on, hook on.

HOSTESS. Will you have Doll Tearsheet meet you at supper?

FALSTAFF. No more words; let's have her.

Exeunt HOSTESS, BARDOLPH, and OFFICERS.

CHIEF JUSTICE. I have heard better news.

FALSTAFF. What's the news, my lord?

CHIEF JUSTICE. Where lay the King to-night?

GOWER. At Basingstoke, my lord.

FALSTAFF. I hope, my lord, all's well. What is the news, my lord?

CHIEF JUSTICE. Come all his forces back?

GOWER. No; fifteen hundred foot, five hundred horse,
Are march'd up to my Lord of Lancaster,
Against Northumberland and the Archbishop.

FALSTAFF. Comes the King back from Wales, my noble lord?

CHIEF JUSTICE. You shall have letters of me presently.
Come, go along with me, good Master Gower.

FALSTAFF. My lord!

CHIEF JUSTICE. What's the matter?

FALSTAFF. Master Gower, shall I entreat you with me to dinner?

GOWER. I must wait upon my good lord here, I thank you, good Sir John.

CHIEF JUSTICE. Sir John, you loiter here too long, being you are to take soldiers up in counties as you go.

FALSTAFF. Will you sup with me, Master Gower?

CHIEF JUSTICE. What foolish master taught you these manners, Sir John?

FALSTAFF. Master Gower, if they become me not, he was a fool that taught them me. This is the right fencing grace, my lord; tap for tap, and so part fair.

CHIEF JUSTICE. Now, the Lord lighten thee! Thou art a great fool

Exeunt.

⚜ SCENE II ⚜
London. Another street

Enter PRINCE HENRY and POINS

PRINCE. Before God, I am exceeding weary.

POINS. Is't come to that? I had thought weariness durst not have attach'd one of so high blood.

PRINCE. Faith, it does me; though it discolours the complexion of my greatness to acknowledge it. Doth it not show vilely in me to desire small beer?

POINS. Why, a prince should not be so loosely studied as to remember so weak a composition.

PRINCE. Belike then my appetite was not-princely got; for, by my troth, I do now remember the poor creature, small beer. But indeed these humble considerations make me out of love with my greatness. What a disgrace is it to me to remember thy name, or to know thy face to-morrow, or to take note how many pair of silk stockings thou hast-viz., these, and those that were thy peach-colour'd ones-or to bear the inventory of thy shirts-as, one for superfluity, and another for use! But that the tennis-court-keeper knows better than I; for it is a low ebb of linen with thee when thou keepest not racket there; as thou hast not done a great while, because the rest of thy low countries have made a shift to eat up thy holland. And God knows whether those that bawl out of the ruins of thy linen shall inherit his kingdom; but the midwives say the children are not in the fault; whereupon the world increases, and kindreds are mightily strengthened.

POINS. How ill it follows, after you have laboured so hard, you should talk so idly! Tell me, how many good young princes would do so, their fathers being so sick as yours at this time is?

PRINCE. Shall I tell thee one thing, Poins?

POINS. Yes, faith; and let it be an excellent good thing.

PRINCE. It shall serve among wits of no higher breeding than thine.

POINS. Go to; I stand the push of your one thing that you will tell.

PRINCE. Marry, I tell thee it is not meet that I should be sad, now my father is sick; albeit I could tell to thee-as to one it pleases me, for fault of a better, to call my friend-I could be sad and sad indeed too.

POINS. Very hardly upon such a subject.

PRINCE. By this hand, thou thinkest me as far in the devil's book as thou and Falstaff for obduracy and persistency: let the end try the man. But I tell thee my heart bleeds inwardly that my father is so sick; and keeping such vile company as thou art hath in reason taken from me all ostentation of sorrow.

POINS. The reason?

PRINCE. What wouldst thou think of me if I should weep?

POINS. I would think thee a most princely hypocrite.

PRINCE. It would be every man's thought; and thou art a blessed fellow to think as every man thinks. Never a man's thought in the world keeps the road-way better than thine. Every man would think me an hypocrite indeed. And what accites your most worshipful thought to think so?

POINS. Why, because you have been so lewd and so much engraffed to Falstaff.

PRINCE. And to thee.

POINS. By this light, I am well spoke on; I can hear it with mine own ears. The worst that they can say of me is that I am a second brother and that I am a proper fellow of my hands; and those two things, I confess, I cannot help. By the mass, here comes Bardolph.

Enter BARDOLPH and PAGE

PRINCE. And the boy that I gave Falstaff. 'A had him from me Christian; and look if the fat villain have not transform'd him ape.

BARDOLPH. God save your Grace!

PRINCE. And yours, most noble Bardolph!

POINS. Come, you virtuous ass, you bashful fool, must you be blushing? Wherefore blush you now? What a maidenly man-at-arms are you become! Is't such a matter to get a pottle-pot's maidenhead?

PAGE. 'A calls me e'en now, my lord, through a red lattice, and I could discern no part of his face from the window. At last I spied his eyes; and methought he had made two holes in the alewife's new petticoat, and so peep'd through.

PRINCE. Has not the boy profited?

BARDOLPH. Away, you whoreson upright rabbit, away!

PAGE. Away, you rascally Althaea's dream, away!

PRINCE. Instruct us, boy; what dream, boy?

PAGE. Marry, my lord, Althaea dreamt she was delivered of a firebrand; and therefore I call him her dream.

PRINCE. A crown's worth of good interpretation. There 'tis, boy.

Giving a crown

POINS. O that this blossom could be kept from cankers!
Well, there is sixpence to preserve thee.

BARDOLPH. An you do not make him be hang'd among you, the gallows shall have wrong.

PRINCE. And how doth thy master, Bardolph?

BARDOLPH. Well, my lord. He heard of your Grace's coming to town. There's a letter for you.

POINS. Deliver'd with good respect. And how doth the martlemas, your master?

BARDOLPH. In bodily health, sir.

POINS. Marry, the immortal part needs a physician; but that moves not him. Though that be sick, it dies not.

PRINCE. I do allow this well to be as familiar with me as my dog; and he holds his place, for look you how he writes.

POINS. *[Reads]* 'John Falstaff, knight'-Every man must know that as oft as he has occasion to name himself, even like those that are kin to the King; for they never prick their finger but they say 'There's some of the King's blood spilt.' 'How comes that?' says he that takes upon him not to conceive. The answer is as ready as a borrower's cap: 'I am the King's poor cousin, sir.'

PRINCE. Nay, they will be kin to us, or they will fetch it from Japhet. But the letter:
[Reads] 'Sir John Falstaff, knight, to the son of the King nearest his father, Harry Prince of Wales, greeting.'

POINS. Why, this is a certificate.

PRINCE. Peace! *[Reads]* 'I will imitate the honourable Romans in brevity.'-

POINS. He sure means brevity in breath, short-winded.

PRINCE. *[Reads]* 'I commend me to thee, I commend thee, and I leave thee. Be not too familiar with Poins; for he misuses thy favours so much that he swears thou art to marry his sister Nell. Repent at idle times as thou mayst, and so farewell. Thine, by yea and no-which is as much as to say as thou usest him-JACK FALSTAFF with my familiars, JOHN with my brothers and sisters, and SIR JOHN with all Europe.'

POINS. My lord, I'll steep this letter in sack and make him eat it.

PRINCE. That's to make him eat twenty of his words. But do you use me thus, Ned? Must I marry your sister?

POINS. God send the wench no worse fortune! But I never said so.

PRINCE. Well, thus we play the fools with the time, and the spirits of the wise sit in the clouds and mock us. Is your master here in London?

BARDOLPH. Yea, my lord.

PRINCE. Where sups he? Doth the old boar feed in the old frank?

BARDOLPH. At the old place, my lord,
  in Eastcheap.

PRINCE. What company?

PAGE. Ephesians, my lord, of the old church.

PRINCE. Sup any women with him?

PAGE. None, my lord, but old Mistress Quickly
  and Mistress Doll Tearsheet.

PRINCE. What pagan may that be?

PAGE. A proper gentlewoman, sir, and a
  kinswoman of my master's.

PRINCE. Even such kin as the parish heifers are to
  the town bull. Shall we steal upon them, Ned,
  at supper?

POINS. I am your shadow, my lord; I'll follow you.

PRINCE. Sirrah, you boy, and Bardolph, no word
  to your master that I am yet come to town.
  There's for your silence.

BARDOLPH. I have no tongue, sir.

PAGE. And for mine, sir, I will govern it.

PRINCE. Fare you well; go.

[Exeunt BARDOLPH and PAGE]

This Doll Tearsheet should be some road.

POINS. I warrant you, as common as the way
  between Saint Albans and London.

PRINCE. How might we see Falstaff bestow
  himself to-night in his true colours, and not
  ourselves be seen?

POINS. Put on two leathern jerkins and aprons,
  and wait upon him at his table as drawers.

PRINCE. From a god to a bull? A heavy
  descension! It was Jove's case. From a prince to
  a prentice? A low transformation! That shall be
  mine; for in everything the purpose must weigh
  with the folly. Follow me, Ned.

Exeunt

✿ SCENE III ✿

Warkworth. Before the castle

*Enter NORTHUMBERLAND, LADY
NORTHUMBERLAND, and Lady Percy*

NORTHUMBERLAND. I pray thee, loving wife, and
  gentle daughter,
  Give even way unto my rough affairs;
  Put not you on the visage of the times
  And be, like them, to Percy troublesome.

LADY NORTHUMBERLAND. I have given over, I
  will speak no more.
  Do what you will; your wisdom be your guide.

NORTHUMBERLAND. Alas, sweet wife, my honour
  is at pawn;

And but my going nothing can redeem it.

LADY PERCY. O, yet, for God's sake, go not to
  these wars!
  The time was, father, that you broke your word,
  When you were more endear'd to it than now;
  When your own Percy, when my heart's
    dear Harry,
  Threw many a northward look to see his father
  Bring up his powers; but he did long in vain.
  Who then persuaded you to stay at home?
  There were two honours lost, yours and
    your son's.
  For yours, the God of heaven brighten it!
  For his, it stuck upon him as the sun
  In the grey vault of heaven; and by his light
  Did all the chivalry of England move
  To do brave acts. He was indeed the glass
  Wherein the noble youth did dress themselves.
  He had no legs that practis'd not his gait;
  And speaking thick, which nature made
    his blemish,
  Became the accents of the valiant;
  For those who could speak low and tardily
  Would turn their own perfection to abuse
  To seem like him: so that in speech, in gait,
  In diet, in affections of delight,
  In military rules, humours of blood,
  He was the mark and glass, copy and book,
  That fashion'd others. And him-O
    wondrous him!
  O miracle of men!-him did you leave-
  Second to none, unseconded by you-
  To look upon the hideous god of war
  In disadvantage, to abide a field
  Where nothing but the sound of
    Hotspur's name
  Did seem defensible. So you left him.
  Never, O never, do his ghost the wrong
  To hold your honour more precise and nice
  With others than with him! Let them alone.
  The Marshal and the Archbishop are strong.
  Had my sweet Harry had but half
    their numbers,
  To-day might I, hanging on Hotspur's neck,
  Have talk'd of Monmouth's grave.

NORTHUMBERLAND. Beshrew your heart,
  Fair daughter, you do draw my spirits from me
  With new lamenting ancient oversights.
  But I must go and meet with danger there,
  Or it will seek me in another place,
  And find me worse provided.

LADY NORTHUMBERLAND. O, fly to Scotland
  Till that the nobles and the armed commons

Have of their puissance made a little taste.

LADY PERCY. If they get ground and vantage of
  the King,
  Then join you with them, like a rib of steel,
  To make strength stronger; but, for all our loves,
  First let them try themselves. So did your son;
  He was so suff'red; so came I a widow;
  And never shall have length of life enough
  To rain upon remembrance with mine eyes,
  That it may grow and sprout as high as heaven,
  For recordation to my noble husband.

NORTHUMBERLAND. Come, come, go in with
  me. 'Tis with my mind
  As with the tide swell'd up unto his height,
  That makes a still-stand, running neither way.
  Fain would I go to meet the Archbishop,
  But many thousand reasons hold me back.
  I will resolve for Scotland. There am I,
  Till time and vantage crave my company.

Exeunt.

❧ SCENE IV ❧

London. The Boar's Head Tavern in Eastcheap

Enter FRANCIS and another DRAWER

FRANCIS. What the devil hast thou brought there-
  apple-johns? Thou knowest Sir John cannot
  endure an apple-john.

SECOND DRAWER. Mass, thou say'st true. The
  Prince once set a dish of apple-johns before
  him, and told him there were five more Sir
  Johns; and, putting off his hat, said 'I will now
  take my leave of these six dry, round, old,
  withered knights.' It ang'red him to the heart;
  but he hath forgot that.

FRANCIS. Why, then, cover and set them down;
  and see if thou canst find out Sneak's noise;
  Mistress Tearsheet would fain hear some music.

Enter THIRD DRAWER

THIRD DRAWER. Dispatch! The room where they
  supp'd is too hot; they'll come in straight.

FRANCIS. Sirrah, here will be the Prince and
  Master Poins anon; and they will put on two of
  our jerkins and aprons; and Sir John must not
  know of it. Bardolph hath brought word.

THIRD DRAWER. By the mass, here will be old
  utis; it will be an excellent stratagem.

SECOND DRAWER. I'll see if I can find out Sneak.

Exeunt SECOND and THIRD DRAWERS.

Enter HOSTESS and DOLL TEARSHEET

HOSTESS. I' faith, sweetheart, methinks now
you are in an excellent good temperality. Your
pulsidge beats as extraordinarily as heart would
desire; and your colour, I warrant you, is as
red as any rose, in good truth, la! But, i' faith,
you have drunk too much canaries; and that's
a marvellous searching wine, and it perfumes
the blood ere one can say 'What's this?' How do
you now?

DOLL. Better than I was-hem.

HOSTESS. Why, that's well said; a good heart's
worth gold.
  Lo, here comes Sir John.

Enter FALSTAFF

FALSTAFF. [Singing] 'When Arthur first in court'-
Empty the jordan. [Exit FRANCIS, singing] 'And was
a worthy king'-How now, Mistress Doll!

HOSTESS. Sick of a calm; yea, good faith.

FALSTAFF. So is all her sect; and they be once in a
  calm, they are sick.

DOLL. A pox damn you, you muddy rascal! Is that
all the comfort you give me?

FALSTAFF. You make fat rascals, Mistress Doll.

DOLL. I make them! Gluttony and diseases make
them: I make them not.

FALSTAFF. If the cook help to make the gluttony,
you help to make the diseases, Doll. We catch
of you, Doll, we catch of you; grant that, my
poor virtue, grant that.

DOLL. Yea, joy, our chains and our jewels.

FALSTAFF. 'Your brooches, pearls, and ouches.'
For to serve bravely is to come halting off; you
know, to come off the breach with his pike bent
bravely, and to surgery bravely; to venture upon
the charg'd chambers bravely-

DOLL. Hang yourself, you muddy conger,
hang yourself!

HOSTESS. By my troth, this is the old fashion; you
two never meet but you fall to some discord.
You are both, i' good truth, as rheumatic as two
dry toasts; you cannot one bear with another's
confirmities. What the good-year! one must
bear, and that must be you. You are the weaker
vessel, as as they say, the emptier vessel.

DOLL. Can a weak empty vessel bear such a huge
full hogs-head? There's a whole merchant's
venture of Bourdeaux stuff in him; you have not
seen a hulk better stuff'd in the hold. Come, I'll
be friends with thee, Jack. Thou art going to the
wars; and whether I shall ever see thee again or
no, there is nobody cares.

Re-enter FRANCIS

FRANCIS. Sir, Ancient Pistol's below and would
speak with you.

DOLL. Hang him, swaggering rascal! Let him not come hither; it is the foul-mouth'dst rogue in England.

HOSTESS. If he swagger, let him not come here. No, by my faith! I must live among my neighbours; I'll no swaggerers. I am in good name and fame with the very best. Shut the door. There comes no swaggerers here; I have not liv'd all this while to have swaggering now. Shut the door, I pray you.

FALSTAFF. Dost thou hear, hostess?

HOSTESS. Pray ye, pacify yourself, Sir John; there comes no swaggerers here.

FALSTAFF. Dost thou hear? It is mine ancient.

HOSTESS. Tilly-fally, Sir John, ne'er tell me; and your ancient swagg'rer comes not in my doors. I was before Master Tisick, the debuty, t' other day; and, as he said to me-'twas no longer ago than Wednesday last, i' good faith!-'Neighbour Quickly', says he-Master Dumbe, our minister, was by then-'Neighbour Quickly,' says he, 'receive those that are civil, for,' said he, 'you are in an ill name.' Now 'a said so, I can tell whereupon. 'For,' says he, 'you are an honest woman and well thought on, therefore take heed what guests you receive. Receive,' says he, 'no swaggering companions.' There comes none here. You would bless you to hear what he said. No, I'll no swagg'rers.

FALSTAFF. He's no swagg'rer, hostess; a tame cheater, i' faith; you may stroke him as gently as a puppy greyhound. He'll not swagger with a Barbary hen, if her feathers turn back in any show of resistance. Call him up, drawer.

Exit FRANCIS.

HOSTESS. Cheater, call you him? I will bar no honest man my house, nor no cheater; but I do not love swaggering, by my troth. I am the worse when one says 'swagger'. Feel, masters, how I shake; look you, I warrant you.

DOLL. So you do, hostess.

HOSTESS. Do I? Yea, in very truth, do I, an 'twere an aspen leaf. I cannot abide swagg'rers.

Enter PISTOL, BARDOLPH, and PAGE

PISTOL. God save you, Sir John!

FALSTAFF. Welcome, Ancient Pistol. Here, Pistol, I charge you with a cup of sack; do you discharge upon mine hostess.

PISTOL. I will discharge upon her, Sir John, with two bullets.

FALSTAFF. She is pistol-proof, sir; you shall not hardly offend her.

HOSTESS. Come, I'll drink no proofs nor no bullets. I'll drink no more than will do me good, for no man's pleasure, I.

PISTOL. Then to you, Mistress Dorothy; I will charge you.

DOLL. Charge me! I scorn you, scurvy companion. What! you poor, base, rascally, cheating, lack-linen mate! Away, you mouldy rogue, away! I am meat for your master.

PISTOL. I know you, Mistress Dorothy.

DOLL. Away, you cut-purse rascal! you filthy bung, away! By this wine, I'll thrust my knife in your mouldy chaps, an you play the saucy cuttle with me. Away, you bottle-ale rascal! you basket-hilt stale juggler, you! Since when, I pray you, sir? God's light, with two points on your shoulder? Much!

PISTOL. God let me not live but I will murder your ruff for this.

FALSTAFF. No more, Pistol; I would not have you go off here. Discharge yourself of our company, Pistol.

HOSTESS. No, good Captain Pistol; not here, sweet captain.

DOLL. Captain! Thou abominable damn'd cheater, art thou not ashamed to be called captain? An captains were of my mind, they would truncheon you out, for taking their names upon you before you have earn'd them. You a captain! you slave, for what? For tearing a poor whore's ruff in a bawdy-house? He a captain! hang him, rogue! He lives upon mouldy stew'd prunes and dried cakes. A captain! God's light, these villains will make the word as odious as the word 'occupy'; which was an excellent good word before it was ill sorted. Therefore captains had need look to't.

BARDOLPH. Pray thee go down, good ancient.

FALSTAFF. Hark thee hither, Mistress Doll.

PISTOL. Not I! I tell thee what, Corporal Bardolph, I could tear her; I'll be reveng'd of her.

PAGE. Pray thee go down.

PISTOL. I'll see her damn'd first; to Pluto's damn'd lake, by this hand, to th' infernal deep, with Erebus and tortures vile also. Hold hook and line, say I. Down, down, dogs! down, faitors! Have we not Hiren here?

HOSTESS. Good Captain Peesel, be quiet; 'tis very late, i' faith; I beseek you now, aggravate your choler.

PISTOL. These be good humours, indeed! Shall packhorses, And hollow pamper'd jades of Asia, Which cannot go but thirty mile a day,

Compare with Caesars, and with Cannibals,
And Troiant Greeks? Nay, rather damn
  them with
King Cerberus; and let the welkin roar.
Shall we fall foul for toys?

HOSTESS. By my troth, Captain, these are very
  bitter words.

BARDOLPH. Be gone, good ancient; this will grow
  to a brawl anon.

PISTOL. Die men like dogs! Give crowns like pins!
  Have we not Hiren here?

HOSTESS. O' my word, Captain, there's none
  such here. What the good-year! do you think I
  would deny her? For God's sake, be quiet.

PISTOL. Then feed and be fat, my fair Calipolis.
  Come, give's some sack.
  'Si fortune me tormente sperato me contento.'
  Fear we broadsides? No, let the fiend give fire.
  Give me some sack; and, sweetheart, lie thou
  there. [Laying down his sword]
  Come we to full points here, and are
  etceteras nothings?

FALSTAFF. Pistol, I would be quiet.

PISTOL. Sweet knight, I kiss thy neaf. What! we
  have seen the seven stars.

DOLL. For God's sake thrust him down stairs; I
  cannot endure such a fustian rascal.

PISTOL. Thrust him down stairs! Know we not
  Galloway nags?

FALSTAFF. Quoit him down, Bardolph, like a
  shove-groat shilling. Nay, an 'a do nothing but
  speak nothing, 'a shall be nothing here.

BARDOLPH. Come, get you down stairs.

PISTOL. What! shall we have incision? Shall we
  imbrue?[Snatching up his sword]
  Then death rock me asleep, abridge my
  doleful days!
  Why, then, let grievous, ghastly, gaping wounds
  Untwine the Sisters Three! Come, Atropos, I say!

HOSTESS. Here's goodly stuff toward!

FALSTAFF. Give me my rapier, boy.

DOLL. I pray thee, Jack, I pray thee, do not draw.

FALSTAFF. Get you down stairs.

Drawing and driving PISTOL out

HOSTESS. Here's a goodly tumult! I'll forswear
  keeping house afore I'll be in these tirrits and
  frights. So; murder, I warrant now. Alas, alas!
  put up your naked weapons, put up your
  naked weapons.

Exeunt PISTOL and BARDOLPH.

DOLL. I pray thee, Jack, be quiet; the rascal's
  gone. Ah, you whoreson little valiant
  villain, you!

HOSTESS. Are you not hurt i' th' groin?
  Methought 'a made a shrewd thrust at
  your belly.

Re-enter BARDOLPH

FALSTAFF. Have you turn'd him out a doors?

BARDOLPH. Yea, sir. The rascal's drunk. You have
  hurt him, sir, i' th' shoulder.

FALSTAFF. A rascal! to brave me!

DOLL. Ah, you sweet little rogue, you! Alas, poor
  ape, how thou sweat'st! Come, let me wipe
  thy face. Come on, you whoreson chops. Ah,
  rogue! i' faith, I love thee. Thou art as valorous
  as Hector of Troy, worth five of Agamemnon,
  and ten times better than the Nine Worthies.
  Ah, villain!

FALSTAFF. A rascally slave! I will toss the rogue in
  a blanket.

DOLL. Do, an thou dar'st for thy heart. An thou
  dost, I'll canvass thee between a pair of sheets.

Enter Musicians

PAGE. The music is come, sir.

FALSTAFF. Let them play. Play, sirs. Sit on my
  knee, Don. A rascal bragging slave! The rogue
  fled from me like quick-silver.

DOLL. I' faith, and thou follow'dst him like a
  church. Thou whoreson little tidy Bartholomew
  boar-pig, when wilt thou leave fighting a days
  and foining a nights, and begin to patch up
  thine old body for heaven?

Enter, PRINCE HENRY and POINS disguised as drawers

FALSTAFF. Peace, good Doll! Do not speak like
  a death's-head; do not bid me remember
  mine end.

DOLL. Sirrah, what humour's the Prince of?

FALSTAFF. A good shallow young fellow. 'A would
  have made a good pantler; 'a would ha' chipp'd
  bread well.

DOLL. They say Poins has a good wit.

FALSTAFF. He a good wit! hang him, baboon! His
  wit's as thick as Tewksbury mustard; there's no
  more conceit in him than is in a mallet.

DOLL. Why does the Prince love him so, then?

FALSTAFF. Because their legs are both of a
  bigness, and 'a plays at quoits well, and eats
  conger and fennel, and drinks off candles' ends
  for flap-dragons, and rides the wild mare with
  the boys, and jumps upon join'd-stools, and
  swears with a good grace, and wears his boots
  very smooth, like unto the sign of the Leg, and
  breeds no bate with telling of discreet stories;
  and such other gambol faculties 'a has, that
  show a weak mind and an able body, for the
  which the Prince admits him. For the Prince

himself is such another; the weight of a hair will turn the scales between their avoirdupois.

PRINCE. Would not this nave of a wheel have his ears cut off?

POINS. Let's beat him before his whore.

PRINCE. Look whe'er the wither'd elder hath not his poll claw'd like a parrot.

POINS. Is it not strange that desire should so many years outlive performance?

FALSTAFF. Kiss me, Doll.

PRINCE. Saturn and Venus this year in conjunction! What says th' almanac to that?

POINS. And look whether the fiery Trigon, his man, be not lisping to his master's old tables, his note-book, his counsel-keeper.

FALSTAFF. Thou dost give me flattering busses.

DOLL. By my troth, I kiss thee with a most constant heart.

FALSTAFF. I am old, I am old.

DOLL. I love thee better than I love e'er a scurvy young boy of them all.

FALSTAFF. What stuff wilt have a kirtle of? I shall receive money a Thursday. Shalt have a cap to-morrow. A merry song, come. 'A grows late; we'll to bed. Thou't forget me when I am gone.

DOLL. By my troth, thou't set me a-weeping, an thou say'st so. Prove that ever I dress myself handsome till thy return. Well, hearken a' th' end.

FALSTAFF. Some sack, Francis.

PRINCE and POINS. Anon, anon, sir. *Advancing*

FALSTAFF. Ha! a bastard son of the King's? And art thou not Poins his brother?

PRINCE. Why, thou globe of sinful continents, what a life dost thou lead!

FALSTAFF. A better than thou. I am a gentleman: thou art a drawer.

PRINCE. Very true, sir, and I come to draw you out by the ears.

HOSTESS. O, the Lord preserve thy Grace! By my troth, welcome to London. Now the Lord bless that sweet face of thine. O Jesu, are you come from Wales?

FALSTAFF. Thou whoreson mad compound of majesty, by this light flesh and corrupt blood, thou art welcome. *Leaning his hand upon DOLL*

DOLL. How, you fat fool! I scorn you.

POINS. My lord, he will drive you out of your revenge and turn all to a merriment, if you take not the heat.

PRINCE. You whoreson candle-mine, you, how vilely did you speak of me even now before this honest, virtuous, civil gentlewoman!

HOSTESS. God's blessing of your good heart! and so she is, by my troth.

FALSTAFF. Didst thou hear me?

PRINCE. Yea; and you knew me, as you did when you ran away by Gadshill. You knew I was at your back, and spoke it on purpose to try my patience.

FALSTAFF. No, no, no; not so; I did not think thou wast within hearing.

PRINCE. I shall drive you then to confess the wilful abuse, and then I know how to handle you.

FALSTAFF. No abuse, Hal, o' mine honour; no abuse.

PRINCE. Not to dispraise me, and call me pander, and bread-chipper, and I know not what!

FALSTAFF. No abuse, Hal.

POINS. No abuse!

FALSTAFF. No abuse, Ned, i' th' world; honest Ned, none. I disprais'd him before the wicked-that the wicked might not fall in love with thee; in which doing, I have done the part of a careful friend and a true subject; and thy father is to give me thanks for it. No abuse, Hal; none, Ned, none; no, faith, boys, none.

PRINCE. See now, whether pure fear and entire cowardice doth not make thee wrong this virtuous gentlewoman to close with us? Is she of the wicked? Is thine hostess here of the wicked? Or is thy boy of the wicked? Or honest Bardolph, whose zeal burns in his nose, of the wicked?

POINS. Answer, thou dead elm, answer.

FALSTAFF. The fiend hath prick'd down Bardolph irrecoverable; and his face is Lucifer's privy-kitchen, where he doth nothing but roast malt-worms. For the boy-there is a good angel about him; but the devil outbids him too.

PRINCE. For the women?

FALSTAFF. For one of them-she's in hell already, and burns poor souls. For th' other-I owe her money; and whether she be damn'd for that, I know not.

HOSTESS. No, I warrant you.

FALSTAFF. No, I think thou art not; I think thou art quit for that. Marry, there is another indictment upon thee for suffering flesh to be eaten in thy house, contrary to the law; for the which I think thou wilt howl.

HOSTESS. All vict'lers do so. What's a joint of mutton or two in a whole Lent?

PRINCE. You, gentlewoman-

DOLL. What says your Grace?

FALSTAFF. His Grace says that which his flesh rebels against.

Knocking within

HOSTESS. Who knocks so loud at door? Look to th' door there, Francis.

Enter PETO

PRINCE. Peto, how now! What news?

PETO. The King your father is at Westminster;
And there are twenty weak and wearied posts
Come from the north; and as I came along
I met and overtook a dozen captains,
Bare-headed, sweating, knocking at the taverns,
And asking every one for Sir John Falstaff.

PRINCE. By heaven, Poins, I feel me much
  to blame
So idly to profane the precious time,
When tempest of commotion, like the south,
Borne with black vapour, doth begin to melt
And drop upon our bare unarmed heads.
Give me my sword and cloak. Falstaff,
  good night.

Exeunt PRINCE, POINS, PETO, and BARDOLPH

FALSTAFF. Now comes in the sweetest morsel
of the night, and we must hence, and leave
it unpick'd. *[Knocking within]* More knocking at
the door!

Re-enter BARDOLPH

How now! What's the matter?

BARDOLPH. You must away to court,
  sir, presently;
A dozen captains stay at door for you.

FALSTAFF. *[To the PAGE]* Pay the musicians, sirrah.-
Farewell, hostess; farewell, Doll. You see, my
good wenches, how men of merit are sought
after; the undeserver may sleep, when the man
of action is call'd on. Farewell, good wenches.
If I be not sent away post, I will see you again
ere I go.

DOLL. I cannot speak. If my heart be not ready to
burst! Well, sweet Jack, have a care of thyself.

FALSTAFF. Farewell, farewell.

Exeunt FALSTAFF and BARDOLPH

HOSTESS. Well, fare thee well. I have known thee
these twenty-nine years, come peascod-time;
but an honester and truer-hearted man-well
fare thee well.

BARDOLPH. *[Within]* Mistress Tearsheet!

HOSTESS. What's the matter?

BARDOLPH. *[Within]* Bid Mistress Tearsheet come
to my master.

HOSTESS. O, run Doll, run, run, good Come. *[To
BARDOLPH]* She comes blubber'd.-Yea, will you
come, Doll?

Exeunt

ACT III

✦ SCENE I ✦
Westminster. The palace

Enter the KING in his nightgown, with a PAGE

KING. Go call the Earls of Surrey and of Warwick;
  But, ere they come, bid them o'er-read
    these letters
  And well consider of them. Make good speed.

Exit PAGE

How many thousands of my poorest subjects
Are at this hour asleep! O sleep, O gentle sleep,
Nature's soft nurse, how have I frighted thee,
That thou no more will weigh my eyelids down,
And steep my senses in forgetfulness?
Why rather, sleep, liest thou in smoky cribs,
Upon uneasy pallets stretching thee,
And hush'd with buzzing night-flies to
  thy slumber,
Than in the perfum'd chambers of the great,
Under the canopies of costly state,
And lull'd with sound of sweetest melody?
O thou dull god, why liest thou with the vile
In loathsome beds, and leav'st the kingly couch
A watch-case or a common 'larum-bell?
Wilt thou upon the high and giddy mast
Seal up the ship-boy's eyes, and rock his brains
In cradle of the rude imperious surge,
And in the visitation of the winds,
Who take the ruffian billows by the top,
Curling their monstrous heads, and
  hanging them
With deafing clamour in the slippery clouds,
That with the hurly death itself awakes?
Canst thou, O partial sleep, give thy repose
To the wet sea-boy in an hour so rude;
And in the calmest and most stillest night,
With all appliances and means to boot,
Deny it to a king? Then, happy low, lie down!
Uneasy lies the head that wears a crown.

Enter WARWICK and SURREY

WARWICK. Many good morrows to your Majesty!

KING. Is it good morrow, lords?

WARWICK. 'Tis one o'clock, and past.

KING. Why then, good morrow to you all,
  my lords.
Have you read o'er the letters that I sent you?

WARWICK. We have, my liege.

KING. Then you perceive the body of
  our kingdom
  How foul it is; what rank diseases grow,
  And with what danger, near the heart of it.
WARWICK. It is but as a body yet distemper'd;
  Which to his former strength may be restored
  With good advice and little medicine.
  My Lord Northumberland will soon be cool'd.
KING. O God! that one might read the book
  of fate,
  And see the revolution of the times
  Make mountains level, and the continent,
  Weary of solid firmness, melt itself
  Into the sea; and other times to see
  The beachy girdle of the ocean
  Too wide for Neptune's hips; how
    chances mock,
  And changes fill the cup of alteration
  With divers liquors! O, if this were seen,
  The happiest youth, viewing his
    progress through,
  What perils past, what crosses to ensue,
  Would shut the book and sit him down and die.
  'Tis not ten years gone
  Since Richard and Northumberland,
    great friends,
  Did feast together, and in two years after
  Were they at wars. It is but eight years since
  This Percy was the man nearest my soul;
  Who like a brother toil'd in my affairs
  And laid his love and life under my foot;
  Yea, for my sake, even to the eyes of Richard
  Gave him defiance. But which of you was by-
  [To Warwick] You, cousin Nevil, as I
    may remember-
  When Richard, with his eye brim full of tears,
  Then check'd and rated by Northumberland,
  Did speak these words, now prov'd a prophecy?
  'Northumberland, thou ladder by the which
  My cousin Bolingbroke ascends my throne'-
  Though then, God knows, I had no such intent
  But that necessity so bow'd the state
  That I and greatness were compell'd to kiss-
  'The time shall come'-thus did he follow it-
  'The time will come that foul sin,
    gathering head,
  Shall break into corruption'-so went on,
  Foretelling this same time's condition
  And the division of our amity.
WARWICK. There is a history in all men's lives,
  Figuring the natures of the times deceas'd;
  The which observ'd, a man may prophesy,
  With a near aim, of the main chance of things

As yet not come to life, who in their seeds
  And weak beginning lie intreasured.
  Such things become the hatch and brood
  of time;
  And, by the necessary form of this,
  King Richard might create a perfect guess
  That great Northumberland, then false to him,
  Would of that seed grow to a greater falseness;
  Which should not find a ground to root upon
  Unless on you.
KING. Are these things then necessities?
  Then let us meet them like necessities;
  And that same word even now cries out on us.
  They say the Bishop and Northumberland
  Are fifty thousand strong.
WARWICK. It cannot be, my lord.
  Rumour doth double, like the voice and echo,
  The numbers of the feared. Please it your Grace
  To go to bed. Upon my soul, my lord,
  The powers that you already have sent forth
  Shall bring this prize in very easily.
  To comfort you the more, I have receiv'd
  A certain instance that Glendower is dead.
  Your Majesty hath been this fortnight ill;
  And these unseasoned hours perforce must add
  Unto your sickness.
KING. I will take your counsel.
  And, were these inward wars once out of hand,
  We would, dear lords, unto the Holy Land.

Exeunt.

✤ SCENE II ✤

Gloucestershire. Before Justice SHALLOW'S house

Enter SHALLOW and SILENCE, meeting; MOULDY,
SHADOW, WART, FEEBLE, BULLCALF, and
SERVANTS behind

SHALLOW. Come on, come on, come on; give me
  your hand, sir; give me your hand, sir. An early
  stirrer, by the rood! And how doth my good
  cousin Silence?
SILENCE. Good morrow, good cousin Shallow.
SHALLOW. And how doth my cousin, your bed-
  fellow? and your fairest daughter and mine, my
  god-daughter Ellen?
SILENCE. Alas, a black ousel, cousin Shallow!
SHALLOW. By yea and no, sir. I dare say my cousin
  William is become a good scholar; he is at
  Oxford still, is he not?
SILENCE. Indeed, sir, to my cost.
SHALLOW. 'A must, then, to the Inns o' Court

shortly. I was once of Clement's Inn; where I
think they will talk of mad Shallow yet.

SILENCE. You were call'd 'lusty Shallow'
then, cousin.

SHALLOW. By the mass, I was call'd anything;
and I would have done anything indeed
too, and roundly too. There was I, and little
John Doit of Staffordshire, and black George
Barnes, and Francis Pickbone, and Will Squele
a Cotsole man-you had not four such swinge-
bucklers in all the Inns of Court again. And
I may say to you we knew where the bona-
robas were, and had the best of them all at
commandment. Then was Jack Falstaff, now
Sir John, boy, and page to Thomas Mowbray,
Duke of Norfolk.

SILENCE. This Sir John, cousin, that comes hither
anon about soldiers?

SHALLOW. The same Sir John, the very same. I
see him break Scoggin's head at the court gate,
when 'a was a crack not thus high; and the
very same day did I fight with one Sampson
Stockfish, a fruiterer, behind Gray's Inn. Jesu,
Jesu, the mad days that I have spent! and to see
how many of my old acquaintance are dead!

SILENCE. We shall all follow, cousin.

SHALLOW. Certain, 'tis certain; very sure, very
sure. Death, as the Psalmist saith, is certain to
all; all shall die. How a good yoke of bullocks at
Stamford fair?

SILENCE. By my troth, I was not there.

SHALLOW. Death is certain. Is old Double of your
town living yet?

SILENCE. Dead, sir.

SHALLOW. Jesu, Jesu, dead! drew a good bow;
and dead! 'A shot a fine shoot. John a Gaunt
loved him well, and betted much money on his
head. Dead! 'A would have clapp'd i' th' clout at
twelve score, and carried you a forehand shaft a
fourteen and fourteen and a half, that it would
have done a man's heart good to see. How a
score of ewes now?

SILENCE. Thereafter as they be-a score of good
ewes may be worth ten pounds.

SHALLOW. And is old Double dead?

Enter BARDOLPH, and One with him

SILENCE. Here come two of Sir John Falstaff's
men, as I think.

SHALLOW. Good morrow, honest gentlemen.

BARDOLPH. I beseech you, which is
Justice Shallow?

SHALLOW. I am Robert Shallow, sir, a poor
esquire of this county, and one of the King's
justices of the peace. What is your good
pleasure with me?

BARDOLPH. My captain, sir, commends him
to you; my captain, Sir John Falstaff-a
tall gentleman, by heaven, and a most
gallant leader.

SHALLOW. He greets me well, sir; I knew him
a good back-sword man. How doth the good
knight? May I ask how my lady his wife doth?

BARDOLPH. Sir, pardon; a soldier is better
accommodated than with a wife.

SHALLOW. It is well said, in faith, sir; and it is
well said indeed too. 'Better accommodated!'
It is good; yea, indeed, is it. Good phrases are
surely, and ever were, very commendable.
'Accommodated!' It comes of accommodo.
Very good; a good phrase.

BARDOLPH. Pardon, sir; I have heard the word.
'Phrase' call you it? By this day, I know not
the phrase; but I will maintain the word
with my sword to be a soldier-like word,
and a word of exceeding good command,
by heaven. Accommodated: that is, when
a man is, as they say, accommodated; or,
when a man is being-whereby 'a may be
thought to be accommodated; which is an
excellent thing.

Enter FALSTAFF

SHALLOW. It is very just. Look, here comes
good Sir John. Give me your good hand, give
me your worship's good hand. By my troth,
you like well and bear your years very well.
Welcome, good Sir John.

FALSTAFF. I am glad to see you well, good
Master Robert Shallow. Master Surecard, as
I think?

SHALLOW. No, Sir John; it is my cousin Silence,
in commission with me.

FALSTAFF. Good Master Silence, it well befits
you should be of the peace.

SILENCE. Your good worship is welcome.

FALSTAFF. Fie! this is hot weather. Gentlemen,
have you provided me here half a dozen
sufficient men?

SHALLOW. Marry, have we, sir. Will you sit?

FALSTAFF. Let me see them, I beseech you.

SHALLOW. Where's the roll? Where's the roll?
Where's the roll? Let me see, let me see,
let me see. So, so, so, so,-so, so-yea, marry,
sir. Rafe Mouldy! Let them appear as I call;
let them do so, let them do so. Let me see;
where is Mouldy?

MOULDY. Here, an't please you.

SHALLOW. What think you, Sir John? A good-limb'd fellow; young, strong, and of good friends.

FALSTAFF. Is thy name Mouldy?

MOULDY. Yea, an't please you.

FALSTAFF. 'Tis the more time thou wert us'd.

SHALLOW. Ha, ha, ha! most excellent, i' faith! Things that are mouldy lack use. Very singular good! In faith, well said, Sir John; very well said.

FALSTAFF. Prick him.

MOULDY. I was prick'd well enough before, an you could have let me alone. My old dame will be undone now for one to do her husbandry and her drudgery. You need not to have prick'd me; there are other men fitter to go out than I.

FALSTAFF. Go to; peace, Mouldy; you shall go. Mouldy, it is time you were spent.

MOULDY. Spent!

SHALLOW. Peace, fellow, peace; stand aside; know you where you are? For th' other, Sir John-let me see. Simon Shadow!

FALSTAFF. Yea, marry, let me have him to sit under. He's like to be a cold soldier.

SHALLOW. Where's Shadow?

SHADOW. Here, sir.

FALSTAFF. Shadow, whose son art thou?

SHADOW. My mother's son, sir.

FALSTAFF. Thy mother's son! Like enough; and thy father's shadow. So the son of the female is the shadow of the male. It is often so indeed; but much of the father's substance!

SHALLOW. Do you like him, Sir John?

FALSTAFF. Shadow will serve for summer. Prick him; for we have a number of shadows fill up the muster-book.

SHALLOW. Thomas Wart!

FALSTAFF. Where's he?

WART. Here, sir.

FALSTAFF. Is thy name Wart?

WART. Yea, sir.

FALSTAFF. Thou art a very ragged wart.

SHALLOW. Shall I prick him, Sir John?

FALSTAFF. It were superfluous; for his apparel is built upon his back, and the whole frame stands upon pins. Prick him no more.

SHALLOW. Ha, ha, ha! You can do it, sir; you can do it. I commend you well. Francis Feeble!

FEEBLE. Here, sir.

FALSTAFF. What trade art thou, Feeble?

FEEBLE. A woman's tailor, sir.

SHALLOW. Shall I prick him, sir?

FALSTAFF. You may; but if he had been a man's tailor, he'd ha' prick'd you. Wilt thou make as many holes in an enemy's battle as thou hast done in a woman's petticoat?

FEEBLE. I will do my good will, sir; you can have no more.

FALSTAFF. Well said, good woman's tailor! well said, courageous Feeble! Thou wilt be as valiant as the wrathful dove or most magnanimous mouse. Prick the woman's tailor-well, Master Shallow, deep, Master Shallow.

FEEBLE. I would Wart might have gone, sir.

FALSTAFF. I would thou wert a man's tailor, that thou mightst mend him and make him fit to go. I cannot put him to a private soldier, that is the leader of so many thousands. Let that suffice, most forcible Feeble.

FEEBLE. It shall suffice, sir.

FALSTAFF. I am bound to thee, reverend Feeble. Who is next?

SHALLOW. Peter Bullcalf o' th' green!

FALSTAFF. Yea, marry, let's see Bullcalf.

BULLCALF. Here, sir.

FALSTAFF. Fore God, a likely fellow! Come, prick me Bullcalf till he roar again.

BULLCALF. O Lord! good my lord captain-

FALSTAFF. What, dost thou roar before thou art prick'd?

BULLCALF. O Lord, sir! I am a diseased man.

FALSTAFF. What disease hast thou?

BULLCALF. A whoreson cold, sir, a cough, sir, which I caught with ringing in the King's affairs upon his coronation day, sir.

FALSTAFF. Come, thou shalt go to the wars in a gown. We will have away thy cold; and I will take such order that thy friends shall ring for thee. Is here all?

SHALLOW. Here is two more call'd than your number. You must have but four here, sir; and so, I pray you, go in with me to dinner.

FALSTAFF. Come, I will go drink with you, but I cannot tarry dinner. I am glad to see you, by my troth, Master Shallow.

SHALLOW. O, Sir John, do you remember since we lay all night in the windmill in Saint George's Field?

FALSTAFF. No more of that, Master Shallow, no more of that.

SHALLOW. Ha, 'twas a merry night. And is Jane Nightwork alive?

FALSTAFF. She lives, Master Shallow.

SHALLOW. She never could away with me.

FALSTAFF. Never, never; she would always say she could not abide Master Shallow.

SHALLOW. By the mass, I could anger her to th'

heart. She was then a bona-roba. Doth she hold her own well?

FALSTAFF. Old, old, Master Shallow.

SHALLOW. Nay, she must be old; she cannot choose but be old; certain she's old; and had Robin Nightwork, by old Nightwork, before I came to Clement's Inn.

SILENCE. That's fifty-five year ago.

SHALLOW. Ha, cousin Silence, that thou hadst seen that that this knight and I have seen! Ha, Sir John, said I well?

FALSTAFF. We have heard the chimes at midnight, Master Shallow.

SHALLOW. That we have, that we have, that we have; in faith, Sir John, we have. Our watchword was 'Hem, boys!' Come, let's to dinner; come, let's to dinner. Jesus, the days that we have seen! Come, come.

Exeunt FALSTAFF and the JUSTICES

BULLCALF. Good Master Corporate Bardolph, stand my friend; and there's four Harry ten shillings in French crowns for you. In very truth, sir, I had as lief be hang'd, sir, as go. And yet, for mine own part, sir, I do not care; but rather because I am unwilling and, for mine own part, have a desire to stay with my friends; else, sir, I did not care for mine own part so much.

BARDOLPH. Go to; stand aside.

MOULDY. And, good Master Corporal Captain, for my old dame's sake, stand my friend. She has nobody to do anything about her when I am gone; and she is old, and cannot help herself. You shall have forty, sir.

BARDOLPH. Go to; stand aside.

FEEBLE. By my troth, I care not; a man can die but once; we owe God a death. I'll ne'er bear a base mind. An't be my destiny, so; an't be not, so. No man's too good to serve 's Prince; and, let it go which way it will, he that dies this year is quit for the next.

BARDOLPH. Well said; th'art a good fellow.

FEEBLE. Faith, I'll bear no base mind.

Re-enter FALSTAFF and the JUSTICES

FALSTAFF. Come, sir, which men shall I have?

SHALLOW. Four of which you please.

BARDOLPH. Sir, a word with you. I have three pound to free Mouldy and Bullcalf.

FALSTAFF. Go to; well.

SHALLOW. Come, Sir John, which four will you have?

FALSTAFF. Do you choose for me.

SHALLOW. Marry, then-Mouldy, Bullcalf, Feeble, and Shadow.

FALSTAFF. Mouldy and Bullcalf: for you, Mouldy, stay at home till you are past service; and for your part, Bullcalf, grow you come unto it. I will none of you.

SHALLOW. Sir John, Sir John, do not yourself wrong. They are your likeliest men, and I would have you serv'd with the best.

FALSTAFF. Will you tell me, Master Shallow, how to choose a man? Care I for the limb, the thews, the stature, bulk, and big assemblance of a man! Give me the spirit, Master Shallow. Here's Wart; you see what a ragged appearance it is. 'A shall charge you and discharge you with the motion of a pewterer's hammer, come off and on swifter than he that gibbets on the brewer's bucket. And this same half-fac'd fellow, Shadow-give me this man. He presents no mark to the enemy; the foeman may with as great aim level at the edge of a penknife. And, for a retreat-how swiftly will this Feeble, the woman's tailor, run off! O, give me the spare men, and spare me the great ones. Put me a caliver into Wart's hand, Bardolph.

BARDOLPH. Hold, Wart. Traverse-thus, thus, thus.

FALSTAFF. Come, manage me your caliver. So-very well. Go to; very good; exceeding good. O, give me always a little, lean, old, chopt, bald shot. Well said, i' faith, Wart; th'art a good scab. Hold, there's a tester for thee.

SHALLOW. He is not his craft's master, he doth not do it right. I remember at Mile-end Green, when I lay at Clement's Inn-I was then Sir Dagonet in Arthur's show-there was a little quiver fellow, and 'a would manage you his piece thus; and 'a would about and about, and come you in and come you in. 'Rah, tah, tah!' would 'a say; 'Bounce!' would 'a say; and away again would 'a go, and again would 'a come. I shall ne'er see such a fellow.

FALSTAFF. These fellows will do well. Master Shallow, God keep you! Master Silence, I will not use many words with you: Fare you well! Gentlemen both, I thank you. I must a dozen mile to-night. Bardolph, give the soldiers coats.

SHALLOW. Sir John, the Lord bless you; God prosper your affairs; God send us peace! At your return, visit our house; let our old acquaintance be renewed. Peradventure I will with ye to the court.

FALSTAFF. Fore God, would you would.

SHALLOW. Go to; I have spoke at a word. God keep you.

FALSTAFF. Fare you well, gentle gentlemen.

[Exeunt JUSTICES] On, Bardolph; lead the men away. *[Exeunt all but FALSTAFF]* As I return, I will fetch off these justices. I do see the bottom of justice Shallow. Lord, Lord, how subject we old men are to this vice of lying! This same starv'd justice hath done nothing but prate to me of the wildness of his youth and the feats he hath done about Turnbull Street; and every third word a lie, duer paid to the hearer than the Turk's tribute. I do remember him at Clement's Inn, like a man made after supper of a cheese-paring. When 'a was naked, he was for all the world like a fork'd radish, with a head fantastically carved upon it with a knife. 'A was so forlorn that his dimensions to any thick sight were invisible. 'A was the very genius of famine; yet lecherous as a monkey, and the whores call'd him mandrake. 'A came ever in the rearward of the fashion, and sung those tunes to the overscutch'd huswifes that he heard the carmen whistle, and sware they were his fancies or his good-nights. And now is this Vice's dagger become a squire, and talks as familiarly of John a Gaunt as if he had been sworn brother to him; and I'll be sworn 'a ne'er saw him but once in the Tiltyard; and then he burst his head for crowding among the marshal's men. I saw it, and told John a Gaunt he beat his own name; for you might have thrust him and all his apparel into an eel-skin; the case of a treble hautboy was a mansion for him, a court-and now has he land and beeves. Well, I'll be acquainted with him if I return; and 't shall go hard but I'll make him a philosopher's two stones to me. If the young dace be a bait for the old pike, I see no reason in the law of nature but I may snap at him. Let time shape, and there an end.

Exit.

ACT IV

SCENE I

Yorkshire. Within the Forest of Gaultree

Enter the ARCHBISHOP OF YORK, MOWBRAY, HASTINGS, and Others

ARCHBISHOP. What is this forest call'd
HASTINGS. 'Tis Gaultree Forest, an't shall please your Grace.

ARCHBISHOP. Here stand, my lords, and send discoverers forth
　To know the numbers of our enemies.
HASTINGS. We have sent forth already.
ARCHBISHOP. 'Tis well done.
　My friends and brethren in these great affairs,
　I must acquaint you that I have receiv'd
　New-dated letters from Northumberland;
　Their cold intent, tenor, and substance, thus:
　Here doth he wish his person, with
　　such powers
　As might hold sortance with his quality,
　The which he could not levy; whereupon
　He is retir'd, to ripe his growing fortunes,
　To Scotland; and concludes in hearty prayers
　That your attempts may overlive the hazard
　And fearful meeting of their opposite.
MOWBRAY. Thus do the hopes we have in him touch ground
　And dash themselves to pieces.

Enter a MESSENGER

HASTINGS. Now, what news?
MESSENGER. West of this forest, scarcely off
　　a mile,
　In goodly form comes on the enemy;
　And, by the ground they hide, I judge
　　their number
　Upon or near the rate of thirty thousand.
MOWBRAY. The just proportion that we gave them out.
　Let us sway on and face them in the field.

Enter WESTMORELAND

ARCHBISHOP. What well-appointed leader fronts us here?
MOWBRAY. I think it is my Lord
　of Westmoreland.
WESTMORELAND. Health and fair greeting from our general,
　The Prince, Lord John and Duke of Lancaster.
ARCHBISHOP. Say on, my Lord of Westmoreland, in peace,
　What doth concern your coming.
WESTMORELAND. Then, my lord,
　Unto your Grace do I in chief address
　The substance of my speech. If that rebellion
　Came like itself, in base and abject routs,
　Led on by bloody youth, guarded with rags,
　And countenanc'd by boys and beggary-
　I say, if damn'd commotion so appear'd
　In his true, native, and most proper shape,
　You, reverend father, and these noble lords,
　Had not been here to dress the ugly form
　Of base and bloody insurrection

With your fair honours. You, Lord Archbishop,
Whose see is by a civil peace maintain'd,
Whose beard the silver hand of peace
 hath touch'd,
Whose learning and good letters peace
 hath tutor'd,
Whose white investments figure innocence,
The dove, and very blessed spirit of peace-
Wherefore you do so ill translate yourself
Out of the speech of peace, that bears
 such grace,
Into the harsh and boist'rous tongue of war;
Turning your books to graves, your ink to blood,
Your pens to lances, and your tongue divine
To a loud trumpet and a point of war?
ARCHBISHOP. Wherefore do I this? So the
 question stands.
Briefly to this end: we are all diseas'd
And with our surfeiting and wanton hours
Have brought ourselves into a burning fever,
And we must bleed for it; of which disease
Our late King, Richard, being infected, died.
But, my most noble Lord of Westmoreland,
I take not on me here as a physician;
Nor do I as an enemy to peace
Troop in the throngs of military men;
But rather show awhile like fearful war
To diet rank minds sick of happiness,
And purge th' obstructions which begin to stop
Our very veins of life. Hear me more plainly.
I have in equal balance justly weigh'd
What wrongs our arms may do, what wrongs
 we suffer,
And find our griefs heavier than our offences.
We see which way the stream of time doth run
And are enforc'd from our most quiet there
By the rough torrent of occasion;
And have the summary of all our griefs,
When time shall serve, to show in articles;
Which long ere this we offer'd to the King,
And might by no suit gain our audience:
When we are wrong'd, and would unfold
 our griefs,
We are denied access unto his person,
Even by those men that most have done
 us wrong.
The dangers of the days but newly gone,
Whose memory is written on the earth
With yet appearing blood, and the examples
Of every minute's instance, present now,
Hath put us in these ill-beseeming arms;
Not to break peace, or any branch of it,
But to establish here a peace indeed,

Concurring both in name and quality.
WESTMORELAND. When ever yet was your
 appeal denied;
Wherein have you been galled by the King;
What peer hath been suborn'd to grate on you
That you should seal this lawless bloody book
Of forg'd rebellion with a seal divine,
And consecrate commotion's bitter edge?
ARCHBISHOP. My brother general,
 the commonwealth,
To brother born an household cruelty,
I make my quarrel in particular.
WESTMORELAND. There is no need of any
 such redress;
Or if there were, it not belongs to you.
MOWBRAY. Why not to him in part, and to us all
That feel the bruises of the days before,
And suffer the condition of these times
To lay a heavy and unequal hand
Upon our honours?
WESTMORELAND. O my good Lord Mowbray,
Construe the times to their necessities,
And you shall say, indeed, it is the time,
And not the King, that doth you injuries.
Yet, for your part, it not appears to me,
Either from the King or in the present time,
That you should have an inch of any ground
To build a grief on. Were you not restor'd
To all the Duke of Norfolk's signiories,
Your noble and right well-rememb'red father's?
MOWBRAY. What thing, in honour, had my
 father lost
That need to be reviv'd and breath'd in me?
The King that lov'd him, as the state stood then,
Was force perforce compell'd to banish him,
And then that Henry Bolingbroke and he,
Being mounted and both roused in their seats,
Their neighing coursers daring of the spur,
Their armed staves in charge, their
 beavers down,
Their eyes of fire sparkling through sights
 of steel,
And the loud trumpet blowing them together-
Then, then, when there was nothing could
 have stay'd
My father from the breast of Bolingbroke,
O, when the King did throw his warder down-
His own life hung upon the staff he threw-
Then threw he down himself, and all their lives
That by indictment and by dint of sword
Have since miscarried under Bolingbroke.
WESTMORELAND. You speak, Lord Mowbray,
 now you know not what.

The Earl of Hereford was reputed then
In England the most valiant gentleman.
Who knows on whom fortune would then
 have smil'd?
But if your father had been victor there,
He ne'er had borne it out of Coventry;
For all the country, in a general voice,
Cried hate upon him; and all their prayers
 and love
Were set on Hereford, whom they doted on,
And bless'd and grac'd indeed more than
 the King.
But this is mere digression from my purpose.
Here come I from our princely general
To know your griefs; to tell you from his Grace
That he will give you audience; and wherein
It shall appear that your demands are just,
You shall enjoy them, everything set off
That might so much as think you enemies.
MOWBRAY. But he hath forc'd us to compel
 this offer;
And it proceeds from policy, not love.
WESTMORELAND. Mowbray, you overween to
 take it so.
This offer comes from mercy, not from fear;
For, lo! within a ken our army lies-
Upon mine honour, all too confident
To give admittance to a thought of fear.
Our battle is more full of names than yours,
Our men more perfect in the use of arms,
Our armour all as strong, our cause the best;
Then reason will our hearts should be as good.
Say you not, then, our offer is compell'd.
MOWBRAY. Well, by my will we shall admit
 no parley.
WESTMORELAND. That argues but the shame of
 your offence:
A rotten case abides no handling.
HASTINGS. Hath the Prince John a
 full commission,
In very ample virtue of his father,
To hear and absolutely to determine
Of what conditions we shall stand upon?
WESTMORELAND. That is intended in the
 general's name.
I muse you make so slight a question.
ARCHBISHOP. Then take, my Lord of
 Westmoreland, this schedule,
For this contains our general grievances.
Each several article herein redress'd,
All members of our cause, both here
 and hence,
That are insinewed to this action,

Acquitted by a true substantial form,
And present execution of our wills
To us and to our purposes confin'd-
We come within our awful banks again,
And knit our powers to the arm of peace.
WESTMORELAND. This will I show the general.
 Please you, lords,
In sight of both our battles we may meet;
And either end in peace-which God so frame!-
Or to the place of diff'rence call the swords
Which must decide it.
ARCHBISHOP. My lord, we will do so.

Exit WESTMORELAND.

MOWBRAY. There is a thing within my bosom
 tells me
That no conditions of our peace can stand.
HASTINGS. Fear you not that: if we can make
 our peace
Upon such large terms and so absolute
As our conditions shall consist upon,
Our peace shall stand as firm as
 rocky mountains.
MOWBRAY. Yea, but our valuation shall be such
That every slight and false-derived cause,
Yea, every idle, nice, and wanton reason,
Shall to the King taste of this action;
That, were our royal faiths martyrs in love,
We shall be winnow'd with so rough a wind
That even our corn shall seem as light as chaff,
And good from bad find no partition.
ARCHBISHOP. No, no, my lord. Note this: the
 King is weary
Of dainty and such picking grievances;
For he hath found to end one doubt by death
Revives two greater in the heirs of life;
And therefore will he wipe his tables clean,
And keep no tell-tale to his memory
That may repeat and history his loss
To new remembrance. For full well he knows
He cannot so precisely weed this land
As his misdoubts present occasion:
His foes are so enrooted with his friends
That, plucking to unfix an enemy,
He doth unfasten so and shake a friend.
So that this land, like an offensive wife
That hath enrag'd him on to offer strokes,
As he is striking, holds his infant up,
And hangs resolv'd correction in the arm
That was uprear'd to execution.
HASTINGS. Besides, the King hath wasted all
 his rods
On late offenders, that he now doth lack
The very instruments of chastisement;

So that his power, like to a fangless lion,
  May offer, but not hold.
ARCHBISHOP. 'Tis very true;
  And therefore be assur'd, my good Lord Marshal,
  If we do now make our atonement well,
  Our peace will, like a broken limb united,
  Grow stronger for the breaking.
MOWBRAY. Be it so.
  Here is return'd my Lord of Westmoreland.

Re-enter WESTMORELAND

WESTMORELAND. The Prince is here at hand.
  Pleaseth your lordship
  To meet his Grace just distance 'tween
  our armies?
MOWBRAY. Your Grace of York, in God's name
  then, set forward.
ARCHBISHOP. Before, and greet his Grace. My
  lord, we come.   *Exeunt*

✤ SCENE II ✤

Another part of the forest

*Enter, from one side, MOWBRAY, attended; afterwards, the
ARCHBISHOP, HASTINGS, and Others; from the other side,
PRINCE JOHN of LANCASTER, WESTMORELAND,
OFFICERS, and Others*

PRINCE JOHN. You are well encount'red here, my
  cousin Mowbray.
  Good day to you, gentle Lord Archbishop;
  And so to you, Lord Hastings, and to all.
  My Lord of York, it better show'd with you
  When that your flock, assembled by the bell,
  Encircled you to hear with reverence
  Your exposition on the holy text
  Than now to see you here an iron man,
  Cheering a rout of rebels with your drum,
  Turning the word to sword, and life to death.
  That man that sits within a monarch's heart
  And ripens in the sunshine of his favour,
  Would he abuse the countenance of the king,
  Alack, what mischiefs might he set abroach
  In shadow of such greatness! With you,
  Lord Bishop,
  It is even so. Who hath not heard it spoken
  How deep you were within the books of God?
  To us the speaker in His parliament,
  To us th' imagin'd voice of God himself,
  The very opener and intelligencer
  Between the grace, the sanctities of heaven,
  And our dull workings. O, who shall believe
  But you misuse the reverence of your place,

Employ the countenance and grace of heav'n
  As a false favourite doth his prince's name,
  In deeds dishonourable? You have ta'en up,
  Under the counterfeited zeal of God,
  The subjects of His substitute, my father,
  And both against the peace of heaven and him
  Have here up-swarm'd them.
ARCHBISHOP. Good my Lord of Lancaster,
  I am not here against your father's peace;
  But, as I told my Lord of Westmoreland,
  The time misord'red doth, in common sense,
  Crowd us and crush us to this monstrous form
  To hold our safety up. I sent your Grace
  The parcels and particulars of our grief,
  The which hath been with scorn shov'd from
  the court,
  Whereon this hydra son of war is born;
  Whose dangerous eyes may well be
  charm'd asleep
  With grant of our most just and right desires;
  And true obedience, of this madness cur'd,
  Stoop tamely to the foot of majesty.
MOWBRAY. If not, we ready are to try our fortunes
  To the last man.
HASTINGS. And though we here fall down,
  We have supplies to second our attempt.
  If they miscarry, theirs shall second them;
  And so success of mischief shall be born,
  And heir from heir shall hold this quarrel up
  Whiles England shall have generation.
PRINCE JOHN. You are too shallow, Hastings,
  much to shallow,
  To sound the bottom of the after-times.
WESTMORELAND. Pleaseth your Grace to answer
  them directly
  How far forth you do like their articles.
PRINCE JOHN. I like them all and do allow
  them well;
  And swear here, by the honour of my blood,
  My father's purposes have been mistook;
  And some about him have too lavishly
  Wrested his meaning and authority.
  My lord, these griefs shall be with
  speed redress'd;
  Upon my soul, they shall. If this may please you,
  Discharge your powers unto their
  several counties,
  As we will ours; and here, between the armies,
  Let's drink together friendly and embrace,
  That all their eyes may bear those tokens home
  Of our restored love and amity.
ARCHBISHOP. I take your princely word for
  these redresses.

PRINCE JOHN. I give it you, and will maintain
my word;
And thereupon I drink unto your Grace.
HASTINGS. Go, Captain, and deliver to the army
This news of peace. Let them have pay,
and part.
I know it will please them. Hie thee, Captain.
Exit OFFICER
ARCHBISHOP. To you, my noble Lord of
Westmoreland.
WESTMORELAND. I pledge your Grace; and if
you knew what pains
I have bestow'd to breed this present peace,
You would drink freely; but my love to ye
Shall show itself more openly hereafter.
ARCHBISHOP. I do not doubt you.
WESTMORELAND. I am glad of it.
Health to my lord and gentle cousin, Mowbray.
MOWBRAY. You wish me health in very
happy season,
For I am on the sudden something ill.
ARCHBISHOP. Against ill chances men are
ever merry;
But heaviness foreruns the good event.
WESTMORELAND. Therefore be merry, coz;
since sudden sorrow
Serves to say thus, 'Some good thing comes to-
morrow.'
ARCHBISHOP. Believe me, I am passing light
in spirit.
MOWBRAY. So much the worse, if your own rule
be true.   *Shouts within*
PRINCE JOHN. The word of peace is rend'red.
Hark, how they shout!
MOWBRAY. This had been cheerful after victory.
ARCHBISHOP. A peace is of the nature of
a conquest;
For then both parties nobly are subdu'd,
And neither party loser.
PRINCE JOHN. Go, my lord,
And let our army be discharged too.
Exit WESTMORELAND.
And, good my lord, so please you let our trains
March by us, that we may peruse the men
We should have cop'd withal.
ARCHBISHOP. Go, good Lord Hastings,
And, ere they be dismiss'd, let them march by.
Exit HASTINGS.
PRINCE JOHN. I trust, lords, we shall lie to-
night together.
Re-enter WESTMORELAND
Now, cousin, wherefore stands our army still?
WESTMORELAND. The leaders, having charge

from you to stand,
Will not go off until they hear you speak.
PRINCE JOHN. They know their duties.
Re-enter HASTINGS
HASTINGS. My lord, our army is
dispers'd already.
Like youthful steers unyok'd, they take
their courses
East, west, north, south; or like a school
broke up,
Each hurries toward his home and sporting-
place.
WESTMORELAND. Good tidings, my Lord
Hastings; for the which
I do arrest thee, traitor, of high treason;
And you, Lord Archbishop, and you,
Lord Mowbray,
Of capital treason I attach you both.
MOWBRAY. Is this proceeding just
and honourable?
WESTMORELAND. Is your assembly so?
ARCHBISHOP. Will you thus break your faith?
PRINCE JOHN. I pawn'd thee none:
I promis'd you redress of these same grievances
Whereof you did complain; which, by
mine honour,
I will perform with a most Christian care.
But for you, rebels-look to taste the due
Meet for rebellion and such acts as yours.
Most shallowly did you these arms commence,
Fondly brought here, and foolishly sent hence.
Strike up our drums, pursue the scatt'red stray.
God, and not we, hath safely fought to-day.
Some guard these traitors to the block
of death,
Treason's true bed and yielder-up of breath.
Exeunt.

❧ SCENE III ❧
Another part of the forest

*Alarum; excursions. Enter FALSTAFF and
COLVILLE, meeting*

FALSTAFF. What's your name, sir? Of what
condition are you, and of what place, I pray?
COLVILLE. I am a knight sir; and my name is
Colville of the Dale.
FALSTAFF. Well then, Colville is your name, a
knight is your degree, and your place the Dale.
Colville shall still be your name, a traitor your
degree, and the dungeon your place-a place

deep enough; so shall you be still Colville of
the Dale.

COLVILLE. Are not you Sir John Falstaff?

FALSTAFF. As good a man as he, sir, whoe'er I
am. Do you yield, sir, or shall I sweat for you?
If I do sweat, they are the drops of thy lovers,
and they weep for thy death; therefore rouse
up fear and trembling, and do observance to
my mercy.

COLVILLE. I think you are Sir John Falstaff, and
in that thought yield me.

FALSTAFF. I have a whole school of tongues in
this belly of mine; and not a tongue of them
all speaks any other word but my name. An
I had but a belly of any indifferency, I were
simply the most active fellow in Europe. My
womb, my womb, my womb undoes me.
Here comes our general.

Enter PRINCE JOHN OF LANCASTER,
WESTMORELAND, BLUNT, and Others

PRINCE JOHN. The heat is past; follow no
further now.
Call in the powers, good
cousin Westmoreland.

Exit WESTMORELAND

Now, Falstaff, where have you been all
this while?
When everything is ended, then you come.
These tardy tricks of yours will, on my life,
One time or other break some gallows' back.

FALSTAFF. I would be sorry, my lord, but it
should be thus: I never knew yet but rebuke
and check was the reward of valour. Do you
think me a swallow, an arrow, or a bullet?
Have I, in my poor and old motion, the
expedition of thought? I have speeded hither
with the very extremest inch of possibility;
I have found'red nine score and odd posts;
and here, travel-tainted as I am, have, in my
pure and immaculate valour, taken Sir John
Colville of the Dale, a most furious knight and
valorous enemy. But what of that? He saw
me, and yielded; that I may justly say with
the hook-nos'd fellow of Rome-I came, saw,
and overcame.

PRINCE JOHN. It was more of his courtesy than
your deserving.

FALSTAFF. I know not. Here he is, and here I
yield him; and I beseech your Grace, let it be
book'd with the rest of this day's deeds; or,
by the Lord, I will have it in a particular ballad
else, with mine own picture on the top on't,
Colville kissing my foot; to the which course

if I be enforc'd, if you do not all show like gilt
twopences to me, and I, in the clear sky of
fame, o'ershine you as much as the full moon
doth the cinders of the element, which show
like pins' heads to her, believe not the word
of the noble. Therefore let me have right, and
let desert mount.

PRINCE JOHN. Thine's too heavy to mount.

FALSTAFF. Let it shine, then.

PRINCE JOHN. Thine's too thick to shine.

FALSTAFF. Let it do something, my good lord,
that may do me good, and call it what you will.

PRINCE JOHN. Is thy name Colville?

COLVILLE. It is, my lord.

PRINCE JOHN. A famous rebel art thou, Colville.

FALSTAFF. And a famous true subject took him.

COLVILLE. I am, my lord, but as my betters are
That led me hither. Had they been rul'd
by me,
You should have won them dearer than
you have.

FALSTAFF. I know not how they sold
themselves; but thou, like a kind fellow,
gavest thyself away gratis; and I thank thee
for thee.

Re-enter WESTMORELAND

PRINCE JOHN. Now, have you left pursuit?

WESTMORELAND. Retreat is made, and
execution stay'd.

PRINCE JOHN. Send Colville, with
his confederates,
To York, to present execution.
Blunt, lead him hence; and see you guard
him sure.

Exeunt BLUNT and Others

And now dispatch we toward the court,
my lords.
I hear the King my father is sore sick.
Our news shall go before us to his Majesty,
Which, cousin, you shall bear to comfort him
And we with sober speed will follow you.

FALSTAFF. My lord, I beseech you, give me
leave to go through Gloucestershire; and,
when you come to court, stand my good lord,
pray, in your good report.

PRINCE JOHN. Fare you well, Falstaff. I, in
my condition,
Shall better speak of you than you deserve.

Exeunt all but FALSTAFF

FALSTAFF. I would you had but the wit; 'twere
better than your dukedom. Good faith, this
same young sober-blooded boy doth not love
me; nor a man cannot make him laugh-but

that's no marvel; he drinks no wine. There's
never none of these demure boys come to
any proof; for thin drink doth so over-cool
their blood, and making many fish-meals,
that they fall into a kind of male green-
sickness; and then, when they marry, they
get wenches. They are generally fools and
cowards-which some of us should be too,
but for inflammation. A good sherris-sack
hath a two-fold operation in it. It ascends
me into the brain; dries me there all the
foolish and dull and crudy vapours which
environ it; makes it apprehensive, quick,
forgetive, full of nimble, fiery, and delectable
shapes; which delivered o'er to the voice, the
tongue, which is the birth, becomes excellent
wit. The second property of your excellent
sherris is the warming of the blood; which
before, cold and settled, left the liver white
and pale, which is the badge of pusillanimity
and cowardice; but the sherris warms it,
and makes it course from the inwards to the
parts extremes. It illumineth the face, which,
as a beacon, gives warning to all the rest of
this little kingdom, man, to arm; and then
the vital commoners and inland petty spirits
muster me all to their captain, the heart, who,
great and puff'd up with this retinue, doth
any deed of courage-and this valour comes
of sherris. So that skill in the weapon is
nothing without sack, for that sets it a-work;
and learning, a mere hoard of gold kept by a
devil till sack commences it and sets it in act
and use. Hereof comes it that Prince Harry
is valiant; for the cold blood he did naturally
inherit of his father, he hath, like lean, sterile,
and bare land, manured, husbanded, and
till'd, with excellent endeavour of drinking
good and good store of fertile sherris, that
he is become very hot and valiant. If I had a
thousand sons, the first humane principle I
would teach them should be to forswear thin
potations and to addict themselves to sack.

Enter BARDOLPH

How now, Bardolph!

BARDOLPH. The army is discharged all
and gone.

FALSTAFF. Let them go. I'll through
Gloucestershire, and there will I visit
Master Robert Shallow, Esquire. I have him
already temp'ring between my finger and
my thumb, and shortly will I seal with him.
Come away.   *Exeunt*

⚜ SCENE IV ⚜
Westminster. The Jerusalem Chamber

*Enter the KING, PRINCE THOMAS OF CLARENCE,
PRINCE HUMPHREY OF GLOUCESTER, WARWICK,
and Others*

KING. Now, lords, if God doth give successful end
To this debate that bleedeth at our doors,
We will our youth lead on to higher fields,
And draw no swords but what are sanctified.
Our navy is address'd, our power connected,
Our substitutes in absence well invested,
And everything lies level to our wish.
Only we want a little personal strength;
And pause us till these rebels, now afoot,
Come underneath the yoke of government.

WARWICK. Both which we doubt not but
your Majesty
Shall soon enjoy.

KING. Humphrey, my son of Gloucester,
Where is the Prince your brother?

PRINCE HUMPHREY. I think he's gone to hunt,
my lord, at Windsor.

KING. And how accompanied?

PRINCE HUMPHREY. I do not know, my lord.

KING. Is not his brother, Thomas of Clarence,
with him?

PRINCE HUMPHREY. No, my good lord, he is in
presence here.

CLARENCE. What would my lord and father?

KING. Nothing but well to thee, Thomas
of Clarence.
How chance thou art not with the Prince
thy brother?
He loves thee, and thou dost neglect
him, Thomas.
Thou hast a better place in his affection
Than all thy brothers; cherish it, my boy,
And noble offices thou mayst effect
Of mediation, after I am dead,
Between his greatness and thy other brethren.
Therefore omit him not; blunt not his love,
Nor lose the good advantage of his grace
By seeming cold or careless of his will;
For he is gracious if he be observ'd.
He hath a tear for pity and a hand
Open as day for melting charity;
Yet notwithstanding, being incens'd, he is flint;
As humorous as winter, and as sudden
As flaws congealed in the spring of day.
His temper, therefore, must be well observ'd.

Chide him for faults, and do it reverently,
When you perceive his blood inclin'd to mirth;
But, being moody, give him line and scope
Till that his passions, like a whale on ground,
Confound themselves with working. Learn
this, Thomas,
And thou shalt prove a shelter to thy friends,
A hoop of gold to bind thy brothers in,
That the united vessel of their blood,
Mingled with venom of suggestion-
As, force perforce, the age will pour it in-
Shall never leak, though it do work as strong
As aconitum or rash gunpowder.

CLARENCE. I shall observe him with all care
and love.

KING. Why art thou not at Windsor with
him, Thomas?

CLARENCE. He is not there to-day; he dines
in London.

KING. And how accompanied? Canst thou
tell that?

CLARENCE. With Poins, and other his
continual followers.

KING. Most subject is the fattest soil to weeds;
And he, the noble image of my youth,
Is overspread with them; therefore my grief
Stretches itself beyond the hour of death.
The blood weeps from my heart when I
do shape,
In forms imaginary, th' unguided days
And rotten times that you shall look upon
When I am sleeping with my ancestors.
For when his headstrong riot hath no curb,
When rage and hot blood are his counsellors
When means and lavish manners meet together,
O, with what wings shall his affections fly
Towards fronting peril and oppos'd decay!

WARWICK. My gracious lord, you look beyond
him quite.
The Prince but studies his companions
Like a strange tongue, wherein, to gain
the language,
'Tis needful that the most immodest word
Be look'd upon and learnt; which once attain'd,
Your Highness knows, comes to no further use
But to be known and hated. So, like gross terms,
The Prince will, in the perfectness of time,
Cast off his followers; and their memory
Shall as a pattern or a measure live
By which his Grace must mete the lives of other,
Turning past evils to advantages.

KING. 'Tis seldom when the bee doth leave
her comb

In the dead carrion.

Enter WESTMORELAND

Who's here? Westmoreland?

WESTMORELAND. Health to my sovereign, and
new happiness
Added to that that I am to deliver!
Prince John, your son, doth kiss your
Grace's hand.
Mowbray, the Bishop Scroop, Hastings, and all,
Are brought to the correction of your law.
There is not now a rebel's sword unsheath'd,
But Peace puts forth her olive everywhere.
The manner how this action hath been borne
Here at more leisure may your Highness read,
With every course in his particular.

KING. O Westmoreland, thou art a summer bird,
Which ever in the haunch of winter sings
The lifting up of day.

Enter HARCOURT

Look, here's more news.

HARCOURT. From enemies heaven keep
your Majesty;
And, when they stand against you, may they fall
As those that I am come to tell you of!
The Earl Northumberland and the
Lord Bardolph,
With a great power of English and of Scots,
Are by the shrieve of Yorkshire overthrown.
The manner and true order of the fight
This packet, please it you, contains at large.

KING. And wherefore should these good news
make me sick?
Will Fortune never come with both hands full,
But write her fair words still in foulest letters?
She either gives a stomach and no food-
Such are the poor, in health-or else a feast,
And takes away the stomach-such are the rich
That have abundance and enjoy it not.
I should rejoice now at this happy news;
And now my sight fails, and my brain is giddy.
O me! come near me now. I am much ill.

PRINCE HUMPHREY. Comfort, your Majesty!

CLARENCE. O my royal father!

WESTMORELAND. My sovereign lord, cheer up
yourself, look up.

WARWICK. Be patient, Princes; you do know
these fits
Are with his Highness very ordinary.
Stand from him, give him air; he'll straight
be well.

CLARENCE. No, no; he cannot long hold out
these pangs.
Th' incessant care and labour of his mind

Hath wrought the mure that should confine it in
So thin that life looks through, and will
  break out.
PRINCE HUMPHREY. The people fear me; for they
  do observe
Unfather'd heirs and loathly births of nature.
The seasons change their manners, as the year
Had found some months asleep, and leapt
  them over.
CLARENCE. The river hath thrice flow'd, no
  ebb between;
  And the old folk, Time's doting chronicles,
  Say it did so a little time before
  That our great grandsire, Edward, sick'd
  and died.
WARWICK. Speak lower, Princes, for the
  King recovers.
PRINCE HUMPHREY. This apoplexy will certain be
  his end.
KING. I pray you take me up, and bear me hence
Into some other chamber. Softly, pray. *Exeunt.*

☙ SCENE V ☙
Westminster. Another chamber

The KING lying on a bed; CLARENCE, GLOUCESTER,
WARWICK, and Others in attendance

KING. Let there be no noise made, my
  gentle friends;
Unless some dull and favourable hand
Will whisper music to my weary spirit.
WARWICK. Call for the music in the other room.
KING. Set me the crown upon my pillow here.
CLARENCE. His eye is hollow, and he
  ·changes much.
WARWICK. Less noise! less noise!
            Enter PRINCE HENRY
PRINCE. Who saw the Duke of Clarence?
CLARENCE. I am here, brother, full of heaviness.
PRINCE. How now! Rain within doors, and
  none abroad!
  How doth the King?
PRINCE HUMPHREY. Exceeding ill.
PRINCE. Heard he the good news yet? Tell it him.
PRINCE HUMPHREY. He alt'red much upon the
  hearing it.
PRINCE. If he be sick with joy, he'll recover
  without physic.
WARWICK. Not so much noise, my lords. Sweet
  Prince, speak low;
  The King your father is dispos'd to sleep.

CLARENCE. Let us withdraw into the other room.
WARWICK. Will't please your Grace to go along
  with us?
PRINCE. No; I will sit and watch here by the King.
            Exeunt all but the PRINCE.
Why doth the crown lie there upon his pillow,
Being so troublesome a bedfellow?
O polish'd perturbation! golden care!
That keep'st the ports of slumber open wide
To many a watchful night! Sleep with it now!
Yet not so sound and half so deeply sweet
As he whose brow with homely biggen bound
Snores out the watch of night. O majesty!
When thou dost pinch thy bearer, thou dost sit
Like a rich armour worn in heat of day
That scald'st with safety. By his gates of breath
There lies a downy feather which stirs not.
Did he suspire, that light and weightless down
Perforce must move. My gracious lord! my father!
This sleep is sound indeed; this is a sleep
That from this golden rigol hath divorc'd
So many English kings. Thy due from me
Is tears and heavy sorrows of the blood
Which nature, love, and filial tenderness,
Shall, O dear father, pay thee plenteously.
My due from thee is this imperial crown,
Which, as immediate from thy place and blood,
Derives itself to me. [*Putting on the crown*] Lo where
  it sits-
Which God shall guard; and put the world's
  whole strength
Into one giant arm, it shall not force
This lineal honour from me. This from thee
Will I to mine leave as 'tis left to me. *Exit.*
KING. Warwick! Gloucester! Clarence!
       Re-enter WARWICK, GLOUCESTER, CLARENCE
CLARENCE. Doth the King call?
WARWICK. What would your Majesty? How fares
  your Grace?
KING. Why did you leave me here alone, my lords?
CLARENCE. We left the Prince my brother here,
  my liege,
  Who undertook to sit and watch by you.
KING. The Prince of Wales! Where is he? Let me
  see him.
  He is not here.
WARWICK. This door is open; he is gone this way.
PRINCE HUMPHREY. He came not through the
  chamber where we stay'd.
KING. Where is the crown? Who took it from
  my pillow?
WARWICK. When we withdrew, my liege, we left
  it here.

KING. The Prince hath ta'en it hence. Go, seek
  him out.
  Is he so hasty that he doth suppose
  My sleep my death?
  Find him, my lord of Warwick; chide
  him hither.

               Exit WARWICK.

  This part of his conjoins with my disease
  And helps to end me. See, sons, what things
  you are!
  How quickly nature falls into revolt
  When gold becomes her object!
  For this the foolish over-careful fathers
  Have broke their sleep with thoughts,
  Their brains with care, their bones
  with industry;
  For this they have engrossed and pil'd up
  The cank'red heaps of strange-achieved gold;
  For this they have been thoughtful to invest
  Their sons with arts and martial exercises;
  When, like the bee, tolling from every flower
  The virtuous sweets,
  Our thighs with wax, our mouths with
  honey pack'd,
  We bring it to the hive, and, like the bees,
  Are murd'red for our pains. This bitter taste
  Yields his engrossments to the ending father.

        Re-enter WARWICK

  Now where is he that will not stay so long
  Till his friend sickness hath determin'd me?
WARWICK. My lord, I found the Prince in the
  next room,
  Washing with kindly tears his gentle cheeks,
  With such a deep demeanour in great sorrow,
  That tyranny, which never quaff'd but blood,
  Would, by beholding him, have wash'd his knife
  With gentle eye-drops. He is coming hither.
KING. But wherefore did he take away
  the crown?

      Re-enter PRINCE HENRY

  Lo where he comes. Come hither to me, Harry.
  Depart the chamber, leave us here alone.

     Exeunt all but the KING and the PRINCE.

PRINCE. I never thought to hear you speak again.
KING. Thy wish was father, Harry, to
  that thought.
  I stay too long by thee, I weary thee.
  Dost thou so hunger for mine empty chair
  That thou wilt needs invest thee with
  my honours
  Before thy hour be ripe? O foolish youth!
  Thou seek'st the greatness that will
  overwhelm thee.

  Stay but a little, for my cloud of dignity
  Is held from falling with so weak a wind
  That it will quickly drop; my day is dim.
  Thou hast stol'n that which, after some
  few hours,
  Were thine without offence; and at my death
  Thou hast seal'd up my expectation.
  Thy life did manifest thou lov'dst me not,
  And thou wilt have me die assur'd of it.
  Thou hid'st a thousand daggers in thy thoughts,
  Which thou hast whetted on thy stony heart,
  To stab at half an hour of my life.
  What, canst thou not forbear me half an hour?
  Then get thee gone, and dig my grave thyself;
  And bid the merry bells ring to thine ear
  That thou art crowned, not that I am dead.
  Let all the tears that should bedew my hearse
  Be drops of balm to sanctify thy head;
  Only compound me with forgotten dust;
  Give that which gave thee life unto the worms.
  Pluck down my officers, break my decrees;
  For now a time is come to mock at form-
  Harry the Fifth is crown'd. Up, vanity:
  Down, royal state. All you sage counsellors,
  hence.
  And to the English court assemble now,
  From every region, apes of idleness.
  Now, neighbour confines, purge you of
  your scum.
  Have you a ruffian that will swear, drink, dance,
  Revel the night, rob, murder, and commit
  The oldest sins the newest kind of ways?
  Be happy, he will trouble you no more.
  England shall double gild his treble guilt;
  England shall give him office, honour, might;
  For the fifth Harry from curb'd licence plucks
  The muzzle of restraint, and the wild dog
  Shall flesh his tooth on every innocent.
  O my poor kingdom, sick with civil blows!
  When that my care could not withhold thy riots,
  What wilt thou do when riot is thy care?
  O, thou wilt be a wilderness again.
  Peopled with wolves, thy old inhabitants!
PRINCE. O, pardon me, my liege! But for my tears,
  The moist impediments unto my speech,
  I had forestall'd this dear and deep rebuke
  Ere you with grief had spoke and I had heard
  The course of it so far. There is your crown,
  And he that wears the crown immortally
  Long guard it yours! *[Kneeling]* If I affect it more
  Than as your honour and as your renown,
  Let me no more from this obedience rise,
  Which my most inward true and duteous spirit

Teacheth this prostrate and exterior bending!
God witness with me, when I here came in
And found no course of breath within
   your Majesty,
How cold it struck my heart! If I do feign,
O, let me in my present wildness die,
And never live to show th' incredulous world
The noble change that I have purposed!
Coming to look on you, thinking you dead-
And dead almost, my liege, to think you were-
I spake unto this crown as having sense,
And thus upbraided it: 'The care on
   thee depending
Hath fed upon the body of my father;
Therefore thou best of gold art worst of gold.
Other, less fine in carat, is more precious,
Preserving life in med'cine potable;
But thou, most fine, most honour'd,
   most renown'd,
Hast eat thy bearer up.' Thus, my most
   royal liege,
Accusing it, I put it on my head,
To try with it-as with an enemy
That had before my face murd'red my father-
The quarrel of a true inheritor.
But if it did infect my blood with joy,
Or swell my thoughts to any strain of pride;
If any rebel or vain spirit of mine
Did with the least affection of a welcome
Give entertainment to the might of it,
Let God for ever keep it from my head,
And make me as the poorest vassal is,
That doth with awe and terror kneel to it!
KING. O my son,
God put it in thy mind to take it hence,
That thou mightst win the more thy
   father's love,
Pleading so wisely in excuse of it!
Come hither, Harry; sit thou by my bed,
And hear, I think, the very latest counsel
That ever I shall breathe. God knows, my son,
By what by-paths and indirect crook'd ways
I met this crown; and I myself know well
How troublesome it sat upon my head:
To thee it shall descend with better quiet,
Better opinion, better confirmation;
For all the soil of the achievement goes
With me into the earth. It seem'd in me
But as an honour snatch'd with boist'rous hand;
And I had many living to upbraid
My gain of it by their assistances;
Which daily grew to quarrel and to bloodshed,
Wounding supposed peace. All these bold fears

Thou seest with peril I have answered;
For all my reign hath been but as a scene
Acting that argument. And now my death
Changes the mood; for what in me
   was purchas'd
Falls upon thee in a more fairer sort;
So thou the garland wear'st successively.
Yet, though thou stand'st more sure than I
   could do,
Thou art not firm enough, since griefs are green;
And all my friends, which thou must make
   thy friends,
Have but their stings and teeth newly ta'en out;
By whose fell working I was first advanc'd,
And by whose power I well might lodge a fear
To be again displac'd; which to avoid,
I cut them off; and had a purpose now
To lead out many to the Holy Land,
Lest rest and lying still might make them look
Too near unto my state. Therefore, my Harry,
Be it thy course to busy giddy minds
With foreign quarrels, that action, hence
   borne out,
May waste the memory of the former days.
More would I, but my lungs are wasted so
That strength of speech is utterly denied me.
How I came by the crown, O God, forgive;
And grant it may with thee in true peace live!
PRINCE. My gracious liege,
   You won it, wore it, kept it, gave it me;
   Then plain and right must my possession be;
   Which I with more than with a common pain
   'Gainst all the world will rightfully maintain.
         Enter PRINCE JOHN OF LANCASTER, WARWICK,
                  LORDS, and Others
KING. Look, look, here comes my John
   of Lancaster.
PRINCE JOHN. Health, peace, and happiness, to
   my royal father!
KING. Thou bring'st me happiness and peace,
   son John;
   But health, alack, with youthful wings is flown
   From this bare wither'd trunk. Upon thy sight
   My worldly business makes a period.
   Where is my Lord of Warwick?
PRINCE. My Lord of Warwick!
KING. Doth any name particular belong
   Unto the lodging where I first did swoon?
WARWICK. 'Tis call'd Jerusalem, my noble lord.
KING. Laud be to God! Even there my life
   must end.
   It hath been prophesied to me many years,
   I should not die but in Jerusalem;

Which vainly I suppos'd the Holy Land.
But bear me to that chamber; there I'll lie;
In that Jerusalem shall Harry die.

Exeunt.

ACT V

SCENE I
Gloucestershire. SHALLOW'S house

Enter SHALLOW, FALSTAFF, BARDOLPH, and PAGE

SHALLOW. By cock and pie, sir, you shall not away
to-night. What, Davy, I say!

FALSTAFF. You must excuse me, Master
Robert Shallow.

SHALLOW. I will not excuse you; you shall not be
excus'd; excuses shall not be admitted; there is
no excuse shall serve; you shall not be excus'd.
Why, Davy!

Enter DAVY

DAVY. Here, sir.

SHALLOW. Davy, Davy, Davy, Davy; let me see,
Davy; let me see, Davy; let me see-yea, marry,
William cook, bid him come hither. Sir John,
you shall not be excus'd.

DAVY. Marry, sir, thus: those precepts cannot
be served; and, again, sir-shall we sow the
headland with wheat?

SHALLOW. With red wheat, Davy. But for William
cook-are there no young pigeons?

DAVY. Yes, sir. Here is now the smith's note for
shoeing and plough-irons.

SHALLOW. Let it be cast, and paid. Sir John, you
shall not be excused.

DAVY. Now, sir, a new link to the bucket must
needs be had; and, sir, do you mean to stop any
of William's wages about the sack he lost the
other day at Hinckley fair?

SHALLOW. 'A shall answer it. Some pigeons,
Davy, a couple of short-legg'd hens, a joint of
mutton, and any pretty little tiny kickshaws, tell
William cook.

DAVY. Doth the man of war stay all night, sir?

SHALLOW. Yea, Davy; I will use him well. A friend
i' th' court is better than a penny in purse. Use
his men well, Davy; for they are arrant knaves
and will backbite.

DAVY. No worse than they are backbitten, sir; for
they have marvellous foul linen.

SHALLOW. Well conceited, Davy-about thy
business, Davy.

DAVY. I beseech you, sir, to countenance William
Visor of Woncot against Clement Perkes o'
th' hill.

SHALLOW. There is many complaints, Davy,
against that Visor. That Visor is an arrant knave,
on my knowledge.

DAVY. I grant your worship that he is a knave,
sir; but yet God forbid, sir, but a knave
should have some countenance at his friend's
request. An honest man, sir, is able to speak
for himself, when a knave is not. I have serv'd
your worship truly, sir, this eight years; and if
I cannot once or twice in a quarter bear out a
knave against an honest man, I have but a very
little credit with your worship. The knave is
mine honest friend, sir; therefore, I beseech
you, let him be countenanc'd.

SHALLOW. Go to; I say he shall have no wrong.
Look about, Davy. *[Exit DAVY]* Where are you,
Sir John? Come, come, come, off with your
boots. Give me your hand, Master Bardolph.

BARDOLPH. I am glad to see your worship.

SHALLOW. I thank thee with all my heart, kind
Master Bardolph. *[To the PAGE]* And welcome, my
tall fellow. Come, Sir John.

FALSTAFF. I'll follow you, good Master Robert
Shallow. *[Exit SHALLOW]* Bardolph, look to
our horses. *[Exeunt BARDOLPH and PAGE]* If I
were sawed into quantities, I should make
four dozen of such bearded hermits' staves
as Master Shallow. It is a wonderful thing to
see the semblable coherence of his men's
spirits and his. They, by observing of him,
do bear themselves like foolish justices: he,
by conversing with them, is turned into a
justice-like serving-man. Their spirits are so
married in conjunction with the participation
of society that they flock together in consent,
like so many wild geese. If I had a suit to
Master Shallow, I would humour his men
with the imputation of being near their
master; if to his men, I would curry with
Master Shallow that no man could better
command his servants. It is certain that either
wise bearing or ignorant carriage is caught, as
men take diseases, one of another; therefore
let men take heed of their company. I will
devise matter enough out of this Shallow to
keep Prince Harry in continual laughter the
wearing out of six fashions, which is four
terms, or two actions; and 'a shall laugh

without intervallums. O, it is much that a lie
with a slight oath, and a jest with a sad brow
will do with a fellow that never had the ache
in his shoulders! O, you shall see him laugh
till his face be like a wet cloak ill laid up!

SHALLOW. [Within] Sir John!

FALSTAFF. I come, Master Shallow; I come,
Master Shallow.   Exit.

⚜ SCENE II ⚜
Westminster. The palace

Enter, severally, WARWICK, and the LORD CHIEF
JUSTICE

WARWICK. How now, my Lord Chief Justice;
whither away?

CHIEF JUSTICE. How doth the King?

WARWICK. Exceeding well; his cares are now
all ended.

CHIEF JUSTICE. I hope, not dead.

WARWICK. He's walk'd the way of nature;
And to our purposes he lives no more.

CHIEF JUSTICE. I would his Majesty had call'd me
with him.
The service that I truly did his life
Hath left me open to all injuries.

WARWICK. Indeed, I think the young King loves
you not.

CHIEF JUSTICE. I know he doth not, and do
arm myself
To welcome the condition of the time,
Which cannot look more hideously upon me
Than I have drawn it in my fantasy.

Enter LANCASTER, CLARENCE, GLOUCESTER,
WESTMORELAND, and Others

WARWICK. Here comes the heavy issue of
dead Harry.
O that the living Harry had the temper
Of he, the worst of these three gentlemen!
How many nobles then should hold their places
That must strike sail to spirits of vile sort!

CHIEF JUSTICE. O God, I fear all will
be overturn'd.

PRINCE JOHN. Good morrow, cousin Warwick,
good morrow.

GLOUCESTER and CLARENCE. Good
morrow, cousin.

PRINCE JOHN. We meet like men that had forgot
to speak.

WARWICK. We do remember; but our argument
Is all too heavy to admit much talk.

PRINCE JOHN. Well, peace be with him that hath
made us heavy!

CHIEF JUSTICE. Peace be with us, lest we
be heavier!

PRINCE HUMPHREY. O, good my lord, you have
lost a friend indeed;
And I dare swear you borrow not that face
Of seeming sorrow-it is sure your own.

PRINCE JOHN. Though no man be assur'd what
grace to find,
You stand in coldest expectation.
I am the sorrier; would 'twere otherwise.

CLARENCE. Well, you must now speak Sir John
Falstaff fair;
Which swims against your stream of quality.

CHIEF JUSTICE. Sweet Princes, what I did, I did
in honour,
Led by th' impartial conduct of my soul;
And never shall you see that I will beg
A ragged and forestall'd remission.
If truth and upright innocency fail me,
I'll to the King my master that is dead,
And tell him who hath sent me after him.

WARWICK. Here comes the Prince.

Enter KING HENRY THE FIFTH, attended

CHIEF JUSTICE. Good morrow, and God save
your Majesty!

KING. This new and gorgeous garment, majesty,
Sits not so easy on me as you think.
Brothers, you mix your sadness with some fear.
This is the English, not the Turkish court;
Not Amurath an Amurath succeeds,
But Harry Harry. Yet be sad, good brothers,
For, by my faith, it very well becomes you.
Sorrow so royally in you appears
That I will deeply put the fashion on,
And wear it in my heart. Why, then, be sad;
But entertain no more of it, good brothers,
Than a joint burden laid upon us all.
For me, by heaven, I bid you be assur'd,
I'll be your father and your brother too;
Let me but bear your love, I'll bear your cares.
Yet weep that Harry's dead, and so will I;
But Harry lives that shall convert those tears
By number into hours of happiness.

BROTHERS. We hope no otherwise from
your Majesty.

KING. You all look strangely on me; and you most.
You are, I think, assur'd I love you not.

CHIEF JUSTICE. I am assur'd, if I be
measur'd rightly,
Your Majesty hath no just cause to hate me.

KING. No?

How might a prince of my great hopes forget
So great indignities you laid upon me?
What, rate, rebuke, and roughly send to prison,
Th' immediate heir of England! Was this easy?
May this be wash'd in Lethe and forgotten?
CHIEF JUSTICE. I then did use the person of
  your father;
The image of his power lay then in me;
And in th' administration of his law,
Whiles I was busy for the commonwealth,
Your Highness pleased to forget my place,
The majesty and power of law and justice,
The image of the King whom I presented,
And struck me in my very seat of judgment;
Whereon, as an offender to your father,
I gave bold way to my authority
And did commit you. If the deed were ill,
Be you contented, wearing now the garland,
To have a son set your decrees at nought,
To pluck down justice from your awful bench,
To trip the course of law, and blunt the sword
That guards the peace and safety of your person;
Nay, more, to spurn at your most royal image,
And mock your workings in a second body.
Question your royal thoughts, make the
  case yours;
Be now the father, and propose a son;
Hear your own dignity so much profan'd,
See your most dreadful laws so loosely slighted,
Behold yourself so by a son disdain'd;
And then imagine me taking your part
And, in your power, soft silencing your son.
After this cold considerance, sentence me;
And, as you are a king, speak in your state
What I have done that misbecame my place,
My person, or my liege's sovereignty.
KING. You are right, Justice, and you weigh this well;
Therefore still bear the balance and the sword;
And I do wish your honours may increase
Till you do live to see a son of mine
Offend you, and obey you, as I did.
So shall I live to speak my father's words:
'Happy am I that have a man so bold
That dares do justice on my proper son;
And not less happy, having such a son
That would deliver up his greatness so
Into the hands of justice.' You did commit me;
For which I do commit into your hand
Th' unstained sword that you have us'd to bear;
With this remembrance-that you use the same
With the like bold, just, and impartial spirit
As you have done 'gainst me. There is my hand.
You shall be as a father to my youth;

My voice shall sound as you do prompt
  mine ear;
And I will stoop and humble my intents
To your well-practis'd wise directions.
And, Princes all, believe me, I beseech you,
My father is gone wild into his grave,
For in his tomb lie my affections;
And with his spirits sadly I survive,
To mock the expectation of the world,
To frustrate prophecies, and to raze out
Rotten opinion, who hath writ me down
After my seeming. The tide of blood in me
Hath proudly flow'd in vanity till now.
Now doth it turn and ebb back to the sea,
Where it shall mingle with the state of floods,
And flow henceforth in formal majesty.
Now call we our high court of parliament;
And let us choose such limbs of noble counsel,
That the great body of our state may go
In equal rank with the best govern'd nation;
That war, or peace, or both at once, may be
As things acquainted and familiar to us;
In which you, father, shall have foremost hand.
Our coronation done, we will accite,
As I before rememb'red, all our state;
And-God consigning to my good intents-
No prince nor peer shall have just cause to say,
God shorten Harry's happy life one day.

Exeunt.

⚜ SCENE III ⚜
Gloucestershire. SHALLOW'S orchard

Enter FALSTAFF, SHALLOW, SILENCE, BARDOLPH,
the PAGE, and DAVY

SHALLOW. Nay, you shall see my orchard, where,
  in an arbour, we will eat a last year's pippin
  of mine own graffing, with a dish of caraways,
  and so forth. Come, cousin Silence. And then
  to bed.
FALSTAFF. Fore God, you have here a goodly
  dwelling and rich.
SHALLOW. Barren, barren, barren; beggars all,
  beggars all, Sir John-marry, good air. Spread,
  Davy, spread, Davy; well said, Davy.
FALSTAFF. This Davy serves you for good uses; he
  is your serving-man and your husband.
SHALLOW. A good varlet, a good varlet, a very
  good varlet, Sir John. By the mass, I have drunk
  too much sack at supper. A good varlet. Now sit
  down, now sit down; come, cousin.

SILENCE. Ah, sirrah! quoth-a-we shall [Singing]
    Do nothing but eat and make good cheer,
    And praise God for the merry year;
    When flesh is cheap and females dear,
    And lusty lads roam here and there,
      So merrily,
    And ever among so merrily.

FALSTAFF. There's a merry heart! Good Master
  Silence, I'll give you a health for that anon.

SHALLOW. Give Master Bardolph some
  wine, Davy.

DAVY. Sweet sir, sit; I'll be with you anon; most
  sweet sir, sit. Master Page, good Master Page,
  sit. Proface! What you want in meat, we'll have
  in drink. But you must bear; the heart's all.
                             Exit.

SHALLOW. Be merry, Master Bardolph; and, my
  little soldier there, be merry.

SILENCE. [Singing]
    Be merry, be merry, my wife has all;
    For women are shrews, both short and tall;
    'Tis merry in hall when beards wag all;
      And welcome merry Shrove-tide.
    Be merry, be merry.

FALSTAFF. I did not think Master Silence had
  been a man of this mettle.

SILENCE. Who, I? I have been merry twice and
  once ere now.

             Re-enter DAVY

DAVY. [To BARDOLPH] There's a dish of leather-
  coats for you.

SHALLOW. Davy!

DAVY. Your worship! I'll be with you straight. [To
  BARDOLPH] A cup of wine, sir?

SILENCE. [Singing]
    A cup of wine that's brisk and fine,
    And drink unto the leman mine;
      And a merry heart lives long-a.

FALSTAFF. Well said, Master Silence.

SILENCE. An we shall be merry, now comes in the
  sweet o' th' night.

FALSTAFF. Health and long life to you, Master
  Silence!

SILENCE. [Singing]
    Fill the cup, and let it come,
    I'll pledge you a mile to th' bottom.

SHALLOW. Honest Bardolph, welcome; if
  thou want'st anything and wilt not call,
  beshrew thy heart. Welcome, my little tiny
  thief, and welcome indeed too. I'll drink to
  Master Bardolph, and to all the cabileros
  about London.

DAVY. I hope to see London once ere I die.

BARDOLPH. An I might see you there, Davy!

SHALLOW. By the mass, you'll crack a quart
  together-ha! will you not, Master Bardolph?

BARDOLPH. Yea, sir, in a pottle-pot.

SHALLOW. By God's liggens, I thank thee. The
  knave will stick by thee, I can assure thee that.
  'A will not out, 'a; 'tis true bred.

BARDOLPH. And I'll stick by him, sir.

SHALLOW. Why, there spoke a king. Lack nothing;
  be merry. [One knocks at door] Look who's at door
  there, ho! Who knocks?   Exit DAVY.

FALSTAFF. [To SILENCE, who has drunk a bumper] Why,
  now you have done me right.

SILENCE. [Singing]
    Do me right,
    And dub me knight.
      Samingo.
  Is't not so?

FALSTAFF. 'Tis so.

SILENCE. Is't so? Why then, say an old man can
  do somewhat.

             Re-enter DAVY

DAVY. An't please your worship, there's one Pistol
  come from the court with news.

FALSTAFF. From the court? Let him come in.

            Enter PISTOL

  How now, Pistol?

PISTOL. Sir John, God save you!

FALSTAFF. What wind blew you hither, Pistol?

PISTOL. Not the ill wind which blows no man to
  good. Sweet knight, thou art now one of the
  greatest men in this realm.

SILENCE. By'r Lady, I think 'a be, but goodman
  Puff of Barson.

PISTOL. Puff!
  Puff in thy teeth, most recreant coward base!
  Sir John, I am thy Pistol and thy friend,
  And helter-skelter have I rode to thee;
  And tidings do I bring, and lucky joys,
  And golden times, and happy news of price.

FALSTAFF. I pray thee now, deliver them like a
  man of this world.

PISTOL. A foutra for the world and
  worldlings base!
  I speak of Africa and golden joys.

FALSTAFF. O base Assyrian knight, what is
  thy news?
  Let King Cophetua know the truth thereof.

SILENCE. [Singing] And Robin Hood, Scarlet,
  and John.

PISTOL. Shall dunghill curs confront the Helicons?
  And shall good news be baffled?
  Then, Pistol, lay thy head in Furies' lap.

SHALLOW. Honest gentleman, I know not
your breeding.

PISTOL. Why, then, lament therefore.

SHALLOW. Give me pardon, sir. If, sir, you come
with news from the court, I take it there's but
two ways-either to utter them or conceal them.
I am, sir, under the King, in some authority.

PISTOL. Under which king, Bezonian? Speak,
or die.

SHALLOW. Under King Harry.

PISTOL. Harry the Fourth-or Fifth?

SHALLOW. Harry the Fourth.

PISTOL. A foutra for thine office!
Sir John, thy tender lambkin now is King;
Harry the Fifth's the man. I speak the truth.
When Pistol lies, do this; and fig me, like
The bragging Spaniard.

FALSTAFF. What, is the old King dead?

PISTOL. As nail in door. The things I speak
are just.

FALSTAFF. Away, Bardolph! saddle my horse.
Master Robert Shallow, choose what office thou
wilt in the land, 'tis thine. Pistol, I will double-
charge thee with dignities.

BARDOLPH. O joyful day!
I would not take a knighthood for my fortune.

PISTOL. What, I do bring good news?

FALSTAFF. Carry Master Silence to bed. Master
Shallow, my Lord Shallow, be what thou wilt-I
am Fortune's steward. Get on thy boots; we'll
ride all night. O sweet Pistol! Away, Bardolph!
[Exit BARDOLPH] Come, Pistol, utter more to
me; and withal devise something to do thyself
good. Boot, boot, Master Shallow! I know
the young King is sick for me. Let us take any
man's horses: the laws of England are at my
commandment. Blessed are they that have been
my friends; and woe to my Lord Chief Justice!

PISTOL. Let vultures vile seize on his lungs also!
'Where is the life that late I led?' say they.
Why, here it is; welcome these pleasant days!
Exeunt.

✿ SCENE IV ✿
London. A street

*Enter BEADLES, dragging in HOSTESS QUICKLY and
DOLL TEARSHEET*

HOSTESS. No, thou arrant knave; I would to God
that I might die, that I might have thee hang'd.
Thou hast drawn my shoulder out of joint.

FIRST BEADLE. The constables have delivered her
over to me; and she shall have whipping-cheer
enough, I warrant her. There hath been a man
or two lately kill'd about her.

DOLL. Nut-hook, nut-hook, you lie. Come on; I'll
tell thee what, thou damn'd tripe-visag'd rascal,
an the child I now go with do miscarry, thou
wert better thou hadst struck thy mother, thou
paper-fac'd villain.

HOSTESS. O the Lord, that Sir John were come!
He would make this a bloody day to somebody.
But I pray God the fruit of her womb miscarry!

FIRST BEADLE. If it do, you shall have a dozen
of cushions again; you have but eleven now.
Come, I charge you both go with me; for
the man is dead that you and Pistol beat
amongst you.

DOLL. I'll tell you what, you thin man in a censer,
I will have you as soundly swing'd for this-
you blue-bottle rogue, you filthy famish'd
correctioner, if you be not swing'd, I'll
forswear half-kirtles.

FIRST BEADLE. Come, come, you she knight-
errant, come.

HOSTESS. O God, that right should thus
overcome might! Well, of sufferance
comes ease.

DOLL. Come, you rogue, come; bring me to
a justice.

HOSTESS. Ay, come, you starv'd bloodhound.

DOLL. Goodman death, goodman bones!

HOSTESS. Thou atomy, thou!

DOLL. Come, you thin thing! come, you rascal!

FIRST BEADLE. Very well.
Exeunt.

✿ SCENE V ✿
Westminster. Near the Abbey

Enter GROOMS, strewing rushes

FIRST GROOM. More rushes, more rushes!

SECOND GROOM. The trumpets have
sounded twice.

THIRD GROOM. 'Twill be two o'clock ere
they come from the coronation. Dispatch,
dispatch. *Exeunt.*
*Trumpets sound, and the KING and his Train pass over the
stage. After them enter FALSTAFF, SHALLOW, PISTOL,
BARDOLPH, and PAGE*

FALSTAFF. Stand here by me, Master Robert
Shallow; I will make the King do you grace. I

will leer upon him, as 'a comes by; and do but
mark the countenance that he will give me.

PISTOL. God bless thy lungs, good knight!

FALSTAFF. Come here, Pistol; stand behind me.
[To SHALLOW] O, if I had had to have made new
liveries, I would have bestowed the thousand
pound I borrowed of you. But 'tis no matter;
this poor show doth better; this doth infer the
zeal I had to see him.

SHALLOW. It doth so.

FALSTAFF. It shows my earnestness of affection-

SHALLOW. It doth so.

FALSTAFF. My devotion-

SHALLOW. It doth, it doth, it doth.

FALSTAFF. As it were, to ride day and night; and
not to deliberate, not to remember, not to have
patience to shift me-

SHALLOW. It is best, certain.

FALSTAFF. But to stand stained with travel, and
sweating with desire to see him; thinking of
nothing else, putting all affairs else in oblivion,
as if there were nothing else to be done but to
see him.

PISTOL. 'Tis 'semper idem' for 'obsque hoc nihil
est.' 'Tis all in every part.

SHALLOW. 'Tis so, indeed.

PISTOL. My knight, I will inflame thy noble liver
And make thee rage.
Thy Doll, and Helen of thy noble thoughts,
Is in base durance and contagious prison;
Hal'd thither
By most mechanical and dirty hand.
Rouse up revenge from ebon den with fell
Alecto's snake,
For Doll is in. Pistol speaks nought but truth.

FALSTAFF. I will deliver her.

Shouts, within, and the trumpets sound

PISTOL. There roar'd the sea, and trumpet-
clangor sounds.

*Enter the KING and his train, the LORD CHIEF JUSTICE
among them*

FALSTAFF. God save thy Grace, King Hal; my
royal Hal!

PISTOL. The heavens thee guard and keep, most
royal imp of fame!

FALSTAFF. God save thee, my sweet boy!

KING. My Lord Chief Justice, speak to that vain man.

CHIEF JUSTICE. Have you your wits? Know you
what 'tis you speak?

FALSTAFF. My king! my Jove! I speak to thee,
my heart!

KING. I know thee not, old man. Fall to
thy prayers.

How ill white hairs become a fool and jester!
I have long dreamt of such a kind of man,
So surfeit-swell'd, so old, and so profane;
But being awak'd, I do despise my dream.
Make less thy body hence, and more thy grace;
Leave gormandizing; know the grave doth gape
For thee thrice wider than for other men-
Reply not to me with a fool-born jest;
Presume not that I am the thing I was,
For God doth know, so shall the world perceive,
That I have turn'd away my former self;
So will I those that kept me company.
When thou dost hear I am as I have been,
Approach me, and thou shalt be as thou wast,
The tutor and the feeder of my riots.
Till then I banish thee, on pain of death,
As I have done the rest of my misleaders,
Not to come near our person by ten mile.
For competence of life I will allow you,
That lack of means enforce you not to evils;
And, as we hear you do reform yourselves,
We will, according to your strengths
and qualities,
Give you advancement. Be it your charge,
my lord,
To see perform'd the tenor of our word.
Set on.   *Exeunt the KING and his Train.*

FALSTAFF. Master Shallow, I owe you a
thousand pounds.

SHALLOW. Yea, marry, Sir John; which I beseech
you to let me have home with me.

FALSTAFF. That can hardly be, Master Shallow.
Do not you grieve at this; I shall be sent for in
private to him. Look you, he must seem thus to
the world. Fear not your advancements; I will
be the man yet that shall make you great.

SHALLOW. I cannot perceive how, unless you give
me your doublet, and stuff me out with straw.
I beseech you, good Sir John, let me have five
hundred of my thousand.

FALSTAFF. Sir, I will be as good as my word. This
that you heard was but a colour.

SHALLOW. A colour that I fear you will die in, Sir John.

FALSTAFF. Fear no colours; go with me to dinner.
Come, Lieutenant Pistol; come, Bardolph. I
shall be sent for soon at night.

*Re-enter PRINCE JOHN, the LORD CHIEF JUSTICE, with
OFFICERS*

CHIEF JUSTICE. Go, carry Sir John Falstaff to the
Fleet; Take all his company along with him.

FALSTAFF. My lord, my lord-

CHIEF JUSTICE. I cannot now speak. I will hear
you soon. Take them away.

PISTOL. Si fortuna me tormenta, spero
me contenta.

Exeunt all but PRINCE JOHN and the LORD CHIEF
JUSTICE.

PRINCE JOHN. I like this fair proceeding of
the King's.
He hath intent his wonted followers
Shall all be very well provided for;
But all are banish'd till their conversations
Appear more wise and modest to the world.
CHIEF JUSTICE. And so they are.
PRINCE JOHN. The King hath call'd his
parliament, my lord.
CHIEF JUSTICE. He hath.
PRINCE JOHN. I will lay odds that, ere this
year expire,
We bear our civil swords and native fire
As far as France. I heard a bird so sing,
Whose music, to my thinking, pleas'd the King.
Come, will you hence?

Exeunt.

EPILOGUE

First my fear, then my curtsy, last my speech.

My fear, is your displeasure; my curtsy, my
duty; and my speech, to beg your pardons. If
you look for a good speech now, you undo me;
for what I have to say is of mine own making;
and what, indeed, I should say will, I doubt,
prove mine own marring. But to the purpose,
and so to the venture. Be it known to you, as
it is very well, I was lately here in the end of a
displeasing play, to pray your patience for it and
to promise you a better. I meant, indeed, to pay
you with this; which if like an ill venture it come
unluckily home, I break, and you, my gentle
creditors, lose. Here I promis'd you I would be,
and here I commit my body to your mercies.
Bate me some, and I will pay you some, and, as
most debtors do, promise you infinitely; and so
I kneel down before you-but, indeed, to pray
for the Queen.

If my tongue cannot entreat you to acquit me,
will you command me to use my legs? And yet
that were but light payment-to dance out of
your debt. But a good conscience will make
any possible satisfaction, and so would I. All
the gentlewomen here have forgiven me. If the
gentlemen will not, then the gentlemen do not
agree with the gentlewomen, which was never
seen before in such an assembly.

One word more, I beseech you. If you be not
too much cloy'd with fat meat, our humble
author will continue the story, with Sir John
in it, and make you merry with fair Katherine
of France; where, for anything I know, Falstaff
shall die of a sweat, unless already 'a be killed
with your hard opinions; for Oldcastle died
a martyr and this is not the man. My tongue
is weary; when my legs are too, I will bid you
good night.

The End

1599

King
Henry V

Dramatis Personae

CHORUS
KING HENRY THE FIFTH

Brothers to the King:
DUKE OF GLOUCESTER
DUKE OF BEDFORD

DUKE OF EXETER, Uncle to the King
DUKE OF YORK, cousin to the King
EARL OF SALISBURY
EARL OF WESTMORELAND
EARL OF WARWICK
ARCHBISHOP OF CANTERBURY
BISHOP OF ELY

Conspirators against King:
EARL OF CAMBRIDGE, LORD SCROOP,
SIR THOMAS GREY

Officers in the King's army:
SIR THOMAS ERPINGHAM, GOWER, FLUELLEN,
MACMORRIS, JAMY

Soldiers in the King's army:
BATES, COURT, WILLIAMS

NYM, BARDOLPH, PISTOL
BOY
A HERALD

CHARLES THE SIXTH, King of France
LEWIS, the Dauphin
DUKE OF BURGUNDY
DUKE OF ORLEANS
DUKE OF BRITAINE
DUKE OF BOURBON
THE CONSTABLE OF FRANCE
RAMBURES and GRANDPRE, French Lords
GOVERNOR OF HARFLEUR

MONTJOY, a French herald
AMBASSADORS to the King of England

ISABEL, Queen of France
KATHERINE, daughter to Charles and Isabel
ALICE, a lady attending her
HOSTESS of the Boar's Head, Eastcheap; formerly
Mrs. Quickly, now married to Pistol

Lords, Duke of Berri, Ladies, Officers, Soldiers,
Messengers, Attendants

SCENE
England and France

PROLOGUE

Enter CHORUS

CHORUS. O for a Muse of fire, that would ascend
The brightest heaven of invention,
A kingdom for a stage, princes to act,
And monarchs to behold the swelling scene.
Then should the warlike Harry, like himself,
Assume the port of Mars; and at his heels,
Leash'd in like hounds, should famine, sword,
 and fire,
Crouch for employment. But pardon,
 gentles all,
The flat unraised spirits that hath dar'd
On this unworthy scaffold to bring forth
So great an object. Can this cockpit hold
The vasty fields of France? Or may we cram
Within this wooden O the very casques
That did affright the air at Agincourt?
O, pardon! since a crooked figure may
Attest in little place a million;
And let us, ciphers to this great accompt,
On your imaginary forces work.
Suppose within the girdle of these walls
Are now confin'd two mighty monarchies,
Whose high upreared and abutting fronts
The perilous narrow ocean parts asunder.
Piece out our imperfections with your thoughts:
Into a thousand parts divide one man,
And make imaginary puissance;
Think, when we talk of horses, that you
 see them
Printing their proud hoofs i' th' receiving earth;

For 'tis your thoughts that now must deck
  our kings,
Carry them here and there, jumping o'er times,
Turning th' accomplishment of many years
Into an hour-glass; for the which supply,
Admit me Chorus to this history;
Who prologue-like your humble patience pray
Gently to hear, kindly to judge, our play. *Exit*

ACT I

SCENE I

London. An ante-chamber in the KING'S palace

Enter the ARCHBISHOP OF CANTERBURY and the
BISHOP OF ELY

CANTERBURY. My lord, I'll tell you: that self bill
  is urg'd
  Which in th' eleventh year of the last king's reign
  Was like, and had indeed against us pass'd
  But that the scambling and unquiet time
  Did push it out of farther question.
ELY. But how, my lord, shall we resist it now?
CANTERBURY. It must be thought on. If it pass
  against us,
  We lose the better half of our possession;
  For all the temporal lands which men devout
  By testament have given to the church
  Would they strip from us; being valu'd thus-
  As much as would maintain, to the
  King's honour,
  Full fifteen earls and fifteen hundred knights,
  Six thousand and two hundred good esquires;
  And, to relief of lazars and weak age,
  Of indigent faint souls, past corporal toil,
  A hundred alms-houses right well supplied;
  And to the coffers of the King, beside,
  A thousand pounds by th' year: thus runs
  the bill.
ELY. This would drink deep.
CANTERBURY. 'T would drink the cup and all.
ELY. But what prevention?
CANTERBURY. The King is full of grace and
  fair regard.
ELY. And a true lover of the holy Church.
CANTERBURY. The courses of his youth promis'd
  it not.
  The breath no sooner left his father's body
  But that his wildness, mortified in him,

Seem'd to die too; yea, at that very moment,
Consideration like an angel came
And whipp'd th' offending Adam out of him,
Leaving his body as a paradise
T'envelop and contain celestial spirits.
Never was such a sudden scholar made;
Never came reformation in a flood,
With such a heady currance, scouring faults;
Nor never Hydra-headed wilfulnes
So soon did lose his seat, and all at once,
As in this king.
ELY. We are blessed in the change.
CANTERBURY. Hear him but reason in divinity,
  And, all-admiring, with an inward wish
  You would desire the King were made a prelate;
  Hear him debate of commonwealth affairs,
  You would say it hath been all in all his study;
  List his discourse of war, and you shall hear
  A fearful battle rend'red you in music.
  Turn him to any cause of policy,
  The Gordian knot of it he will unloose,
  Familiar as his garter; that, when he speaks,
  The air, a charter'd libertine, is still,
  And the mute wonder lurketh in men's ears
  To steal his sweet and honey'd sentences;
  So that the art and practic part of life
  Must be the mistress to this theoric;
  Which is a wonder how his Grace should
  glean it,
  Since his addiction was to courses vain,
  His companies unletter'd, rude, and shallow,
  His hours fill'd up with riots, banquets, sports;
  And never noted in him any study,
  Any retirement, any sequestration
  From open haunts and popularity.
ELY. The strawberry grows underneath the nettle,
  And wholesome berries thrive and ripen best
  Neighbour'd by fruit of baser quality;
  And so the Prince obscur'd his contemplation
  Under the veil of wildness; which, no doubt,
  Grew like the summer grass, fastest by night,
  Unseen, yet crescive in his faculty.
CANTERBURY. It must be so; for miracles
  are ceas'd;
  And therefore we must needs admit the means
  How things are perfected.
ELY. But, my good lord,
  How now for mitigation of this bill
  Urg'd by the Commons? Doth his Majesty
  Incline to it, or no?
CANTERBURY. He seems indifferent
  Or rather swaying more upon our part
  Than cherishing th' exhibiters against us;

For I have made an offer to his Majesty-
Upon our spiritual convocation
And in regard of causes now in hand,
Which I have open'd to his Grace at large,
As touching France-to give a greater sum
Than ever at one time the clergy yet
Did to his predecessors part withal.
ELY. How did this offer seem receiv'd, my lord?
CANTERBURY. With good acceptance of
  his Majesty;
Save that there was not time enough to hear,
As I perceiv'd his Grace would fain have done,
The severals and unhidden passages
Of his true tides to some certain dukedoms,
And generally to the crown and seat of France,
Deriv'd from Edward, his great-grandfather.
ELY. What was th' impediment that broke this off?
CANTERBURY. The French ambassador upon
  that instant
Crav'd audience; and the hour, I think, is come
To give him hearing: is it four o'clock?
ELY. It is.
CANTERBURY. Then go we in, to know
  his embassy;
Which I could with a ready guess declare,
Before the Frenchman speak a word of it.
ELY. I'll wait upon you, and I long to hear it.

Exeunt.

⚘ SCENE II ⚘

**London. The Presence Chamber in the
KING'S palace**

*Enter the KING, GLOUCESTER, BEDFORD, EXETER,
WARWICK, WESTMORELAND, and Attendants*

KING HENRY. Where is my gracious Lord
  of Canterbury?
EXETER. Not here in presence.
KING HENRY. Send for him, good uncle.
WESTMORELAND. Shall we call in th' ambassador,
  my liege?
KING HENRY. Not yet, my cousin; we would
  be resolv'd,
Before we hear him, of some things of weight
That task our thoughts, concerning us
  and France.

*Enter the ARCHBISHOP OF CANTERBURY and the
BISHOP OF ELY*

CANTERBURY. God and his angels guard your
  sacred throne,
And make you long become it!

KING HENRY. Sure, we thank you.
My learned lord, we pray you to proceed,
And justly and religiously unfold
Why the law Salique, that they have in France,
Or should or should not bar us in our claim;
And God forbid, my dear and faithful lord,
That you should fashion, wrest, or bow
  your reading,
Or nicely charge your understanding soul
With opening titles miscreate whose right
Suits not in native colours with the truth;
For God doth know how many, now in health,
Shall drop their blood in approbation
Of what your reverence shall incite us to.
Therefore take heed how you impawn
  our person,
How you awake our sleeping sword of war-
We charge you, in the name of God, take heed;
For never two such kingdoms did contend
Without much fall of blood; whose
  guiltless drops
Are every one a woe, a sore complaint,
'Gainst him whose wrongs gives edge unto
  the swords
That makes such waste in brief mortality.
Under this conjuration speak, my lord;
For we will hear, note, and believe in heart,
That what you speak is in your
  conscience wash'd
As pure as sin with baptism.
CANTERBURY. Then hear me, gracious sovereign,
  and you peers,
That owe yourselves, your lives, and services,
To this imperial throne. There is no bar
To make against your Highness' claim to France
But this, which they produce from Pharamond:
'In terram Salicam mulieres ne succedant'-
'No woman shall succeed in Salique land';
Which Salique land the French unjustly gloze
To be the realm of France, and Pharamond
The founder of this law and female bar.
Yet their own authors faithfully affirm
That the land Salique is in Germany,
Between the floods of Sala and of Elbe;
Where Charles the Great, having subdu'd
  the Saxons,
There left behind and settled certain French;
Who, holding in disdain the German women
For some dishonest manners of their life,
Establish'd then this law: to wit, no female
Should be inheritrix in Salique land;
Which Salique, as I said, 'twixt Elbe and Sala,
Is at this day in Germany call'd Meisen.

Then doth it well appear the Salique law
Was not devised for the realm of France;
Nor did the French possess the Salique land
Until four hundred one and twenty years
After defunction of King Pharamond,
Idly suppos'd the founder of this law;
Who died within the year of our redemption
Four hundred twenty-six; and Charles the Great
Subdu'd the Saxons, and did seat the French
Beyond the river Sala, in the year
Eight hundred five. Besides, their writers say,
King Pepin, which deposed Childeric,
Did, as heir general, being descended
Of Blithild, which was daughter to
 King Clothair,
Make claim and title to the crown of France.
Hugh Capet also, who usurp'd the crown
Of Charles the Duke of Lorraine, sole heir male
Of the true line and stock of Charles the Great,
To find his title with some shows of truth-
Though in pure truth it was corrupt
 and naught-
Convey'd himself as th' heir to th' Lady Lingare,
Daughter to Charlemain, who was the son
To Lewis the Emperor, and Lewis the son
Of Charles the Great. Also King Lewis
 the Tenth,
Who was sole heir to the usurper Capet,
Could not keep quiet in his conscience,
Wearing the crown of France, till satisfied
That fair Queen Isabel, his grandmother,
Was lineal of the Lady Ermengare,
Daughter to Charles the foresaid Duke
 of Lorraine;
By the which marriage the line of Charles
 the Great
Was re-united to the Crown of France.
So that, as clear as is the summer's sun,
King Pepin's title, and Hugh Capet's claim,
King Lewis his satisfaction, all appear
To hold in right and tide of the female;
So do the kings of France unto this day,
Howbeit they would hold up this Salique law
To bar your Highness claiming from the female;
And rather choose to hide them in a net
Than amply to imbar their crooked tides
Usurp'd from you and your progenitors.
KING HENRY. May I with right and conscience
 make this claim?
CANTERBURY. The sin upon my head,
 dread sovereign!
For in the book of Numbers is it writ,
When the man dies, let the inheritance

Descend unto the daughter. Gracious lord,
Stand for your own, unwind your bloody flag,
Look back into your mighty ancestors.
Go, my dread lord, to your great-
 grandsire's tomb,
From whom you claim; invoke his warlike spirit,
And your great-uncle's, Edward the Black Prince,
Who on the French ground play'd a tragedy,
Making defeat on the full power of France,
Whiles his most mighty father on a hill
Stood smiling to behold his lion's whelp
Forage in blood of French nobility.
O noble English, that could entertain
With half their forces the full pride of France,
And let another half stand laughing by,
All out of work and cold for action!
ELY. Awake remembrance of these valiant dead,
 And with your puissant arm renew their feats.
 You are their heir; you sit upon their throne;
 The blood and courage that renowned them
 Runs in your veins; and my thrice-puissant liege
 Is in the very May-morn of his youth,
 Ripe for exploits and mighty enterprises.
EXETER. Your brother kings and monarchs of
 the earth
 Do all expect that you should rouse yourself,
 As did the former lions of your blood.
WESTMORELAND. They know your Grace hath
 cause and means and might-
 So hath your Highness; never King of England
 Had nobles richer and more loyal subjects,
 Whose hearts have left their bodies here
 in England
 And lie pavilion'd in the fields of France.
CANTERBURY. O, let their bodies follow, my
 dear liege,
 With blood and sword and fire to win your right!
 In aid whereof we of the spiritualty
 Will raise your Highness such a mighty sum
 As never did the clergy at one time
 Bring in to any of your ancestors.
KING HENRY. We must not only arm t' invade
 the French,
 But lay down our proportions to defend
 Against the Scot, who will make road upon us
 With all advantages.
CANTERBURY. They of those marches,
 gracious sovereign,
 Shall be a wall sufficient to defend
 Our inland from the pilfering borderers.
KING HENRY. We do not mean the coursing
 snatchers only,
 But fear the main intendment of the Scot,

Who hath been still a giddy neighbour to us;
For you shall read that my great-grandfather
Never went with his forces into France
But that the Scot on his unfurnish'd kingdom
Came pouring, like the tide into a breach,
With ample and brim fulness of his force,
Galling the gleaned land with hot assays,
Girdling with grievous siege castles and towns;
That England, being empty of defence,
Hath shook and trembled at th' ·
 ill neighbourhood.
CANTERBURY. She hath been then more fear'd
 than harm'd, my liege;
For hear her but exampled by herself:
When all her chivalry hath been in France,
And she a mourning widow of her nobles,
She hath herself not only well defended
But taken and impounded as a stray
The King of Scots; whom she did send
 to France,
To fill King Edward's fame with prisoner kings,
And make her chronicle as rich with praise
As is the ooze and bottom of the sea
With sunken wreck and sumless treasuries.
WESTMORELAND. But there's a saying, very old
 and true:
   'If that you will France win,
   Then with Scotland first begin.'
For once the eagle England being in prey,
To her unguarded nest the weasel Scot
Comes sneaking, and so sucks her
 princely eggs,
Playing the mouse in absence of the cat,
To tear and havoc more than she can eat.
EXETER. It follows, then, the cat must stay
 at home;
Yet that is but a crush'd necessity,
Since we have locks to safeguard necessaries
And pretty traps to catch the petty thieves.
While that the armed hand doth fight abroad,
Th' advised head defends itself at home;
For government, though high, and low,
 and lower,
Put into parts, doth keep in one consent,
Congreeing in a full and natural close,
Like music.
CANTERBURY. Therefore doth heaven divide
The state of man in divers functions,
Setting endeavour in continual motion;
To which is fixed as an aim or but
Obedience; for so work the honey bees,
Creatures that by a rule in nature teach
The act of order to a peopled kingdom.

They have a king, and officers of sorts,
Where some like magistrates correct at home;
Others like merchants venture trade abroad;
Others like soldiers, armed in their stings,
Make boot upon the summer's velvet buds,
Which pillage they with merry march
 bring home
To the tent-royal of their emperor;
Who, busied in his majesty, surveys
The singing masons building roofs of gold,
The civil citizens kneading up the honey,
The poor mechanic porters crowding in
Their heavy burdens at his narrow gate,
The sad-ey'd justice, with his surly hum,
Delivering o'er to executors pale
The lazy yawning drone. I this infer,
That many things, having full reference
To one consent, may work contrariously;
As many arrows loosed several ways
Come to one mark, as many ways meet in
 one town,
As many fresh streams meet in one salt sea,
As many lines close in the dial's centre;
So many a thousand actions, once afoot,
End in one purpose, and be all well home
Without defeat. Therefore to France, my liege.
Divide your happy England into four;
Whereof take you one quarter into France,
And you withal shall make all Gallia shake.
If we, with thrice such powers left at home,
Cannot defend our own doors from the dog,
Let us be worried, and our nation lose
The name of hardiness and policy.
KING HENRY. Call in the messengers sent from
 the Dauphin.
                              Exeunt some Attendants.
Now are we well resolv'd; and, by God's help
And yours, the noble sinews of our power,
France being ours, we'll bend it to our awe,
Or break it all to pieces; or there we'll sit,
Ruling in large and ample empery
O'er France and all her almost kingly dukedoms,
Or lay these bones in an unworthy urn,
Tombless, with no remembrance over them.
Either our history shall with full mouth
Speak freely of our acts, or else our grave,
Like Turkish mute, shall have a
 tongueless mouth,
Not worshipp'd with a waxen epitaph.
                    Enter AMBASSADORS of France
Now are we well prepar'd to know the pleasure
Of our fair cousin Dauphin; for we hear
Your greeting is from him, not from the King.

AMBASSADOR. May't please your Majesty to give
  us leave
  Freely to render what we have in charge;
  Or shall we sparingly show you far of
  The Dauphin's meaning and our embassy?
KING HENRY. We are no tyrant, but a
  Christian king,
  Unto whose grace our passion is as subject
  As are our wretches fett'red in our prisons;
  Therefore with frank and with
  uncurbed plainness
  Tell us the Dauphin's mind.
AMBASSADOR. Thus then, in few.
  Your Highness, lately sending into France,
  Did claim some certain dukedoms in the right
  Of your great predecessor, King Edward
  the Third.
  In answer of which claim, the Prince our master
  Says that you savour too much of your youth,
  And bids you be advis'd there's nought
  in France
  That can be with a nimble galliard won;
  You cannot revel into dukedoms there.
  He therefore sends you, meeter for your spirit,
  This tun of treasure; and, in lieu of this,
  Desires you let the dukedoms that you claim
  Hear no more of you. This the Dauphin speaks.
KING HENRY. What treasure, uncle?
EXETER. Tennis-balls, my liege.
KING HENRY. We are glad the Dauphin is so
  pleasant with us;
  His present and your pains we thank you for.
  When we have match'd our rackets to
  these balls,
  We will in France, by God's grace, play a set
  Shall strike his father's crown into the hazard.
  Tell him he hath made a match with such
  a wrangler
  That all the courts of France will be disturb'd
  With chaces. And we understand him well,
  How he comes o'er us with our wilder days,
  Not measuring what use we made of them.
  We never valu'd this poor seat of England;
  And therefore, living hence, did give ourself
  To barbarous licence; as 'tis ever common
  That men are merriest when they are
  from home.
  But tell the Dauphin I will keep my state,
  Be like a king, and show my sail of greatness,
  When I do rouse me in my throne of France;
  For that I have laid by my majesty
  And plodded like a man for working-days;
  But I will rise there with so full a glory

That I will dazzle all the eyes of France,
  Yea, strike the Dauphin blind to look on us.
  And tell the pleasant Prince this mock of his
  Hath turn'd his balls to gun-stones, and his soul
  Shall stand sore charged for the
  wasteful vengeance
  That shall fly with them; for many a
  thousand widows
  Shall this his mock mock of their dear husbands;
  Mock mothers from their sons, mock
  castles down;
  And some are yet ungotten and unborn
  That shall have cause to curse the
  Dauphin's scorn.
  But this lies all within the will of God,
  To whom I do appeal; and in whose name,
  Tell you the Dauphin, I am coming on,
  To venge me as I may and to put forth
  My rightful hand in a well-hallow'd cause.
  So get you hence in peace; and tell the Dauphin
  His jest will savour but of shallow wit,
  When thousands weep more than did laugh at it.
  Convey them with safe conduct. Fare you well.
                    Exeunt AMBASSADORS.
EXETER. This was a merry message.
KING HENRY. We hope to make the sender
  blush at it.
  Therefore, my lords, omit no happy hour
  That may give furth'rance to our expedition;
  For we have now no thought in us but France,
  Save those to God, that run before our business.
  Therefore let our proportions for these wars
  Be soon collected, and all things thought upon
  That may with reasonable swiftness ad
  More feathers to our wings; for, God before,
  We'll chide this Dauphin at his father's door.
  Therefore let every man now task his thought
  That this fair action may on foot be brought.
                    Exeunt.

❧ ACT II ❧

PROLOGUE

Flourish. Enter CHORUS

CHORUS. Now all the youth of England are
  on fire,
  And silken dalliance in the wardrobe lies;
  Now thrive the armourers, and
  honour's thought

Reigns solely in the breast of every man;
They sell the pasture now to buy the horse,
Following the mirror of all Christian kings
With winged heels, as English Mercuries.
For now sits Expectation in the air,
And hides a sword from hilts unto the point
With crowns imperial, crowns, and coronets,
Promis'd to Harry and his followers.
The French, advis'd by good intelligence
Of this most dreadful preparation,
Shake in their fear and with pale policy
Seek to divert the English purposes.
O England! model to thy inward greatness,
Like little body with a mighty heart,
What mightst thou do that honour would
    thee do,
Were all thy children kind and natural!
But see thy fault! France hath in thee found out
A nest of hollow bosoms, which he fills
With treacherous crowns; and three
    corrupted men-
One, Richard Earl of Cambridge, and the second,
Henry Lord Scroop of Masham, and the third,
Sir Thomas Grey, knight, of Northumberland,
Have, for the gilt of France-O guilt indeed!-
Confirm'd conspiracy with fearful France;
And by their hands this grace of kings must die-
If hell and treason hold their promises,
Ere he take ship for France-and in Southampton.
Linger your patience on, and we'll digest
Th' abuse of distance, force a play.
The sum is paid, the traitors are agreed,
The King is set from London, and the scene
Is now transported, gentles, to Southampton;
There is the play-house now, there must you sit,
And thence to France shall we convey you safe
And bring you back, charming the narrow seas
To give you gentle pass; for, if we may,
We'll not offend one stomach with our play.
But, till the King come forth, and not till then,
Unto Southampton do we shift our scene

Exit.

✵ SCENE I ✵

London. Before the Boar's Head Tavern, Eastcheap

Enter CORPORAL NYM and
LIEUTENANT BARDOLPH

BARDOLPH. Well met, Corporal Nym.
NYM. Good morrow, Lieutenant Bardolph.

BARDOLPH. What, are Ancient Pistol and you
    friends yet?
NYM. For my part, I care not; I say little, but when
    time shall serve, there shall be smiles-but that
    shall be as it may. I dare not fight; but I will
    wink and hold out mine iron. It is a simple one;
    but what though? It will toast cheese, and it will
    endure cold as another man's sword will; and
    there's an end.
BARDOLPH. I will bestow a breakfast to make you
    friends; and we'll be all three sworn brothers to
    France. Let't be so, good Corporal Nym.
NYM. Faith, I will live so long as I may, that's the
    certain of it; and when I cannot live any longer,
    I will do as I may. That is my rest, that is the
    rendezvous of it.
BARDOLPH. It is certain, Corporal, that he is
    married to Nell Quickly; and certainly she did
    you wrong, for you were troth-plight to her.
NYM. I cannot tell; things must be as they may.
    Men may sleep, and they may have their
    throats about them at that time; and some say
    knives have edges. It must be as it may; though
    patience be a tired mare, yet she will plod.
    There must be conclusions. Well, I cannot tell.

Enter PISTOL and HOSTESS

BARDOLPH. Here comes Ancient Pistol and his
    wife. Good Corporal, be patient here.
NYM. How now, mine host Pistol!
PISTOL. Base tike, call'st thou me host?
    Now by this hand, I swear I scorn the term;
    Nor shall my Nell keep lodgers.
HOSTESS. No, by my troth, not long; for we
    cannot lodge and board a dozen or fourteen
    gentlewomen that live honestly by the prick of
    their needles, but it will be thought we keep
    a bawdy-house straight. *[NYM draws]* O well-a-
    day, Lady, if he be not drawn! Now we shall see
    wilful adultery and murder committed.
BARDOLPH. Good Lieutenant, good Corporal,
    offer nothing here.
NYM. Pish!
PISTOL. Pish for thee, Iceland dog! thou prick-
    ear'd cur of Iceland!
HOSTESS. Good Corporal Nym, show thy valour,
    and put up your sword.
NYM. Will you shog off? I would have you solus.
PISTOL. 'Solus', egregious dog? O viper vile!
    The 'solus' in thy most mervailous face;
    The 'solus' in thy teeth, and in thy throat,
    And in thy hateful lungs, yea, in thy maw, perdy;
    And, which is worse, within thy nasty mouth!
    I do retort the 'solus' in thy bowels;

For I can take, and Pistol's cock is up,
And flashing fire will follow.

NYM. I am not Barbason: you cannot conjure me.
I have an humour to knock you indifferently
well. If you grow foul with me, Pistol, I will
scour you with my rapier, as I may, in fair terms;
if you would walk off I would prick your guts
a little, in good terms, as I may, and thaes the
humour of it.

PISTOL. O braggart vile and damned
furious wight!
The grave doth gape and doting death is near;
Therefore exhale.   *PISTOL draws*

BARDOLPH. Hear me, hear me what I say: he that
strikes the first stroke I'll run him up to the
hilts, as I am a soldier.   *Draws*

PISTOL. An oath of mickle might; and fury shall
abate. *[PISTOL and NYM sheathe their swords]*
Give me thy fist, thy fore-foot to me give;
Thy spirits are most tall.

NYM. I will cut thy throat one time or other, in fair
terms; that is the humour of it.

PISTOL. 'Couple a gorge!'
That is the word. I thee defy again.
O hound of Crete, think'st thou my spouse
to get?
No; to the spital go,
And from the powd'ring tub of infamy
Fetch forth the lazar kite of Cressid's kind,
Doll Tearsheet she by name, and her espouse.
I have, and I will hold, the quondam Quickly
For the only she; and-pauca, there's enough.
Go to.

Enter the BOY

BOY. Mine host Pistol, you must come to my
master; and your hostess-he is very sick, and
would to bed. Good Bardolph, put thy face
between his sheets, and do the office of a
warming-pan. Faith, he's very ill.

BARDOLPH. Away, you rogue.

HOSTESS. By my troth, he'll yield the crow
a pudding one of these days: the King
has kill'd his heart. Good husband, come
home presently.

Exeunt HOSTESS and BOY.

BARDOLPH. Come, shall I make you two
friends? We must to France together; why
the devil should we keep knives to cut one
another's throats?

PISTOL. Let floods o'erswell, and fiends for food
howl on!

NYM. You'll pay me the eight shillings I won of
you at betting?

PISTOL. Base is the slave that pays.

NYM. That now I will have; that's the humour of it.

PISTOL. As manhood shall compound:
push home.

PISTOL and NYM draw

BARDOLPH. By this sword, he that makes the first
thrust I'll kill him; by this sword, I will.

PISTOL. Sword is an oath, and oaths must have
their course.   *Sheathes his sword*

BARDOLPH. Corporal Nym, an thou wilt be
friends, be friends; an thou wilt not, why then
be enemies with me too. Prithee put up.

NYM. I shall have my eight shillings I won of you
at betting?

PISTOL. A noble shalt thou have, and present pay;
And liquor likewise will I give to thee,
And friendship shall combine, and brotherhood.
I'll live by Nym and Nym shall live by me.
Is not this just? For I shall sutler be
Unto the camp, and profits will accrue.
Give me thy hand.

NYM. *[Sheathing his sword]* I shall have my noble?

PISTOL. In cash most justly paid.

NYM. *[Shaking hands]* Well, then, that's the
humour of't.

Re-enter HOSTESS

HOSTESS. As ever you come of women, come
in quickly to Sir John. Ah, poor heart! he is so
shak'd of a burning quotidian tertian that it is
most lamentable to behold. Sweet men, come
to him.

NYM. The King hath run bad humours on the
knight; that's the even of it.

PISTOL. Nym, thou hast spoke the right;
His heart is fracted and corroborate.

NYM. The King is a good king, but it must be as it
may; he passes some humours and careers.

PISTOL. Let us condole the knight; for, lambkins,
we will live.   *Exeunt.*

❧ SCENE II ❧
Southampton. A council-chamber

Enter EXETER, BEDFORD, and WESTMORELAND

BEDFORD. Fore God, his Grace is bold, to trust
these traitors.

EXETER. They shall be apprehended by and by.

WESTMORELAND. How smooth and even they do
bear themselves,
As if allegiance in their bosoms sat,
Crowned with faith and constant loyalty!

BEDFORD. The King hath note of all that
  they intend,
  By interception which they dream not of.
EXETER. Nay, but the man that was his bedfellow,
  Whom he hath dull'd and cloy'd with
    gracious favours-
  That he should, for a foreign purse, so sell
  His sovereign's life to death and treachery!

Trumpets sound. Enter the KING, SCROOP, CAMBRIDGE,
GREY, and Attendants

KING HENRY. Now sits the wind fair, and we
  will aboard.
  My Lord of Cambridge, and my kind Lord of
    Masham,
  And you, my gentle knight, give me
    your thoughts.
  Think you not that the pow'rs we bear with us
  Will cut their passage through the force
    of France,
  Doing the execution and the act
  For which we have in head assembled them?
SCROOP. No doubt, my liege, if each man do
  his best.
KING HENRY. I doubt not that, since we are
  well persuaded
  We carry not a heart with us from hence
  That grows not in a fair consent with ours;
  Nor leave not one behind that doth not wish
  Success and conquest to attend on us.
CAMBRIDGE. Never was monarch better fear'd
  and lov'd
  Than is your Majesty. There's not, I think,
    a subject
  That sits in heart-grief and uneasiness
  Under the sweet shade of your government.
GREY. True: those that were your father's enemies
  Have steep'd their galls in honey, and do
    serve you
  With hearts create of duty and of zeal.
KING HENRY. We therefore have great cause
  of thankfulness,
  And shall forget the office of our hand
  Sooner than quittance of desert and merit
  According to the weight and worthiness.
SCROOP. So service shall with steeled sinews toil,
  And labour shall refresh itself with hope,
  To do your Grace incessant services.
KING HENRY. We judge no less. Uncle of Exeter,
  Enlarge the man committed yesterday
  That rail'd against our person. We consider
  It was excess of wine that set him on;
  And on his more advice we pardon him.
SCROOP. That's mercy, but too much security.

Let him be punish'd, sovereign, lest example
  Breed, by his sufferance, more of such a kind.
KING HENRY. O, let us yet be merciful!
CAMBRIDGE. So may your Highness, and yet
  punish too.
GREY. Sir,
  You show great mercy if you give him life,
  After the taste of much correction.
KING HENRY. Alas, your too much love and care
  of me
  Are heavy orisons 'gainst this poor wretch!
  If little faults proceeding on distemper
  Shall not be wink'd at, how shall we stretch
    our eye
  When capital crimes, chew'd, swallow'd,
    and digested,
  Appear before us? We'll yet enlarge that man,
  Though Cambridge, Scroop, and Grey, in their
    dear care
  And tender preservation of our person,
  Would have him punish'd. And now to our
    French causes:
  Who are the late commissioners?
CAMBRIDGE. I one, my lord.
  Your Highness bade me ask for it to-day.
SCROOP. So did you me, my liege.
GREY. And I, my royal sovereign.
KING HENRY. Then, Richard Earl of Cambridge,
  there is yours;
  There yours, Lord Scroop of Masham; and,
    Sir Knight,
  Grey of Northumberland, this same is yours.
  Read them, and know I know your worthiness.
  My Lord of Westmoreland, and uncle Exeter,
  We will aboard to-night. Why, how
    now, gentlemen?
  What see you in those papers, that you lose
  So much complexion? Look ye how they change!
  Their cheeks are paper. Why, what read
    you there
  That have so cowarded and chas'd your blood
  Out of appearance?
CAMBRIDGE. I do confess my fault,
  And do submit me to your Highness' mercy.
GREY, SCROOP. To which we all appeal.
KING HENRY. The mercy that was quick in us
  but late
  By your own counsel is suppress'd and kill'd.
  You must not dare, for shame, to talk of mercy;
  For your own reasons turn into your bosoms
  As dogs upon their masters, worrying you.
  See you, my princes and my noble peers,
  These English monsters! My Lord of

Cambridge here-
You know how apt our love was to accord
To furnish him with all appertinents
Belonging to his honour; and this man
Hath, for a few light crowns, lightly conspir'd,
And sworn unto the practices of France
To kill us here in Hampton; to the which
This knight, no less for bounty bound to us
Than Cambridge is, hath likewise sworn. But, O,
What shall I say to thee, Lord Scroop, thou cruel,
Ingrateful, savage, and inhuman creature?
Thou that didst bear the key of all my counsels,
That knew'st the very bottom of my soul,
That almost mightst have coin'd me into gold,
Wouldst thou have practis'd on me for thy use-
May it be possible that foreign hire
Could out of thee extract one spark of evil
That might annoy my finger? 'Tis so strange
That, though the truth of it stands off as gross
As black and white, my eye will scarcely see it.
Treason and murder ever kept together,
As two yoke-devils sworn to either's purpose,
Working so grossly in a natural cause
That admiration did not whoop at them;
But thou, 'gainst all proportion, didst bring in
Wonder to wait on treason and on murder;
And whatsoever cunning fiend it was
That wrought upon thee so preposterously
Hath got the voice in hell for excellence;
And other devils that suggest by treasons
Do botch and bungle up damnation
With patches, colours, and with forms,
 being fetch'd
From glist'ring semblances of piety;
But he that temper'd thee bade thee stand up,
Gave thee no instance why thou shouldst
 do treason,
Unless to dub thee with the name of traitor.
If that same demon that hath gull'd thee thus
Should with his lion gait walk the whole world,
He might return to vasty Tartar back,
And tell the legions 'I can never win
A soul so easy as that Englishman's.'
O, how hast thou with jealousy infected
The sweetness of affiance! Show men dutiful?
Why, so didst thou. Seem they grave
 and learned?
Why, so didst thou. Come they of noble family?
Why, so didst thou. Seem they religious?
Why, so didst thou. Or are they spare in diet,
Free from gross passion or of mirth or anger,
Constant in spirit, not swerving with the blood,
Garnish'd and deck'd in modest complement,

Not working with the eye without the ear,
And but in purged judgment trusting neither?
Such and so finely bolted didst thou seem;
And thus thy fall hath left a kind of blot
To mark the full-fraught man and best indued
With some suspicion. I will weep for thee;
For this revolt of thine, methinks, is like
Another fall of man. Their faults are open.
Arrest them to the answer of the law;
And God acquit them of their practices!
EXETER. I arrest thee of high treason, by the
 name of Richard Earl of Cambridge. I arrest
 thee of high treason, by the name of Henry
 Lord Scroop of Masham. I arrest thee of high
 treason, by the name of Thomas Grey, knight,
 of Northumberland.
SCROOP. Our purposes God justly
 hath discover'd,
And I repent my fault more than my death;
Which I beseech your Highness to forgive,
Although my body pay the price of it.
CAMBRIDGE. For me, the gold of France did
 not seduce,
Although I did admit it as a motive
The sooner to effect what I intended;
But God be thanked for prevention,
Which I in sufferance heartily will rejoice,
Beseeching God and you to pardon me.
GREY. Never did faithful subject more rejoice
 At the discovery of most dangerous treason
Than I do at this hour joy o'er myself,
Prevented from a damned enterprise.
My fault, but not my body, pardon, sovereign.
KING HENRY. God quit you in his mercy! Hear
 your sentence.
You have conspir'd against our royal person,
Join'd with an enemy proclaim'd, and from
 his coffers
Receiv'd the golden earnest of our death;
Wherein you would have sold your King
 to slaughter,
His princes and his peers to servitude,
His subjects to oppression and contempt,
And his whole kingdom into desolation.
Touching our person seek we no revenge;
But we our kingdom's safety must so tender,
Whose ruin you have sought, that to her laws
We do deliver you. Get you therefore hence,
Poor miserable wretches, to your death;
The taste whereof God of his mercy give
You patience to endure, and true repentance
Of all your dear offences. Bear them hence.
 Exeunt CAMBRIDGE, SCROOP, and GREY, guarded.

Now, lords, for France; the enterprise whereof
Shall be to you as us like glorious.
We doubt not of a fair and lucky war,
Since God so graciously hath brought to light
This dangerous treason, lurking in our way
To hinder our beginnings; we doubt not now
But every rub is smoothed on our way.
Then, forth, dear countrymen; let us deliver
Our puissance into the hand of God,
Putting it straight in expedition.
Cheerly to sea; the signs of war advance;
No king of England, if not king of France!

Flourish. Exeunt.

❧ SCENE III ❧
Eastcheap. Before the Boar's Head tavern

Enter PISTOL, HOSTESS, NYM, BARDOLPH, and BOY

HOSTESS. Prithee, honey-sweet husband, let me
  bring thee to Staines.
PISTOL. No; for my manly heart doth earn.
  Bardolph, be blithe; Nym, rouse thy
  vaunting veins;
  Boy, bristle thy courage up. For Falstaff he
  is dead,
  And we must earn therefore.
BARDOLPH. Would I were with him,
  wheresome'er he is, either in heaven or in hell!
HOSTESS. Nay, sure, he's not in hell: he's in
  Arthur's bosom, if ever man went to Arthur's
  bosom. 'A made a finer end, and went away
  an it had been any christom child; 'a parted
  ev'n just between twelve and one, ev'n at the
  turning o' th' tide; for after I saw him fumble
  with the sheets, and play with flowers, and
  smile upon his fingers' end, I knew there was
  but one way; for his nose was as sharp as a pen,
  and 'a babbl'd of green fields. 'How now, Sir
  John!' quoth I, 'What, man, be o' good cheer.'
  So 'a cried out 'God, God, God!' three or four
  times. Now I, to comfort him, bid him 'a should
  not think of God; I hop'd there was no need
  to trouble himself with any such thoughts yet.
  So 'a bade me lay more clothes on his feet; I
  put my hand into the bed and felt them, and
  they were as cold as any stone; then I felt to his
  knees, and so upward and upward, and all was
  as cold as any stone.
NYM. They say he cried out of sack.
HOSTESS. Ay, that 'a did.
BARDOLPH. And of women.

HOSTESS. Nay, that 'a did not.
BOY. Yes, that 'a did, and said they were
  devils incarnate.
HOSTESS. 'A could never abide carnation; 'twas a
  colour he never liked.
BOY. 'A said once the devil would have him
  about women.
HOSTESS. 'A did in some sort, indeed, handle
  women; but then he was rheumatic, and talk'd
  of the Whore of Babylon.
BOY. Do you not remember 'a saw a flea stick
  upon Bardolph's nose, and 'a said it was a black
  soul burning in hell?
BARDOLPH. Well, the fuel is gone that maintain'd
  that fire: that's all the riches I got in his service.
NYM. Shall we shog? The King will be gone
  from Southampton.
PISTOL. Come, let's away. My love, give me
  thy lips.
  Look to my chattles and my moveables;
  Let senses rule. The word is 'Pitch and Pay'.
  Trust none;
  For oaths are straws, men's faiths are wafer-
  cakes,
  And Holdfast is the only dog, my duck.
  Therefore, Caveto be thy counsellor.
  Go, clear thy crystals. Yoke-fellows in arms,
  Let us to France, like horse-leeches, my boys,
  To suck, to suck, the very blood to suck.
BOY. And that's but unwholesome food, they say.
PISTOL. Touch her soft mouth and march.
BARDOLPH. Farewell, hostess. *Kissing her*
NYM. I cannot kiss, that is the humour of it;
  but adieu.
PISTOL. Let housewifery appear; keep close, I
  thee command.
HOSTESS. Farewell; adieu. *Exeunt.*

❧ SCENE IV ❧
France. The KING'S palace

*Flourish. Enter the FRENCH KING, the DAUPHIN, the
DUKES OF BERRI and BRITAINE, the CONSTABLE,
and Others*

FRENCH KING. Thus comes the English with full
  power upon us;
  And more than carefully it us concerns
  To answer royally in our defences.
  Therefore the Dukes of Berri and of Britaine,
  Of Brabant and of Orleans, shall make forth,
  And you, Prince Dauphin, with all swift dispatch,

To line and new repair our towns of war
With men of courage and with means defendant;
For England his approaches makes as fierce
As waters to the sucking of a gulf.
It fits us, then, to be as provident
As fear may teach us, out of late examples
Left by the fatal and neglected English
Upon our fields.

DAUPHIN. My most redoubted father,
It is most meet we arm us 'gainst the foe;
For peace itself should not so dull a kingdom,
Though war nor no known quarrel were
in question,
But that defences, musters, preparations,
Should be maintain'd, assembled, and collected,
As were a war in expectation.
Therefore, I say, 'tis meet we all go forth
To view the sick and feeble parts of France;
And let us do it with no show of fear-
No, with no more than if we heard that England
Were busied with a Whitsun morris-dance;
For, my good liege, she is so idly king'd,
Her sceptre so fantastically borne
By a vain, giddy, shallow, humorous youth,
That fear attends her not.

CONSTABLE. O peace, Prince Dauphin!
You are too much mistaken in this king.
Question your Grace the late ambassadors
With what great state he heard their embassy,
How well supplied with noble counsellors,
How modest in exception, and withal
How terrible in constant resolution,
And you shall find his vanities forespent
Were but the outside of the Roman Brutus,
Covering discretion with a coat of folly;
As gardeners do with ordure hide those roots
That shall first spring and be most delicate.

DAUPHIN. Well, 'tis not so, my Lord
High Constable;
But though we think it so, it is no matter.
In cases of defence 'tis best to weigh
The enemy more mighty than he seems;
So the proportions of defence are fill'd;
Which of a weak and niggardly projection
Doth like a miser spoil his coat with scanting
A little cloth.

FRENCH KING. Think we King Harry strong;
And, Princes, look you strongly arm to meet him.
The kindred of him hath been flesh'd upon us;
And he is bred out of that bloody strain
That haunted us in our familiar paths.
Witness our too much memorable shame
When Cressy battle fatally was struck,

And all our princes captiv'd by the hand
Of that black name, Edward, Black Prince
of Wales;
Whiles that his mountain sire-on
mountain standing,
Up in the air, crown'd with the golden sun-
Saw his heroical seed, and smil'd to see him,
Mangle the work of nature, and deface
The patterns that by God and by French fathers
Had twenty years been made. This is a stem
Of that victorious stock; and let us fear
The native mightiness and fate of him.

Enter a MESSENGER

MESSENGER. Ambassadors from Harry King
of England
Do crave admittance to your Majesty.

FRENCH KING. We'll give them present audience.
Go and bring them.

Exeunt MESSENGER and certain LORDS.

You see this chase is hotly followed, friends.

DAUPHIN. Turn head and stop pursuit; for
coward dogs
Most spend their mouths when what they seem
to threaten
Runs far before them. Good my sovereign,
Take up the English short, and let them know
Of what a monarchy you are the head.
Self-love, my liege, is not so vile a sin
As self-neglecting.

Re-enter LORDS, with EXETER and train

FRENCH KING. From our brother of England?

EXETER. From him, and thus he greets
your Majesty:
He wills you, in the name of God Almighty,
That you divest yourself, and lay apart
The borrowed glories that by gift of heaven,
By law of nature and of nations, 'longs
To him and to his heirs-namely, the crown,
And all wide-stretched honours that pertain,
By custom and the ordinance of times,
Unto the crown of France. That you may know
'Tis no sinister nor no awkward claim,
Pick'd from the worm-holes of long-
vanish'd days,
Nor from the dust of old oblivion rak'd,
He sends you this most memorable line, *[Gives
a paper]*
In every branch truly demonstrative;
Willing you overlook this pedigree.
And when you find him evenly deriv'd
From his most fam'd of famous ancestors,
Edward the Third, he bids you then resign
Your crown and kingdom, indirectly held

From him, the native and true challenger.

FRENCH KING. Or else what follows?

EXETER. Bloody constraint; for if you hide
the crown
Even in your hearts, there will he rake for it.
Therefore in fierce tempest is he coming,
In thunder and in earthquake, like a Jove,
That if requiring fail, he will compel;
And bids you, in the bowels of the Lord,
Deliver up the crown; and to take mercy
On the poor souls for whom this hungry war
Opens his vasty jaws; and on your head
Turning the widows' tears, the orphans' cries,
The dead men's blood, the privy
maidens' groans,
For husbands, fathers, and betrothed lovers,
That shall be swallowed in this controversy.
This is his claim, his threat'ning, and
my message;
Unless the Dauphin be in presence here,
To whom expressly I bring greeting too.

FRENCH KING. For us, we will consider of
this further;
To-morrow shall you bear our full intent
Back to our brother of England.

DAUPHIN. For the Dauphin:
I stand here for him. What to him from England?

EXETER. Scorn and defiance, slight
regard, contempt,
And anything that may not misbecome
The mighty sender, doth he prize you at.
Thus says my King: an if your father's Highness
Do not, in grant of all demands at large,
Sweeten the bitter mock you sent his Majesty,
He'll call you to so hot an answer of it
That caves and womby vaultages of France
Shall chide your trespass and return your mock
In second accent of his ordinance.

DAUPHIN. Say, if my father render fair return,
It is against my will; for I desire
Nothing but odds with England. To that end,
As matching to his youth and vanity,
I did present him with the Paris balls.

EXETER. He'll make your Paris Louvre shake for it,
Were it the mistress court of mighty Europe;
And be assur'd you'll find a difference,
As we his subjects have in wonder found,
Between the promise of his greener days
And these he masters now. Now he weighs time
Even to the utmost grain; that you shall read
In your own losses, if he stay in France.

FRENCH KING. To-morrow shall you know our
mind at full.

EXETER. Dispatch us with all speed, lest that
our King
Come here himself to question our delay;
For he is footed in this land already.

FRENCH KING. You shall be soon dispatch'd with
fair conditions.
A night is but small breath and little pause
To answer matters of this consequence.

Flourish. Exeunt.

❧ ACT III ❧

PROLOGUE

Flourish. Enter CHORUS

CHORUS. Thus with imagin'd wing our swift
scene flies,
In motion of no less celerity
Than that of thought. Suppose that you
have seen
The well-appointed King at Hampton pier
Embark his royalty; and his brave fleet
With silken streamers the young
Phoebus fanning.
Play with your fancies; and in them behold
Upon the hempen tackle ship-boys climbing;
Hear the shrill whistle which doth order give
To sounds confus'd; behold the threaden sails,
Borne with th' invisible and creeping wind,
Draw the huge bottoms through the
furrowed sea,
Breasting the lofty surge. O, do but think
You stand upon the rivage and behold
A city on th' inconstant billows dancing;
For so appears this fleet majestical,
Holding due course to Harfleur. Follow, follow!
Grapple your minds to sternage of this navy
And leave your England as dead midnight still,
Guarded with grandsires, babies, and old women,
Either past or not arriv'd to pith and puissance;
For who is he whose chin is but enrich'd
With one appearing hair that will not follow
These cull'd and choice-drawn cavaliers
to France?
Work, work your thoughts, and therein see
a siege;
Behold the ordnance on their carriages,
With fatal mouths gaping on girded Harfleur.
Suppose th' ambassador from the French
comes back;

Tells Harry that the King doth offer him
Katherine his daughter, and with her to dowry
Some petty and unprofitable dukedoms.
The offer likes not; and the nimble gunner
With linstock now the devilish cannon touches,

[Alarum, and chambers go off]

And down goes an before them. Still be kind,
And eke out our performance with your mind.

Exit.

✤ SCENE I ✤
France. Before Harfleur

*Alarum. Enter the KING, EXETER, BEDFORD,
GLOUCESTER, and Soldiers with scaling-ladders*

KING. Once more unto the breach, dear friends,
  once more;
  Or close the wall up with our English dead.
  In peace there's nothing so becomes a man
  As modest stillness and humility;
  But when the blast of war blows in our ears,
  Then imitate the action of the tiger:
  Stiffen the sinews, summon up the blood,
  Disguise fair nature with hard-favour'd rage;
  Then lend the eye a terrible aspect;
  Let it pry through the portage of the head
  Like the brass cannon: let the brow o'erwhelm it
  As fearfully as doth a galled rock
  O'erhang and jutty his confounded base,
  Swill'd with the wild and wasteful ocean.
  Now set the teeth and stretch the nostril wide;
  Hold hard the breath, and bend up every spirit
  To his full height. On, on, you noblest English,
  Whose blood is fet from fathers of war-proof-
  Fathers that like so many Alexanders
  Have in these parts from morn till
   even fought,
  And sheath'd their swords for lack
   of argument.
  Dishonour not your mothers; now attest
  That those whom you call'd fathers did
   beget you.
  Be copy now to men of grosser blood,
  And teach them how to war. And you,
   good yeomen,
  Whose limbs were made in England, show
   us here
  The mettle of your pasture; let us swear
  That you are worth your breeding-which I
   doubt not;
  For there is none of you so mean and base

That hath not noble lustre in your eyes.
I see you stand like greyhounds in the slips,
Straining upon the start. The game's afoot:
Follow your spirit; and upon this charge
Cry 'God for Harry, England, and Saint George!'

Exeunt. Alarum, and chambers go off

✤ SCENE II ✤
Before Harfleur

Enter NYM, BARDOLPH, PISTOL, and BOY

BARDOLPH. On, on, on, on, on! to the breach, to
  the breach!
NYM. Pray thee, Corporal, stay; the knocks are too
  hot, and for mine own part I have not a case
  of lives. The humour of it is too hot; that is the
  very plain-song of it.
PISTOL. The plain-song is most just; for humours
  do abound:
      Knocks go and come; God's vassals drop
          and die;
        And sword and shield
        In bloody field
      Doth win immortal fame.
BOY. Would I were in an alehouse in London!
  I would give all my fame for a pot of ale
  and safety.
PISTOL. And I:
      If wishes would prevail with me,
      My purpose should not fail with me,
        But thither would I hie.
BOY. As duly, but not as truly,
        As bird doth sing on bough.

Enter FLUELLEN

FLUELLEN. Up to the breach, you dogs!
  Avaunt, you cullions! *Driving them forward*
PISTOL. Be merciful, great duke, to men of mould.
  Abate thy rage, abate thy manly rage;
  Abate thy rage, great duke.
  Good bawcock, bate thy rage. Use lenity,
  sweet chuck.
NYM. These be good humours. Your honour wins
  bad humours. *Exeunt all but BOY.*
BOY. As young as I am, I have observ'd these
  three swashers. I am boy to them all three;
  but all they three, though they would serve
  me, could not be man to me; for indeed three
  such antics do not amount to a man. For
  Bardolph, he is white-liver'd and red-fac'd; by
  the means whereof 'a faces it out, but fights
  not. For Pistol, he hath a killing tongue and a

quiet sword; by the means whereof 'a breaks words and keeps whole weapons. For Nym, he hath heard that men of few words are the best men, and therefore he scorns to say his prayers lest 'a should be thought a coward; but his few bad words are match'd with as few good deeds; for 'a never broke any man's head but his own, and that was against a post when he was drunk. They will steal anything, and call it purchase. Bardolph stole a lute-case, bore it twelve leagues, and sold it for three halfpence. Nym and Bardolph are sworn brothers in filching, and in Calais they stole a fire-shovel; I knew by that piece of service the men would carry coals. They would have me as familiar with men's pockets as their gloves or their handkerchers; which makes much against my manhood, if I should take from another's pocket to put into mine; for it is plain pocketing up of wrongs. I must leave them and seek some better service; their villainy goes against my weak stomach, and therefore I must cast it up. *Exit.*

Re-enter FLUELLEN, GOWER following

GOWER. Captain Fluellen, you must come presently to the mines; the Duke of Gloucester would speak with you.

FLUELLEN. To the mines! Tell you the Duke it is not so good to come to the mines; for, look you, the mines is not according to the disciplines of the war; the concavities of it is not sufficient. For, look you, th' athversary-you may discuss unto the Duke, look you-is digt himself four yard under the countermines; by Cheshu, I think 'a will plow up all, if there is not better directions.

GOWER. The Duke of Gloucester, to whom the order of the siege is given, is altogether directed by an Irishman-a very vallant gentleman, i' faith.

FLUELLEN. It is Captain Macmorris, is it not?

GOWER. I think it be.

FLUELLEN. By Cheshu, he is an ass, as in the world: I will verify as much in his beard; he has no more directions in the true disciplines of the wars, look you, of the Roman disciplines, than is a puppy-dog.

Enter MACMORRIS and CAPTAIN JAMY

GOWER. Here 'a comes; and the Scots captain, Captain Jamy, with him.

FLUELLEN. Captain Jamy is a marvellous falorous gentleman, that is certain, and of great expedition and knowledge in th' aunchient wars, upon my particular knowledge of his directions. By Cheshu, he will maintain his argument as well as any military man in the world, in the disciplines of the pristine wars of the Romans.

JAMY. I say gud day, Captain Fluellen.

FLUELLEN. God-den to your worship, good Captain James.

GOWER. How now, Captain Macmorris! Have you quit the mines? Have the pioneers given o'er?

MACMORRIS. By Chrish, la, tish ill done! The work ish give over, the trompet sound the retreat. By my hand, I swear, and my father's soul, the work ish ill done; it ish give over; I would have blowed up the town, so Chrish save me, la, in an hour. O, tish ill done, tish ill done; by my hand, tish ill done!

FLUELLEN. Captain Macmorris, I beseech you now, will you voutsafe me, look you, a few disputations with you, as partly touching or concerning the disciplines of the war, the Roman wars, in the way of argument, look you, and friendly communication; partly to satisfy my opinion, and partly for the satisfaction, look you, of my mind, as touching the direction of the military discipline, that is the point.

JAMY. It sall be vary gud, gud feith, gud captains bath; and I sall quit you with gud leve, as I may pick occasion; that sall I, marry.

MACMORRIS. It is no time to discourse, so Chrish save me. The day is hot, and the weather, and the wars, and the King, and the Dukes; it is no time to discourse. The town is beseech'd, and the trumpet call us to the breach; and we talk and, be Chrish, do nothing. 'Tis shame for us all, so God sa' me, 'tis shame to stand still; it is shame, by my hand; and there is throats to be cut, and works to be done; and there ish nothing done, so Chrish sa' me, la.

JAMY. By the mess, ere theise eyes of mine take themselves to slomber, ay'll de gud service, or I'll lig i' th' grund for it; ay, or go to death. And I'll pay't as valorously as I may, that sall I suerly do, that is the breff and the long. Marry, I wad full fain heard some question 'tween you tway.

FLUELLEN. Captain Macmorris, I think, look you, under your correction, there is not many of your nation-

MACMORRIS. Of my nation? What ish my nation? Ish a villain, and a bastard, and a knave, and

a rascal. What ish my nation? Who talks of
my nation?
FLUELLEN. Look you, if you take the matter
otherwise than is meant, Captain Macmorris,
peradventure I shall think you do not use
me with that affability as in discretion you
ought to use me, look you; being as good
a man as yourself, both in the disciplines of
war and in the derivation of my birth, and in
other particularities.
MACMORRIS. I do not know you so good a man
as myself; so Chrish save me, I will cut off
your head.
GOWER. Gentlemen both, you will mistake
each other.
JAMY. Ah! that's a foul fault. *A parley sounded*
GOWER. The town sounds a parley.
FLUELLEN. Captain Macmorris, when there is
more better opportunity to be required, look
you, I will be so bold as to tell you I know the
disciplines of war; and there is an end. *Exeunt.*

✥ SCENE III ✥
Before the gates of Harfleur

Enter the GOVERNOR and some Citizens on the walls. Enter
the KING and all his train before the gates

KING HENRY. How yet resolves the Governor of
the town?
This is the latest parle we will admit;
Therefore to our best mercy give yourselves,
Or, like to men proud of destruction,
Defy us to our worst; for, as I am a soldier,
A name that in my thoughts becomes me best,
If I begin the batt'ry once again,
I will not leave the half-achieved Harfleur
Till in her ashes she lie buried.
The gates of mercy shall be all shut up,
And the flesh'd soldier, rough and hard of heart,
In liberty of bloody hand shall range
With conscience wide as hell, mowing like grass
Your fresh fair virgins and your flow'ring infants.
What is it then to me if impious war,
Array'd in flames, like to the prince of fiends,
Do, with his smirch'd complexion, all fell feats
Enlink'd to waste and desolation?
What is't to me when you yourselves are cause,
If your pure maidens fall into the hand
Of hot and forcing violation?
What rein can hold licentious wickednes
When down the hill he holds his fierce career?

We may as bootless spend our vain command
Upon th' enraged soldiers in their spoil,
As send precepts to the Leviathan
To come ashore. Therefore, you men
of Harfleur,
Take pity of your town and of your people
Whiles yet my soldiers are in my command;
Whiles yet the cool and temperate wind of grace
O'erblows the filthy and contagious clouds
Of heady murder, spoil, and villainy.
If not-why, in a moment look to see
The blind and bloody with foul hand
Defile the locks of your shrill-
shrieking daughters;
Your fathers taken by the silver beards,
And their most reverend heads dash'd to the
walls;
Your naked infants spitted upon pikes,
Whiles the mad mothers with their
howls confus'd
Do break the clouds, as did the wives of Jewry
At Herod's bloody-hunting slaughtermen.
What say you? Will you yield, and this avoid?
Or, guilty in defence, be thus destroy'd?
GOVERNOR. Our expectation hath this day
an end:
The Dauphin, whom of succours we entreated,
Returns us that his powers are yet not ready
To raise so great a siege. Therefore, great King,
We yield our town and lives to thy soft mercy.
Enter our gates; dispose of us and ours;
For we no longer are defensible.
KING HENRY. Open your gates. [*Exit GOVERNOR*]
Come, uncle Exeter,
Go you and enter Harfleur; there remain,
And fortify it strongly 'gainst the French;
Use mercy to them all. For us, dear uncle,
The winter coming on, and sickness growing
Upon our soldiers, we will retire to Calais.
To-night in Harfleur will we be your guest;
To-morrow for the march are we addrest.
Flourish. The KING and his train enter the town

✥ SCENE IV ✥
Rouen. The FRENCH KING'S palace

Enter KATHERINE and ALICE

KATHERINE. Alice, tu as été en Angleterre, et tu
parles bien le langage.
ALICE. Un peu, madame.
KATHERINE. Je te prie, m'enseignez; il faut que

j'apprenne à parler. Comment appelez-vous la main en Anglais?

ALICE. La main? Elle est appelée de hand.

KATHERINE. De hand. Et les doigts?

ALICE. Les doigts? Ma foi, j'oublie les doigts; mais je me souviendrai. Les doigts? Je pense qu'ils sont appelés de fingres; oui, de fingres.

KATHERINE. La main, de hand; les doigts, de fingres. Je pense que je suis le bon écolier; j'ai gagné deux mots d'Anglais vitement. Comment appelez-vous les ongles?

ALICE. Les ongles? Nous les appelons de nails.

KATHERINE. De nails. Ecoutez; dites-moi si je parle bien: de hand, de fingres, et de nails.

ALICE. C'est bien dit, madame; il est fort bon Anglais.

KATHERINE. Dites-moi l'Anglais pour le bras.

ALICE. De arm, madame.

KATHERINE. Et le coude?

ALICE. D'elbow.

KATHERINE. D'elbow. Je m'en fais la répétition de tous les mots que vous m'avez appris dès à present.

ALICE. Il est trop difficile, madame, comme je pense.

KATHERINE. Excusez-moi, Alice; écoutez: d'hand, de fingre, de nails, d'arma, de bilbow.

ALICE. D'elbow, madame.

KATHERINE. O Seigneur Dieu, je m'en oublie! D'elbow. Comment appelez-vous le col?

ALICE. De nick, madame.

KATHERINE. De nick. Et le menton?

ALICE. De chin.

KATHERINE. De sin. Le col, de nick; le menton, de sin.

ALICE. Oui. Sauf votre honneur, en vérité, vous prononcez les mots aussi droit que les natifs d'Angleterre.

KATHERINE. Je ne doute point d'apprendre, par la grace de Dieu, et en peu de temps.

ALICE. N'avez-vous pas deja oublié ce que je vous ai enseigné?

KATHERINE. Non, je réciterai à vous promptement: d'hand, de fingre, de mails-

ALICE. De nails, madame.

KATHERINE. De nails, de arm, de ilbow.

ALICE. Sauf votre honneur, d'elbow.

KATHERINE. Ainsi dis-je; d'elbow, de nick, et de sin. Comment appelez-vous le pied et la robe?

ALICE. Le foot, madame; et le count.

KATHERINE. Le foot et le count. O Seigneur Dieu! ils sont mots de son mauvais, corruptible, gros, et impudique, et non pour les dames

d'honneur d'user: je ne voudrais prononcer ces mots devant les seigneurs de France pour tout le monde. Foh! le foot et le count! Néanmoins, je réciterai une autre fois ma leçon ensemble: d'hand, de fingre, de nails, d'arm, d'elbow, de nick, de sin, de foot, le count.

ALICE. Excellent, madame!

KATHERINE. C'est assez pour une fois: allons-nous à diner. *Exeunt.*

☙ SCENE V ❧
The FRENCH KING'S palace

Enter the KING OF FRANCE, the DAUPHIN, DUKE OF BRITAINE, the CONSTABLE OF FRANCE, and Others

FRENCH KING. 'Tis certain he hath pass'd the river Somme.

CONSTABLE. And if he be not fought withal, my lord,
Let us not live in France; let us quit all,
And give our vineyards to a barbarous people.

DAUPHIN. O Dieu vivant! Shall a few sprays of us,
The emptying of our fathers' luxury,
Our scions, put in wild and savage stock,
Spirt up so suddenly into the clouds,
And overlook their grafters?

BRITAINE. Normans, but bastard Normans, Norman bastards!
Mort Dieu, ma vie! if they march along
Unfought withal, but I will sell my dukedom
To buy a slobb'ry and a dirty farm
In that nook-shotten isle of Albion.

CONSTABLE. Dieu de batailles! where have they this mettle?
Is not their climate foggy, raw, and dull;
On whom, as in despite, the sun looks pale,
Killing their fruit with frowns? Can sodden water,
A drench for sur-rein'd jades, their barley-broth,
Decoct their cold blood to such valiant heat?
And shall our quick blood, spirited with wine,
Seem frosty? O, for honour of our land,
Let us not hang like roping icicles
Upon our houses' thatch, whiles a more frosty people
Sweat drops of gallant youth in our rich fields-
Poor we call them in their native lords!

DAUPHIN. By faith and honour,
Our madams mock at us and plainly say

Our mettle is bred out, and they will give
Their bodies to the lust of English youth
To new-store France with bastard warriors.

BRITAINE. They bid us to the English dancing-schools
And teach lavoltas high and swift corantos,
Saying our grace is only in our heels
And that we are most lofty runaways.

FRENCH KING. Where is Montjoy the herald? Speed him hence;
Let him greet England with our sharp defiance.
Up, Princes, and, with spirit of honour edged
More sharper than your swords, hie to the field:
Charles Delabreth, High Constable of France;
You Dukes of Orleans, Bourbon, and of Berri,
Alengon, Brabant, Bar, and Burgundy;
Jaques Chatillon, Rambures, Vaudemont,
Beaumont, Grandpre, Roussi, and Fauconbridge,
Foix, Lestrake, Bouciqualt, and Charolois;
High dukes, great princes, barons, lords, and knights,
For your great seats now quit you of great shames.
Bar Harry England, that sweeps through our land
With pennons painted in the blood of Harfleur.
Rush on his host as doth the melted snow
Upon the valleys, whose low vassal seat
The Alps doth spit and void his rheum upon;
Go down upon him, you have power enough,
And in a captive chariot into Rouen
Bring him our prisoner.

CONSTABLE. This becomes the great.
Sorry am I his numbers are so few,
His soldiers sick and famish'd in their march;
For I am sure, when he shall see our army,
He'll drop his heart into the sink of fear,
And for achievement offer us his ransom.

FRENCH KING. Therefore, Lord Constable, haste on Montjoy,
And let him say to England that we send
To know what willing ransom he will give.
Prince Dauphin, you shall stay with us in Rouen.

DAUPHIN. Not so, I do beseech your Majesty.

FRENCH KING. Be patient, for you shall remain with us.
Now forth, Lord Constable and Princes all,
And quickly bring us word of England's fall.

Exeunt

SCENE VI

The English camp in Picardy

Enter CAPTAINS, English and Welsh, GOWER, and FLUELLEN

GOWER. How now, Captain Fluellen! Come you from the bridge?

FLUELLEN. I assure you there is very excellent services committed at the bridge.

GOWER. Is the Duke of Exeter safe?

FLUELLEN. The Duke of Exeter is as magnanimous as Agamemnon; and a man that I love and honour with my soul, and my heart, and my duty, and my life, and my living, and my uttermost power. He is not-God be praised and blessed!-any hurt in the world, but keeps the bridge most valiantly, with excellent discipline. There is an aunchient Lieutenant there at the bridge-I think in my very conscience he is as valiant a man as Mark Antony; and he is man of no estimation in the world; but I did see him do as gallant service.

GOWER. What do you call him?

FLUELLEN. He is call'd Aunchient Pistol.

GOWER. I know him not.

Enter PISTOL

FLUELLEN. Here is the man.

PISTOL. Captain, I thee beseech to do me favours.
The Duke of Exeter doth love thee well.

FLUELLEN. Ay, I praise God; and I have merited some love at his hands.

PISTOL. Bardolph, a soldier, firm and sound of heart,
And of buxom valour, hath by cruel fate
And giddy Fortune's furious fickle wheel,
That goddess blind,
That stands upon the rolling restless stone-

FLUELLEN. By your patience, Aunchient Pistol. Fortune is painted blind, with a muffler afore her eyes, to signify to you that Fortune is blind; and she is painted also with a wheel, to signify to you, which is the moral of it, that she is turning, and inconstant, and mutability, and variation; and her foot, look you, is fixed upon a spherical stone, which rolls, and rolls, and rolls. In good truth, the poet makes a most excellent description of it: Fortune is an excellent moral.

PISTOL. Fortune is Bardolph's foe, and frowns on him;

For he hath stol'n a pax, and hanged must 'a be-
A damned death!
Let gallows gape for dog; let man go free,
And let not hemp his windpipe suffocate.
But Exeter hath given the doom of death
For pax of little price.
Therefore, go speak-the Duke will hear
 thy voice;
And let not Bardolph's vital thread be cut
With edge of penny cord and vile reproach.
Speak, Captain, for his life, and I will
 thee requite.

FLUELLEN. Aunchient Pistol, I do partly
 understand your meaning.

PISTOL. Why then, rejoice therefore.

FLUELLEN. Certainly, Aunchient, it is not a thing
 to rejoice at; for if, look you, he were my
 brother, I would desire the Duke to use his
 good pleasure, and put him to execution; for
 discipline ought to be used.

PISTOL. Die and be damn'd! and figo for
 thy friendship!

FLUELLEN. It is well.

PISTOL. The fig of Spain!   *Exit.*

FLUELLEN. Very good.

GOWER. Why, this is an arrant counterfeit rascal; I
 remember him now-a bawd, a cutpurse.

FLUELLEN. I'll assure you, 'a utt'red as prave
 words at the pridge as you shall see in a
 summer's day. But it is very well; what he has
 spoke to me, that is well, I warrant you, when
 time is serve.

GOWER. Why, 'tis a gull a fool a rogue, that now
 and then goes to the wars to grace himself,
 at his return into London, under the form of
 a soldier. And such fellows are perfect in the
 great commanders' names; and they will learn
 you by rote where services were done-at such
 and such a sconce, at such a breach, at such a
 convoy; who came off bravely, who was shot,
 who disgrac'd, what terms the enemy stood
 on; and this they con perfectly in the phrase of
 war, which they trick up with new-tuned oaths;
 and what a beard of the General's cut and a
 horrid suit of the camp will do among foaming
 bottles and ale-wash'd wits is wonderful to
 be thought on. But you must learn to know
 such slanders of the age, or else you may be
 marvellously mistook.

FLUELLEN. I tell you what, Captain Gower, I do
 perceive he is not the man that he would gladly
 make show to the world he is; if I find a hole
 in his coat I will tell him my mind. *[Drum within]*

Hark you, the King is coming; and I must speak
 with him from the pridge. *[Drum and colours]*
Enter the KING and his poor Soldiers, and GLOUCESTER
God pless your Majesty!

KING HENRY. How now, Fluellen! Cam'st thou
 from the bridge?

FLUELLEN. Ay, so please your Majesty. The
 Duke of Exeter has very gallantly maintain'd
 the pridge; the French is gone off, look you,
 and there is gallant and most prave passages.
 Marry, th' athversary was have possession of
 the pridge; but he is enforced to retire, and the
 Duke of Exeter is master of the pridge; I can tell
 your Majesty the Duke is a prave man.

KING HENRY. What men have you lost, Fluellen!

FLUELLEN. The perdition of th' athversary hath
 been very great, reasonable great; marry, for my
 part, I think the Duke hath lost never a man,
 but one that is like to be executed for robbing a
 church-one Bardolph, if your Majesty know the
 man; his face is all bubukles, and whelks, and
 knobs, and flames o' fire; and his lips blows at
 his nose, and it is like a coal of fire, sometimes
 plue and sometimes red; but his nose is
 executed and his fire's out.

KING HENRY. We would have all such offenders
 so cut off. And we give express charge that
 in our marches through the country there be
 nothing compell'd from the villages, nothing
 taken but paid for, none of the French
 upbraided or abused in disdainful language; for
 when lenity and cruelty play for a kingdom the
 gentler gamester is the soonest winner.

 Tucket. Enter MONTJOY

MONTJOY. You know me by my habit.

KING HENRY. Well then, I know thee; what shall I
 know of thee?

MONTJOY. My master's mind.

KING HENRY. Unfold it.

MONTJOY. Thus says my King. Say thou to Harry
 of England: Though we seem'd dead we did
 but sleep; advantage is a better soldier than
 rashness. Tell him we could have rebuk'd him
 at Harfleur, but that we thought not good to
 bruise an injury till it were full ripe. Now we
 speak upon our cue, and our voice is imperial:
 England shall repent his folly, see his weakness,
 and admire our sufferance. Bid him therefore
 consider of his ransom, which must proportion
 the losses we have borne, the subjects we have
 lost, the disgrace we have digested; which, in
 weight to re-answer, his pettiness would bow
 under. For our losses his exchequer is too

poor; for th' effusion of our blood, the muster
of his kingdom too faint a number; and for
our disgrace, his own person kneeling at our
feet but a weak and worthless satisfaction. To
this add defiance; and tell him, for conclusion,
he hath betrayed his followers, whose
condemnation is pronounc'd. So far my King
and master; so much my office.
KING HENRY. What is thy name? I know
thy quality.
MONTJOY. Montjoy.
KING HENRY. Thou dost thy office fairly. Turn
thee back,
And tell thy King I do not seek him now,
But could be willing to march on to Calais
Without impeachment; for, to say the sooth-
Though 'tis no wisdom to confess so much
Unto an enemy of craft and vantage-
My people are with sickness much enfeebled;
My numbers lessen'd; and those few I have
Almost no better than so many French;
Who when they were in health, I tell
thee, herald,
I thought upon one pair of English legs
Did march three Frenchmen. Yet forgive
me, God,
That I do brag thus; this your air of France
Hath blown that vice in me; I must repent.
Go, therefore, tell thy master here I am;
My ransom is this frail and worthless trunk;
My army but a weak and sickly guard;
Yet, God before, tell him we will come on,
Though France himself and such another neighbour
Stand in our way. There's for thy
labour, Montjoy.
Go, bid thy master well advise himself.
If we may pass, we will; if we be hind'red,
We shall your tawny ground with your red blood
Discolour; and so, Montjoy, fare you well.
The sum of all our answer is but this:
We would not seek a battle as we are;
Nor as we are, we say, we will not shun it.
So tell your master.
MONTJOY. I shall deliver so. Thanks to your
Highness.   *Exit.*
GLOUCESTER. I hope they will not come upon
us now.
KING HENRY. We are in God's hand, brother, not
in theirs.
March to the bridge, it now draws toward night;
Beyond the river we'll encamp ourselves,
And on to-morrow bid them march away.
Exeunt.

✣ SCENE VII ✣
The French camp near Agincourt

Enter the CONSTABLE OF FRANCE, *the LORD*
RAMBURES, *the* DUKE OF ORLEANS, *the* DAUPHIN,
with Others

CONSTABLE. Tut! I have the best armour of
the world.
Would it were day!
ORLEANS. You have an excellent armour; but let
my horse have his due.
CONSTABLE. It is the best horse of Europe.
ORLEANS. Will it never be morning?
DAUPHIN. My Lord of Orleans and my Lord High
Constable, you talk of horse and armour?
ORLEANS. You are as well provided of both as any
prince in the world.
DAUPHIN. What a long night is this! I will not
change my horse with any that treads but on
four pasterns. Ça, ha! he bounds from the earth
as if his entrails were hairs; le cheval volant,
the Pegasus, chez les narines de feu! When I
bestride him I soar, I am a hawk. He trots the
air; the earth sings when he touches it; the
basest horn of his hoof is more musical than
the pipe of Hermes.
ORLEANS. He's of the colour of the nutmeg.
DAUPHIN. And of the heat of the ginger. It is a
beast for Perseus: he is pure air and fire; and
the dull elements of earth and water never
appear in him, but only in patient stillness while
his rider mounts him; he is indeed a horse, and
all other jades you may call beasts.
CONSTABLE. Indeed, my lord, it is a most
absolute and excellent horse.
DAUPHIN. It is the prince of palfreys; his neigh
is like the bidding of a monarch, and his
countenance enforces homage.
ORLEANS. No more, cousin.
DAUPHIN. Nay, the man hath no wit that cannot,
from the rising of the lark to the lodging of the
lamb, vary deserved praise on my palfrey. It is a
theme as fluent as the sea: turn the sands into
eloquent tongues, and my horse is argument
for them all: 'tis a subject for a sovereign to
reason on, and for a sovereign's sovereign to
ride on; and for the world-familiar to us and
unknown-to lay apart their particular functions
and wonder at him. I once writ a sonnet in his
praise and began thus: 'Wonder of nature'-

ORLEANS. I have heard a sonnet begin so to
one's mistress.

DAUPHIN. Then did they imitate that which
I compos'd to my courser; for my horse is
my mistress.

ORLEANS. Your mistress bears well.

DAUPHIN. Me well; which is the prescript
praise and perfection of a good and
particular mistress.

CONSTABLE. Nay, for methought yesterday your
mistress shrewdly shook your back.

DAUPHIN. So perhaps did yours.

CONSTABLE. Mine was not bridled.

DAUPHIN. O, then belike she was old and gentle;
and you rode like a kern of Ireland, your French
hose off and in your strait strossers.

CONSTABLE. You have good judgment
in horsemanship.

DAUPHIN. Be warn'd by me, then: they that ride
so, and ride not warily, fall into foul bogs. I had
rather have my horse to my mistress.

CONSTABLE. I had as lief have my mistress a jade.

DAUPHIN. I tell thee, Constable, my mistress
wears his own hair.

CONSTABLE. I could make as true a boast as that,
if I had a sow to my mistress.

DAUPHIN. 'Le chien est retourné à son propre
vomissement, et la truie lavée au bourbier.'
Thou mak'st use of anything.

CONSTABLE. Yet do I not use my horse for my
mistress, or any such proverb so little kin to
the purpose.

RAMBURES. My Lord Constable, the armour that I
saw in your tent to-night-are those stars or suns
upon it?

CONSTABLE. Stars, my lord.

DAUPHIN. Some of them will fall to-morrow,
I hope.

CONSTABLE. And yet my sky shall not want.

DAUPHIN. That may be, for you bear a many
superfluously, and 'twere more honour some
were away.

CONSTABLE. Ev'n as your horse bears your
praises, who would trot as well were some of
your brags dismounted.

DAUPHIN. Would I were able to load him with
his desert! Will it never be day? I will trot to-
morrow a mile, and my way shall be paved with
English faces.

CONSTABLE. I will not say so, for fear I should
be fac'd out of my way; but I would it were
morning, for I would fain be about the ears of
the English.

RAMBURES. Who will go to hazard with me for
twenty prisoners?

CONSTABLE. You must first go yourself to hazard
ere you have them.

DAUPHIN. 'Tis midnight; I'll go arm myself. *Exit.*

ORLEANS. The Dauphin longs for morning.

RAMBURES. He longs to eat the English.

CONSTABLE. I think he will eat all he kills.

ORLEANS. By the white hand of my lady, he's a
gallant prince.

CONSTABLE. Swear by her foot, that she may
tread out the oath.

ORLEANS. He is simply the most active gentleman
of France.

CONSTABLE. Doing is activity, and he will still
be doing.

ORLEANS. He never did harm that I heard of.

CONSTABLE. Nor will do none to-morrow: he will
keep that good name still.

ORLEANS. I know him to be valiant.

CONSTABLE. I was told that by one that knows
him better than you.

ORLEANS. What's he?

CONSTABLE. Marry, he told me so himself; and he
said he car'd not who knew it.

ORLEANS. He needs not; it is no hidden virtue
in him.

CONSTABLE. By my faith, sir, but it is; never
anybody saw it but his lackey. 'Tis a hooded
valour, and when it appears it will bate.

ORLEANS. Ill-wind never said well.

CONSTABLE. I will cap that proverb with 'There is
flattery in friendship.'

ORLEANS. And I will take up that with 'Give the
devil his due.'

CONSTABLE. Well plac'd! There stands your
friend for the devil; have at the very eye of that
proverb with 'A pox of the devil!'

ORLEANS. You are the better at proverbs by how
much 'A fool's bolt is soon shot.'

CONSTABLE. You have shot over.

ORLEANS. 'Tis not the first time you
were overshot.

Enter a MESSENGER

MESSENGER. My Lord High Constable, the
English lie within fifteen hundred paces of
your tents.

CONSTABLE. Who hath measur'd the ground?

MESSENGER. The Lord Grandpre.

CONSTABLE. A valiant and most expert
gentleman. Would it were day! Alas, poor Harry
of England! he longs not for the dawning as
we do.

ORLEANS. What a wretched and peevish fellow
is this King of England, to mope with his fat-
brain'd followers so far out of his knowledge!

CONSTABLE. If the English had any apprehension,
they would run away.

ORLEANS. That they lack; for if their heads had
any intellectual armour, they could never wear
such heavy head-pieces.

RAMBURES. That island of England breeds
very valiant creatures; their mastiffs are of
unmatchable courage.

ORLEANS. Foolish curs, that run winking into the
mouth of a Russian bear, and have their heads
crush'd like rotten apples! You may as well say
that's a valiant flea that dare eat his breakfast on
the lip of a lion.

CONSTABLE. Just, just! and the men do
sympathise with the mastiffs in robustious and
rough coming on, leaving their wits with their
wives; and then give them great meals of beef
and iron and steel; they will eat like wolves and
fight like devils.

ORLEANS. Ay, but these English are shrewdly out
of beef.

CONSTABLE. Then shall we find to-morrow they
have only stomachs to eat, and none to fight.
Now is it time to arm. Come, shall we about it?

ORLEANS. It is now two o'clock; but let me
see-by ten
We shall have each a hundred Englishmen.

Exeunt.

⬧ ACT IV ⬧

PROLOGUE

Enter CHORUS

CHORUS. Now entertain conjecture of a time
When creeping murmur and the poring dark
Fills the wide vessel of the universe.
From camp to camp, through the foul womb
  of night,
The hum of either army stilly sounds,
That the fix'd sentinels almost receive
The secret whispers of each other's watch.
Fire answers fire, and through their paly flames
Each battle sees the other's umber'd face;
Steed threatens steed, in high and boastful neighs
Piercing the night's dull ear; and from the tents
The armourers accomplishing the knights,

With busy hammers closing rivets up,
Give dreadful note of preparation.
The country cocks do crow, the clocks do toll,
And the third hour of drowsy morning name.
Proud of their numbers and secure in soul,
The confident and over-lusty French
Do the low-rated English play at dice;
And chide the cripple tardy-gaited night
Who like a foul and ugly witch doth limp
So tediously away. The poor
  condemned English,
Like sacrifices, by their watchful fires
Sit patiently and inly ruminate
The morning's danger; and their gesture sad
Investing lank-lean cheeks and war-worn coats
Presenteth them unto the gazing moon
So many horrid ghosts. O, now, who will behold
The royal captain of this ruin'd band
Walking from watch to watch, from tent to tent,
Let him cry 'Praise and glory on his head!'
For forth he goes and visits all his host;
Bids them good morrow with a modest smile,
And calls them brothers, friends,
  and countrymen.
Upon his royal face there is no note
How dread an army hath enrounded him;
Nor doth he dedicate one jot of colour
Unto the weary and all-watched night;
But freshly looks, and over-bears attaint
With cheerful semblance and sweet majesty;
That every wretch, pining and pale before,
Beholding him, plucks comfort from his looks;
A largess universal, like the sun,
His liberal eye doth give to every one,
Thawing cold fear, that mean and gentle all
Behold, as may unworthiness define,
A little touch of Harry in the night.
And so our scene must to the battle fly;
Where-O for pity!-we shall much disgrace
With four or five most vile and ragged foils,
Right ill-dispos'd in brawl ridiculous,
The name of Agincourt. Yet sit and see,
Minding true things by what their mock'ries be.

Exit.

⚘ SCENE I ⚘
France. The English camp at Agincourt

Enter the KING, BEDFORD, and GLOUCESTER

KING HENRY. Gloucester, 'tis true that we are in
great danger;

The greater therefore should our courage be.
Good morrow, brother Bedford. God Almighty!
There is some soul of goodness in things evil,
Would men observingly distil it out;
For our bad neighbour makes us early stirrers,
Which is both healthful and good husbandry.
Besides, they are our outward consciences
And preachers to us all, admonishing
That we should dress us fairly for our end.
Thus may we gather honey from the weed,
And make a moral of the devil himself.

Enter ERPINGHAM

Good morrow, old Sir Thomas Erpingham:
A good soft pillow for that good white head
Were better than a churlish turf of France.
ERPINGHAM. Not so, my liege; this lodging likes
me better,
Since I may say 'Now lie I like a king.'
KING HENRY. 'Tis good for men to love their
present pains
Upon example; so the spirit is eased;
And when the mind is quick'ned, out of doubt
The organs, though defunct and dead before,
Break up their drowsy grave and newly move
With casted slough and fresh legerity.
Lend me thy cloak, Sir Thomas. Brothers both,
Commend me to the princes in our camp;
Do my good morrow to them, and anon
Desire them all to my pavilion.
GLOUCESTER. We shall, my liege.
ERPINGHAM. Shall I attend your Grace?
KING HENRY. No, my good knight:
Go with my brothers to my lords of England;
I and my bosom must debate awhile,
And then I would no other company.
ERPINGHAM. The Lord in heaven bless thee,
noble Harry!   *Exeunt all but the KING.*
KING HENRY. God-a-mercy, old heart! thou
speak'st cheerfully.

Enter PISTOL

PISTOL. Qui va là?
KING HENRY. A friend.
PISTOL. Discuss unto me: art thou officer,
Or art thou base, common, and popular?
KING HENRY. I am a gentleman of a company.
PISTOL. Trail'st thou the puissant pike?
KING HENRY. Even so. What are you?
PISTOL. As good a gentleman as the Emperor.
KING HENRY. Then you are a better than
the King.
PISTOL. The King's a bawcock and a heart of gold,
A lad of life, an imp of fame;
Of parents good, of fist most valiant.

I kiss his dirty shoe, and from heart-string
I love the lovely bully. What is thy name?
KING HENRY. Harry le Roy.
PISTOL. Le Roy! a Cornish name; art thou of
Cornish crew?
KING HENRY. No, I am a Welshman.
PISTOL. Know'st thou Fluellen?
KING HENRY. Yes.
PISTOL. Tell him I'll knock his leek about his pate
Upon Saint Davy's day.
KING HENRY. Do not you wear your dagger
in your cap that day, lest he knock that
about yours.
PISTOL. Art thou his friend?
KING HENRY. And his kinsman too.
PISTOL. The figo for thee, then!
KING HENRY. I thank you; God be with you!
PISTOL. My name is Pistol call'd.   *Exit.*
KING HENRY. It sorts well with your fierceness.

Enter FLUELLEN and GOWER

GOWER. Captain Fluellen!
FLUELLEN. So! in the name of Jesu Christ, speak
fewer. It is the greatest admiration in the
universal world, when the true and aunchient
prerogatifes and laws of the wars is not kept:
if you would take the pains but to examine
the wars of Pompey the Great, you shall find, I
warrant you, that there is no tiddle-taddle nor
pibble-pabble in Pompey's camp; I warrant
you, you shall find the ceremonies of the wars,
and the cares of it, and the forms of it, and
the sobriety of it, and the modesty of it, to
be otherwise.
GOWER. Why, the enemy is loud; you hear him
all night.
FLUELLEN. If the enemy is an ass, and a fool,
and a prating coxcomb, is it meet, think you,
that we should also, look you, be an ass, and
a fool, and a prating coxcomb? In your own
conscience, now?
GOWER. I will speak lower.
FLUELLEN. I pray you and beseech you that
you will.

Exeunt GOWER and FLUELLEN.

KING HENRY. Though it appear a little out
of fashion,
There is much care and valour in this Welshman.

*Enter three soldiers: JOHN BATES, ALEXANDER COURT,
and MICHAEL WILLIAMS*

COURT. Brother John Bates, is not that the
morning which breaks yonder?
BATES. I think it be; but we have no great cause to
desire the approach of day.

WILLIAMS. We see yonder the beginning of the
day, but I think we shall never see the end of it.
Who goes there?

KING HENRY. A friend.

WILLIAMS. Under what captain serve you?

KING HENRY. Under Sir Thomas Erpingham.

WILLIAMS. A good old commander and a most
kind gentleman. I pray you, what thinks he of
our estate?

KING HENRY. Even as men wreck'd upon a sand,
that look to be wash'd off the next tide.

BATES. He hath not told his thought to the King?

KING HENRY. No; nor it is not meet he should.
For though I speak it to you, I think the King
is but a man as I am: the violet smells to
him as it doth to me; the element shows to
him as it doth to me; all his senses have but
human conditions; his ceremonies laid by,
in his nakedness he appears but a man; and
though his affections are higher mounted
than ours, yet, when they stoop, they stoop
with the like wing. Therefore, when he sees
reason of fears, as we do, his fears, out of
doubt, be of the same relish as ours are; yet,
in reason, no man should possess him with
any appearance of fear, lest he, by showing it,
should dishearten his army.

BATES. He may show what outward courage he
will; but I believe, as cold a night as 'tis, he
could wish himself in Thames up to the neck;
and so I would he were, and I by him, at all
adventures, so we were quit here.

KING HENRY. By my troth, I will speak my
conscience of the King: I think he would not
wish himself anywhere but where he is.

BATES. Then I would he were here alone; so
should he be sure to be ransomed, and a many
poor men's lives saved.

KING HENRY. I dare say you love him not so ill
to wish him here alone, howsoever you speak
this, to feel other men's minds; methinks I
could not die anywhere so contented as in the
King's company, his cause being just and his
quarrel honourable.

WILLIAMS. That's more than we know.

BATES. Ay, or more than we should seek after; for
we know enough if we know we are the King's
subjects. If his cause be wrong, our obedience
to the King wipes the crime of it out of us.

WILLIAMS. But if the cause be not good, the King
himself hath a heavy reckoning to make when
all those legs and arms and heads, chopp'd
off in a battle, shall join together at the latter

day and cry all 'We died at such a place'-some
swearing, some crying for a surgeon, some
upon their wives left poor behind them, some
upon the debts they owe, some upon their
children rawly left. I am afeard there are few
die well that die in a battle; for how can they
charitably dispose of anything when blood is
their argument? Now, if these men do not die
well, it will be a black matter for the King that
led them to it; who to disobey were against all
proportion of subjection.

KING HENRY. So, if a son that is by his
father sent about merchandise do sinfully
miscarry upon the sea, the imputation of his
wickedness, by your rule, should be imposed
upon his father that sent him; or if a servant,
under his master's command transporting a
sum of money, be assailed by robbers and die
in many irreconcil'd iniquities, you may call
the business of the master the author of the
servant's damnation. But this is not so: the
King is not bound to answer the particular
endings of his soldiers, the father of his
son, nor the master of his servant; for they
purpose not their death when they purpose
their services. Besides, there is no king, be
his cause never so spotless, if it come to the
arbitrement of swords, can try it out with
all unspotted soldiers: some peradventure
have on them the guilt of premeditated and
contrived murder; some, of beguiling virgins
with the broken seals of perjury; some,
making the wars their bulwark, that have
before gored the gentle bosom of peace
with pillage and robbery. Now, if these men
have defeated the law and outrun native
punishment, though they can outstrip men
they have no wings to fly from God: war is
His beadle, war is His vengeance; so that
here men are punish'd for before-breach of
the King's laws in now the King's quarrel.
Where they feared the death they have borne
life away; and where they would be safe they
perish. Then if they die unprovided, no more
is the King guilty of their damnation than he
was before guilty of those impieties for the
which they are now visited. Every subject's
duty is the King's; but every subject's soul
is his own. Therefore should every soldier
in the wars do as every sick man in his bed-
wash every mote out of his conscience; and
dying so, death is to him advantage; or not
dying, the time was blessedly lost wherein

such preparation was gained; and in him that escapes it were not sin to think that, making God so free an offer, He let him outlive that day to see His greatness, and to teach others how they should prepare.

WILLIAMS. 'Tis certain, every man that dies ill, the ill upon his own head-the King is not to answer for it.

BATES. I do not desire he should answer for me, and yet I determine to fight lustily for him.

KING HENRY. I myself heard the King say he would not be ransom'd.

WILLIAMS. Ay, he said so, to make us fight cheerfully; but when our throats are cut he may be ransom'd, and we ne'er the wiser.

KING HENRY. If I live to see it, I will never trust his word after.

WILLIAMS. You pay him then! That's a perilous shot out of an elder-gun, that a poor and a private displeasure can do against a monarch! You may as well go about to turn the sun to ice with fanning in his face with a peacock's feather. You'll never trust his word after! Come, 'tis a foolish saying.

KING HENRY. Your reproof is something too round; I should be angry with you, if the time were convenient.

WILLIAMS. Let it be a quarrel between us if you live.

KING HENRY. I embrace it.

WILLIAMS. How shall I know thee again?

KING HENRY. Give me any gage of thine, and I will wear it in my bonnet; then if ever thou dar'st acknowledge it, I will make it my quarrel.

WILLIAMS. Here's my glove; give me another of thine.

KING HENRY. There.

WILLIAMS. This will I also wear in my cap; if ever thou come to me and say, after to-morrow, 'This is my glove', by this hand I will take thee a box on the ear.

KING HENRY. If ever I live to see it, I will challenge it.

WILLIAMS. Thou dar'st as well be hang'd.

KING HENRY. Well, I will do it, though I take thee in the King's company.

WILLIAMS. Keep thy word. Fare thee well.

BATES. Be friends, you English fools, be friends; we have French quarrels enow, if you could tell how to reckon.

KING HENRY. Indeed, the French may lay twenty French crowns to one they will beat us, for they bear them on their shoulders; but it is no English treason to cut French crowns, and to-morrow the King himself will be a clipper.

Exeunt Soldiers.

Upon the King! Let us our lives, our souls,
Our debts, our careful wives,
Our children, and our sins, lay on the King!
We must bear all. O hard condition,
Twin-born with greatness, subject to the breath
Of every fool, whose sense no more can feel
But his own wringing! What infinite heart's ease
Must kings neglect that private men enjoy!
And what have kings that privates have not too,
Save ceremony-save general ceremony?
And what art thou, thou idol Ceremony?
What kind of god art thou, that suffer'st more
Of mortal griefs than do thy worshippers?
What are thy rents? What are thy comings-in?
O Ceremony, show me but thy worth!
What is thy soul of adoration?
Art thou aught else but place, degree, and form,
Creating awe and fear in other men?
Wherein thou art less happy being fear'd
Than they in fearing.
What drink'st thou oft, instead of homage sweet,
But poison'd flattery? O, be sick, great greatness,
And bid thy ceremony give thee cure!
Thinks thou the fiery fever will go out
With titles blown from adulation?
Will it give place to flexure and low bending?
Canst thou, when thou command'st the beggar's knee,
Command the health of it? No, thou proud dream,
That play'st so subtly with a king's repose.
I am a king that find thee; and I know
'Tis not the balm, the sceptre, and the ball,
The sword, the mace, the crown imperial,
The intertissued robe of gold and pearl,
The farced tide running fore the king,
The throne he sits on, nor the tide of pomp
That beats upon the high shore of this world-
No, not all these, thrice gorgeous ceremony,
Not all these, laid in bed majestical,
Can sleep so soundly as the wretched slave
Who, with a body fill'd and vacant mind,
Gets him to rest, cramm'd with distressful bread;
Never sees horrid night, the child of hell;
But, like a lackey, from the rise to set
Sweats in the eye of Phœbus, and all night
Sleeps in Elysium; next day, after dawn,
Doth rise and help Hyperion to his horse;
And follows so the ever-running year
With profitable labour, to his grave.

And but for ceremony, such a wretch,
Winding up days with toil and nights with sleep,
Had the fore-hand and vantage of a king.
The slave, a member of the country's peace,
Enjoys it; but in gross brain little wots'
What watch the king keeps to maintain
  the peace
Whose hours the peasant best advantages.

Enter ERPINGHAM

ERPINGHAM. My lord, your nobles, jealous of
  your absence,
Seek through your camp to find you.
KING. Good old knight,
  Collect them all together at my tent:
  I'll be before thee.
ERPINGHAM. I shall do't, my lord. *Exit.*
KING. O God of battles, steel my soldiers' hearts,
  Possess them not with fear! Take from
    them now
  The sense of reck'ning, if th' opposed numbers
  Pluck their hearts from them! Not to-day,
    O Lord,
  O, not to-day, think not upon the fault
  My father made in compassing the crown!
  I Richard's body have interred new,
  And on it have bestowed more contrite tears
  Than from it issued forced drops of blood;
  Five hundred poor I have in yearly pay,
  Who twice a day their wither'd hands hold up
  Toward heaven, to pardon blood; and I
    have built
  Two chantries, where the sad and solemn priests
  Sing still for Richard's soul. More will I do;
  Though all that I can do is nothing worth,
  Since that my penitence comes after all,
  Imploring pardon.

Enter GLOUCESTER

GLOUCESTER. My liege!
KING HENRY. My brother Gloucester's voice? Ay;
  I know thy errand, I will go with thee;
  The day, my friends, and all things, stay for me.
                                          Exeunt.

⚜ SCENE II ⚜
The French camp

Enter the DAUPHIN, ORLEANS, RAMBURES, and Others

ORLEANS. The sun doth gild our armour; up,
  my lords!
DAUPHIN. Montez à cheval! My horse! Varlet,
  laquais! Ha!

ORLEANS. O brave spirit!
DAUPHIN. Via! Les eaux et la terre-
ORLEANS. Rien puis? L'air et le feu.
DAUPHIN. Ciel! cousin Orleans.

Enter CONSTABLE

  Now, my Lord Constable!
CONSTABLE. Hark how our steeds for present
  service neigh!
DAUPHIN. Mount them, and make incision in
  their hides,
  That their hot blood may spin in English eyes,
  And dout them with superfluous courage, ha!
RAMBURES. What, will you have them weep our
  horses' blood?
  How shall we then behold their natural tears?

Enter a MESSENGER

MESSENGER. The English are embattl'd, you
  French peers.
CONSTABLE. To horse, you gallant Princes!
  straight to horse!
  Do but behold yon poor and starved band,
  And your fair show shall suck away their souls,
  Leaving them but the shales and husks of men.
  There is not work enough for all our hands;
  Scarce blood enough in all their sickly veins
  To give each naked curtle-axe a stain
  That our French gallants shall to-day draw out,
  And sheathe for lack of sport. Let us but blow
    on them,
  The vapour of our valour will o'erturn them.
  'Tis positive 'gainst all exceptions, lords,
  That our superfluous lackeys and our peasants-
  Who in unnecessary action swarm
  About our squares of battle-were enow
  To purge this field of, such a hilding foe;
  Though we upon this mountain's basis by
  Took stand for idle speculation-
  But that our honours must not. What's to say?
  A very little little let us do,
  And all is done. Then let the trumpets sound
  The tucket sonance and the note to mount;
  For our approach shall so much dare the field
  That England shall couch down in fear and yield.

Enter GRANDPRE

GRANDPRE. Why do you stay so long, my lords
  of France?
  Yond island carrions, desperate of their bones,
  Ill-favouredly become the morning field;
  Their ragged curtains poorly are let loose,
  And our air shakes them passing scornfully;
  Big Mars seems bankrupt in their beggar'd host,
  And faintly through a rusty beaver peeps.
  The horsemen sit like fixed candlesticks

With torch-staves in their hand; and their
  poor jades
Lob down their heads, dropping the hides
  and hips,
The gum down-roping from their pale-
  dead eyes,
And in their pale dull mouths the gimmal'd bit
Lies foul with chaw'd grass, still and motionless;
And their executors, the knavish crows,
Fly o'er them, all impatient for their hour.
Description cannot suit itself in words
To demonstrate the life of such a battle
In life so lifeless as it shows itself.
CONSTABLE. They have said their prayers and
  they stay for death.
DAUPHIN. Shall we go send them dinners and
  fresh suits,
And give their fasting horses provender,
And after fight with them?
CONSTABLE. I stay but for my guidon. To
  the field!
I will the banner from a trumpet take,
And use it for my haste. Come, come, away!
The sun is high, and we outwear the day. *Exeunt.*

⚜ SCENE III ⚜
The English camp

Enter GLOUCESTER, BEDFORD, EXETER,
ERPINGHAM, with all his host; SALISBURY and
WESTMORELAND

GLOUCESTER. Where is the King?
BEDFORD. The King himself is rode to view
  their battle.
WESTMORELAND. Of fighting men they have full
  three-score thousand.
EXETER. There's five to one; besides, they all
  are fresh.
SALISBURY. God's arm strike with us! 'tis a
  fearful odds.
  God bye you, Princes all; I'll to my charge.
  If we no more meet till we meet in heaven,
  Then joyfully, my noble Lord of Bedford,
  My dear Lord Gloucester, and my good
    Lord Exeter,
  And my kind kinsman-warriors all, adieu!
BEDFORD. Farewell, good Salisbury; and good
  luck go with thee!
EXETER. Farewell, kind lord. Fight valiantly to-day;
  And yet I do thee wrong to mind thee of it,
  For thou art fram'd of the firm truth of valour.

Exit SALISBURY.
BEDFORD. He is as full of valour as of kindness;
  Princely in both.
Enter the KING
WESTMORELAND. O that we now had here
  But one ten thousand of those men in England
  That do no work to-day!
KING. What's he that wishes so?
  My cousin Westmoreland? No, my fair cousin;
  If we are mark'd to die, we are enow
  To do our country loss; and if to live,
  The fewer men, the greater share of honour.
  God's will! I pray thee, wish not one man more.
  By Jove, I am not covetous for gold,
  Nor care I who doth feed upon my cost;
  It yearns me not if men my garments wear;
  Such outward things dwell not in my desires.
  But if it be a sin to covet honour,
  I am the most offending soul alive.
  No, faith, my coz, wish not a man
    from England.
  God's peace! I would not lose so great an
    honour
  As one man more methinks would share
    from me
  For the best hope I have. O, do not wish
    one more!
  Rather proclaim it, Westmoreland, through
    my host,
  That he which hath no stomach to this fight,
  Let him depart; his passport shall be made,
  And crowns for convoy put into his purse;
  We would not die in that man's company
  That fears his fellowship to die with us.
  This day is call'd the feast of Crispian.
  He that outlives this day, and comes safe home,
  Will stand a tip-toe when this day is nam'd,
  And rouse him at the name of Crispian.
  He that shall live this day, and see old age,
  Will yearly on the vigil feast his neighbours,
  And say 'To-morrow is Saint Crispian.'
  Then will he strip his sleeve and show his scars,
  And say 'These wounds I had on
    Crispian's day.'
  Old men forget; yet all shall be forgot,
  But he'll remember, with advantages,
  What feats he did that day. Then shall our
    names,
  Familiar in his mouth as household words-
  Harry the King, Bedford and Exeter,
  Warwick and Talbot, Salisbury and Gloucester-
  Be in their flowing cups freshly rememb'red.
  This story shall the good man teach his son;

And Crispin Crispian shall ne'er go by,
From this day to the ending of the world,
But we in it shall be remembered-
We few, we happy few, we band of brothers;
For he to-day that sheds his blood with me
Shall be my brother; be he ne'er so vile,
This day shall gentle his condition;
And gentlemen in England now-a-bed
Shall think themselves accurs'd they were
  not here,
And hold their manhoods cheap whiles
  any speaks
That fought with us upon Saint Crispin's day.

Re-enter SALISBURY

SALISBURY. My sovereign lord, bestow yourself
  with speed:
The French are bravely in their battles set,
And will with all expedience charge on us.
KING HENRY. All things are ready, if our minds
  be so.
WESTMORELAND. Perish the man whose mind is
  backward now!
KING HENRY. Thou dost not wish more help
  from England, coz?
WESTMORELAND. God's will, my liege! would
  you and I alone,
Without more help, could fight this royal battle!
KING HENRY. Why, now thou hast unwish'd five
  thousand men;
Which likes me better than to wish us one.
You know your places. God be with you all!

Tucket. Enter MONTJOY

MONTJOY. Once more I come to know of thee,
  King Harry,
If for thy ransom thou wilt now compound,
Before thy most assured overthrow;
For certainly thou art so near the gulf
Thou needs must be englutted. Besides,
  in mercy,
The constable desires thee thou wilt mind
Thy followers of repentance, that their souls
May make a peaceful and a sweet retire
From off these fields, where, wretches, their
  poor bodies
Must lie and fester.
KING HENRY. Who hath sent thee now?
MONTJOY. The Constable of France.
KING HENRY. I pray thee bear my former
  answer back:
Bid them achieve me, and then sell my bones.
Good God! why should they mock poor
  fellows thus?
The man that once did sell the lion's skin

While the beast liv'd was kill'd with
  hunting him.
A many of our bodies shall no doubt
Find native graves; upon the which, I trust,
Shall witness live in brass of this day's work.
And those that leave their valiant bones
  in France,
Dying like men, though buried in
  your dunghills,
They shall be fam'd; for there the sun shall
  greet them
And draw their honours reeking up to heaven,
Leaving their earthly parts to choke your clime,
The smell whereof shall breed a plague
  in France.
Mark then abounding valour in our English,
That, being dead, like to the bullet's grazing
Break out into a second course of mischief,
Killing in relapse of mortality.
Let me speak proudly: tell the Constable
We are but warriors for the working-day;
Our gayness and our gilt are all besmirch'd
With rainy marching in the painful field;
There's not a piece of feather in our host-
Good argument, I hope, we will not fly-
And time hath worn us into slovenry.
But, by the mass, our hearts are in the trim;
And my poor soldiers tell me yet ere night
They'll be in fresher robes, or they will pluck
The gay new coats o'er the French
  soldiers' heads
And turn them out of service. If they do this-
As, if God please, they shall-my ransom then
Will soon be levied. Herald, save thou
  thy labour;
Come thou no more for ransom, gentle herald;
They shall have none, I swear, but these
  my joints;
Which if they have, as I will leave 'em them,
Shall yield them little, tell the Constable.
MONTJOY. I shall, King Harry. And so fare
  thee well:
Thou never shalt hear herald any more. *Exit.*
KING HENRY. I fear thou wilt once more come
  again for a ransom.

Enter the DUKE OF YORK

YORK. My lord, most humbly on my knee I beg
The leading of the vaward.
KING HENRY. Take it, brave York. Now, soldiers,
  march away;
And how thou pleasest, God, dispose the day!

Exeunt.

❧ SCENE IV ❧
The field of battle

Alarum. Excursions. Enter FRENCH SOLDIER,
PISTOL, and BOY

PISTOL. Yield, cur!

FRENCH SOLDIER. Je pense que vous êtes le
gentilhomme de bonne qualité.

PISTOL. Cality! Calen o custure me! Art thou
a gentleman?
What is thy name? Discuss.

FRENCH SOLDIER. O Seigneur Dieu!

PISTOL. O, Signieur Dew should be a gentleman.
Perpend my words, O Signieur Dew, and mark:
O Signieur Dew, thou diest on point of fox,
Except, O Signieur, thou do give to me
Egregious ransom.

FRENCH SOLDIER. O, prenez miséricorde; ayez
pitié de moi!

PISTOL. Moy shall not serve; I will have
forty moys;
Or I will fetch thy rim out at thy throat
In drops of crimson blood.

FRENCH SOLDIER. Est-il impossible d'échapper la
force de ton bras?

PISTOL. Brass, cur?
Thou damned and luxurious mountain-goat,
Offer'st me brass?

FRENCH SOLDIER. O, pardonnez-moi!

PISTOL. Say'st thou me so? Is that a ton of moys?
Come hither, boy; ask me this slave in French
What is his name.

BOY. Ecoutez: comment êtes-vous appelé?

FRENCH SOLDIER. Monsieur le Fer.

BOY. He says his name is Master Fer.

PISTOL. Master Fer! I'll fer him, and firk him,
and ferret him-discuss the same in French
unto him.

BOY. I do not know the French for fer, and ferret,
and firk.

PISTOL. Bid him prepare; for I will cut his throat.

FRENCH SOLDIER. Que dit-il, monsieur?

BOY. Il me commande à vous dire que vous faites
vous prêt; car ce soldat ici est disposé tout à
cette heure de couper votre gorge.

PISTOL. Owy, cuppele gorge, permafoy!
Peasant, unless thou give me crowns,
brave crowns;
Or mangled shalt thou be by this my sword.

FRENCH SOLDIER. O, je vous supplie, pour
l'amour de Dieu, me pardonner! Je suis
gentilhomme de bonne maison. Gardez ma vie,
et je vous donnerai deux cents écus.

PISTOL. What are his words?

BOY. He prays you to save his life; he is a
gentleman of a good house, and for his ransom
he will give you two hundred crowns.

PISTOL. Tell him my fury shall abate, and I
The crowns will take.

FRENCH SOLDIER. Petit monsieur, que dit-il?

BOY. Encore qu'il est contre son jurement de
pardonner aucun prisonnier, néamnoins, pour
les écus que vous l'avez promis, il est content à
vous donner la liberté, le franchisement.

FRENCH SOLDIER. Sur mes genoux je vous donne
mille remercimens; et je m'estime heureux que
je suis tombé entre les mains d'un chevalier, je
pense, le plus brave, vaillant, et très distingué
seigneur d'Angleterre.

PISTOL. Expound unto me, boy.

BOY. He gives you, upon his knees, a thousand
thanks; and he esteems himself happy that he
hath fall'n into the hands of one-as he thinks-
the most brave, valorous, and thrice-worthy
signieur of England.

PISTOL. As I suck blood, I will some mercy show.
Follow me. *Exit.*❧

BOY. Suivez-vous le grand capitaine. *[Exit FRENCH
SOLDIER]* I did never know so full a voice issue
from so empty a heart; but the saying is true-
the empty vessel makes the greatest sound.
Bardolph and Nym had ten times more valour
than this roaring devil i' th' old play, that every
one may pare his nails with a wooden dagger;
and they are both hang'd; and so would this be,
if he durst steal anything adventurously. I must
stay with the lackeys, with the luggage of our
camp. The French might have a good prey of
us, if he knew of it; for there is none to guard it
but boys. *Exit.*❧

❧ SCENE V ❧
Another part of the field of battle

Enter CONSTABLE, ORLEANS, BOURBON, DAUPHIN,
and RAMBURES

CONSTABLE. O diable!

ORLEANS. O Seigneur! le jour est perdu, tout
est perdu!

DAUPHIN. Mort Dieu, ma vie! all is
confounded, all!
Reproach and everlasting shame

Sits mocking in our plumes. *[A short alarum]*
O méchante fortune! Do not run away.
CONSTABLE. Why, all our ranks are broke.
DAUPHIN. O perdurable shame! Let's
  stab ourselves.
  Be these the wretches that we play'd at dice for?
ORLEANS. Is this the king we sent to for
  his ransom?
BOURBON. Shame, and eternal shame, nothing
  but shame!
  Let us die in honour: once more back again;
  And he that will not follow Bourbon now,
  Let him go hence and, with his cap in hand
  Like a base pander, hold the chamber-door
  Whilst by a slave, no gender than my dog,
  His fairest daughter is contaminated.
CONSTABLE. Disorder, that hath spoil'd us, friend
  us now!
  Let us on heaps go offer up our lives.
ORLEANS. We are enow yet living in the field
  To smother up the English in our throngs,
  If any order might be thought upon.
BOURBON. The devil take order now! I'll to
  the throng.
  Let life be short, else shame will be too long.
                                        Exeunt.

✦ SCENE VI ✦

Another part of the field

Alarum. Enter the KING and his train, with prisoners;
EXETER, and Others

KING HENRY. Well have we done, thrice-
  valiant countrymen;
  But all's not done-yet keep the French the field.
EXETER. The Duke of York commends him to
  your Majesty.
KING HENRY. Lives he, good uncle? Thrice within
  this hour
  I saw him down; thrice up again, and fighting;
  From helmet to the spur all blood he was.
EXETER. In which array, brave soldier, doth he lie
  Larding the plain; and by his bloody side,
  Yoke-fellow to his honour-owing wounds,
  The noble Earl of Suffolk also lies.
  Suffolk first died; and York, all haggled over,
  Comes to him, where in gore he lay insteeped,
  And takes him by the beard, kisses the gashes
  That bloodily did yawn upon his face,
  He cries aloud 'Tarry, my cousin Suffolk.
  My soul shall thine keep company to heaven;

Tarry, sweet soul, for mine, then fly abreast;
As in this glorious and well-foughten field
We kept together in our chivalry.'
Upon these words I came and cheer'd him up;
He smil'd me in the face, raught me his hand,
And, with a feeble grip, says 'Dear my lord,
Commend my service to my sovereign.'
So did he turn, and over Suffolk's neck
He threw his wounded arm and kiss'd his lips;
And so, espous'd to death, with blood he seal'd
A testament of noble-ending love.
The pretty and sweet manner of it forc'd
Those waters from me which I would
  have stopp'd;
But I had not so much of man in me,
And all my mother came into mine eyes
And gave me up to tears.
KING HENRY. I blame you not;
For, hearing this, I must perforce compound
With mistful eyes, or they will issue too. *[Alarum]*
But hark! what new alarum is this same?
The French have reinforc'd their scatter'd men.
Then every soldier kill his prisoners;
Give the word through.   *Exeunt.*

✦ SCENE VII ✦

Another part of the field

Enter FLUELLEN and GOWER

FLUELLEN. Kill the poys and the luggage! 'Tis
  expressly against the law of arms; 'tis as arrant
  a piece of knavery, mark you now, as can be
  offert; in your conscience, now, is it not?
GOWER. 'Tis certain there's not a boy left alive;
  and the cowardly rascals that ran from the
  battle ha' done this slaughter; besides, they
  have burned and carried away all that was
  in the King's tent; wherefore the King most
  worthily hath caus'd every soldier to cut his
  prisoner's throat. O, 'tis a gallant King!
FLUELLEN. Ay, he was porn at Monmouth,
  Captain Gower. What call you the town's
  name where Alexander the Pig was born?
GOWER. Alexander the Great.
FLUELLEN. Why, I pray you, is not 'pig' great?
  The pig, or great, or the mighty, or the huge,
  or the magnanimous, are all one reckonings,
  save the phrase is a little variations.
GOWER. I think Alexander the Great was born
  in Macedon; his father was called Philip of

Macedon, as I take it.

FLUELLEN. I think it is in Macedon where
Alexander is porn. I tell you, Captain, if
you look in the maps of the 'orld, I warrant
you sall find, in the comparisons between
Macedon and Monmouth, that the situations,
look you, is both alike. There is a river in
Macedon; and there is also moreover a river
at Monmouth; it is call'd Wye at Monmouth,
but it is out of my prains what is the name
of the other river; but 'tis all one, 'tis alike
as my fingers is to my fingers, and there is
salmons in both. If you mark Alexander's
life well, Harry of Monmouth's life is come
after it indifferent well; for there is figures
in all things. Alexander-God knows, and you
know-in his rages, and his furies, and his
wraths, and his cholers, and his moods, and
his displeasures, and his indignations, and
also being a little intoxicates in his prains,
did, in his ales and his angers, look you, kill
his best friend, Cleitus.

GOWER. Our King is not like him in that: he
never kill'd any of his friends.

FLUELLEN. It is not well done, mark you now,
to take the tales out of my mouth ere it is
made and finished. I speak but in the figures
and comparisons of it; as Alexander kill'd his
friend Cleitus, being in his ales and his cups,
so also Harry Monmouth, being in his right
wits and his good judgments, turn'd away the
fat knight with the great belly doublet; he
was full of jests, and gipes, and knaveries, and
mocks; I have forgot his name.

GOWER. Sir John Falstaff.

FLUELLEN. That is he. I'll tell you there is good
men porn at Monmouth.

GOWER. Here comes his Majesty. *[Alarum.]*

Enter the KING, WARWICK, GLOUCESTER,
EXETER, and Others, with Prisoners. Flourish

KING HENRY. I was not angry since I came
to France
Until this instant. Take a trumpet, herald,
Ride thou unto the horsemen on yond hill;
If they will fight with us, bid them come down
Or void the field; they do offend our sight.
If they'll do neither, we will come to them
And make them skirr away as swift as stones
Enforced from the old Assyrian slings;
Besides, we'll cut the throats of those we
have,
And not a man of them that we shall take
Shall taste our mercy. Go and tell them so.

Enter MONTJOY

EXETER. Here comes the herald of the French,
my liege.

GLOUCESTER. His eyes are humbler than they
us'd to be.

KING HENRY. How now! What means this,
herald? know'st thou not
That I have fin'd these bones of mine
for ransom?
Com'st thou again for ransom?

MONTJOY. No, great King;
I come to thee for charitable licence,
That we may wander o'er this bloody field
To book our dead, and then to bury them;
To sort our nobles from our common men;
For many of our princes-woe the while!-
Lie drown'd and soak'd in mercenary blood;
So do our vulgar drench their peasant limbs
In blood of princes; and their wounded steeds
Fret fetlock deep in gore, and with wild rage
Yerk out their armed heels at their
dead masters,
Killing them twice. O, give us leave,
great King,
To view the field in safety, and dispose
Of their dead bodies!

KING HENRY. I tell thee truly, herald,
I know not if the day be ours or no;
For yet a many of your horsemen peer
And gallop o'er the field.

MONTJOY. The day is yours.

KING HENRY. Praised be God, and not our
strength, for it!
What is this castle call'd that stands hard by?

MONTJOY. They call it Agincourt.

KING HENRY. Then call we this the field
of Agincourt,
Fought on the day of Crispin Crispianus.

FLUELLEN. Your grandfather of famous
memory, an't please your Majesty, and your
great-uncle Edward the Plack Prince of Wales,
as I have read in the chronicles, fought a
most prave pattle here in France.

KING HENRY. They did, Fluellen.

FLUELLEN. Your Majesty says very true; if your
Majesties is remeb'red of it, the Welshmen
did good service in a garden where leeks did
grow, wearing leeks in their Monmouth caps;
which your Majesty know to this hour is an
honourable badge of the service; and I do
believe your Majesty takes no scorn to wear
the leek upon Saint Tavy's day.

KING HENRY. I wear it for a memorable honour;

For I am Welsh, you know, good countryman.

FLUELLEN. All the water in Wye cannot wash your Majesty's Welsh plood out of your pody, I can tell you that. Got pless it and preserve it as long as it pleases his Grace and his Majesty too!

KING HENRY. Thanks, good my countryman.

FLUELLEN. By Jeshu, I am your Majesty's countryman, care not who know it; I will confess it to all the 'orld: I need not be asham'd of your Majesty, praised be Got, so long as your Majesty is an honest man.

Enter WILLIAMS

KING HENRY. God keep me so! Our heralds go with him:
Bring me just notice of the numbers dead
On both our parts. Call yonder fellow hither.

Exeunt HERALDS with MONTJOY.

EXETER. Soldier, you must come to the King.

KING HENRY. Soldier, why wear'st thou that glove in thy cap?

WILLIAMS. An't please your Majesty, 'tis the gage of one that I should fight withal, if he be alive.

KING HENRY. An Englishman?

WILLIAMS. An't please your Majesty, a rascal that swagger'd with me last night; who, if 'a live and ever dare to challenge this glove, I have sworn to take him a box o' th' ear; or if I can see my glove in his cap-which he swore, as he was a soldier, he would wear if alive-I will strike it out soundly.

KING HENRY. What think you, Captain Fluellen, is it fit this soldier keep his oath?

FLUELLEN. He is a craven and a villain else, an't please your Majesty, in my conscience.

KING HENRY. It may be his enemy is a gentlemen of great sort, quite from the answer of his degree.

FLUELLEN. Though he be as good a gentleman as the Devil is, as Lucifer and Belzebub himself, it is necessary, look your Grace, that he keep his vow and his oath; if he be perjur'd, see you now, his reputation is as arrant a villain and a Jacksauce as ever his black shoe trod upon God's ground and his earth, in my conscience, la.

KING HENRY. Then keep thy vow, sirrah, when thou meet'st the fellow.

WILLIAMS. So I will, my liege, as I live.

KING HENRY. Who serv'st thou under?

WILLIAMS. Under Captain Gower, my liege.

FLUELLEN. Gower is a good captain, and is good knowledge and literatured in the wars.

KING HENRY. Call him hither to me, soldier.

WILLIAMS. I will, my liege.   *Exit.*

KING HENRY. Here, Fluellen; wear thou this favour for me, and stick it in thy cap; when Alençon and myself were down together, I pluck'd this glove from his helm. If any man challenge this, he is a friend to Alençon and an enemy to our person; if thou encounter any such, apprehend him, an thou dost me love.

FLUELLEN. Your Grace does me as great honours as can be desir'd in the hearts of his subjects. I would fain see the man that has but two legs that shall find himself aggrief'd at this glove, that is all; but I would fain see it once, an please God of his grace that I might see.

KING HENRY. Know'st thou Gower?

FLUELLEN. He is my dear friend, an please you.

KING HENRY. Pray thee, go seek him, and bring him to my tent.

FLUELLEN. I will fetch him.   *Exit.*

KING HENRY. My Lord of Warwick and my brother Gloucester,
Follow Fluellen closely at the heels;
The glove which I have given him for a favour
May haply purchase him a box o' th' ear.
It is the soldier's: I, by bargain, should
Wear it myself. Follow, good cousin Warwick;
If that the soldier strike him, as I judge
By his blunt bearing he will keep his word,
Some sudden mischief may arise of it;
For I do know Fluellen valiant,
And touch'd with choler, hot as gunpowder,
And quickly will return an injury;
Follow, and see there be no harm
between them.
Go you with me, uncle of Exeter.

Exeunt.

☙ SCENE VIII ❧
Before KING HENRY'S pavilion

Enter GOWER and WILLIAMS

WILLIAMS. I warrant it is to knight you, Captain.

Enter FLUELLEN

FLUELLEN. God's will and his pleasure, Captain, I beseech you now, come apace to the King: there is more good toward you peradventure than is in your knowledge to dream of.

WILLIAMS. Sir, know you this glove?

FLUELLEN. Know the glove? I know the glove is
a glove.

WILLIAMS. I know this; and thus I challenge it.

Strikes him

FLUELLEN. 'Sblood, an arrant traitor as any's
in the universal world, or in France, or
in England!

GOWER. How now, sir! you villain!

WILLIAMS. Do you think I'll be forsworn?

FLUELLEN. Stand away, Captain Gower; I
will give treason his payment into plows, I
warrant you.

WILLIAMS. I am no traitor.

FLUELLEN. That's a lie in thy throat. I charge
you in his Majesty's name, apprehend him:
he's a friend of the Duke Alençon's.

Enter WARWICK and GLOUCESTER

WARWICK. How now! how now! what's
the matter?

FLUELLEN. My Lord of Warwick, here is-praised
be God for it!-a most contagious treason
come to light, look you, as you shall desire in
a summer's day. Here is his Majesty.

Enter the KING and EXETER

KING HENRY. How now! what's the matter?

FLUELLEN. My liege, here is a villain and a
traitor, that, look your Grace, has struck the
glove which your Majesty is take out of the
helmet of Alençon.

WILLIAMS. My liege, this was my glove: here
is the fellow of it; and he that I gave it to
in change promis'd to wear it in his cap; I
promis'd to strike him if he did; I met this
man with my glove in his cap, and I have
been as good as my word.

FLUELLEN. Your Majesty hear now, saving your
Majesty's manhood, what an arrant, rascally,
beggarly, lousy knave it is; I hope your
Majesty is pear me testimony and witness,
and will avouchment, that this is the glove of
Alençon that your Majesty is give me; in your
conscience, now.

KING HENRY. Give me thy glove, soldier; look,
here is the fellow of it. 'Twas I, indeed, thou
promised'st to strike, And thou hast given me
most bitter terms.

FLUELLEN. An please your Majesty, let his neck
answer for it, if there is any martial law in
the world.

KING HENRY. How canst thou make
me satisfaction?

WILLIAMS. All offences, my lord, come from the
heart; never came any from mine that might
offend your Majesty.

KING HENRY. It was ourself thou didst abuse.

WILLIAMS. Your Majesty came not like yourself:
you appear'd to me but as a common man;
witness the night, your garments, your
lowliness; and what your Highness suffer'd
under that shape I beseech you take it for your
own fault, and not mine; for had you been as
I took you for, I made no offence; therefore, I
beseech your Highness pardon me.

KING HENRY. Here, uncle Exeter, fill this glove
with crowns,

And give it to this fellow. Keep it, fellow;

And wear it for an honour in thy cap

Till I do challenge it. Give him the crowns;

And, Captain, you must needs be friends

with him.

FLUELLEN. By this day and this light, the fellow
has mettle enough in his belly: hold, there
is twelve pence for you; and I pray you to
serve God, and keep you out of prawls, and
prabbles, and quarrels, and dissensions, and,
I warrant you, it is the better for you.

WILLIAMS. I will none of your money.

FLUELLEN. It is with a good will; I can tell you
it will serve you to mend your shoes. Come,
wherefore should you be so pashful? Your
shoes is not so good. 'Tis a good silling, I
warrant you, or I will change it.

Enter an ENGLISH HERALD

KING HENRY. Now, herald, are the dead
numb'red?

HERALD. Here is the number of the slaught'red
French.   *Gives a paper.*

KING HENRY. What prisoners of good sort are
taken, uncle?

EXETER. Charles Duke of Orleans, nephew to
the King;

John Duke of Bourbon, and Lord Bouciqualt;

Of other lords and barons, knights
and squires,

Full fifteen hundred, besides common men.

KING HENRY. This note doth tell me of ten
thousand French

That in the field lie slain; of princes in
this number,

And nobles bearing banners, there lie dead

One hundred twenty-six; added to these,

Of knights, esquires, and gallant gentlemen,

Eight thousand and four hundred; of
the which

Five hundred were but yesterday
  dubb'd knights.
So that, in these ten thousand they have lost,
There are but sixteen hundred mercenaries;
The rest are princes, barons, lords,
  knights, squires,
And gentlemen of blood and quality.
The names of those their nobles that lie dead:
Charles Delabreth, High Constable of France;
Jaques of Chatillon, Admiral of France;
The master of the cross-bows, Lord Rambures;
Great Master of France, the brave Sir
  Guichard Dolphin;
John Duke of Alençon; Antony Duke
  of Brabant,
The brother to the Duke of Burgundy;
And Edward Duke of Bar. Of lusty earls,
Grandpre and Roussi, Fauconbridge and Foix,
Beaumont and Marle, Vaudemont
  and Lestrake.
Here was a royal fellowship of death!
Where is the number of our English dead?
  [HERALD presents another paper]
Edward the Duke of York, the Earl of Suffolk,
Sir Richard Kikely, Davy Gam, Esquire;
None else of name; and of all other men
But five and twenty. O God, thy arm was here!
And not to us, but to thy arm alone,
Ascribe we all. When, without stratagem,
But in plain shock and even play of battle,
Was ever known so great and little loss
On one part and on th' other? Take it, God,
For it is none but thine.
EXETER. 'Tis wonderful!
KING HENRY. Come, go we in procession to
  the village;
And be it death proclaimed through our host
To boast of this or take that praise from God
Which is his only.
FLUELLEN. Is it not lawful, an please your
  Majesty, to tell how many is kill'd?
KING HENRY. Yes, Captain; but with
  this acknowledgment,
  That God fought for us.
FLUELLEN. Yes, my conscience, he did us
  great good.
KING HENRY. Do we all holy rites:
  Let there be sung 'Non nobis' and 'Te Deum';
  The dead with charity enclos'd in clay-
  And then to Calais; and to England then;
  Where ne'er from France arriv'd more
  happy men.
  Exeunt.

ACT V

PROLOGUE

Enter CHORUS

CHORUS. Vouchsafe to those that have not read
  the story
That I may prompt them; and of such as have,
I humbly pray them to admit th' excuse
Of time, of numbers, and due course of things,
Which cannot in their huge and proper life
Be here presented. Now we bear the King
Toward Calais. Grant him there. There seen,
Heave him away upon your winged thoughts
Athwart the sea. Behold, the English beach
Pales in the flood with men, with wives,
  and boys,
Whose shouts and claps out-voice the deep-
  mouth'd sea,
Which, like a mighty whiffler, fore the King
Seems to prepare his way. So let him land,
And solemnly see him set on to London.
So swift a pace hath thought that even now
You may imagine him upon Blackheath;
Where that his lords desire him to have borne
His bruised helmet and his bended sword
Before him through the city. He forbids it,
Being free from vainness and self-glorious pride;
Giving full trophy, signal, and ostent,
Quite from himself to God. But now behold
In the quick forge and working-house
  of thought,
How London doth pour out her citizens!
The mayor and all his brethren in best sort-
Like to the senators of th' antique Rome,
With the plebeians swarming at their heels-
Go forth and fetch their conqu'ring Caesar in;
As, by a lower but loving likelihood,
Were now the General of our gracious Empress-
As in good time he may-from Ireland coming,
Bringing rebellion broached on his sword,
How many would the peaceful city quit
To welcome him! Much more, and much
  more cause,
Did they this Harry. Now in London place him-
As yet the lamentation of the French
Invites the King of England's stay at home;
The Emperor's coming in behalf of France
To order peace between them; and omit

All the occurrences, whatever chanc'd,
Till Harry's back-return again to France.
There must we bring him; and myself
have play'd
The interim, by rememb'ring you 'tis past.
Then brook abridgment; and your eyes advance,
After your thoughts, straight back again
to France.

Exit.

✣ SCENE I ✣
France. The English camp

Enter FLUELLEN and GOWER

GOWER. Nay, that's right; but why wear you your
leek to-day? Saint Davy's day is past.

FLUELLEN. There is occasions and causes why
and wherefore in all things. I will tell you, ass
my friend, Captain Gower: the rascally, scald,
beggarly, lousy, pragging knave, Pistol-which
you and yourself and all the world know to be
no petter than a fellow, look you now, of no
merits-he is come to me, and prings me pread
and salt yesterday, look you, and bid me eat
my leek; it was in a place where I could not
breed no contendon with him; but I will be so
bold as to wear it in my cap till I see him once
again, and then I will tell him a little piece of
my desires.

Enter PISTOL

GOWER. Why, here he comes, swelling like
a turkey-cock.

FLUELLEN. 'Tis no matter for his swellings nor his
turkey-cocks. God pless you, Aunchient Pistol!
you scurvy, lousy knave, God pless you!

PISTOL. Ha! art thou bedlam? Dost thou thirst,
base Troyan,
To have me fold up Parca's fatal web?
Hence! I am qualmish at the smell of leek.

FLUELLEN. I peseech you heartily, scurvy,
lousy knave, at my desires, and my requests,
and my petitions, to eat, look you, this leek;
because, look you, you do not love it, nor
your affections, and your appetites, and your
digestions, does not agree with it, I would
desire you to eat it.

PISTOL. Not for Cadwallader and all his goats.

FLUELLEN. There is one goat for you. *[Strikes him]*
Will you be so good, scald knave, as eat it?

PISTOL. Base Troyan, thou shalt die.

FLUELLEN. You say very true, scald knave-when

God's will is. I will desire you to live in the
meantime, and eat your victuals; come, there
is sauce for it. *[Striking him again]* You call'd me
yesterday mountain-squire; but I will make you
to-day a squire of low degree. I pray you fall to;
if you can mock a leek, you can eat a leek.

GOWER. Enough, Captain, you have astonish'd
him.

FLUELLEN. I say I will make him eat some part of
my leek, or I will peat his pate four days. Bite, I
pray you, it is good for your green wound and
your ploody coxcomb.

PISTOL. Must I bite?

FLUELLEN. Yes, certainly, and out of doubt, and
out of question too, and ambiguides.

PISTOL. By this leek, I will most horribly revenge-I
eat and eat, I swear-

FLUELLEN. Eat, I pray you; will you have some
more sauce to your leek? There is not enough
leek to swear by.

PISTOL. Quiet thy cudgel: thou dost see I eat.

FLUELLEN. Much good do you, scald knave,
heartily. Nay, pray you throw none away; the
skin is good for your broken coxcomb. When
you take occasions to see leeks hereafter, I pray
you mock at 'em; that is all.

PISTOL. Good.

FLUELLEN. Ay, leeks is good. Hold you, there is a
groat to heal your pate.

PISTOL. Me a groat!

FLUELLEN. Yes, verily and in truth, you shall take
it; or I have another leek in my pocket which
you shall eat.

PISTOL. I take thy groat in earnest of revenge.

FLUELLEN. If I owe you anything I will pay you in
cudgels; you shall be a woodmonger, and buy
nothing of me but cudgels. God bye you, and
keep you, and heal your pate. *Exit.*

PISTOL. All hell shall stir for this.

GOWER. Go, go: you are a counterfeit cowardly
knave. Will you mock at an ancient tradition,
begun upon an honourable respect, and worn
as a memorable trophy of predeceased valour,
and dare not avouch in your deeds any of your
words? I have seen you gleeking and galling at
this gentleman twice or thrice. You thought,
because he could not speak English in the
native garb, he could not therefore handle
an English cudgel; you find it otherwise, and
henceforth let a Welsh correction teach you a
good English condition. Fare ye well.*Exit.*

PISTOL. Doth Fortune play the huswife with
me now?

News have I that my Nell is dead i' th' spital
Of malady of France;
And there my rendezvous is quite cut off.
Old I do wax; and from my weary limbs
Honour is cudgell'd. Well, bawd I'll turn,
And something lean to cutpurse of quick hand.
To England will I steal, and there I'll steal;
And patches will I get unto these cudgell'd scars,
And swear I got them in the Gallia wars. *Exit.*

❧ SCENE II ❧
France. The FRENCH KING'S palace

Enter at one door, KING HENRY, EXETER, BEDFORD,
GLOUCESTER, WARWICK, WESTMORELAND, and
other LORDS; at another, the FRENCH KING, QUEEN
ISABEL, the PRINCESS KATHERINE, ALICE, and other
LADIES; the DUKE OF BURGUNDY, and his Train

KING HENRY. Peace to this meeting, wherefore
  we are met!
Unto our brother France, and to our sister,
Health and fair time of day; joy and good wishes
To our most fair and princely cousin Katherine.
And, as a branch and member of this royalty,
By whom this great assembly is contriv'd,
We do salute you, Duke of Burgundy.
And, princes French, and peers, health to
  you all!
FRENCH KING. Right joyous are we to behold
  your face,
Most worthy brother England; fairly met!
So are you, princes English, every one.
QUEEN ISABEL. So happy be the issue,
  brother England,
Of this good day and of this gracious meeting
As we are now glad to behold your eyes-
Your eyes, which hitherto have home in them,
Against the French that met them in their bent,
The fatal balls of murdering basilisks;
The venom of such looks, we fairly hope,
Have lost their quality; and that this day
Shall change all griefs and quarrels into love.
KING HENRY. To cry amen to that, thus
  we appear.
QUEEN ISABEL. You English princes all, I do
  salute you.
BURGUNDY. My duty to you both, on equal love,
  Great Kings of France and England! That I
  have labour'd
With all my wits, my pains, and
  strong endeavours,

To bring your most imperial Majesties
Unto this bar and royal interview,
Your mightiness on both parts best can witness.
Since then my office hath so far prevail'd
That face to face and royal eye to eye
You have congreeted, let it not disgrace me
If I demand, before this royal view,
What rub or what impediment there is
Why that the naked, poor, and mangled Peace,
Dear nurse of arts, plenties, and joyful births,
Should not in this best garden of the world,
Our fertile France, put up her lovely visage?
Alas, she hath from France too long been chas'd!
And all her husbandry doth lie on heaps,
Corrupting in it own fertility.
Her vine, the merry cheerer of the heart,
Unpruned dies; her hedges even-pleach'd,
Like prisoners wildly overgrown with hair,
Put forth disorder'd twigs; her fallow leas
The darnel, hemlock, and rank fumitory,
Doth root upon, while that the coulter rusts
That should deracinate such savagery;
The even mead, that erst brought sweetly forth
The freckled cowslip, burnet, and green clover,
Wanting the scythe, all uncorrected, rank,
Conceives by idleness, and nothing teems
But hateful docks, rough thistles, kecksies, burs,
Losing both beauty and utility.
And as our vineyards, fallows, meads,
  and hedges,
Defective in their natures, grow to wildness;
Even so our houses and ourselves and children
Have lost, or do not learn for want of time,
The sciences that should become our country;
But grow, like savages-as soldiers will,
That nothing do but meditate on blood-
To swearing and stern looks, diffus'd attire,
And everything that seems unnatural.
Which to reduce into our former favour
You are assembled; and my speech entreats
That I may know the let why gentle Peace
Should not expel these inconveniences
And bless us with her former qualities.
KING HENRY. If, Duke of Burgundy, you would
  the peace
Whose want gives growth to th' imperfections
Which you have cited, you must buy that peace
With full accord to all our just demands;
Whose tenours and particular effects
You have, enschedul'd briefly, in your hands.
BURGUNDY. The King hath heard them; to the
  which as yet
There is no answer made.

KING HENRY. Well then, the peace,
Which you before so urg'd, lies in his answer.

FRENCH KING. I have but with a cursorary eye
O'erglanced the articles; pleaseth your Grace
To appoint some of your council presently
To sit with us once more, with better heed
To re-survey them, we will suddenly
Pass our accept and peremptory answer.

KING HENRY. Brother, we shall. Go, uncle Exeter,
And brother Clarence, and you,
  brother Gloucester,
Warwick, and Huntington, go with the King;
And take with you free power to ratify,
Augment, or alter, as your wisdoms best
Shall see advantageable for our dignity,
Any thing in or out of our demands;
And we'll consign thereto. Will you, fair sister,
Go with the princes or stay here with us?

QUEEN ISABEL. Our gracious brother, I will go
with them;
Haply a woman's voice may do some good,
When articles too nicely urg'd be stood on.

KING HENRY. Yet leave our cousin Katherine here
with us;
She is our capital demand, compris'd
Within the fore-rank of our articles.

QUEEN ISABEL. She hath good leave.

Exeunt all but the KING, KATHERINE, and ALICE.

KING HENRY. Fair Katherine, and most fair,
Will you vouchsafe to teach a soldier terms
Such as will enter at a lady's ear,
And plead his love-suit to her gentle heart?

KATHERINE. Your Majesty shall mock me; I
cannot speak your England.

KING HENRY. O fair Katherine, if you will love me
soundly with your French heart, I will be glad to
hear you confess it brokenly with your English
tongue. Do you like me, Kate?

KATHERINE. Pardonnez-moi, I cannot tell vat is
like me.

KING HENRY. An angel is like you, Kate, and you
are like an angel.

KATHERINE. Que dit-il? que je suis semblable à
les anges?

ALICE. Oui, vraiment, sauf votre grace, ainsi dit-il.

KING HENRY. I said so, dear Katherine, and I
must not blush to affirm it.

KATHERINE. O bon Dieu! les langues des
hommes sont pleines de tromperies.

KING HENRY. What says she, fair one? that the
tongues of men are full of deceits?

ALICE. Oui, dat de tongues of de mans is be full of
deceits-dat is de Princess.

KING HENRY. The Princess is the better English-
woman. I' faith, Kate, my wooing is fit for thy
understanding: I am glad thou canst speak no
better English; for if thou couldst, thou wouldst
find me such a plain king that thou wouldst
think I had sold my farm to buy my crown. I
know no ways to mince it in love, but directly
to say 'I love you.' Then, if you urge me farther
than to say 'Do you in faith?' I wear out my suit.
Give me your answer; i' faith, do; and so clap
hands and a bargain. How say you, lady?

KATHERINE. Sauf votre honneur, me
understand well.

KING HENRY. Marry, if you would put me to
verses or to dance for your sake, Kate, why you
undid me; for the one I have neither words
nor measure, and for the other I have no
strength in measure, yet a reasonable measure
in strength. If I could win a lady at leap-frog, or
by vaulting into my saddle with my armour on
my back, under the correction of bragging be
it spoken, I should quickly leap into wife. Or if
I might buffet for my love, or bound my horse
for her favours, I could lay on like a butcher,
and sit like a jack-an-apes, never off. But, before
God, Kate, I cannot look greenly, nor gasp
out my eloquence, nor I have no cunning in
protestation; only downright oaths, which I
never use till urg'd, nor never break for urging.
If thou canst love a fellow of this temper, Kate,
whose face is not worth sunburning, that never
looks in his glass for love of anything he sees
there, let thine eye be thy cook. I speak to thee
plain soldier. If thou canst love me for this,
take me; if not, to say to thee that I shall die
is true-but for thy love, by the Lord, no; yet I
love thee too. And while thou liv'st, dear Kate,
take a fellow of plain and uncoined constancy;
for he perforce must do thee right, because
he hath not the gift to woo in other places; for
these fellows of infinite tongue, that can rhyme
themselves into ladies' favours, they do always
reason themselves out again. What! a speaker is
but a prater: a rhyme is but a ballad. A good leg
will fall; a straight back will stoop; a black beard
will turn white; a curl'd pate will grow bald; a
fair face will wither; a full eye will wax hollow.
But a good heart, Kate, is the sun and the
moon; or, rather, the sun, and not the moon-
for it shines bright and never changes, but
keeps his course truly. If thou would have such
a one, take me; and take me, take a soldier;
take a soldier, take a king. And what say'st thou,

then, to my love? Speak, my fair, and fairly, I pray thee.

KATHERINE. Is it possible dat I sould love de enemy of France?

KING HENRY. No, it is not possible you should love the enemy of France, Kate, but in loving me you should love the friend of France; for I love France so well that I will not part with a village of it; I will have it all mine. And, Kate, when France is mine and I am yours, then yours is France and you are mine.

KATHERINE. I cannot tell vat is dat.

KING HENRY. No, Kate? I will tell thee in French, which I am sure will hang upon my tongue like a new-married wife about her husband's neck, hardly to be shook off. Je quand sur le possession de France, et quand vous avez le possession de moi-let me see, what then? Saint Denis be my speed!-donc votre est France et vous êtes mienne. It is as easy for me, Kate, to conquer the kingdom as to speak so much more French: I shall never move thee in French, unless it be to laugh at me.

KATHERINE. Sauf votre honneur, le Français que vous parlez, il est meilleur que l'Anglais lequel je parle.

KING HENRY. No, faith, is't not, Kate; but thy speaking of my tongue, and I thine, most truly falsely, must needs be granted to be much at one. But, Kate, dost thou understand thus much English-Canst thou love me?

KATHERINE. I cannot tell.

KING HENRY. Can any of your neighbours tell, Kate? I'll ask them. Come, I know thou lovest me; and at night, when you come into your closet, you'll question this gentlewoman about me; and I know, Kate, you will to her dispraise those parts in me that you love with your heart. But, good Kate, mock me mercifully; the rather, gentle Princess, because I love thee cruelly. If ever thou beest mine, Kate, as I have a saving faith within me tells me thou shalt, I get thee with scambling, and thou must therefore needs prove a good soldier-breeder. Shall not thou and I, between Saint Denis and Saint George, compound a boy, half French, half English, that shall go to Constantinople and take the Turk by the beard? Shall we not? What say'st thou, my fair flower-de-luce?

KATHERINE. I do not know dat.

KING HENRY. No: 'tis hereafter to know, but now to promise; do but now promise, Kate, you will endeavour for your French part of such a boy; and for my English moiety take the word of a king and a bachelor. How answer you, la plus belle Katherine du monde, mon très cher et divin déesse?

KATHERINE. Your Majestee ave fausse French enough to deceive de most sage damoiselle dat is en France.

KING HENRY. Now, fie upon my false French! By mine honour, in true English, I love thee, Kate; by which honour I dare not swear thou lovest me; yet my blood begins to flatter me that thou dost, notwithstanding the poor and untempering effect of my visage. Now beshrew my father's ambition! He was thinking of civil wars when he got me; therefore was I created with a stubborn outside, with an aspect of iron, that when I come to woo ladies I fright them. But, in faith, Kate, the elder I wax, the better I shall appear: my comfort is, that old age, that ill layer-up of beauty, can do no more spoil upon my face; thou hast me, if thou hast me, at the worst; and thou shalt wear me, if thou wear me, better and better. And therefore tell me, most fair Katherine, will you have me? Put off your maiden blushes; avouch the thoughts of your heart with the looks of an empress; take me by the hand and say 'Harry of England, I am thine.' Which word thou shalt no sooner bless mine ear withal but I will tell thee aloud 'England is thine, Ireland is thine, France is thine, and Henry Plantagenet is thine'; who, though I speak it before his face, if he be not fellow with the best king, thou shalt find the best king of good fellows. Come, your answer in broken music-for thy voice is music and thy English broken; therefore, Queen of all, Katherine, break thy mind to me in broken English, wilt thou have me?

KATHERINE. Dat is as it shall please de roi mon père.

KING HENRY. Nay, it will please him well, Kate-it shall please him, Kate.

KATHERINE. Den it sall also content me.

KING HENRY. Upon that I kiss your hand, and I can you my queen.

KATHERINE. Laissez, mon seigneur, laissez, laissez! Ma foi, je ne veux point que vous abaissiez votre grandeur en baisant la main d'une, notre seigneur, indigne serviteur;

excusez-moi, je vous supplie, mon très
puissant seigneur.

KING HENRY. Then I will kiss your lips, Kate.

KATHERINE. Les dames et demoiselles pour
être baisées devant leur noces, il n'est pas la
coutume de France.

KING HENRY. Madame my interpreter, what
says she?

ALICE. Dat it is not be de fashion pour le ladies of
France-I cannot tell vat is baiser en Anglish.

KING HENRY. To kiss.

ALICE. Your Majestee entendre bettre que moi.

KING HENRY. It is not a fashion for the maids in
France to kiss before they are married, would
she say?

ALICE. Oui, vraiment.

KING HENRY. O Kate, nice customs curtsy to
great kings. Dear Kate, you and I cannot be
confin'd within the weak list of a country's
fashion; we are the makers of manners, Kate;
and the liberty that follows our places stops
the mouth of all find-faults-as I will do yours
for upholding the nice fashion of your country
in denying me a kiss; therefore, patiently and
yielding. *[Kissing her]* You have witchcraft in
your lips, Kate: there is more eloquence in a
sugar touch of them than in the tongues of
the French council; and they should sooner
persuade Henry of England than a general
petition of monarchs. Here comes your father.

Enter the French Power and the English LORDS

BURGUNDY. God save your Majesty! My
royal cousin,
  Teach you our princess English?

KING HENRY. I would have her learn, my fair
cousin, how perfectly I love her; and that is
good English.

BURGUNDY. Is she not apt?

KING HENRY. Our tongue is rough, coz, and my
condition is not smooth; so that, having neither
the voice nor the heart of flattery about me, I
cannot so conjure up the spirit of love in her
that he will appear in his true likeness.

BURGUNDY. Pardon the frankness of my mirth,
if I answer you for that. If you would conjure
in her, you must make a circle; if conjure up
love in her in his true likeness, he must appear
naked and blind. Can you blame her, then,
being a maid yet ros'd over with the virgin
crimson of modesty, if she deny the appearance
of a naked blind boy in her naked seeing self?
It were, my lord, a hard condition for a maid to
consign to.

KING HENRY. Yet they do wink and yield, as love
is blind and enforces.

BURGUNDY. They are then excus'd, my lord,
when they see not what they do.

KING HENRY. Then, good my lord, teach your
cousin to consent winking.

BURGUNDY. I will wink on her to consent, my
lord, if you will teach her to know my meaning;
for maids well summer'd and warm kept are
like flies at Bartholomew-tide, blind, though
they have their eyes; and then they will endure
handling, which before would not abide
looking on.

KING HENRY. This moral ties me over to time
and a hot summer; and so I shall catch the fly,
your cousin, in the latter end, and she must be
blind too.

BURGUNDY. As love is, my lord, before it loves.

KING HENRY. It is so; and you may, some of you,
thank love for my blindness, who cannot see
many a fair French city for one fair French maid
that stands in my way.

FRENCH KING. Yes, my lord, you see them
perspectively, the cities turned into a maid; for
they are all girdled with maiden walls that war
hath never ent'red.

KING HENRY. Shall Kate be my wife?

FRENCH KING. So please you.

KING HENRY. I am content, so the maiden cities
you talk of may wait on her; so the maid that
stood in the way for my wish shall show me the
way to my will.

FRENCH KING. We have consented to all terms
of reason.

KING HENRY. Is't so, my lords of England?

WESTMORELAND. The King hath granted
every article:
  His daughter first; and then in sequel, all,
  According to their firm proposed natures.

EXETER. Only he hath not yet subscribed this:
Where your Majesty demands that the King
of France, having any occasion to write for
matter of grant, shall name your Highness in
this form and with this addition, in French,
Notre très cher fils Henri, Roi d'Angleterre,
Héritier de France; and thus in Latin,
Praeclarissimus filius noster Henricus, Rex
Angliae et Haeres Franciae.

FRENCH KING. Nor this I have not, brother, so
denied
  But our request shall make me let it pass.

KING HENRY. I pray you, then, in love and
dear alliance,

Let that one article rank with the rest;
And thereupon give me your daughter.
FRENCH KING. Take her, fair son, and from her
  blood raise up
Issue to me; that the contending kingdoms
Of France and England, whose very shores
  look pale
With envy of each other's happiness,
May cease their hatred; and this
  dear conjunction
Plant neighbourhood and Christian-like accord
In their sweet bosoms, that never war advance
His bleeding sword 'twixt England and
  fair France.
LORDS. Amen!
KING HENRY. Now, welcome, Kate; and bear me
  witness all,
That here I kiss her as my sovereign queen.

Flourish

QUEEN ISABEL. God, the best maker of
  all marriages,
Combine your hearts in one, your realms in one!
As man and wife, being two, are one in love,
So be there 'twixt your kingdoms such a spousal
That never may ill office or fell jealousy,
Which troubles oft the bed of blessed marriage,
Thrust in between the paction of
  these kingdoms,
To make divorce of their incorporate league;
That English may as French, French Englishmen,
Receive each other. God speak this Amen!
ALL. Amen!
KING HENRY. Prepare we for our marriage; on
  which day,
My Lord of Burgundy, we'll take your oath,
And all the peers', for surety of our leagues.
Then shall I swear to Kate, and you to me,
And may our oaths well kept and prosp'rous be!

Sennet. Exeunt.

EPILOGUE

Enter CHORUS

CHORUS. Thus far, with rough and all-unable pen,
Our bending author hath pursu'd the story,
In little room confining mighty men,
Mangling by starts the full course of their glory.
Small time, but, in that small, most greatly lived
This star of England. Fortune made his sword;
By which the world's best garden he achieved,
And of it left his son imperial lord.

Henry the Sixth, in infant bands crown'd King
Of France and England, did this King succeed;
Whose state so many had the managing
That they lost France and made his
  England bleed;
Which oft our stage hath shown; and, for
  their sake,
In your fair minds let this acceptance take. *Exit.*

The End

King Henry VI, Part I

Dramatis Personae

KING HENRY THE SIXTH
DUKE OF GLOUCESTER, uncle to the King, and Protector
DUKE OF BEDFORD, uncle to the King, and Regent of France
THOMAS BEAUFORT, DUKE OF EXETER, great-uncle to the king
HENRY BEAUFORT, great-uncle to the King, BISHOP OF WINCHESTER, and afterwards CARDINAL
JOHN BEAUFORT, EARL OF SOMERSET, afterwards Duke
RICHARD PLANTAGENET, son of Richard, late Earl of Cambridge, afterwards DUKE OF YORK
EARL OF WARWICK
EARL OF SALISBURY
EARL OF SUFFOLK
LORD TALBOT, afterwards EARL OF SHREWSBURY
JOHN TALBOT, his son
EDMUND MORTIMER, EARL OF MARCH
SIR JOHN FASTOLFE
SIR WILLIAM LUCY
SIR WILLIAM GLANSDALE
SIR THOMAS GARGRAVE
MAYOR of LONDON
WOODVILLE, Lieutenant of the Tower
VERNON, of the White Rose or York faction
BASSET, of the Red Rose or Lancaster faction
A LAWYER
GAOLERS, to Mortimer
CHARLES, Dauphin, and afterwards King of France
REIGNIER, DUKE OF ANJOU, and titular King of Naples
DUKE OF BURGUNDY
DUKE OF ALENÇON
BASTARD OF ORLEANS
GOVERNOR OF PARIS
MASTER-GUNNER OF ORLEANS, and his SON
GENERAL OF THE FRENCH FORCES in Bordeaux
A FRENCH SERGEANT
A PORTER
AN OLD SHEPHERD, father to Joan la Pucelle
MARGARET, daughter to Reignier, afterwards married to King Henry
COUNTESS OF AUVERGNE
JOAN LA PUCELLE, commonly called JOAN OF ARC

Lords, Warders of the Tower, Heralds, Officers, Soldier, Messengers, English and French Attendants. Fiends appearing to La Pucelle

SCENE
England and France

❊

◆ ACT I ◆

❧ SCENE I ❧
Westminster Abbey

Dead March. Enter the funeral of KING HENRY THE FIFTH, attended on by the DUKE OF BEDFORD, Regent of France, the DUKE OF GLOUCESTER, Protector, the DUKE OF EXETER, the EARL OF WARWICK, the BISHOP OF WINCHESTER

BEDFORD. Hung be the heavens with black, yield day to night!
Comets, importing change of times and states,
Brandish your crystal tresses in the sky
And with them scourge the bad revolting stars
That have consented unto Henry's death!
King Henry the Fifth, too famous to live long!
England ne'er lost a king of so much worth.
GLOUCESTER. England ne'er had a king until his time.
Virtue he had, deserving to command;
His brandish'd sword did blind men with his beams;
His arms spread wider than a dragon's wings;
His sparkling eyes, replete with wrathful fire,
More dazzled and drove back his enemies
Than mid-day sun fierce bent against their faces.

What should I say? His deeds exceed all speech:
He ne'er lift up his hand but conquered.
EXETER. We mourn in black; why mourn we not
  in blood?
Henry is dead and never shall revive.
Upon a wooden coffin we attend;
And death's dishonourable victory
We with our stately presence glorify,
Like captives bound to a triumphant car.
What! shall we curse the planets of mishap
That plotted thus our glory's overthrow?
Or shall we think the subtle-witted French
Conjurers and sorcerers, that, afraid of him,
By magic verses have contriv'd his end?
WINCHESTER. He was a king bless'd of the King
  of kings;
Unto the French the dreadful judgment-day
So dreadful will not be as was his sight.
The battles of the Lord of Hosts he fought;
The Church's prayers made him so prosperous.
GLOUCESTER. The Church! Where is it? Had not
  churchmen pray'd,
His thread of life had not so soon decay'd.
None do you like but an effeminate prince,
Whom like a school-boy you may overawe.
WINCHESTER. Gloucester, whate'er we like, thou
  art Protector
And lookest to command the Prince and realm.
Thy wife is proud; she holdeth thee in awe
More than God or religious churchmen may.
GLOUCESTER. Name not religion, for thou lov'st
  the flesh;
And ne'er throughout the year to church
  thou go'st,
Except it be to pray against thy foes.
BEDFORD. Cease, cease these jars and rest your
  minds in peace;
Let's to the altar. Heralds, wait on us.
Instead of gold, we'll offer up our arms,
Since arms avail not, now that Henry's dead.
Posterity, await for wretched years,
When at their mothers' moist'ned eyes babes
  shall suck,
Our isle be made a nourish of salt tears,
And none but women left to wail the dead.
Henry the Fifth, thy ghost I invocate:
Prosper this realm, keep it from civil broils,
Combat with adverse planets in the heavens.
A far more glorious star thy soul will make
Than Julius Caesar or bright-
    Enter a MESSENGER
MESSENGER. My honourable lords, health to
  you all!

Sad tidings bring I to you out of France,
Of loss, of slaughter, and discomfiture:
Guienne, Champagne, Rheims, Orleans,
Paris, Guysors, Poictiers, are all quite lost.
BEDFORD. What say'st thou, man, before dead
  Henry's corse?
Speak softly, or the loss of those great towns
Will make him burst his lead and rise
  from death.
GLOUCESTER. Is Paris lost? Is Rouen yielded up?
If Henry were recall'd to life again,
These news would cause him once more yield
  the ghost.
EXETER. How were they lost? What treachery
  was us'd?
MESSENGER. No treachery, but want of men
  and money.
Amongst the soldiers this is muttered
That here you maintain several factions;
And whilst a field should be dispatch'd
  and fought,
You are disputing of your generals:
One would have ling'ring wars, with little cost;
Another would fly swift, but wanteth wings;
A third thinks, without expense at all,
By guileful fair words peace may be obtain'd.
Awake, awake, English nobility!
Let not sloth dim your honours, new-begot.
Cropp'd are the flower-de-luces in your arms;
Of England's coat one half is cut away.
EXETER. Were our tears wanting to this funeral,
These tidings would call forth their flowing tides.
BEDFORD. Me they concern; Regent I am
  of France.
Give me my steeled coat; I'll fight for France.
Away with these disgraceful wailing robes!
Wounds will I lend the French instead of eyes,
To weep their intermissive miseries.
    Enter a second MESSENGER
SECOND MESSENGER. Lords, view these letters
  full of bad mischance.
France is revolted from the English quite,
Except some petty towns of no import.
The Dauphin Charles is crowned king in Rheims;
The Bastard of Orleans with him is join'd;
Reignier, Duke of Anjou, doth take his part;
The Duke of Alençon flieth to his side.
EXETER. The Dauphin crowned king! all fly
  to him!
O, whither shall we fly from this reproach?
GLOUCESTER. We will not fly but to our
  enemies' throats.
Bedford, if thou be slack I'll fight it out.

BEDFORD. Gloucester, why doubt'st thou of
  my forwardness?
An army have I muster'd in my thoughts,
Wherewith already France is overrun.

Enter a third MESSENGER

THIRD MESSENGER. My gracious lords, to add to
  your laments,
Wherewith you now bedew King Henry's hearse,
I must inform you of a dismal fight
Betwixt the stout Lord Talbot and the French.
WINCHESTER. What! Wherein Talbot overcame?
  Is't so?
THIRD MESSENGER. O, no; wherein Lord Talbot
  was o'erthrown.
The circumstance I'll tell you more at large.
The tenth of August last this dreadful lord,
Retiring from the siege of Orleans,
Having full scarce six thousand in his troop,
By three and twenty thousand of the French
Was round encompassed and set upon.
No leisure had he to enrank his men;
He wanted pikes to set before his archers;
Instead whereof sharp stakes pluck'd out
  of hedges
They pitched in the ground confusedly
To keep the horsemen off from breaking in.
More than three hours the fight continued;
Where valiant Talbot, above human thought,
Enacted wonders with his sword and lance:
Hundreds he sent to hell, and none durst
  stand him;
Here, there, and everywhere, enrag'd he slew
The French exclaim'd the devil was in arms;
All the whole army stood agaz'd on him.
His soldiers, spying his undaunted spirit,
'A Talbot! a Talbot!' cried out amain,
And rush'd into the bowels of the battle.
Here had the conquest fully been seal'd up
If Sir John Fastolfe had not play'd the coward.
He, being in the vaward plac'd behind
With purpose to relieve and follow them-
Cowardly fled, not having struck one stroke;
Hence grew the general wreck and massacre.
Enclosed were they with their enemies.
A base Walloon, to win the Dauphin's grace,
Thrust Talbot with a spear into the back;
Whom all France, with their chief
  assembled strength,
Durst not presume to look once in the face.
BEDFORD. Is Talbot slain? Then I will slay myself,
For living idly here in pomp and ease,
Whilst such a worthy leader, wanting aid,
Unto his dastard foemen is betray'd.

THIRD MESSENGER. O no, he lives, but is
  took prisoner,
And Lord Scales with him, and Lord Hungerford;
Most of the rest slaughter'd or took likewise.
BEDFORD. His ransom there is none but I
  shall pay.
I'll hale the Dauphin headlong from his throne;
His crown shall be the ransom of my friend;
Four of their lords I'll change for one of ours.
Farewell, my masters; to my task will I;
Bonfires in France forthwith I am to make
To keep our great Saint George's feast withal.
Ten thousand soldiers with me I will take,
Whose bloody deeds shall make an
  Europe quake.
THIRD MESSENGER. So you had need; for
  Orleans is besieg'd;
The English army is grown weak and faint;
The Earl of Salisbury craveth supply
And hardly keeps his men from mutiny,
Since they, so few, watch such a multitude.
EXETER. Remember, lords, your oaths to
  Henry sworn,
Either to quell the Dauphin utterly,
Or bring him in obedience to your yoke.
BEDFORD. I do remember it, and here take
  my leave
To go about my preparation.   *Exit.*
GLOUCESTER. I'll to the Tower with all the haste
  I can
To view th' artillery and munition;
And then I will proclaim young Henry king.*Exit.*
EXETER. To Eltham will I, where the young
  King is,
Being ordain'd his special governor;
And for his safety there I'll best devise.   *Exit.*
WINCHESTER. *[Aside]* Each hath his place and
  function to attend:
I am left out; for me nothing remains.
But long I will not be Jack out of office.
The King from Eltham I intend to steal,
And sit at chiefest stern of public weal.*Exeunt.*

♯ SCENE II ♯
France. Before Orleans

Sound a Flourish. Enter CHARLES THE DAUPHIN,
ALENÇON, and REIGNIER, marching with drum and
SOLDIERS

CHARLES. Mars his true moving, even as in
  the heavens

So in the earth, to this day is not known.
Late did he shine upon the English side;
Now we are victors, upon us he smiles.
What towns of any moment but we have?
At pleasure here we lie near Orleans;
Otherwhiles the famish'd English, like
  pale ghosts,
Faintly besiege us one hour in a month.
ALENÇON. They want their porridge and their fat
  bull beeves.
Either they must be dieted like mules
And have their provender tied to their mouths,
Or piteous they will look, like drowned mice.
REIGNIER. Let's raise the siege. Why live we
  idly here?
Talbot is taken, whom we wont to fear;
Remaineth none but mad-brain'd Salisbury,
And he may well in fretting spend his gall
Nor men nor money hath he to make war.
CHARLES. Sound, sound alarum; we will rush
  on them.
Now for the honour of the forlorn French!
Him I forgive my death that killeth me,
When he sees me go back one foot or flee.

Exeunt.

Here alarum. They are beaten back by the English, with great
  loss.
Re-enter CHARLES, ALENÇON, and REIGNIER

CHARLES. Who ever saw the like? What men
  have I!
Dogs! cowards! dastards! I would ne'er have fled
But that they left me midst my enemies.
REIGNIER. Salisbury is a desperate homicide;
He fighteth as one weary of his life.
The other lords, like lions wanting food,
Do rush upon us as their hungry prey.
ALENÇON. Froissart, a countryman of
  ours, records
England all Olivers and Rowlands bred
During the time Edward the Third did reign.
More truly now may this be verified;
For none but Samsons and Goliases
It sendeth forth to skirmish. One to ten!
Lean raw-bon'd rascals! Who would e'er suppose
They had such courage and audacity?
CHARLES. Let's leave this town; for they are hare-
  brain'd slaves,
And hunger will enforce them to be more eager.
Of old I know them; rather with their teeth
The walls they'll tear down than forsake
  the siege.
REIGNIER. I think by some odd gimmers or device
Their arms are set, like clocks, still to strike on;

Else ne'er could they hold out so as they do.
By my consent, we'll even let them alone.
ALENÇON. Be it so.

Enter the BASTARD OF ORLEANS

BASTARD. Where's the Prince Dauphin? I have
  news for him.
CHARLES. Bastard of Orleans, thrice welcome
  to us.
BASTARD. Methinks your looks are sad, your
  cheer appall'd.
Hath the late overthrow wrought this offence?
Be not dismay'd, for succour is at hand.
A holy maid hither with me I bring,
Which, by a vision sent to her from heaven,
Ordained is to raise this tedious siege
And drive the English forth the bounds
  of France.
The spirit of deep prophecy she hath,
Exceeding the nine sibyls of old Rome:
What's past and what's to come she can descry.
Speak, shall I call her in? Believe my words,
For they are certain and unfallible.
CHARLES. Go, call her in. *[Exit BASTARD]*
But first, to try her skill,
Reignier, stand thou as Dauphin in my place;
Question her proudly; let thy looks be stern;
By this means shall we sound what skill
  she hath.

Re-enter the BASTARD OF ORLEANS with JOAN LA
  PUCELLE

REIGNIER. Fair maid, is 't thou wilt do these
  wondrous feats?
PUCELLE. Reignier, is 't thou that thinkest to
  beguile me?
Where is the Dauphin? Come, come
  from behind;
I know thee well, though never seen before.
Be not amaz'd, there's nothing hid from me.
In private will I talk with thee apart.
Stand back, you lords, and give us leave awhile.
REIGNIER. She takes upon her bravely at
  first dash.
PUCELLE. Dauphin, I am by birth a
  shepherd's daughter,
My wit untrain'd in any kind of art.
Heaven and our Lady gracious hath it pleas'd
To shine on my contemptible estate.
Lo, whilst I waited on my tender lambs
And to sun's parching heat display'd my cheeks,
God's Mother deigned to appear to me,
And in a vision full of majesty
Will'd me to leave my base vocation
And free my country from calamity

Her aid she promis'd and assur'd success.
In complete glory she reveal'd herself;
And whereas I was black and swart before,
With those clear rays which she infus'd on me
That beauty am I bless'd with which you
may see.
Ask me what question thou canst possible,
And I will answer unpremeditated.
My courage try by combat if thou dar'st,
And thou shalt find that I exceed my sex.
Resolve on this: thou shalt be fortunate
If thou receive me for thy warlike mate.
CHARLES. Thou hast astonish'd me with thy
high terms.
Only this proof I'll of thy valour make
In single combat thou shalt buckle with me;
And if thou vanquishest, thy words are true;
Otherwise I renounce all confidence.
PUCELLE. I am prepar'd; here is my keen-
edg'd sword,
Deck'd with five flower-de-luces on each side,
The which at Touraine, in Saint
Katherine's churchyard,
Out of a great deal of old iron I chose forth.
CHARLES. Then come, o' God's name; I fear
no woman.
PUCELLE. And while I live I'll ne'er fly from
a man.
Here they fight and JOAN LA PUCELLE overcomes
CHARLES. Stay, stay thy hands; thou art
an Amazon,
And fightest with the sword of Deborah.
PUCELLE. Christ's Mother helps me, else I were
too weak.
CHARLES. Whoe'er helps thee, 'tis thou that
must help me.
Impatiently I burn with thy desire;
My heart and hands thou hast at once subdu'd.
Excellent Pucelle, if thy name be so,
Let me thy servant and not sovereign be.
'Tis the French Dauphin sueth to thee thus.
PUCELLE. I must not yield to any rites of love,
For my profession's sacred from above.
When I have chased all thy foes from hence,
Then will I think upon a recompense.
CHARLES. Meantime look gracious on thy
prostrate thrall.
REIGNIER. My lord, methinks, is very long in talk.
ALENÇON. Doubtless he shrives this woman to
her smock;
Else ne'er could he so long protract his speech.
REIGNIER. Shall we disturb him, since he keeps
no mean?

ALENÇON. He may mean more than we poor
men do know;
These women are shrewd tempters with
their tongues.
REIGNIER. My lord, where are you? What devise
you on?
Shall we give o'er Orleans, or no?
PUCELLE. Why, no, I say; distrustful recreants!
Fight till the last gasp; I will be your guard.
CHARLES. What she says I'll confirm; we'll fight
it out.
PUCELLE. Assign'd am I to be the
English scourge.
This night the siege assuredly I'll raise.
Expect Saint Martin's summer, halcyon days,
Since I have entered into these wars.
Glory is like a circle in the water,
Which never ceaseth to enlarge itself
Till by broad spreading it disperse to nought.
With Henry's death the English circle ends;
Dispersed are the glories it included.
Now am I like that proud insulting ship
Which Caesar and his fortune bare at once.
CHARLES. Was Mahomet inspired with a dove?
Thou with an eagle art inspired then.
Helen, the mother of great Constantine,
Nor yet Saint Philip's daughters were like thee.
Bright star of Venus, fall'n down on the earth,
How may I reverently worship thee enough?
ALENÇON. Leave off delays, and let us raise
the siege.
REIGNIER. Woman, do what thou canst to save
our honours;
Drive them from Orleans, and be immortaliz'd.
CHARLES. Presently we'll try. Come, let's away
about it.
No prophet will I trust if she prove false.

Exeunt.

✒ SCENE III ✒

London. Before the tower gates

Enter the DUKE OF GLOUCESTER, with his SERVING-
MEN in blue coats

GLOUCESTER. I am come to survey the Tower
this day;
Since Henry's death, I fear, there is conveyance.
Where be these warders that they wait not here?
Open the gates; 'tis Gloucester that calls.
FIRST WARDER. *[Within]* Who's there that knocks
so imperiously?

FIRST SERVING-MAN. It is the noble Duke
of Gloucester.
SECOND WARDER. *[Within]* Whoe'er he be, you
may not be let in.
FIRST SERVING-MAN. Villains, answer you so the
Lord Protector?
FIRST WARDER. *[Within]* The Lord protect him! so
we answer him.
We do not otherwise than we are will'd.
GLOUCESTER. Who willed you, or whose will
stands but mine?
There's none Protector of the realm but I.
Break up the gates, I'll be your warrantize.
Shall I be flouted thus by dunghill grooms?
GLOUCESTER'S men rush at the Tower gates, and
WOODVILLE the Lieutenant speaks within
WOODVILLE. *[Within]* What noise is this? What
traitors have we here?
GLOUCESTER. Lieutenant, is it you whose voice
I hear?
Open the gates; here's Gloucester that
would enter.
WOODVILLE. *[Within]* Have patience, noble Duke,
I may not open;
The Cardinal of Winchester forbids.
From him I have express commandment
That thou nor none of thine shall be let in.
GLOUCESTER. Faint-hearted Woodville, prizest
him fore me?
Arrogant Winchester, that haughty prelate
Whom Henry, our late sovereign, ne'er
could brook!
Thou art no friend to God or to the King.
Open the gates, or I'll shut thee out shortly.
SERVING-MEN. Open the gates unto the
Lord Protector,
Or we'll burst them open, if that you come
not quickly.
Enter to the PROTECTOR at the Tower gates
WINCHESTER and his men in tawny coats
WINCHESTER. How now, ambitious Humphrey!
What means this?
GLOUCESTER. Peel'd priest, dost thou command
me to be shut out?
WINCHESTER. I do, thou most usurping proditor,
And not Protector of the King or realm.
GLOUCESTER. Stand back, thou
manifest conspirator,
Thou that contrived'st to murder our
dead lord;
Thou that giv'st whores indulgences to sin.
I'll canvass thee in thy broad cardinal's hat,
If thou proceed in this thy insolence.

WINCHESTER. Nay, stand thou back; I will not
budge a foot.
This be Damascus; be thou cursed Cain,
To slay thy brother Abel, if thou wilt.
GLOUCESTER. I will not slay thee, but I'll drive
thee back.
Thy scarlet robes as a child's bearing-cloth
I'll use to carry thee out of this place.
WINCHESTER. Do what thou dar'st; I beard thee
to thy face.
GLOUCESTER. What! am I dar'd and bearded to
my face?
Draw, men, for all this privileged place;
Blue-coats to tawny-coats. Priest, beware
your beard;
I mean to tug it, and to cuff you soundly;
Under my feet I stamp thy cardinal's hat;
In spite of Pope or dignities of church,
Here by the cheeks I'll drag thee up and down.
WINCHESTER. Gloucester, thou wilt answer this
before the Pope.
GLOUCESTER. Winchester goose! I cry 'A rope,
a rope!'
Now beat them hence; why do you let
them stay?
Thee I'll chase hence, thou wolf in sheep's array.
Out, tawny-coats! Out, scarlet hypocrite!
Here GLOUCESTER'S men beat out the CARDINAL'S men;
and enter in the hurly-burly the MAYOR OF LONDON and
his OFFICERS
MAYOR. Fie, lords! that you, being
supreme magistrates,
Thus contumeliously should break the peace!
GLOUCESTER. Peace, Mayor! thou know'st little
of my wrongs:
Here's Beaufort, that regards nor God nor King,
Hath here distrain'd the Tower to his use.
WINCHESTER. Here's Gloucester, a foe
to citizens;
One that still motions war and never peace,
O'ercharging your free purses with large fines;
That seeks to overthrow religion,
Because he is Protector of the realm,
And would have armour here out of the Tower,
To crown himself King and suppress the Prince.
GLOUCESTER. I will not answer thee with words,
but blows.
Here they skirmish again
MAYOR. Nought rests for me in this
tumultuous strife
But to make open proclamation.
Come, officer, as loud as e'er thou canst,
Cry.

OFFICER. *[Cries]* All manner of men assembled
  here in arms this day against God's peace
  and the King's, we charge and command
  you, in his Highness' name, to repair to your
  several dwelling-places; and not to wear,
  handle, or use any sword, weapon, or dagger,
  henceforward, upon pain of death.
GLOUCESTER. Cardinal, I'll be no breaker of
  the law; But we shall meet and break our
  minds at large.
WINCHESTER. Gloucester, we'll meet to thy
  cost, be sure;   .
  Thy heart-blood I will have for this day's work.
MAYOR. I'll call for clubs if you will not away.
  This Cardinal's more haughty than the devil.
GLOUCESTER. Mayor, farewell; thou dost but
  what thou mayst.
WINCHESTER. Abominable Gloucester, guard
  thy head,
  For I intend to have it ere long.
            Exeunt, severally, GLOUCESTER *and* WINCHESTER
                                  with their servants.
MAYOR. See the coast clear'd, and then we
  will depart.
  Good God, these nobles should such
  stomachs bear!
  I myself fight not once in forty year.*Exeunt.*

⚜ SCENE IV ⚜
France. Before Orleans

Enter, on the walls, the MASTER-GUNNER OF ORLEANS
and his BOY

MASTER-GUNNER. Sirrah, thou know'st how
  Orleans is besieg'd,
  And how the English have the suburbs won.
BOY. Father, I know; and oft have shot at them,
  Howe'er, unfortunate, I miss'd my aim.
MASTER-GUNNER. But now thou shalt not. Be
  thou rul'd by me.
  Chief master-gunner am I of this town;
  Something I must do to procure me grace.
  The Prince's espials have informed me
  How the English, in the suburbs
  close intrench'd,
  Wont, through a secret grate of iron bars
  In yonder tower, to overpeer the city,
  And thence discover how with most advantage
  They may vex us with shot or with assault.
  To intercept this inconvenience,
  A piece of ordnance 'gainst it I have plac'd;

And even these three days have I watch'd
If I could see them. Now do thou watch,
For I can stay no longer.
If thou spy'st any, run and bring me word;
And thou shalt find me at the Governor's.
                                        Exit.
BOY. Father, I warrant you; take you no care;
  I'll never trouble you, if I may spy them.*Exit.*
Enter SALISBURY *and* TALBOT *on the turrets, with* SIR
    WILLIAM GLANSDALE, SIR THOMAS
          GARGRAVE, *and Others*
SALISBURY. Talbot, my life, my joy,
  again return'd!
  How wert thou handled being prisoner?
  Or by what means got'st thou to be releas'd?
  Discourse, I prithee, on this turret's top.
TALBOT. The Earl of Bedford had a prisoner
  Call'd the brave Lord Ponton de Santrailles;
  For him was I exchang'd and ransomed.
  But with a baser man of arms by far
  Once, in contempt, they would have
  barter'd me;
  Which I disdaining scorn'd, and craved death
  Rather than I would be so vile esteem'd.
  In fine, redeem'd I was as I desir'd.
  But, O! the treacherous Fastolfe wounds
  my heart
  Whom with my bare fists I would execute,
  If I now had him brought into my power.
SALISBURY. Yet tell'st thou not how thou
  wert entertain'd.
TALBOT. With scoffs, and scorns, and
  contumelious taunts,
  In open market-place produc'd they me
  To be a public spectacle to all;
  Here, said they, is the terror of the French,
  The scarecrow that affrights our children so.
  Then broke I from the officers that led me,
  And with my nails digg'd stones out of
  the ground
  To hurl at the beholders of my shame;
  My grisly countenance made others fly;
  None durst come near for fear of
  sudden death.
  In iron walls they deem'd me not secure;
  So great fear of my name 'mongst them
  was spread
  That they suppos'd I could rend bars of steel
  And spurn in pieces posts of adamant;
  Wherefore a guard of chosen shot I had
  That walk'd about me every minute-while;
  And if I did but stir out of my bed,
  Ready they were to shoot me to the heart.

Enter the BOY with a linstock

SALISBURY. I grieve to hear what torments
  you endur'd;
  But we will be reveng'd sufficiently.
  Now it is supper-time in Orleans:
  Here, through this grate, I count each one
  And view the Frenchmen how they fortify.
  Let us look in; the sight will much delight thee.
  Sir Thomas Gargrave and Sir William Glansdale,
  Let me have your express opinions
  Where is best place to make our batt'ry next.
GARGRAVE. I think at the North Gate; for there
  stand lords.
GLANSDALE. And I here, at the bulwark of
  the bridge.
TALBOT. For aught I see, this city must
  be famish'd,
  Or with light skirmishes enfeebled.

Here they shoot and SALISBURY and GARGRAVE fall down

SALISBURY. O Lord, have mercy on us,
  wretched sinners!
GARGRAVE. O Lord, have mercy on me,
  woeful man!
TALBOT. What chance is this that suddenly hath
  cross'd us?
  Speak, Salisbury; at least, if thou canst speak.
  How far'st thou, mirror of all martial men?
  One of thy eyes and thy cheek's side struck off!
  Accursed tower! accursed fatal hand
  That hath contriv'd this woeful tragedy!
  In thirteen battles Salisbury o'ercame;
  Henry the Fifth he first train'd to the wars;
  Whilst any trump did sound or drum struck up,
  His sword did ne'er leave striking in the field.
  Yet liv'st thou, Salisbury? Though thy speech
  doth fail,
  One eye thou hast to look to heaven for grace;
  The sun with one eye vieweth all the world.
  Heaven, be thou gracious to none alive
  If Salisbury wants mercy at thy hands!
  Bear hence his body; I will help to bury it.
  Sir Thomas Gargrave, hast thou any life?
  Speak unto Talbot; nay, look up to him.
  Salisbury, cheer thy spirit with this comfort,
  Thou shalt not die whiles-
  He beckons with his hand and smiles on me,
  As who should say, 'When I am dead and gone,
  Remember to avenge me on the French.'
  Plantagenet, I will; and like thee, Nero,
  Play on the lute, beholding the towns burn.
  Wretched shall France be only in my name. *[Here*
  an alarum, and it thunders and lightens]
  What stir is this? What tumult's in the heavens?

Whence cometh this alarum and the noise?

Enter a MESSENGER

MESSENGER. My lord, my lord, the French have
  gather'd head.
  The Dauphin, with one Joan la Pucelle join'd,
  A holy prophetess new risen up,
  Is come with a great power to raise the siege.

[Here SALISBURY lifteth himself up and groans]

TALBOT. Hear, hear how dying Salisbury
  doth groan.
  It irks his heart he cannot be reveng'd.
  Frenchmen, I'll be a Salisbury to you.
  Pucelle or puzzel, dolphin or dogfish,
  Your hearts I'll stamp out with my horse's heels
  And make a quagmire of your mingled brains.
  Convey me Salisbury into his tent,
  And then we'll try what these dastard
  Frenchmen dare.

Alarum. Exeunt

SCENE V
Before Orleans

Here an alarum again, and TALBOT pursueth the DAUPHIN
and driveth him. Then enter JOAN LA PUCELLE driving
Englishmen before her. Then enter TALBOT

TALBOT. Where is my strength, my valour, and
  my force?
  Our English troops retire, I cannot stay them;
  A woman clad in armour chaseth them.

Re-enter LA PUCELLE

  Here, here she comes. I'll have a bout with thee.
  Devil or devil's dam, I'll conjure thee;
  Blood will I draw on thee-thou art a witch
  And straightway give thy soul to him
  thou serv'st.
PUCELLE. Come, come, 'tis only I that must
  disgrace thee.

Here they fight

TALBOT. Heavens, can you suffer hell so
  to prevail?
  My breast I'll burst with straining of my courage.
  And from my shoulders crack my arms asunder,
  But I will chastise this high-minded strumpet.

They fight again

PUCELLE. Talbot, farewell; thy hour is not
  yet come.
  I must go victual Orleans forthwith. *[A short alarum;*
  then enter the town with soldiers]
  O'ertake me if thou canst; I scorn thy strength.
  Go, go, cheer up thy hungry starved men;

Help Salisbury to make his testament.
This day is ours, as many more shall be. *Exit.*
TALBOT. My thoughts are whirled like a
 potter's wheel;
I know not where I am nor what I do.
A witch by fear, not force, like Hannibal,
Drives back our troops and conquers as
 she lists.
So bees with smoke and doves with
 noisome stench
Are from their hives and houses driven away.
They call'd us, for our fierceness, English dogs;
Now like to whelps we crying run away. *[A*
 short alarum]
Hark, countrymen! Either renew the fight
Or tear the lions out of England's coat;
Renounce your soil, give sheep in lions' stead:
Sheep run not half so treacherous from the wolf,
Or horse or oxen from the leopard,
As you fly from your oft-subdued slaves. *[Alarum.*
 Here another skirmish]
It will not be-retire into your trenches.
You all consented unto Salisbury's death,
For none would strike a stroke in his revenge.
Pucelle is ent'red into Orleans
In spite of us or aught that we could do.
O, would I were to die with Salisbury!
The shame hereof will make me hide my head.

  Exit TALBOT. *Alarum; retreat*

☙ SCENE VI ☙
Orleans

Flourish. Enter on the walls, LA PUCELLE, CHARLES,
REIGNIER, ALENÇON, and SOLDIERS

PUCELLE. Advance our waving colours on
 the walls;
Rescu'd is Orleans from the English.
Thus Joan la Pucelle hath perform'd her word.
CHARLES. Divinest creature, Astraea's daughter,
How shall I honour thee for this success?
Thy promises are like Adonis' gardens,
That one day bloom'd and fruitful were
 the next.
France, triumph in thy glorious prophetess.
Recover'd is the town of Orleans.
More blessed hap did ne'er befall our state.
REIGNIER. Why ring not out the bells aloud
 throughout the town?
Dauphin, command the citizens make bonfires
And feast and banquet in the open streets

To celebrate the joy that God hath given us.
ALENÇON. All France will be replete with mirth
 and joy
When they shall hear how we have play'd the men.
CHARLES. 'Tis Joan, not we, by whom the day
 is won;
For which I will divide my crown with her;
And all the priests and friars in my realm
Shall in procession sing her endless praise.
A statelier pyramis to her I'll rear
Than Rhodope's of Memphis ever was.
In memory of her, when she is dead,
Her ashes, in an urn more precious
Than the rich jewel'd coffer of Darius,
Transported shall be at high festivals
Before the kings and queens of France.
No longer on Saint Denis will we cry,
But Joan la Pucelle shall be France's saint.
Come in, and let us banquet royally
After this golden day of victory.

  Flourish. Exeunt.

❧ ACT II ❧

☙ SCENE I ☙
Before Orleans

Enter a FRENCH SERGEANT and two SENTINELS

SERGEANT. Sirs, take your places and be vigilant.
If any noise or soldier you perceive
Near to the walls, by some apparent sign
Let us have knowledge at the court of guard.
FIRST SENTINEL. Sergeant, you shall.
 [Exit SERGEANT]
Thus are poor servitors,
When others sleep upon their quiet beds,
Constrain'd to watch in darkness, rain, and cold.
Enter TALBOT, BEDFORD, BURGUNDY, and Forces, with
 scaling-ladders; their drums beating a dead march
TALBOT. Lord Regent, and redoubted Burgundy,
By whose approach the regions of Artois,
Wallon, and Picardy, are friends to us,
This happy night the Frenchmen are secure,
Having all day carous'd and banqueted;
Embrace we then this opportunity,
As fitting best to quittance their deceit,
Contriv'd by art and baleful sorcery.
BEDFORD. Coward of France, how much he
 wrongs his fame,
Despairing of his own arm's fortitude,

To join with witches and the help of hell!

BURGUNDY. Traitors have never other company.
But what's that Pucelle whom they term so pure?

TALBOT. A maid, they say.

BEDFORD. A maid! and be so martial!

BURGUNDY. Pray God she prove not masculine
ere long,
If underneath the standard of the French
She carry armour as she hath begun.

TALBOT. Well, let them practise and converse
with spirits:
God is our fortress, in whose conquering name
Let us resolve to scale their flinty bulwarks.

BEDFORD. Ascend, brave Talbot; we will
follow thee.

TALBOT. Not all together; better far, I guess,
That we do make our entrance several ways;
That if it chance the one of us do fail
The other yet may rise against their force.

BEDFORD. Agreed; I'll to yond corner.

BURGUNDY. And I to this.

TALBOT. And here will Talbot mount or make
his grave.
Now, Salisbury, for thee, and for the right
Of English Henry, shall this night appear
How much in duty I am bound to both.

The English scale the walls and cry, 'Saint George! a Talbot!'

SENTINEL. Arm! arm! The enemy doth
make assault.

The French leap o'er the walls in their shirts.

Enter, several ways, BASTARD, ALENÇON, REIGNIER,
half ready and half unready

ALENÇON. How now, my lords? What, all
unready so?

BASTARD. Unready! Ay, and glad we 'scap'd
so well.

REIGNIER. 'Twas time, I trow, to wake and leave
our beds,
Hearing alarums at our chamber doors.

ALENÇON. Of all exploits since first I
follow'd arms,
Ne'er heard I of a warlike enterprise
More venturous or desperate than this.

BASTARD. I think this Talbot be a fiend of hell.

REIGNIER. If not of hell, the heavens, sure,
favour him

ALENÇON. Here cometh Charles; I marvel how
he sped.

Enter CHARLES and LA PUCELLE

BASTARD. Tut! holy Joan was his defensive guard.

CHARLES. Is this thy cunning, thou
deceitful dame?
Didst thou at first, to flatter us withal,

Make us partakers of a little gain
That now our loss might be ten times so much?

PUCELLE. Wherefore is Charles impatient with
his friend?
At all times will you have my power alike?
Sleeping or waking, must I still prevail
Or will you blame and lay the fault on me?
Improvident soldiers! Had your watch
been good,
This sudden mischief never could have fall'n.

CHARLES. Duke of Alençon, this was your default
That, being captain of the watch to-night,
Did look no better to that weighty charge.

ALENÇON. Had all your quarters been as
safely kept
As that whereof I had the government,
We had not been thus shamefully surpris'd.

BASTARD. Mine was secure.

REIGNIER. And so was mine, my lord.

CHARLES. And, for myself, most part of all
this night,
Within her quarter and mine own precinct
I was employ'd in passing to and fro
About relieving of the sentinels.
Then how or which way should they first
break in?

PUCELLE. Question, my lords, no further of
the case,
How or which way; 'tis sure they found
some place
But weakly guarded, where the breach
was made.
And now there rests no other shift but this
To gather our soldiers, scatter'd and dispers'd,
And lay new platforms to endamage them.

Alarum. Enter an ENGLISH SOLDIER, crying 'A Talbot! A
Talbot!' They fly, leaving their clothes behind

SOLDIER. I'll be so bold to take what they
have left.
The cry of Talbot serves me for a sword;
For I have loaden me with many spoils,
Using no other weapon but his name. *Exit.*

☙ SCENE II ☙
ORLEANS. Within the town

Enter TALBOT, BEDFORD, BURGUNDY,
a CAPTAIN, and others

BEDFORD. The day begins to break, and night
is fled
Whose pitchy mantle over-veil'd the earth.

Here sound retreat and cease our hot pursuit.

Retreat sounded

TALBOT. Bring forth the body of old Salisbury
  And here advance it in the market-place,
  The middle centre of this cursed town.
  Now have I paid my vow unto his soul;
  For every drop of blood was drawn from him
  There hath at least five Frenchmen died to-night.
  And that hereafter ages may behold
  What ruin happen'd in revenge of him,
  Within their chiefest temple I'll erect
  A tomb, wherein his corpse shall be interr'd;
  Upon the which, that every one may read,
  Shall be engrav'd the sack of Orleans,
  The treacherous manner of his mournful death,
  And what a terror he had been to France.
  But, lords, in all our bloody massacre,
  I muse we met not with the Dauphin's grace,
  His new-come champion, virtuous Joan of Arc,
  Nor any of his false confederates.
BEDFORD. 'Tis thought, Lord Talbot, when the
  fight began,
  Rous'd on the sudden from their drowsy beds,
  They did amongst the troops of armed men
  Leap o'er the walls for refuge in the field.
BURGUNDY. Myself, as far as I could well discern
  For smoke and dusky vapours of the night,
  Am sure I scar'd the Dauphin and his trull,
  When arm in arm they both came
  swiftly running,
  Like to a pair of loving turtle-doves
  That could not live asunder day or night.
  After that things are set in order here,
  We'll follow them with all the power we have.

Enter a MESSENGER

MESSENGER. All hail, my lords! Which of this
  princely train
  Call ye the warlike Talbot, for his acts
  So much applauded through the realm
  of France?
TALBOT. Here is the Talbot; who would speak
  with him?
MESSENGER. The virtuous lady, Countess
  of Auvergne,
  With modesty admiring thy renown,
  By me entreats, great lord, thou
  wouldst vouchsafe
  To visit her poor castle where she lies,
  That she may boast she hath beheld the man
  Whose glory fills the world with loud report.
BURGUNDY. Is it even so? Nay, then I see
  our wars
  Will turn into a peaceful comic sport,

When ladies crave to be encount'red with.
  You may not, my lord, despise her gentle suit.
TALBOT. Ne'er trust me then; for when a world
  of men
  Could not prevail with all their oratory,
  Yet hath a woman's kindness overrul'd;
  And therefore tell her I return great thanks
  And in submission will attend on her.
  Will not your honours bear me company?
BEDFORD. No, truly; 'tis more than manners will;
  And I have heard it said unbidden guests
  Are often welcomest when they are gone.
TALBOT. Well then, alone, since there's
  no remedy,
  I mean to prove this lady's courtesy.
  Come hither, Captain. *[Whispers]* You perceive
  my mind?
CAPTAIN. I do, my lord, and mean accordingly.

Exeunt.

✣ SCENE III ✣
AUVERGNE. The castle

Enter the COUNTESS and her PORTER

COUNTESS. Porter, remember what I gave
  in charge;
  And when you have done so, bring the keys
  to me.
PORTER. Madam, I will.
COUNTESS. The plot is laid; if all things fall
  out right,
  I shall as famous be by this exploit,
  As Scythian Tomyris by Cyrus' death.
  Great is the rumour of this dreadful knight,
  And his achievements of no less account.
  Fain would mine eyes be witness with mine ears
  To give their censure of these rare reports.

Enter MESSENGER and TALBOT

MESSENGER. Madam, according as your
  ladyship desir'd,
  By message crav'd, so is Lord Talbot come.
COUNTESS. And he is welcome. What! is this
  the man?
MESSENGER. Madam, it is.
COUNTESS. Is this the scourge of France?
  Is this Talbot, so much fear'd abroad
  That with his name the mothers still their babes?
  I see report is fabulous and false.
  I thought I should have seen some Hercules,
  A second Hector, for his grim aspect
  And large proportion of his strong-knit limbs.

Alas, this is a child, a silly dwarf!
It cannot be this weak and writhled shrimp
Should strike such terror to his enemies.
TALBOT. Madam, I have been bold to trouble you;
But since your ladyship is not at leisure,
I'll sort some other time to visit you. *Going*
COUNTESS. What means he now? Go ask him
whither he goes.
MESSENGER. Stay, my Lord Talbot; for my
lady craves
To know the cause of your abrupt departure.
TALBOT. Marry, for that she's in a wrong belief,
I go to certify her Talbot's here.
Re-enter PORTER with keys
COUNTESS. If thou be he, then art thou prisoner.
TALBOT. Prisoner! To whom?
COUNTESS. To me, blood-thirsty lord,
And for that cause I train'd thee to my house.
Long time thy shadow hath been thrall to me,
For in my gallery thy picture hangs;
But now the substance shall endure the like
And I will chain these legs and arms of thine
That hast by tyranny these many years
Wasted our country, slain our citizens,
And sent our sons and husbands captive.
TALBOT. Ha, ha, ha!
COUNTESS. Laughest thou, wretch? Thy mirth
shall turn to moan.
TALBOT. I laugh to see your ladyship so fond
To think that you have aught but
Talbot's shadow
Whereon to practise your severity.
COUNTESS. Why, art not thou the man?
TALBOT. I am indeed.
COUNTESS. Then have I substance too.
TALBOT. No, no, I am but shadow of myself.
You are deceiv'd, my substance is not here;
For what you see is but the smallest part
And least proportion of humanity.
I tell you, madam, were the whole frame here,
It is of such a spacious lofty pitch
Your roof were not sufficient to contain 't.
COUNTESS. This is a riddling merchant for
the nonce;
He will be here, and yet he is not here.
How can these contrarieties agree?
TALBOT. That will I show you presently. *[Winds his*
horn; drums strike up; a peal of ordnance.]
Enter SOLDIERS
How say you, madam? Are you now persuaded
That Talbot is but shadow of himself?
These are his substance, sinews, arms,
and strength,

With which he yoketh your rebellious necks,
Razeth your cities, and subverts your towns,
And in a moment makes them desolate.
COUNTESS. Victorious Talbot! pardon my abuse.
I find thou art no less than fame hath bruited,
And more than may be gather'd by thy shape.
Let my presumption not provoke thy wrath,
For I am sorry that with reverence
I did not entertain thee as thou art.
TALBOT. Be not dismay'd, fair lady;
nor misconster
The mind of Talbot as you did mistake
The outward composition of his body.
What you have done hath not offended me.
Nor other satisfaction do I crave
But only, with your patience, that we may
Taste of your wine and see what cates you have,
For soldiers' stomachs always serve them well.
COUNTESS. With all my heart, and think
me honoured
To feast so great a warrior in my house. *Exeunt.*

✣ SCENE IV ✣

London. The temple garden

Enter the EARLS OF SOMERSET, SUFFOLK, and
WARWICK; RICHARD PLANTAGENET, VERNON,
and a LAWYER

PLANTAGENET. Great lords and gentlemen, what
means this silence?
Dare no man answer in a case of truth?
SUFFOLK. Within the Temple Hall we were
too loud;
The garden here is more convenient.
PLANTAGENET. Then say at once if I maintain'd
the truth;
Or else was wrangling Somerset in th' error?
SUFFOLK. Faith, I have been a truant in the law
And never yet could frame my will to it;
And therefore frame the law unto my will.
SOMERSET. Judge you, my Lord of Warwick, then,
between us.
WARWICK. Between two hawks, which flies the
higher pitch;
Between two dogs, which hath the
deeper mouth;
Between two blades, which bears the
better temper;
Between two horses, which doth bear him best;
Between two girls, which hath the merriest eye
I have perhaps some shallow spirit of judgment;

But in these nice sharp quillets of the law,
Good faith, I am no wiser than a daw.
PLANTAGENET. Tut, tut, here is a
mannerly forbearance:
The truth appears so naked on my side
That any purblind eye may find it out.
SOMERSET. And on my side it is so
well apparell'd,
So clear, so shining, and so evident,
That it will glimmer through a blind man's eye.
PLANTAGENET. Since you are tongue-tied and so
loath to speak,
In dumb significants proclaim your thoughts.
Let him that is a true-born gentleman
And stands upon the honour of his birth,
If he suppose that I have pleaded truth,
From off this brier pluck a white rose with me.
SOMERSET. Let him that is no coward nor
no flatterer,
But dare maintain the party of the truth,
Pluck a red rose from off this thorn with me.
WARWICK. I love no colours; and, without
all colour
Of base insinuating flattery,
I pluck this white rose with Plantagenet.
SUFFOLK. I pluck this red rose with
young Somerset,
And say withal I think he held the right.
VERNON. Stay, lords and gentlemen, and pluck
no more
Till you conclude that he upon whose side
The fewest roses are cropp'd from the tree
Shall yield the other in the right opinion.
SOMERSET. Good Master Vernon, it is
well objected;
If I have fewest, I subscribe in silence.
PLANTAGENET. And I.
VERNON. Then, for the truth and plainness of
the case,
I pluck this pale and maiden blossom here,
Giving my verdict on the white rose side.
SOMERSET. Prick not your finger as you pluck
it off,
Lest, bleeding, you do paint the white rose red,
And fall on my side so, against your will.
VERNON. If I, my lord, for my opinion bleed,
Opinion shall be surgeon to my hurt
And keep me on the side where still I am.
SOMERSET. Well, well, come on; who else?
LAWYER. *[To Somerset]* Unless my study and my
books be false,
The argument you held was wrong in you;
In sign whereof I pluck a white rose too.

PLANTAGENET. Now, Somerset, where is
your argument?
SOMERSET. Here in my scabbard, meditating that,
Shall dye your white rose in a bloody red.
PLANTAGENET. Meantime your cheeks do
counterfeit our roses;
For pale they look with fear, as witnessing
The truth on our side.
SOMERSET. No, Plantagenet,
'Tis not for fear but anger that thy cheeks
Blush for pure shame to counterfeit our roses,
And yet thy tongue will not confess thy error.
PLANTAGENET. Hath not thy rose a
canker, Somerset?
SOMERSET. Hath not thy rose a
thorn, Plantagenet?
PLANTAGENET. Ay, sharp and piercing, to
maintain his truth;
Whiles thy consuming canker eats his falsehood.
SOMERSET. Well, I'll find friends to wear my
bleeding roses,
That shall maintain what I have said is true,
Where false Plantagenet dare not be seen.
PLANTAGENET. Now, by this maiden blossom in
my hand,
I scorn thee and thy fashion, peevish boy.
SUFFOLK. Turn not thy scorns this
way, Plantagenet.
PLANTAGENET. Proud Pole, I will, and scorn both
him and thee.
SUFFOLK. I'll turn my part thereof into thy throat.
SOMERSET. Away, away, good William de la Pole!
We grace the yeoman by conversing with him.
WARWICK. Now, by God's will, thou wrong'st
him, Somerset;
His grandfather was Lionel Duke of Clarence,
Third son to the third Edward, King of England.
Spring crestless yeomen from so deep a root?
PLANTAGENET. He bears him on the
place's privilege,
Or durst not for his craven heart say thus.
SOMERSET. By Him that made me, I'll maintain
my words
On any plot of ground in Christendom.
Was not thy father, Richard Earl of Cambridge,
For treason executed in our late king's days?
And by his treason stand'st not thou attainted,
Corrupted, and exempt from ancient gentry?
His trespass yet lives guilty in thy blood;
And till thou be restor'd thou art a yeoman.
PLANTAGENET. My father was attached,
not attainted;
Condemn'd to die for treason, but no traitor;

And that I'll prove on better men than Somerset,
Were growing time once ripen'd to my will.
For your partaker Pole, and you yourself,
I'll note you in my book of memory
To scourge you for this apprehension.
Look to it well, and say you are well warn'd.
SOMERSET. Ay, thou shalt find us ready for
  thee still;
And know us by these colours for thy foes,
For these, my friends, in spite of thee shall wear.
PLANTAGENET. And, by my soul, this pale and
  angry rose,
As cognizance of my blood-drinking hate,
Will I for ever, and my faction, wear,
Until it wither with me to my grave,
Or flourish to the height of my degree.
SUFFOLK. Go forward, and be chok'd with
  thy ambition!
And so farewell until I meet thee next. *Exit.*
SOMERSET. Have with thee, Pole. Farewell,
  ambitious Richard.   *Exit.*
PLANTAGENET. How I am brav'd, and must
  perforce endure it!
WARWICK. This blot that they object against
  your house
Shall be wip'd out in the next Parliament,
Call'd for the truce of Winchester and Gloucester;
And if thou be not then created York,
I will not live to be accounted Warwick.
Meantime, in signal of my love to thee,
Against proud Somerset and William Pole,
Will I upon thy party wear this rose;
And here I prophesy: this brawl to-day,
Grown to this faction in the Temple Garden,
Shall send between the Red Rose and the White
A thousand souls to death and deadly night.
PLANTAGENET. Good Master Vernon, I am bound
  to you
That you on my behalf would pluck a flower.
VERNON. In your behalf still will I wear the same.
LAWYER. And so will I.
PLANTAGENET. Thanks, gentle sir.
Come, let us four to dinner. I dare say
This quarrel will drink blood another day. *Exeunt.*

⚜ SCENE V ⚜
The Tower of London

Enter MORTIMER, brought in a chair, and GAOLERS

MORTIMER. Kind keepers of my weak
  decaying age,
Let dying Mortimer here rest himself.
Even like a man new haled from the rack,
So fare my limbs with long imprisonment;
And these grey locks, the pursuivants
  of death,
Nestor-like aged in an age of care,
Argue the end of Edmund Mortimer.
These eyes, like lamps whose wasting oil
  is spent,
Wax dim, as drawing to their exigent;
Weak shoulders, overborne with
  burdening grief,
And pithless arms, like to a wither'd vine
That droops his sapless branches to
  the ground.
Yet are these feet, whose strengthless stay
  is numb,
Unable to support this lump of clay,
Swift-winged with desire to get a grave,
As witting I no other comfort have.
But tell me, keeper, will my nephew come?
FIRST KEEPER. Richard Plantagenet, my lord,
  will come.
We sent unto the Temple, unto his chamber;
And answer was return'd that he will come.
MORTIMER. Enough; my soul shall then
  be satisfied.
Poor gentleman! his wrong doth equal mine.
Since Henry Monmouth first began to reign,
Before whose glory I was great in arms,
This loathsome sequestration have I had;
And even since then hath Richard
  been obscur'd,
Depriv'd of honour and inheritance.
But now the arbitrator of despairs,
Just Death, kind umpire of men's miseries,
With sweet enlargement doth dismiss
  me hence.
I would his troubles likewise were expir'd,
That so he might recover what was lost.
  Enter RICHARD PLANTAGENET
FIRST KEEPER. My lord, your loving nephew
  now is come.
MORTIMER. Richard Plantagenet, my friend, is
  he come?
PLANTAGENET. Ay, noble uncle, thus
  ignobly us'd,
Your nephew, late despised Richard, comes.
MORTIMER. Direct mine arms I may embrace
  his neck
And in his bosom spend my latter gasp.
O, tell me when my lips do touch his cheeks,
That I may kindly give one fainting kiss.

And now declare, sweet stem from York's
great stock,
Why didst thou say of late thou wert despis'd?
PLANTAGENET. First, lean thine aged back
against mine arm;
And, in that ease, I'll tell thee my disease.
This day, in argument upon a case,
Some words there grew 'twixt Somerset
and me;
Among which terms he us'd his lavish tongue
And did upbraid me with my father's death;
Which obloquy set bars before my tongue,
Else with the like I had requited him.
Therefore, good uncle, for my father's sake,
In honour of a true Plantagenet,
And for alliance sake, declare the cause
My father, Earl of Cambridge, lost his head.
MORTIMER. That cause, fair nephew, that
imprison'd me
And hath detain'd me all my flow'ring youth
Within a loathsome dungeon, there to pine,
Was cursed instrument of his decease.
PLANTAGENET. Discover more at large what
cause that was,
For I am ignorant and cannot guess.
MORTIMER. I will, if that my fading
breath permit
And death approach not ere my tale be done.
Henry the Fourth, grandfather to this king,
Depos'd his nephew Richard, Edward's son,
The first-begotten and the lawful heir
Of Edward king, the third of that descent;
During whose reign the Percies of the north,
Finding his usurpation most unjust,
Endeavour'd my advancement to the throne.
The reason mov'd these warlike lords to this
Was, for that young Richard thus remov'd,
Leaving no heir begotten of his body-
I was the next by birth and parentage;
For by my mother I derived am
From Lionel Duke of Clarence, third son
To King Edward the Third; whereas he
From John of Gaunt doth bring his pedigree,
Being but fourth of that heroic line.
But mark: as in this haughty great attempt
They laboured to plant the rightful heir,
I lost my liberty, and they their lives.
Long after this, when Henry the Fifth,
Succeeding his father Bolingbroke, did reign,
Thy father, Earl of Cambridge, then deriv'd
From famous Edmund Langley, Duke of York,
Marrying my sister, that thy mother was,
Again, in pity of my hard distress,

Levied an army, weening to redeem
And have install'd me in the diadem;
But, as the rest, so fell that noble earl,
And was beheaded. Thus the Mortimers,
In whom the title rested, were suppress'd.
PLANTAGENET. Of which, my lord, your honour
is the last.
MORTIMER. True; and thou seest that I no
issue have,
And that my fainting words do warrant death.
Thou art my heir; the rest I wish thee gather;
But yet be wary in thy studious care.
PLANTAGENET. Thy grave admonishments
prevail with me.
But yet methinks my father's execution
Was nothing less than bloody tyranny.
MORTIMER. With silence, nephew, be
thou politic;
Strong fixed is the house of Lancaster
And like a mountain not to be remov'd.
But now thy uncle is removing hence,
As princes do their courts when they
are cloy'd
With long continuance in a settled place.
PLANTAGENET. O uncle, would some part of
my young years
Might but redeem the passage of your age!
MORTIMER. Thou dost then wrong me, as that
slaughterer doth,
Which giveth many wounds when one will kill.
Mourn not, except thou sorrow for my good;
Only give order for my funeral.
And so, farewell; and fair be all thy hopes,
And prosperous be thy life in peace and
war!   *Dies.*
PLANTAGENET. And peace, no war, befall thy
parting soul!
In prison hast thou spent a pilgrimage,
And like a hermit overpass'd thy days.
Well, I will lock his counsel in my breast;
And what I do imagine, let that rest.
Keepers, convey him hence; and I myself
Will see his burial better than his life.
Exeunt GAOLERS, bearing out the body of MORTIMER.
Here dies the dusky torch of Mortimer,
Chok'd with ambition of the meaner sort;
And for those wrongs, those bitter injuries,
Which Somerset hath offer'd to my house,
I doubt not but with honour to redress;
And therefore haste I to the Parliament,
Either to be restored to my blood,
Or make my ill th' advantage of my good.
Exit.

ACT III

SCENE I

London. The Parliament House

Flourish. Enter the KING, EXETER, GLOUCESTER, WARWICK, SOMERSET, and SUFFOLK; the BISHOP OF WINCHESTER, RICHARD PLANTAGENET, and Others. GLOUCESTER offers to put up a bill; WINCHESTER snatches it, and tears it

WINCHESTER. Com'st thou with deep
  premeditated lines,
  With written pamphlets studiously devis'd?
  Humphrey of Gloucester, if thou canst accuse
  Or aught intend'st to lay unto my charge,
  Do it without invention, suddenly;
  I with sudden and extemporal speech
  Purpose to answer what thou canst object.
GLOUCESTER. Presumptuous priest, this place
  commands my patience,
  Or thou shouldst find thou hast dishonour'd me.
  Think not, although in writing I preferr'd
  The manner of thy vile outrageous crimes,
  That therefore I have forg'd, or am not able
  Verbatim to rehearse the method of my pen.
  No, prelate; such is thy audacious wickedness,
  Thy lewd, pestiferous, and dissentious pranks,
  As very infants prattle of thy pride.
  Thou art a most pernicious usurer;
  Froward by nature, enemy to peace;
  Lascivious, wanton, more than well beseems
  A man of thy profession and degree;
  And for thy treachery, what's more manifest
  In that thou laid'st a trap to take my life,
  As well at London Bridge as at the Tower?
  Beside, I fear me, if thy thoughts were sifted,
  The King, thy sovereign, is not quite exempt
  From envious malice of thy swelling heart.
WINCHESTER. Gloucester, I do defy thee.
  Lords, vouchsafe
  To give me hearing what I shall reply.
  If I were covetous, ambitious, or perverse,
  As he will have me, how am I so poor?
  Or how haps it I seek not to advance
  Or raise myself, but keep my wonted calling?
  And for dissension, who preferreth peace
  More than I do, except I be provok'd?
  No, my good lords, it is not that offends;
  It is not that that hath incens'd the Duke:

It is because no one should sway but he;
No one but he should be about the King;
And that engenders thunder in his breast
And makes him roar these accusations forth.
But he shall know I am as good-
GLOUCESTER. As good!
Thou bastard of my grandfather!
WINCHESTER. Ay, lordly sir; for what are you,
  I pray,
  But one imperious in another's throne?
GLOUCESTER. Am I not Protector, saucy priest?
WINCHESTER. And am not I a prelate of
  the church?
GLOUCESTER. Yes, as an outlaw in a castle keeps,
  And useth it to patronage his theft.
WINCHESTER. Unreverent Gloucester!
GLOUCESTER. Thou art reverend
  Touching thy spiritual function, not thy life.
WINCHESTER. Rome shall remedy this.
WARWICK. Roam thither then.
SOMERSET. My lord, it were your duty to forbear.
WARWICK. Ay, see the bishop be not overborne.
SOMERSET. Methinks my lord should be religious,
  And know the office that belongs to such.
WARWICK. Methinks his lordship should
  be humbler;
  It fitteth not a prelate so to plead.
SOMERSET. Yes, when his holy state is touch'd
  so near.
WARWICK. State holy or unhallow'd, what of that?
  Is not his Grace Protector to the King?
PLANTAGENET. *[Aside]* Plantagenet, I see, must
  hold his tongue,
  Lest it be said 'Speak, sirrah, when you should;
  Must your bold verdict enter talk with lords?'
  Else would I have a fling at Winchester.
KING HENRY. Uncles of Gloucester and
  of Winchester,
  The special watchmen of our English weal,
  I would prevail, if prayers might prevail
  To join your hearts in love and amity.
  O, what a scandal is it to our crown
  That two such noble peers as ye should jar!
  Believe me, lords, my tender years can tell
  Civil dissension is a viperous worm
  That gnaws the bowels of the commonwealth. *[A
  noise within: 'Down with the tawny coats!']*
  What tumult's this?
WARWICK. An uproar, I dare warrant,
  Begun through malice of the Bishop's men.
    A noise again: 'Stones! Stones!'
    Enter the MAYOR OF LONDON, attended
MAYOR. O, my good lords, and virtuous Henry,

Pity the city of London, pity us!
The Bishop and the Duke of Gloucester's men,
Forbidden late to carry any weapon,
Have fill'd their pockets full of pebble stones
And, banding themselves in contrary parts,
Do pelt so fast at one another's pate
That many have their giddy brains knock'd out.
Our windows are broke down in every street,
And we for fear compell'd to shut our shops.

Enter in skirmish, the retainers of GLOUCESTER and
WINCHESTER, with bloody pates

KING HENRY. We charge you, on allegiance
to ourself,
To hold your slaught'ring hands and keep
the peace.
Pray, uncle Gloucester, mitigate this strife.

FIRST SERVING-MAN. Nay, if we be forbidden
stones, we'll fall to it with our teeth.

SECOND SERVING-MAN. Do what ye dare, we are
as resolute.

Skirmish again

GLOUCESTER. You of my household, leave this
peevish broil,
And set this unaccustom'd fight aside.

THIRD SERVING-MAN. My lord, we know your
Grace to be a man
Just and upright, and for your royal birth
Inferior to none but to his Majesty;
And ere that we will suffer such a prince,
So kind a father of the commonweal,
To be disgraced by an inkhorn mate,
We and our wives and children all will fight
And have our bodies slaught'red by thy foes.

FIRST SERVING-MAN. Ay, and the very parings of
our nails
Shall pitch a field when we are dead.*Begin again*

GLOUCESTER. Stay, stay, I say!
And if you love me, as you say you do,
Let me persuade you to forbear awhile.

KING HENRY. O, how this discord doth afflict
my soul!
Can you, my Lord of Winchester, behold
My sighs and tears and will not once relent?
Who should be pitiful, if you be not?
Or who should study to prefer a peace,
If holy churchmen take delight in broils?

WARWICK. Yield, my Lord Protector;
yield, Winchester;
Except you mean with obstinate repulse
To slay your sovereign and destroy the realm.
You see what mischief, and what murder too,
Hath been enacted through your enmity;
Then be at peace, except ye thirst for blood.

WINCHESTER. He shall submit, or I will
never yield.

GLOUCESTER. Compassion on the King
commands me stoop,
Or I would see his heart out ere the priest
Should ever get that privilege of me.

WARWICK. Behold, my Lord of Winchester,
the Duke
Hath banish'd moody discontented fury,
As by his smoothed brows it doth appear;
Why look you still so stern and tragical?

GLOUCESTER. Here, Winchester, I offer thee
my hand.

KING HENRY. Fie, uncle Beaufort! I have heard
you preach
That malice was a great and grievous sin;
And will not you maintain the thing you teach,
But prove a chief offender in the same?

WARWICK. Sweet King! The Bishop hath a
kindly gird.
For shame, my Lord of Winchester, relent;
What, shall a child instruct you what to do?

WINCHESTER. Well, Duke of Gloucester, I will
yield to thee;
Love for thy love and hand for hand I give.

GLOUCESTER [Aside] Ay, but, I fear me, with a
hollow heart.
See here, my friends and loving countrymen:
This token serveth for a flag of truce
Betwixt ourselves and all our followers.
So help me God, as I dissemble not!

WINCHESTER [Aside] So help me God, as I intend
it not!

KING HENRY. O loving uncle, kind Duke
of Gloucester,
How joyful am I made by this contract!
Away, my masters! trouble us no more;
But join in friendship, as your lords have done.

FIRST SERVING-MAN. Content: I'll to
the surgeon's.

SECOND SERVING-MAN. And so will I.

THIRD SERVING-MAN. And I will see what physic
the tavern affords.

Exeunt servants, MAYOR, etc.

WARWICK. Accept this scroll, most
gracious sovereign;
Which in the right of Richard Plantagenet
We do exhibit to your Majesty.

GLOUCESTER. Well urg'd, my Lord of Warwick;
for, sweet prince,
An if your Grace mark every circumstance,
You have great reason to do Richard right;
Especially for those occasions

At Eltham Place I told your Majesty.

KING HENRY. And those occasions, uncle, were
   of force;
   Therefore, my loving lords, our pleasure is
   That Richard be restored to his blood.

WARWICK. Let Richard be restored to his blood;
   So shall his father's wrongs be recompens'd.

WINCHESTER. As will the rest, so
   willeth Winchester.

KING HENRY. If Richard will be true, not
   that alone
   But all the whole inheritance I give
   That doth belong unto the house of York,
   From whence you spring by lineal descent.

PLANTAGENET. Thy humble servant
   vows obedience
   And humble service till the point of death.

KING HENRY. Stoop then and set your knee
   against my foot;
   And in reguerdon of that duty done
   I girt thee with the valiant sword of York.
   Rise, Richard, like a true Plantagenet,
   And rise created princely Duke of York.

PLANTAGENET. And so thrive Richard as thy foes
   may fall!
   And as my duty springs, so perish they
   That grudge one thought against your Majesty!

ALL. Welcome, high Prince, the mighty Duke
   of York!

SOMERSET. [Aside] Perish, base Prince, ignoble
   Duke of York!

GLOUCESTER. Now will it best avail your Majesty
   To cross the seas and to be crown'd in France:
   The presence of a king engenders love
   Amongst his subjects and his loyal friends,
   As it disanimates his enemies.

KING HENRY. When Gloucester says the word,
   King Henry goes;
   For friendly counsel cuts off many foes.

GLOUCESTER. Your ships already are
   in readiness.

   Sennet. Flourish. Exeunt all but EXETER.

EXETER. Ay, we may march in England or
   in France,
   Not seeing what is likely to ensue.
   This late dissension grown betwixt the peers
   Burns under feigned ashes of forg'd love
   And will at last break out into a flame;
   As fest'red members rot but by degree
   Till bones and flesh and sinews fall away,
   So will this base and envious discord breed.
   And now I fear that fatal prophecy.
   Which in the time of Henry nam'd the Fifth

Was in the mouth of every sucking babe:
That Henry born at Monmouth should win all,
And Henry born at Windsor should lose all.
Which is so plain that Exeter doth wish
His days may finish ere that hapless time. *Exit.*

❧ SCENE II ❧

France. Before Rouen

*Enter LA PUCELLE disguis'd, with four SOLDIERS dressed
like countrymen, with sacks upon their backs*

PUCELLE. These are the city gates, the gates
   of Rouen,
   Through which our policy must make a breach.
   Take heed, be wary how you place your words;
   Talk like the vulgar sort of market-men
   That come to gather money for their corn.
   If we have entrance, as I hope we shall,
   And that we find the slothful watch but weak,
   I'll by a sign give notice to our friends,
   That Charles the Dauphin may encounter them.

FIRST SOLDIER. Our sacks shall be a mean to sack
   the city,
   And we be lords and rulers over Rouen;
   Therefore we'll knock.   *Knocks*

WATCH. [*Within*] Qui est la?

PUCELLE. Paysans, pauvres gens de France
   Poor market-folks that come to sell their corn.

WATCH. Enter, go in; the market-bell is rung.

PUCELLE. Now, Rouen, I'll shake thy bulwarks to
   the ground.

   LA PUCELLE, etc., enter the town

   *Enter CHARLES, BASTARD, ALENÇON, REIGNIER,
   and forces*

CHARLES. Saint Denis bless this happy stratagem!
   And once again we'll sleep secure in Rouen.

BASTARD. Here ent'red Pucelle and
   her practisants;
   Now she is there, how will she specify
   Here is the best and safest passage in?

ALENÇON. By thrusting out a torch from
   yonder tower;
   Which once discern'd shows that her meaning is
   No way to that, for weakness, which she ent'red.

   Enter LA PUCELLE, on the top, thrusting out a torch burning

PUCELLE. Behold, this is the happy wedding torch
   That joineth Rouen unto her countrymen,
   But burning fatal to the Talbotites. *Exit.*

BASTARD. See, noble Charles, the beacon of
   our friend;
   The burning torch in yonder turret stands.

CHARLES. Now shine it like a comet of revenge,
A prophet to the fall of all our foes!
ALENÇON. Defer no time, delays have
dangerous ends;
Enter, and cry 'The Dauphin!' presently,

And then do execution on the watch.

Alarum. Exeunt.

An Alarum. Enter TALBOT in an excursion

TALBOT. France, thou shalt rue this treason with
thy tears,
If Talbot but survive thy treachery.
Pucelle, that witch, that damned sorceress,
Hath wrought this hellish mischief unawares,
That hardly we escap'd the pride of France.

Exit.

An alarum; excursions. BEDFORD brought in sick in a chair.
Enter TALBOT and BURGUNDY without; within, LA
PUCELLE, CHARLES, BASTARD, ALENÇON, and
REIGNIER, on the walls

PUCELLE. Good morrow, gallants! Want ye corn
for bread?
I think the Duke of Burgundy will fast
Before he'll buy again at such a rate.
'Twas full of darnel-do you like the taste?
BURGUNDY. Scoff on, vile fiend and
shameless courtesan.
I trust ere long to choke thee with thine own,
And make thee curse the harvest of that corn.
CHARLES. Your Grace may starve, perhaps, before
that time.
BEDFORD. O, let no words, but deeds, revenge
this treason!
PUCELLE. What you do, good grey beard? Break
a lance,
And run a tilt at death within a chair?
TALBOT. Foul fiend of France and hag of
all despite,
Encompass'd with thy lustful paramours,
Becomes it thee to taunt his valiant age
And twit with cowardice a man half dead?
Damsel, I'll have a bout with you again,
Or else let Talbot perish with this shame.
PUCELLE. Are ye so hot, sir? Yet, Pucelle, hold
thy peace;
If Talbot do but thunder, rain will follow.

[The English party whisper together in council]

God speed the parliament! Who shall be
the Speaker?
TALBOT. Dare ye come forth and meet us in
the field?
PUCELLE. Belike your lordship takes us then
for fools,
To try if that our own be ours or no.

TALBOT. I speak not to that railing Hecate,
But unto thee, Alençon, and the rest.
Will ye, like soldiers, come and fight it out?
ALENÇON. Signior, no.
TALBOT. Signior, hang! Base muleteers of France!
Like peasant foot-boys do they keep the walls,
And dare not take up arms like gentlemen.
PUCELLE. Away, captains! Let's get us from
the walls;
For Talbot means no goodness by his looks.
God b'uy, my lord; we came but to tell you
That we are here. *Exeunt from the walls.*
TALBOT. And there will we be too, ere it be long,
Or else reproach be Talbot's greatest fame!
Vow, Burgundy, by honour of thy house,
Prick'd on by public wrongs sustain'd in France,
Either to get the town again or die;
And I, as sure as English Henry lives
And as his father here was conqueror,
As sure as in this late betrayed town
Great Coeur-de-lion's heart was buried
So sure I swear to get the town or die.
BURGUNDY. My vows are equal partners with
thy vows.
TALBOT. But ere we go, regard this dying prince,
The valiant Duke of Bedford. Come, my lord,
We will bestow you in some better place,
Fitter for sickness and for crazy age.
BEDFORD. Lord Talbot, do not so dishonour me;
Here will I sit before the walls of Rouen,
And will be partner of your weal or woe.
BURGUNDY. Courageous Bedford, let us now
persuade you.
BEDFORD. Not to be gone from hence; for once
I read
That stout Pendragon in his litter sick
Came to the field, and vanquished his foes.
Methinks I should revive the soldiers' hearts,
Because I ever found them as myself.
TALBOT. Undaunted spirit in a dying breast!
Then be it so. Heavens keep old Bedford safe!
And now no more ado, brave Burgundy,
But gather we our forces out of hand
And set upon our boasting enemy.

Exeunt against the town all but BEDFORD and Attendants.
An alarum; excursions. Enter SIR JOHN FASTOLFE, and a
CAPTAIN

CAPTAIN. Whither away, Sir John Fastolfe, in
such haste?
FASTOLFE. Whither away? To save myself
by flight:
We are like to have the overthrow again.
CAPTAIN. What! Will you fly and leave

Lord Talbot?

FASTOLFE. Ay,

All the Talbots in the world, to save my life. *Exit.*

CAPTAIN. Cowardly knight! ill fortune follow thee!

Exit into the town.

Retreat; excursions. LA PUCELLE, ALENÇON, and
CHARLES fly.

BEDFORD. Now, quiet soul, depart when
heaven please,

For I have seen our enemies' overthrow.

What is the trust or strength of foolish man?

They that of late were daring with their scoffs

Are glad and fain by flight to save themselves.

BEDFORD dies and is carried in by two in his chair
An alarum. Re-enter TALBOT, BURGUNDY, and the rest

TALBOT. Lost and recover'd in a day again!

This is a double honour, Burgundy.

Yet heavens have glory for this victory!

BURGUNDY. Warlike and martial

Talbot, Burgundy

Enshrines thee in his heart, and there erects

Thy noble deeds as valour's monuments.

TALBOT. Thanks, gentle Duke. But where is
Pucelle now?

I think her old familiar is asleep.

Now where's the Bastard's braves, and Charles
his gleeks?

What, all amort? Rouen hangs her head for grief

That such a valiant company are fled.

Now will we take some order in the town,

Placing therein some expert officers;

And then depart to Paris to the King,

For there young Henry with his nobles lie.

BURGUNDY. What wills Lord Talbot
pleaseth Burgundy.

TALBOT. But yet, before we go, let's not forget

The noble Duke of Bedford, late deceas'd,

But see his exequies fulfill'd in Rouen.

A braver soldier never couched lance,

A gentler heart did never sway in court;

But kings and mightiest potentates must die,

For that's the end of human misery.

Exeunt.

✿ SCENE III ✿

The plains near Rouen

Enter CHARLES, the BASTARD, ALENÇON, LA
PUCELLE, and Forces

PUCELLE. Dismay not, Princes, at this accident,

Nor grieve that Rouen is so recovered.

Care is no cure, but rather corrosive,

For things that are not to be remedied.

Let frantic Talbot triumph for a while

And like a peacock sweep along his tail;

We'll pull his plumes and take away his train,

If Dauphin and the rest will be but rul'd.

CHARLES. We have been guided by thee hitherto,

And of thy cunning had no diffidence;

One sudden foil shall never breed distrust

BASTARD. Search out thy wit for secret policies,

And we will make thee famous through
the world.

ALENÇON. We'll set thy statue in some holy place,

And have thee reverenc'd like a blessed saint.

Employ thee, then, sweet virgin, for our good.

PUCELLE. Then thus it must be; this doth
Joan devise:

By fair persuasions, mix'd with sug'red words,

We will entice the Duke of Burgundy

To leave the Talbot and to follow us.

CHARLES. Ay, marry, sweeting, if we could
do that,

France were no place for Henry's warriors;

Nor should that nation boast it so with us,

But be extirped from our provinces.

ALENÇON. For ever should they be expuls'd
from France,

And not have tide of an earldom here.

PUCELLE. Your honours shall perceive how I
will work

To bring this matter to the wished end.

[Drum sounds afar off] Hark! by the sound of drum
you may perceive

Their powers are marching unto Paris-ward. *[Here*
sound an English march.]

Enter, and pass over at a distance, TALBOT and his forces

There goes the Talbot, with his colours spread,

And all the troops of English after him.

[French march]

Enter the DUKE OF BURGUNDY and his Forces

Now in the rearward comes the Duke and his.

Fortune in favour makes him lag behind.

Summon a parley; we will talk with him.

Trumpets sound a parley

CHARLES. A parley with the Duke of Burgundy!

BURGUNDY. Who craves a parley with
the Burgundy?

PUCELLE. The princely Charles of France,
thy countryman.

BURGUNDY. What say'st thou, Charles? for I am
marching hence.

CHARLES. Speak, Pucelle, and enchant him with
thy words.

PUCELLE. Brave Burgundy, undoubted hope
  of France!
  Stay, let thy humble handmaid speak to thee.
BURGUNDY. Speak on; but be not over-tedious.
PUCELLE. Look on thy country, look on
  fertile France,
  And see the cities and the towns defac'd
  By wasting ruin of the cruel foe;
  As looks the mother on her lowly babe
  When death doth close his tender dying eyes,
  See, see the pining malady of France;
  Behold the wounds, the most unnatural wounds,
  Which thou thyself hast given her woeful breast.
  O, turn thy edged sword another way;
  Strike those that hurt, and hurt not those
  that help!
  One drop of blood drawn from thy
  country's bosom
  Should grieve thee more than streams of
  foreign gore.
  Return thee therefore with a flood of tears,
  And wash away thy country's stained spots.
BURGUNDY. Either she hath bewitch'd me with
  her words,
  Or nature makes me suddenly relent.
PUCELLE. Besides, all French and France exclaims
  on thee,
  Doubting thy birth and lawful progeny.
  Who join'st thou with but with a lordly nation
  That will not trust thee but for profit's sake?
  When Talbot hath set footing once in France,
  And fashion'd thee that instrument of ill,
  Who then but English Henry will be lord,
  And thou be thrust out like a fugitive?
  Call we to mind-and mark but this for proof:
  Was not the Duke of Orleans thy foe?
  And was he not in England prisoner?
  But when they heard he was thine enemy
  They set him free without his ransom paid,
  In spite of Burgundy and all his friends.
  See then, thou fight'st against thy countrymen,
  And join'st with them will be thy slaughtermen.
  Come, come, return; return, thou
  wand'ring lord;
  Charles and the rest will take thee in their arms.
BURGUNDY. I am vanquished; these haughty
  words of hers
  Have batt'red me like roaring cannon-shot
  And made me almost yield upon my knees.
  Forgive me, country, and sweet countrymen
  And, lords, accept this hearty kind embrace.
  My forces and my power of men are yours;
  So, farewell, Talbot; I'll no longer trust thee.

PUCELLE. Done like a Frenchman- [Aside] turn and
  turn again.
CHARLES. Welcome, brave Duke! Thy friendship
  makes us fresh.
BASTARD. And doth beget new courage in
  our breasts.
ALENÇON. Pucelle hath bravely play'd her part
  in this,
  And doth deserve a coronet of gold.
CHARLES. Now let us on, my lords, and join
  our powers,
  And seek how we may prejudice the foe.

                                  Exeunt.

⚜ SCENE IV ⚜
Paris. The palace

Enter the KING, GLOUCESTER, WINCHESTER,
YORK, SUFFOLK, SOMERSET, WARWICK, EXETER,
VERNON, BASSET, and others. To them, with his
SOLDIERS, TALBOT

TALBOT. My gracious Prince, and
  honourable peers,
  Hearing of your arrival in this realm,
  I have awhile given truce unto my wars
  To do my duty to my sovereign;
  In sign whereof, this arm that hath reclaim'd
  To your obedience fifty fortresses,
  Twelve cities, and seven walled towns
  of strength,
  Beside five hundred prisoners of esteem,
  Lets fall his sword before your Highness' feet,
  And with submissive loyalty of heart
  Ascribes the glory of his conquest got
  First to my God and next unto your
  Grace. [Kneels]
KING HENRY. Is this the Lord Talbot,
  uncle Gloucester,
  That hath so long been resident in France?
GLOUCESTER. Yes, if it please your Majesty,
  my liege.
KING HENRY. Welcome, brave captain and
  victorious lord!
  When I was young, as yet I am not old,
  I do remember how my father said
  A stouter champion never handled sword.
  Long since we were resolved of your truth,
  Your faithful service, and your toil in war;
  Yet never have you tasted our reward,
  Or been reguerdon'd with so much as thanks,
  Because till now we never saw your face.
  Therefore stand up; and for these good deserts
  We here create you Earl of Shrewsbury;

And in our coronation take your place.

Sennet. Flourish. Exeunt all but VERNON and BASSET.

VERNON. Now, sir, to you, that were so hot at sea,
Disgracing of these colours that I wear
In honour of my noble Lord of York
Dar'st thou maintain the former words
thou spak'st?

BASSET. Yes, sir; as well as you dare patronage
The envious barking of your saucy tongue
Against my lord the Duke of Somerset.

VERNON. Sirrah, thy lord I honour as he is.

BASSET. Why, what is he? As good a man as York!

VERNON. Hark ye: not so. In witness, take ye that.

Strikes him

BASSET. Villain, thou knowest the law of arms
is such
That whoso draws a sword 'tis present death,
Or else this blow should broach thy
dearest blood.
But I'll unto his Majesty and crave
I may have liberty to venge this wrong;
When thou shalt see I'll meet thee to thy cost.

VERNON. Well, miscreant, I'll be there as soon
as you;
And, after, meet you sooner than you would.

Exeunt.

ACT IV

SCENE I
Paris. The palace

Enter the KING, GLOUCESTER, WINCHESTER,
YORK, SUFFOLK, SOMERSET, WARWICK, TALBOT,
EXETER, the GOVERNOR OF PARIS, and others

GLOUCESTER. Lord Bishop, set the crown upon
his head.

WINCHESTER. God save King Henry, of that name
the Sixth!

GLOUCESTER. Now, Governor of Paris, take your
oath [*GOVERNOR kneels*]
That you elect no other king but him,
Esteem none friends but such as are his friends,
And none your foes but such as shall pretend
Malicious practices against his state.
This shall ye do, so help you righteous God!

Exeunt GOVERNOR and his train.
Enter SIR JOHN FASTOLFE

FASTOLFE. My gracious sovereign, as I rode

from Calais,
To haste unto your coronation,
A letter was deliver'd to my hands,
Writ to your Grace from th' Duke of Burgundy.

TALBOT. Shame to the Duke of Burgundy
and thee!
I vow'd, base knight, when I did meet thee next
To tear the Garter from thy craven's leg, [*Plucking
it off*]
Which I have done, because unworthily
Thou wast installed in that high degree.
Pardon me, princely Henry, and the rest:
This dastard, at the battle of Patay,
When but in all I was six thousand strong,
And that the French were almost ten to one,
Before we met or that a stroke was given,
Like to a trusty squire did run away;
In which assault we lost twelve hundred men;
Myself and divers gentlemen beside
Were there surpris'd and taken prisoners.
Then judge, great lords, if I have done amiss,
Or whether that such cowards ought to wear
This ornament of knighthood-yea or no.

GLOUCESTER. To say the truth, this fact
was infamous
And ill beseeming any common man,
Much more a knight, a captain, and a leader.

TALBOT. When first this order was ordain'd,
my lords,
Knights of the Garter were of noble birth,
Valiant and virtuous, full of haughty courage,
Such as were grown to credit by the wars;
Not fearing death nor shrinking for distress,
But always resolute in most extremes.
He then that is not furnish'd in this sort
Doth but usurp the sacred name of knight,
Profaning this most honourable order,
And should, if I were worthy to be judge,
Be quite degraded, like a hedge-born swain
That doth presume to boast of gentle blood.

KING HENRY. Stain to thy countrymen, thou
hear'st thy doom.
Be packing, therefore, thou that wast a knight;
Henceforth we banish thee on pain of death.

Exit FASTOLFE.

And now, my Lord Protector, view the letter
Sent from our uncle Duke of Burgundy.

GLOUCESTER. [*Viewing the superscription*] What
means his
Grace, that he hath chang'd his style?
No more but plain and bluntly 'To the King!'
Hath he forgot he is his sovereign?
Or doth this churlish superscription

Pretend some alteration in good will?
What's here? [Reads] 'I have, upon especial cause,
Mov'd with compassion of my country's wreck,
Together with the pitiful complaints
Of such as your oppression feeds upon,
Forsaken your pernicious faction,
And join'd with Charles, the rightful King
of France.'
O monstrous treachery! Can this be so
That in alliance, amity, and oaths,
There should be found such false
dissembling guile?
KING HENRY. What! Doth my uncle
Burgundy revolt?
GLOUCESTER. He doth, my lord, and is become
your foe.
KING HENRY. Is that the worst this letter
doth contain?
GLOUCESTER. It is the worst, and all, my lord,
he writes.
KING HENRY. Why then Lord Talbot there shall
talk with him
And give him chastisement for this abuse.
How say you, my lord, are you not content?
TALBOT. Content, my liege! Yes; but that I
am prevented,
I should have begg'd I might have
been employ'd.
KING HENRY. Then gather strength and march
unto him straight;
Let him perceive how ill we brook his treason.
And what offence it is to flout his friends.
TALBOT. I go, my lord, in heart desiring still
You may behold confusion of your foes. *Exit.*

Enter VERNON and BASSET

VERNON. Grant me the combat,
gracious sovereign.
BASSET. And me, my lord, grant me the
combat too.
YORK. This is my servant: hear him, noble Prince.
SOMERSET. And this is mine: sweet Henry,
favour him.
KING HENRY. Be patient, lords, and give them
leave to speak.
Say, gentlemen, what makes you thus exclaim,
And wherefore crave you combat, or
with whom?
VERNON. With him, my lord; for he hath done
me wrong.
BASSET. And I with him; for he hath done
me wrong.
KING HENRY. What is that wrong whereof
you both

complain? First let me know, and then I'll
answer you.
BASSET. Crossing the sea from England
into France,
This fellow here, with envious carping tongue,
Upbraided me about the rose I wear,
Saying the sanguine colour of the leaves
Did represent my master's blushing cheeks
When stubbornly he did repugn the truth
About a certain question in the law
Argu'd betwixt the Duke of York and him;
With other vile and ignominious terms
In confutation of which rude reproach
And in defence of my lord's worthiness,
I crave the benefit of law of arms.
VERNON. And that is my petition, noble lord;
For though he seem with forged quaint conceit
To set a gloss upon his bold intent,
Yet know, my lord, I was provok'd by him,
And he first took exceptions at this badge,
Pronouncing that the paleness of this flower
Bewray'd the faintness of my master's heart.
YORK. Will not this malice, Somerset, be left?
SOMERSET. Your private grudge, my Lord of York,
will out,
Though ne'er so cunningly you smother it.
KING HENRY. Good Lord, what madness rules in
brainsick men,
When for so slight and frivolous a cause
Such factious emulations shall arise!
Good cousins both, of York and Somerset,
Quiet yourselves, I pray, and be at peace.
YORK. Let this dissension first be tried by fight,
And then your Highness shall command a peace.
SOMERSET. The quarrel toucheth none but
us alone;
Betwixt ourselves let us decide it then.
YORK. There is my pledge; accept it, Somerset.
VERNON. Nay, let it rest where it began at first.
BASSET. Confirm it so, mine honourable lord.
GLOUCESTER. Confirm it so? Confounded be
your strife;
And perish ye, with your audacious prate!
Presumptuous vassals, are you not asham'd
With this immodest clamorous outrage
To trouble and disturb the King and us?
And you, my lords-methinks you do not well
To bear with their perverse objections,
Much less to take occasion from their mouths
To raise a mutiny betwixt yourselves.
Let me persuade you take a better course.
EXETER. It grieves his Highness. Good my lords,
be friends.

KING HENRY. Come hither, you that would
  be combatants:
Henceforth I charge you, as you love
  our favour,
Quite to forget this quarrel and the cause.
And you, my lords, remember where we are:
In France, amongst a fickle wavering nation;
If they perceive dissension in our looks
And that within ourselves we disagree,
How will their grudging stomachs be provok'd
To wilful disobedience, and rebel!
Beside, what infamy will there arise
When foreign princes shall be certified
That for a toy, a thing of no regard,
King Henry's peers and chief nobility
Destroy'd themselves and lost the realm
  of France!
O, think upon the conquest of my father,
My tender years; and let us not forgo
That for a trifle that was bought with blood!
Let me be umpire in this doubtful strife.
I see no reason, if I wear this rose, *[Putting on a*
red rose]
That any one should therefore be suspicious
I more incline to Somerset than York:
Both are my kinsmen, and I love them both.
As well they may upbraid me with my crown,
Because, forsooth, the King of Scots is crown'd.
But your discretions better can persuade
Than I am able to instruct or teach;
And, therefore, as we hither came in peace,
So let us still continue peace and love.
Cousin of York, we institute your Grace
To be our Regent in these parts of France.
And, good my Lord of Somerset, unite
Your troops of horsemen with his bands
  of foot;
And like true subjects, sons of
  your progenitors,
Go cheerfully together and digest
Your angry choler on your enemies.
Ourself, my Lord Protector, and the rest,
After some respite will return to Calais;
From thence to England, where I hope ere long
To be presented by your victories
With Charles, Alençon, and that traitorous rout.
    Flourish. Exeunt all but YORK, WARWICK, EXETER,
                   VERNON.
WARWICK. My Lord of York, I promise you,
  the King
Prettily, methought, did play the orator.
YORK. And so he did; but yet I like it not,
  In that he wears the badge of Somerset.

WARWICK. Tush, that was but his fancy; blame
  him not;
I dare presume, sweet prince, he thought
  no harm.
YORK. An if I wist he did—but let it rest;
  Other affairs must now be managed.
                Exeunt all but EXETER.
EXETER. Well didst thou, Richard, to suppress
  thy voice;
For had the passions of thy heart burst out,
I fear we should have seen decipher'd there
More rancorous spite, more furious
  raging broils,
Than yet can be imagin'd or suppos'd.
But howsoe'er, no simple man that sees
This jarring discord of nobility,
This shouldering of each other in the court,
This factious bandying of their favourites,
But that it doth presage some ill event.
'Tis much when sceptres are in children's hands;
But more when envy breeds unkind division:
There comes the ruin, there begins confusion.
                    Exit.

❧ SCENE II ❧
France. Before Bordeaux

Enter TALBOT, with trump and drum

TALBOT. Go to the gates of Bordeaux, trumpeter;
  Summon their general unto the wall. *[Trumpet*
sounds a parley.]
  Enter, aloft, the GENERAL OF THE FRENCH, and Others
English John Talbot, Captains, calls you forth,
Servant in arms to Harry King of England;
And thus he would open your city gates,
Be humble to us, call my sovereign yours
And do him homage as obedient subjects,
And I'll withdraw me and my bloody power;
But if you frown upon this proffer'd peace,
You tempt the fury of my three attendants,
Lean famine, quartering steel, and climbing fire;
Who in a moment even with the earth
Shall lay your stately and air-braving towers,
If you forsake the offer of their love.
GENERAL OF THE FRENCH. Thou ominous and
  fearful owl of death,
Our nation's terror and their bloody scourge!
The period of thy tyranny approacheth.
On us thou canst not enter but by death;
For, I protest, we are well fortified,
And strong enough to issue out and fight.

If thou retire, the Dauphin, well appointed,
Stands with the snares of war to tangle thee.
On either hand thee there are squadrons pitch'd
To wall thee from the liberty of flight,
And no way canst thou turn thee for redress
But death doth front thee with apparent spoil
And pale destruction meets thee in the face.
Ten thousand French have ta'en the sacrament
To rive their dangerous artillery
Upon no Christian soul but English Talbot.
Lo, there thou stand'st, a breathing valiant man,
Of an invincible unconquer'd spirit!
This is the latest glory of thy praise
That I, thy enemy, due thee withal;
For ere the glass that now begins to run
Finish the process of his sandy hour,
These eyes that see thee now well coloured
Shall see thee withered, bloody, pale, and dead.
    [Drum afar off]
Hark! hark! The Dauphin's drum, a warning bell,
Sings heavy music to thy timorous soul;
And mine shall ring thy dire departure out. *Exit.*
TALBOT. He fables not; I hear the enemy.
  Out, some light horsemen, and peruse
    their wings.
  O, negligent and heedless discipline!
  How are we park'd and bounded in a pale,
  A little herd of England's timorous deer,
  Maz'd with a yelping kennel of French curs!
  If we be English deer, be then in blood;
  Not rascal-like to fall down with a pinch,
  But rather, moody-mad and desperate stags,
  Turn on the bloody hounds with heads of steel
  And make the cowards stand aloof at bay.
  Sell every man his life as dear as mine,
  And they shall find dear deer of us, my friends.
  God and Saint George, Talbot and
    England's right,
  Prosper our colours in this dangerous fight!
                              Exeunt.

✣ SCENE III ✣
Plains in Gascony

Enter YORK, with trumpet and many SOLDIERS. A
MESSENGER meets him

YORK. Are not the speedy scouts return'd again
  That dogg'd the mighty army of the Dauphin?
MESSENGER. They are return'd, my lord, and give
    it out
  That he is march'd to Bordeaux with his power

To fight with Talbot; as he march'd along,
  By your espials were discovered
  Two mightier troops than that the Dauphin led,
  Which join'd with him and made their march
    for Bordeaux.
YORK. A plague upon that villain Somerset
  That thus delays my promised supply
  Of horsemen that were levied for this siege!
  Renowned Talbot doth expect my aid,
  And I am louted by a traitor villain
  And cannot help the noble chevalier.
  God comfort him in this necessity!
  If he miscarry, farewell wars in France.
                  Enter SIR WILLIAM LUCY
LUCY. Thou princely leader of our
    English strength,
  Never so needful on the earth of France,
  Spur to the rescue of the noble Talbot,
  Who now is girdled with a waist of iron
  And hemm'd about with grim destruction.
  To Bordeaux, warlike Duke! to Bordeaux, York!
  Else, farewell Talbot, France, and
    England's honour.
YORK. O God, that Somerset, who in proud heart
  Doth stop my cornets, were in Talbot's place!
  So should we save a valiant gentleman
  By forfeiting a traitor and a coward.
  Mad ire and wrathful fury makes me weep
  That thus we die while remiss traitors sleep.
LUCY. O, send some succour to the
    distress'd lord!
YORK. He dies; we lose; I break my warlike word.
  We mourn: France smiles. We lose: they
    daily get-
  All 'long of this vile traitor Somerset.
LUCY. Then God take mercy on brave
    Talbot's soul,
  And on his son, young John, who two
    hours since
  I met in travel toward his warlike father.
  This seven years did not Talbot see his son;
  And now they meet where both their lives
    are done.
YORK. Alas, what joy shall noble Talbot have
  To bid his young son welcome to his grave?
  Away! vexation almost stops my breath,
  That sund'red friends greet in the hour of death.
  Lucy, farewell; no more my fortune can
  But curse the cause I cannot aid the man.
  Maine, Blois, Poictiers, and Tours, are won away
  Long all of Somerset and his delay.
                          Exit with forces.
LUCY. Thus, while the vulture of sedition

Feeds in the bosom of such great commanders,
Sleeping neglection doth betray to loss
The conquest of our scarce-cold conqueror,
That ever-living man of memory,
Henry the Fifth. Whiles they each other cross,
Lives, honours, lands, and all, hurry to loss.*Exit.*

✿ SCENE IV ✿
Other plains of Gascony

*Enter SOMERSET, with his Forces; an OFFICER of
TALBOT'S with him*

SOMERSET. It is too late; I cannot send them now.
  This expedition was by York and Talbot
  Too rashly plotted; all our general force
  Might with a sally of the very town
  Be buckled with. The over-daring Talbot
  Hath sullied all his gloss of former honour
  By this unheedful, desperate, wild adventure.
  York set him on to fight and die in shame.
  That, Talbot dead, great York might bear the name.
OFFICER. Here is Sir William Lucy, who with me
  Set from our o'er-match'd forces forth for aid.
            Enter SIR WILLIAM LUCY
SOMERSET. How now, Sir William! Whither were
  you sent?
LUCY. Whither, my lord! From bought and sold
  Lord Talbot,
  Who, ring'd about with bold adversity,
  Cries out for noble York and Somerset
  To beat assailing death from his weak legions;
  And whiles the honourable captain there
  Drops bloody sweat from his war-wearied limbs
  And, in advantage ling'ring, looks for rescue,
  You, his false hopes, the trust of
  England's honour,
  Keep off aloof with worthless emulation.
  Let not your private discord keep away
  The levied succours that should lend him aid,
  While he, renowned noble gentleman,
  Yield up his life unto a world of odds.
  Orleans the Bastard, Charles, Burgundy,
  Alençon, Reignier, compass him about,
  And Talbot perisheth by your default.
SOMERSET. York set him on; York should have
  sent him aid.
LUCY. And York as fast upon your Grace exclaims,
  Swearing that you withhold his levied host,
  Collected for this expedition.
SOMERSET. York lies; he might have sent and had
  the horse.

I owe him little duty and less love,
  And take foul scorn to fawn on him by sending.
LUCY. The fraud of England, not the force
  of France,
  Hath now entrapp'd the noble-minded Talbot.
  Never to England shall he bear his life,
  But dies betray'd to fortune by your strife.
SOMERSET. Come, go; I will dispatch the
  horsemen straight;
  Within six hours they will be at his aid.
LUCY. Too late comes rescue; he is ta'en or slain,
  For fly he could not if he would have fled;
  And fly would Talbot never, though he might.
SOMERSET. If he be dead, brave Talbot,
  then, adieu!
LUCY. His fame lives in the world, his shame
  in you.
                              Exeunt.

✿ SCENE V ✿
The English camp near Bordeaux

Enter TALBOT and JOHN his son

TALBOT. O young John Talbot! I did send for thee
  To tutor thee in stratagems of war,
  That Talbot's name might be in thee reviv'd
  When sapless age and weak unable limbs
  Should bring thy father to his drooping chair.
  But, O malignant and ill-boding stars!
  Now thou art come unto a feast of death,
  A terrible and unavoided danger;
  Therefore, dear boy, mount on my
  swiftest horse,
  And I'll direct thee how thou shalt escape
  By sudden flight. Come, dally not, be gone.
JOHN. Is my name Talbot, and am I your son?
  And shall I fly? O, if you love my mother,
  Dishonour not her honourable name,
  To make a bastard and a slave of me!
  The world will say he is not Talbot's blood
  That basely fled when noble Talbot stood.
TALBOT. Fly to revenge my death, if I be slain.
JOHN. He that flies so will ne'er return again.
TALBOT. If we both stay, we both are sure to die.
JOHN. Then let me stay; and, father, do you fly.
  Your loss is great, so your regard should be;
  My worth unknown, no loss is known in me;
  Upon my death the French can little boast;
  In yours they will, in you all hopes are lost.
  Flight cannot stain the honour you have won;
  But mine it will, that no exploit have done;

You fled for vantage, every one will swear;
But if I bow, they'll say it was for fear.
There is no hope that ever I will stay
If the first hour I shrink and run away.
Here, on my knee, I beg mortality,
Rather than life preserv'd with infamy.

TALBOT. Shall all thy mother's hopes lie in
one tomb?

JOHN. Ay, rather than I'll shame my
mother's womb.

TALBOT. Upon my blessing I command thee go.

JOHN. To fight I will, but not to fly the foe.

TALBOT. Part of thy father may be sav'd in thee.

JOHN. No part of him but will be shame in me.

TALBOT. Thou never hadst renown, nor canst not
lose it.

JOHN. Yes, your renowned name; shall flight
abuse it?

TALBOT. Thy father's charge shall clear thee from
that stain.

JOHN. You cannot witness for me, being slain.
If death be so apparent, then both fly.

TALBOT. And leave my followers here to fight
and die?
My age was never tainted with such shame.

JOHN. And shall my youth be guilty of
such blame?
No more can I be severed from your side
Than can yourself yourself in twain divide.
Stay, go, do what you will, the like do I;
For live I will not if my father die.

TALBOT. Then here I take my leave of thee,
fair son,
Born to eclipse thy life this afternoon.
Come, side by side together live and die;
And soul with soul from France to heaven fly.

Exeunt.

✣ SCENE VI ✣
A field of battle

*Alarum: excursions wherein JOHN TALBOT is hemm'd about,
and TALBOT rescues him*

TALBOT. Saint George and victory! Fight,
soldiers, fight.
The Regent hath with Talbot broke his word
And left us to the rage of France his sword.
Where is John Talbot? Pause and take thy breath;
I gave thee life and rescu'd thee from death.

JOHN. O, twice my father, twice am I thy son!
The life thou gav'st me first was lost and done

Till with thy warlike sword, despite of fate,
To my determin'd time thou gav'st new date.

TALBOT. When from the Dauphin's crest thy
sword struck fire,
It warm'd thy father's heart with proud desire
Of bold-fac'd victory. Then leaden age,
Quicken'd with youthful spleen and
warlike rage,
Beat down Alençon, Orleans, Burgundy,
And from the pride of Gallia rescued thee.
The ireful bastard Orleans, that drew blood
From thee, my boy, and had the maidenhood
Of thy first fight, I soon encountered
And, interchanging blows, I quickly shed
Some of his bastard blood; and in disgrace
Bespoke him thus: 'Contaminated, base,
And misbegotten blood I spill of thine,
Mean and right poor, for that pure blood
of mine
Which thou didst force from Talbot, my
brave boy.'
Here purposing the Bastard to destroy,
Came in strong rescue. Speak, thy father's care;
Art thou not weary, John? How dost thou fare?
Wilt thou yet leave the battle, boy, and fly,
Now thou art seal'd the son of chivalry?
Fly, to revenge my death when I am dead:
The help of one stands me in little stead.
O, too much folly is it, well I wot,
To hazard all our lives in one small boat!
If I to-day die not with Frenchmen's rage,
To-morrow I shall die with mickle age.
By me they nothing gain an if I stay:
'Tis but the short'ning of my life one day.
In thee thy mother dies, our household's name,
My death's revenge, thy youth, and
England's fame.
All these and more we hazard by thy stay;
All these are sav'd if thou wilt fly away.

JOHN. The sword of Orleans hath not made
me smart;
These words of yours draw life-blood from
my heart.
On that advantage, bought with such a shame,
To save a paltry life and slay bright fame,
Before young Talbot from old Talbot fly,
The coward horse that bears me fall and die!
And like me to the peasant boys of France,
To be shame's scorn and subject of mischance!
Surely, by all the glory you have won,
An if I fly, I am not Talbot's son;
Then talk no more of flight, it is no boot;
If son to Talbot, die at Talbot's foot.

TALBOT. Then follow thou thy desp'rate sire
  of Crete,
  Thou Icarus; thy life to me is sweet.
  If thou wilt fight, fight by thy father's side;
  And, commendable prov'd, let's die in pride.

  Exeunt.

✦ SCENE VII ✦
Another part of the field

Alarum; excursions. Enter old TALBOT led by a SERVANT

TALBOT. Where is my other life? Mine own
  is gone.
  O, where's young Talbot? Where is valiant John?
  Triumphant death, smear'd with captivity,
  Young Talbot's valour makes me smile at thee.
  When he perceiv'd me shrink and on my knee,
  His bloody sword he brandish'd over me,
  And like a hungry lion did commence
  Rough deeds of rage and stern impatience;
  But when my angry guardant stood alone,
  Tend'ring my ruin and assail'd of none,
  Dizzy-ey'd fury and great rage of heart
  Suddenly made him from my side to start
  Into the clust'ring battle of the French;
  And in that sea of blood my boy did drench
  His overmounting spirit; and there died,
  My Icarus, my blossom, in his pride.

Enter soldiers, bearing the body of JOHN TALBOT

SERVANT. O my dear lord, lo where your son
  is borne!
TALBOT. Thou antic Death, which laugh'st us
  here to scorn,
  Anon, from thy insulting tyranny,
  Coupled in bonds of perpetuity,
  Two Talbots, winged through the lither sky,
  In thy despite shall 'scape mortality.
  O thou whose wounds become hard-
  favoured Death,
  Speak to thy father ere thou yield thy breath!
  Brave Death by speaking, whether he will or no;
  Imagine him a Frenchman and thy foe.
  Poor boy! he smiles, methinks, as who
  should say,
  Had Death been French, then Death had
  died to-day.
  Come, come, and lay him in his father's arms.
  My spirit can no longer bear these harms.
  Soldiers, adieu! I have what I would have,
  Now my old arms are young John Talbot's grave.

  Dies.

Enter CHARLES, ALENÇON, BURGUNDY, BASTARD,
LA PUCELLE, and Forces

CHARLES. Had York and Somerset brought
  rescue in,
  We should have found a bloody day of this.
BASTARD. How the young whelp of Talbot's,
  raging wood,
  Did flesh his puny sword in
  Frenchmen's blood!
PUCELLE. Once I encount'red him, and thus I said:
  'Thou maiden youth, be vanquish'd by a maid.'
  But with a proud majestical high scorn
  He answer'd thus: 'Young Talbot was not born
  To be the pillage of a giglot wench.'
  So, rushing in the bowels of the French,
  He left me proudly, as unworthy fight.
BURGUNDY. Doubtless he would have made a
  noble knight.
  See where he lies inhearsed in the arms
  Of the most bloody nurser of his harms!
BASTARD. Hew them to pieces, hack their
  bones asunder,
  Whose life was England's glory, Gallia's wonder.
CHARLES. O, no; forbear! For that which we
  have fled
  During the life, let us not wrong it dead.

Enter SIR WILLIAM Lucy, attended; a FRENCH
Herald preceding

LUCY. Herald, conduct me to the Dauphin's tent,
  To know who hath obtain'd the glory of
  the day.
CHARLES. On what submissive message art
  thou sent?
LUCY. Submission, Dauphin! 'Tis a mere
  French word:
  We English warriors wot not what it means.
  I come to know what prisoners thou hast ta'en,
  And to survey the bodies of the dead.
CHARLES. For prisoners ask'st thou? Hell our
  prison is.
  But tell me whom thou seek'st.
LUCY. But where's the great Alcides of the field,
  Valiant Lord Talbot, Earl of Shrewsbury,
  Created for his rare success in arms
  Great Earl of Washford, Waterford, and Valence,
  Lord Talbot of Goodrig and Urchinfield,
  Lord Strange of Blackmere, Lord Verdun
  of Alton,
  Lord Cromwell of Wingfield, Lord Furnival
  of Sheffield,
  The thrice victorious Lord of Falconbridge,
  Knight of the noble order of Saint George,
  Worthy Saint Michael, and the Golden Fleece,

Great Marshal to Henry the Sixth
Of all his wars within the realm of France?
PUCELLE. Here's a silly-stately style indeed!
  The Turk, that two-and-fifty kingdoms hath,
  Writes not so tedious a style as this.
  Him that thou magnifi'st with all these tides,
  Stinking and fly-blown lies here at our feet.
LUCY. Is Talbot slain-the Frenchmen's
  only scourge,
  Your kingdom's terror and black Nemesis?
  O, were mine eye-balls into bullets turn'd,
  That I in rage might shoot them at your faces!
  O that I could but call these dead to life!
  It were enough to fright the realm of France.
  Were but his picture left amongst you here,
  It would amaze the proudest of you all.
  Give me their bodies, that I may bear
  them hence
  And give them burial as beseems their worth.
PUCELLE. I think this upstart is old Talbot's ghost,
  He speaks with such a proud commanding spirit.
  For God's sake, let him have them; to keep
  them here,
  They would but stink, and putrefy the air.
CHARLES. Go, take their bodies hence.
LUCY. I'll bear them hence; but from their ashes
  shall be rear'd
  A phoenix that shall make all France afeard.
CHARLES. So we be rid of them, do with them
  what thou wilt.
  And now to Paris in this conquering vein!
  All will be ours, now bloody Talbot's slain.

Exeunt.

ACT V

SCENE I
London. The palace

Sennet. Enter the KING, GLOUCESTER, and EXETER

KING HENRY. Have you perus'd the letters from
  the Pope,
  The Emperor, and the Earl of Armagnac?
GLOUCESTER. I have, my lord; and their intent
  is this:
  They humbly sue unto your Excellence
  To have a godly peace concluded of
  Between the realms of England and of France.
KING HENRY. How doth your Grace affect
  their motion?

GLOUCESTER. Well, my good lord, and as the
  only means
  To stop effusion of our Christian blood
  And stablish quietness on every side.
KING HENRY. Ay, marry, uncle; for I
  always thought
  It was both impious and unnatural
  That such immanity and bloody strife
  Should reign among professors of one faith.
GLOUCESTER. Beside, my lord, the sooner
  to effect
  And surer bind this knot of amity,
  The Earl of Armagnac, near knit to Charles,
  A man of great authority in France,
  Proffers his only daughter to your Grace
  In marriage, with a large and sumptuous dowry.
KING HENRY. Marriage, uncle! Alas, my years
  are young
  And fitter is my study and my books
  Than wanton dalliance with a paramour.
  Yet call th' ambassadors, and, as you please,
  So let them have their answers every one.
  I shall be well content with any choice
  Tends to God's glory and my country's weal.

*Enter in Cardinal's habit BEAUFORT, the PAPAL LEGATE,
and two AMBASSADORS*

EXETER. What! Is my Lord of Winchester install'd
  And call'd unto a cardinal's degree?
  Then I perceive that will be verified
  Henry the Fifth did sometime prophesy:
  'If once he come to be a cardinal,
  He'll make his cap co-equal with the crown.'
KING HENRY. My Lords Ambassadors, your
  several suits
  Have been consider'd and debated on.
  Your purpose is both good and reasonable,
  And therefore are we certainly resolv'd
  To draw conditions of a friendly peace,
  Which by my Lord of Winchester we mean
  Shall be transported presently to France.
GLOUCESTER. And for the proffer of my lord
  your master,
  I have inform'd his Highness so at large,
  As, liking of the lady's virtuous gifts,
  Her beauty, and the value of her dower,
  He doth intend she shall be England's Queen.
KING HENRY. *[To AMBASSADOR]* In argument and
  proof of which contract,
  Bear her this jewel, pledge of my affection.
  And so, my Lord Protector, see them guarded
  And safely brought to Dover; where inshipp'd,
  Commit them to the fortune of the sea.

Exeunt all but WINCHESTER and the LEGATE.

WINCHESTER. Stay, my Lord Legate; you shall
  first receive
  The sum of money which I promised
  Should be delivered to his Holiness
  For clothing me in these grave ornaments.
LEGATE. I will attend upon your
  lordship's leisure.
WINCHESTER. [Aside] Now Winchester will not
  submit, I trow,
  Or be inferior to the proudest peer.
  Humphrey of Gloucester, thou shalt
  well perceive
  That neither in birth or for authority
  The Bishop will be overborne by thee.
  I'll either make thee stoop and bend thy knee,
  Or sack this country with a mutiny.   Exeunt.

⚘ SCENE II ⚘
France. Plains in Anjou

*Enter CHARLES, BURGUNDY, ALENÇON, BASTARD,
REIGNIER, LA PUCELLE, and Forces*

CHARLES. These news, my lords, may cheer our
  drooping spirits:
  'Tis said the stout Parisians do revolt
  And turn again unto the warlike French.
ALENÇON. Then march to Paris, royal Charles
  of France,
  And keep not back your powers in dalliance.
PUCELLE. Peace be amongst them, if they turn
  to us;
  Else ruin combat with their palaces!
          Enter a SCOUT
SCOUT. Success unto our valiant general,
  And happiness to his accomplices!
CHARLES. What tidings send our scouts? I
  prithee speak.
SCOUT. The English army, that divided was
  Into two parties, is now conjoin'd in one,
  And means to give you battle presently.
CHARLES. Somewhat too sudden, sirs, the
  warning is;
  But we will presently provide for them.
BURGUNDY. I trust the ghost of Talbot is
  not there.
  Now he is gone, my lord, you need not fear.
PUCELLE. Of all base passions, fear is
  most accurs'd.
  Command the conquest, Charles, it shall
  be thine,
  Let Henry fret and all the world repine.

CHARLES. Then on, my lords; and France be
  fortunate!
                    Exeunt.

⚘ SCENE III ⚘
Before Angiers

Alarum, excursions. Enter LA PUCELLE

PUCELLE. The Regent conquers and the
  Frenchmen fly.
  Now help, ye charming spells and periapts;
  And ye choice spirits that admonish me
  And give me signs of future accidents; [Thunder]
  You speedy helpers that are substitutes
  Under the lordly monarch of the north,
  Appear and aid me in this enterprise!
            Enter FIENDS
  This speedy and quick appearance argues proof
  Of your accustom'd diligence to me.
  Now, ye familiar spirits that are cull'd
  Out of the powerful regions under earth,
  Help me this once, that France may get the field.
  [They walk and speak not]
  O, hold me not with silence over-long!
  Where I was wont to feed you with my blood,
  I'll lop a member off and give it you
  In earnest of a further benefit,
  So you do condescend to help me now. [They hang
    their heads]
  No hope to have redress? My body shall
  Pay recompense, if you will grant my suit. [They
    shake their heads]
  Cannot my body nor blood sacrifice
  Entreat you to your wonted furtherance?
  Then take my soul-my body, soul, and all,
  Before that England give the French the foil.
  [They depart]
  See! they forsake me. Now the time is come
  That France must vail her lofty-plumed crest
  And let her head fall into England's lap.
  My ancient incantations are too weak,
  And hell too strong for me to buckle with.
  Now, France, thy glory droopeth to the dust.
                    Exit.
    *Excursions. Enter French and English, fighting.
    LA PUCELLE and YORK fight hand to hand;
      LA PUCELLE is taken. The French fly.*
YORK. Damsel of France, I think I have you fast.
  Unchain your spirits now with spelling charms,
  And try if they can gain your liberty.
  A goodly prize, fit for the devil's grace!
  See how the ugly witch doth bend her brows

As if, with Circe, she would change my shape!

PUCELLE. Chang'd to a worser shape thou canst
  not be.

YORK. O, Charles the Dauphin is a proper man:
  No shape but his can please your dainty eye.

PUCELLE. A plaguing mischief fight on Charles
  and thee!
  And may ye both be suddenly surpris'd
  By bloody hands, in sleeping on your beds!

YORK. Fell banning hag; enchantress, hold
  thy tongue.

PUCELLE. I prithee give me leave to curse awhile.

YORK. Curse, miscreant, when thou comest to
  the stake.   *Exeunt.*
   Alarum. Enter SUFFOLK, with MARGARET in his hand

SUFFOLK. Be what thou wilt, thou art my
  prisoner. *[Gazes on her]*
  O fairest beauty, do not fear nor fly!
  For I will touch thee but with reverent hands;
  I kiss these fingers for eternal peace,
  And lay them gently on thy tender side.
  Who art thou? Say, that I may honour thee.

MARGARET. Margaret my name, and daughter to
  a king,
  The King of Naples-whosoe'er thou art.

SUFFOLK. An earl I am, and Suffolk am I call'd.
  Be not offended, nature's miracle,
  Thou art allotted to be ta'en by me.
  So doth the swan her downy cygnets save,
  Keeping them prisoner underneath her wings.
  Yet, if this servile usage once offend,
  Go and be free again as Suffolk's friend. *[She is going]*
  O, stay! *[Aside]* I have no power to let her pass;
  My hand would free her, but my heart says no.
  As plays the sun upon the glassy streams,
  Twinkling another counterfeited beam,
  So seems this gorgeous beauty to mine eyes.
  Fain would I woo her, yet I dare not speak.
  I'll call for pen and ink, and write my mind.
  Fie, de la Pole! disable not thyself;
  Hast not a tongue? Is she not here thy prisoner?
  Wilt thou be daunted at a woman's sight?
  Ay, beauty's princely majesty is such
  Confounds the tongue and makes the
  senses rough.

MARGARET. Say, Earl of Suffolk, if thy name be so,
  What ransom must I pay before I pass?
  For I perceive I am thy prisoner.

SUFFOLK. *[Aside]* How canst thou tell she will deny
  thy suit,
  Before thou make a trial of her love?

MARGARET. Why speak'st thou not? What ransom
  must I pay?

SUFFOLK. *[Aside]* She's beautiful, and therefore to
  be woo'd;
  She is a woman, therefore to be won.

MARGARET. Wilt thou accept of ransom-yea
  or no?

SUFFOLK. *[Aside]* Fond man, remember that thou
  hast a wife;
  Then how can Margaret be thy paramour?

MARGARET. I were best leave him, for he will
  not hear.

SUFFOLK. *[Aside]* There all is marr'd; there lies a
  cooling card.

MARGARET. He talks at random; sure, the man
  is mad.

SUFFOLK. *[Aside]* And yet a dispensation may
  be had.

MARGARET. And yet I would that you would
  answer me.

SUFFOLK. *[Aside]* I'll win this Lady Margaret.
  For whom?
  Why, for my King! Tush, that's a wooden thing!

MARGARET. He talks of wood. It is
  some carpenter.

SUFFOLK. *[Aside]* Yet so my fancy may be satisfied,
  And peace established between these realms.
  But there remains a scruple in that too;
  For though her father be the King of Naples,
  Duke of Anjou and Maine, yet is he poor,
  And our nobility will scorn the match.

MARGARET. Hear ye, Captain-are you not
  at leisure?

SUFFOLK. *[Aside]* It shall be so, disdain they ne'er
  so much.
  Henry is youthful, and will quickly yield.
  Madam, I have a secret to reveal.

MARGARET. *[Aside]* What though I be enthrall'd?
  He seems a knight,
  And will not any way dishonour me.

SUFFOLK. Lady, vouchsafe to listen what I say.

MARGARET. *[Aside]* Perhaps I shall be rescu'd by
  the French;
  And then I need not crave his courtesy.

SUFFOLK. Sweet madam, give me hearing in
  a cause-

MARGARET. *[Aside]* Tush! women have been
  captivate ere now.

SUFFOLK. Lady, wherefore talk you so?

MARGARET. I cry you mercy, 'tis but quid for quo.

SUFFOLK. Say, gentle Princess, would you
  not suppose
  Your bondage happy, to be made a queen?

MARGARET. To be a queen in bondage is
  more vile

Than is a slave in base servility;
For princes should be free.
SUFFOLK. And so shall you,
  If happy England's royal king be free.
MARGARET. Why, what concerns his freedom
  unto me?
SUFFOLK. I'll undertake to make thee
  Henry's queen,
  To put a golden sceptre in thy hand
  And set a precious crown upon thy head,
  If thou wilt condescend to be my-
MARGARET. What?
SUFFOLK. His love.
MARGARET. I am unworthy to be Henry's wife.
SUFFOLK. No, gentle madam; I unworthy am
  To woo so fair a dame to be his wife
  And have no portion in the choice myself.
  How say you, madam? Are ye so content?
MARGARET. An if my father please, I am content.
SUFFOLK. Then call our captains and our
  colours forth!
  And, madam, at your father's castle walls
  We'll crave a parley to confer with him.
    Sound a parley. Enter REIGNIER on the walls
  See, Reignier, see, thy daughter prisoner!
REIGNIER. To whom?
SUFFOLK. To me.
REIGNIER. Suffolk, what remedy?
  I am a soldier and unapt to weep
  Or to exclaim on fortune's fickleness.
SUFFOLK. Yes, there is remedy enough, my lord.
  Consent, and for thy honour give consent,
  Thy daughter shall be wedded to my king,
  Whom I with pain have woo'd and won thereto;
  And this her easy-held imprisonment
  Hath gain'd thy daughter princely liberty.
REIGNIER. Speaks Suffolk as he thinks?
SUFFOLK. Fair Margaret knows
  That Suffolk doth not flatter, face, or feign.
REIGNIER. Upon thy princely warrant I descend
  To give thee answer of thy just demand.
    Exit REIGNIER from the walls
SUFFOLK. And here I will expect thy coming.
    Trumpets sound. Enter REIGNIER below
REIGNIER. Welcome, brave Earl, into our territories;
  Command in Anjou what your Honour pleases.
SUFFOLK. Thanks, Reignier, happy for so sweet
  a child,
  Fit to be made companion with a king.
  What answer makes your Grace unto my suit?
REIGNIER. Since thou dost deign to woo her
  little worth
  To be the princely bride of such a lord,

Upon condition I may quietly
Enjoy mine own, the country Maine and Anjou,
Free from oppression or the stroke of war,
My daughter shall be Henry's, if he please.
SUFFOLK. That is her ransom; I deliver her.
  And those two counties I will undertake
  Your Grace shall well and quietly enjoy.
REIGNIER. And I again, in Henry's royal name,
  As deputy unto that gracious king,
  Give thee her hand for sign of plighted faith.
SUFFOLK. Reignier of France, I give thee
  kingly thanks,
  Because this is in traffic of a king.
  [*Aside*] And yet, methinks, I could be well content
  To be mine own attorney in this case.
  I'll over then to England with this news,
  And make this marriage to be solemnis'd.
  So, farewell, Reignier. Set this diamond safe
  In golden palaces, as it becomes.
REIGNIER. I do embrace thee as I would embrace
  The Christian prince, King Henry, were he here.
MARGARET. Farewell, my lord. Good wishes,
  praise, and prayers,
  Shall Suffolk ever have of Margaret. *She is going*
SUFFOLK. Farewell, sweet madam. But hark
  you, Margaret
  No princely commendations to my king?
MARGARET. Such commendations as becomes
  a maid,
  A virgin, and his servant, say to him.
SUFFOLK. Words sweetly plac'd and
  modestly directed.
  But, madam, I must trouble you again,
  No loving token to his Majesty?
MARGARET. Yes, my good lord: a pure
  unspotted heart,
  Never yet taint with love, I send the King.
SUFFOLK. And this withal.   *Kisses her*
MARGARET. That for thyself, I will not so presume
  To send such peevish tokens to a king.
    Exeunt REIGNIER and MARGARET.
SUFFOLK. O, wert thou for myself! But,
  Suffolk, stay;
  Thou mayst not wander in that labyrinth:
  There Minotaurs and ugly treasons lurk.
  Solicit Henry with her wondrous praise.
  Bethink thee on her virtues that surmount,
  And natural graces that extinguish art;
  Repeat their semblance often on the seas,
  That, when thou com'st to kneel at Henry's feet,
  Thou mayst bereave him of his wits
  with wonder.
    Exit.

✱ SCENE IV ✱
Camp of the DUKE OF YORK in Anjou

Enter YORK, WARWICK, and Others

YORK. Bring forth that sorceress, condemn'd
  to burn.

Enter LA PUCELLE, guarded, and a SHEPHERD

SHEPHERD. Ah, Joan, this kills thy father's
  heart outright!
  Have I sought every country far and near,
  And, now it is my chance to find thee out,
  Must I behold thy timeless cruel death?
  Ah, Joan, sweet daughter Joan, I'll die with thee!

PUCELLE. Decrepit miser! base ignoble wretch!
  I am descended of a gentler blood;
  Thou art no father nor no friend of mine.

SHEPHERD. Out, out! My lords, an please you, 'tis
  not so;
  I did beget her, all the parish knows.
  Her mother liveth yet, can testify
  She was the first fruit of my bach'lorship.

WARWICK. Graceless, wilt thou deny thy
  parentage?

YORK. This argues what her kind of life hath been-
  Wicked and vile; and so her death concludes.

SHEPHERD. Fie, Joan, that thou wilt be
  so obstacle!
  God knows thou art a collop of my flesh;
  And for thy sake have I shed many a tear.
  Deny me not, I prithee, gentle Joan.

PUCELLE. Peasant, avaunt! You have suborn'd
  this man
  Of purpose to obscure my noble birth.

SHEPHERD. 'Tis true, I gave a noble to the priest
  The morn that I was wedded to her mother.
  Kneel down and take my blessing, good my girl.
  Wilt thou not stoop? Now cursed be the time
  Of thy nativity. I would the milk
  Thy mother gave thee when thou suck'dst
  her breast
  Had been a little ratsbane for thy sake.
  Or else, when thou didst keep my lambs afield,
  I wish some ravenous wolf had eaten thee.
  Dost thou deny thy father, cursed drab?
  O, burn her, burn her! Hanging is too
  good. *Exit*

YORK. Take her away; for she hath liv'd too long,
  To fill the world with vicious qualities.

PUCELLE. First let me tell you whom you
  have condemn'd:
  Not me begotten of a shepherd swain,
  But issued from the progeny of kings;
  Virtuous and holy, chosen from above
  By inspiration of celestial grace,
  To work exceeding miracles on earth.
  I never had to do with wicked spirits.
  But you, that are polluted with your lusts,
  Stain'd with the guiltless blood of innocents,
  Corrupt and tainted with a thousand vices,
  Because you want the grace that others have,
  You judge it straight a thing impossible
  To compass wonders but by help of devils.
  No, misconceived! Joan of Arc hath been
  A virgin from her tender infancy,
  Chaste and immaculate in very thought;
  Whose maiden blood, thus rigorously effus'd,
  Will cry for vengeance at the gates of heaven.

YORK. Ay, ay. Away with her to execution!

WARWICK. And hark ye, sirs; because she is
  a maid,
  Spare for no fagots, let there be enow.
  Place barrels of pitch upon the fatal stake,
  That so her torture may be shortened.

PUCELLE. Will nothing turn your
  unrelenting hearts?
  Then, Joan, discover thine infirmity
  That warranteth by law to be thy privilege:
  I am with child, ye bloody homicides;
  Murder not then the fruit within my womb,
  Although ye hale me to a violent death.

YORK. Now heaven forfend! The holy maid
  with child!

WARWICK. The greatest miracle that e'er
  ye wrought:
  Is all your strict preciseness come to this?

YORK. She and the Dauphin have been juggling.
  I did imagine what would be her refuge.

WARWICK. Well, go to; we'll have no bastards live;
  Especially since Charles must father it.

PUCELLE. You are deceiv'd; my child is none
  of his:
  It was Alençon that enjoy'd my love.

YORK. Alençon, that notorious Machiavel!
  It dies, an if it had a thousand lives.

PUCELLE. O, give me leave, I have deluded you.
  'Twas neither Charles nor yet the Duke I nam'd,
  But Reignier, King of Naples, that prevail'd.

WARWICK. A married man! That's
  most intolerable.

YORK. Why, here's a girl! I think she knows
  not well
  There were so many-whom she may accuse.

WARWICK. It's sign she hath been liberal and free.

YORK. And yet, forsooth, she is a virgin pure.
  Strumpet, thy words condemn thy brat and thee.
  Use no entreaty, for it is in vain.
PUCELLE. Then lead me hence—with whom I leave
  my curse:
  May never glorious sun reflex his beams
  Upon the country where you make abode;
  But darkness and the gloomy shade of death
  Environ you, till mischief and despair
  Drive you to break your necks or
  hang yourselves!

Exit, guarded.

YORK. Break thou in pieces and consume
  to ashes,
  Thou foul accursed minister of hell!

Enter CARDINAL BEAUFORT, attended

CARDINAL. Lord Regent, I do greet
  your Excellence
  With letters of commission from the King.
  For know, my lords, the states of Christendom,
  Mov'd with remorse of these outrageous broils,
  Have earnestly implor'd a general peace
  Betwixt our nation and the aspiring French;
  And here at hand the Dauphin and his train
  Approacheth, to confer about some matter.
YORK. Is all our travail turn'd to this effect?
  After the slaughter of so many peers,
  So many captains, gentlemen, and soldiers,
  That in this quarrel have been overthrown
  And sold their bodies for their country's benefit,
  Shall we at last conclude effeminate peace?
  Have we not lost most part of all the towns,
  By treason, falsehood, and by treachery,
  Our great progenitors had conquered?
  O Warwick, Warwick! I foresee with grief
  The utter loss of all the realm of France.
WARWICK. Be patient, York. If we conclude
  a peace,
  It shall be with such strict and severe covenants
  As little shall the Frenchmen gain thereby.

Enter CHARLES, ALENÇON, BASTARD, REIGNIER,
and Others

CHARLES. Since, lords of England, it is thus agreed
  That peaceful truce shall be proclaim'd
  in France,
  We come to be informed by yourselves
  What the conditions of that league must be.
YORK. Speak, Winchester; for boiling
  choler chokes
  The hollow passage of my poison'd voice,
  By sight of these our baleful enemies.
CARDINAL. Charles, and the rest, it is
  enacted thus:

That, in regard King Henry gives consent,
  Of mere compassion and of lenity,
  To ease your country of distressful war,
  An suffer you to breathe in fruitful peace,
  You shall become true liegemen to his crown;
  And, Charles, upon condition thou wilt swear
  To pay him tribute and submit thyself,
  Thou shalt be plac'd as viceroy under him,
  And still enjoy thy regal dignity.
ALENÇON. Must he be then as shadow of himself?
  Adorn his temples with a coronet
  And yet, in substance and authority,
  Retain but privilege of a private man?
  This proffer is absurd and reasonless.
CHARLES. 'Tis known already that I am possess'd
  With more than half the Gallian territories,
  And therein reverenc'd for their lawful king.
  Shall I, for lucre of the rest unvanquish'd,
  Detract so much from that prerogative
  As to be call'd but viceroy of the whole?
  No, Lord Ambassador; I'll rather keep
  That which I have than, coveting for more,
  Be cast from possibility of all.
YORK. Insulting Charles! Hast thou by
  secret means
  Us'd intercession to obtain a league,
  And now the matter grows to compromise
  Stand'st thou aloof upon comparison?
  Either accept the title thou usurp'st,
  Of benefit proceeding from our king
  And not of any challenge of desert,
  Or we will plague thee with incessant wars.
REIGNIER. *[To CHARLES]* My lord, you do not well
  in obstinacy
  To cavil in the course of this contract.
  If once it be neglected, ten to one
  We shall not find like opportunity.
ALENÇON. *[To CHARLES]* To say the truth, it is
  your policy
  To save your subjects from such massacre
  And ruthless slaughters as are daily seen
  By our proceeding in hostility;
  And therefore take this compact of a truce,
  Although you break it when your
  pleasure serves.
WARWICK. How say'st thou, Charles? Shall our
  condition stand?
CHARLES. It shall;
  Only reserv'd, you claim no interest
  In any of our towns of garrison.
YORK. Then swear allegiance to his Majesty:
  As thou art knight, never to disobey
  Nor be rebellious to the crown of England,

Thou, nor thy nobles, to the crown of England.

[CHARLES and the rest give tokens of fealty]

So, now dismiss your army when ye please;
Hang up your ensigns, let your drums be still,
For here we entertain a solemn peace.

Exeunt.

⚜ SCENE V ⚜

London. The palace

Enter SUFFOLK, in conference with the KING,
GLOUCESTER and EXETER

KING HENRY. Your wondrous rare description,
   noble Earl,
   Of beauteous Margaret hath astonish'd me.
   Her virtues, graced with external gifts,
   Do breed love's settled passions in my heart;
   And like as rigour of tempestuous gusts
   Provokes the mightiest hulk against the tide,
   So am I driven by breath of her renown
   Either to suffer shipwreck or arrive
   Where I may have fruition of her love.
SUFFOLK. Tush, my good lord! This
   superficial tale
   Is but a preface of her worthy praise.
   The chief perfections of that lovely dame,
   Had I sufficient skill to utter them,
   Would make a volume of enticing lines,
   Able to ravish any dull conceit;
   And, which is more, she is not so divine,
   So full-replete with choice of all delights,
   But with as humble lowliness of mind
   She is content to be at your command;
   Command, I mean, of virtuous intents,
   To love and honour Henry as her lord.
KING HENRY. And otherwise will Henry
   ne'er presume.
   Therefore, my Lord Protector, give consent
   That Margaret may be England's royal Queen.
GLOUCESTER. So should I give consent to
   flatter sin.
   You know, my lord, your Highness is betroth'd
   Unto another lady of esteem.
   How shall we then dispense with that contract,
   And not deface your honour with reproach?
SUFFOLK. As doth a ruler with unlawful oaths;
   Or one that at a triumph, having vow'd
   To try his strength, forsaketh yet the lists
   By reason of his adversary's odds:
   A poor earl's daughter is unequal odds,
   And therefore may be broke without offence.

GLOUCESTER. Why, what, I pray, is Margaret
   more than that?
   Her father is no better than an earl,
   Although in glorious titles he excel.
SUFFOLK. Yes, my lord, her father is a king,
   The King of Naples and Jerusalem;
   And of such great authority in France
   As his alliance will confirm our peace,
   And keep the Frenchmen in allegiance.
GLOUCESTER. And so the Earl of Armagnac
   may do,
   Because he is near kinsman unto Charles.
EXETER. Beside, his wealth doth warrant a
   liberal dower;
   Where Reignier sooner will receive than give.
SUFFOLK. A dow'r, my lords! Disgrace not so
   your king,
   That he should be so abject, base, and poor,
   To choose for wealth and not for perfect love.
   Henry is able to enrich his queen,
   And not to seek a queen to make him rich.
   So worthless peasants bargain for their wives,
   As market-men for oxen, sheep, or horse.
   Marriage is a matter of more worth
   Than to be dealt in by attorneyship;
   Not whom we will, but whom his Grace affects,
   Must be companion of his nuptial bed.
   And therefore, lords, since he affects her most,
   It most of all these reasons bindeth us
   In our opinions she should be preferr'd;
   For what is wedlock forced but a hell,
   An age of discord and continual strife?
   Whereas the contrary bringeth bliss,
   And is a pattern of celestial peace.
   Whom should we match with Henry, being
    a king,
   But Margaret, that is daughter to a king?
   Her peerless feature, joined with her birth,
   Approves her fit for none but for a king;
   Her valiant courage and undaunted spirit,
   More than in women commonly is seen,
   Will answer our hope in issue of a king;
   For Henry, son unto a conqueror,
   Is likely to beget more conquerors,
   If with a lady of so high resolve
   As is fair Margaret he be link'd in love.
   Then yield, my lords; and here conclude
   with me
   That Margaret shall be Queen, and none but she.
KING HENRY. Whether it be through force of
   your report,
   My noble Lord of Suffolk, or for that
   My tender youth was never yet attaint

With any passion of inflaming love,
I cannot tell; but this I am assur'd,
I feel such sharp dissension in my breast,
Such fierce alarums both of hope and fear,
As I am sick with working of my thoughts.
Take therefore shipping; post, my lord,
  to France;
Agree to any covenants; and procure
That Lady Margaret do vouchsafe to come
To cross the seas to England, and be crown'd
King Henry's faithful and anointed queen.
For your expenses and sufficient charge,
Among the people gather up a tenth.
Be gone, I say; for till you do return
I rest perplexed with a thousand cares.
And you, good uncle, banish all offence:
If you do censure me by what you were,
Not what you are, I know it will excuse
This sudden execution of my will.
And so conduct me where, from company,
I may revolve and ruminate my grief. *Exit.*
GLOUCESTER. Ay, grief, I fear me, both at first
  and last. *Exeunt GLOUCESTER and EXETER.*
SUFFOLK. Thus Suffolk hath prevail'd; and thus
  he goes,
As did the youthful Paris once to Greece,
With hope to find the like event in love
But prosper better than the Troyan did.
Margaret shall now be Queen, and rule the King;
But I will rule both her, the King, and realm.

Exit.

The End

King Henry VI, Part II

Dramatis Personae

KING HENRY THE SIXTH
HUMPHREY, DUKE OF GLOUCESTER, his uncle
CARDINAL BEAUFORT, BISHOP OF
WINCHESTER, great-uncle to the King
RICHARD PLANTAGENET, DUKE OF YORK
EDWARD and RICHARD, his sons
DUKE OF SOMERSET
DUKE OF SUFFOLK
DUKE OF BUCKINGHAM
LORD CLIFFORD
YOUNG CLIFFORD, his son
EARL OF SALISBURY
EARL OF WARWICK
LORD SCALES
LORD SAY
SIR HUMPHREY STAFFORD
WILLIAM STAFFORD, his brother
SIR JOHN STANLEY
VAUX
MATTHEW GOFFE
A LIEUTENANT; a SHIPMASTER; a MASTER'S
MATE; and WALTER WHITMORE
TWO GENTLEMEN, prisoners with Suffolk
JOHN HUME and JOHN SOUTHWELL, two priests
ROGER BOLINGBROKE, a conjurer
A SPIRIT raised by him
THOMAS HORNER, an armourer
PETER, his man
CLERK OF CHATHAM
MAYOR OF SAINT ALBANS
SAUNDER SIMPCOX, an impostor
ALEXANDER IDEN, a Kentish gentleman
JACK CADE, a rebel
GEORGE BEVIS; JOHN HOLLAND; DICK THE
BUTCHER; SMITH THE WEAVER;
MICHAEL; etc., followers of Cade
TWO MURDERERS

MARGARET, Queen to King Henry
ELEANOR, Duchess of Gloucester
MARGERY JOURDAIN, a witch
WIFE to SIMPCOX

Lords, Ladies, and Attendants; Petitioners,
Aldermen, a Herald, a Beadle, a Sheriff, Officers,
Citizens, Prentices, Falconers, Guards, Soldiers,
Messengers, etc.

SCENE
England

ACT I

⚘ SCENE I ⚘
London. The palace

Flourish of trumpets; then hautboys. Enter the KING,
DUKE HUMPHREY OF GLOUCESTER, SALISBURY,
WARWICK, and CARDINAL BEAUFORT, on the one
side; the QUEEN, SUFFOLK, YORK, SOMERSET, and
BUCKINGHAM, on the other

SUFFOLK. As by your high imperial Majesty
I had in charge at my depart for France,
As procurator to your Excellence,
To marry Princess Margaret for your Grace;
So, in the famous ancient city Tours,
In presence of the Kings of France and Sicil,
The Dukes of Orleans, Calaber, Bretagne,
  and Alençon,
Seven earls, twelve barons, and twenty
  reverend bishops,
I have perform'd my task, and was espous'd;
And humbly now upon my bended knee,
In sight of England and her lordly peers,
Deliver up my title in the Queen
To your most gracious hands, that are
  the substance
Of that great shadow I did represent:
The happiest gift that ever marquis gave,
The fairest queen that ever king receiv'd.
KING HENRY. Suffolk, arise. Welcome,
  Queen Margaret:
I can express no kinder sign of love
Than this kind kiss. O Lord, that lends me life,

Lend me a heart replete with thankfulness!
For thou hast given me in this beauteous face
A world of earthly blessings to my soul,
If sympathy of love unite our thoughts.
QUEEN. Great King of England, and my
  gracious lord,
The mutual conference that my mind hath had,
By day, by night, waking and in my dreams,
In courtly company or at my beads,
With you, mine alder-liefest sovereign,
Makes me the bolder to salute my king
With ruder terms, such as my wit affords
And over-joy of heart doth minister.
KING HENRY. Her sight did ravish, but her grace
  in speech,
Her words y-clad with wisdom's majesty,
Makes me from wond'ring fall to weeping joys,
Such is the fulness of my heart's content.
Lords, with one cheerful voice welcome my love.
ALL. [Kneeling] Long live Queen Margaret,
  England's happiness!
QUEEN. We thank you all.   [Flourish]
SUFFOLK. My Lord Protector, so it please
  your Grace,
Here are the articles of contracted peace
Between our sovereign and the French
  King Charles,
For eighteen months concluded by consent.
GLOUCESTER. [Reads] 'Imprimis: It is agreed
  between the French King Charles and William
  de la Pole, Marquess of Suffolk, ambassador
  for Henry King of England, that the said Henry
  shall espouse the Lady Margaret, daughter
  unto Reignier King of Naples, Sicilia, and
  Jerusalem, and crown her Queen of England
  ere the thirtieth of May next ensuing. Item: That
  the duchy of Anjou and the county of Maine
  shall be released and delivered to the King
  her father'-

Lets the paper fall

KING HENRY. Uncle, how now!
GLOUCESTER. Pardon me, gracious lord;
  Some sudden qualm hath struck me at the heart,
  And dimm'd mine eyes, that I can read
  no further.
KING HENRY. Uncle of Winchester, I pray
  read on.
CARDINAL. [Reads] 'Item: It is further agreed
  between them that the duchies of Anjou and
  Maine shall be released and delivered over to
  the King her father, and she sent over of the
  King of England's own proper cost and charges,
  without having any dowry.'

KING HENRY. They please us well. Lord Marquess,
   kneel down.
We here create thee the first Duke of Suffolk,
And girt thee with the sword. Cousin of York,
We here discharge your Grace from
   being Regent
I' th' parts of France, till term of
   eighteen months
Be full expir'd. Thanks, uncle Winchester,
Gloucester, York, Buckingham, Somerset,
Salisbury, and Warwick;
We thank you all for this great favour done
In entertainment to my princely queen.
Come, let us in, and with all speed provide
To see her coronation be perform'd.
                Exeunt KING, QUEEN, and SUFFOLK.
GLOUCESTER. Brave peers of England, pillars of
   the state,
To you Duke Humphrey must unload his grief-
Your grief, the common grief of all the land.
What! did my brother Henry spend his youth,
His valour, coin, and people, in the wars?
Did he so often lodge in open field,
In winter's cold and summer's parching heat,
To conquer France, his true inheritance?
And did my brother Bedford toil his wits
To keep by policy what Henry got?
Have you yourselves, Somerset, Buckingham,
Brave York, Salisbury, and victorious Warwick,
Receiv'd deep scars in France and Normandy?
Or hath mine uncle Beaufort and myself,
With all the learned Council of the realm,
Studied so long, sat in the Council House
Early and late, debating to and fro
How France and Frenchmen might be kept
   in awe?
And had his Highness in his infancy
Crowned in Paris, in despite of foes?
And shall these labours and these honours die?
Shall Henry's conquest, Bedford's vigilance,
Your deeds of war, and all our counsel die?
O peers of England, shameful is this league!
Fatal this marriage, cancelling your fame,
Blotting your names from books of memory,
Razing the characters of your renown,
Defacing monuments of conquer'd France,
Undoing all, as all had never been!
CARDINAL. Nephew, what means this
   passionate discourse,
This peroration with such circumstance?
For France, 'tis ours; and we will keep it still.
GLOUCESTER. Ay, uncle, we will keep it if we can;
But now it is impossible we should.

Suffolk, the new-made duke that rules the roast,
Hath given the duchy of Anjou and Maine
Unto the poor King Reignier, whose large style
Agrees not with the leanness of his purse.
SALISBURY. Now, by the death of Him that died
   for all,
These counties were the keys of Normandy!
But wherefore weeps Warwick, my valiant son?
WARWICK. For grief that they are past recovery;
For were there hope to conquer them again
My sword should shed hot blood, mine eyes
   no tears.
Anjou and Maine! myself did win them both;
Those provinces these arms of mine
   did conquer;
And are the cities that I got with wounds
Deliver'd up again with peaceful words?
Mort Dieu!
YORK. For Suffolk's duke, may he be suffocate,
That dims the honour of this warlike isle!
France should have torn and rent my very heart
Before I would have yielded to this league.
I never read but England's kings have had
Large sums of gold and dowries with their wives;
And our King Henry gives away his own
To match with her that brings no vantages.
GLOUCESTER. A proper jest, and never
   heard before,
That Suffolk should demand a whole fifteenth
For costs and charges in transporting her!
She should have stay'd in France, and starv'd in
   France,
Before-
CARDINAL. My Lord of Gloucester, now ye grow
   too hot:
It was the pleasure of my lord the King.
GLOUCESTER. My Lord of Winchester, I know
   your mind;
'Tis not my speeches that you do mislike,
But 'tis my presence that doth trouble ye.
Rancour will out: proud prelate, in thy face
I see thy fury; if I longer stay
We shall begin our ancient bickerings.
Lordings, farewell; and say, when I am gone,
I prophesied France will be lost ere long.*Exit.*
CARDINAL. So, there goes our Protector in a rage.
'Tis known to you he is mine enemy;
Nay, more, an enemy unto you all,
And no great friend, I fear me, to the King.
Consider, lords, he is the next of blood
And heir apparent to the English crown.
Had Henry got an empire by his marriage
And all the wealthy kingdoms of the west,

There's reason he should be displeas'd at it.
Look to it, lords; let not his smoothing words
Bewitch your hearts; be wise and circumspect.
What though the common people favour him,
Calling him 'Humphrey, the good Duke
  of Gloucester',
Clapping their hands, and crying with loud voice
'Jesu maintain your royal excellence!'
With 'God preserve the good Duke Humphrey!'
I fear me, lords, for all this flattering gloss,
He will be found a dangerous Protector.
BUCKINGHAM. Why should he then protect
  our sovereign,
He being of age to govern of himself?
Cousin of Somerset, join you with me,
And all together, with the Duke of Suffolk,
We'll quickly hoise Duke Humphrey from
  his seat.
CARDINAL. This weighty business will not
  brook delay;
I'll to the Duke of Suffolk presently.   *Exit.*
SOMERSET. Cousin of Buckingham, though
  Humphrey's pride
And greatness of his place be grief to us,
Yet let us watch the haughty cardinal;
His insolence is more intolerable
Than all the princes in the land beside;
If Gloucester be displac'd, he'll be Protector.
BUCKINGHAM. Or thou or I, Somerset, will
  be Protector,
Despite Duke Humphrey or the Cardinal.
           Exeunt BUCKINGHAM and SOMERSET.
SALISBURY. Pride went before, ambition
  follows him.
While these do labour for their own preferment,
Behoves it us to labour for the realm.
I never saw but Humphrey Duke of Gloucester
Did bear him like a noble gentleman.
Oft have I seen the haughty Cardinal-
More like a soldier than a man o' th' church,
As stout and proud as he were lord of all-
Swear like a ruffian and demean himself
Unlike the ruler of a commonweal.
Warwick my son, the comfort of my age,
Thy deeds, thy plainness, and thy housekeeping,
Hath won the greatest favour of the commons,
Excepting none but good Duke Humphrey.
And, brother York, thy acts in Ireland,
In bringing them to civil discipline,
Thy late exploits done in the heart of France
When thou wert Regent for our sovereign,
Have made thee fear'd and honour'd of
  the people:

Join we together for the public good,
In what we can, to bridle and suppress
The pride of Suffolk and the Cardinal,
With Somerset's and Buckingham's ambition;
And, as we may, cherish Duke
  Humphrey's deeds
While they do tend the profit of the land.
WARWICK. So God help Warwick, as he loves
  the land
And common profit of his country!
YORK. And so says York- *[Aside]* for he hath
  greatest cause.
SALISBURY. Then let's make haste away and look
  unto the main.
WARWICK. Unto the main! O father, Maine is lost-
That Maine which by main force Warwick
  did win,
And would have kept so long as breath did last.
Main chance, father, you meant; but I
  meant Maine,
Which I will win from France, or else be slain.
           Exeunt WARWICK and SALISBURY.
YORK. Anjou and Maine are given to the French;
Paris is lost; the state of Normandy
Stands on a tickle point now they are gone.
Suffolk concluded on the articles;
The peers agreed; and Henry was well pleas'd
To change two dukedoms for a duke's
  fair daughter.
I cannot blame them all: what is't to them?
'Tis thine they give away, and not their own.
Pirates may make cheap pennyworths of
  their pillage,
And purchase friends, and give to courtesans,
Still revelling like lords till all be gone;
While as the silly owner of the goods
Weeps over them and wrings his hapless hands
And shakes his head and trembling
  stands aloof,
While all is shar'd and all is borne away,
Ready to starve and dare not touch his own.
So York must sit and fret and bite his tongue,
While his own lands are bargain'd for and sold.
Methinks the realms of England, France,
  and Ireland,
Bear that proportion to my flesh and blood
As did the fatal brand Althaea burnt
Unto the prince's heart of Calydon.
Anjou and Maine both given unto the French!
Cold news for me, for I had hope of France,
Even as I have of fertile England's soil.
A day will come when York shall claim his own;
And therefore I will take the Nevils' parts,

And make a show of love to proud
 Duke Humphrey,
And when I spy advantage, claim the crown,
For that's the golden mark I seek to hit.
Nor shall proud Lancaster usurp my right,
Nor hold the sceptre in his childish fist,
Nor wear the diadem upon his head,
Whose church-like humours fits not for a crown.
Then, York, be still awhile, till time do serve;
Watch thou and wake, when others be asleep,
To pry into the secrets of the state;
Till Henry, surfeiting in joys of love
With his new bride and England's dear-
 bought queen,
And Humphrey with the peers be fall'n at jars;
Then will I raise aloft the milk-white rose,
With whose sweet smell the air shall
 be perfum'd,
And in my standard bear the arms of York,
To grapple with the house of Lancaster;
And force perforce I'll make him yield
 the crown,
Whose bookish rule hath pull'd fair
 England down.

Exit.

⚜ SCENE II ⚜
The DUKE OF GLOUCESTER'S house

Enter DUKE and his wife ELEANOR

DUCHESS. Why droops my lord, like over-
 ripen'd corn
 Hanging the head at Ceres' plenteous load?
 Why doth the great Duke Humphrey knit
 his brows,
 As frowning at the favours of the world?
 Why are thine eyes fix'd to the sullen earth,
 Gazing on that which seems to dim thy sight?
 What see'st thou there? King Henry's diadem,
 Enchas'd with all the honours of the world?
 If so, gaze on, and grovel on thy face
 Until thy head be circled with the same.
 Put forth thy hand, reach at the glorious gold.
 What, is't too short? I'll lengthen it with mine;
 And having both together heav'd it up,
 We'll both together lift our heads to heaven,
 And never more abase our sight so low
 As to vouchsafe one glance unto the ground.
GLOUCESTER. O Nell, sweet Nell, if thou dost
 love thy lord,
 Banish the canker of ambitious thoughts!

And may that thought, when I imagine ill
Against my king and nephew, virtuous Henry,
Be my last breathing in this mortal world!
My troublous dreams this night doth make
 me sad.
DUCHESS. What dream'd my lord? Tell me, and
 I'll requite it
 With sweet rehearsal of my morning's dream.
GLOUCESTER. Methought this staff, mine office-
 badge in court,
 Was broke in twain; by whom I have forgot,
 But, as I think, it was by th' Cardinal;
 And on the pieces of the broken wand
 Were plac'd the heads of Edmund Duke
 of Somerset
 And William de la Pole, first Duke of Suffolk.
 This was my dream; what it doth bode,
 God knows.
DUCHESS. Tut, this was nothing but an argument
 That he that breaks a stick of Gloucester's grove
 Shall lose his head for his presumption.
 But list to me, my Humphrey, my sweet Duke:
 Methought I sat in seat of majesty
 In the cathedral church of Westminster,
 And in that chair where kings and queens
 were crown'd;
 Where Henry and Dame Margaret kneel'd to me,
 And on my head did set the diadem.
GLOUCESTER. Nay, Eleanor, then must I
 chide outright.
 Presumptuous dame, ill-nurtur'd Eleanor!
 Art thou not second woman in the realm,
 And the Protector's wife, belov'd of him?
 Hast thou not worldly pleasure at command
 Above the reach or compass of thy thought?
 And wilt thou still be hammering treachery
 To tumble down thy husband and thyself
 From top of honour to disgrace's feet?
 Away from me, and let me hear no more!
DUCHESS. What, what, my lord! Are you
 so choleric
 With Eleanor for telling but her dream?
 Next time I'll keep my dreams unto myself
 And not be check'd.
GLOUCESTER. Nay, be not angry; I am
 pleas'd again.

Enter a MESSENGER

MESSENGER. My Lord Protector, 'tis his
 Highness' pleasure
 You do prepare to ride unto Saint Albans,
 Where as the King and Queen do mean to hawk.
GLOUCESTER. I go. Come, Nell, thou wilt ride
 with us?

DUCHESS. Yes, my good lord, I'll follow presently.

Exeunt GLOUCESTER and MESSENGER

Follow I must; I cannot go before,
While Gloucester bears this base and
  humble mind.
Were I a man, a duke, and next of blood,
I would remove these tedious stumbling-blocks
And smooth my way upon their headless necks;
And, being a woman, I will not be slack
To play my part in Fortune's pageant.
Where are you there, Sir John? Nay, fear
  not, man,
We are alone; here's none but thee and I.

Enter HUME

HUME. Jesus preserve your royal Majesty!
DUCHESS. What say'st thou? Majesty! I am
  but Grace.
HUME. But, by the grace of God and
  Hume's advice,
Your Grace's title shall be multiplied.
DUCHESS. What say'st thou, man? Hast thou as
  yet conferr'd
With Margery Jourdain, the cunning witch of Eie,
With Roger Bolingbroke, the conjurer?
And will they undertake to do me good?
HUME. This they have promised, to show
  your Highness
A spirit rais'd from depth of underground
That shall make answer to such questions
As by your Grace shall be propounded him
DUCHESS. It is enough; I'll think upon
  the questions;
When from Saint Albans we do make return
We'll see these things effected to the full.
Here, Hume, take this reward; make
  merry, man,
With thy confederates in this weighty cause.

Exit

HUME. Hume must make merry with the
  Duchess' gold;
Marry, and shall. But, how now, Sir John Hume!
Seal up your lips and give no words but mum:
The business asketh silent secrecy.
Dame Eleanor gives gold to bring the witch:
Gold cannot come amiss were she a devil.
Yet have I gold flies from another coast-
I dare not say from the rich Cardinal,
And from the great and new-made Duke
  of Suffolk;
Yet I do find it so; for, to be plain,
They, knowing Dame Eleanor's aspiring humour,
Have hired me to undermine the Duchess,
And buzz these conjurations in her brain.

They say 'A crafty knave does need no broker';
Yet am I Suffolk and the Cardinal's broker.
Hume, if you take not heed, you shall go near
To call them both a pair of crafty knaves.
Well, so it stands; and thus, I fear, at last
Hume's knavery will be the Duchess' wreck,
And her attainture will be Humphrey's fall.
Sort how it will, I shall have gold for all. *Exit*

⚘ SCENE III ⚘

London. The palace

Enter three or four PETITIONERS, PETER, the Armourer's man, being one

FIRST PETITIONER. My masters, let's stand close;
  my Lord Protector will come this way by and
  by, and then we may deliver our supplications
  in the quill.
SECOND PETITIONER. Marry, the Lord protect
  him, for he's a good man, Jesu bless him!

Enter SUFFOLK and QUEEN

FIRST PETITIONER. Here 'a comes, methinks, and
  the Queen with him. I'll be the first, sure.
SECOND PETITIONER. Come back, fool; this is
  the Duke of Suffolk and not my Lord Protector.
SUFFOLK. How now, fellow! Wouldst anything
  with me?
FIRST PETITIONER. I pray, my lord, pardon me; I
  took ye for my Lord Protector.
QUEEN. *[Reads]* 'To my Lord Protector'! Are your
  supplications to his lordship? Let me see them.
  What is thine?
FIRST PETITIONER. Mine is, an't please your
  Grace, against John Goodman, my Lord
  Cardinal's man, for keeping my house and
  lands, and wife and all, from me.
SUFFOLK. Thy wife too! That's some wrong
  indeed. What's yours? What's here! *[Reads]*
  'Against the Duke of Suffolk, for enclosing the
  commons of Melford.' How now, sir knave!
SECOND PETITIONER. Alas, sir, I am but a poor
  petitioner of our whole township.
PETER. *[Presenting his petition]* Against my master,
  Thomas Horner, for saying that the Duke of
  York was rightful heir to the crown.
QUEEN. What say'st thou? Did the Duke of York
  say he was rightful heir to the crown?
PETER. That my master was? No, forsooth. My
  master said that he was, and that the King was
  an usurper.
SUFFOLK. Who is there?

Enter servant

Take this fellow in, and send for his master with
a pursuivant presently. We'll hear more of your
matter before the King.

Exit servant with PETER

QUEEN. And as for you, that love to be protected
Under the wings of our Protector's grace,
Begin your suits anew, and sue to him. [*Tears
the supplications*]
Away, base cullions! Suffolk, let them go.

ALL. Come, let's be gone. *Exeunt*

QUEEN. My Lord of Suffolk, say, is this
the guise,
Is this the fashions in the court of England?
Is this the government of Britain's isle,
And this the royalty of Albion's king?
What, shall King Henry be a pupil still,
Under the surly Gloucester's governance?
Am I a queen in title and in style,
And must be made a subject to a duke?
I tell thee, Pole, when in the city Tours
Thou ran'st a tilt in honour of my love
And stol'st away the ladies' hearts of France,
I thought King Henry had resembled thee
In courage, courtship, and proportion;
But all his mind is bent to holiness,
To number Ave-Maries on his beads;
His champions are the prophets and apostles;
His weapons, holy saws of sacred writ;
His study is his tilt-yard, and his loves
Are brazen images of canonised saints.
I would the college of the Cardinals
Would choose him Pope, and carry him
to Rome,
And set the triple crown upon his head;
That were a state fit for his holiness.

SUFFOLK. Madam, be patient. As I was cause
Your Highness came to England, so will I
In England work your Grace's full content.

QUEEN. Beside the haughty Protector, have
we Beaufort
The imperious churchman;
Somerset, Buckingham,
And grumbling York; and not the least of these
But can do more in England than the King.

SUFFOLK. And he of these that can do most of all
Cannot do more in England than the Nevils;
Salisbury and Warwick are no simple peers.

QUEEN. Not all these lords do vex me half
so much
As that proud dame, the Lord Protector's wife.
She sweeps it through the court with troops
of ladies,
More like an empress than Duke
Humphrey's wife.
Strangers in court do take her for the Queen.
She bears a duke's revenues on her back,
And in her heart she scorns our poverty;
Shall I not live to be aveng'd on her?
Contemptuous base-born callet as she is,
She vaunted 'mongst her minions t' other day
The very train of her worst wearing gown
Was better worth than all my father's lands,
Till Suffolk gave two dukedoms for
his daughter.

SUFFOLK. Madam, myself have lim'd a bush
for her,
And plac'd a quire of such enticing birds
That she will light to listen to the lays,
And never mount to trouble you again.
So, let her rest. And, madam, list to me,
For I am bold to counsel you in this:
Although we fancy not the Cardinal,
Yet must we join with him and with the lords,
Till we have brought Duke Humphrey in
disgrace.
As for the Duke of York, this late complaint
Will make but little for his benefit.
So one by one we'll weed them all at last,
And you yourself shall steer the happy helm.

Sound a sennet. Enter the KING, DUKE HUMPHREY,
CARDINAL BEAUFORT, BUCKINGHAM, YORK,
SOMERSET, SALISBURY, WARWICK, *and the*
DUCHESS OF GLOUCESTER

KING HENRY. For my part, noble lords, I care
not which:
Or Somerset or York, all's one to me.

YORK. If York have ill demean'd himself in France,
Then let him be denay'd the regentship.

SOMERSET. If Somerset be unworthy of the place,
Let York be Regent; I will yield to him.

WARWICK. Whether your Grace be worthy, yea
or no,
Dispute not that; York is the worthier.

CARDINAL. Ambitious Warwick, let thy
betters speak.

WARWICK. The Cardinal's not my better in
the field.

BUCKINGHAM. All in this presence are thy
betters, Warwick.

WARWICK. Warwick may live to be the best of all.

SALISBURY. Peace, son! And show some
reason, Buckingham,
Why Somerset should be preferr'd in this.

QUEEN. Because the King, forsooth, will have
it so.

GLOUCESTER. Madam, the King is old
enough himself
  To give his censure. These are no
  women's matters.
QUEEN. If he be old enough, what needs
your Grace
  To be Protector of his Excellence?
GLOUCESTER. Madam, I am Protector of
the realm;
  And at his pleasure will resign my place.
SUFFOLK. Resign it then, and leave
thine insolence.
  Since thou wert king-as who is king but thou?-
  The commonwealth hath daily run to wrack,
  The Dauphin hath prevail'd beyond the seas,
  And all the peers and nobles of the realm
  Have been as bondmen to thy sovereignty.
CARDINAL. The commons hast thou rack'd; the
clergy's bags
  Are lank and lean with thy extortions.
SOMERSET. Thy sumptuous buildings and thy
wife's attire
  Have cost a mass of public treasury.
BUCKINGHAM. Thy cruelty in execution
  Upon offenders hath exceeded law,
  And left thee to the mercy of the law.
QUEEN. Thy sale of offices and towns in France,
  If they were known, as the suspect is great,
  Would make thee quickly hop without thy head.
  [Exit GLOUCESTER. The QUEEN drops her fan]
  Give me my fan. What, minion, can ye not? *[She
  gives the DUCHESS a box on the ear]*
  I cry your mercy, madam; was it you?
DUCHESS. Was't I? Yea, I it was,
proud Frenchwoman.
  Could I come near your beauty with my nails,
  I could set my ten commandments in your face.
KING HENRY. Sweet aunt, be quiet; 'twas against
her will.
DUCHESS. Against her will, good King? Look to
't in time;
  She'll hamper thee and dandle thee like a baby.
  Though in this place most master wear
  no breeches,
  She shall not strike Dame Eleanor unreveng'd.
  Exit
BUCKINGHAM. Lord Cardinal, I will
follow Eleanor,
  And listen after Humphrey, how he proceeds.
  She's tickled now; her fume needs no spurs,
  She'll gallop far enough to her destruction.
  Exit

  Re-enter GLOUCESTER

GLOUCESTER. Now, lords, my choler
being overblown
  With walking once about the quadrangle,
  I come to talk of commonwealth affairs.
  As for your spiteful false objections,
  Prove them, and I lie open to the law;
  But God in mercy so deal with my soul
  As I in duty love my king and country!
  But to the matter that we have in hand:
  I say, my sovereign, York is meetest man
  To be your Regent in the realm of France.
SUFFOLK. Before we make election, give me leave
  To show some reason, of no little force,
  That York is most unmeet of any man.
YORK. I'll tell thee, Suffolk, why I am unmeet:
  First, for I cannot flatter thee in pride;
  Next, if I be appointed for the place,
  My Lord of Somerset will keep me here
  Without discharge, money, or furniture,
  Till France be won into the Dauphin's hands.
  Last time I danc'd attendance on his will
  Till Paris was besieg'd, famish'd, and lost.
WARWICK. That can I witness; and a fouler fact
  Did never traitor in the land commit.
SUFFOLK. Peace, headstrong Warwick!
WARWICK. Image of pride, why should I hold
my peace?
  Enter HORNER, the Armourer, and his man PETER, guarded
SUFFOLK. Because here is a man accus'd
of treason:
  Pray God the Duke of York excuse himself!
YORK. Doth any one accuse York for a traitor?
KING HENRY. What mean'st thou, Suffolk? Tell
me, what are these?
SUFFOLK. Please it your Majesty, this is the man
  That doth accuse his master of high treason;
  His words were these: that Richard Duke of York
  Was rightful heir unto the English crown,
  And that your Majesty was an usurper.
KING HENRY. Say, man, were these thy words?
HORNER. An't shall please your Majesty, I never
  said nor thought any such matter. God is my
  witness, I am falsely accus'd by the villain.
PETER. *[Holding up his hands]* By these ten bones, my
  lords, he did speak them to me in the garret
  one night, as we were scouring my Lord of
  York's armour.
YORK. Base dunghill villain and mechanical,
  I'll have thy head for this thy traitor's speech.
  I do beseech your royal Majesty,
  Let him have all the rigour of the law.
HORNER. Alas, my lord, hang me if ever I spake
  the words. My accuser is my prentice; and when

I did correct him for his fault the other day,
he did vow upon his knees he would be even
with me. I have good witness of this; therefore
I beseech your Majesty, do not cast away an
honest man for a villain's accusation.
KING HENRY. Uncle, what shall we say to this
in law?
GLOUCESTER. This doom, my lord, if I
may judge:
Let Somerset be Regent o'er the French,
Because in York this breeds suspicion;
And let these have a day appointed them
For single combat in convenient place,
For he hath witness of his servant's malice.
This is the law, and this Duke
Humphrey's doom.
SOMERSET. I humbly thank your royal Majesty.
HORNER. And I accept the combat willingly.
PETER. Alas, my lord, I cannot fight; for God's
sake, pity my case! The spite of man prevaileth
against me. O Lord, have mercy upon me, I
shall never be able to fight a blow! O Lord,
my heart!
GLOUCESTER. Sirrah, or you must fight or else
be hang'd.
KING HENRY. Away with them to prison; and
the day of combat shall be the last of the
next month. Come, Somerset, we'll see thee
sent away.

Flourish. Exeunt.

✣ SCENE IV ✣
London. The DUKE OF GLOUCESTER'S garden

*Enter MARGERY JOURDAIN, the witch; the two priests,
HUME and SOUTHWELL; and BOLINGBROKE*

HUME. Come, my masters; the Duchess, I tell
you, expects
performance of your promises.
BOLINGBROKE. Master Hume, we are therefore
provided; will her ladyship behold and hear
our exorcisms?
HUME. Ay, what else? Fear you not her courage.
BOLINGBROKE. I have heard her reported to be
a woman of an invincible spirit; but it shall be
convenient, Master Hume, that you be by her
aloft while we be busy below; and so I pray you
go, in God's name, and leave us. *[Exit HUME]*
Mother Jourdain, be you prostrate and grovel
on the earth; John Southwell, read you; and let
us to our work.

Enter DUCHESS aloft, followed by HUME

DUCHESS. Well said, my masters; and welcome
all. To this gear, the sooner the better.
BOLINGBROKE. Patience, good lady; wizards
know their times:
Deep night, dark night, the silent of the night,
The time of night when Troy was set on fire;
The time when screech-owls cry and ban-
dogs howl,
And spirits walk and ghosts break up
their graves-
That time best fits the work we have in hand.
Madam, sit you, and fear not: whom we raise
We will make fast within a hallow'd verge.
*[Here they do the ceremonies belonging, and make the circle;
BOLINGBROKE or SOUTHWELL reads: 'Conjuro te,' etc.
It thunders and lightens terribly; then the SPIRIT riseth]*
SPIRIT. Adsum.
MARGERY JOURDAIN. Asmath,
By the eternal God, whose name and power
Thou tremblest at, answer that I shall ask;
For till thou speak thou shalt not pass
from hence.
SPIRIT. Ask what thou wilt; that I had said
and done.
BOLINGBROKE. *[Reads]* 'First of the king: what
shall of him become?'
SPIRIT. The Duke yet lives that Henry
shall depose;
But him outlive, and die a violent death.
As the SPIRIT speaks, SOUTHWELL writes the answer
BOLINGBROKE. 'What fates await the Duke
of Suffolk?'
SPIRIT. By water shall he die and take his end.
BOLINGBROKE. 'What shall befall the Duke
of Somerset?'
SPIRIT. Let him shun castles:
Safer shall he be upon the sandy plains
Than where castles mounted stand.
Have done, for more I hardly can endure.
BOLINGBROKE. Descend to darkness and the
burning lake;
False fiend, avoid! *Thunder and lightning. Exit
SPIRIT*
*Enter the DUKE OF YORK and the DUKE OF
BUCKINGHAM with guard, and break in*
YORK. Lay hands upon these traitors and
their trash.
Beldam, I think we watch'd you at an inch.
What, madam, are you there? The King
and commonweal
Are deeply indebted for this piece of pains;
My Lord Protector will, I doubt it not,

See you well guerdon'd for these
good deserts.

DUCHESS. Not half so bad as thine to
England's king,
Injurious Duke, that threatest where's
no cause.

BUCKINGHAM. True, madam, none at all. What
can you this?
Away with them! let them be clapp'd up close,
And kept asunder. You, madam, shall with us.
Stafford, take her to thee.
We'll see your trinkets here all forthcoming.
All, away!

Exeunt, above, DUCHESS and HUME, guarded; below,
WITCH, SOUTHWELL and BOLINGBROKE,
guarded.

YORK. Lord Buckingham, methinks you watch'd
her well.
A pretty plot, well chosen to build upon!
Now, pray, my lord, let's see the devil's writ.
What have we here?
[Reads] 'The duke yet lives that Henry
shall depose;
But him outlive, and die a violent death.'
Why, this is just
'Aio te, Aeacida, Romanos vincere posse.'
Well, to the rest:
'Tell me what fate awaits the Duke of Suffolk?'
'By water shall he die and take his end.'
'What shall betide the Duke of Somerset?'
'Let him shun castles;
Safer shall he be upon the sandy plains
Than where castles mounted stand.'
Come, come, my lords;
These oracles are hardly attain'd,
And hardly understood.
The King is now in progress towards
Saint Albans,
With him the husband of this lovely lady;
Thither go these news as fast as horse can
carry them-
A sorry breakfast for my Lord Protector.

BUCKINGHAM. Your Grace shall give me leave,
my Lord of York,
To be the post, in hope of his reward.

YORK. At your pleasure, my good lord.
Who's within there, ho?

Enter a serving-man

Invite my Lords of Salisbury and Warwick
To sup with me to-morrow night. Away!

Exeunt.

ACT II

SCENE I
Saint Albans

Enter the KING, QUEEN, GLOUCESTER, CARDINAL,
and SUFFOLK, with Falconers halloing

QUEEN. Believe me, lords, for flying at the brook,
I saw not better sport these seven years' day;
Yet, by your leave, the wind was very high,
And ten to one old Joan had not gone out.

KING HENRY. But what a point, my lord, your
falcon made,
And what a pitch she flew above the rest!
To see how God in all His creatures works!
Yea, man and birds are fain of climbing high.

SUFFOLK. No marvel, an it like your Majesty,
My Lord Protector's hawks do tow'r so well;
They know their master loves to be aloft,
And bears his thoughts above his falcon's pitch.

GLOUCESTER. My lord, 'tis but a base
ignoble mind
That mounts no higher than a bird can soar.

CARDINAL. I thought as much; he would be above
the clouds.

GLOUCESTER. Ay, my lord Cardinal, how think
you by that?
Were it not good your Grace could fly to heaven?

KING HENRY. The treasury of everlasting joy!

CARDINAL. Thy heaven is on earth; thine eyes
and thoughts
Beat on a crown, the treasure of thy heart;
Pernicious Protector, dangerous peer,
That smooth'st it so with King
and commonweal.

GLOUCESTER. What, Cardinal, is your priesthood
grown peremptory?
Tantaene animis coelestibus irae?
Churchmen so hot? Good uncle, hide
such malice;
With such holiness can you do it?

SUFFOLK. No malice, sir; no more than
well becomes
So good a quarrel and so bad a peer.

GLOUCESTER. As who, my lord?

SUFFOLK. Why, as you, my lord,
An't like your lordly Lord's Protectorship.

GLOUCESTER. Why, Suffolk, England knows
thine insolence.

QUEEN. And thy ambition, Gloucester.

KING HENRY. I prithee, peace,
  Good Queen, and whet not on these
    furious peers;
  For blessed are the peacemakers on earth.

CARDINAL. Let me be blessed for the peace
    I make
  Against this proud Protector with my sword!

GLOUCESTER. [Aside to CARDINAL] Faith, holy
  uncle, would 'twere come to that!

CARDINAL. [Aside to GLOUCESTER] Marry, when
  thou dar'st.

GLOUCESTER. [Aside to CARDINAL] Make up no
  factious numbers for the matter; In thine own
  person answer thy abuse.

CARDINAL. [Aside to GLOUCESTER] Ay, where thou
  dar'st not peep; an if thou dar'st, This evening
  on the east side of the grove.

KING HENRY. How now, my lords!

CARDINAL. Believe me, cousin Gloucester,
  Had not your man put up the fowl so suddenly,
  We had had more sport. [Aside to GLOUCESTER]
  Come with thy two-hand sword.

GLOUCESTER. True, uncle.

CARDINAL. [Aside to GLOUCESTER] Are ye advis'd?
  The east side of the grove?

GLOUCESTER. [Aside to CARDINAL] Cardinal, I am
  with you.

KING HENRY. Why, how now, uncle Gloucester!

GLOUCESTER. Talking of hawking; nothing else,
  my lord.
  [Aside to CARDINAL] Now, by God's Mother, priest,
  I'll shave your crown for this,
  Or all my fence shall fail.

CARDINAL. [Aside to GLOUCESTER] Medice, teipsum;
  Protector, see to't well; protect yourself.

KING HENRY. The winds grow high; so do your
    stomachs, lords.
  How irksome is this music to my heart!
  When such strings jar, what hope of harmony?
  I pray, my lords, let me compound this strife.
    Enter a TOWNSMAN of Saint Albans, crying 'A miracle!'

GLOUCESTER. What means this noise?
  Fellow, what miracle dost thou proclaim?

TOWNSMAN. A miracle! A miracle!

SUFFOLK. Come to the King, and tell him
    what miracle.

TOWNSMAN. Forsooth, a blind man at Saint
    Albans shrine
  Within this half hour hath receiv'd his sight;
  A man that ne'er saw in his life before.

KING HENRY. Now God be prais'd that to
    believing souls

Gives light in darkness, comfort in despair!
    Enter the MAYOR OF SAINT ALBANS and his brethren,
    bearing Simpcox between two in a chair; his WIFE and a
    multitude following

CARDINAL. Here come the townsmen
    on procession
  To present your Highness with the man.

KING HENRY. Great is his comfort in this
    earthly vale,
  Although by his sight his sin be multiplied.

GLOUCESTER. Stand by, my masters; bring him
    near the King;
  His Highness' pleasure is to talk with him.

KING HENRY. Good fellow, tell us here
    the circumstance,
  That we for thee may glorify the Lord.
  What, hast thou been long blind and
    now restor'd?

SIMPCOX. Born blind, an't please your Grace.

WIFE. Ay indeed was he.

SUFFOLK. What woman is this?

WIFE. His wife, an't like your worship.

GLOUCESTER. Hadst thou been his mother, thou
    couldst have better told.

KING HENRY. Where wert thou born?

SIMPCOX. At Berwick in the north, an't like
    your Grace.

KING HENRY. Poor soul, God's goodness hath
    been great to thee.
  Let never day nor night unhallowed pass,
  But still remember what the Lord hath done.

QUEEN. Tell me, good fellow, cam'st thou here
    by chance,
  Or of devotion, to this holy shrine?

SIMPCOX. God knows, of pure devotion;
    being call'd
  A hundred times and oft'ner, in my sleep,
  By good Saint Alban, who said 'Simpcox, come,
  Come, offer at my shrine, and I will help thee.'

WIFE. Most true, forsooth; and many time and oft
  Myself have heard a voice to call him so.

CARDINAL. What, art thou lame?

SIMPCOX. Ay, God Almighty help me!

SUFFOLK. How cam'st thou so?

SIMPCOX. A fall off of a tree.

WIFE. A plum tree, master.

GLOUCESTER. How long hast thou been blind?

SIMPCOX. O, born so, master!

GLOUCESTER. What, and wouldst climb a tree?

SIMPCOX. But that in all my life, when I was
    a youth.

WIFE. Too true; and bought his climbing
    very dear.

GLOUCESTER. Mass, thou lov'dst plums well, that
wouldst venture so.

SIMPCOX. Alas, good master, my wife desir'd
some damsons
And made me climb, with danger of my life.

GLOUCESTER. A subtle knave! But yet it shall
not serve:
Let me see thine eyes; wink now; now
open them;
In my opinion yet thou seest not well.

SIMPCOX. Yes, master, clear as day, I thank God
and Saint Alban.

GLOUCESTER. Say'st thou me so? What colour is
this cloak of?

SIMPCOX. Red, master; red as blood.

GLOUCESTER. Why, that's well said. What colour
is my gown of?

SIMPCOX. Black, forsooth; coal-black as jet.

KING HENRY. Why, then, thou know'st what
colour jet is of?

SUFFOLK. And yet, I think, jet did he never see.

GLOUCESTER. But cloaks and gowns before this
day a many.

WIFE. Never before this day in all his life.

GLOUCESTER. Tell me, sirrah, what's my name?

SIMPCOX. Alas, master, I know not.

GLOUCESTER. What's his name?

SIMPCOX. I know not.

GLOUCESTER. Nor his?

SIMPCOX. No, indeed, master.

GLOUCESTER. What's thine own name?

SIMPCOX. Saunder Simpcox, an if it please
you, master.

GLOUCESTER. Then, Saunder, sit there, the
lying'st knave in Christendom. If thou
hadst been born blind, thou mightst as
well have known all our names as thus to
name the several colours we do wear. Sight
may distinguish of colours; but suddenly
to nominate them all, it is impossible. My
lords, Saint Alban here hath done a miracle;
and would ye not think his cunning to be
great that could restore this cripple to his
legs again?

SIMPCOX. O master, that you could!

GLOUCESTER. My masters of Saint Albans, have
you not beadles in your town, and things
call'd whips?

MAYOR. Yes, my lord, if it please your Grace.

GLOUCESTER. Then send for one presently.

MAYOR. Sirrah, go fetch the beadle hither straight.
Exit an Attendant.

GLOUCESTER. Now fetch me a stool hither by
and by. *[A stool brought]* Now, sirrah, if you mean to
save yourself from whipping, leap me over this
stool and run away.

SIMPCOX. Alas, master, I am not able to
stand alone!
You go about to torture me in vain.
Enter a BEADLE with whips

GLOUCESTER. Well, sir, we must have you find
your legs. Sirrah beadle, whip him till he leap
over that same stool.

BEADLE. I will, my lord. Come on, sirrah; off
with your doublet quickly.

SIMPCOX. Alas, master, what shall I do? I am
not able to stand.
*After the BEADLE hath hit him once, he leaps over the stool
and runs away; and they follow and cry 'A miracle!'*

KING HENRY. O God, seest Thou this, and
bearest so long?

QUEEN. It made me laugh to see the villain run.

GLOUCESTER. Follow the knave, and take this
drab away.

WIFE. Alas, sir, we did it for pure need!

GLOUCESTER. Let them be whipp'd through
every market town till they come to Berwick,
from whence they came.
Exeunt MAYOR, BEADLE, WIFE, etc.

CARDINAL. Duke Humphrey has done a
miracle to-day.

SUFFOLK. True; made the lame to leap and
fly away.

GLOUCESTER. But you have done more
miracles than I:
You made in a day, my lord, whole towns
to fly.
Enter BUCKINGHAM

KING HENRY. What tidings with our
cousin Buckingham?

BUCKINGHAM. Such as my heart doth tremble
to unfold:
A sort of naughty persons, lewdly bent,
Under the countenance and confederacy
Of Lady Eleanor, the Protector's wife,
The ringleader and head of all this rout,
Have practis'd dangerously against your state,
Dealing with witches and with conjurers,
Whom we have apprehended in the fact,
Raising up wicked spirits from under ground,
Demanding of King Henry's life and death
And other of your Highness' Privy Council,
As more at large your Grace shall understand.

CARDINAL. And so, my Lord Protector, by
this means
Your lady is forthcoming yet at London.

This news, I think, hath turn'd your
  weapon's edge;
'Tis like, my lord, you will not keep your hour.
GLOUCESTER. Ambitious churchman, leave to
  afflict my heart.
  Sorrow and grief have vanquish'd all my powers;
  And, vanquish'd as I am, I yield to thee
  Or to the meanest groom.
KING HENRY. O God, what mischiefs work the
  wicked ones,
  Heaping confusion on their own heads thereby!
QUEEN. Gloucester, see here the tainture of
  thy nest;
  And look thyself be faultless, thou wert best.
GLOUCESTER. Madam, for myself, to heaven I
  do appeal
  How I have lov'd my King and commonweal;
  And for my wife I know not how it stands.
  Sorry I am to hear what I have heard.
  Noble she is; but if she have forgot
  Honour and virtue, and convers'd with such
  As, like to pitch, defile nobility,
  I banish her my bed and company
  And give her as a prey to law and shame,
  That hath dishonoured Gloucester's
  honest name.
KING HENRY. Well, for this night we will repose
  us here.
  To-morrow toward London back again
  To look into this business thoroughly
  And call these foul offenders to their answers,
  And poise the cause in justice' equal scales,
  Whose beam stands sure, whose rightful
  cause prevails.

                                    Flourish. Exeunt.

✤ SCENE II ✤
London. The DUKE OF YORK'S garden

Enter YORK, SALISBURY, and WARWICK

YORK. Now, my good Lords of Salisbury
  and Warwick,
  Our simple supper ended, give me leave
  In this close walk to satisfy myself
  In craving your opinion of my tide,
  Which is infallible, to England's crown.
SALISBURY. My lord, I long to hear it at full.
WARWICK. Sweet York, begin; and if thy claim
  be good,
  The Nevils are thy subjects to command.
YORK. Then thus:

Edward the Third, my lords, had seven sons;
  The first, Edward the Black Prince, Prince
  of Wales;
  The second, William of Hatfield; and the third,
  Lionel Duke of Clarence; next to whom
  Was John of Gaunt, the Duke of Lancaster;
  The fifth was Edmund Langley, Duke of York;
  The sixth was Thomas of Woodstock, Duke
  of Gloucester;
  William of Windsor was the seventh and last.
  Edward the Black Prince died before his father
  And left behind him Richard, his only son,
  Who, after Edward the Third's death, reign'd
  as king
  Till Henry Bolingbroke, Duke of Lancaster,
  The eldest son and heir of John of Gaunt,
  Crown'd by the name of Henry the Fourth,
  Seiz'd on the realm, depos'd the rightful king,
  Sent his poor queen to France, from whence
  she came.
  And him to Pomfret, where, as all you know,
  Harmless Richard was murdered traitorously.
WARWICK. Father, the Duke hath told the truth;
  Thus got the house of Lancaster the crown.
YORK. Which now they hold by force, and not
  by right;
  For Richard, the first son's heir, being dead,
  The issue of the next son should have reign'd.
SALISBURY. But William of Hatfield died without
  an heir.
YORK. The third son, Duke of Clarence, from
  whose line
  I claim the crown, had issue Philippe,
  a daughter,
  Who married Edmund Mortimer, Earl of March;
  Edmund had issue, Roger Earl of March;
  Roger had issue, Edmund, Anne, and Eleanor.
SALISBURY. This Edmund, in the reign
  of Bolingbroke,
  As I have read, laid claim unto the crown;
  And, but for Owen Glendower, had been king,
  Who kept him in captivity till he died.
  But, to the rest.
YORK. His eldest sister, Anne,
  My mother, being heir unto the crown,
  Married Richard Earl of Cambridge, who was
  To Edmund Langley, Edward the Third's fifth
  son, son.
  By her I claim the kingdom: she was heir
  To Roger Earl of March, who was the son
  Of Edmund Mortimer, who married Philippe,
  Sole daughter unto Lionel Duke of Clarence;
  So, if the issue of the elder son

Succeed before the younger, I am King.

WARWICK. What plain proceedings is more plain
  than this?

Henry doth claim the crown from John of Gaunt,
The fourth son: York claims it from the third.
Till Lionel's issue fails, his should not reign.
It fails not yet, but flourishes in thee
And in thy sons, fair slips of such a stock.
Then, father Salisbury, kneel we together,
And in this private plot be we the first
That shall salute our rightful sovereign
With honour of his birthright to the crown.

BOTH. Long live our sovereign Richard,
  England's King!

YORK. We thank you, lords. But I am not
  your king
Till I be crown'd, and that my sword be stain'd
With heart-blood of the house of Lancaster;
And that's not suddenly to be perform'd,
But with advice and silent secrecy.
Do you as I do in these dangerous days:
Wink at the Duke of Suffolk's insolence,
At Beaufort's pride, at Somerset's ambition,
At Buckingham, and all the crew of them,
Till they have snar'd the shepherd of the flock,
That virtuous prince, the good Duke Humphrey;
'Tis that they seek; and they, in seeking that,
Shall find their deaths, if York can prophesy.

SALISBURY. My lord, break we off; we know your
  mind at full.

WARWICK. My heart assures me that the Earl
  of Warwick
Shall one day make the Duke of York a king.

YORK. And, Nevil, this I do assure myself,
Richard shall live to make the Earl of Warwick
The greatest man in England but the King.

Exeunt.⬧

⚜ SCENE III ⚜
London. A hall of justice

*Sound trumpets. Enter the KING and State: the QUEEN,
GLOUCESTER, YORK, SUFFOLK, and SALISBURY,
with guard, to banish the DUCHESS. Enter, guarded, the
DUCHESS OF GLOUCESTER, MARGERY JOURDAIN,
HUME, SOUTHWELL, and BOLINGBROKE*

KING HENRY. Stand forth, Dame Eleanor
  Cobham, Gloucester's wife:
In sight of God and us, your guilt is great;
Receive the sentence of the law for sins
Such as by God's book are adjudg'd to death.

You four, from hence to prison back again;
From thence unto the place of execution:
The witch in Smithfield shall be burnt to ashes,
And you three shall be strangled on the gallows.
You, madam, for you are more nobly born,
Despoiled of your honour in your life,
Shall, after three days' open penance done,
Live in your country here in banishment
With Sir John Stanley in the Isle of Man.

DUCHESS. Welcome is banishment; welcome
  were my death.

GLOUCESTER. Eleanor, the law, thou seest, hath
  judged thee.
I cannot justify whom the law condemns.

Exeunt the DUCHESS and the other prisoners, guarded.⬧

Mine eyes are full of tears, my heart of grief.
Ah, Humphrey, this dishonour in thine age
Will bring thy head with sorrow to the ground!
I beseech your Majesty give me leave to go;
Sorrow would solace, and mine age would ease.

KING HENRY. Stay, Humphrey Duke of
  Gloucester; ere thou go,
Give up thy staff; Henry will to himself
Protector be; and God shall be my hope,
My stay, my guide, and lantern to my feet.
And go in peace, Humphrey, no less belov'd
Than when thou wert Protector to thy King.

QUEEN. I see no reason why a king of years
Should be to be protected like a child.
God and King Henry govern England's realm!
Give up your staff, sir, and the King his realm.

GLOUCESTER. My staff! Here, noble Henry, is
  my staff.
As willingly do I the same resign
As ere thy father Henry made it mine;
And even as willingly at thy feet I leave it
As others would ambitiously receive it.
Farewell, good King; when I am dead and gone,
May honourable peace attend thy throne!*Exit.⬧*

QUEEN. Why, now is Henry King, and
  Margaret Queen,
And Humphrey Duke of Gloucester
  scarce himself,
That bears so shrewd a maim: two pulls at once-
His lady banish'd and a limb lopp'd off.
This staff of honour raught, there let it stand
Where it best fits to be, in Henry's hand.

SUFFOLK. Thus droops this lofty pine and hangs
  his sprays;
Thus Eleanor's pride dies in her youngest days.

YORK. Lords, let him go. Please it your Majesty,
This is the day appointed for the combat;
And ready are the appellant and defendant,

The armourer and his man, to enter the lists,
So please your Highness to behold the fight.
QUEEN. Ay, good my lord; for purposely therefore
Left I the court, to see this quarrel tried.
KING HENRY. A God's name, see the lists and all
things fit;
Here let them end it, and God defend the right!
YORK. I never saw a fellow worse bested,
Or more afraid to fight, than is the appellant,
The servant of his armourer, my lords.

Enter at one door, HORNER, the Armourer, and his
NEIGHBOURS, drinking to him so much that he is drunk; and
he enters with a drum before him and his staff with a sand-bag
fastened to it; and at the other door PETER, his man, with a
drum and sand-bag, and PRENTICES drinking to him

FIRST NEIGHBOUR. Here, neighbour Horner,
I drink to you in a cup of sack; and fear not,
neighbour, you shall do well enough.
SECOND NEIGHBOUR. And here, neighbour,
here's a cup of charneco.
THIRD NEIGHBOUR. And here's a pot of good
double beer, neighbour; drink, and fear not
your man.
HORNER. Let it come, i' faith, and I'll pledge you
all; and a fig for Peter!
FIRST PRENTICE. Here, Peter, I drink to thee; and
be not afraid.
SECOND PRENTICE. Be merry, Peter, and fear not
thy master: fight for credit of the prentices.
PETER. I thank you all. Drink, and pray for me,
I pray you; for I think I have taken my last
draught in this world. Here, Robin, an if I die, I
give thee my apron; and, Will, thou shalt have
my hammer; and here, Tom, take all the money
that I have. O Lord bless me, I pray God! for I
am never able to deal with my master, he hath
learnt so much fence already.
SALISBURY. Come, leave your drinking and fall to
blows. Sirrah, what's thy name?
PETER. Peter, forsooth.
SALISBURY. Peter? What more?
PETER. Thump.
SALISBURY. Thump? Then see thou thump thy
master well.
HORNER. Masters, I am come hither, as it were,
upon my man's instigation, to prove him a
knave and myself an honest man; and touching
the Duke of York, I will take my death I never
meant him any ill, nor the King, nor the Queen;
and therefore, Peter, have at thee with a
downright blow!
YORK. Dispatch-this knave's tongue begins
to double.

Sound, trumpets, alarum to the combatants!

Alarum. They fight and PETER strikes him down

HORNER. Hold, Peter, hold! I confess, I confess
treason.   *Dies.*
YORK. Take away his weapon. Fellow, thank God,
and the good wine in thy master's way.
PETER. O God, have I overcome mine enemies
in this presence? O Peter, thou hast prevail'd
in right!
KING HENRY. Go, take hence that traitor from
our sight,
For by his death we do perceive his guilt;
And God in justice hath reveal'd to us
The truth and innocence of this poor fellow,
Which he had thought to have
murder'd wrongfully.
Come, fellow, follow us for thy reward.

Sound a flourish. Exeunt.

✿ SCENE IV ✿
London. A street

Enter HUMPHREY, DUKE OF GLOUCESTER and his
Men, in mourning cloaks

GLOUCESTER. Thus sometimes hath the brightest
day a cloud,
And after summer evermore succeeds
Barren winter, with his wrathful nipping cold;
So cares and joys abound, as seasons fleet.
Sirs, what's o'clock?
SERVING-MAN. Ten, my lord.
GLOUCESTER. Ten is the hour that was
appointed me
To watch the coming of my punish'd duchess.
Uneath may she endure the flinty streets
To tread them with her tender-feeling feet.
Sweet Nell, ill can thy noble mind abrook
The abject people gazing on thy face,
With envious looks, laughing at thy shame,
That erst did follow thy proud chariot wheels
When thou didst ride in triumph through
the streets.
But, soft! I think she comes, and I'll prepare
My tear-stain'd eyes to see her miseries.

Enter the DUCHESS OF GLOUCESTER in a white sheet,
and a taper burning in her hand, with SIR JOHN STANLEY,
the SHERIFF, and Officers

SERVING-MAN. So please your Grace, we'll take
her from the sheriff.
GLOUCESTER. No, stir not for your lives; let her
pass by.

DUCHESS. Come you, my lord, to see my
open shame?
Now thou dost penance too. Look how
they gaze!
See how the giddy multitude do point
And nod their heads and throw their eyes
on thee;
Ah, Gloucester, hide thee from their
hateful looks,
And, in thy closet pent up, rue my shame
And ban thine enemies, both mine and thine!
GLOUCESTER. Be patient, gentle Nell; forget
this grief.
DUCHESS. Ah, Gloucester, teach me to
forget myself!
For whilst I think I am thy married wife
And thou a prince, Protector of this land,
Methinks I should not thus be led along,
Mail'd up in shame, with papers on my back,
And follow'd with a rabble that rejoice
To see my tears and hear my deep-fet groans.
The ruthless flint doth cut my tender feet,
And when I start, the envious people laugh
And bid me be advised how I tread.
Ah, Humphrey, can I bear this shameful yoke?
Trow'st thou that e'er I'll look upon the world
Or count them happy that enjoy the sun?
No; dark shall be my light and night my day;
To think upon my pomp shall be my hell.
Sometimes I'll say I am Duke Humphrey's wife,
And he a prince, and ruler of the land;
Yet so he rul'd, and such a prince he was,
As he stood by whilst I, his forlorn duchess,
Was made a wonder and a pointing-stock
To every idle rascal follower.
But be thou mild, and blush not at my shame,
Nor stir at nothing till the axe of death
Hang over thee, as sure it shortly will.
For Suffolk-he that can do all in all
With her that hateth thee and hates us all-
And York, and impious Beaufort, that
false priest,
Have all lim'd bushes to betray thy wings,
And, fly thou how thou canst, they'll tangle thee.
But fear not thou until thy foot be snar'd,
Nor never seek prevention of thy foes.
GLOUCESTER. Ah, Nell, forbear! Thou aimest
all awry.
I must offend before I be attainted;
And had I twenty times so many foes,
And each of them had twenty times their power,
All these could not procure me any scathe
So long as I am loyal, true, and crimeless.

Wouldst have me rescue thee from
this reproach?
Why, yet thy scandal were not wip'd away,
But I in danger for the breach of law.
Thy greatest help is quiet, gentle Nell.
I pray thee sort thy heart to patience;
These few days' wonder will be quickly worn.

Enter a HERALD

HERALD. I summon your Grace to his
Majesty's Parliament,
Holden at Bury the first of this next month.
GLOUCESTER. And my consent ne'er ask'd
herein before!
This is close dealing. Well, I will be there. *[Exit
HERALD]*
My Nell, I take my leave-and, master sheriff,
Let not her penance exceed the
King's commission.
SHERIFF. An't please your Grace, here my
commission stays;
And Sir John Stanley is appointed now
To take her with him to the Isle of Man.
GLOUCESTER. Must you, Sir John, protect my
lady here?
STANLEY. So am I given in charge, may't please
your Grace.
GLOUCESTER. Entreat her not the worse in that
I pray
You use her well; the world may laugh again,
And I may live to do you kindness if
You do it her. And so, Sir John, farewell.
DUCHESS. What, gone, my lord, and bid me
not farewell!
GLOUCESTER. Witness my tears, I cannot stay
to speak.

Exeunt GLOUCESTER and SERVANTS

DUCHESS. Art thou gone too? All comfort go with
thee!
For none abides with me. My joy is death-
Death, at whose name I oft have been afeard,
Because I wish'd this world's eternity.
Stanley, I prithee go, and take me hence;
I care not whither, for I beg no favour,
Only convey me where thou art commanded.
STANLEY. Why, madam, that is to the Isle of Man,
There to be us'd according to your state.
DUCHESS. That's bad enough, for I am
but reproach-
And shall I then be us'd reproachfully?
STANLEY. Like to a duchess and Duke
Humphrey's lady;
According to that state you shall be us'd.
DUCHESS. Sheriff, farewell, and better than I fare,

Although thou hast been conduct of my shame.
SHERIFF. It is my office; and, madam, pardon me.
DUCHESS. Ay, ay, farewell; thy office is discharg'd.
Come, Stanley, shall we go?
STANLEY. Madam, your penance done, throw off
this sheet,
And go we to attire you for our journey.
DUCHESS. My shame will not be shifted with
my sheet.
No, it will hang upon my richest robes
And show itself, attire me how I can.
Go, lead the way; I long to see my prison.

Exeunt.

◈ ACT III ◈

ꙮ SCENE I ꙮ
The Abbey at Bury St. Edmunds

Sound a sennet. Enter the KING, the QUEEN, CARDINAL,
SUFFOLK, YORK, BUCKINGHAM, SALISBURY, and
WARWICK, to the Parliament

KING HENRY. I muse my Lord of Gloucester is
not come.
'Tis not his wont to be the hindmost man,
Whate'er occasion keeps him from us now.
QUEEN. Can you not see, or will ye not observe
The strangeness of his alter'd countenance?
With what a majesty he bears himself;
How insolent of late he is become,
How proud, how peremptory, and
unlike himself?
We know the time since he was mild and affable,
And if we did but glance a far-off look
Immediately he was upon his knee,
That all the court admir'd him for submission.
But meet him now and be it in the morn,
When every one will give the time of day,
He knits his brow and shows an angry eye
And passeth by with stiff unbowed knee,
Disdaining duty that to us belongs.
Small curs are not regarded when they grin,
But great men tremble when the lion roars,
And Humphrey is no little man in England.
First note that he is near you in descent,
And should you fall, he is the next will mount;
Me seemeth, then, it is no policy-
Respecting what a rancorous mind he bears,
And his advantage following your decease-
That he should come about your royal person

Or be admitted to your Highness' Council.
By flattery hath he won the commons' hearts;
And when he please to make commotion,
'Tis to be fear'd they all will follow him.
Now 'tis the spring, and weeds are shallow-
rooted;
Suffer them now, and they'll o'ergrow
the garden
And choke the herbs for want of husbandry.
The reverent care I bear unto my lord
Made me collect these dangers in the Duke.
If it be fond, call it a woman's fear;
Which fear if better reasons can supplant,
I will subscribe, and say I wrong'd the Duke.
My Lord of Suffolk, Buckingham, and York,
Reprove my allegation if you can,
Or else conclude my words effectual.
SUFFOLK. Well hath your Highness seen into
this duke;
And had I first been put to speak my mind,
I think I should have told your Grace's tale.
The Duchess, by his subornation,
Upon my life, began her devilish practices;
Or if he were not privy to those faults,
Yet by reputing of his high descent-
As next the King he was successive heir-
And such high vaunts of his nobility,
Did instigate the bedlam brainsick Duchess
By wicked means to frame our sovereign's fall.
Smooth runs the water where the brook is deep,
And in his simple show he harbours treason.
The fox barks not when he would steal
the lamb.
No, no, my sovereign, Gloucester is a man
Unsounded yet, and full of deep deceit.
CARDINAL. Did he not, contrary to form of law,
Devise strange deaths for small offences done?
YORK. And did he not, in his protectorship,
Levy great sums of money through the realm
For soldiers' pay in France, and never sent it?
By means whereof the towns each day revolted.
BUCKINGHAM. Tut, these are petty faults to
faults unknown
Which time will bring to light in smooth
Duke Humphrey.
KING HENRY. My lords, at once: the care you
have of us,
To mow down thorns that would annoy
our foot,
Is worthy praise; but shall I speak
my conscience?
Our kinsman Gloucester is as innocent
From meaning treason to our royal person

As is the sucking lamb or harmless dove:
The Duke is virtuous, mild, and too well given
To dream on evil or to work my downfall.
QUEEN. Ah, what's more dangerous than this
    fond affiance?
Seems he a dove? His feathers are but borrow'd,
For he's disposed as the hateful raven.
Is he a lamb? His skin is surely lent him,
For he's inclin'd as is the ravenous wolf.
Who cannot steal a shape that means deceit?
Take heed, my lord; the welfare of us all
Hangs on the cutting short that fraudful man.

Enter SOMERSET

SOMERSET. All health unto my
    gracious sovereign!
KING HENRY. Welcome, Lord Somerset. What
    news from France?
SOMERSET. That all your interest in
    those territories
Is utterly bereft you; all is lost.
KING HENRY. Cold news, Lord Somerset; but
    God's will be done!
YORK. *[Aside]* Cold news for me; for I had hope
    of France
As firmly as I hope for fertile England.
Thus are my blossoms blasted in the bud,
And caterpillars eat my leaves away;
But I will remedy this gear ere long,
Or sell my title for a glorious grave.

Enter GLOUCESTER

GLOUCESTER. All happiness unto my lord
    the King!
Pardon, my liege, that I have stay'd so long.
SUFFOLK. Nay, Gloucester, know that thou art
    come too soon,
Unless thou wert more loyal than thou art.
I do arrest thee of high treason here.
GLOUCESTER. Well, Suffolk, thou shalt not see
    me blush
Nor change my countenance for this arrest:
A heart unspotted is not easily daunted.
The purest spring is not so free from mud
As I am clear from treason to my sovereign.
Who can accuse me? Wherein am I guilty?
YORK. 'Tis thought, my lord, that you took bribes
    of France
And, being Protector, stay'd the soldiers' pay;
By means whereof his Highness hath
    lost France.
GLOUCESTER. Is it but thought so? What are they
    that think it?
I never robb'd the soldiers of their pay
Nor ever had one penny bribe from France.

So help me God, as I have watch'd the night-
Ay, night by night-in studying good for England!
That doit that e'er I wrested from the King,
Or any groat I hoarded to my use,
Be brought against me at my trial-day!
No; many a pound of mine own proper store,
Because I would not tax the needy commons,
Have I dispursed to the garrisons,
And never ask'd for restitution.
CARDINAL. It serves you well, my lord, to say
    so much.
GLOUCESTER. I say no more than truth, so help
    me God!
YORK. In your protectorship you did devise
Strange tortures for offenders, never heard of,
That England was defam'd by tyranny.
GLOUCESTER. Why, 'tis well known that whiles I
    was Protector
Pity was all the fault that was in me;
For I should melt at an offender's tears,
And lowly words were ransom for their fault.
Unless it were a bloody murderer,
Or foul felonious thief that fleec'd
    poor passengers,
I never gave them condign punishment.
Murder indeed, that bloody sin, I tortur'd
Above the felon or what trespass else.
SUFFOLK. My lord, these faults are easy,
    quickly answer'd;
But mightier crimes are laid unto your charge,
Whereof you cannot easily purge yourself.
I do arrest you in His Highness' name,
And here commit you to my Lord Cardinal
To keep until your further time of trial.
KING HENRY. My Lord of Gloucester, 'tis my
    special hope
That you will clear yourself from all suspense.
My conscience tells me you are innocent.
GLOUCESTER. Ah, gracious lord, these days
    are dangerous!
Virtue is chok'd with foul ambition,
And charity chas'd hence by rancour's hand;
Foul subornation is predominant,
And equity exil'd your Highness' land.
I know their complot is to have my life;
And if my death might make this island happy
And prove the period of their tyranny,
I would expend it with all willingness.
But mine is made the prologue to their play;
For thousands more that yet suspect no peril
Will not conclude their plotted tragedy.
Beaufort's red sparkling eyes blab his
    heart's malice,

And Suffolk's cloudy brow his stormy hate;
Sharp Buckingham unburdens with his tongue
The envious load that lies upon his heart;
And dogged York, that reaches at the moon,
Whose overweening arm I have pluck'd back,
By false accuse doth level at my life.
And you, my sovereign lady, with the rest,
Causeless have laid disgraces on my head,
And with your best endeavour have stirr'd up
My liefest liege to be mine enemy;
Ay, all of you have laid your heads together-
Myself had notice of your conventicles-
And all to make away my guiltless life.
I shall not want false witness to condemn me
Nor store of treasons to augment my guilt.
The ancient proverb will be well effected:
'A staff is quickly found to beat a dog.'
CARDINAL. My liege, his railing is intolerable.
　If those that care to keep your royal person
　From treason's secret knife and traitor's rage
　Be thus upbraided, chid, and rated at,
　And the offender granted scope of speech,
　'Twill make them cool in zeal unto your Grace.
SUFFOLK. Hath he not twit our sovereign
　lady here
　With ignominious words, though
　clerkly couch'd,
　As if she had suborned some to swear
　False allegations to o'erthrow his state?
QUEEN. But I can give the loser leave to chide.
GLOUCESTER. Far truer spoke than meant: I
　lose indeed.
　Beshrew the winners, for they play'd me false!
　And well such losers may have leave to speak.
BUCKINGHAM. He'll wrest the sense, and hold us
　here all day.
　Lord Cardinal, he is your prisoner.
CARDINAL. Sirs, take away the Duke, and guard
　him sure.
GLOUCESTER. Ah, thus King Henry throws away
　his crutch
　Before his legs be firm to bear his body!
　Thus is the shepherd beaten from thy side,
　And wolves are gnarling who shall gnaw
　thee first.
　Ah, that my fear were false! ah, that it were!
　For, good King Henry, thy decay I fear.
　　　　　　　　　　　　　　　Exit, guarded.
KING HENRY. My lords, what to your wisdoms
　seemeth best
　Do or undo, as if ourself were here.
QUEEN. What, will your Highness leave
　the Parliament?

KING HENRY. Ay, Margaret; my heart is drown'd
　with grief,
　Whose flood begins to flow within mine eyes;
　My body round engirt with misery-
　For what's more miserable than discontent?
　Ah, uncle Humphrey, in thy face I see
　The map of honour, truth, and loyalty!
　And yet, good Humphrey, is the hour to come
　That e'er I prov'd thee false or fear'd thy faith.
　What louring star now envies thy estate
　That these great lords, and Margaret
　our Queen,
　Do seek subversion of thy harmless life?
　Thou never didst them wrong, nor no
　man wrong;
　And as the butcher takes away the calf,
　And binds the wretch, and beats it when
　it strays,
　Bearing it to the bloody slaughter-house,
　Even so, remorseless, have they borne
　him hence;
　And as the dam runs lowing up and down,
　Looking the way her harmless young one went,
　And can do nought but wail her darling's loss,
　Even so myself bewails good Gloucester's case
　With sad unhelpful tears, and with dimm'd eyes
　Look after him, and cannot do him good,
　So mighty are his vowed enemies.
　His fortunes I will weep, and 'twixt each groan
　Say 'Who's a traitor? Gloucester he is none.'
　　　　　　　　　　　　　　　Exit.
QUEEN. Free lords, cold snow melts with the
　sun's hot beams:
　Henry my lord is cold in great affairs,
　Too full of foolish pity; and Gloucester's show
　Beguiles him as the mournful crocodile
　With sorrow snares relenting passengers;
　Or as the snake, roll'd in a flow'ring bank,
　With shining checker'd slough, doth sting a child
　That for the beauty thinks it excellent.
　Believe me, lords, were none more wise than I-
　And yet herein I judge mine own wit good-
　This Gloucester should be quickly rid the world
　To rid us from the fear we have of him.
CARDINAL. That he should die is worthy policy;
　But yet we want a colour for his death.
　'Tis meet he be condemn'd by course of law.
SUFFOLK. But, in my mind, that were no policy:
　The King will labour still to save his life;
　The commons haply rise to save his life;
　And yet we have but trivial argument,
　More than mistrust, that shows him
　worthy death.

YORK. So that, by this, you would not have
   him die.
SUFFOLK. Ah, York, no man alive so fain as I!
YORK. 'Tis York that hath more reason for
   his death.
   But, my Lord Cardinal, and you, my Lord
    of Suffolk,
   Say as you think, and speak it from your souls:
   Were't not all one, an empty eagle were set
   To guard the chicken from a hungry kite
   As place Duke Humphrey for the King's
    Protector?
QUEEN. So the poor chicken should be sure
   of death.
SUFFOLK. Madam, 'tis true; and were't not
   madness then
   To make the fox surveyor of the fold?
   Who being accus'd a crafty murderer,
   His guilt should be but idly posted over,
   Because his purpose is not executed.
   No; let him die, in that he is a fox,
   By nature prov'd an enemy to the flock,
   Before his chaps be stain'd with crimson blood,
   As Humphrey, prov'd by reasons, to my liege.
   And do not stand on quillets how to slay him;
   Be it by gins, by snares, by subtlety,
   Sleeping or waking, 'tis no matter how,
   So he be dead; for that is good deceit
   Which mates him first that first intends deceit.
QUEEN. Thrice-noble Suffolk, 'tis
   resolutely spoke.
SUFFOLK. Not resolute, except so much
   were done,
   For things are often spoke and seldom meant;
   But that my heart accordeth with my tongue,
   Seeing the deed is meritorious,
   And to preserve my sovereign from his foe,
   Say but the word, and I will be his priest.
CARDINAL. But I would have him dead, my Lord
   of Suffolk,
   Ere you can take due orders for a priest;
   Say you consent and censure well the deed,
   And I'll provide his executioner-
   I tender so the safety of my liege.
SUFFOLK. Here is my hand, the deed is
   worthy doing.
QUEEN. And so say I.
YORK. And I. And now we three have spoke it,
   It skills not greatly who impugns our doom.

       Enter a POST

POST. Great lords, from Ireland am I come amain
   To signify that rebels there are up
   And put the Englishmen unto the sword.

   Send succours, lords, and stop the rage betime,
   Before the wound do grow uncurable;
   For, being green, there is great hope of help.
CARDINAL. A breach that craves a quick
   expedient stop!
   What counsel give you in this weighty cause?
YORK. That Somerset be sent as Regent thither;
   'Tis meet that lucky ruler be employ'd,
   Witness the fortune he hath had in France.
SOMERSET. If York, with all his far-fet policy,
   Had been the Regent there instead of me,
   He never would have stay'd in France so long.
YORK. No, not to lose it all as thou hast done.
   I rather would have lost my life betimes
   Than bring a burden of dishonour home
   By staying there so long till all were lost.
   Show me one scar character'd on thy skin:
   Men's flesh preserv'd so whole do seldom win.
QUEEN. Nay then, this spark will prove a
   raging fire,
   If wind and fuel be brought to feed it with;
   No more, good York; sweet Somerset, be still.
   Thy fortune, York, hadst thou been
    Regent there,
   Might happily have prov'd far worse than his.
YORK. What, worse than nought? Nay, then a
   shame take all!
SOMERSET. And in the number, thee that
   wishest shame!
CARDINAL. My Lord of York, try what your
   fortune is.
   Th' uncivil kerns of Ireland are in arms
   And temper clay with blood of Englishmen;
   To Ireland will you lead a band of men,
   Collected choicely, from each county some,
   And try your hap against the Irishmen?
YORK. I will, my lord, so please his Majesty.
SUFFOLK. Why, our authority is his consent,
   And what we do establish he confirms;
   Then, noble York, take thou this task in hand.
YORK. I am content; provide me soldiers, lords,
   Whiles I take order for mine own affairs.
SUFFOLK. A charge, Lord York, that I will
   see perform'd.
   But now return we to the false Duke Humphrey.
CARDINAL. No more of him; for I will deal
   with him
   That henceforth he shall trouble us no more.
   And so break off; the day is almost spent.
   Lord Suffolk, you and I must talk of that event.
YORK. My Lord of Suffolk, within fourteen days
   At Bristol I expect my soldiers;
   For there I'll ship them all for Ireland.

SUFFOLK. I'll see it truly done, my Lord of York.

Exeunt all but YORK.

YORK. Now, York, or never, steel thy
  fearful thoughts
  And change misdoubt to resolution;
  Be that thou hop'st to be; or what thou art
  Resign to death-it is not worth th' enjoying.
  Let pale-fac'd fear keep with the mean-born man
  And find no harbour in a royal heart.
  Faster than spring-time show'rs comes thought
    on thought,
  And not a thought but thinks on dignity.
  My brain, more busy than the labouring spider,
  Weaves tedious snares to trap mine enemies.
  Well, nobles, well, 'tis politicly done
  To send me packing with an host of men.
  I fear me you but warm the starved snake,
  Who, cherish'd in your breasts, will sting
    your hearts.
  'Twas men I lack'd, and you will give them me;
  I take it kindly. Yet be well assur'd
  You put sharp weapons in a madman's hands.
  Whiles I in Ireland nourish a mighty band,
  I will stir up in England some black storm
  Shall blow ten thousand souls to heaven or hell;
  And this fell tempest shall not cease to rage
  Until the golden circuit on my head,
  Like to the glorious sun's transparent beams,
  Do calm the fury of this mad-bred flaw.
  And for a minister of my intent
  I have seduc'd a headstrong Kentishman,
  John Cade of Ashford,
  To make commotion, as full well he can,
  Under the tide of John Mortimer.
  In Ireland have I seen this stubborn Cade
  Oppose himself against a troop of kerns,
  And fought so long till that his thighs with darts
  Were almost like a sharp-quill'd porpentine;
  And in the end being rescu'd, I have seen
  Him caper upright like a wild Morisco,
  Shaking the bloody darts as he his bells.
  Full often, like a shag-hair'd crafty kern,
  Hath he conversed with the enemy,
  And undiscover'd come to me again
  And given me notice of their villainies.
  This devil here shall be my substitute;
  For that John Mortimer, which now is dead,
  In face, in gait, in speech, he doth resemble.
  By this I shall perceive the commons' mind,
  How they affect the house and claim of York.
  Say he be taken, rack'd, and tortured;
  I know no pain they can inflict upon him
  Will make him say I mov'd him to those arms.

Say that he thrive, as 'tis great like he will,
  Why, then from Ireland come I with my strength,
  And reap the harvest which that rascal sow'd;
  For Humphrey being dead, as he shall be,
  And Henry put apart, the next for me.

Exit.

✱ SCENE II ✿
Bury St. Edmunds. A room of state

*Enter two or three MURDERERS running over the stage, from
the murder of GLOUCESTER*

FIRST MURDERER. Run to my Lord of Suffolk; let
  him know
  We have dispatch'd the Duke, as
  he commanded.
SECOND MURDERER. O that it were to do! What
  have we done?
  Didst ever hear a man so penitent?

Enter SUFFOLK

FIRST MURDERER. Here comes my lord.
SUFFOLK. Now, sirs, have you dispatch'd
  this thing?
FIRST MURDERER. Ay, my good lord, he's dead.
SUFFOLK. Why, that's well said. Go, get you to
  my house;
  I will reward you for this venturous deed.
  The King and all the peers are here at hand.
  Have you laid fair the bed? Is all things well,
  According as I gave directions?
FIRST MURDERER. 'Tis, my good lord.
SUFFOLK. Away! be gone. *Exeunt MURDERERS.*

*Sound trumpets. Enter the KING, the QUEEN, CARDINAL,
SOMERSET, with Attendants*

KING HENRY. Go call our uncle to our
  presence straight;
  Say we intend to try his Grace to-day,
  If he be guilty, as 'tis published.
SUFFOLK. I'll call him presently, my noble lord.

Exit.

KING HENRY. Lords, take your places; and, I pray
  you all,
  Proceed no straiter 'gainst our uncle Gloucester
  Than from true evidence, of good esteem,
  He be approv'd in practice culpable.
QUEEN. God forbid any malice should prevail
  That faultless may condemn a nobleman!
  Pray God he may acquit him of suspicion!
KING HENRY. I thank thee, Meg; these words
  content me much.

Re-enter SUFFOLK

How now! Why look'st thou pale? Why
    tremblest thou?
Where is our uncle? What's the matter, Suffolk?
SUFFOLK. Dead in his bed, my lord; Gloucester
    is dead.
QUEEN. Marry, God forfend!
CARDINAL. God's secret judgment! I did
    dream to-night
    The Duke was dumb and could not speak
    a word.

            The KING *swoons*

QUEEN. How fares my lord? Help, lords! The King
    is dead.
SOMERSET. Rear up his body; wring him by
    the nose.
QUEEN. Run, go, help, help! O Henry, ope
    thine eyes!
SUFFOLK. He doth revive again; madam,
    be patient.
KING. O heavenly God!
QUEEN. How fares my gracious lord?
SUFFOLK. Comfort, my sovereign! Gracious
    Henry, comfort!
KING HENRY. What, doth my Lord of Suffolk
    comfort me?
    Came he right now to sing a raven's note,
    Whose dismal tune bereft my vital pow'rs;
    And thinks he that the chirping of a wren,
    By crying comfort from a hollow breast,
    Can chase away the first conceived sound?
    Hide not thy poison with such sug'red words;
    Lay not thy hands on me; forbear, I say,
    Their touch affrights me as a serpent's sting.
    Thou baleful messenger, out of my sight!
    Upon thy eye-balls murderous tyranny
    Sits in grim majesty to fright the world.
    Look not upon me, for thine eyes are wounding;
    Yet do not go away; come, basilisk,
    And kill the innocent gazer with thy sight;
    For in the shade of death I shall find joy-
    In life but double death,now Gloucester's dead.
QUEEN. Why do you rate my Lord of Suffolk thus?
    Although the Duke was enemy to him,
    Yet he most Christian-like laments his death;
    And for myself-foe as he was to me-
    Might liquid tears, or heart-offending groans,
    Or blood-consuming sighs, recall his life,
    I would be blind with weeping, sick with groans,
    Look pale as primrose with blood-drinking sighs,
    And all to have the noble Duke alive.
    What know I how the world may deem of me?
    For it is known we were but hollow friends:
    It may be judg'd I made the Duke away;

So shall my name with slander's tongue
    be wounded,
And princes' courts be fill'd with my reproach.
This get I by his death. Ay me, unhappy!
To be a queen and crown'd with infamy!
KING HENRY. Ah, woe is me for Gloucester,
    wretched man!
QUEEN. Be woe for me, more wretched than
    he is.
    What, dost thou turn away, and hide thy face?
    I am no loathsome leper-look on me.
    What, art thou like the adder waxen deaf?
    Be poisonous too, and kill thy forlorn Queen.
    Is all thy comfort shut in Gloucester's tomb?
    Why, then Dame Margaret was ne'er thy joy.
    Erect his statue and worship it,
    And make my image but an alehouse sign.
    Was I for this nigh wreck'd upon the sea,
    And twice by awkward wind from England's bank
    Drove back again unto my native clime?
    What boded this but well-forewarning wind
    Did seem to say 'Seek not a scorpion's nest,
    Nor set no footing on this unkind shore'?
    What did I then but curs'd the gentle gusts,
    And he that loos'd them forth their brazen caves;
    And bid them blow towards England's
    blessed shore,
    Or turn our stern upon a dreadful rock?
    Yet Aeolus would not be a murderer,
    But left that hateful office unto thee.
    The pretty-vaulting sea refus'd to drown me,
    Knowing that thou wouldst have me drown'd
    on shore
    With tears as salt as sea through thy unkindness;
    The splitting rocks cow'r'd in the sinking sands
    And would not dash me with their ragged sides,
    Because thy flinty heart, more hard than they,
    Might in thy palace perish Margaret.
    As far as I could ken thy chalky cliffs,
    When from thy shore the tempest beat us back,
    I stood upon the hatches in the storm;
    And when the dusky sky began to rob
    My earnest-gaping sight of thy land's view,
    I took a costly jewel from my neck-
    A heart it was, bound in with diamonds-
    And threw it towards thy land. The sea
    receiv'd it;
    And so I wish'd thy body might my heart.
    And even with this I lost fair England's view,
    And bid mine eyes be packing with my heart,
    And call'd them blind and dusky spectacles
    For losing ken of Albion's wished coast.
    How often have I tempted Suffolk's tongue-

The agent of thy foul inconstancy-
To sit and witch me, as Ascanius did
When he to madding Dido would unfold
His father's acts commenc'd in burning Troy!
Am I not witch'd like her? Or thou not false
  like him?
Ay me, I can no more! Die, Margaret,
For Henry weeps that thou dost live so long.

Noise within. Enter WARWICK, SALISBURY, and many
commons

WARWICK. It is reported, mighty sovereign,
  That good Duke Humphrey traitorously
    is murd'red
  By Suffolk and the Cardinal Beaufort's means.
  The commons, like an angry hive of bees
  That want their leader, scatter up and down
  And care not who they sting in his revenge.
  Myself have calm'd their spleenful mutiny
  Until they hear the order of his death.
KING HENRY. That he is dead, good Warwick, 'tis
  too true;
  But how he died God knows, not Henry.
  Enter his chamber, view his breathless corpse,
  And comment then upon his sudden death.
WARWICK. That shall I do, my liege.
  Stay, Salisbury,
  With the rude multitude till I return. *Exit.*

Exit SALISBURY with the commons.

KING HENRY. O Thou that judgest all things, stay
  my thoughts-
  My thoughts that labour to persuade my soul
  Some violent hands were laid on
    Humphrey's life!
  If my suspect be false, forgive me, God;
  For judgment only doth belong to Thee.
  Fain would I go to chafe his paly lips
  With twenty thousand kisses and to drain
  Upon his face an ocean of salt tears
  To tell my love unto his dumb deaf trunk;
  And with my fingers feel his hand un-feeling;
  But all in vain are these mean obsequies;
  And to survey his dead and earthy image,
  What were it but to make my sorrow greater?

Bed put forth with the body. Enter WARWICK

WARWICK. Come hither, gracious sovereign, view
  this body.
KING HENRY. That is to see how deep my grave
  is made;
  For with his soul fled all my worldly solace,
  For, seeing him, I see my life in death.
WARWICK. As surely as my soul intends to live
  With that dread King that took our state
    upon Him

To free us from his Father's wrathful curse,
  I do believe that violent hands were laid
  Upon the life of this thrice-famed Duke.
SUFFOLK. A dreadful oath, sworn with a
  solemn tongue!
  What instance gives Lord Warwick for his vow?
WARWICK. See how the blood is settled in
  his face.
  Oft have I seen a timely-parted ghost,
  Of ashy semblance, meagre, pale, and bloodless,
  Being all descended to the labouring heart,
  Who, in the conflict that it holds with death,
  Attracts the same for aidance 'gainst the enemy,
  Which with the heart there cools, and
    ne'er returneth
  To blush and beautify the cheek again.
  But see, his face is black and full of blood;
  His eye-balls further out than when he liv'd,
  Staring full ghastly like a strangled man;
  His hair uprear'd, his nostrils stretch'd
    with struggling;
  His hands abroad display'd, as one that grasp'd
  And tugg'd for life, and was by strength subdu'd.
  Look, on the sheets his hair, you see, is sticking;
  His well-proportion'd beard made rough
    and rugged,
  Like to the summer's corn by tempest lodged.
  It cannot be but he was murd'red here:
  The least of all these signs were probable.
SUFFOLK. Why, Warwick, who should do the
  Duke to death?
  Myself and Beaufort had him in protection;
  And we, I hope, sir, are no murderers.
WARWICK. But both of you were vow'd Duke
  Humphrey's foes;
  And you, forsooth, had the good Duke to keep.
  'Tis like you would not feast him like a friend;
  And 'tis well seen he found an enemy.
QUEEN. Then you, belike, suspect
  these noblemen
  As guilty of Duke Humphrey's timeless death.
WARWICK. Who finds the heifer dead and
  bleeding fresh,
  And sees fast by a butcher with an axe,
  But will suspect 'twas he that made
    the slaughter?
  Who finds the partridge in the puttock's nest
  But may imagine how the bird was dead,
  Although the kite soar with unbloodied beak?
  Even so suspicious is this tragedy.
QUEEN. Are you the butcher, Suffolk? Where's
  your knife?
  Is Beaufort term'd a kite? Where are his talons?

SUFFOLK. I wear no knife to slaughter
    sleeping men;
  But here's a vengeful sword, rusted with ease,
  That shall be scoured in his rancorous heart
  That slanders me with murder's crimson badge.
  Say if thou dar'st, proud Lord of Warwickshire,
  That I am faulty in Duke Humphrey's death.
      Exeunt CARDINAL, SOMERSET, and Others.

WARWICK. What dares not Warwick, if false
    Suffolk dare him?

QUEEN. He dares not calm his
    contumelious spirit,
  Nor cease to be an arrogant controller,
  Though Suffolk dare him twenty
    thousand times.

WARWICK. Madam, be still-with reverence may
    I say;
  For every word you speak in his behalf
  Is slander to your royal dignity.

SUFFOLK. Blunt-witted lord, ignoble
    in demeanour,
  If ever lady wrong'd her lord so much,
  Thy mother took into her blameful bed
  Some stern untutor'd churl, and noble stock
  Was graft with crab-tree slip, whose fruit
    thou art,
  And never of the Nevils' noble race.

WARWICK. But that the guilt of murder
    bucklers thee,
  And I should rob the deathsman of his fee,
  Quitting thee thereby of ten thousand shames,
  And that my sovereign's presence makes
    me mild,
  I would, false murd'rous coward, on thy knee
  Make thee beg pardon for thy passed speech
  And say it was thy mother that thou meant'st,
  That thou thyself was born in bastardy;
  And, after all this fearful homage done,
  Give thee thy hire and send thy soul to hell,
  Pernicious blood-sucker of sleeping men.

SUFFOLK. Thou shalt be waking while I shed
    thy blood,
  If from this presence thou dar'st go with me.

WARWICK. Away even now, or I will drag
    thee hence.
  Unworthy though thou art, I'll cope with thee,
  And do some service to Duke
    Humphrey's ghost.
      Exeunt SUFFOLK and WARWICK.

KING HENRY. What stronger breastplate than a
    heart untainted?
  Thrice is he arm'd that hath his quarrel just;
  And he but naked, though lock'd up in steel,

  Whose conscience with injustice is corrupted.
      A noise within

QUEEN. What noise is this?
    Re-enter SUFFOLK and WARWICK, with their weapons
        drawn

KING. Why, how now, lords, your wrathful
    weapons drawn
  Here in our presence! Dare you be so bold?
  Why, what tumultuous clamour have we here?

SUFFOLK. The trait'rous Warwick, with the men
    of Bury,
  Set all upon me, mighty sovereign.
      Re-enter SALISBURY

SALISBURY. *[To the Commons within]* Sirs, stand apart,
    the King shall know your mind.
  Dread lord, the commons send you word by me
  Unless Lord Suffolk straight be done to death,
  Or banished fair England's territories,
  They will by violence tear him from your palace
  And torture him with grievous ling'ring death.
  They say by him the good Duke Humphrey died;
  They say in him they fear your Highness' death;
  And mere instinct of love and loyalty,
  Free from a stubborn opposite intent,
  As being thought to contradict your liking,
  Makes them thus forward in his banishment.
  They say, in care of your most royal person,
  That if your Highness should intend to sleep
  And charge that no man should disturb
    your rest,
  In pain of your dislike or pain of death,
  Yet, notwithstanding such a strait edict,
  Were there a serpent seen with forked tongue
  That slily glided towards your Majesty,
  It were but necessary you were wak'd,
  Lest, being suffer'd in that harmful slumber,
  The mortal worm might make the sleep eternal.
  And therefore do they cry, though you forbid,
  That they will guard you, whe'er you will or no,
  From such fell serpents as false Suffolk is;
  With whose envenomed and fatal sting
  Your loving uncle, twenty times his worth,
  They say, is shamefully bereft of life.

COMMONS. *[Within]* An answer from the King, my
    Lord of Salisbury!

SUFFOLK. 'Tis like the commons, rude
    unpolish'd hinds,
  Could send such message to their sovereign;
  But you, my lord, were glad to be employ'd,
  To show how quaint an orator you are.
  But all the honour Salisbury hath won
  Is that he was the lord ambassador
  Sent from a sort of tinkers to the King.

COMMONS. [*Within*] An answer from the King, or
  we will all break in!
KING HENRY. Go, Salisbury, and tell them all
  from me
  I thank them for their tender loving care;
  And had I not been cited so by them,
  Yet did I purpose as they do entreat;
  For sure my thoughts do hourly prophesy
  Mischance unto my state by Suffolk's means.
  And therefore by His Majesty I swear,
  Whose far unworthy deputy I am,
  He shall not breathe infection in this air
  But three days longer, on the pain of death.
                    Exit SALISBURY.
QUEEN. O Henry, let me plead for gentle Suffolk!
KING HENRY. Ungentle Queen, to call him
  gentle Suffolk!
  No more, I say; if thou dost plead for him,
  Thou wilt but add increase unto my wrath.
  Had I but said, I would have kept my word;
  But when I swear, it is irrevocable.
  If after three days' space thou here be'st found
  On any ground that I am ruler of,
  The world shall not be ransom for thy life.
  Come, Warwick, come, good Warwick, go
  with me;
  I have great matters to impart to thee.
         Exeunt all but the QUEEN and SUFFOLK.
QUEEN. Mischance and sorrow go along with you!
  Heart's discontent and sour affliction
  Be playfellows to keep you company!
  There's two of you; the devil make a third,
  And threefold vengeance tend upon your steps!
SUFFOLK. Cease, gentle Queen, these execrations,
  And let thy Suffolk take his heavy leave.
QUEEN. Fie, coward woman and soft-
  hearted wretch,
  Has thou not spirit to curse thine enemy?
SUFFOLK. A plague upon them! Wherefore should
  I curse them?
  Would curses kill as doth the mandrake's groan,
  I would invent as bitter searching terms,
  As curst, as harsh, and horrible to hear,
  Deliver'd strongly through my fixed teeth,
  With full as many signs of deadly hate,
  As lean-fac'd Envy in her loathsome cave.
  My tongue should stumble in mine
  earnest words,
  Mine eyes should sparkle like the beaten flint,
  Mine hair be fix'd on end, as one distract;
  Ay, every joint should seem to curse and ban;
  And even now my burden'd heart would break,
  Should I not curse them. Poison be their drink!

  Gall, worse than gall, the daintiest that
  they taste!
  Their sweetest shade a grove of cypress trees!
  Their chiefest prospect murd'ring basilisks!
  Their softest touch as smart as lizards' stings!
  Their music frightful as the serpent's hiss,
  And boding screech-owls make the consort full!
  All the foul terrors in dark-seated hell-
QUEEN. Enough, sweet Suffolk, thou
  torment'st thyself;
  And these dread curses, like the sun
  'gainst glass,
  Or like an overcharged gun, recoil,
  And turns the force of them upon thyself.
SUFFOLK. You bade me ban, and will you bid
  me leave?
  Now, by the ground that I am banish'd from,
  Well could I curse away a winter's night,
  Though standing naked on a mountain top
  Where biting cold would never let grass grow,
  And think it but a minute spent in sport.
QUEEN. O, let me entreat thee cease! Give me
  thy hand,
  That I may dew it with my mournful tears;
  Nor let the rain of heaven wet this place
  To wash away my woeful monuments.
  O, could this kiss be printed in thy hand,
  That thou might'st think upon these by the seal,
  Through whom a thousand sighs are breath'd
  for thee!
  So, get thee gone, that I may know my grief;
  'Tis but surmis'd whiles thou art standing by,
  As one that surfeits thinking on a want.
  I will repeal thee or, be well assur'd,
  Adventure to be banished myself;
  And banished I am, if but from thee.
  Go, speak not to me; even now be gone.
  O, go not yet! Even thus two friends condemn'd
  Embrace, and kiss, and take ten thousand leaves,
  Loather a hundred times to part than die.
  Yet now, farewell; and farewell life with thee!
SUFFOLK. Thus is poor Suffolk ten
  times banished,
  Once by the King and three times thrice by thee,
  'Tis not the land I care for, wert thou thence;
  A wilderness is populous enough,
  So Suffolk had thy heavenly company;
  For where thou art, there is the world itself,
  With every several pleasure in the world;
  And where thou art not, desolation.
  I can no more: Live thou to joy thy life;
  Myself no joy in nought but that thou liv'st.
                     Enter VAUX

QUEEN. Whither goes Vaux so fast? What news,
  I prithee?
VAUX. To signify unto his Majesty
  That Cardinal Beaufort is at point of death;
  For suddenly a grievous sickness took him
  That makes him gasp, and stare, and catch
    the air,
  Blaspheming God, and cursing men on earth.
  Sometime he talks as if Duke Humphrey's ghost
  Were by his side; sometime he calls the King
  And whispers to his pillow, as to him,
  The secrets of his overcharged soul;
  And I am sent to tell his Majesty
  That even now he cries aloud for him.
QUEEN. Go tell this heavy message to the King.
                                    Exit VAUX
  Ay me! What is this world! What news are these!
  But wherefore grieve I at an hour's poor loss,
  Omitting Suffolk's exile, my soul's treasure?
  Why only, Suffolk, mourn I not for thee,
  And with the southern clouds contend in tears-
  Theirs for the earth's increase, mine for
    my sorrows?
  Now get thee hence: the King, thou know'st,
    is coming;
  If thou be found by me, thou art but dead.
SUFFOLK. If I depart from thee I cannot live;
  And in thy sight to die, what were it else
  But like a pleasant slumber in thy lap?
  Here could I breathe my soul into the air,
  As mild and gentle as the cradle-babe
  Dying with mother's dug between its lips;
  Where, from thy sight, I should be raging mad
  And cry out for thee to close up mine eyes,
  To have thee with thy lips to stop my mouth;
  So shouldst thou either turn my flying soul,
  Or I should breathe it so into thy body,
  And then it liv'd in sweet Elysium.
  To die by thee were but to die in jest:
  From thee to die were torture more than death.
  O, let me stay, befall what may befall!
QUEEN. Away! Though parting be a
    fretful corrosive,
  It is applied to a deathful wound.
  To France, sweet Suffolk. Let me hear from thee;
  For whereso'er thou art in this world's globe
  I'll have an Iris that shall find thee out.
SUFFOLK. I go.
QUEEN. And take my heart with thee.
                          She kisses him
SUFFOLK. A jewel, lock'd into the woeful'st cask
  That ever did contain a thing of worth.
  Even as a splitted bark, so sunder we:

This way fall I to death.
QUEEN. This way for me.
                              Exeunt severally

✦ SCENE III ✦
London. CARDINAL BEAUFORT'S bedchamber

*Enter the KING, SALISBURY, and WARWICK, to the
CARDINAL in bed*

KING HENRY. How fares my lord? Speak,
  Beaufort, to thy sovereign.
CARDINAL. If thou be'st Death I'll give thee
    England's treasure,
  Enough to purchase such another island,
  So thou wilt let me live and feel no pain.
KING HENRY. Ah, what a sign it is of evil life
  Where death's approach is seen so terrible!
WARWICK. Beaufort, it is thy sovereign speaks
  to thee.
CARDINAL. Bring me unto my trial when you will.
  Died he not in his bed? Where should he die?
  Can I make men live, whe'er they will or no?
  O, torture me no more! I will confess.
  Alive again? Then show me where he is;
  I'll give a thousand pound to look upon him.
  He hath no eyes, the dust hath blinded them.
  Comb down his hair; look, look! it stands upright,
  Like lime-twigs set to catch my winged soul!
  Give me some drink; and bid the apothecary
  Bring the strong poison that I bought of him.
KING HENRY. O Thou eternal Mover of
    the heavens,
  Look with a gentle eye upon this wretch!
  O, beat away the busy meddling fiend
  That lays strong siege unto this wretch's soul,
  And from his bosom purge this black despair!
WARWICK. See how the pangs of death do make
  him grin.
SALISBURY. Disturb him not, let him
  pass peaceably.
KING HENRY. Peace to his soul, if God's good
  pleasure be!
  Lord Card'nal, if thou think'st on heaven's bliss,
  Hold up thy hand, make signal of thy hope.
  He dies, and makes no sign: O God, forgive him!
WARWICK. So bad a death argues a
  monstrous life.
KING HENRY. Forbear to judge, for we are
  sinners all.
  Close up his eyes, and draw the curtain close;
  And let us all to meditation.   *Exeunt*

❧ ACT IV ❧

❧ SCENE I ❧
The coast of Kent

Alarum. Fight at sea. Ordnance goes off. Enter a
LIEUTENANT, a SHIPMASTER and his MATE, and
WALTER WHITMORE, with Sailors; SUFFOLK and other
GENTLEMEN, as Prisoners

LIEUTENANT. The gaudy, blabbing, and
  remorseful day
  Is crept into the bosom of the sea;
  And now loud-howling wolves arouse the jades
  That drag the tragic melancholy night;
  Who with their drowsy, slow, and
    flagging wings
  Clip dead men's graves, and from their
    misty jaws
  Breathe foul contagious darkness in the air.
  Therefore bring forth the soldiers of our prize;
  For, whilst our pinnace anchors in the Downs,
  Here shall they make their ransom on
    the sand,
  Or with their blood stain this
    discoloured shore.
  Master, this prisoner freely give I thee;
  And thou that art his mate make boot of this;
  The other, Walter Whitmore, is thy share.
FIRST GENTLEMAN. What is my ransom,
  master, let me know?
MASTER. A thousand crowns, or else lay down
  your head.
MATE. And so much shall you give, or off
  goes yours.
LIEUTENANT. What, think you much to pay two
  thousand crowns,
  And bear the name and port of gentlemen?
  Cut both the villains' throats-for die you shall;
  The lives of those which we have lost in fight
  Be counterpois'd with such a petty sum!
FIRST GENTLEMAN. I'll give it, sir: and therefore
  spare my life.
SECOND GENTLEMAN. And so will I, and write
  home for it straight.
WHITMORE. I lost mine eye in laying the
  prize aboard,
  [To SUFFOLK] And therefore, to revenge it, shalt
  thou die;
  And so should these, if I might have my will.

LIEUTENANT. Be not so rash; take ransom, let
  him live.
SUFFOLK. Look on my George, I am a gentleman:
  Rate me at what thou wilt, thou shalt be paid.
WHITMORE. And so am I: my name is
  Walter Whitmore.
  How now! Why start'st thou? What, doth
  death affright?
SUFFOLK. Thy name affrights me, in whose sound
  is death.
  A cunning man did calculate my birth
  And told me that by water I should die;
  Yet let not this make thee be bloody-minded;
  Thy name is Gaultier, being rightly sounded.
WHITMORE. Gualtier or Walter, which it is I
  care not:
  Never yet did base dishonour blur our name,
  But with our sword we wip'd away the blot;
  Therefore, when merchant-like I sell revenge,
  Broke be my sword, my arms torn and defac'd,
  And I proclaim'd a coward through the world.
SUFFOLK. Stay, Whitmore, for thy prisoner is
  a prince,
  The Duke of Suffolk, William de la Pole.
WHITMORE. The Duke of Suffolk muffled up
  in rags?
SUFFOLK. Ay, but these rags are no part of
  the Duke:
  Jove sometime went disguis'd, and why not I?
LIEUTENANT. But Jove was never slain, as thou
  shalt be.
SUFFOLK. Obscure and lowly swain, King
  Henry's blood,
  The honourable blood of Lancaster,
  Must not be shed by such a jaded groom.
  Hast thou not kiss'd thy hand and held
  my stirrup,
  Bareheaded plodded by my foot-cloth mule,
  And thought thee happy when I shook my head?
  How often hast thou waited at my cup,
  Fed from my trencher, kneel'd down at
  the board,
  When I have feasted with Queen Margaret?
  Remember it, and let it make thee crestfall'n,
  Ay, and allay thus thy abortive pride,
  How in our voiding-lobby hast thou stood
  And duly waited for my coming forth.
  This hand of mine hath writ in thy behalf,
  And therefore shall it charm thy riotous tongue.
WHITMORE. Speak, Captain, shall I stab the
  forlorn swain?
LIEUTENANT. First let my words stab him, as he
  hath me.

SUFFOLK. Base slave, thy words are blunt, and so
  art thou.
LIEUTENANT. Convey him hence, and on our
  longboat's side
  Strike off his head.
SUFFOLK. Thou dar'st not, for thy own.
LIEUTENANT. Poole!
SUFFOLK. Poole?
LIEUTENANT. Ay, kennel, puddle, sink, whose
  filth and dirt
  Troubles the silver spring where England drinks;
  Now will I dam up this thy yawning mouth
  For swallowing the treasure of the realm.
  Thy lips, that kiss'd the Queen, shall sweep
  the ground;
  And thou that smil'dst at good Duke
  Humphrey's death
  Against the senseless winds shalt grin in vain,
  Who in contempt shall hiss at thee again;
  And wedded be thou to the hags of hell
  For daring to affy a mighty lord
  Unto the daughter of a worthless king,
  Having neither subject, wealth, nor diadem.
  By devilish policy art thou grown great,
  And, like ambitious Sylla, overgorg'd
  With gobbets of thy mother's bleeding heart.
  By thee Anjou and Maine were sold to France;
  The false revolting Normans thorough thee
  Disdain to call us lord; and Picardy
  Hath slain their governors, surpris'd our forts,
  And sent the ragged soldiers wounded home.
  The princely Warwick, and the Nevils all,
  Whose dreadful swords were never drawn
  in vain,
  As hating thee, are rising up in arms;
  And now the house of York-thrust from the crown
  By shameful murder of a guiltless king
  And lofty proud encroaching tyranny-
  Burns with revenging fire, whose
  hopeful colours
  Advance our half-fac'd sun, striving to shine,
  Under the which is writ 'Invitis nubibus.'
  The commons here in Kent are up in arms;
  And to conclude, reproach and beggary
  Is crept into the palace of our King,
  And all by thee. Away! convey him hence.
SUFFOLK. O that I were a god, to shoot
  forth thunder
  Upon these paltry, servile, abject drudges!
  Small things make base men proud: this
  villain here,
  Being captain of a pinnace, threatens more
  Than Bargulus, the strong Illyrian pirate.

Drones suck not eagles' blood, but rob beehives.
It is impossible that I should die
By such a lowly vassal as thyself.
Thy words move rage and not remorse in me.
I go of message from the Queen to France:
I charge thee waft me safely cross the Channel.
LIEUTENANT. Walter-
WHITMORE. Come, Suffolk, I must waft thee to
  thy death.
SUFFOLK. Gelidus timor occupat artus: it is thee
  I fear.
WHITMORE. Thou shalt have cause to fear before
  I leave thee.
  What, are ye daunted now? Now will ye stoop?
FIRST GENTLEMAN. My gracious lord, entreat
  him, speak him fair.
SUFFOLK. Suffolk's imperial tongue is stern
  and rough,
  Us'd to command, untaught to plead for favour.
  Far be it we should honour such as these
  With humble suit: no, rather let my head
  Stoop to the block than these knees bow to any
  Save to the God of heaven and to my king;
  And sooner dance upon a bloody pole
  Than stand uncover'd to the vulgar groom.
  True nobility is exempt from fear:
  More can I bear than you dare execute.
LIEUTENANT. Hale him away, and let him talk
  no more.
SUFFOLK. Come, soldiers, show what cruelty
  ye can,
  That this my death may never be forgot-
  Great men oft die by vile bezonians:
  A Roman sworder and banditto slave
  Murder'd sweet Tully; Brutus' bastard hand
  Stabb'd Julius Caesar; savage islanders
  Pompey the Great; and Suffolk dies by pirates.
        Exit WALTER with SUFFOLK.
LIEUTENANT. And as for these, whose ransom we
  have set,
  It is our pleasure one of them depart;
  Therefore come you with us, and let him go.
        Exeunt all but the FIRST GENTLEMAN.
      Re-enter WHITMORE with SUFFOLK'S body
WHITMORE. There let his head and lifeless
  body lie,
  Until the Queen his mistress bury it.   *Exit.*
FIRST GENTLEMAN. O barbarous and
  bloody spectacle!
  His body will I bear unto the King.
  If he revenge it not, yet will his friends;
  So will the Queen, that living held him dear.
        Exit with the body.

✒ SCENE II ✒
Blackheath

Enter GEORGE BEVIS and JOHN HOLLAND

GEORGE. Come and get thee a sword, though made of a lath; they have been up these two days.

JOHN. They have the more need to sleep now, then.

GEORGE. I tell thee, Jack Cade the clothier means to dress the commonwealth, and turn it, and set a new nap upon it.

JOHN. So he had need, for 'tis threadbare. Well, I say it was never merry world in England since gentlemen came up.

GEORGE. O miserable age! Virtue is not regarded in handicraftsmen.

JOHN. The nobility think scorn to go in leather aprons.

GEORGE. Nay, more, the King's Council are no good workmen.

JOHN. True; and yet it is said 'Labour in thy vocation'; which is as much to say as 'Let the magistrates be labouring men'; and therefore should we be magistrates.

GEORGE. Thou hast hit it; for there's no better sign of a brave mind than a hard hand.

JOHN. I see them! I see them! There's Best's son, the tanner of Wingham-

GEORGE. He shall have the skins of our enemies to make dog's leather of.

JOHN. And Dick the butcher-

GEORGE. Then is sin struck down, like an ox, and iniquity's throat cut like a calf.

JOHN. And Smith the weaver-

GEORGE. Argo, their thread of life is spun.

JOHN. Come, come, let's fall in with them.

Drum. Enter CADE, DICK THE BUTCHER, SMITH THE WEAVER, and a SAWYER, with infinite numbers

CADE. We John Cade, so term'd of our supposed father-

DICK. *[Aside]* Or rather, of stealing a cade of herrings.

CADE. For our enemies shall fall before us, inspired with the spirit of putting down kings and princes-command silence.

DICK. Silence!

CADE. My father was a Mortimer-

DICK. *[Aside]* He was an honest man and a good bricklayer.

CADE. My mother a Plantagenet-

DICK. *[Aside]* I knew her well; she was a midwife.

CADE. My wife descended of the Lacies-

DICK. *[Aside]* She was, indeed, a pedlar's daughter, and sold many laces.

SMITH. *[Aside]* But now of late, not able to travel with her furr'd pack, she washes bucks here at home.

CADE. Therefore am I of an honourable house.

DICK. *[Aside]* Ay, by my faith, the field is honourable, and there was he born, under a hedge, for his father had never a house but the cage.

CADE. Valiant I am.

SMITH. *[Aside]* 'A must needs; for beggary is valiant.

CADE. I am able to endure much.

DICK. *[Aside]* No question of that; for I have seen him whipt three market days together.

CADE. I fear neither sword nor fire.

SMITH. *[Aside]* He need not fear the sword, for his coat is of proof.

DICK. *[Aside]* But methinks he should stand in fear of fire, being burnt i' th' hand for stealing of sheep.

CADE. Be brave, then, for your captain is brave, and vows reformation. There shall be in England seven halfpenny loaves sold for a penny; the three-hoop'd pot shall have ten hoops; and I will make it felony to drink small beer. All the realm shall be in common, and in Cheapside shall my palfrey go to grass. And when I am king-as king I will be-

ALL. God save your Majesty!

CADE. I thank you, good people-there shall be no money; all shall eat and drink on my score, and I will apparel them all in one livery, that they may agree like brothers and worship me their lord.

DICK. The first thing we do, let's kill all the lawyers.

CADE. Nay, that I mean to do. Is not this a lamentable thing, that of the skin of an innocent lamb should be made parchment? That parchment, being scribbl'd o'er, should undo a man? Some say the bee stings; but I say 'tis the bee's wax; for I did but seal once to a thing, and I was never mine own man since. How now! Who's there?

Enter some, bringing in the CLERK OF CHATHAM

SMITH. The clerk of Chatham. He can write and read and cast accompt.

CADE. O monstrous!

SMITH. We took him setting of boys' copies.

CADE. Here's a villain!

SMITH. Has a book in his pocket with red
letters in't.

CADE. Nay, then he is a conjurer.

DICK. Nay, he can make obligations and
write court-hand.

CADE. I am sorry for't; the man is a proper man,
of mine honour; unless I find him guilty, he
shall not die. Come hither, sirrah, I must
examine thee. What is thy name?

CLERK. Emmanuel.

DICK. They use to write it on the top of letters;
'twill go hard with you.

CADE. Let me alone. Dost thou use to write thy
name, or hast thou a mark to thyself, like a
honest plain-dealing man?

CLERK. Sir, I thank God, I have been so well
brought up that I can write my name.

ALL. He hath confess'd. Away with him! He's a
villain and a traitor.

CADE. Away with him, I say! Hang him with his
pen and inkhorn about his neck.

Exit one with the CLERK.

Enter MICHAEL

MICHAEL. Where's our General?

CADE. Here I am, thou particular fellow.

MICHAEL. Fly, fly, fly! Sir Humphrey Stafford and
his brother are hard by, with the King's forces.

CADE. Stand, villain, stand, or I'll fell thee down.
He shall be encount'red with a man as good as
himself. He is but a knight, is 'a?

MICHAEL. No.

CADE. To equal him, I will make myself a knight
presently. *[Kneels]* Rise up, Sir John Mortimer.
[Rises] Now have at him!

*Enter SIR HUMPHREY STAFFORD and WILLIAM his
brother, with drum and SOLDIERS*

STAFFORD. Rebellious hinds, the filth and scum
of Kent,
Mark'd for the gallows, lay your weapons down;
Home to your cottages, forsake this groom;
The King is merciful if you revolt.

WILLIAM STAFFORD. But angry, wrathful, and
inclin'd to blood,
If you go forward; therefore yield or die.

CADE. As for these silken-coated slaves, I pass not;
It is to you, good people, that I speak,
O'er whom, in time to come, I hope to reign;
For I am rightful heir unto the crown.

STAFFORD. Villain, thy father was a plasterer;
And thou thyself a shearman, art thou not?

CADE. And Adam was a gardener.

WILLIAM STAFFORD. And what of that?

CADE. Marry, this: Edmund Mortimer, Earl
of March,
Married the Duke of Clarence' daughter, did
he not?

STAFFORD. Ay, sir.

CADE. By her he had two children at one birth.

WILLIAM STAFFORD. That's false.

CADE. Ay, there's the question; but I say 'tis true.
The elder of them being put to nurse,
Was by a beggar-woman stol'n away,
And, ignorant of his birth and parentage,
Became a bricklayer when he came to age.
His son am I; deny it if you can.

DICK. Nay, 'tis too true; therefore he shall be king.

SMITH. Sir, he made a chimney in my father's
house, and the bricks are alive at this day to
testify it; therefore deny it not.

STAFFORD. And will you credit this base
drudge's words
That speaks he knows not what?

ALL. Ay, marry, will we; therefore get ye gone.

WILLIAM STAFFORD. Jack Cade, the Duke of York
hath taught you this.

CADE. *[Aside]* He lies, for I invented it myself-Go
to, sirrah, tell the King from me that for his
father's sake, Henry the Fifth, in whose time
boys went to span-counter for French crowns, I
am content he shall reign; but I'll be Protector
over him.

DICK. And furthermore, we'll have the Lord Say's
head for selling the dukedom of Maine.

CADE. And good reason; for thereby is England
main'd and fain to go with a staff, but that
my puissance holds it up. Fellow kings, I
tell you that that Lord Say hath gelded the
commonwealth and made it an eunuch; and
more than that, he can speak French, and
therefore he is a traitor.

STAFFORD. O gross and miserable ignorance!

CADE. Nay, answer if you can; the Frenchmen are
our enemies. Go to, then, I ask but this: can he
that speaks with the tongue of an enemy be a
good counsellor, or no?

ALL. No, no; and therefore we'll have his head.

WILLIAM STAFFORD. Well, seeing gentle words
will not prevail,
Assail them with the army of the King.

STAFFORD. Herald, away; and throughout
every town
Proclaim them traitors that are up with Cade;
That those which fly before the battle ends
May, even in their wives' and children's sight,
Be hang'd up for example at their doors.

And you that be the King's friends, follow me.

Exeunt the TWO STAFFORDS and soldiers.

CADE. And you that love the commons follow me.
Now show yourselves men; 'tis for liberty.
We will not leave one lord, one gentleman;
Spare none but such as go in clouted shoon,
For they are thrifty honest men and such
As would-but that they dare not-take our parts.

DICK. They are all in order, and march toward us.

CADE. But then are we in order when we are most
out of order. Come, march forward. *Exeunt.*

SCENE III

Another part of Blackheath

*Alarums to the fight, wherein both the STAFFORDS are slain.
Enter CADE and the rest*

CADE. Where's Dick, the butcher of Ashford?

DICK. Here, sir.

CADE. They fell before thee like sheep and oxen,
and thou behavedst thyself as if thou hadst
been in thine own slaughter-house; therefore
thus will I reward thee-the Lent shall be as long
again as it is, and thou shalt have a licence to
kill for a hundred lacking one.

DICK. I desire no more.

CADE. And, to speak truth, thou deserv'st no
less. *[Putting on SIR HUMPHREY'S brigandine]* This
monument of the victory will I bear, and the
bodies shall be dragged at my horse heels till
I do come to London, where we will have the
mayor's sword borne before us.

DICK. If we mean to thrive and do good, break
open the gaols and let out the prisoners.

CADE. Fear not that, I warrant thee. Come, let's
march towards London. *Exeunt.*

SCENE IV

London. The palace

*Enter the KING with a supplication, and the QUEEN with
SUFFOLK'S head; the DUKE OF BUCKINGHAM, and the
LORD SAY*

QUEEN. Oft have I heard that grief softens
the mind
And makes it fearful and degenerate;
Think therefore on revenge and cease to weep.
But who can cease to weep, and look on this?
Here may his head lie on my throbbing breast;

But where's the body that I should embrace?

BUCKINGHAM. What answer makes your Grace to
the rebels' supplication?

KING HENRY. I'll send some holy bishop
to entreat;
For God forbid so many simple souls
Should perish by the sword! And I myself,
Rather than bloody war shall cut them short,
Will parley with Jack Cade their general.
But stay, I'll read it over once again.

QUEEN. Ah, barbarous villains! Hath this
lovely face
Rul'd like a wandering planet over me,
And could it not enforce them to relent
That were unworthy to behold the same?

KING HENRY. Lord Say, Jack Cade hath sworn to
have thy head.

SAY. Ay, but I hope your Highness shall have his.

KING HENRY. How now, madam!
Still lamenting and mourning for Suffolk's death?
I fear me, love, if that I had been dead,
Thou wouldst not have mourn'd so much
for me.

QUEEN. No, my love, I should not mourn, but die
for thee.

Enter A MESSENGER

KING HENRY. How now! What news? Why com'st
thou in such haste?

MESSENGER. The rebels are in Southwark; fly,
my lord!
Jack Cade proclaims himself Lord Mortimer,
Descended from the Duke of Clarence' house,
And calls your Grace usurper, openly,
And vows to crown himself in Westminster.
His army is a ragged multitude
Of hinds and peasants, rude and merciless;
Sir Humphrey Stafford and his brother's death
Hath given them heart and courage to proceed.
All scholars, lawyers, courtiers, gentlemen,
They call false caterpillars and intend
their death.

KING HENRY. O graceless men! they know not
what they do.

BUCKINGHAM. My gracious lord, retire
to Killingworth
Until a power be rais'd to put them down.

QUEEN. Ah, were the Duke of Suffolk now alive,
These Kentish rebels would be soon appeas'd!

KING HENRY. Lord Say, the traitors hate thee;
Therefore away with us to Killingworth.

SAY. So might your Grace's person be in danger.
The sight of me is odious in their eyes;
And therefore in this city will I stay

And live alone as secret as I may.

Enter another MESSENGER

SECOND MESSENGER. Jack Cade hath gotten
London Bridge.
The citizens fly and forsake their houses;
The rascal people, thirsting after prey,
Join with the traitor; and they jointly swear
To spoil the city and your royal court.

BUCKINGHAM. Then linger not, my lord; away,
take horse.

KING HENRY. Come Margaret; God, our hope,
will succour us.

QUEEN. My hope is gone, now Suffolk is deceas'd.

KING HENRY. *[To LORD SAY]* Farewell, my lord,
trust not the Kentish rebels.

BUCKINGHAM. Trust nobody, for fear you
be betray'd.

SAY. The trust I have is in mine innocence,
And therefore am I bold and resolute. *Exeunt.*

✿ SCENE V ✿
London. The Tower

*Enter LORD SCALES upon the Tower, walking. Then enter
two or three CITIZENS, below*

SCALES. How now! Is Jack Cade slain?

FIRST CITIZEN. No, my lord, nor likely to be slain;
for they have won the bridge, killing all those
that withstand them. The Lord Mayor craves aid
of your honour from the Tower, to defend the
city from the rebels.

SCALES. Such aid as I can spare you shall command,
But I am troubled here with them myself;
The rebels have assay'd to win the Tower.
But get you to Smithfield, and gather head,
And thither I will send you Matthew Goffe;
Fight for your King, your country, and your lives;
And so, farewell, for I must hence again. *Exeunt.*

✿ SCENE VI ✿
London. Cannon Street

*Enter JACK CADE and the rest, and strikes his staff on
London Stone*

CADE. Now is Mortimer lord of this city. And
here, sitting upon London Stone, I charge and
command that, of the city's cost, the pissing
conduit run nothing but claret wine this first
year of our reign. And now henceforward it

shall be treason for any that calls me other than
Lord Mortimer.

Enter a SOLDIER, running

SOLDIER. Jack Cade! Jack Cade!

CADE. Knock him down there. *They kill him*

SMITH. If this fellow be wise, he'll never call
ye Jack Cade more; I think he hath a very
fair warning.

DICK. My lord, there's an army gathered together
in Smithfield.

CADE. Come then, let's go fight with them. But
first go and set London Bridge on fire; and,
if you can, burn down the Tower too. Come,
let's away.

Exeunt.

✿ SCENE VII ✿
London. Smithfield

*Alarums. MATTHEW GOFFE is slain, and all the rest. Then
enter JACK CADE, with his company*

CADE. So, sirs. Now go some and pull down the
Savoy; others to th' Inns of Court; down with
them all.

DICK. I have a suit unto your lordship.

CADE. Be it a lordship, thou shalt have it for
that word.

DICK. Only that the laws of England may come
out of your mouth.

JOHN. *[Aside]* Mass, 'twill be sore law then; for he
was thrust in the mouth with a spear, and 'tis
not whole yet.

SMITH. *[Aside]* Nay, John, it will be stinking law; for
his breath stinks with eating toasted cheese.

CADE. I have thought upon it; it shall be so. Away,
burn all the records of the realm. My mouth
shall be the Parliament of England.

JOHN. *[Aside]* Then we are like to have biting
statutes, unless his teeth be pull'd out.

CADE. And henceforward all things shall be
in common.

Enter a MESSENGER

MESSENGER. My lord, a prize, a prize! Here's the
Lord Say, which sold the towns in France; he
that made us pay one and twenty fifteens, and
one shining to the pound, the last subsidy.

Enter GEORGE BEVIS, with the LORD SAY

CADE. Well, he shall be beheaded for it ten times.
Ah, thou say, thou serge, nay, thou buckram
lord! Now art thou within point blank of our
jurisdiction regal. What canst thou answer to

my Majesty for giving up of Normandy unto
Mounsieur Basimecu the Dauphin of France?
Be it known unto thee by these presence, even
the presence of Lord Mortimer, that I am the
besom that must sweep the court clean of such
filth as thou art. Thou hast most traitorously
corrupted the youth of the realm in erecting
a grammar school; and whereas, before, our
forefathers had no other books but the score
and the tally, thou hast caused printing to be
us'd, and, contrary to the King, his crown, and
dignity, thou hast built a paper-mill. It will be
proved to thy face that thou hast men about
thee that usually talk of a noun and a verb,
and such abominable words as no Christian
ear can endure to hear. Thou hast appointed
justices of peace, to call poor men before them
about matters they were not able to answer.
Moreover, thou hast put them in prison, and
because they could not read, thou hast hang'd
them, when, indeed, only for that cause they
have been most worthy to live. Thou dost ride
in a foot-cloth, dost thou not?

SAY. What of that?

CADE. Marry, thou ought'st not to let thy horse
wear a cloak, when honester men than thou go
in their hose and doublets.

DICK. And work in their shirt too, as myself, for
example, that am a butcher.

SAY. You men of Kent-

DICK. What say you of Kent?

SAY. Nothing but this: 'tis 'bona terra, mala gens.'

CADE. Away with him, away with him! He
speaks Latin.

SAY. Hear me but speak, and bear me where
you will.
Kent, in the Commentaries Caesar writ,
Is term'd the civil'st place of all this isle.
Sweet is the country, because full of riches;
The people liberal valiant, active, wealthy;
Which makes me hope you are not void of pity.
I sold not Maine, I lost not Normandy;
Yet, to recover them, would lose my life.
Justice with favour have I always done;
Pray'rs and tears have mov'd me, gifts
could never.
When have I aught exacted at your hands,
But to maintain the King, the realm, and you?
Large gifts have I bestow'd on learned clerks,
Because my book preferr'd me to the King,
And seeing ignorance is the curse of God,
Knowledge the wing wherewith we fly
to heaven,

Unless you be possess'd with devilish spirits
You cannot but forbear to murder me.
This tongue hath parley'd unto foreign kings
For your behoof.

CADE. Tut, when struck'st thou one blow in
the field?

SAY. Great men have reaching hands. Oft have
I struck
Those that I never saw, and struck them dead.

GEORGE. O monstrous coward! What, to come
behind folks?

SAY. These cheeks are pale for watching for
your good.

CADE. Give him a box o' th' ear, and that will
make 'em red again.

SAY. Long sitting to determine poor men's causes
Hath made me full of sickness and diseases.

CADE. Ye shall have a hempen caudle then, and
the help of hatchet.

DICK. Why dost thou quiver, man?

SAY. The palsy, and not fear, provokes me.

CADE. Nay, he nods at us, as who should say 'I'll
be even with you'; I'll see if his head will stand
steadier on a pole, or no. Take him away, and
behead him.

SAY. Tell me: wherein have I offended most?
Have I affected wealth or honour? Speak.
Are my chests fill'd up with extorted gold?
Is my apparel sumptuous to behold?
Whom have I injur'd, that ye seek my death?
These hands are free from
guiltless bloodshedding,
This breast from harbouring foul
deceitful thoughts.
O, let me live!

CADE. [Aside] I feel remorse in myself with his
words; but I'll bridle it. He shall die, an it be
but for pleading so well for his life.-Away with
him! He has a familiar under his tongue; he
speaks not o' God's name. Go, take him away, I
say, and strike off his head presently, and then
break into his son-in-law's house, Sir James
Cromer, and strike off his head, and bring them
both upon two poles hither.

ALL. It shall be done.

SAY. Ah, countrymen! if when you make
your pray'rs,
God should be so obdurate as yourselves,
How would it fare with your departed souls?
And therefore yet relent and save my life.

CADE. Away with him, and do as I command
ye. [Exeunt some with LORD SAY] The proudest
peer in the realm shall not wear a head on his

shoulders, unless he pay me tribute; there
shall not a maid be married, but she shall pay
to me her maidenhead ere they have it. Men
shall hold of me in capite; and we charge and
command that their wives be as free as heart
can wish or tongue can tell.

DICK. My lord, when shall we go to Cheapside,
and take up commodities upon our bills?

CADE. Marry, presently.

ALL. O, brave!

Re-enter one with the heads

CADE. But is not this braver? Let them kiss one
another, for they lov'd well when they were
alive. Now part them again, lest they consult
about the giving up of some more towns in
France. Soldiers, defer the spoil of the city until
night; for with these borne before us instead of
maces will we ride through the streets, and at
every corner have them kiss. Away! *Exeunt.*

❧ SCENE VIII ❧
Southwark

Alarum and retreat. Enter again CADE and all his rabblement

CADE. Up Fish Street! down Saint Magnus'
Corner! Kill and knock down! Throw them into
Thames! *[Sound a parley]* What noise is this I hear?
Dare any be so bold to sound retreat or parley
when I command them kill?

Enter BUCKINGHAM and old CLIFFORD, attended

BUCKINGHAM. Ay, here they be that dare and will
disturb thee.
And therefore yet relent, and save my life.
Know, Cade, we come ambassadors from
the King
Unto the commons whom thou hast misled;
And here pronounce free pardon to them all
That will forsake thee and go home in peace.

CLIFFORD. What say ye, countrymen? Will
ye relent
And yield to mercy whilst 'tis offer'd you,
Or let a rebel lead you to your deaths?
Who loves the King, and will embrace his
pardon,
Fling up his cap and say 'God save his Majesty!'
Who hateth him and honours not his father,
Henry the Fifth, that made all France to quake,
Shake he his weapon at us and pass by.

ALL. God save the King! God save the King!

CADE. What, Buckingham and Clifford, are ye so
brave? And you, base peasants, do ye believe
him? Will you needs be hang'd with your
pardons about your necks? Hath my sword
therefore broke through London gates, that
you should leave me at the White Hart in
Southwark? I thought ye would never have
given out these arms till you had recovered
your ancient freedom. But you are all recreants
and dastards, and delight to live in slavery to
the nobility. Let them break your backs with
burdens, take your houses over your heads,
ravish your wives and daughters before your
faces. For me, I will make shift for one; and so
God's curse light upon you all!

ALL. We'll follow Cade, we'll follow Cade!

CLIFFORD. Is Cade the son of Henry the Fifth,
That thus you do exclaim you'll go with him?
Will he conduct you through the heart of
France,
And make the meanest of you earls and dukes?
Alas, he hath no home, no place to fly to;
Nor knows he how to live but by the spoil,
Unless by robbing of your friends and us.
Were't not a shame that whilst you live at jar,
The fearful French, whom you late vanquished,
Should make a start o'er seas and vanquish you?
Methinks already in this civil broil
I see them lording it in London streets,
Crying 'Villiago!' unto all they meet.
Better ten thousand base-born Cades miscarry
Than you should stoop unto a
Frenchman's mercy.
To France, to France, and get what you
have lost;
Spare England, for it is your native coast.
Henry hath money; you are strong and manly.
God on our side, doubt not of victory.

ALL. A Clifford! a Clifford! We'll follow the King
and Clifford.

CADE. Was ever feather so lightly blown to and
fro as this multitude? The name of Henry the
Fifth hales them to an hundred mischiefs, and
makes them leave me desolate. I see them lay
their heads together to surprise me. My sword
make way for me, for here is no staying. In
despite of the devils and hell, have through the
very middest of you! and heavens and honour
be witness that no want of resolution in me,
but only my followers' base and ignominious
treasons, makes me betake me to my heels.
Exit.

BUCKINGHAM. What, is he fled? Go some, and
follow him;
And he that brings his head unto the King

Shall have a thousand crowns for his reward.

Exeunt some of them.

Follow me, soldiers; we'll devise a mean
To reconcile you all unto the King. *Exeunt.*

✣ SCENE IX ✣
Kenilworth Castle

Sound trumpets. Enter KING, QUEEN, and SOMERSET,
on the terrace

KING HENRY. Was ever king that joy'd an
  earthly throne
  And could command no more content than I?
  No sooner was I crept out of my cradle
  But I was made a king, at nine months old.
  Was never subject long'd to be a King
  As I do long and wish to be a subject.

Enter BUCKINGHAM and old CLIFFORD

BUCKINGHAM. Health and glad tidings to
  your Majesty!
KING HENRY. Why, Buckingham, is the traitor
  Cade surpris'd? Or is he but retir'd to make
  him strong?

Enter, below, multitudes, with halters about their necks

CLIFFORD. He is fled, my lord, and all his powers
  do yield,
  And humbly thus, with halters on their necks,
  Expect your Highness' doom of life or death.
KING HENRY. Then, heaven, set ope thy
  everlasting gates,
  To entertain my vows of thanks and praise!
  Soldiers, this day have you redeem'd your lives,
  And show'd how well you love your Prince
  and country.
  Continue still in this so good a mind,
  And Henry, though he be infortunate,
  Assure yourselves, will never be unkind.
  And so, with thanks and pardon to you all,
  I do dismiss you to your several countries.
ALL. God save the King! God save the King!

Enter a MESSENGER

MESSENGER. Please it your Grace to be advertised
  The Duke of York is newly come from Ireland
  And with a puissant and a mighty power
  Of gallowglasses and stout kerns
  Is marching hitherward in proud array,
  And still proclaimeth, as he comes along,
  His arms are only to remove from thee
  The Duke of Somerset, whom he terms a traitor.
KING HENRY. Thus stands my state, 'twixt Cade
  and York distress'd;

Like to a ship that, having scap'd a tempest,
Is straightway calm'd, and boarded with a pirate;
But now is Cade driven back, his men dispers'd,
And now is York in arms to second him.
I pray thee, Buckingham, go and meet him
And ask him what's the reason of these arms.
Tell him I'll send Duke Edmund to the Tower-
And Somerset, we will commit thee thither
Until his army be dismiss'd from him.
SOMERSET. My lord,
  I'll yield myself to prison willingly,
  Or unto death, to do my country good.
KING HENRY. In any case be not too rough
  in terms,
  For he is fierce and cannot brook hard language.
BUCKINGHAM. I will, my lord, and doubt not so
  to deal
  As all things shall redound unto your good.
KING HENRY. Come, wife, let's in, and learn to
  govern better;
  For yet may England curse my wretched reign.

Flourish. Exeunt.

✣ SCENE X ✣
Kent. Iden's garden

Enter CADE

CADE. Fie on ambitions! Fie on myself, that have
a sword and yet am ready to famish! These five
days have I hid me in these woods and durst
not peep out, for all the country is laid for me;
but now am I so hungry that, if I might have
a lease of my life for a thousand years, I could
stay no longer. Wherefore, on a brick wall have
I climb'd into this garden, to see if I can eat
grass or pick a sallet another while, which is not
amiss to cool a man's stomach this hot weather.
And I think this word 'sallet' was born to do
me good; for many a time, but for a sallet, my
brain-pain had been cleft with a brown bill; and
many a time, when I have been dry, and bravely
marching, it hath serv'd me instead of a quart-
pot to drink in; and now the word 'sallet' must
serve me to feed on.

Enter IDEN

IDEN. Lord, who would live turmoiled in the court
And may enjoy such quiet walks as these?
This small inheritance my father left me
Contenteth me, and worth a monarchy.
I seek not to wax great by others' waning
Or gather wealth I care not with what envy;

Sufficeth that I have maintains my state,
And sends the poor well pleased from my gate.

CADE. Here's the lord of the soil come to seize
me for a stray, for entering his fee-simple
without leave. Ah, villain, thou wilt betray me,
and get a thousand crowns of the King by
carrying my head to him; but I'll make thee eat
iron like an ostrich and swallow my sword like a
great pin ere thou and I part.

IDEN. Why, rude companion, whatsoe'er thou be,
I know thee not; why then should I betray thee?
Is't not enough to break into my garden
And like a thief to come to rob my grounds,
Climbing my walls in spite of me the owner,
But thou wilt brave me with these saucy terms?

CADE. Brave thee? Ay, by the best blood that
ever was broach'd, and beard thee too. Look
on me well: I have eat no meat these five days,
yet come thou and thy five men and if I do not
leave you all as dead as a door-nail, I pray God I
may never eat grass more.

IDEN. Nay, it shall ne'er be said, while
England stands,
That Alexander Iden, an esquire of Kent,
Took odds to combat a poor famish'd man.
Oppose thy steadfast-gazing eyes to mine;
See if thou canst outface me with thy looks;
Set limb to limb, and thou art far the lesser;
Thy hand is but a finger to my fist,
Thy leg a stick compared with this truncheon;
My foot shall fight with all the strength
thou hast,
And if mine arm be heaved in the air,
Thy grave is digg'd already in the earth.
As for words, whose greatness answers words,
Let this my sword report what speech forbears.

CADE. By my valour, the most complete
champion that ever I heard! Steel, if thou turn
the edge, or cut not out the burly-bon'd clown
in chines of beef ere thou sleep in thy sheath, I
beseech God on my knees thou mayst be turn'd
to hobnails. *[Here they fight; CADE falls]* O, I am slain!
famine and no other hath slain me. Let ten
thousand devils come against me, and give me
but the ten meals I have lost, and I'd defy them
all. Wither, garden, and be henceforth a burying
place to all that do dwell in this house, because
the unconquered soul of Cade is fled.

IDEN. Is't Cade that I have slain, that
monstrous traitor?
Sword, I will hallow thee for this thy deed
And hang thee o'er my tomb when I am dead.
Ne'er shall this blood be wiped from thy point,

But thou shalt wear it as a herald's coat
To emblaze the honour that thy master got.

CADE. Iden, farewell; and be proud of thy victory.
Tell Kent from me she hath lost her best man,
and exhort all the world to be cowards; for
I, that never feared any, am vanquished by
famine, not by valour.

Dies.

IDEN. How much thou wrong'st me, heaven be
my judge.
Die, damned wretch, the curse of her that
bare thee!
And as I thrust thy body in with my sword,
So wish I, I might thrust thy soul to hell.
Hence will I drag thee headlong by the heels
Unto a dunghill, which shall be thy grave,
And there cut off thy most ungracious head,
Which I will bear in triumph to the King,
Leaving thy trunk for crows to feed upon.

Exit.

ACT V

SCENE I

Fields between Dartford and Blackheath

Enter YORK, and his army of Irish, with drum and colours

YORK. From Ireland thus comes York to claim
his right
And pluck the crown from feeble Henry's head:
Ring bells aloud, burn bonfires clear and bright,
To entertain great England's lawful king.
Ah, sancta majestas! who would not buy thee dear?
Let them obey that knows not how to rule;
This hand was made to handle nought but gold.
I cannot give due action to my words
Except a sword or sceptre balance it.
A sceptre shall it have, have I a soul
On which I'll toss the flower-de-luce of France.

Enter BUCKINGHAM

[Aside] Whom have we here? Buckingham, to
disturb me?
The King hath sent him, sure: I must dissemble.

BUCKINGHAM. York, if thou meanest well, I greet
thee well.

YORK. Humphrey of Buckingham, I accept
thy greeting.
Art thou a messenger, or come of pleasure?

BUCKINGHAM. A messenger from Henry, our
dread liege,

To know the reason of these arms in peace;
Or why thou, being a subject as I am,
Against thy oath and true allegiance sworn,
Should raise so great a power without his leave,
Or dare to bring thy force so near the court.
YORK. *[Aside]* Scarce can I speak, my choler is
  so great.
O, I could hew up rocks and fight with flint,
I am so angry at these abject terms;
And now, like Ajax Telamonius,
On sheep or oxen could I spend my fury.
I am far better born than is the King,
More like a king, more kingly in my thoughts;
But I must make fair weather yet awhile,
Till Henry be more weak and I more strong.-
Buckingham, I prithee, pardon me
That I have given no answer all this while;
My mind was troubled with deep melancholy.
The cause why I have brought this army hither
Is to remove proud Somerset from the King,
Seditious to his Grace and to the state.
BUCKINGHAM. That is too much presumption on
  thy part;
But if thy arms be to no other end,
The King hath yielded unto thy demand:
The Duke of Somerset is in the Tower.
YORK. Upon thine honour, is he prisoner?
BUCKINGHAM. Upon mine honour, he
  is prisoner.
YORK. Then, Buckingham, I do dismiss
  my pow'rs.
Soldiers, I thank you all; disperse yourselves;
Meet me to-morrow in Saint George's field,
You shall have pay and everything you wish.
And let my sovereign, virtuous Henry,
Command my eldest son, nay, all my sons,
As pledges of my fealty and love.
I'll send them all as willing as I live:
Lands, goods, horse, armour, anything I have,
Is his to use, so Somerset may die.
BUCKINGHAM. York, I commend this kind
  submission.
We twain will go into his Highness' tent.
  Enter the KING, and Attendants
KING HENRY. Buckingham, doth York intend no
  harm to us,
That thus he marcheth with thee arm in arm?
YORK. In all submission and humility
York doth present himself unto your Highness.
KING HENRY. Then what intends these forces
  thou dost bring?
YORK. To heave the traitor Somerset from hence,
And fight against that monstrous rebel Cade,

Who since I heard to be discomfited.
  Enter IDEN, with CADE's head
IDEN. If one so rude and of so mean condition
May pass into the presence of a king,
Lo, I present your Grace a traitor's head,
The head of Cade, whom I in combat slew.
KING HENRY. The head of Cade! Great God, how
  just art Thou!
O, let me view his visage, being dead,
That living wrought me such exceeding trouble.
Tell me, my friend, art thou the man that
  slew him?
IDEN. I was, an't like your Majesty.
KING HENRY. How art thou call'd? And what is
  thy degree?
IDEN. Alexander Iden, that's my name;
A poor esquire of Kent that loves his king.
BUCKINGHAM. So please it you, my lord, 'twere
  not amiss
He were created knight for his good service.
KING HENRY. Iden, kneel down. *[He kneels]* Rise up
  a knight.
We give thee for reward a thousand marks,
And will that thou thenceforth attend on us.
IDEN. May Iden live to merit such a bounty,
And never live but true unto his liege!
  Enter the QUEEN and SOMERSET
KING HENRY. See, Buckingham! Somerset comes
  with th' Queen:
Go, bid her hide him quickly from the Duke.
QUEEN. For thousand Yorks he shall not hide
  his head,
But boldly stand and front him to his face.
YORK. How now! Is Somerset at liberty?
Then, York, unloose thy long-
  imprisoned thoughts
And let thy tongue be equal with thy heart.
Shall I endure the sight of Somerset?
False king, why hast thou broken faith with me,
Knowing how hardly I can brook abuse?
King did I call thee? No, thou art not king;
Not fit to govern and rule multitudes,
Which dar'st not, no, nor canst not rule a traitor.
That head of thine doth not become a crown;
Thy hand is made to grasp a palmer's staff,
And not to grace an awful princely sceptre.
That gold must round engirt these brows of mine,
Whose smile and frown, like to Achilles' spear,
Is able with the change to kill and cure.
Here is a hand to hold a sceptre up,
And with the same to act controlling laws.
Give place. By heaven, thou shalt rule no more
O'er him whom heaven created for thy ruler.

SOMERSET. O monstrous traitor! I arrest
thee, York,
Of capital treason 'gainst the King and crown.
Obey, audacious traitor; kneel for grace.
YORK. Wouldst have me kneel? First let me ask
of these,
If they can brook I bow a knee to man.
Sirrah, call in my sons to be my bail: *Exit*
Attendant.
I know, ere thy will have me go to ward,
They'll pawn their swords for
my enfranchisement.
QUEEN. Call hither Clifford; bid him come amain,
To say if that the bastard boys of York
Shall be the surety for their traitor father.
Exit BUCKINGHAM.
YORK. O blood-bespotted Neapolitan,
Outcast of Naples, England's bloody scourge!
The sons of York, thy betters in their birth,
Shall be their father's bail; and bane to those
That for my surety will refuse the boys!
Enter EDWARD and RICHARD PLANTAGENET
See where they come: I'll warrant they'll make
it good.
Enter CLIFFORD and his SON
QUEEN. And here comes Clifford to deny
their bail.
CLIFFORD. Health and all happiness to my lord
the King! *Kneels*
YORK. I thank thee, Clifford. Say, what news
with thee?
Nay, do not fright us with an angry look.
We are thy sovereign, Clifford, kneel again;
For thy mistaking so, we pardon thee.
CLIFFORD. This is my King, York, I do
not mistake;
But thou mistakes me much to think I do.
To Bedlam with him! Is the man grown mad?
KING HENRY. Ay, Clifford; a bedlam and
ambitious humour
Makes him oppose himself against his king.
CLIFFORD. He is a traitor; let him to the Tower,
And chop away that factious pate of his.
QUEEN. He is arrested, but will not obey;
His sons, he says, shall give their words for him.
YORK. Will you not, sons?
EDWARD. Ay, noble father, if our words will serve.
RICHARD. And if words will not, then our
weapons shall.
CLIFFORD. Why, what a brood of traitors have
we here!
YORK. Look in a glass, and call thy image so:
I am thy king, and thou a false-heart traitor.

Call hither to the stake my two brave bears,
That with the very shaking of their chains
They may astonish these fell-lurking curs.
Bid Salisbury and Warwick come to me.
Enter the EARLS OF WARWICK and SALISBURY
CLIFFORD. Are these thy bears? We'll bait thy
bears to death,
And manacle the berard in their chains,
If thou dar'st bring them to the baiting-place.
RICHARD. Oft have I seen a hot o'er-weening cur
Run back and bite, because he was withheld;
Who, being suffer'd, with the bear's fell paw,
Hath clapp'd his tail between his legs and cried;
And such a piece of service will you do,
If you oppose yourselves to match
Lord Warwick.
CLIFFORD. Hence, heap of wrath, foul
indigested lump,
As crooked in thy manners as thy shape!
YORK. Nay, we shall heat you thoroughly anon.
CLIFFORD. Take heed, lest by your heat you
burn yourselves.
KING HENRY. Why, Warwick, hath thy knee forgot
to bow?
Old Salisbury, shame to thy silver hair,
Thou mad misleader of thy brainsick son!
What, wilt thou on thy death-bed play the ruffian
And seek for sorrow with thy spectacles?
O, where is faith? O, where is loyalty?
If it be banish'd from the frosty head,
Where shall it find a harbour in the earth?
Wilt thou go dig a grave to find out war
And shame thine honourable age with blood?
Why art thou old, and want'st experience?
Or wherefore dost abuse it, if thou hast it?
For shame! In duty bend thy knee to me,
That bows unto the grave with mickle age.
SALISBURY. My lord, I have considered
with myself
The title of this most renowned duke,
And in my conscience do repute his Grace
The rightful heir to England's royal seat.
KING HENRY. Hast thou not sworn allegiance
unto me?
SALISBURY. I have.
KING HENRY. Canst thou dispense with heaven
for such an oath?
SALISBURY. It is great sin to swear unto a sin;
But greater sin to keep a sinful oath.
Who can be bound by any solemn vow
To do a murd'rous deed, to rob a man,
To force a spotless virgin's chastity,
To reave the orphan of his patrimony,

To wring the widow from her custom'd right,
And have no other reason for this wrong
But that he was bound by a solemn oath?
QUEEN. A subtle traitor needs no sophister.
KING HENRY. Call Buckingham, and bid him
arm himself.
YORK. Call Buckingham, and all the friends
thou hast,
I am resolv'd for death or dignity.
CLIFFORD. The first I warrant thee, if dreams
prove true.
WARWICK. You were best to go to bed and
dream again
To keep thee from the tempest of the field.
CLIFFORD. I am resolv'd to bear a greater storm
Than any thou canst conjure up to-day;
And that I'll write upon thy burgonet,
Might I but know thee by thy household badge.
WARWICK. Now, by my father's badge, old
Nevil's crest,
The rampant bear chain'd to the ragged staff,
This day I'll wear aloft my burgonet,
As on a mountain-top the cedar shows,
That keeps his leaves in spite of any storm,
Even to affright thee with the view thereof.
CLIFFORD. And from thy burgonet I'll rend
thy bear
And tread it under foot with all contempt,
Despite the berard that protects the bear.
YOUNG CLIFFORD. And so to arms,
victorious father,
To quell the rebels and their complices.
RICHARD. Fie! charity, for shame! Speak not
in spite,
For you shall sup with Jesu Christ to-night.
YOUNG CLIFFORD. Foul stigmatic, that's more
than thou canst tell.
RICHARD. If not in heaven, you'll surely sup
in hell.

Exeunt severally.

ꙮ SCENE II ꙮ
Saint Albans

Alarums to the battle. Enter WARWICK

WARWICK. Clifford of Cumberland, 'tis
Warwick calls;
And if thou dost not hide thee from the bear,
Now, when the angry trumpet sounds alarum
And dead men's cries do fill the empty air,
Clifford, I say, come forth and fight with me.

Proud northern lord, Clifford of Cumberland,
Warwick is hoarse with calling thee to arms.
Enter YORK
How now, my noble lord! what, all a-foot?
YORK. The deadly-handed Clifford slew my steed;
But match to match I have encount'red him,
And made a prey for carrion kites and crows
Even of the bonny beast he lov'd so well.
Enter OLD CLIFFORD
WARWICK. Of one or both of us the time is come.
YORK. Hold, Warwick, seek thee out some
other chase,
For I myself must hunt this deer to death.
WARWICK. Then, nobly, York; 'tis for a crown
thou fight'st.
As I intend, Clifford, to thrive to-day,
It grieves my soul to leave thee unassail'd. *Exit.*
CLIFFORD. What seest thou in me, York? Why
dost thou pause?
YORK. With thy brave bearing should I be in love
But that thou art so fast mine enemy.
CLIFFORD. Nor should thy prowess want praise
and esteem
But that 'tis shown ignobly and in treason.
YORK. So let it help me now against thy sword,
As I in justice and true right express it!
CLIFFORD. My soul and body on the action both!
YORK. A dreadful lay! Address thee instantly.
They fight and CLIFFORD falls
CLIFFORD. La fin couronne les oeuvres. *Dies.*
YORK. Thus war hath given thee peace, for thou
art still.
Peace with his soul, heaven, if it be thy will! *Exit*
Enter YOUNG CLIFFORD
YOUNG CLIFFORD. Shame and confusion! All is
on the rout;
Fear frames disorder, and disorder wounds
Where it should guard. O war, thou son of hell,
Whom angry heavens do make their minister,
Throw in the frozen bosoms of our part
Hot coals of vengeance! Let no soldier fly.
He that is truly dedicate to war
Hath no self-love; nor he that loves himself
Hath not essentially, but by circumstance,
The name of valour. *[Sees his father's body]*
O, let the vile world end
And the premised flames of the last day
Knit earth and heaven together!
Now let the general trumpet blow his blast,
Particularities and petty sounds
To cease! Wast thou ordain'd, dear father,
To lose thy youth in peace and to achieve
The silver livery of advised age,

And in thy reverence and thy chair-days thus
To die in ruffian battle? Even at this sight
My heart is turn'd to stone; and while 'tis mine
It shall be stony. York not our old men spares;
No more will I their babes. Tears virginal
Shall be to me even as the dew to fire;
And beauty, that the tyrant oft reclaims,
Shall to my flaming wrath be oil and flax.
Henceforth I will not have to do with pity:
Meet I an infant of the house of York,
Into as many gobbets will I cut it
As wild Medea young Absyrtus did;
In cruelty will I seek out my fame.
Come, thou new ruin of old Clifford's house;
As did Aeneas old Anchises bear,
So bear I thee upon my manly shoulders;
But then Aeneas bare a living load,
Nothing so heavy as these woes of mine.

Exit with the body.

Enter RICHARD and SOMERSET to fight. SOMERSET
is killed

RICHARD. So, lie thou there;
For underneath an alehouse' paltry sign,
The Castle in Saint Albans, Somerset
Hath made the wizard famous in his death.
Sword, hold thy temper; heart, be wrathful still:
Priests pray for enemies, but princes kill.*Exit.*

Fight. Excursions. Enter KING, QUEEN, and Others

QUEEN. Away, my lord! You are slow; for
shame, away!
KING HENRY. Can we outrun the heavens? Good
Margaret, stay.
QUEEN. What are you made of? You'll nor fight
nor fly.
Now is it manhood, wisdom, and defence,
To give the enemy way, and to secure us
By what we can, which can no more but fly.
[Alarum afar off]
If you be ta'en, we then should see the bottom
Of all our fortunes; but if we haply scape-
As well we may, if not through your neglect-
We shall to London get, where you are lov'd,
And where this breach now in our fortunes made
May readily be stopp'd.

Re-enter YOUNG CLIFFORD

YOUNG CLIFFORD. But that my heart's on future
mischief set,
I would speak blasphemy ere bid you fly;
But fly you must; uncurable discomfit
Reigns in the hearts of all our present parts.
Away, for your relief! and we will live
To see their day and them our fortune give.
Away, my lord, away!   *Exeunt.*

⚜ SCENE III ⚜
Fields near Saint Albans

Alarum. Retreat. Enter YORK, RICHARD, WARWICK,
and soldiers, with drum and colours

YORK. Of Salisbury, who can report of him,
That winter lion, who in rage forgets
Aged contusions and all brush of time
And, like a gallant in the brow of youth,
Repairs him with occasion? This happy day
Is not itself, nor have we won one foot,
If Salisbury be lost.
RICHARD. My noble father,
Three times to-day I holp him to his horse,
Three times bestrid him, thrice I led him off,
Persuaded him from any further act;
But still where danger was, still there I met him;
And like rich hangings in a homely house,
So was his will in his old feeble body.
But, noble as he is, look where he comes.

Enter SALISBURY

SALISBURY. Now, by my sword, well hast thou
fought to-day!
By th' mass, so did we all. I thank you, Richard:
God knows how long it is I have to live,
And it hath pleas'd Him that three times to-day
You have defended me from imminent death.
Well, lords, we have not got that which we have;
'Tis not enough our foes are this time fled,
Being opposites of such repairing nature.
YORK. I know our safety is to follow them;
For, as I hear, the King is fled to London
To call a present court of Parliament.
Let us pursue him ere the writs go forth.
What says Lord Warwick? Shall we after them?
WARWICK. After them? Nay, before them, if
we can.
Now, by my faith, lords, 'twas a glorious day:
Saint Albans' battle, won by famous York,
Shall be eterniz'd in all age to come.
Sound drum and trumpets and to London all;
And more such days as these to us befall!

Exeunt.

The End

1592

King Henry VI, Part III

Dramatis Personae

KING HENRY THE SIXTH
EDWARD, PRINCE OF WALES, his son
LEWIS XI, King of France
DUKE OF SOMERSET
DUKE OF EXETER
EARL OF OXFORD
EARL OF NORTHUMBERLAND
EARL OF WESTMORELAND
LORD CLIFFORD
RICHARD PLANTAGENET, DUKE OF YORK
EDWARD, EARL OF MARCH, afterwards KING
EDWARD IV, his son
EDMUND, EARL OF RUTLAND, his son
GEORGE, afterwards DUKE OF CLARENCE,
his son
RICHARD, afterwards DUKE OF GLOUCESTER,
his son
DUKE OF NORFOLK
MARQUIS OF MONTAGUE
EARL OF WARWICK
EARL OF PEMBROKE
LORD HASTINGS
LORD STAFFORD

Uncles to the Duke of York:
SIR JOHN MORTIMER
SIR HUGH MORTIMER

HENRY, EARL OF RICHMOND, a youth
LORD RIVERS, brother to Lady Grey
SIR WILLIAM STANLEY
SIR JOHN MONTGOMERY
SIR JOHN SOMERVILLE
TUTOR, to Rutland
MAYOR OF YORK
LIEUTENANT OF THE TOWER
A NOBLEMAN

TWO KEEPERS
A HUNTSMAN
A SON that has killed his father
A FATHER that has killed his son

QUEEN MARGARET
LADY GREY, afterwards QUEEN to Edward IV
BONA, sister to the French Queen

Soldiers, Attendants, Messengers,
Watchmen, etc.

SCENE
England and France

ACT I

SCENE I
London. The Parliament House

*Alarum. Enter DUKE OF YORK, EDWARD, RICHARD,
NORFOLK, MONTAGUE, WARWICK, and soldiers, with
white roses in their hats*

WARWICK. I wonder how the King escap'd
  our hands.
YORK. While we pursu'd the horsemen of
  the north,
  He slily stole away and left his men;
  Whereat the great Lord of Northumberland,
  Whose warlike ears could never brook retreat,
  Cheer'd up the drooping army, and himself,
  Lord Clifford, and Lord Stafford, all abreast,
  Charg'd our main battle's front, and, breaking in,
  Were by the swords of common soldiers slain.
EDWARD. Lord Stafford's father, Duke
  of Buckingham,
  Is either slain or wounded dangerous;
  I cleft his beaver with a downright blow.
  That this is true, father, behold his blood.
MONTAGUE. And, brother, here's the Earl of
  Wiltshire's blood,
  Whom I encount'red as the battles join'd.
RICHARD. Speak thou for me, and tell them what
  I did.
  Throwing down SOMERSET'S head

YORK. Richard hath best deserv'd of all my sons.
But is your Grace dead, my Lord of Somerset?
NORFOLK. Such hope have all the line of John
of Gaunt!
RICHARD. Thus do I hope to shake King
Henry's head.
WARWICK. And so do I. Victorious Prince of York,
Before I see thee seated in that throne
Which now the house of Lancaster usurps,
I vow by heaven these eyes shall never close.
This is the palace of the fearful King,
And this the regal seat. Possess it, York;
For this is thine, and not King Henry's heirs'.
YORK. Assist me then, sweet Warwick, and I will;
For hither we have broken in by force.
NORFOLK. We'll all assist you; he that flies
shall die.
YORK. Thanks, gentle Norfolk. Stay by me,
my lords;
And, soldiers, stay and lodge by me this night.
They go up
WARWICK. And when the King comes, offer him
no violence.
Unless he seek to thrust you out perforce.
YORK. The Queen this day here holds
her parliament,
But little thinks we shall be of her council.
By words or blows here let us win our right.
RICHARD. Arm'd as we are, let's stay within
this house.
WARWICK. The bloody parliament shall this
be call'd,
Unless Plantagenet, Duke of York, be King,
And bashful Henry depos'd, whose cowardice
Hath made us by-words to our enemies.
YORK. Then leave me not, my lords; be resolute:
I mean to take possession of my right.
WARWICK. Neither the King, nor he that loves
him best,
The proudest he that holds up Lancaster,
Dares stir a wing if Warwick shake his bells.
I'll plant Plantagenet, root him up who dares.
Resolve thee, Richard; claim the English crown.
YORK occupies the throne
Flourish. Enter KING HENRY, CLIFFORD,
NORTHUMBERLAND, WESTMORELAND, EXETER,
and others, with red roses in their hats
KING HENRY. My lords, look where the sturdy
rebel sits,
Even in the chair of state! Belike he means,
Back'd by the power of Warwick, that false peer,
To aspire unto the crown and reign as king.
Earl of Northumberland, he slew thy father;

And thine, Lord Clifford; and you both have
vow'd revenge
On him, his sons, his favourites, and his friends.
NORTHUMBERLAND. If I be not, heavens be
reveng'd on me!
CLIFFORD. The hope thereof makes Clifford
mourn in steel.
WESTMORELAND. What, shall we suffer this? Let's
pluck him down;
My heart for anger burns; I cannot brook it.
KING HENRY. Be patient, gentle Earl
of Westmoreland.
CLIFFORD. Patience is for poltroons such as he;
He durst not sit there had your father liv'd.
My gracious lord, here in the parliament
Let us assail the family of York.
NORTHUMBERLAND. Well hast thou spoken,
cousin; be it so.
KING HENRY. Ah, know you not the city
favours them,
And they have troops of soldiers at their beck?
EXETER. But when the Duke is slain they'll
quickly fly.
KING HENRY. Far be the thought of this from
Henry's heart,
To make a shambles of the parliament house!
Cousin of Exeter, frowns, words, and threats,
Shall be the war that Henry means to use.
Thou factious Duke of York, descend my throne
And kneel for grace and mercy at my feet;
I am thy sovereign.
YORK. I am thine.
EXETER. For shame, come down; he made thee
Duke of York.
YORK. 'Twas my inheritance, as the earldom was.
EXETER. Thy father was a traitor to the crown.
WARWICK. Exeter, thou art a traitor to the crown
In following this usurping Henry.
CLIFFORD. Whom should he follow but his
natural king?
WARWICK. True, Clifford; and that's Richard Duke
of York.
KING HENRY. And shall I stand, and thou sit in
my throne?
YORK. It must and shall be so; content thyself.
WARWICK. Be Duke of Lancaster; let him be King.
WESTMORELAND. He is both King and Duke
of Lancaster;
And that the Lord of Westmoreland
shall maintain.
WARWICK. And Warwick shall disprove it. You forget
That we are those which chas'd you from
the field,

And slew your fathers, and with colours spread
March'd through the city to the palace gates.
NORTHUMBERLAND. Yes, Warwick, I remember
  it to my grief;
And, by his soul, thou and thy house shall rue it.
WESTMORELAND. Plantagenet, of thee, and these
  thy sons,
Thy kinsmen, and thy friends, I'll have
  more lives
Than drops of blood were in my father's veins.
CLIFFORD. Urge it no more; lest that instead
  of words
I send thee, Warwick, such a messenger
As shall revenge his death before I stir.
WARWICK. Poor Clifford, how I scorn his
  worthless threats!
YORK. Will you we show our title to the crown?
If not, our swords shall plead it in the field.
KING HENRY. What title hast thou, traitor, to
  the crown?
Thy father was, as thou art, Duke of York;
Thy grandfather, Roger Mortimer, Earl of March:
I am the son of Henry the Fifth,
Who made the Dauphin and the French to stoop,
And seiz'd upon their towns and provinces.
WARWICK. Talk not of France, sith thou hast lost
  it all.
KING HENRY. The Lord Protector lost it, and
  not I:
When I was crown'd, I was but nine months old.
RICHARD. You are old enough now, and yet
  methinks you lose.
Father, tear the crown from the usurper's head.
EDWARD. Sweet father, do so; set it on your head.
MONTAGUE. Good brother, as thou lov'st and
  honourest arms,
Let's fight it out and not stand cavilling thus.
RICHARD. Sound drums and trumpets, and the
  King will fly.
YORK. Sons, peace!
KING HENRY. Peace thou! and give King Henry
  leave to speak.
WARWICK. Plantagenet shall speak first. Hear
  him, lords;
And be you silent and attentive too,
For he that interrupts him shall not live.
KING HENRY. Think'st thou that I will leave my
  kingly throne,
Wherein my grandsire and my father sat?
No; first shall war unpeople this my realm;
Ay, and their colours, often borne in France,
And now in England to our heart's great sorrow,
Shall be my winding-sheet. Why faint you, lords?

My title's good, and better far than his.
WARWICK. Prove it, Henry, and thou shalt
  be King.
KING HENRY. Henry the Fourth by conquest got
  the crown.
YORK. 'Twas by rebellion against his king.
KING HENRY. [Aside] I know not what to say; my
  title's weak.-
Tell me, may not a king adopt an heir?
YORK. What then?
KING HENRY. An if he may, then am I lawful King;
For Richard, in the view of many lords,
Resign'd the crown to Henry the Fourth,
Whose heir my father was, and I am his.
YORK. He rose against him, being his sovereign,
And made him to resign his crown perforce.
WARWICK. Suppose, my lords, he did
  it unconstrain'd,
Think you 'twere prejudicial to his crown?
EXETER. No; for he could not so resign his crown
But that the next heir should succeed and reign.
KING HENRY. Art thou against us, Duke of Exeter?
EXETER. His is the right, and therefore
  pardon me.
YORK. Why whisper you, my lords, and
  answer not?
EXETER. My conscience tells me he is lawful King.
KING HENRY. [Aside] All will revolt from me, and
  turn to him.
NORTHUMBERLAND. Plantagenet, for all the
  claim thou lay'st,
Think not that Henry shall be so depos'd.
WARWICK. Depos'd he shall be, in despite of all.
NORTHUMBERLAND. Thou art deceiv'd. 'Tis not
  thy southern power
Of Essex, Norfolk, Suffolk, nor of Kent,
Which makes thee thus presumptuous
  and proud,
Can set the Duke up in despite of me.
CLIFFORD. King Henry, be thy title right
  or wrong,
Lord Clifford vows to fight in thy defence.
May that ground gape, and swallow me alive,
Where I shall kneel to him that slew my father!
KING HENRY. O Clifford, how thy words revive
  my heart!
YORK. Henry of Lancaster, resign thy crown.
What mutter you, or what conspire you, lords?
WARWICK. Do right unto this princely Duke
  of York;
Or I will fill the house with armed men,
And o'er the chair of state, where now he sits,
Write up his title with usurping blood.

He stamps with his foot and the soldiers show themselves

KING HENRY. My Lord of Warwick, hear but
one word:
Let me for this my life-time reign as king.

YORK. Confirm the crown to me and to
mine heirs,
And thou shalt reign in quiet while thou liv'st.

KING HENRY. I am content. Richard Plantagenet,
Enjoy the kingdom after my decease.

CLIFFORD. What wrong is this unto the Prince
your son!

WARWICK. What good is this to England
and himself!

WESTMORELAND. Base, fearful, and
despairing Henry!

CLIFFORD. How hast thou injur'd both thyself
and us!

WESTMORELAND. I cannot stay to hear
these articles.

NORTHUMBERLAND. Nor I.

CLIFFORD. Come, cousin, let us tell the Queen
these news.

WESTMORELAND. Farewell, faint-hearted and
degenerate king,
In whose cold blood no spark of honour bides.

NORTHUMBERLAND. Be thou a prey unto the
house of York
And die in bands for this unmanly deed!

CLIFFORD. In dreadful war mayst thou
be overcome,
Or live in peace abandon'd and despis'd!

*Exeunt NORTHUMBERLAND, CLIFFORD, and
WESTMORELAND.*

WARWICK. Turn this way, Henry, and regard
them not.

EXETER. They seek revenge, and therefore will
not yield.

KING HENRY. Ah, Exeter!

WARWICK. Why should you sigh, my lord?

KING HENRY. Not for myself, Lord Warwick, but
my son,
Whom I unnaturally shall disinherit.
But be it as it may. *[To YORK]* I here entail
The crown to thee and to thine heirs for ever;
Conditionally, that here thou take an oath
To cease this civil war, and, whilst I live,
To honour me as thy king and sovereign,
And neither by treason nor hostility
To seek to put me down and reign thyself.

YORK. This oath I willingly take, and will perform.

Coming from the throne

WARWICK. Long live King Henry! Plantagenet,
embrace him.

KING HENRY. And long live thou, and these thy
forward sons!

YORK. Now York and Lancaster are reconcil'd.

EXETER. Accurs'd be he that seeks to make
them foes!

Sennet. Here they come down

YORK. Farewell, my gracious lord; I'll to my castle.

WARWICK. And I'll keep London with my soldiers.

NORFOLK. And I to Norfolk with my followers.

MONTAGUE. And I unto the sea, from whence
I came.   *Exeunt the YORKISTS.*

KING HENRY. And I, with grief and sorrow, to
the court.

Enter QUEEN MARGARET and the PRINCE OF WALES

EXETER. Here comes the Queen, whose looks
bewray her anger.
I'll steal away.

KING HENRY. Exeter, so will I.

QUEEN MARGARET. Nay, go not from me; I will
follow thee.

KING HENRY. Be patient, gentle queen, and I will
stay.

QUEEN MARGARET. Who can be patient in
such extremes?
Ah, wretched man! Would I had died a maid,
And never seen thee, never borne thee son,
Seeing thou hast prov'd so unnatural a father!
Hath he deserv'd to lose his birthright thus?
Hadst thou but lov'd him half so well as I,
Or felt that pain which I did for him once,
Or nourish'd him as I did with my blood,
Thou wouldst have left thy dearest heart-
blood there
Rather than have made that savage duke
thine heir,
And disinherited thine only son.

PRINCE OF WALES. Father, you cannot
disinherit me.
If you be King, why should not I succeed?

KING HENRY. Pardon me, Margaret; pardon me,
sweet son.
The Earl of Warwick and the Duke enforc'd me.

QUEEN MARGARET. Enforc'd thee! Art thou King
and wilt be forc'd?
I shame to hear thee speak. Ah,
timorous wretch!
Thou hast undone thyself, thy son, and me;
And giv'n unto the house of York such head
As thou shalt reign but by their sufferance.
To entail him and his heirs unto the crown,
What is it but to make thy sepulchre
And creep into it far before thy time?
Warwick is Chancellor and the lord of Calais;

Stern Falconbridge commands the narrow seas;
The Duke is made Protector of the realm;
And yet shalt thou be safe? Such safety finds
The trembling lamb environed with wolves.
Had I been there, which am a silly woman,
The soldiers should have toss'd me on their pikes
Before I would have granted to that act.
But thou prefer'st thy life before thine honour;
And seeing thou dost, I here divorce myself,
Both from thy table, Henry, and thy bed,
Until that act of parliament be repeal'd
Whereby my son is disinherited.
The northern lords that have forsworn thy colours
Will follow mine, if once they see them spread;
And spread they shall be, to thy foul disgrace
And utter ruin of the house of York.
Thus do I leave thee. Come, son, let's away;
Our army is ready; come, we'll after them.
KING HENRY. Stay, gentle Margaret, and hear
  me speak.
QUEEN MARGARET. Thou hast spoke too much
  already; get thee gone.
KING HENRY. Gentle son Edward, thou wilt stay
  with me?
QUEEN MARGARET. Ay, to be murder'd by
  his enemies.
PRINCE OF WALES. When I return with victory from
  the field
  I'll see your Grace; till then I'll follow her.
QUEEN MARGARET. Come, son, away; we may not
  linger thus.
      Exeunt QUEEN MARGARET *and the* PRINCE.
KING HENRY. Poor queen! How love to me and
  to her son
  Hath made her break out into terms of rage!
  Reveng'd may she be on that hateful Duke,
  Whose haughty spirit, winged with desire,
  Will cost my crown, and like an empty eagle
  Tire on the flesh of me and of my son!
  The loss of those three lords torments my heart.
  I'll write unto them, and entreat them fair;
  Come, cousin, you shall be the messenger.
EXETER. And I, I hope, shall reconcile them all.
      Exeunt.

✿ SCENE II ✿

Sandal Castle, near Wakefield, in Yorkshire

Flourish. Enter EDWARD, RICHARD, *and* MONTAGUE

RICHARD. Brother, though I be youngest, give
  me leave.

EDWARD. No, I can better play the orator.
MONTAGUE. But I have reasons strong
  and forcible.
      Enter the DUKE OF YORK
YORK. Why, how now, sons and brother! at
  a strife?
  What is your quarrel? How began it first?
EDWARD. No quarrel, but a slight contention.
YORK. About what?
RICHARD. About that which concerns your Grace
  and us-
  The crown of England, father, which is yours.
YORK. Mine, boy? Not till King Henry be dead.
RICHARD. Your right depends not on his life
  or death.
EDWARD. Now you are heir, therefore enjoy
  it now.
  By giving the house of Lancaster leave
  to breathe,
  It will outrun you, father, in the end.
YORK. I took an oath that he should quietly reign.
EDWARD. But for a kingdom any oath may
  be broken:
  I would break a thousand oaths to reign
  one year.
RICHARD. No; God forbid your Grace should
  be forsworn.
YORK. I shall be, if I claim by open war.
RICHARD. I'll prove the contrary, if you'll hear
  me speak.
YORK. Thou canst not, son; it is impossible.
RICHARD. An oath is of no moment, being
  not took
  Before a true and lawful magistrate
  That hath authority over him that swears.
  Henry had none, but did usurp the place;
  Then, seeing 'twas he that made you to depose,
  Your oath, my lord, is vain and frivolous.
  Therefore, to arms. And, father, do but think
  How sweet a thing it is to wear a crown,
  Within whose circuit is Elysium
  And all that poets feign of bliss and joy.
  Why do we linger thus? I cannot rest
  Until the white rose that I wear be dy'd
  Even in the lukewarm blood of Henry's heart.
YORK. Richard, enough; I will be King, or die.
  Brother, thou shalt to London presently
  And whet on Warwick to this enterprise.
  Thou, Richard, shalt to the Duke of Norfolk
  And tell him privily of our intent.
  You, Edward, shall unto my Lord Cobham,
  With whom the Kentishmen will willingly rise;
  In them I trust, for they are soldiers,

Witty, courteous, liberal, full of spirit.
While you are thus employ'd, what resteth more
But that I seek occasion how to rise,
And yet the King not privy to my drift,
Nor any of the house of Lancaster?

Enter a MESSENGER

But, stay. What news? Why com'st thou in
such post?
MESSENGER. The Queen with all the northern
earls and lords
Intend here to besiege you in your castle.
She is hard by with twenty thousand men;
And therefore fortify your hold, my lord.
YORK. Ay, with my sword. What! think'st thou that
we fear them?
Edward and Richard, you shall stay with me;
My brother Montague shall post to London.
Let noble Warwick, Cobham, and the rest,
Whom we have left protectors of the King,
With pow'rful policy strengthen themselves
And trust not simple Henry nor his oaths.
MONTAGUE. Brother, I go; I'll win them, fear it not.
And thus most humbly I do take my leave. *Exit.*

Enter SIR JOHN and SIR HUGH MORTIMER

YORK. Sir John and Sir Hugh Mortimer,
mine uncles!
You are come to Sandal in a happy hour;
The army of the Queen mean to besiege us.
SIR JOHN. She shall not need; we'll meet her in
the field.
YORK. What, with five thousand men?
RICHARD. Ay, with five hundred, father, for a need.
A woman's general; what should we fear?

A march afar off

EDWARD. I hear their drums. Let's set our men
in order,
And issue forth and bid them battle straight.
YORK. Five men to twenty! Though the odds
be great,
I doubt not, uncle, of our victory.
Many a battle have I won in France,
When as the enemy hath been ten to one;
Why should I not now have the like success?

Exeunt.

✿ SCENE III ✿

Field of battle between Sandal Castle and Wakefield

Alarum. Enter RUTLAND and his TUTOR

RUTLAND. Ah, whither shall I fly to scape
their hands?

Ah, tutor, look where bloody Clifford comes!

Enter CLIFFORD and SOLDIERS

CLIFFORD. Chaplain, away! Thy priesthood saves
thy life.
As for the brat of this accursed duke,
Whose father slew my father, he shall die.
TUTOR. And I, my lord, will bear him company.
CLIFFORD. Soldiers, away with him!
TUTOR. Ah, Clifford, murder not this
innocent child,
Lest thou be hated both of God and man.

Exit, forced off by SOLDIERS.

CLIFFORD. How now, is he dead already? Or is
it fear
That makes him close his eyes? I'll open them.
RUTLAND. So looks the pent-up lion o'er
the wretch
That trembles under his devouring paws;
And so he walks, insulting o'er his prey,
And so he comes, to rend his limbs asunder.
Ah, gentle Clifford, kill me with thy sword,
And not with such a cruel threat'ning look!
Sweet Clifford, hear me speak before I die.
I am too mean a subject for thy wrath;
Be thou reveng'd on men, and let me live.
CLIFFORD. In vain thou speak'st, poor boy; my
father's blood
Hath stopp'd the passage where thy words
should enter.
RUTLAND. Then let my father's blood open
it again:
He is a man, and, Clifford, cope with him.
CLIFFORD. Had I thy brethren here, their lives
and thine
Were not revenge sufficient for me;
No, if I digg'd up thy forefathers' graves
And hung their rotten coffins up in chains,
It could not slake mine ire nor ease my heart.
The sight of any of the house of York
Is as a fury to torment my soul;
And till I root out their accursed line
And leave not one alive, I live in hell.
Therefore-
RUTLAND. O, let me pray before I take my death!
To thee I pray: sweet Clifford, pity me.
CLIFFORD. Such pity as my rapier's point affords.
RUTLAND. I never did thee harm; why wilt thou
slay me?
CLIFFORD. Thy father hath.
RUTLAND. But 'twas ere I was born.
Thou hast one son; for his sake pity me,
Lest in revenge thereof, sith God is just,
He be as miserably slain as I.

Ah, let me live in prison all my days;
And when I give occasion of offence
Then let me die, for now thou hast no cause.
CLIFFORD. No cause!
　Thy father slew my father; therefore, die.*Stabs him*
RUTLAND. Di faciant laudis summa sit ista tuae!
Dies

CLIFFORD. Plantagenet, I come, Plantagenet;
And this thy son's blood cleaving to my blade
Shall rust upon my weapon, till thy blood,
Congeal'd with this, do make me wipe off both.
Exit

❧ SCENE IV ❧
Another part of the field

Alarum. Enter the DUKE OF YORK

YORK. The army of the Queen hath got the field.
My uncles both are slain in rescuing me;
And all my followers to the eager foe
Turn back and fly, like ships before the wind,
Or lambs pursu'd by hunger-starved wolves.
My sons-God knows what hath bechanced them;
But this I know-they have demean'd themselves
Like men born to renown by life or death.
Three times did Richard make a lane to me,
And thrice cried 'Courage, father! fight it out'.
And full as oft came Edward to my side
With purple falchion, painted to the hilt
In blood of those that had encount'red him.
And when the hardiest warriors did retire,
Richard cried 'Charge, and give no foot
of ground!'
And cried 'A crown, or else a glorious tomb!
A sceptre, or an earthly sepulchre!'
With this we charg'd again; but out alas!
We bodg'd again; as I have seen a swan
With bootless labour swim against the tide
And spend her strength with over-matching
waves. *[A short alarum within]*
Ah, hark! The fatal followers do pursue,
And I am faint and cannot fly their fury;
And were I strong, I would not shun their fury.
The sands are numb'red that make up my life;
Here must I stay, and here my life must end.
Enter QUEEN MARGARET, CLIFFORD,
NORTHUMBERLAND, the PRINCE OF WALES, and
SOLDIERS
Come, bloody Clifford, rough Northumberland,
I dare your quenchless fury to more rage;
I am your butt, and I abide your shot.

NORTHUMBERLAND. Yield to our mercy,
proud Plantagenet.
CLIFFORD. Ay, to such mercy as his ruthless arm
With downright payment show'd unto
my father.
Now Phaethon hath tumbled from his car,
And made an evening at the noontide prick.
YORK. My ashes, as the phoenix, may bring forth
A bird that will revenge upon you all;
And in that hope I throw mine eyes to heaven,
Scorning whate'er you can afflict me with.
Why come you not? What! multitudes, and fear?
CLIFFORD. So cowards fight when they can fly
no further;
So doves do peck the falcon's piercing talons;
So desperate thieves, all hopeless of their lives,
Breathe out invectives 'gainst the officers.
YORK. O Clifford, but bethink thee once again,
And in thy thought o'errun my former time;
And, if thou canst for blushing, view this face,
And bite thy tongue that slanders him
with cowardice
Whose frown hath made thee faint and fly
ere this!
CLIFFORD. I will not bandy with thee word
for word,
But buckler with thee blows, twice two for one.
QUEEN MARGARET. Hold, valiant Clifford; for a
thousand causes
I would prolong awhile the traitor's life.
Wrath makes him deaf; speak
thou, Northumberland.
NORTHUMBERLAND. Hold, Clifford! do not
honour him so much
To prick thy finger, though to wound his heart.
What valour were it, when a cur doth grin,
For one to thrust his hand between his teeth,
When he might spurn him with his foot away?
It is war's prize to take all vantages;
And ten to one is no impeach of valour.
They lay hands on YORK, who struggles
CLIFFORD. Ay, ay, so strives the woodcock with
the gin.
NORTHUMBERLAND. So doth the cony struggle
in the net.
YORK. So triumph thieves upon their
conquer'd booty;
So true men yield, with robbers so o'er-
match'd.
NORTHUMBERLAND. What would your Grace
have done unto him now?
QUEEN MARGARET. Brave warriors, Clifford
and Northumberland,

Come, make him stand upon this molehill here
That raught at mountains with
 outstretched arms,
Yet parted but the shadow with his hand.
What, was it you that would be England's king?
Was't you that revell'd in our parliament
And made a preachment of your high descent?
Where are your mess of sons to back you now?
The wanton Edward and the lusty George?
And where's that valiant crook-back prodigy,
Dicky your boy, that with his grumbling voice
Was wont to cheer his dad in mutinies?
Or, with the rest, where is your darling Rutland?
Look, York: I stain'd this napkin with the blood
That valiant Clifford with his rapier's point
Made issue from the bosom of the boy;
And if thine eyes can water for his death,
I give thee this to dry thy cheeks withal.
Alas, poor York! but that I hate thee deadly,
I should lament thy miserable state.
I prithee grieve to make me merry, York.
What, hath thy fiery heart so parch'd
 thine entrails
That not a tear can fall for Rutland's death?
Why art thou patient, man? Thou shouldst
 be mad;
And I to make thee mad do mock thee thus.
Stamp, rave, and fret, that I may sing and dance.
Thou wouldst be fee'd, I see, to make me sport;
York cannot speak unless he wear a crown.
A crown for York!-and, lords, bow low to him.
Hold you his hands whilst I do set it on. *[Putting a
paper crown on his head]*
Ay, marry, sir, now looks he like a king!
Ay, this is he that took King Henry's chair,
And this is he was his adopted heir.
But how is it that great Plantagenet
Is crown'd so soon and broke his solemn oath?
As I bethink me, you should not be King
Till our King Henry had shook hands with death.
And will you pale your head in Henry's glory,
And rob his temples of the diadem,
Now in his life, against your holy oath?
O, 'tis a fault too too unpardonable.
Off with the crown and with the crown his head;
And, whilst we breathe, take time to do him dead.
CLIFFORD. That is my office, for my father's sake.
QUEEN MARGARET. Nay, stay; let's hear the
 orisons he makes.
YORK. She-wolf of France, but worse than wolves
 of France,
Whose tongue more poisons than the
 adder's tooth!
How ill-beseeming is it in thy sex
To triumph like an Amazonian trull
Upon their woes whom fortune captivates!
But that thy face is visard-like, unchanging,
Made impudent with use of evil deeds,
I would assay, proud queen, to make
 thee blush.
To tell thee whence thou cam'st, of
 whom deriv'd,
Were shame enough to shame thee, wert thou
 not shameless.
Thy father bears the type of King of Naples,
Of both the Sicils and Jerusalem,
Yet not so wealthy as an English yeoman.
Hath that poor monarch taught thee to insult?
It needs not, nor it boots thee not,
 proud queen;
Unless the adage must be verified,
That beggars mounted run their horse
 to death.
'Tis beauty that doth oft make women proud;
But, God He knows, thy share thereof is small.
'Tis virtue that doth make them most admir'd;
The contrary doth make thee wond'red at.
'Tis government that makes them seem divine;
The want thereof makes thee abominable.
Thou art as opposite to every good
As the Antipodes are unto us,
Or as the south to the septentrion.
O tiger's heart wrapp'd in a woman's hide!
How couldst thou drain the life-blood of
 the child,
To bid the father wipe his eyes withal,
And yet be seen to bear a woman's face?
Women are soft, mild, pitiful, and flexible:
Thou stern, obdurate, flinty,
 rough, remorseless.
Bid'st thou me rage? Why, now thou hast
 thy wish;
Wouldst have me weep? Why, now thou hast
 thy will;
For raging wind blows up incessant showers,
And when the rage allays, the rain begins.
These tears are my sweet Rutland's obsequies;
And every drop cries vengeance for his death
'Gainst thee, fell Clifford, and thee,
 false Frenchwoman.
NORTHUMBERLAND. Beshrew me, but his
 passions move me so
That hardly can I check my eyes from tears.
YORK. That face of his the hungry cannibals
Would not have touch'd, would not have
 stain'd with blood;

But you are more inhuman, more inexorable-
O, ten times more-than tigers of Hyrcania.
See, ruthless queen, a hapless father's tears.
This cloth thou dipp'dst in blood of my
   sweet boy,
And I with tears do wash the blood away.
Keep thou the napkin, and go boast of this;
And if thou tell'st the heavy story right,
Upon my soul, the hearers will shed tears;
Yea, even my foes will shed fast-falling tears
And say 'Alas, it was a piteous deed!'
There, take the crown, and with the crown
   my curse;
And in thy need such comfort come to thee
As now I reap at thy too cruel hand!
Hard-hearted Clifford, take me from the world;
My soul to heaven, my blood upon your heads!
NORTHUMBERLAND. Had he been slaughter-man
   to all my kin,
I should not for my life but weep with him,
To see how inly sorrow gripes his soul.
QUEEN MARGARET. What, weeping-ripe, my
   Lord Northumberland?
Think but upon the wrong he did us all,
And that will quickly dry thy melting tears.
CLIFFORD. Here's for my oath, here's for my
   father's death.
                           Stabbing him
QUEEN MARGARET. And here's to right our
   gentle-hearted king.
                           Stabbing him
YORK. Open Thy gate of mercy, gracious God!
My soul flies through these wounds to seek
   out Thee.
                           Dies
QUEEN MARGARET. Off with his head, and set it
   on York gates;
So York may overlook the town of York.
                           Flourish. Exeunt

ACT II

SCENE I

A plain near Mortimer's Cross in Herefordshire

A march. Enter EDWARD, RICHARD, and their Power

EDWARD. I wonder how our princely father scap'd,
Or whether he be scap'd away or no
From Clifford's and Northumberland's pursuit.
Had he been ta'en, we should have heard
   the news;

Had he been slain, we should have heard
   the news;
Or had he scap'd, methinks we should
   have heard
The happy tidings of his good escape.
How fares my brother? Why is he so sad?
RICHARD. I cannot joy until I be resolv'd
Where our right valiant father is become.
I saw him in the battle range about,
And watch'd him how he singled Clifford forth.
Methought he bore him in the thickest troop
As doth a lion in a herd of neat;
Or as a bear, encompass'd round with dogs,
Who having pinch'd a few and made them cry,
The rest stand all aloof and bark at him.
So far'd our father with his enemies;
So fled his enemies my warlike father.
Methinks 'tis prize enough to be his son.
See how the morning opes her golden gates
And takes her farewell of the glorious sun.
How well resembles it the prime of youth,
Trimm'd like a younker prancing to his love!
EDWARD. Dazzle mine eyes, or do I see
   three suns?
RICHARD. Three glorious suns, each one a
   perfect sun;
Not separated with the racking clouds,
But sever'd in a pale clear-shining sky.
See, see! they join, embrace, and seem to kiss,
As if they vow'd some league inviolable.
Now are they but one lamp, one light, one sun.
In this the heaven figures some event.
EDWARD. 'Tis wondrous strange, the like yet
   never heard of.
I think it cites us, brother, to the field,
That we, the sons of brave Plantagenet,
Each one already blazing by our meeds,
Should notwithstanding join our lights together
And overshine the earth, as this the world.
Whate'er it bodes, henceforward will I bear
Upon my target three fair shining suns.
RICHARD. Nay, bear three daughters-by your
   leave I speak it,
You love the breeder better than the male.
                    Enter a MESSENGER, blowing
But what art thou, whose heavy looks foretell
Some dreadful story hanging on thy tongue?
MESSENGER. Ah, one that was a woeful looker-on
When as the noble Duke of York was slain,
Your princely father and my loving lord!
EDWARD. O, speak no more! for I have heard
   too much.
RICHARD. Say how he died, for I will hear it all.

MESSENGER. Environed he was with many foes,
And stood against them as the hope of Troy
Against the Greeks that would have
ent'red Troy.
But Hercules himself must yield to odds;
And many strokes, though with a little axe,
Hews down and fells the hardest-timber'd oak.
By many hands your father was subdu'd;
But only slaught'red by the ireful arm
Of unrelenting Clifford and the Queen,
Who crown'd the gracious Duke in high despite,
Laugh'd in his face; and when with grief
he wept,
The ruthless Queen gave him to dry his cheeks
A napkin steeped in the harmless blood
Of sweet young Rutland, by rough Clifford slain;
And after many scorns, many foul taunts,
They took his head, and on the gates of York
They set the same; and there it doth remain,
The saddest spectacle that e'er I view'd.
EDWARD. Sweet Duke of York, our prop to
lean upon,
Now thou art gone, we have no staff, no stay.
O Clifford, boist'rous Clifford, thou hast slain
The flow'r of Europe for his chivalry;
And treacherously hast thou vanquish'd him,
For hand to hand he would have
vanquish'd thee.
Now my soul's palace is become a prison.
Ah, would she break from hence, that this
my body
Might in the ground be closed up in rest!
For never henceforth shall I joy again;
Never, O never, shall I see more joy.
RICHARD. I cannot weep, for all my
body's moisture
Scarce serves to quench my furnace-
burning heart;
Nor can my tongue unload my heart's
great burden,
For self-same wind that I should speak withal
Is kindling coals that fires all my breast,
And burns me up with flames that tears
would quench.
To weep is to make less the depth of grief.
Tears then for babes; blows and revenge for me!
Richard, I bear thy name; I'll venge thy death,
Or die renowned by attempting it.
EDWARD. His name that valiant duke hath left
with thee;
His dukedom and his chair with me is left.
RICHARD. Nay, if thou be that princely
eagle's bird,

Show thy descent by gazing 'gainst the sun;
For chair and dukedom, throne and
kingdom, say:
Either that is thine, or else thou wert not his.
March. Enter WARWICK, MONTAGUE, and their Army
WARWICK. How now, fair lords! What fare? What
news abroad?
RICHARD. Great Lord of Warwick, if we
should recount
Our baleful news and at each word's deliverance
Stab poinards in our flesh till all were told,
The words would add more anguish than
the wounds.
O valiant lord, the Duke of York is slain!
EDWARD. O Warwick, Warwick! that Plantagenet
Which held thee dearly as his soul's redemption
Is by the stern Lord Clifford done to death.
WARWICK. Ten days ago I drown'd these news
in tears;
And now, to add more measure to your woes,
I come to tell you things sith then befall'n.
After the bloody fray at Wakefield fought,
Where your brave father breath'd his latest gasp,
Tidings, as swiftly as the posts could run,
Were brought me of your loss and his depart.
I, then in London, keeper of the King,
Muster'd my soldiers, gathered flocks of friends,
And very well appointed, as I thought,
March'd toward Saint Albans to intercept
the Queen,
Bearing the King in my behalf along;
For by my scouts I was advertised
That she was coming with a full intent
To dash our late decree in parliament
Touching King Henry's oath and
your succession.
Short tale to make-we at Saint Albans met,
Our battles join'd, and both sides fiercely fought;
But whether 'twas the coldness of the King,
Who look'd full gently on his warlike queen,
That robb'd my soldiers of their heated spleen,
Or whether 'twas report of her success,
Or more than common fear of Clifford's rigour,
Who thunders to his captives blood and death,
I cannot judge; but, to conclude with truth,
Their weapons like to lightning came and went:
Our soldiers', like the night-owl's lazy flight
Or like an idle thresher with a flail,
Fell gently down, as if they struck their friends.
I cheer'd them up with justice of our cause,
With promise of high pay and great rewards,
But all in vain; they had no heart to fight,
And we in them no hope to win the day;

So that we fled: the King unto the Queen;
Lord George your brother, Norfolk,
 and myself,
In haste post-haste are come to join with you;
For in the marches here we heard you were
Making another head to fight again.
EDWARD. Where is the Duke of Norfolk,
 gentle Warwick?
And when came George from Burgundy
 to England?
WARWICK. Some six miles off the Duke is with
 the soldiers;
And for your brother, he was lately sent
From your kind aunt, Duchess of Burgundy,
With aid of soldiers to this needful war.
RICHARD. 'Twas odds, belike, when valiant
 Warwick fled.
Oft have I heard his praises in pursuit,
But ne'er till now his scandal of retire.
WARWICK. Nor now my scandal, Richard, dost
 thou hear;
For thou shalt know this strong right hand
 of mine
Can pluck the diadem from faint Henry's head
And wring the awful sceptre from his fist,
Were he as famous and as bold in war
As he is fam'd for mildness, peace, and prayer.
RICHARD. I know it well, Lord Warwick; blame
 me not.
'Tis love I bear thy glories makes me speak.
But in this troublous time what's to be done?
Shall we go throw away our coats of steel
And wrap our bodies in black mourning-gowns,
Numb'ring our Ave-Maries with our beads?
Or shall we on the helmets of our foes
Tell our devotion with revengeful arms?
If for the last, say 'Ay', and to it, lords.
WARWICK. Why, therefore Warwick came to
 seek you out;
And therefore comes my brother Montague.
Attend me, lords. The proud insulting Queen,
With Clifford and the haught Northumberland,
And of their feather many moe proud birds,
Have wrought the easy-melting King like wax.
He swore consent to your succession,
His oath enrolled in the parliament;
And now to London all the crew are gone
To frustrate both his oath and what beside
May make against the house of Lancaster.
Their power, I think, is thirty thousand strong.
Now if the help of Norfolk and myself,
With all the friends that thou, brave Earl
 of March,

Amongst the loving Welshmen canst procure,
Will but amount to five and twenty thousand,
Why, Via! to London will we march amain,
And once again bestride our foaming steeds,
And once again cry 'Charge upon our foes!'
But never once again turn back and fly.
RICHARD. Ay, now methinks I hear great
 Warwick speak.
Ne'er may he live to see a sunshine day
That cries 'Retire!' if Warwick bid him stay.
EDWARD. Lord Warwick, on thy shoulder will
 I lean;
And when thou fail'st-as God forbid the hour!-
Must Edward fall, which peril heaven forfend.
WARWICK. No longer Earl of March, but Duke
 of York;
The next degree is England's royal throne,
For King of England shalt thou be proclaim'd
In every borough as we pass along;
And he that throws not up his cap for joy
Shall for the fault make forfeit of his head.
King Edward, valiant Richard, Montague,
Stay we no longer, dreaming of renown,
But sound the trumpets and about our task.
RICHARD. Then, Clifford, were thy heart as hard
 as steel,
As thou hast shown it flinty by thy deeds,
I come to pierce it or to give thee mine.
EDWARD. Then strike up drums. God and Saint
 George for us!

Enter a MESSENGER

WARWICK. How now! what news?
MESSENGER. The Duke of Norfolk sends you
 word by me
The Queen is coming with a puissant host,
And craves your company for speedy counsel.
WARWICK. Why, then it sorts; brave warriors,
 let's away.   *Exeunt*

✿ SCENE II ✿
Before York

Flourish. Enter KING HENRY, QUEEN
MARGARET, the PRINCE OF WALES, CLIFFORD,
NORTHUMBERLAND, with drum and trumpets

QUEEN MARGARET. Welcome, my lord, to this
 brave town of York.
Yonder's the head of that arch-enemy
That sought to be encompass'd with
 your crown.
Doth not the object cheer your heart, my lord?

KING HENRY. Ay, as the rocks cheer them that
 fear their wreck-
To see this sight, it irks my very soul.
Withhold revenge, dear God; 'tis not my fault,
Nor wittingly have I infring'd my vow.
CLIFFORD. My gracious liege, this too much lenity
And harmful pity must be laid aside.
To whom do lions cast their gentle looks?
Not to the beast that would usurp their den.
Whose hand is that the forest bear doth lick?
Not his that spoils her young before her face.
Who scapes the lurking serpent's mortal sting?
Not he that sets his foot upon her back,
The smallest worm will turn, being trodden on,
And doves will peck in safeguard of their brood.
Ambitious York did level at thy crown,
Thou smiling while he knit his angry brows.
He, but a Duke, would have his son a king,
And raise his issue like a loving sire:
Thou, being a king, bless'd with a goodly son,
Didst yield consent to disinherit him,
Which argued thee a most unloving father.
Unreasonable creatures feed their young;
And though man's face be fearful to their eyes,
Yet, in protection of their tender ones,
Who hath not seen them-even with those wings
Which sometime they have us'd with
 fearful flight-
Make war with him that climb'd unto their nest,
Offering their own lives in their young's defence?
For shame, my liege, make them
 your precedent!
Were it not pity that this goodly boy
Should lose his birthright by his father's fault,
And long hereafter say unto his child
'What my great-grandfather and grandsire got
My careless father fondly gave away'?
Ah, what a shame were this! Look on the boy;
And let his manly face, which promiseth
Successful fortune, steel thy melting heart
To hold thine own and leave thine own
 with him.
KING HENRY. Full well hath Clifford play'd
 the orator,
Inferring arguments of mighty force.
But, Clifford, tell me, didst thou never hear
That things ill got had ever bad success?
And happy always was it for that son
Whose father for his hoarding went to hell?
I'll leave my son my virtuous deeds behind;
And would my father had left me no more!
For all the rest is held at such a rate
As brings a thousand-fold more care to keep

Than in possession any jot of pleasure.
Ah, cousin York! would thy best friends
 did know
How it doth grieve me that thy head is here!
QUEEN MARGARET. My lord, cheer up your
 spirits; our foes are nigh,
And this soft courage makes your followers faint.
You promis'd knighthood to our forward son:
Unsheathe your sword and dub him presently.
Edward, kneel down.
KING HENRY. Edward Plantagenet, arise a knight;
And learn this lesson: Draw thy sword in right.
PRINCE OF WALES. My gracious father, by your
 kingly leave,
I'll draw it as apparent to the crown,
And in that quarrel use it to the death.
CLIFFORD. Why, that is spoken like a
 toward prince.

Enter a MESSENGER

MESSENGER. Royal commanders, be in readiness;
For with a band of thirty thousand men
Comes Warwick, backing of the Duke of York,
And in the towns, as they do march along,
Proclaims him king, and many fly to him.
Darraign your battle, for they are at hand.
CLIFFORD. I would your Highness would depart
 the field:
The Queen hath best success when you
 are absent.
QUEEN MARGARET. Ay, good my lord, and leave
 us to our fortune.
KING HENRY. Why, that's my fortune too;
 therefore I'll stay.
NORTHUMBERLAND. Be it with resolution, then,
 to fight.
PRINCE OF WALES. My royal father, cheer these
 noble lords,
And hearten those that fight in your defence.
Unsheathe your sword, good father; cry
 'Saint George!'

March. Enter EDWARD, GEORGE, RICHARD,
WARWICK, NORFOLK, MONTAGUE, and SOLDIERS

EDWARD. Now, perjur'd Henry, wilt thou kneel
 for grace
And set thy diadem upon my head,
Or bide the mortal fortune of the field?
QUEEN MARGARET. Go rate thy minions, proud
 insulting boy.
Becomes it thee to be thus bold in terms
Before thy sovereign and thy lawful king?
EDWARD. I am his king, and he should bow
 his knee.
I was adopted heir by his consent:

Since when, his oath is broke; for, as I hear,
You that are King, though he do wear the crown,
Have caus'd him by new act of parliament
To blot out me and put his own son in.

CLIFFORD. And reason too:
Who should succeed the father but the son?

RICHARD. Are you there, butcher? O, I
cannot speak!

CLIFFORD. Ay, crook-back, here I stand to
answer thee,
Or any he, the proudest of thy sort.

RICHARD. 'Twas you that kill'd young Rutland,
was it not?

CLIFFORD. Ay, and old York, and yet not satisfied.

RICHARD. For God's sake, lords, give signal to
the fight.

WARWICK. What say'st thou, Henry? Wilt thou
yield the crown?

QUEEN MARGARET. Why, how now, long-tongu'd
Warwick! Dare you speak?
When you and I met at Saint Albans last
Your legs did better service than your hands.

WARWICK. Then 'twas my turn to fly, and now
'tis thine.

CLIFFORD. You said so much before, and yet
you fled.

WARWICK. 'Twas not your valour, Clifford, drove
me thence.

NORTHUMBERLAND. No, nor your manhood that
durst make you stay.

RICHARD. Northumberland, I hold
thee reverently.
Break off the parley; for scarce I can refrain
The execution of my big-swol'n heart
Upon that Clifford, that cruel child-killer.

CLIFFORD. I slew thy father; call'st thou him
a child?

RICHARD. Ay, like a dastard and a
treacherous coward,
As thou didst kill our tender brother Rutland;
But ere sunset I'll make thee curse the deed.

KING HENRY. Have done with words, my lords,
and hear me speak.

QUEEN MARGARET. Defy them then, or else hold
close thy lips.

KING HENRY. I prithee give no limits to
my tongue:
I am a king, and privileg'd to speak.

CLIFFORD. My liege, the wound that bred this
meeting here
Cannot be cur'd by words; therefore be still.

RICHARD. Then, executioner, unsheathe
thy sword.

By Him that made us all, I am resolv'd
That Clifford's manhood lies upon his tongue.

EDWARD. Say, Henry, shall I have my right, or no?
A thousand men have broke their fasts to-day
That ne'er shall dine unless thou yield the crown.

WARWICK. If thou deny, their blood upon
thy head;
For York in justice puts his armour on.

PRINCE OF WALES. If that be right which Warwick
says is right,
There is no wrong, but every thing is right.

RICHARD. Whoever got thee, there thy
mother stands;
For well I wot thou hast thy mother's tongue.

QUEEN MARGARET. But thou art neither like thy
sire nor dam;
But like a foul misshapen stigmatic,
Mark'd by the destinies to be avoided,
As venom toads or lizards' dreadful stings.

RICHARD. Iron of Naples hid with English gilt,
Whose father bears the title of a king-
As if a channel should be call'd the sea-
Sham'st thou not, knowing whence thou
art extraught,
To let thy tongue detect thy base-born heart?

EDWARD. A wisp of straw were worth a
thousand crowns
To make this shameless callet know herself.
Helen of Greece was fairer far than thou,
Although thy husband may be Menelaus;
And ne'er was Agamemnon's brother wrong'd
By that false woman as this king by thee.
His father revell'd in the heart of France,
And tam'd the King, and made the
Dauphin stoop;
And had he match'd according to his state,
He might have kept that glory to this day;
But when he took a beggar to his bed
And grac'd thy poor sire with his bridal day,
Even then that sunshine brew'd a show'r for him
That wash'd his father's fortunes forth of France
And heap'd sedition on his crown at home.
For what hath broach'd this tumult but
thy pride?
Hadst thou been meek, our title still had slept;
And we, in pity of the gentle King,
Had slipp'd our claim until another age.

GEORGE. But when we saw our sunshine made
thy spring,
And that thy summer bred us no increase,
We set the axe to thy usurping root;
And though the edge hath something
hit ourselves,

Yet know thou, since we have begun to strike,
We'll never leave till we have hewn thee down,
Or bath'd thy growing with our heated bloods.

EDWARD. And in this resolution I defy thee;
Not willing any longer conference,
Since thou deniest the gentle King to speak.
Sound trumpets; let our bloody colours wave,
And either victory or else a grave!

QUEEN MARGARET. Stay, Edward.

EDWARD. No, wrangling woman, we'll no
longer stay;
These words will cost ten thousand lives
this day.

Exeunt.

⚔ SCENE III ⚔

A field of battle between Towton and Saxton, in Yorkshire

Alarum; excursions. Enter WARWICK

WARWICK. Forspent with toil, as runners with
a race,
I lay me down a little while to breathe;
For strokes receiv'd and many blows repaid
Have robb'd my strong-knit sinews of
their strength,
And spite of spite needs must I rest awhile.

Enter EDWARD, running

EDWARD. Smile, gentle heaven, or strike,
ungentle death;
For this world frowns, and Edward's sun
is clouded.

WARWICK. How now, my lord. What hap? What
hope of good?

Enter GEORGE

GEORGE. Our hap is lost, our hope but
sad despair;
Our ranks are broke, and ruin follows us.
What counsel give you? Whither shall we fly?

EDWARD. Bootless is flight: they follow us
with wings;
And weak we are, and cannot shun pursuit.

Enter RICHARD

RICHARD. Ah, Warwick, why hast thou
withdrawn thyself?
Thy brother's blood the thirsty earth hath drunk,
Broach'd with the steely point of Clifford's lance;
And in the very pangs of death he cried,
Like to a dismal clangor heard from far,
'Warwick, revenge! Brother, revenge my death'.
So, underneath the belly of their steeds,

That stain'd their fetlocks in his smoking blood,
The noble gentleman gave up the ghost.

WARWICK. Then let the earth be drunken with
our blood.
I'll kill my horse, because I will not fly.
Why stand we like soft-hearted women here,
Wailing our losses, whiles the foe doth rage,
And look upon, as if the tragedy
Were play'd in jest by counterfeiting actors?
Here on my knee I vow to God above
I'll never pause again, never stand still,
Till either death hath clos'd these eyes of mine
Or fortune given me measure of revenge.

EDWARD. O Warwick, I do bend my knee
with thine,
And in this vow do chain my soul to thine!
And ere my knee rise from the earth's cold face
I throw my hands, mine eyes, my heart to Thee,
Thou setter-up and plucker-down of kings,
Beseeching Thee, if with Thy will it stands
That to my foes this body must be prey,
Yet that Thy brazen gates of heaven may ope
And give sweet passage to my sinful soul.
Now, lords, take leave until we meet again,
Where'er it be, in heaven or in earth.

RICHARD. Brother, give me thy hand; and,
gentle Warwick,
Let me embrace thee in my weary arms.
I that did never weep now melt with woe
That winter should cut off our spring-time so.

WARWICK. Away, away! Once more, sweet
lords, farewell.

GEORGE. Yet let us all together to our troops,
And give them leave to fly that will not stay,
And call them pillars that will stand to us;
And if we thrive, promise them such rewards
As victors wear at the Olympian games.
This may plant courage in their quailing breasts,
For yet is hope of life and victory.
Forslow no longer; make we hence amain.

Exeunt.

⚔ SCENE IV ⚔

Another part of the field

Excursions. Enter RICHARD and CLIFFORD

RICHARD. Now, Clifford, I have singled
thee alone.
Suppose this arm is for the Duke of York,
And this for Rutland; both bound to revenge,
Wert thou environ'd with a brazen wall.

CLIFFORD. Now, Richard, I am with thee
  here alone.
  This is the hand that stabbed thy father York;
  And this the hand that slew thy brother Rutland;
  And here's the heart that triumphs in their death
  And cheers these hands that slew thy sire
  and brother
  To execute the like upon thyself;
  And so, have at thee!   *They fight*
      Enter WARWICK; CLIFFORD flies.
RICHARD. Nay, Warwick, single out some
  other chase;
  For I myself will hunt this wolf to death.*Exeunt.*

✿ SCENE V ✿
Another part of the field

Alarum. Enter KING HENRY alone

KING HENRY. This battle fares like to the
  morning's war,
  When dying clouds contend with growing light,
  What time the shepherd, blowing of his nails,
  Can neither call it perfect day nor night.
  Now sways it this way, like a mighty sea
  Forc'd by the tide to combat with the wind;
  Now sways it that way, like the selfsame sea
  Forc'd to retire by fury of the wind.
  Sometime the flood prevails, and then the wind;
  Now one the better, then another best;
  Both tugging to be victors, breast to breast,
  Yet neither conqueror nor conquered.
  So is the equal poise of this fell war.
  Here on this molehill will I sit me down.
  To whom God will, there be the victory!
  For Margaret my queen, and Clifford too,
  Have chid me from the battle, swearing both
  They prosper best of all when I am thence.
  Would I were dead, if God's good will were so!
  For what is in this world but grief and woe?
  O God! methinks it were a happy life
  To be no better than a homely swain;
  To sit upon a hill, as I do now,
  To carve out dials quaintly, point by point,
  Thereby to see the minutes how they run-
  How many makes the hour full complete,
  How many hours brings about the day,
  How many days will finish up the year,
  How many years a mortal man may live.
  When this is known, then to divide the times-
  So many hours must I tend my flock;
  So many hours must I take my rest;

So many hours must I contemplate;
So many hours must I sport myself;
So many days my ewes have been with young;
So many weeks ere the poor fools will ean;
So many years ere I shall shear the fleece:
So minutes, hours, days, months, and years,
Pass'd over to the end they were created,
Would bring white hairs unto a quiet grave.
Ah, what a life were this! how sweet! how lovely!
Gives not the hawthorn bush a sweeter shade
To shepherds looking on their silly sheep,
Than doth a rich embroider'd canopy
To kings that fear their subjects' treachery?
O yes, it doth; a thousand-fold it doth.
And to conclude: the shepherd's homely curds,
His cold thin drink out of his leather bottle,
His wonted sleep under a fresh tree's shade,
All which secure and sweetly he enjoys,
Is far beyond a prince's delicates-
His viands sparkling in a golden cup,
His body couched in a curious bed,
When care, mistrust, and treason waits on him.
    Alarum. Enter a SON that hath kill'd his Father, at one door;
     and a FATHER that hath kill'd his Son, at another door
SON. Ill blows the wind that profits nobody.
  This man whom hand to hand I slew in fight
  May be possessed with some store of crowns;
  And I, that haply take them from him now,
  May yet ere night yield both my life and them
  To some man else, as this dead man doth me.
  Who's this? O God! It is my father's face,
  Whom in this conflict I unwares have kill'd.
  O heavy times, begetting such events!
  From London by the King was I press'd forth;
  My father, being the Earl of Warwick's man,
  Came on the part of York, press'd by his master;
  And I, who at his hands receiv'd my life,
  Have by my hands of life bereaved him.
  Pardon me, God, I knew not what I did.
  And pardon, father, for I knew not thee.
  My tears shall wipe away these bloody marks;
  And no more words till they have flow'd
  their fill.
KING HENRY. O piteous spectacle! O
  bloody times!
  Whiles lions war and battle for their dens,
  Poor harmless lambs abide their enmity.
  Weep, wretched man; I'll aid thee tear for tear;
  And let our hearts and eyes, like civil war,
  Be blind with tears and break o'ercharg'd
  with grief.
     Enter FATHER, bearing of his SON
FATHER. Thou that so stoutly hath resisted me,

Give me thy gold, if thou hast any gold;
For I have bought it with an hundred blows.
But let me see. Is this our foeman's face?
Ah, no, no, no, it is mine only son!
Ah, boy, if any life be left in thee,
Throw up thine eye! See, see what show'rs arise,
Blown with the windy tempest of my heart
Upon thy wounds, that kills mine eye and heart!
O, pity, God, this miserable age!
What stratagems, how fell, how butcherly,
Erroneous, mutinous, and unnatural,
This deadly quarrel daily doth beget!
O boy, thy father gave thee life too soon,
And hath bereft thee of thy life too late!

KING HENRY. Woe above woe! grief more than
  common grief!
O that my death would stay these ruthful deeds!
O pity, pity, gentle heaven, pity!
The red rose and the white are on his face,
The fatal colours of our striving houses:
The one his purple blood right well resembles;
The other his pale cheeks, methinks, presenteth.
Wither one rose, and let the other flourish!
If you contend, a thousand lives must perish.

SON. How will my mother for a father's death
Take on with me, and ne'er be satisfied!

FATHER. How will my wife for slaughter of my son
Shed seas of tears, and ne'er be satisfied!

KING HENRY. How will the country for these
  woeful chances
Misthink the King, and not be satisfied!

SON. Was ever son so rued a father's death?

FATHER. Was ever father so bemoan'd his son?

KING HENRY. Was ever king so griev'd for
  subjects' woe?
Much is your sorrow; mine ten times so much.

SON. I'll bear thee hence, where I may weep
  my fill.
Exit with the body.

FATHER. These arms of mine shall be thy winding-
sheet;
My heart, sweet boy, shall be thy sepulchre,
For from my heart thine image ne'er shall go;
My sighing breast shall be thy funeral bell;
And so obsequious will thy father be,
Even for the loss of thee, having no more,
As Priam was for all his valiant sons.
I'll bear thee hence; and let them fight that will,
For I have murdered where I should not kill.
Exit with the body.

KING HENRY. Sad-hearted men, much overgone
  with care,
Here sits a king more woeful than you are.

*Alarums, excursions. Enter QUEEN MARGARET, PRINCE
OF WALES, and EXETER*

PRINCE OF WALES. Fly, father, fly; for all your
  friends are fled,
And Warwick rages like a chafed bull.
Away! for death doth hold us in pursuit.

QUEEN MARGARET. Mount you, my lord; towards
  Berwick post amain.
Edward and Richard, like a brace of greyhounds
Having the fearful flying hare in sight,
With fiery eyes sparkling for very wrath,
And bloody steel grasp'd in their ireful hands,
Are at our backs; and therefore hence amain.

EXETER. Away! for vengeance comes along
  with them.
Nay, stay not to expostulate; make speed;
Or else come after. I'll away before.

KING HENRY. Nay, take me with thee, good
  sweet Exeter.
Not that I fear to stay, but love to go
Whither the Queen intends. Forward; away!
Exeunt.

❧ SCENE VI ❧
Another part of the field

A loud alarum. Enter CLIFFORD, wounded

CLIFFORD. Here burns my candle out; ay, here
  it dies,
Which, whiles it lasted, gave King Henry light.
O Lancaster, I fear thy overthrow
More than my body's parting with my soul!
My love and fear glu'd many friends to thee;
And, now I fall, thy tough commixture melts,
Impairing Henry, strength'ning
  misproud York.
The common people swarm like summer flies;
And whither fly the gnats but to the sun?
And who shines now but Henry's enemies?
O Phoebus, hadst thou never given consent
That Phaethon should check thy fiery steeds,
Thy burning car never had scorch'd the earth!
And, Henry, hadst thou sway'd as kings
  should do,
Or as thy father and his father did,
Giving no ground unto the house of York,
They never then had sprung like summer flies;
I and ten thousand in this luckless realm
Had left no mourning widows for our death;
And thou this day hadst kept thy chair
  in peace.

For what doth cherish weeds but gentle air?
And what makes robbers bold but too
  much lenity?
Bootless are plaints, and cureless are
  my wounds.
No way to fly, nor strength to hold out flight.
The foe is merciless and will not pity;
For at their hands I have deserv'd no pity.
The air hath got into my deadly wounds,
And much effuse of blood doth make me faint.
Come, York and Richard, Warwick and the rest;
I stabb'd your fathers' bosoms: split my breast.

He faints

Alarum and retreat. Enter EDWARD, GEORGE,
RICHARD, MONTAGUE, WARWICK, and soldiers

EDWARD. Now breathe we, lords. Good fortune
  bids us pause
And smooth the frowns of war with peaceful
  looks.
Some troops pursue the bloody-minded Queen
That led calm Henry, though he were a king,
As doth a sail, fill'd with a fretting gust,
Command an argosy to stem the waves.
But think you, lords, that Clifford fled
  with them?
WARWICK. No, 'tis impossible he should escape;
For, though before his face I speak the words,
Your brother Richard mark'd him for the grave;
And, whereso'er he is, he's surely dead.

CLIFFORD groans, and dies.

RICHARD. Whose soul is that which takes her
  heavy leave?
A deadly groan, like life and death's departing.
See who it is.
EDWARD. And now the battle's ended,
If friend or foe, let him be gently used.
RICHARD. Revoke that doom of mercy, for
  'tis Clifford;
Who not contented that he lopp'd the branch
In hewing Rutland when his leaves put forth,
But set his murd'ring knife unto the root
From whence that tender spray did sweetly spring-
I mean our princely father, Duke of York.
WARWICK. From off the gates of York fetch down
  the head,
Your father's head, which Clifford placed there;
Instead whereof let this supply the room.
Measure for measure must be answered.
EDWARD. Bring forth that fatal screech-owl to
  our house,
That nothing sung but death to us and ours.
Now death shall stop his dismal
  threat'ning sound,

And his ill-boding tongue no more shall speak.
WARWICK. I think his understanding is bereft.
Speak, Clifford, dost thou know who speaks
  to thee?
Dark cloudy death o'ershades his beams of life,
And he nor sees nor hears us what we say.
RICHARD. O, would he did! and so, perhaps,
  he doth.
'Tis but his policy to counterfeit,
Because he would avoid such bitter taunts
Which in the time of death he gave our father.
GEORGE. If so thou think'st, vex him with
  eager words.
RICHARD. Clifford, ask mercy and obtain
  no grace.
EDWARD. Clifford, repent in bootless penitence.
WARWICK. Clifford, devise excuses for thy faults.
GEORGE. While we devise fell tortures for
  thy faults.
RICHARD. Thou didst love York, and I am son
  to York.
EDWARD. Thou pitied'st Rutland, I will pity thee.
GEORGE. Where's Captain Margaret, to fence
  you now?
WARWICK. They mock thee, Clifford; swear as
  thou wast wont.
RICHARD. What, not an oath? Nay, then the world
  goes hard
When Clifford cannot spare his friends an oath.
I know by that he's dead; and by my soul,
If this right hand would buy two hours' life,
That I in all despite might rail at him,
This hand should chop it off, and with the
  issuing blood
Stifle the villain whose unstanched thirst
York and young Rutland could not satisfy.
WARWICK. Ay, but he's dead. Off with the
  traitor's head,
And rear it in the place your father's stands.
And now to London with triumphant march,
There to be crowned England's royal King;
From whence shall Warwick cut the sea
  to France,
And ask the Lady Bona for thy queen.
So shalt thou sinew both these lands together;
And, having France thy friend, thou shalt
  not dread
The scatt'red foe that hopes to rise again;
For though they cannot greatly sting to hurt,
Yet look to have them buzz to offend thine ears.
First will I see the coronation;
And then to Brittany I'll cross the sea
To effect this marriage, so it please my lord.

EDWARD. Even as thou wilt, sweet Warwick, let
  it be;
  For in thy shoulder do I build my seat,
  And never will I undertake the thing
  Wherein thy counsel and consent is wanting.
  Richard, I will create thee Duke of Gloucester;
  And George, of Clarence; Warwick, as ourself,
  Shall do and undo as him pleaseth best.
RICHARD. Let me be Duke of Clarence, George
  of Gloucester;
  For Gloucester's dukedom is too ominous.
WARWICK. Tut, that's a foolish observation.
  Richard, be Duke of Gloucester. Now to London
  To see these honours in possession.

Exeunt.

ACT III

✦ SCENE I ✦
A chase in the north of England

Enter two KEEPERS, with cross-bows in their hands

FIRST KEEPER. Under this thick-grown brake we'll
  shroud ourselves,
  For through this laund anon the deer will come;
  And in this covert will we make our stand,
  Culling the principal of all the deer.
SECOND KEEPER. I'll stay above the hill, so both
  may shoot.
FIRST KEEPER. That cannot be; the noise of
  thy cross-bow
  Will scare the herd, and so my shoot is lost.
  Here stand we both, and aim we at the best;
  And, for the time shall not seem tedious,
  I'll tell thee what befell me on a day
  In this self-place where now we mean to stand.
SECOND KEEPER. Here comes a man; let's stay till
  he be past.

Enter KING HENRY, disguised, with a prayer-book

KING HENRY. From Scotland am I stol'n, even of
  pure love,
  To greet mine own land with my wishful sight.
  No, Harry, Harry, 'tis no land of thine;
  Thy place is fill'd, thy sceptre wrung from thee,
  Thy balm wash'd off wherewith thou
  wast anointed.
  No bending knee will call thee Caesar now,
  No humble suitors press to speak for right,
  No, not a man comes for redress of thee;
  For how can I help them and not myself?

FIRST KEEPER. Ay, here's a deer whose skin's a
  keeper's fee.
  This is the quondam King; let's seize upon him.
KING HENRY. Let me embrace thee,
  sour adversity,
  For wise men say it is the wisest course.
SECOND KEEPER. Why linger we? let us lay hands
  upon him.
FIRST KEEPER. Forbear awhile; we'll hear a
  little more.
KING HENRY. My Queen and son are gone to
  France for aid;
  And, as I hear, the great commanding Warwick
  Is thither gone to crave the French King's sister
  To wife for Edward. If this news be true,
  Poor Queen and son, your labour is but lost;
  For Warwick is a subtle orator,
  And Lewis a prince soon won with
  moving words.
  By this account, then, Margaret may win him;
  For she's a woman to be pitied much.
  Her sighs will make a batt'ry in his breast;
  Her tears will pierce into a marble heart;
  The tiger will be mild whiles she doth mourn;
  And Nero will be tainted with remorse
  To hear and see her plaints, her brinish tears.
  Ay, but she's come to beg: Warwick, to give.
  She, on his left side, craving aid for Henry:
  He, on his right, asking a wife for Edward.
  She weeps, and says her Henry is depos'd:
  He smiles, and says his Edward is install'd;
  That she, poor wretch, for grief can speak
  no more;
  Whiles Warwick tells his title, smooths
  the wrong,
  Inferreth arguments of mighty strength,
  And in conclusion wins the King from her
  With promise of his sister, and what else,
  To strengthen and support King Edward's place.
  O Margaret, thus 'twill be; and thou, poor soul,
  Art then forsaken, as thou went'st forlorn!
SECOND KEEPER. Say, what art thou that talk'st of
  kings and queens?
KING HENRY. More than I seem, and less than I
  was born to:
  A man at least, for less I should not be;
  And men may talk of kings, and why not I?
SECOND KEEPER. Ay, but thou talk'st as if thou
  wert a king.
KING HENRY. Why, so I am-in mind; and
  that's enough.
SECOND KEEPER. But, if thou be a king, where is
  thy crown?

KING HENRY. My crown is in my heart, not on
my head;
Not deck'd with diamonds and Indian stones,
Not to be seen. My crown is call'd content;
A crown it is that seldom kings enjoy.
SECOND KEEPER. Well, if you be a king crown'd
with content,
Your crown content and you must be contented
To go along with us; for as we think,
You are the king King Edward hath depos'd;
And we his subjects, sworn in all allegiance,
Will apprehend you as his enemy.
KING HENRY. But did you never swear, and break
an oath?
SECOND KEEPER. No, never such an oath; nor
will not now.
KING HENRY. Where did you dwell when I was
King of England?
SECOND KEEPER. Here in this country, where we
now remain.
KING HENRY. I was anointed king at nine
months old;
My father and my grandfather were kings;
And you were sworn true subjects unto me;
And tell me, then, have you not broke your oaths?
FIRST KEEPER. No;
For we were subjects but while you were king.
KING HENRY. Why, am I dead? Do I not breathe
a man?
Ah, simple men, you know not what you swear!
Look, as I blow this feather from my face,
And as the air blows it to me again,
Obeying with my wind when I do blow,
And yielding to another when it blows,
Commanded always by the greater gust,
Such is the lightness of you common men.
But do not break your oaths; for of that sin
My mild entreaty shall not make you guilty.
Go where you will, the King shall
be commanded;
And be you kings: command, and I'll obey.
FIRST KEEPER. We are true subjects to the King,
King Edward.
KING HENRY. So would you be again to Henry,
If he were seated as King Edward is.
FIRST KEEPER. We charge you, in God's name
and the King's,
To go with us unto the officers.
KING HENRY. In God's name, lead; your King's
name be obey'd;
And what God will, that let your King perform;
And what he will, I humbly yield unto.

Exeunt.

❧ SCENE II ❧
London. The palace

*Enter KING EDWARD, GLOUCESTER, CLARENCE,
and LADY GREY*

KING EDWARD. Brother of Gloucester, at Saint
Albans' field
This lady's husband, Sir Richard Grey, was slain,
His land then seiz'd on by the conqueror.
Her suit is now to repossess those lands;
Which we in justice cannot well deny,
Because in quarrel of the house of York
The worthy gentleman did lose his life.
GLOUCESTER. Your Highness shall do well to
grant her suit;
It were dishonour to deny it her.
KING EDWARD. It were no less; but yet I'll make
a pause.
GLOUCESTER. [*Aside to CLARENCE*] Yea, is it so?
I see the lady hath a thing to grant,
Before the King will grant her humble suit.
CLARENCE. [*Aside to GLOUCESTER*] He knows the
game; how true he keeps the wind!
GLOUCESTER. [*Aside to CLARENCE*] Silence!
KING EDWARD. Widow, we will consider of
your suit;
And come some other time to know our mind.
LADY GREY. Right gracious lord, I cannot
brook delay.
May it please your Highness to resolve me now;
And what your pleasure is shall satisfy me.
GLOUCESTER. [*Aside*] Ay, widow? Then I'll warrant
you all your lands,
An if what pleases him shall pleasure you.
Fight closer or, good faith, you'll catch a blow.
CLARENCE. [*Aside to GLOUCESTER*] I fear her not,
unless she chance to fall.
GLOUCESTER. [*Aside to CLARENCE*] God forbid that,
for he'll take vantages.
KING EDWARD. How many children hast thou,
widow, tell me.
CLARENCE. [*Aside to GLOUCESTER*] I think he means
to beg a child of her.
GLOUCESTER. [*Aside to CLARENCE*] Nay, then whip
me; he'll rather give her two.
LADY GREY. Three, my most gracious lord.
GLOUCESTER. [*Aside*] You shall have four if you'll
be rul'd by him.
KING EDWARD. 'Twere pity they should lose their
father's lands.

LADY GREY. Be pitiful, dread lord, and grant
it, then.

KING EDWARD. Lords, give us leave; I'll try this
widow's wit.

GLOUCESTER. [Aside] Ay, good leave have you; for
you will have leave
Till youth take leave and leave you to the crutch.

GLOUCESTER and CLARENCE withdraw.

KING EDWARD. Now tell me, madam, do you love
your children?

LADY GREY. Ay, full as dearly as I love myself.

KING EDWARD. And would you not do much to
do them good?

LADY GREY. To do them good I would sustain
some harm.

KING EDWARD. Then get your husband's lands,
to do them good.

LADY GREY. Therefore I came unto your Majesty.

KING EDWARD. I'll tell you how these lands are
to be got.

LADY GREY. So shall you bind me to your
Highness' service.

KING EDWARD. What service wilt thou do me if I
give them?

LADY GREY. What you command that rests in me
to do.

KING EDWARD. But you will take exceptions to
my boon.

LADY GREY. No, gracious lord, except I cannot
do it.

KING EDWARD. Ay, but thou canst do what I
mean to ask.

LADY GREY. Why, then I will do what your Grace
commands.

GLOUCESTER. He plies her hard; and much rain
wears the marble.

CLARENCE. As red as fire! Nay, then her wax
must melt.

LADY GREY. Why stops my lord? Shall I not hear
my task?

KING EDWARD. An easy task; 'tis but to love a king.

LADY GREY. That's soon perform'd, because I am
a subject.

KING EDWARD. Why, then, thy husband's lands I
freely give thee.

LADY GREY. I take my leave with many
thousand thanks.

GLOUCESTER. The match is made; she seals it
with a curtsy.

KING EDWARD. But stay thee—'tis the fruits of love
I mean.

LADY GREY. The fruits of love I mean, my
loving liege.

KING EDWARD. Ay, but, I fear me, in
another sense.
What love, thinkst thou, I sue so much to get?

LADY GREY. My love till death, my humble thanks,
my prayers;
That love which virtue begs and virtue grants.

KING EDWARD. No, by my troth, I did not mean
such love.

LADY GREY. Why, then you mean not as I thought
you did.

KING EDWARD. But now you partly may perceive
my mind.

LADY GREY. My mind will never grant what
I perceive
Your Highness aims at, if I aim aright.

KING EDWARD. To tell thee plain, I aim to lie with
thee.

LADY GREY. To tell you plain, I had rather lie
in prison.

KING EDWARD. Why, then thou shalt not have
thy husband's lands.

LADY GREY. Why, then mine honesty shall be
my dower;
For by that loss I will not purchase them.

KING EDWARD. Therein thou wrong'st thy
children mightily.

LADY GREY. Herein your Highness wrongs both
them and me.
But, mighty lord, this merry inclination
Accords not with the sadness of my suit.
Please you dismiss me, either with ay or no.

KING EDWARD. Ay, if thou wilt say ay to
my request;
No, if thou dost say no to my demand.

LADY GREY. Then, no, my lord. My suit is at
an end.

GLOUCESTER. The widow likes him not; she knits
her brows.

CLARENCE. He is the bluntest wooer
in Christendom.

KING EDWARD. [Aside] Her looks doth argue her
replete with modesty;
Her words doth show her wit incomparable;
All her perfections challenge sovereignty.
One way or other, she is for a king;
And she shall be my love, or else my queen.
Say that King Edward take thee for his queen?

LADY GREY. 'Tis better said than done, my
gracious lord.
I am a subject fit to jest withal,
But far unfit to be a sovereign.

KING EDWARD. Sweet widow, by my state I swear
to thee

I speak no more than what my soul intends;
And that is to enjoy thee for my love.
LADY GREY. And that is more than I will
  yield unto.
I know I am too mean to be your queen,
And yet too good to be your concubine.
KING EDWARD. You cavil, widow; I did mean
  my queen.
LADY GREY. 'Twill grieve your Grace my sons
  should call you father.
KING EDWARD. No more than when my
  daughters call thee mother.
  Thou art a widow, and thou hast some children;
  And, by God's Mother, I, being but a bachelor,
  Have other some. Why, 'tis a happy thing
  To be the father unto many sons.
  Answer no more, for thou shalt be my queen.
GLOUCESTER. The ghostly father now hath done
  his shrift.
CLARENCE. When he was made a shriver, 'twas
  for shrift.
KING EDWARD. Brothers, you muse what chat we
  two have had.
GLOUCESTER. The widow likes it not, for she
  looks very sad.
KING EDWARD. You'd think it strange if I should
  marry her.
CLARENCE. To whom, my lord?
KING EDWARD. Why, Clarence, to myself.
GLOUCESTER. That would be ten days' wonder
  at the least.
CLARENCE. That's a day longer than a wonder lasts.
GLOUCESTER. By so much is the wonder
  in extremes.
KING EDWARD. Well, jest on, brothers; I can tell
  you both
  Her suit is granted for her husband's lands.

Enter a NOBLEMAN

NOBLEMAN. My gracious lord, Henry your foe
  is taken
  And brought your prisoner to your palace gate.
KING EDWARD. See that he be convey'd unto
  the Tower.
  And go we, brothers, to the man that took him
  To question of his apprehension.
  Widow, go you along. Lords, use
  her honourably.

Exeunt all but GLOUCESTER

GLOUCESTER. Ay, Edward will use women
  honourably.
  Would he were wasted, marrow, bones, and all,
  That from his loins no hopeful branch
  may spring

To cross me from the golden time I look for!
And yet, between my soul's desire and me-
The lustful Edward's title buried-
Is Clarence, Henry, and his son young Edward,
And all the unlook'd-for issue of their bodies,
To take their rooms ere I can place myself.
A cold premeditation for my purpose!
Why, then I do but dream on sovereignty;
Like one that stands upon a promontory
And spies a far-off shore where he would tread,
Wishing his foot were equal with his eye;
And chides the sea that sunders him
  from thence,
Saying he'll lade it dry to have his way-
So do I wish the crown, being so far off;
And so I chide the means that keeps me from it;
And so I say I'll cut the causes off,
Flattering me with impossibilities.
My eye's too quick, my heart o'erweens
  too much,
Unless my hand and strength could equal them.
Well, say there is no kingdom then for Richard;
What other pleasure can the world afford?
I'll make my heaven in a lady's lap,
And deck my body in gay ornaments,
And witch sweet ladies with my words and looks.
O miserable thought! and more unlikely
Than to accomplish twenty golden crowns.
Why, love forswore me in my mother's womb;
And, for I should not deal in her soft laws,
She did corrupt frail nature with some bribe
To shrink mine arm up like a wither'd shrub
To make an envious mountain on my back,
Where sits deformity to mock my body;
To shape my legs of an unequal size;
To disproportion me in every part,
Like to a chaos, or an unlick'd bear-whelp
That carries no impression like the dam.
And am I, then, a man to be belov'd?
O monstrous fault to harbour such a thought!
Then, since this earth affords no joy to me
But to command, to check, to o'erbear such
As are of better person than myself,
I'll make my heaven to dream upon the crown,
And whiles I live t' account this world but hell,
Until my misshap'd trunk that bear this head
Be round impaled with a glorious crown.
And yet I know not how to get the crown,
For many lives stand between me and home;
And I-like one lost in a thorny wood
That rents the thorns and is rent with
  the thorns,
Seeking a way and straying from the way;

Not knowing how to find the open air,
But toiling desperately to find it out-
Torment myself to catch the English crown;
And from that torment I will free myself
Or hew my way out with a bloody axe.
Why, I can smile, and murder whiles I smile,
And cry 'Content!' to that which grieves
  my heart,
And wet my cheeks with artificial tears,
And frame my face to all occasions.
I'll drown more sailors than the mermaid shall;
I'll slay more gazers than the basilisk;
I'll play the orator as well as Nestor,
Deceive more slily than Ulysses could,
And, like a Sinon, take another Troy.
I can add colours to the chameleon,
Change shapes with Protheus for advantages,
And set the murderous Machiavel to school.
Can I do this, and cannot get a crown?
Tut, were it farther off, I'll pluck it down.

Exit.

❧ SCENE III ❧
France. The KING'S palace

*Flourish. Enter LEWIS the French King, his sister BONA, his
Admiral call'd BOURBON; PRINCE EDWARD, QUEEN
MARGARET, and the EARL OF OXFORD. LEWIS sits,
and riseth up again*

LEWIS. Fair Queen of England, worthy Margaret,
  Sit down with us. It ill befits thy state
  And birth that thou shouldst stand while Lewis
  doth sit.
QUEEN MARGARET. No, mighty King of France.
  Now Margaret
  Must strike her sail and learn a while to serve
  Where kings command. I was, I must confess,
  Great Albion's Queen in former golden days;
  But now mischance hath trod my title down
  And with dishonour laid me on the ground,
  Where I must take like seat unto my fortune,
  And to my humble seat conform myself.
LEWIS. Why, say, fair Queen, whence springs this
  deep despair?
QUEEN MARGARET. From such a cause as fills
  mine eyes with tears
  And stops my tongue, while heart is drown'd in
  cares.
LEWIS. Whate'er it be, be thou still like thyself,
  And sit thee by our side. *[Seats her by him]* Yield not
  thy neck
  To fortune's yoke, but let thy dauntless mind
  Still ride in triumph over all mischance.

Be plain, Queen Margaret, and tell thy grief;
  It shall be eas'd, if France can yield relief.
QUEEN MARGARET. Those gracious words
  revive my drooping thoughts
  And give my tongue-tied sorrows leave
  to speak.
  Now therefore be it known to noble Lewis
  That Henry, sole possessor of my love,
  Is, of a king, become a banish'd man,
  And forc'd to live in Scotland a forlorn;
  While proud ambitious Edward Duke of York
  Usurps the regal title and the seat
  Of England's true-anointed lawful King.
  This is the cause that I, poor Margaret,
  With this my son, Prince Edward, Henry's heir,
  Am come to crave thy just and lawful aid;
  And if thou fail us, all our hope is done.
  Scotland hath will to help, but cannot help;
  Our people and our peers are both misled,
  Our treasure seiz'd, our soldiers put to flight,
  And, as thou seest, ourselves in heavy plight.
LEWIS. Renowned Queen, with patience calm
  the storm,
  While we bethink a means to break it off.
QUEEN MARGARET. The more we stay, the
  stronger grows our foe.
LEWIS. The more I stay, the more I'll
  succour thee.
QUEEN MARGARET. O, but impatience waiteth on
  true sorrow.
  And see where comes the breeder of my sorrow!
Enter WARWICK
LEWIS. What's he approacheth boldly to
  our presence?
QUEEN MARGARET. Our Earl of Warwick,
  Edward's greatest friend.
LEWIS. Welcome, brave Warwick! What brings
  thee to France?
He descends. She ariseth
QUEEN MARGARET. Ay, now begins a second
  storm to rise;
  For this is he that moves both wind and tide.
WARWICK. From worthy Edward, King of Albion,
  My lord and sovereign, and thy vowed friend,
  I come, in kindness and unfeigned love,
  First to do greetings to thy royal person,
  And then to crave a league of amity,
  And lastly to confirm that amity
  With nuptial knot, if thou vouchsafe to grant
  That virtuous Lady Bona, thy fair sister,
  To England's King in lawful marriage.
QUEEN MARGARET. *[Aside]* If that go forward,
  Henry's hope is done.

WARWICK. *[To BONA]* And, gracious madam, in
  our king's behalf,
I am commanded, with your leave and favour,
Humbly to kiss your hand, and with my tongue
To tell the passion of my sovereign's heart;
Where fame, late ent'ring at his heedful ears,
Hath plac'd thy beauty's image and thy virtue.
QUEEN MARGARET. King Lewis and Lady Bona,
  hear me speak
Before you answer Warwick. His demand
Springs not from Edward's well-meant
  honest love,
But from deceit bred by necessity;
For how can tyrants safely govern home
Unless abroad they purchase great alliance?
To prove him tyrant this reason may suffice,
That Henry liveth still; but were he dead,
Yet here Prince Edward stands, King
  Henry's son.
Look therefore, Lewis, that by this league
  and marriage
Thou draw not on thy danger and dishonour;
For though usurpers sway the rule a while
Yet heav'ns are just, and time
  suppresseth wrongs.
WARWICK. Injurious Margaret!
PRINCE OF WALES. And why not Queen?
WARWICK. Because thy father Henry did usurp;
And thou no more art prince than she is queen.
OXFORD. Then Warwick disannuls great John
  of Gaunt,
Which did subdue the greatest part of Spain;
And, after John of Gaunt, Henry the Fourth,
Whose wisdom was a mirror to the wisest;
And, after that wise prince, Henry the Fifth,
Who by his prowess conquered all France.
From these our Henry lineally descends.
WARWICK. Oxford, how haps it in this
  smooth discourse
You told not how Henry the Sixth hath lost
All that which Henry the Fifth had gotten?
Methinks these peers of France should smile
  at that.
But for the rest: you tell a pedigree
Of threescore and two years-a silly time
To make prescription for a kingdom's worth.
OXFORD. Why, Warwick, canst thou speak
  against thy liege,
Whom thou obeyed'st thirty and six years,
And not betray thy treason with a blush?
WARWICK. Can Oxford that did ever fence
  the right
Now buckler falsehood with a pedigree?

For shame! Leave Henry, and call Edward king.
OXFORD. Call him my king by whose
  injurious doom
My elder brother, the Lord Aubrey Vere,
Was done to death; and more than so,
  my father,
Even in the downfall of his mellow'd years,
When nature brought him to the door of death?
No, Warwick, no; while life upholds this arm,
This arm upholds the house of Lancaster.
WARWICK. And I the house of York.
LEWIS. Queen Margaret, Prince Edward, and
  Oxford,
Vouchsafe at our request to stand aside
While I use further conference with Warwick.

                  They stand aloof

QUEEN MARGARET. Heavens grant that Warwick's
  words bewitch him not!
LEWIS. Now, Warwick, tell me, even upon
  thy conscience,
Is Edward your true king? for I were loath
To link with him that were not lawful chosen.
WARWICK. Thereon I pawn my credit and
  mine honour.
LEWIS. But is he gracious in the people's eye?
WARWICK. The more that Henry was unfortunate.
LEWIS. Then further: all dissembling set aside,
  Tell me for truth the measure of his love
Unto our sister Bona.
WARWICK. Such it seems
As may beseem a monarch like himself.
Myself have often heard him say and swear
That this his love was an eternal plant
Whereof the root was fix'd in virtue's ground,
The leaves and fruit maintain'd with
  beauty's sun,
Exempt from envy, but not from disdain,
Unless the Lady Bona quit his pain.
LEWIS. Now, sister, let us hear your firm resolve.
BONA. Your grant or your denial shall be mine.
  [To WARWICK] Yet I confess that often ere
  this day,
When I have heard your king's desert recounted,
Mine ear hath tempted judgment to desire.
LEWIS. Then, Warwick, thus: our sister shall
  be Edward's.
And now forthwith shall articles be drawn
Touching the jointure that your king must make,
Which with her dowry shall be counterpois'd.
Draw near, Queen Margaret, and be a witness
That Bona shall be wife to the English king.
PRINCE OF WALES. To Edward, but not to the
  English king.

QUEEN MARGARET. Deceitful Warwick, it was
thy device
By this alliance to make void my suit.
Before thy coming, Lewis was Henry's friend.
LEWIS. And still is friend to him and Margaret.
But if your title to the crown be weak,
As may appear by Edward's good success,
Then 'tis but reason that I be releas'd
From giving aid which late I promised.
Yet shall you have all kindness at my hand
That your estate requires and mine can yield.
WARWICK. Henry now lives in Scotland at
his ease,
Where having nothing, nothing can he lose.
And as for you yourself, our quondam queen,
You have a father able to maintain you,
And better 'twere you troubled him
than France.
QUEEN MARGARET. Peace, impudent and
shameless Warwick,
Proud setter up and puller down of kings!
I will not hence till with my talk and tears,
Both full of truth, I make King Lewis behold
Thy sly conveyance and thy lord's false love;
For both of you are birds of self-same feather.

POST blowing a horn within

LEWIS. Warwick, this is some post to us or thee.

Enter the POST

POST. My lord ambassador, these letters are
for you,
Sent from your brother, Marquis Montague.
These from our King unto your Majesty.
And, madam, these for you; from whom I
know not.

They all read their letters

OXFORD. I like it well that our fair Queen
and mistress
Smiles at her news, while Warwick frowns
at his.
PRINCE OF WALES. Nay, mark how Lewis stamps
as he were nettled. I hope all's for the best.
LEWIS. Warwick, what are thy news? And yours,
fair Queen?
QUEEN MARGARET. Mine such as fill my heart
with unhop'd joys.
WARWICK. Mine, full of sorrow and
heart's discontent.
LEWIS. What, has your king married the
Lady Grey?
And now, to soothe your forgery and his,
Sends me a paper to persuade me patience?
Is this th' alliance that he seeks with France?
Dare he presume to scorn us in this manner?

QUEEN MARGARET. I told your Majesty as
much before.
This proveth Edward's love and
Warwick's honesty.
WARWICK. King Lewis, I here protest in sight
of heaven,
And by the hope I have of heavenly bliss,
That I am clear from this misdeed of Edward's—
No more my king, for he dishonours me,
But most himself, if he could see his shame.
Did I forget that by the house of York
My father came untimely to his death?
Did I let pass th' abuse done to my niece?
Did I impale him with the regal crown?
Did I put Henry from his native right?
And am I guerdon'd at the last with shame?
Shame on himself! for my desert is honour;
And to repair my honour lost for him
I here renounce him and return to Henry.
My noble Queen, let former grudges pass,
And henceforth I am thy true servitor.
I will revenge his wrong to Lady Bona,
And replant Henry in his former state.
QUEEN MARGARET. Warwick, these words have
turn'd my hate to love;
And I forgive and quite forget old faults,
And joy that thou becom'st King Henry's friend.
WARWICK. So much his friend, ay, his unfeigned
friend,
That if King Lewis vouchsafe to furnish us
With some few bands of chosen soldiers,
I'll undertake to land them on our coast
And force the tyrant from his seat by war.
'Tis not his new-made bride shall succour him;
And as for Clarence, as my letters tell me,
He's very likely now to fall from him
For matching more for wanton lust than honour
Or than for strength and safety of our country.
BONA. Dear brother, how shall Bona be reveng'd
But by thy help to this distressed queen?
QUEEN MARGARET. Renowned Prince, how shall
poor Henry live
Unless thou rescue him from foul despair?
BONA. My quarrel and this English queen's
are one.
WARWICK. And mine, fair Lady Bona, joins
with yours.
LEWIS. And mine with hers, and thine,
and Margaret's.
Therefore, at last, I firmly am resolv'd
You shall have aid.
QUEEN MARGARET. Let me give humble thanks
for all at once.

LEWIS. Then, England's messenger, return in post
  And tell false Edward, thy supposed king,
  That Lewis of France is sending over masquers
  To revel it with him and his new bride.
  Thou seest what's past; go fear thy king withal.
BONA. Tell him, in hope he'll prove a
  widower shortly,
  I'll wear the willow-garland for his sake.
QUEEN MARGARET. Tell him my mourning weeds
  are laid aside,
  And I am ready to put armour on.
WARWICK. Tell him from me that he hath done
  me wrong,
  And therefore I'll uncrown him ere't be long.
  There's thy reward; be gone. *Exit POST.*
LEWIS. But, Warwick,
  Thou and Oxford, with five thousand men,
  Shall cross the seas and bid false Edward battle:
  And, as occasion serves, this noble Queen
  And Prince shall follow with a fresh supply.
  Yet, ere thou go, but answer me one doubt:
  What pledge have we of thy firm loyalty?
WARWICK. This shall assure my constant loyalty:
  That if our Queen and this young Prince agree,
  I'll join mine eldest daughter and my joy
  To him forthwith in holy wedlock bands.
QUEEN MARGARET. Yes, I agree, and thank you
  for your motion.
  Son Edward, she is fair and virtuous,
  Therefore delay not-give thy hand to Warwick;
  And with thy hand thy faith irrevocable
  That only Warwick's daughter shall be thine.
PRINCE OF WALES. Yes, I accept her, for she well
  deserves it;
  And here, to pledge my vow, I give my hand.
    He gives his hand to WARWICK
LEWIS. Why stay we now? These soldiers shall
  be levied;
  And thou, Lord Bourbon, our High Admiral,
  Shall waft them over with our royal fleet.
  I long till Edward fall by war's mischance
  For mocking marriage with a dame of France.
    Exeunt all but WARWICK.
WARWICK. I came from Edward as ambassador,
  But I return his sworn and mortal foe.
  Matter of marriage was the charge he gave me,
  But dreadful war shall answer his demand.
  Had he none else to make a stale but me?
  Then none but I shall turn his jest to sorrow.
  I was the chief that rais'd him to the crown,
  And I'll be chief to bring him down again;
  Not that I pity Henry's misery,
  But seek revenge on Edward's mockery. *Exit.*

ACT IV

✦ SCENE I ✦
London. The palace

*Enter GLOUCESTER, CLARENCE, SOMERSET, and
MONTAGUE*

GLOUCESTER. Now tell me, brother Clarence,
  what think you
  Of this new marriage with the Lady Grey?
  Hath not our brother made a worthy choice?
CLARENCE. Alas, you know 'tis far from hence
  to France!
  How could he stay till Warwick made return?
SOMERSET. My lords, forbear this talk; here
  comes the King.
    *Flourish. Enter KING EDWARD, attended; LADY GREY,
    as Queen; PEMBROKE, STAFFORD, HASTINGS, and
    Others. Four stand on one side, and four on the other*
GLOUCESTER. And his well-chosen bride.
CLARENCE. I mind to tell him plainly what I think.
KING EDWARD. Now, brother of Clarence, how
  like you our choice
  That you stand pensive as half malcontent?
CLARENCE. As well as Lewis of France or the Earl
  of Warwick,
  Which are so weak of courage and in judgment
  That they'll take no offence at our abuse.
KING EDWARD. Suppose they take offence
  without a cause;
  They are but Lewis and Warwick: I am Edward,
  Your King and Warwick's and must have my will.
GLOUCESTER. And shall have your will, because
  our King.
  Yet hasty marriage seldom proveth well.
KING EDWARD. Yea, brother Richard, are you
  offended too?
GLOUCESTER. Not I.
  No, God forbid that I should wish them sever'd
  Whom God hath join'd together; ay, and
  'twere pity
  To sunder them that yoke so well together.
KING EDWARD. Setting your scorns and your
  mislike aside,
  Tell me some reason why the Lady Grey
  Should not become my wife and
  England's Queen.
  And you too, Somerset and Montague,
  Speak freely what you think.

CLARENCE. Then this is mine opinion: that
King Lewis
Becomes your enemy for mocking him
About the marriage of the Lady Bona.
GLOUCESTER. And Warwick, doing what you gave
in charge,
Is now dishonoured by this new marriage.
KING EDWARD. What if both Lewis and Warwick
be appeas'd
By such invention as I can devise?
MONTAGUE. Yet to have join'd with France in
such alliance
Would more have strength'ned this
our commonwealth
'Gainst foreign storms than any home-
bred marriage.
HASTINGS. Why, knows not Montague that
of itself
England is safe, if true within itself?
MONTAGUE. But the safer when 'tis back'd
with France.
HASTINGS. 'Tis better using France than
trusting France.
Let us be back'd with God, and with the seas
Which He hath giv'n for fence impregnable,
And with their helps only defend ourselves.
In them and in ourselves our safety lies.
CLARENCE. For this one speech Lord Hastings
well deserves
To have the heir of the Lord Hungerford.
KING EDWARD. Ay, what of that? it was my will
and grant;
And for this once my will shall stand for law.
GLOUCESTER. And yet methinks your Grace hath
not done well
To give the heir and daughter of Lord Scales
Unto the brother of your loving bride.
She better would have fitted me or Clarence;
But in your bride you bury brotherhood.
CLARENCE. Or else you would not have bestow'd
the heir
Of the Lord Bonville on your new wife's son,
And leave your brothers to go speed elsewhere.
KING EDWARD. Alas, poor Clarence! Is it for a wife
That thou art malcontent? I will provide thee.
CLARENCE. In choosing for yourself you show'd
your judgment,
Which being shallow, you shall give me leave
To play the broker in mine own behalf;
And to that end I shortly mind to leave you.
KING EDWARD. Leave me or tarry, Edward will
be King,
And not be tied unto his brother's will.

QUEEN ELIZABETH. My lords, before it pleas'd
his Majesty
To raise my state to title of a queen,
Do me but right, and you must all confess
That I was not ignoble of descent:
And meaner than myself have had like fortune.
But as this title honours me and mine,
So your dislikes, to whom I would be pleasing,
Doth cloud my joys with danger and
with sorrow.
KING EDWARD. My love, forbear to fawn upon
their frowns.
What danger or what sorrow can befall thee,
So long as Edward is thy constant friend
And their true sovereign whom they must obey?
Nay, whom they shall obey, and love thee too,
Unless they seek for hatred at my hands;
Which if they do, yet will I keep thee safe,
And they shall feel the vengeance of my wrath.
GLOUCESTER. [Aside] I hear, yet say not much, but
think the more.

Enter a POST

KING EDWARD. Now, messenger, what letters or
what news
From France?
MESSENGER. My sovereign liege, no letters, and
few words,
But such as I, without your special pardon,
Dare not relate.
KING EDWARD. Go to, we pardon thee;
therefore, in brief,
Tell me their words as near as thou canst
guess them.
What answer makes King Lewis unto our letters?
MESSENGER. At my depart, these were his
very words:
'Go tell false Edward, the supposed king,
That Lewis of France is sending over masquers
To revel it with him and his new bride.'
KING EDWARD. Is Lewis so brave? Belike he
thinks me Henry.
But what said Lady Bona to my marriage?
MESSENGER. These were her words, utt'red with
mild disdain:
'Tell him, in hope he'll prove a widower shortly,
I'll wear the willow-garland for his sake.'
KING EDWARD. I blame not her: she could say
little less;
She had the wrong. But what said
Henry's queen?
For I have heard that she was there in place.
MESSENGER. 'Tell him' quoth she 'my mourning
weeds are done,

And I am ready to put armour on.'
KING EDWARD. Belike she minds to play
  the Amazon.
But what said Warwick to these injuries?
MESSENGER. He, more incens'd against
  your Majesty
Than all the rest, discharg'd me with these
  words:
'Tell him from me that he hath done
  me wrong;
And therefore I'll uncrown him ere't be long.'
KING EDWARD. Ha! durst the traitor breathe
  out so proud words?
Well, I will arm me, being thus forewarn'd.
They shall have wars and pay for
  their presumption.
But say, is Warwick friends with Margaret?
MESSENGER. Ay, gracious sovereign; they are
  so link'd in friendship
That young Prince Edward marries
  Warwick's daughter.
CLARENCE. Belike the elder; Clarence will have
  the younger.
Now, brother king, farewell, and sit you fast,
For I will hence to Warwick's other daughter;
That, though I want a kingdom, yet
  in marriage
I may not prove inferior to yourself.
You that love me and Warwick, follow me.
            Exit, and SOMERSET follows
GLOUCESTER. [Aside] Not I.
My thoughts aim at a further matter; I
Stay not for the love of Edward but the crown.
KING EDWARD. Clarence and Somerset both
  gone to Warwick!
Yet am I arm'd against the worst can happen;
And haste is needful in this desp'rate case.
Pembroke and Stafford, you in our behalf
Go levy men and make prepare for war;
They are already, or quickly will be landed.
Myself in person will straight follow you.
         Exeunt PEMBROKE and STAFFORD
But ere I go, Hastings and Montague,
Resolve my doubt. You twain, of all the rest,
Are near to Warwick by blood and by alliance.
Tell me if you love Warwick more than me?
If it be so, then both depart to him:
I rather wish you foes than hollow friends.
But if you mind to hold your true obedience,
Give me assurance with some friendly vow,
That I may never have you in suspect.
MONTAGUE. So God help Montague as he
  proves true!

HASTINGS. And Hastings as he favours
  Edward's cause!
KING EDWARD. Now, brother Richard, will you
  stand by us?
GLOUCESTER. Ay, in despite of all that shall
  withstand you.
KING EDWARD. Why, so! then am I sure
  of victory.
Now therefore let us hence, and lose no hour
Till we meet Warwick with his foreign pow'r.
                    Exeunt

✲ SCENE II ✲
A plain in Warwickshire

Enter WARWICK and OXFORD, with French soldiers

WARWICK. Trust me, my lord, all hitherto
  goes well;
The common people by numbers swarm to us.
         Enter CLARENCE and SOMERSET
But see where Somerset and Clarence comes.
Speak suddenly, my lords-are we all friends?
CLARENCE. Fear not that, my lord.
WARWICK. Then, gentle Clarence, welcome
  unto Warwick;
And welcome, Somerset. I hold it cowardice
To rest mistrustful where a noble heart
Hath pawn'd an open hand in sign of love;
Else might I think that Clarence,
  Edward's brother,
Were but a feigned friend to our proceedings.
But welcome, sweet Clarence; my daughter shall
  be thine.
And now what rests but, in night's coverture,
Thy brother being carelessly encamp'd,
His soldiers lurking in the towns about,
And but attended by a simple guard,
We may surprise and take him at our pleasure?
Our scouts have found the adventure very easy;
That as Ulysses and stout Diomede
With sleight and manhood stole to Rhesus' tents,
And brought from thence the Thracian
  fatal steeds,
So we, well cover'd with the night's
  black mantle,
At unawares may beat down Edward's guard
And seize himself-I say not 'slaughter him',
For I intend but only to surprise him.
You that will follow me to this attempt,
Applaud the name of Henry with your leader.
         They all cry 'Henry!'

Why then, let's on our way in silent sort.
For Warwick and his friends, God and
   Saint George!

                    Exeunt.

✿ SCENE III ✿
Edward's camp, near Warwick

Enter three WATCHMEN, to guard the KING'S tent

FIRST WATCHMAN. Come on, my masters, each
   man take his stand;
The King by this is set him down to sleep.
SECOND WATCHMAN. What, will he not to bed?
FIRST WATCHMAN. Why, no; for he hath made a
   solemn vow
Never to lie and take his natural rest
Till Warwick or himself be quite suppress'd.
SECOND WATCHMAN. To-morrow then, belike,
   shall be the day,
If Warwick be so near as men report.
THIRD WATCHMAN. But say, I pray, what
   nobleman is that
That with the King here resteth in his tent?
FIRST WATCHMAN. 'Tis the Lord Hastings, the
   King's chiefest friend.
THIRD WATCHMAN. O, is it so? But why
   commands the King
That his chief followers lodge in towns
   about him,
While he himself keeps in the cold field?
SECOND WATCHMAN. 'Tis the more honour,
   because more dangerous.
THIRD WATCHMAN. Ay, but give me worship
   and quietness;
I like it better than dangerous honour.
If Warwick knew in what estate he stands,
'Tis to be doubted he would waken him.
FIRST WATCHMAN. Unless our halberds did shut
   up his passage.
SECOND WATCHMAN. Ay, wherefore else guard
   we his royal tent
But to defend his person from night-foes?
Enter WARWICK, CLARENCE, OXFORD, SOMERSET,
and French soldiers, silent all
WARWICK. This is his tent; and see where stand
   his guard.
Courage, my masters! Honour now or never!
But follow me, and Edward shall be ours.
FIRST WATCHMAN. Who goes there?
SECOND WATCHMAN. Stay, or thou diest.
WARWICK and the rest cry all 'Warwick! Warwick!' and set

upon the guard, who fly, crying 'Arm! Arm!' WARWICK and
                  the rest following them
The drum playing and trumpet sounding, re-enter WARWICK
and the rest, bringing the KING out in his gown, sitting in a
   chair. GLOUCESTER and HASTINGS fly over the stage
SOMERSET. What are they that fly there?
WARWICK. Richard and Hastings. Let them go;
   here is the Duke.
KING EDWARD. The Duke! Why, Warwick, when
   we parted,
Thou call'dst me King?
WARWICK. Ay, but the case is alter'd.
When you disgrac'd me in my embassade,
Then I degraded you from being King,
And come now to create you Duke of York.
Alas, how should you govern any kingdom
That know not how to use ambassadors,
Nor how to be contented with one wife,
Nor how to use your brothers brotherly,
Nor how to study for the people's welfare,
Nor how to shroud yourself from enemies?
KING EDWARD. Yea, brother of Clarence, art thou
   here too?
Nay, then I see that Edward needs must down.
Yet, Warwick, in despite of all mischance,
Of thee thyself and all thy complices,
Edward will always bear himself as King.
Though fortune's malice overthrow my state,
My mind exceeds the compass of her wheel.
WARWICK. Then, for his mind, be Edward
   England's king; *[Takes off his crown]*
But Henry now shall wear the English crown
And be true King indeed; thou but the shadow.
My Lord of Somerset, at my request,
See that forthwith Duke Edward be convey'd
Unto my brother, Archbishop of York.
When I have fought with Pembroke and
   his fellows,
I'll follow you and tell what answer
Lewis and the Lady Bona send to him.
Now for a while farewell, good Duke of York.
KING EDWARD. What fates impose, that men
   must needs abide;
It boots not to resist both wind and tide.
                    They lead him out forcibly.
OXFORD. What now remains, my lords, for us
   to do
But march to London with our soldiers?
WARWICK. Ay, that's the first thing that we have
   to do;
To free King Henry from imprisonment,
And see him seated in the regal throne.
                    Exeunt.

✦ SCENE IV ✦
London. The palace

Enter QUEEN ELIZABETH and RIVERS

RIVERS. Madam, what makes you in this
  sudden change?
QUEEN ELIZABETH. Why, brother Rivers, are you
  yet to learn
What late misfortune is befall'n King Edward?
RIVERS. What, loss of some pitch'd battle
  against Warwick?
QUEEN ELIZABETH. No, but the loss of his own
  royal person.
RIVERS. Then is my sovereign slain?
QUEEN ELIZABETH. Ay, almost slain, for he is
  taken prisoner;
Either betray'd by falsehood of his guard
Or by his foe surpris'd at unawares;
And, as I further have to understand,
Is new committed to the Bishop of York,
Fell Warwick's brother, and by that our foe.
RIVERS. These news, I must confess, are full
  of grief;
Yet, gracious madam, bear it as you may:
Warwick may lose that now hath won the day.
QUEEN ELIZABETH. Till then, fair hope must
  hinder life's decay.
And I the rather wean me from despair
For love of Edward's offspring in my womb.
This is it that makes me bridle passion
And bear with mildness my misfortune's cross;
Ay, ay, for this I draw in many a tear
And stop the rising of blood-sucking sighs,
Lest with my sighs or tears I blast or drown
King Edward's fruit, true heir to th'
  English crown.
RIVERS. But, madam, where is Warwick
  then become?
QUEEN ELIZABETH. I am inform'd that he comes
  towards London
To set the crown once more on Henry's head.
Guess thou the rest: King Edward's friends
  must down.
But to prevent the tyrant's violence-
For trust not him that hath once broken faith-
I'll hence forthwith unto the sanctuary
To save at least the heir of Edward's right.
There shall I rest secure from force and fraud.
Come, therefore, let us fly while we may fly:
If Warwick take us, we are sure to die.

Exeunt✦

✦ SCENE V ✦
A park near Middleham Castle in Yorkshire

*Enter GLOUCESTER, LORD HASTINGS, SIR
WILLIAM STANLEY, and others*

GLOUCESTER. Now, my Lord Hastings and Sir
  William Stanley,
Leave off to wonder why I drew you hither
Into this chiefest thicket of the park.
Thus stands the case: you know our King,
  my brother,
Is prisoner to the Bishop here, at whose hands
He hath good usage and great liberty;
And often but attended with weak guard
Comes hunting this way to disport himself.
I have advertis'd him by secret means
That if about this hour he make this way,
Under the colour of his usual game,
He shall here find his friends, with horse
  and men,
To set him free from his captivity.

Enter KING EDWARD and a HUNTSMAN with him

HUNTSMAN. This way, my lord; for this way lies
  the game.
KING EDWARD. Nay, this way, man. See where
  the huntsmen stand.
Now, brother of Gloucester, Lord Hastings, and
  the rest,
Stand you thus close to steal the Bishop's deer?
GLOUCESTER. Brother, the time and case
  requireth haste;
Your horse stands ready at the park corner.
KING EDWARD. But whither shall we then?
HASTINGS. To Lynn, my lord; and shipt from
  thence to Flanders.
GLOUCESTER. Well guess'd, believe me; for that
  was my meaning.
KING EDWARD. Stanley, I will requite
  thy forwardness.
GLOUCESTER. But wherefore stay we? 'Tis no
  time to talk.
KING EDWARD. Huntsman, what say'st thou? Wilt
  thou go along?
HUNTSMAN. Better do so than tarry and
  be hang'd.
GLOUCESTER. Come then, away; let's ha' no
  more ado.
KING EDWARD. Bishop, farewell. Shield thee
  from Warwick's frown,
And pray that I may repossess the crown.

Exeunt✦

✤ SCENE VI ✤
London. The Tower

Flourish. Enter KING HENRY, CLARENCE, WARWICK,
SOMERSET, young HENRY, EARL OF RICHMOND,
OXFORD, MONTAGUE, LIEUTENANT OF THE
TOWER, and Attendants

KING HENRY. Master Lieutenant, now that God
and friends
Have shaken Edward from the regal seat
And turn'd my captive state to liberty,
My fear to hope, my sorrows unto joys,
At our enlargement what are thy due fees?
LIEUTENANT. Subjects may challenge nothing of
their sov'reigns;
But if an humble prayer may prevail,
I then crave pardon of your Majesty.
KING HENRY. For what, Lieutenant? For well
using me?
Nay, be thou sure I'll well requite thy kindness,
For that it made my imprisonment a pleasure;
Ay, such a pleasure as incaged birds
Conceive when, after many moody thoughts,
At last by notes of household harmony
They quite forget their loss of liberty.
But, Warwick, after God, thou set'st me free,
And chiefly therefore I thank God and thee;
He was the author, thou the instrument.
Therefore, that I may conquer fortune's spite
By living low where fortune cannot hurt me,
And that the people of this blessed land
May not be punish'd with my thwarting stars,
Warwick, although my head still wear
the crown,
I here resign my government to thee,
For thou art fortunate in all thy deeds.
WARWICK. Your Grace hath still been fam'd
for virtuous,
And now may seem as wise as virtuous
By spying and avoiding fortune's malice,
For few men rightly temper with the stars;
Yet in this one thing let me blame your Grace,
For choosing me when Clarence is in place.
CLARENCE. No, Warwick, thou art worthy of
the sway,
To whom the heav'ns in thy nativity
Adjudg'd an olive branch and laurel crown,
As likely to be blest in peace and war;
And therefore I yield thee my free consent.
WARWICK. And I choose Clarence only
for Protector.

KING HENRY. Warwick and Clarence, give me
both your hands.
Now join your hands, and with your hands
your hearts,
That no dissension hinder government.
I make you both Protectors of this land,
While I myself will lead a private life
And in devotion spend my latter days,
To sin's rebuke and my Creator's praise.
WARWICK. What answers Clarence to his
sovereign's will?
CLARENCE. That he consents, if Warwick
yield consent,
For on thy fortune I repose myself.
WARWICK. Why, then, though loath, yet must I
be content.
We'll yoke together, like a double shadow
To Henry's body, and supply his place;
I mean, in bearing weight of government,
While he enjoys the honour and his ease.
And, Clarence, now then it is more than needful
Forthwith that Edward be pronounc'd a traitor,
And all his lands and goods confiscated.
CLARENCE. What else? And that succession
be determin'd.
WARWICK. Ay, therein Clarence shall not want
his part.
KING HENRY. But, with the first of all your
chief affairs,
Let me entreat-for I command no more-
That Margaret your Queen and my son Edward
Be sent for to return from France with speed;
For till I see them here, by doubtful fear
My joy of liberty is half eclips'd.
CLARENCE. It shall be done, my sovereign, with
all speed.
KING HENRY. My Lord of Somerset, what youth
is that,
Of whom you seem to have so tender care?
SOMERSET. My liege, it is young Henry, Earl
of Richmond.
KING HENRY. Come hither, England's hope. *[Lays*
his hand on his head]
If secret powers
Suggest but truth to my divining thoughts,
This pretty lad will prove our country's bliss.
His looks are full of peaceful majesty;
His head by nature fram'd to wear a crown,
His hand to wield a sceptre; and himself
Likely in time to bless a regal throne.
Make much of him, my lords; for this is he
Must help you more than you are hurt by me.
Enter a POST

WARWICK. What news, my friend?

POST. That Edward is escaped from your brother
  And fled, as he hears since, to Burgundy.

WARWICK. Unsavoury news! But how made
  he escape?

POST. He was convey'd by Richard Duke
  of Gloucester
  And the Lord Hastings, who attended him
  In secret ambush on the forest side
  And from the Bishop's huntsmen rescu'd him;
  For hunting was his daily exercise.

WARWICK. My brother was too careless of
  his charge.
  But let us hence, my sovereign, to provide
  A salve for any sore that may betide.

Exeunt all but SOMERSET, RICHMOND, and OXFORD.

SOMERSET. My lord, I like not of this flight of
  Edward's;
  For doubtless Burgundy will yield him help,
  And we shall have more wars befor't be long.
  As Henry's late presaging prophecy
  Did glad my heart with hope of this
  young Richmond,
  So doth my heart misgive me, in these conflicts,
  What may befall him to his harm and ours.
  Therefore, Lord Oxford, to prevent the worst,
  Forthwith we'll send him hence to Brittany,
  Till storms be past of civil enmity.

OXFORD. Ay, for if Edward repossess the crown,
  'Tis like that Richmond with the rest shall down.

SOMERSET. It shall be so; he shall to Brittany.
  Come therefore, let's about it speedily. *Exeunt.*

✿ SCENE VII ✿
Before York

*Flourish. Enter KING EDWARD, GLOUCESTER,
HASTINGS, and SOLDIERS*

KING EDWARD. Now, brother Richard, Lord
  Hastings, and the rest,
  Yet thus far fortune maketh us amends,
  And says that once more I shall interchange
  My waned state for Henry's regal crown.
  Well have we pass'd and now repass'd the seas,
  And brought desired help from Burgundy;
  What then remains, we being thus arriv'd
  From Ravenspurgh haven before the gates
  of York,
  But that we enter, as into our dukedom?

GLOUCESTER. The gates made fast! Brother, I like
  not this;

For many men that stumble at the threshold
Are well foretold that danger lurks within.

KING EDWARD. Tush, man, abodements must not
  now affright us.
  By fair or foul means we must enter in,
  For hither will our friends repair to us.

HASTINGS. My liege, I'll knock once more to
  summon them.

Enter, on the walls, the MAYOR OF YORK and his Brethren

MAYOR. My lords, we were forewarned of
  your coming
  And shut the gates for safety of ourselves,
  For now we owe allegiance unto Henry.

KING EDWARD. But, Master Mayor, if Henry be
  your King,
  Yet Edward at the least is Duke of York.

MAYOR. True, my good lord; I know you for
  no less.

KING EDWARD. Why, and I challenge nothing but
  my dukedom,
  As being well content with that alone.

GLOUCESTER. *[Aside]* But when the fox hath once
  got in his nose,
  He'll soon find means to make the body follow.

HASTINGS. Why, Master Mayor, why stand you in
  a doubt?
  Open the gates; we are King Henry's friends.

MAYOR. Ay, say you so? The gates shall then
  be open'd.

He descends

GLOUCESTER. A wise stout captain, and
  soon persuaded!

HASTINGS. The good old man would fain that all
  were well,
  So 'twere not long of him; but being ent'red,
  I doubt not, I, but we shall soon persuade
  Both him and all his brothers unto reason.

Enter, below, the MAYOR and two ALDERMEN

KING EDWARD. So, Master Mayor. These gates
  must not be shut
  But in the night or in the time of war.
  What! fear not, man, but yield me up the keys;
  [Takes his keys]
  For Edward will defend the town and thee,
  And all those friends that deign to follow me.

March. Enter MONTGOMERY with drum and SOLDIERS

GLOUCESTER. Brother, this is Sir
  John Montgomery,
  Our trusty friend, unless I be deceiv'd.

KING EDWARD. Welcome, Sir John! But why
  come you in arms?

MONTGOMERY. To help King Edward in his time
of storm,
As every loyal subject ought to do.
KING EDWARD. Thanks, good Montgomery; but
we now forget
Our title to the crown, and only claim
Our dukedom till God please to send the rest.
MONTGOMERY. Then fare you well, for I will
hence again.
I came to serve a king and not a duke.
Drummer, strike up, and let us march away.

The drum begins to march

KING EDWARD. Nay, stay, Sir John, a while, and
we'll debate
By what safe means the crown may be recover'd.
MONTGOMERY. What talk you of debating? In
few words:
If you'll not here proclaim yourself our King,
I'll leave you to your fortune and be gone
To keep them back that come to succour you.
Why shall we fight, if you pretend no title?
GLOUCESTER. Why, brother, wherefore stand you
on nice points?
KING EDWARD. When we grow stronger, then
we'll make our claim;
Till then 'tis wisdom to conceal our meaning.
HASTINGS. Away with scrupulous wit! Now arms
must rule.
GLOUCESTER. And fearless minds climb soonest
unto crowns.
Brother, we will proclaim you out of hand;
The bruit thereof will bring you many friends.
KING EDWARD. Then be it as you will; for 'tis
my right,
And Henry but usurps the diadem.
MONTGOMERY. Ay, now my sovereign speaketh
like himself;
And now will I be Edward's champion.
HASTINGS. Sound trumpet; Edward shall be
here proclaim'd.
Come, fellow soldier, make thou proclamation.

Gives him a paper. Flourish

SOLDIER. [*Reads*] 'Edward the Fourth, by the grace
of God,
King of England and France, and Lord of
Ireland, etc.'
MONTGOMERY. And whoso'er gainsays King
Edward's right,
By this I challenge him to single fight.

[*Throws down gauntlet*]

ALL. Long live Edward the Fourth!
KING EDWARD. Thanks, brave Montgomery, and
thanks unto you all;

If fortune serve me, I'll requite this kindness.
Now for this night let's harbour here in York;
And when the morning sun shall raise his car
Above the border of this horizon,
We'll forward towards Warwick and his mates;
For well I wot that Henry is no soldier.
Ah, froward Clarence, how evil it beseems thee
To flatter Henry and forsake thy brother!
Yet, as we may, we'll meet both thee
and Warwick.
Come on, brave soldiers; doubt not of the day,
And, that once gotten, doubt not of large pay.

Exeunt

✣ SCENE VIII ✣
London. The palace

Flourish. Enter KING HENRY, WARWICK,
MONTAGUE, CLARENCE, OXFORD, and EXETER

WARWICK. What counsel, lords? Edward
from Belgia,
With hasty Germans and blunt Hollanders,
Hath pass'd in safety through the narrow seas
And with his troops doth march amain
to London;
And many giddy people flock to him.
KING HENRY. Let's levy men and beat him
back again.
CLARENCE. A little fire is quickly trodden out,
Which, being suffer'd, rivers cannot quench.
WARWICK. In Warwickshire I have true-
hearted friends,
Not mutinous in peace, yet bold in war;
Those will I muster up, and thou, son Clarence,
Shalt stir up in Suffolk, Norfolk, and in Kent,
The knights and gentlemen to come with thee.
Thou, brother Montague, in Buckingham,
Northampton, and in Leicestershire, shalt find
Men well inclin'd to hear what thou command'st.
And thou, brave Oxford, wondrous well belov'd,
In Oxfordshire shalt muster up thy friends.
My sovereign, with the loving citizens,
Like to his island girt in with the ocean
Or modest Dian circled with her nymphs,
Shall rest in London till we come to him.
Fair lords, take leave and stand not to reply.
Farewell, my sovereign.
KING HENRY. Farewell, my Hector and my Troy's
true hope.
CLARENCE. In sign of truth, I kiss your
Highness' hand.

KING HENRY. Well-minded Clarence, be
 thou fortunate!
MONTAGUE. Comfort, my lord; and so I take
 my leave.
OXFORD. *[Kissing the KING'S hand]* And thus I seal my
 truth and bid adieu.
KING HENRY. Sweet Oxford, and my
 loving Montague,
 And all at once, once more a happy farewell.
WARWICK. Farewell, sweet lords; let's meet
 at Coventry.
 Exeunt all but the KING and EXETER
KING HENRY. Here at the palace will I rest
 a while.
 Cousin of Exeter, what thinks your lordship?
 Methinks the power that Edward hath in field
 Should not be able to encounter mine.
EXETER. The doubt is that he will seduce the rest.
KING HENRY. That's not my fear; my meed hath
 got me fame:
 I have not stopp'd mine ears to their demands,
 Nor posted off their suits with slow delays;
 My pity hath been balm to heal their wounds,
 My mildness hath allay'd their swelling griefs,
 My mercy dried their water-flowing tears;
 I have not been desirous of their wealth,
 Nor much oppress'd them with great subsidies,
 Nor forward of revenge, though they
 much err'd.
 Then why should they love Edward more
 than me?
 No, Exeter, these graces challenge grace;
 And, when the lion fawns upon the lamb,
 The lamb will never cease to follow him.
 Shout within 'A Lancaster! A Lancaster!'
EXETER. Hark, hark, my lord! What shouts
 are these?
 Enter KING EDWARD, GLOUCESTER, and SOLDIERS
KING EDWARD. Seize on the shame-fac'd Henry,
 bear him hence;
 And once again proclaim us King of England.
 You are the fount that makes small brooks
 to flow.
 Now stops thy spring; my sea shall suck
 them dry,
 And swell so much the higher by their ebb.
 Hence with him to the Tower: let him not speak.
 Exeunt some with KING HENRY
 And, lords, towards Coventry bend we
 our course,
 Where peremptory Warwick now remains.
 The sun shines hot; and, if we use delay,
 Cold biting winter mars our hop'd-for hay.

GLOUCESTER. Away betimes, before his
 forces join,
 And take the great-grown traitor unawares.
 Brave warriors, march amain towards Coventry.
 Exeunt

ACT V

SCENE I
Coventry

*Enter WARWICK, the MAYOR OF COVENTRY, two
MESSENGERS, and Others upon the walls*

WARWICK. Where is the post that came from
 valiant Oxford?
 How far hence is thy lord, mine honest fellow?
FIRST MESSENGER. By this at Dunsmore,
 marching hitherward.
WARWICK. How far off is our brother Montague?
 Where is the post that came from Montague?
SECOND MESSENGER. By this at Daintry, with a
 puissant troop.
 Enter SIR JOHN SOMERVILLE
WARWICK. Say, Somerville, what says my
 loving son?
 And by thy guess how nigh is Clarence now?
SOMERVILLE. At Southam I did leave him with
 his forces,
 And do expect him here some two hours hence.
 Drum heard
WARWICK. Then Clarence is at hand; I hear
 his drum.
SOMERVILLE. It is not his, my lord; here Southam
 lies.
 The drum your Honour hears marcheth
 from Warwick.
WARWICK. Who should that be? Belike unlook'd-
 for friends.
SOMERVILLE. They are at hand, and you shall
 quickly know.
 *March. Flourish. Enter KING EDWARD, GLOUCESTER,
 and SOLDIERS*
KING EDWARD. Go, trumpet, to the walls, and
 sound a parle.
GLOUCESTER. See how the surly Warwick mans
 the wall.
WARWICK. O unbid spite! Is sportful
 Edward come?
 Where slept our scouts or how are they seduc'd
 That we could hear no news of his repair?

KING EDWARD. Now, Warwick, wilt thou ope the
city gates,
Speak gentle words, and humbly bend thy knee,
Call Edward King, and at his hands beg mercy?
And he shall pardon thee these outrages.
WARWICK. Nay, rather, wilt thou draw thy
forces hence,
Confess who set thee up and pluck'd thee down,
Call Warwick patron, and be penitent?
And thou shalt still remain the Duke of York.
GLOUCESTER. I thought, at least, he would have
said the King;
Or did he make the jest against his will?
WARWICK. Is not a dukedom, sir, a goodly gift?
GLOUCESTER. Ay, by my faith, for a poor earl
to give.
I'll do thee service for so good a gift.
WARWICK. 'Twas I that gave the kingdom to
thy brother.
KING EDWARD. Why then 'tis mine, if but by
Warwick's gift.
WARWICK. Thou art no Atlas for so great a weight;
And, weakling, Warwick takes his gift again;
And Henry is my King, Warwick his subject.
KING EDWARD. But Warwick's king is
Edward's prisoner.
And, gallant Warwick, do but answer this:
What is the body when the head is off?
GLOUCESTER. Alas, that Warwick had no
more forecast,
But, whiles he thought to steal the single ten,
The king was slily finger'd from the deck!
You left poor Henry at the Bishop's palace,
And ten to one you'll meet him in the Tower.
KING EDWARD. 'Tis even so; yet you are
Warwick still.
GLOUCESTER. Come, Warwick, take the time;
kneel down, kneel down.
Nay, when? Strike now, or else the iron cools.
WARWICK. I had rather chop this hand off at
a blow,
And with the other fling it at thy face,
Than bear so low a sail to strike to thee.
KING EDWARD. Sail how thou canst, have wind
and tide thy friend,
This hand, fast wound about thy coal-black hair,
Shall, whiles thy head is warm and new cut off,
Write in the dust this sentence with thy blood:
'Wind-changing Warwick now can change
no more.'
Enter OXFORD, with drum and colours
WARWICK. O cheerful colours! See where
Oxford comes.

OXFORD. Oxford, Oxford, for Lancaster!
He and his Forces enter the city
GLOUCESTER. The gates are open, let us
enter too.
KING EDWARD. So other foes may set upon
our backs.
Stand we in good array, for they no doubt
Will issue out again and bid us battle;
If not, the city being but of small defence,
We'll quietly rouse the traitors in the same.
WARWICK. O, welcome, Oxford! for we want
thy help.
Enter MONTAGUE, with drum and colours
MONTAGUE. Montague, Montague, for Lancaster!
He and his Forces enter the city
GLOUCESTER. Thou and thy brother both shall
buy this treason
Even with the dearest blood your bodies bear.
KING EDWARD. The harder match'd, the
greater victory.
My mind presageth happy gain and conquest.
Enter SOMERSET, with drum and colours
SOMERSET. Somerset, Somerset, for Lancaster!
He and his Forces enter the city
GLOUCESTER. Two of thy name, both Dukes
of Somerset,
Have sold their lives unto the house of York;
And thou shalt be the third, if this sword hold.
Enter CLARENCE, with drum and colours
WARWICK. And lo where George of Clarence
sweeps along,
Of force enough to bid his brother battle;
With whom an upright zeal to right prevails
More than the nature of a brother's love.
CLARENCE. Clarence, Clarence, for Lancaster!
KING EDWARD. Et tu Brute-wilt thou stab
Caesar too?
A parley, sirrah, to George of Clarence.
Sound a parley. RICHARD and CLARENCE whisper
WARWICK. Come, Clarence, come. Thou wilt if
Warwick call.
CLARENCE. *[Taking the red rose from his hat and throwing it at
WARWICK]* Father of Warwick, know you what
this means?
Look here, I throw my infamy at thee.
I will not ruinate my father's house,
Who gave his blood to lime the stones together,
And set up Lancaster. Why, trowest
thou, Warwick,
That Clarence is so harsh, so blunt, unnatural,
To bend the fatal instruments of war
Against his brother and his lawful King?
Perhaps thou wilt object my holy oath.

To keep that oath were more impiety
Than Jephtha when he sacrific'd his daughter.
I am so sorry for my trespass made
That, to deserve well at my brother's hands,
I here proclaim myself thy mortal foe;
With resolution whereso'er I meet thee-
As I will meet thee, if thou stir abroad-
To plague thee for thy foul misleading me.
And so, proud-hearted Warwick, I defy thee,
And to my brother turn my blushing cheeks.
Pardon me, Edward, I will make amends;
And, Richard, do not frown upon my faults,
For I will henceforth be no more unconstant.
KING EDWARD. Now welcome more, and ten
  times more belov'd,
Than if thou never hadst deserv'd our hate.
GLOUCESTER. Welcome, good Clarence; this
  is brother-like.
WARWICK. O passing traitor, perjur'd and unjust!
KING EDWARD. What, Warwick, wilt thou leave
  the town and fight?
Or shall we beat the stones about thine ears?
WARWICK. Alas, I am not coop'd here for defence!
  I will away towards Barnet presently
  And bid thee battle, Edward, if thou dar'st.
KING EDWARD. Yes, Warwick, Edward dares and
  leads the way.
  Lords, to the field; Saint George and victory!
    Exeunt YORKISTS. March. WARWICK and his company
    follow

✿ SCENE II ✿
A field of battle near Barnet

Alarum and excursions. Enter KING EDWARD, bringing
forth WARWICK, wounded

KING EDWARD. So, lie thou there. Die thou, and
  die our fear;
  For Warwick was a bug that fear'd us all.
  Now, Montague, sit fast; I seek for thee,
  That Warwick's bones may keep thine company.
    Exit
WARWICK. Ah, who is nigh? Come to me, friend
  or foe,
  And tell me who is victor, York or Warwick?
  Why ask I that? My mangled body shows,
  My blood, my want of strength, my sick
  heart shows,
  That I must yield my body to the earth
  And, by my fall, the conquest to my foe.
  Thus yields the cedar to the axe's edge,

Whose arms gave shelter to the princely eagle,
Under whose shade the ramping lion slept,
Whose top-branch overpeer'd Jove's
  spreading tree
And kept low shrubs from winter's
  pow'rful wind.
These eyes, that now are dimm'd with death's
  black veil,
Have been as piercing as the mid-day sun
To search the secret treasons of the world;
The wrinkles in my brows, now fill'd with blood,
Were lik'ned oft to kingly sepulchres;
For who liv'd King, but I could dig his grave?
And who durst smile when Warwick bent
  his brow?
Lo now my glory smear'd in dust and blood!
My parks, my walks, my manors, that I had,
Even now forsake me; and of all my lands
Is nothing left me but my body's length.
Why, what is pomp, rule, reign, but earth
  and dust?
And live we how we can, yet die we must.
    Enter OXFORD and SOMERSET
SOMERSET. Ah, Warwick, Warwick! wert thou as
  we are,
We might recover all our loss again.
The Queen from France hath brought a
  puissant power;
Even now we heard the news. Ah, couldst
  thou fly!
WARWICK. Why then, I would not fly. Ah,
  Montague,
If thou be there, sweet brother, take my hand,
And with thy lips keep in my soul a while!
Thou lov'st me not; for, brother, if thou didst,
Thy tears would wash this cold congealed blood
That glues my lips and will not let me speak.
Come quickly, Montague, or I am dead.
SOMERSET. Ah, Warwick! Montague hath breath'd
  his last;
And to the latest gasp cried out for Warwick,
And said 'Commend me to my valiant brother.'
And more he would have said; and more
  he spoke,
Which sounded like a clamour in a vault,
That mought not be distinguish'd; but at last,
I well might hear, delivered with a groan,
'O farewell, Warwick!'
WARWICK. Sweet rest his soul! Fly, lords, and
  save yourselves:
For Warwick bids you all farewell, to meet
  in heaven.
    Dies

OXFORD. Away, away, to meet the Queen's
  great power!

Here they bear away his body.

✿ SCENE III ✿
Another part of the field

*Flourish. Enter KING EDWARD in triumph; with
GLOUCESTER, CLARENCE, and the rest*

KING EDWARD. Thus far our fortune keeps an
  upward course,
  And we are grac'd with wreaths of victory.
  But in the midst of this bright-shining day
  I spy a black, suspicious, threat'ning cloud
  That will encounter with our glorious sun
  Ere he attain his easeful western bed-
  I mean, my lords, those powers that the Queen
  Hath rais'd in Gallia have arriv'd our coast
  And, as we hear, march on to fight with us.
CLARENCE. A little gale will soon disperse
  that cloud
  And blow it to the source from whence it came;
  Thy very beams will dry those vapours up,
  For every cloud engenders not a storm.
GLOUCESTER. The Queen is valued thirty
  thousand strong,
  And Somerset, with Oxford, fled to her.
  If she have time to breathe, be well assur'd
  Her faction will be full as strong as ours.
KING EDWARD. We are advertis'd by our
  loving friends
  That they do hold their course
  toward Tewksbury;
  We, having now the best at Barnet field,
  Will thither straight, for willingness rids way;
  And as we march our strength will
  be augmented
  In every county as we go along.
  Strike up the drum; cry 'Courage!' and away.

Exeunt.

✿ SCENE IV ✿
Plains near Tewksbury

*Flourish. March. Enter QUEEN MARGARET, PRINCE
EDWARD, SOMERSET, OXFORD, and SOLDIERS*

QUEEN MARGARET. Great lords, wise men ne'er
  sit and wail their loss,
  But cheerly seek how to redress their harms.
  What though the mast be now
  blown overboard,
  The cable broke, the holding-anchor lost,
  And half our sailors swallow'd in the flood;
  Yet lives our pilot still. Is't meet that he
  Should leave the helm and, like a fearful lad,
  With tearful eyes add water to the sea
  And give more strength to that which hath
  too much;
  Whiles, in his moan, the ship splits on the rock,
  Which industry and courage might have sav'd?
  Ah, what a shame! ah, what a fault were this!
  Say Warwick was our anchor; what of that?
  And Montague our top-mast; what of him?
  Our slaught'red friends the tackles; what of
  these?
  Why, is not Oxford here another anchor?
  And Somerset another goodly mast?
  The friends of France our shrouds
  and tacklings?
  And, though unskilful, why not Ned and I
  For once allow'd the skilful pilot's charge?
  We will not from the helm to sit and weep,
  But keep our course, though the rough wind
  say no,
  From shelves and rocks that threaten us
  with wreck,
  As good to chide the waves as speak them fair.
  And what is Edward but a ruthless sea?
  What Clarence but a quicksand of deceit?
  And Richard but a ragged fatal rock?
  All these the enemies to our poor bark.
  Say you can swim; alas, 'tis but a while!
  Tread on the sand; why, there you quickly sink.
  Bestride the rock; the tide will wash you off,
  Or else you famish-that's a threefold death.
  This speak I, lords, to let you understand,
  If case some one of you would fly from us,
  That there's no hop'd-for mercy with the
  brothers
  More than with ruthless waves, with sands,
  and rocks.
  Why, courage then! What cannot be avoided
  'Twere childish weakness to lament or fear.
PRINCE OF WALES. Methinks a woman of this
  valiant spirit
  Should, if a coward hear her speak
  these words,
  Infuse his breast with magnanimity
  And make him naked foil a man-at-arms.
  I speak not this as doubting any here;
  For did I but suspect a fearful man,
  He should have leave to go away betimes,

Lest in our need he might infect another
And make him of the like spirit to himself.
If any such be here-as God forbid!-
Let him depart before we need his help.
OXFORD. Women and children of so high
a courage,
And warriors faint! Why, 'twere
perpetual shame.
O brave young Prince! thy
famous grandfather
Doth live again in thee. Long mayst thou live
To bear his image and renew his glories!
SOMERSET. And he that will not fight for such
a hope,
Go home to bed and, like the owl by day,
If he arise, be mock'd and wond'red at.
QUEEN MARGARET. Thanks, gentle Somerset;
sweet Oxford, thanks.
PRINCE OF WALES. And take his thanks that
yet hath nothing else.

Enter a MESSENGER

MESSENGER. Prepare you, lords, for Edward is
at hand
Ready to fight; therefore be resolute.
OXFORD. I thought no less. It is his policy
To haste thus fast, to find us unprovided.
SOMERSET. But he's deceiv'd; we are
in readiness.
QUEEN MARGARET. This cheers my heart, to
see your forwardness.
OXFORD. Here pitch our battle; hence we will
not budge.

Flourish and march. Enter, at a distance, KING
EDWARD, GLOUCESTER, CLARENCE, and
SOLDIERS

KING EDWARD. Brave followers, yonder stands
the thorny wood
Which, by the heavens' assistance and your
strength,
Must by the roots be hewn up yet ere night.
I need not add more fuel to your fire,
For well I wot ye blaze to burn them out.
Give signal to the fight, and to it, lords.
QUEEN MARGARET. Lords, knights, and
gentlemen, what I should say
My tears gainsay; for every word I speak,
Ye see, I drink the water of my eye.
Therefore, no more but this: Henry,
your sovereign,
Is prisoner to the foe; his state usurp'd,
His realm a slaughter-house, his
subjects slain,
His statutes cancell'd, and his treasure spent;

And yonder is the wolf that makes this spoil.
You fight in justice. Then, in God's name, lords,
Be valiant, and give signal to the fight.

Alarum, retreat, excursions. Exeunt.

✤ SCENE V ✤
Another part of the field

Flourish. Enter KING EDWARD, GLOUCESTER,
CLARENCE, and Forces, with QUEEN MARGARET,
OXFORD, and SOMERSET, prisoners

KING EDWARD. Now here a period of
tumultuous broils.
Away with Oxford to Hames Castle straight;
For Somerset, off with his guilty head.
Go, bear them hence; I will not hear
them speak.
OXFORD. For my part, I'll not trouble thee
with words.
SOMERSET. Nor I, but stoop with patience to
my fortune.

Exeunt OXFORD and SOMERSET, guarded.

QUEEN MARGARET. So part we sadly in this
troublous world,
To meet with joy in sweet Jerusalem.
KING EDWARD. Is proclamation made that who
finds Edward
Shall have a high reward, and he his life?
GLOUCESTER. It is; and lo where youthful
Edward comes.

Enter soldiers, with PRINCE EDWARD

KING EDWARD. Bring forth the gallant; let us
hear him speak.
What, can so young a man begin to prick?
Edward, what satisfaction canst thou make
For bearing arms, for stirring up my subjects,
And all the trouble thou hast turn'd me to?
PRINCE OF WALES. Speak like a subject, proud
ambitious York.
Suppose that I am now my father's mouth;
Resign thy chair, and where I stand kneel thou,
Whilst I propose the self-same words to thee
Which, traitor, thou wouldst have me
answer to.
QUEEN MARGARET. Ah, that thy father had been
so resolv'd!
GLOUCESTER. That you might still have worn
the petticoat
And ne'er have stol'n the breech from Lancaster.
PRINCE OF WALES. Let Aesop fable in a winter's night;
His currish riddles sort not with this place.

GLOUCESTER. By heaven, brat, I'll plague ye for
that word.
QUEEN MARGARET. Ay, thou wast born to be a
plague to men.
GLOUCESTER. For God's sake, take away this
captive scold.
PRINCE OF WALES. Nay, take away this scolding
crookback rather.
KING EDWARD. Peace, wilful boy, or I will charm
your tongue.
CLARENCE. Untutor'd lad, thou art too malapert.
PRINCE OF WALES. I know my duty; you are
all undutiful.
Lascivious Edward, and thou perjur'd George,
And thou misshapen Dick, I tell ye all
I am your better, traitors as ye are;
And thou usurp'st my father's right and mine.
KING EDWARD. Take that, the likeness of this
railer here.   *Stabs him*
GLOUCESTER. Sprawl'st thou? Take that, to end
thy agony.   *Stabs him*
CLARENCE. And there's for twitting me with
perjury.   *Stabs him*
QUEEN MARGARET. O, kill me too!
GLOUCESTER. Marry, and shall. *Offers to kill her*
KING EDWARD. Hold, Richard, hold; for we have
done too much.
GLOUCESTER. Why should she live to fill the
world with words?
KING EDWARD. What, doth she swoon? Use
means for her recovery.
GLOUCESTER. Clarence, excuse me to the King
my brother.
I'll hence to London on a serious matter;
Ere ye come there, be sure to hear some news.
CLARENCE. What? what?
GLOUCESTER. The Tower! the Tower!   *Exit.*
QUEEN MARGARET. O Ned, sweet Ned, speak to
thy mother, boy!
Canst thou not speak? O traitors! murderers!
They that stabb'd Caesar shed no blood at all,
Did not offend, nor were not worthy blame,
If this foul deed were by to equal it.
He was a man: this, in respect, a child;
And men ne'er spend their fury on a child.
What's worse than murderer, that I may name it?
No, no, my heart will burst, an if I speak-
And I will speak, that so my heart may burst.
Butchers and villains! bloody cannibals!
How sweet a plant have you untimely cropp'd!
You have no children, butchers, if you had,
The thought of them would have stirr'd
up remorse.

But if you ever chance to have a child,
Look in his youth to have him so cut off
As, deathsmen, you have rid this sweet
young prince!
KING EDWARD. Away with her; go, bear her
hence perforce.
QUEEN MARGARET. Nay, never bear me hence;
dispatch me here.
Here sheathe thy sword; I'll pardon thee
my death.
What, wilt thou not? Then, Clarence, do it thou.
CLARENCE. By heaven, I will not do thee so
much ease.
QUEEN MARGARET. Good Clarence, do; sweet
Clarence, do thou do it.
CLARENCE. Didst thou not hear me swear I would
not do it?
QUEEN MARGARET. Ay, but thou usest to
forswear thyself.
'Twas sin before, but now 'tis charity.
What! wilt thou not? Where is that
devil's butcher,
Hard-favour'd Richard? Richard, where art thou?
Thou art not here. Murder is thy alms-deed;
Petitioners for blood thou ne'er put'st back.
KING EDWARD. Away, I say; I charge ye bear
her hence.
QUEEN MARGARET. So come to you and yours as
to this prince.   *Exit, led out forcibly.*
KING EDWARD. Where's Richard gone?
CLARENCE. To London, all in post; and, as I guess,
To make a bloody supper in the Tower.
KING EDWARD. He's sudden, if a thing comes in
his head.
Now march we hence. Discharge the
common sort
With pay and thanks; and let's away to London
And see our gentle queen how well she fares.
By this, I hope, she hath a son for me.
          Exeunt.

✿ SCENE VI ✿
London. The Tower

*Enter KING HENRY and GLOUCESTER with the
LIEUTENANT, on the walls*

GLOUCESTER. Good day, my lord. What, at your
book so hard?
KING HENRY. Ay, my good lord-my lord, I should
say rather.
'Tis sin to flatter; 'good' was little better.

'Good Gloucester' and 'good devil' were alike,
And both preposterous; therefore, not 'good lord'.
GLOUCESTER. Sirrah, leave us to ourselves; we
  must confer.   *Exit LIEUTENANT.*
KING HENRY. So flies the reckless shepherd from
  the wolf;
  So first the harmless sheep doth yield his fleece,
  And next his throat unto the butcher's knife.
  What scene of death hath Roscius now to act?
GLOUCESTER. Suspicion always haunts the
  guilty mind:
  The thief doth fear each bush an officer.
KING HENRY. The bird that hath been limed in
  a bush
  With trembling wings misdoubteth every bush;
  And I, the hapless male to one sweet bird,
  Have now the fatal object in my eye
  Where my poor young was lim'd, was caught,
  and kill'd.
GLOUCESTER. Why, what a peevish fool was that
  of Crete
  That taught his son the office of a fowl!
  And yet, for all his wings, the fool was drown'd.
KING HENRY. I, Daedalus; my poor boy, Icarus;
  Thy father, Minos, that denied our course;
  The sun that sear'd the wings of my sweet boy,
  Thy brother Edward; and thyself, the sea
  Whose envious gulf did swallow up his life.
  Ah, kill me with thy weapon, not with words!
  My breast can better brook thy dagger's point
  Than can my ears that tragic history.
  But wherefore dost thou come? Is't for my life?
GLOUCESTER. Think'st thou I am an executioner?
KING HENRY. A persecutor I am sure thou art.
  If murdering innocents be executing,
  Why, then thou art an executioner.
GLOUCESTER. Thy son I kill'd for his presumption.
KING HENRY. Hadst thou been kill'd when first
  thou didst presume,
  Thou hadst not liv'd to kill a son of mine.
  And thus I prophesy, that many a thousand
  Which now mistrust no parcel of my fear,
  And many an old man's sigh, and many a widow's,
  And many an orphan's water-standing eye-
  Men for their sons, wives for their husbands,
  Orphans for their parents' timeless death-
  Shall rue the hour that ever thou wast born.
  The owl shriek'd at thy birth-an evil sign;
  The night-crow cried, aboding luckless time;
  Dogs howl'd, and hideous tempest shook
  down trees;
  The raven rook'd her on the chimney's top,
  And chatt'ring pies in dismal discords sung;

Thy mother felt more than a mother's pain,
And yet brought forth less than a mother's hope,
To wit, an indigest deformed lump,
Not like the fruit of such a goodly tree.
Teeth hadst thou in thy head when thou
  wast born,
To signify thou cam'st to bite the world;
And if the rest be true which I have heard,
Thou cam'st-
GLOUCESTER. I'll hear no more. Die, prophet, in
  thy speech. *[Stabs him]*
  For this, amongst the rest, was I ordain'd.
KING HENRY. Ay, and for much more slaughter
  after this.
  O, God forgive my sins and pardon thee! *Dies*
GLOUCESTER. What, will the aspiring blood
  of Lancaster
  Sink in the ground? I thought it would
  have mounted.
  See how my sword weeps for the poor
  King's death.
  O, may such purple tears be always shed
  From those that wish the downfall of our house!
  If any spark of life be yet remaining,
  Down, down to hell; and say I sent thee thither-
    [Stabs him again]
  I, that have neither pity, love, nor fear.
  Indeed, 'tis true that Henry told me of;
  For I have often heard my mother say
  I came into the world with my legs forward.
  Had I not reason, think ye, to make haste
  And seek their ruin that usurp'd our right?
  The midwife wonder'd; and the women cried
  'O, Jesus bless us, he is born with teeth!'
  And so I was, which plainly signified
  That I should snarl, and bite, and play the dog.
  Then, since the heavens have shap'd my
  body so,
  Let hell make crook'd my mind to answer it.
  I have no brother, I am like no brother;
  And this word 'love', which greybeards
  call divine,
  Be resident in men like one another,
  And not in me! I am myself alone.
  Clarence, beware; thou keep'st me from
  the light,
  But I will sort a pitchy day for thee;
  For I will buzz abroad such prophecies
  That Edward shall be fearful of his life;
  And then to purge his fear, I'll be thy death.
  King Henry and the Prince his son are gone.
  Clarence, thy turn is next, and then the rest;
  Counting myself but bad till I be best.

I'll throw thy body in another room,
And triumph, Henry, in thy day of doom.

Exit with the body.

⚜ SCENE VII ⚜
London. The palace

*Flourish. Enter KING EDWARD, QUEEN ELIZABETH,
CLARENCE, GLOUCESTER, HASTINGS, NURSE, with
the Young PRINCE, and Attendants*

KING EDWARD. Once more we sit in England's
  royal throne,
Repurchas'd with the blood of enemies.
What valiant foemen, like to autumn's corn,
Have we mow'd down in tops of all their pride!
Three Dukes of Somerset, threefold renown'd
For hardy and undoubted champions;
Two Cliffords, as the father and the son;
And two Northumberlands-two braver men
Ne'er spurr'd their coursers at the
  trumpet's sound;
With them the two brave bears, Warwick
  and Montague,
That in their chains fetter'd the kingly lion
And made the forest tremble when they roar'd.
Thus have we swept suspicion from our seat
And made our footstool of security.
Come hither, Bess, and let me kiss my boy.
Young Ned, for thee thine uncles and myself
Have in our armours watch'd the winter's night,
Went all afoot in summer's scalding heat,
That thou might'st repossess the crown
  in peace;
And of our labours thou shalt reap the gain.
GLOUCESTER. *[Aside]* I'll blast his harvest if your
  head were laid;
For yet I am not look'd on in the world.
This shoulder was ordain'd so thick to heave;
And heave it shall some weight or break
  my back.
Work thou the way-and that shall execute.
KING EDWARD. Clarence and Gloucester, love my
  lovely queen;
And kiss your princely nephew, brothers both.
CLARENCE. The duty that I owe unto your Majesty
I seal upon the lips of this sweet babe.
KING EDWARD. Thanks, noble Clarence; worthy
  brother, thanks.
GLOUCESTER. And that I love the tree from
  whence thou sprang'st,

Witness the loving kiss I give the fruit.
  [Aside] To say the truth, so Judas kiss'd his master
  And cried 'All hail!' when as he meant all harm.
KING EDWARD. Now am I seated as my soul
  delights,
Having my country's peace and brothers' loves.
CLARENCE. What will your Grace have done
  with Margaret?
Reignier, her father, to the King of France
Hath pawn'd the Sicils and Jerusalem,
And hither have they sent it for her ransom.
KING EDWARD. Away with her, and waft her
  hence to France.
And now what rests but that we spend the time
With stately triumphs, mirthful comic shows,
Such as befits the pleasure of the court?
Sound drums and trumpets. Farewell,
  sour annoy!
For here, I hope, begins our lasting joy.

Exeunt.

The End

King Richard III

Dramatis Personae

EDWARD THE FOURTH

Sons to the King:
EDWARD, PRINCE OF WALES, afterwards KING
EDWARD V
RICHARD, DUKE OF YORK

Brothers to the King:
GEORGE, DUKE OF CLARENCE
RICHARD, DUKE OF GLOUCESTER, afterwards
KING RICHARD III

A YOUNG SON OF CLARENCE (Edward, Earl
of Warwick)
HENRY, EARL OF RICHMOND, afterwards KING
HENRY VII
CARDINAL BOURCHIER, ARCHBISHOP
OF CANTERBURY
THOMAS ROTHERHAM, ARCHBISHOP OF YORK
JOHN MORTON, BISHOP OF ELY
DUKE OF BUCKINGHAM
DUKE OF NORFOLK
EARL OF SURREY, his son
EARL RIVERS, brother to King Edward's Queen
MARQUIS OF DORSET and LORD GREY, her sons
EARL OF OXFORD
LORD HASTINGS
LORD LOVEL
LORD STANLEY, called also EARL OF DERBY
SIR THOMAS VAUGHAN
SIR RICHARD RATCLIFF
SIR WILLIAM CATESBY
SIR JAMES TYRREL
SIR JAMES BLOUNT
SIR WALTER HERBERT
SIR WILLIAM BRANDON
SIR ROBERT BRAKENBURY, Lieutenant of
the Tower
CHRISTOPHER URSWICK, a priest

LORD MAYOR OF LONDON
SHERIFF OF WILTSHIRE
HASTINGS, a PURSUIVANT
TRESSEL and BERKELEY, gentlemen attending on
Lady Anne
ELIZABETH, Queen to King Edward IV
MARGARET, widow of King Henry VI
DUCHESS OF YORK, mother to King Edward IV
LADY ANNE, widow of Edward, Prince of Wales,
son to King Henry VI; afterwards married to the
Duke of Gloucester
A YOUNG DAUGHTER OF CLARENCE (Margaret
Plantagenet, Countess of Salisbury)
GHOSTS of Richard's victims
Lords, Gentlemen, and Attendants; Priest,
Scrivener, Page, Bishops, Aldermen, Citizens,
Soldiers, Messengers, Murderers, Keeper

SCENE
England

ACT I

SCENE I
London. A street

Enter RICHARD, DUKE OF GLOUCESTER, solus

GLOUCESTER. Now is the winter of
  our discontent
Made glorious summer by this sun of York;
And all the clouds that lour'd upon our house
In the deep bosom of the ocean buried.
Now are our brows bound with
  victorious wreaths;
Our bruised arms hung up for monuments;
Our stern alarums chang'd to merry meetings,
Our dreadful marches to delightful measures.
Grim-visag'd war hath smooth'd his
  wrinkled front,
And now, instead of mounting barbed steeds
To fright the souls of fearful adversaries,
He capers nimbly in a lady's chamber
To the lascivious pleasing of a lute.
But I-that am not shap'd for sportive tricks,
Nor made to court an amorous looking-glass-

I-that am rudely stamp'd, and want
  love's majesty
To strut before a wanton ambling nymph-
I-that am curtail'd of this fair proportion,
Cheated of feature by dissembling nature,
Deform'd, unfinish'd, sent before my time
Into this breathing world scarce half made up,
And that so lamely and unfashionable
That dogs bark at me as I halt by them-
Why, I, in this weak piping time of peace,
Have no delight to pass away the time,
Unless to spy my shadow in the sun
And descant on mine own deformity.
And therefore, since I cannot prove a lover
To entertain these fair well-spoken days,
I am determined to prove a villain
And hate the idle pleasures of these days.
Plots have I laid, inductions dangerous,
By drunken prophecies, libels, and dreams,
To set my brother Clarence and the King
In deadly hate the one against the other;
And if King Edward be as true and just
As I am subtle, false, and treacherous,
This day should Clarence closely be mew'd up-
About a prophecy which says that G
Of Edward's heirs the murderer shall be.
Dive, thoughts, down to my soul. Here
  Clarence comes.

    Enter CLARENCE, guarded, and BRAKENBURY
Brother, good day. What means this
  armed guard
That waits upon your Grace?
CLARENCE. His Majesty,
  Tend'ring my person's safety, hath appointed
  This conduct to convey me to th' Tower.
GLOUCESTER. Upon what cause?
CLARENCE. Because my name is George.
GLOUCESTER. Alack, my lord, that fault is none
  of yours:
  He should, for that, commit your godfathers.
  O, belike his Majesty hath some intent
  That you should be new-christ'ned in
    the Tower.
  But what's the matter, Clarence? May I know?
CLARENCE. Yea, Richard, when I know; for I
  protest
  As yet I do not; but, as I can learn,
  He hearkens after prophecies and dreams,
  And from the cross-row plucks the letter G,
  And says a wizard told him that by G
  His issue disinherited should be;
  And, for my name of George begins with G,
  It follows in his thought that I am he.

These, as I learn, and such like toys as these
Hath mov'd his Highness to commit me now.
GLOUCESTER. Why, this it is when men are rul'd
  by women:
  'Tis not the King that sends you to the Tower;
  My Lady Grey his wife, Clarence, 'tis she
  That tempers him to this extremity.
  Was it not she and that good man of worship,
  Antony Woodville, her brother there,
  That made him send Lord Hastings to
    the Tower,
  From whence this present day he is delivered?
  We are not safe, Clarence; we are not safe.
CLARENCE. By heaven, I think there is no
  man secure
  But the Queen's kindred, and night-walking
  heralds
  That trudge betwixt the King and Mistress Shore.
  Heard you not what an humble suppliant
  Lord Hastings was, for her delivery?
GLOUCESTER. Humbly complaining to her deity
  Got my Lord Chamberlain his liberty.
  I'll tell you what-I think it is our way,
  If we will keep in favour with the King,
  To be her men and wear her livery:
  The jealous o'er-worn widow, and herself,
  Since that our brother dubb'd
    them gentlewomen,
  Are mighty gossips in our monarchy.
BRAKENBURY. I beseech your Graces both to
  pardon me:
  His Majesty hath straitly given in charge
  That no man shall have private conference,
  Of what degree soever, with your brother.
GLOUCESTER. Even so; an't please your
  worship, Brakenbury,
  You may partake of any thing we say:
  We speak no treason, man; we say the King
  Is wise and virtuous, and his noble queen
  Well struck in years, fair, and not jealous;
  We say that Shore's wife hath a pretty foot,
  A cherry lip, a bonny eye, a passing
    pleasing tongue;
  And that the Queen's kindred are
    made gentlefolks.
  How say you, sir? Can you deny all this?
BRAKENBURY. With this, my lord, myself have
  naught to do.
GLOUCESTER. Naught to do with Mistress Shore!
  I tell thee, fellow,
  He that doth naught with her, excepting one,
  Were best to do it secretly alone.
BRAKENBURY. What one, my lord?

GLOUCESTER. Her husband, knave! Wouldst
  thou betray me?
BRAKENBURY. I do beseech your Grace to
  pardon me, and withal
Forbear your conference with the noble Duke.
CLARENCE. We know thy charge, Brakenbury,
  and will obey.
GLOUCESTER. We are the Queen's abjects and
  must obey.
Brother, farewell; I will unto the King;
And whatsoe'er you will employ me in-
Were it to call King Edward's widow sister-
I will perform it to enfranchise you.
Meantime, this deep disgrace in brotherhood
Touches me deeper than you can imagine.
CLARENCE. I know it pleaseth neither of
  us well.
GLOUCESTER. Well, your imprisonment shall
  not be long;
I will deliver or else lie for you.
Meantime, have patience.
CLARENCE. I must perforce. Farewell.
    Exeunt CLARENCE, BRAKENBURY, and guard.
GLOUCESTER. Go tread the path that thou shalt
  ne'er return.
Simple, plain Clarence, I do love thee so
That I will shortly send thy soul to heaven,
If heaven will take the present at our hands.
But who comes here? The new-
  delivered Hastings?
    Enter LORD HASTINGS
HASTINGS. Good time of day unto my
  gracious lord!
GLOUCESTER. As much unto my good
  Lord Chamberlain!
Well are you welcome to the open air.
How hath your lordship
  brook'd imprisonment?
HASTINGS. With patience, noble lord, as
  prisoners must;
But I shall live, my lord, to give them thanks
That were the cause of my imprisonment.
GLOUCESTER. No doubt, no doubt; and so shall
  Clarence too;
For they that were your enemies are his,
And have prevail'd as much on him as you.
HASTINGS. More pity that the eagles should
  be mew'd
Whiles kites and buzzards prey at liberty.
GLOUCESTER. What news abroad?
HASTINGS. No news so bad abroad as this
  at home:
The King is sickly, weak, and melancholy,

And his physicians fear him mightily.
GLOUCESTER. Now, by Saint John, that news is
  bad indeed.
O, he hath kept an evil diet long
And overmuch consum'd his royal person!
'Tis very grievous to be thought upon.
Where is he? In his bed?
HASTINGS. He is.
GLOUCESTER. Go you before, and I will follow
  you. *[Exit HASTINGS]*
He cannot live, I hope, and must not die
Till George be pack'd with posthorse up
  to heaven.
I'll in to urge his hatred more to Clarence
With lies well steel'd with weighty arguments;
And, if I fail not in my deep intent,
Clarence hath not another day to live;
Which done, God take King Edward to
  his mercy,
And leave the world for me to bustle in!
For then I'll marry Warwick's
  youngest daughter.
What though I kill'd her husband and
  her father?
The readiest way to make the wench amends
Is to become her husband and her father;
The which will I-not all so much for love
As for another secret close intent
By marrying her which I must reach unto.
But yet I run before my horse to market.
Clarence still breathes; Edward still lives
  and reigns;
When they are gone, then must I count
  my gains.
                              Exit.

✦ SCENE II ✦
London. Another street

*Enter corpse of KING HENRY THE SIXTH, with Halberds
to guard it; LADY ANNE being the mourner, attended by
TRESSEL and BERKELEY*

ANNE. Set down, set down your honourable load-
If honour may be shrouded in a hearse;
Whilst I awhile obsequiously lament
Th' untimely fall of virtuous Lancaster.
Poor key-cold figure of a holy king!
Pale ashes of the house of Lancaster!
Thou bloodless remnant of that royal blood!
Be it lawful that I invocate thy ghost
To hear the lamentations of poor Anne,

Wife to thy Edward, to thy slaughtered son,
Stabb'd by the self-same hand that made
  these wounds.
Lo, in these windows that let forth thy life
I pour the helpless balm of my poor eyes.
O, cursed be the hand that made these holes!
Cursed the heart that had the heart to do it!
Cursed the blood that let this blood from hence!
More direful hap betide that hated wretch
That makes us wretched by the death of thee
Than I can wish to adders, spiders, toads,
Or any creeping venom'd thing that lives!
If ever he have child, abortive be it,
Prodigious, and untimely brought to light,
Whose ugly and unnatural aspect
May fright the hopeful mother at the view,
And that be heir to his unhappiness!
If ever he have wife, let her be made
More miserable by the death of him
Than I am made by my young lord and thee!
Come, now towards Chertsey with your
  holy load,
Taken from Paul's to be interred there;
And still as you are weary of this weight
Rest you, whiles I lament King Henry's corse.

The bearers take up the coffin

Enter GLOUCESTER

GLOUCESTER. Stay, you that bear the corse, and
  set it down.
ANNE. What black magician conjures up this fiend
  To stop devoted charitable deeds?
GLOUCESTER. Villains, set down the corse; or, by
  Saint Paul,
  I'll make a corse of him that disobeys!
FIRST GENTLEMAN. My lord, stand back, and let
  the coffin pass.
GLOUCESTER. Unmanner'd dog! Stand thou,
  when I command.
  Advance thy halberd higher than my breast,
  Or, by Saint Paul, I'll strike thee to my foot
  And spurn upon thee, beggar, for thy boldness.

The bearers set down the coffin

ANNE. What, do you tremble? Are you all afraid?
  Alas, I blame you not, for you are mortal,
  And mortal eyes cannot endure the devil.
  Avaunt, thou dreadful minister of hell!
  Thou hadst but power over his mortal body,
  His soul thou canst not have; therefore, be gone.
GLOUCESTER. Sweet saint, for charity, be not
  so curst.
ANNE. Foul devil, for God's sake, hence and
  trouble us not;
  For thou hast made the happy earth thy hell,

Fill'd it with cursing cries and deep exclaims.
If thou delight to view thy heinous deeds,
Behold this pattern of thy butcheries.
O, gentlemen, see, see! Dead Henry's wounds
Open their congeal'd mouths and bleed afresh.
Blush, blush, thou lump of foul deformity,
For 'tis thy presence that exhales this blood
From cold and empty veins where no
  blood dwells;
Thy deeds inhuman and unnatural
Provokes this deluge most unnatural.
O God, which this blood mad'st, revenge
  his death!
O earth, which this blood drink'st, revenge
  his death!
Either, heav'n, with lightning strike the
  murd'rer dead;
Or, earth, gape open wide and eat him quick,
As thou dost swallow up this good king's blood,
Which his hell-govern'd arm hath butchered.
GLOUCESTER. Lady, you know no rules of charity,
  Which renders good for bad, blessings
  for curses.
ANNE. Villain, thou knowest nor law of God
  nor man:
  No beast so fierce but knows some touch of pity.
GLOUCESTER. But I know none, and therefore
  am no beast.
ANNE. O wonderful, when devils tell the truth!
GLOUCESTER. More wonderful when angels are
  so angry.
  Vouchsafe, divine perfection of a woman,
  Of these supposed crimes to give me leave
  By circumstance but to acquit myself.
ANNE. Vouchsafe, diffus'd infection of a man,
  Of these known evils but to give me leave
  By circumstance to accuse thy cursed self.
GLOUCESTER. Fairer than tongue can name thee,
  let me have
  Some patient leisure to excuse myself.
ANNE. Fouler than heart can think thee, thou
  canst make
  No excuse current but to hang thyself.
GLOUCESTER. By such despair I should
  accuse myself.
ANNE. And by despairing shalt thou stand excused
  For doing worthy vengeance on thyself
  That didst unworthy slaughter upon others.
GLOUCESTER. Say that I slew them not?
ANNE. Then say they were not slain.
  But dead they are, and, devilish slave, by thee.
GLOUCESTER. I did not kill your husband.
ANNE. Why, then he is alive.

GLOUCESTER. Nay, he is dead, and slain by
  Edward's hands.
ANNE. In thy foul throat thou liest: Queen
  Margaret saw
  Thy murd'rous falchion smoking in his blood;
  The which thou once didst bend against
    her breast,
  But that thy brothers beat aside the point.
GLOUCESTER. I was provoked by her
  sland'rous tongue
  That laid their guilt upon my guiltless shoulders.
ANNE. Thou wast provoked by thy bloody mind,
  That never dream'st on aught but butcheries.
  Didst thou not kill this king?
GLOUCESTER. I grant ye.
ANNE. Dost grant me, hedgehog? Then, God
  grant me too
  Thou mayst be damned for that wicked deed!
  O, he was gentle, mild, and virtuous!
GLOUCESTER. The better for the King of Heaven,
  that hath him.
ANNE. He is in heaven, where thou shalt
  never come.
GLOUCESTER. Let him thank me that holp to
  send him thither,
  For he was fitter for that place than earth.
ANNE. And thou unfit for any place but hell.
GLOUCESTER. Yes, one place else, if you will hear
  me name it.
ANNE. Some dungeon.
GLOUCESTER. Your bed-chamber.
ANNE. Ill rest betide the chamber where
  thou liest!
GLOUCESTER. So will it, madam, till I lie with you.
ANNE. I hope so.
GLOUCESTER. I know so. But, gentle Lady Anne,
  To leave this keen encounter of our wits,
  And fall something into a slower method-
  Is not the causer of the timeless deaths
  Of these Plantagenets, Henry and Edward,
  As blameful as the executioner?
ANNE. Thou wast the cause and most
  accurs'd effect.
GLOUCESTER. Your beauty was the cause of
  that effect-
  Your beauty that did haunt me in my sleep
  To undertake the death of all the world
  So I might live one hour in your sweet bosom.
ANNE. If I thought that, I tell thee, homicide,
  These nails should rend that beauty from
    my cheeks.
GLOUCESTER. These eyes could not endure that
  beauty's wreck;

You should not blemish it if I stood by.
  As all the world is cheered by the sun,
  So I by that; it is my day, my life.
ANNE. Black night o'ershade thy day, and death
  thy life!
GLOUCESTER. Curse not thyself, fair creature;
  thou art both.
ANNE. I would I were, to be reveng'd on thee.
GLOUCESTER. It is a quarrel most unnatural,
  To be reveng'd on him that loveth thee.
ANNE. It is a quarrel just and reasonable,
  To be reveng'd on him that kill'd my husband.
GLOUCESTER. He that bereft thee, lady, of
  thy husband
  Did it to help thee to a better husband.
ANNE. His better doth not breathe upon
  the earth.
GLOUCESTER. He lives that loves thee better than
  he could.
ANNE. Name him.
GLOUCESTER. Plantagenet.
ANNE. Why, that was he.
GLOUCESTER. The self-same name, but one of
  better nature.
ANNE. Where is he?
GLOUCESTER. Here. [She spits at him] Why dost
  thou spit at me?
ANNE. Would it were mortal poison, for thy sake!
GLOUCESTER. Never came poison from so sweet
  a place.
ANNE. Never hung poison on a fouler toad.
  Out of my sight! Thou dost infect mine eyes.
GLOUCESTER. Thine eyes, sweet lady, have
  infected mine.
ANNE. Would they were basilisks to strike
  thee dead!
GLOUCESTER. I would they were, that I might
  die at once;
  For now they kill me with a living death.
  Those eyes of thine from mine have drawn
    salt tears,
  Sham'd their aspects with store of
    childish drops-
  These eyes, which never shed remorseful tear,
  No, when my father York and Edward wept
  To hear the piteous moan that Rutland made
  When black-fac'd Clifford shook his sword
    at him;
  Nor when thy warlike father, like a child,
  Told the sad story of my father's death,
  And twenty times made pause to sob and weep
  That all the standers-by had wet their cheeks
  Like trees bedash'd with rain-in that sad time

My manly eyes did scorn an humble tear;
And what these sorrows could not
thence exhale
Thy beauty hath, and made them blind
with weeping.
I never sued to friend nor enemy;
My tongue could never learn sweet
smoothing word;
But, now thy beauty is propos'd my fee,
My proud heart sues, and prompts my tongue
to speak. *[She looks scornfully at him]*
Teach not thy lip such scorn; for it was made
For kissing, lady, not for such contempt.
If thy revengeful heart cannot forgive,
Lo here I lend thee this sharp-pointed sword;
Which if thou please to hide in this true breast
And let the soul forth that adoreth thee,
I lay it naked to the deadly stroke,
And humbly beg the death upon my knee. *[He
lays his breast open; she offers at it with his sword]*
Nay, do not pause; for I did kill King Henry-
But 'twas thy beauty that provoked me.
Nay, now dispatch; 'twas I that stabb'd
young Edward-
But 'twas thy heavenly face that set me on. *[She
falls the sword]*
Take up the sword again, or take up me.
ANNE. Arise, dissembler; though I wish thy death,
I will not be thy executioner.
GLOUCESTER. Then bid me kill myself, and I will
do it;
ANNE. I have already.
GLOUCESTER. That was in thy rage.
Speak it again, and even with the word
This hand, which for thy love did kill thy love,
Shall for thy love kill a far truer love;
To both their deaths shalt thou be accessary.
ANNE. I would I knew thy heart.
GLOUCESTER. 'Tis figur'd in my tongue.
ANNE. I fear me both are false.
GLOUCESTER. Then never was man true.
ANNE. Well, well put up your sword.
GLOUCESTER. Say, then, my peace is made.
ANNE. That shalt thou know hereafter.
GLOUCESTER. But shall I live in hope?
ANNE. All men, I hope, live so.
GLOUCESTER. Vouchsafe to wear this ring.
ANNE. To take is not to give. *Puts on the ring*
GLOUCESTER. Look how my ring encompasseth
thy finger,
Even so thy breast encloseth my poor heart;
Wear both of them, for both of them are thine.
And if thy poor devoted servant may

But beg one favour at thy gracious hand,
Thou dost confirm his happiness for ever.
ANNE. What is it?
GLOUCESTER. That it may please you leave these
sad designs
To him that hath most cause to be a mourner,
And presently repair to Crosby House;
Where-after I have solemnly interr'd
At Chertsey monast'ry this noble king,
And wet his grave with my repentant tears-
I will with all expedient duty see you.
For divers unknown reasons, I beseech you,
Grant me this boon.
ANNE. With all my heart; and much it joys me too
To see you are become so penitent.
Tressel and Berkeley, go along with me.
GLOUCESTER. Bid me farewell.
ANNE. 'Tis more than you deserve;
But since you teach me how to flatter you,
Imagine I have said farewell already.
Exeunt two GENTLEMEN with LADY ANNE.
GLOUCESTER. Sirs, take up the corse.
GENTLEMEN. Towards Chertsey, noble lord?
GLOUCESTER. No, to White Friars; there attend
my coming. *[Exeunt all but GLOUCESTER]*
Was ever woman in this humour woo'd?
Was ever woman in this humour won?
I'll have her; but I will not keep her long.
What! I that kill'd her husband and his father-
To take her in her heart's extremest hate,
With curses in her mouth, tears in her eyes,
The bleeding witness of my hatred by;
Having God, her conscience, and these bars
against me,
And I no friends to back my suit at all
But the plain devil and dissembling looks,
And yet to win her, all the world to nothing!
Ha!
Hath she forgot already that brave prince,
Edward, her lord, whom I, some three
months since,
Stabb'd in my angry mood at Tewksbury?
A sweeter and a lovelier gentleman-
Fram'd in the prodigality of nature,
Young, valiant, wise, and no doubt right royal-
The spacious world cannot again afford;
And will she yet abase her eyes on me,
That cropp'd the golden prime of this
sweet prince
And made her widow to a woeful bed?
On me, whose all not equals Edward's moiety?
On me, that halts and am misshapen thus?
My dukedom to a beggarly denier,

I do mistake my person all this while.
Upon my life, she finds, although I cannot,
Myself to be a marv'llous proper man.
I'll be at charges for a looking-glass,
And entertain a score or two of tailors
To study fashions to adorn my body.
Since I am crept in favour with myself,
I will maintain it with some little cost.
But first I'll turn yon fellow in his grave,
And then return lamenting to my love.
Shine out, fair sun, till I have bought a glass,
That I may see my shadow as I pass. *Exit.*

✤ SCENE III ✤
London. The palace

Enter QUEEN ELIZABETH, LORD RIVERS,
and LORD GREY

RIVERS. Have patience, madam; there's no doubt
his Majesty
Will soon recover his accustom'd health.
GREY. In that you brook it ill, it makes
him worse;
Therefore, for God's sake, entertain
good comfort,
And cheer his Grace with quick and merry eyes.
QUEEN ELIZABETH. If he were dead, what
would betide on me?
GREY. No other harm but loss of such a lord.
QUEEN ELIZABETH. The loss of such a lord
includes all harms.
GREY. The heavens have bless'd you with a
goodly son
To be your comforter when he is gone.
QUEEN ELIZABETH. Ah, he is young; and
his minority
Is put unto the trust of Richard Gloucester,
A man that loves not me, nor none of you.
RIVERS. Is it concluded he shall be Protector?
QUEEN ELIZABETH. It is determin'd, not
concluded yet;
But so it must be, if the King miscarry.
Enter BUCKINGHAM and DERBY
GREY. Here come the Lords of Buckingham
and Derby.
BUCKINGHAM. Good time of day unto your
royal Grace!
DERBY. God make your Majesty joyful as you
have been.
QUEEN ELIZABETH. The Countess Richmond,
good my Lord of Derby,

To your good prayer will scarcely say amen.
Yet, Derby, notwithstanding she's your wife
And loves not me, be you, good lord, assur'd
I hate not you for her proud arrogance.
DERBY. I do beseech you, either not believe
The envious slanders of her false accusers;
Or, if she be accus'd on true report,
Bear with her weakness, which I think proceeds
From wayward sickness and no
grounded malice.
QUEEN ELIZABETH. Saw you the King to-day, my
Lord of Derby?
DERBY. But now the Duke of Buckingham and I
Are come from visiting his Majesty.
QUEEN ELIZABETH. What likelihood of his
amendment, Lords?
BUCKINGHAM. Madam, good hope; his Grace
speaks cheerfully.
QUEEN ELIZABETH. God grant him health! Did
you confer with him?
BUCKINGHAM. Ay, madam; he desires to
make atonement
Between the Duke of Gloucester and
your brothers,
And between them and my Lord Chamberlain;
And sent to warn them to his royal presence.
QUEEN ELIZABETH. Would all were well! But
that will never be.
I fear our happiness is at the height.
Enter GLOUCESTER, HASTINGS, and DORSET
GLOUCESTER. They do me wrong, and I will not
endure it.
Who is it that complains unto the King
That I, forsooth, am stern and love them not?
By holy Paul, they love his Grace but lightly
That fill his ears with such dissentious rumours.
Because I cannot flatter and look fair,
Smile in men's faces, smooth, deceive, and cog,
Duck with French nods and apish courtesy,
I must be held a rancorous enemy.
Cannot a plain man live and think no harm
But thus his simple truth must be abus'd
With silken, sly, insinuating Jacks?
GREY. To who in all this presence speaks
your Grace?
GLOUCESTER. To thee, that hast nor honesty
nor grace.
When have I injur'd thee? when done
thee wrong,
Or thee, or thee, or any of your faction?
A plague upon you all! His royal Grace-
Whom God preserve better than you
would wish!-

Cannot be quiet scarce a breathing while
But you must trouble him with lewd complaints.
QUEEN ELIZABETH. Brother of Gloucester, you
mistake the matter.
The King, on his own royal disposition
And not provok'd by any suitor else-
Aiming, belike, at your interior hatred
That in your outward action shows itself
Against my children, brothers, and myself-
Makes him to send that he may learn
the ground.
GLOUCESTER. I cannot tell; the world is grown
so bad
That wrens make prey where eagles dare
not perch.
Since every Jack became a gentleman,
There's many a gentle person made a Jack.
QUEEN ELIZABETH. Come, come, we know your
meaning, brother Gloucester:
You envy my advancement and my friends';
God grant we never may have need of you!
GLOUCESTER. Meantime, God grants that I have
need of you.
Our brother is imprison'd by your means,
Myself disgrac'd, and the nobility
Held in contempt; while great promotions
Are daily given to ennoble those
That scarce some two days since were worth
a noble.
QUEEN ELIZABETH. By Him that rais'd me to this
careful height
From that contented hap which I enjoy'd,
I never did incense his Majesty
Against the Duke of Clarence, but have been
An earnest advocate to plead for him.
My lord, you do me shameful injury
Falsely to draw me in these vile suspects.
GLOUCESTER. You may deny that you were not
the mean
Of my Lord Hastings' late imprisonment.
RIVERS. She may, my lord; for-
GLOUCESTER. She may, Lord Rivers? Why, who
knows not so?
She may do more, sir, than denying that:
She may help you to many fair preferments
And then deny her aiding hand therein,
And lay those honours on your high desert.
What may she not? She may-ay, marry, may she-
RIVERS. What, marry, may she?
GLOUCESTER. What, marry, may she? Marry with
a king,
A bachelor, and a handsome stripling too.
I wis your grandam had a worser match.

QUEEN ELIZABETH. My Lord of Gloucester, I
have too long borne
Your blunt upbraidings and your bitter scoffs.
By heaven, I will acquaint his Majesty
Of those gross taunts that oft I have endur'd.
I had rather be a country servant-maid
Than a great queen with this condition-
To be so baited, scorn'd, and stormed at.

Enter old QUEEN MARGARET, behind

Small joy have I in being England's Queen.
QUEEN MARGARET. And less'ned be that small,
God, I beseech Him!
Thy honour, state, and seat, is due to me.
GLOUCESTER. What! Threat you me with telling
of the King?
Tell him and spare not. Look what I have said
I will avouch't in presence of the King.
I dare adventure to be sent to th' Tow'r.
'Tis time to speak-my pains are quite forgot.
QUEEN MARGARET. Out, devil! I do remember
them too well:
Thou kill'dst my husband Henry in the Tower,
And Edward, my poor son, at Tewksbury.
GLOUCESTER. Ere you were queen, ay, or your
husband king,
I was a pack-horse in his great affairs,
A weeder-out of his proud adversaries,
A liberal rewarder of his friends;
To royalize his blood I spent mine own.
QUEEN MARGARET. Ay, and much better blood
than his or thine.
GLOUCESTER. In all which time you and your
husband Grey
Were factious for the house of Lancaster;
And, Rivers, so were you. Was not
your husband
In Margaret's battle at Saint Albans slain?
Let me put in your minds, if you forget,
What you have been ere this, and what you are;
Withal, what I have been, and what I am.
QUEEN MARGARET. A murd'rous villain, and so
still thou art.
GLOUCESTER. Poor Clarence did forsake his
father, Warwick,
Ay, and forswore himself-which Jesu pardon!-
QUEEN MARGARET. Which God revenge!
GLOUCESTER. To fight on Edward's party for
the crown;
And for his meed, poor lord, he is mewed up.
I would to God my heart were flint
like Edward's,
Or Edward's soft and pitiful like mine.
I am too childish-foolish for this world.

QUEEN MARGARET. Hie thee to hell for shame
  and leave this world,
  Thou cacodemon; there thy kingdom is.
RIVERS. My Lord of Gloucester, in those
  busy days
  Which here you urge to prove us enemies,
  We follow'd then our lord, our sovereign king.
  So should we you, if you should be our king.
GLOUCESTER. If I should be! I had rather be a
  pedlar.
  Far be it from my heart, the thought thereof!
QUEEN ELIZABETH. As little joy, my lord, as
  you suppose
  You should enjoy were you this country's king,
  As little joy you may suppose in me
  That I enjoy, being the Queen thereof.
QUEEN MARGARET. As little joy enjoys the
  Queen thereof;
  For I am she, and altogether joyless.
  I can no longer hold me patient. [Advancing]
  Hear me, you wrangling pirates, that fall out
  In sharing that which you have pill'd from me.
  Which of you trembles not that looks on me?
  If not that, I am Queen, you bow like subjects,
  Yet that, by you depos'd, you quake
  like rebels?
  Ah, gentle villain, do not turn away!
GLOUCESTER. Foul wrinkled witch, what mak'st
  thou in my sight?
QUEEN MARGARET. But repetition of what thou
  hast marr'd,
  That will I make before I let thee go.
GLOUCESTER. Wert thou not banished on pain
  of death?
QUEEN MARGARET. I was; but I do find more
  pain in banishment
  Than death can yield me here by my abode.
  A husband and a son thou ow'st to me;
  And thou a kingdom; all of you allegiance.
  This sorrow that I have by right is yours;
  And all the pleasures you usurp are mine.
GLOUCESTER. The curse my noble father laid
  on thee,
  When thou didst crown his warlike brows
  with paper
  And with thy scorns drew'st rivers from
  his eyes,
  And then to dry them gav'st the Duke a clout
  Steep'd in the faultless blood of
  pretty Rutland-
  His curses then from bitterness of soul
  Denounc'd against thee are all fall'n
  upon thee;

And God, not we, hath plagu'd thy
  bloody deed.
QUEEN ELIZABETH. So just is God to right
  the innocent.
HASTINGS. O, 'twas the foulest deed to slay
  that babe,
  And the most merciless that e'er was heard of!
RIVERS. Tyrants themselves wept when it
  was reported.
DORSET. No man but prophesied revenge for it.
BUCKINGHAM. Northumberland, then present,
  wept to see it.
QUEEN MARGARET. What, were you snarling all
  before I came,
  Ready to catch each other by the throat,
  And turn you all your hatred now on me?
  Did York's dread curse prevail so much
  with heaven
  That Henry's death, my lovely Edward's death,
  Their kingdom's loss, my woeful banishment,
  Should all but answer for that peevish brat?
  Can curses pierce the clouds and
  enter heaven?
  Why then, give way, dull clouds, to my
  quick curses!
  Though not by war, by surfeit die your king,
  As ours by murder, to make him a king!
  Edward thy son, that now is Prince of Wales,
  For Edward our son, that was Prince of Wales,
  Die in his youth by like untimely violence!
  Thyself a queen, for me that was a queen,
  Outlive thy glory, like my wretched self!
  Long mayest thou live to wail thy
  children's death,
  And see another, as I see thee now,
  Deck'd in thy rights, as thou art stall'd
  in mine!
  Long die thy happy days before thy death;
  And, after many length'ned hours of grief,
  Die neither mother, wife, nor
  England's Queen!
  Rivers and Dorset, you were standers by,
  And so wast thou, Lord Hastings, when my son
  Was stabb'd with bloody daggers. God, I
  pray him,
  That none of you may live his natural age,
  But by some unlook'd accident cut off!
GLOUCESTER. Have done thy charm, thou
  hateful wither'd hag.
QUEEN MARGARET. And leave out thee? Stay,
  dog, for thou shalt hear me.
  If heaven have any grievous plague in store
  Exceeding those that I can wish upon thee,

O, let them keep it till thy sins be ripe,
And then hurl down their indignation
On thee, the troubler of the poor
  world's peace!
The worm of conscience still be-gnaw thy soul!
Thy friends suspect for traitors while
  thou liv'st,
And take deep traitors for thy dearest friends!
No sleep close up that deadly eye of thine,
Unless it be while some tormenting dream
Affrights thee with a hell of ugly devils!
Thou elvish-mark'd, abortive, rooting hog,
Thou that wast seal'd in thy nativity
The slave of nature and the son of hell,
Thou slander of thy heavy mother's womb,
Thou loathed issue of thy father's loins,
Thou rag of honour, thou detested-
GLOUCESTER. Margaret!
QUEEN MARGARET. Richard!
GLOUCESTER. Ha?
QUEEN MARGARET. I call thee not.
GLOUCESTER. I cry thee mercy then, for I
  did think
  That thou hadst call'd me all these
  bitter names.
QUEEN MARGARET. Why, so I did, but look'd
  for no reply.
  O, let me make the period to my curse!
GLOUCESTER. 'Tis done by me, and ends in-
  Margaret.
QUEEN ELIZABETH. Thus have you breath'd
  your curse against yourself.
QUEEN MARGARET. Poor painted queen, vain
  flourish of my fortune!
Why strew'st thou sugar on that bottled spider
Whose deadly web ensnareth thee about?
Fool, fool! thou whet'st a knife to kill thyself.
The day will come that thou shalt wish for me
To help thee curse this poisonous bunch-
  back'd toad.
HASTINGS. False-boding woman, end thy
  frantic curse,
  Lest to thy harm thou move our patience.
QUEEN MARGARET. Foul shame upon you! you
  have all mov'd mine.
RIVERS. Were you well serv'd, you would be
  taught your duty.
QUEEN MARGARET. To serve me well you all
  should do me duty,
  Teach me to be your queen and you
  my subjects.
  O, serve me well, and teach yourselves
  that duty!

DORSET. Dispute not with her; she is lunatic.
QUEEN MARGARET. Peace, Master Marquis, you
  are malapert;
  Your fire-new stamp of honour is
  scarce current.
  O, that your young nobility could judge
  What 'twere to lose it and be miserable!
  They that stand high have many blasts to
  shake them,
  And if they fall they dash themselves to pieces.
GLOUCESTER. Good counsel, marry; learn it,
  learn it, Marquis.
DORSET. It touches you, my lord, as much
  as me.
GLOUCESTER. Ay, and much more; but I was
  born so high,
  Our aery buildeth in the cedar's top,
  And dallies with the wind, and scorns the sun.
QUEEN MARGARET. And turns the sun to shade-
  alas! alas!
  Witness my son, now in the shade of death,
  Whose bright out-shining beams thy
  cloudy wrath
  Hath in eternal darkness folded up.
  Your aery buildeth in our aery's nest.
  O God that seest it, do not suffer it;
  As it is won with blood, lost be it so!
BUCKINGHAM. Peace, peace, for shame, if not
  for charity!
QUEEN MARGARET. Urge neither charity nor
  shame to me.
  Uncharitably with me have you dealt,
  And shamefully my hopes by you are butcher'd.
  My charity is outrage, life my shame;
  And in that shame still live my sorrow's rage!
BUCKINGHAM. Have done, have done.
QUEEN MARGARET. O princely Buckingham, I'll
  kiss thy hand
  In sign of league and amity with thee.
  Now fair befall thee and thy noble house!
  Thy garments are not spotted with our blood,
  Nor thou within the compass of my curse.
BUCKINGHAM. Nor no one here; for curses
  never pass
  The lips of those that breathe them in the air.
QUEEN MARGARET. I will not think but they
  ascend the sky
  And there awake God's gentle-sleeping peace.
  O Buckingham, take heed of yonder dog!
  Look when he fawns, he bites; and when
  he bites,
  His venom tooth will rankle to the death:
  Have not to do with him, beware of him;

Sin, death, and hell, have set their marks on him,
And all their ministers attend on him.
GLOUCESTER. What doth she say, my Lord
  of Buckingham?
BUCKINGHAM. Nothing that I respect, my
  gracious lord.
QUEEN MARGARET. What, dost thou scorn me for
  my gentle counsel,
  And soothe the devil that I warn thee from?
  O, but remember this another day,
  When he shall split thy very heart with sorrow,
  And say poor Margaret was a prophetess!
  Live each of you the subjects to his hate,
  And he to yours, and all of you to God's! *Exit.*
BUCKINGHAM. My hair doth stand an end to hear
  her curses.
RIVERS. And so doth mine. I muse why she's
  at liberty.
GLOUCESTER. I cannot blame her; by God's
  holy Mother,
  She hath had too much wrong; and I repent
  My part thereof that I have done to her.
QUEEN ELIZABETH. I never did her any to
  my knowledge.
GLOUCESTER. Yet you have all the vantage of
  her wrong.
  I was too hot to do somebody good
  That is too cold in thinking of it now.
  Marry, as for Clarence, he is well repaid;
  He is frank'd up to fatting for his pains;
  God pardon them that are the cause thereof!
RIVERS. A virtuous and a Christian-like conclusion,
  To pray for them that have done scathe to us!
GLOUCESTER. So do I ever- *[Aside]* being
  well advis'd;
  For had I curs'd now, I had curs'd myself.
                Enter CATESBY
CATESBY. Madam, his Majesty doth call for you,
  And for your Grace, and you, my gracious lords.
QUEEN ELIZABETH. Catesby, I come. Lords, will
  you go with me?
RIVERS. We wait upon your Grace.
              Exeunt all but GLOUCESTER.
GLOUCESTER. I do the wrong, and first begin
  to brawl.
  The secret mischiefs that I set abroach
  I lay unto the grievous charge of others.
  Clarence, who I indeed have cast in darkness,
  I do beweep to many simple gulls;
  Namely, to Derby, Hastings, Buckingham;
  And tell them 'tis the Queen and her allies
  That stir the King against the Duke my brother.
  Now they believe it, and withal whet me

To be reveng'd on Rivers, Dorset, Grey;
  But then I sigh and, with a piece of Scripture,
  Tell them that God bids us do good for evil.
  And thus I clothe my naked villainy
  With odd old ends stol'n forth of holy writ,
  And seem a saint when most I play the devil.
                Enter two MURDERERS
  But, soft, here come my executioners.
  How now, my hardy stout resolved mates!
  Are you now going to dispatch this thing?
FIRST MURDERER. We are, my lord, and come to
  have the warrant,
  That we may be admitted where he is.
GLOUCESTER. Well thought upon; I have it here
  about me. *[Gives the warrant]*
  When you have done, repair to Crosby Place.
  But, sirs, be sudden in the execution,
  Withal obdurate, do not hear him plead;
  For Clarence is well-spoken, and perhaps
  May move your hearts to pity, if you mark him.
FIRST MURDERER. Tut, tut, my lord, we will not
  stand to prate;
  Talkers are no good doers. Be assur'd
  We go to use our hands and not our tongues.
GLOUCESTER. Your eyes drop millstones when
  fools' eyes fall tears.
  I like you, lads; about your business straight;
  Go, go, dispatch.
FIRST MURDERER. We will, my noble lord.
                          Exeunt.

✣ SCENE IV ✣
London. The Tower

Enter CLARENCE and KEEPER

KEEPER. Why looks your Grace so heavily to-day?
CLARENCE. O, I have pass'd a miserable night,
  So full of fearful dreams, of ugly sights,
  That, as I am a Christian faithful man,
  I would not spend another such a night
  Though 'twere to buy a world of happy days-
  So full of dismal terror was the time!
KEEPER. What was your dream, my lord? I pray
  you tell me.
CLARENCE. Methoughts that I had broken from
  the Tower
  And was embark'd to cross to Burgundy;
  And in my company my brother Gloucester,
  Who from my cabin tempted me to walk
  Upon the hatches. Thence we look'd
    toward England,

And cited up a thousand heavy times,
During the wars of York and Lancaster,
That had befall'n us. As we pac'd along
Upon the giddy footing of the hatches,
Methought that Gloucester stumbled, and
in falling
Struck me, that thought to stay him, overboard
Into the tumbling billows of the main.
O Lord, methought what pain it was to drown,
What dreadful noise of waters in my ears,
What sights of ugly death within my eyes!
Methoughts I saw a thousand fearful wrecks,
A thousand men that fishes gnaw'd upon,
Wedges of gold, great anchors, heaps of pearl,
Inestimable stones, unvalued jewels,
All scatt'red in the bottom of the sea;
Some lay in dead men's skulls, and in the holes
Where eyes did once inhabit there were crept,
As 'twere in scorn of eyes, reflecting gems,
That woo'd the slimy bottom of the deep
And mock'd the dead bones that lay
scatt'red by.
KEEPER. Had you such leisure in the time
of death
To gaze upon these secrets of the deep?
CLARENCE. Methought I had; and often did
I strive
To yield the ghost, but still the envious flood
Stopp'd in my soul and would not let it forth
To find the empty, vast, and wand'ring air;
But smother'd it within my panting bulk,
Who almost burst to belch it in the sea.
KEEPER. Awak'd you not in this sore agony?
CLARENCE. No, no, my dream was lengthen'd
after life.
O, then began the tempest to my soul!
I pass'd, methought, the melancholy flood
With that sour ferryman which poets write of,
Unto the kingdom of perpetual night.
The first that there did greet my stranger soul
Was my great father-in-law, renowned Warwick,
Who spake aloud 'What scourge for perjury
Can this dark monarchy afford false Clarence?'
And so he vanish'd. Then came wand'ring by
A shadow like an angel, with bright hair
Dabbled in blood, and he shriek'd out aloud
'Clarence is come-false, fleeting,
perjur'd Clarence,
That stabb'd me in the field by Tewksbury.
Seize on him, Furies, take him unto torment!'
With that, methoughts, a legion of foul fiends
Environ'd me, and howled in mine ears
Such hideous cries that, with the very noise,

I trembling wak'd, and for a season after
Could not believe but that I was in hell,
Such terrible impression made my dream.
KEEPER. No marvel, lord, though it
affrighted you;
I am afraid, methinks, to hear you tell it.
CLARENCE. Ah, Keeper, Keeper, I have done
these things
That now give evidence against my soul
For Edward's sake, and see how he
requites me!
O God! If my deep prayers cannot
appease Thee,
But Thou wilt be aveng'd on my misdeeds,
Yet execute Thy wrath in me alone;
O, spare my guiltless wife and my
poor children!
Keeper, I prithee sit by me awhile;
My soul is heavy, and I fain would sleep.
KEEPER. I will, my lord. God give your Grace
good rest.   *CLARENCE sleeps*
Enter BRAKENBURY the Lieutenant
BRAKENBURY. Sorrow breaks seasons and
reposing hours,
Makes the night morning and the
noontide night.
Princes have but their titles for their glories,
An outward honour for an inward toil;
And for unfelt imaginations
They often feel a world of restless cares,
So that between their tides and low name
There's nothing differs but the outward fame.
Enter the two MURDERERS
FIRST MURDERER. Ho! who's here?
BRAKENBURY. What wouldst thou, fellow, and
how cam'st thou hither?
FIRST MURDERER. I would speak with Clarence,
and I came hither on my legs.
BRAKENBURY. What, so brief?
SECOND MURDERER. 'Tis better, sir, than to be
tedious. Let him see our commission and talk
no more.   *RAKENBURY reads it*
BRAKENBURY. I am, in this, commanded
to deliver
The noble Duke of Clarence to your hands.
I will not reason what is meant hereby,
Because I will be guiltless from the meaning.
There lies the Duke asleep; and there the keys.
I'll to the King and signify to him
That thus I have resign'd to you my charge.
FIRST MURDERER. You may, sir; 'tis a point of
wisdom. Fare you well.
Exeunt BRAKENBURY and KEEPER

SECOND MURDERER. What, shall I stab him as he sleeps?

FIRST MURDERER. No; he'll say 'twas done cowardly, when he wakes.

SECOND MURDERER. Why, he shall never wake until the great judgment-day.

FIRST MURDERER. Why, then he'll say we stabb'd him sleeping.

SECOND MURDERER. The urging of that word 'judgment' hath bred a kind of remorse in me.

FIRST MURDERER. What, art thou afraid?

SECOND MURDERER. Not to kill him, having a warrant; but to be damn'd for killing him, from the which no warrant can defend me.

FIRST MURDERER. I thought thou hadst been resolute.

SECOND MURDERER. So I am, to let him live.

FIRST MURDERER. I'll back to the Duke of Gloucester and tell him so.

SECOND MURDERER. Nay, I prithee, stay a little. I hope this passionate humour of mine will change; it was wont to hold me but while one tells twenty.

FIRST MURDERER. How dost thou feel thyself now?

SECOND MURDERER. Faith, some certain dregs of conscience are yet within me.

FIRST MURDERER. Remember our reward, when the deed's done.

SECOND MURDERER. Zounds, he dies; I had forgot the reward.

FIRST MURDERER. Where's thy conscience now?

SECOND MURDERER. O, in the Duke of Gloucester's purse!

FIRST MURDERER. When he opens his purse to give us our reward, thy conscience flies out.

SECOND MURDERER. 'Tis no matter; let it go; there's few or none will entertain it.

FIRST MURDERER. What if it come to thee again?

SECOND MURDERER. I'll not meddle with it-it makes a man coward: a man cannot steal, but it accuseth him; a man cannot swear, but it checks him; a man cannot lie with his neighbour's wife, but it detects him. 'Tis a blushing shame-fac'd spirit that mutinies in a man's bosom; it fills a man full of obstacles: it made me once restore a purse of gold that-by chance I found. It beggars any man that keeps it. It is turn'd out of towns and cities for a dangerous thing; and every man that means to live well endeavours to trust to himself and live without it.

FIRST MURDERER. Zounds, 'tis even now at my elbow, persuading me not to kill the Duke.

SECOND MURDERER. Take the devil in thy mind and believe him not; he would insinuate with thee but to make thee sigh.

FIRST MURDERER. I am strong-fram'd; he cannot prevail with me.

SECOND MURDERER. Spoke like a tall man that respects thy reputation. Come, shall we fall to work?

FIRST MURDERER. Take him on the costard with the hilts of thy sword, and then chop him in the malmsey-butt in the next room.

SECOND MURDERER. O excellent device! and make a sop of him.

FIRST MURDERER. Soft! he wakes.

SECOND MURDERER. Strike!

FIRST MURDERER. No, we'll reason with him.

CLARENCE. Where art thou, Keeper? Give me a cup of wine.

SECOND MURDERER. You shall have wine enough, my lord, anon.

CLARENCE. In God's name, what art thou?

FIRST MURDERER. A man, as you are.

CLARENCE. But not as I am, royal.

SECOND MURDERER. Nor you as we are, loyal.

CLARENCE. Thy voice is thunder, but thy looks are humble.

FIRST MURDERER. My voice is now the King's, my looks mine own.

CLARENCE. How darkly and how deadly dost thou speak!
    Your eyes do menace me. Why look you pale?
    Who sent you hither? Wherefore do you come?

SECOND MURDERER. To, to, to-

CLARENCE. To murder me?

BOTH MURDERERS. Ay, ay.

CLARENCE. You scarcely have the hearts to tell me so,
    And therefore cannot have the hearts to do it.
    Wherein, my friends, have I offended you?

FIRST MURDERER. Offended us you have not, but the King.

CLARENCE. I shall be reconcil'd to him again.

SECOND MURDERER. Never, my lord; therefore prepare to die.

CLARENCE. Are you drawn forth among a world of men
    To slay the innocent? What is my offence?
    Where is the evidence that doth accuse me?
    What lawful quest have given their verdict up
    Unto the frowning judge, or who pronounc'd
    The bitter sentence of poor Clarence' death?

Before I be convict by course of law,
To threaten me with death is most unlawful.
I charge you, as you hope to have redemption
By Christ's dear blood shed for our
grievous sins,
That you depart and lay no hands on me.
The deed you undertake is damnable.
FIRST MURDERER. What we will do, we do
upon command.
SECOND MURDERER. And he that hath
commanded is our King.
CLARENCE. Erroneous vassals! the great King
of kings
Hath in the tables of his law commanded
That thou shalt do no murder. Will you then
Spurn at his edict and fulfil a man's?
Take heed; for he holds vengeance in his hand
To hurl upon their heads that break his law.
SECOND MURDERER. And that same vengeance
doth he hurl on thee
For false forswearing, and for murder too;
Thou didst receive the sacrament to fight
In quarrel of the house of Lancaster.
FIRST MURDERER. And like a traitor to the name
of God
Didst break that vow; and with thy
treacherous blade
Unripp'dst the bowels of thy sov'reign's son.
SECOND MURDERER. Whom thou wast sworn to
cherish and defend.
FIRST MURDERER. How canst thou urge God's
dreadful law to us,
When thou hast broke it in such dear degree?
CLARENCE. Alas! for whose sake did I that
ill deed?
For Edward, for my brother, for his sake.
He sends you not to murder me for this,
For in that sin he is as deep as I.
If God will be avenged for the deed,
O, know you yet He doth it publicly.
Take not the quarrel from His pow'rful arm;
He needs no indirect or lawless course
To cut off those that have offended Him.
FIRST MURDERER. Who made thee then a
bloody minister
When gallant-springing brave Plantagenet,
That princely novice, was struck dead by thee?
CLARENCE. My brother's love, the devil, and my rage.
FIRST MURDERER. Thy brother's love, our duty,
and thy faults,
Provoke us hither now to slaughter thee.
CLARENCE. If you do love my brother, hate
not me;

I am his brother, and I love him well.
If you are hir'd for meed, go back again,
And I will send you to my brother Gloucester,
Who shall reward you better for my life
Than Edward will for tidings of my death.
SECOND MURDERER. You are deceiv'd: your
brother Gloucester hates you.
CLARENCE. O, no, he loves me, and he holds
me dear.
Go you to him from me.
FIRST MURDERER. Ay, so we will.
CLARENCE. Tell him when that our princely
father York
Bless'd his three sons with his victorious arm
And charg'd us from his soul to love each other,
He little thought of this divided friendship.
Bid Gloucester think of this, and he will weep.
FIRST MURDERER. Ay, millstones; as he lesson'd
us to weep.
CLARENCE. O, do not slander him, for he is kind.
FIRST MURDERER. Right, as snow in harvest.
Come, you deceive yourself:
'Tis he that sends us to destroy you here.
CLARENCE. It cannot be; for he bewept
my fortune
And hugg'd me in his arms, and swore with sobs
That he would labour my delivery.
FIRST MURDERER. Why, so he doth, when he
delivers you
From this earth's thraldom to the joys of heaven.
SECOND MURDERER. Make peace with God, for
you must die, my lord.
CLARENCE. Have you that holy feeling in
your souls
To counsel me to make my peace with God,
And are you yet to your own souls so blind
That you will war with God by murd'ring me?
O, sirs, consider: they that set you on
To do this deed will hate you for the deed.
SECOND MURDERER. What shall we do?
CLARENCE. Relent, and save your souls.
FIRST MURDERER. Relent! No, 'tis cowardly
and womanish.
CLARENCE. Not to relent is beastly,
savage, devilish.
Which of you, if you were a prince's son,
Being pent from liberty as I am now,
If two such murderers as yourselves came
to you,
Would not entreat for life?
My friend, I spy some pity in thy looks;
O, if thine eye be not a flatterer,
Come thou on my side and entreat for me-

As you would beg were you in my distress.
A begging prince what beggar pities not?
SECOND MURDERER. Look behind you, my lord.
FIRST MURDERER. *[Stabbing him]* Take that, and that.
If all this will not do,
I'll drown you in the malmsey-butt within.
Exit with the body.

SECOND MURDERER. A bloody deed, and
desperately dispatch'd!
How fain, like Pilate, would I wash my hands
Of this most grievous murder!
Re-enter FIRST MURDERER

FIRST MURDERER. How now, what mean'st thou
that thou help'st me not?
By heavens, the Duke shall know how slack you
have been!
SECOND MURDERER. I would he knew that I had
sav'd his brother!
Take thou the fee, and tell him what I say;
For I repent me that the Duke is slain. *Exit.*
FIRST MURDERER. So do not I. Go, coward as
thou art.
Well, I'll go hide the body in some hole,
Till that the Duke give order for his burial;
And when I have my meed, I will away;
For this will out, and then I must not stay. *Exit.*

 ACT II

SCENE I
London. The palace

Flourish. Enter KING EDWARD, sick, QUEEN
ELIZABETH, DORSET, RIVERS, HASTINGS,
BUCKINGHAM, GREY, and Others

KING EDWARD. Why, so. Now have I done a good
day's work.
You peers, continue this united league.
I every day expect an embassage
From my Redeemer to redeem me hence;
And more at peace my soul shall part to heaven,
Since I have made my friends at peace on earth.
Hastings and Rivers, take each other's hand;
Dissemble not your hatred, swear your love.
RIVERS. By heaven, my soul is purg'd from
grudging hate;
And with my hand I seal my true heart's love.
HASTINGS. So thrive I, as I truly swear the like!
KING EDWARD. Take heed you dally not before
your king;

Lest He that is the supreme King of kings
Confound your hidden falsehood and award
Either of you to be the other's end.
HASTINGS. So prosper I, as I swear perfect love!
RIVERS. And I, as I love Hastings with my heart!
KING EDWARD. Madam, yourself is not exempt
from this;
Nor you, son Dorset; Buckingham, nor you:
You have been factious one against the other.
Wife, love Lord Hastings, let him kiss your hand;
And what you do, do it unfeignedly.
QUEEN ELIZABETH. There, Hastings; I will never
more remember
Our former hatred, so thrive I and mine!
KING EDWARD. Dorset, embrace him; Hastings,
love Lord Marquis.
DORSET. This interchange of love, I here protest,
Upon my part shall be inviolable.
HASTINGS. And so swear I. *They embrace*
KING EDWARD. Now, princely Buckingham, seal
thou this league
With thy embracements to my wife's allies,
And make me happy in your unity.
BUCKINGHAM. *[To the QUEEN]* Whenever
Buckingham doth turn his hate
Upon your Grace, but with all duteous love
Doth cherish you and yours, God punish me
With hate in those where I expect most love!
When I have most need to employ a friend
And most assured that he is a friend,
Deep, hollow, treacherous, and full of guile,
Be he unto me! This do I beg of God
When I am cold in love to you or yours.
They embrace
KING EDWARD. A pleasing cordial,
princely Buckingham,
Is this thy vow unto my sickly heart.
There wanteth now our brother Gloucester here
To make the blessed period of this peace.
BUCKINGHAM. And, in good time,
Here comes Sir Richard Ratcliff and the Duke.
Enter GLOUCESTER and RATCLIFF
GLOUCESTER. Good morrow to my sovereign
king and Queen;
And, princely peers, a happy time of day!
KING EDWARD. Happy, indeed, as we have spent
the day.
Gloucester, we have done deeds of charity,
Made peace of enmity, fair love of hate,
Between these swelling wrong-incensed peers.
GLOUCESTER. A blessed labour, my most
sovereign lord.
Among this princely heap, if any here,

By false intelligence or wrong surmise,
Hold me a foe-
If I unwittingly, or in my rage,
Have aught committed that is hardly borne
To any in this presence, I desire
To reconcile me to his friendly peace:
'Tis death to me to be at enmity;
I hate it, and desire all good men's love.
First, madam, I entreat true peace of you,
Which I will purchase with my duteous service;
Of you, my noble cousin Buckingham,
If ever any grudge were lodg'd between us;
Of you, and you, Lord Rivers, and of Dorset,
That all without desert have frown'd on me;
Of you, Lord Woodville, and, Lord Scales, of you;
Dukes, earls, lords, gentlemen-indeed, of all.
I do not know that Englishman alive
With whom my soul is any jot at odds
More than the infant that is born to-night.
I thank my God for my humility.
QUEEN ELIZABETH. A holy day shall this be
  kept hereafter.
I would to God all strifes were
  well compounded.
My sovereign lord, I do beseech your Highness
To take our brother Clarence to your grace.
GLOUCESTER. Why, madam, have I off'red love
  for this,
To be so flouted in this royal presence?
Who knows not that the gentle Duke is dead?
  [They all start]
You do him injury to scorn his corse.
KING EDWARD. Who knows not he is dead! Who
  knows he is?
QUEEN ELIZABETH. All-seeing heaven, what a
  world is this!
BUCKINGHAM. Look I so pale, Lord Dorset, as
  the rest?
DORSET. Ay, my good lord; and no man in
  the presence
But his red colour hath forsook his cheeks.
KING EDWARD. Is Clarence dead? The order
  was revers'd.
GLOUCESTER. But he, poor man, by your first
  order died,
And that a winged Mercury did bear;
Some tardy cripple bare the countermand
That came too lag to see him buried.
God grant that some, less noble and less loyal,
Nearer in bloody thoughts, an not in blood,
Deserve not worse than wretched Clarence did,
And yet go current from suspicion!
  Enter DERBY

DERBY. A boon, my sovereign, for my
  service done!
KING EDWARD. I prithee, peace; my soul is full
  of sorrow.
DERBY. I will not rise unless your Highness
  hear me.
KING EDWARD. Then say at once what is it thou
  requests.
DERBY. The forfeit, sovereign, of my servant's life;
  Who slew to-day a riotous gentleman
  Lately attendant on the Duke of Norfolk.
KING EDWARD. Have I a tongue to doom my
  brother's death,
And shall that tongue give pardon to a slave?
My brother killed no man-his fault was thought,
And yet his punishment was bitter death.
Who sued to me for him? Who, in my wrath,
Kneel'd at my feet, and bid me be advis'd?
Who spoke of brotherhood? Who spoke of love?
Who told me how the poor soul did forsake
The mighty Warwick and did fight for me?
Who told me, in the field at Tewksbury
When Oxford had me down, he rescued me
And said 'Dear Brother, live, and be a king'?
Who told me, when we both lay in the field
Frozen almost to death, how he did lap me
Even in his garments, and did give himself,
All thin and naked, to the numb cold night?
All this from my remembrance brutish wrath
Sinfully pluck'd, and not a man of you
Had so much grace to put it in my mind.
But when your carters or your waiting-vassals
Have done a drunken slaughter and defac'd
The precious image of our dear Redeemer,
You straight are on your knees for
  pardon, pardon;
And I, unjustly too, must grant it you.
  [DERBY rises]
But for my brother not a man would speak;
Nor I, ungracious, speak unto myself
For him, poor soul. The proudest of you all
Have been beholding to him in his life;
Yet none of you would once beg for his life.
O God, I fear thy justice will take hold
On me, and you, and mine, and yours, for this!
Come, Hastings, help me to my closet. Ah,
  poor Clarence!
  Exeunt some with KING and QUEEN
GLOUCESTER. This is the fruits of rashness.
  Mark'd you not
How that the guilty kindred of the Queen
Look'd pale when they did hear of
  Clarence' death?

O, they did urge it still unto the King!
God will revenge it. Come, lords, will you go
To comfort Edward with our company?
BUCKINGHAM. We wait upon your Grace. *Exeunt*

✦ SCENE II ✦
London. The palace

Enter the old DUCHESS OF YORK, with the SON and
DAUGHTER of CLARENCE

SON. Good grandam, tell us, is our father dead?
DUCHESS. No, boy.
DAUGHTER. Why do you weep so oft, and beat
  your breast,
  And cry 'O Clarence, my unhappy son!'?
SON. Why do you look on us, and shake
  your head,
  And call us orphans, wretches, castaways,
  If that our noble father were alive?
DUCHESS. My pretty cousins, you mistake
  me both;
  I do lament the sickness of the King,
  As loath to lose him, not your father's death;
  It were lost sorrow to wail one that's lost.
SON. Then you conclude, my grandam, he
  is dead.
  The King mine uncle is to blame for it.
  God will revenge it; whom I will importune
  With earnest prayers all to that effect.
DAUGHTER. And so will I.
DUCHESS. Peace, children, peace! The King doth
  love you well.
  Incapable and shallow innocents,
  You cannot guess who caus'd your
  father's death.
SON. Grandam, we can; for my good
  uncle Gloucester
  Told me the King, provok'd to it by the Queen,
  Devis'd impeachments to imprison him.
  And when my uncle told me so, he wept,
  And pitied me, and kindly kiss'd my cheek;
  Bade me rely on him as on my father,
  And he would love me dearly as a child.
DUCHESS. Ah, that deceit should steal such
  gentle shape,
  And with a virtuous vizor hide deep vice!
  He is my son; ay, and therein my shame;
  Yet from my dugs he drew not this deceit.
SON. Think you my uncle did
  dissemble, grandam?
DUCHESS. Ay, boy.

SON. I cannot think it. Hark! what noise is this?
Enter QUEEN ELIZABETH, with her hair about her ears;
  RIVERS and DORSET after her
QUEEN ELIZABETH. Ah, who shall hinder me to
  wail and weep,
  To chide my fortune, and torment myself?
  I'll join with black despair against my soul
  And to myself become an enemy.
DUCHESS. What means this scene of
  rude impatience?
QUEEN ELIZABETH. To make an act of
  tragic violence.
  Edward, my lord, thy son, our king, is dead.
  Why grow the branches when the root is gone?
  Why wither not the leaves that want their sap?
  If you will live, lament; if die, be brief,
  That our swift-winged souls may catch
  the King's,
  Or like obedient subjects follow him
  To his new kingdom of ne'er-changing night.
DUCHESS. Ah, so much interest have I in
  thy sorrow
  As I had title in thy noble husband!
  I have bewept a worthy husband's death,
  And liv'd with looking on his images;
  But now two mirrors of his princely semblance
  Are crack'd in pieces by malignant death,
  And I for comfort have but one false glass,
  That grieves me when I see my shame in him.
  Thou art a widow, yet thou art a mother
  And hast the comfort of thy children left;
  But death hath snatch'd my husband from
  mine arms
  And pluck'd two crutches from my
  feeble hands-
  Clarence and Edward. O, what cause have I-
  Thine being but a moiety of my moan-
  To overgo thy woes and drown thy cries?
SON. Ah, aunt, you wept not for our
  father's death!
  How can we aid you with our kindred tears?
DAUGHTER. Our fatherless distress was
  left unmoan'd;
  Your widow-dolour likewise be unwept!
QUEEN ELIZABETH. Give me no help
  in lamentation;
  I am not barren to bring forth complaints.
  All springs reduce their currents to mine eyes
  That I, being govern'd by the watery moon,
  May send forth plenteous tears to drown the
  world!
  Ah for my husband, for my dear Lord Edward!
CHILDREN. Ah for our father, for our dear

Lord Clarence!

DUCHESS. Alas for both, both mine, Edward
and Clarence!

QUEEN ELIZABETH. What stay had I but Edward?
and he's gone.

CHILDREN. What stay had we but Clarence? and
he's gone.

DUCHESS. What stays had I but they? and they
are gone.

QUEEN ELIZABETH. Was never widow had so
dear a loss.

CHILDREN. Were never orphans had so dear
a loss.

DUCHESS. Was never mother had so dear a loss.
Alas, I am the mother of these griefs!
Their woes are parcell'd, mine is general.
She for an Edward weeps, and so do I:
I for a Clarence weep, so doth not she.
These babes for Clarence weep, and so do I:
I for an Edward weep, so do not they.
Alas, you three on me, threefold distress'd,
Pour all your tears! I am your sorrow's nurse,
And I will pamper it with lamentation.

DORSET. Comfort, dear mother. God is much
displeas'd
That you take with unthankfulness his doing.
In common worldly things 'tis called ungrateful
With dull unwillingness to repay a debt
Which with a bounteous hand was kindly lent;
Much more to be thus opposite with heaven,
For it requires the royal debt it lent you.

RIVERS. Madam, bethink you, like a
careful mother,
Of the young prince your son. Send straight
for him;
Let him be crown'd; in him your comfort lives.
Drown desperate sorrow in dead
Edward's grave,
And plant your joys in living Edward's throne.

Enter GLOUCESTER, BUCKINGHAM, DERBY,
HASTINGS, and RATCLIFF

GLOUCESTER. Sister, have comfort. All of us
have cause
To wail the dimming of our shining star;
But none can help our harms by wailing them.
Madam, my mother, I do cry you mercy;
I did not see your Grace. Humbly on my knee
I crave your blessing.

DUCHESS. God bless thee; and put meekness in
thy breast,
Love, charity, obedience, and true duty!

GLOUCESTER. Amen! *[Aside]* And make me die a
good old man!

That is the butt end of a mother's blessing;
I marvel that her Grace did leave it out.

BUCKINGHAM. You cloudy princes and heart-
sorrowing peers,
That bear this heavy mutual load of moan,
Now cheer each other in each other's love.
Though we have spent our harvest of this king,
We are to reap the harvest of his son.
The broken rancour of your high-swol'n hearts,
But lately splinter'd, knit, and join'd together,
Must gently be preserv'd, cherish'd, and kept.
Me seemeth good that, with some little train,
Forthwith from Ludlow the young prince be fet
Hither to London, to be crown'd our King.

RIVERS. Why with some little train, my Lord of
Buckingham?

BUCKINGHAM. Marry, my lord, lest by a multitude
The new-heal'd wound of malice should
break out,
Which would be so much the more dangerous
By how much the estate is green and
yet ungovern'd;
Where every horse bears his commanding rein
And may direct his course as please himself,
As well the fear of harm as harm apparent,
In my opinion, ought to be prevented.

GLOUCESTER. I hope the King made peace with
all of us;
And the compact is firm and true in me.

RIVERS. And so in me; and so, I think, in all.
Yet, since it is but green, it should be put
To no apparent likelihood of breach,
Which haply by much company might be urg'd;
Therefore I say with noble Buckingham
That it is meet so few should fetch the Prince.

HASTINGS. And so say I.

GLOUCESTER. Then be it so; and go we
to determine
Who they shall be that straight shall post to
Ludlow.
Madam, and you, my sister, will you go
To give your censures in this business?

Exeunt all but BUCKINGHAM and GLOUCESTER

BUCKINGHAM. My lord, whoever journeys to
the Prince,
For God's sake, let not us two stay at home;
For by the way I'll sort occasion,
As index to the story we late talk'd of,
To part the Queen's proud kindred from
the Prince.

GLOUCESTER. My other self, my
counsel's consistory,
My oracle, my prophet, my dear cousin,

I, as a child, will go by thy direction.
Toward Ludlow then, for we'll not stay behind.

Exeunt.

✦ SCENE III ✦
London. A street

Enter one CITIZEN at one door, and another at the other

FIRST CITIZEN. Good morrow, neighbour.
Whither away so fast?
SECOND CITIZEN. I promise you, I scarcely
know myself.
Hear you the news abroad?
FIRST CITIZEN. Yes, that the King is dead.
SECOND CITIZEN. Ill news, by'r lady; seldom
comes the better. I fear, I fear 'twill prove a
giddy world.

Enter another CITIZEN

THIRD CITIZEN. Neighbours, God speed!
FIRST CITIZEN. Give you good morrow, sir.
THIRD CITIZEN. Doth the news hold of good
King Edward's death?
SECOND CITIZEN. Ay, sir, it is too true; God help
the while!
THIRD CITIZEN. Then, masters, look to see a
troublous world.
FIRST CITIZEN. No, no; by God's good grace, his
son shall reign.
THIRD CITIZEN. Woe to that land that's govern'd
by a child.
SECOND CITIZEN. In him there is a hope
of government,
Which, in his nonage, council under him,
And, in his full and ripened years, himself,
No doubt, shall then, and till then, govern well.
FIRST CITIZEN. So stood the state when Henry
the Sixth
Was crown'd in Paris but at nine months old.
THIRD CITIZEN. Stood the state so? No, no, good
friends, God wot;
For then this land was famously enrich'd
With politic grave counsel; then the King
Had virtuous uncles to protect his Grace.
FIRST CITIZEN. Why, so hath this, both by his
father and mother.
THIRD CITIZEN. Better it were they all came by
his father,
Or by his father there were none at all;
For emulation who shall now be nearest
Will touch us all too near, if God prevent not.
O, full of danger is the Duke of Gloucester!

And the Queen's sons and brothers haught
and proud;
And were they to be rul'd, and not to rule,
This sickly land might solace as before.
FIRST CITIZEN. Come, come, we fear the worst;
all will be well.
THIRD CITIZEN. When clouds are seen, wise men
put on their cloaks;
When great leaves fall, then winter is at hand;
When the sun sets, who doth not look for night?
Untimely storms make men expect a dearth.
All may be well; but, if God sort it so,
'Tis more than we deserve or I expect.
SECOND CITIZEN. Truly, the hearts of men are
full of fear.
You cannot reason almost with a man
That looks not heavily and full of dread.
THIRD CITIZEN. Before the days of change, still
is it so;
By a divine instinct men's minds mistrust
Ensuing danger; as by proof we see
The water swell before a boist'rous storm.
But leave it all to God. Whither away?
SECOND CITIZEN. Marry, we were sent for to
the justices.
THIRD CITIZEN. And so was I; I'll bear
you company

Exeunt.

✦ SCENE IV ✦
London. The palace

*Enter the ARCHBISHOP OF YORK, the young DUKE OF
YORK, QUEEN ELIZABETH, and the DUCHESS OF
YORK*

ARCHBISHOP. Last night, I hear, they lay at
Stony Stratford,
And at Northampton they do rest to-night;
To-morrow or next day they will be here.
DUCHESS. I long with all my heart to see
the Prince.
I hope he is much grown since last I saw him.
QUEEN ELIZABETH. But I hear no; they say my
son of York
Has almost overta'en him in his growth.
YORK. Ay, mother; but I would not have it so.
DUCHESS. Why, my good cousin, it is good
to grow.
YORK. Grandam, one night as we did sit
at supper,
My uncle Rivers talk'd how I did grow

More than my brother. 'Ay', quoth my
  uncle Gloucester
'Small herbs have grace: great weeds do
  grow apace.'
And since, methinks, I would not grow so fast,
Because sweet flow'rs are slow and weeds make
  haste.
DUCHESS. Good faith, good faith, the saying did
  not hold
In him that did object the same to thee.
He was the wretched'st thing when he
  was young,
So long a-growing and so leisurely
That, if his rule were true, he should
  be gracious.
ARCHBISHOP. And so no doubt he is, my
  gracious madam.
DUCHESS. I hope he is; but yet let
  mothers doubt.
YORK. Now, by my troth, if I had
  been rememb'red,
I could have given my uncle's Grace a flout
To touch his growth nearer than he
  touch'd mine.
DUCHESS. How, my young York? I prithee let me
  hear it.
YORK. Marry, they say my uncle grew so fast
That he could gnaw a crust at two hours old.
'Twas full two years ere I could get a tooth.
Grandam, this would have been a biting jest.
DUCHESS. I prithee, pretty York, who told
  thee this?
YORK. Grandam, his nurse.
DUCHESS. His nurse! Why she was dead ere thou
  wast born.
YORK. If 'twere not she, I cannot tell who told me.
QUEEN ELIZABETH. A parlous boy! Go to, you are
  too shrewd.
ARCHBISHOP. Good madam, be not angry with
  the child.
QUEEN ELIZABETH. Pitchers have ears.

Enter a MESSENGER

ARCHBISHOP. Here comes a messenger.
  What news?
MESSENGER. Such news, my lord, as grieves me
  to report.
QUEEN ELIZABETH. How doth the Prince?
MESSENGER. Well, madam, and in health.
DUCHESS. What is thy news?
MESSENGER. Lord Rivers and Lord Grey
  Are sent to Pomfret, and with them
  Sir Thomas Vaughan, prisoners.
DUCHESS. Who hath committed them?

MESSENGER. The mighty Dukes, Gloucester
  and Buckingham.
ARCHBISHOP. For what offence?
MESSENGER. The sum of all I can, I
  have disclos'd.
  Why or for what the nobles were committed
  Is all unknown to me, my gracious lord.
QUEEN ELIZABETH. Ay me, I see the ruin of
  my house!
  The tiger now hath seiz'd the gentle hind;
  Insulting tyranny begins to jet
  Upon the innocent and aweless throne.
  Welcome, destruction, blood, and massacre!
  I see, as in a map, the end of all.
DUCHESS. Accursed and unquiet wrangling days,
  How many of you have mine eyes beheld!
  My husband lost his life to get the crown;
  And often up and down my sons were toss'd
  For me to joy and weep their gain and loss;
  And being seated, and domestic broils
  Clean over-blown, themselves the conquerors
  Make war upon themselves-brother to brother,
  Blood to blood, self against self. O, preposterous
  And frantic outrage, end thy damned spleen,
  Or let me die, to look on death no more!
QUEEN ELIZABETH. Come, come, my boy; we will
  to sanctuary. Madam, farewell.
DUCHESS. Stay, I will go with you.
QUEEN ELIZABETH. You have no cause.
ARCHBISHOP. *[To the QUEEN]* My gracious lady, go.
  And thither bear your treasure and your goods.
  For my part, I'll resign unto your Grace
  The seal I keep; and so betide to me
  As well I tender you and all of yours!
  Go, I'll conduct you to the sanctuary. *Exeunt*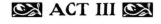

ACT III

SCENE I
London. A street

The trumpets sound. Enter the PRINCE OF WALES,
GLOUCESTER, BUCKINGHAM, CATESBY,
CARDINAL BOURCHIER, and Others

BUCKINGHAM. Welcome, sweet Prince, to
  London, to your chamber.
GLOUCESTER. Welcome, dear cousin, my
  thoughts' sovereign.
  The weary way hath made you melancholy.
PRINCE. No, uncle; but our crosses on the way

Have made it tedious, wearisome, and heavy.
I want more uncles here to welcome me.

GLOUCESTER. Sweet Prince, the untainted
  virtue of your years
  Hath not yet div'd into the world's deceit;
  Nor more can you distinguish of a man
  Than of his outward show; which, God
  He knows,
  Seldom or never jumpeth with the heart.
  Those uncles which you want were dangerous;
  Your Grace attended to their sug'red words
  But look'd not on the poison of their hearts.
  God keep you from them and from such
  false friends!

PRINCE. God keep me from false friends! but
  they were none.

GLOUCESTER. My lord, the Mayor of London
  comes to greet you.

  Enter the LORD MAYOR and his Train

MAYOR. God bless your Grace with health and
  happy days!

PRINCE. I thank you, good my lord, and thank
  you all.
  I thought my mother and my brother York
  Would long ere this have met us on the way.
  Fie, what a slug is Hastings, that he comes not
  To tell us whether they will come or no!

  Enter LORD HASTINGS

BUCKINGHAM. And, in good time, here comes
  the sweating Lord.

PRINCE. Welcome, my lord. What, will our
  mother come?

HASTINGS. On what occasion, God He knows,
  not I,
  The Queen your mother and your
  brother York
  Have taken sanctuary. The tender Prince
  Would fain have come with me to meet
  your Grace,
  But by his mother was perforce withheld.

BUCKINGHAM. Fie, what an indirect and
  peevish course
  Is this of hers! Lord Cardinal, will your Grace
  Persuade the Queen to send the Duke of York
  Unto his princely brother presently?
  If she deny, Lord Hastings, go with him
  And from her jealous arms pluck him perforce.

CARDINAL. My Lord of Buckingham, if my
  weak oratory
  Can from his mother win the Duke of York,
  Anon expect him here; but if she be obdurate
  To mild entreaties, God in heaven forbid
  We should infringe the holy privilege

Of blessed sanctuary! Not for all this land
Would I be guilty of so deep a sin.

BUCKINGHAM. You are too senseless-obstinate,
  my lord,
  Too ceremonious and traditional.
  Weigh it but with the grossness of this age,
  You break not sanctuary in seizing him.
  The benefit thereof is always granted
  To those whose dealings have deserv'd
  the place
  And those who have the wit to claim the place.
  This Prince hath neither claim'd it nor
  deserv'd it,
  And therefore, in mine opinion, cannot have it.
  Then, taking him from thence that is
  not there,
  You break no privilege nor charter there.
  Oft have I heard of sanctuary men;
  But sanctuary children never till now.

CARDINAL. My lord, you shall o'errule my mind
  for once.
  Come on, Lord Hastings, will you go with me?

HASTINGS. I go, my lord.

PRINCE. Good lords, make all the speedy haste
  you may.

  Exeunt CARDINAL and HASTINGS.

Say, uncle Gloucester, if our brother come,
Where shall we sojourn till our coronation?

GLOUCESTER. Where it seems best unto your
  royal self.
  If I may counsel you, some day or two
  Your Highness shall repose you at the Tower,
  Then where you please and shall be thought
  most fit
  For your best health and recreation.

PRINCE. I do not like the Tower, of any place.
  Did Julius Caesar build that place, my lord?

BUCKINGHAM. He did, my gracious lord, begin
  that place,
  Which, since, succeeding ages have re-edified.

PRINCE. Is it upon record, or else reported
  Successively from age to age, he built it?

BUCKINGHAM. Upon record, my gracious lord.

PRINCE. But say, my lord, it were not regist'red,
  Methinks the truth should lice from age
  to age,
  As 'twere retail'd to all posterity,
  Even to the general all-ending day.

GLOUCESTER. [*Aside*] So wise so young, they
  say, do never live long.

PRINCE. What say you, uncle?

GLOUCESTER. I say, without characters, fame
  lives long.

[Aside] Thus, like the formal vice, Iniquity,
I moralize two meanings in one word.
PRINCE. That Julius Caesar was a famous man;
With what his valour did enrich his wit,
His wit set down to make his valour live.
Death makes no conquest of this conqueror;
For now he lives in fame, though not in life.
I'll tell you what, my cousin Buckingham-
BUCKINGHAM. What, my gracious lord?
PRINCE. An if I live until I be a man,
I'll win our ancient right in France again,
Or die a soldier as I liv'd a king.
GLOUCESTER. *[Aside]* Short summers lightly
have a forward spring.
Enter HASTINGS, young YORK, and the CARDINAL
BUCKINGHAM. Now, in good time, here comes
the Duke of York.
PRINCE. Richard of York, how fares our
loving brother?
YORK. Well, my dread lord; so must I call
you now.
PRINCE. Ay brother, to our grief, as it is yours.
Too late he died that might have kept
that title,
Which by his death hath lost much majesty.
GLOUCESTER. How fares our cousin, noble
Lord of York?
YORK. I thank you, gentle uncle. O, my lord,
You said that idle weeds are fast in growth.
The Prince my brother hath outgrown me far.
GLOUCESTER. He hath, my lord.
YORK. And therefore is he idle?
GLOUCESTER. O, my fair cousin, I must not say so.
YORK. Then he is more beholding to you than I.
GLOUCESTER. He may command me as
my sovereign;
But you have power in me as in a kinsman.
YORK. I pray you, uncle, give me this dagger.
GLOUCESTER. My dagger, little cousin? With all
my heart!
PRINCE. A beggar, brother?
YORK. Of my kind uncle, that I know will give,
And being but a toy, which is no grief to give.
GLOUCESTER. A greater gift than that I'll give
my cousin.
YORK. A greater gift! O, that's the sword to it!
GLOUCESTER. Ay, gentle cousin, were it
light enough.
YORK. O, then, I see you will part but with
light gifts:
In weightier things you'll say a beggar nay.
GLOUCESTER. It is too heavy for your Grace
to wear.

YORK. I weigh it lightly, were it heavier.
GLOUCESTER. What, would you have my
weapon, little Lord?
YORK. I would, that I might thank you as you
call me.
GLOUCESTER. How?
YORK. Little.
PRINCE. My Lord of York will still be cross in talk.
Uncle, your Grace knows how to bear with him.
YORK. You mean, to bear me, not to bear
with me.
Uncle, my brother mocks both you and me;
Because that I am little, like an ape,
He thinks that you should bear me on
your shoulders.
BUCKINGHAM. With what a sharp-provided wit
he reasons!
To mitigate the scorn he gives his uncle
He prettily and aptly taunts himself.
So cunning and so young is wonderful.
GLOUCESTER. My lord, will't please you
pass along?
Myself and my good cousin Buckingham
Will to your mother, to entreat of her
To meet you at the Tower and welcome you.
YORK. What, will you go unto the Tower, my lord?
PRINCE. My Lord Protector needs will have it so.
YORK. I shall not sleep in quiet at the Tower.
GLOUCESTER. Why, what should you fear?
YORK. Marry, my uncle Clarence' angry ghost.
My grandam told me he was murder'd there.
PRINCE. I fear no uncles dead.
GLOUCESTER. Nor none that live, I hope.
PRINCE. An if they live, I hope I need not fear.
But come, my lord; and with a heavy heart,
Thinking on them, go I unto the Tower.
A sennet.
Exeunt all but GLOUCESTER,
BUCKINGHAM, and CATESBY
BUCKINGHAM. Think you, my lord, this little
prating York
Was not incensed by his subtle mother
To taunt and scorn you thus opprobriously?
GLOUCESTER. No doubt, no doubt. O, 'tis a
perilous boy;
Bold, quick, ingenious, forward, capable.
He is all the mother's, from the top to toe.
BUCKINGHAM. Well, let them rest. Come
hither, Catesby.
Thou art sworn as deeply to effect what
we intend
As closely to conceal what we impart.
Thou know'st our reasons urg'd upon the way.

What think'st thou? Is it not an easy matter
To make William Lord Hastings of our mind,
For the instalment of this noble Duke
In the seat royal of this famous isle?
CATESBY. He for his father's sake so loves
the Prince
That he will not be won to aught against him.
BUCKINGHAM. What think'st thou then of
Stanley? Will not he?
CATESBY. He will do all in all as Hastings doth.
BUCKINGHAM. Well then, no more but this: go,
gentle Catesby,
And, as it were far off, sound thou Lord Hastings
How he doth stand affected to our purpose;
And summon him to-morrow to the Tower,
To sit about the coronation.
If thou dost find him tractable to us,
Encourage him, and tell him all our reasons;
If he be leaden, icy, cold, unwilling,
Be thou so too, and so break off the talk,
And give us notice of his inclination;
For we to-morrow hold divided councils,
Wherein thyself shalt highly be employ'd.
GLOUCESTER. Commend me to Lord William.
Tell him, Catesby,
His ancient knot of dangerous adversaries
To-morrow are let blood at Pomfret Castle;
And bid my lord, for joy of this good news,
Give Mistress Shore one gentle kiss the more.
BUCKINGHAM. Good Catesby, go effect this
business soundly.
CATESBY. My good lords both, with all the heed
I can.
GLOUCESTER. Shall we hear from you, Catesby,
ere we sleep?
CATESBY. You shall, my lord.
GLOUCESTER. At Crosby House, there shall you
find us both.   *Exit CATESBY*
BUCKINGHAM. Now, my lord, what shall we do if
we perceive
Lord Hastings will not yield to our complots?
GLOUCESTER. Chop off his head-something we
will determine.
And, look when I am King, claim thou of me
The earldom of Hereford and all the movables
Whereof the King my brother was possess'd.
BUCKINGHAM. I'll claim that promise at your
Grace's hand.
GLOUCESTER. And look to have it yielded with
all kindness.
Come, let us sup betimes, that afterwards
We may digest our complots in some form.
Exeunt.

⚜ SCENE II ⚜
Before LORD HASTINGS' house

Enter a MESSENGER to the door of HASTINGS

MESSENGER. My lord, my lord! *[Knocking]*
HASTINGS. *[Within]* Who knocks?
MESSENGER. One from the Lord Stanley.
HASTINGS. *[Within]* What is't o'clock?
MESSENGER. Upon the stroke of four.
Enter LORD HASTINGS
HASTINGS. Cannot my Lord Stanley sleep these
tedious nights?
MESSENGER. So it appears by that I have to say.
First, he commends him to your noble self.
HASTINGS. What then?
MESSENGER. Then certifies your lordship that
this night
He dreamt the boar had razed off his helm.
Besides, he says there are two councils kept,
And that may be determin'd at the one
Which may make you and him to rue at
th' other.
Therefore he sends to know your
lordship's pleasure-
If you will presently take horse with him
And with all speed post with him toward
the north
To shun the danger that his soul divines.
HASTINGS. Go, fellow, go, return unto thy lord;
Bid him not fear the separated council:
His honour and myself are at the one,
And at the other is my good friend Catesby;
Where nothing can proceed that toucheth us
Whereof I shall not have intelligence.
Tell him his fears are shallow, without instance;
And for his dreams, I wonder he's so simple
To trust the mock'ry of unquiet slumbers.
To fly the boar before the boar pursues
Were to incense the boar to follow us
And make pursuit where he did mean no chase.
Go, bid thy master rise and come to me;
And we will both together to the Tower,
Where, he shall see, the boar will use us kindly.
MESSENGER. I'll go, my lord, and tell him what
you say.   *Exit.*
Enter CATESBY
CATESBY. Many good morrows to my noble lord!
HASTINGS. Good morrow, Catesby; you are
early stirring.
What news, what news, in this our tott'ring state?

CATESBY. It is a reeling world indeed, my lord;
  And I believe will never stand upright
  Till Richard wear the garland of the realm.
HASTINGS. How, wear the garland! Dost thou
  mean the crown?
CATESBY. Ay, my good lord.
HASTINGS. I'll have this crown of mine cut from
  my shoulders
  Before I'll see the crown so foul misplac'd.
  But canst thou guess that he doth aim at it?
CATESBY. Ay, on my life; and hopes to find
  you forward
  Upon his party for the gain thereof;
  And thereupon he sends you this good news,
  That this same very day your enemies,
  The kindred of the Queen, must die at Pomfret.
HASTINGS. Indeed, I am no mourner for
  that news,
  Because they have been still my adversaries;
  But that I'll give my voice on Richard's side
  To bar my master's heirs in true descent,
  God knows I will not do it to the death.
CATESBY. God keep your lordship in that
  gracious mind!
HASTINGS. But I shall laugh at this a twelve
  month hence,
  That they which brought me in my
  master's hate,
  I live to look upon their tragedy.
  Well, Catesby, ere a fortnight make me older,
  I'll send some packing that yet think not on't.
CATESBY. 'Tis a vile thing to die, my
  gracious lord,
  When men are unprepar'd and look not for it.
HASTINGS. O monstrous, monstrous! And so
  falls it out
  With Rivers, Vaughan, Grey; and so 'twill do
  With some men else that think themselves
  as safe
  As thou and I, who, as thou knowest, are dear
  To princely Richard and to Buckingham.
CATESBY. The Princes both make high account
  of you-
  [Aside] For they account his head upon
  the bridge.
HASTINGS. I know they do, and I have well
  deserv'd it.

          Enter LORD STANLEY

Come on, come on; where is your boar-
  spear, man?
Fear you the boar, and go so unprovided?
STANLEY. My lord, good morrow; good
  morrow, Catesby.

You may jest on, but, by the holy rood,
I do not like these several councils, I.
HASTINGS. My lord, I hold my life as dear
  as yours,
And never in my days, I do protest,
Was it so precious to me as 'tis now.
Think you, but that I know our state secure,
I would be so triumphant as I am?
STANLEY. The lords at Pomfret, when they rode
  from London,
Were jocund and suppos'd their states were
  sure,
And they indeed had no cause to mistrust;
But yet you see how soon the day o'ercast.
This sudden stab of rancour I misdoubt;
Pray God, I say, I prove a needless coward.
What, shall we toward the Tower? The day
  is spent.
HASTINGS. Come, come, have with you. Wot you
  what, my Lord?
To-day the lords you talk'd of are beheaded.
STANLEY. They, for their truth, might better wear
  their heads
Than some that have accus'd them wear
  their hats.
But come, my lord, let's away.

          Enter HASTINGS, a PURSUIVANT

HASTINGS. Go on before; I'll talk with this
  good fellow.

          Exeunt STANLEY and CATESBY.

How now, Hastings! How goes the world
  with thee?
PURSUIVANT. The better that your lordship
  please to ask.
HASTINGS. I tell thee, man, 'tis better with me now
  Than when thou met'st me last where now
  we meet:
  Then was I going prisoner to the Tower
  By the suggestion of the Queen's allies;
  But now, I tell thee-keep it to thyself-
  This day those enemies are put to death,
  And I in better state than e'er I was.
PURSUIVANT. God hold it, to your honour's
  good content!
HASTINGS. Gramercy, Hastings; there, drink that
  for me.

          Throws him his purse

PURSUIVANT. I thank your honour. *Exit.*

          Enter a PRIEST

PRIEST. Well met, my lord; I am glad to see
  your honour.
HASTINGS. I thank thee, good Sir John, with all
  my heart.

I am in your debt for your last exercise;
Come the next Sabbath, and I will content you.

He whispers in his ear

PRIEST. I'll wait upon your lordship.

Enter BUCKINGHAM

BUCKINGHAM. What, talking with a priest,
Lord Chamberlain!
Your friends at Pomfret, they do need the priest:
Your honour hath no shriving work in hand.

HASTINGS. Good faith, and when I met this
holy man,
The men you talk of came into my mind.
What, go you toward the Tower?

BUCKINGHAM. I do, my lord, but long I cannot
stay there;
I shall return before your lordship thence.

HASTINGS. Nay, like enough, for I stay
dinner there.

BUCKINGHAM. *[Aside]* And supper too, although
thou knowest it not.-
Come, will you go?

HASTINGS. I'll wait upon your lordship.

Exeunt.

⚜ SCENE III ⚜
Pomfret Castle

*Enter SIR RICHARD RATCLIFF, with Halberds, carrying
the Nobles, RIVERS, GREY, and VAUGHAN, to death*

RIVERS. Sir Richard Ratcliff, let me tell thee this:
To-day shalt thou behold a subject die
For truth, for duty, and for loyalty.

GREY. God bless the Prince from all the pack
of you!
A knot you are of damned blood-suckers.

VAUGHAN. You live that shall cry woe for
this hereafter.

RATCLIFF. Dispatch; the limit of your lives is out.

RIVERS. O Pomfret, Pomfret! O thou
bloody prison,
Fatal and ominous to noble peers!
Within the guilty closure of thy walls
Richard the Second here was hack'd to death;
And for more slander to thy dismal seat,
We give to thee our guiltless blood to drink.

GREY. Now Margaret's curse is fall'n upon
our heads,
When she exclaim'd on Hastings, you, and I,
For standing by when Richard stabb'd her son.

RIVERS. Then curs'd she Richard, then curs'd
she Buckingham,

Then curs'd she Hastings. O, remember, God,
To hear her prayer for them, as now for us!
And for my sister, and her princely sons,
Be satisfied, dear God, with our true blood,
Which, as thou know'st, unjustly must be spilt.

RATCLIFF. Make haste; the hour of death
is expiate.

RIVERS. Come, Grey; come, Vaughan; let us
here embrace.
Farewell, until we meet again in heaven.

Exeunt.

⚜ SCENE IV ⚜
London. The Tower

*Enter BUCKINGHAM, DERBY, HASTINGS, the
BISHOP OF ELY, RATCLIFF, LOVEL, with Others and seat
themselves at a table*

HASTINGS. Now, noble peers, the cause why we
are met
Is to determine of the coronation.
In God's name speak-when is the royal day?

BUCKINGHAM. Is all things ready for the
royal time?

DERBY. It is, and wants but nomination.

BISHOP OF ELY. To-morrow then I judge a
happy day.

BUCKINGHAM. Who knows the Lord Protector's
mind herein?
Who is most inward with the noble Duke?

BISHOP OF ELY. Your Grace, we think, should
soonest know his mind.

BUCKINGHAM. We know each other's faces; for
our hearts,
He knows no more of mine than I of yours;
Or I of his, my lord, than you of mine.
Lord Hastings, you and he are near in love.

HASTINGS. I thank his Grace, I know he loves
me well;
But for his purpose in the coronation
I have not sounded him, nor he deliver'd
His gracious pleasure any way therein.
But you, my honourable lords, may name
the time;
And in the Duke's behalf I'll give my voice,
Which, I presume, he'll take in gentle part.

Enter GLOUCESTER

BISHOP OF ELY. In happy time, here comes the
Duke himself.

GLOUCESTER. My noble lords and cousins all,
good morrow.

I have been long a sleeper, but I trust
My absence doth neglect no great design
Which by my presence might have
    been concluded.
BUCKINGHAM. Had you not come upon your
    cue, my lord,
William Lord Hastings had pronounc'd
    your part-
I mean, your voice for crowning of the King.
GLOUCESTER. Than my Lord Hastings no man
    might be bolder;
His lordship knows me well and loves me well.
My lord of Ely, when I was last in Holborn
I saw good strawberries in your garden there.
I do beseech you send for some of them.
BISHOP OF ELY. Marry and will, my lord, with all
    my heart.   *Exit*
GLOUCESTER. Cousin of Buckingham, a word
    with you. [*Takes him aside*]
Catesby hath sounded Hastings in our business,
And finds the testy gentleman so hot
That he will lose his head ere give consent
His master's child, as worshipfully he terms it,
Shall lose the royalty of England's throne.
BUCKINGHAM. Withdraw yourself awhile; I'll go
    with you.
            Exeunt GLOUCESTER and BUCKINGHAM.
DERBY. We have not yet set down this day
    of triumph.
To-morrow, in my judgment, is too sudden;
For I myself am not so well provided
As else I would be, were the day prolong'd.
            Re-enter the BISHOP OF ELY
BISHOP OF ELY. Where is my lord the Duke
    of Gloucester?
I have sent for these strawberries.
HASTINGS. His Grace looks cheerfully and
    smooth this morning;
There's some conceit or other likes him well
When that he bids good morrow with
    such spirit.
I think there's never a man in Christendom
Can lesser hide his love or hate than he;
For by his face straight shall you know
    his heart.
DERBY. What of his heart perceive you in his face
By any livelihood he show'd to-day?
HASTINGS. Marry, that with no man here he
    is offended;
For, were he, he had shown it in his looks.
            Re-enter GLOUCESTER and BUCKINGHAM
GLOUCESTER. I pray you all, tell me what
    they deserve

That do conspire my death with devilish plots
Of damned witchcraft, and that have prevail'd
Upon my body with their hellish charms?
HASTINGS. The tender love I bear your Grace,
    my lord,
Makes me most forward in this
    princely presence
To doom th' offenders, whosoe'er they be.
I say, my lord, they have deserved death.
GLOUCESTER. Then be your eyes the witness of
    their evil.
Look how I am bewitch'd; behold, mine arm
Is like a blasted sapling wither'd up.
And this is Edward's wife, that monstrous witch,
Consorted with that harlot strumpet Shore,
That by their witchcraft thus have marked me.
HASTINGS. If they have done this deed, my
    noble lord-
GLOUCESTER. If?-thou protector of this
    damned strumpet,
Talk'st thou to me of ifs? Thou art a traitor.
Off with his head! Now by Saint Paul I swear
I will not dine until I see the same.
Lovel and Ratcliff, look that it be done.
The rest that love me, rise and follow me.
        Exeunt all but HASTINGS, LOVEL, and RATCLIFF.
HASTINGS. Woe, woe, for England! not a whit
    for me;
For I, too fond, might have prevented this.
Stanley did dream the boar did raze our helms,
And I did scorn it and disdain to fly.
Three times to-day my foot-cloth horse
    did stumble,
And started when he look'd upon the Tower,
As loath to bear me to the slaughter-house.
O, now I need the priest that spake to me!
I now repent I told the pursuivant,
As too triumphing, how mine enemies
To-day at Pomfret bloodily were butcher'd,
And I myself secure in grace and favour.
O Margaret, Margaret, now thy heavy curse
Is lighted on poor Hastings' wretched head!
RATCLIFF. Come, come, dispatch; the Duke
    would be at dinner.
Make a short shrift; he longs to see your head.
HASTINGS. O momentary grace of mortal men,
Which we more hunt for than the grace of God!
Who builds his hope in air of your good looks
Lives like a drunken sailor on a mast,
Ready with every nod to tumble down
Into the fatal bowels of the deep.
LOVEL. Come, come, dispatch; 'tis bootless
    to exclaim.

HASTINGS. O bloody Richard! Miserable England!
  I prophesy the fearfull'st time to thee
  That ever wretched age hath look'd upon.
  Come, lead me to the block; bear him my head.
  They smile at me who shortly shall be dead.

                                        Exeunt.

✦ SCENE V ✦
London. The Tower-walls

*Enter GLOUCESTER and BUCKINGHAM in rotten
armour, marvellous ill-favoured*

GLOUCESTER. Come, cousin, canst thou quake
    and change thy colour,
  Murder thy breath in middle of a word,
  And then again begin, and stop again,
  As if thou were distraught and mad
    with terror?
BUCKINGHAM. Tut, I can counterfeit the
    deep tragedian;
  Speak and look back, and pry on every side,
  Tremble and start at wagging of a straw,
  Intending deep suspicion. Ghastly looks
  Are at my service, like enforced smiles;
  And both are ready in their offices
  At any time to grace my stratagems.
  But what, is Catesby gone?
GLOUCESTER. He is; and, see, he brings the
    mayor along.

        Enter the LORD MAYOR and CATESBY

BUCKINGHAM. Lord Mayor-
GLOUCESTER. Look to the drawbridge there!
BUCKINGHAM. Hark! a drum.
GLOUCESTER. Catesby, o'erlook the walls.
BUCKINGHAM. Lord Mayor, the reason we
    have sent-
GLOUCESTER. Look back, defend thee; here
    are enemies.
BUCKINGHAM. God and our innocence defend
    and guard us!

        Enter LOVEL and RATCLIFF, with HASTINGS' head

GLOUCESTER. Be patient; they are friends-
    Ratcliff and Lovel.
LOVEL. Here is the head of that ignoble traitor,
  The dangerous and unsuspected Hastings.
GLOUCESTER. So dear I lov'd the man that I
    must weep.
  I took him for the plainest harmless creature
  That breath'd upon the earth a Christian;
  Made him my book, wherein my soul recorded
  The history of all her secret thoughts.

So smooth he daub'd his vice with show
    of virtue
  That, his apparent open guilt omitted,
  I mean his conversation with Shore's wife-
  He liv'd from all attainder of suspects.
BUCKINGHAM. Well, well, he was the covert'st
    shelt'red traitor
  That ever liv'd
  Would you imagine, or almost believe-
  Were't not that by great preservation
  We live to tell it-that the subtle traitor
  This day had plotted, in the council-house,
  To murder me and my good Lord
    of Gloucester.
MAYOR. Had he done so?
GLOUCESTER. What! think you we are Turks
    or Infidels?
  Or that we would, against the form of law,
  Proceed thus rashly in the villain's death
  But that the extreme peril of the case,
  The peace of England and our persons' safety,
  Enforc'd us to this execution?
MAYOR. Now, fair befall you! He deserv'd
    his death;
  And your good Graces both have well
    proceeded
  To warn false traitors from the like attempts.
  I never look'd for better at his hands
  After he once fell in with Mistress Shore.
BUCKINGHAM. Yet had we not determin'd he
    should die
  Until your lordship came to see his end-
  Which now the loving haste of these
    our friends,
  Something against our meanings,
    have prevented-
  Because, my lord, I would have had you heard
  The traitor speak, and timorously confess
  The manner and the purpose of his treasons:
  That you might well have signified the same
  Unto the citizens, who haply may
  Misconster us in him and wail his death.
MAYOR. But, my good lord, your Grace's words
    shall serve
  As well as I had seen and heard him speak;
  And do not doubt, right noble Princes both,
  But I'll acquaint our duteous citizens
  With all your just proceedings in this cause.
GLOUCESTER. And to that end we wish'd your
    lordship here,
  T' avoid the censures of the carping world.
BUCKINGHAM. Which since you come too late
    of our intent,

Yet witness what you hear we did intend.
And so, my good Lord Mayor, we bid farewell.
Exit LORD MAYOR.
GLOUCESTER. Go, after, after,
    cousin Buckingham.
The Mayor towards Guildhall hies him in
    all post.
There, at your meet'st advantage of the time,
Infer the bastardy of Edward's children.
Tell them how Edward put to death a citizen
Only for saying he would make his son
Heir to the crown-meaning indeed his house,
Which by the sign thereof was termed so.
Moreover, urge his hateful luxury
And bestial appetite in change of lust,
Which stretch'd unto their servants,
    daughters, wives,
Even where his raging eye or savage heart
Without control lusted to make a prey.
Nay, for a need, thus far come near my person:
Tell them, when that my mother went
    with child
Of that insatiate Edward, noble York
My princely father then had wars in France
And, by true computation of the time,
Found that the issue was not his begot;
Which well appeared in his lineaments,
Being nothing like the noble Duke my father.
Yet touch this sparingly, as 'twere far off;
Because, my lord, you know my mother lives.
BUCKINGHAM. Doubt not, my lord, I'll play
    the orator
As if the golden fee for which I plead
Were for myself; and so, my lord, adieu.
GLOUCESTER. If you thrive well, bring them to
    Baynard's Castle;
Where you shall find me well accompanied
With reverend fathers and well
    learned bishops.
BUCKINGHAM. I go; and towards three or
    four o'clock
Look for the news that the Guildhall affords.
    Exit.
GLOUCESTER. Go, Lovel, with all speed to
    Doctor Shaw.
    [To CATESBY] Go thou to Friar Penker. Bid
    them both
    Meet me within this hour at Baynard's Castle.
        Exeunt all but GLOUCESTER.
Now will I go to take some privy order
To draw the brats of Clarence out of sight,
And to give order that no manner person
Have any time recourse unto the Princes.*Exit.*

❧ SCENE VI ❧
London. A street

Enter a SCRIVENER

SCRIVENER. Here is the indictment of the good
    Lord Hastings;
Which in a set hand fairly is engross'd
That it may be to-day read o'er in Paul's.
And mark how well the sequel hangs together:
Eleven hours I have spent to write it over,
For yesternight by Catesby was it sent me;
The precedent was full as long a-doing;
And yet within these five hours Hastings liv'd,
Untainted, unexamin'd, free, at liberty.
Here's a good world the while! Who is so gross
That cannot see this palpable device?
Yet who's so bold but says he sees it not?
Bad is the world; and all will come to nought,
When such ill dealing must be seen in thought.
    Exit.

❧ SCENE VII ❧
London. Baynard's Castle

Enter GLOUCESTER and BUCKINGHAM, at several doors

GLOUCESTER. How now, how now! What say
    the citizens?
BUCKINGHAM. Now, by the holy Mother of
    our Lord,
The citizens are mum, say not a word.
GLOUCESTER. Touch'd you the bastardy of
    Edward's children?
BUCKINGHAM. I did; with his contract with
    Lady Lucy,
And his contract by deputy in France;
Th' insatiate greediness of his desire,
And his enforcement of the city wives;
His tyranny for trifles; his own bastardy,
As being got, your father then in France,
And his resemblance, being not like the Duke.
Withal I did infer your lineaments,
Being the right idea of your father,
Both in your form and nobleness of mind;
Laid open all your victories in Scotland,
Your discipline in war, wisdom in peace,
Your bounty, virtue, fair humility;
Indeed, left nothing fitting for your purpose
Untouch'd or slightly handled in discourse.

And when mine oratory drew toward end
I bid them that did love their country's good
Cry 'God save Richard, England's royal King!'
GLOUCESTER. And did they so?
BUCKINGHAM. No, so God help me, they spake
   not a word;
But, like dumb statues or breathing stones,
Star'd each on other, and look'd deadly pale.
Which when I saw, I reprehended them,
And ask'd the Mayor what meant this
   wilful silence.
His answer was, the people were not used
To be spoke to but by the Recorder.
Then he was urg'd to tell my tale again.
'Thus saith the Duke, thus hath the
   Duke inferr'd'-
But nothing spoke in warrant from himself.
When he had done, some followers of mine own
At lower end of the hall hurl'd up their caps,
And some ten voices cried 'God save King
   Richard!'
And thus I took the vantage of those few-
'Thanks, gentle citizens and friends', quoth I
'This general applause and cheerful shout
Argues your wisdoms and your love to Richard.'
And even here brake off and came away.
GLOUCESTER. What, tongueless blocks were
   they? Would they not speak?
Will not the Mayor then and his brethren come?
BUCKINGHAM. The Mayor is here at hand. Intend
   some fear;
Be not you spoke with but by mighty suit;
And look you get a prayer-book in your hand,
And stand between two churchmen, good
   my lord;
For on that ground I'll make a holy descant;
And be not easily won to our requests.
Play the maid's part: still answer nay, and take it.
GLOUCESTER. I go; and if you plead as well
   for them
As I can say nay to thee for myself,
No doubt we bring it to a happy issue.
BUCKINGHAM. Go, go, up to the leads; the Lord
   Mayor knocks. [Exit GLOUCESTER]
Enter the LORD MAYOR, ALDERMEN, and CITIZENS
Welcome, my lord. I dance attendance here;
I think the Duke will not be spoke withal.
            Enter CATESBY
Now, Catesby, what says your lord to
   my request?
CATESBY. He doth entreat your Grace, my
   noble lord,
To visit him to-morrow or next day.

He is within, with two right reverend fathers,
Divinely bent to meditation;
And in no worldly suits would he be mov'd,
To draw him from his holy exercise.
BUCKINGHAM. Return, good Catesby, to the
   gracious Duke;
Tell him, myself, the Mayor and Aldermen,
In deep designs, in matter of great moment,
No less importing than our general good,
Are come to have some conference with his
   Grace.
CATESBY. I'll signify so much unto him straight.
                                          Exit.
BUCKINGHAM. Ah ha, my lord, this prince is not
   an Edward!
He is not lolling on a lewd love-bed,
But on his knees at meditation;
Not dallying with a brace of courtesans,
But meditating with two deep divines;
Not sleeping, to engross his idle body,
But praying, to enrich his watchful soul.
Happy were England would this virtuous prince
Take on his Grace the sovereignty thereof;
But, sure, I fear we shall not win him to it.
MAYOR. Marry, God defend his Grace should say
   us nay!
BUCKINGHAM. I fear he will. Here Catesby
   comes again.
            Re-enter CATESBY
Now, Catesby, what says his Grace?
CATESBY. My lord,
He wonders to what end you have assembled
Such troops of citizens to come to him.
His Grace not being warn'd thereof before,
He fears, my lord, you mean no good to him.
BUCKINGHAM. Sorry I am my noble
   cousin should
Suspect me that I mean no good to him.
By heaven, we come to him in perfect love;
And so once more return and tell his Grace.
                                   Exit CATESBY
When holy and devout religious men
Are at their beads, 'tis much to draw
   them thence,
So sweet is zealous contemplation.
      Enter GLOUCESTER aloft, between two BISHOPS.
            CATESBY returns
MAYOR. See where his Grace stands 'tween
   two clergymen!
BUCKINGHAM. Two props of virtue for a
   Christian prince,
To stay him from the fall of vanity;
And, see, a book of prayer in his hand,

True ornaments to know a holy man.
Famous Plantagenet, most gracious Prince,
Lend favourable ear to our requests,
And pardon us the interruption
Of thy devotion and right Christian zeal.
GLOUCESTER. My lord, there needs no
    such apology:
I do beseech your Grace to pardon me,
Who, earnest in the service of my God,
Deferr'd the visitation of my friends.
But, leaving this, what is your Grace's pleasure?
BUCKINGHAM. Even that, I hope, which pleaseth
    God above,
And all good men of this ungovern'd isle.
GLOUCESTER. I do suspect I have done
    some offence
That seems disgracious in the city's eye,
And that you come to reprehend my ignorance.
BUCKINGHAM. You have, my lord. Would it might
    please your Grace,
On our entreaties, to amend your fault!
GLOUCESTER. Else wherefore breathe I in a
    Christian land?
BUCKINGHAM. Know then, it is your fault that
    you resign
The supreme seat, the throne majestical,
The scept'red office of your ancestors,
Your state of fortune and your due of birth,
The lineal glory of your royal house,
To the corruption of a blemish'd stock;
Whiles in the mildness of your sleepy thoughts,
Which here we waken to our country's good,
The noble isle doth want her proper limbs;
Her face defac'd with scars of infamy,
Her royal stock graft with ignoble plants,
And almost should'red in the swallowing gulf
Of dark forgetfulness and deep oblivion.
Which to recure, we heartily solicit
Your gracious self to take on you the charge
And kingly government of this your land-
Not as protector, steward, substitute,
Or lowly factor for another's gain;
But as successively, from blood to blood,
Your right of birth, your empery, your own.
For this, consorted with the citizens,
Your very worshipful and loving friends,
And by their vehement instigation,
In this just cause come I to move your Grace.
GLOUCESTER. I cannot tell if to depart in silence
    Or bitterly to speak in your reproof
Best fitteth my degree or your condition.
If not to answer, you might haply think
Tongue-tied ambition, not replying, yielded

To bear the golden yoke of sovereignty,
Which fondly you would here impose on me;
If to reprove you for this suit of yours,
So season'd with your faithful love to me,
Then, on the other side, I check'd my friends.
Therefore-to speak, and to avoid the first,
And then, in speaking, not to incur the last-
Definitively thus I answer you:
Your love deserves my thanks, but my desert
Unmeritable shuns your high request.
First, if all obstacles were cut away,
And that my path were even to the crown,
As the ripe revenue and due of birth,
Yet so much is my poverty of spirit,
So mighty and so many my defects,
That I would rather hide me from my greatness-
Being a bark to brook no mighty sea-
Than in my greatness covet to be hid,
And in the vapour of my glory smother'd.
But, God be thank'd, there is no need of me-
And much I need to help you, were there need.
The royal tree hath left us royal fruit
Which, mellow'd by the stealing hours of time,
Will well become the seat of majesty
And make, no doubt, us happy by his reign.
On him I lay that you would lay on me-
The right and fortune of his happy stars,
Which God defend that I should wring
    from him.
BUCKINGHAM. My lord, this argues conscience in
    your Grace;
But the respects thereof are nice and trivial,
All circumstances well considered.
You say that Edward is your brother's son.
So say we too, but not by Edward's wife;
For first was he contract to Lady Lucy-
Your mother lives a witness to his vow-
And afterward by substitute betroth'd
To Bona, sister to the King of France.
These both put off, a poor petitioner,
A care-craz'd mother to a many sons,
A beauty-waning and distressed widow,
Even in the afternoon of her best days,
Made prize and purchase of his wanton eye,
Seduc'd the pitch and height of his degree
To base declension and loath'd bigamy.
By her, in his unlawful bed, he got
This Edward, whom our manners call the Prince.
More bitterly could I expostulate,
Save that, for reverence to some alive,
I give a sparing limit to my tongue.
Then, good my lord, take to your royal self
This proffer'd benefit of dignity;

If not to bless us and the land withal,
Yet to draw forth your noble ancestry
From the corruption of abusing times
Unto a lineal true-derived course.
MAYOR. Do, good my lord; your citizens
entreat you.
BUCKINGHAM. Refuse not, mighty lord, this
proffer'd love.
CATESBY. O, make them joyful, grant their
lawful suit!
GLOUCESTER. Alas, why would you heap this care
on me?
I am unfit for state and majesty.
I do beseech you, take it not amiss:
I cannot nor I will not yield to you.
BUCKINGHAM. If you refuse it-as, in love and zeal,
Loath to depose the child, your brother's son;
As well we know your tenderness of heart
And gentle, kind, effeminate remorse,
Which we have noted in you to your kindred
And egally indeed to all estates-
Yet know, whe'er you accept our suit or no,
Your brother's son shall never reign our king;
But we will plant some other in the throne
To the disgrace and downfall of your house;
And in this resolution here we leave you.
Come, citizens. Zounds, I'll entreat no more.
GLOUCESTER. O, do not swear, my lord
of Buckingham.
Exeunt BUCKINGHAM, MAYOR, and citizens.
CATESBY. Call him again, sweet Prince, accept
their suit.
If you deny them, all the land will rue it.
GLOUCESTER. Will you enforce me to a world
of cares?
Call them again. I am not made of stones,
But penetrable to your kind entreaties,
Albeit against my conscience and my soul.
Re-enter BUCKINGHAM and the rest
Cousin of Buckingham, and sage grave men,
Since you will buckle fortune on my back,
To bear her burden, whe'er I will or no,
I must have patience to endure the load;
But if black scandal or foul-fac'd reproach
Attend the sequel of your imposition,
Your mere enforcement shall acquittance me
From all the impure blots and stains thereof;
For God doth know, and you may partly see,
How far I am from the desire of this.
MAYOR. God bless your Grace! We see it, and will
say it.
GLOUCESTER. In saying so, you shall but say
the truth.

BUCKINGHAM. Then I salute you with this
royal title-
Long live King Richard, England's worthy King!
ALL. Amen.
BUCKINGHAM. To-morrow may it please you to
be crown'd?
GLOUCESTER. Even when you please, for you will
have it so.
BUCKINGHAM. To-morrow, then, we will attend
your Grace;
And so, most joyfully, we take our leave.
GLOUCESTER. *[To the BISHOPS]* Come, let us to our
holy work again.
Farewell, my cousin; farewell, gentle friends.
Exeunt.

ACT IV

SCENE I
London. Before the Tower

*Enter QUEEN ELIZABETH, DUCHESS OF YORK, and
MARQUIS OF DORSET, at one door; ANNE, DUCHESS
OF GLOUCESTER, leading LADY MARGARET
PLANTAGENET, CLARENCE's young daughter,
at another door*

DUCHESS. Who meets us here? My
niece Plantagenet,
Led in the hand of her kind aunt of Gloucester?
Now, for my life, she's wand'ring to the Tower,
On pure heart's love, to greet the
tender Princes.
Daughter, well met.
ANNE. God give your Graces both
A happy and a joyful time of day!
QUEEN ELIZABETH. As much to you, good
sister! Whither away?
ANNE. No farther than the Tower; and, as
I guess,
Upon the like devotion as yourselves,
To gratulate the gentle Princes there.
QUEEN ELIZABETH. Kind sister, thanks; we'll
enter all together.
Enter BRAKENBURY
And in good time, here the lieutenant comes.
Master Lieutenant, pray you, by your leave,
How doth the Prince, and my young son
of York?
BRAKENBURY. Right well, dear madam. By
your patience,

I may not suffer you to visit them.
The King hath strictly charg'd the contrary.
QUEEN ELIZABETH. The King! Who's that?
BRAKENBURY. I mean the Lord Protector.
QUEEN ELIZABETH. The Lord protect him from
that kingly title!
Hath he set bounds between their love and me?
I am their mother; who shall bar me from them?
DUCHESS. I am their father's mother; I will
see them.
ANNE. Their aunt I am in law, in love
their mother.
Then bring me to their sights; I'll bear
thy blame,
And take thy office from thee on my peril.
BRAKENBURY. No, madam, no. I may not leave
it so;
I am bound by oath, and therefore pardon me.

Exit

Enter STANLEY

STANLEY. Let me but meet you, ladies, one
hour hence,
And I'll salute your Grace of York as mother
And reverend looker-on of two fair queens.
[To ANNE] Come, madam, you must straight
to Westminster,
There to be crowned Richard's royal queen.
QUEEN ELIZABETH. Ah, cut my lace asunder
That my pent heart may have some scope
to beat,
Or else I swoon with this dead-killing news!
ANNE. Despiteful tidings! O unpleasing news!
DORSET. Be of good cheer; mother, how fares
your Grace?
QUEEN ELIZABETH. O Dorset, speak not to me,
get thee gone!
Death and destruction dogs thee at thy heels;
Thy mother's name is ominous to children.
If thou wilt outstrip death, go cross the seas,
And live with Richmond, from the reach
of hell.
Go, hie thee, hie thee from this slaughter-house,
Lest thou increase the number of the dead,
And make me die the thrall of Margaret's curse,
Nor mother, wife, nor England's
counted queen.
STANLEY. Full of wise care is this your
counsel, madam.
Take all the swift advantage of the hours;
You shall have letters from me to my son
In your behalf, to meet you on the way.
Be not ta'en tardy by unwise delay.
DUCHESS. O ill-dispersing wind of misery!

O my accursed womb, the bed of death!
A cockatrice hast thou hatch'd to the world,
Whose unavoided eye is murderous.
STANLEY. Come, madam, come; I in all haste
was sent.
ANNE. And I with all unwillingness will go.
O, would to God that the inclusive verge
Of golden metal that must round my brow
Were red-hot steel, to sear me to the brains!
Anointed let me be with deadly venom,
And die ere men can say 'God save the Queen!'
QUEEN ELIZABETH. Go, go, poor soul; I envy not
thy glory.
To feed my humour, wish thyself no harm.
ANNE. No, why? When he that is my husband now
Came to me, as I follow'd Henry's corse;
When scarce the blood was well wash'd from
his hands
Which issued from my other angel husband,
And that dear saint which then I
weeping follow'd-
O, when, I say, I look'd on Richard's face,
This was my wish: 'Be thou' quoth I 'accurs'd
For making me, so young, so old a widow;
And when thou wed'st, let sorrow haunt
thy bed;
And be thy wife, if any be so mad,
More miserable by the life of thee
Than thou hast made me by my dear
lord's death.'
Lo, ere I can repeat this curse again,
Within so small a time, my woman's heart
Grossly grew captive to his honey words
And prov'd the subject of mine own soul's curse,
Which hitherto hath held my eyes from rest;
For never yet one hour in his bed
Did I enjoy the golden dew of sleep,
But with his timorous dreams was still awak'd.
Besides, he hates me for my father Warwick;
And will, no doubt, shortly be rid of me.
QUEEN ELIZABETH. Poor heart, adieu! I pity
thy complaining.
ANNE. No more than with my soul I mourn
for yours.
DORSET. Farewell, thou woeful welcomer
of glory!
ANNE. Adieu, poor soul, that tak'st thy leave of it!
DUCHESS. *[To DORSET]* Go thou to Richmond,
and good fortune guide thee! *[To ANNE]*
Go thou to Richard, and good angels tend thee!
[To QUEEN ELIZABETH]
Go thou to sanctuary, and good thoughts
possess thee!

I to my grave, where peace and rest lie with me!
Eighty odd years of sorrow have I seen,
And each hour's joy wreck'd with a week
    of teen.
QUEEN ELIZABETH. Stay, yet look back with me
    unto the Tower.
Pity, you ancient stones, those tender babes
Whom envy hath immur'd within your walls,
Rough cradle for such little pretty ones.
Rude ragged nurse, old sullen playfellow
For tender princes, use my babies well.
So foolish sorrows bids your stones farewell.

                                    Exeunt.

✣ SCENE II ✣

London. The palace

Sound a sennet. Enter RICHARD, in pomp, as KING;
BUCKINGHAM, CATESBY, RATCLIFF, LOVEL,
a PAGE, and Others

KING RICHARD. Stand all apart. Cousin
    of Buckingham!
BUCKINGHAM. My gracious sovereign?
KING RICHARD. Give me thy hand. [*Here he ascendeth*
    the throne. Sound a sennet.]
Thus high, by thy advice
And thy assistance, is King Richard seated.
But shall we wear these glories for a day;
Or shall they last, and we rejoice in them?
BUCKINGHAM. Still live they, and for ever let
    them last!
KING RICHARD. Ah, Buckingham, now do I play
    the touch,
To try if thou be current gold indeed.
Young Edward lives-think now what I
    would speak.
BUCKINGHAM. Say on, my loving lord.
KING RICHARD. Why, Buckingham, I say I would
    be King.
BUCKINGHAM. Why, so you are, my thrice-
    renowned lord.
KING RICHARD. Ha! am I King? 'Tis so; but
    Edward lives.
BUCKINGHAM. True, noble Prince.
KING RICHARD. O bitter consequence:
That Edward still should live-true, noble Prince!
Cousin, thou wast not wont to be so dull.
Shall I be plain? I wish the bastards dead.
And I would have it suddenly perform'd.
What say'st thou now? Speak suddenly, be brief.
BUCKINGHAM. Your Grace may do your pleasure.

KING RICHARD. Tut, tut, thou art all ice; thy
    kindness freezes.
Say, have I thy consent that they shall die?
BUCKINGHAM. Give me some little breath, some
    pause, dear Lord,
Before I positively speak in this.
I will resolve you herein presently.*Exit.*
CATESBY. [*Aside to another*] The King is angry; see, he
    gnaws his lip.
KING RICHARD. I will converse with iron-witted
    fools [*Descends from the throne*]
And unrespective boys; none are for me
That look into me with considerate eyes.
High-reaching Buckingham grows circumspect.
Boy!
PAGE. My lord?
KING RICHARD. Know'st thou not any whom
    corrupting gold
Will tempt unto a close exploit of death?
PAGE. I know a discontented gentleman
Whose humble means match not his
    haughty spirit.
Gold were as good as twenty orators,
And will, no doubt, tempt him to anything.
KING RICHARD. What is his name?
PAGE. His name, my lord, is Tyrrel.
KING RICHARD. I partly know the man. Go, call
    him hither, boy.   *Exit PAGE.*
The deep-revolving witty Buckingham
No more shall be the neighbour to my counsels.
Hath he so long held out with me, untir'd,
And stops he now for breath? Well, be it so.

                        Enter STANLEY

How now, Lord Stanley! What's the news?
STANLEY. Know, my loving lord,
The Marquis Dorset, as I hear, is fled
To Richmond, in the parts where he abides.
    Stands apart
KING RICHARD. Come hither, Catesby. Rumour
    it abroad
That Anne, my wife, is very grievous sick;
I will take order for her keeping close.
Inquire me out some mean poor gentleman,
Whom I will marry straight to
    Clarence' daughter-
The boy is foolish, and I fear not him.
Look how thou dream'st! I say again, give out
That Anne, my queen, is sick and like to die.
About it; for it stands me much upon
To stop all hopes whose growth may damage
    me. [*Exit CATESBY*]
I must be married to my brother's daughter,
Or else my kingdom stands on brittle glass.

Murder her brothers, and then marry her!
Uncertain way of gain! But I am in
So far in blood that sin will pluck on sin.
Tear-falling pity dwells not in this eye.

Re-enter PAGE, with TYRREL

Is thy name Tyrrel?

TYRREL. James Tyrrel, and your most
obedient subject.

KING RICHARD. Art thou, indeed?

TYRREL. Prove me, my gracious lord.

KING RICHARD. Dar'st thou resolve to kill a
friend of mine?

TYRREL. Please you;
But I had rather kill two enemies.

KING RICHARD. Why, then thou hast it. Two
deep enemies,
Foes to my rest, and my sweet sleep's disturbers,
Are they that I would have thee deal upon.
Tyrrel, I mean those bastards in the Tower.

TYRREL. Let me have open means to come
to them,
And soon I'll rid you from the fear of them.

KING RICHARD. Thou sing'st sweet music. Hark,
come hither, Tyrrel.
Go, by this token. Rise, and lend thine
ear. *[Whispers]*
There is no more but so: say it is done,
And I will love thee and prefer thee for it.

TYRREL. I will dispatch it straight. *Exit.*

Re-enter BUCKINGHAM

BUCKINGHAM. My lord, I have consider'd in
my mind
The late request that you did sound me in.

KING RICHARD. Well, let that rest. Dorset is fled
to Richmond.

BUCKINGHAM. I hear the news, my lord.

KING RICHARD. Stanley, he is your wife's son:
well, look unto it.

BUCKINGHAM. My lord, I claim the gift, my due
by promise,
For which your honour and your faith is pawn'd:
Th' earldom of Hereford and the movables
Which you have promised I shall possess.

KING RICHARD. Stanley, look to your wife; if she
convey
Letters to Richmond, you shall answer it.

BUCKINGHAM. What says your Highness to my
just request?

KING RICHARD. I do remember me: Henry
the Sixth
Did prophesy that Richmond should be King,
When Richmond was a little peevish boy.
A king!-perhaps-

BUCKINGHAM. My lord-

KING RICHARD. How chance the prophet could
not at that time
Have told me, I being by, that I should kill him?

BUCKINGHAM. My lord, your promise for
the earldom-

KING RICHARD. Richmond! When last I was
at Exeter,
The mayor in courtesy show'd me the castle
And call'd it Rugemount, at which name
I started,
Because a bard of Ireland told me once
I should not live long after I saw Richmond.

BUCKINGHAM. My lord-

KING RICHARD. Ay, what's o'clock?

BUCKINGHAM. I am thus bold to put your Grace
in mind
Of what you promis'd me.

KING RICHARD. Well, but o'clock?

BUCKINGHAM. Upon the stroke of ten.

KING RICHARD. Well, let it strike.

BUCKINGHAM. Why let it strike?

KING RICHARD. Because that like a Jack thou
keep'st the stroke
Betwixt thy begging and my meditation.
I am not in the giving vein to-day.

BUCKINGHAM. May it please you to resolve me
in my suit.

KING RICHARD. Thou troublest me; I am not in
the vein.

Exeunt all but Buckingham.

BUCKINGHAM. And is it thus? Repays he my
deep service
With such contempt? Made I him King for this?
O, let me think on Hastings, and be gone
To Brecknock while my fearful head is on!

Exit.

❦ SCENE III ❦
London. The palace

Enter TYRREL

TYRREL. The tyrannous and bloody act is done,
The most arch deed of piteous massacre
That ever yet this land was guilty of.
Dighton and Forrest, who I did suborn
To do this piece of ruthless butchery,
Albeit they were flesh'd villains, bloody dogs,
Melted with tenderness and mild compassion,
Wept like two children in their deaths' sad story.
'O, thus' quoth Dighton 'lay the gentle babes'-

'Thus, thus', quoth Forrest 'girdling one another
Within their alabaster innocent arms.
Their lips were four red roses on a stalk,
And in their summer beauty kiss'd each other.
A book of prayers on their pillow lay;
Which once', quoth Forrest 'almost chang'd
my mind;
But, O, the devil'-there the villain stopp'd;
When Dighton thus told on: 'We smothered
The most replenished sweet work of nature
That from the prime creation e'er she framed.'
Hence both are gone with conscience
and remorse
They could not speak; and so I left them both,
To bear this tidings to the bloody King.

Enter KING RICHARD

And here he comes. All health, my
sovereign lord!
KING RICHARD. Kind Tyrrel, am I happy in
thy news?
TYRREL. If to have done the thing you gave
in charge
Beget your happiness, be happy then,
For it is done.
KING RICHARD. But didst thou see them dead?
TYRREL. I did, my lord.
KING RICHARD. And buried, gentle Tyrrel?
TYRREL. The chaplain of the Tower hath
buried them;
But where, to say the truth, I do not know.
KING RICHARD. Come to me, Tyrrel, soon at
after supper,
When thou shalt tell the process of their death.
Meantime, but think how I may do thee good
And be inheritor of thy desire.
Farewell till then.
TYRREL. I humbly take my leave.   *Exit.*
KING RICHARD. The son of Clarence have I pent
up close;
His daughter meanly have I match'd in marriage;
The sons of Edward sleep in Abraham's bosom,
And Anne my wife hath bid this world
good night.
Now, for I know the Britaine Richmond aims
At young Elizabeth, my brother's daughter,
And by that knot looks proudly on the crown,
To her go I, a jolly thriving wooer.

Enter RATCLIFF

RATCLIFF. My lord!
KING RICHARD. Good or bad news, that thou
com'st in so bluntly?
RATCLIFF. Bad news, my lord: Morton is fled
to Richmond;

And Buckingham, back'd with the hardy
Welshmen,
Is in the field, and still his power increaseth.
KING RICHARD. Ely with Richmond troubles me
more near
Than Buckingham and his rash-
levied strength.
Come, I have learn'd that fearful commenting
Is leaden servitor to dull delay;
Delay leads impotent and snail-pac'd beggary.
Then fiery expedition be my wing,
Jove's Mercury, and herald for a king!
Go, muster men. My counsel is my shield.
We must be brief when traitors brave the field.

Exeunt.

✲ SCENE IV ✲
London. Before the palace

Enter old QUEEN MARGARET

QUEEN MARGARET. So now prosperity begins
to mellow
And drop into the rotten mouth of death.
Here in these confines slily have I lurk'd
To watch the waning of mine enemies.
A dire induction am I witness to,
And will to France, hoping the consequence
Will prove as bitter, black, and tragical.
Withdraw thee, wretched Margaret. Who
comes here?

Retires.

Enter QUEEN ELIZABETH and the DUCHESS OF YORK

QUEEN ELIZABETH. Ah, my poor princes! ah, my
tender babes!
My unblown flowers, new-appearing sweets!
If yet your gentle souls fly in the air
And be not fix'd in doom perpetual,
Hover about me with your airy wings
And hear your mother's lamentation.
QUEEN MARGARET. Hover about her; say that
right for right
Hath dimm'd your infant morn to aged night.
DUCHESS. So many miseries have craz'd my voice
That my woe-wearied tongue is still and mute.
Edward Plantagenet, why art thou dead?
QUEEN MARGARET. Plantagenet doth
quit Plantagenet,
Edward for Edward pays a dying debt.
QUEEN ELIZABETH. Wilt thou, O God, fly from
such gentle lambs
And throw them in the entrails of the wolf?

When didst thou sleep when such a deed
  was done?
QUEEN MARGARET. When holy Harry died, and
  my sweet son.
DUCHESS. Dead life, blind sight, poor mortal
  living ghost,
  Woe's scene, world's shame, grave's due by
   life usurp'd,
  Brief abstract and record of tedious days,
  Rest thy unrest on England's lawful
   earth,*[Sitting down]*
  Unlawfully made drunk with innocent blood.
QUEEN ELIZABETH. Ah, that thou wouldst as
  soon afford a grave
  As thou canst yield a melancholy seat!
  Then would I hide my bones, not rest
   them here.
  Ah, who hath any cause to mourn but we?
            Sitting down by her
QUEEN MARGARET. *[Coming forward]* If ancient
  sorrow be most reverend,
  Give mine the benefit of seniory,
  And let my griefs frown on the upper hand.
  If sorrow can admit society, *[Sitting down with them]*
  Tell o'er your woes again by viewing mine.
  I had an Edward, till a Richard kill'd him;
  I had a husband, till a Richard kill'd him:
  Thou hadst an Edward, till a Richard kill'd him;
  Thou hadst a Richard, till a Richard kill'd him.
DUCHESS. I had a Richard too, and thou didst
  kill him;
  I had a Rutland too, thou holp'st to kill him.
QUEEN MARGARET. Thou hadst a Clarence too,
  and Richard kill'd him.
  From forth the kennel of thy womb hath crept
  A hell-hound that doth hunt us all to death.
  That dog, that had his teeth before his eyes
  To worry lambs and lap their gentle blood,
  That foul defacer of God's handiwork,
  That excellent grand tyrant of the earth
  That reigns in galled eyes of weeping souls,
  Thy womb let loose to chase us to our graves.
  O upright, just, and true-disposing God,
  How do I thank thee that this carnal cur
  Preys on the issue of his mother's body
  And makes her pew-fellow with others' moan!
DUCHESS. O Harry's wife, triumph not in
  my woes!
  God witness with me, I have wept for thine.
QUEEN MARGARET. Bear with me; I am hungry
  for revenge,
  And now I cloy me with beholding it.
  Thy Edward he is dead, that kill'd my Edward;

The other Edward dead, to quit my Edward;
Young York he is but boot, because both they
Match'd not the high perfection of my loss.
Thy Clarence he is dead that stabb'd my Edward;
And the beholders of this frantic play,
Th' adulterate Hastings, Rivers, Vaughan, Grey,
Untimely smother'd in their dusky graves.
Richard yet lives, hell's black intelligencer;
Only reserv'd their factor to buy souls
And send them thither. But at hand, at hand,
Ensues his piteous and unpitied end.
Earth gapes, hell burns, fiends roar, saints pray,
To have him suddenly convey'd from hence.
Cancel his bond of life, dear God, I pray,
That I may live and say 'The dog is dead'.
QUEEN ELIZABETH. O, thou didst prophesy the
  time would come
  That I should wish for thee to help me curse
  That bottled spider, that foul bunch-back'd toad!
QUEEN MARGARET. I call'd thee then vain
  flourish of my fortune;
  I call'd thee then poor shadow, painted queen,
  The presentation of but what I was,
  The flattering index of a direful pageant,
  One heav'd a-high to be hurl'd down below,
  A mother only mock'd with two fair babes,
  A dream of what thou wast, a garish flag
  To be the aim of every dangerous shot,
  A sign of dignity, a breath, a bubble,
  A queen in jest, only to fill the scene.
  Where is thy husband now? Where be
   thy brothers?
  Where be thy two sons? Wherein dost
   thou joy?
  Who sues, and kneels, and says 'God save
   the Queen'?
  Where be the bending peers that
   flattered thee?
  Where be the thronging troops that
   followed thee?
  Decline all this, and see what now thou art:
  For happy wife, a most distressed widow;
  For joyful mother, one that wails the name;
  For one being su'd to, one that humbly sues;
  For Queen, a very caitiff crown'd with care;
  For she that scorn'd at me, now scorn'd of me;
  For she being fear'd of all, now fearing one;
  For she commanding all, obey'd of none.
  Thus hath the course of justice whirl'd about
  And left thee but a very prey to time,
  Having no more but thought of what
   thou wast
  To torture thee the more, being what thou art.

Thou didst usurp my place, and dost thou not
Usurp the just proportion of my sorrow?
Now thy proud neck bears half my
  burden'd yoke,
From which even here I slip my weary head
And leave the burden of it all on thee.
Farewell, York's wife, and queen of
  sad mischance;
These English woes shall make me smile
  in France.

QUEEN ELIZABETH. O thou well skill'd in curses,
  stay awhile
And teach me how to curse mine enemies!

QUEEN MARGARET. Forbear to sleep the nights,
  and fast the days;
Compare dead happiness with living woe;
Think that thy babes were sweeter than
  they were,
And he that slew them fouler than he is.
Bett'ring thy loss makes the bad-causer worse;
Revolving this will teach thee how to curse.

QUEEN ELIZABETH. My words are dull; O,
  quicken them with thine!

QUEEN MARGARET. Thy woes will make them
  sharp and pierce like mine.   Exit.

DUCHESS. Why should calamity be full of words?

QUEEN ELIZABETH. Windy attorneys to their
  client woes,
Airy succeeders of intestate joys,
Poor breathing orators of miseries,
Let them have scope; though what they
  will impart
Help nothing else, yet do they ease the heart.

DUCHESS. If so, then be not tongue-tied. Go
  with me,
And in the breath of bitter words let's smother
My damned son that thy two sweet
  sons smother'd.
The trumpet sounds; be copious in exclaims.

*Enter KING RICHARD and his Train, marching with drums
  and trumpets*

KING RICHARD. Who intercepts me in
  my expedition?

DUCHESS. O, she that might have intercepted thee,
By strangling thee in her accursed womb,
From all the slaughters, wretch, that thou
  hast done!

QUEEN ELIZABETH. Hidest thou that forehead
  with a golden crown
Where't should be branded, if that right
  were right,
The slaughter of the Prince that ow'd
  that crown,

And the dire death of my poor sons
  and brothers?
Tell me, thou villain slave, where are
  my children?

DUCHESS. Thou toad, thou toad, where is thy
  brother Clarence?
And little Ned Plantagenet, his son?

QUEEN ELIZABETH. Where is the gentle Rivers,
  Vaughan, Grey?

DUCHESS. Where is kind Hastings?

KING RICHARD. A flourish, trumpets! Strike
  alarum, drums!
Let not the heavens hear these tell-tale women
Rail on the Lord's anointed. Strike, I say!

[Flourish. Alarums]

Either be patient and entreat me fair,
Or with the clamorous report of war
Thus will I drown your exclamations.

DUCHESS. Art thou my son?

KING RICHARD. Ay, I thank God, my father,
  and yourself.

DUCHESS. Then patiently hear my impatience.

KING RICHARD. Madam, I have a touch of
  your condition
That cannot brook the accent of reproof.

DUCHESS. O, let me speak!

KING RICHARD. Do, then; but I'll not hear.

DUCHESS. I will be mild and gentle in my words.

KING RICHARD. And brief, good mother; for I am
  in haste.

DUCHESS. Art thou so hasty? I have stay'd
  for thee,
God knows, in torment and in agony.

KING RICHARD. And came I not at last to
  comfort you?

DUCHESS. No, by the holy rood, thou know'st
  it well
Thou cam'st on earth to make the earth my hell.
A grievous burden was thy birth to me;
Tetchy and wayward was thy infancy;
Thy school-days frightful, desp'rate, wild,
  and furious;
Thy prime of manhood daring, bold,
  and venturous;
Thy age confirm'd, proud, subtle, sly, and
  bloody,
More mild, but yet more harmful-kind in hatred.
What comfortable hour canst thou name
That ever grac'd me with thy company?

KING RICHARD. Faith, none but Humphrey Hour,
  that call'd your Grace
To breakfast once forth of my company.
If I be so disgracious in your eye,

Let me march on and not offend you, madam.
Strike up the drum.
DUCHESS. I prithee hear me speak.
KING RICHARD. You speak too bitterly.
DUCHESS. Hear me a word;
For I shall never speak to thee again.
KING RICHARD. So.
DUCHESS. Either thou wilt die by God's
just ordinance
Ere from this war thou turn a conqueror;
Or I with grief and extreme age shall perish
And never more behold thy face again.
Therefore take with thee my most
grievous curse,
Which in the day of battle tire thee more
Than all the complete armour that thou wear'st!
My prayers on the adverse party fight;
And there the little souls of Edward's children
Whisper the spirits of thine enemies
And promise them success and victory.
Bloody thou art; bloody will be thy end.
Shame serves thy life and doth thy death attend.

Exit.

QUEEN ELIZABETH. Though far more cause, yet
much less spirit to curse
Abides in me; I say amen to her.
KING RICHARD. Stay, madam, I must talk a word
with you.
QUEEN ELIZABETH. I have no moe sons of the
royal blood
For thee to slaughter. For my
daughters, Richard,
They shall be praying nuns, not weeping queens;
And therefore level not to hit their lives.
KING RICHARD. You have a daughter
call'd Elizabeth.
Virtuous and fair, royal and gracious.
QUEEN ELIZABETH. And must she die for this? O,
let her live,
And I'll corrupt her manners, stain her beauty,
Slander myself as false to Edward's bed,
Throw over her the veil of infamy;
So she may live unscarr'd of bleeding slaughter,
I will confess she was not Edward's daughter.
KING RICHARD. Wrong not her birth; she is a
royal Princess.
QUEEN ELIZABETH. To save her life I'll say she is
not so.
KING RICHARD. Her life is safest only in her birth.
QUEEN ELIZABETH. And only in that safety died
her brothers.
KING RICHARD. Lo, at their birth good stars
were opposite.

QUEEN ELIZABETH. No, to their lives ill friends
were contrary.
KING RICHARD. All unavoided is the doom
of destiny.
QUEEN ELIZABETH. True, when avoided grace
makes destiny.
My babes were destin'd to a fairer death,
If grace had bless'd thee with a fairer life.
KING RICHARD. You speak as if that I had slain
my cousins.
QUEEN ELIZABETH. Cousins, indeed; and by their
uncle cozen'd
Of comfort, kingdom, kindred, freedom, life.
Whose hand soever lanc'd their tender hearts,
Thy head, an indirectly, gave direction.
No doubt the murd'rous knife was dull and blunt
Till it was whetted on thy stone-hard heart
To revel in the entrails of my lambs.
But that stiff use of grief makes wild grief tame,
My tongue should to thy ears not name my boys
Till that my nails were anchor'd in thine eyes;
And I, in such a desp'rate bay of death,
Like a poor bark, of sails and tackling reft,
Rush all to pieces on thy rocky bosom.
KING RICHARD. Madam, so thrive I in
my enterprise
And dangerous success of bloody wars,
As I intend more good to you and yours
Than ever you or yours by me were harm'd!
QUEEN ELIZABETH. What good is cover'd with
the face of heaven,
To be discover'd, that can do me good?
KING RICHARD. Th' advancement of your
children, gentle lady.
QUEEN ELIZABETH. Up to some scaffold, there to
lose their heads?
KING RICHARD. Unto the dignity and height
of Fortune,
The high imperial type of this earth's glory.
QUEEN ELIZABETH. Flatter my sorrow with
report of it;
Tell me what state, what dignity, what honour,
Canst thou demise to any child of mine?
KING RICHARD. Even all I have-ay, and myself
and all
Will I withal endow a child of thine;
So in the Lethe of thy angry soul
Thou drown the sad remembrance of
those wrongs
Which thou supposest I have done to thee.
QUEEN ELIZABETH. Be brief, lest that the process
of thy kindness
Last longer telling than thy kindness' date.

KING RICHARD. Then know, that from my soul I
  love thy daughter.
QUEEN ELIZABETH. My daughter's mother thinks
  it with her soul.
KING RICHARD. What do you think?
QUEEN ELIZABETH. That thou dost love my
  daughter from thy soul.
  So from thy soul's love didst thou love
    her brothers,
  And from my heart's love I do thank thee for it.
KING RICHARD. Be not so hasty to confound
  my meaning.
  I mean that with my soul I love thy daughter
  And do intend to make her Queen of England.
QUEEN ELIZABETH. Well, then, who dost thou
  mean shall be her king?
KING RICHARD. Even he that makes her Queen.
  Who else should be?
QUEEN ELIZABETH. What, thou?
KING RICHARD. Even so. How think you of it?
QUEEN ELIZABETH. How canst thou woo her?
KING RICHARD. That would I learn of you,
  As one being best acquainted with her humour.
QUEEN ELIZABETH. And wilt thou learn of me?
KING RICHARD. Madam, with all my heart.
QUEEN ELIZABETH. Send to her, by the man that
  slew her brothers,
  A pair of bleeding hearts; thereon engrave
  'Edward' and 'York'. Then haply will she weep;
  Therefore present to her-as sometimes Margaret
  Did to thy father, steep'd in Rutland's blood-
  A handkerchief; which, say to her, did drain
  The purple sap from her sweet brother's body,
  And bid her wipe her weeping eyes withal.
  If this inducement move her not to love,
  Send her a letter of thy noble deeds;
  Tell her thou mad'st away her uncle Clarence,
  Her uncle Rivers; ay, and for her sake
  Mad'st quick conveyance with her good
    aunt Anne.
KING RICHARD. You mock me, madam; this is
  not the way
  To win your daughter.
QUEEN ELIZABETH. There is no other way;
  Unless thou couldst put on some other shape
  And not be Richard that hath done all this.
KING RICHARD. Say that I did all this for love
  of her.
QUEEN ELIZABETH. Nay, then indeed she cannot
  choose but hate thee,
  Having bought love with such a bloody spoil.
KING RICHARD. Look what is done cannot be
  now amended.

Men shall deal unadvisedly sometimes,
Which after-hours gives leisure to repent.
If I did take the kingdom from your sons,
To make amends I'll give it to your daughter.
If I have kill'd the issue of your womb,
To quicken your increase I will beget
Mine issue of your blood upon your daughter.
A grandam's name is little less in love
Than is the doating title of a mother;
They are as children but one step below,
Even of your metal, of your very blood;
Of all one pain, save for a night of groans
Endur'd of her, for whom you bid like sorrow.
Your children were vexation to your youth;
But mine shall be a comfort to your age.
The loss you have is but a son being King,
And by that loss your daughter is made
  Queen.
I cannot make you what amends I would,
Therefore accept such kindness as I can.
Dorset your son, that with a fearful soul
Leads discontented steps in foreign soil,
This fair alliance quickly shall call home
To high promotions and great dignity.
The King, that calls your beauteous
  daughter wife,
Familiarly shall call thy Dorset brother;
Again shall you be mother to a king,
And all the ruins of distressful times
Repair'd with double riches of content.
What! we have many goodly days to see.
The liquid drops of tears that you have shed
Shall come again, transform'd to orient pearl,
Advantaging their loan with interest
Of ten times double gain of happiness.
Go, then, my mother, to thy daughter go;
Make bold her bashful years with
  your experience;
Prepare her ears to hear a wooer's tale;
Put in her tender heart th' aspiring flame
Of golden sovereignty; acquaint the Princes
With the sweet silent hours of marriage joys.
And when this arm of mine hath chastised
The petty rebel, dull-brain'd Buckingham,
Bound with triumphant garlands will I come,
And lead thy daughter to a conqueror's bed;
To whom I will retail my conquest won,
And she shall be sole victoress,
  Caesar's Caesar.
QUEEN ELIZABETH. What were I best to say? Her
  father's brother
  Would be her lord? Or shall I say her uncle?
  Or he that slew her brothers and her uncles?

Under what title shall I woo for thee
That God, the law, my honour, and her love
Can make seem pleasing to her tender years?
KING RICHARD. Infer fair England's peace by
this alliance.
QUEEN ELIZABETH. Which she shall purchase
with still-lasting war.
KING RICHARD. Tell her the King, that may
command, entreats.
QUEEN ELIZABETH. That at her hands which the
King's King forbids.
KING RICHARD. Say she shall be a high and
mighty queen.
QUEEN ELIZABETH. To wail the title, as her
mother doth.
KING RICHARD. Say I will love her everlastingly.
QUEEN ELIZABETH. But how long shall that title
'ever' last?
KING RICHARD. Sweetly in force unto her fair
life's end.
QUEEN ELIZABETH. But how long fairly shall her
sweet life last?
KING RICHARD. As long as heaven and nature
lengthens it.
QUEEN ELIZABETH. As long as hell and Richard
likes of it.
KING RICHARD. Say I, her sovereign, am her
subject low.
QUEEN ELIZABETH. But she, your subject,
loathes such sovereignty.
KING RICHARD. Be eloquent in my behalf to her.
QUEEN ELIZABETH. An honest tale speeds best
being plainly told.
KING RICHARD. Then plainly to her tell my
loving tale.
QUEEN ELIZABETH. Plain and not honest is too
harsh a style.
KING RICHARD. Your reasons are too shallow and
too quick.
QUEEN ELIZABETH. O, no, my reasons are too
deep and dead-
Too deep and dead, poor infants, in their graves.
KING RICHARD. Harp not on that string, madam;
that is past.
QUEEN ELIZABETH. Harp on it still shall I till
heartstrings break.
KING RICHARD. Now, by my George, my garter,
and my crown-
QUEEN ELIZABETH. Profan'd, dishonour'd, and
the third usurp'd.
KING RICHARD. I swear-
QUEEN ELIZABETH. By nothing; for this is
no oath:

Thy George, profan'd, hath lost his
lordly honour;
Thy garter, blemish'd, pawn'd his
knightly virtue;
Thy crown, usurp'd, disgrac'd his kingly glory.
If something thou wouldst swear to be believ'd,
Swear then by something that thou hast
not wrong'd.
KING RICHARD. Then, by my self-
QUEEN ELIZABETH. Thy self is self-misus'd.
KING RICHARD. Now, by the world-
QUEEN ELIZABETH. 'Tis full of thy foul wrongs.
KING RICHARD. My father's death-
QUEEN ELIZABETH. Thy life hath it dishonour'd.
KING RICHARD. Why, then, by God-
QUEEN ELIZABETH. God's wrong is most of all.
If thou didst fear to break an oath with Him,
The unity the King my husband made
Thou hadst not broken, nor my brothers died.
If thou hadst fear'd to break an oath by Him,
Th' imperial metal, circling now thy head,
Had grac'd the tender temples of my child;
And both the Princes had been breathing here,
Which now, two tender bedfellows for dust,
Thy broken faith hath made the prey for worms.
What canst thou swear by now?
KING RICHARD. The time to come.
QUEEN ELIZABETH. That thou hast wronged in
the time o'erpast;
For I myself have many tears to wash
Hereafter time, for time past wrong'd by thee.
The children live whose fathers thou
hast slaughter'd,
Ungovern'd youth, to wail it in their age;
The parents live whose children thou
hast butcher'd,
Old barren plants, to wail it with their age.
Swear not by time to come; for that thou hast
Misus'd ere us'd, by times ill-us'd o'erpast.
KING RICHARD. As I intend to prosper
and repent,
So thrive I in my dangerous affairs
Of hostile arms! Myself myself confound!
Heaven and fortune bar me happy hours!
Day, yield me not thy light; nor, night, thy rest!
Be opposite all planets of good luck
To my proceeding!-if, with dear heart's love,
Immaculate devotion, holy thoughts,
I tender not thy beauteous princely daughter.
In her consists my happiness and thine;
Without her, follows to myself and thee,
Herself, the land, and many a Christian soul,
Death, desolation, ruin, and decay.

It cannot be avoided but by this;
It will not be avoided but by this.
Therefore, dear mother-I must call you so-
Be the attorney of my love to her;
Plead what I will be, not what I have been;
Not my deserts, but what I will deserve.
Urge the necessity and state of times,
And be not peevish-fond in great designs.

QUEEN ELIZABETH. Shall I be tempted of the
devil thus?

KING RICHARD. Ay, if the devil tempt you to
do good.

QUEEN ELIZABETH. Shall I forget myself to
be myself?

KING RICHARD. Ay, if your self's remembrance
wrong yourself.

QUEEN ELIZABETH. Yet thou didst kill
my children.

KING RICHARD. But in your daughter's womb I
bury them;
Where, in that nest of spicery, they will breed
Selves of themselves, to your recomforture.

QUEEN ELIZABETH. Shall I go win my daughter
to thy will?

KING RICHARD. And be a happy mother by
the deed.

QUEEN ELIZABETH. I go. Write to me
very shortly,
And you shall understand from me her mind.

KING RICHARD. Bear her my true love's
kiss; and so, farewell. *[Kissing her. Exit QUEEN ELIZABETH]*
Relenting fool, and shallow, changing woman!
Enter RATCLIFF; CATESBY following
How now! what news?

RATCLIFF. Most mighty sovereign, on the
western coast
Rideth a puissant navy; to our shores
Throng many doubtful hollow-hearted friends,
Unarm'd, and unresolv'd to beat them back.
'Tis thought that Richmond is their admiral;
And there they hull, expecting but the aid
Of Buckingham to welcome them ashore.

KING RICHARD. Some light-foot friend post to
the Duke of Norfolk.
Ratcliff, thyself-or Catesby; where is he?

CATESBY. Here, my good lord.

KING RICHARD. Catesby, fly to the Duke.

CATESBY. I will my lord, with all convenient
haste.

KING RICHARD. Ratcliff, come hither. Post
to Salisbury;
When thou com'st thither- *[To CATESBY]* Dull,

unmindful villain,
Why stay'st thou here, and go'st not to
the Duke?

CATESBY. First, mighty liege, tell me your
Highness' pleasure,
What from your Grace I shall deliver to him.

KING RICHARD. O, true, good Catesby. Bid him
levy straight
The greatest strength and power that he
can make
And meet me suddenly at Salisbury.

CATESBY. I go. *Exit.*

RATCLIFF. What, may it please you, shall I do
at Salisbury?

KING RICHARD. Why, what wouldst thou do
there before I go?

RATCLIFF. Your Highness told me I should
post before.

KING RICHARD. My mind is chang'd.
Enter LORD STANLEY
Stanley, what news with you?

STANLEY. None good, my liege, to please you
with the hearing;
Nor none so bad but well may be reported.

KING RICHARD. Hoyday, a riddle! neither good
nor bad!
What need'st thou run so many miles about,
When thou mayest tell thy tale the nearest way?
Once more, what news?

STANLEY. Richmond is on the seas.

KING RICHARD. There let him sink, and be the
seas on him!
White-liver'd runagate, what doth he there?

STANLEY. I know not, mighty sovereign, but
by guess.

KING RICHARD. Well, as you guess?

STANLEY. Stirr'd up by Dorset, Buckingham,
and Morton,
He makes for England here to claim the crown.

KING RICHARD. Is the chair empty? Is the
sword unsway'd?
Is the King dead, the empire unpossess'd?
What heir of York is there alive but we?
And who is England's King but great York's heir?
Then tell me what makes he upon the seas.

STANLEY. Unless for that, my liege, I cannot guess.

KING RICHARD. Unless for that he comes to be
your liege,
You cannot guess wherefore the
Welshman comes.
Thou wilt revolt and fly to him, I fear.

STANLEY. No, my good lord; therefore mistrust
me not.

KING RICHARD. Where is thy power then, to beat
  him back?
  Where be thy tenants and thy followers?
  Are they not now upon the western shore,
  Safe-conducting the rebels from their ships?
STANLEY. No, my good lord, my friends are in
  the north.
KING RICHARD. Cold friends to me. What do they
  in the north,
  When they should serve their sovereign in
  the west?
STANLEY. They have not been commanded,
  mighty King.
  Pleaseth your Majesty to give me leave,
  I'll muster up my friends and meet your Grace
  Where and what time your Majesty shall please.
KING RICHARD. Ay, ay, thou wouldst be gone to
  join with Richmond;
  But I'll not trust thee.
STANLEY. Most mighty sovereign,
  You have no cause to hold my friendship
  doubtful.
  I never was nor never will be false.
KING RICHARD. Go, then, and muster men. But
  leave behind
  Your son, George Stanley. Look your heart
  be firm,
  Or else his head's assurance is but frail.
STANLEY. So deal with him as I prove true to you.
                                              Exit.

                Enter a MESSENGER

MESSENGER. My gracious sovereign, now
  in Devonshire,
  As I by friends am well advertised,
  Sir Edward Courtney and the haughty prelate,
  Bishop of Exeter, his elder brother,
  With many moe confederates, are in arms.

            Enter another MESSENGER

SECOND MESSENGER. In Kent, my liege, the
  Guilfords are in arms;
  And every hour more competitors
  Flock to the rebels, and their power
  grows strong.

            Enter another MESSENGER

THIRD MESSENGER. My lord, the army of
  great Buckingham-
KING RICHARD. Out on you, owls! Nothing but
  songs of death? [*He strikes him*]
  There, take thou that till thou bring better news.
THIRD MESSENGER. The news I have to tell
  your Majesty
  Is that by sudden floods and fall of waters
  Buckingham's army is dispers'd and scatter'd;

And he himself wand'red away alone,
  No man knows whither.
KING RICHARD. I cry thee mercy.
  There is my purse to cure that blow of thine.
  Hath any well-advised friend proclaim'd
  Reward to him that brings the traitor in?
THIRD MESSENGER. Such proclamation hath
  been made, my Lord.

            Enter another MESSENGER

FOURTH MESSENGER. Sir Thomas Lovel and Lord
  Marquis Dorset,
  'Tis said, my liege, in Yorkshire are in arms.
  But this good comfort bring I to your Highness-
  The Britaine navy is dispers'd by tempest.
  Richmond in Dorsetshire sent out a boat
  Unto the shore, to ask those on the banks
  If they were his assistants, yea or no;
  Who answer'd him they came from Buckingham
  Upon his party. He, mistrusting them,
  Hois'd sail, and made his course again
  for Britaine.
KING RICHARD. March on, march on, since we
  are up in arms;
  If not to fight with foreign enemies,
  Yet to beat down these rebels here at home.

              Re-enter CATESBY

CATESBY. My liege, the Duke of Buckingham
  is taken-
  That is the best news. That the Earl of Richmond
  Is with a mighty power landed at Milford
  Is colder tidings, yet they must be told.
KING RICHARD. Away towards Salisbury! While
  we reason here
  A royal battle might be won and lost.
  Some one take order Buckingham be brought
  To Salisbury; the rest march on with me.
                              Flourish. Exeunt.

              ✿ SCENE V ✿
            LORD STANLEY'S house

      Enter STANLEY and SIR CHRISTOPHER URSWICK

STANLEY. Sir Christopher, tell Richmond this
  from me:
  That in the sty of the most deadly boar
  My son George Stanley is frank'd up in hold;
  If I revolt, off goes young George's head;
  The fear of that holds off my present aid.
  So, get thee gone; commend me to thy lord.
  Withal say that the Queen hath
  heartily consented

He should espouse Elizabeth her daughter.
But tell me, where is princely Richmond now?
CHRISTOPHER. At Pembroke, or at Ha'rford
  west in Wales.
STANLEY. What men of name resort to him?
CHRISTOPHER. Sir Walter Herbert, a
  renowned soldier;
  Sir Gilbert Talbot, Sir William Stanley,
  Oxford, redoubted Pembroke, Sir James Blunt,
  And Rice ap Thomas, with a valiant crew;
  And many other of great name and worth;
  And towards London do they bend
    their power,
  If by the way they be not fought withal.
STANLEY. Well, hie thee to thy lord; I kiss
  his hand;
  My letter will resolve him of my mind.
  Farewell.   *Exeunt.*

ACT V

✸ SCENE I ✸
Salisbury. An open place

*Enter the SHERIFF and Guard, with BUCKINGHAM, led
to execution*

BUCKINGHAM. Will not King Richard let me
  speak with him?
SHERIFF. No, my good lord; therefore be patient.
BUCKINGHAM. Hastings, and Edward's children,
  Grey, and Rivers,
  Holy King Henry, and thy fair son Edward,
  Vaughan, and all that have miscarried
  By underhand corrupted foul injustice,
  If that your moody discontented souls
  Do through the clouds behold this present hour,
  Even for revenge mock my destruction!
  This is All-Souls' day, fellow, is it not?
SHERIFF. It is, my lord.
BUCKINGHAM. Why, then All-Souls' day is my
  body's doomsday.
  This is the day which in King Edward's time
  I wish'd might fall on me when I was found
  False to his children and his wife's allies;
  This is the day wherein I wish'd to fall
  By the false faith of him whom most I trusted;
  This, this All-Souls' day to my fearful soul
  Is the determin'd respite of my wrongs;
  That high All-Seer which I dallied with
  Hath turn'd my feigned prayer on my head

And given in earnest what I begg'd in jest.
Thus doth He force the swords of wicked men
To turn their own points in their
  masters' bosoms.
Thus Margaret's curse falls heavy on my neck.
'When he' quoth she 'shall split thy heart
  with sorrow,
Remember Margaret was a prophetess.'
Come lead me, officers, to the block of shame;
Wrong hath but wrong, and blame the due
  of blame.
                              Exeunt.

✸ SCENE II ✸
Camp near Tamworth

*Enter RICHMOND, OXFORD, SIR JAMES BLUNT, SIR
WALTER HERBERT, and Others, with drum and colours*

RICHMOND. Fellows in arms, and my most
  loving friends,
  Bruis'd underneath the yoke of tyranny,
  Thus far into the bowels of the land
  Have we march'd on without impediment;
  And here receive we from our father Stanley
  Lines of fair comfort and encouragement.
  The wretched, bloody, and usurping boar,
  That spoil'd your summer fields and
    fruitful vines,
  Swills your warm blood like wash, and makes
    his trough
  In your embowell'd bosoms-this foul swine
  Is now even in the centre of this isle,
  Near to the town of Leicester, as we learn.
  From Tamworth thither is but one day's march.
  In God's name cheerly on, courageous friends,
  To reap the harvest of perpetual peace
  By this one bloody trial of sharp war.
OXFORD. Every man's conscience is a
  thousand men,
  To fight against this guilty homicide.
HERBERT. I doubt not but his friends will turn
  to us.
BLUNT. He hath no friends but what are friends
  for fear,
  Which in his dearest need will fly from him.
RICHMOND. All for our vantage. Then in God's
  name march.
  True hope is swift and flies with swallow's wings;
  Kings it makes gods, and meaner
    creatures kings.
                              Exeunt.

⚜ SCENE III ⚜
Bosworth Field

Enter KING RICHARD in arms, with NORFOLK,
RATCLIFF, the EARL OF SURREY and Others

KING RICHARD. Here pitch our tent, even here in
  Bosworth field.
  My Lord of Surrey, why look you so sad?
SURREY. My heart is ten times lighter than
  my looks.
KING RICHARD. My Lord of Norfolk!
NORFOLK. Here, most gracious liege.
KING RICHARD. Norfolk, we must have knocks;
  ha! must we not?
NORFOLK. We must both give and take, my
  loving lord.
KING RICHARD. Up with my tent! Here will I
  lie to-night;
        Soldiers begin to set up the KING'S tent
  But where to-morrow? Well, all's one for that.
  Who hath descried the number of the traitors?
NORFOLK. Six or seven thousand is their
  utmost power.
KING RICHARD. Why, our battalia trebles
  that account;
  Besides, the King's name is a tower of strength,
  Which they upon the adverse faction want.
  Up with the tent! Come, noble gentlemen,
  Let us survey the vantage of the ground.
  Call for some men of sound direction.
  Let's lack no discipline, make no delay;
  For, lords, to-morrow is a busy day. *Exeunt.⚜*
    Enter, on the other side of the field, RICHMOND, SIR
  WILLIAM BRANDON, OXFORD, DORSET, and Others.
      Some pitch RICHMOND'S tent
RICHMOND. The weary sun hath made a golden set,
  And by the bright tract of his fiery car
  Gives token of a goodly day to-morrow.
  Sir William Brandon, you shall bear my standard.
  Give me some ink and paper in my tent.
  I'll draw the form and model of our battle,
  Limit each leader to his several charge,
  And part in just proportion our small power.
  My Lord of Oxford-you, Sir William Brandon-
  And you, Sir Walter Herbert-stay with me.
  The Earl of Pembroke keeps his regiment;
  Good Captain Blunt, bear my good night to him,
  And by the second hour in the morning
  Desire the Earl to see me in my tent.
  Yet one thing more, good Captain, do for me-
  Where is Lord Stanley quarter'd, do you know?

BLUNT. Unless I have mista'en his colours much-
  Which well I am assur'd I have not done-
  His regiment lies half a mile at least
  South from the mighty power of the King.
RICHMOND. If without peril it be possible,
  Sweet Blunt, make some good means to speak
    with him
  And give him from me this most needful note.
BLUNT. Upon my life, my lord, I'll undertake it;
  And so, God give you quiet rest to-night!
RICHMOND. Good night, good Captain Blunt.
  Come, gentlemen,
  Let us consult upon to-morrow's business.
  In to my tent; the dew is raw and cold.
            They withdraw into the tent.⚜
    Enter, to his tent, KING RICHARD, NORFOLK,
        RATCLIFF, and CATESBY

KING RICHARD. What is't o'clock?
CATESBY. It's supper-time, my lord;
  It's nine o'clock.
KING RICHARD. I will not sup to-night.
  Give me some ink and paper.
  What, is my beaver easier than it was?
  And all my armour laid into my tent?
CATESBY. It is, my liege; and all things are
  in readiness.
KING RICHARD. Good Norfolk, hie thee to
  thy charge;
  Use careful watch, choose trusty sentinels.
NORFOLK. I go, my lord.
KING RICHARD. Stir with the lark to-morrow,
  gentle Norfolk.
NORFOLK. I warrant you, my lord. *Exit.⚜*
KING RICHARD. Catesby!
CATESBY. My lord?
KING RICHARD. Send out a pursuivant-at-arms
  To Stanley's regiment; bid him bring his power
  Before sunrising, lest his son George fall
  Into the blind cave of eternal night. [*Exit*
  CATESBY]
  Fill me a bowl of wine. Give me a watch.
  Saddle white Surrey for the field to-morrow.
  Look that my staves be sound, and not too heavy.
  Ratcliff!
RATCLIFF. My lord?
KING RICHARD. Saw'st thou the melancholy Lord
  Northumberland?
RATCLIFF. Thomas the Earl of Surrey and himself,
  Much about cock-shut time, from troop to troop
  Went through the army, cheering up
    the soldiers.
KING RICHARD. So, I am satisfied. Give me a bowl
  of wine.

I have not that alacrity of spirit
Nor cheer of mind that I was wont to have.
Set it down. Is ink and paper ready?
RATCLIFF. It is, my lord.
KING RICHARD. Bid my guard watch; leave me.
RATCLIFF, about the mid of night come to
my tent
And help to arm me. Leave me, I say.

Exit RATCLIFF. RICHARD sleeps
Enter STANLEY to RICHMOND in his tent; LORDS
attending

STANLEY. Fortune and victory sit on thy helm!
RICHMOND. All comfort that the dark night
can afford
Be to thy person, noble father-in-law!
Tell me, how fares our loving mother?
STANLEY. I, by attorney, bless thee from
thy mother,
Who prays continually for Richmond's good.
So much for that. The silent hours steal on,
And flaky darkness breaks within the east.
In brief, for so the season bids us be,
Prepare thy battle early in the morning,
And put thy fortune to the arbitrement
Of bloody strokes and mortal-staring war.
I, as I may-that which I would I cannot-
With best advantage will deceive the time
And aid thee in this doubtful shock of arms;
But on thy side I may not be too forward,
Lest, being seen, thy brother, tender George,
Be executed in his father's sight.
Farewell; the leisure and the fearful time
Cuts off the ceremonious vows of love
And ample interchange of sweet discourse
Which so-long-sund'red friends should
dwell upon.
God give us leisure for these rites of love!
Once more, adieu; be valiant, and speed well!
RICHMOND. Good lords, conduct him to
his regiment.
I'll strive with troubled thoughts to take a nap,
Lest leaden slumber peise me down to-morrow
When I should mount with wings of victory.
Once more, good night, kind lords
and gentlemen.

Exeunt all but RICHMOND.

O Thou, whose captain I account myself,
Look on my forces with a gracious eye;
Put in their hands Thy bruising irons of wrath,
That they may crush down with a heavy fall
The usurping helmets of our adversaries!
Make us Thy ministers of chastisement,
That we may praise Thee in the victory!

To Thee I do commend my watchful soul
Ere I let fall the windows of mine eyes.
Sleeping and waking, O, defend me still! *Sleeps*
Enter the GHOST Of YOUNG PRINCE EDWARD, son to
HENRY THE SIXTH

GHOST. *[To RICHARD]* Let me sit heavy on thy
soul to-morrow!
Think how thou stabb'dst me in my prime
of youth
At Tewksbury; despair, therefore, and die!
[To RICHMOND] Be cheerful, Richmond; for the
wronged souls
Of butcher'd princes fight in thy behalf.
King Henry's issue, Richmond, comforts thee.
Enter the GHOST OF HENRY THE SIXTH

GHOST. *[To RICHARD]* When I was mortal, my
anointed body
By thee was punched full of deadly holes.
Think on the Tower and me. Despair, and die.
Harry the Sixth bids thee despair and die.
[To RICHMOND] Virtuous and holy, be
thou conqueror!
Harry, that prophesied thou shouldst be King,
Doth comfort thee in thy sleep. Live
and flourish!
Enter the GHOST OF CLARENCE

GHOST. *[To RICHARD]* Let me sit heavy in thy soul
to-morrow! I that was wash'd to death with
fulsome wine,
Poor Clarence, by thy guile betray'd to death!
To-morrow in the battle think on me,
And fall thy edgeless sword. Despair and die!
[To RICHMOND] Thou offspring of the house
of Lancaster,
The wronged heirs of York do pray for thee.
Good angels guard thy battle! Live and flourish!
Enter the GHOSTS OF RIVERS, GREY, and VAUGHAN

GHOST OF RIVERS. *[To RICHARD]* Let me sit heavy
in thy soul to-morrow,
Rivers that died at Pomfret! Despair and die!
GHOST OF GREY. *[To RICHARD]* Think upon Grey,
and let thy soul despair!
GHOST OF VAUGHAN. *[To RICHARD]* Think upon
Vaughan, and with guilty fear
Let fall thy lance. Despair and die!
ALL. *[To RICHMOND]* Awake, and think our wrongs
in Richard's bosom
Will conquer him. Awake and win the day.
Enter the GHOST OF HASTINGS

GHOST. *[To RICHARD]* Bloody and guilty,
guiltily awake,
And in a bloody battle end thy days!
Think on Lord Hastings. Despair and die.

[*To* RICHMOND] Quiet untroubled soul,
awake, awake!
Arm, fight, and conquer, for fair England's sake!

Enter the GHOSTS *of the two young* PRINCES

GHOSTS. [*To* RICHARD] Dream on thy cousins
smothered in the Tower.
Let us be lead within thy bosom, Richard,
And weigh thee down to ruin, shame, and death!
Thy nephews' souls bid thee despair and die.
[*To* RICHMOND] Sleep, Richmond, sleep in peace,
and wake in joy;
Good angels guard thee from the boar's annoy!
Live, and beget a happy race of kings!
Edward's unhappy sons do bid thee flourish.

Enter the GHOST OF LADY ANNE, *his wife*

GHOST. [*To* RICHARD] Richard, thy wife, that
wretched Anne thy wife
That never slept a quiet hour with thee
Now fills thy sleep with perturbations.
To-morrow in the battle think on me,
And fall thy edgeless sword. Despair and die.
[*To* RICHMOND] Thou quiet soul, sleep thou a
quiet sleep;
Dream of success and happy victory.
Thy adversary's wife doth pray for thee.

Enter the GHOST OF BUCKINGHAM

GHOST. [*To* RICHARD] The first was I that help'd
thee to the crown;
The last was I that felt thy tyranny.
O, in the battle think on Buckingham,
And die in terror of thy guiltiness!
Dream on, dream on of bloody deeds and death;
Fainting, despair; despairing, yield thy breath!
[*To* RICHMOND] I died for hope ere I could lend
thee aid;
But cheer thy heart and be thou not dismay'd:
God and good angels fight on Richmond's side;
And Richard falls in height of all his pride.

The GHOSTS *vanish.* ✍ RICHARD *starts out of his dream*

KING RICHARD. Give me another horse. Bind up
my wounds.
Have mercy, Jesu! Soft! I did but dream.
O coward conscience, how dost thou afflict me!
The lights burn blue. It is now dead midnight.
Cold fearful drops stand on my trembling flesh.
What do I fear? Myself? There's none else by.
Richard loves Richard; that is, I am I.
Is there a murderer here? No-yes, I am.
Then fly. What, from myself? Great reason why-
Lest I revenge. What, myself upon myself!
Alack, I love myself. Wherefore? For any good
That I myself have done unto myself?
O, no! Alas, I rather hate myself

For hateful deeds committed by myself!
I am a villain; yet I lie, I am not.
Fool, of thyself speak well. Fool, do not flatter.
My conscience hath a thousand several tongues,
And every tongue brings in a several tale,
And every tale condemns me for a villain.
Perjury, perjury, in the high'st degree;
Murder, stern murder, in the dir'st degree;
All several sins, all us'd in each degree,
Throng to the bar, crying all 'Guilty! guilty!'
I shall despair. There is no creature loves me;
And if I die no soul will pity me:
And wherefore should they, since that I myself
Find in myself no pity to myself?
Methought the souls of all that I had murder'd
Came to my tent, and every one did threat
To-morrow's vengeance on the head of Richard.

Enter RATCLIFF

RATCLIFF. My lord!
KING RICHARD. Zounds, who is there?
RATCLIFF. Ratcliff, my lord; 'tis I. The early village-
cock
Hath twice done salutation to the morn;
Your friends are up and buckle on their armour.
KING RICHARD. O Ratcliff, I have dream'd a
fearful dream!
What think'st thou-will our friends prove
all true?
RATCLIFF. No doubt, my lord.
KING RICHARD. O Ratcliff, I fear, I fear.
RATCLIFF. Nay, good my lord, be not afraid
of shadows.
KING RICHARD. By the apostle Paul, shadows to-
night
Have stuck more terror to the soul of Richard
Than can the substance of ten thousand soldiers
Armed in proof and led by shallow Richmond.
'Tis not yet near day. Come, go with me;
Under our tents I'll play the eaves-dropper,
To see if any mean to shrink from me. *Exeunt.* ✍

Enter the LORDS *to* RICHMOND *sitting in his tent*

LORDS. Good morrow, Richmond!
RICHMOND. Cry mercy, lords and
watchful gentlemen,
That you have ta'en a tardy sluggard here.
LORDS. How have you slept, my lord?
RICHMOND. The sweetest sleep and fairest-
boding dreams
That ever ent'red in a drowsy head
Have I since your departure had, my lords.
Methought their souls whose bodies
Richard murder'd
Came to my tent and cried on victory.

I promise you my soul is very jocund
In the remembrance of so fair a dream.
How far into the morning is it, lords?
LORDS. Upon the stroke of four.
RICHMOND. Why, then 'tis time to arm and give
    direction. [His Oration to his Soldiers]
More than I have said, loving countrymen,
The leisure and enforcement of the time
Forbids to dwell upon; yet remember this:
God and our good cause fight upon our side;
The prayers of holy saints and wronged souls,
Like high-rear'd bulwarks, stand before
    our faces;
Richard except, those whom we fight against
Had rather have us win than him they follow.
For what is he they follow? Truly, gentlemen,
A bloody tyrant and a homicide;
One rais'd in blood, and one in
    blood establish'd;
One that made means to come by what he hath,
And slaughtered those that were the means to
    help him;
A base foul stone, made precious by the foil
Of England's chair, where he is falsely set;
One that hath ever been God's enemy.
Then if you fight against God's enemy,
God will in justice ward you as his soldiers;
If you do sweat to put a tyrant down,
You sleep in peace, the tyrant being slain;
If you do fight against your country's foes,
Your country's foes shall pay your pains the hire;
If you do fight in safeguard of your wives,
Your wives shall welcome home the conquerors;
If you do free your children from the sword,
Your children's children quit it in your age.
Then, in the name of God and all these rights,
Advance your standards, draw your
    willing swords.
For me, the ransom of my bold attempt
Shall be this cold corpse on the earth's cold face;
But if I thrive, the gain of my attempt
The least of you shall share his part thereof.
Sound drums and trumpets boldly
    and cheerfully;
God and Saint George! Richmond and victory!
                                    Exeunt.

Re-enter KING RICHARD, RATCLIFF, Attendants, and
                        Forces
KING RICHARD. What said Northumberland as
    touching Richmond?
RATCLIFF. That he was never trained up in arms.
KING RICHARD. He said the truth; and what said
    Surrey then?

RATCLIFF. He smil'd, and said 'The better for
    our purpose.'
KING He was in the right; and so indeed it is.
    [Clock strikes]
Tell the clock there. Give me a calendar.
Who saw the sun to-day?
RATCLIFF. Not I, my lord.
KING RICHARD. Then he disdains to shine; for by
    the book
He should have brav'd the east an hour ago.
A black day will it be to somebody.
Ratcliff!
RATCLIFF. My lord?
KING RICHARD. The sun will not be seen to-day;
The sky doth frown and lour upon our army.
I would these dewy tears were from the ground.
Not shine to-day! Why, what is that to me
More than to Richmond? For the
    selfsame heaven
That frowns on me looks sadly upon him.
                        Enter NORFOLK
NORFOLK. Arm, arm, my lord; the foe vaunts in
    the field.
KING RICHARD. Come, bustle, bustle; caparison
    my horse;
Call up Lord Stanley, bid him bring his power.
I will lead forth my soldiers to the plain,
And thus my battle shall be ordered:
My foreward shall be drawn out all in length,
Consisting equally of horse and foot;
Our archers shall be placed in the midst.
John Duke of Norfolk, Thomas Earl of Surrey,
Shall have the leading of this foot and horse.
They thus directed, we will follow
In the main battle, whose puissance on
    either side
Shall be well winged with our chiefest horse.
This, and Saint George to boot! What
    think'st thou,
Norfolk?
NORFOLK. A good direction, warlike sovereign.
This found I on my tent this morning.
                    He sheweth him a paper
KING RICHARD. [Reads] 'Jockey of Norfolk, be not
    so bold,
For Dickon thy master is bought and sold.'
A thing devised by the enemy.
Go, gentlemen, every man unto his charge.
Let not our babbling dreams affright our souls;
Conscience is but a word that cowards use,
Devis'd at first to keep the strong in awe.
Our strong arms be our conscience, swords
    our law.

March on, join bravely, let us to it pell-mell;
If not to heaven, then hand in hand to hell. [His
    Oration to his Army]
What shall I say more than I have inferr'd?
Remember whom you are to cope withal-
A sort of vagabonds, rascals, and runaways,
A scum of Britaines, and base lackey peasants,
Whom their o'er-cloyed country vomits forth
To desperate adventures and
    assur'd destruction.
You sleeping safe, they bring to you unrest;
You having lands, and bless'd with
    beauteous wives,
They would restrain the one, distain the other.
And who doth lead them but a paltry fellow,
Long kept in Britaine at our mother's cost?
A milk-sop, one that never in his life
Felt so much cold as over shoes in snow?
Let's whip these stragglers o'er the seas again;
Lash hence these over-weening rags of France,
These famish'd beggars, weary of their lives;
Who, but for dreaming on this fond exploit,
For want of means, poor rats, had
    hang'd themselves.
If we be conquered, let men conquer us,
And not these bastard Britaines, whom
    our fathers
Have in their own land beaten, bobb'd,
    and thump'd,
And, in record, left them the heirs of shame.
Shall these enjoy our lands? lie with our wives,
Ravish our daughters? [Drum afar off] Hark! I hear
    their drum.
Fight, gentlemen of England! Fight, bold yeomen!
Draw, archers, draw your arrows to the head!
Spur your proud horses hard, and ride
    in blood;
Amaze the welkin with your broken staves!
            Enter a MESSENGER
What says Lord Stanley? Will he bring
    his power?
MESSENGER. My lord, he doth deny to come.
KING RICHARD. Off with his son George's head!
NORFOLK. My lord, the enemy is pass'd
    the marsh.
After the battle let George Stanley die.
KING RICHARD. A thousand hearts are great
    within my bosom.
Advance our standards, set upon our foes;
Our ancient word of courage, fair Saint George,
Inspire us with the spleen of fiery dragons!
Upon them! Victory sits on our helms.
                        Exeunt.

⚜ SCENE IV ⚜
Another part of the field

Alarum; excursions.
Enter NORFOLK and Forces; to him CATESBY

CATESBY. Rescue, my Lord of Norfolk,
    rescue, rescue!
The King enacts more wonders than a man,
Daring an opposite to every danger.
His horse is slain, and all on foot he fights,
Seeking for Richmond in the throat of death.
Rescue, fair lord, or else the day is lost.
        Alarums. Enter KING RICHARD
KING RICHARD. A horse! a horse! my kingdom
    for a horse!
CATESBY. Withdraw, my lord! I'll help you to
    a horse.
KING RICHARD. Slave, I have set my life upon
    a cast
And I will stand the hazard of the die.
I think there be six Richmonds in the field;
Five have I slain to-day instead of him.
A horse! a horse! my kingdom for a horse!
                        Exeunt.

⚜ SCENE V ⚜
Another part of the field

Alarum. Enter RICHARD and RICHMOND; they fight;
RICHARD is slain. Retreat and flourish. Enter RICHMOND,
STANLEY bearing the crown, with other Lords

RICHMOND. God and your arms be prais'd,
    victorious friends;
The day is ours, the bloody dog is dead.
STANLEY. Courageous Richmond, well hast thou
    acquit thee!
Lo, here, this long-usurped royalty
From the dead temples of this bloody wretch
Have I pluck'd off, to grace thy brows withal.
Wear it, enjoy it, and make much of it.
RICHMOND. Great God of heaven, say Amen to all!
But, tell me is young George Stanley living?
STANLEY . He is, my lord, and safe in
    Leicester town,
Whither, if it please you, we may now
    withdraw us.
RICHMOND. What men of name are slain on
    either side?

STANLEY . John Duke of Norfolk, Walter
  Lord Ferrers,
  Sir Robert Brakenbury, and Sir William Brandon.
RICHMOND. Inter their bodies as becomes
  their births.
  Proclaim a pardon to the soldiers fled
  That in submission will return to us.
  And then, as we have ta'en the sacrament,
  We will unite the white rose and the red.
  Smile heaven upon this fair conjunction,
  That long have frown'd upon their enmity!
  What traitor hears me, and says not Amen?
  England hath long been mad, and
   scarr'd herself;
  The brother blindly shed the brother's blood,
  The father rashly slaughter'd his own son,
  The son, compell'd, been butcher to the sire;
  All this divided York and Lancaster,
  Divided in their dire division,
  O, now let Richmond and Elizabeth,
  The true succeeders of each royal house,
  By God's fair ordinance conjoin together!
  And let their heirs, God, if thy will be so,
  Enrich the time to come with smooth-
   fac'd peace,
  With smiling plenty, and fair prosperous days!
  Abate the edge of traitors, gracious Lord,
  That would reduce these bloody days again
  And make poor England weep in streams
   of blood!
  Let them not live to taste this land's increase
  That would with treason wound this fair
   land's peace!
  Now civil wounds are stopp'd, peace lives again-
  That she may long live here, God say Amen!

Exeunt.

The End

1611

King
Henry VIII

Dramatis Personae

KING HENRY THE EIGHTH
CARDINAL WOLSEY
CARDINAL CAMPEIUS
CAPUCIUS, Ambassador from the Emperor
Charles V
CRANMER, ARCHBISHOP OF CANTERBURY
DUKE OF NORFOLK
DUKE OF BUCKINGHAM
DUKE OF SUFFOLK
EARL OF SURREY
LORD CHAMBERLAIN
LORD CHANCELLOR
GARDINER, BISHOP OF WINCHESTER
BISHOP OF LINCOLN
LORD ABERGAVENNY
LORD SANDYS
SIR HENRY GUILDFORD
SIR THOMAS LOVELL
SIR ANTHONY DENNY
SIR NICHOLAS VAUX
SECRETARIES to Wolsey
CROMWELL, servant to Wolsey
GRIFFITH, gentleman-usher to Queen Katharine
THREE GENTLEMEN
DOCTOR BUTTS, physician to the King
GARTER KING-AT-ARMS
SURVEYOR to the Duke of Buckingham
BRANDON, and a SERGEANT-AT-ARMS
DOORKEEPER of the Council chamber
PORTER, and his MAN
PAGE to Gardiner
A CRIER

QUEEN KATHARINE, wife to King Henry,
afterwards divorced
ANNE BULLEN, her Maid of Honour,
afterwards Queen
AN OLD LADY, friend to Anne Bullen
PATIENCE, woman to Queen Katharine

Lord Mayor, Aldermen, Lords and Ladies in
the Dumb Shows; Women attending upon the
Queen; Scribes, Officers, Guards, and other
Attendants; Spirits

SCENE
London: Westminster: Kimbolton

PROLOGUE

I come no more to make you laugh; things now
That bear a weighty and a serious brow,
Sad, high, and working, full of state and woe,
Such noble scenes as draw the eye to flow,
We now present. Those that can pity here
May, if they think it well, let fall a tear:
The subject will deserve it. Such as give
Their money out of hope they may believe
May here find truth too. Those that come to see
Only a show or two, and so agree
The play may pass, if they be still and willing,
I'll undertake may see away their shilling
Richly in two short hours. Only they
That come to hear a merry bawdy play,
A noise of targets, or to see a fellow
In a long motley coat guarded with yellow,
Will be deceiv'd; for, gentle hearers, know,
To rank our chosen truth with such a show
As fool and fight is, beside forfeiting
Our own brains, and the opinion that we bring
To make that only true we now intend,
Will leave us never an understanding friend.
Therefore, for goodness sake, and as you
  are known
The first and happiest hearers of the town,
Be sad, as we would make ye. Think ye see
The very persons of our noble story
As they were living; think you see them great,
And follow'd with the general throng and sweat
Of thousand friends; then, in a moment, see
How soon this mightiness meets misery.
And if you can be merry then, I'll say
A man may weep upon his wedding-day.

ACT I

SCENE I
London. The palace

*Enter the DUKE OF NORFOLK at one door; at the
other, the DUKE OF BUCKINGHAM and the LORD
ABERGAVENNY*

BUCKINGHAM. Good morrow, and well met.
  How have ye done
  Since last we saw in France?
NORFOLK. I thank your Grace,
  Healthful; and ever since a fresh admirer
  Of what I saw there.
BUCKINGHAM. An untimely ague
  Stay'd me a prisoner in my chamber when
  Those suns of glory, those two lights of men,
  Met in the vale of Andren.
NORFOLK. 'Twixt Guynes and Arde-
  I was then present, saw them salute
    on horseback;
  Beheld them, when they lighted, how
    they clung
  In their embracement, as they grew together;
  Which had they, what four thron'd ones could
    have weigh'd
  Such a compounded one?
BUCKINGHAM. All the whole time
  I was my chamber's prisoner.
NORFOLK. Then you lost
  The view of earthly glory; men might say,
  Till this time pomp was single, but now married
  To one above itself. Each following day
  Became the next day's master, till the last
  Made former wonders its. To-day the French,
  All clinquant, all in gold, like heathen gods,
  Shone down the English; and to-morrow they
  Made Britain India: every man that stood
  Show'd like a mine. Their dwarfish pages were
  As cherubins, all gilt; the madams too,
  Not us'd to toil, did almost sweat to bear
  The pride upon them, that their very labour
  Was to them as a painting. Now this masque
  Was cried incomparable; and th' ensuing night
  Made it a fool and beggar. The two kings,
  Equal in lustre, were now best, now worst,
  As presence did present them: him in eye
  Still him in praise; and being present both,
  'Twas said they saw but one, and no discerner

Durst wag his tongue in censure. When
  these suns-
For so they phrase 'em-by their
  heralds challeng'd
The noble spirits to arms, they did perform
Beyond thought's compass, that former
  fabulous story,
Being now seen possible enough, got credit,
That Bevis was believ'd.

BUCKINGHAM. O, you go far!

NORFOLK. As I belong to worship, and affect
  In honour honesty, the tract of ev'rything
  Would by a good discourser lose some life
  Which action's self was tongue to. All
    was royal:
  To the disposing of it nought rebell'd;
  Order gave each thing view. The office did
  Distinctly his full function.

BUCKINGHAM. Who did guide-
  I mean, who set the body and the limbs
  Of this great sport together, as you guess?

NORFOLK. One, certes, that promises
    no element
  In such a business.

BUCKINGHAM. I pray you, who, my lord?

NORFOLK. All this was ord'red by the
    good discretion
  Of the right reverend Cardinal of York.

BUCKINGHAM. The devil speed him! No man's
    pie is freed
  From his ambitious finger. What had he
  To do in these fierce vanities? I wonder
  That such a keech can with his very bulk
  Take up the rays o' th' beneficial sun,
  And keep it from the earth.

NORFOLK. Surely, sir,
  There's in him stuff that puts him to
    these ends;
  For, being not propp'd by ancestry,
    whose grace
  Chalks successors their way, nor call'd upon
  For high feats done to th' crown, neither allied
  To eminent assistants, but spider-like,
  Out of his self-drawing web, 'a gives us note
  The force of his own merit makes his way-
  A gift that heaven gives for him, which buys
  A place next to the King.

ABERGAVENNY. I cannot tell
  What heaven hath given him-let some
    graver eye
  Pierce into that; but I can see his pride
  Peep through each part of him. Whence has
  he that?

If not from hell, the devil is a niggard
  Or has given all before, and he begins
  A new hell in himself.

BUCKINGHAM. Why the devil,
  Upon this French going out, took he
    upon him-
  Without the privity o' th' King-t' appoint
  Who should attend on him? He makes up
    the file
  Of all the gentry; for the most part such
  To whom as great a charge as little honour
  He meant to lay upon; and his own letter,
  The honourable board of council out,
  Must fetch him in he papers.

ABERGAVENNY. I do know
  Kinsmen of mine, three at the least, that have
  By this so sicken'd their estates that never
  They shall abound as formerly.

BUCKINGHAM. O, many
  Have broke their backs with laying manors
    on 'em
  For this great journey. What did this vanity
  But minister communication of
  A most poor issue?

NORFOLK. Grievingly I think
  The peace between the French and us
    not values
  The cost that did conclude it.

BUCKINGHAM. Every man,
  After the hideous storm that follow'd, was
  A thing inspir'd, and, not consulting, broke
  Into a general prophecy-that this tempest,
  Dashing the garment of this peace, aboded
  The sudden breach on't.

NORFOLK. Which is budded out;
  For France hath flaw'd the league, and
    hath attach'd
  Our merchants' goods at Bordeaux.

ABERGAVENNY. Is it therefore
  Th' ambassador is silenc'd?

NORFOLK. Marry, is't.

ABERGAVENNY. A proper tide of a peace,
    and purchas'd
  At a superfluous rate!

BUCKINGHAM. Why, all this business
  Our reverend Cardinal carried.

NORFOLK. Like it your Grace,
  The state takes notice of the private difference
  Betwixt you and the Cardinal. I advise you-
  And take it from a heart that wishes
    towards you
  Honour and plenteous safety-that you read
  The Cardinal's malice and his potency

Together; to consider further, that
What his high hatred would effect wants not
A minister in his power. You know his nature,
That he's revengeful; and I know his sword
Hath a sharp edge-it's long and't may be said
It reaches far, and where 'twill not extend,
Thither he darts it. Bosom up my counsel
You'll find it wholesome. Lo, where comes
  that rock
That I advise your shunning.

Enter CARDINAL WOLSEY, the purse borne before
him, certain of the Guard, and two SECRETARIES with
papers. The CARDINAL in his passage fixeth his eye on
BUCKINGHAM, and BUCKINGHAM on him, both full
                                    of disdain

WOLSEY. The Duke of Buckingham's
  surveyor? Ha!
  Where's his examination?
SECRETARY. Here, so please you.
WOLSEY. Is he in person ready?
SECRETARY. Ay, please your Grace.
WOLSEY. Well, we shall then know more,
  and Buckingham
  Shall lessen this big look.

                    Exeunt WOLSEY and his train.

BUCKINGHAM. This butcher's cur is venom-
  mouth'd, and I
  Have not the power to muzzle him;
    therefore best
  Not wake him in his slumber. A beggar's book
  Outworths a noble's blood.
NORFOLK. What, are you chaf'd?
  Ask God for temp'rance; that's th'
    appliance only
  Which your disease requires.
BUCKINGHAM. I read in's looks
  Matter against me, and his eye revil'd
  Me as his abject object. At this instant
  He bores me with some trick. He's gone to
    th' King;
  I'll follow, and outstare him.
NORFOLK. Stay, my lord,
  And let your reason with your choler question
  What 'tis you go about. To climb steep hills
  Requires slow pace at first. Anger is like
  A full hot horse, who being allow'd his way,
  Self-mettle tires him. Not a man in England
  Can advise me like you; be to yourself
  As you would to your friend.
BUCKINGHAM. I'll to the King,
  And from a mouth of honour quite cry down
  This Ipswich fellow's insolence; or proclaim
  There's difference in no persons.

NORFOLK. Be advis'd:
  Heat not a furnace for your foe so hot
  That it do singe yourself. We may outrun
  By violent swiftness that which we run at,
  And lose by over-running. Know you not
  The fire that mounts the liquor till't run o'er
  In seeming to augment it wastes it? Be advis'd.
  I say again there is no English soul
  More stronger to direct you than yourself,
  If with the sap of reason you would quench
  Or but allay the fire of passion.
BUCKINGHAM. Sir,
  I am thankful to you, and I'll go along
  By your prescription; but this
    top-proud fellow-
  Whom from the flow of gall I name not, but
  From sincere motions, by intelligence,
  And proofs as clear as founts in July when
  We see each grain of gravel-I do know
  To be corrupt and treasonous.
NORFOLK. Say not treasonous.
BUCKINGHAM. To th' King I'll say't, and make
    my vouch as strong
  As shore of rock. Attend: this holy fox,
  Or wolf, or both-for he is equal rav'nous
  As he is subtle, and as prone to mischief
  As able to perform't, his mind and place
  Infecting one another, yea, reciprocally-
  Only to show his pomp as well in France
  As here at home, suggests the King our master
  To this last costly treaty, th' interview
  That swallowed so much treasure and like
    a glass
  Did break i' th' wrenching.
NORFOLK. Faith, and so it did.
BUCKINGHAM. Pray, give me favour, sir; this
    cunning cardinal
  The articles o' th' combination drew
  As himself pleas'd; and they were ratified
  As he cried 'Thus let be' to as much end
  As give a crutch to th' dead. But our Count-
    Cardinal
  Has done this, and 'tis well; for worthy Wolsey,
  Who cannot err, he did it. Now this follows,
  Which, as I take it, is a kind of puppy
  To th' old dam treason: Charles the Emperor,
  Under pretence to see the Queen his aunt-
  For 'twas indeed his colour, but he came
  To whisper Wolsey-here makes visitation-
  His fears were that the interview betwixt
  England and France might through their amity
  Breed him some prejudice; for from
    this league

Peep'd harms that menac'd him-privily
Deals with our Cardinal; and, as I trow-
Which I do well, for I am sure the Emperor
Paid ere he promis'd; whereby his suit
 was granted
Ere it was ask'd-but when the way was made,
And pav'd with gold, the Emperor
 thus desir'd,
That he would please to alter the
 King's course,
And break the foresaid peace. Let the
 King know,
As soon he shall by me, that thus the Cardinal
Does buy and sell his honour as he pleases,
And for his own advantage.

NORFOLK. I am sorry
To hear this of him, and could wish he were
Something mistaken in't.

BUCKINGHAM. No, not a syllable:
I do pronounce him in that very shape
He shall appear in proof.

*Enter BRANDON, a SERGEANT-AT-ARMS before him,
and two or three of the Guard*

BRANDON. Your office, sergeant: execute it.

SERGEANT. Sir,
My lord the Duke of Buckingham, and Earl
Of Hereford, Stafford, and Northampton, I
Arrest thee of high treason, in the name
Of our most sovereign King.

BUCKINGHAM. Lo you, my lord,
The net has fall'n upon me! I shall perish
Under device and practice.

BRANDON. I am sorry
To see you ta'en from liberty, to look on
The business present; 'tis his
 Highness' pleasure
You shall to th' Tower.

BUCKINGHAM. It will help nothing
To plead mine innocence; for that dye is
 on me
Which makes my whit'st part black. The will
 of heav'n
Be done in this and all things! I obey.
O my Lord Aberga'ny, fare you well!

BRANDON. Nay, he must bear you company.
[To ABERGAVENNY] The King
Is pleas'd you shall to th' Tower, till you know
How he determines further.

ABERGAVENNY. As the Duke said,
The will of heaven be done, and the
 King's pleasure
By me obey'd.

BRANDON. Here is warrant from

The King t' attach Lord Montacute and
 the bodies
Of the Duke's confessor, John de la Car,
One Gilbert Peck, his chancellor-

BUCKINGHAM. So, so!
These are the limbs o' th' plot; no more,
 I hope.

BRANDON. A monk o' th' Chartreux.

BUCKINGHAM. O, Nicholas Hopkins?

BRANDON. He.

BUCKINGHAM. My surveyor is false. The o'er-
 great Cardinal
Hath show'd him gold; my life is
 spann'd already.
I am the shadow of poor Buckingham,
Whose figure even this instant cloud puts on
By dark'ning my clear sun. My lord, farewell.

Exeunt.

✣ SCENE II ✣
London. The Council Chamber

*Cornets. Enter KING HENRY, leaning on the CARDINAL'S
shoulder, the NOBLES, and SIR THOMAS LOVELL, with
Others. The CARDINAL places himself under the KING'S feet
on his right side*

KING. My life itself, and the best heart of it,
Thanks you for this great care; I stood i'
 th' level
Of a full-charg'd confederacy, and give thanks
To you that chok'd it. Let be call'd before us
That gentleman of Buckingham's. In person
I'll hear his confessions justify;
And point by point the treasons of his master
He shall again relate.

*A noise within, crying 'Room for the Queen!' Enter the
QUEEN, usher'd by the DUKES OF NORFOLK and
SUFFOLK; she kneels. The KING riseth from his state, takes
her up, kisses and placeth her by him*

QUEEN KATHARINE. Nay, we must longer kneel:
I am a suitor.

KING. Arise, and take place by us. Half your suit
Never name to us: you have half our power.
The other moiety ere you ask is given;
Repeat your will, and take it.

QUEEN KATHARINE. Thank your Majesty.
That you would love yourself, and in that love
Not unconsidered leave your honour nor
The dignity of your office, is the point
Of my petition.

KING. Lady mine, proceed.

QUEEN KATHARINE. I am solicited, not by a few,
  And those of true condition, that your subjects
  Are in great grievance: there have
    been commissions
  Sent down among 'em which hath flaw'd
    the heart
  Of all their loyalties; wherein, although,
  My good Lord Cardinal, they vent reproaches
  Most bitterly on you as putter-on
  Of these exactions, yet the King our master-
  Whose honour Heaven shield from soil!-even
    he escapes not
  Language unmannerly; yea, such which breaks
  The sides of loyalty, and almost appears
  In loud rebellion.
NORFOLK. Not almost appears-
  It doth appear; for, upon these taxations,
  The clothiers all, not able to maintain
  The many to them 'longing, have put off
  The spinsters, carders, fullers, weavers, who
  Unfit for other life, compell'd by hunger
  And lack of other means, in desperate manner
  Daring th' event to th' teeth, are all in uproar,
  And danger serves among them.
KING. Taxation!
  Wherein? and what taxation? My Lord Cardinal,
  You that are blam'd for it alike with us,
  Know you of this taxation?
WOLSEY. Please you, sir,
  I know but of a single part in aught
  Pertains to th' state, and front but in that file
  Where others tell steps with me.
QUEEN KATHARINE. No, my lord!
  You know no more than others! But you frame
  Things that are known alike, which are
    not wholesome
  To those which would not know them, and
    yet must
  Perforce be their acquaintance.
    These exactions,
  Whereof my sovereign would have note,
    they are
  Most pestilent to th' hearing; and to bear 'em
  The back is sacrifice to th' load. They say
  They are devis'd by you, or else you suffer
  Too hard an exclamation.
KING. Still exaction!
  The nature of it? In what kind, let's know,
  Is this exaction?
QUEEN KATHARINE. I am much too venturous
  In tempting of your patience, but am bold'ned
  Under your promis'd pardon. The
    subjects' grief

Comes through commissions, which compels
    from each
  The sixth part of his substance, to be levied
  Without delay; and the pretence for this
  Is nam'd your wars in France. This makes
    bold mouths;
  Tongues spit their duties out, and cold
    hearts freeze
  Allegiance in them; their curses now
  Live where their prayers did; and it's come
    to pass
  This tractable obedience is a slave
  To each incensed will. I would your Highness
  Would give it quick consideration, for
  There is no primer business.
KING. By my life,
  This is against our pleasure.
WOLSEY. And for me,
  I have no further gone in this than by
  A single voice; and that not pass'd me but
  By learned approbation of the judges. If I am
  Traduc'd by ignorant tongues, which
    neither know
  My faculties nor person, yet will be
  The chronicles of my doing, let me say
  'Tis but the fate of place, and the rough brake
  That virtue must go through. We must not stint
  Our necessary actions in the fear
  To cope malicious censurers, which ever
  As rav'nous fishes do a vessel follow
  That is new-trimm'd, but benefit no further
  Than vainly longing. What we oft do best,
  By sick interpreters, once weak ones, is
  Not ours, or not allow'd; what worst, as oft
  Hitting a grosser quality, is cried up
  For our best act. If we shall stand still,
  In fear our motion will be mock'd or carp'd at,
  We should take root here where we sit, or sit
  State-statues only.
KING. Things done well
  And with a care exempt themselves from fear:
  Things done without example, in their issue
  Are to be fear'd. Have you a precedent
  Of this commission? I believe, not any.
  We must not rend our subjects from our laws,
  And stick them in our will. Sixth part of each?
  A trembling contribution! Why, we take
  From every tree lop, bark, and part o'
    th' timber;
  And though we leave it with a root,
    thus hack'd,
  The air will drink the sap. To every county
  Where this is question'd send our letters with

Free pardon to each man that has denied
The force of this commission. Pray, look to't;
I put it to your care.
WOLSEY. *[Aside to the SECRETARY]* A word
  with you.
Let there be letters writ to every shire
Of the King's grace and pardon. The
  grieved commons
Hardly conceive of me-let it be nois'd
That through our intercession
  this revokement
And pardon comes. I shall anon advise you
Further in the proceeding. *Exit SECRETARY*
     Enter SURVEYOR
QUEEN KATHARINE. I am sorry that the Duke
  of Buckingham
Is run in your displeasure.
KING. It grieves many.
The gentleman is learn'd and a most
  rare speaker;
To nature none more bound; his training such
That he may furnish and instruct
  great teachers
And never seek for aid out of himself. Yet see,
When these so noble benefits shall prove
Not well dispos'd, the mind growing
  once corrupt,
They turn to vicious forms, ten times
  more ugly
Than ever they were fair. This man
  so complete,
Who was enroll'd 'mongst wonders, and
  when we,
Almost with ravish'd list'ning, could not find
His hour of speech a minute-he, my lady,
Hath into monstrous habits put the graces
That once were his, and is become as black
As if besmear'd in hell. Sit by us; you
  shall hear-
This was his gentleman in trust-of him
Things to strike honour sad. Bid him recount
The fore-recited practices, whereof
We cannot feel too little, hear too much.
WOLSEY. Stand forth, and with bold spirit relate
  what you,
Most like a careful subject, have collected
Out of the Duke of Buckingham.
KING. Speak freely.
SURVEYOR. First, it was usual with him-
  every day
It would infect his speech-that if the King
Should without issue die, he'll carry it so
To make the sceptre his. These very words

I've heard him utter to his son-in-law,
Lord Aberga'ny, to whom by oath he menac'd
Revenge upon the Cardinal.
WOLSEY. Please your Highness, note
This dangerous conception in this point:
Not friended by his wish, to your high person
His will is most malignant, and it stretches
Beyond you to your friends.
QUEEN KATHARINE. My learn'd Lord Cardinal,
  Deliver all with charity.
KING. Speak on.
How grounded he his title to the crown
Upon our fail? To this point hast thou
  heard him
At any time speak aught?
SURVEYOR. He was brought to this
By a vain prophecy of Nicholas Henton.
KING. What was that Henton?
SURVEYOR. Sir, a Chartreux friar,
His confessor, who fed him every minute
With words of sovereignty.
KING. How know'st thou this?
SURVEYOR. Not long before your Highness
  sped to France,
The Duke being at the Rose, within the parish
Saint Lawrence Poultney, did of me demand
What was the speech among the Londoners
Concerning the French journey. I replied
Men fear'd the French would prove perfidious,
To the King's danger. Presently the Duke
Said 'twas the fear indeed and that he doubted
'Twould prove the verity of certain words
Spoke by a holy monk 'that oft', says he,
'Hath sent to me, wishing me to permit
John de la Car, my chaplain, a choice hour
To hear from him a matter of some moment;
Whom after under the confession's seal
He solemnly had sworn that what he spoke
My chaplain to no creature living but
To me should utter, with demure confidence
This pausingly ensu'd: "Neither the King
  nor's heirs,
Tell you the Duke, shall prosper; bid
  him strive
To gain the love o' th' commonalty; the Duke
Shall govern England." '
QUEEN KATHARINE. If I know you well,
You were the Duke's surveyor, and lost
  your office
On the complaint o' th' tenants. Take good heed
You charge not in your spleen a noble person
And spoil your nobler soul. I say, take heed;
Yes, heartily beseech you.

KING. Let him on.
Go forward.
SURVEYOR. On my soul, I'll speak but truth.
I told my lord the Duke, by th' devil's illusions
The monk might be deceiv'd, and that 'twas
dangerous for him
To ruminate on this so far, until
It forg'd him some design, which,
being believ'd,
It was much like to do. He answer'd 'Tush,
It can do me no damage'; adding further
That, had the King in his last sickness fail'd,
The Cardinal's and Sir Thomas Lovell's heads
Should have gone off.
KING. Ha! what, so rank? Ah ha!
There's mischief in this man. Canst thou
say further?
SURVEYOR. I can, my liege.
KING. Proceed.
SURVEYOR. Being at Greenwich,
After your Highness had reprov'd the Duke
About Sir William Bulmer-
KING. I remember
Of such a time: being my sworn servant,
The Duke retain'd him his. But on:
what hence?
SURVEYOR. 'If' quoth he 'I for this had
been committed-
As to the Tower I thought-I would have play'd
The part my father meant to act upon
Th' usurper Richard; who, being at Salisbury,
Made suit to come in's presence, which
if granted,
As he made semblance of his duty, would
Have put his knife into him.'
KING. A giant traitor!
WOLSEY. Now, madam, may his Highness live
in freedom,
And this man out of prison?
QUEEN KATHARINE. God mend all!
KING. There's something more would out of
thee: what say'st?
SURVEYOR. After 'the Duke his father' with
the 'knife',
He stretch'd him, and, with one hand on
his dagger,
Another spread on's breast, mounting
his eyes,
He did discharge a horrible oath,
whose tenour
Was, were he evil us'd, he would outgo
His father by as much as a performance
Does an irresolute purpose.

KING. There's his period,
To sheath his knife in us. He is attach'd;
Call him to present trial. If he may
Find mercy in the law, 'tis his; if none,
Let him not seek't of us. By day and night!
He's traitor to th' height.

Exeunt.

✿ SCENE III ✿
London. The palace

Enter the LORD CHAMBERLAIN and LORD SANDYS

CHAMBERLAIN. Is't possible the spells of France
should juggle
Men into such strange mysteries?
SANDYS. New customs,
Though they be never so ridiculous,
Nay, let 'em be unmanly, yet are follow'd.
CHAMBERLAIN. As far as I see, all the good
our English
Have got by the late voyage is but merely
A fit or two o' th' face; but they are shrewd ones;
For when they hold 'em, you would
swear directly
Their very noses had been counsellors
To Pepin or Clotharius, they keep state so.
SANDYS. They have all new legs, and lame ones.
One would take it,
That never saw 'em pace before, the spavin
Or springhalt reign'd among 'em.
CHAMBERLAIN. Death! my lord,
Their clothes are after such a pagan cut to't,
That sure th' have worn out Christendom.

Enter SIR THOMAS LOVELL

How now?
What news, Sir Thomas Lovell?
LOVELL. Faith, my lord,
I hear of none but the new proclamation
That's clapp'd upon the court gate.
CHAMBERLAIN. What is't for?
LOVELL. The reformation of our travell'd gallants,
That fill the court with quarrels, talk, and tailors.
CHAMBERLAIN. I am glad 'tis there. Now I would
pray our monsieurs
To think an English courtier may be wise,
And never see the Louvre.
LOVELL. They must either,
For so run the conditions, leave those remnants
Of fool and feather that they got in France,
With all their honourable points of ignorance
Pertaining thereunto-as fights and fireworks;

Abusing better men than they can be,
Out of a foreign wisdom-renouncing clean
The faith they have in tennis, and tall stockings,
Short blist'red breeches, and those types
    of travel
And understand again like honest men,
Or pack to their old playfellows. There, I
    take it,
They may, cum privilegio, wear away
The lag end of their lewdness and be
    laugh'd at.
SANDYS. 'Tis time to give 'em physic,
    their diseases
Are grown so catching.
CHAMBERLAIN. What a loss our ladies
Will have of these trim vanities!
LOVELL. Ay, marry,
There will be woe indeed, lords: the
    sly whoresons
Have got a speeding trick to lay down ladies.
A French song and a fiddle has no fellow.
SANDYS. The devil fiddle 'em! I am glad they
    are going,
For sure there's no converting 'em. Now
An honest country lord, as I am, beaten
A long time out of play, may bring his
    plainsong
And have an hour of hearing; and, by'r Lady,
Held current music too.
CHAMBERLAIN. Well said, Lord Sandys;
Your colt's tooth is not cast yet.
SANDYS. No, my lord,
Nor shall not while I have a stump.
CHAMBERLAIN. Sir Thomas,
Whither were you a-going?
LOVELL. To the Cardinal's;
Your lordship is a guest too.
CHAMBERLAIN. O, 'tis true;
This night he makes a supper, and a great one,
To many lords and ladies; there will be
The beauty of this kingdom, I'll assure you.
LOVELL. That churchman bears a bounteous
    mind indeed,
A hand as fruitful as the land that feeds us;
His dews fall everywhere.
CHAMBERLAIN. No doubt he's noble;
He had a black mouth that said other of him.
SANDYS. He may, my lord; has wherewithal.
    In him
Sparing would show a worse sin than
    ill doctrine:
Men of his way should be most liberal,
They are set here for examples.

CHAMBERLAIN. True, they are so;
But few now give so great ones. My
    barge stays;
Your lordship shall along. Come, good
    Sir Thomas,
We shall be late else; which I would not be,
For I was spoke to, with Sir Henry Guildford,
This night to be comptrollers.
SANDYS. I am your lordship's.

Exeunt.

❧ SCENE IV ❧
London. The Presence Chamber in York Place

*Hautboys. A small table under a state for the Cardinal, a longer
table for the guests. Then enter ANNE BULLEN, and divers
other Ladies and Gentlemen, as guests, at one door; at another
door enter SIR HENRY GUILDFORD*

GUILDFORD. Ladies, a general welcome from
    his Grace
Salutes ye all; this night he dedicates
To fair content and you. None here, he hopes,
In all this noble bevy, has brought with her
One care abroad; he would have all as merry
As, first, good company, good wine,
    good welcome,
Can make good people.
    *Enter LORD CHAMBERLAIN, LORD SANDYS, and
            SIR THOMAS LOVELL*
O, my lord, y'are tardy,
The very thought of this fair company
Clapp'd wings to me.
CHAMBERLAIN. You are young, Sir
    Harry Guildford.
SANDYS. Sir Thomas Lovell, had the Cardinal
But half my lay thoughts in him, some of these
Should find a running banquet ere they rested
I think would better please 'em. By my life,
They are a sweet society of fair ones.
LOVELL. O that your lordship were but
    now confessor
To one or two of these!
SANDYS. I would I were;
They should find easy penance.
LOVELL. Faith, how easy?
SANDYS. As easy as a down bed would afford it.
CHAMBERLAIN. Sweet ladies, will it please you
    sit? Sir Harry,
Place you that side; I'll take the charge of this.
His Grace is ent'ring. Nay, you must
    not freeze:

Two women plac'd together makes
   cold weather.
My Lord Sandys, you are one will keep
   'em waking:
Pray sit between these ladies.
SANDYS. By my faith,
   And thank your lordship. By your leave, sweet
      ladies. *[Seats himself between ANNE BULLEN and
      another lady]*
   If I chance to talk a little wild, forgive me;
   I had it from my father.
ANNE. Was he mad, sir?
SANDYS. O, very mad, exceeding mad, in
   love too.
   But he would bite none; just as I do now,
   He would kiss you twenty with a breath.
                     Kisses her
CHAMBERLAIN. Well said, my lord.
   So, now y'are fairly seated. Gentlemen,
   The penance lies on you if these fair ladies
   Pass away frowning.
SANDYS. For my little cure,
   Let me alone.
        *Hautboys. Enter CARDINAL WOLSEY, attended; and
                     takes his state*
WOLSEY. Y'are welcome, my fair guests. That
   noble lady
   Or gentleman that is not freely merry
   Is not my friend. This, to confirm my welcome-
   And to you all, good health!   *Drinks*
SANDYS. Your Grace is noble.
   Let me have such a bowl may hold my thanks
   And save me so much talking.
WOLSEY. My Lord Sandys,
   I am beholding to you. Cheer
      your neighbours.
   Ladies, you are not merry. Gentlemen,
   Whose fault is this?
SANDYS. The red wine first must rise
   In their fair cheeks, my lord; then we shall
      have 'em
   Talk us to silence.
ANNE. You are a merry gamester,
   My Lord Sandys.
SANDYS. Yes, if I make my play.
   Here's to your ladyship; and pledge it, madam,
   For 'tis to such a thing-
ANNE. You cannot show me.
SANDYS. I told your Grace they would
   talk anon.
             Drum and trumpet. Chambers discharg'd
WOLSEY. What's that?
CHAMBERLAIN. Look out there, some of ye.

                                   Exit a SERVANT
WOLSEY. What warlike voice,
   And to what end, is this? Nay, ladies, fear not:
   By all the laws of war y'are privileg'd.
                     Re-enter SERVANT
CHAMBERLAIN. How now! what is't?
SERVANT. A noble troop of strangers-
   For so they seem. Th' have left their barge
      and landed,
   And hither make, as great ambassadors
   From foreign princes.
WOLSEY. Good Lord Chamberlain,
   Go, give 'em welcome; you can speak the
      French tongue;
   And pray receive 'em nobly and conduct 'em
   Into our presence, where this heaven
      of beauty
   Shall shine at full upon them. Some
      attend him.
                Exit CHAMBERLAIN attended.
              All rise, and tables remov'd
You have now a broken banquet, but we'll
   mend it.
A good digestion to you all; and once more
I show'r a welcome on ye; welcome all.
   *Hautboys. Enter the KING, and Others, as maskers, habited
   like shepherds, usher'd by the LORD CHAMBERLAIN.
   They pass directly before the CARDINAL, and gracefully
                     salute him*
A noble company! What are their pleasures?
CHAMBERLAIN. Because they speak no English,
   thus they pray'd
To tell your Grace, that, having heard by fame
Of this so noble and so fair assembly
This night to meet here, they could do no less,
Out of the great respect they bear to beauty,
But leave their flocks and, under your
   fair conduct,
Crave leave to view these ladies and entreat
An hour of revels with 'em.
WOLSEY. Say, Lord Chamberlain,
   They have done my poor house grace; for
      which I pay 'em
   A thousand thanks, and pray 'em take
      their pleasures.
   They choose ladies. The KING chooses ANNE BULLEN
KING. The fairest hand I ever touch'd! O beauty,
   Till now I never knew thee! *Music. Dance*
WOLSEY. My lord!
CHAMBERLAIN. Your Grace?
WOLSEY. Pray tell 'em thus much from me:
   There should be one amongst 'em, by
      his person,

More worthy this place than myself; to whom,
If I but knew him, with my love and duty
I would surrender it.
CHAMBERLAIN. I will, my lord.

He whispers to the maskers

WOLSEY. What say they?
CHAMBERLAIN. Such a one, they all confess,
There is indeed; which they would have
  your Grace
Find out, and he will take it.
WOLSEY. Let me see, then. *[Comes from his state]*
By all your good leaves, gentlemen, here
  I'll make
My royal choice.
KING. *[Unmasking]* Ye have found him, Cardinal.
You hold a fair assembly; you do well, lord.
You are a churchman, or, I'll tell you, Cardinal,
I should judge now unhappily.
WOLSEY. I am glad
Your Grace is grown so pleasant.
KING. My Lord Chamberlain,
Prithee come hither: what fair lady's that?
CHAMBERLAIN. An't please your Grace, Sir
  Thomas Bullen's daughter-
The Viscount Rochford-one of her
  Highness' women.
KING. By heaven, she is a dainty one.
  Sweet heart,
I were unmannerly to take you out
And not to kiss you. A health, gentlemen!
Let it go round.
WOLSEY. Sir Thomas Lovell, is the
  banquet ready
I' th' privy chamber?
LOVELL. Yes, my lord.
WOLSEY. Your Grace,
I fear, with dancing is a little heated.
KING. I fear, too much.
WOLSEY. There's fresher air, my lord,
In the next chamber.
KING. Lead in your ladies, ev'ry one.
  Sweet partner,
I must not yet forsake you. Let's be merry:
Good my Lord Cardinal, I have half a
  dozen healths
To drink to these fair ladies, and a measure
To lead 'em once again; and then let's dream
Who's best in favour. Let the music knock it.

Exeunt, with trumpets.

ACT II

SCENE I
Westminster. A street

Enter two GENTLEMEN, at several doors

FIRST GENTLEMAN. Whither away so fast?
SECOND GENTLEMAN. O, God save ye!
  Ev'n to the Hall, to hear what shall become
  Of the great Duke of Buckingham.
FIRST GENTLEMAN. I'll save you
  That labour, sir. All's now done but
  the ceremony
  Of bringing back the prisoner.
SECOND GENTLEMAN. Were you there?
FIRST GENTLEMAN. Yes, indeed, was I.
SECOND GENTLEMAN. Pray, speak what
  has happen'd.
FIRST GENTLEMAN. You may guess quickly what.
SECOND GENTLEMAN. Is he found guilty?
FIRST GENTLEMAN. Yes, truly is he, and
  condemn'd upon't.
SECOND GENTLEMAN. I am sorry for't.
FIRST GENTLEMAN. So are a number more.
SECOND GENTLEMAN. But, pray, how pass'd it?
FIRST GENTLEMAN. I'll tell you in a little. The
  great Duke.
  Came to the bar; where to his accusations
  He pleaded still not guilty, and alleged
  Many sharp reasons to defeat the law.
  The King's attorney, on the contrary,
  Urg'd on the examinations, proofs, confessions,
  Of divers witnesses; which the Duke desir'd
  To have brought, viva voce, to his face;
  At which appear'd against him his surveyor,
  Sir Gilbert Peck his chancellor, and John Car,
  Confessor to him, with that devil-monk,
  Hopkins, that made this mischief.
SECOND GENTLEMAN. That was he
  That fed him with his prophecies?
FIRST GENTLEMAN. The same.
  All these accus'd him strongly, which he fain
  Would have flung from him; but indeed he
  could not;
  And so his peers, upon this evidence,
  Have found him guilty of high treason. Much
  He spoke, and learnedly, for life; but all
  Was either pitied in him or forgotten.
SECOND GENTLEMAN. After all this, how did he
  bear himself?
FIRST GENTLEMAN. When he was brought again

to th' bar to hear
His knell rung out, his judgment, he was stirr'd
With such an agony he sweat extremely,
And something spoke in choler, ill and hasty;
But he fell to himself again, and sweetly
In all the rest show'd a most noble patience.
SECOND GENTLEMAN. I do not think he
  fears death.
FIRST GENTLEMAN. Sure, he does not;
He never was so womanish; the cause
He may a little grieve at.
SECOND GENTLEMAN. Certainly
The Cardinal is the end of this.
FIRST GENTLEMAN. 'Tis likely,
By all conjectures: first, Kildare's attainder,
Then deputy of Ireland, who remov'd,
Earl Surrey was sent thither, and in haste too,
Lest he should help his father.
SECOND GENTLEMAN. That trick of state
Was a deep envious one.
FIRST GENTLEMAN. At his return
No doubt he will requite it. This is noted,
And generally: whoever the King favours
The Cardinal instantly will find employment,
And far enough from court too.
SECOND GENTLEMAN. All the commons
Hate him perniciously, and, o' my conscience,
Wish him ten fathom deep: this Duke as much
They love and dote on; call him
  bounteous Buckingham,
The mirror of all courtesy-

Enter BUCKINGHAM from his arraignment, tip-staves
before him; the axe with the edge towards him; Halberds on
each side; accompanied with SIR THOMAS LOVELL,
SIR NICHOLAS VAUX, SIR WILLIAM SANDYS, and
Common people, etc.

FIRST GENTLEMAN. Stay there, sir,
And see the noble ruin'd man you speak of.
SECOND GENTLEMAN. Let's stand close, and
  behold him.
BUCKINGHAM. All good people,
You that thus far have come to pity me,
Hear what I say, and then go home and lose me.
I have this day receiv'd a traitor's judgment,
And by that name must die; yet, heaven
  bear witness,
And if I have a conscience, let it sink me
Even as the axe falls, if I be not faithful!
The law I bear no malice for my death:
'T has done, upon the premises, but justice.
But those that sought it I could wish
  more Christians.
Be what they will, I heartily forgive 'em;

Yet let 'em look they glory not in mischief
Nor build their evils on the graves of great men,
For then my guiltless blood must cry
  against 'em.
For further life in this world I ne'er hope
Nor will I sue, although the King have mercies
More than I dare make faults. You few that
  lov'd me
And dare be bold to weep for Buckingham,
His noble friends and fellows, whom to leave
Is only bitter to him, only dying,
Go with me like good angels to my end;
And as the long divorce of steel falls on me
Make of your prayers one sweet sacrifice,
And lift my soul to heaven. Lead on, o'
  God's name.
LOVELL. I do beseech your Grace, for charity,
If ever any malice in your heart
Were hid against me, now to forgive me frankly.
BUCKINGHAM. Sir Thomas Lovell, I as free
  forgive you
As I would be forgiven. I forgive all.
There cannot be those numberless offences
'Gainst me that I cannot take peace with. No
  black envy
Shall mark my grave. Commend me to his Grace;
And if he speak of Buckingham, pray tell him
You met him half in heaven. My vows
  and prayers
Yet are the King's, and, till my soul forsake,
Shall cry for blessings on him. May he live
Longer than I have time to tell his years;
Ever belov'd and loving may his rule be;
And when old time shall lead him to his end,
Goodness and he fill up one monument!
LOVELL. To th' water side I must conduct
  your Grace;
Then give my charge up to Sir Nicholas Vaux,
Who undertakes you to your end.
VAUX. Prepare there;
The Duke is coming; see the barge be ready;
And fit it with such furniture as suits
The greatness of his person.
BUCKINGHAM. Nay, Sir Nicholas,
Let it alone; my state now will but mock me.
When I came hither I was Lord High Constable
And Duke of Buckingham; now, poor
  Edward Bohun.
Yet I am richer than my base accusers
That never knew what truth meant; I now seal it;
And with that blood will make 'em one day
  groan fort.
My noble father, Henry of Buckingham,

Who first rais'd head against usurping Richard,
Flying for succour to his servant Banister,
Being distress'd, was by that wretch betray'd
And without trial fell; God's peace be with him!
Henry the Seventh succeeding, truly pitying
My father's loss, like a most royal prince,
Restor'd me to my honours, and out of ruins
Made my name once more noble. Now his son,
Henry the Eighth, life, honour, name, and all
That made me happy, at one stroke has taken
For ever from the world. I had my trial,
And must needs say a noble one; which
  makes me
A little happier than my wretched father;
Yet thus far we are one in fortunes: both
Fell by our servants, by those men we
  lov'd most-
A most unnatural and faithless service.
Heaven has an end in all. Yet, you that hear me,
This from a dying man receive as certain:
Where you are liberal of your loves and counsels,
Be sure you be not loose; for those you
  make friends
And give your hearts to, when they
  once perceive
The least rub in your fortunes, fall away
Like water from ye, never found again
But where they mean to sink ye. All good
  people,
Pray for me! I must now forsake ye; the last hour
Of my long weary life is come upon me.
Farewell;
And when you would say something that is sad,
Speak how I fell. I have done; and God
  forgive me!

Exeunt BUCKINGHAM and Train.

FIRST GENTLEMAN. O, this is full of pity! Sir,
  it calls,
I fear, too many curses on their heads
That were the authors.
SECOND GENTLEMAN. If the Duke be guiltless,
'Tis full of woe; yet I can give you inkling
Of an ensuing evil, if it fall,
Greater than this.
FIRST GENTLEMAN. Good angels keep it from us!
What may it be? You do not doubt my faith, sir?
SECOND GENTLEMAN. This secret is so weighty,
  'twill require
A strong faith to conceal it.
FIRST GENTLEMAN. Let me have it;
  I do not talk much.
SECOND GENTLEMAN. I am confident.
You shall, sir. Did you not of late days hear

A buzzing of a separation
Between the King and Katharine?
FIRST GENTLEMAN. Yes, but it held not;
For when the King once heard it, out of anger
He sent command to the Lord Mayor straight
To stop the rumour and allay those tongues
That durst disperse it.
SECOND GENTLEMAN. But that slander, sir,
Is found a truth now; for it grows again
Fresher than e'er it was, and held for certain
The King will venture at it. Either the Cardinal
Or some about him near have, out of malice
To the good Queen, possess'd him with
  a scruple
That will undo her. To confirm this too,
Cardinal Campeius is arriv'd and lately;
As all think, for this business.
FIRST GENTLEMAN. 'Tis the Cardinal;
And merely to revenge him on the Emperor
For not bestowing on him at his asking
The archbishopric of Toledo, this is purpos'd.
SECOND GENTLEMAN. I think you have hit the
  mark; but is't not cruel
That she should feel the smart of this?
  The Cardinal
Will have his will, and she must fall.
FIRST GENTLEMAN. 'Tis woeful.
We are too open here to argue this;
Let's think in private more.   *Exeunt.*

SCENE II

London. The palace

Enter the LORD CHAMBERLAIN reading this letter

CHAMBERLAIN. 'My lord, the horses your
  lordship sent for, with all the care had, I saw
  well chosen, ridden, and furnish'd. They were
  young and handsome, and of the best breed
  in the north. When they were ready to set out
  for London, a man of my Lord Cardinal's, by
  commission, and main power, took 'em from
  me, with this reason: his master would be
  serv'd before a subject, if not before the King;
  which stopp'd our mouths, sir.'
I fear he will indeed. Well, let him have them.
He will have all, I think.

*Enter to the LORD CHAMBERLAIN the DUKES OF
NORFOLK and SUFFOLK*

NORFOLK. Well met, my Lord Chamberlain.
CHAMBERLAIN. Good day to both your Graces.
SUFFOLK. How is the King employ'd?

CHAMBERLAIN. I left him private,
Full of sad thoughts and troubles.

NORFOLK. What's the cause?

CHAMBERLAIN. It seems the marriage with his
brother's wife
Has crept too near his conscience.

SUFFOLK. No, his conscience
Has crept too near another lady.

NORFOLK. 'Tis so;
This is the Cardinal's doing; the King-Cardinal,
That blind priest, like the eldest son of fortune,
Turns what he list. The King will know him
one day.

SUFFOLK. Pray God he do! He'll never know
himself else.

NORFOLK. How holily he works in all
his business!
And with what zeal! For, now he has crack'd
the league
Between us and the Emperor, the Queen's
great nephew,
He dives into the King's soul and there scatters
Dangers, doubts, wringing of the conscience,
Fears, and despairs-and all these for his
marriage;
And out of all these to restore the King,
He counsels a divorce, a loss of her
That like a jewel has hung twenty years
About his neck, yet never lost her lustre;
Of her that loves him with that excellence
That angels love good men with; even of her
That, when the greatest stroke of fortune falls,
Will bless the King-and is not this course pious?

CHAMBERLAIN. Heaven keep me from such
counsel! 'Tis most true
These news are everywhere; every tongue
speaks 'em,
And every true heart weeps for 't. All that dare
Look into these affairs see this main end-
The French King's sister. Heaven will one
day open
The King's eyes, that so long have slept upon
This bold bad man.

SUFFOLK. And free us from his slavery.

NORFOLK. We had need pray, and heartily, for
our deliverance;
Or this imperious man will work us all
From princes into pages. All men's honours
Lie like one lump before him, to be fashion'd
Into what pitch he please.

SUFFOLK. For me, my lords,
I love him not, nor fear him-there's my creed;
As I am made without him, so I'll stand,
If the King please; his curses and his blessings
Touch me alike; th' are breath I not believe in.
I knew him, and I know him; so I leave him
To him that made him proud-the Pope.

NORFOLK. Let's in;
And with some other business put the King
From these sad thoughts that work too much
upon him.
My lord, you'll bear us company?

CHAMBERLAIN. Excuse me,
The King has sent me otherwhere; besides,
You'll find a most unfit time to disturb him.
Health to your lordships!

NORFOLK. Thanks, my good Lord Chamberlain.

Exit LORD CHAMBERLAIN

The KING draws the curtain and sits reading pensively

SUFFOLK. How sad he looks; sure, he is much
afflicted.

KING. Who's there, ha?

NORFOLK. Pray God he be not angry.

KING HENRY. Who's there, I say? How dare you
thrust yourselves
Into my private meditations?
Who am I, ha?

NORFOLK. A gracious king that pardons
all offences
Malice ne'er meant. Our breach of duty this way
Is business of estate, in which we come
To know your royal pleasure.

KING. Ye are too bold.
Go to; I'll make ye know your times of business.
Is this an hour for temporal affairs, ha?

Enter WOLSEY and CAMPEIUS with a commission

Who's there? My good Lord Cardinal? O
my Wolsey,
The quiet of my wounded conscience,
Thou art a cure fit for a King. *[To CAMPEIUS]*
You're welcome,
Most learned reverend sir, into our kingdom.
Use us and it. *[To WOLSEY]* My good lord, have
great care
I be not found a talker.

WOLSEY. Sir, you cannot.
I would your Grace would give us but an hour
Of private conference.

KING. *[To NORFOLK and SUFFOLK]* We are busy; go.

NORFOLK. *[Aside to SUFFOLK]* This priest has no
pride in him!

SUFFOLK. *[Aside to NORFOLK]* Not to speak of!
I would not be so sick though for his place.
But this cannot continue.

NORFOLK. *[Aside to SUFFOLK]* If it do,
I'll venture one have-at-him.

SUFFOLK. *[Aside to NORFOLK]* I another.

Exeunt NORFOLK and SUFFOLK

WOLSEY. Your Grace has given a precedent
  of wisdom
  Above all princes, in committing freely
  Your scruple to the voice of Christendom.
  Who can be angry now? What envy reach you?
  The Spaniard, tied by blood and favour to her,
  Must now confess, if they have any goodness,
  The trial just and noble. All the clerks,
  I mean the learned ones, in Christian kingdoms
  Have their free voices. Rome the nurse
  of judgment,
  Invited by your noble self, hath sent
  One general tongue unto us, this good man,
  This just and learned priest, Cardinal Campeius,
  Whom once more I present unto your Highness.

KING. And once more in mine arms I bid
  him welcome,
  And thank the holy conclave for their loves.
  They have sent me such a man I would have
  wish'd for.

CAMPEIUS. Your Grace must needs deserve all
  strangers' loves,
  You are so noble. To your Highness' hand
  I tender my commission; by whose virtue-
  The court of Rome commanding-you, my Lord
  Cardinal of York, are join'd with me their servant
  In the unpartial judging of this business.

KING. Two equal men. The Queen shall
  be acquainted
  Forthwith for what you come. Where's Gardiner?

WOLSEY. I know your Majesty has always lov'd her
  So dear in heart not to deny her that
  A woman of less place might ask by law-
  Scholars allow'd freely to argue for her.

KING. Ay, and the best she shall have; and
  my favour
  To him that does best. God forbid else. Cardinal,
  Prithee call Gardiner to me, my new secretary;
  I find him a fit fellow.   *Exit WOLSEY*

Re-enter WOLSEY with GARDINER

WOLSEY. *[Aside to GARDINER]* Give me your hand:
  much joy and favour to you;
  You are the King's now.

GARDINER. *[Aside to WOLSEY]* But to
  be commanded
  For ever by your Grace, whose hand has
  rais'd me.

KING. Come hither, Gardiner. *Walks and whispers*

CAMPEIUS. My Lord of York, was not one
  Doctor Pace
  In this man's place before him?

WOLSEY. Yes, he was.

CAMPEIUS. Was he not held a learned man?

WOLSEY. Yes, surely.

CAMPEIUS. Believe me, there's an ill opinion
  spread then,
  Even of yourself, Lord Cardinal.

WOLSEY. How! Of me?

CAMPEIUS. They will not stick to say you
  envied him
  And, fearing he would rise, he was so virtuous,
  Kept him a foreign man still; which so
  griev'd him
  That he ran mad and died.

WOLSEY. Heav'n's peace be with him!
  That's Christian care enough. For
  living murmurers
  There's places of rebuke. He was a fool,
  For he would needs be virtuous: that
  good fellow,
  If I command him, follows my appointment.
  I will have none so near else. Learn this, brother,
  We live not to be grip'd by meaner persons.

KING. Deliver this with modesty to th' Queen.

Exit GARDINER

  The most convenient place that I can think of
  For such receipt of learning is Blackfriars;
  There ye shall meet about this weighty business-
  My Wolsey, see it furnish'd. O, my lord,
  Would it not grieve an able man to leave
  So sweet a bedfellow? But,
  conscience, conscience!
  O, 'tis a tender place! and I must leave her.

Exeunt

✦ SCENE III ✦
London. The palace

Enter ANNE BULLEN and an OLD LADY

ANNE. Not for that neither. Here's the pang
  that pinches:
  His Highness having liv'd so long with her,
  and she
  So good a lady that no tongue could ever
  Pronounce dishonour of her-by my life,
  She never knew harm-doing-O, now, after
  So many courses of the sun enthroned,
  Still growing in a majesty and pomp, the which
  To leave a thousand-fold more bitter than
  'Tis sweet at first t' acquire-after this process,
  To give her the avaunt, it is a pity
  Would move a monster.

OLD LADY. Hearts of most hard temper
Melt and lament for her.

ANNE. O, God's will! much better
She ne'er had known pomp; though't
be temporal,
Yet, if that quarrel, fortune, do divorce
It from the bearer, 'tis a sufferance panging
As soul and body's severing.

OLD LADY. Alas, poor lady!
She's a stranger now again.

ANNE. So much the more
Must pity drop upon her. Verily,
I swear 'tis better to be lowly born
And range with humble livers in content
Than to be perk'd up in a glist'ring grief
And wear a golden sorrow.

OLD LADY. Our content
Is our best having.

ANNE. By my troth and maidenhead,
I would not be a queen.

OLD LADY. Beshrew me, I would,
And venture maidenhead for 't; and so
would you,
For all this spice of your hypocrisy.
You that have so fair parts of woman on you
Have too a woman's heart, which ever yet
Affected eminence, wealth, sovereignty;
Which, to say sooth, are blessings; and
which gifts,
Saving your mincing, the capacity
Of your soft cheveril conscience would receive
If you might please to stretch it.

ANNE. Nay, good troth.

OLD LADY. Yes, troth and troth. You would not
be a queen?

ANNE. No, not for all the riches under heaven.

OLD LADY. 'Tis strange: a threepence bow'd
would hire me,
Old as I am, to queen it. But, I pray you,
What think you of a duchess? Have you limbs
To bear that load of title?

ANNE. No, in truth.

OLD LADY. Then you are weakly made. Pluck off
a little;
I would not be a young count in your way
For more than blushing comes to. If your back
Cannot vouchsafe this burden, 'tis too weak
Ever to get a boy.

ANNE. How you do talk!
I swear again I would not be a queen
For all the world.

OLD LADY. In faith, for little England
You'd venture an emballing. I myself

Would for Carnarvonshire, although there long'd
No more to th' crown but that. Lo, who
comes here?

Enter the LORD CHAMBERLAIN

CHAMBERLAIN. Good morrow, ladies. What
were't worth to know
The secret of your conference?

ANNE. My good lord,
Not your demand; it values not your asking.
Our mistress' sorrows we were pitying.

CHAMBERLAIN. It was a gentle business
and becoming
The action of good women; there is hope
All will be well.

ANNE. Now, I pray God, amen!

CHAMBERLAIN. You bear a gentle mind, and
heav'nly blessings
Follow such creatures. That you may, fair lady,
Perceive I speak sincerely and high notes
Ta'en of your many virtues, the King's Majesty
Commends his good opinion of you to you, and
Does purpose honour to you no less flowing
Than Marchioness of Pembroke; to which tide
A thousand pound a year, annual support,
Out of his grace he adds.

ANNE. I do not know
What kind of my obedience I should tender;
More than my all is nothing, nor my prayers
Are not words duly hallowed, nor my wishes
More worth than empty vanities; yet prayers
and wishes
Are all I can return. Beseech your lordship,
Vouchsafe to speak my thanks and
my obedience,
As from a blushing handmaid, to his Highness;
Whose health and royalty I pray for.

CHAMBERLAIN. Lady,
I shall not fail t' approve the fair conceit
The King hath of you. *[Aside]* I have perus'd
her well:
Beauty and honour in her are so mingled
That they have caught the King; and who
knows yet
But from this lady may proceed a gem
To lighten all this isle?-I'll to the King
And say I spoke with you.

ANNE. My honour'd lord!

Exit LORD CHAMBERLAIN

OLD LADY. Why, this it is: see, see!
I have been begging sixteen years in court-
Am yet a courtier beggarly-nor could
Come pat betwixt too early and too late
For any suit of pounds; and you, O fate!

A very fresh-fish here-fie, fie, fie upon
This compell'd fortune!-have your mouth
fill'd up
Before you open it.
ANNE. This is strange to me.
OLD LADY. How tastes it? Is it bitter? Forty
pence, no.
There was a lady once-'tis an old story-
That would not be a queen, that would she not,
For all the mud in Egypt. Have you heard it?
ANNE. Come, you are pleasant.
OLD LADY. With your theme I could
O'ermount the lark. The Marchioness
of Pembroke!
A thousand pounds a year for pure respect!
No other obligation! By my life,
That promises moe thousands: honour's train
Is longer than his foreskirt. By this time
I know your back will bear a duchess. Say,
Are you not stronger than you were?
ANNE. Good lady,
Make yourself mirth with your particular fancy,
And leave me out on't. Would I had no being,
If this salute my blood a jot; it faints me
To think what follows.
The Queen is comfortless, and we forgetful
In our long absence. Pray, do not deliver
What here y' have heard to her.
OLD LADY. What do you think me?*Exeunt.*

✿ SCENE IV ✿
London. A hall in Blackfriars

*Trumpets, sennet, and cornets. Enter two Vergers, with short
silver wands; next them, two SCRIBES, in the habit of doctors;
after them, the ARCHBISHOP OF CANTERBURY alone;
after him, the BISHOPS OF LINCOLN, Ely, Rochester,
and Saint Asaph; next them, with some small distance, follows
a Gentleman bearing the purse, with the great seal, and a
cardinal's hat; then two Priests, bearing each a silver cross; then
a GENTLEMAN USHER, bareheaded, accompanied with
a SERGEANT-AT-ARMS bearing a silver mace; then two
Gentlemen bearing two great silver pillars; after them, side by
side, the two CARDINALS, WOLSEY and CAMPEIUS;
two Noblemen with the sword and mace. Then enter the KING
and QUEEN and their Trains. The KING takes place under
the cloth of state; the two CARDINALS sit under him as judges.
The QUEEN takes place some distance from the KING. The
BISHOPS place themselves on each side of the court, in manner
of consistory; below them the SCRIBES. The Lords sit next the
BISHOPS. The rest of the Attendants stand in convenient order
about the stage*

WOLSEY. Whilst our commission from Rome
is read,
Let silence be commanded.
KING. What's the need?
It hath already publicly been read,
And on all sides th' authority allow'd;
You may then spare that time.
WOLSEY. Be't so; proceed.
SCRIBE. Say 'Henry King of England, come into
the court.'
CRIER. Henry King of England, etc.
KING. Here.
SCRIBE. Say 'Katharine Queen of England, come
into the court.'
CRIER. Katharine Queen of England, etc.
*The QUEEN makes no answer, rises out of her chair, goes about
the court, comes to the KING, and kneels at his feet; then speaks*
QUEEN KATHARINE. Sir, I desire you do me right
and justice,
And to bestow your pity on me; for
I am a most poor woman and a stranger,
Born out of your dominions, having here
No judge indifferent, nor no more assurance
Of equal friendship and proceeding. Alas, sir,
In what have I offended you? What cause
Hath my behaviour given to your displeasure
That thus you should proceed to put me off
And take your good grace from me?
Heaven witness,
I have been to you a true and humble wife,
At all times to your will conformable,
Ever in fear to kindle your dislike,
Yea, subject to your countenance-glad or sorry
As I saw it inclin'd. When was the hour
I ever contradicted your desire
Or made it not mine too? Or which of
your friends
Have I not strove to love, although I knew
He were mine enemy? What friend of mine
That had to him deriv'd your anger did
Continue in my liking? Nay, gave notice
He was from thence discharg'd? Sir, call to mind
That I have been your wife in this obedience
Upward of twenty years, and have been blest
With many children by you. If, in the course
And process of this time, you can report,
And prove it too against mine honour, aught,
My bond to wedlock or my love and duty,
Against your sacred person, in God's name,
Turn me away and let the foul'st contempt
Shut door upon me, and so give me up
To the sharp'st kind of justice. Please you, sir,
The King, your father, was reputed for

A prince most prudent, of an excellent
And unmatch'd wit and judgment; Ferdinand,
My father, King of Spain, was reckon'd one
The wisest prince that there had reign'd
  by many
A year before. It is not to be question'd
That they had gather'd a wise council to them
Of every realm, that did debate this business,
Who deem'd our marriage lawful. Wherefore
  I humbly
Beseech you, sir, to spare me till I may
Be by my friends in Spain advis'd, whose counsel
I will implore. If not, i' th' name of God,
Your pleasure be fulfill'd!
WOLSEY. You have here, lady,
  And of your choice, these reverend fathers-men
  Of singular integrity and learning,
  Yea, the elect o' th' land, who are assembled
  To plead your cause. It shall be
    therefore bootless
  That longer you desire the court, as well
  For your own quiet as to rectify
  What is unsettled in the King.
CAMPEIUS. His Grace
  Hath spoken well and justly; therefore, madam,
  It's fit this royal session do proceed
  And that, without delay, their arguments
  Be now produc'd and heard.
QUEEN KATHARINE. Lord Cardinal,
  To you I speak.
WOLSEY. Your pleasure, madam?
QUEEN KATHARINE. Sir,
  I am about to weep; but, thinking that
  We are a queen, or long have dream'd so, certain
  The daughter of a king, my drops of tears
  I'll turn to sparks of fire.
WOLSEY. Be patient yet.
QUEEN KATHARINE. I will, when you are humble;
    nay, before
  Or God will punish me. I do believe,
  Induc'd by potent circumstances, that
  You are mine enemy, and make my challenge
  You shall not be my judge; for it is you
  Have blown this coal betwixt my lord and me-
  Which God's dew quench! Therefore I say again,
  I utterly abhor, yea, from my soul
  Refuse you for my judge, whom yet once more
  I hold my most malicious foe and think not
  At all a friend to truth.
WOLSEY. I do profess
  You speak not like yourself, who ever yet
  Have stood to charity and display'd th' effects
  Of disposition gentle and of wisdom

O'ertopping woman's pow'r. Madam, you do
  me wrong:
I have no spleen against you, nor injustice
For you or any; how far I have proceeded,
Or how far further shall, is warranted
By a commission from the Consistory,
Yea, the whole Consistory of Rome. You
  charge me
That I have blown this coal: I do deny it.
The King is present; if it be known to him
That I gainsay my deed, how may he wound,
And worthily, my falsehood! Yea, as much
As you have done my truth. If he know
That I am free of your report, he knows
I am not of your wrong. Therefore in him
It lies to cure me, and the cure is to
Remove these thoughts from you; the
  which before
His Highness shall speak in, I do beseech
You, gracious madam, to unthink your speaking
And to say so no more.
QUEEN KATHARINE. My lord, my lord,
  I am a simple woman, much too weak
  T' oppose your cunning. Y'are meek
    and humble-mouth'd;
  You sign your place and calling, in full seeming,
  With meekness and humility; but your heart
  Is cramm'd with arrogancy, spleen, and pride.
  You have, by fortune and his Highness' favours,
  Gone slightly o'er low steps, and now
    are mounted
  Where pow'rs are your retainers, and
    your words,
  Domestics to you, serve your will as't please
  Yourself pronounce their office. I must tell you
  You tender more your person's honour than
  Your high profession spiritual; that again
  I do refuse you for my judge and here,
  Before you all, appeal unto the Pope,
  To bring my whole cause 'fore his Holiness
  And to be judg'd by him.

She curtsies to the KING, and offers to depart

CAMPEIUS. The Queen is obstinate,
  Stubborn to justice, apt to accuse it, and
  Disdainful to be tried by't; 'tis not well.
  She's going away.
KING. Call her again.
CRIER. Katharine Queen of England, come into
  the court.
GENTLEMAN USHER. Madam, you are call'd back.
QUEEN KATHARINE. What need you note it? Pray
  you keep your way;
  When you are call'd, return. Now the Lord help!

They vex me past my patience. Pray you pass on.
I will not tarry; no, nor ever more
Upon this business my appearance make
In any of their courts.

Exeunt QUEEN and her Attendants.

KING. Go thy ways, Kate.
That man i' th' world who shall report he has
A better wife, let him in nought be trusted
For speaking false in that. Thou art, alone-
If thy rare qualities, sweet gentleness,
Thy meekness saint-like, wife-like government,
Obeying in commanding, and thy parts
Sovereign and pious else, could speak thee out-
The queen of earthly queens. She's noble born;
And like her true nobility she has
Carried herself towards me.

WOLSEY. Most gracious sir,
In humblest manner I require your Highness
That it shall please you to declare in hearing
Of all these ears-for where I am robb'd
and bound,
There must I be unloos'd, although not there
At once and fully satisfied-whether ever I
Did broach this business to your Highness, or
Laid any scruple in your way which might
Induce you to the question on't, or ever
Have to you, but with thanks to God for such
A royal lady, spake one the least word that might
Be to the prejudice of her present state,
Or touch of her good person?

KING. My Lord Cardinal,
I do excuse you; yea, upon mine honour,
I free you from't. You are not to be taught
That you have many enemies that know not
Why they are so, but, like to village curs,
Bark when their fellows do. By some of these
The Queen is put in anger. Y'are excus'd.
But will you be more justified? You ever
Have wish'd the sleeping of this business;
never desir'd
It to be stirr'd; but oft have hind'red, oft,
The passages made toward it. On my honour,
I speak my good Lord Cardinal to this point,
And thus far clear him. Now, what mov'd
me to't,
I will be bold with time and your attention.
Then mark th' inducement. Thus it came-give
heed to't:
My conscience first receiv'd a tenderness,
Scruple, and prick, on certain speeches utter'd
By th' Bishop of Bayonne, then
French ambassador,
Who had been hither sent on the debating

A marriage 'twixt the Duke of Orleans and
Our daughter Mary. I' th' progress of
this business,
Ere a determinate resolution, he-
I mean the Bishop-did require a respite
Wherein he might the King his lord advertise
Whether our daughter were legitimate,
Respecting this our marriage with the dowager,
Sometimes our brother's wife. This
respite shook
The bosom of my conscience, enter'd me,
Yea, with a splitting power, and made to tremble
The region of my breast, which forc'd such way
That many maz'd considerings did throng
And press'd in with this caution.
First, methought
I stood not in the smile of heaven, who had
Commanded nature that my lady's womb,
If it conceiv'd a male child by me, should
Do no more offices of life to't than
The grave does to the dead; for her male issue
Or died where they were made, or shortly after
This world had air'd them. Hence I took
a thought
This was a judgment on me, that my kingdom,
Well worthy the best heir o' th' world,
should not
Be gladded in't by me. Then follows that
I weigh'd the danger which my realms stood in
By this my issue's fail, and that gave to me
Many a groaning throe. Thus hulling in
The wild sea of my conscience, I did steer
Toward this remedy, whereupon we are
Now present here together; that's to say
I meant to rectify my conscience, which
I then did feel full sick, and yet not well,
By all the reverend fathers of the land
And doctors learn'd. First, I began in private
With you, my Lord of Lincoln; you remember
How under my oppression I did reek,
When I first mov'd you.

LINCOLN. Very well, my liege.

KING. I have spoke long; be pleas'd yourself to say
How far you satisfied me.

LINCOLN. So please your Highness,
The question did at first so stagger me-
Bearing a state of mighty moment in't
And consequence of dread-that I committed
The daring'st counsel which I had to doubt,
And did entreat your Highness to this course
Which you are running here.

KING. I then mov'd you,
My Lord of Canterbury, and got your leave

To make this present summons. Unsolicited
I left no reverend person in this court,
But by particular consent proceeded
Under your hands and seals; therefore, go on,
For no dislike i' th' world against the person
Of the good Queen, but the sharp thorny points
Of my alleged reasons, drives this forward.
Prove but our marriage lawful, by my life
And kingly dignity, we are contented
To wear our moral state to come with her,
Katharine our queen, before the
  primest creature
That's paragon'd o' th' world.
CAMPEIUS. So please your Highness,
The Queen being absent, 'tis a needful fitness
That we adjourn this court till further day;
Meanwhile must be an earnest motion
Made to the Queen to call back her appeal
She intends unto his Holiness.
KING. *[Aside]* I may perceive
These cardinals trifle with me. I abhor
This dilatory sloth and tricks of Rome.
My learn'd and well-beloved servant, Cranmer,
Prithee return. With thy approach I know
My comfort comes along.-Break up the court;
I say, set on.*Exeunt in manner as they entered.*

❧ ACT III ❧

❧ SCENE I ❧
London. The QUEEN'S apartments

Enter the QUEEN and her Women, as at work

QUEEN KATHARINE. Take thy lute, wench. My
  soul grows sad with troubles;
Sing and disperse 'em, if thou canst.
  Leave working.

SONG
  Orpheus with his lute made trees,
  And the mountain tops that freeze,
    Bow themselves when he did sing;
  To his music plants and flowers
  Ever sprung, as sun and showers
    There had made a lasting spring.
  Every thing that heard him play,
  Even the billows of the sea,
    Hung their heads and then lay by.
  In sweet music is such art,
  Killing care and grief of heart

Fall asleep or hearing die.
Enter a GENTLEMAN
QUEEN KATHARINE. How now?
GENTLEMAN. An't please your Grace, the two
  great Cardinals
  Wait in the presence.
QUEEN KATHARINE. Would they speak with me?
GENTLEMAN. They will'd me say so, madam.
QUEEN KATHARINE. Pray their Graces
  To come near. *[Exit GENTLEMAN]* What can be
    their business
  With me, a poor weak woman, fall'n from favour?
  I do not like their coming. Now I think on't,
  They should be good men, their affairs
    as righteous;
  But all hoods make not monks.
Enter the two CARDINALS, WOLSEY and CAMPEIUS
WOLSEY. Peace to your Highness!
QUEEN KATHARINE. Your Graces find me here
  part of housewife;
  I would be all, against the worst may happen.
  What are your pleasures with me,
    reverend lords?
WOLSEY. May it please you, noble madam,
  to withdraw
  Into your private chamber, we shall give you
  The full cause of our coming.
QUEEN KATHARINE. Speak it here;
  There's nothing I have done yet, o'
    my conscience,
  Deserves a corner. Would all other women
  Could speak this with as free a soul as I do!
  My lords, I care not-so much I am happy
  Above a number-if my actions
  Were tried by ev'ry tongue, ev'ry eye saw 'em,
  Envy and base opinion set against 'em,
  I know my life so even. If your business
  Seek me out, and that way I am wife in,
  Out with it boldly; truth loves open dealing.
WOLSEY. Tanta est erga te mentis integritas,
  regina serenissima-
QUEEN KATHARINE. O, good my lord, no Latin!
  I am not such a truant since my coming,
  As not to know the language I have liv'd in;
  A strange tongue makes my cause more
    strange, suspicious;
  Pray speak in English. Here are some will
    thank you,
  If you speak truth, for their poor mistress' sake:
  Believe me, she has had much wrong.
    Lord Cardinal,
  The willing'st sin I ever yet committed
  May be absolv'd in English.

WOLSEY. Noble lady,
  I am sorry my integrity should breed,
  And service to his Majesty and you,
  So deep suspicion, where all faith was meant.
  We come not by the way of accusation
  To taint that honour every good tongue blesses,
  Nor to betray you any way to sorrow-
  You have too much, good lady; but to know
  How you stand minded in the weighty difference
  Between the King and you, and to deliver,
  Like free and honest men, our just opinions
  And comforts to your cause.
CAMPEIUS. Most honour'd madam,
  My Lord of York, out of his noble nature,
  Zeal and obedience he still bore your Grace,
  Forgetting, like a good man, your late censure
  Both of his truth and him-which was too far-
  Offers, as I do, in a sign of peace,
  His service and his counsel.
QUEEN KATHARINE. *[Aside]* To betray me.-
  My lords, I thank you both for your good wills;
  Ye speak like honest men-pray God ye prove so!
  But how to make ye suddenly an answer,
  In such a point of weight, so near mine honour,
  More near my life, I fear, with my weak wit,
  And to such men of gravity and learning,
  In truth I know not. I was set at work
  Among my maids, full little, God knows, looking
  Either for such men or such business.
  For her sake that I have been-for I feel
  The last fit of my greatness-good your Graces,
  Let me have time and counsel for my cause.
  Alas, I am a woman, friendless, hopeless!
WOLSEY. Madam, you wrong the King's love with
  these fears;
  Your hopes and friends are infinite.
QUEEN KATHARINE. In England
  But little for my profit; can you think, lords,
  That any Englishman dare give me counsel?
  Or be a known friend, 'gainst his
  Highness' pleasure-
  Though he be grown so desperate to be honest-
  And live a subject? Nay, forsooth, my friends,
  They that must weigh out my afflictions,
  They that my trust must grow to, live not here;
  They are, as all my other comforts, far hence,
  In mine own country, lords.
CAMPEIUS. I would your Grace
  Would leave your griefs, and take my counsel.
QUEEN KATHARINE. How, sir?
CAMPEIUS. Put your main cause into the
  King's protection;
  He's loving and most gracious. 'Twill be much

Both for your honour better and your cause;
  For if the trial of the law o'ertake ye
  You'll part away disgrac'd.
WOLSEY. He tells you rightly.
QUEEN KATHARINE. Ye tell me what ye wish for
  both-my ruin.
  Is this your Christian counsel? Out upon ye!
  Heaven is above all yet: there sits a Judge
  That no king can corrupt.
CAMPEIUS. Your rage mistakes us.
QUEEN KATHARINE. The more shame for ye; holy
  men I thought ye,
  Upon my soul, two reverend cardinal virtues;
  But cardinal sins and hollow hearts I fear ye.
  Mend 'em, for shame, my lords. Is this
  your comfort?
  The cordial that ye bring a wretched lady-
  A woman lost among ye, laugh'd at, scorn'd?
  I will not wish ye half my miseries:
  I have more charity; but say I warned ye.
  Take heed, for heaven's sake take heed, lest
  at once
  The burden of my sorrows fall upon ye.
WOLSEY. Madam, this is a mere distraction;
  You turn the good we offer into envy.
QUEEN KATHARINE. Ye turn me into nothing.
  Woe upon ye,
  And all such false professors! Would you
  have me-
  If you have any justice, any pity,
  If ye be any thing but churchmen's habits-
  Put my sick cause into his hands that hates me?
  Alas! has banish'd me his bed already,
  His love too long ago! I am old, my lords,
  And all the fellowship I hold now with him
  Is only my obedience. What can happen
  To me above this wretchedness? All your studies
  Make me a curse like this.
CAMPEIUS. Your fears are worse.
QUEEN KATHARINE. Have I liv'd thus long-let me
  speak myself,
  Since virtue finds no friends-a wife, a true one?
  A woman, I dare say without vain-glory,
  Never yet branded with suspicion?
  Have I with all my full affections
  Still met the King, lov'd him next heav'n,
  obey'd him,
  Been, out of fondness, superstitious to him,
  Almost forgot my prayers to content him,
  And am I thus rewarded? 'Tis not well, lords.
  Bring me a constant woman to her husband,
  One that ne'er dream'd a joy beyond
  his pleasure,

And to that woman, when she has done most,
Yet will I add an honour-a great patience.

WOLSEY. Madam, you wander from the good we
aim at.

QUEEN KATHARINE. My lord, I dare not make
myself so guilty,
To give up willingly that noble title
Your master wed me to: nothing but death
Shall e'er divorce my dignities.

WOLSEY. Pray hear me.

QUEEN KATHARINE. Would I had never trod this
English earth,
Or felt the flatteries that grow upon it!
Ye have angels' faces, but heaven knows
your hearts.
What will become of me now, wretched lady?
I am the most unhappy woman living.
[To her WOMEN] Alas, poor wenches, where are
now your fortunes?
Shipwreck'd upon a kingdom, where no pity,
No friends, no hope; no kindred weep for me;
Almost no grave allow'd me. Like the lily,
That once was mistress of the field,
and flourish'd,
I'll hang my head and perish.

WOLSEY. If your Grace
Could but be brought to know our ends
are honest,
You'd feel more comfort. Why should we,
good lady,
Upon what cause, wrong you? Alas, our places,
The way of our profession is against it;
We are to cure such sorrows, not to sow 'em.
For goodness' sake, consider what you do;
How you may hurt yourself, ay, utterly
Grow from the King's acquaintance, by
this carriage.
The hearts of princes kiss obedience,
So much they love it; but to stubborn spirits
They swell and grow as terrible as storms.
I know you have a gentle, noble temper,
A soul as even as a calm. Pray think us
Those we profess, peace-makers, friends,
and servants.

CAMPEIUS. Madam, you'll find it so. You wrong
your virtues
With these weak women's fears. A noble spirit,
As yours was put into you, ever casts
Such doubts as false coin from it. The King
loves you;
Beware you lose it not. For us, if you please
To trust us in your business, we are ready
To use our utmost studies in your service.

QUEEN KATHARINE. Do what ye will my lords;
and pray forgive me
If I have us'd myself unmannerly;
You know I am a woman, lacking wit
To make a seemly answer to such persons.
Pray do my service to his Majesty;
He has my heart yet, and shall have my prayers
While I shall have my life. Come,
reverend fathers,
Bestow your counsels on me; she now begs
That little thought, when she set footing here,
She should have bought her dignities so
dear.

Exeunt.

✣ SCENE II ✣
London. The palace

*Enter the DUKE OF NORFOLK, the DUKE OF
SUFFOLK, the EARL OF SURREY, and the LORD
CHAMBERLAIN*

NORFOLK. If you will now unite in
your complaints
And force them with a constancy, the Cardinal
Cannot stand under them: if you omit
The offer of this time, I cannot promise
But that you shall sustain moe new disgraces
With these you bear already.

SURREY. I am joyful
To meet the least occasion that may give me
Remembrance of my father-in-law, the Duke,
To be reveng'd on him.

SUFFOLK. Which of the peers
Have uncontemn'd gone by him, or at least
Strangely neglected? When did he regard
The stamp of nobleness in any person
Out of himself?

CHAMBERLAIN. My lords, you speak
your pleasures.
What he deserves of you and me I know;
What we can do to him-though now the time
Gives way to us-I much fear. If you cannot
Bar his access to th' King, never attempt
Anything on him; for he hath a witchcraft
Over the King in's tongue.

NORFOLK. O, fear him not!
His spell in that is out; the King hath found
Matter against him that for ever mars
The honey of his language. No, he's settled,
Not to come off, in his displeasure.

SURREY. Sir,
I should be glad to hear such news as this
Once every hour.

NORFOLK. Believe it, this is true:
 In the divorce his contrary proceedings
 Are all unfolded; wherein he appears
 As I would wish mine enemy.
SURREY. How came
 His practices to light?
SUFFOLK. Most strangely.
SURREY. O, how, how?
SUFFOLK. The Cardinal's letters to the
 Pope miscarried,
 And came to th' eye o' th' King; wherein
 was read
 How that the Cardinal did entreat his Holiness
 To stay the judgment o' th' divorce; for if
 It did take place, 'I do' quoth he 'perceive
 My king is tangled in affection to
 A creature of the Queen's, Lady Anne Bullen.'
SURREY. Has the King this?
SUFFOLK. Believe it.
SURREY. Will this work?
CHAMBERLAIN. The King in this perceives him
 how he coasts
 And hedges his own way. But in this point
 All his tricks founder, and he brings his physic
 After his patient's death: the King already
 Hath married the fair lady.
SURREY. Would he had!
SUFFOLK. May you be happy in your wish,
 my lord!
 For, I profess, you have it.
SURREY. Now, all my joy
 Trace the conjunction!
SUFFOLK. My amen to't!
NORFOLK. All men's!
SUFFOLK. There's order given for her coronation;
 Marry, this is yet but young, and may be left
 To some ears unrecounted. But, my lords,
 She is a gallant creature, and complete
 In mind and feature. I persuade me from her
 Will fall some blessing to this land, which shall
 In it be memoris'd.
SURREY. But will the King
 Digest this letter of the Cardinal's?
 The Lord forbid!
NORFOLK. Marry, amen!
SUFFOLK. No, no;
 There be moe wasps that buzz about his nose
 Will make this sting the sooner.
  Cardinal Campeius
 Is stol'n away to Rome; hath ta'en no leave;
 Has left the cause o' th' King unhandled, and
 Is posted, as the agent of our Cardinal,
 To second all his plot. I do assure you

 The King cried 'Ha!' at this.
CHAMBERLAIN. Now, God incense him,
 And let him cry 'Ha!' louder!
NORFOLK. But, my lord,
 When returns Cranmer?
SUFFOLK. He is return'd in his opinions; which
 Have satisfied the King for his divorce,
 Together with all famous colleges
 Almost in Christendom. Shortly, I believe,
 His second marriage shall be publish'd, and
 Her coronation. Katharine no more
 Shall be call'd queen, but princess dowager
 And widow to Prince Arthur.
NORFOLK. This same Cranmer's
 A worthy fellow, and hath ta'en much pain
 In the King's business.
SUFFOLK. He has; and we shall see him
 For it an archbishop.
NORFOLK. So I hear.
SUFFOLK. 'Tis so.
    Enter WOLSEY and CROMWELL
 The Cardinal!
NORFOLK. Observe, observe, he's moody.
WOLSEY. The packet, Cromwell,
 Gave't you the King?
CROMWELL. To his own hand, in's bedchamber.
WOLSEY. Look'd he o' th' inside of the paper?
CROMWELL. Presently
 He did unseal them; and the first he view'd,
 He did it with a serious mind; a heed
 Was in his countenance. You he bade
 Attend him here this morning.
WOLSEY. Is he ready
 To come abroad?
CROMWELL. I think by this he is.
WOLSEY. Leave me awhile. *[Exit CROMWELL]*
 [Aside] It shall be to the Duchess of Alençon,
 The French King's sister; he shall marry her.
 Anne Bullen! No, I'll no Anne Bullens for him;
 There's more in't than fair visage. Bullen!
 No, we'll no Bullens. Speedily I wish
 To hear from Rome. The Marchioness
 of Pembroke!
NORFOLK. He's discontented.
SUFFOLK. May be he hears the King
 Does whet his anger to him.
SURREY. Sharp enough,
 Lord, for thy justice!
WOLSEY. *[Aside]* The late Queen's gentlewoman, a
 knight's daughter,
 To be her mistress' mistress! The
 Queen's queen!
 This candle burns not clear. 'Tis I must snuff it;

Then out it goes. What though I know
  her virtuous
And well deserving? Yet I know her for
A spleeny Lutheran; and not wholesome to
Our cause that she should lie i' th' bosom of
Our hard-rul'd King. Again, there is sprung up
An heretic, an arch one, Cranmer; one
Hath crawl'd into the favour of the King,
And is his oracle.
NORFOLK. He is vex'd at something.

  Enter the KING, reading of a schedule, and LOVELL

SURREY. I would 'twere something that would fret
  the string,
  The master-cord on's heart!
SUFFOLK. The King, the King!
KING. What piles of wealth hath he accumulated
  To his own portion! And what expense by
  th' hour
  Seems to flow from him! How, i' th' name
  of thrift,
  Does he rake this together?-Now, my lords,
  Saw you the Cardinal?
NORFOLK. My lord, we have
  Stood here observing him. Some
  strange commotion
  Is in his brain: he bites his lip and starts,
  Stops on a sudden, looks upon the ground,
  Then lays his finger on his temple; straight
  Springs out into fast gait; then stops again,
  Strikes his breast hard; and anon he casts
  His eye against the moon. In most
  strange postures
  We have seen him set himself.
KING. It may well be
  There is a mutiny in's mind. This morning
  Papers of state he sent me to peruse,
  As I requir'd; and wot you what I found
  There-on my conscience, put unwittingly?
  Forsooth, an inventory, thus importing
  The several parcels of his plate, his treasure,
  Rich stuffs, and ornaments of household; which
  I find at such proud rate that it outspeaks
  Possession of a subject.
NORFOLK. It's heaven's will;
  Some spirit put this paper in the packet
  To bless your eye withal.
KING. If we did think
  His contemplation were above the earth
  And fix'd on spiritual object, he should still
  Dwell in his musings; but I am afraid
  His thinkings are below the moon, not worth
  His serious considering.

  The KING takes his seat and whispers LOVELL, who goes to

  the CARDINAL

WOLSEY. Heaven forgive me!
  Ever God bless your Highness!
KING. Good, my lord,
  You are full of heavenly stuff, and bear
  the inventory
  Of your best graces in your mind; the which
  You were now running o'er. You have
  scarce time
  To steal from spiritual leisure a brief span
  To keep your earthly audit; sure, in that
  I deem you an ill husband, and am glad
  To have you therein my companion.
WOLSEY. Sir,
  For holy offices I have a time; a time
  To think upon the part of business which
  I bear i' th' state; and nature does require
  Her times of preservation, which perforce
  I, her frail son, amongst my brethren mortal,
  Must give my tendance to.
KING. You have said well.
WOLSEY. And ever may your Highness
  yoke together,
  As I will lend you cause, my doing well
  With my well saying!
KING. 'Tis well said again;
  And 'tis a kind of good deed to say well;
  And yet words are no deeds. My father lov'd you:
  He said he did; and with his deed did crown
  His word upon you. Since I had my office
  I have kept you next my heart; have not alone
  Employ'd you where high profits might
  come home,
  But par'd my present havings to bestow
  My bounties upon you.
WOLSEY. *[Aside]* What should this mean?
SURREY. *[Aside]* The Lord increase this business!
KING. Have I not made you
  The prime man of the state? I pray you tell me
  If what I now pronounce you have found true;
  And, if you may confess it, say withal
  If you are bound to us or no. What say you?
WOLSEY. My sovereign, I confess your
  royal graces,
  Show'r'd on me daily, have been more
  than could
  My studied purposes requite; which went
  Beyond all man's endeavours. My endeavours,
  Have ever come too short of my desires,
  Yet fil'd with my abilities; mine own ends
  Have been mine so that evermore they pointed
  To th' good of your most sacred person and
  The profit of the state. For your great graces

Heap'd upon me, poor undeserver, I
Can nothing render but allegiant thanks;
My pray'rs to heaven for you; my loyalty,
Which ever has and ever shall be growing,
Till death, that winter, kill it.
KING. Fairly answer'd!
A loyal and obedient subject is
Therein illustrated; the honour of it
Does pay the act of it, as, i' th' contrary,
The foulness is the punishment. I presume
That, as my hand has open'd bounty to you,
My heart dropp'd love, my pow'r rain'd
honour, more
On you than any, so your hand and heart,
Your brain, and every function of your power,
Should, notwithstanding that your bond of duty,
As 'twere in love's particular, be more
To me, your friend, than any.
WOLSEY. I do profess
That for your Highness' good I ever labour'd
More than mine own; that am, have, and will be-
Though all the world should crack their duty
to you,
And throw it from their soul; though perils did
Abound as thick as thought could make 'em, and
Appear in forms more horrid-yet my duty,
As doth a rock against the chiding flood,
Should the approach of this wild river break,
And stand unshaken yours.
KING. 'Tis nobly spoken.
Take notice, lords, he has a loyal breast,
For you have seen him open 't. Read o'er this;
[Giving him papers]
And after, this; and then to breakfast with
What appetite you have.
Exit the KING, frowning upon the CARDINAL; the Nobles
throng after him, smiling and whispering
WOLSEY. What should this mean?
What sudden anger's this? How have I reap'd it?
He parted frowning from me, as if ruin
Leap'd from his eyes; so looks the chafed lion
Upon the daring huntsman that has gall'd him-
Then makes him nothing. I must read
this paper;
I fear, the story of his anger. 'Tis so;
This paper has undone me. 'Tis th' account
Of all that world of wealth I have drawn together
For mine own ends; indeed to gain
the popedom,
And fee my friends in Rome. O negligence,
Fit for a fool to fall by! What cross devil
Made me put this main secret in the packet
I sent the King? Is there no way to cure this?

No new device to beat this from his brains?
I know 'twill stir him strongly; yet I know
A way, if it take right, in spite of fortune,
Will bring me off again. What's this? 'To
th' Pope'.
The letter, as I live, with all the business
I writ to's Holiness. Nay then, farewell!
I have touch'd the highest point of all
my greatness,
And from that full meridian of my glory
I haste now to my setting. I shall fall
Like a bright exhalation in the evening,
And no man see me more.
Re-enter to WOLSEY the DUKES OF NORFOLK and
SUFFOLK, the EARL OF SURREY, and the LORD
CHAMBERLAIN
NORFOLK. Hear the King's pleasure, Cardinal,
who commands you
To render up the great seal presently
Into our hands, and to confine yourself
To Asher House, my Lord of Winchester's,
Till you hear further from his Highness.
WOLSEY. Stay:
Where's your commission, lords? Words
cannot carry
Authority so weighty.
SUFFOLK. Who dares cross 'em,
Bearing the King's will from his
mouth expressly?
WOLSEY. Till I find more than will or words to
do it-
I mean your malice-know, officious lords,
I dare and must deny it. Now I feel
Of what coarse metal ye are moulded-envy;
How eagerly ye follow my disgraces,
As if it fed ye; and how sleek and wanton
Ye appear in every thing may bring my ruin!
Follow your envious courses, men of malice;
You have Christian warrant for 'em, and
no doubt
In time will find their fit rewards. That seal
You ask with such a violence, the King-
Mine and your master-with his own hand
gave me;
Bade me enjoy it, with the place and honours,
During my life; and, to confirm his goodness,
Tied it by letters-patents. Now, who'll take it?
SURREY. The King, that gave it.
WOLSEY. It must be himself then.
SURREY. Thou art a proud traitor, priest.
WOLSEY. Proud lord, thou liest.
Within these forty hours Surrey durst better
Have burnt that tongue than said so.

SURREY. Thy ambition,
  Thou scarlet sin, robb'd this bewailing land
  Of noble Buckingham, my father-in-law.
  The heads of all thy brother cardinals,
  With thee and all thy best parts bound together,
  Weigh'd not a hair of his. Plague of your policy!
  You sent me deputy for Ireland;
  Far from his succour, from the King, from all
  That might have mercy on the fault thou
    gav'st him;
  Whilst your great goodness, out of holy pity,
  Absolv'd him with an axe.
WOLSEY. This, and all else
  This talking lord can lay upon my credit,
  I answer is most false. The Duke by law
  Found his deserts; how innocent I was
  From any private malice in his end,
  His noble jury and foul cause can witness.
  If I lov'd many words, lord, I should tell you
  You have as little honesty as honour,
  That in the way of loyalty and truth
  Toward the King, my ever royal master,
  Dare mate a sounder man than Surrey can be
  And all that love his follies.
SURREY. By my soul,
  Your long coat, priest, protects you; thou
    shouldst feel
  My sword i' the life-blood of thee else. My lords
  Can ye endure to hear this arrogance?
  And from this fellow? If we live thus tamely,
  To be thus jaded by a piece of scarlet,
  Farewell nobility! Let his Grace go forward
  And dare us with his cap like larks.
WOLSEY. All goodness
  Is poison to thy stomach.
SURREY. Yes, that goodness
  Of gleaning all the land's wealth into one,
  Into your own hands, Cardinal, by extortion;
  The goodness of your intercepted packets
  You writ to th' Pope against the King;
    your goodness,
  Since you provoke me, shall be most notorious.
  My Lord of Norfolk, as you are truly noble,
  As you respect the common good, the state
  Of our despis'd nobility, our issues,
  Whom, if he live, will scarce be gentlemen-
  Produce the grand sum of his sins, the articles
  Collected from his life. I'll startle you
  Worse than the sacring bell, when the
    brown wench
  Lay kissing in your arms, Lord Cardinal.
WOLSEY. How much, methinks, I could despise
  this man,

But that I am bound in charity against it!
NORFOLK. Those articles, my lord, are in the
  King's hand;
  But, thus much, they are foul ones.
WOLSEY. So much fairer
  And spotless shall mine innocence arise,
  When the King knows my truth.
SURREY. This cannot save you.
  I thank my memory I yet remember
  Some of these articles; and out they shall.
  Now, if you can blush and cry guilty, Cardinal,
  You'll show a little honesty.
WOLSEY. Speak on, sir;
  I dare your worst objections. If I blush,
  It is to see a nobleman want manners.
SURREY. I had rather want those than my head.
  Have at you!
  First, that without the King's assent
    or knowledge
  You wrought to be a legate; by which power
  You maim'd the jurisdiction of all bishops.
NORFOLK. Then, that in all you writ to Rome,
  or else
  To foreign princes, 'Ego et Rex meus'
  Was still inscrib'd; in which you brought
    the King
  To be your servant.
SUFFOLK. Then, that without the knowledge
  Either of King or Council, when you went
  Ambassador to the Emperor, you made bold
  To carry into Flanders the great seal.
SURREY. Item, you sent a large commission
  To Gregory de Cassado, to conclude,
  Without the King's will or the state's allowance,
  A league between his Highness and Ferrara.
SUFFOLK. That out of mere ambition you
  have caus'd
  Your holy hat to be stamp'd on the King's coin.
SURREY. Then, that you have sent
  innumerable substance,
  By what means got I leave to your
    own conscience,
  To furnish Rome and to prepare the ways
  You have for dignities, to the mere undoing
  Of all the kingdom. Many more there are,
  Which, since they are of you, and odious,
  I will not taint my mouth with.
CHAMBERLAIN. O my lord,
  Press not a falling man too far! 'Tis virtue.
  His faults lie open to the laws; let them,
  Not you, correct him. My heart weeps to see him
  So little of his great self.
SURREY. I forgive him.

SUFFOLK. Lord Cardinal, the King's further
  pleasure is-
Because all those things you have done of late,
By your power legatine within this kingdom,
Fall into th' compass of a praemunire-
That therefore such a writ be sued against you:
To forfeit all your goods, lands, tenements,
Chattels, and whatsoever, and to be
Out of the King's protection. This is my charge.
NORFOLK. And so we'll leave you to
  your meditations
How to live better. For your stubborn answer
About the giving back the great seal to us,
The King shall know it, and, no doubt, shall
  thank you.
So fare you well, my little good Lord Cardinal.
            Exeunt all but WOLSEY
WOLSEY. So farewell to the little good you
  bear me.
Farewell, a long farewell, to all my greatness!
This is the state of man: to-day he puts forth
The tender leaves of hopes; to-morrow blossoms
And bears his blushing honours thick upon him;
The third day comes a frost, a killing frost,
And when he thinks, good easy man, full surely
His greatness is a-ripening, nips his root,
And then he falls, as I do. I have ventur'd,
Like little wanton boys that swim on bladders,
This many summers in a sea of glory;
But far beyond my depth. My high-blown pride
At length broke under me, and now has left me,
Weary and old with service, to the mercy
Of a rude stream, that must for ever hide me.
Vain pomp and glory of this world, I hate ye;
I feel my heart new open'd. O, how wretched
Is that poor man that hangs on princes' favours!
There is betwixt that smile we would aspire to,
That sweet aspect of princes, and their ruin
More pangs and fears than wars or women have;
And when he falls, he falls like Lucifer,
Never to hope again.
      Enter CROMWELL, standing amazed
Why, how now, Cromwell!
CROMWELL. I have no power to speak, sir.
WOLSEY. What, amaz'd
At my misfortunes? Can thy spirit wonder
A great man should decline? Nay, an you weep,
I am fall'n indeed.
CROMWELL. How does your Grace?
WOLSEY. Why, well;
Never so truly happy, my good Cromwell.
I know myself now, and I feel within me
A peace above all earthly dignities,

A still and quiet conscience. The King has
  cur'd me,
I humbly thank his Grace; and from
  these shoulders,
These ruin'd pillars, out of pity, taken
A load would sink a navy-too much honour.
O, 'tis a burden, Cromwell, 'tis a burden
Too heavy for a man that hopes for heaven!
CROMWELL. I am glad your Grace has made that
  right use of it.
WOLSEY. I hope I have. I am able now, methinks,
Out of a fortitude of soul I feel,
To endure more miseries and greater far
Than my weak-hearted enemies dare offer.
What news abroad?
CROMWELL. The heaviest and the worst
Is your displeasure with the King.
WOLSEY. God bless him!
CROMWELL. The next is that Sir Thomas More
  is chosen
Lord Chancellor in your place.
WOLSEY. That's somewhat sudden.
But he's a learned man. May he continue
Long in his Highness' favour, and do justice
For truth's sake and his conscience; that
  his bones
When he has run his course and sleeps
  in blessings,
May have a tomb of orphans' tears wept on him!
What more?
CROMWELL. That Cranmer is return'd
  with welcome,
Install'd Lord Archbishop of Canterbury.
WOLSEY. That's news indeed.
CROMWELL. Last, that the Lady Anne,
Whom the King hath in secrecy long married,
This day was view'd in open as his queen,
Going to chapel; and the voice is now
Only about her coronation.
WOLSEY. There was the weight that pull'd me
  down.O Cromwell,
The King has gone beyond me. All my glories
In that one woman I have lost for ever.
No sun shall ever usher forth mine honours,
Or gild again the noble troops that waited
Upon my smiles. Go get thee from
  me, Cromwell;
I am a poor fall'n man, unworthy now
To be thy lord and master. Seek the King;
That sun, I pray, may never set! I have told him
What and how true thou art. He will
  advance thee;
Some little memory of me will stir him-

I know his noble nature-not to let
Thy hopeful service perish too. Good Cromwell,
Neglect him not; make use now, and provide
For thine own future safety.

CROMWELL. O my lord,
Must I then leave you? Must I needs forgo
So good, so noble, and so true a master?
Bear witness, all that have not hearts of iron,
With what a sorrow Cromwell leaves his lord.
The King shall have my service; but my prayers
For ever and for ever shall be yours.

WOLSEY. Cromwell, I did not think to shed a tear
In all my miseries; but thou hast forc'd me,
Out of thy honest truth, to play the woman.
Let's dry our eyes; and thus far hear
  me, Cromwell,
And when I am forgotten, as I shall be,
And sleep in dull cold marble, where no mention
Of me more must be heard of, say I taught thee-
Say Wolsey, that once trod the ways of glory,
And sounded all the depths and shoals
  of honour,
Found thee a way, out of his wreck, to rise in-
A sure and safe one, though thy master miss'd it.
Mark but my fall and that that ruin'd me.
Cromwell, I charge thee, fling away ambition:
By that sin fell the angels. How can man then,
The image of his Maker, hope to win by it?
Love thyself last; cherish those hearts that
  hate thee;
Corruption wins not more than honesty.
Still in thy right hand carry gentle peace
To silence envious tongues. Be just, and
  fear not;
Let all the ends thou aim'st at be thy country's,
Thy God's, and truth's; then, if thou fall'st,
  O Cromwell,
Thou fall'st a blessed martyr!
Serve the King, and-prithee lead me in.
There take an inventory of all I have
To the last penny; 'tis the King's. My robe,
And my integrity to heaven, is all
I dare now call mine own. O
  Cromwell, Cromwell!
Had I but serv'd my God with half the zeal
I serv'd my King, he would not in mine age
Have left me naked to mine enemies.

CROMWELL. Good sir, have patience.

WOLSEY. So I have. Farewell
The hopes of court! My hopes in heaven
  do dwell.

Exeunt.

 **ACT IV**

✦ SCENE I ✦
A street in Westminster

Enter two GENTLEMEN, meeting one another

FIRST GENTLEMAN. Y'are well met once again.

SECOND GENTLEMAN. So are you.

FIRST GENTLEMAN. You come to take your
  stand here, and behold
  The Lady Anne pass from her coronation?

SECOND GENTLEMAN. 'Tis all my business. At
  our last encounter
  The Duke of Buckingham came from his trial.

FIRST GENTLEMAN. 'Tis very true. But that time
  offer'd sorrow;
  This, general joy.

SECOND GENTLEMAN. 'Tis well. The citizens,
  I am sure, have shown at full their
  royal minds-
  As, let 'em have their rights, they are
  ever forward-
  In celebration of this day with shows,
  Pageants, and sights of honour.

FIRST GENTLEMAN. Never greater,
  Nor, I'll assure you, better taken, sir.

SECOND GENTLEMAN. May I be bold to ask
  what that contains,
  That paper in your hand?

FIRST GENTLEMAN. Yes; 'tis the list
  Of those that claim their offices this day,
  By custom of the coronation.
  The Duke of Suffolk is the first, and claims
  To be High Steward; next, the Duke of Norfolk,
  He to be Earl Marshal. You may read the rest.

SECOND GENTLEMAN. I thank you, sir; had I
  not known those customs,
  I should have been beholding to your paper.
  But, I beseech you, what's become
  of Katharine,
  The Princess Dowager? How goes
  her business?

FIRST GENTLEMAN. That I can tell you too.
  The Archbishop
  Of Canterbury, accompanied with other
  Learned and reverend fathers of his order,
  Held a late court at Dunstable, six miles off
  From Ampthill, where the Princess lay;
  to which
  She was often cited by them, but appear'd not.
  And, to be short, for not appearance and

The King's late scruple, by the main assent
Of all these learned men, she was divorc'd,
And the late marriage made of none effect;
Since which she was removed to Kimbolton,
Where she remains now sick.
SECOND GENTLEMAN. Alas, good lady! *[Trumpets]*
The trumpets sound. Stand close, the Queen
is coming.

Hautboys
THE ORDER OF THE CORONATION.
1. *A lively flourish of trumpets.*
2. *Then two JUDGES.*
3. *LORD CHANCELLOR, with purse and mace before him.*
4. *CHORISTERS singing. Music*
5. *MAYOR OF LONDON, bearing the mace. Then
   GARTER, in his coat of arms, and on his head a gilt
   copper crown.*
6. *MARQUIS DORSET, bearing a sceptre of gold, on his head
   a demi-coronal of gold. With him, the EARL OF SURREY,
   bearing the rod of silver with the dove, crowned with an earl's
   coronet. Collars of Esses.*
7. *DUKE OF SUFFOLK, in his robe of estate, his coronet
   on his head, bearing a long white wand, as High Steward.
   With him, the DUKE OF NORFOLK, with the rod of
   marshalship, a coronet on his head. Collars of Esses.*
8. *A canopy borne by four of the CINQUE-PORTS; under
   it the QUEEN in her robe; in her hair richly adorned
   with pearl, crowned. On each side her, the BISHOPS OF
   LONDON and WINCHESTER.*
9. *The old DUCHESS OF NORFOLK, in a coronal of gold
   wrought with flowers, bearing the QUEEN'S train.*
10. *Certain LADIES or COUNTESSES, with plain circlets of
    gold without flowers.*
   *Exeunt, first passing over the stage in order and state, and then a
   great flourish of trumpets.*

SECOND GENTLEMAN. A royal train, believe
me. These I know. Who's that that bears
the sceptre?
FIRST GENTLEMAN. Marquis Dorset;
And that the Earl of Surrey, with the rod.
SECOND GENTLEMAN. A bold brave gentleman.
That should be the Duke of Suffolk?
FIRST GENTLEMAN. 'Tis the same-High Steward.
SECOND GENTLEMAN. And that my Lord
of Norfolk?
FIRST GENTLEMAN. Yes.
SECOND GENTLEMAN. *[Looking on the QUEEN]*
Heaven bless thee!
Thou hast the sweetest face I ever look'd on.
Sir, as I have a soul, she is an angel;
Our king has all the Indies in his arms,
And more and richer, when he strains that lady;
I cannot blame his conscience.

FIRST GENTLEMAN. They that bear
The cloth of honour over her are four barons
Of the Cinque-ports.
SECOND GENTLEMAN. Those men are happy;
and so are all are near her.
I take it she that carries up the train
Is that old noble lady, Duchess of Norfolk.
FIRST GENTLEMAN. It is; and all the rest
are countesses.
SECOND GENTLEMAN. Their coronets say so.
These are stars indeed,
And sometimes falling ones.
FIRST GENTLEMAN. No more of that.
   Exit Procession, with a great flourish of trumpets.
   Enter a third GENTLEMAN
God save you, sir! Where have you
been broiling?
THIRD GENTLEMAN. Among the crowds i' th'
Abbey, where a finger
Could not be wedg'd in more; I am stifled
With the mere rankness of their joy.
SECOND GENTLEMAN. You saw
The ceremony?
THIRD GENTLEMAN. That I did.
FIRST GENTLEMAN. How was it?
THIRD GENTLEMAN. Well worth the seeing.
SECOND GENTLEMAN. Good sir, speak it to us.
THIRD GENTLEMAN. As well as I am able. The
rich stream
Of lords and ladies, having brought the Queen
To a prepar'd place in the choir, fell off
A distance from her, while her Grace sat down
To rest awhile, some half an hour or so,
In a rich chair of state, opposing freely
The beauty of her person to the people.
Believe me, sir, she is the goodliest woman
That ever lay by man; which when the people
Had the full view of, such a noise arose
As the shrouds make at sea in a stiff tempest,
As loud, and to as many tunes; hats, cloaks-
Doublets, I think-flew up, and had their faces
Been loose, this day they had been lost.
Such joy
I never saw before. Great-bellied women,
That had not half a week to go, like rams
In the old time of war, would shake the press,
And make 'em reel before 'em. No man living
Could say 'This is my wife' there, all
were woven
So strangely in one piece.
SECOND GENTLEMAN. But what follow'd?
THIRD GENTLEMAN. At length her Grace rose,
and with modest paces

Came to the altar, where she kneel'd,
  and saintlike
Cast her fair eyes to heaven, and
  pray'd devoutly.
Then rose again, and bow'd her to the people;
When by the Archbishop of Canterbury
She had all the royal makings of a queen:
As holy oil, Edward Confessor's crown,
The rod, and bird of peace, and all
  such emblems
Laid nobly on her; which perform'd, the choir,
With all the choicest music of the kingdom,
Together sung 'Te Deum'. So she parted,
And with the same full state pac'd back again
To York Place, where the feast is held.
FIRST GENTLEMAN. Sir,
  You must no more call it York Place: that's past:
  For since the Cardinal fell that title's lost.
  'Tis now the King's, and called Whitehall.
THIRD GENTLEMAN. I know it;
  But 'tis so lately alter'd that the old name
  Is fresh about me.
SECOND GENTLEMAN. What two
  reverend bishops
  Were those that went on each side of
  the Queen?
THIRD GENTLEMAN. Stokesly and Gardiner: the
  one of Winchester,
  Newly preferr'd from the King's secretary;
  The other, London.
SECOND GENTLEMAN. He of Winchester
  Is held no great good lover of the Archbishop's,
  The virtuous Cranmer.
THIRD GENTLEMAN. All the land knows that;
  However, yet there is no great breach. When
  it comes,
  Cranmer will find a friend will not shrink
  from him.
SECOND GENTLEMAN. Who may that be, I
  pray you?
THIRD GENTLEMAN. Thomas Cromwell,
  A man in much esteem with th' King, and truly
  A worthy friend. The King has made him Master
  O' th' Jewel House,
  And one, already, of the Privy Council.
SECOND GENTLEMAN. He will deserve more.
THIRD GENTLEMAN. Yes, without all doubt.
  Come, gentlemen, ye shall go my way, which
  Is to th' court, and there ye shall be
  my guests:
  Something I can command. As I walk thither,
  I'll tell ye more.
BOTH. You may command us, sir. *Exeunt.*

✒ SCENE II ✒
Kimbolton

Enter KATHARINE, Dowager, sick; led between GRIFFITH,
her Gentleman Usher, and PATIENCE, her woman

GRIFFITH. How does your Grace?
KATHARINE. O Griffith, sick to death!
  My legs like loaden branches bow to th' earth,
  Willing to leave their burden. Reach a chair.
  So-now, methinks, I feel a little ease.
  Didst thou not tell me, Griffith, as thou
  led'st me,
  That the great child of honour, Cardinal Wolsey,
  Was dead?
GRIFFITH. Yes, madam; but I think your Grace,
  Out of the pain you suffer'd, gave no ear to't.
KATHARINE. Prithee, good Griffith, tell me how
  he died.
  If well, he stepp'd before me, happily,
  For my example.
GRIFFITH. Well, the voice goes, madam;
  For after the stout Earl Northumberland
  Arrested him at York and brought him forward,
  As a man sorely tainted, to his answer,
  He fell sick suddenly, and grew so ill
  He could not sit his mule.
KATHARINE. Alas, poor man!
GRIFFITH. At last, with easy roads, he came
  to Leicester,
  Lodg'd in the abbey; where the reverend abbot,
  With all his covent, honourably receiv'd him;
  To whom he gave these words: 'O father Abbot,
  An old man, broken with the storms of state,
  Is come to lay his weary bones among ye;
  Give him a little earth for charity!'
  So went to bed; where eagerly his sickness
  Pursu'd him still. And three nights after this,
  About the hour of eight-which he himself
  Foretold should be his last-full of repentance,
  Continual meditations, tears, and sorrows,
  He gave his honours to the world again,
  His blessed part to heaven, and slept in peace.
KATHARINE. So may he rest; his faults lie gently
  on him!
  Yet thus far, Griffith, give me leave to speak him,
  And yet with charity. He was a man
  Of an unbounded stomach, ever ranking
  Himself with princes; one that, by suggestion,
  Tied all the kingdom. Simony was fair play;
  His own opinion was his law. I' th' presence

He would say untruths, and be ever double
Both in his words and meaning. He was never,
But where he meant to ruin, pitiful.
His promises were, as he then was, mighty;
But his performance, as he is now, nothing.
Of his own body he was ill, and gave
The clergy ill example.

GRIFFITH. Noble madam,
Men's evil manners live in brass: their virtues
We write in water. May it please your Highness
To hear me speak his good now?

KATHARINE. Yes, good Griffith;
I were malicious else.

GRIFFITH. This Cardinal,
Though from an humble stock, undoubtedly
Was fashion'd to much honour from
  his cradle.
He was a scholar, and a ripe and good one;
Exceeding wise, fair-spoken, and persuading;
Lofty and sour to them that lov'd him not,
But to those men that sought him sweet
  as summer.
And though he were unsatisfied in getting-
Which was a sin-yet in bestowing, madam,
He was most princely: ever witness for him
Those twins of learning that he rais'd in you,
Ipswich and Oxford! One of which fell with him,
Unwilling to outlive the good that did it;
The other, though unfinish'd, yet so famous,
So excellent in art, and still so rising,
That Christendom shall ever speak his virtue.
His overthrow heap'd happiness upon him;
For then, and not till then, he felt himself,
And found the blessedness of being little.
And, to add greater honours to his age
Than man could give him, he died fearing God.

KATHARINE. After my death I wish no
  other herald,
No other speaker of my living actions,
To keep mine honour from corruption,
But such an honest chronicler as Griffith.
Whom I most hated living, thou hast made me,
With thy religious truth and modesty,
Now in his ashes honour. Peace be with him!
Patience, be near me still, and set me lower:
I have not long to trouble thee. Good Griffith,
Cause the musicians play me that sad note
I nam'd my knell, whilst I sit meditating
On that celestial harmony I go to.

Sad and solemn music

GRIFFITH. She is asleep. Good wench, let's sit
  down quiet,
For fear we wake her. Softly, gentle Patience.

THE VISION.

*Enter, solemnly tripping one after another, six Personages clad in
white robes, wearing on their heads garlands of bays, and golden
vizards on their faces; branches of bays or palm in their hands. They
first congee unto her, then dance; and, at certain changes, the first
two hold a spare garland over her head, at which the other four make
reverent curtsies. Then the two that held the garland deliver the same
to the other next two, who observe the same order in their changes,
and holding the garland over her head; which done, they deliver the
same garland to the last two, who likewise observe the same order;
at which, as it were by inspiration, she makes in her sleep signs
of rejoicing, and holdeth up her hands to heaven. And so in their
dancing vanish, carrying the garland with them. The music continues*

KATHARINE. Spirits of peace, where are ye? Are
  ye all gone?
And leave me here in wretchedness behind ye?

GRIFFITH. Madam, we are here.

KATHARINE. It is not you I call for.
Saw ye none enter since I slept?

GRIFFITH. None, madam.

KATHARINE. No? Saw you not, even now, a
  blessed troop
Invite me to a banquet; whose bright faces
Cast thousand beams upon me, like the sun?
They promis'd me eternal happiness,
And brought me garlands, Griffith, which I feel
I am not worthy yet to wear. I shall, assuredly.

GRIFFITH. I am most joyful, madam, such
  good dreams
Possess your fancy.

KATHARINE. Bid the music leave,
They are harsh and heavy to me. *Music ceases*

PATIENCE. Do you note
How much her Grace is alter'd on the sudden?
How long her face is drawn! How pale she looks,
And of an earthly cold! Mark her eyes.

GRIFFITH. She is going, wench. Pray, pray.

PATIENCE. Heaven comfort her!

Enter a MESSENGER

MESSENGER. An't like your Grace-

KATHARINE. You are a saucy fellow.
Deserve we no more reverence?

GRIFFITH. You are to blame,
Knowing she will not lose her wonted greatness,
To use so rude behaviour. Go to, kneel.

MESSENGER. I humbly do entreat your
  Highness' pardon;
My haste made me unmannerly. There is staying
A gentleman, sent from the King, to see you.

KATHARINE. Admit him entrance, Griffith; but
  this fellow
Let me ne'er see again. *Exit MESSENGER*

Enter LORD CAPUCIUS

If my sight fail not,
You should be Lord Ambassador from
  the Emperor,
My royal nephew, and your name Capucius.
CAPUCIUS. Madam, the same-your servant.
KATHARINE. O, my Lord,
  The times and titles now are alter'd strangely
  With me since first you knew me. But, I pray you,
  What is your pleasure with me?
CAPUCIUS. Noble lady,
  First, mine own service to your Grace; the next,
  The King's request that I would visit you,
  Who grieves much for your weakness, and
  by me
  Sends you his princely commendations
  And heartily entreats you take good comfort.
KATHARINE. O my good lord, that comfort comes
  too late,
  'Tis like a pardon after execution:
  That gentle physic, given in time, had cur'd me;
  But now I am past all comforts here, but prayers.
  How does his Highness?
CAPUCIUS. Madam, in good health.
KATHARINE. So may he ever do! and ever flourish
  When I shall dwell with worms, and my
  poor name
  Banish'd the kingdom! Patience, is that letter
  I caus'd you write yet sent away?
PATIENCE. No, madam.*Giving it to KATHARINE*
KATHARINE. Sir, I most humbly pray you
  to deliver
  This to my lord the King.
CAPUCIUS. Most willing, madam.
KATHARINE. In which I have commended to
  his goodness
  The model of our chaste loves, his
  young daughter-
  The dews of heaven fall thick in blessings
  on her!-
  Beseeching him to give her virtuous breeding-
  She is young, and of a noble modest nature;
  I hope she will deserve well-and a little
  To love her for her mother's sake, that
  lov'd him,
  Heaven knows how dearly. My next
  poor petition
  Is that his noble Grace would have some pity
  Upon my wretched women that so long
  Have follow'd both my fortunes faithfully;
  Of which there is not one, I dare avow-
  And now I should not lie-but will deserve,
  For virtue and true beauty of the soul,
  For honesty and decent carriage,

A right good husband, let him be a noble;
And sure those men are happy that shall have
  'em.
The last is for my men-they are the poorest,
But poverty could never draw 'em from me-
That they may have their wages duly paid 'em,
And something over to remember me by.
If heaven had pleas'd to have given me
  longer life
And able means, we had not parted thus.
These are the whole contents; and, good
  my lord,
By that you love the dearest in this world,
As you wish Christian peace to souls departed,
Stand these poor people's friend, and urge
  the King
To do me this last right.
CAPUCIUS. By heaven, I will,
  Or let me lose the fashion of a man!
KATHARINE. I thank you, honest lord.
  Remember me
  In all humility unto his Highness;
  Say his long trouble now is passing
  Out of this world. Tell him in death I
  bless'd him,
  For so I will. Mine eyes grow dim. Farewell,
  My lord. Griffith, farewell. Nay, Patience,
  You must not leave me yet. I must to bed;
  Call in more women. When I am dead,
  good wench,
  Let me be us'd with honour; strew me over
  With maiden flowers, that all the world
  may know
  I was a chaste wife to my grave. Embalm me,
  Then lay me forth; although unqueen'd, yet like
  A queen, and daughter to a king, inter me.
  I can no more.*Exeunt, leading KATHARINE*

❧ ACT V ❧

✒ SCENE I ✒
London. A gallery in the palace

*Enter GARDINER, BISHOP OF WINCHESTER, a PAGE
with a torch before him, met by SIR THOMAS LOVELL*

GARDINER. It's one o'clock, boy, is't not?
BOY. It hath struck.
GARDINER. These should be hours for necessities,
  Not for delights; times to repair our nature
  With comforting repose, and not for us

To waste these times. Good hour of night,
Sir Thomas!
Whither so late?
LOVELL. Came you from the King, my lord?
GARDINER. I did, Sir Thomas, and left him
at primero
With the Duke of Suffolk.
LOVELL. I must to him too,
Before he go to bed. I'll take my leave.
GARDINER. Not yet, Sir Thomas Lovell. What's
the matter?
It seems you are in haste. An if there be
No great offence belongs to't, give your friend
Some touch of your late business. Affairs
that walk-
As they say spirits do-at midnight, have
In them a wilder nature than the business
That seeks despatch by day.
LOVELL. My lord, I love you;
And durst commend a secret to your ear
Much weightier than this work. The Queen's
in labour,
They say in great extremity, and fear'd
She'll with the labour end.
GARDINER. The fruit she goes with
I pray for heartily, that it may find
Good time, and live; but for the stock,
Sir Thomas,
I wish it grubb'd up now.
LOVELL. Methinks I could
Cry thee amen; and yet my conscience says
She's a good creature, and, sweet lady, does
Deserve our better wishes.
GARDINER. But, sir, sir-
Hear me, Sir Thomas. Y'are a gentleman
Of mine own way; I know you wise, religious;
And, let me tell you, it will ne'er be well-
'Twill not, Sir Thomas Lovell, take't of me-
Till Cranmer, Cromwell, her two hands, and she,
Sleep in their graves.
LOVELL. Now, sir, you speak of two
The most remark'd i' th' kingdom. As
for Cromwell,
Beside that of the Jewel House, is made Master
O' th' Rolls, and the King's secretary; further, sir,
Stands in the gap and trade of moe preferments,
With which the time will load him.
Th' Archbishop
Is the King's hand and tongue, and who
dare speak
One syllable against him?
GARDINER. Yes, yes, Sir Thomas,
There are that dare; and I myself have ventur'd

To speak my mind of him; and indeed
this day,
Sir-I may tell it you-I think I have
Incens'd the lords o' th' Council, that he is-
For so I know he is, they know he is-
A most arch heretic, a pestilence
That does infect the land; with which
they moved
Have broken with the King, who hath so far
Given ear to our complaint-of his great grace
And princely care, foreseeing those
fell mischiefs
Our reasons laid before him-hath commanded
To-morrow morning to the Council board
He be convented. He's a rank weed,
Sir Thomas,
And we must root him out. From your affairs
I hinder you too long-good night, Sir Thomas.
LOVELL. Many good nights, my lord; I rest your
servant. *Exeunt GARDINER and PAGE.*
Enter the KING and the DUKE OF SUFFOLK
KING. Charles, I will play no more to-night;
My mind's not on't; you are too hard for me.
SUFFOLK. Sir, I did never win of you before.
KING. But little, Charles;
Nor shall not, when my fancy's on my play.
Now, Lovell, from the Queen what is the news?
LOVELL. I could not personally deliver to her
What you commanded me, but by her woman
I sent your message; who return'd her thanks
In the great'st humbleness, and desir'd
your Highness
Most heartily to pray for her.
KING. What say'st thou, ha?
To pray for her? What, is she crying out?
LOVELL. So said her woman; and that her
suff'rance made
Almost each pang a death.
KING. Alas, good lady!
SUFFOLK. God safely quit her of her
burden, and
With gentle travail, to the gladding of
Your Highness with an heir!
KING. 'Tis midnight, Charles;
Prithee to bed; and in thy pray'rs remember
Th' estate of my poor queen. Leave me alone,
For I must think of that which company
Will not be friendly to.
SUFFOLK. I wish your Highness
A quiet night, and my good mistress will
Remember in my prayers.
KING. Charles, good night. *Exit SUFFOLK.*
Enter SIR ANTHONY DENNY

Well, sir, what follows?

DENNY. Sir, I have brought my lord
the Archbishop,
As you commanded me.

KING. Ha! Canterbury?

DENNY. Ay, my good lord.

KING. 'Tis true. Where is he, Denny?

DENNY. He attends your Highness' pleasure.

KING. Bring him to us.   *Exit DENNY.*

LOVELL. *[Aside]* This is about that which the
bishop spake.
I am happily come hither.
                    Re-enter DENNY, with CRANMER

KING. Avoid the gallery. *[LOVELL seems to stay]*
Ha! I have said. Be gone.
What!   *Exeunt LOVELL and DENNY.*

CRANMER. *[Aside]* I am fearful-wherefore frowns
he thus?
'Tis his aspect of terror. All's not well.

KING. How now, my lord? You do desire to know
Wherefore I sent for you.

CRANMER. *[Kneeling]* It is my duty
T'attend your Highness' pleasure.

KING. Pray you, arise,
My good and gracious Lord of Canterbury.
Come, you and I must walk a turn together;
I have news to tell you; come, come, give me
your hand.
Ah, my good lord, I grieve at what I speak,
And am right sorry to repeat what follows.
I have, and most unwillingly, of late
Heard many grievous-I do say, my lord,
Grievous-complaints of you; which,
being consider'd,
Have mov'd us and our Council that you shall
This morning come before us; where I know
You cannot with such freedom purge yourself
But that, till further trial in those charges
Which will require your answer, you must take
Your patience to you and be well contented
To make your house our Tow'r. You a brother
of us,
It fits we thus proceed, or else no witness
Would come against you.

CRANMER. I humbly thank your Highness
And am right glad to catch this good occasion
Most throughly to be winnowed where my chaff
And corn shall fly asunder; for I know
There's none stands under more
calumnious tongues
Than I myself, poor man.

KING. Stand up, good Canterbury;
Thy truth and thy integrity is rooted

In us, thy friend. Give me thy hand, stand up;
Prithee let's walk. Now, by my holidame,
What manner of man are you? My lord, I look'd
You would have given me your petition that
I should have ta'en some pains to bring together
Yourself and your accusers, and to have
heard you
Without indurance further.

CRANMER. Most dread liege,
The good I stand on is my truth and honesty;
If they shall fail, I with mine enemies
Will triumph o'er my person; which I weigh not,
Being of those virtues vacant. I fear nothing
What can be said against me.

KING. Know you not
How your state stands i' th' world, with the
whole world?
Your enemies are many, and not small;
their practices
Must bear the same proportion; and not ever
The justice and the truth o' th' question carries
The due o' th' verdict with it; at what ease
Might corrupt minds procure knaves as corrupt
To swear against you? Such things have
been done.
You are potently oppos'd, and with a malice
Of as great size. Ween you of better luck,
I mean in perjur'd witness, than your Master,
Whose minister you are, whiles here He liv'd
Upon this naughty earth? Go to, go to;
You take a precipice for no leap of danger,
And woo your own destruction.

CRANMER. God and your Majesty
Protect mine innocence, or I fall into
The trap is laid for me!

KING. Be of good cheer;
They shall no more prevail than we give way to.
Keep comfort to you, and this morning see
You do appear before them; if they shall chance,
In charging you with matters, to commit you,
The best persuasions to the contrary
Fail not to use, and with what vehemency
Th' occasion shall instruct you. If entreaties
Will render you no remedy, this ring
Deliver them, and your appeal to us
There make before them. Look, the good
man weeps!
He's honest, on mine honour. God's
blest Mother!
I swear he is true-hearted, and a soul
None better in my kingdom. Get you gone,
And do as I have bid you. *Exit CRANMER.*
He has strangled his language in his tears.

Enter OLD LADY

GENTLEMAN. *[Within]* Come back; what mean you?

OLD LADY. I'll not come back; the tidings that
  I bring
  Will make my boldness manners. Now,
    good angels
  Fly o'er thy royal head, and shade thy person
  Under their blessed wings!

KING. Now, by thy looks
  I guess thy message. Is the Queen deliver'd?
  Say ay, and of a boy.

OLD LADY. Ay, ay, my liege;
  And of a lovely boy. The God of Heaven
  Both now and ever bless her! 'Tis a girl,
  Promises boys hereafter. Sir, your queen
  Desires your visitation, and to be
  Acquainted with this stranger; 'tis as like you
  As cherry is to cherry.

KING. Lovell!

Enter LOVELL

LOVELL. Sir?

KING. Give her an hundred marks. I'll to the
  Queen.

Exit.

OLD LADY. An hundred marks? By this light, I'll
  ha' more!
  An ordinary groom is for such payment.
  I will have more, or scold it out of him.
  Said I for this the girl was like to him! I'll
  Have more, or else unsay't; and now, while
  'tis hot,
  I'll put it to the issue.

Exeunt.

✎ SCENE II ✎

Lobby before the Council Chamber

Enter CRANMER, ARCHBISHOP OF CANTERBURY

CRANMER. I hope I am not too late; and yet
  the gentleman
  That was sent to me from the Council pray'd me
  To make great haste. All fast? What means
  this? Ho!
  Who waits there? Sure you know me?

Enter KEEPER

KEEPER. Yes, my lord;
  But yet I cannot help you.

CRANMER. Why?

KEEPER. Your Grace must wait till you be
  call'd for.

Enter DOCTOR BUTTS

CRANMER. So.

BUTTS. *[Aside]* This is a piece of malice. I am glad
  I came this way so happily; the King
  Shall understand it presently.

Exit.

CRANMER. *[Aside]* 'Tis Butts,
  The King's physician; as he pass'd along,
  How earnestly he cast his eyes upon me!
  Pray heaven he sound not my disgrace!
    For certain,
  This is of purpose laid by some that hate me-
  God turn their hearts! I never sought
    their malice-
  To quench mine honour; they would shame to
    make me
  Wait else at door, a fellow councillor,
  'Mong boys, grooms, and lackeys. But
    their pleasures
  Must be fulfill'd, and I attend with patience.

Enter the KING and BUTTS at window above

BUTTS. I'll show your Grace the strangest sight-

KING. What's that, Butts?

BUTTS. I think your Highness saw this many
  a day.

KING. Body a me, where is it?

BUTTS. There my lord:
  The high promotion of his Grace of Canterbury;
  Who holds his state at door,
    'mongst pursuivants,
  Pages, and footboys.

KING. Ha, 'tis he indeed.
  Is this the honour they do one another?
  'Tis well there's one above 'em yet. I
    had thought
  They had parted so much honesty among 'em-
  At least good manners-as not thus to suffer
  A man of his place, and so near our favour,
  To dance attendance on their
    lordships' pleasures,
  And at the door too, like a post with packets.
  By holy Mary, Butts, there's knavery!
  Let 'em alone, and draw the curtain close;
  We shall hear more anon.

Exeunt.

✎ SCENE III ✎

The Council Chamber

*A Council table brought in, with chairs and stools, and placed
under the state. Enter LORD CHANCELLOR, who places
himself at the upper end of the table on the left hand, a seat
being left void above him, as for Canterbury's seat. DUKE OF
SUFFOLK, DUKE OF NORFOLK, SURREY, LORD
CHAMBERLAIN, GARDINER, seat themselves in order
on each side; CROMWELL at the lower end, as secretary.*

KEEPER at the door

CHANCELLOR. Speak to the business,
  master secretary;
  Why are we met in council?
CROMWELL. Please your honours,
  The chief cause concerns his Grace
  of Canterbury.
GARDINER. Has he had knowledge of it?
CROMWELL. Yes.
NORFOLK. Who waits there?
KEEPER. Without, my noble lords?
GARDINER. Yes.
KEEPER. My Lord Archbishop;
  And has done half an hour, to know
  your pleasures.
CHANCELLOR. Let him come in.
KEEPER. Your Grace may enter now.
    CRANMER approaches the Council table
CHANCELLOR. My good Lord Archbishop, I am
  very sorry
  To sit here at this present, and behold
  That chair stand empty; but we all are men,
  In our own natures frail and capable
  Of our flesh; few are angels; out of which frailty
  And want of wisdom, you, that best should
  teach us,
  Have misdemean'd yourself, and not a little,
  Toward the King first, then his laws, in filling
  The whole realm by your teaching and
  your chaplains-
  For so we are inform'd-with new opinions,
  Divers and dangerous; which are heresies,
  And, not reform'd, may prove pernicious.
GARDINER. Which reformation must be
  sudden too,
  My noble lords; for those that tame wild horses
  Pace 'em not in their hands to make 'em gentle,
  But stop their mouth with stubborn bits and
  spur 'em
  Till they obey the manage. If we suffer,
  Out of our easiness and childish pity
  To one man's honour, this contagious sickness,
  Farewell all physic; and what follows then?
  Commotions, uproars, with a general taint
  Of the whole state; as of late days
  our neighbours,
  The upper Germany, can dearly witness,
  Yet freshly pitied in our memories.
CRANMER. My good lords, hitherto in all
  the progress
  Both of my life and office, I have labour'd,
  And with no little study, that my teaching

And the strong course of my authority
Might go one way, and safely; and the end
Was ever to do well. Nor is there living-
I speak it with a single heart, my lords-
A man that more detests, more stirs against,
Both in his private conscience and his place,
Defacers of a public peace than I do.
Pray heaven the King may never find a heart
With less allegiance in it! Men that make
Envy and crooked malice nourishment
Dare bite the best. I do beseech your lordships
That, in this case of justice, my accusers,
Be what they will, may stand forth face to face
And freely urge against me.
SUFFOLK. Nay, my lord,
  That cannot be; you are a councillor,
  And by that virtue no man dare accuse you.
GARDINER. My lord, because we have business of
  more moment,
  We will be short with you. 'Tis his
  Highness' pleasure
  And our consent, for better trial of you,
  From hence you be committed to the Tower;
  Where, being but a private man again,
  You shall know many dare accuse you boldly,
  More than, I fear, you are provided for.
CRANMER. Ah, my good Lord of Winchester, I
  thank you;
  You are always my good friend; if your will pass,
  I shall both find your lordship judge and juror,
  You are so merciful. I see your end-
  'Tis my undoing. Love and meekness, lord,
  Become a churchman better than ambition;
  Win straying souls with modesty again,
  Cast none away. That I shall clear myself,
  Lay all the weight ye can upon my patience,
  I make as little doubt as you do conscience
  In doing daily wrongs. I could say more,
  But reverence to your calling makes me modest.
GARDINER. My lord, my lord, you are a sectary;
  That's the plain truth. Your painted
  gloss discovers,
  To men that understand you, words
  and weakness.
CROMWELL. My Lord of Winchester, y'are a little,
  By your good favour, too sharp; men so noble,
  However faulty, yet should find respect
  For what they have been; 'tis a cruelty
  To load a falling man.
GARDINER. Good Master Secretary,
  I cry your honour mercy; you may, worst
  Of all this table, say so.
CROMWELL. Why, my lord?

GARDINER. Do not I know you for a favourer
  Of this new sect? Ye are not sound.
CROMWELL. Not sound?
GARDINER. Not sound, I say.
CROMWELL. Would you were half so honest!
  Men's prayers then would seek you, not
    their fears.
GARDINER. I shall remember this bold language.
CROMWELL. Do.
  Remember your bold life too.
CHANCELLOR. This is too much;
  Forbear, for shame, my lords.
GARDINER. I have done.
CROMWELL. And I.
CHANCELLOR. Then thus for you, my lord: it
  stands agreed,
  I take it, by all voices, that forthwith
  You be convey'd to th' Tower a prisoner;
  There to remain till the King's further pleasure
  Be known unto us. Are you all agreed, lords?
ALL. We are.
CRANMER. Is there no other way of mercy,
  But I must needs to th' Tower, my lords?
GARDINER. What other
  Would you expect? You are
  strangely troublesome.
  Let some o' th' guard be ready there.

Enter the guard

CRANMER. For me?
  Must I go like a traitor thither?
GARDINER. Receive him,
  And see him safe i' th' Tower.
CRANMER. Stay, good my lords,
  I have a little yet to say. Look there, my lords;
  By virtue of that ring I take my cause
  Out of the gripes of cruel men and give it
  To a most noble judge, the King my master.
CHAMBERLAIN. This is the King's ring.
SURREY. 'Tis no counterfeit.
SUFFOLK. 'Tis the right ring, by heav'n. I told
  ye all,
  When we first put this dangerous stone a-rolling,
  'Twould fall upon ourselves.
NORFOLK. Do you think, my lords,
  The King will suffer but the little finger
  Of this man to be vex'd?
CHAMBERLAIN. 'Tis now too certain;
  How much more is his life in value with him!
  Would I were fairly out on't!
CROMWELL. My mind gave me,
  In seeking tales and informations
  Against this man-whose honesty the devil
  And his disciples only envy at-

Ye blew the fire that burns ye. Now have at ye!

Enter the KING frowning on them; he takes his seat

GARDINER. Dread sovereign, how much are we
  bound to heaven
  In daily thanks, that gave us such a prince;
  Not only good and wise but most religious;
  One that in all obedience makes the church
  The chief aim of his honour and, to strengthen
  That holy duty, out of dear respect,
  His royal self in judgment comes to hear
  The cause betwixt her and this great offender.
KING. You were ever good at
  sudden commendations,
  Bishop of Winchester. But know I come not
  To hear such flattery now, and in my presence
  They are too thin and bare to hide offences.
  To me you cannot reach you play the spaniel,
  And think with wagging of your tongue to
  win me;
  But whatsoe'er thou tak'st me for, I'm sure
  Thou hast a cruel nature and a bloody.
  [*To CRANMER*] Good man, sit down. Now let me
  see the proudest
  He that dares most but wag his finger at thee.
  By all that's holy, he had better starve
  Than but once think this place becomes
  thee not.
SURREY. May it please your Grace-
KING. No, sir, it does not please me.
  I had thought I had had men of some
  understanding
  And wisdom of my Council; but I find none.
  Was it discretion, lords, to let this man,
  This good man-few of you deserve that title-
  This honest man, wait like a lousy footboy
  At chamber door? and one as great as you are?
  Why, what a shame was this! Did my commission
  Bid ye so far forget yourselves? I gave ye
  Power as he was a councillor to try him,
  Not as a groom. There's some of ye, I see,
  More out of malice than integrity,
  Would try him to the utmost, had ye mean;
  Which ye shall never have while I live.
CHANCELLOR. Thus far,
  My most dread sovereign, may it like your Grace
  To let my tongue excuse all. What was purpos'd
  Concerning his imprisonment was rather-
  If there be faith in men-meant for his trial
  And fair purgation to the world, than malice,
  I'm sure, in me.
KING. Well, well, my lords, respect him;
  Take him, and use him well, he's worthy of it.
  I will say thus much for him: if a prince

May be beholding to a subject, I
Am for his love and service so to him.
Make me no more ado, but all embrace him;
Be friends, for shame, my lords! My Lord
  of Canterbury,
I have a suit which you must not deny me:
That is, a fair young maid that yet wants baptism;
You must be godfather, and answer for her.
CRANMER. The greatest monarch now alive
  may glory
In such an honour; how may I deserve it,
That am a poor and humble subject to you?
KING. Come, come, my lord, you'd spare your
  spoons. You shall have two noble partners
  with you: the old Duchess of Norfolk and Lady
  Marquis Dorset. Will these please you?
Once more, my Lord of Winchester, I
  charge you,
Embrace and love this man.
GARDINER. With a true heart
And brother-love I do it.
CRANMER. And let heaven
Witness how dear I hold this confirmation.
KING. Good man, those joyful tears show thy
  true heart.
The common voice, I see, is verified
Of thee, which says thus: 'Do my Lord
  of Canterbury
A shrewd turn and he's your friend for ever'.
Come, lords, we trifle time away; I long
To have this young one made a Christian.
As I have made ye one, lords, one remain;
So I grow stronger, you more honour gain.

                                    Exeunt.

✿ SCENE IV ✿
The palace yard

Noise and tumult within. Enter PORTER and his MAN

PORTER. You'll leave your noise anon, ye rascals.
  Do you take the court for Paris garden? Ye rude
  slaves, leave your gaping.
[*Within*] Good master porter, I belong to th' larder.
PORTER. Belong to th' gallows, and be hang'd,
  ye rogue! Is this a place to roar in? Fetch me a
  dozen crab-tree staves, and strong ones; these
  are but switches to 'em. I'll scratch your heads.
  You must be seeing christenings? Do you look
  for ale and cakes here, you rude rascals?
MAN. Pray, sir, be patient; 'tis as much impossible,
  Unless we sweep 'em from the door

with cannons,
  To scatter 'em as 'tis to make 'em sleep
  On May-day morning; which will never be.
  We may as well push against Paul's as stir 'em.
PORTER. How got they in, and be hang'd?
MAN. Alas, I know not: how gets the tide in?
  As much as one sound cudgel of four foot—
  You see the poor remainder—could distribute,
  I made no spare, sir.
PORTER. You did nothing, sir.
MAN. I am not Samson, nor Sir Guy, nor Colbrand,
  To mow 'em down before me; but if I spar'd any
  That had a head to hit, either young or old,
  He or she, cuckold or cuckold-maker,
  Let me ne'er hope to see a chine again;
  And that I would not for a cow, God save her!
  [*Within*] Do you hear, master porter?
PORTER. I shall be with you presently, good
  master puppy.
  Keep the door close, sirrah.
MAN. What would you have me do?
PORTER. What should you do, but knock 'em
  down by th' dozens? Is this Moorfields to
  muster in? Or have we some strange Indian
  with the great tool come to court, the
  women so besiege us? Bless me, what a fry
  of fornication is at door! On my Christian
  conscience, this one christening will beget a
  thousand: here will be father, godfather, and
  all together.
MAN. The spoons will be the bigger, sir. There is
  a fellow somewhat near the door, he should
  be a brazier by his face, for, o' my conscience,
  twenty of the dog-days now reign in's nose; all
  that stand about him are under the line, they
  need no other penance. That fire-drake did I
  hit three times on the head, and three times
  was his nose discharged against me; he stands
  there like a mortar-piece, to blow us. There
  was a haberdasher's wife of small wit near him,
  that rail'd upon me till her pink'd porringer fell
  off her head, for kindling such a combustion
  in the state. I miss'd the meteor once, and hit
  that woman, who cried out 'Clubs!' when I
  might see from far some forty truncheoners
  draw to her succour, which were the hope o'
  th' Strand, where she was quartered. They fell
  on; I made good my place. At length they came
  to th' broomstaff to me; I defied 'em still; when
  suddenly a file of boys behind 'em, loose shot,
  deliver'd such a show'r of pebbles that I was
  fain to draw mine honour in and let 'em win the
  work: the devil was amongst 'em, I think surely.

PORTER. These are the youths that thunder at a
  playhouse and fight for bitten apples; that no
  audience but the tribulation of Tower-hill or
  the limbs of Limehouse, their dear brothers, are
  able to endure. I have some of 'em in Limbo
  Patrum, and there they are like to dance these
  three days; besides the running banquet of two
  beadles that is to come.

Enter the LORD CHAMBERLAIN

CHAMBERLAIN. Mercy o' me, what a multitude
  are here!
  They grow still too; from all parts they
  are coming,
  As if we kept a fair here! Where are
  these porters,
  These lazy knaves? Y'have made a fine
  hand, fellows.
  There's a trim rabble let in: are all these
  Your faithful friends o' th' suburbs? We
  shall have
  Great store of room, no doubt, left for the ladies,
  When they pass back from the christening.

PORTER. An't please your honour,
  We are but men; and what so many may do,
  Not being torn a pieces, we have done.
  An army cannot rule 'em.

CHAMBERLAIN. As I live,
  If the King blame me for't, I'll lay ye all
  By th' heels, and suddenly; and on your heads
  Clap round fines for neglect. Y'are lazy knaves;
  And here ye lie baiting of bombards, when
  Ye should do service. Hark! the trumpets sound;
  Th' are come already from the christening.
  Go break among the press and find a way out
  To let the troops pass fairly, or I'll find
  A Marshalsea shall hold ye play these
  two months.

PORTER. Make way there for the Princess.

MAN. You great fellow,
  Stand close up, or I'll make your head ache.

PORTER. You i' th' camlet, get up o' th' rail;
  I'll peck you o'er the pales else.   *Exeunt.*

✣ SCENE V ✣

The palace

Enter TRUMPETS, sounding; then two Aldermen, LORD
MAYOR, GARTER, CRANMER, DUKE OF NORFOLK,
with his marshal's staff, DUKE OF SUFFOLK, two Noblemen
bearing great standing-bowls for the christening gifts; then four
Noblemen bearing a canopy, under which the DUCHESS
OF NORFOLK, godmother, bearing the Child richly habited

in a mantle, etc., train borne by a Lady; then follows the
MARCHIONESS DORSET, the other godmother, and Ladies.
The troop pass once about the stage, and GARTER speaks.

GARTER. Heaven, from thy endless goodness,
  send prosperous life, long and ever-
  happy, to the high and mighty Princess of
  England, Elizabeth!

Flourish. Enter KING and guard

CRANMER. [Kneeling] And to your royal Grace and
  the good Queen!
  My noble partners and myself thus pray:
  All comfort, joy, in this most gracious lady,
  Heaven ever laid up to make parents happy,
  May hourly fall upon ye!

KING. Thank you, good Lord Archbishop.
  What is her name?

CRANMER. Elizabeth.

KING. Stand up, lord. [The KING kisses the child]
  With this kiss take my blessing: God
  protect thee!
  Into whose hand I give thy life.

CRANMER. Amen.

KING. My noble gossips, y'have been too prodigal;
  I thank ye heartily. So shall this lady,
  When she has so much English.

CRANMER. Let me speak, sir,
  For heaven now bids me; and the words I utter
  Let none think flattery, for they'll find 'em truth.
  This royal infant-heaven still move about her!-
  Though in her cradle, yet now promises
  Upon this land a thousand blessings,
  Which time shall bring to ripeness. She shall be-
  But few now living can behold that goodness-
  A pattern to all princes living with her,
  And all that shall succeed. Saba was never
  More covetous of wisdom and fair virtue
  Than this pure soul shall be. All princely graces
  That mould up such a mighty piece as this is,
  With all the virtues that attend the good,
  Shall still be doubled on her. Truth shall
  nurse her,
  Holy and heavenly thoughts still counsel her;
  She shall be lov'd and fear'd. Her own shall
  bless her:
  Her foes shake like a field of beaten corn,
  And hang their heads with sorrow. Good grows
  with her;
  In her days every man shall eat in safety
  Under his own vine what he plants, and sing
  The merry songs of peace to all his neighbours.
  God shall be truly known; and those about her
  From her shall read the perfect ways of honour,

And by those claim their greatness, not by blood.
Nor shall this peace sleep with her; but as when
The bird of wonder dies, the maiden phoenix
Her ashes new create another heir
As great in admiration as herself,
So shall she leave her blessedness to one-
When heaven shall call her from this cloud
  of darkness-
Who from the sacred ashes of her honour
Shall star-like rise, as great in fame as she was,
And so stand fix'd. Peace, plenty, love,
  truth, terror,
That were the servants to this chosen infant,
Shall then be his, and like a vine grow to him;
Wherever the bright sun of heaven shall shine,
His honour and the greatness of his name
Shall be, and make new nations; he
  shall flourish,
And like a mountain cedar reach his branches
To all the plains about him; our
  children's children
Shall see this and bless heaven.
KING. Thou speakest wonders.
CRANMER. She shall be, to the happiness of
  England,
An aged princess; many days shall see her,
And yet no day without a deed to crown it.
Would I had known no more! But she must die-
She must, the saints must have her-yet a virgin;
A most unspotted lily shall she pass
To th' ground, and all the world shall
  mourn her.
KING. O Lord Archbishop,
Thou hast made me now a man; never before
This happy child did I get anything.
This oracle of comfort has so pleas'd me
That when I am in heaven I shall desire
To see what this child does, and praise
  my Maker.
I thank ye all. To you, my good Lord Mayor,
And you, good brethren, I am much beholding;
I have receiv'd much honour by your presence,
And ye shall find me thankful. Lead the
  way, lords;
Ye must all see the Queen, and she must
  thank ye,
She will be sick else. This day, no man think
Has business at his house; for all shall stay.
This little one shall make it holiday.

Exeunt.

EPILOGUE

'Tis ten to one this play can never please
All that are here. Some come to take their ease
And sleep an act or two; but those, we fear,
W'have frighted with our trumpets; so, 'tis clear,
They'll say 'tis nought; others to hear the city
Abus'd extremely, and to cry 'That's witty!'
Which we have not done neither; that, I fear,
All the expected good w'are like to hear
For this play at this time is only in
The merciful construction of good women;
For such a one we show'd 'em. If they smile
And say 'twill do, I know within a while
All the best men are ours; for 'tis ill hap
If they hold when their ladies bid 'em clap.

The End

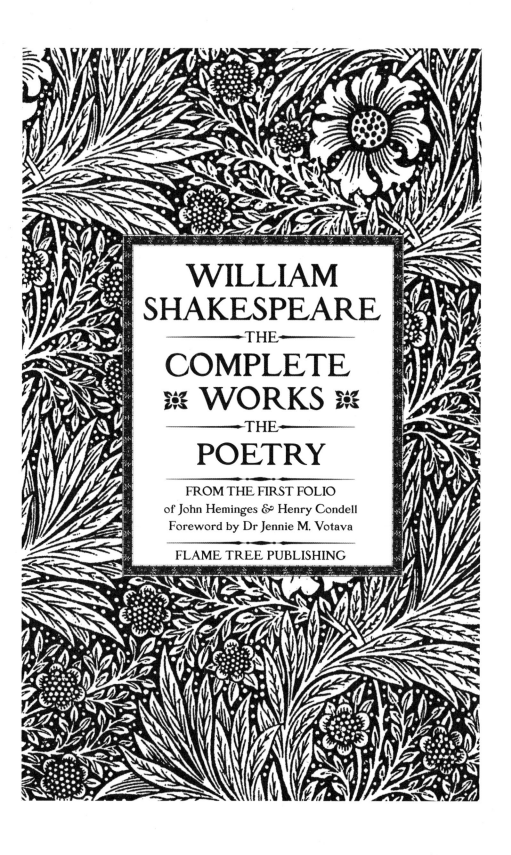

WILLIAM SHAKESPEARE

— THE —

COMPLETE
❋ WORKS ❋

— THE —

POETRY

FROM THE FIRST FOLIO
of John Heminges & Henry Condell
Foreword by Dr Jennie M. Votava

FLAME TREE PUBLISHING

1609

The Sonnets

❧ 1 ❧

From fairest creatures we desire increase,
That thereby beauty's rose might never die,
But as the riper should by time decease,
His tender heir might bear his memory:
But thou contracted to thine own bright eyes,
Feed'st thy light's flame with self-substantial fuel,
Making a famine where abundance lies,
Thy self thy foe, to thy sweet self too cruel:
Thou that art now the world's fresh ornament,
And only herald to the gaudy spring,
Within thine own bud buriest thy content,
And tender churl mak'st waste in niggarding:
　Pity the world, or else this glutton be,
　　To eat the world's due, by the grave and thee.

❧ 2 ❧

When forty winters shall besiege thy brow,
And dig deep trenches in thy beauty's field,
Thy youth's proud livery so gazed on now,
Will be a tattered weed of small worth held:
Then being asked, where all thy beauty lies,
Where all the treasure of thy lusty days;
To say within thine own deep sunken eyes,
Were an all-eating shame, and thriftless praise.
How much more praise deserved thy beauty's use,
If thou couldst answer 'This fair child of mine
Shall sum my count, and make my old excuse'
Proving his beauty by succession thine.
　This were to be new made when thou art old,
　　And see thy blood warm when thou feel'st
　　　it cold.

❧ 3 ❧

Look in thy glass and tell the face thou viewest,
Now is the time that face should form another,
Whose fresh repair if now thou not renewest,
Thou dost beguile the world, unbless
　some mother.
For where is she so fair whose uneared womb
Disdains the tillage of thy husbandry?
Or who is he so fond will be the tomb,
Of his self-love to stop posterity?
Thou art thy mother's glass and she in thee
Calls back the lovely April of her prime,
So thou through windows of thine age shalt see,
Despite of wrinkles this thy golden time.
　But if thou live remembered not to be,
　　Die single and thine image dies with thee.

❧ 4 ❧

Unthrifty loveliness why dost thou spend,
Upon thy self thy beauty's legacy?
Nature's bequest gives nothing but doth lend,
And being frank she lends to those are free:
Then beauteous niggard why dost thou abuse,
The bounteous largess given thee to give?
Profitless usurer why dost thou use
So great a sum of sums yet canst not live?
For having traffic with thy self alone,
Thou of thy self thy sweet self dost deceive,
Then how when nature calls thee to be gone,
What acceptable audit canst thou leave?
　Thy unused beauty must be tombed with thee,
　　Which used lives th' executor to be.

❧ 5 ❧

Those hours that with gentle work did frame
The lovely gaze where every eye doth dwell
Will play the tyrants to the very same,
And that unfair which fairly doth excel:
For never-resting time leads summer on
To hideous winter and confounds him there,
Sap checked with frost and lusty leaves quite gone,
Beauty o'er-snowed and bareness every where:
Then were not summer's distillation left
A liquid prisoner pent in walls of glass,
Beauty's effect with beauty were bereft,
Nor it nor no remembrance what it was.
　But flowers distilled though they with winter meet,
　　Leese but their show; their substance still
　　　lives sweet.

🖾 6 🖾

Then let not winter's ragged hand deface,
In thee thy summer ere thou be distilled:
Make sweet some vial; treasure thou some place,
With beauty's treasure ere it be self-killed:
That use is not forbidden usury,
Which happies those that pay the willing loan;
That's for thy self to breed another thee,
Or ten times happier be it ten for one,
Ten times thy self were happier than thou art,
If ten of thine ten times refigured thee:
Then what could death do if thou shouldst depart,
Leaving thee living in posterity?
  Be not self-willed for thou art much too fair,
  To be death's conquest and make worms
    thine heir.

🖾 7 🖾

Lo in the orient when the gracious light
Lifts up his burning head, each under eye
Doth homage to his new-appearing sight,
Serving with looks his sacred majesty,
And having climbed the steep-up heavenly hill,
Resembling strong youth in his middle age,
Yet mortal looks adore his beauty still,
Attending on his golden pilgrimage:
But when from highmost pitch with weary car,
Like feeble age he reeleth from the day,
The eyes ('fore duteous) now converted are
From his low tract and look another way:
  So thou, thy self out-going in thy noon:
  Unlooked on diest unless thou get a son.

🖾 8 🖾

Music to hear, why hear'st thou music sadly?
Sweets with sweets war not, joy delights in joy:
Why lov'st thou that which thou receiv'st not gladly,
Or else receiv'st with pleasure thine annoy?
If the true concord of well-tuned sounds,
By unions married do offend thine ear,
They do but sweetly chide thee, who confounds
In singleness the parts that thou shouldst bear:
Mark how one string sweet husband to another,
Strikes each in each by mutual ordering;
Resembling sire, and child, and happy mother,
Who all in one, one pleasing note do sing:
  Whose speechless song being many, seeming one,
  Sings this to thee, 'Thou single wilt prove none'.

🖾 9 🖾

Is it for fear to wet a widow's eye,
That thou consum'st thy self in single life?
Ah, if thou issueless shalt hap to die,
The world will wail thee like a makeless wife,
The world will be thy widow and still weep,
That thou no form of thee hast left behind,
When every private widow well may keep,
By children's eyes, her husband's shape in mind:
Look what an unthrift in the world doth spend
Shifts but his place, for still the world enjoys it;
But beauty's waste hath in the world an end,
And kept unused the user so destroys it:
  No love toward others in that bosom sits
  That on himself such murd'rous
    shame commits.

🖾 10 🖾

For shame deny that thou bear'st love to any
Who for thy self art so unprovident.
Grant if thou wilt, thou art beloved of many,
But that thou none lov'st is most evident:
For thou art so possessed with murd'rous hate,
That 'gainst thy self thou stick'st not to conspire,
Seeking that beauteous roof to ruinate
Which to repair should be thy chief desire:
O change thy thought, that I may change my mind,
Shall hate be fairer lodged than gentle love?
Be as thy presence is gracious and kind,
Or to thy self at least kind-hearted prove,
  Make thee another self for love of me,
  That beauty still may live in thine or thee.

❦ 11 ❦

As fast as thou shalt wane so fast thou grow'st,
In one of thine, from that which thou departest,
And that fresh blood which youngly thou bestow'st,
Thou mayst call thine, when thou from
　youth convertest,
Herein lives wisdom, beauty, and increase,
Without this folly, age, and cold decay,
If all were minded so, the times should cease,
And threescore year would make the world away:
Let those whom nature hath not made for store,
Harsh, featureless, and rude, barrenly perish:
Look whom she best endowed, she gave thee more;
Which bounteous gift thou shouldst in
　bounty cherish:
　She carved thee for her seal, and meant thereby,
　Thou shouldst print more, not let that copy die.

❦ 12 ❦

When I do count the clock that tells the time,
And see the brave day sunk in hideous night,
When I behold the violet past prime,
And sable curls all silvered o'er with white:
When lofty trees I see barren of leaves,
Which erst from heat did canopy the herd
And summer's green all girded up in sheaves
Borne on the bier with white and bristly beard:
Then of thy beauty do I question make
That thou among the wastes of time must go,
Since sweets and beauties do themselves forsake,
And die as fast as they see others grow,
　And nothing 'gainst Time's scythe can
　make defence
　Save breed to brave him, when he takes
　thee hence.

❦ 13 ❦

O that you were your self, but love you are
No longer yours, than you your self here live,
Against this coming end you should prepare,
And your sweet semblance to some other give.
So should that beauty which you hold in lease
Find no determination, then you were
Your self again after your self's decease,
When your sweet issue your sweet form should bear.
Who lets so fair a house fall to decay,
Which husbandry in honour might uphold,
Against the stormy gusts of winter's day
And barren rage of death's eternal cold?
　O none but unthrifts, dear my love you know,
　You had a father, let your son say so.

❦ 14 ❦

Not from the stars do I my judgment pluck,
And yet methinks I have astronomy,
But not to tell of good, or evil luck,
Of plagues, of dearths, or seasons' quality,
Nor can I fortune to brief minutes tell;
Pointing to each his thunder, rain and wind,
Or say with princes if it shall go well
By oft predict that I in heaven find.
But from thine eyes my knowledge I derive,
And constant stars in them I read such art
As truth and beauty shall together thrive
If from thy self, to store thou wouldst convert:
　Or else of thee this I prognosticate,
　Thy end is truth's and beauty's doom and date.

❦ 15 ❦

When I consider every thing that grows
Holds in perfection but a little moment.
That this huge stage presenteth nought but shows
Whereon the stars in secret influence comment.
When I perceive that men as plants increase,
Cheered and checked even by the self-same sky:
Vaunt in their youthful sap, at height decrease,
And wear their brave state out of memory.
Then the conceit of this inconstant stay,
Sets you most rich in youth before my sight,
Where wasteful time debateth with decay
To change your day of youth to sullied night,
　And all in war with Time for love of you,
　As he takes from you, I engraft you new.

❦ 16 ❦

But wherefore do not you a mightier way
Make war upon this bloody tyrant Time?
And fortify your self in your decay
With means more blessed than my barren rhyme?
Now stand you on the top of happy hours,
And many maiden gardens yet unset,
With virtuous wish would bear you living flowers,
Much liker than your painted counterfeit:
So should the lines of life that life repair
Which this (Time's pencil) or my pupil pen
Neither in inward worth nor outward fair
Can make you live your self in eyes of men.
　To give away your self, keeps your self still,
　And you must live drawn by your own
　sweet skill.

❧ 17 ❧

Who will believe my verse in time to come
If it were filled with your most high deserts?
Though yet heaven knows it is but as a tomb
Which hides your life, and shows not half your parts:
If I could write the beauty of your eyes,
And in fresh numbers number all your graces,
The age to come would say this poet lies,
Such heavenly touches ne'er touched earthly faces.
So should my papers (yellowed with their age)
Be scorned, like old men of less truth than tongue,
And your true rights be termed a poet's rage,
And stretched metre of an antique song.
    But were some child of yours alive that time,
    You should live twice in it, and in my rhyme.

❧ 20 ❧

A woman's face with nature's own hand painted,
Hast thou the master mistress of my passion,
A woman's gentle heart but not acquainted
With shifting change as is false women's fashion,
An eye more bright than theirs, less false in rolling:
Gilding the object whereupon it gazeth,
A man in hue all hues in his controlling,
Which steals men's eyes and women's souls amazeth.
And for a woman wert thou first created,
Till nature as she wrought thee fell a-doting,
And by addition me of thee defeated,
By adding one thing to my purpose nothing.
    But since she pricked thee out for women's pleasure,
    Mine be thy love and thy love's use their treasure.

❧ 18 ❧

Shall I compare thee to a summer's day?
Thou art more lovely and more temperate:
Rough winds do shake the darling buds of May,
And summer's lease hath all too short a date:
Sometime too hot the eye of heaven shines,
And often is his gold complexion dimmed,
And every fair from fair sometime declines,
By chance, or nature's changing course untrimmed:
But thy eternal summer shall not fade,
Nor lose possession of that fair thou ow'st,
Nor shall death brag thou wand'rest in his shade,
When in eternal lines to time thou grow'st,
    So long as men can breathe or eyes can see,
    So long lives this, and this gives life to thee.

❧ 19 ❧

Devouring Time blunt thou the lion's paws,
And make the earth devour her own sweet brood,
Pluck the keen teeth from the fierce tiger's jaws,
And burn the long-lived phoenix, in her blood,
Make glad and sorry seasons as thou fleet'st,
And do whate'er thou wilt swift-footed Time
To the wide world and all her fading sweets:
But I forbid thee one most heinous crime,
O carve not with thy hours my love's fair brow,
Nor draw no lines there with thine antique pen,
Him in thy course untainted do allow,
For beauty's pattern to succeeding men.
    Yet do thy worst old Time: despite thy wrong,
    My love shall in my verse ever live young.

❧ 21 ❧

So is it not with me as with that muse,
Stirred by a painted beauty to his verse,
Who heaven it self for ornament doth use,
And every fair with his fair doth rehearse,
Making a couplement of proud compare
With sun and moon, with earth and sea's rich gems:
With April's first-born flowers and all things rare,
That heaven's air in this huge rondure hems.
O let me true in love but truly write,
And then believe me, my love is as fair,
As any mother's child, though not so bright
As those gold candles fixed in heaven's air:
    Let them say more that like of hearsay well,
    I will not praise that purpose not to sell.

22

My glass shall not persuade me I am old,
So long as youth and thou are of one date,
But when in thee time's furrows I behold,
Then look I death my days should expiate.
For all that beauty that doth cover thee,
Is but the seemly raiment of my heart,
Which in thy breast doth live, as thine in me,
How can I then be elder than thou art?
O therefore love be of thyself so wary,
As I not for my self, but for thee will,
Bearing thy heart which I will keep so chary
As tender nurse her babe from faring ill.
  Presume not on thy heart when mine is slain,
  Thou gav'st me thine not to give back again.

23

As an unperfect actor on the stage,
Who with his fear is put beside his part,
Or some fierce thing replete with too much rage,
Whose strength's abundance weakens his own heart;
So I for fear of trust, forget to say,
The perfect ceremony of love's rite,
And in mine own love's strength seem to decay,
O'ercharged with burthen of mine own love's might:
O let my looks be then the eloquence,
And dumb presagers of my speaking breast,
Who plead for love, and look for recompense,
More than that tongue that more hath
  more expressed.
  O learn to read what silent love hath writ,
  To hear with eyes belongs to love's fine wit.

24

Mine eye hath played the painter and hath stelled,
Thy beauty's form in table of my heart,
My body is the frame wherein 'tis held,
And perspective it is best painter's art.
For through the painter must you see his skill,
To find where your true image pictured lies,
Which in my bosom's shop is hanging still,
That hath his windows glazed with thine eyes:
Now see what good turns eyes for eyes have done,
Mine eyes have drawn thy shape, and thine for me
Are windows to my breast, where-through the sun
Delights to peep, to gaze therein on thee;
  Yet eyes this cunning want to grace their art,
  They draw but what they see, know not
    the heart.

25

Let those who are in favour with their stars,
Of public honour and proud titles boast,
Whilst I whom fortune of such triumph bars
Unlooked for joy in that I honour most;
Great princes' favourites their fair leaves spread,
But as the marigold at the sun's eye,
And in themselves their pride lies buried,
For at a frown they in their glory die.
The painful warrior famoused for fight,
After a thousand victories once foiled,
Is from the book of honour razed quite,
And all the rest forgot for which he toiled:
  Then happy I that love and am beloved
  Where I may not remove nor be removed.

26

Lord of my love, to whom in vassalage
Thy merit hath my duty strongly knit;
To thee I send this written embassage
To witness duty, not to show my wit.
Duty so great, which wit so poor as mine
May make seem bare, in wanting words to show it;
But that I hope some good conceit of thine
In thy soul's thought (all naked) will bestow it:
Till whatsoever star that guides my moving,
Points on me graciously with fair aspect,
And puts apparel on my tattered loving,
To show me worthy of thy sweet respect,
  Then may I dare to boast how I do love thee,
  Till then, not show my head where thou mayst
    prove me.

27

Weary with toil, I haste me to my bed,
The dear respose for limbs with travel tired,
But then begins a journey in my head
To work my mind, when body's work's expired.
For then my thoughts (from far where I abide)
Intend a zealous pilgrimage to thee,
And keep my drooping eyelids open wide,
Looking on darkness which the blind do see.
Save that my soul's imaginary sight
Presents thy shadow to my sightless view,
Which like a jewel (hung in ghastly night)
Makes black night beauteous, and her old face new.
  Lo thus by day my limbs, by night my mind,
  For thee, and for my self, no quiet find.

28

How can I then return in happy plight
That am debarred the benefit of rest?
When day's oppression is not eased by night,
But day by night and night by day oppressed.
And each (though enemies to either's reign)
Do in consent shake hands to torture me,
The one by toil, the other to complain
How far I toil, still farther off from thee.
I tell the day to please him thou art bright,
And dost him grace when clouds do blot the heaven:
So flatter I the swart-complexioned night,
When sparkling stars twire not thou gild'st the even.
  But day doth daily draw my sorrows longer,
  And night doth nightly make grief's length
    seem stronger

29

When in disgrace with Fortune and men's eyes,
I all alone beweep my outcast state,
And trouble deaf heaven with my bootless cries,
And look upon my self and curse my fate,
Wishing me like to one more rich in hope,
Featured like him, like him with
  friends possessed,
Desiring this man's art, and that man's scope,
With what I most enjoy contented least,
Yet in these thoughts my self almost despising,
Haply I think on thee, and then my state,
(Like to the lark at break of day arising
From sullen earth) sings hymns at heaven's gate,
  For thy sweet love remembered such wealth brings,
  That then I scorn to change my state with kings.

30

When to the sessions of sweet silent thought,
I summon up remembrance of things past,
I sigh the lack of many a thing I sought,
And with old woes new wail my dear time's waste:
Then can I drown an eye (unused to flow)
For precious friends hid in death's dateless night,
And weep afresh love's long-since cancelled woe,
And moan th' expense of many a vanished sight.
Then can I grieve at grievances foregone,
And heavily from woe to woe tell o'er
The sad account of fore-bemoaned moan,
Which I new pay as if not paid before.
  But if the while I think on thee (dear friend)
  All losses are restored, and sorrows end.

31

Thy bosom is endeared with all hearts,
Which I by lacking have supposed dead,
And there reigns love and all love's loving parts,
And all those friends which I thought buried.
How many a holy and obsequious tear
Hath dear religious love stol'n from mine eye,
As interest of the dead, which now appear,
But things removed that hidden in thee lie.
Thou art the grave where buried love doth live,
Hung with the trophies of my lovers gone,
Who all their parts of me to thee did give,
That due of many, now is thine alone.
  Their images I loved, I view in thee,
  And thou (all they) hast all the all of me.

32

If thou survive my well-contented day,
When that churl Death my bones with dust shall cover
And shalt by fortune once more re-survey
These poor rude lines of thy deceased lover:
Compare them with the bett'ring of the time,
And though they be outstripped by every pen,
Reserve them for my love, not for their rhyme,
Exceeded by the height of happier men.
O then vouchsafe me but this loving thought,
'Had my friend's Muse grown with this growing age,
A dearer birth than this his love had brought
To march in ranks of better equipage:
  But since he died and poets better prove,
  Theirs for their style I'll read, his for his love'.

❧ 33 ❧

Full many a glorious morning have I seen,
Flatter the mountain tops with sovereign eye,
Kissing with golden face the meadows green;
Gilding pale streams with heavenly alchemy:
Anon permit the basest clouds to ride,
With ugly rack on his celestial face,
And from the forlorn world his visage hide
Stealing unseen to west with this disgrace:
Even so my sun one early morn did shine,
With all triumphant splendour on my brow,
But out alack, he was but one hour mine,
The region cloud hath masked him from me now.
  Yet him for this, my love no whit disdaineth,
  Suns of the world may stain, when heaven's
    sun staineth.

❧ 34 ❧

Why didst thou promise such a beauteous day,
And make me travel forth without my cloak,
To let base clouds o'ertake me in my way,
Hiding thy brav'ry in their rotten smoke?
'Tis not enough that through the cloud thou break,
To dry the rain on my storm-beaten face,
For no man well of such a salve can speak,
That heals the wound, and cures not the disgrace:
Nor can thy shame give physic to my grief,
Though thou repent, yet I have still the loss,
Th' offender's sorrow lends but weak relief
To him that bears the strong offence's cross.
  Ah but those tears are pearl which thy love sheds,
  And they are rich, and ransom all ill deeds.

❧ 35 ❧

No more be grieved at that which thou hast done,
Roses have thorns, and silver fountains mud,
Clouds and eclipses stain both moon and sun,
And loathsome canker lives in sweetest bud.
All men make faults, and even I in this,
Authorizing thy trespass with compare,
My self corrupting salving thy amiss,
Excusing thy sins more than thy sins are:
For to thy sensual fault I bring in sense,
Thy adverse party is thy advocate,
And 'gainst my self a lawful plea commence:
Such civil war is in my love and hate,
  That I an accessary needs must be,
  To that sweet thief which sourly robs from me.

❧ 36 ❧

Let me confess that we two must be twain,
Although our undivided loves are one:
So shall those blots that do with me remain,
Without thy help, by me be borne alone.
In our two loves there is but one respect,
Though in our lives a separable spite,
Which though it alter not love's sole effect,
Yet doth it steal sweet hours from love's delight.
I may not evermore acknowledge thee,
Lest my bewailed guilt should do thee shame,
Nor thou with public kindness honour me,
Unless thou take that honour from thy name:
  But do not so, I love thee in such sort,
  As thou being mine, mine is thy good report.

❧ 37 ❧

As a decrepit father takes delight,
To see his active child do deeds of youth,
So I, made lame by Fortune's dearest spite
Take all my comfort of thy worth and truth.
For whether beauty, birth, or wealth, or wit,
Or any of these all, or all, or more
Entitled in thy parts, do crowned sit,
I make my love engrafted to this store:
So then I am not lame, poor, nor despised,
Whilst that this shadow doth such substance give,
That I in thy abundance am sufficed,
And by a part of all thy glory live:
  Look what is best, that best I wish in thee,
  This wish I have, then ten times happy me.

❧ 38 ❧

How can my Muse want subject to invent
While thou dost breathe that pour'st into
    my verse,
Thine own sweet argument, too excellent,
For every vulgar paper to rehearse?
O give thy self the thanks if aught in me,
Worthy perusal stand against thy sight,
For who's so dumb that cannot write to thee,
When thou thy self dost give invention light?
Be thou the tenth Muse, ten times more in worth
Than those old nine which rhymers invocate,
And he that calls on thee, let him bring forth
Eternal numbers to outlive long date.
  If my slight muse do please these curious days,
  The pain be mine, but thine shall be the praise.

❧ 39 ❧

O how thy worth with manners may I sing,
When thou art all the better part of me?
What can mine own praise to mine own self bring:
And what is't but mine own when I praise thee?
Even for this, let us divided live,
And our dear love lose name of single one,
That by this separation I may give:
That due to thee which thou deserv'st alone:
O absence what a torment wouldst thou prove,
Were it not thy sour leisure gave sweet leave,
To entertain the time with thoughts of love,
Which time and thoughts so sweetly doth deceive.
  And that thou teachest how to make one twain,
  By praising him here who doth hence remain.

❧ 40 ❧

Take all my loves, my love, yea take them all,
What hast thou then more than thou
    hadst before?
No love, my love, that thou mayst true love call,
All mine was thine, before thou hadst this more:
Then if for my love, thou my love receivest,
I cannot blame thee, for my love thou usest,
But yet be blamed, if thou thy self deceivest
By wilful taste of what thy self refusest.
I do forgive thy robbery, gentle thief
Although thou steal thee all my poverty:
And yet love knows it is a greater grief
To bear greater wrong, than hate's known injury.
  Lascivious grace, in whom all ill well shows,
  Kill me with spites yet we must not be foes.

❧ 41 ❧

Those pretty wrongs that liberty commits,
When I am sometime absent from thy heart,
Thy beauty, and thy years full well befits,
For still temptation follows where thou art.
Gentle thou art, and therefore to be won,
Beauteous thou art, therefore to be assailed.
And when a woman woos, what woman's son
Will sourly leave her till he have prevailed?
Ay me, but yet thou mightst my seat forbear,
And chide thy beauty, and thy straying youth,
Who lead thee in their riot even there
Where thou art forced to break a twofold truth:
  Hers, by thy beauty tempting her to thee,
  Thine, by thy beauty being false to me.

❧ 42 ❧

That thou hast her it is not all my grief,
And yet it may be said I loved her dearly,
That she hath thee is of my wailing chief,
A loss in love that touches me more nearly.
Loving offenders thus I will excuse ye,
Thou dost love her, because thou know'st I love her,
And for my sake even so doth she abuse me,
Suff'ring my friend for my sake to approve her.
If I lose thee, my loss is my love's gain,
And losing her, my friend hath found that loss,
Both find each other, and I lose both twain,
And both for my sake lay on me this cross,
  But here's the joy, my friend and I are one,
  Sweet flattery, then she loves but me alone.

❧ 43 ❧

When most I wink then do mine eyes best see,
For all the day they view things unrespected,
But when I sleep, in dreams they look on thee,
And darkly bright, are bright in dark directed.
Then thou whose shadow shadows doth make bright
How would thy shadow's form, form happy show,
To the clear day with thy much clearer light,
When to unseeing eyes thy shade shines so!
How would (I say) mine eyes be blessed made,
By looking on thee in the living day,
When in dead night thy fair imperfect shade,
Through heavy sleep on sightless eyes doth stay!
  All days are nights to see till I see thee,
  And nights bright days when dreams do show
    thee me.

❧ 44 ❧

If the dull substance of my flesh were thought,
Injurious distance should not stop my way,
For then despite of space I would be brought,
From limits far remote, where thou dost stay,
No matter then although my foot did stand
Upon the farthest earth removed from thee,
For nimble thought can jump both sea and land,
As soon as think the place where he would be.
But ah, thought kills me that I am not thought
To leap large lengths of miles when thou art gone,
But that so much of earth and water wrought,
I must attend, time's leisure with my moan.
  Receiving nought by elements so slow,
  But heavy tears, badges of either's woe.

❧ 45 ❧

The other two, slight air, and purging fire,
Are both with thee, wherever I abide;
The first my thought, the other my desire,
These present-absent with swift motion slide.
For when these quicker elements are gone
In tender embassy of love to thee,
My life being made of four, with two alone,
Sinks down to death, oppressed with melancholy.
Until life's composition be recured,
By those swift messengers returned from thee,
Who even but now come back again assured,
Of thy fair health, recounting it to me.
  This told, I joy, but then no longer glad,
  I send them back again and straight grow sad.

❧ 46 ❧

Mine eye and heart are at a mortal war,
How to divide the conquest of thy sight,
Mine eye, my heart thy picture's sight would bar,
My heart, mine eye the freedom of that right,
My heart doth plead that thou in him dost lie,
(A closet never pierced with crystal eyes)
But the defendant doth that plea deny,
And says in him thy fair appearance lies.
To side this title is impanelled
A quest of thoughts, all tenants to the heart,
And by their verdict is determined
The clear eye's moiety, and the dear heart's part.
  As thus, mine eye's due is thy outward part,
  And my heart's right, thy inward love of heart.

❧ 47 ❧

Betwixt mine eye and heart a league is took,
And each doth good turns now unto the other,
When that mine eye is famished for a look,
Or heart in love with sighs himself doth smother;
With my love's picture then my eye doth feast,
And to the painted banquet bids my heart:
Another time mine eye is my heart's guest,
And in his thoughts of love doth share a part.
So either by thy picture or my love,
Thy self away art present still with me,
For thou not farther than my thoughts canst move,
And I am still with them, and they with thee.
  Or if they sleep, thy picture in my sight
  Awakes my heart, to heart's and eye's delight.

❧ 48 ❧

How careful was I when I took my way,
Each trifle under truest bars to thrust,
That to my use it might unused stay
From hands of falsehood, in sure wards of trust!
But thou, to whom my jewels trifles are,
Most worthy comfort, now my greatest grief,
Thou best of dearest, and mine only care,
Art left the prey of every vulgar thief.
Thee have I not locked up in any chest,
Save where thou art not, though I feel thou art,
Within the gentle closure of my breast,
From whence at pleasure thou mayst come
  and part,
  And even thence thou wilt be stol'n I fear,
  For truth proves thievish for a prize so dear.

❧ 49 ❧

Against that time (if ever that time come)
When I shall see thee frown on my defects,
When as thy love hath cast his utmost sum,
Called to that audit by advised respects,
Against that time when thou shalt strangely pass,
And scarcely greet me with that sun thine eye,
When love converted from the thing it was
Shall reasons find of settled gravity;
Against that time do I ensconce me here
Within the knowledge of mine own desert,
And this my hand, against my self uprear,
To guard the lawful reasons on thy part,
  To leave poor me, thou hast the strength of laws,
  Since why to love, I can allege no cause.

❦ 50 ❦

How heavy do I journey on the way,
When what I seek (my weary travel's end)
Doth teach that case and that repose to say
'Thus far the miles are measured from thy friend.'
The beast that bears me, tired with my woe,
Plods dully on, to bear that weight in me,
As if by some instinct the wretch did know
His rider loved not speed being made from thee:
The bloody spur cannot provoke him on,
That sometimes anger thrusts into his hide,
Which heavily he answers with a groan,
More sharp to me than spurring to his side,
  For that same groan doth put this in my mind,
  My grief lies onward and my joy behind.

❦ 51 ❦

Thus can my love excuse the slow offence,
Of my dull bearer, when from thee I speed,
From where thou art, why should I haste
  me thence?
Till I return of posting is no need.
O what excuse will my poor beast then find,
When swift extremity can seem but slow?
Then should I spur though mounted on the wind,
In winged speed no motion shall I know,
Then can no horse with my desire keep pace,
Therefore desire (of perfect'st love being made)
Shall neigh (no dull flesh) in his fiery race,
But love, for love, thus shall excuse my jade,
  Since from thee going, he went wilful-slow,
  Towards thee I'll run, and give him leave to go.

❦ 52 ❦

So am I as the rich whose blessed key,
Can bring him to his sweet up-locked treasure,
The which he will not every hour survey,
For blunting the fine point of seldom pleasure.
Therefore are feasts so solemn and so rare,
Since seldom coming in that long year set,
Like stones of worth they thinly placed are,
Or captain jewels in the carcanet.
So is the time that keeps you as my chest
Or as the wardrobe which the robe doth hide,
To make some special instant special-blest,
By new unfolding his imprisoned pride.
  Blessed are you whose worthiness gives scope,
  Being had to triumph, being lacked to hope.

❦ 53 ❦

What is your substance, whereof are you made,
That millions of strange shadows on you tend?
Since every one, hath every one, one shade,
And you but one, can every shadow lend:
Describe Adonis and the counterfeit,
Is poorly imitated after you,
On Helen's cheek all art of beauty set,
And you in Grecian tires are painted new:
Speak of the spring, and foison of the year,
The one doth shadow of your beauty show,
The other as your bounty doth appear,
And you in every blessed shape we know.
  In all external grace you have some part,
  But you like none, none you for constant heart.

❦ 54 ❦

O how much more doth beauty beauteous seem,
By that sweet ornament which truth doth give!
The rose looks fair, but fairer we it deem
For that sweet odour, which doth in it live:
The canker blooms have full as deep a dye,
As the perfumed tincture of the roses,
Hang on such thorns, and play as wantonly,
When summer's breath their masked buds discloses:
But for their virtue only is their show,
They live unwooed, and unrespected fade,
Die to themselves. Sweet roses do not so,
Of their sweet deaths, are sweetest odours made:
  And so of you, beauteous and lovely youth,
  When that shall vade, by verse distills your truth.

55

Not marble, nor the gilded monuments
Of princes shall outlive this powerful rhyme,
But you shall shine more bright in these contents
Than unswept stone, besmeared with
    sluttish time.
When wasteful war shall statues overturn,
And broils root out the work of masonry,
Nor Mars his sword, nor war's quick fire shall burn
The living record of your memory.
'Gainst death, and all-oblivious enmity
Shall you pace forth, your praise shall still find room,
Even in the eyes of all posterity
That wear this world out to the ending doom.
    So till the judgment that your self arise,
    You live in this, and dwell in lovers' eyes.

56

Sweet love renew thy force, be it not said
Thy edge should blunter be than appetite,
Which but to-day by feeding is allayed,
To-morrow sharpened in his former might.
So love be thou, although to-day thou fill
Thy hungry eyes, even till they wink with fulness,
To-morrow see again, and do not kill
The spirit of love, with a perpetual dulness:
Let this sad interim like the ocean be
Which parts the shore, where two contracted new
Come daily to the banks, that when they see
Return of love, more blest may be the view.
    Or call it winter, which being full of care,
    Makes summer's welcome, thrice more wished,
        more rare.

57

Being your slave what should I do but tend,
Upon the hours, and times of your desire?
I have no precious time at all to spend;
Nor services to do till you require.
Nor dare I chide the world-without-end hour,
Whilst I (my sovereign) watch the clock for you,
Nor think the bitterness of absence sour,
When you have bid your servant once adieu.
Nor dare I question with my jealous thought,
Where you may be, or your affairs suppose,
But like a sad slave stay and think of nought
Save where you are, how happy you make those.
    So true a fool is love, that in your will,
    (Though you do any thing) he thinks no ill.

58

That God forbid, that made me first your slave,
I should in thought control your times
    of pleasure,
Or at your hand th' account of hours to crave,
Being your vassal bound to stay your leisure.
O let me suffer (being at your beck)
Th' imprisoned absence of your liberty,
And patience tame to sufferance bide each check,
Without accusing you of injury.
Be where you list, your charter is so strong,
That you your self may privilege your time
To what you will, to you it doth belong,
Your self to pardon of self-doing crime.
    I am to wait, though waiting so be hell,
    Not blame your pleasure be it ill or well.

59

If there be nothing new, but that which is
Hath been before, how are our brains beguiled,
Which labouring for invention bear amis
The second burthen of a former child!
O that record could with a backward look,
Even of five hundred courses of the sun,
Show me your image in some antique book,
Since mind at first in character was done.
That I might see what the old world could say,
To this composed wonder of your frame,
Whether we are mended, or where better they,
Or whether revolution be the same.
    O sure I am the wits of former days,
    To subjects worse have given admiring praise.

60

Like as the waves make towards the
    pebbled shore,
So do our minutes hasten to their end,
Each changing place with that which goes before,
In sequent toil all forwards do contend.
Nativity once in the main of light,
Crawls to maturity, wherewith being crowned,
Crooked eclipses 'gainst his glory fight,
And Time that gave, doth now his gift confound.
Time doth transfix the flourish set on youth,
And delves the parallels in beauty's brow,
Feeds on the rarities of nature's truth,
And nothing stands but for his scythe to mow.
    And yet to times in hope, my verse shall stand
    Praising thy worth, despite his cruel hand.

61

Is it thy will, thy image should keep open
My heavy eyelids to the weary night?
Dost thou desire my slumbers should be broken,
While shadows like to thee do mock my sight?
Is it thy spirit that thou send'st from thee
So far from home into my deeds to pry,
To find out shames and idle hours in me,
The scope and tenure of thy jealousy?
O no, thy love though much, is not so great,
It is my love that keeps mine eye awake,
Mine own true love that doth my rest defeat,
To play the watchman ever for thy sake.
  For thee watch I, whilst thou dost
    wake elsewhere,
  From me far off, with others all too near.

62

Sin of self-love possesseth all mine eye,
And all my soul, and all my every part;
And for this sin there is no remedy,
It is so grounded inward in my heart.
Methinks no face so gracious is as mine,
No shape so true, no truth of such account,
And for my self mine own worth do define,
As I all other in all worths surmount.
But when my glass shows me my self indeed
Beated and chopt with tanned antiquity,
Mine own self-love quite contrary I read:
Self, so self-loving were iniquity.
  'Tis thee (my self) that for my self I praise,
  Painting my age with beauty of thy days.

63

Against my love shall be as I am now
With Time's injurious hand crushed and o'erworn,
When hours have drained his blood and filled
    his brow
With lines and wrinkles, when his youthful morn
Hath travelled on to age's steepy night,
And all those beauties whereof now he's king
Are vanishing, or vanished out of sight,
Stealing away the treasure of his spring:
For such a time do I now fortify
Against confounding age's cruel knife,
That he shall never cut from memory
My sweet love's beauty, though my lover's life.
  His beauty shall in these black lines be seen,
  And they shall live, and he in them still green.

64

When I have seen by Time's fell hand defaced
The rich-proud cost of outworn buried age,
When sometime lofty towers I see down-rased,
And brass eternal slave to mortal rage.
When I have seen the hungry ocean gain
Advantage on the kingdom of the shore,
And the firm soil win of the watery main,
Increasing store with loss, and loss with store.
When I have seen such interchange of state,
Or state it self confounded, to decay,
Ruin hath taught me thus to ruminate
That Time will come and take my love away.
  This thought is as a death which cannot choose
  But weep to have that which it fears to lose.

65

Since brass, nor stone, nor earth, nor
    boundless sea,
But sad mortality o'ersways their power,
How with this rage shall beauty hold a plea,
Whose action is no stronger than a flower?
O how shall summer's honey breath hold out,
Against the wrackful siege of batt'ring days,
When rocks impregnable are not so stout,
Nor gates of steel so strong but time decays?
O fearful meditation, where alack,
Shall Time's best jewel from Time's chest lie hid?
Or what strong hand can hold his swift foot back,
Or who his spoil of beauty can forbid?
  O none, unless this miracle have might,
  That in black ink my love may still shine bright.

❦ 66 ❦

Tired with all these for restful death I cry,
As to behold desert a beggar born,
And needy nothing trimmed in jollity,
And purest faith unhappily forsworn,
And gilded honour shamefully misplaced,
And maiden virtue rudely strumpeted,
And right perfection wrongfully disgraced,
And strength by limping sway disabled
And art made tongue-tied by authority,
And folly (doctor-like) controlling skill,
And simple truth miscalled simplicity,
And captive good attending captain ill.
  Tired with all these, from these would I be gone,
  Save that to die, I leave my love alone.

❦ 67 ❦

Ah wherefore with infection should he live,
And with his presence grace impiety,
That sin by him advantage should achieve,
And lace it self with his society?
Why should false painting imitate his cheek,
And steal dead seeming of his living hue?
Why should poor beauty indirectly seek,
Roses of shadow, since his rose is true?
Why should he live, now Nature bankrupt is,
Beggared of blood to blush through lively veins,
For she hath no exchequer now but his,
And proud of many, lives upon his gains?
  O him she stores, to show what wealth she had,
  In days long since, before these last so bad.

❦ 68 ❦

Thus is his cheek the map of days outworn,
When beauty lived and died as flowers do now,
Before these bastard signs of fair were born,
Or durst inhabit on a living brow:
Before the golden tresses of the dead,
The right of sepulchres, were shorn away,
To live a second life on second head,
Ere beauty's dead fleece made another gay:
In him those holy antique hours are seen,
Without all ornament, it self and true,
Making no summer of another's green,
Robbing no old to dress his beauty new,
  And him as for a map doth Nature store,
  To show false Art what beauty was of yore.

❦ 69 ❦

Those parts of thee that the world's eye doth view,
Want nothing that the thought of hearts can mend:
All tongues (the voice of souls) give thee that due,
Uttering bare truth, even so as foes commend.
Thy outward thus with outward praise is crowned,
But those same tongues that give thee so thine own,
In other accents do this praise confound
By seeing farther than the eye hath shown.
They look into the beauty of thy mind,
And that in guess they measure by thy deeds,
Then churls their thoughts (although their eyes
    were kind)
To thy fair flower add the rank smell of weeds:
  But why thy odour matcheth not thy show,
  The soil is this, that thou dost common grow.

❦ 70 ❦

That thou art blamed shall not be thy defect,
For slander's mark was ever yet the fair,
The ornament of beauty is suspect,
A crow that flies in heaven's sweetest air.
So thou be good, slander doth but approve,
Thy worth the greater being wooed of time,
For canker vice the sweetest buds doth love,
And thou present'st a pure unstained prime.
Thou hast passed by the ambush of young days,
Either not assailed, or victor being charged,
Yet this thy praise cannot be so thy praise,
To tie up envy, evermore enlarged,
  If some suspect of ill masked not thy show,
  Then thou alone kingdoms of hearts
    shouldst owe.

❦ 71 ❦

No longer mourn for me when I am dead,
Than you shall hear the surly sullen bell
Give warning to the world that I am fled
From this vile world with vilest worms to dwell:
Nay if you read this line, remember not,
The hand that writ it, for I love you so,
That I in your sweet thoughts would be forgot,
If thinking on me then should make you woe.
O if (I say) you look upon this verse,
When I (perhaps) compounded am with clay,
Do not so much as my poor name rehearse;
But let your love even with my life decay.
  Lest the wise world should look into your moan,
  And mock you with me after I am gone.

❧ 72 ❧

O lest the world should task you to recite,
What merit lived in me that you should love
After my death (dear love) forget me quite,
For you in me can nothing worthy prove.
Unless you would devise some virtuous lie,
To do more for me than mine own desert,
And hang more praise upon deceased I,
Than niggard truth would willingly impart:
O lest your true love may seem false in this,
That you for love speak well of me untrue,
My name be buried where my body is,
And live no more to shame nor me, nor you.
  For I am shamed by that which I bring forth,
  And so should you, to love things nothing worth.

❧ 75 ❧

So are you to my thoughts as food to life,
Or as sweet-seasoned showers are to the ground;
And for the peace of you I hold such strife
As 'twixt a miser and his wealth is found.
Now proud as an enjoyer, and anon
Doubting the filching age will steal his treasure,
Now counting best to be with you alone,
Then bettered that the world may see
  my pleasure,
Sometime all full with feasting on your sight,
And by and by clean starved for a look,
Possessing or pursuing no delight
Save what is had, or must from you be took.
  Thus do I pine and surfeit day by day,
  Or gluttoning on all, or all away.

❧ 73 ❧

That time of year thou mayst in me behold,
When yellow leaves, or none, or few do hang
Upon those boughs which shake against the cold,
Bare ruined choirs, where late the sweet birds sang.
In me thou seest the twilight of such day,
As after sunset fadeth in the west,
Which by and by black night doth take away,
Death's second self that seals up all in rest.
In me thou seest the glowing of such fire,
That on the ashes of his youth doth lie,
As the death-bed, whereon it must expire,
Consumed with that which it was nourished by.
  This thou perceiv'st, which makes thy love
    more strong,
  To love that well, which thou must leave ere long.

❧ 74 ❧

But be contented when that fell arrest,
Without all bail shall carry me away,
My life hath in this line some interest,
Which for memorial still with thee shall stay.
When thou reviewest this, thou dost review,
The very part was consecrate to thee,
The earth can have but earth, which is his due,
My spirit is thine the better part of me,
So then thou hast but lost the dregs of life,
The prey of worms, my body being dead,
The coward conquest of a wretch's knife,
Too base of thee to be remembered,
  The worth of that, is that which it contains,
  And that is this, and this with thee remains.

❧ 76 ❧

Why is my verse so barren of new pride?
So far from variation or quick change?
Why with the time do I not glance aside
To new-found methods, and to
  compounds strange?
Why write I still all one, ever the same,
And keep invention in a noted weed,
That every word doth almost tell my name,
Showing their birth, and where they did proceed?
O know sweet love I always write of you,
And you and love are still my argument:
So all my best is dressing old words new,
Spending again what is already spent:
  For as the sun is daily new and old,
  So is my love still telling what is told.

🔖 77 🔖

Thy glass will show thee how thy beauties wear,
Thy dial how thy precious minutes waste,
These vacant leaves thy mind's imprint will bear,
And of this book, this learning mayst thou taste.
The wrinkles which thy glass will truly show,
Of mouthed graves will give thee memory,
Thou by thy dial's shady stealth mayst know,
Time's thievish progress to eternity.
Look what thy memory cannot contain,
Commit to these waste blanks, and thou shalt find
Those children nursed, delivered from thy brain,
To take a new acquaintance of thy mind.
  These offices, so oft as thou wilt look,
  Shall profit thee, and much enrich thy book.

🔖 78 🔖

So oft have I invoked thee for my muse,
And found such fair assistance in my verse,
As every alien pen hath got my use,
And under thee their poesy disperse.
Thine eyes, that taught the dumb on high to sing,
And heavy ignorance aloft to fly,
Have added feathers to the learned's wing,
And given grace a double majesty.
Yet be most proud of that which I compile,
Whose influence is thine, and born of thee,
In others' works thou dost but mend the style,
And arts with thy sweet graces graced be.
  But thou art all my art, and dost advance
  As high as learning, my rude ignorance.

🔖 79 🔖

Whilst I alone did call upon thy aid,
My verse alone had all thy gentle grace,
But now my gracious numbers are decayed,
And my sick muse doth give another place.
I grant (sweet love) thy lovely argument
Deserves the travail of a worthier pen,
Yet what of thee thy poet doth invent,
He robs thee of, and pays it thee again,
He lends thee virtue, and he stole that word,
From thy behaviour, beauty doth he give
And found it in thy cheek: he can afford
No praise to thee, but what in thee doth live.
  Then thank him not for that which he doth say,
  Since what he owes thee, thou thy self dost pay.

🔖 80 🔖

O how I faint when I of you do write,
Knowing a better spirit doth use your name,
And in the praise thereof spends all his might,
To make me tongue-tied speaking of your fame.
But since your worth (wide as the ocean is)
The humble as the proudest sail doth bear,
My saucy bark (inferior far to his)
On your broad main doth wilfully appear.
Your shallowest help will hold me up afloat,
Whilst he upon your soundless deep doth ride,
Or (being wrecked) I am a worthless boat,
He of tall building, and of goodly pride.
  Then if he thrive and I be cast away,
  The worst was this, my love was my decay.

🔖 81 🔖

Or I shall live your epitaph to make,
Or you survive when I in earth am rotten,
From hence your memory death cannot take,
Although in me each part will be forgotten.
Your name from hence immortal life shall have,
Though I (once gone) to all the world must die,
The earth can yield me but a common grave,
When you entombed in men's eyes shall lie,
Your monument shall be my gentle verse,
Which eyes not yet created shall o'er-read,
And tongues to be, your being shall rehearse,
When all the breathers of this world are dead,
  You still shall live (such virtue hath my pen)
  Where breath most breathes, even in the
    mouths of men.

🔖 82 🔖

I grant thou wert not married to my muse,
And therefore mayst without attaint o'erlook
The dedicated words which writers use
Of their fair subject, blessing every book.
Thou art as fair in knowledge as in hue,
Finding thy worth a limit past my praise,
And therefore art enforced to seek anew,
Some fresher stamp of the time-bettering days.
And do so love, yet when they have devised,
What strained touches rhetoric can lend,
Thou truly fair, wert truly sympathized,
In true plain words, by thy true-telling friend.
  And their gross painting might be better used,
  Where cheeks need blood, in thee it is abused.

🖾 83 🖾

I never saw that you did painting need,
And therefore to your fair no painting set,
I found (or thought I found) you did exceed,
That barren tender of a poet's debt:
And therefore have I slept in your report,
That you your self being extant well might show,
How far a modern quill doth come too short,
Speaking of worth, what worth in you doth grow.
This silence for my sin you did impute,
Which shall be most my glory being dumb,
For I impair not beauty being mute,
When others would give life, and bring a tomb.
　There lives more life in one of your fair eyes,
　Than both your poets can in praise devise.

🖾 84 🖾

Who is it that says most, which can say more,
Than this rich praise, that you alone, are you?
In whose confine immured is the store,
Which should example where your equal grew.
Lean penury within that pen doth dwell,
That to his subject lends not some small glory,
But he that writes of you, if he can tell,
That you are you, so dignifies his story.
Let him but copy what in you is writ,
Not making worse what nature made so clear,
And such a counterpart shall fame his wit,
Making his style admired every where.
　You to your beauteous blessings add a curse,
　Being fond on praise, which makes your
　　praises worse.

🖾 85 🖾

My tongue-tied Muse in manners holds her still,
While comments of your praise richly compiled,
Reserve their character with golden quill,
And precious phrase by all the Muses filed.
I think good thoughts, whilst other write
　good words,
And like unlettered clerk still cry 'Amen',
To every hymn that able spirit affords,
In polished form of well refined pen.
Hearing you praised, I say 'tis so, 'tis true,
And to the most of praise add something more,
But that is in my thought, whose love to you
(Though words come hindmost) holds his
　rank before,
　Then others, for the breath of words respect,
　Me for my dumb thoughts, speaking in effect.

🖾 86 🖾

Was it the proud full sail of his great verse,
Bound for the prize of (all too precious) you,
That did my ripe thoughts in my brain inhearse,
Making their tomb the womb wherein they grew?
Was it his spirit, by spirits taught to write,
Above a mortal pitch, that struck me dead?
No, neither he, nor his compeers by night
Giving him aid, my verse astonished.
He nor that affable familiar ghost
Which nightly gulls him with intelligence,
As victors of my silence cannot boast,
I was not sick of any fear from thence.
　But when your countenance filled up his line,
　Then lacked I matter, that enfeebled mine.

🖾 87 🖾

Farewell! thou art too dear for my possessing,
And like enough thou know'st thy estimate,
The charter of thy worth gives thee releasing:
My bonds in thee are all determinate.
For how do I hold thee but by thy granting,
And for that riches where is my deserving?
The cause of this fair gift in me is wanting,
And so my patent back again is swerving.
Thy self thou gav'st, thy own worth then
　not knowing,
Or me to whom thou gav'st it, else mistaking,
So thy great gift upon misprision growing,
Comes home again, on better judgment making.
　Thus have I had thee as a dream doth flatter,
　In sleep a king, but waking no such matter.

❧ 88 ❧

When thou shalt be disposed to set me light,
And place my merit in the eye of scorn,
Upon thy side, against my self I'll fight,
And prove thee virtuous, though thou
    art forsworn:
With mine own weakness being best acquainted,
Upon thy part I can set down a story
Of faults concealed, wherein I am attainted:
That thou in losing me, shalt win much glory:
And I by this will be a gainer too,
For bending all my loving thoughts on thee,
The injuries that to my self I do,
Doing thee vantage, double-vantage me.
  Such is my love, to thee I so belong,
  That for thy right, my self will bear all wrong.

❧ 89 ❧

Say that thou didst forsake me for some fault,
And I will comment upon that offence,
Speak of my lameness, and I straight will halt:
Against thy reasons making no defence.
Thou canst not (love) disgrace me half so ill,
To set a form upon desired change,
As I'll my self disgrace, knowing thy will,
I will acquaintance strangle and look strange:
Be absent from thy walks and in my tongue,
Thy sweet beloved name no more shall dwell,
Lest I (too much profane) should do it wrong:
And haply of our old acquaintance tell.
  For thee, against my self I'll vow debate,
  For I must ne'er love him whom thou dost hate.

❧ 90 ❧

Then hate me when thou wilt, if ever, now,
Now while the world is bent my deeds to cross,
Join with the spite of fortune, make me bow,
And do not drop in for an after-loss:
Ah do not, when my heart hath 'scaped
  this sorrow,
Come in the rearward of a conquered woe,
Give not a windy night a rainy morrow,
To linger out a purposed overthrow.
If thou wilt leave me, do not leave me last,
When other petty griefs have done their spite,
But in the onset come, so shall I taste
At first the very worst of fortune's might.
  And other strains of woe, which now seem woe,
  Compared with loss of thee, will not seem so.

❧ 91 ❧

Some glory in their birth, some in their skill,
Some in their wealth, some in their body's force,
Some in their garments though new-fangled ill:
Some in their hawks and hounds, some in
  their horse.
And every humour hath his adjunct pleasure,
Wherein it finds a joy above the rest,
But these particulars are not my measure,
All these I better in one general best.
Thy love is better than high birth to me,
Richer than wealth, prouder than garments' costs,
Of more delight than hawks and horses be:
And having thee, of all men's pride I boast.
  Wretched in this alone, that thou mayst take,
  All this away, and me most wretchcd make.

❧ 92 ❧

But do thy worst to steal thy self away,
For term of life thou art assured mine,
And life no longer than thy love will stay,
For it depends upon that love of thine.
Then need I not to fear the worst of wrongs,
When in the least of them my life hath end,
I see a better state to me belongs
Than that, which on thy humour doth depend.
Thou canst not vex me with inconstant mind,
Since that my life on thy revolt doth lie,
O what a happy title do I find,
Happy to have thy love, happy to die!
  But what's so blessed-fair that fears no blot?
  Thou mayst be false, and yet I know it not.

❧ 93 ❧

So shall I live, supposing thou art true,
Like a deceived husband, so love's face,
May still seem love to me, though altered new:
Thy looks with me, thy heart in other place.
For there can live no hatred in thine eye,
Therefore in that I cannot know thy change,
In many's looks, the false heart's history
Is writ in moods and frowns and wrinkles strange.
But heaven in thy creation did decree,
That in thy face sweet love should ever dwell,
Whate'er thy thoughts, or thy heart's workings be,
Thy looks should nothing thence, but
  sweetness tell.
  How like Eve's apple doth thy beauty grow,
  If thy sweet virtue answer not thy show.

94

They that have power to hurt, and will do none,
That do not do the thing, they most do show,
Who moving others, are themselves as stone,
Unmoved, cold, and to temptation slow:
They rightly do inherit heaven's graces,
And husband nature's riches from expense,
They are the lords and owners of their faces,
Others, but stewards of their excellence:
The summer's flower is to the summer sweet,
Though to it self, it only live and die,
But if that flower with base infection meet,
The basest weed outbraves his dignity:
  For sweetest things turn sourest by their deeds,
  Lilies that fester, smell far worse than weeds.

95

How sweet and lovely dost thou make the shame,
Which like a canker in the fragrant rose,
Doth spot the beauty of thy budding name!
O in what sweets dost thou thy sins enclose!
That tongue that tells the story of thy days,
(Making lascivious comments on thy sport)
Cannot dispraise, but in a kind of praise,
Naming thy name, blesses an ill report.
O what a mansion have those vices got,
Which for their habitation chose out thee,
Where beauty's veil doth cover every blot,
And all things turns to fair, that eyes can see!
  Take heed (dear heart) of this large privilege,
  The hardest knife ill-used doth lose his edge.

96

Some say thy fault is youth, some wantonness,
Some say thy grace is youth and gentle sport,
Both grace and faults are loved of more and less:
Thou mak'st faults graces, that to thee resort:
As on the finger of a throned queen,
The basest jewel will be well esteemed:
So are those errors that in thee are seen,
To truths translated, and for true things deemed.
How many lambs might the stern wolf betray,
If like a lamb he could his looks translate!
How many gazers mightst thou lead away,
If thou wouldst use the strength of all thy state!
  But do not so, I love thee in such sort,
  As thou being mine, mine is thy good report.

97

How like a winter hath my absence been
From thee, the pleasure of the fleeting year!
What freezings have I felt, what dark days seen!
What old December's bareness everywhere!
And yet this time removed was summer's time,
The teeming autumn big with rich increase,
Bearing the wanton burden of the prime,
Like widowed wombs after their lords' decease:
Yet this abundant issue seemed to me
But hope of orphans, and unfathered fruit,
For summer and his pleasures wait on thee,
And thou away, the very birds are mute.
  Or if they sing, 'tis with so dull a cheer,
  That leaves look pale, dreading the
    winter's near.

98

From you have I been absent in the spring,
When proud-pied April (dressed in all his trim)
Hath put a spirit of youth in every thing:
That heavy Saturn laughed and leaped with him.
Yet nor the lays of birds, nor the sweet smell
Of different flowers in odour and in hue,
Could make me any summer's story tell:
Or from their proud lap pluck them where they grew:
Nor did I wonder at the lily's white,
Nor praise the deep vermilion in the rose,
They were but sweet, but figures of delight:
Drawn after you, you pattern of all those.
  Yet seemed it winter still, and you away,
  As with your shadow I with these did play.

❦ 99 ❦

The forward violet thus did I chide,
Sweet thief, whence didst thou steal thy sweet
    that smells,
If not from my love's breath? The purple pride
Which on thy soft cheek for complexion dwells,
In my love's veins thou hast too grossly dyed.
The lily I condemned for thy hand,
And buds of marjoram had stol'n thy hair,
The roses fearfully on thorns did stand,
One blushing shame, another white despair:
A third nor red, nor white, had stol'n of both,
And to his robbery had annexed thy breath,
But for his theft in pride of all his growth
A vengeful canker eat him up to death.
    More flowers I noted, yet I none could see,
    But sweet, or colour it had stol'n from thee.

❦ 100 ❦

Where art thou Muse that thou forget'st so long,
To speak of that which gives thee all thy might?
Spend'st thou thy fury on some worthless song,
Darkening thy power to lend base subjects light?
Return forgetful Muse, and straight redeem,
In gentle numbers time so idly spent,
Sing to the ear that doth thy lays esteem,
And gives thy pen both skill and argument.
Rise resty Muse, my love's sweet face survey,
If Time have any wrinkle graven there,
If any, be a satire to decay,
And make Time's spoils despised everywhere.
    Give my love fame faster than Time wastes life,
    So thou prevent'st his scythe, and crooked knife.

❦ 101 ❦

O truant Muse what shall be thy amends,
For thy neglect of truth in beauty dyed?
Both truth and beauty on my love depends:
So dost thou too, and therein dignified:
Make answer Muse, wilt thou not haply say,
'Truth needs no colour with his colour fixed,
Beauty no pencil, beauty's truth to lay:
But best is best, if never intermixed'?
Because he needs no praise, wilt thou be dumb?
Excuse not silence so, for't lies in thee,
To make him much outlive a gilded tomb:
And to be praised of ages yet to be.
    Then do thy office Muse, I teach thee how,
    To make him seem long hence, as he shows now.

❦ 102 ❦

My love is strengthened though more weak
    in seeming,
I love not less, though less the show appear,
That love is merchandized, whose rich esteeming,
The owner's tongue doth publish every where.
Our love was new, and then but in the spring,
When I was wont to greet it with my lays,
As Philomel in summer's front doth sing,
And stops her pipe in growth of riper days:
Not that the summer is less pleasant now
Than when her mournful hymns did hush the night,
But that wild music burthens every bough,
And sweets grown common lose their dear delight.
    Therefore like her, I sometime hold my tongue:
    Because I would not dull you with my song.

❦ 103 ❦

Alack what poverty my Muse brings forth,
That having such a scope to show her pride,
The argument all bare is of more worth
Than when it hath my added praise beside.
O blame me not if I no more can write!
Look in your glass and there appears a face,
That over-goes my blunt invention quite,
Dulling my lines, and doing me disgrace.
Were it not sinful then striving to mend,
To mar the subject that before was well?
For to no other pass my verses tend,
Than of your graces and your gifts to tell.
    And more, much more than in my verse can sit,
    Your own glass shows you, when you look in it.

❦ 104 ❦

To me fair friend you never can be old,
For as you were when first your eye I eyed,
Such seems your beauty still: three winters cold,
Have from the forests shook three summers' pride,
Three beauteous springs to yellow autumn turned,
In process of the seasons have I seen,
Three April perfumes in three hot Junes burned,
Since first I saw you fresh which yet are green.
Ah yet doth beauty like a dial hand,
Steal from his figure, and no pace perceived,
So your sweet hue, which methinks still doth stand
Hath motion, and mine eye may be deceived.
    For fear of which, hear this thou age unbred,
    Ere you were born was beauty's summer dead.

105

Let not my love be called idolatry,
Nor my beloved as an idol show,
Since all alike my songs and praises be
To one, of one, still such, and ever so.
Kind is my love to-day, to-morrow kind,
Still constant in a wondrous excellence,
Therefore my verse to constancy confined,
One thing expressing, leaves out difference.
Fair, kind, and true, is all my argument,
Fair, kind, and true, varying to other words,
And in this change is my invention spent,
Three themes in one, which wondrous scope affords.
    Fair, kind, and true, have often lived alone.
    Which three till now, never kept seat in one.

106

When in the chronicle of wasted time,
I see descriptions of the fairest wights,
And beauty making beautiful old rhyme,
In praise of ladies dead, and lovely knights,
Then in the blazon of sweet beauty's best,
Of hand, of foot, of lip, of eye, of brow,
I see their antique pen would have expressed,
Even such a beauty as you master now.
So all their praises are but prophecies
Of this our time, all you prefiguring,
And for they looked but with divining eyes,
They had not skill enough your worth to sing:
    For we which now behold these present days,
    Have eyes to wonder, but lack tongues to praise.

107

Not mine own fears, nor the prophetic soul,
Of the wide world, dreaming on things to come,
Can yet the lease of my true love control,
Supposed as forfeit to a confined doom.
The mortal moon hath her eclipse endured,
And the sad augurs mock their own presage,
Incertainties now crown themselves assured,
And peace proclaims olives of endless age.
Now with the drops of this most balmy time,
My love looks fresh, and death to me subscribes,
Since spite of him I'll live in this poor rhyme,
While he insults o'er dull and speechless tribes.
    And thou in this shalt find thy monument,
    When tyrants' crests and tombs of brass
    are spent.

108

What's in the brain that ink may character,
Which hath not figured to thee my true spirit,
What's new to speak, what now to register,
That may express my love, or thy dear merit?
Nothing sweet boy, but yet like prayers divine,
I must each day say o'er the very same,
Counting no old thing old, thou mine, I thine,
Even as when first I hallowed thy fair name.
So that eternal love in love's fresh case,
Weighs not the dust and injury of age,
Nor gives to necessary wrinkles place,
But makes antiquity for aye his page,
    Finding the first conceit of love there bred,
    Where time and outward form would show it dead.

109

O never say that I was false of heart,
Though absence seemed my flame to qualify,
As easy might I from my self depart,
As from my soul which in thy breast doth lie:
That is my home of love, if I have ranged,
Like him that travels I return again,
Just to the time, not with the time exchanged,
So that my self bring water for my stain,
Never believe though in my nature reigned,
All frailties that besiege all kinds of blood,
That it could so preposterously be stained,
To leave for nothing all thy sum of good:
    For nothing this wide universe I call,
    Save thou my rose, in it thou art my all.

❧ 110 ❧

Alas 'tis true, I have gone here and there,
And made my self a motley to the view,
Gored mine own thoughts, sold cheap what is
    most dear,
Made old offences of affections new.
Most true it is, that I have looked on truth
Askance and strangely: but by all above,
These blenches gave my heart another youth,
And worse essays proved thee my best of love.
Now all is done, have what shall have no end,
Mine appetite I never more will grind
On newer proof, to try an older friend,
A god in love, to whom I am confined.
    Then give me welcome, next my heaven the best,
    Even to thy pure and most most loving breast.

❧ 111 ❧

O for my sake do you with Fortune chide,
The guilty goddess of my harmful deeds,
That did not better for my life provide,
Than public means which public manners breeds.
Thence comes it that my name receives a brand,
And almost thence my nature is subdued
To what it works in, like the dyer's hand:
Pity me then, and wish I were renewed,
Whilst like a willing patient I will drink,
Potions of eisel 'gainst my strong infection,
No bitterness that I will bitter think,
Nor double penance to correct correction.
    Pity me then dear friend, and I assure ye,
    Even that your pity is enough to cure me.

❧ 112 ❧

Your love and pity doth th' impression fill,
Which vulgar scandal stamped upon my brow,
For what care I who calls me well or ill,
So you o'er-green my bad, my good allow?
You are my all the world, and I must strive,
To know my shames and praises from
    your tongue,
None else to me, nor I to none alive,
That my steeled sense or changes right or wrong.
In so profound abysm I throw all care
Of others' voices, that my adder's sense,
To critic and to flatterer stopped are:
Mark how with my neglect I do dispense.
    You are so strongly in my purpose bred,
    That all the world besides methinks are dead.

❧ 113 ❧

Since I left you, mine eye is in my mind,
And that which governs me to go about,
Doth part his function, and is partly blind,
Seems seeing, but effectually is out:
For it no form delivers to the heart
Of bird, of flower, or shape which it doth latch,
Of his quick objects hath the mind no part,
Nor his own vision holds what it doth catch:
For if it see the rud'st or gentlest sight,
The most sweet favour or deformed'st creature,
The mountain, or the sea, the day, or night:
The crow, or dove, it shapes them to your feature.
    Incapable of more, replete with you,
    My most true mind thus maketh mine untrue.

❧ 114 ❧

Or whether doth my mind being crowned with you
Drink up the monarch's plague this flattery?
Or whether shall I say mine eye saith true,
And that your love taught it this alchemy?
To make of monsters, and things indigest,
Such cherubins as your sweet self resemble,
Creating every bad a perfect best
As fast as objects to his beams assemble:
O 'tis the first, 'tis flattery in my seeing,
And my great mind most kingly drinks it up,
Mine eye well knows what with his gust is 'greeing,
And to his palate doth prepare the cup.
    If it be poisoned, 'tis the lesser sin,
    That mine eye loves it and doth first begin.

❧ 115 ❧

Those lines that I before have writ do lie,
Even those that said I could not love you dearer,
Yet then my judgment knew no reason why,
My most full flame should afterwards burn clearer,
But reckoning time, whose millioned accidents
Creep in 'twixt vows, and change decrees of kings,
Tan sacred beauty, blunt the sharp'st intents,
Divert strong minds to the course of alt'ring things:
Alas why fearing of time's tyranny,
Might I not then say 'Now I love you best,'
When I was certain o'er incertainty,
Crowning the present, doubting of the rest?
    Love is a babe, then might I not say so
    To give full growth to that which still doth grow.

🔖 116 🔖

Let me not to the marriage of true minds
Admit impediments. Love is not love
Which alters when it alteration finds,
Or bends with the remover to remove.
O no, it is an ever-fixed mark
That looks on tempests and is never shaken;
It is the star to every wand'ring bark,
Whose worth's unknown, although his height
  be taken.
Love's not Time's fool, though rosy lips and cheeks
Within his bending sickle's compass come,
Love alters not with his brief hours and weeks,
But bears it out even to the edge of doom:
  If this be error and upon me proved,
  I never writ, nor no man ever loved.

🔖 117 🔖

Accuse me thus, that I have scanted all,
Wherein I should your great deserts repay,
Forgot upon your dearest love to call,
Whereto all bonds do tie me day by day,
That I have frequent been with unknown minds,
And given to time your own dear-purchased right,
That I have hoisted sail to all the winds
Which should transport me farthest from your sight.
Book both my wilfulness and errors down,
And on just proof surmise, accumulate,
Bring me within the level of your frown,
But shoot not at me in your wakened hate:
  Since my appeal says I did strive to prove
  The constancy and virtue of your love.

🔖 118 🔖

Like as to make our appetite more keen
With eager compounds we our palate urge,
As to prevent our maladies unseen,
We sicken to shun sickness when we purge.
Even so being full of your ne'er-cloying sweetness,
To bitter sauces did I frame my feeding;
And sick of welfare found a kind of meetness,
To be diseased ere that there was true needing.
Thus policy in love t' anticipate
The ills that were not, grew to faults assured,
And brought to medicine a healthful state
Which rank of goodness would by ill be cured.
  But thence I learn and find the lesson true,
  Drugs poison him that so fell sick of you.

🔖 119 🔖

What potions have I drunk of Siren tears
Distilled from limbecks foul as hell within,
Applying fears to hopes, and hopes to fears,
Still losing when I saw my self to win!
What wretched errors hath my heart committed,
Whilst it hath thought it self so blessed never!
How have mine eyes out of their spheres
  been fitted
In the distraction of this madding fever!
O benefit of ill, now I find true
That better is by evil still made better.
And ruined love when it is built anew
Grows fairer than at first, more strong, far greater.
  So I return rebuked to my content,
  And gain by ills thrice more than I have spent.

🔖 120 🔖

That you were once unkind befriends me now,
And for that sorrow, which I then did feel,
Needs must I under my transgression bow,
Unless my nerves were brass or hammered steel.
For if you were by my unkindness shaken
As I by yours, y'have passed a hell of time,
And I a tyrant have no leisure taken
To weigh how once I suffered in your crime.
O that our night of woe might have remembered
My deepest sense, how hard true sorrow hits,
And soon to you, as you to me then tendered
The humble salve, which wounded bosoms fits!
  But that your trespass now becomes a fee,
  Mine ransoms yours, and yours must
    ransom me.

❧ 121 ❧

'Tis better to be vile than vile esteemed,
When not to be, receives reproach of being,
And the just pleasure lost, which is so deemed,
Not by our feeling, but by others' seeing.
For why should others' false adulterate eyes
Give salutation to my sportive blood?
Or on my frailties why are frailer spies,
Which in their wills count bad what I think good?
No, I am that I am, and they that level
At my abuses, reckon up their own,
I may be straight though they themselves be bevel;
By their rank thoughts, my deeds must not
  be shown
  Unless this general evil they maintain,
  All men are bad and in their badness reign.

❧ 122 ❧

Thy gift, thy tables, are within my brain
Full charactered with lasting memory,
Which shall above that idle rank remain
Beyond all date even to eternity.
Or at the least, so long as brain and heart
Have faculty by nature to subsist,
Till each to razed oblivion yield his part
Of thee, thy record never can be missed:
That poor retention could not so much hold,
Nor need I tallies thy dear love to score,
Therefore to give them from me was I bold,
To trust those tables that receive thee more:
  To keep an adjunct to remember thee
  Were to import forgetfulness in me.

❧ 123 ❧

No! Time, thou shalt not boast that I do change,
Thy pyramids built up with newer might
To me are nothing novel, nothing strange,
They are but dressings of a former sight:
Our dates are brief, and therefore we admire,
What thou dost foist upon us that is old,
And rather make them born to our desire,
Than think that we before have heard them told:
Thy registers and thee I both defy,
Not wond'ring at the present, nor the past,
For thy records, and what we see doth lie,
Made more or less by thy continual haste:
  This I do vow and this shall ever be,
  I will be true despite thy scythe and thee.

❧ 124 ❧

If my dear love were but the child of state,
It might for Fortune's bastard be unfathered,
As subject to Time's love or to Time's hate,
Weeds among weeds, or flowers with
  flowers gathered.
No it was builded far from accident,
It suffers not in smiling pomp, nor falls
Under the blow of thralled discontent,
Whereto th' inviting time our fashion calls:
It fears not policy that heretic,
Which works on leases of short-numbered hours,
But all alone stands hugely politic,
That it nor grows with heat, nor drowns with showers.
  To this I witness call the fools of time,
  Which die for goodness, who have lived for crime.

❧ 125 ❧

Were't aught to me I bore the canopy,
With my extern the outward honouring,
Or laid great bases for eternity,
Which proves more short than waste or ruining?
Have I not seen dwellers on form and favour
Lose all, and more by paying too much rent
For compound sweet; forgoing simple savour,
Pitiful thrivers in their gazing spent?
No, let me be obsequious in thy heart,
And take thou my oblation, poor but free,
Which is not mixed with seconds, knows no art,
But mutual render, only me for thee.
  Hence, thou suborned informer, a true soul
  When most impeached, stands least in
   thy control.

❧ 126 ❧

O thou my lovely boy who in thy power,
Dost hold Time's fickle glass his fickle hour:
Who hast by waning grown, and therein show'st,
Thy lovers withering, as thy sweet self grow'st.
If Nature (sovereign mistress over wrack)
As thou goest onwards still will pluck thee back,
She keeps thee to this purpose, that her skill
May time disgrace, and wretched minutes kill.
Yet fear her O thou minion of her pleasure,
She may detain, but not still keep her treasure!
  Her audit (though delayed) answered must be,
  And her quietus is to render thee.

127

In the old age black was not counted fair,
Or if it were it bore not beauty's name:
But now is black beauty's successive heir,
And beauty slandered with a bastard shame,
For since each hand hath put on nature's power,
Fairing the foul with art's false borrowed face,
Sweet beauty hath no name no holy bower,
But is profaned, if not lives in disgrace.
Therefore my mistress' eyes are raven black,
Her eyes so suited, and they mourners seem,
At such who not born fair no beauty lack,
Slandering creation with a false esteem,
  Yet so they mourn becoming of their woe,
  That every tongue says beauty should look so.

130

My mistress' eyes are nothing like the sun,
Coral is far more red, than her lips red,
If snow be white, why then her breasts are dun:
If hairs be wires, black wires grow on her head:
I have seen roses damasked, red and white,
But no such roses see I in her cheeks,
And in some perfumes is there more delight,
Than in the breath that from my mistress reeks.
I love to hear her speak, yet well I know,
That music hath a far more pleasing sound:
I grant I never saw a goddess go,
My mistress when she walks treads on the ground.
  And yet by heaven I think my love as rare,
  As any she belied with false compare.

128

How oft when thou, my music, music play'st,
Upon that blessed wood whose motion sounds
With thy sweet fingers when thou gently sway'st
The wiry concord that mine ear confounds,
Do I envy those jacks that nimble leap,
To kiss the tender inward of thy hand,
Whilst my poor lips which should that harvest reap,
At the wood's boldness by thee blushing stand.
To be so tickled they would change their state
And situation with those dancing chips,
O'er whom thy fingers walk with gentle gait,
Making dead wood more blest than living lips,
  Since saucy jacks so happy are in this,
  Give them thy fingers, me thy lips to kiss.

129

Th' expense of spirit in a waste of shame
Is lust in action, and till action, lust
Is perjured, murd'rous, bloody full of blame,
Savage, extreme, rude, cruel, not to trust,
Enjoyed no sooner but despised straight,
Past reason hunted, and no sooner had
Past reason hated as a swallowed bait,
On purpose laid to make the taker mad.
Mad in pursuit and in possession so,
Had, having, and in quest, to have extreme,
A bliss in proof and proved, a very woe,
Before a joy proposed behind a dream.
  All this the world well knows yet none knows well,
  To shun the heaven that leads men to this hell.

131

Thou art as tyrannous, so as thou art,
As those whose beauties proudly make them cruel;
For well thou know'st to my dear doting heart
Thou art the fairest and most precious jewel.
Yet in good faith some say that thee behold,
Thy face hath not the power to make love groan;
To say they err, I dare not be so bold,
Although I swear it to my self alone.
And to be sure that is not false I swear,
A thousand groans but thinking on thy face,
One on another's neck do witness bear
Thy black is fairest in my judgment's place.
  In nothing art thou black save in thy deeds,
  And thence this slander as I think proceeds.

☒ 132 ☒

Thine eyes I love, and they as pitying me,
Knowing thy heart torment me with disdain,
Have put on black, and loving mourners be,
Looking with pretty ruth upon my pain.
And truly not the morning sun of heaven
Better becomes the grey cheeks of the east,
Nor that full star that ushers in the even
Doth half that glory to the sober west
As those two mourning eyes become thy face:
O let it then as well beseem thy heart
To mourn for me since mourning doth thee grace,
And suit thy pity like in every part.
  Then will I swear beauty herself is black,
  And all they foul that thy complexion lack.

☒ 133 ☒

Beshrew that heart that makes my heart to groan
For that deep wound it gives my friend and me;
Is't not enough to torture me alone,
But slave to slavery my sweet'st friend must be?
Me from my self thy cruel eye hath taken,
And my next self thou harder hast engrossed,
Of him, my self, and thee I am forsaken,
A torment thrice three-fold thus to be crossed:
Prison my heart in thy steel bosom's ward,
But then my friend's heart let my poor heart bail,
Whoe'er keeps me, let my heart be his guard,
Thou canst not then use rigour in my gaol.
  And yet thou wilt, for I being pent in thee,
  Perforce am thine and all that is in me.

☒ 134 ☒

So now I have confessed that he is thine,
And I my self am mortgaged to thy will,
My self I'll forfeit, so that other mine,
Thou wilt restore to be my comfort still:
But thou wilt not, nor he will not be free,
For thou art covetous, and he is kind,
He learned but surety-like to write for me,
Under that bond that him as fast doth bind.
The statute of thy beauty thou wilt take,
Thou usurer that put'st forth all to use,
And sue a friend, came debtor for my sake,
So him I lose through my unkind abuse.
  Him have I lost, thou hast both him and me,
  He pays the whole, and yet am I not free.

☒ 135 ☒

Whoever hath her wish, thou hast thy 'Will',
And 'Will' to boot, and 'Will' in over-plus,
More than enough am I that vex thee still,
To thy sweet will making addition thus.
Wilt thou whose will is large and spacious,
Not once vouchsafe to hide my will in thine?
Shall will in others seem right gracious,
And in my will no fair acceptance shine?
The sea all water, yet receives rain still,
And in abundance addeth to his store,
So thou being rich in 'Will' add to thy 'Will'
One will of mine to make thy large will more.
  Let no unkind, no fair beseechers kill,
  Think all but one, and me in that one 'Will.'

☒ 136 ☒

If thy soul check thee that I come so near,
Swear to thy blind soul that I was thy 'Will',
And will thy soul knows is admitted there,
Thus far for love, my love-suit sweet fulfil.
'Will' will fulfil the treasure of thy love,
Ay, fill it full with wills, and my will one,
In things of great receipt with ease we prove,
Among a number one is reckoned none.
Then in the number let me pass untold,
Though in thy store's account I one must be,
For nothing hold me, so it please thee hold,
That nothing me, a something sweet to thee.
  Make but my name thy love, and love that still,
  And then thou lov'st me for my name is 'Will'.

☒ 137 ☒

Thou blind fool Love, what dost thou to mine eyes,
That they behold and see not what they see?
They know what beauty is, see where it lies,
Yet what the best is, take the worst to be.
If eyes corrupt by over-partial looks,
Be anchored in the bay where all men ride,
Why of eyes' falsehood hast thou forged hooks,
Whereto the judgment of my heart is tied?
Why should my heart think that a several plot,
Which my heart knows the wide world's
  common place?
Or mine eyes seeing this, say this is not
To put fair truth upon so foul a face?
  In things right true my heart and eyes have erred,
  And to this false plague are they
    now transferred.

138

When my love swears that she is made of truth,
I do believe her though I know she lies,
That she might think me some untutored youth,
Unlearned in the world's false subtleties.
Thus vainly thinking that she thinks me young,
Although she knows my days are past the best,
Simply I credit her false-speaking tongue,
On both sides thus is simple truth suppressed:
But wherefore says she not she is unjust?
And wherefore say not I that I am old?
O love's best habit is in seeming trust,
And age in love, loves not to have years told.
  Therefore I lie with her, and she with me,
  And in our faults by lies we flattered be.

139

O call not me to justify the wrong,
That thy unkindness lays upon my heart,
Wound me not with thine eye but with thy tongue,
Use power with power, and slay me not by art,
Tell me thou lov'st elsewhere; but in my sight,
Dear heart forbear to glance thine eye aside,
What need'st thou wound with cunning when
   thy might
Is more than my o'erpressed defence can bide?
Let me excuse thee, ah my love well knows,
Her pretty looks have been mine enemies,
And therefore from my face she turns my foes,
That they elsewhere might dart their injuries:
  Yet do not so, but since I am near slain,
  Kill me outright with looks, and rid my pain.

140

Be wise as thou art cruel, do not press
My tongue-tied patience with too much disdain:
Lest sorrow lend me words and words express,
The manner of my pity-wanting pain.
If I might teach thee wit better it were,
Though not to love, yet love to tell me so,
As testy sick men when their deaths be near,
No news but health from their physicians know.
For if I should despair I should grow mad,
And in my madness might speak ill of thee,
Now this ill-wresting world is grown so bad,
Mad slanderers by mad ears believed be.
  That I may not be so, nor thou belied,
  Bear thine eyes straight, though thy proud heart
  go wide.

141

In faith I do not love thee with mine eyes,
For they in thee a thousand errors note,
But 'tis my heart that loves what they despise,
Who in despite of view is pleased to dote.
Nor are mine ears with thy tongue's
   tune delighted,
Nor tender feeling to base touches prone,
Nor taste, nor smell, desire to be invited
To any sensual feast with thee alone:
But my five wits, nor my five senses can
Dissuade one foolish heart from serving thee,
Who leaves unswayed the likeness of a man,
Thy proud heart's slave and vassal wretch to be:
  Only my plague thus far I count my gain,
  That she that makes me sin, awards me pain.

142

Love is my sin, and thy dear virtue hate,
Hate of my sin, grounded on sinful loving,
O but with mine, compare thou thine own state,
And thou shalt find it merits not reproving,
Or if it do, not from those lips of thine,
That have profaned their scarlet ornaments,
And sealed false bonds of love as oft as mine,
Robbed others' beds' revenues of their rents.
Be it lawful I love thee as thou lov'st those,
Whom thine eyes woo as mine importune thee,
Root pity in thy heart that when it grows,
Thy pity may deserve to pitied be.
  If thou dost seek to have what thou dost hide,
  By self-example mayst thou be denied.

❧ 143 ❧

Lo as a careful huswife runs to catch,
One of her feathered creatures broke away,
Sets down her babe and makes all swift dispatch
In pursuit of the thing she would have stay:
Whilst her neglected child holds her in chase,
Cries to catch her whose busy care is bent,
To follow that which flies before her face:
Not prizing her poor infant's discontent;
So run'st thou after that which flies from thee,
Whilst I thy babe chase thee afar behind,
But if thou catch thy hope turn back to me:
And play the mother's part, kiss me, be kind.
  So will I pray that thou mayst have thy 'Will',
  If thou turn back and my loud crying still.

❧ 144 ❧

Two loves I have of comfort and despair,
Which like two spirits do suggest me still,
The better angel is a man right fair:
The worser spirit a woman coloured ill.
To win me soon to hell my female evil,
Tempteth my better angel from my side,
And would corrupt my saint to be a devil:
Wooing his purity with her foul pride.
And whether that my angel be turned fiend,
Suspect I may, yet not directly tell,
But being both from me both to each friend,
I guess one angel in another's hell.
  Yet this shall I ne'er know but live in doubt,
  Till my bad angel fire my good one out.

❧ 145 ❧

Those lips that Love's own hand did make,
Breathed forth the sound that said 'I hate',
To me that languished for her sake:
But when she saw my woeful state,
Straight in her heart did mercy come,
Chiding that tongue that ever sweet,
Was used in giving gentle doom:
And taught it thus anew to greet:
'I hate' she altered with an end,
That followed it as gentle day,
Doth follow night who like a fiend
From heaven to hell is flown away.
  'I hate', from hate away she threw,
  And saved my life saying 'not you'.

❧ 146 ❧

Poor soul the centre of my sinful earth,
My sinful earth these rebel powers array,
Why dost thou pine within and suffer dearth
Painting thy outward walls so costly gay?
Why so large cost having so short a lease,
Dost thou upon thy fading mansion spend?
Shall worms, inheritors of this excess,
Eat up thy charge? is this thy body's end?
Then soul live thou upon thy servant's loss,
And let that pine to aggravate thy store;
Buy terms divine in selling hours of dross;
Within be fed, without be rich no more,
  So shall thou feed on Death, that feeds on men,
  And Death once dead, there's no more
    dying then.

❧ 147 ❧

My love is as a fever longing still,
For that which longer nurseth the disease,
Feeding on that which doth preserve the ill,
Th' uncertain sickly appetite to please:
My reason the physician to my love,
Angry that his prescriptions are not kept
Hath left me, and I desperate now approve,
Desire is death, which physic did except.
Past cure I am, now reason is past care,
And frantic-mad with evermore unrest,
My thoughts and my discourse as mad men's are,
At random from the truth vainly expressed.
  For I have sworn thee fair, and thought
    thee bright,
    Who art as black as hell, as dark as night.

❧ 148 ❧

O me! what eyes hath Love put in my head,
Which have no correspondence with true sight,
Or if they have, where is my judgment fled,
That censures falsely what they see aright?
If that be fair whereon my false eyes dote,
What means the world to say it is not so?
If it be not, then love doth well denote,
Love's eye is not so true as all men's: no,
How can it? O how can Love's eye be true,
That is so vexed with watching and with tears?
No marvel then though I mistake my view,
The sun it self sees not, till heaven clears.
  O cunning Love, with tears thou keep'st
    me blind,
    Lest eyes well-seeing thy foul faults should find.

☙ 149 ☙

Canst thou O cruel, say I love thee not,
When I against my self with thee partake?
Do I not think on thee when I forgot
Am of my self, all-tyrant, for thy sake?
Who hateth thee that I do call my friend,
On whom frown'st thou that I do fawn upon,
Nay if thou lour'st on me do I not spend
Revenge upon my self with present moan?
What merit do I in my self respect,
That is so proud thy service to despise,
When all my best doth worship thy defect,
Commanded by the motion of thine eyes?
  But love hate on for now I know thy mind,
  Those that can see thou lov'st, and I am blind.

☙ 150 ☙

O from what power hast thou this powerful might,
With insufficiency my heart to sway,
To make me give the lie to my true sight,
And swear that brightness doth not grace the day?
Whence hast thou this becoming of things ill,
That in the very refuse of thy deeds,
There is such strength and warrantise of skill,
That in my mind thy worst all best exceeds?
Who taught thee how to make me love thee more,
The more I hear and see just cause of hate?
O though I love what others do abhor,
With others thou shouldst not abhor my state.
  If thy unworthiness raised love in me,
  More worthy I to be beloved of thee.

☙ 151 ☙

Love is too young to know what conscience is,
Yet who knows not conscience is born of love?
Then gentle cheater urge not my amiss,
Lest guilty of my faults thy sweet self prove.
For thou betraying me, I do betray
My nobler part to my gross body's treason,
My soul doth tell my body that he may,
Triumph in love, flesh stays no farther reason,
But rising at thy name doth point out thee,
As his triumphant prize, proud of this pride,
He is contented thy poor drudge to be,
To stand in thy affairs, fall by thy side.
  No want of conscience hold it that I call,
  Her love, for whose dear love I rise and fall.

☙ 152 ☙

In loving thee thou know'st I am forsworn,
But thou art twice forsworn to me love swearing,
In act thy bed-vow broke and new faith torn,
In vowing new hate after new love bearing:
But why of two oaths' breach do I accuse thee,
When I break twenty? I am perjured most,
For all my vows are oaths but to misuse thee:
And all my honest faith in thee is lost.
For I have sworn deep oaths of thy deep kindness:
Oaths of thy love, thy truth, thy constancy,
And to enlighten thee gave eyes to blindness,
Or made them swear against the thing they see.
  For I have sworn thee fair: more perjured I,
  To swear against the truth so foul a lie.

☙ 153 ☙

Cupid laid by his brand and fell asleep,
A maid of Dian's this advantage found,
And his love-kindling fire did quickly steep
In a cold valley-fountain of that ground:
Which borrowed from this holy fire of Love,
A dateless lively heat still to endure,
And grew a seething bath which yet men prove,
Against strange maladies a sovereign cure:
But at my mistress' eye Love's brand new-fired,
The boy for trial needs would touch my breast,
I sick withal the help of bath desired,
And thither hied a sad distempered guest.
  But found no cure, the bath for my help lies,
  Where Cupid got new fire; my mistress' eyes.

☙ 154 ☙

The little Love-god lying once asleep,
Laid by his side his heart-inflaming brand,
Whilst many nymphs that vowed chaste life
  to keep,
Came tripping by, but in her maiden hand,
The fairest votary took up that fire,
Which many legions of true hearts had warmed,
And so the general of hot desire,
Was sleeping by a virgin hand disarmed.
This brand she quenched in a cool well by,
Which from Love's fire took heat perpetual,
Growing a bath and healthful remedy,
For men discased, but I my mistress' thrall,
  Came there for cure and this by that I prove,
  Love's fire heats water, water cools not love.

A Lover's Complaint

From off a hill whose concave womb reworded
A plaintful story from a sist'ring vale,
My spirits t'attend this double voice accorded,
And down I laid to list the sad-tuned tale,
Ere long espied a fickle maid full pale,
Tearing of papers, breaking rings atwain,
Storming her world with sorrow's wind and rain.

Upon her head a platted hive of straw,
Which fortified her visage from the sun,
Whereon the thought might think sometime it saw
The carcase of a beauty spent and done.
Time had not scythed all that youth begun,
Nor youth all quit, but spite of heaven's fell rage
Some beauty peeped through lattice of
    seared age.

Oft did she heave her napkin to her eyne,
Which on it had conceited characters,
Laund'ring the silken figures in the brine
That seasoned woe had pelleted in tears,
And often reading what contents it bears;
As often shrieking undistinguished woe,
In clamours of all size, both high and low.

Sometimes her levelled eyes their carriage ride,
As they did batt'ry to the spheres intend;
Sometime diverted their poor balls are tied
To th' orbed earth; sometimes they do extend
Their view right on; anon their gazes lend
To every place at once, and nowhere fixed,
The mind and sight distractedly commixed.

Her hair, nor loose nor tied in formal plat,
Proclaimed in her a careless hand of pride;
For some, untucked, descended her sheaved hat,
Hanging her pale and pined cheek beside;
Some in her threaden fillet still did bide,

And, true to bondage, would not break
    from thence,
Though slackly braided in loose negligence.

A thousand favours from a maund she drew
Of amber, crystal, and of beaded jet,
Which one by one she in a river threw,
Upon whose weeping margent she was set;
Like usury applying wet to wet,
Or monarchs' hands that lets not bounty fall
Where want cries some, but where excess begs all.

Of folded schedules had she many a one,
Which she perused, sighed, tore, and gave
    the flood;
Cracked many a ring of posied gold and bone,
Bidding them find their sepulchres in mud;
Found yet moe letters sadly penned in blood,
With sleided silk feat and affectedly
Enswathed and sealed to curious secrecy.

These often bathed she in her fluxive eyes,
And often kissed, and often 'gan to tear;
Cried, 'O false blood, thou register of lies,
What unapproved witness dost thou bear!
Ink would have seemed more black and
    damned here!'
This said, in top of rage the lines she rents,
Big discontent so breaking their contents.

A reverend man that grazed his cattle nigh,
Sometime a blusterer that the ruffle knew
Of court, of city, and had let go by
The swiftest hours observed as they flew,
Towards this afflicted fancy fastly drew;
And, privileged by age, desires to know
In brief the grounds and motives of her woe.

So slides he down upon his grained bat,
And comely distant sits he by her side;
When he again desires her, being sat,
Her grievance with his hearing to divide.
If that from him there may be aught applied
Which may her suffering ecstasy assuage,
'Tis promised in the charity of age.

'Father,' she says, 'though in me you behold
The injury of many a blasting hour,
Let it not tell your judgment I am old:
Not age, but sorrow, over me hath power.
I might as yet have been a spreading flower,
Fresh to myself, if I had self-applied
Love to myself, and to no love beside.

'But woe is me! too early I attended
A youthful suit-it was to gain my grace-
O, one by nature's outwards so commended
That maidens' eyes stuck over all his face.
Love lacked a dwelling and made him her place;
And when in his fair parts she did abide,
She was new lodged and newly deified.

'His browny locks did hang in crooked curls;
And every light occasion of the wind
Upon his lips their silken parcels hurls.
What's sweet to do, to do will aptly find:
Each eye that saw him did enchant the mind;
For on his visage was in little drawn
What largeness thinks in Paradise was sawn.

'Small show of man was yet upon his chin;
His phoenix down began but to appear,
Like unshorn velvet, on that termless skin,
Whose bare out-bragged the web it seemed
     to wear:
Yet showed his visage by that cost more dear;
And nice affections wavering stood in doubt
If best were as it was, or best without.

'His qualities were beauteous as his form,
For maiden-tongued he was, and thereof free;
Yet if men moved him, was he such a storm
As oft 'twixt May and April is to see,
When winds breathe sweet, unruly though
     they be.
His rudeness so with his authorised youth
Did livery falseness in a pride of truth.

'Well could he ride, and often men would say,
"That horse his mettle from his rider takes:
Proud of subjection, noble by the sway,
What rounds, what bounds, what course, what
     stop he makes!"
And controversy hence a question takes
Whether the horse by him became his deed,
Or he his manage by th' well-doing steed.

'But quickly on this side the verdict went:
His real habitude gave life and grace
To appertainings and to ornament,
Accomplished in himself, not in his case,
All aids, themselves made fairer by their place,
Came for additions; yet their purposed trim
Pierced not his grace, but were all graced by him.

'So on the tip of his subduing tongue
All kind of arguments and question deep,

All replication prompt, and reason strong,
For his advantage still did wake and sleep.
To make the weeper laugh, the laugher weep,
He had the dialect and different skill,
Catching all passions in his craft of will,

'That he did in the general bosom reign
Of young, of old, and sexes both enchanted,
To dwell with him in thoughts, or to remain
In personal duty, following where he haunted.
Consents bewitched, ere he desire, have granted,
And dialogued for him what he would say,
Asked their own wills, and made their wills obey.

'Many there were that did his picture get,
To serve their eyes, and in it put their mind;
Like fools that in th' imagination set
The goodly objects which abroad they find
Of lands and mansions, theirs in thought assigned;
And labouring in moe pleasures to bestow them
Than the true gouty landlord which doth owe them.

'So many have, that never touched his hand,
Sweetly supposed them mistress of his heart.
My woeful self, that did in freedom stand,
And was my own fee-simple, not in part,
What with his art in youth, and youth in art,
Threw my affections in his charmed power
Reserved the stalk and gave him all my flower.

'Yet did I not, as some my equals did,
Demand of him, nor being desired yielded;
Finding myself in honour so forbid,
With safest distance I mine honour shielded.
Experience for me many bulwarks builded
Of proofs new-bleeding, which remained the foil
Of this false jewel, and his amorous spoil.

'But ah, who ever shunned by precedent
The destined ill she must herself assay?
Or forced examples, 'gainst her own content,
To put the by-past perils in her way?
Counsel may stop awhile what will not stay;
For when we rage, advice is often seen
By blunting us to make our wits more keen.

'Nor gives it satisfaction to our blood
That we must curb it upon others' proof,
To be forbod the sweets that seem so good
For fear of harms that preach in our behoof.
O appetite, from judgment stand aloof!
The one a palate hath that needs will taste,
Though Reason weep, and cry it is thy last.

For further I could say this man's untrue,
And knew the patterns of his foul beguiling;
Heard where his plants in others' orchards grew;
Saw how deceits were gilded in his smiling;
Knew vows were ever brokers to defiling;
Thought characters and words merely but art,
And bastards of his foul adulterate heart.

'And long upon these terms I held my city,
Till thus he 'gan besiege me: "Gentle maid,
Have of my suffering youth some feeling pity,
And be not of my holy vows afraid.
That's to ye sworn to none was ever said;
For feasts of love I have been called unto,
Till now did ne'er invite nor never woo.

'"All my offences that abroad you see
Are errors of the blood, none of the mind;
Love made them not; with acture they may be,
Where neither party is nor true nor kind.
They sought their shame that so their shame
   did find;
And so much less of shame in me remains
By how much of me their reproach contains.

'"Among the many that mine eyes have seen,
Not one whose flame my heart so much
   as warmed,
Or my affection put to th' smallest teen,
Or any of my leisures ever charmed.
Harm have I done to them, but ne'er was harmed;
Kept hearts in liveries, but mine own was free,
And reigned commanding in his monarchy.

'"Look here what tributes wounded fancies
   sent me,
Of paled pearls and rubies red as blood;
Figuring that they their passions likewise lent me
Of grief and blushes, aptly understood
In bloodless white and the encrimsoned mood-
Effects of terror and dear modesty,
Encamped in hearts, but fighting outwardly.

'"And, lo, behold these talents of their hair,
With twisted metal amorously empleached,
I have receiv'd from many a several fair,
Their kind acceptance weepingly beseeched,
With the annexions of fair gems enriched,
And deep-brained sonnets that did amplify
Each stone's dear nature, worth, and quality.

'"The diamond? why, 'twas beautiful and hard,
Whereto his invised properties did tend;

The deep-green em'rald, in whose fresh regard
Weak sights their sickly radiance do amend;
The heaven-hued sapphire and the opal blend
With objects manifold; each several stone,
With wit well blazoned, smiled, or made some moan.

'"Lo, all these trophies of affections hot,
Of pensived and subdued desires the tender,
Nature hath charged me that I hoard them not,
But yield them up where I myself must render-
That is, to you, my origin and ender;
For these, of force, must your oblations be,
Since I their altar, you enpatron me.

'"O then advance of yours that phraseless hand
Whose white weighs down the airy scale of praise;
Take all these similes to your own command,
Hallowed with sighs that burning lungs did raise;
What me your minister for you obeys
Works under you; and to your audit comes
Their distract parcels in combined sums.

'"Lo, this device was sent me from a nun,
Or sister sanctified, of holiest note,
Which late her noble suit in court did shun,
Whose rarest havings made the blossoms dote;
For she was sought by spirits of richest coat,
But kept cold distance, and did thence remove
To spend her living in eternal love.

'"But, O my sweet, what labour is't to leave
The thing we have not, mast'ring what not strives,
Playing the place which did no form receive,
Playing patient sports in unconstrained gyves!
She that her fame so to herself contrives,
The scars of battle scapeth by the flight,
And makes her absence valiant, not her might.

'"O pardon me in that my boast is true!
The accident which brought me to her eye
Upon the moment did her force subdue,
And now she would the caged cloister fly.
Religious love put out Religion's eye.
Not to be tempted, would she be immured,
And now to tempt all liberty procured.

'"How mighty then you are, O hear me tell!
The broken bosoms that to me belong
Have emptied all their fountains in my well,
And mine I pour your ocean all among.
I strong o'er them, and you o'er me being strong,
Must for your victory us all congest,
As compound love to physic your cold breast.

'"My parts had pow'r to charm a sacred nun,
Who, disciplined, ay, dieted in grace,
Believed her eyes when they t'assail begun,
All vows and consecrations giving place,
O most potential love, vow, bond, nor space,
In thee hath neither sting, knot, nor confine,
For thou art all, and all things else are thine.

'"When thou impressest, what are precepts worth
Of stale example? When thou wilt inflame,
How coldly those impediments stand forth,
Of wealth, of filial fear, law, kindred, fame!
Love's arms are peace, 'gainst rule, 'gainst sense,
   'gainst shame.
And sweetens, in the suff'ring pangs it bears,
The aloes of all forces, shocks and fears.

'"Now all these hearts that do on mine depend,
Feeling it break, with bleeding groans they pine,
And supplicant their sighs to you extend,
To leave the batt'ry that you make 'gainst mine,
Lending soft audience to my sweet design,
And credent soul to that strong-bonded oath,
That shall prefer and undertake my troth."

'This said, his wat'ry eyes he did dismount,
Whose sights till then were levelled on my face;
Each cheek a river running from a fount
With brinish current downward flowed apace.
O, how the channel to the stream gave grace!
Who glazed with crystal gate the glowing roses
That flame through water which their
   hue encloses.

'O father, what a hell of witchcraft lies
In the small orb of one particular tear!
But with the inundation of the eyes
What rocky heart to water will not wear?
What breast so cold that is not warmed here?
O cleft effect! cold modesty, hot wrath,
Both fire from hence and chill extincture hath.

'For lo, his passion, but an art of craft,
Even there resolved my reason into tears;
There my white stole of chastity I daffed,
Shook off my sober guards and civil fears;
Appear to him as he to me appears,
All melting; though our drops this diff'rence bore:
His poisoned me, and mine did him restore.

'In him a plenitude of subtle matter,
Applied to cautels, all strange forms receives,
Of burning blushes or of weeping water,

Or swooning paleness; and he takes and leaves,
In either's aptness, as it best deceives,
To blush at speeches rank, to weep at woes,
Or to turn white and swoon at tragic shows;

'That not a heart which in his level came
Could scape the hail of his all-hurting aim,
Showing fair nature is both kind and tame;
And, veiled in them, did win whom he
   would maim.
Against the thing he sought he would exclaim;
When he most burned in heart-wished luxury,
He preached pure maid and praised cold chastity.

'Thus merely with the garment of a Grace
The naked and concealed fiend he covered,
That th' unexperient gave the tempter place,
Which, like a cherubin, above them hovered.
Who, young and simple, would not be so lovered?
Ay me, I fell, and yet do question make
What I should do again for such a sake.

'O, that infected moisture of his eye,
O, that false fire which in his cheek so glowed,
O, that forced thunder from his heart did fly,
O, that sad breath his spongy lungs bestowed,
O, all that borrowed motion, seeming owed,
Would yet again betray the fore-betrayed,
And new pervert a reconciled maid.'

The End

The Rape of Lucrece

DEDICATION

TO THE RIGHT HONOURABLE HENRY
WRIOTHESLY, Earl of Southampton, and Baron
of Tichfield.

THE love I dedicate to your lordship is without
end; whereof this pamphlet, without beginning,
is but a superfluous moiety. The warrant I have of
your honourable disposition, not the worth of my
untutored lines, makes it assured of acceptance.
What I have done is yours; what I have to do is
yours; being part in all I have, devoted yours.
Were my worth greater, my duty would show
greater; meantime, as it is, it is bound to your
lordship, to whom I wish long life, still lengthened
with all happiness.

Your lordship's in all duty,
William Shakespeare

THE ARGUMENT

Lucius Tarquinius, for his excessive pride
surnamed Superbus, after he had caused his
own father-in-law Servius Tullius to be cruelly
murdered, and, contrary to the Roman laws
and customs, not requiring or staying for the
people's suffrages, had possessed himself of
the kingdom, went, accompanied with his sons
and other noblemen of Rome, to besiege Ardea.
During which siege the principal men of the
army meeting one evening at the tent of Sextus
Tarquinius, the king's son, in their discourses
after supper every one commended the virtues
of his own wife: among whom Collatinus extolled
the incomparable chastity of his wife Lucretia. In
that pleasant humour they posted to Rome; and
intending, by their secret and sudden arrival, to
make trial of that which every one had before
avouched, only Collatinus finds his wife, though
it were late in the night, spinning amongst her
maids: the other ladies were all found dancing
and revelling, or in several disports. Whereupon
the noblemen yielded Collatinus the victory, and
his wife the fame. At that time Sextus Tarquinius
being inflamed with Lucrece' beauty, yet
smothering his passions for the present, departed
with the rest back to the camp; from whence he
shortly after privily withdrew himself, and was,
according to his estate, royally entertained and
lodged by Lucrece at Collatium. The same night
he treacherously stealeth into her chamber,
violently ravished her, and early in the morning
speedeth away. Lucrece, in this lamentable
plight, hastily dispatcheth messengers, one to
Rome for her father, another to the camp for
Collatine. They came, the one accompanied with
Junius Brutus, the other with Publius Valerius;
and finding Lucrece attired in mourning habit,
demanded the cause of her sorrow. She, first
taking an oath of them for her revenge, revealed
the actor, and whole manner of his dealing, and
withal suddenly stabbed herself. Which done,
with one consent they all vowed to root out the
whole hated family of the Tarquins; and bearing
the dead body to Rome, Brutus acquainted the
people with the doer and manner of the vile deed,
with a bitter invective against the tyranny of the
king: wherewith the people were so moved, that
with one consent and a general acclamation the
Tarquins were all exiled, and the state government
changed from kings to consuls.

FROM the besieged Ardea all in post,
Borne by the trustless wings of false desire,
Lust-breathed Tarquin leaves the Roman host,
And to Collatium bears the lightless fire
Which, in pale embers hid, lurks to aspire
  And girdle with embracing flames the waist
  Of Collatine's fair love, Lucrece the chaste.

Haply that name of 'chaste' unhappily set
This bateless edge on his keen appetite;
When Collatine unwisely did not let
To praise the clear unmatched red and white
Which triumph'd in that sky of his delight,
  Where mortal stars, as bright as
    heaven's beauties,
  With pure aspects did him peculiar duties.

For he the night before, in Tarquin's tent,
Unlock'd the treasure of his happy state;
What priceless wealth the heavens had him lent
In the possession of his beauteous mate;
Reckoning his fortune at such high-proud rate,
  That kings might be espoused to more fame,
  But king nor peer to such a peerless dame.

O happiness enjoy'd but of a few!
And, if possess'd, as soon decay'd and done
As is the morning's silver-melting dew
Against the golden splendour of the sun!
An expired date, cancell'd ere well begun:
  Honour and beauty, in the owner's arms,
  Are weakly fortress'd from a world of harms.

Beauty itself doth of itself persuade
The eyes of men without an orator;
What needeth then apologies be made,
To set forth that which is so singular?
Or why is Collatine the publisher
  Of that rich jewel he should keep unknown
  From thievish ears, because it is his own?

Perchance his boast of Lucrece' sovereignty
Suggested this proud issue of a king;
For by our ears our hearts oft tainted be:
Perchance that envy of so rich a thing,
Braving compare, disdainfully did sting
  His high-pitch'd thoughts, that meaner men
    should vaunt
  That golden hap which their superiors want.

But some untimely thought did instigate
His all-too-timeless speed, if none of those:
His honour, his affairs, his friends, his state,

Neglected all, with swift intent he goes
To quench the coal which in his liver glows.
  O rash false heat, wrapp'd in repentant cold,
  Thy hasty spring still blasts, and ne'er grows old!

When at Collatium this false lord arrived,
Well was he welcomed by the Roman dame,
Within whose face beauty and virtue strived
Which of them both should underprop her fame:
When virtue bragg'd, beauty would blush
    for shame;
  When beauty boasted blushes, in despite
  Virtue would stain that o'er with silver white.

But beauty, in that white intituled,
From Venus' doves doth challenge that fair field:
Then virtue claims from beauty beauty's red,
Which virtue gave the golden age to gild
Their silver cheeks, and call'd it then their shield;
  Teaching them thus to use it in the fight,
  When shame assail'd, the red should fence
  the white.

This heraldry in Lucrece' face was seen,
Argued by beauty's red and virtue's white
Of either's colour was the other queen,
Proving from world's minority their right:
Yet their ambition makes them still to fight;
  The sovereignty of either being so great,
  That oft they interchange each other's seat.

Their silent war of lilies and of roses,
Which Tarquin view'd in her fair face's field,
In their pure ranks his traitor eye encloses;
Where, lest between them both it should be kill'd,
The coward captive vanquished doth yield
  To those two armies that would let him go,
  Rather than triumph in so false a foe.

Now thinks he that her husband's
    shallow tongue,—
The niggard prodigal that praised her so,—
In that high task hath done her beauty wrong,
Which far exceeds his barren skill to show:
Therefore that praise which Collatine doth owe
  Enchanted Tarquin answers with surmise,
  In silent wonder of still-gazing eyes.

This earthly saint, adored by this devil,
Little suspecteth the false worshipper;
For unstain'd thoughts do seldom dream
  on evil;
Birds never limed no secret bushes fear:

So guiltless she securely gives good cheer
  And reverend welcome to her princely guest,
  Whose inward ill no outward harm express'd:

For that he colour'd with his high estate,
Hiding base sin in plaits of majesty;
That nothing in him seem'd inordinate,
Save something too much wonder of his eye,
Which, having all, all could not satisfy;
  But, poorly rich, so wanteth in his store,
  That, cloy'd with much, he pineth still for more.

But she, that never coped with stranger eyes,
Could pick no meaning from their parling looks,
Nor read the subtle-shining secrecies
Writ in the glassy margents of such books:
She touch'd no unknown baits, nor fear'd
  no hooks;
  Nor could she moralise his wanton sight,
  More than his eyes were open'd to the light.

He stories to her ears her husband's fame,
Won in the fields of fruitful Italy;
And decks with praises Collatine's high name,
Made glorious by his manly chivalry
With bruised arms and wreaths of victory:
  Her joy with heaved-up hand she doth express,
  And, wordless, so greets heaven for his success.

Far from the purpose of his coming hither,
He makes excuses for his being there:
No cloudy show of stormy blustering weather
Doth yet in his fair welkin once appear;
Till sable Night, mother of Dread and Fear,
  Upon the world dim darkness doth display,
  And in her vaulty prison stows the Day.

For then is Tarquin brought unto his bed,
Intending weariness with heavy spright;
For, after supper, long he questioned
With modest Lucrece, and wore out the night:
Now leaden slumber with life's strength
  doth fight;
  And every one to rest themselves betake,
  Save thieves, and cares, and troubled minds,
  that wake.

As one of which doth Tarquin lie revolving
The sundry dangers of his will's obtaining;
Yet ever to obtain his will resolving,
Though weak-built hopes persuade him
  to abstaining:
Despair to gain doth traffic oft for gaining;

And when great treasure is the meed proposed,
  Though death be adjunct, there's no
    death supposed.

Those that much covet are with gain so fond,
For what they have not, that which they possess
They scatter and unloose it from their bond,
And so, by hoping more, they have but less;
Or, gaining more, the profit of excess
  Is but to surfeit, and such griefs sustain,
  That they prove bankrupt in this poor-rich gain.

The aim of all is but to nurse the life
With honour, wealth, and ease, in waning age;
And in this aim there is such thwarting strife,
That one for all, or all for one we gage;
As life for honour in fell battle's rage;
  Honour for wealth; and oft that wealth doth cost
  The death of all, and all together lost.

So that in venturing ill we leave to be
The things we are for that which we expect;
And this ambitious foul infirmity,
In having much, torments us with defect
Of that we have: so then we do neglect
  The thing we have; and, all for want of wit,
  Make something nothing by augmenting it.

Such hazard now must doting Tarquin make,
Pawning his honour to obtain his lust;
And for himself himself be must forsake:
Then where is truth, if there be no self-trust?
When shall he think to find a stranger just,
  When he himself himself confounds, betrays
  To slanderous tongues and wretched
    hateful days?

Now stole upon the time the dead of night,
When heavy sleep had closed up mortal eyes:
No comfortable star did lend his light,
No noise but owls' and wolves' death-
  boding cries;
Now serves the season that they may surprise
  The silly lambs: pure thoughts are dead and still,
  While lust and murder wake to stain and kill.

And now this lustful lord leap'd from his bed,
Throwing his mantle rudely o'er his arm;
Is madly toss'd between desire and dread;
Th' one sweetly flatters, th' other feareth harm;
But honest fear, bewitch'd with lust's foul charm,
  Doth too too oft betake him to retire,
  Beaten away by brain-sick rude desire.

His falchion on a flint he softly smiteth,
That from the cold stone sparks of fire do fly;
Whereat a waxen torch forthwith he lighteth,
Which must be lode-star to his lustful eye;
And to the flame thus speaks advisedly,
  'As from this cold flint I enforced this fire,
  So Lucrece must I force to my desire.'

Here pale with fear he doth premeditate
The dangers of his loathsome enterprise,
And in his inward mind he doth debate
What following sorrow may on this arise:
Then looking scornfully, he doth despise
  His naked armour of still-slaughter'd lust,
  And justly thus controls his thoughts unjust:

'Fair torch, burn out thy light, and lend it not
To darken her whose light excelleth thine:
And die, unhallow'd thoughts, before you blot
With your uncleanness that which is divine;
Offer pure incense to so pure a shrine:
  Let fair humanity abhor the deed
  That spots and stains love's modest snow-
    white weed.

'O shame to knighthood and to shining arms!
O foul dishonour to my household's grave!
O impious act, including all foul harms!
A martial man to be soft fancy's slave!
True valour still a true respect should have;
  Then my digression is so vile, so base,
  That it will live engraven in my face.

'Yea, though I die, the scandal will survive,
And be an eye-sore in my golden coat;
Some loathsome dash the herald will contrive,
To cipher me how fondly I did dote;
That my posterity, shamed with the note
  Shall curse my bones, and hold it for no sin
  To wish that I their father had not bin.

'What win I, if I gain the thing I seek?
A dream, a breath, a froth of fleeting joy.
Who buys a minute's mirth to wail a week?
Or sells eternity to get a toy?
For one sweet grape who will the vine destroy?
  Or what fond beggar, but to touch the crown,
  Would with the sceptre straight be
    strucken down?

'If Collatinus dream of my intent,
Will he not wake, and in a desperate rage
Post hither, this vile purpose to prevent?

This siege that hath engirt his marriage,
This blur to youth, this sorrow to the sage,
  This dying virtue, this surviving shame,
  Whose crime will bear an ever-during blame?

'O, what excuse can my invention make,
When thou shalt charge me with so black a deed?
Will not my tongue be mute, my frail joints shake,
Mine eyes forego their light, my false heart bleed?
The guilt being great, the fear doth still exceed;
  And extreme fear can neither fight nor fly,
  But coward-like with trembling terror die.

'Had Collatinus kill'd my son or sire,
Or lain in ambush to betray my life,
Or were he not my dear friend, this desire
Might have excuse to work upon his wife,
As in revenge or quittal of such strife:
  But as he is my kinsman, my dear friend,
  The shame and fault finds no excuse nor end.

'Shameful it is; ay, if the fact be known:
Hateful it is; there is no hate in loving:
I'll beg her love; but she is own:
The worst is but denial and reproving:
My will is strong, past reason's weak removing.
  Who fears a sentence or an old man's saw
  Shall by a painted cloth be kept in awe.'

Thus, graceless, holds he disputation
'Tween frozen conscience and hot-burning will,
And with good thoughts make dispensation,
Urging the worser sense for vantage still;
Which in a moment doth confound and kill
  All pure effects, and doth so far proceed,
  That what is vile shows like a virtuous deed.

Quoth he, 'She took me kindly by the hand,
And gazed for tidings in my eager eyes,
Fearing some hard news from the
    warlike band,
Where her beloved Collatinus lies.
O, how her fear did make her colour rise!
  First red as roses that on lawn we lay,
  Then white as lawn, the roses took away.

'And how her hand, in my hand being lock'd
Forced it to tremble with her loyal fear!
Which struck her sad, and then it faster rock'd,
Until her husband's welfare she did hear;
Whereat she smiled with so sweet a cheer,
  That had Narcissus seen her as she stood,
  Self-love had never drown'd him in the flood.

'Why hunt I then for colour or excuses?
All orators are dumb when beauty pleadeth;
Poor wretches have remorse in poor abuses;
Love thrives not in the heart that
    shadows dreadeth:
Affection is my captain, and he leadeth;
  And when his gaudy banner is display'd,
  The coward fights and will not be dismay'd.

'Then, childish fear, avaunt! debating, die!
Respect and reason, wait on wrinkled age!
My heart shall never countermand mine eye:
Sad pause and deep regard beseem the sage;
My part is youth, and beats these from the stage:
  Desire my pilot is, beauty my prize;
  Then who fears sinking where such
    treasure lies?'

As corn o'ergrown by weeds, so heedful fear
Is almost choked by unresisted lust.
Away he steals with open listening ear,
Full of foul hope and full of fond mistrust;
Both which, as servitors to the unjust,
  So cross him with their opposite persuasion,
  That now he vows a league, and now invasion.

Within his thought her heavenly image sits,
And in the self-same seat sits Collatine:
That eye which looks on her confounds his wits;
That eye which him beholds, as more divine,
Unto a view so false will not incline;
  But with a pure appeal seeks to the heart,
  Which once corrupted takes the worser part;

And therein heartens up his servile powers,
Who, flatter'd by their leader's jocund show,
Stuff up his lust, as minutes fill up hours;
And as their captain, so their pride doth grow,
Paying more slavish tribute than they owe.
  By reprobate desire thus madly led,
  The Roman lord marcheth to Lucrece' bed.

The locks between her chamber and his will,
Each one by him enforced, retires his ward;
But, as they open, they all rate his ill,
Which drives the creeping thief to some regard:
The threshold grates the door to have him heard;
  Night-wandering weasels shriek to see
  him there;
  They fright him, yet he still pursues his fear.

As each unwilling portal yields him way,
Through little vents and crannies of the place

The wind wars with his torch to make him stay,
And blows the smoke of it into his face,
Extinguishing his conduct in this case;
  But his hot heart, which fond desire
  doth scorch,
  Puffs forth another wind that fires the torch:

And being lighted, by the light he spies
Lucretia's glove, wherein her needle sticks:
He takes it from the rushes where it lies,
And griping it, the needle his finger pricks;
As who should say 'This glove to wanton tricks
  Is not inured; return again in haste;
  Thou see'st our mistress' ornaments are chaste.'

But all these poor forbiddings could not stay him;
He in the worst sense construes their denial:
The doors, the wind, the glove, that did delay him,
He takes for accidental things of trial;
Or as those bars which stop the hourly dial,
  Who with a lingering slay his course doth let,
  Till every minute pays the hour his debt.

'So, so,' quoth he, 'these lets attend the time,
Like little frosts that sometime threat the spring,
To add a more rejoicing to the prime,
And give the sneaped birds more cause to sing.
Pain pays the income of each precious thing;
  Huge rocks, high winds, strong pirates, shelves
  and sands,
  The merchant fears, ere rich at home he lands.'

Now is he come unto the chamber-door,
That shuts him from the heaven of his thought,
Which with a yielding latch, and with no more,
Hath barr'd him from the blessed thing be sought.
So from himself impiety hath wrought,
  That for his prey to pray he doth begin,
  As if the heavens should countenance his sin.

But in the midst of his unfruitful prayer,
Having solicited th' eternal power
That his foul thoughts might compass his fair fair,
And they would stand auspicious to the hour,
Even there he starts: quoth he, 'I must deflower:
  The powers to whom I pray abhor this fact,
  How can they then assist me in the act?

'Then Love and Fortune be my gods, my guide!
My will is back'd with resolution:
Thoughts are but dreams till their effects be tried;
The blackest sin is clear'd with absolution;
Against love's fire fear's frost hath dissolution.

The eye of heaven is out, and misty night
Covers the shame that follows sweet delight.'

This said, his guilty hand pluck'd up the latch,
And with his knee the door he opens wide.
The dove sleeps fast that this night-owl will catch:
Thus treason works ere traitors be espied.
Who sees the lurking serpent steps aside;
  But she, sound sleeping, fearing no such thing,
  Lies at the mercy of his mortal sting.

Into the chamber wickedly he stalks,
And gazeth on her yet unstained bed.
The curtains being close, about he walks,
Rolling his greedy eyeballs in his head:
By their high treason is his heart misled;
  Which gives the watch-word to his hand
    full soon
  To draw the cloud that hides the silver moon.

Look, as the fair and fiery-pointed sun,
Rushing from forth a cloud, bereaves our sight;
Even so, the curtain drawn, his eyes begun
To wink, being blinded with a greater light:
Whether it is that she reflects so bright,
  That dazzleth them, or else some
    shame supposed;
  But blind they are, and keep
    themselves enclosed.

O, had they in that darksome prison died!
Then had they seen the period of their ill;
Then Collatine again, by Lucrece' side,
In his clear bed might have reposed still:
But they must ope, this blessed league to kill;
  And holy-thoughted Lucrece to their sight
  Must sell her joy, her life, her world's delight.

Her lily hand her rosy cheek lies under,
Cozening the pillow of a lawful kiss;
Who, therefore angry, seems to part in sunder,
Swelling on either side to want his bliss;
Between whose hills her head entombed is:
  Where, like a virtuous monument, she lies,
  To be admired of lewd unhallow'd eyes.

Without the bed her other fair hand was,
On the green coverlet; whose perfect white
Show'd like an April daisy on the grass,
With pearly sweat, resembling dew of night.
Her eyes, like marigolds, had sheathed their light,
  And canopied in darkness sweetly lay,
  Till they might open to adorn the day.

Her hair, like golden threads, play'd with
  her breath;
O modest wantons! wanton modesty!
Showing life's triumph in the map of death,
And death's dim look in life's mortality:
Each in her sleep themselves so beautify,
  As if between them twain there were no strife,
  But that life lived in death, and death in life.

Her breasts, like ivory globes circled with blue,
A pair of maiden worlds unconquered,
Save of their lord no bearing yoke they knew,
And him by oath they truly honoured.
These worlds in Tarquin new ambition bred;
  Who, like a foul usurper, went about
  From this fair throne to heave the owner out.

What could he see but mightily he noted?
What did he note but strongly he desired?
What he beheld, on that he firmly doted,
And in his will his wilful eye he tired.
With more than admiration he admired
  Her azure veins, her alabaster skin,
  Her coral lips, her snow-white dimpled chin.

As the grim lion fawneth o'er his prey,
Sharp hunger by the conquest satisfied,
So o'er this sleeping soul doth Tarquin stay,
His rage of lust by gazing qualified;
Slack'd, not suppress'd; for standing by her side,
  His eye, which late this mutiny restrains,
  Unto a greater uproar tempts his veins:

And they, like straggling slaves for
  pillage fighting,
Obdurate vassals fell exploits effecting,
In bloody death and ravishment delighting,
Nor children's tears nor mothers'
  groans respecting,
Swell in their pride, the onset still expecting:
  Anon his beating heart, alarum striking,
  Gives the hot charge and bids them do
    their liking.

His drumming heart cheers up his burning eye,
His eye commends the leading to his hand;
His hand, as proud of such a dignity,
Smoking with pride, march'd on to make
  his stand
On her bare breast, the heart of all her land;
  Whose ranks of blue veins, as his hand
    did scale,
  Left there round turrets destitute and pale.

They, mustering to the quiet cabinet
Where their dear governess and lady lies,
Do tell her she is dreadfully beset,
And fright her with confusion of their cries:
She, much amazed, breaks ope her lock'd-up eyes,
  Who, peeping forth this tumult to behold,
  Are by his flaming torch dimm'd and controll'd.

Imagine her as one in dead of night
From forth dull sleep by dreadful fancy waking,
That thinks she hath beheld some ghastly sprite,
Whose grim aspect sets every joint a-shaking;
What terror or 'tis! but she, in worser taking,
  From sleep disturbed, heedfully doth view
  The sight which makes supposed terror true.

Wrapp'd and confounded in a thousand fears,
Like to a new-kill'd bird she trembling lies;
She dares not look; yet, winking, there appears
Quick-shifting antics, ugly in her eyes:
Such shadows are the weak brain's forgeries;
  Who, angry that the eyes fly from their lights,
  In darkness daunts them with more
    dreadful sights.

His hand, that yet remains upon her breast,—
Rude ram, to batter such an ivory wall!—
May feel her heart-poor citizen!—distress'd,
Wounding itself to death, rise up and fall,
Beating her bulk, that his hand shakes withal.
  This moves in him more rage and lesser pity,
  To make the breach and enter this sweet city.

First, like a trumpet, doth his tongue begin
To sound a parley to his heartless foe;
Who o'er the white sheet peers her whiter chin,
The reason of this rash alarm to know,
Which he by dumb demeanour seeks to show;
  But she with vehement prayers urgeth still
  Under what colour he commits this ill.

Thus he replies: 'The colour in thy face,
That even for anger makes the lily pale,
And the red rose blush at her own disgrace,
Shall plead for me and tell my loving tale:
Under that colour am I come to scale
  Thy never-conquer'd fort: the fault is thine,
  For those thine eyes betray thee unto mine.

'Thus I forestall thee, if thou mean to chide:
Thy beauty hath ensnared thee to this night,
Where thou with patience must my will abide;
My will that marks thee for my earth's delight,
Which I to conquer sought with all my might;
  But as reproof and reason beat it dead,
  By thy bright beauty was it newly bred.

'I see what crosses my attempt will bring;
I know what thorns the growing rose defends;
I think the honey guarded with a sting;
All this beforehand counsel comprehends:
But will is deaf and hears no heedful friends;
  Only he hath an eye to gaze on beauty,
  And dotes on what he looks, 'gainst law
    or duty.

'I have debated, even in my soul,
What wrong, what shame, what sorrow I
    shall breed;
But nothing can affection's course control,
Or stop the headlong fury of his speed.
I know repentant tears ensue the deed,
  Reproach, disdain, and deadly enmity;
  Yet strive I to embrace mine infamy.'

This said, he shakes aloft his Roman blade,
Which, like a falcon towering in the skies,
Coucheth the fowl below with his wings' shade,
Whose crooked beak threats if he mount he dies:
So under his insulting falchion lies
  Harmless Lucretia, marking what he tells
  With trembling fear, as fowl hear falcon's bells.

'Lucrece,' quoth he, 'this night I must enjoy thee:
If thou deny, then force must work my way,
For in thy bed I purpose to destroy thee:
That done, some worthless slave of thine I'll slay,
To kill thine honour with thy life's decay;
  And in thy dead arms do I mean to place him,
  Swearing I slew him, seeing thee embrace him.

'So thy surviving husband shall remain
The scornful mark of every open eye;
Thy kinsmen hang their heads at this disdain,
Thy issue blurr'd with nameless bastardy:
And thou, the author of their obloquy,
  Shalt have thy trespass cited up in rhymes,
  And sung by children in succeeding times.

'But if thou yield, I rest thy secret friend:
The fault unknown is as a thought unacted;
A little harm done to a great good end
For lawful policy remains enacted.
The poisonous simple sometimes is compacted
  In a pure compound; being so applied,
  His venom in effect is purified.

'Then, for thy husband and thy children's sake,
Tender my suit: bequeath not to their lot
The shame that from them no device can take,
The blemish that will never be forgot;
Worse than a slavish wipe or birth-hour's blot:
　For marks descried in men's nativity
　Are nature's faults, not their own infamy.'

Here with a cockatrice' dead-killing eye
He rouseth up himself and makes a pause;
While she, the picture of pure piety,
Like a white hind under the gripe's sharp claws,
Pleads, in a wilderness where are no laws,
　To the rough beast that knows no gentle right,
　Nor aught obeys but his foul appetite.

But when a black-faced cloud the world
　　doth threat,
In his dim mist the aspiring mountains hiding,
From earth's dark womb some gentle gust
　　doth get,
Which blows these pitchy vapours from
　　their bidding,
Hindering their present fall by this dividing;
　So his unhallow'd haste her words delays,
　And moody Pluto winks while Orpheus plays.

Yet, foul night-waking cat, he doth but dally,
While in his hold-fast foot the weak
　　mouse panteth:
Her sad behaviour feeds his vulture folly,
A swallowing gulf that even in plenty wanteth:
His ear her prayers admits, but his heart granteth
　No penetrable entrance to her plaining:
　Tears harden lust, though marble wear
　　with raining.

Her pity-pleading eyes are sadly fix'd
In the remorseless wrinkles of his face;
Her modest eloquence with sighs is mix'd,
Which to her oratory adds more grace.
She puts the period often from his place;
　And midst the sentence so her accent breaks,
　That twice she doth begin ere once she speaks.

She conjures him by high almighty Jove,
By knighthood, gentry, and sweet
　　friendship's oath,
By her untimely tears, her husband's love,
By holy human law, and common troth,
By heaven and earth, and all the power of both,
　That to his borrow'd bed he make retire,
　And stoop to honour, not to foul desire.

Quoth she, 'Reward not hospitality
With such black payment as thou hast pretended;
Mud not the fountain that gave drink to thee;
Mar not the thing that cannot be amended;
End thy ill aim before thy shoot be ended;
　He is no woodman that doth bend his bow
　To strike a poor unseasonable doe.

'My husband is thy friend; for his sake spare me:
Thyself art mighty; for thine own sake leave me:
Myself a weakling; do not then ensnare me:
Thou look'st not like deceit; do not deceive me.
My sighs, like whirlwinds, labour hence to
　　heave thee:
　If ever man were moved with woman moans,
　Be moved with my tears, my sighs, my groans:

'All which together, like a troubled ocean,
Beat at thy rocky and wreck-threatening heart,
To soften it with their continual motion;
For stones dissolved to water do convert.
O, if no harder than a stone thou art,
　Melt at my tears, and be compassionate!
　Soft pity enters at an iron gate.

'In Tarquin's likeness I did entertain thee:
Hast thou put on his shape to do him shame?
To all the host of heaven I complain me,
Thou wrong'st his honour, wound'st his
　　princely name.
Thou art not what thou seem'st; and if the same,
　Thou seem'st not what thou art, a god, a king;
　For kings like gods should govern everything.

'How will thy shame be seeded in thine age,
When thus thy vices bud before thy spring!
If in thy hope thou darest do such outrage,
What darest thou not when once thou art a king?
O, be remember'd, no outrageous thing
　From vassal actors can be wiped away;
　Then kings' misdeeds cannot be hid in clay.

'This deed will make thee only loved for fear;
But happy monarchs still are fear'd for love:
With foul offenders thou perforce must bear,
When they in thee the like offences prove:
If but for fear of this, thy will remove;
　For princes are the glass, the school, the book,
　Where subjects' eyes do learn, do read, do look.

'And wilt thou be the school where Lust
　　shall learn?
Must he in thee read lectures of such shame?

Wilt thou be glass wherein it shall discern
Authority for sin, warrant for blame,
To privilege dishonour in thy name?
   Thou black'st reproach against long-living laud,
   And makest fair reputation but a bawd.

Hast thou command? by him that gave it thee,
From a pure heart command thy rebel will:
Draw not thy sword to guard iniquity,
For it was lent thee all that brood to kill.
Thy princely office how canst thou fulfil,
   When, pattern'd by thy fault, foul sin may say,
   He learn'd to sin, and thou didst teach the way?

'Think but how vile a spectacle it were,
To view thy present trespass in another.
Men's faults do seldom to themselves appear;
Their own transgressions partially they smother:
This guilt would seem death-worthy in
   thy brother.
   O, how are they wrapp'd in with infamies
   That from their own misdeeds askance
   their eyes!

'To thee, to thee, my heaved-up hands appeal,
Not to seducing lust, thy rash relier:
I sue for exiled majesty's repeal;
Let him return, and flattering thoughts retire:
His true respect will prison false desire,
   And wipe the dim mist from thy doting eyne,
   That thou shalt see thy state and pity mine.'

'Have done,' quoth he: 'my uncontrolled tide
Turns not, but swells the higher by this let.
Small lights are soon blown out, huge fires abide,
And with the wind in greater fury fret:
The petty streams that pay a daily debt
   To their salt sovereign, with their fresh
   falls' haste
   Add to his flow, but alter not his taste.'

'Thou art,' quoth she, 'a sea, a sovereign king;
And, lo, there falls into thy boundless flood
Black lust, dishonour, shame, misgoverning,
Who seek to stain the ocean of thy blood.
If all these pretty ills shall change thy good,
   Thy sea within a puddle's womb is hearsed,
   And not the puddle in thy sea dispersed.

'So shall these slaves be king, and thou their slave;
Thou nobly base, they basely dignified;
Thou their fair life, and they thy fouler grave:
Thou loathed in their shame, they in thy pride:
   The lesser thing should not the greater hide;
   The cedar stoops not to the base shrub's foot,
   But low shrubs wither at the cedar's root.

'So let thy thoughts, low vassals to thy state'—
'No more,' quoth he; 'by heaven, I will not
   hear thee:
Yield to my love; if not, enforced hate,
Instead of love's coy touch, shall rudely tear thee;
That done, despitefully I mean to bear thee
   Unto the base bed of some rascal groom,
   To be thy partner in this shameful doom.'

This said, he sets his foot upon the light,
For light and lust are deadly enemies:
Shame folded up in blind concealing night,
When most unseen, then most doth tyrannise.
The wolf hath seized his prey, the poor lamb cries;
   Till with her own white fleece her
   voice controll'd
   Entombs her outcry in her lips' sweet fold:

For with the nightly linen that she wears
He pens her piteous clamours in her head;
Cooling his hot face in the chastest tears
That ever modest eyes with sorrow shed.
O, that prone lust should stain so pure a bed!
   The spots whereof could weeping purify,
   Her tears should drop on them perpetually.

But she hath lost a dearer thing than life,
And he hath won what he would lose again:
This forced league doth force a further strife;
This momentary joy breeds months of pain;
This hot desire converts to cold disdain:
   Pure Chastity is rifled of her store,
   And Lust, the thief, far poorer than before.

Look, as the full-fed hound or gorged hawk,
Unapt for tender smell or speedy flight,
Make slow pursuit, or altogether balk
The prey wherein by nature they delight;
So surfeit-taking Tarquin fares this night:
   His taste delicious, in digestion souring,
   Devours his will, that lived by foul devouring.

O, deeper sin than bottomless conceit
Can comprehend in still imagination!
Drunken Desire must vomit his receipt,
Ere he can see his own abomination.
While Lust is in his pride, no exclamation
   Can curb his heat or rein his rash desire,
   Till, like a jade, self-will himself doth tire.

And then with lank and lean discolour'd cheek,
With heavy eye, knit brow, and strengthless pace,
Feeble Desire, all recreant, poor, and meek,
Like to a bankrupt beggar wails his case:
The flesh being proud, Desire doth fight
    with Grace,
  For there it revels; and when that decays,
  The guilty rebel for remission prays.

So fares it with this faultful lord of Rome,
Who this accomplishment so hotly chased;
For now against himself he sounds this doom,
That through the length of times he
    stands disgraced:
Besides, his soul's fair temple is defaced;
  To whose weak ruins muster troops of cares,
  To ask the spotted princess how she fares.

She says, her subjects with foul insurrection
Have batter'd down her consecrated wall,
And by their mortal fault brought in subjection
Her immortality, and made her thrall
To living death and pain perpetual:
  Which in her prescience she controlled still,
  But her foresight could not forestall their will.

Even in this thought through the dark night
    he stealeth,
A captive victor that hath lost in gain;
Bearing away the wound that nothing healeth,
The scar that will, despite of cure, remain;
Leaving his spoil perplex'd in greater pain.
  She bears the load of lust he left behind,
  And he the burden of a guilty mind.

He like a thievish dog creeps sadly thence;
She like a wearied lamb lies panting there;
He scowls and hates himself for his offence;
She, desperate, with her nails her flesh
    doth tear;
He faintly flies, sneaking with guilty fear;
  She stays, exclaiming on the direful night;
  He runs, and chides his vanish'd,
    loathed delight.

He thence departs a heavy convertite;
She there remains a hopeless castaway;
He in his speed looks for the morning light;
She prays she never may behold the day,
'For day,' quoth she, 'nights scapes doth
    open lay,
  And my true eyes have never practised how
  To cloak offences with a cunning brow.

'They think not but that every eye can see
The same disgrace which they themselves behold;
And therefore would they still in darkness be,
To have their unseen sin remain untold;
For they their guilt with weeping will unfold,
  And grave, like water that doth eat in steel,
  Upon my cheeks what helpless shame I feel.'

Here she exclaims against repose and rest,
And bids her eyes hereafter still be blind.
She wakes her heart by beating on her breast,
And bids it leap from thence, where it may find
Some purer chest to close so pure a mind.
  Frantic with grief thus breathes she forth
    her spite
  Against the unseen secrecy of night:

'O comfort-killing Night, image of hell!
Dim register and notary of shame!
Black stage for tragedies and murders fell!
Vast sin-concealing chaos! nurse of blame!
Blind muffled bawd! dark harbour for defame!
  Grim cave of death! whispering conspirator
  With close-tongued treason and the ravisher!

'O hateful, vaporous, and foggy Night!
Since thou art guilty of my cureless crime,
Muster thy mists to meet the eastern light,
Make war against proportion'd course of time;
Or if thou wilt permit the sun to climb
  His wonted height, yet ere he go to bed,
  Knit poisonous clouds about his golden head.

'With rotten damps ravish the morning air;
Let their exhaled unwholesome breaths make sick
The life of purity, the supreme fair,
Ere he arrive his weary noon-tide prick;
And let thy misty vapours march so thick,
  That in their smoky ranks his smother'd light
  May set at noon and make perpetual night.

'Were Tarquin Night, as he is but Night's child,
The silver-shining queen he would distain;
Her twinkling handmaids too, by him defiled,
Through Night's black bosom should not
    peep again:
So should I have co-partners in my pain;
  And fellowship in woe doth woe assuage,
  As palmers' chat makes short their pilgrimage.

'Where now I have no one to blush with me,
To cross their arms and hang their heads
    with mine,

To mask their brows and hide their infamy;
But I alone alone must sit and pine,
Seasoning the earth with showers of silver brine,
  Mingling my talk with tears, my grief
    with groans,
  Poor wasting monuments of lasting moans.

'O Night, thou furnace of foul-reeking smoke,
Let not the jealous Day behold that face
Which underneath thy black all-hiding cloak
Immodestly lies martyr'd with disgrace!
Keep still possession of thy gloomy place,
  That all the faults which in thy reign are made
  May likewise be sepulchred in thy shade!

'Make me not object to the tell-tale Day!
The light will show, character'd in my brow,
The story of sweet chastity's decay,
The impious breach of holy wedlock vow:
Yea the illiterate, that know not how
  To cipher what is writ in learned books,
  Will quote my loathsome trespass in my looks.

'The nurse, to still her child, will tell my story,
And fright her crying babe with Tarquin's name;
The orator, to deck his oratory,
Will couple my reproach to Tarquin's shame;
Feast-finding minstrels, tuning my defame,
  Will tie the hearers to attend each line,
  How Tarquin wronged me, I Collatine.

'Let my good name, that senseless reputation,
For Collatine's dear love be kept unspotted:
If that be made a theme for disputation,
The branches of another root are rotted,
And undeserved reproach to him allotted
  That is as clear from this attaint of mine
  As I, ere this, was pure to Collatine.

'O unseen shame! invisible disgrace!
O unfelt sore! crest-wounding, private scar!
Reproach is stamp'd in Collatinus' face,
And Tarquin's eye may read the mot afar,
How he in peace is wounded, not in war.
  Alas, how many bear such shameful blows,
  Which not themselves, but he that gives
    them knows!

'If, Collatine, thine honour lay in me,
From me by strong assault it is bereft.
My honour lost, and I, a drone-like bee,
Have no perfection of my summer left,
But robb'd and ransack'd by injurious theft:

In thy weak hive a wandering wasp hath crept,
  And suck'd the honey which thy chaste
    bee kept.

'Yet am I guilty of thy honour's wrack;
Yet for thy honour did I entertain him;
Coming from thee, I could not put him back,
For it had been dishonour to disdain him:
Besides, of weariness he did complain him,
  And talk'd of virtue: O unlook'd-for evil,
  When virtue is profaned in such a devil!

'Why should the worm intrude the maiden bud?
Or hateful cuckoos hatch in sparrows' nests?
Or toads infect fair founts with venom mud?
Or tyrant folly lurk in gentle breasts?
Or kings be breakers of their own behests?
  But no perfection is so absolute, That some
  impurity doth not pollute.

'The aged man that coffers-up his gold
Is plagued with cramps and gouts and
    painful fits;
And scarce hath eyes his treasure to behold,
But like still-pining Tantalus he sits,
And useless barns the harvest of his wits;
  Having no other pleasure of his gain
  But torment that it cannot cure his pain.

'So then he hath it when he cannot use it,
And leaves it to be master'd by his young;
Who in their pride do presently abuse it:
Their father was too weak, and they too strong,
To hold their cursed-blessed fortune long.
  The sweets we wish for turn to loathed sours
  Even in the moment that we call them ours.

'Unruly blasts wait on the tender spring;
Unwholesome weeds take root with
    precious flowers;
The adder hisses where the sweet birds sing;
What virtue breeds iniquity devours:
We have no good that we can say is ours,
  But ill-annexed Opportunity
  Or kills his life or else his quality.

'O Opportunity, thy guilt is great!
'Tis thou that executest the traitor's treason:
Thou set'st the wolf where he the lamb may get;
Whoever plots the sin, thou 'point'st the season;
'Tis thou that spurn'st at right, at law, at reason;
  And in thy shady cell, where none may spy him,
  Sits Sin, to seize the souls that wander by him.

'Thou makest the vestal violate her oath;
Thou blow'st the fire when temperance is thaw'd;
Thou smother'st honesty, thou murder'st troth;
Thou foul abettor! thou notorious bawd!
Thou plantest scandal and displacest laud:
  Thou ravisher, thou traitor, thou false thief,
  Thy honey turns to gall, thy joy to grief!

'Thy secret pleasure turns to open shame,
Thy private feasting to a public fast,
Thy smoothing titles to a ragged name,
Thy sugar'd tongue to bitter wormwood taste:
Thy violent vanities can never last.
  How comes it then, vile Opportunity,
  Being so bad, such numbers seek for thee?

'When wilt thou be the humble suppliant's friend,
And bring him where his suit may be obtain'd?
When wilt thou sort an hour great strifes to end?
Or free that soul which wretchedness
  hath chain'd?
Give physic to the sick, ease to the pain'd?
  The poor, lame, blind, halt, creep, cry out
  for thee;
  But they ne'er meet with Opportunity.

'The patient dies while the physician sleeps;
The orphan pines while the oppressor feeds;
Justice is feasting while the widow weeps;
Advice is sporting while infection breeds:
Thou grant'st no time for charitable deeds:
  Wrath, envy, treason, rape, and murder's rages,
  Thy heinous hours wait on them as their pages.

'When Truth and Virtue have to do with thee,
A thousand crosses keep them from thy aid:
They buy thy help; but Sin ne'er gives a fee,
He gratis comes; and thou art well appaid
As well to hear as grant what he hath said.
  My Collatine would else have come to me
  When Tarquin did, but he was stay'd by thee.

'Guilty thou art of murder and of theft,
Guilty of perjury and subornation,
Guilty of treason, forgery, and shift,
Guilty of incest, that abomination;
An accessary by thine inclination
  To all sins past, and all that are to come,
  From the creation to the general doom.

'Mis-shapen Time, copesmate of ugly Night,
Swift subtle post, carrier of grisly care,
Eater of youth, false slave to false delight,

Base watch of woes, sin's pack-horse,
  virtue's snare;
Thou nursest all and murder'st all that are:
  O, hear me then, injurious, shifting Time!
  Be guilty of my death, since of my crime.

'Why hath thy servant, Opportunity,
Betray'd the hours thou gavest me to repose,
Cancell'd my fortunes, and enchained me
To endless date of never-ending woes?
Time's office is to fine the hate of foes;
  To eat up errors by opinion bred,
  Not spend the dowry of a lawful bed.

'Time's glory is to calm contending kings,
To unmask falsehood and bring truth to light,
To stamp the seal of time in aged things,
To wake the morn and sentinel the night,
To wrong the wronger till he render right,
  To ruinate proud buildings with thy hours,
  And smear with dust their glittering
  golden towers;

'To fill with worm-holes stately monuments,
To feed oblivion with decay of things,
To blot old books and alter their contents,
To pluck the quills from ancient ravens' wings,
To dry the old oak's sap and cherish springs,
  To spoil antiquities of hammer'd steel,
  And turn the giddy round of Fortune's wheel;

'To show the beldam daughters of her daughter,
To make the child a man, the man a child,
To slay the tiger that doth live by slaughter,
To tame the unicorn and lion wild,
To mock the subtle in themselves beguiled,
  To cheer the ploughman with increaseful crops,
  And waste huge stones with little water drops.

'Why work'st thou mischief in thy pilgrimage,
Unless thou couldst return to make amends?
One poor retiring minute in an age
Would purchase thee a thousand
  thousand friends,
Lending him wit that to bad debtors lends:
  O, this dread night, wouldst thou one hour
  come back,
  I could prevent this storm and shun thy wrack!

'Thou ceaseless lackey to eternity,
With some mischance cross Tarquin in his flight:
Devise extremes beyond extremity,
To make him curse this cursed crimeful night:

Let ghastly shadows his lewd eyes affright;
  And the dire thought of his committed evil
  Shape every bush a hideous shapeless devil.

'Disturb his hours of rest with restless trances,
Afflict him in his bed with bedrid groans;
Let there bechance him pitiful mischances,
To make him moan; but pity not his moans:
Stone him with harden'd hearts harder
    than stones;
  And let mild women to him lose their mildness,
  Wilder to him than tigers in their wildness.

'Let him have time to tear his curled hair,
Let him have time against himself to rave,
Let him have time of Time's help to despair,
Let him have time to live a loathed slave,
Let him have time a beggar's orts to crave,
  And time to see one that by alms doth live
  Disdain to him disdained scraps to give.

'Let him have time to see his friends his foes,
And merry fools to mock at him resort;
Let him have time to mark how slow time goes
In time of sorrow, and how swift and short
His time of folly and his time of sport;
  And ever let his unrecalling crime
  Have time to wail th' abusing of his time.

'O Time, thou tutor both to good and bad,
Teach me to curse him that thou taught'st
    this ill!
At his own shadow let the thief run mad,
Himself himself seek every hour to kill!
Such wretched hands such wretched blood
    should spill;
  For who so base would such an office have
  As slanderous death's-man to so base a slave?

'The baser is he, coming from a king,
To shame his hope with deeds degenerate:
The mightier man, the mightier is the thing
That makes him honour'd, or begets him hate;
For greatest scandal waits on greatest state.
  The moon being clouded presently is miss'd,
  But little stars may hide them when they list.

'The crow may bathe his coal-black wings in mire,
And unperceived fly with the filth away;
But if the like the snow-white swan desire,
The stain upon his silver down will stay.
Poor grooms are sightless night, kings
    glorious day:

Gnats are unnoted wheresoe'er they fly,
But eagles gazed upon with every eye.

'Out, idle words, servants to shallow fools!
Unprofitable sounds, weak arbitrators!
Busy yourselves in skill-contending schools;
Debate where leisure serves with dull debaters;
To trembling clients be you mediators:
  For me, I force not argument a straw,
  Since that my case is past the help of law.

'In vain I rail at Opportunity,
At Time, at Tarquin, and uncheerful Night;
In vain I cavil with mine infamy,
In vain I spurn at my confirm'd despite:
This helpless smoke of words doth me no right.
  The remedy indeed to do me good
  Is to let forth my foul-defiled blood.

'Poor hand, why quiver'st thou at this decree?
Honour thyself to rid me of this shame:
For if I die, my honour lives in thee;
But if I live, thou livest in my defame:
Since thou couldst not defend thy loyal dame,
  And wast afeard to scratch her wicked foe,
  Kill both thyself and her for yielding so.'

This said, from her be-tumbled couch she starteth,
To find some desperate instrument of death:
But this no slaughterhouse no tool imparteth
To make more vent for passage of her breath;
Which, thronging through her lips, so vanisheth
  As smoke from Ætna, that in air consumes,
  Or that which from discharged cannon fumes.

'In vain,' quoth she, 'I live, and seek in vain
Some happy mean to end a hapless life.
I fear'd by Tarquin's falchion to be slain,
Yet for the self-same purpose seek a knife:
But when I fear'd I was a loyal wife:
  So am I now: O no, that cannot be;
  Of that true type hath Tarquin rifled me.

'O, that is gone for which I sought to live,
And therefore now I need not fear to die.
To clear this spot by death, at least I give
A badge of fame to slander's livery;
A dying life to living infamy:
  Poor helpless help, the treasure stol'n away,
  To burn the guiltless casket where it lay!

'Well, well, dear Collatine, thou shalt not know
The stained taste of violated troth;

I will not wrong thy true affection so,
To flatter thee with an infringed oath;
This bastard graff shall never come to growth:
  He shall not boast who did thy stock pollute
  That thou art doting father of his fruit.

'Nor shall he smile at thee in secret thought,
Nor laugh with his companions at thy state:
But thou shalt know thy interest was not bought
Basely with gold, but stol'n from forth thy gate.
For me, I am the mistress of my fate,
  And with my trespass never will dispense,
  Till life to death acquit my forced offence.

'I will not poison thee with my attaint,
Nor fold my fault in cleanly-coin'd excuses;
My sable ground of sin I will not paint,
To hide the truth of this false night's abuses:
My tongue shall utter all; mine eyes, like sluices,
  As from a mountain-spring that feeds a dale,
  Shall gush pure streams to purge my
    impure tale.'

By this, lamenting Philomel had ended
The well-tuned warble of her nightly sorrow,
And solemn night with slow sad gait descended
To ugly hell; when, lo, the blushing morrow
Lends light to all fair eyes that light will borrow:
  But cloudy Lucrece shames herself to see,
  And therefore still in night would cloister'd be.

Revealing day through every cranny spies,
And seems to point her out where she
  sits weeping;
To whom she sobbing speaks: 'O eye of eyes,
Why pry'st thou through my window? leave
  thy peeping:
Mock with thy tickling beams eyes that
  are sleeping:
  Brand not my forehead with thy piercing light,
  For day hath nought to do what's done
    by night.'

Thus cavils she with every thing she sees:
True grief is fond and testy as a child,
Who wayward once, his mood with nought agrees:
Old woes, not infant sorrows, bear them mild;
Continuance tames the one; the other wild,
  Like an unpractised swimmer plunging still,
  With too much labour drowns for want of skill.

So she, deep-drenched in a sea of care,
Holds disputation with each thing she views,

And to herself all sorrow doth compare;
No object but her passion's strength renews;
And as one shifts, another straight ensues:
  Sometime her grief is dumb and hath no words;
  Sometime 'tis mad and too much talk affords.

The little birds that tune their morning's joy
Make her moans mad with their sweet melody:
For mirth doth search the bottom of annoy;
Sad souls are slain in merry company;
Grief best is pleased with grief's society:
  True sorrow then is feelingly sufficed
  When with like semblance it is sympathised.

'Tis double death to drown in ken of shore;
He ten times pines that pines beholding food;
To see the salve doth make the wound ache more;
Great grief grieves most at that would do it good;
Deep woes roll forward like a gentle flood,
  Who being stopp'd, the bounding
    banks o'erflows;
  Grief dallied with nor law nor limit knows.

'You mocking-birds,' quoth she, 'your
  tunes entomb
Within your hollow-swelling feather'd breasts,
And in my hearing be you mute and dumb:
My restless discord loves no stops nor rests;
A woeful hostess brooks not merry guests:
  Relish your nimble notes to pleasing ears;
  Distress likes dumps when time is kept
    with tears.

'Come, Philomel, that sing'st of ravishment,
Make thy sad grove in my dishevell'd hair:
As the dank earth weeps at thy languishment,
So I at each sad strain will strain a tear,
And with deep groans the diapason bear;
  For burden-wise I'll hum on Tarquin still,
  While thou on Tereus descant'st better skill.

'And whiles against a thorn thou bear'st thy part,
To keep thy sharp woes waking, wretched I,
To imitate thee well, against my heart
Will fix a sharp knife to affright mine eye;
Who, if it wink, shall thereon fall and die.
  These means, as frets upon an instrument,
  Shall tune our heart-strings to
    true languishment.

'And for, poor bird, thou sing'st not in the day,
As shaming any eye should thee behold,
Some dark deep desert, seated from the way,

That knows not parching heat nor freezing cold,
Will we find out; and there we will unfold
  To creatures stern sad tunes, to change
    their kinds:
  Since men prove beasts, let beasts bear
    gentle minds.'

As the poor frighted deer, that stands at gaze,
Wildly determining which way to fly,
Or one encompass'd with a winding maze,
That cannot tread the way out readily;
So with herself is she in mutiny,
  To live or die which of the twain were better,
  When life is shamed, and death
    reproach's debtor.

'To kill myself,' quoth she, 'alack, what were it,
But with my body my poor soul's pollution?
They that lose half with greater patience bear it
Than they whose whole is swallow'd in confusion.
That mother tries a merciless conclusion
  Who, having two sweet babes, when death
    takes one,
  Will slay the other and be nurse to none.

'My body or my soul, which was the dearer,
When the one pure, the other made divine?
Whose love of either to myself was nearer,
When both were kept for heaven and Collatine?
Ay me! the bark peel'd from the lofty pine,
  His leaves will wither and his sap decay;
  So must my soul, her bark being peel'd away.

'Her house is sack'd, her quiet interrupted,
Her mansion batter'd by the enemy;
Her sacred temple spotted, spoil'd, corrupted,
Grossly engirt with daring infamy:
Then let it not be call'd impiety,
  If in this blemish'd fort I make some hole
  Through which I may convey this troubled soul.

'Yet die I will not till my Collatine
Have heard the cause of my untimely death;
That he may vow, in that sad hour of mine,
Revenge on him that made me stop my breath.
My stained blood to Tarquin I'll bequeath,
  Which by him tainted shall for him be spent,
  And as his due writ in my testament.

'My honour I'll bequeath unto the knife
That wounds my body so dishonoured.
'Tis honour to deprive dishonour'd life;
The one will live, the other being dead:

So of shame's ashes shall my fame be bred;
  For in my death I murder shameful scorn:
  My shame so dead, mine honour is new-born.

'Dear lord of that dear jewel I have lost,
What legacy shall I bequeath to thee?
My resolution, love, shall be thy boast,
By whose example thou revenged mayest be.
How Tarquin must be used, read it in me:
  Myself, thy friend, will kill myself, thy foe,
  And for my sake serve thou false Tarquin so.

'This brief abridgment of my will I make:
My soul and body to the skies and ground;
My resolution, husband, do thou take;
Mine honour be the knife's that makes
  my wound;
My shame be his that did my fame confound;
  And all my fame that lives disbursed be
  To those that live, and think no shame of me.

'Thou, Collatine, shalt oversee this will;
How was I overseen that thou shalt see it!
My blood shall wash the slander of mine ill;
My life's foul deed, my life's fair end shall free it.
Faint not, faint heart, but stoutly say "So be it:"
  Yield to my hand; my hand shall conquer thee:
  Thou dead, both die, and both shall victors be.'

This plot of death when sadly she had laid,
And wiped the brinish pearl from her bright eyes,
With untuned tongue she hoarsely calls her maid,
Whose swift obedience to her mistress hies;
For fleet-wing'd duty with thought's feathers flies.
  Poor Lucrece' cheeks unto her maid seem so
  As winter meads when sun doth melt their snow.

Her mistress she doth give demure good-morrow,
With soft-slow tongue, true mark of modesty,
And sorts a sad look to her lady's sorrow,
For why her face wore sorrow's livery;
But durst not ask of her audaciously
  Why her two suns were cloud-eclipsed so,
  Nor why her fair cheeks over-wash'd with woe.

But as the earth doth weep, the sun being set,
Each flower moisten'd like a melting eye;
Even so the maid with swelling drops gan wet
Her circled eyne, enforced by sympathy
Of those fair suns set in her mistress' sky,
  Who in a salt-waved ocean quench their light,
  Which makes the maid weep like the
    dewy night.

A pretty while these pretty creatures stand,
Like ivory conduits coral cisterns filling:
One justly weeps; the other takes in hand
No cause, but company, of her drops spilling:
Their gentle sex to weep are often willing;
  Grieving themselves to guess at others' smarts,
  And then they drown their eyes or break
    their hearts.

For men have marble, women waxen, minds,
And therefore are they form'd as marble will;
The weak oppress'd, the impression of
    strange kinds
Is form'd in them by force, by fraud, or skill:
Then call them not the authors of their ill,
  No more than wax shall be accounted evil
  Wherein is stamp'd the semblance of a devil.

Their smoothness, like a goodly champaign plain,
Lays open all the little worms that creep;
In men, as in a rough-grown grove, remain
Cave-keeping evils that obscurely sleep:
Through crystal walls each little mote will peep:
  Though men can cover crimes with bold
    stern looks,
  Poor women's faces are their own fault's books.

No man inveigh against the wither'd flower,
But chide rough winter that the flower hath kill'd:
Not that devour'd, but that which doth devour,
Is worthy blame. O, let it not be hild
Poor women's faults, that they are so fulfill'd
  With men's abuses: those proud lords, to blame,
  Make weak-made women tenants to
    their shame.

The precedent whereof in Lucrece view,
Assail'd by night with circumstances strong
Of present death, and shame that might ensue
By that her death, to do her husband wrong:
Such danger to resistance did belong,
  That dying fear through all her body spread;
  And who cannot abuse a body dead?

By this, mild patience bid fair Lucrece speak
To the poor counterfeit of her complaining:
'My girl,' quoth she, 'on what occasion break
Those tears from thee, that down thy cheeks
    are raining?
If thou dost weep for grief of my sustaining,
  Know, gentle wench, it small avails my mood:
  If tears could help, mine own would do
    me good.

'But tell me, girl, when went'—and there
    she stay'd
Till after a deep groan—'Tarquin from hence?'
'Madam, ere I was up,' replied the maid,
'The more to blame my sluggard negligence:
Yet with the fault I thus far can dispense;
  Myself was stirring ere the break of day,
  And, ere I rose, was Tarquin gone away.

'But, lady, if your maid may be so bold,
She would request to know your heaviness.'
'O, peace!' quoth Lucrece: 'if it should be told,
The repetition cannot make it less;
For more it is than I can well express:
  And that deep torture may be call'd a hell
  When more is felt than one hath power to tell.

'Go, get me hither paper, ink, and pen:
Yet save that labour, for I have them here.
What should I say? One of my husband's men
Bid thou be ready, by and by, to bear
A letter to my lord, my love, my dear;
  Bid him with speed prepare to carry it;
  The cause craves haste, and it will soon be writ.'

Her maid is gone, and she prepares to write,
First hovering o'er the paper with her quill:
Conceit and grief an eager combat fight;
What wit sets down is blotted straight with will;
This is too curious-good, this blunt and ill:
  Much like a press of people at a door,
  Throng her inventions, which shall go before.

At last she thus begins: 'Thou worthy lord
Of that unworthy wife that greeteth thee,
Health to thy person! next vouchsafe t' afford—
If ever, love, thy Lucrece thou wilt see—
Some present speed to come and visit me.
  So, I commend me from our house in grief:
  My woes are tedious, though my words
    are brief.'

Here folds she up the tenor of her woe,
Her certain sorrow writ uncertainly.
By this short schedule Collatine may know
Her grief, but not her grief's true quality:
She dares not thereof make discovery,
  Lest he should hold it her own gross abuse,
  Ere she with blood had stain'd her
    stain'd excuse.

Besides, the life and feeling of her passion
She hoards, to spend when he is by to hear her:

When sighs and groans and tears may grace
  the fashion
Of her disgrace, the better so to clear her
From that suspicion which the world might
  bear her.
  To shun this blot, she would not blot the letter
  With words, till action might become
    them better.

To see sad sights moves more than hear
  them told;
For then eye interprets to the ear
The heavy motion that it doth behold,
When every part a part of woe doth bear.
'Tis but a part of sorrow that we hear:
  Deep sounds make lesser noise than
    shallow fords,
  And sorrow ebbs, being blown with wind
    of words.

Her letter now is seal'd, and on it writ
'At Ardea to my lord with more than haste.'
The post attends, and she delivers it,
Charging the sour-faced groom to hie as fast
As lagging fowls before the northern blast:
  Speed more than speed but dull and slow
    she deems:
  Extremity still urgeth such extremes.

The homely villain court'sies to her low;
And, blushing on her, with a steadfast eye
Receives the scroll without or yea or no,
And forth with bashful innocence doth hie.
But they whose guilt within their bosoms lie
  Imagine every eye beholds their blame;
  For Lucrece thought he blush'd to her
    see shame:

When, silly groom! God wot, it was defect
Of spirit, Life, and bold audacity.
Such harmless creatures have a true respect
To talk in deeds, while others saucily
Promise more speed, but do it leisurely:
  Even so this pattern of the worn-out age
  Pawn'd honest looks, but laid no words
    to gage.

His kindled duty kindled her mistrust,
That two red fires in both their faces blazed;
She thought he blush'd, as knowing
  Tarquin's lust,
And, blushing with him, wistly on him gazed;
Her earnest eye did make him more amazed:

The more she saw the blood his
  cheeks replenish,
The more she thought he spied in her
  some blemish.

But long she thinks till he return again,
And yet the duteous vassal scarce is gone.
The weary time she cannot entertain,
For now 'tis stale to sigh, to weep, and groan:
So woe hath wearied woe, moan tired moan,
  That she her plaints a little while doth stay,
  Pausing for means to mourn some newer way.

At last she calls to mind where hangs a piece
Of skilful painting, made for Priam's Troy:
Before the which is drawn the power of Greece.
For Helen's rape the city to destroy,
Threatening cloud-kissing Ilion with annoy;
  Which the conceited painter drew so proud,
  As heaven, it seem'd, to kiss the turrets bow'd.

A thousand lamentable objects there,
In scorn of nature, art gave lifeless life:
Many a dry drop seem'd a weeping tear,
Shed for the slaughter'd husband by the wife:
The red blood reek'd, to show the painter's strife;
  And dying eyes gleam'd forth their ashy lights,
  Like dying coals burnt out in tedious nights.

There might you see the labouring pioneer
Begrimed with sweat, and smeared all with dust;
And from the towers of Troy there would appear
The very eyes of men through loop-holes thrust,
Gazing upon the Greeks with little lust:
  Such sweet observance in this work was had,
  That one might see those far-off eyes look sad.

In great commanders grace and majesty
You might behold, triumphing in their faces;
In youth, quick bearing and dexterity;
And here and there the painter interlaces
Pale cowards, marching on with trembling paces;
  Which heartless peasants did so well resemble,
  That one would swear he saw them quake
    and tremble.

In Ajax and Ulysses, O, what art
Of physiognomy might one behold!
The face of either cipher'd either's heart;
Their face their manners most expressly told:
In Ajax' eyes blunt rage and rigour roll'd;
  But the mild glance that sly Ulysses lent
  Show'd deep regard and smiling government.

There pleading might you see grave Nestor stand,
As 'twere encouraging the Greeks to fight;
Making such sober action with his hand,
That it beguiled attention, charm'd the sight:
In speech, it seem'd, his beard, all silver white,
    Wagg'd up and down, and from his lips did fly
    Thin winding breath, which purl'd up to the sky.

About him were a press of gaping faces,
Which seem'd to swallow up his sound advice;
All jointly listening, but with several graces,
As if some mermaid did their ears entice,
Some high, some low, the painter was so nice;
    The scalps of many, almost hid behind,
    To jump up higher seem'd, to mock the mind.

Here one man's hand lean'd on another's head,
His nose being shadow'd by his neighbour's ear;
Here one being throng'd bears back, all boll'n
    and red;
Another smother'd seems to pelt and swear;
And in their rage such signs of rage they bear,
    As, but for loss of Nestor's golden words,
    It seem'd they would debate with angry swords.

For much imaginary work was there;
Conceit deceitful, so compact, so kind,
That for Achilles' image stood his spear,
Griped in an armed hand; himself, behind,
Was left unseen, save to the eye of mind:
    A hand, a foot, a face, a leg, a head,
    Stood for the whole to be imagined.

And from the walls of strong-besieged Troy
When their brave hope, bold Hector, march'd
    to field,
Stood many Trojan mothers, sharing joy
To see their youthful sons bright weapons wield;
And to their hope they such odd action yield,
    That through their light joy seemed to appear,
    Like bright things stain'd, a kind of heavy fear.

And from the strand of Dardan, where
    they fought,
To Simois' reedy banks the red blood ran,
Whose waves to imitate the battle sought
With swelling ridges; and their ranks began
To break upon the galled shore, and than
    Retire again, till, meeting greater ranks,
    They join and shoot their foam at Simois' banks.

To this well-painted piece is Lucrece come,
To find a face where all distress is stell'd.

Many she sees where cares have carved some,
But none where all distress and dolour dwell'd,
Till she despairing Hecuba beheld,
    Staring on Priam's wounds with her old eyes,
    Which bleeding under Pyrrhus' proud foot lies.

In her the painter had anatomized
Time's ruin, beauty's wreck, and grim care's reign:
Her cheeks with chaps and wrinkles
    were disguised;
Of what she was no semblance did remain:
Her blue blood changed to black in every vein,
    Wanting the spring that those shrunk pipes
    had fed,
    Show'd life imprison'd in a body dead.

On this sad shadow Lucrece spends her eyes,
And shapes her sorrow to the beldam's woes,
Who nothing wants to answer her but cries,
And bitter words to ban her cruel foes:
The painter was no god to lend her those;
    And therefore Lucrece swears he did her wrong,
    To give her so much grief and not a tongue.

'Poor instrument,' quoth she, 'without a sound,
I'll tune thy woes with my lamenting tongue;
And drop sweet balm in Priam's painted wound,
And rail on Pyrrhus that hath done him wrong;
And with my tears quench Troy that burns
    so long;
    And with my knife scratch out the angry eyes
    Of all the Greeks that are thine enemies.

'Show me the strumpet that began this stir,
That with my nails her beauty I may tear.
Thy heat of lust, fond Paris, did incur
This load of wrath that burning Troy doth bear:
Thy eye kindled the fire that burneth here;
    And here in Troy, for trespass of thine eye,
    The sire, the son, the dame, and daughter die.

'Why should the private pleasure of some one
Become the public plague of many moe?
Let sin, alone committed, light alone
Upon his head that hath transgressed so;
Let guiltless souls be freed from guilty woe:
    For one's offence why should so many fall,
    To plague a private sin in general?

'Lo, here weeps Hecuba, here Priam dies,
Here manly Hector faints, here Troilus swounds,
Here friend by friend in bloody channel lies,
And friend to friend gives unadvised wounds,

And one man's lust these many lives confounds:
  Had doting Priam check'd his son's desire,
  Troy had been bright with fame and not
    with fire.'

Here feelingly she weeps Troy's painted woes:
For sorrow, like a heavy-hanging bell,
Once set on ringing, with his own weight goes;
Then little strength rings out the doleful knell:
So Lucrece, set a-work, sad tales doth tell
  To pencill'd pensiveness and colour'd sorrow;
  She lends them words, and she their looks
    doth borrow.

She throws her eyes about the painting round,
And whom she finds forlorn she doth lament.
At last she sees a wretched image bound,
That piteous looks to Phrygian shepherds lent:
His face, though full of cares, yet show'd content;
  Onward to Troy with the blunt swains he goes,
  So mild, that Patience seem'd to scorn his woes.

In him the painter labour'd with his skill
To hide deceit, and give the harmless show
An humble gait, calm looks, eyes wailing still,
A brow unbent, that seem'd to welcome woe;
Cheeks neither red nor pale, but mingled so
  That blushing red no guilty instance gave,
  Nor ashy pale the fear that false hearts have.

But, like a constant and confirmed devil,
He entertain'd a show so seeming just,
And therein so ensconced his secret evil,
That jealousy itself could not mistrust
False-creeping craft and perjury should thrust
  Into so bright a day such black-faced storms,
  Or blot with hell-born sin such saint-like forms.

The well-skill'd workman this mild image drew
For perjured Sinon, whose enchanting story
The credulous old Priam after slew;
Whose words like wildfire burnt the
    shining glory
Of rich-built Ilion, that the skies were sorry,
  And little stars shot from their fixed places,
  When their glass fell wherein they view'd
    their faces.

This picture she advisedly perused,
And chid the painter for his wondrous skill,
Saying, some shape in Sinon's was abused;
So fair a form lodged not a mind so ill:
And still on him she gazed; and gazing still,

Such signs of truth in his plain face she spied,
That she concludes the picture was belied.

'It cannot be,' quoth she, 'that so much guile'—
She would have said 'can lurk in such a look;'
But Tarquin's shape came in her mind the while,
And from her tongue 'can lurk' from 'cannot' took:
'It cannot be' she in that sense forsook,
  And turn'd it thus, 'It cannot be, I find,
  But such a face should bear a wicked mind.

'For even as subtle Sinon here is painted.
So sober-sad, so weary, and so mild,
As if with grief or travail he had fainted,
To me came Tarquin armed; so beguiled
With outward honesty, but yet defiled
  With inward vice: as Priam him did cherish,
  So did I Tarquin; so my Troy did perish.

'Look, look, how listening Priam wets his eyes,
To see those borrow'd tears that Sinon sheds!
Priam, why art thou old and yet not wise?
For every tear he falls a Trojan bleeds:
His eye drops fire, no water thence proceeds;
  Those round clear pearls of his, that move
    thy pity,
  Are balls of quenchless fire to burn thy city.

'Such devils steal effects from lightless hell;
For Sinon in his fire doth quake with cold,
And in that cold hot-burning fire doth dwell;
These contraries such unity do hold,
Only to flatter fools and make them bold:
  So Priam's trust false Sinon's tears doth flatter,
  That he finds means to burn his Troy
    with water.'

Here, all enraged, such passion her assails,
That patience is quite beaten from her breast.
She tears the senseless Sinon with her nails,
Comparing him to that unhappy guest
Whose deed hath made herself herself detest:
  At last she smilingly with this gives o'er;
  'Fool, fool!' quoth she, 'his wounds will not
    be sore.'

Thus ebbs and flows the current of her sorrow,
And time doth weary time with her complaining.
She looks for night, and then she longs
    for morrow,
And both she thinks too long with her remaining:
Short time seems long in sorrow's
    sharp sustaining:

Though woe be heavy, yet it seldom sleeps,
And they that watch see time how slow
   it creeps.

Which all this time hath overslipp'd her thought,
That she with painted images hath spent;
Being from the feeling of her own grief brought
By deep surmise of others' detriment;
Losing her woes in shows of discontent.
  It easeth some, though none it ever cured,
  To think their dolour others have endured.

But now the mindful messenger, come back,
Brings home his lord and other company;
Who finds his Lucrece clad in mourning black:
And round about her tear-stained eye
Blue circles stream'd; like rainbows in the sky:
  These water-galls in her dim element
  Foretell new storms to those already spent.

Which when her sad-beholding husband saw,
Amazedly in her sad face he stares:
Her eyes, though sod in tears, look'd red
  and raw,
Her lively colour kill'd with deadly cares.
He hath no power to ask her how she fares:
  Both stood, like old acquaintance in a trance,
  Met far from home, wondering each
    other's chance.

At last he takes her by the bloodless hand,
And thus begins: 'What uncouth ill event
Hath thee befall'n, that thou dost trembling stand?
Sweet love, what spite hath thy fair colour spent?
Why art thou thus attired in discontent?
  Unmask, dear dear, this moody heaviness,
  And tell thy grief, that we may give redress.'

Three times with sighs she gives her sorrow fire,
Ere once she can discharge one word of woe:
At length address'd to answer his desire,
She modestly prepares to let them know
Her honour is ta'en prisoner by the foe;
  While Collatine and his consorted lords
  With sad attention long to hear her words.

And now this pale swan in her watery nest
Begins the sad dirge of her certain ending;
'Few words,' quoth she, 'Shall fit the trespass best,
Where no excuse can give the fault amending:
In me moe woes than words are now depending;
  And my laments would be drawn out too long,
  To tell them all with one poor tired tongue.

'Then be this all the task it hath to say
Dear husband, in the interest of thy bed
A stranger came, and on that pillow lay
Where thou was wont to rest thy weary head;
And what wrong else may be imagined
  By foul enforcement might be done to me,
  From that, alas, thy Lucrece is not free.

'For in the dreadful dead of dark midnight,
With shining falchion in my chamber came
A creeping creature, with a flaming light,
And softly cried 'Awake, thou Roman dame,
And entertain my love; else lasting shame
  On thee and thine this night I will inflict,
  If thou my love's desire do contradict.

'"For some hard-favour'd groom of thine"',
  quoth he,
"Unless thou yoke thy liking to my will,
I'll murder straight, and then I'll slaughter thee
And swear I found you where you did fulfil
The loathsome act of lust, and so did kill
  The lechers in their deed: this act will be
  My fame and thy perpetual infamy".

'With this, I did begin to start and cry;
And then against my heart he sets his sword,
Swearing, unless I took all patiently,
I should not live to speak another word;
So should my shame still rest upon record,
  And never be forgot in mighty Rome
  Th' adulterate death of Lucrece and her groom.

'Mine enemy was strong, my poor self weak,
And far the weaker with so strong a fear:
My bloody judge forbade my tongue to speak;
No rightful plea might plead for justice there:
His scarlet lust came evidence to swear
  That my poor beauty had purloin'd his eyes;
  And when the judge is robb'd the
    prisoner dies.

'O, teach me how to make mine own excuse!
Or at the least this refuge let me find;
Though my gross blood be stain'd with this abuse,
Immaculate and spotless is my mind;
That was not forced; that never was inclined
  To accessary yieldings, but still pure
  Doth in her poison'd closet yet endure.'

Lo, here, the hopeless merchant of this loss,
With head declined, and voice damm'd up
  with woe,

With sad set eyes, and wretched arms across,
From lips new-waxen pale begins to blow
The grief away that stops his answer so:
  But, wretched as he is, he strives in vain;
  What he breathes out his breath drinks
    up again.

As through an arch the violent roaring tide
Outruns the eye that doth behold his haste,
Yet in the eddy boundeth in his pride
Back to the strait that forced him on so fast;
In rage sent out, recall'd in rage, being past:
  Even so his sighs, his sorrows, make a saw,
  To push grief on, and back the same grief draw.

Which speechless woe of his poor she attendeth,
And his untimely frenzy thus awaketh:
'Dear lord, thy sorrow to my sorrow lendeth
Another power; no flood by raining slaketh.
My woe too sensible thy passion maketh
  More feeling-painful: let it then suffice
  To drown one woe, one pair of weeping eyes.

'And for my sake, when I might charm thee so,
For she that was thy Lucrece, now attend me:
Be suddenly revenged on my foe,
Thine, mine, his own: suppose thou dost
    defend me
From what is past: the help that thou shalt
    lend me
  Comes all too late, yet let the traitor die;
  For sparing justice feeds iniquity.

'But ere I name him, you fair lords,' quoth she,
Speaking to those that came with Collatine,
'Shall plight your honourable faiths to me,
With swift pursuit to venge this wrong of mine;
For 'tis a meritorious fair design
  To chase injustice with revengeful arms:
  Knights, by their oaths, should right poor
    ladies' harms.'

At this request, with noble disposition
Each present lord began to promise aid,
As bound in knighthood to her imposition,
Longing to hear the hateful foe bewray'd.
But she, that yet her sad task hath not said,
  The protestation stops. 'O, speak, 'quoth she,
  'How may this forced stain be wiped from me?

'What is the quality of mine offence,
Being constrain'd with dreadful circumstance?
May my pure mind with the foul act dispense,
My low-declined honour to advance?
May any terms acquit me from this chance?
  The poison'd fountain clears itself again;
  And why not I from this compelled stain?'

With this, they all at once began to say,
Her body's stain her mind untainted clears;
While with a joyless smile she turns away
The face, that map which deep impression bears
Of hard misfortune, carved in it with tears.
  'No, no,' quoth she, 'no dame, hereafter living,
  By my excuse shall claim excuse's giving.'

Here with a sigh, as if her heart would break,
She throws forth Tarquin's name; 'He, he,'
    she says,
But more than 'he' her poor tongue could
    not speak;
Till after many accents and delays,
Untimely breathings, sick and short assays,
  She utters this, 'He, he, fair lords, 'tis he,
  That guides this hand to give this wound to me.'

Even here she sheathed in her harmless breast
A harmful knife, that thence her
    soul unsheathed:
That blow did that it from the deep unrest
Of that polluted prison where it breathed:
Her contrite sighs unto the clouds bequeath'd
  Her winged sprite, and through her wounds
    doth fly
  Life's lasting date from cancell'd destiny.

Stone-still, astonish'd with this deadly deed,
Stood Collatine and all his lordly crew;
Till Lucrece' father, that beholds her bleed,
Himself on her self-slaughter'd body threw;
And from the purple fountain Brutus drew
  The murderous knife, and, as it left the place,
  Her blood, in poor revenge, held it in chase;

And bubbling from her breast, it doth divide
In two slow rivers, that the crimson blood
Circles her body in on every side,
Who, like a late-sack'd island, vastly stood
Bare and unpeopled in this fearful flood.
  Some of her blood still pure and red remain'd,
  And some look'd black, and that false
    Tarquin stain'd.

About the mourning and congealed face
Of that black blood a watery rigol goes,
Which seems to weep upon the tainted place:

And ever since, as pitying Lucrece' woes,
Corrupted blood some watery token shows;
  And blood untainted still doth red abide,
  Blushing at that which is so putrified.

'Daughter, dear daughter,' old Lucretius cries,
'That life was mine which thou hast
  here deprived.
If in the child the father's image lies,
Where shall I live now Lucrece is unlived?
Thou wast not to this end from me derived.
  If children predecease progenitors,
  We are their offspring, and they none of ours.

'Poor broken glass, I often did behold
In thy sweet semblance my old age new born;
But now that fresh fair mirror, dim and old,
Shows me a bare-boned death by time
  out-worn:
O, from thy cheeks my image thou hast torn,
  And shivered all the beauty of my glass,
  That I no more can see what once I was!

'O time, cease thou thy course and last
  no longer,
If they surcease to be that should survive.
Shall rotten death make conquest of
  the stronger
And leave the faltering feeble souls alive?
The old bees die, the young possess their hive:
  Then live, sweet Lucrece, live again and see
  Thy father die, and not thy father thee!

By this, starts Collatine as from a dream,
And bids Lucretius give his sorrow place;
And then in key-cold Lucrece' bleeding stream
He falls, and bathes the pale fear in his face,
And counterfeits to die with her a space;
  Till manly shame bids him possess his breath
  And live to be revenged on her death.

The deep vexation of his inward soul
Hath served a dumb arrest upon his tongue;
Who, mad that sorrow should his use control,
Or keep him from heart-easing words so long,
Begins to talk; but through his lips do throng
  Weak words, so thick come in his poor
    heart's aid,
  That no man could distinguish what he said.

Yet sometime 'Tarquin' was pronounced plain,
But through his teeth, as if the name he tore.
This windy tempest, till it blow up rain,

Held back his sorrow's tide, to make it more;
At last it rains, and busy winds give o'er:
  Then son and father weep with equal strife
  Who should weep most, for daughter or
    for wife.

The one doth call her his, the other his,
Yet neither may possess the claim they lay.
The father says 'She's mine.' 'O, mine she is,'
Replies her husband: 'do not take away
My sorrow's interest; let no mourner say
  He weeps for her, for she was only mine,
  And only must be wail'd by Collatine.'

'O,' quoth Lucretius,' I did give that life
Which she too early and too late hath spill'd.'
'Woe, woe,' quoth Collatine, 'she was my wife,
I owed her, and 'tis mine that she hath kill'd.'
'My daughter' and 'my wife' with clamours fill'd
  The dispersed air, who, holding Lucrece' life,
  Answer'd their cries, 'my daughter' and
    'my wife.'

Brutus, who pluck'd the knife from Lucrece' side,
Seeing such emulation in their woe,
Began to clothe his wit in state and pride,
Burying in Lucrece' wound his folly's show.
He with the Romans was esteemed so
  As silly-jeering idiots are with kings,
  For sportive words and uttering foolish things:

But now he throws that shallow habit by,
Wherein deep policy did him disguise;
And arm'd his long-hid wits advisedly,
To check the tears in Collatinus' eyes.
'Thou wronged lord of Rome,' quoth he, 'arise:
  Let my unsounded self, supposed a fool,
  Now set thy long-experienced wit to school.

'Why, Collatine, is woe the cure for woe?
Do wounds help wounds, or grief help
  grievous deeds?
Is it revenge to give thyself a blow
For his foul act by whom thy fair wife bleeds?
Such childish humour from weak
  minds proceeds:
  Thy wretched wife mistook the matter so,
  To slay herself, that should have slain her foe.

'Courageous Roman, do not steep thy heart
In such relenting dew of lamentations;
But kneel with me and help to bear thy part,
To rouse our Roman gods with invocations,

That they will suffer these abominations,
  Since Rome herself in them doth
    stand disgraced,
  By our strong arms from forth her fair
    streets chased.

'Now, by the Capitol that we adore,
And by this chaste blood so unjustly stain'd,
By heaven's fair sun that breeds the fat
    earth's store,
By all our country rights in Rome maintain'd,
And by chaste Lucrece' soul that late complain'd
  Her wrongs to us, and by this bloody knife,
  We will revenge the death of this true wife.'

This said, he struck his hand upon his breast,
And kiss'd the fatal knife, to end his vow;
And to his protestation urged the rest,
Who, wondering at him, did his words allow:
Then jointly to the ground their knees they bow;
  And that deep vow, which Brutus made before,
  He doth again repeat, and that they swore.

When they had sworn to this advised doom,
They did conclude to bear dead Lucrece thence;
To show her bleeding body thorough Rome,
And so to publish Tarquin's foul offence:
Which being done with speedy diligence,
  The Romans plausibly did give consent
  To Tarquin's everlasting banishment.

The End

1592

Venus and Adonis

'Vilia miretur vulgus; mihi flavus Apollo
Pocula Castalia plena ministret aqua.'

DEDICATION

TO THE RIGHT HONOURABLE
HENRY WRIOTHESLY,
Earl of Southampton, and Baron of Tichfield.

RIGHT HONOURABLE,
I KNOW not how I shall offend in dedicating my
unpolished lines to your lordship, nor how the
world will censure me for choosing so strong a
prop to support so weak a burden only, if your
honour seem but pleased, I account myself
highly praised, and vow to take advantage of all
idle hours, till I have honoured you with some
graver labour. But if the first heir of my invention
prove deformed, I shall be sorry it had so noble
a god-father, and never after ear so barren a
land, for fear it yield me still so bad a harvest.
I leave it to your honourable survey, and your
honour to your heart's content; which I wish may
always answer your own wish and the world's
hopeful expectation.

Your honour's in all duty,
William Shakespeare

EVEN as the sun with purple-colour'd face
Had ta'en his last leave of the weeping morn,
Rose-cheek'd Adonis hied him to the chase;
Hunting he loved, but love he laugh'd to scorn;
  Sick-thoughted Venus makes amain unto him,
  And like a bold-faced suitor 'gins to woo him.

'Thrice-fairer than myself,' thus she began,
'The field's chief flower, sweet above compare,
Stain to all nymphs, more lovely than a man,
More white and red than doves or roses are;
  Nature that made thee, with herself at strife,
  Saith that the world hath ending with thy life.

'Vouchsafe, thou wonder, to alight thy steed,
And rein his proud head to the saddle-bow;
If thou wilt deign this favour, for thy meed
A thousand honey secrets shalt thou know:
  Here come and sit, where never serpent hisses,
  And being set, I'll smother thee with kisses;

'And yet not cloy thy lips with loathed satiety,
But rather famish them amid their plenty,
Making them red and pale with fresh variety,
Ten kisses short as one, one long as twenty:
  A summer's day will seem an hour but short,
  Being wasted in such time-beguiling sport.'

With this she seizeth on his sweating palm,
The precedent of pith and livelihood,
And trembling in her passion, calls it balm,
Earth's sovereign salve to do a goddess good:
  Being so enraged, desire doth lend her force
  Courageously to pluck him from his horse.

Over one arm the lusty courser's rein,
Under her other was the tender boy,
Who blush'd and pouted in a dull disdain,
With leaden appetite, unapt to toy;
  She red and hot as coals of glowing fire,
  He red for shame, but frosty in desire.

The studded bridle on a ragged bough
Nimbly she fastens: – O, how quick is love! –
The steed is stalled up, and even now
To tie the rider she begins to prove:
  Backward she push'd him, as she would
    be thrust,
  And govern'd him in strength, though not
    in lust.

So soon was she along as he was down,
Each leaning on their elbows and their hips:

Now doth she stroke his cheek, now doth
  he frown,
And 'gins to chide, but soon she stops his lips;
  And kissing speaks, with lustful language broken,
  'If thou wilt chide, thy lips shall never open.'

He burns with bashful shame: she with her tears
Doth quench the maiden burning of his cheeks;
Then with her windy sighs and golden hairs
To fan and blow them dry again she seeks:
  He saith she is immodest, blames her 'miss;
  What follows more she murders with a kiss.

Even as an empty eagle, sharp by fast,
Tires with her beak on feathers, flesh and bone,
Shaking her wings, devouring all in haste,
Till either gorge be stuff'd or prey be gone;
  Even so she kissed his brow, his cheek, his chin,
  And where she ends she doth anew begin.

Forced to content, but never to obey,
Panting he lies and breatheth in her face;
She feedeth on the steam as on a prey,
And calls it heavenly moisture, air of grace;
  Wishing her cheeks were gardens full of flowers,
  So they were dew'd with such distilling showers.

Look, how a bird lies tangled in a net,
So fasten'd in her arms Adonis lies;
Pure shame and awed resistance made him fret,
Which bred more beauty in his angry eyes:
  Rain added to a river that is rank
  Perforce will force it overflow the bank.

Still she entreats, and prettily entreats,
For to a pretty ear she tunes her tale;
Still is he sullen, still he lours and frets,
'Twixt crimson shame and anger ashy-pale:
  Being red, she loves him best; and being white,
  Her best is better'd with a more delight.

Look how he can, she cannot choose but love;
And by her fair immortal hand she swears,
From his soft bosom never to remove,
Till he take truce with her contending tears,
  Which long have rain'd, making her cheeks
    all wet;
  And one sweet kiss shall pay this countless debt.

Upon this promise did he raise his chin,
Like a dive-dapper peering through a wave,
Who, being look'd on, ducks as quickly in;
So offers he to give what she did crave;

But when her lips were ready for his pay,
He winks, and turns his lips another way.

Never did passenger in summer's heat
More thirst for drink than she for this good turn.
Her help she sees, but help she cannot get;
She bathes in water, yet her fire must burn:
  'O, pity,' 'gan she cry, 'flint-hearted boy!
  'Tis but a kiss I beg; why art thou coy?

'I have been woo'd, as I entreat thee now,
Even by the stern and direful god of war,
Whose sinewy neck in battle ne'er did bow,
Who conquers where he comes in every jar;
  Yet hath he been my captive and my slave,
  And begg'd for that which thou unask'd
    shalt have.

'Over my altars hath he hung his lance,
His batter'd shield, his uncontrolled crest,
And for my sake hath learn'd to sport and dance,
To toy, to wanton, dally, smile and jest,
  Scorning his churlish drum and ensign red,
  Making my arms his field, his tent my bed.

'Thus he that overruled I oversway'd,
Leading him prisoner in a red-rose chain:
Strong-tempered steel his stronger
    strength obey'd,
Yet was he servile to my coy disdain.
  O, be not proud, nor brag not of thy might,
  For mastering her that foil'd the god of fight!

'Touch but my lips with those fair lips of thine, –
Though mine be not so fair, yet are they red –
The kiss shall be thine own as well as mine.
What seest thou in the ground? hold up thy head:
  Look in mine eye-balls, there thy beauty lies;
  Then why not lips on lips, since eyes in eyes?

'Art thou ashamed to kiss? then wink again,
And I will wink; so shall the day seem night;
Love keeps his revels where they are but twain;
Be bold to play, our sport is not in sight:
  These blue-vein'd violets whereon we lean
  Never can blab, nor know not what we mean.

'The tender spring upon thy tempting lip
Shows thee unripe; yet mayst thou well be tasted:
Make use of time, let not advantage slip;
Beauty within itself should not be wasted:
  Fair flowers that are not gather'd in their prime
  Rot and consume themselves in little time.

'Were I hard-favour'd, foul, or wrinkled-old,
Ill-nurtured, crooked, churlish, harsh in voice,
O'erworn, despised, rheumatic and cold,
Thick-sighted, barren, lean and lacking juice,
  Then mightst thou pause, for then I were not
    for thee
  But having no defects, why dost abhor me?

'Thou canst not see one wrinkle in my brow;
Mine eyes are grey and bright and quick
  in turning:
My beauty as the spring doth yearly grow,
My flesh is soft and plump, my marrow burning;
  My smooth moist hand, were it with thy
    hand felt,
  Would in thy palm dissolve, or seem to melt.

'Bid me discourse, I will enchant thine ear,
Or, like a fairy, trip upon the green,
Or, like a nymph, with long dishevell'd hair,
Dance on the sands, and yet no footing seen.
  Love is a spirit all compact of fire,
  Not gross to sink, but light, and will aspire.

'Witness this primrose bank whereon I lie;
These forceless flowers like sturdy trees
  support me;
Two strengthless doves will draw me through
  the sky,
From morn till night, even where I list to
  sport me:
  Is love so light, sweet boy, and may it be
  That thou shouldst think it heavy unto thee?

'Is thine own heart to thine own face affected?
Can thy right hand seize love upon thy left?
Then woo thyself, be of thyself rejected,
Steal thine own freedom and complain on theft.
  Narcissus so himself himself forsook,
  And died to kiss his shadow in the brook.

'Torches are made to light, jewels to wear,
Dainties to taste, fresh beauty for the use,
Herbs for their smell, and sappy plants to bear:
Things growing to themselves are growth's abuse:
  Seeds spring from seeds and beauty
    breedeth beauty;
  Thou wast begot; to get it is thy duty.

'Upon the earth's increase why shouldst
  thou feed,
Unless the earth with thy increase be fed?
By law of nature thou art bound to breed,

That thine may live when thou thyself art dead;
  And so, in spite of death, thou dost survive,
  In that thy likeness still is left alive.'

By this the love-sick queen began to sweat,
For where they lay the shadow had forsook them,
And Titan, tired in the mid-day heat,
With burning eye did hotly overlook them;
  Wishing Adonis had his team to guide,
  So he were like him and by Venus' side.

And now Adonis, with a lazy spright,
And with a heavy, dark, disliking eye,
His louring brows o'erwhelming his fair sight,
Like misty vapours when they blot the sky,
  Souring his cheeks cries, 'Fie, no more of love!
  The sun doth burn my face: I must remove.'

'Ay me,' quoth Venus, 'young, and so unkind?
What bare excuses makest thou to be gone!
I'll sigh celestial breath, whose gentle wind
Shall cool the heat of this descending sun:
  I'll make a shadow for thee of my hairs;
  If they burn too, I'll quench them with
    my tears.

'The sun that shines from heaven shines
  but warm,
And, lo, I lie between that sun and thee:
The heat I have from thence doth little harm,
Thine eye darts forth the fire that burneth me;
  And were I not immortal, life were done
  Between this heavenly and earthly sun.

'Art thou obdurate, flinty, hard as steel,
Nay, more than flint, for stone at rain relenteth?
Art thou a woman's son, and canst not feel
What 'tis to love? how want of love tormenteth?
  O, had thy mother borne so hard a mind,
  She had not brought forth thee, but
    died unkind.

'What am I, that thou shouldst contemn me this?
Or what great danger dwells upon my suit?
What were thy lips the worse for one poor kiss?
Speak, fair; but speak fair words, or else be mute:
  Give me one kiss, I'll give it thee again,
  And one for interest, if thou wilt have twain.

'Fie, lifeless picture, cold and senseless stone,
Well-painted idol, image dun and dead,
Statue contenting but the eye alone,
Thing like a man, but of no woman bred!

Thou art no man, though of a
  man's complexion,
For men will kiss even by their own direction.'

This said, impatience chokes her
  pleading tongue,
And swelling passion doth provoke a pause;
Red cheeks and fiery eyes blaze forth he wrong;
Being judge in love, she cannot right her cause:
  And now she weeps, and now she fain
    would speak,
  And now her sobs do her intendments break.

Sometimes she shakes her head and then
  his hand,
Now gazeth she on him, now on the ground;
Sometimes her arms infold him like a band:
She would, he will not in her arms be bound;
  And when from thence he struggles to
    be gone,
  She locks her lily fingers one in one.

'Fondling,' she saith, 'since I have hemm'd
  thee here
Within the circuit of this ivory pale,
I'll be a park, and thou shalt be my deer;
Feed where thou wilt, on mountain or in dale:
  Graze on my lips; and if those hills be dry,
  Stray lower, where the pleasant fountains lie.

'Within this limit is relief enough,
Sweet bottom-grass and high delightful plain,
Round rising hillocks, brakes obscure and rough,
To shelter thee from tempest and from rain
  Then be my deer, since I am such a park;
  No dog shall rouse thee, though a
    thousand bark.'

At this Adonis smiles as in disdain,
That in each cheek appears a pretty dimple:
Love made those hollows, if himself were slain,
He might be buried in a tomb so simple;
  Foreknowing well, if there he came to lie,
  Why, there Love lived and there he could
    not die.

These lovely caves, these round enchanting pits,
Open'd their mouths to swallow Venus' liking.
Being mad before, how doth she now for wits?
Struck dead at first, what needs a
  second striking?
  Poor queen of love, in thine own law forlorn,
  To love a cheek that smiles at thee in scorn!

Now which way shall she turn? what shall she say?
Her words are done, her woes are
  more increasing;
The time is spent, her object will away,
And from her twining arms doth urge releasing.
  'Pity,' she cries, 'some favour, some remorse!'
  Away he springs and hasteth to his horse.

But, lo, from forth a copse that neighbours by,
A breeding jennet, lusty, young and proud,
Adonis' trampling courser doth espy,
And forth she rushes, snorts and neighs aloud:
  The strong-neck'd steed, being tied unto a tree,
  Breaketh his rein, and to her straight goes he.

Imperiously he leaps, he neighs, he bounds,
And now his woven girths he breaks asunder;
The bearing earth with his hard hoof he wounds,
Whose hollow womb resounds like
  heaven's thunder;
  The iron bit he crusheth 'tween his teeth,
  Controlling what he was controlled with.

His ears up-prick'd; his braided hanging mane
Upon his compass'd crest now stand on end;
His nostrils drink the air, and forth again,
As from a furnace, vapours doth he send:
  His eye, which scornfully glisters like fire,
  Shows his hot courage and his high desire.

Sometime he trots, as if he told the steps,
With gentle majesty and modest pride;
Anon he rears upright, curvets and leaps,
As who should say, 'Lo, thus my strength is tried,
  And this I do to captivate the eye
  Of the fair breeder that is standing by.'

What recketh he his rider's angry stir,
His flattering 'Holla,' or his 'Stand, I say'?
What cares he now for curb or pricking spur?
For rich caparisons or trapping gay?
  He sees his love, and nothing else he sees,
  For nothing else with his proud sight agrees.

Look, when a painter would surpass the life,
In limning out a well-proportion'd steed,
His art with nature's workmanship at strife,
As if the dead the living should exceed;
  So did this horse excel a common one
  In shape, in courage, colour, pace and bone.

Round-hoof'd, short-jointed, fetlocks shag
  and long,

Broad breast, full eye, small head and nostril wide,
High crest, short ears, straight legs and
　　passing strong,
Thin mane, thick tail, broad buttock, tender hide:
　Look, what a horse should have he did not lack,
　Save a proud rider on so proud a back.

Sometime he scuds far off and there he stares;
Anon he starts at stirring of a feather;
To bid the wind a base he now prepares,
And whether he run or fly they know not whether;
　For through his mane and tail the high
　　wind sings,
　Fanning the hairs, who wave like
　　feather'd wings.

He looks upon his love and neighs unto her;
She answers him as if she knew his mind:
Being proud, as females are, to see him woo her,
She puts on outward strangeness, seems unkind,
　Spurns at his love and scorns the heat he feels,
　Beating his kind embracements with her heels.

Then, like a melancholy malcontent,
He veils his tail that, like a falling plume,
Cool shadow to his melting buttock lent:
He stamps and bites the poor flies in his fume.
　His love, perceiving how he is enraged,
　Grew kinder, and his fury was assuaged.

His testy master goeth about to take him;
When, lo, the unback'd breeder, full of fear,
Jealous of catching, swiftly doth forsake him,
With her the horse, and left Adonis there:
　As they were mad, unto the wood they hie them,
　Out-stripping crows that strive to over-fly them.

All swoln with chafing, down Adonis sits,
Banning his boisterous and unruly beast:
And now the happy season once more fits,
That love-sick Love by pleading may be blest;
　For lovers say, the heart hath treble wrong
　When it is barr'd the aidance of the tongue.

An oven that is stopp'd, or river stay'd,
Burneth more hotly, swelleth with more rage:
So of concealed sorrow may be said;
Free vent of words love's fire doth assuage;
　But when the heart's attorney once is mute,
　The client breaks, as desperate in his suit.

He sees her coming, and begins to glow,
Even as a dying coal revives with wind,

And with his bonnet hides his angry brow;
Looks on the dull earth with disturbed mind,
　Taking no notice that she is so nigh,
　For all askance he holds her in his eye.

O, what a sight it was, wistly to view
How she came stealing to the wayward boy!
To note the fighting conflict of her hue,
How white and red each other did destroy!
　But now her cheek was pale, and by and by
　It flash'd forth fire, as lightning from the sky.

Now was she just before him as he sat,
And like a lowly lover down she kneels;
With one fair hand she heaveth up his hat,
Her other tender hand his fair cheek feels:
　His tenderer cheek receives her soft
　　hand's print,
　As apt as new-fall'n snow takes any dint.

O, what a war of looks was then between them!
Her eyes petitioners to his eyes suing;
His eyes saw her eyes as they had not seen them;
Her eyes woo'd still, his eyes disdain'd
　　the wooing:
　And all this dumb play had his acts made plain
　With tears, which, chorus-like, her eyes
　　did rain.

Full gently now she takes him by the hand,
A lily prison'd in a gaol of snow,
Or ivory in an alabaster band;
So white a friend engirts so white a foe:
　This beauteous combat, wilful and unwilling,
　Show'd like two silver doves that sit a-billing.

Once more the engine of her thoughts began:
'O fairest mover on this mortal round,
Would thou wert as I am, and I a man,
My heart all whole as thine, thy heart my wound;
　For one sweet look thy help I would
　　assure thee,
　Though nothing but my body's bane would
　　cure thee!'

'Give me my hand,' saith he, 'why dost thou
　feel it?'
'Give me my heart,' saith she, 'and thou shalt
　have it:
O, give it me, lest thy hard heart do steel it,
And being steel'd, soft sighs can never grave it:
　Then love's deep groans I never shall regard,
　Because Adonis' heart hath made mine hard.'

'For shame,' he cries, 'let go, and let me go;
My day's delight is past, my horse is gone,
And 'tis your fault I am bereft him so:
I pray you hence, and leave me here alone;
    For all my mind, my thought, my busy care,
    Is how to get my palfrey from the mare.'

Thus she replies: 'Thy palfrey, as he should,
Welcomes the warm approach of sweet desire:
Affection is a coal that must be cool'd;
Else, suffer'd, it will set the heart on fire:
    The sea hath bounds, but deep desire
        hath none;
    Therefore no marvel though thy horse
        be gone.

'How like a jade he stood, tied to the tree,
Servilely master'd with a leathern rein!
But when he saw his love, his youth's fair fee,
He held such petty bondage in disdain;
    Throwing the base thong from his bending crest,
    Enfranchising his mouth, his back, his breast.

'Who sees his true-love in her naked bed,
Teaching the sheets a whiter hue than white,
But, when his glutton eye so full hath fed,
His other agents aim at like delight?
    Who is so faint, that dare not be so bold
    To touch the fire, the weather being cold?

'Let me excuse thy courser, gentle boy;
And learn of him, I heartily beseech thee,
To take advantage on presented joy;
Though I were dumb, yet his proceedings
        teach thee;
    O, learn to love; the lesson is but plain,
    And once made perfect, never lost again.'

'I know not love,' quoth he, 'nor will not
        know it,
Unless it be a boar, and then I chase it;
'Tis much to borrow, and I will not owe it;
My love to love is love but to disgrace it;
    For I have heard it is a life in death,
    That laughs and weeps, and all but with
        a breath.

'Who wears a garment shapeless and unfinish'd?
Who plucks the bud before one leaf put forth?
If springing things be any jot diminish'd,
They wither in their prime, prove nothing worth:
    The colt that's back'd and burden'd being young
    Loseth his pride and never waxeth strong.

'You hurt my hand with wringing; let us part,
And leave this idle theme, this bootless chat:
Remove your siege from my unyielding heart;
To love's alarms it will not ope the gate:
    Dismiss your vows, your feigned tears,
        your flattery;
    For where a heart is hard they make no battery.'

'What! canst thou talk?' quoth she, 'hast thou
        a tongue?
O, would thou hadst not, or I had no hearing!
Thy mermaid's voice hath done me double wrong;
I had my load before, now press'd with bearing:
    Melodious discord, heavenly tune
        harsh sounding,
    Ear's deep-sweet music, and heart's deep-
        sore wounding.

'Had I no eyes but ears, my ears would love
That inward beauty and invisible;
Or were I deaf, thy outward parts would move
Each part in me that were but sensible:
    Though neither eyes nor ears, to hear nor see,
    Yet should I be in love by touching thee.

'Say, that the sense of feeling were bereft me,
And that I could not see, nor hear, nor touch,
And nothing but the very smell were left me,
Yet would my love to thee be still as much;
    For from the stillitory of thy face excelling
    Comes breath perfumed that breedeth love
        by smelling.

'But, O, what banquet wert thou to the taste,
Being nurse and feeder of the other four!
Would they not wish the feast might ever last,
And bid Suspicion double-lock the door,
    Lest Jealousy, that sour unwelcome guest,
    Should, by his stealing in, disturb the feast?'

Once more the ruby-colour'd portal open'd,
Which to his speech did honey passage yield;
Like a red morn, that ever yet betoken'd
Wreck to the seaman, tempest to the field,
    Sorrow to shepherds, woe unto the birds,
    Gusts and foul flaws to herdmen and to herds.

This ill presage advisedly she marketh:
Even as the wind is hush'd before it raineth,
Or as the wolf doth grin before he barketh,
Or as the berry breaks before it staineth,
    Or like the deadly bullet of a gun,
    His meaning struck her ere his words begun.

And at his look she flatly falleth down,
For looks kill love and love by looks reviveth;
A smile recures the wounding of a frown;
But blessed bankrupt, that by love so thriveth!
 The silly boy, believing she is dead,
  Claps her pale cheek, till clapping makes it red;

And all amazed brake off his late intent,
For sharply he did think to reprehend her,
Which cunning love did wittily prevent:
Fair fall the wit that can so well defend her!
 For on the grass she lies as she were slain,
  Till his breath breatheth life in her again.

He wrings her nose, he strikes her on the cheeks,
He bends her fingers, holds her pulses hard,
He chafes her lips; a thousand ways he seeks
To mend the hurt that his unkindness marr'd:
 He kisses her; and she, by her good will,
  Will never rise, so he will kiss her still.

The night of sorrow now is turn'd to day:
Her two blue windows faintly she up-heaveth,
Like the fair sun, when in his fresh array
He cheers the morn and all the earth relieveth;
 And as the bright sun glorifies the sky,
  So is her face illumined with her eye;

Whose beams upon his hairless face are fix'd,
As if from thence they borrow'd all their shine.
Were never four such lamps together mix'd,
Had not his clouded with his brow's repine;
 But hers, which through the crystal tears
  gave light,
  Shone like the moon in water seen by night.

'O, where am I?' quoth she, 'in earth or heaven,
Or in the ocean drench'd, or in the fire?
What hour is this? or morn or weary even?
Do I delight to die, or life desire?
 But now I lived, and life was death's annoy;
  But now I died, and death was lively joy.

'O, thou didst kill me: kill me once again:
Thy eyes' shrewd tutor, that hard heart of thine,
Hath taught them scornful tricks and such disdain
That they have murder'd this poor heart of mine;
 And these mine eyes, true leaders to
  their queen,
  But for thy piteous lips no more had seen.

'Long may they kiss each other, for this cure!
O, never let their crimson liveries wear!

And as they last, their verdure still endure,
To drive infection from the dangerous year!
 That the star-gazers, having writ on death,
  May say, the plague is banish'd by thy breath.

'Pure lips, sweet seals in my soft lips imprinted,
What bargains may I make, still to be sealing?
To sell myself I can be well contented,
So thou wilt buy and pay and use good dealing;
 Which purchase if thou make, for fear of slips
  Set thy seal-manual on my wax-red lips.

'A thousand kisses buys my heart from me;
And pay them at thy leisure, one by one.
What is ten hundred touches unto thee?
Are they not quickly told and quickly gone?
 Say, for non-payment that the debt
  should double,
  Is twenty hundred kisses such a trouble?

'Fair queen,' quoth he, 'if any love you owe me,
Measure my strangeness with my unripe years:
Before I know myself, seek not to know me;
No fisher but the ungrown fry forbears:
 The mellow plum doth fall, the green sticks fast,
  Or being early pluck'd is sour to taste.

'Look, the world's comforter, with weary gait,
His day's hot task hath ended in the west;
The owl, night's herald, shrieks, "'Tis very late;"
The sheep are gone to fold, birds to their nest,
 And coal-black clouds that shadow
  heaven's light
  Do summon us to part and bid good night.

'Now let me say "Good night," and so say you;
If you will say so, you shall have a kiss.'
'Good night,' quoth she, and, ere he says 'Adieu,'
The honey fee of parting tender'd is:
 Her arms do lend his neck a sweet embrace;
  Incorporate then they seem; face grows to face.

Till, breathless, he disjoin'd, and backward drew
The heavenly moisture, that sweet coral mouth,
Whose precious taste her thirsty lips well knew,
Whereon they surfeit, yet complain on drouth:
 He with her plenty press'd, she faint with dearth
  Their lips together glued, fall to the earth.

Now quick desire hath caught the yielding prey,
And glutton-like she feeds, yet never filleth;
Her lips are conquerors, his lips obey,
Paying what ransom the insulter willeth;

Whose vulture thought doth pitch the price
  so high,
That she will draw his lips' rich treasure dry:

And having felt the sweetness of the spoil,
With blindfold fury she begins to forage;
Her face doth reek and smoke, her blood
  doth boil,
And careless lust stirs up a desperate courage,
  Planting oblivion, beating reason back,
  Forgetting shame's pure blush and
  honour's wrack.

Hot, faint, and weary, with her hard embracing,
Like a wild bird being tamed with too
  much handling,
Or as the fleet-foot roe that's tired with chasing,
Or like the froward infant still'd with dandling,
  He now obeys, and now no more resisteth,
  While she takes all she can, not all she listeth.

What wax so frozen but dissolves with tempering,
And yields at last to every light impression?
Things out of hope are compass'd oft
  with venturing,
Chiefly in love, whose leave exceeds commission:
  Affection faints not like a pale-faced coward,
  But then woos best when most his choice
  is froward.

When he did frown, O, had she then gave over,
Such nectar from his lips she had not suck'd.
Foul words and frowns must not repel a lover;
What though the rose have prickles, yet
  'tis pluck'd:
  Were beauty under twenty locks kept fast,
  Yet love breaks through and picks them all
  at last.

For pity now she can no more detain him;
The poor fool prays her that he may depart:
She is resolved no longer to restrain him;
Bids him farewell, and look well to her heart,
  The which, by Cupid's bow she doth protest,
  He carries thence incaged in his breast.

'Sweet boy,' she says, 'this night I'll waste
  in sorrow,
For my sick heart commands mine eyes to watch.
Tell me, Love's master, shall we meet to-morrow?
Say, shall we? shall we? wilt thou make the match?'
  He tells her, no; to-morrow he intends
  To hunt the boar with certain of his friends

'The boar!' quoth she; whereat a sudden pale,
Like lawn being spread upon the blushing rose,
Usurps her cheek; she trembles at his tale,
And on his neck her yoking arms she throws:
  She sinketh down, still hanging by his neck,
  He on her belly falls, she on her back.

Now is she in the very lists of love,
Her champion mounted for the hot encounter:
All is imaginary she doth prove,
He will not manage her, although he mount her;
  That worse than Tantalus' is her annoy,
  To clip Elysium and to lack her joy.

Even as poor birds, deceived with painted grapes,
Do surfeit by the eye and pine the maw,
Even so she languisheth in her mishaps,
As those poor birds that helpless berries saw.
  The warm effects which she in him
  finds missing
  She seeks to kindle with continual kissing.

But all in vain; good queen, it will not be:
She hath assay'd as much as may be proved;
Her pleading hath deserved a greater fee;
She's Love, she loves, and yet she is not loved.
  'Fie, fie,' he says, 'you crush me; let me go;
  You have no reason to withhold me so.'

'Thou hadst been gone,' quoth she, 'sweet boy,
  ere this,
But that thou told'st me thou wouldst hunt
  the boar.
O, be advised! thou know'st not what it is
With javelin's point a churlish swine to gore,
  Whose tushes never sheathed he whetteth still,
  Like to a mortal butcher bent to kill.

'On his bow-back he hath a battle set
Of bristly pikes, that ever threat his foes;
His eyes, like glow-worms, shine when he
  doth fret;
His snout digs sepulchres where'er he goes;
  Being moved, he strikes whate'er is in his way,
  And whom he strikes his cruel tushes slay.

'His brawny sides, with hairy bristles arm'd,
Are better proof than thy spear's point can enter;
His short thick neck cannot be easily harm'd;
Being ireful, on the lion he will venture:
  The thorny brambles and embracing bushes,
  As fearful of him, part, through whom
  he rushes.

'Alas, he nought esteems that face of thine,
To which Love's eyes pay tributary gazes;
Nor thy soft hands, sweet lips and crystal eyne,
Whose full perfection all the world amazes;
    But having thee at vantage, – wondrous dread! –
    Would root these beauties as he roots the mead.

'O, let him keep his loathsome cabin still;
Beauty hath nought to do with such foul fiends:
Come not within his danger by thy will;
They that thrive well take counsel of their friends.
    When thou didst name the boar, not
        to dissemble,
    I fear'd thy fortune, and my joints did tremble.

'Didst thou not mark my face? was it not white?
Saw'st thou not signs of fear lurk in mine eye?
Grew I not faint? and fell I not downright?
Within my bosom, whereon thou dost lie,
    My boding heart pants, beats, and takes no rest,
    But, like an earthquake, shakes thee on
        my breast.

'For where Love reigns, disturbing Jealousy
Doth call himself Affection's sentinel;
Gives false alarms, suggesteth mutiny,
And in a peaceful hour doth cry, "Kill, kill!"
    Distempering gentle Love in his desire,
    As air and water do abate the fire.

'This sour informer, this bate-breeding spy,
This canker that eats up Love's tender spring,
This carry-tale, dissentious Jealousy,
That sometime true news, sometime false
        doth bring,
    Knocks at my heart and whispers in mine ear
    That if I love thee, I thy death should fear:

'And more than so, presenteth to mine eye
The picture of an angry-chafing boar,
Under whose sharp fangs on his back doth lie
An image like thyself, all stain'd with gore;
    Whose blood upon the fresh flowers
        being shed
    Doth make them droop with grief and hang
        the head.

'What should I do, seeing thee so indeed,
That tremble at the imagination?
The thought of it doth make my faint heart bleed,
And fear doth teach it divination:
    I prophesy thy death, my living sorrow,
    If thou encounter with the boar to-morrow.

'But if thou needs wilt hunt, be ruled by me;
Uncouple at the timorous flying hare,
Or at the fox which lives by subtlety,
Or at the roe which no encounter dare:
    Pursue these fearful creatures o'er the downs,
    And on thy well-breath'd horse keep with
        thy hounds.

'And when thou hast on foot the purblind hare,
Mark the poor wretch, to overshoot his troubles
How he outruns the wind and with what care
He cranks and crosses with a thousand doubles:
    The many musets through the which he goes
    Are like a labyrinth to amaze his foes.

'Sometime he runs among a flock of sheep,
To make the cunning hounds mistake their smell,
And sometime where earth-delving conies keep,
To stop the loud pursuers in their yell,
    And sometime sorteth with a herd of deer:
    Danger deviseth shifts; wit waits on fear:

'For there his smell with others being mingled,
The hot scent-snuffing hounds are driven
        to doubt,
Ceasing their clamorous cry till they have singled
With much ado the cold fault cleanly out;
    Then do they spend their mouths: Echo replies,
    As if another chase were in the skies.

'By this, poor Wat, far off upon a hill,
Stands on his hinder legs with listening ear,
To harken if his foes pursue him still:
Anon their loud alarums he doth hear;
    And now his grief may be compared well
    To one sore sick that hears the passing-bell.

'Then shalt thou see the dew-bedabbled wretch
Turn, and return, indenting with the way;
Each envious briar his weary legs doth scratch,
Each shadow makes him stop, each murmur stay:
    For misery is trodden on by many,
    And being low never relieved by any.

'Lie quietly, and hear a little more;
Nay, do not struggle, for thou shalt not rise:
To make thee hate the hunting of the boar,
Unlike myself thou hear'st me moralise,
    Applying this to that, and so to so;
    For love can comment upon every woe.

'Where did I leave?' 'No matter where,' quoth he,
'Leave me, and then the story aptly ends:

The night is spent.' 'Why, what of that?' quoth she.
'I am,' quoth he, 'expected of my friends;
  And now 'tis dark, and going I shall fall.'
  'In night,' quoth she, 'desire sees best of all

'But if thou fall, O, then imagine this,
The earth, in love with thee, thy footing trips,
And all is but to rob thee of a kiss.
Rich preys make true men thieves; so do thy lips
  Make modest Dian cloudy and forlorn,
  Lest she should steal a kiss and die forsworn.

'Now of this dark night I perceive the reason:
Cynthia for shame obscures her silver shine,
Till forging Nature be condemn'd of treason,
For stealing moulds from heaven that were divine;
  Wherein she framed thee in high
    heaven's despite,
  To shame the sun by day and her by night.

'And therefore hath she bribed the Destinies
To cross the curious workmanship of nature,
To mingle beauty with infirmities,
And pure perfection with impure defeature,
  Making it subject to the tyranny
  Of mad mischances and much misery;

'As burning fevers, agues pale and faint,
Life-poisoning pestilence and frenzies wood,
The marrow-eating sickness, whose attaint
Disorder breeds by heating of the blood:
  Surfeits, imposthumes, grief, and
    damn'd despair,
  Swear Nature's death for framing thee so fair.

'And not the least of all these maladies
But in one minute's fight brings beauty under:
Both favour, savour, hue and qualities,
Whereat the impartial gazer late did wonder,
  Are on the sudden wasted, thaw'd and done,
  As mountain-snow melts with the mid-day sun.

'Therefore, despite of fruitless chastity,
Love-lacking vestals and self-loving nuns,
That on the earth would breed a scarcity
And barren dearth of daughters and of sons,
  Be prodigal: the lamp that burns by night
  Dries up his oil to lend the world his light.

'What is thy body but a swallowing grave,
Seeming to bury that posterity
Which by the rights of time thou needs must have,
If thou destroy them not in dark obscurity?

If so, the world will hold thee in disdain,
  Sith in thy pride so fair a hope is slain.

'So in thyself thyself art made away;
A mischief worse than civil home-bred strife,
Or theirs whose desperate hands themselves
  do slay,
Or butcher-sire that reaves his son of life.
  Foul-cankering rust the hidden treasure frets,
  But gold that's put to use more gold begets.'

'Nay, then,' quoth Adon, 'you will fall again
Into your idle over-handled theme:
The kiss I gave you is bestow'd in vain,
And all in vain you strive against the stream;
  For, by this black-faced night, desire's foul nurse,
  Your treatise makes me like you worse
    and worse.

'If love have lent you twenty thousand tongues,
And every tongue more moving than your own,
Bewitching like the wanton mermaid's songs,
Yet from mine ear the tempting tune is blown
  For know, my heart stands armed in mine ear,
  And will not let a false sound enter there;

'Lest the deceiving harmony should run
Into the quiet closure of my breast;
And then my little heart were quite undone,
In his bedchamber to be barr'd of rest.
  No, lady, no; my heart longs not to groan,
  But soundly sleeps, while now it sleeps alone.

'What have you urged that I cannot reprove?
The path is smooth that leadeth on to danger:
I hate not love, but your device in love,
That lends embracements unto every stranger.
  You do it for increase: O strange excuse,
  When reason is the bawd to lust's abuse!

'Call it not love, for Love to heaven is fled,
Since sweating Lust on earth usurp'd his name;
Under whose simple semblance he hath fed
Upon fresh beauty, blotting it with blame;
  Which the hot tyrant stains and soon bereaves,
  As caterpillars do the tender leaves.

'Love comforteth like sunshine after rain,
But Lust's effect is tempest after sun;
Love's gentle spring doth always fresh remain,
Lust's winter comes ere summer half be done;
  Love surfeits not, Lust like a glutton dies;
  Love is all truth, Lust full of forged lies.

'More I could tell, but more I dare not say;
The text is old, the orator too green.
Therefore, in sadness, now I will away;
My face is full of shame, my heart of teen:
　Mine ears, that to your wanton talk attended,
　Do burn themselves for having so offended.'

With this, he breaketh from the sweet embrace,
Of those fair arms which bound him to her breast,
And homeward through the dark laund
　runs apace;
Leaves Love upon her back deeply distress'd.
　Look, how a bright star shooteth from the sky,
　So glides he in the night from Venus' eye.

Which after him she darts, as one on shore
Gazing upon a late-embarked friend,
Till the wild waves will have him seen no more,
Whose ridges with the meeting clouds contend:
　So did the merciless and pitchy night
　Fold in the object that did feed her sight.

Whereat amazed, as one that unaware
Hath dropp'd a precious jewel in the flood,
Or stonish'd as night-wanderers often are,
Their light blown out in some mistrustful wood,
　Even so confounded in the dark she lay,
　Having lost the fair discovery of her way.

And now she beats her heart, whereat it groans,
That all the neighbour caves, as seeming troubled,
Make verbal repetition of her moans;
Passion on passion deeply is redoubled:
　'Ay me!' she cries, and twenty times, 'Woe, woe!'
　And twenty echoes twenty times cry so.

She marking them begins a wailing note
And sings extemporally a woeful ditty;
How love makes young men thrall and old
　men dote;
How love is wise in folly, foolish-witty:
　Her heavy anthem still concludes in woe,
　And still the choir of echoes answer so.

Her song was tedious and outwore the night,
For lovers' hours are long, though seeming short:
If pleased themselves, others, they think, delight
In such-like circumstance, with suchlike sport:
　Their copious stories oftentimes begun
　End without audience and are never done.

For who hath she to spend the night withal
But idle sounds resembling parasites,

Like shrill-tongued tapsters answering every call,
Soothing the humour of fantastic wits?
　She says, ''Tis so:' they answer all, ''Tis so;'
　And would say after her, if she said 'No.'

Lo, here the gentle lark, weary of rest,
From his moist cabinet mounts up on high,
And wakes the morning, from whose silver breast
The sun ariseth in his majesty;
　Who doth the world so gloriously behold
　That cedar-tops and hills seem burnish'd gold.

Venus salutes him with this fair good-morrow:
'O thou clear god, and patron of all light,
From whom each lamp and shining star
　doth borrow
The beauteous influence that makes him bright,
　There lives a son that suck'd an earthly mother,
　May lend thee light, as thou dost lend to other.'

This said, she hasteth to a myrtle grove,
Musing the morning is so much o'erworn,
And yet she hears no tidings of her love:
She hearkens for his hounds and for his horn:
　Anon she hears them chant it lustily,
　And all in haste she coasteth to the cry.

And as she runs, the bushes in the way
Some catch her by the neck, some kiss her face,
Some twine about her thigh to make her stay:
She wildly breaketh from their strict embrace,
　Like a milch doe, whose swelling dugs do ache,
　Hasting to feed her fawn hid in some brake.

By this, she hears the hounds are at a bay;
Whereat she starts, like one that spies an adder
Wreathed up in fatal folds just in his way,
The fear whereof doth make him shake
　and shudder;
　Even so the timorous yelping of the hounds
　Appals her senses and her spirit confounds.

For now she knows it is no gentle chase,
But the blunt boar, rough bear, or lion proud,
Because the cry remaineth in one place,
Where fearfully the dogs exclaim aloud:
　Finding their enemy to be so curst,
　They all strain courtesy who shall cope him first.

This dismal cry rings sadly in her ear,
Through which it enters to surprise her heart;
Who, overcome by doubt and bloodless fear,
With cold-pale weakness numbs each feeling part:

Like soldiers, when their captain once
   doth yield,
They basely fly and dare not stay the field.

Thus stands she in a trembling ecstasy;
Till, cheering up her senses all dismay'd,
She tells them 'tis a causeless fantasy,
And childish error, that they are afraid;
   Bids them leave quaking, bids them fear no
     more: –
   And with that word she spied the hunted boar,

Whose frothy mouth, bepainted all with red,
Like milk and blood being mingled both together,
A second fear through all her sinews spread,
Which madly hurries her she knows not whither:
   This way runs, and now she will no further,
   But back retires to rate the boar for murther.

A thousand spleens bear her a thousand ways;
She treads the path that she untreads again;
Her more than haste is mated with delays,
Like the proceedings of a drunken brain,
   Full of respects, yet nought at all respecting;
   In hand with all things, nought at all effecting.

Here kennell'd in a brake she finds a hound,
And asks the weary caitiff for his master,
And there another licking of his wound,
'Gainst venom'd sores the only sovereign plaster;
   And here she meets another sadly scowling,
   To whom she speaks, and he replies
     with howling.

When he hath ceased his ill-resounding noise,
Another flap-mouth'd mourner, black and grim,
Against the welkin volleys out his voice;
Another and another answer him,
   Clapping their proud tails to the ground below,
   Shaking their scratch'd ears, bleeding as they go.

Look, how the world's poor people are amazed
At apparitions, signs and prodigies,
Whereon with fearful eyes they long have gazed,
Infusing them with dreadful prophecies;
   So she at these sad signs draws up her breath
   And sighing it again, exclaims on Death.

'Hard-favour'd tyrant, ugly, meagre, lean,
Hateful divorce of love,' – thus chides she
   Death, –
'Grim-grinning ghost, earth's worm, what dost
   thou mean

To stifle beauty and to steal his breath,
   Who when he lived, his breath and beauty set
   Gloss on the rose, smell to the violet?

'If he be dead, – O no, it cannot be,
Seeing his beauty, thou shouldst strike at it: –
O yes, it may; thou hast no eyes to see,
But hatefully at random dost thou hit.
   Thy mark is feeble age, but thy false dart
   Mistakes that aim and cleaves an infant's heart.

'Hadst thou but bid beware, then he had spoke,
And, hearing him, thy power had lost his power.
The Destinies will curse thee for this stroke;
They bid thee crop a weed, thou pluck'st a flower:
   Love's golden arrow at him should have fled,
   And not Death's ebon dart, to strike him dead.

'Dost thou drink tears, that thou provokest
   such weeping?
What may a heavy groan advantage thee?
Why hast thou cast into eternal sleeping
Those eyes that taught all other eyes to see?
   Now Nature cares not for thy mortal vigour,
   Since her best work is ruin'd with thy rigour.'

Here overcome, as one full of despair,
She vail'd her eyelids, who, like sluices, stopt
The crystal tide that from her two cheeks fair
In the sweet channel of her bosom dropt;
   But through the flood-gates breaks the
     silver rain,
   And with his strong course opens them again.

O, how her eyes and tears did lend and borrow!
Her eyes seen in the tears, tears in her eye;
Both crystals, where they view'd each
   other's sorrow,
Sorrow that friendly sighs sought still to dry;
   But like a stormy day, now wind, now rain,
   Sighs dry her cheeks, tears make them
     wet again.

Variable passions throng her constant woe,
As striving who should best become her grief;
All entertain'd, each passion labours so,
That every present sorrow seemeth chief,
   But none is best: then join they all together,
   Like many clouds consulting for foul weather.

By this, far off she hears some huntsman hollo;
A nurse's song ne'er pleased her babe so well:
The dire imagination she did follow

This sound of hope doth labour to expel;
  For now reviving joy bids her rejoice,
  And flatters her it is Adonis' voice.

Whereat her tears began to turn their tide,
Being prison'd in her eye like pearls in glass;
Yet sometimes falls an orient drop beside,
Which her cheek melts, as scorning it should pass,
  To wash the foul face of the sluttish ground,
  Who is but drunken when she seemeth drown'd.

O hard-believing love, how strange it seems
Not to believe, and yet too credulous!
Thy weal and woe are both of them extremes;
Despair and hope makes thee ridiculous:
  The one doth flatter thee in thoughts unlikely,
  In likely thoughts the other kills thee quickly.

Now she unweaves the web that she
    hath wrought;
Adonis lives, and Death is not to blame;
It was not she that call'd him, all-to naught:
Now she adds honours to his hateful name;
  She clepes him king of graves and grave
    for kings,
  Imperious supreme of all mortal things.

'No, no,' quoth she, 'sweet Death, I did but jest;
Yet pardon me I felt a kind of fear
When as I met the boar, that bloody beast,
Which knows no pity, but is still severe;
  Then, gentle shadow, – truth I must confess, –
  I rail'd on thee, fearing my love's decease.

''Tis not my fault: the boar provoked my tongue;
Be wreak'd on him, invisible commander;
'Tis he, foul creature, that hath done thee wrong;
I did but act, he's author of thy slander:
  Grief hath two tongues, and never woman yet
  Could rule them both without ten women's wit.'

Thus hoping that Adonis is alive,
Her rash suspect she doth extenuate;
And that his beauty may the better thrive,
With Death she humbly doth insinuate;
  Tells him of trophies, statues, tombs,
    and stories
  His victories, his triumphs and his glories.

'O Jove,' quoth she, 'how much a fool was I
To be of such a weak and silly mind
To wail his death who lives and must not die
Till mutual overthrow of mortal kind!

For he being dead, with him is beauty slain,
And, beauty dead, black chaos comes again.

'Fie, fie, fond love, thou art so full of fear
As one with treasure laden, hemm'd with thieves;
Trifles, unwitnessed with eye or ear,
Thy coward heart with false bethinking grieves.'
  Even at this word she hears a merry horn,
  Whereat she leaps that was but late forlorn.

As falcon to the lure, away she flies;
The grass stoops not, she treads on it so light;
And in her haste unfortunately spies
The foul boar's conquest on her fair delight;
  Which seen, her eyes, as murder'd with the view,
  Like stars ashamed of day, themselves withdrew;

Or, as the snail, whose tender horns being hit,
Shrinks backward in his shelly cave with pain,
And there, all smother'd up, in shade doth sit,
Long after fearing to creep forth again;
  So, at his bloody view, her eyes are fled
  Into the deep dark cabins of her head:

Where they resign their office and their light
To the disposing of her troubled brain;
Who bids them still consort with ugly night,
And never wound the heart with looks again;
  Who like a king perplexed in his throne,
  By their suggestion gives a deadly groan,

Whereat each tributary subject quakes;
As when the wind, imprison'd in the ground,
Struggling for passage, earth's foundation shakes,
Which with cold terror doth men's
    minds confound.
  This mutiny each part doth so surprise
  That from their dark beds once more leap
    her eyes;

And, being open'd, threw unwilling light
Upon the wide wound that the boar had trench'd
In his soft flank; whose wonted lily white
With purple tears, that his wound wept,
    was drench'd:
  No flower was nigh, no grass, herb, leaf,
    or weed,
  But stole his blood and seem'd with him
    to bleed.

This solemn sympathy poor Venus noteth;
Over one shoulder doth she hang her head;
Dumbly she passions, franticly she doteth;

She thinks he could not die, he is not dead:
  Her voice is stopt, her joints forget to bow;
  Her eyes are mad that they have wept til now.

Upon his hurt she looks so steadfastly,
That her sight dazzling makes the wound seem three;
And then she reprehends her mangling eye,
That makes more gashes where no breach
    should be:
  His face seems twain, each several limb
    is doubled;
  For oft the eye mistakes, the brain
    being troubled.

'My tongue cannot express my grief for one,
And yet,' quoth she, 'behold two Adons dead!
My sighs are blown away, my salt tears gone,
Mine eyes are turn'd to fire, my heart to lead:
  Heavy heart's lead, melt at mine eyes' red fire!
  So shall I die by drops of hot desire.

'Alas, poor world, what treasure hast thou lost!
What face remains alive that's worth the viewing?
Whose tongue is music now? what canst
    thou boast
Of things long since, or any thing ensuing?
  The flowers are sweet, their colours fresh
    and trim;
  But true-sweet beauty lived and died with him.

'Bonnet nor veil henceforth no creature wear!
Nor sun nor wind will ever strive to kiss you:
Having no fair to lose, you need not fear;
The sun doth scorn you and the wind doth
    hiss you:
  But when Adonis lived, sun and sharp air
  Lurk'd like two thieves, to rob him of his fair:

'And therefore would he put his bonnet on,
Under whose brim the gaudy sun would peep;
The wind would blow it off and, being gone,
Play with his locks: then would Adonis weep;
  And straight, in pity of his tender years,
  They both would strive who first should dry
    his tears.

'To see his face the lion walk'd along
Behind some hedge, because he would not
    fear him;
To recreate himself when he hath sung,
The tiger would be tame and gently hear him;
  If he had spoke, the wolf would leave his prey
  And never fright the silly lamb that day.

'When he beheld his shadow in the brook,
The fishes spread on it their golden gills;
When he was by, the birds such pleasure took,
That some would sing, some other in their bills
  Would bring him mulberries and ripe-
    red cherries;
  He fed them with his sight, they him
    with berries.

'But this foul, grim, and urchin-snouted boar,
Whose downward eye still looketh for a grave,
Ne'er saw the beauteous livery that he wore,
Witness the entertainment that he gave:
  If he did see his face, why then I know
  He thought to kiss him, and hath kill'd him so.

''Tis true, 'tis true; thus was Adonis slain:
He ran upon the boar with his sharp spear,
Who did not whet his teeth at him again,
But by a kiss thought to persuade him there;
  And nuzzling in his flank, the loving swine
  Sheathed unaware the tusk in his soft groin.

'Had I been tooth'd like him, I must confess,
With kissing him I should have kill'd him first;
But he is dead, and never did he bless
My youth with his; the more am I accurst.'
  With this, she falleth in the place she stood,
  And stains her face with his congealed blood.

She looks upon his lips, and they are pale;
She takes him by the hand, and that is cold;
She whispers in his ears a heavy tale,
As if they heard the woeful words she told;
  She lifts the coffer-lids that close his eyes,
  Where, lo, two lamps, burnt out, in
    darkness lies;

Two glasses, where herself herself beheld
A thousand times, and now no more reflect;
Their virtue lost, wherein they late excell'd,
And every beauty robb'd of his effect:
  'Wonder of time,' quoth she, 'this is my spite,
  That, thou being dead, the day should yet
    be light.

'Since thou art dead, lo, here I prophesy:
Sorrow on love hereafter shall attend:
It shall be waited on with jealousy,
Find sweet beginning, but unsavoury end,
  Ne'er settled equally, but high or low,
  That all love's pleasure shall not match
    his woe.

'It shall be fickle, false and full of fraud,
Bud and be blasted in a breathing-while;
The bottom poison, and the top o'erstraw'd
With sweets that shall the truest sight beguile:
  The strongest body shall it make most weak,
  Strike the wise dumb and teach the fool
    to speak.

'It shall be sparing and too full of riot,
Teaching decrepit age to tread the measures;
The staring ruffian shall it keep in quiet,
Pluck down the rich, enrich the poor
  with treasures;
  It shall be raging-mad and silly-mild,
  Make the young old, the old become a child.

'It shall suspect where is no cause of fear;
It shall not fear where it should most mistrust;
It shall be merciful and too severe,
And most deceiving when it seems most just;
  Perverse it shall be where it shows
    most toward,
  Put fear to valour, courage to the coward.

'It shall be cause of war and dire events,
And set dissension 'twixt the son and sire;
Subject and servile to all discontents,
As dry combustious matter is to fire:
  Sith in his prime Death doth my love destroy,
  They that love best their loves shall not enjoy.'

By this, the boy that by her side lay kill'd
Was melted like a vapour from her sight,
And in his blood that on the ground lay spill'd,
A purple flower sprung up, chequer'd
  with white,
  Resembling well his pale cheeks and the blood
  Which in round drops upon their
    whiteness stood.

She bows her head, the new-sprung flower
  to smell,
Comparing it to her Adonis' breath,
And says, within her bosom it shall dwell,
Since he himself is reft from her by death:
  She crops the stalk, and in the breach appears
  Green dropping sap, which she compares
    to tears.

'Poor flower,' quoth she, 'this was thy
    father's guise –
Sweet issue of a more sweet-smelling sire –
For every little grief to wet his eyes:

To grow unto himself was his desire,
  And so 'tis thine; but know, it is as good
  To wither in my breast as in his blood.

'Here was thy father's bed, here in my breast;
Thou art the next of blood, and 'tis thy right:
Lo, in this hollow cradle take thy rest,
My throbbing heart shall rock thee day and night:
  There shall not be one minute in an hour
  Wherein I will not kiss my sweet love's flower.'

Thus weary of the world, away she hies,
And yokes her silver doves; by whose swift aid
Their mistress mounted through the empty skies
In her light chariot quickly is convey'd;
  Holding their course to Paphos, where
    their queen
  Means to immure herself and not be seen.

The End

1601

The Phoenix
and the Turtle

Let the bird of loudest lay,
On the sole Arabian tree,
Herald sad and trumpet be,
To whose sound chaste wings obey.

But thou, shrieking harbinger,
Foul pre-currer of the fiend,
Augur of the fever's end,
To this troop come thou not near.

From this session interdict
Every fowl of tyrant wing,
Save the eagle, feather'd king:
Keep the obsequy so strict.

Let the priest in surplice white,
That defunctive music can,
Be the death-divining swan,
Lest the requiem lack his right.

And thou, treble-dated crow,
That thy sable gender mak'st
With the breath thou giv'st and tak'st,
'Mongst our mourners shalt thou go.

Here the anthem doth commence:
Love and constancy is dead;
Phoenix and the turtle fled
In a mutual flame from hence.

So they lov'd, as love in twain
Had the essence but in one;
Two distincts, division none:
Number there in love was slain.

Hearts remote, yet not asunder;
Distance, and no space was seen
'Twixt the turtle and his queen;
But in them it were a wonder.

So between them love did shine,
That the turtle saw his right
Flaming in the phoenix' sight:
Either was the other's mine.

Property was thus appall'd,
That the self was not the same;
Single nature's double name
Neither two nor one was call'd.

Reason, in itself confounded,
Saw division grow together;
To themselves yet either-neither,
Simple were so well compounded

That it cried how true a twain
Seemeth this concordant one!
Love hath reason, reason none
If what parts can so remain.

Whereupon it made this threne
To the phoenix and the dove,
Co-supreme and stars of love;
As chorus to their tragic scene.

THRENOS

Beauty, truth, and rarity.
Grace in all simplicity,
Here enclos'd in cinders lie.

Death is now the phoenix' nest;
And the turtle's loyal breast
To eternity doth rest,

Leaving no posterity:-
'Twas not their infirmity,
It was married chastity.

Truth may seem, but cannot be:
Beauty brag, but 'tis not she;
Truth and beauty buried be.

To this urn let those repair
That are either true or fair;
For these dead birds sigh a prayer.

The End

Biographies

William Shakespeare

Possibly the most famous writer in the world, Willliam Shakespeare (1564–1616) remains one of the most quoted and influential English authors of all time. His genius and his impact on both culture and language cannot be underestimated.

Born in Stratford-upon-Avon, England, to John Shakespeare and Mary Arden, William's date of birth is celebrated on 23 April, St George's Day – coincidentally the same date as his death in 1616. The third of eight children, Shakespeare attended the King's New School in Stratford and probably studied the Greek and Latin classics, the influence of which can be seen in his plays.

Little factual evidence exists about his early life apart from his marriage to Anne Hathaway, then 26 years old, in 1582 when he was just 18. Anne gave birth to their first child, Susanna, just six months later. Twins Judith and Hamnet followed in 1585, but Shakespeare's only son died in 1596 of unknown causes.

Around this time, Shakespeare began to establish himself in London as a playwright and actor. He is thought to have written 39 plays, although theories abound on whether he authored them all.

Shakespeare's plays were likely influenced by fashions in theatre and important historical or political events of the day. They can be largely split into the four genres of histories, including *Henry VI* and *Richard III*, comedies such as *A Midsummer Night's Dream* and *Twelfth Night*, tragedies including *Hamlet*, *Macbeth* and *Romeo and Juliet*, and tragicomedies or romances, such as *The Tempest* and *The Winter's Tale*, a list which gives just a sample of the range and scope of his genius.

No matter the genre, Shakespeare used his masterful, authentic and often flawed characters to explore universal themes such as love, revenge, ambition and morality, which remain just as relevant to modern audiences as they were when first performed.

In addition to his plays, Shakespeare wrote 154 sonnets and three narrative poems. His sonnets often feature a 'dark lady' or 'fair youth', sparking rumours on Shakespeare's sexuality and how autobiographical his poems may have been. As Shakespeare was skilled at creating drama, he may have enjoyed toying with his audience in his poems just as much as he did in his plays and it is likely that we will never know the true inspiration behind his poignant sonnets.

Shakespeare is thought to have invented words by combining parts of existing words or using parts of speech in different ways, such as using nouns as verbs. Examples of words attributed to him include 'traditional', 'fashionable' and 'lonely'. A number of well-known British expressions were coined by Shakespeare including 'cruel to be kind', 'green-eyed monster' and 'eaten me out of house and home'. Who could fail to enjoy such biting insults as 'I do desire we may be better strangers' or 'I'll beat thee, but I should infect my hands'? His publications also helped to standardize the English language, which prior to his works was often inconsistent.

Shakespeare died in Stratford at the age of 52. He is buried at the Holy Trinity Church and his grave bears a dramatic epitaph that threatens to curse anyone who disturbs his bones.

From the first publications of his works, Shakespeare's influence on literature, the media, music, art and language has been colossal. His works have been translated into 80 languages and have sold over four billion copies since his death.

A man as legendary as his characters, he is perhaps best remembered by the playwright Ben Jonson's quotation as being 'not of an age, but for all time'.

Dr Jennie M. Votava
(Foreword)

Dr Jennie M. Votava (Foreword) is an Associate Professor of English at Allegheny College. She received her BA in English and MD from Harvard University in 1997 and 2001, respectively, and her PhD from New York University in 2012. Her book *Shakespeare's Histories on Screen: Adaptation, Race, and Intersectionality* was published by Arden in 2023. She has also published essays in *Renaissance Drama, Shakespeare Survey* and *Shakespeare Bulletin*, as well as in the edited collections *Contagion and the Shakespearean Stage* (Palgrave Macmillan, 2019) and *Shakespeare, Race, and Anglophone Popular Culture* (Bloomsbury, under contract).

William Morris
(Decorations)

Born in Kent, William Morris (1834 –96) was an outstanding character of many talents, being an architect, writer, social campaigner, artist and, with his Kelmscott Press, an important figure of the Arts and Crafts movement. Many of us perhaps know him best for his superb furnishings and textile designs, intricately weaving together natural motifs in a highly stylized two-dimensional fashion influenced by medieval conventions, but his passion for ancient and medieval texts combined with his skills at ornamentation mean that his typographical achievements and decorations for book printing have left a treasure trove of pattern elements perfectly suited to editions such as this.

Louis Rhead
(Illustrations from *Tales of Shakespeare* by Charles Lamb and Mary Lamb, 1918)

Born in Staffordshire, England, Louis John Rhead (1857–1926) studied art in Paris before attending the National Art Training School in London. Emigrating to America in 1883, he became art director at D. Appleton's publishing house in New York City before working as a successful poster artist. From the early 1900s, Rhead illustrated a number of children's books including works by Daniel Defoe, Robert Louis Stevenson and Charles and Mary Lamb.

Florence Harrison
(Illustrations from *Early Poems of William Morris*, 1914)

The illustrator Florence Susan Harrison (1877–1955) is sometimes confused with the English artist Emma Florence Harrison. Hailing from Brisbane, Australia, Harrison came to England and worked for Blackie & Son publishers. As well as illustrating tomes by William Morris, Christina Rossetti and Alfred Lord Tennyson, she wrote and illustrated her own book of verse named *Elfin Song* (1912). Her vivid and assured illustrations combine elements of the Art Nouveau and Pre-Raphaelite styles.

FLAME TREE PUBLISHING

Beautiful Books, Timeless Storytelling

The Flame Tree Complete Works of Shakespeare, based on the First Folio edition of 1623 is published in three volumes:

The Comedies, *The Histories* (with the poetry) and *The Tragedies*.

Other titles in our wide range of epic and world literature include:

The Aeneid • *The Decameron* • *The Divine Comedy* • *I Ching* • *The Odyssey and the Iliad* • *Japanese Myths & Tales* • *King Arthur & The Knights of the Round Table* *Ramayana* • *African Myths & Tales* • *Paradise Lost* • *Persian Myths & Tales*

Flame Tree's companion Gothic Fantasy books offer a carefully curated series of new titles, each with combinations of original and classic writing for new new and established authors. Titles include:

American Gothic • *Chilling Horror* • *Chilling Ghost* • *Asian Ghost* • *Murder Mayhem*• *Crime & Mystery* • *Swords & Steam* • *Dystopia Utopia* • *Supernatural Horror* • *Time Travel* • *Heroic Fantasy* • *Agents & Spies* • *Robots & AI* • *Lost Souls* • *Haunted House* • *Cosy Crime* • *Urban Crime* • *Epic Fantasy* • *Detective Thrillers* • *Footsteps in the Dark* • *Strange Lands* • *Weird Horror* • *Lost Atlantis* • *Lovecraft Mythos* • *Terrifying Ghosts* • *Black Sci-Fi* • *Chilling Crime* • *Compelling Science Fiction* • *First Peoples Shared Stories* • *Alternate History* • *Immigrant Sci-Fi* • *Spirits & Ghouls*

Available from all good bookstores, worldwide, and online at
flametreepublishing.com

Join our monthly newsletter with offers, submissions and stories:
FLAME TREE FICTION NEWSLETTER
flametreepress.com